# The Brunist Day of Wrath

# ROBERT COOVER

# The Brunist Day of Wrath

DZANC BOOKS

5220 Dexter Ann Arbor Rd.
Ann Arbor, MI 48103
www.dzancbooks.org



Book design by Steven Seighman

Published 2014 by Dzanc Books
ISBN: 978-1-938604-38-6
First edition: March 2014

This project is supported in part by the National Endowment for the Arts and the MCACA.

Printed in the United States of America



10 9 8 7 6 5 4 3 2 1

For James Ballowe, who was here well before page one.
And in memory of Sol Yurick, generous and uncompromising sharer of our first-book annealings.

*The Kingdom is at war, besieged by a roving band of demented Cretin Wizards who have stirred up the forest wild things and aroused the demonic within the commoners. Undermined by intrigue and stupidity, its battlements crumbling, the Kingdom is about to capitulate. The King and his minions cannot save it. But Beauty can try.*

—Sally Elliott, *Against the Cretins*

# PROLOGUE

## Tuesday 7 July

"Jesus loves me, this I know, For the Bible tells me so…" The young Reverend Joshua J. Jenkins, candidate for the West Condon Presbyterian ministry, whushing along through the rain-drenched countryside, the bus nosing out of lush farmlands and dark wet forests onto the gently undulant and somewhat barren coal basin that is to be, if his interview goes well, his new home, finds himself meditating upon his church's Great Awakening—a great disaster, as he was taught (he himself is just awaking from a thick early morning doze, his head fallen against the bus window, muddled dreams of collegial dispute)—and upon the sequence of disruptive church schisms and rationalist heresies that followed upon the Awakening's excessive evangelism through the convulsions of the American nineteenth century, so shaped by Presbyterian thought (and, one might say, confused by it as well), out of which musings he hopes to craft his inaugural sermon, and humming meanwhile that children's hymn of simple faith…"Little ones to Him belong, They are weak, but He is strong…" He does not know why this old Sunday school tune has sprung to mind, but perhaps it is a subconscious reminder that he will not be addressing fellow intellectuals in this remote little coaltown, and must therefore keep his message, however profound at the root, simple and direct in its expression.

Not his forte, as his professors have often remarked. He has the ability, which he perceives as a virtue but others more often as a fault, of holding several contrary ideas in his head at the same time, acting on each as if they were independent, even while being fully aware of their relative veracity or utility. On the one hand, for example, the Biblical account of the creation of the universe some six thousand years ago, and, on the other, what we know about the half billion years it has taken to produce the landscape the bus is now rolling through (a landscape, as seen through the smear of streaming rain on the window, increasingly scarred by the grotesquerie of strip mining: man's impact on nature is more dynamic than geological processes, about which he also holds various conflicting views). Glaciers left their mark on this area as recently as some twelve thousand years ago, but the primordial swamps that nourished the vegetation which ultimately became the coal now being mined here, powering a nation but fostering much local violence and misery, existed at least three hundred million years ago, he knows that; yet he also knows that God, in His omnipotence and wisdom, can play with time as man might play with a ball of string, so that such so-called scientific facts do not exclude, even if they superficially contradict, the sacred stories in the Bible. There are various modes of discourse, Joshua believes—narrative, analytical, rhetorical—and each proceeds toward a truth of its own kind. He personally prefers (usually) that which leads, not to further disputation, but to action, the social or moral mode, as one might call it—"Jesus loves me when I'm good, When I do the things I should…"—and it is that way of thinking that has brought him aboard the bus this morning. He was in fact contemplating missionary work in Africa or in the poorer nations in Latin America when the offer of a pastorate in an impoverished and depressed coalmining community came along, thanks to a professor who had not previously been very supportive ("Jesus loves me when I'm bad, Though it makes Him very sad…"), and he recognized it as the perfect challenge with which to launch his ministerial career, though the professor may well have thought of it as a way of getting rid of him. Joshua has a deep instinctive sympathy with the unemployed, with the less privileged, the minorities, the illiterate, the maimed, and not excluding overworked and underpaid coalminers. Not many of whom are apt to be Presbyterians, of course, but still there is a mission here. He understands that currently there are divisive eschatological issues in this community, and he believes he will have something constructive to contribute to the discussion of them, having both an ecumenical tolerance for confused and heretical beliefs and an unbending faith in doctrinal orthodoxy, not to mention a profound distaste for emotional revivalism such as that which characterized the Presbyterian Great Awakening—a distaste, as he discovered in a telephone conversation, that he shares with church elder Theodore Cavanaugh, chairman of the Board of Deacons. Yes, this will be the right place for him. Intellectually engaged and socially concerned though he is, however, ultimately it is his simple love for Jesus that is his mainstay. Jesus is his master and his guide, but he is also his friend, a friend he has talked with daily ever since his earliest days in the Sunday School Brigade. Young Reverend Jenkins has few friends, but he does not need them, for his is to be—as designed, he believes, by God Himself—a lonely, austere, and singular passage through life's mazy uncertainties. He has a friend in Jesus, and that's enough. Which is why, in reality (whatever *that* is; many possibilities), he is humming this simple song. "Yes, Jesus loves me! Yes, Jesus loves me…!" In his zeal, he is singing aloud and, to his embarrassment, someone at the back of the bus joins in: "The Bible tells me so!"

After bus stops at a progression of small wet towns, eerily empty and haunted by the skeletons of abandoned mine tipples, Joshua arrives in West Condon at last. The rain has stopped and the sun is surging from behind the clouds, welcoming him to his new life. One of his companions on the bus, perhaps the one who had sung along with him earlier, asks as he steps down behind him: "Are you a defender, brother?" A big man in a billed cap, plaid shirt, and hunting boots. "Of the faith, you mean…? Yes, of course." "Better git a gun, then," he says and lifts his rifle in demonstration. The man and his two friends rattle off in somebody's pickup truck before young Reverend Jenkins can reply (repartee is also not his forte) that, no (though why did he ask?), he is a man of peace. It is the message of the New Testament (one of them; militancy is another of course, though a peaceful militancy, mostly peaceful), a message he will try to incorporate in his inaugural sermon. So that they will know who he is, what he stands for. Peace. Faith. Charity. And so on.

The bus pulls out with a gassy wheeze, leaving him standing alone on an empty street. He is surprised that no one has come to meet him. In the inside jacket pocket of his new three-piece corduroy suit he bears the flattering letter from Mr. Cavanaugh and the First Presbyterian Board of Deacons, which suggested that Mr. Cavanaugh himself would be waiting here for him. Inside the little one-story corner bus station, he finds the manager complaining about a power outage. "You get a half sprinkle in this damn forsooken town and ain't nothin' works," he says, adding an unnecessary vulgarism or two. When Joshua inquires, he is told that, no, no one has been asking for him. Impatient fellow, rather rude and rough of tongue. Almost certainly not a Presbyterian. Joshua supposes Mr. Cavanaugh's bank cannot be far away, but he decides, now that the sun is coming out (he is perhaps a bit overdressed for July, but he knows the importance of first impressions), that this might be a fortunate opportunity to examine his prospective new town and church on his own, without a local booster at his elbow. As the four beasts of the Apocalypse say: Come and see. So he shall. He has the bank's phone number; he will call later to explain why, having been "forsooken," he chose not to bother Mr. Cavanaugh but to make his way on his own. According to the map Mr. Cavanaugh sent him, the town, though free-form in shape, is laid out on a simple grid, numbers running one direction, trees, flowers, and American and local patriots the other; the church—soon to be *his* church—is marked on the map with red pencil and should be easy to find. He deposits his heavy bag, overweighted with his cherished books, with the station manager, who drags it disdainfully behind the counter, kicking it back against the wall, and he sets off on his exploration.

Joshua has hardly left the bus station before he is out of the commercial district, there being so little of it, though the residential neighborhoods are not free of the occasional shop or repair facility as well as small homespun enterprises announced by hand-lettered signs in the windows. An unzoned blurring of private and working lives, profoundly American. The wet street is aglitter with the sun shining on it and, though people are beginning to emerge from their doors, it is peaceful yet, as if newly created, and largely free of traffic. He had expected to feel out of place, but he does not. He can make a home here. The town is not as impoverished as he had imagined, though of course this is the Presbyterian side of it, so to speak (he is passing a quite monumental Baptist church even as he has this thought), and probably not where most of the miners live. He will visit those neighborhoods and discover their needs and bring the power of Christian love and the charitable weight of his own church to bear upon them. Here on these dripping tree-lined streets (he walks on the sunny side) there is the charm of the ordinary: brick houses with broad porches bearded with flowering shrubbery, white frame houses with mock shutters and screen porches and carports, others brightly painted, yellow, pale blue, rose. American flags fly, and in many of the yards there are portable barbecue grills and cedar picnic tables, bejeweled still with raindrops, poised for homely smalltown family pleasures. There are no fences; the yards are one shared yard. People greet each other from their porches. "Are your lights working?" a woman calls to another. "No, they must be out on the whole street." "I hope my freezer don't melt!" Some have well-tended lawns and colorful flower gardens, others are scruffier with balls and toys and tricycles in the front yard, rusting bicycles leaning against porch posts, a tire swing hanging from a tree branch, a dented pickup truck on cement blocks. Dogs have been let out and are chasing each other. In a house somewhere, a child is being scolded. Dandelions proliferate between the sidewalk and the street. Where a bent hubcap lies in the gutter near a clogged drain. Is all this beautiful? It must be. God is the first author of beauty and all his handiwork is a priori perfect, and thus good and true and also necessarily beautiful. It cannot be otherwise. Instead, one asks of all one sees: wherein *lies* its beauty? His inaugural sermon, as yet unwritten, is entitled "An Old Evangel for a New Day," and perhaps that will be the theme, one of them: Seeking the extraordinary in the ordinary, the uncommon in the common. He feels quite wise and rich with insight, touched as it were by something holy ("Just a closer walk with thee," he is humming as he strolls, "grant it, Jesus, is my plea…"), the world behaving as a theater for his inmost thoughts.

A block before the Presbyterian church, a convoy of three Army trucks full of soldiers comes rolling by as if conjured up from the puddles in the street. They are certainly not conjured up from his thoughts; they surprise them. The trucks pause and the driver of the lead vehicle leans from his window and calls out: "Hey, chubby! Can you tell me how to find the high school?" "I'm afraid I am not yet from here," he replies, then realizes that will not be easily understood. "But I have a map." He hands it up to the driver, who studies it. A young officer is sitting beside him, staring straight ahead. There are impolite comments from the back of the truck about the manner of Joshua's dress. "Right," says the driver. "Mind if I keep this?" "Well—" "Thanks, chief." And they go rumbling on down the street, spewing black exhaust and rude remarks. A curious and, given his present transcendent state of mind, somewhat jarring apparition. Perhaps it was to remind him that that "peace in the valley" he longs for is not without its obligatory sacrifices. That there are those for whom peace is not a first priority. He knows them; they were the bane of his childhood. He is reminded of the line from Luke: And when ye shall see Jerusalem compassed with armies, then know that the desolation thereof is nigh. But he, young Reverend Joshua J. Jenkins, is a man of peace, yes, he is, through and through. He would outlaw all the world's armies, if he could; he will never ask his congregation to sing "Onward, Christian Soldiers." A man of peace like Christ Jesus and his Gospel of Love. His friend. His best friend. Yes, what a friend I have in Jesus! He is humming to himself again.

Again, an old Sunday school song. In spite of his aptitude for abstruse and complex thought, so convoluted at times that he baffles his listeners and even sometimes gets lost himself, it is the simple songs that Joshua loves most, songs like the one he is humming now, standing before the church that is to be his home, his platform, his testing ground, and his awesome pastoral responsibility, tunefully murmured like a kind of prayer to Jesus: Precious Lord, take my hand, lead me on…

The church is less impressive than in the photograph they sent him, a modest brick structure, vaguely modernist in style, far less grand than the Baptist church near the town center and not so classic a house of worship as the stone Lutheran church he passed a couple of blocks back with its solid square bell tower and big double doors; but just as Joshua loves the simple songs, so does he love the simple Christian virtues, which people in this country in their ignorance think of as American virtues, and this church in its honest friendly dignity stands as a quiet monument to them. It suits him. It suits Presbyterianism and its democratic community spirit.

As the church is presently without a minister, he fears the doors may be locked, but they are not. He removes his felt hat and wipes his brow. "I'm tired, I'm weak, I'm alone; through the storm, through the night, lead me on to the light, take my hand, precious Lord, lead me home!"

"You have arrived, Mr. Jenkins. Mr. Joshua *J.* Jenkins."

"Why, yes—!" He has been thinking so much about his friend Jesus that young Reverend Jenkins is not altogether surprised to see him standing at the pulpit. Sunlight enters the church through the high windows in clearly defined beams. Jesus is standing in one of them, exactly as he appears in the frontispiece of Joshua's favorite book of Bible stories for children. It is an astonishing sight. Jesus wants me for a sunbeam, Joshua is thinking, somewhat madly, the melody tinkling in his head as if played on glass bells. "But how did you—?"

"Your résumé, Mr. Jenkins."

"My résumé—?"

"And what does the middle 'J' stand for, Mr. Jenkins? Not my name, I hope."

*"No!"* He has been anticipating this visit to his new church with such excitement, perhaps he is only dreaming about it and the bus not yet arrived. That would explain the nightmarish army trucks. He touches his breast pocket; no, the map is gone. But dreaming is another mode of discourse, similar to the narrative mode but freed from some mimetic conventions. The map, for example, can be there and not be there at the same time. When he wakes, he will take notes. They will make for an interesting sermon. Perhaps his inaugural one. What happened to me on my way into West Condon. On the other hand, if he is not dreaming, and he probably is not, it can't be Jesus, and in the realization of that he understands the terrible shallowness of his faith. Though in one part of his mind, that part he takes most comfort in, he is having a personal encounter with Christ; in the larger part, wherein his reason resides like the house demon, he knows it is not possible. "It's…it's Jehoshaphat. My grandfather…"

"Jehoshaphat! A king! 'I am as thou art, my people as thy people, my horses as thy horses!' Hah! What a memory! Not all of us are so lucky to have such a grandfather. Or even a grandfather at all. On my paternal side, it is something of a mystery." Joshua is nodding at all this, hat in hand, but he's not sure what he's affirming. "Yes, I know you wrote a paper on it. I thank you for your contribution."

"Pardon? Paper—?"

"He was reminding me that he wrote an essay on the old fellow, your namesake, getting diddled by the king of Israel. He got a B-plus for it. I was acknowledging that."

"Oh yes, I see." But he doesn't. Who got a B-plus? He feels as he often feels when lost in his own theological conundrums, and wonders if he should go out and come in again.

"Who, Mr. Joshua Jehoshaphat Jenkins, do you say that I am?"

"Well, hah…you *look* a bit like Christ Jesus, but—!"

"Looks, Mr. Jenkins, are not always deceiving." The man smiles benignly down upon him, stroking his beard. "We were talking, I believe, about the end of the world."

"We were?"

"Everybody is. It is, I am afraid, the topic of the day. By many it is expected imminently. Perhaps before lunch. But the end of the world, Mr. Jenkins, is not an event. It is a kind of knowledge. And therefore, at least for those in the know, it has already happened. And those who are not in the know are living in sin, for ignorance is sin—the worst sin, am I right?"

"Well…"

"Of course I am. As soon as it was imagined, it was a done deal, I told you that millennia ago, don't you remember?"

"I-I wasn't—"

"'But if it is by the finger of God that I drive out the devils,' I said," he says, pointing a finger down at Joshua as if probing for more demons, "'then be sure the Kingdom of God has *already* come upon you.' That's what I said. 'Repent ye, for the Kingdom of Heaven is at hand.' My very words, repeated hundreds of times. They wrote them down. 'But I tell you of a truth, there be some standing here, which shall not taste of death, till they see the kingdom of God.' You're a man of the Good Book, as it is called in the trade. You have read it. Would I lie to you?"

"No! But—"

"Shut up! Apart from me you can do nothing!"

"I-I'm sorry—?"

"He was telling me I lie all the time."

"He—?"

"That business of driving out devils like chasing hair lice, for example, he meant. Not exactly true, I admit it, but it was the way we talked back then."

A lady enters. Like Jesus, she is also dressed in a flowing gown. A flimsy thing the color of fresh peaches. She seems almost to float. Is she walking on her toes? "Jesus! Those awful people are marching up that hill again! And they all have *guns!* I was watching it on TV until the lights went off. I don't know *what's* going to happen! I heard some very loud noises! I think we should excuse this gentleman and hurry back to the basement!"

"On the contrary, my dear. We too shall proceed to the infamous hill. I believe they are waiting for me."

"No! They don't know *what* they are waiting for! They're completely *crazy!* Come with me now! *Please!*"

Jesus, or whoever he is (she *called* him Jesus!), only smiles calmly and raises one hand in a kind of blessing. Which would be completely convincing were he not scratching himself with the other. "We shall take Mr. Joshua J. Jenkins with us. He is the grandson of a king. He will protect us." He winks at Joshua. Is he supposed to wink back? What people is she talking about? What infamous hill? Why do they need protection? Perhaps he should have waited for Mr. Cavanaugh at the bus station. "Come! Follow me!"

# BOOK I

And I saw when the Lamb opened one of the seals,
and I heard, as it were the noise of thunder,
one of the four beasts saying, Come and see.
And I saw, and behold a white horse:
and he that sat on him had a bow;
and a crown was given unto him:
and he went forth conquering, and to conquer.

—*The Book of Revelation 6.1-2*

# I.I

## Easter Sunday 29 March

It is the hour of dawn, but the skies are black and stormy, curtaining the sun's emergence from the catacombs of night. A small party of climbers is struggling up the muddy slope of a steep man-made hogback ridge toward the pale wet light at the top, ghostly figures wrapped up against the elements when viewed from atop the ridge, black featureless silhouettes when seen from below against the dull nimbus, ribboned with rain, at the crest. Some lose their footing, drop to their hands and knees in the mud, swallowing down the curses that rise to their throats, mindful on this most holy morning that the stakes are high: nothing short of everlasting life. The source of which is death. That is the message of the day. For on this day, they say, exactly at dawn nearly two thousand years ago, one who died arose and walked again, promising a similar reward for all who would follow him, an easement against the anguish of death's hard passage. "For as in Adam all men die, so in Christ all will be made to live." *Stirb und werde*, as the Trinity Lutheran pastor intends to put it up here in the opening prayer he has been invited to deliver. Die and come to life—die and *be*—the meaning of this moment.

This the incentive for the community's long tradition of witnessing at a prayerful sunrise service the breaking of Easter's dawn, though never before from such a place as this: a high artificial ridge of disturbed heaped-up earth at the South County Coal Company strip mine, the easternmost of a parallel set of such ridges. For nearly half a century, the Presbyterians have held their Easter sunrise service on Inspiration Point at their No-Name Wilderness church camp, gradually expanding it over the years into an ecumenical occasion as the town population and church memberships declined; but this year, the camp was mysteriously unavailable, rumored to have been sold to a developer, and this site was chosen in its stead by the West Condon Ministerial Association as the setting for the annual celebration of the Dawn Resurrection. The light at the top of the ridge is provided by battery-operated mine lamps mounted on stanchions, which do not so much light up the area as cast a pale otherworldly glow upon it, through which the rain falls as if upon a rubbly forsaken stage, one seeded with coal chips and bits of gravel, and barren except for weedy grasses that have taken root here and there. The giant claws that sculpted this strange terrain lurk in the pooled black waters below like skeletal creatures of the netherworld, mute witnesses to the sacred ceremonies at the top.

The pastors of several different denominations are clustered under umbrellas up here, each with a few brave members of their congregations, though the minister of the First Presbyterian Church, traditional host of this event, has not yet arrived; they await him with what patience they can muster, as the remaining stragglers slowly make their way up the slippery slope to join them, feeling somewhat martyred by their own righteousness, many with hands and knees muddied and umbrellas broken. To fill the time, the Presbyterian choirmaster, huddled with his wife under a large striped umbrella with a handkerchief at his nose, is leading them all through some Easter morning hymns that no one can hear, the voices, even their own, drowned out in the lashing rain. "His Cheering Message from the Grave." "A Brighter Dawn Is Breaking."

When Inspiration Point at the Presbyterian church camp became unavailable, alternative locations for the sunrise service were few, the land around here being generally flat and uninspiring. One of the highest points in the area is the mine hill out at the Greater Deepwater Coal Company, an old slag heap from earlier in the century, now part of the landscape, but since the terrible disaster out there five years ago and the Brunist cult's temporary appropriation of it for its own heretical purposes, it has acquired an unholy aura, for which reason it was not even considered. The rise at the sixth tee at the country club golf course was proposed, but not only was it deemed a secular and elitist location, there was also drinking out there and dancing and card playing and other even more un-Christian behavior. So when the wealthy owner of South County Coal and former member of the Church of the Nazarene congregation offered this ridge, it was hastily and gratefully accepted. There was some talk about canceling the event when foul weather was predicted, but as several pastors declared: What if Mary and Magdalene had stayed home on the day of Christ's rising merely because of a few showers?

Easter sunrise services being a modern invention of American Protestant churches, there are no Roman Catholics in attendance—indeed, they have not even been invited—but there are also many Protestant denominations whose spiritual leaders oppose the very idea of ecumenism as a dilution of the true faith and a liberal corruption of the Word of God and who have discouraged their congregations from participating in this service, offering them pancake prayer breakfasts in their church basements in its stead. One world, one church: this is not the American way, and it is not God's way. There are those who are with God and those who are not, and there always have been and always will be until Judgment Day. It is by our differences that we know one another, and those differences divide and cannot be denied. Some will be welcomed into the Promised Land, but most will not, and that's a plain fact, the Bible says so. It's either/or: step up and take your pick, brothers and sisters. It's your eternity. A sign outside the First Baptist Church says as much.

Others, however, including the Presbyterian hosts, take a more generous view of their fellow religionists and welcome these opportunities for interdenominational Christian fellowship. Chief among them is the pastor of Trinity Lutheran, whose grand vision is of a global one-world, one-church ecumenical order focused on social reformulation, a contemporary articulation of meditation, contemplation, and prayer, and a recovery of the Holy Scriptures while embracing secular spirituality, for God is good and everywhere. He has written about this, though none here have read his writings, nor would they likely understand them should they try to do so. His parishioners have occasionally heard such thoughts expressed in the pastor's Sunday sermons, but they have not understood them there either.

The black-bearded South County Coal Company manager, whose task it has been to prepare the site for the morning's service at his boss's request, detests this entire pagan event as an unholy abomination. He has stood sullenly on the shadowy slope in his black slicker, a lit cigarillo dangling under his rainhat, hands resting on the butts of his holstered guns, watching the fools slip and fall on their climb but helping none of them. They are the condemned; let them get used to falling. The so-called Christian church is not Christian at all; it is an evil and degenerate institution, infiltrated and controlled by Satan, who, as the Holy Book says, deceiveth the whole world. The *whole* world. Christ was not crucified on a Friday, did not rise on a Sunday. Can they not read their own Bible? Do they not have fingers on which to count? The very notion of Easter, absorbed into Christianity by the early church fathers, so-called, in their corrupt lust for power and named after a whorish pagan goddess, is obscenely ludicrous. Sunrise services, Easter parades, chocolate bunnies and colored eggs: all vile impurities, idolatrous humanist perversions. The Great Conspiracy, as he calls it. The church's pact with the Devil. He loathes them all.

The Presbyterian minister appears on the slope at last, hatless, coatless, unshaven, floundering about in the mud. He is met partway up by the town banker, a Presbyterian stalwart, dressed in heavy boots and the sort of rain gear worn by hunters and fishermen, and helped up the rest of the way, the banker asking why he has only one shoe on. *"What? What? Am I not free?"* he shouts in reply. *"Where am I? There is a darkness on the land!"* The Lutheran pastor steps forward to lead them all in prayer, but he is interrupted by the Presbyterian minister who, upon reaching the top, plants his stockinged foot in a murky puddle and without prayer or preamble ("Oh no!" squeaks the choirmaster's wife) raises his face to the downpour and, shaking his fist at it, cries out: *"Blessed are those who are free from the infection of angels! What? What are you saying? I know, I know! A people laden with iniquity! Woe upon them all! But what about me? I am filled with bitterness! Get out, damn you! Out!"* Whereupon, there is a sudden blinding flash and a ground-rocking blast of thunder and everyone flees, slipping and sliding urgently down the greasy slope.

Last down is the town banker, guiding the confused and increasingly incoherent Presbyterian minister, the banker picking his steps out carefully with the help of one of the mine lamps lifted from its stanchion, avoiding the slick tracks laid down by those who had lost their footing and, with yelps of alarm, feet flying, had slid down on their backsides. The Presbyterian minister, soaked through, stumbling unsteadily, one shoe off, one shoe on, babbles on. *"No! Not one jot or one tittle! Not an iota, not a dot!"* The sky flares again with lightning—*"Can you hear me? Who do they say that I am?"* the man yells at the storm, and his knees buckle and down he goes, nearly pulling the banker down with him. "God *damn* you!" the banker mutters under his breath, fully aware of the peculiarly precise power of such an oath on such a day. But too much is awry for propriety. He hauls the minister to his feet and, slapping through the ankle-deep water at the bottom, bundles him into his Lincoln Continental and heads in a fury, kicking up mud, for the church manse.

It is in such browbeating weather that West Condon prodigal son (there is an army of them) Georgie Lucci steps down off the bus from the city on his first return in nearly five years to the scene of his youthful indiscretions, somewhat nauseous from the long overnight ride, having sucked up half a case of cheap beer en route and fallen dead asleep only an hour before pulling in. He hardly knows where he is, only that he is getting fucking wet. At this unholy hour, the old corner bus station, where once he reigned as pinball king, is closed (he decorates its doorway with a pool of vomit, just for old times' sake: Ciao, bambini, Georgie's home!), as is the rest of the downtown, which he examines in a brief futile stagger, seeking shelter and a bite of breakfast, wearing his duffel bag as a ponderous rainhat. Not a soul on the streets, everything dark as midnight and shut up tight, some shops boarded up as though forever, the cold rain bombing down, the thunder and lightning giving him a headache. Fuck off, he groans, though to no one in particular, being no blasphemer, at least not by intent. None of his crimes have been, they've just happened. He tries the door up to the Legion Hall above the Woolworths, hoping some old pal might be sleeping it off on a couch up there, but that door too is closed to him, so he pisses on it, adding his bit to the flow flooding the earth. There are a few cars parked on the street in front of the broken penny parking meters, their junky antiquity bespeaking the town's present economic circumstances. He tries their handles, no luck, the mistrustful bastards, so he breaks into a rusty old Ford station wagon and crawls inside, strips off his wet clothes and wraps himself in the woolly blanket he finds in the back. He still has a couple of beers in his bag, so it's hair of the dog for breakfast or as a nightcap, whatever. Not for the first time in his long and unkempt life.

That's about all Georgie remembers of time's recent passage when he is jostled awake by the police chief, Dee Romano, and asked what the hell he's doing there. "Ah, the welcoming committee has arrived," he growls froggily. "You've unloosed some pretty unfriendly weather on me here in old Wet Condom, Demetrio, I had to get in outa the storm to save my life. Whose car is this, by the way?" "It's *my* car, you stupid stronzo." "I shoulda guessed. Only you could own a blanket that smells this bad." "It's my dog's. He won't appreciate that remark. And what have you done, thrown up in it? Merda! I may have to turn him loose on you." "Well, I'm pretty hungry, it might be an even scrap. Why don't you do the right thing, compagno, and go bring your honored guest some scrambled eggs and coffee?" "C'mon. Outa there,

Giorgio. I got no time for wiseasses; I got too many problems. We're shorthanded with Old Willie gone, our cruisers are falling apart and no money from the city to fix them, broken streets full of drunks and thieves, the damn Brunists back in town, trouble at the school—" "A chi lo dice! The Brunists! Them rain dancers are back?" "Yeah, they're setting up shop out in the old summer camp on the road to Tucker City. From what I hear, you should be dressed just about right for them. But here in town it's against the law. So get them rags back on and haul your ugly culo outa there. *Now!*" "Them rags is cold and wet, Dee. Listen, do me a favor. Arrest me and lock me up in a warm dry cell for a few hours. I deserve it." "You want a roof over your head, Georgie, go to Mass." "Mass? Is it Sunday?" "It's Easter, you fucking cretino. Now move it!" "Okay, okay. Good idea, Dee. I'll go to Mass. Easter. Whaddaya know. I'll go confess to old Bags all the evil things I done, give him a rise. I got stories from the city that'll burn his hang-dog flappers off. But first gimme a lift over to my old lady's so's I can borrow her tub and clothes dryer."

So that's how it is that, in due course, the explosive news about the Brunists detonates upon the broad well-worn steps of St. Stephen's Roman Catholic Church on this Easter morning. Several of the worshippers have gathered there before High Mass during a break in the thunderstorm, grabbing a quick smoke and grousing about the economy, the kids, the corruption at city hall, the weather, what's ailing them, what's ailing West Condon, the rest of the world, the cosmos, etc., and what can be done about it; namely, nothing. The plagued town, still mourning its dead from the mine disaster of five years ago, is in a state of terminal decay and depression, so broke it can't fix the winter potholes or pick up the garbage. It has been bypassed by the new interstate, all the deep-shaft coalmines are closed, the downtown is emptying out and the car dealers are shutting down, the only hotel is an empty derelict, subsidence is sinking home values as if they could sink any lower, strip mines have torn up the countryside and polluted the water, the high school basketball team has won two games all season, the old coal-burning power plant is unstable and blackouts are frequent, prices are up, wages down for those who have jobs (not many), families are breaking up, friends are dying, the local newspaper has folded, TV reception is poor and there's nothing on it but protests, wars, assassinations, corruption, riots, quiz shows and beer ads. Sal Ferrero and one-armed Bert Martini have been out at the hospital this week visiting fellow ex-miner Big Pete Chigi, who's dying of black lung or something worse, and Sal reports that he's in a respirator now. "Big Pete ain't so big no more," says Bert. "Damn coal dust," is another's mutter. "It's not just the dust, it's also them coffin nails," says Guido Mello, grinding his out under heel, and Sal, staring dolefully with baggy eyes at the cigarette from which he's just taken a drag, says, "I'm quitting tomorrow." Mickey DeMars, whose downtown sandwich joint is closed for the day (the high price of meat has been the subject of his previous discourse, which aroused some surprise among his interlocutors that his hamburgers actually contain such an ingredient), says he heard on the radio that fully one-fifth of the nation was living in abject poverty. "That ain't bad odds," growls Vince Bonali, wallowing a dead cigar in his jowls. "Wish it was that good here." Vince has recently lost his wife, has long since lost his job, and it's said he's drinking more than he's eating these days. There's a rumble of thunder and, peering up at the black sky, Carlo Juliano says, "It don't stop. Better go home and build a ark." "I would," says Bonali, "but I can't afford the mortgage."

Which is when errant native son Georgie Lucci is spotted (he gets a welcoming shout) hurrying their way over the puddly potholed street and broken sidewalk like a tall clownish bird, bearing glad tidings, bad breath, lurid tales of nightlife in the city, empty pockets (cousin Carlo, when pressed, reluctantly loans him a five-spot), and the news that the Brunists are back, reportedly up to their old tricks out at the edge of town. This evangel draws a large eager audience, so Georgie, always the crowd-pleaser, elaborates on it, describing the Brunists' ecstatic and diabolical rites in fulgid colors, details supplied by a stag movie he saw up in the city about a secret orgy society, and using the chief of police as the horse's mouth. The ladies in the crowd peel away to spread the word among the others ("Monsignor Baglione must know!"

gasps Mrs. Abruzzi, hurrying off in her sparse orange hair and the black widow's garb she has worn for thirty years) and Carlo says maybe they ought to hide the Pincushion, popular name for their statue of St. Stephen, so the Brunists don't steal it again.

So they're back. Vince Bonali, gazing off toward the rainsoaked streets as though pondering their bleak future, feels a stirring of something commingled of nostalgia, excitement, mortification, and anticipation. When that insane cult first started up here, he helped his old high school teammate and town banker Ted Cavanaugh create the Common Sense Committee to try to put the brakes on. After the mine disaster, West Condon was in deep shit, and that end-of-the-world lunacy was the wrong story to send out to the world—Vince said as much in his famous "rockdusting" speech at the first big rally, and Ted loved it. Ted runs this town, and Vince became his righthand man. He was at the center of things and welcomed all over town, his pals were even calling him "the Mayor"—except for his days as second-team all-state tackle, it was the proudest moment of his life. And, after his stupid fuckup, the worst. Total humiliation. From king of the hill to the bottomless pit. Thinking about it still made Vince sick to his stomach, and he feels sick now. He's not happy to see Georgie back in town. Georgie was there for it all, witness to his most shameful moments. Georgie has no pride. Sooner or later all those old stories are going to get retold. Just for laughs. Sick jokes from the past. Even now they're yattering on about that mad carnival out at the mine ("At least we felt alive then," someone says), the day he sank the lowest. But he has changed since then. Stupidity sometimes has more to do with heart than head. His refound faith has centered him, put his reason right. Most know that and respect him for it. "You remember when old Red Baxter tried to lay into our altar with a mining pick?" "It was crazy! He called the church a whore!" When Vince's wife Etta died a couple years back, Ted sent flowers. A sign of forgiveness? Angie works at his bank now. And he and Ted were WCHS teammates after all on the best football team in their division in the state. That's what the big-city papers said. Maybe he should give old pal Ted a call, see if he needs any help. "Yeah, but remember what we done to their prayer barn afterwards!" Maybe he shouldn't.

"Isn't that Joey Castiglione over there, putting a play on your daughter, Vince?" asks Carlo, and Vince grunts in reply. He is well aware of his daughter's dangerous beauty. And her likely misuse of it. Angie is pretty dreamy and out of the human loop of late and she's taking a lot of baths; it's his impression she's putting out on a regular basis. Right now she's cooing over the Piccolottis' baby, who is getting christened today, Joey whispering something in her ear. Joey's all right. College kid, smart, better choice than most. His old man, killed in the mine blast, was a tough union scrapper, and Joey, though just a runt, has a lot of his feisty grit. But Angie's probably too dumb for him. He rather wishes she'd take an interest in the Moroni boy, a good kid more her speed upstairs, decent footballer in his day, Ange and Concetta's only boy, named after his crusty old nonno Nazario. Keep it in the family. Five years gone since Deepwater blew up, and he still misses Ange. Damn it. His best pal since kneepants. Got laid together for the first time in the same Waterton whorehouse. In-fucking-separable, to speak in the old way. Young Nazario now wears his dad's old hat, tipped cockily down over his nose the way Ange always wore it playing pinochle or sharing a bottle. Angela is dressed in a new Easter outfit she bought herself with a hemline just under her chin. It's a scandal, everybody's looking at her, but what can he do? With Etta gone, there's no one to talk to her. His daughter gets all her advice from the trashy romance rags she reads. As the family wage-earner, she dismisses him as a tiresome and useless old fool. The older kids have all gone their own ways, she'll be leaving soon, too. He'll be all alone. "That's your daughter?" Georgie asks with a shit-eating grin on his face. Yeah, and keep your fucking hands off her, Vince says to himself, otherwise remaining silent except for an ambiguous grunt. "Hey, where's Etta?" Georgie asks.

Joey *is* smart, Angela knows this. She likes him. Unlike that stupid creep Moron Moroni who is, regrettably, part of her Dark Ages, and still acts like he owns her; at the moment he's staring at her legs from under the brim of his dad's hat, tipped down over his broken nose, and kissing the air. Which is as close as he or any of his rough pals will ever get again. Joey is considerate and sweet and he loves her. He used to fix her bike and help her with her homework and he wrote "To the one and only!" in her yearbook. She would never have made it through math without him, and that helped her get the job at the bank, where everyone says she's really good at numbers. He and his dad were close, it was always Joe and Joey, so it was so sad when his dad got killed in the mine accident. Her heart went out to him. And then, when her mom passed away, Joey was the first to drop by and say how sorry he was and how he knew how she felt. He came home from college, where he's studying to be a mine engineer, just to do that. But, though they've gone to dances together and he's had his hand between her legs, she doesn't love him. Not the way he loves her. It is Tommy Cavanaugh she loves and that makes Joey really mad. Joey saw her in Tommy's car last night and he has called Tommy a very bad name. "Don't use language like that, Joey. You're at church." "An asshole's an asshole wherever you are." "Honestly, Joey, Tommy and me are just friends. We didn't do anything, we just drove around." "Oh sure. That rich fratboy is only interested in hicksville chitchat." She sighs. "You don't understand, Joey." He doesn't. She is having her period. Tommy will have to wait. Until Wednesday.

The news that the Brunists have returned, taking over the old closed-down Presbyterian church camp out by No-Name Creek, is spreading across the waterlogged West Condon church lawns this morning like a storm within a storm, causing alarm, anger, disgust, fear, disdain, curiosity, ridicule. Some say they are squatting illegally, others that they have a rich patron who has bought the camp for them, yet others that they were invited in by the Presbyterians, though none can fathom why the Presbyterians, chief architects of their expulsion five years ago, would do such a thing. Probably has to do with money. With those people, it always does. That those foot-stomping rollabouts were shown up as deluded fools and chased out of town should have been the end of them, but they have apparently been able to find plenty of other gullible saps and are now said to be a full-blown church, nearly as big as the Seventh-Day Adventists, many of whom have joined them. But though Brunist churches may have sprung up across the country—it's said in the magazines in doctors' offices that they're the country's fastest growing new Pentecostal church—they must know they are not welcome here. Their return is a taunt, a slap in the face.

But what to do about it? Some few are willing to live and let live, but most believe the cult must be sent packing, and right away, before they've had time to sink new roots, for as it says in the Old Testament, "Neither shalt thou bring an abomination into thine house, lest thou be a cursed thing like it." Many of the townsfolk were out at the old Deepwater No. 9 coalmine—it was about this same time of year, and it rained then, too—when the Brunists, watched by the whole world, waited for that watching world's fiery end, dancing around in the mud in their wet nightshirts and underwear, whipping each other, crying and screaming for Jesus to come—it was like the storm was egging them on, driving them all berserk, and a lot of locals went crazy and joined in as well. The state police had to be called in, there were brawls and beatings, a lot of people were jailed or hospitalized, including their so-called prophet, who was sent off to the loony bin where he belonged, and in the middle of it all, laid out on the hillside like bait for the angels sent to gather the elect, there was a sickening blue corpse on a folded lawnchair, that sad little Italian girl, her dead body getting rained on while her hand pointed spookily at the sky as though accusing it of something. Some say the cultists themselves killed her in some sort of weird ritual sacrifice, and few would put it past them. For the rest of the world, the end might not have come that day, but for West Condon, it surely did. It was the worst thing that ever happened here and the town has never really recovered from it.

How the Brunists have ended up in their old church camp is something of a mystery even to the Presbyterians themselves. Ted Cavanaugh, head of the Board of Deacons, is having to field a lot of questions about it in a kind of ad hoc gathering of the board on the church lawn during the break between Sunday School and the main church service, the storm having let up for the moment in timely fashion. He explains that the minister and his wife evidently took a number of actions of questionable legality without consulting the board, and that he has already begun the processes that will recover the camp and force the intruders to leave. But privately he knows it is largely his own fault and it won't be easy to get it back. When the Edwardses brought up the idea of selling the old camp a couple of months ago, back when winter was at its worst, Ted thought it was a good idea. The camp had fallen into ruin, and the church could use some immediate revenue. He told them to go ahead and see if they could find a buyer. When the strip mine operator Pat Suggs came forward with a decent offer, he'd seen nothing wrong with it, supposing that Suggs, who owned adjacent lands, was planning to develop the site as an industrial park or strip it for coal or both. Suggs is destroying the countryside, but any investment and source of new jobs in these hard times is welcome, so Ted helped negotiate a tax break and used his connections to get electricity brought over from the closed mine, the camp's old generator having long since given up the ghost with no hope for resurrection. He'd heard there were people living out there in trailers, a construction crew of some sort, and supposed they were Suggs' cheap imported non-union labor. Should have looked into it, should have insisted on a review by the board, but his mind was elsewhere. He finally picked up on the Brunist connection a week or so ago when Clara Collins and Ben Wosznik turned up at the Randolph Junction bank to set up an organizational checking account and he got called for a reference, they having each had accounts at his bank in times past. It was a substantial initial deposit, garnered apparently from donations from the worldwide faithful. They gave the camp as their address and explained that they had a five-year lease on the site at a dollar a year. A side of John P. Suggs he hadn't paid attention to. Hasn't paid attention to a lot of things of late, too much going on in his life, he has let things slide. Edwards' onrushing breakdown, for example.

"Some Easter," Burt Robbins says sourly, scowling at the thick black sky. Burt runs the five-and-dime, is a member of everything, complains often, contributes little, a man amused only by pratfalls and public humiliations. "And now those Armageddon nuts landing on us again. Sorry I didn't get out there to the sunrise service, Ted. But the sun never rose. Thought it must have got canceled."

"Me, too, Ted," the Chamber of Commerce Executive Director Jim Elliott says. "I wasn't even sure where it was this year."

"Out at South County. Pat Suggs set it up."

"That was a friendly gesture," says Elliott with his dippy smile.

"No, it wasn't." Standing up there among the rainsoaked and muddied few, he'd wondered if in fact it had been some kind of practical joke, but he'd discounted it. John P. Suggs is not a humorous man, not even meanly so. It was simply a tactical move. He has tried to pin Suggs down all week, hoping to cut some kind of deal, undo this wretched business somehow; the bank has its hands on properties elsewhere in the state that could be used as a trade. But Suggs was resolutely unavailable. Ted also put pressure on Wes Edwards to renege on the sale, got nowhere. Couldn't even get his attention. Seemed off in some other world. Ted talked to his bank lawyer, Nick Minicozzi, about trying to get an injunction on the grounds that the minister had illegally bypassed the church board; Nick said he could try, but it would be difficult, given Ted's own earlier approval.

"South County Coal," says Robbins, squinting in that general direction, cigarette dangling from the corner of his mouth. "You know, you can probably see the Waterton whorehouses from up there."

"Oh, nice," says Elliott. "Of course, I wouldn't know."

"Serviced at sunrise," Gus Baird says.

Jim and Burt are board members and they and Gus teach Sunday School classes. Ted doubts they've read any more of the Good Book than he has, but he may need them close at hand this morning to help with the rescue operation if Wes Edwards loses it or doesn't show. Full house today. Extra rows of wooden folding chairs and more chairs in the aisles. "Couldn't see anything this morning in that downpour. It was a mess. And so was Wes. Good thing I went out there."

Burt nods. "Ralph says Wes was splashing around crazily in his stocking feet out there and yelling at the rain."

"He was somewhat out of touch."

"Just singin' in the rain," croons Gus Baird, the travel agent and Rotary Club president, and he does a little turn around his umbrella.

Burt laughs dryly and says, "Them two kooks should be locked up, him and his wife both."

"Well..." And, while fresh thunder rumbles overhead, he fills them in on what he found when he got Wes back to the manse, the general disorder, foul smells, things flung about, the spilled milk in the kitchen and the smashed eggs. "Wes said he'd been trying to make breakfast."

"Well, I've dropped a few eggs in my time myself," says Baird amiably.

"On the walls?"

"Oh oh."

"Wait a minute. What do you mean?"

"I mean, his wife's gone."

"Debra? Really?" Elliott turns his dopy gaze toward the manse. "Wow, what do you think? She's gone off with some—?"

"Wait. She wouldn't have anything to do with that damned cult, would she?"

"You can bet on it, Burt. That screwed-up Meredith kid who was in it from the start has been living with them, and he's gone, too."

"Oh boy," says Elliott, flashing his stunned stupid look. "We have a big problem." Ted has a big problem with Elliott. An incompetent drunk, holding the town back. The area still has a lot to offer—cheap energy, old rails still in place, unused land, a workforce desperate for jobs, favorable tax incentives—but Elliott is useless. The Chamber needs new blood, someone with energy and imagination and appeal to get the town back on the commercial map again. Something Stacy could do well if she'd agree to it. She's off visiting family. When she's back, he'll try again.

Robbins strikes a match to light a new cigarette and says, "It's a disaster."

Ted rose this morning before the unseen dawn, a routine now. His emaciated wife has already had a couple of falls trying to get to the bathroom on her own, so he tries to be up in time to take her. Irene's decline infuriates her and she's resentful of his help, insists he shut the bathroom door and leave her alone. He grants her that, but stands by to help her back to bed again. Poor sweet Irene. It's heartbreaking. There'd been a couple of giggling young lovers up at the aborted service who evidently, following the Easter vigil tradition of watching the rising sun dance its bunny-hop to have their loves and lives blessed by it, had stayed up all night before coming, and seeing them Ted had felt a pang of grief, remembering Irene at that age and their own premarital spring. Such a pretty thing she was, and so loving, and so *his*. The girl's wet dress clung provocatively to her body and the boy slipped his hand between the cheeks of her bottom, and then he felt a sudden pang of desire, and a pang of guilt. Whereupon, with equal suddenness, lightning struck.

Across the lawn, through the crowd, he sees his son Tommy, home from university for the Easter break, leaning against the Lincoln. He looks cool, but Ted knows he's hurting. He had given the home care nurse Easter Sunday off, so he let Tommy sleep in and be there if Irene needed anything, and when he got back from dropping Wes off at the manse, he found Tommy trying to help his mother, at her insistence, get dressed for church. The boy was down on his knees, struggling with her nylons, and he looked miserable. "Tommy," he said, "she can't go." Outside the bedroom, they embraced and wept a little.

The sadness of a house saturated with the depressing odor of mortality and decaying connections got to Tommy last night, so he borrowed his dad's car and, on a whim inspired by the home-again Brunist news, gave Angela Bonali a call to get together to talk about her new job at the bank. That conversation lasted a minute or two and then his old high school flame gave him a spectacular blowjob while the rain drummed down on the car roof, best in a long time, nearly brought tears to his eyes. He'll see her again Wednesday when she's off the rag. It's a kind of anniversary. They lost their cherries together on an Easter weekend five years ago and, thanks to a couple of gut courses at university, browsing through the old myths, he now knows how appropriate that was. He has been through those juicy old rituals countless times since then, it would have been easy for her to drop out of the memory stream, but those were pretty unforgettable times. First everythings and all that, but the Brunists also helped make them so. Those apocalyptic lunatics not only stirred things up in town, adding an edge of danger and something bordering on an alien invasion, they also gifted him with a what-if line to score by. Later helped him ace a sociology course too. "Making History by Ending History" was the title of his A-plus term paper, a high-water mark in his academic career. Angie was curvy and cute back then, an inexperienced virgin like he was, but just naturally good at it. Because she liked it. She exemplified his notion of loose hotpants Catholic girls. Perfect for an uptight hotpants Protestant boy earnestly looking to get laid. Now she's a grownup dark-eyed beauty with all the moves, plus a world-class ass and humongous tits. He gets hard just thinking about them. She'll be big as a barn someday, but right now she's gorgeous. And his. She's crazy about him. Complete surrender. No limits.

Sally Elliott, wearing an Easter getup of sneakers without socks, frayed cut-off jeans, and an old stained trenchcoat with torn pockets, pulls up on her bike, leans it against a tree, and comes over to where he's sitting against his dad's car, keeping his distance from the dismaying well-intended remarks of the church congregation ("We're praying for a miracle, Tommy!"), and asks him how his mom's doing. "Not so good." Coming home was a shock, really. Her body all raisined up and twisted, hair gone, her mind mostly somewhere else. She's changed a lot just since Christmas. Weird look in her eyes. Not even remotely the mom he used to know. "She's got very religious. In a crazy kind of way." "What other kind of religion is there?" Sally says. Surprises him. Always thought of Sally as the dumb smalltown Sunday-school type, though he's heard she's turned a bit wild. "The plain truth, Tommy, is life is mostly crap, is very short, and ends badly. Not many people can live with that, so they buy into a happier setup somewhere else, another world where life's what you want it to be and nothing hurts and you don't die. That's religion. Has been since it got invented. Totally insane, but totally human." He's not religious himself, though he doesn't think too much about it. Why break your brains over the unknowable? But he's not exactly an atheist either. When they asked him to read the scripture lesson this morning, he agreed without thinking about it—he'd done it often enough before, a tradition at this little church, he feels comfortable with it—but it isn't the same thing as believing what he reads. Just a way of joining in. He glances across at his father on the other side of the soggy First Presbyterian Church lawn, having a smoke before the service with Sally's dad and other old guys, and no doubt filling them in on the Brunist story. Main news of the day, though his dad's been worrying about it all week. His dad's the reason Tommy is here today; church is not something he does up at school. It's rough for his dad right now, but he's standing tall. Tommy once asked him what he really believed, and he said, the Apostles' Creed, the gospels, the Commandments, that sort of thing, but he wasn't really made for religious or speculative thought. He's a doer not a thinker. So he had to accept the historical weight behind Christianity, the great thinkers who worried out its details. He had to trust that all those really smart guys can't be wrong and believe as they believed, even if he didn't completely understand it. That suits Tommy. "Well," Tommy says now, "you don't have to be crazy to believe in something." "Like Christianity, you mean? Yes, you do. Eat your god, suck his blood, and live forever. I mean, come on! Just look at today. Has to be the wackiest day on the calendar. A zombie horror story with Easter egg hunts. Open up that tomb and let the ghouls go walking, scavenging for chocolate. Weird, man!" He laughs as she staggers about in the grassy muck, her arms out monster-style, her snarly hair falling about her face in wet knotted strings. Or maybe she's hanging from the cross. She's a lanky girl, looks down on a lot of guys, used to look down on him in junior high. They've got some history. They had a flirtation or two back when they were both virgins and he was still a bit desperate. He even tried that apocalyptic line on her back when the Brunists were in town and had her pants down in the back seat, but that's as far as they got. Angela came along, and then others, a parade of them really, then university. Sally went off to some dinky liberal arts college where they taught her to dress like a tramp. They've both moved on. He can't even remember what her ass looked like, and inside the trenchcoat, there's no telling now.

Sally lights up and offers him a cigarette. "Nah. Thanks. Training. Unless you've got a joint." She reaches into a ripped pocket and draws out a little stash bag. He grins, shakes his head. "Just kidding, Sal. Gotta stay cool here in the old hometown." From her other pocket she offers him a hollow chocolate Easter egg, already cracked open, and he breaks off a chunk, brushes away the lint, hands back the glossy remains. The bells are ringing and Sally says: "Hear that? They're dropping eggs picked up in Rome." "Who are?" "The bells. They go to Rome to have supper with the Pope and pick up the eggs they'll drop on their return. Or maybe the Pope knocks them up. Not sure about bells." "Yeah, I think I read that somewhere. We must have taken the same courses. Leads to egg fights. Better than crawling around in bunny shit, I guess." She sucks on the cigarette, exhales slowly, drops the butt into the running gutter. "So, are you staying around this summer?" "Looks like it. I had plans for Europe, but Dad wants me here." "At the bank?" "No. I told him I wanted to stay outside, pool or parks or whatever. No money counting. Keeping books is too much like reading them." Actually, he would have been happy to work at the bank, it's air-conditioned and the work's easy and now Angie's there, but his dad said there was nothing useful for him to do and promised instead to get him on the city payroll in some fashion. Probably his dad wants him to mix more with the hoi polloi, one of his little civics training exercises. Or else he's already heard about him and Angie. "Anyway, I'm dropping econ and business school and going for a PhD in sociology." "No kidding." "It's what I've got the most out of up at the U. Got me thinking about more than decimal points." He's making this up as he goes along, but he likes the sound of it as it comes out. "Now that the Brunists are back in town I may use them as a summer research project." "What? You're shitting me! The Brunists are back?" "Yeah, they're out at No-Name. Where we used to sing 'God Sees the Little Sparrow Fall' around a campfire, remember?" "I remember you put your hand on my butt up on Inspiration Point." "Oh wow! I did? How old was I?" She grins. "About nine. You started young. You pretended it was an accident. So how did those crazies end up in our camp?" "I guess we sold it to them. Some rich guy gave them the money. Looks like they're making it their home base. Dad got blindsided and he's freaking out about it." He fills Sally in on the gossip as picked up this morning from his dad, including stories from the so-called sunrise service, making the most of the lightning bolt that sent everyone skidding down the hill on their asses and the completely nutty behavior of Reverend Edwards, staggering around in the mud like My Son John and spouting gibberish, which gets Sally laughing. "You may get an even daffier Easter story today than usual, Sal." "Oh, I'm not staying. I heard you were in town, figured you'd be here, just wanted to stop by and say hello, ask about your mom. Can't bear this infantile nonsense myself. Have fun in the arms of Jesus, Tommy. See you around."

The church bells are clanging away in concert with the approaching thunder. Time to go back in. "I could use some help," Ted says to the others, flicking his cigarette butt out into the wet street. "Edwards seems to be going through some kind of nervous breakdown, and anything can happen. Before I left him, he'd got into dry clothes and seemed to be getting a grip on himself, but he kept turning his smile on and off like a tic and muttering to himself. When I asked him what he was saying, he said he was practicing his sermon. At one point he blurted out, 'I'm doing my best!', but I don't think he was speaking to me."

"To tell the truth, he's been acting pretty weird for weeks now," Burt says around a final drag. "Almost smart-alecky. Like week before last when he seemed to just sort of blank out and stare up at the rafters when it came time to give his sermon. And what was all that last week about Jesus and the holy ass? Was he trying to be funny, or what?"

"I thought at first it was a dirty joke, but it was probably just craziness," Baird says, rolling his eyes. "Yesterday, I saw him walking down the street talking to himself and waving his arms about like he was directing traffic." He imitates this.

"I know. He has to see a doctor. I gave Connie Dreyer a call over at Trinity Lutheran this morning. We'll move what we can of today's other events over there and postpone the rest, and we'll bring in some guest pastors over the next few weeks. We just have to get through this morning's service somehow. I'll make an announcement about all the changes during church tidings before the scripture reading, and I'd appreciate having you guys down front. After Edwards gets going, if you see me get up and go to the pulpit, I want you to join me. Ditto, if he doesn't turn up at all. Be ready to read the Easter story from the Bible to fill the gap."

"Oh gosh," Elliott gasps. "Which book is that in?"

"A couple of them. Luke, I think. Or John."

"That's in the New Testament, right?"

"Should be. Check the program. Tommy's reading a few lines from it." He glances across the lawn, sees that Elliott's daughter, who has been talking with Tommy, has wandered off. A real handful, that girl, fast and rebellious, her mother's daughter, but Tommy's probably up to the challenge. "I've had a talk with Prissy Tindle. She understands the problem. If she has to, she can play another number or two on the organ to fill time. I'll get Ralph to lead us all in a couple of songs and we'll have a quick prayer and then get everybody out of there."

"Right," says Robbins, dropping his cigarette to the sidewalk and crushing it underfoot as they prepare to re-enter the church. It's starting to rain again. "Roll that stone away."

# I.2

## Easter Sunday 29 March

When that bully Cavanaugh, shouldered round by all his fawning scribes and elders, rises in the middle of the opening prayer like a self-righteous Sadducee to silence Reverend Wesley Edwards (was he shouting? Of course, he was shouting, God is deaf as a stump), neither he nor Jesus is surprised. In fact, they welcome it. Such persecutions are to be expected when what is hidden is revealed, and indeed stand as validation of it. What else is the Easter story about—for *Christ's* sake? Who concurs: As they persecuted me, they'll persecute you. A prophet in his own country, and all that, my son. But rejoice and be glad, your reward is great. His immediate reward is to have to sit beside the pulpit, biting his tongue, staring out on the sad blank faces of his congregation, while the banker, having skipped ahead in the proceedings to the tithes and offerings, money being all he knows (and power, he knows power), speaks of the general good health of the church finances, its immediate needs (an assistant minister, for example—*urgently!*), and Easter as a loving family occasion. No, no, you idiot! It is a time of *rejection* of family, indeed of all earthly connections! Have you no ears? If anyone comes to me and does not hate his own father and mother and wife and children and brothers and sisters, yes, and even his own life, he cannot be my disciple! Leave everything—*everything!*—and follow me! You ignorant fool! Listen to your own son's scripture reading: "But who do you say that I am?" Do you not *know?* It's all Wesley can do to stop another noisy eruption. The indwelling Christ, too, is aboil with indignation, cursing traders and moneychangers and all their abominable progeny. Look at them all up there! Smirking! A den of thieves! They are polluting the temple! Drive them out! He's in a state, they're both in a state.

It has been a trying couple of weeks. The Passion of Wesley Edwards. He's not kidding, he has endured it all in this Passiontide fortnight, from the deathly silence of God and the collapse of his faith, through all the upheavals at home and a plunge into harrowing desolation, a veritable descent into hell, to—finally—a kind of weird convulsive redemption that has left him rattled and confused and not completely in control of himself. Wesley was always a dutiful son and responsible student, and he has tried, all his life long and even now while suffering so, to be a dutiful and responsible pastor and citizen, which is to say a typical West Condon hypocrite, and though the sunrise service didn't go well (all right, so he forgot to put on one of his shoes, what was so important about that? Jesus said: That you had one shoe on was your undoing...), he got himself dried off and properly dressed and dug up one of his old Easter sermons and was prepared to fulfill his parishioners' expectations of him for one more day.

And the service began calmly enough. In spite of the storm, there was a large wet-but-festive crowd, a chirrupy twitter of Easter greetings, colorful floral displays banking the brick walls. Priscilla, accompanied by muffled thunder and the drum of rain on the tiled roof, did something peppily Risen-Sonish on the organ to get things started, there was the usual unsingable hymn ("The Strife Is O'er..."), followed by the Doxology and prayer of confession muttered in unison, a cantata ("Was It a Morning Like This?"), and then the weekly welcome and church tidings. This was normally his task (and what tidings he had!), but Cavanaugh took it over, canceling the rest of Easter. No problem with that. In fact, a great relief. He would never have got through it all, the maddening detail of his ministry—all the weddings and baptisms and funerals and christenings, the bake sales and potluck suppers, sickroom visits, board meetings, Girl Scouts, quilters, the obligatory golf foursomes and service clubs, spiritual counseling, breakfast clubs and Bible study, not to mention just keeping the church clean and the pianos tuned and the lights and toilets working—contributing intimately to his crisis. But then the banker's wiseacre brat read the Easter scripture lesson and reached the part where John says, "In that day you will know that I am in my Father and you in me, and I in you," and he couldn't hold back: "You don't know the half of it!" he cried, and launched into his Job-inspired diatribe in the name of the opening prayer (*"I will not restrain my mouth! I will speak in the anguish of my spirit! I will complain in the bitterness of my soul!"*) and got sat down.

While Cavanaugh carries on with his family values malarkey, thanking his son for the scripture reading and speaking of the church as one big family—there is a suffocating stench worse than the old family farm in the haying season of wet clothing, damp bodies, thick perfume, musty song books, and dead flowers that seems to be rising from the speech itself—Wesley glances over at Prissy sitting at her keyboard and sees that she is staring at him, clearly in shocked pain, but as if trying to console him with her sorrowful but adoring gaze. Jesus asks who she is. Priscilla Tindle. Wife of the choir director. Used to be a dancer.

Hah. You, as we say, know her.

An innocent flirtation. Her husband…

Is impotent.

…is a nice fellow.

Thus, Wesley carries on with what he thinks of as a redemptive dialogue if it is not a damnatory one, trying not to move his lips or yelp out loud, sitting meekly as a lamb while the banker speaks sentimentally of his mortally ill wife, who so longed to be here today, thanking everyone for their Christian expressions of concern and sympathy, and announcing a special fund that Irene is establishing with her own substantial contribution for the purpose of creating a proper well-equipped fellowship hall in the church basement. Irene has fond hopes, he says, that in lieu of gifts and flowers for her, her fellow presbyters will add their own generous offerings to the fund in the hope that she might see the consecration of the hall in her own lifetime. Pledge slips can be dropped in the collection plates being passed.

Money, money, money, groans Jesus. Why don't you drive that viper out? Nothing good dwells in his flesh! Cast him forth!

If I tried to do that, they'd lock me up.

They're going to lock you up anyway. But all right, this is a complete farce, so rise, let us go hence. The place stinks.

And so, stirring a dark muddy murmur through the sluggish sea of gaping faces, Wesley rises, withdrawing his briar pipe and tobacco pouch from his jacket pocket, and steps down into the midst of his congregation. No, not a sea. A stagnant pond, a backwater. Wherein he has been drowning. He nods at each of his parishioners as he strolls up the aisle, eyeing them one by one in search of an understanding spirit (there is none), idly filling his pipe with sweet tobacco, tamping it with his finger. The poor ignorant hypocritical fools. He hates them—he would like to tear their silly bonnets off their heads, strangle them with their own gaudy ties—but he pities them, too, lost as they are in the wilderness of their hand-me-down banalities. Nor can he altogether condemn them, for all too recently has he been of their number.

Why seek ye the living among the dead? Tell them that nothing but eternal hell awaits them!

Shut up, he says to Jesus, I'm in enough trouble as it is, and a lady in a pink hat with flowers says, "I didn't say anything, Reverend Edwards! Are you all right? What trouble?" Not just to Jesus, then.

*Do* something! It is time to wake them from their sleep! It may be your last chance!

A collection plate reaches the aisle up which he walks, threading his way through the added folding chairs. He takes it up, stares into it a moment as though trying to decipher its contents, his pipe clamped between his teeth, then he heaves it across the church, coins and bills and pledges flying. "*Woe to you, hypocrites!*" he bellows, coached from within. "*You desolate whitewashed tombs full of dead men's bones! Woe!*"

That's my good man! Brilliant! Truly, I say unto you, there will not be left here one stone upon another…

"I tell you, there'll be no fellowship hall, no church either! *There will not be left here one stone on another that will not be thrown down!*" He gestures to indicate this wholesale destruction and strides, pleased with the exit he is making (but brick, he corrects himself, not stone), on out of the church and into the waters of chaos awaiting him outside.

Later, he finds himself walking in the downpour at the edge of town along a small gravel road, lined by soggy patches of hardscrabble farmland, a few scraggly sassafras, black locust, and mulberry trees drooping skeletally over the roadside ditch as though contemplating a final exasperated plunge, and, in the near distance, scrimmed by the sheets of rain, the strange combed disturbance of a strip mine, looking like a field harrowed by giants, black water pooling in its long deep furrows. He seems to have forgotten to return to the manse. Perhaps he dreads it. A site of much suffering. He is still clamping the pacifying stem of his pipe between his teeth, though its contents have long since been doused by the rain. His hat is gone, who knows where. Why is he out here? It is not Jesus Christ who asks this question; he asks it of himself. An unconscious return to his boyhood on the family farm? If so, he is being presented with a desperate parody of it—bleak, wasted, lifeless. These muddy yellow plots with their mean little shacks and their collapsing unpainted tin-roofed outbuildings bear no resemblance to his hardworking father's well-kept acres with their rich fields and orchards, red barns, bright white house and sheds, groomed lawn, well-oiled equipment and healthy flocks and herds, except to suggest the inevitable decay and death of all beauty. No, encouraged by his mother, who was not born to a farm, poor woman, Wesley left happily and took up his faith as career to his father's and grandparents' great disappointment, he being not only first-born but also only-born, and never looked back. If he feels nostalgia for anything it is for the comforting old certainties—as embodied in his father's sturdy hickory fences and the black family Bible with its notched carmined edges—to which, all too effortlessly, he has since clung.

No longer. Although his faith was always more an occupational convenience than a mission and tainted from early days by irony (he and Debra were both whimsically amused children of *The Golden Bough*, Eastertide in the early years of their marriage their most ardent season), he had felt at home in it. The routines of it filled his life quite amiably, its language playing on his tongue as easily as that of baseball or the weather—until that Ash Wednesday Rotary Club luncheon forty days ago when everything, with dreadful simplicity, changed. He was asked to give the usual benediction and, in the middle of a prayer he had routinely delivered hundreds of times, he was silenced by the sudden realization: My God! What am I saying? I don't believe any of this! He blinked, cleared his throat, bit his lip, apologized, finished as best he could, fearing with good reason that nothing would ever be the same again. For a month, he plunged into an introspective frenzy, scribbling out page after page of justification for his faith, his calling, his life, his very being (there *was* no justification), rereading all his old course notes and desultory diary entries, his infinitely tedious sermons and lectures, and poring through all the old books that had once meant so much to him, from Augustine and Abelard to Kierkegaard, Kant, Buber and Tillich, books he hadn't looked at in years, not since he moved to West Condon, realizing in his wretchedness that he had never understood any of them, nor would he ever, he wasn't smart enough, or good enough, the Mystery was forever denied him, he was nothing but a hapless dunce living an empty meaningless life. Only Kierkegaard's "sickness unto death" made sense to him. He lost his appetite, developed a sniffle, as much of self-pity as of a cold, suffered sleepless nights and so felt only half-awake by day. He wore the same clothes every day. He stopped taking his vitamins. He didn't want to think about such things. It was actually convenient that that manic orphan boy had returned to keep Debra entertained, he had no time for her or for anything else beyond his most unavoidable pastoral duties and the impassioned soul-searching that possessed him. Who *was* he? What did he really believe? He found he could not reject God entirely, the world seemed unimaginable without Him, but he no longer had the dimmest idea who or what God was or might be or might have been. God as a kingly father figure had vanished years ago along with Santa Claus and the Easter bunny, but his longheld notion that the universe was something like the Spirit expressing itself through matter, the resurrection story a kind of sublime mythology, now seemed vacuous and dishonest. It was too much for him, really. He'd never figure it out. He'd been a poor student, the Bible his only refuge, and now that refuge was denied him. When he tried to explain all this to Debra, she said God had simply found him unworthy. In short, He had turned His back on Wesley. Speaking anthropomorphically. But God owed him more than that, he felt. Wesley had after all, in his fashion, devoted his life to Him. When he'd prayed to Him, he'd always felt God was listening, they were having a kind of conversation. But it was too one-sided. It was time for God to speak to him. If God would only speak, he thought, all would be well. Was that too much to ask?

So on Passion Sunday, known also as Quiet Sunday, he made his appeal during the scripture reading and opening prayer ("*O God, do not keep silence; do not hold Thy peace or be still, O God! Wilt Thou restrain Thyself at these things, O Lord? Wilt Thou keep silent, and afflict us sorely?*") and then stood motionless throughout his notorious "Silent Sermon," head cocked toward the rafters, listening intently. Naturally, there was a lot of restlessness among the congregation. He raised one hand to shush them, cupped the other to his ear. A quarter of an hour passed. Nothing. He lowered his head. Not in prayer, as those in the pews probably thought, but in abject despair. He had no choice. It was not that he would forsake the pulpit; the pulpit was forsaking him. He attempted to express all this last week on Palm Sunday—a day for irrevocable decisions—in his sermon of the "Parable of the Holy Ass," in which, speaking as Jesus spoke ("Is he not a maker of parables?"), he told of all the neglected mules and donkeys of the Bible, from those of Absalom, Abigail, and Abraham to the mounts of Moses and Solomon, and then imagined for the somewhat amazed congregation the fate of the ass that Jesus rode into Jerusalem the Sunday before his execution, after the Prophet had dismounted and gone on to glory, no longer interested in the beast that had served him so humbly and so well. "Jesus rode me, but he rides me no more," he declared, speaking for the abandoned donkey, thus imitating the dumb ass that spoke with human voice and restrained the false prophet Balaam's madness—or, rather, parodying that ass, for here no restraint was at hand. What can one do with a rejected donkey, too clumsy and stupid to make its own way in the world? Rent it out as a circus animal perhaps, a caricature of itself. Come see the ass the Prophet rode, a creature for children to ride, adults to mock and abuse... As ever, he was misunderstood by his congregation. They called it his "funny donkey sermon," and few if any grasped in it his intention to abandon his calling. Or his dismissal by it. Most thought it might be some sort of Sunday School story for the children, as there were many in the audience, waving their little palm branches, and at least he said something, which was better than the nothing of the week before. The organist flashed him a look of wrenching sorrow, though it was hard to know what she meant by it. It was a look she wore as if born with it. At the door he was either avoided or complimented with the usual platitudes. Another failure. Debra was not there. She had left in the middle of the service, looking aggrieved.

Debra, too, has been changing over the years, but in a contrary direction, finding resolve and purpose—one might almost say character—in her intensifying commitment, not just to the Christian ethic (that's easy, they've shared this) but to the fundamental message, the spookier side of the hung-Christ story and its cataclysmic place in human history. Their bed was no longer a frivolous playground, it was a place of prayer. She was increasingly dissatisfied with him, accusing him of smugness and hypocrisy and of playing to privilege (she was right, all this was true), ridiculing his sermons and his pious banalities and his meaningless little pastoral routines, insisting on some transcendent vision alien and inaccessible to him. Back on the Sunday before Lent and that fateful Rotary Club meeting, as if to taunt her—she was totally obsessed by that crazy suicidal boy, Wesley wanted her attention—he used a frivolous golfing metaphor, suggesting that approaching Jesus was like approaching the green in a game of golf. One should "make straight paths for your feet" and strive to enter by the narrow gate that leads to life, but whatever else happens along the way from first tee to journey's end, he announced solemnly, it's all won on the approach shots. You can power your way recklessly down the fairway toward the ultimate goal, knowing that even if you get caught in the devil's sandtraps, slice sinfully into the rough, or hook into a waterhole, there's still time for redemption if you approach the green's blood-flagged tree at the end with the right irons and with sensible and measured swings. He'd hoped Debra would recall their myth-and-folklore days, green the symbolic color of the Risen Son as emanation of the Green God and all that, but though his parishioners loved it, grins on their faces at the church door afterwards, she was furious and she did a very strange thing. She dumped all his golf clubs out in the driveway and drove the car back and forth over them, the mad boy Colin cheering her on, both of them laughing hysterically.

Well. Those two. Wesley traces their marital problems back to the moment during the Brunist troubles when the Meredith boy spent a wildly distraught night at the manse and tried to kill himself. Cavanaugh and his so-called Common Sense Committee had persuaded Wesley to help them try to break up the cult by luring away its weakest members, and consequently he had participated (he is ashamed of this now) in the hotboxing of young Meredith, a vulnerable unstable boy, easy to confuse and persuade, but an unreliable convert. Colin, weeping, agreed to renounce the cult and moved that same night into the manse, under Wesley's protection. It was Debra who found him later, lying naked in the bathroom with his wrists slashed. He was rushed to hospital—Debra managed this, Wesley feeling about as stable as the boy at that moment and facing police and television interviews—and he was released a few days later to the same mental institution the brain-damaged coalminer Giovanni Bruno was later sent. Colin is an orphan. Someone had to sign the committal papers, and Wesley did. Enraging Debra. "We could care for him!" "Oh, Debra, he's very disturbed. He needs professional care." Cavanaugh's phrase. Debra never forgave him that. Nor for what happened after…

You don't want to talk about that.

I don't want to talk about that. Where have you been? I was rather hoping you'd left.

Just resting. Seventh day and all that.

What right do you have to rest? You've created nothing. A bellyache.

Jesus acknowledges this with his silence. A cranky vindictive silence. The turmoil within brings Wesley to a temporary halt at the edge of the road, clutching his stomach. The miserable farms are behind him, now nothing but the bizarre extraterrestrial landscape of inundated strip mines, reminders of this morning's ignominy. God is dead. And has left His Only Begotten buried in him like a gassy tumor. When did this happen? Thursday night, probably. Debra left him that night after offering to prepare for him what she bitingly called a last supper. "It's our anniversary," he said. "Oh, is it? Well, I'm sorry, dear Wesley. Shall I make you an omelet before I go?" "No. What thou doest," he said, quoting his own traditional Thursday sermon on the theme of the betrayal of Judas, one of those annual replays Debra finds so despicable, "do quickly." He wanted to break her neck, but instead accepted her chilling bye-bye kiss ("This is forever, Wesley…") on his forehead. After she'd left, he decided to commune with Jesus' body and blood, consuming the True Vine and Bread of Life, as was the evening's custom. He ate an entire loaf of sliced white bread, washing it down with a half gallon of jug wine, and when that was done, emptied the gin and bourbon bottles, too.

He woke up the next day before dawn on the bathroom floor where he'd fallen, suffering from a splitting headache, his sacred head as if disfigured and crowned with piercing thorn, as someone has said. "O blessèd Head so wounded, reviled and put to scorn…" Thus, deep in hell, he mocked himself. He even had (the passion of Wesley Edwards was complete) a pain in his side and his hands were numb; he worried he might be coming down with multiple sclerosis, though it was most likely due to sleeping all night on the floor. He seemed to remember a crashing tile, but maybe that was himself crashing *on* the tiles. Had he been throwing up? He had been throwing up. He was lying in the evidence. It was Good Friday. He had more services to face, hospital calls, who knows what all. What a season. It never stops. He stripped and crawled on all fours into the shower and scourged himself with stinging lashes of ice-cold water, which woke him up—but he was still desperately sick, and he threw up again, this time finding the great white throne, praise the Lord. Left a sour vinegary taste in his mouth. In the mirror, he saw a skull with some pale greenish skin stretched over it, eyes red like the devil's, its tongue out. He did not stay to study the ghastly apparition, but pulled on his bathrobe, the silky lavender one given him one bygone Christmas by Debra (how she longed for her own little manger event, oh yes, failure upon failure!), and staggered into the kitchen, hoping to find she'd come back and cleaned up his mess. No such luck. It was not a pretty sight, the walls decorated with the eggs he'd thrown at them, milk spilled and sour now, chairs and table overturned, though it was not so bad as the bathroom. He leaned into the sink and drank straight from the tap, consumed by thirst. There were puddles of pale wax here and there. He must have lit some candles. Might have burned the manse down around him. Might have meant to.

In the bedroom he found Debra's old wedding nightgown with the hand-embroidered scarlet hearts ripped to shreds. In grief? Rage? Horror? She's grown heavy, it no longer fits, so maybe just in humiliation. A more intimate grief. Or maybe he found it and tore it up himself. Everything else of hers was gone. All her clothes, shoes, hats, toiletries, personal papers, scarves and kerchiefs, adornments. Her red-rimmed reading glasses. Address book. Her sunflower alarm clock and her makeup mirror. Probably the stuff had been disappearing for weeks; he hadn't noticed. Empty dresser drawers hung open like jaws agape, her closet stripped out like a vacated jail cell, door mournfully ajar. Though he hadn't slept in it, the bed was unmade. A spectacle of hurried flight. No matter. Good riddance. Those who marry will only have worldly troubles; it would have been wiser not to have married in the first place. Which was something not thought so much as heard. It is better to live in a desert land than with a contentious and fretful woman. I know, I know. Wesley, like his mother, often held inner dialogues with himself, responding silently, more or less silently, to his parents, his grandmother, his professors, his coaches, his old girlfriends, Debra, people who challenged him in any way. But who was this? There was a man here in West Condon some years ago with whom he'd had the first serious conversations about religion since seminary. Justin Miller, the newspaperman. An atheist and romantic rationalist. A fundamentalist in his way, infuriatingly aggressive and blockheaded, but smart and well read. Debra liked to say in her damning faint-praise way that Wesley was more interesting when Miller was in town. Miller had departed about the same time the Brunists did, having launched that madness largely with his own perverse evangel and having thereby made himself unwelcome around here, and for some years after, Wesley had continued his conversations with the man in his head, worrying his way through all the arguments Justin had thrown at him. This was not a one-sided dialogue. Wesley often won the point, or convinced himself he did, but sometimes the Miller within was cleverer than he—or, more accurately, closer to a truth Wesley was reluctant to acknowledge. These inward exchanges had eventually faded away, Miller having been dead to him for some time except as an occasional television image from one international war zone or another, but now, during this Lenten crisis, he had arisen once more in Wesley's thoughts like unattended prophecy. Not so much the things Miller had said, but the things he himself had said in reply. A brief period of creative thinking, hinting at dramatic changes in his life, quietly snuffed out with the newsman's departure. On the floor, crumpled up, lay Debra's pithy farewell note: Dear Wesley. I'm leaving you. Love, Debra. Two of her seven last words were at least words of endearment. But used more as nails to the heart than as balm. Never mind. Forget her. Those who have wives should live…? As though they had none, Wesley said aloud, completing the thought. A text he'd never preached upon except in private to himself. So, was this Miller? No. He knew who it was.

He had a white-bread Jesus inside him.

The revelation was sudden and explosive. Almost as though the floor were heaving. Wesley flung off the robe and lurched to the bathroom, where he emptied out violently at both ends, adding to the mess in there and to his despair—a thorough purging, his quaking gut gushing out as did Judas' bowels. As he sat there, letting it rip like the tearing of a veil, he thought of this immediate ordeal, somewhat hopefully, as ridding himself of the invasive Godson, but in fact it was only the debris he expelled, as it were. The residue continued to speak above the eruptions. Hah, it declared. Let the temple be purified! A voice more distinct than ever, as if freed from the muffling crusts and dregs. Whereupon, Wesley, his belly relaxing at last, came to understand the communion service in a way he had not done before.

You let that bully push you around, Jesus Christ says now in the rain. You didn't stand up for me as you ought. You denied me.

No. Should've denied you maybe. Didn't. Only doubted. Your story's so full of holes.

Probably you were reading the wrong people.

Well, the Evangelists…

Like I say. Another generation, never met them. They made up stuff and couldn't get their story straight. And they may have had their reasons, but they changed everything. You can't trust them.

I know that. I wrote a paper on it.

You got a B. It wasn't very good.

How do you know what I got?

What? Am I not the Son of God?

Are you asking me or telling me?

You don't believe in me…

How can I not?

Wesley, all alone in the inhospitable world, is climbing a small rise, snapping his replies out around his bobbing pipe stem, gesticulating in the rain. Which shows no sign of letting up. There are legends of Indian burial mounds in the area. Maybe he's on one. Walking on pagan bones. Dem dry bones. Getting a bath today. He is surrounded by folds of raked land (one of those huge steam shovels, taller than the buildings of West Condon, sits idly in pooling water at the bottom of a giant furrow) and considers that the road he's on with its glossy black chips amid the gravel may be merely an access road for the strip mine. Going nowhere, like himself. He doesn't know why the mines look like that, though he supposes it's not unlike digging up potatoes with a harrow. Though coal doesn't grow in rows. Does it? He's been here for years and knows almost nothing about mining. No miners in his congregation. No owners either, who mostly live elsewhere, one big city or another. An engineer, once. Man who coached the church softball team, but whose main pastime was extended fishing and hunting trips up north. Wife sang in the choir. Had nice legs. Which she showed in a friendly way. He ignores Jesus' remark. He is an innocent man. This has often gone unappreciated. Maybe too innocent. Miller often railed at him on the subject, saying innocence was the main cause of the mess the world was in. Suffer me no little children. Did Miller say that or did Jesus? Jesus, he recalls, rather liked little children. Some say too much. Not Wesley's problem. On the contrary.

From the top of the hump, he can see, some distance off, perched on the side of a hill and silhouetted against the drizzly sky, one of those intricate mine structures for tipping and emptying coal cars. Or were they for loading them? What does he know? It does not look like a cross. It looks more like a crazy assemblage from a child's toybox, but it has the stark lonely aspect of one, and it adds to his melancholy. Must be Deepwater No. 9. He saw it up close only once. The day after the accident. Ninety-eight men dead or buried. Most catastrophic thing to happen to the little town since the early days of the union battles. About which he also knows nothing. He and Debra went out there because it seemed the Christian thing to do. Offer consolation and so on. He felt completely out of place. He knew none of those people and didn't know how to talk to them. They brushed him aside like the clumsy ineffectual intruder he was. The best he could do was commiserate with other ministers he recognized and offer his church facilities, though for what he couldn't imagine. He was grateful to see Justin Miller out there, covering the story for his newspaper. He ached for a connection that would make him feel less an outsider. But Miller was tired and ill-humored and belittled him, calling him, in effect, a complacent ill-informed hypocrite. Which he was. What could he say? He went home, didn't return, though Debra stayed on to serve doughnuts and coffee in the Red Cross canteen. People are suffering, she said when she came home. And we've lost touch with them. His response was a Sunday sermon on the spiritual origin of physical matter: i.e., that the carbon in the coal is not from the soil but from the air. Buried sunlight. He'd discovered this in the set of encyclopedias kept in his church office, frequent source of sermon inspiration. Didn't know why he hadn't looked up "coal" before. It was created, he'd learned, in the carboniferous age when the Earth was seething hot and the air was saturated with the fine dust of carbon atoms, a time when there were dense forests, trees a hundred feet tall, and forty-foot ferns, bats with wingspreads twenty feet, dragonflies as big as vultures (the grandeur fascinated him and he took notes for other sermons)—"And then: the Earth shrank, the crust wrinkled, forests sank into shallow seas, tons of boiling mud buried millions of green trees in the Earth's hot maw, mountains pitched upwards, vomiting floods of lava, earthquakes split mountaintops into jagged peaks, seas bubbled—ah! we live, my friends, in a quiet time: 8,500,000 furious years were needed to press out that one bed of coal out there, which we hack out, bring up, burn in minutes—we live, yes, in a quiet time, but at incredible speed..." Debra called his sermon frivolous, an insult to the dead and bereaved (she said that someone, who was either scandalized or laughing, told her they thought he'd said "in the Earth's hot ma"), and went straight back out to the mine, arriving just as they were bringing up that fellow Bruno, the lone survivor. It's a miracle, she said when she got back. She was clearly moved.

If that is the Deepwater mine, then he's not all that far from the old Presbyterian No-Name Wilderness Church Camp. You could see that same mine structure from Inspiration Point. The Presbyterian kids at camp called it the Gate of Hell and threatened to take the little ones over there and drop them down the bottomless pit. "You just keep falling forever and ever and you can't see anything even with your eyes wide open!" And that hill must be the one where the Brunists gathered to await the end of the world. Another kind of blind forevering. How did he find his way here? To this hump, this vista, this convergence? He reconsiders his abandoned Presbyterian belief in predestination, for he seems to be doing what he has to do, even though he does not know he is doing it. That hill, he knows, is John P. Suggs' next target. He should warn Cavanaugh, but he owes the man no favors. When Suggs approached him back in the early fall with a fair offer on the old abandoned camp, Wesley was interested. Church camps no longer had much appeal among his Presbyterians and it would require a major investment to make it operational again, even as a rental. Except for the occasional church picnic and the annual sunrise service, it had fallen into complete dilapidation. Debra, having a romantic attachment to the place, objected. She had loved it out there, had often spent days at the camp on her own, cleaning it up, making small repairs. Wesley had felt more comfortable in town, hated the flies and mosquitoes, the dark, the straw ticking and old dust, the privies and communal latrines and showers, the constant worry about snakes and ticks, the burrs, thorns and nettles, the lack of books, poor light, bad food; but the rough life excited Debra. She confessed once that she felt like she was naked all the time out there, or wanted to be. She still had fading hopes the camp could be restored in the way that she still had fading hopes they might have a child. She hated strip mining and said it was his moral duty to protect the camp from such a brutal sacrilege. Then suddenly she changed her mind and urged him to complete the sale. They could use the revenue for her halfway house for troubled teenagers, she said. Her pet project. Her abrupt turnaround was a surprise, but suited him. The sale was approved by the synod, and in early February the papers were signed, turning the land over to the coal baron. Whereupon Colin

Meredith turned up with his strange beatific smile and goggle eyes and the conspiratorial whispering between them began.

You were deceived.

It was not something I wanted to think about. I deceived myself.

So what's going on out there now?

I don't know.

You have some idea.

I have some idea. A kind of evangelical commune.

You know what I mean.

She loves that camp. Always has. She's a good camp mom.

Especially for that boy.

He's an orphan. She's the mother he never had.

As he's the child she never had.

Well…

You are filled with remorse about that. And you're jealous.

Nonsense.

Those sexy Easter egg hunts, for example. With the boy around, no time for that. Made you angry.

Not angry. Just…disappointed.

Wesley feels wobbly through the middle. Is Jesus laughing? He's probably imagining all those eggs splattered against the kitchen walls. Easter hilarity. The expulsion of unclean spirits was one of Jesus' best tricks. Wesley needs a similar sort of exorcist to rid himself of the in-dwelling Christ, buried within him for three days now with no sign of rising. Anyway, it's not just that stupid boy. The decline of the egg game has been going on for some time. Though Debra has continued to hide Easter eggs for him each year till this, she had already stopped—well before that end-of-the-world carnival over there—hiding the last one between her thighs. Hiding and revealing. The World-Egg, she used to call it. As was their youthful fancy, her wishful thinking. He didn't object to her withdrawal. It was becoming all too testing anyway. Over the years, she had become less warm to him, more impatient, was adding a chin, her eggnest thighs were spreading, the enticing little gap in there had closed. The bloom, as they say, was off the rose.

The bizarre events of that Sunday gathering of the cult on the mine hill five years ago happened without him. He did not go out there and did not watch the coverage, retreating to his office in the church. He had a sermon to deliver, even if to a half-empty auditorium. No doubt another pretty piece of his trademark nonsense. Maybe he looked up "delusions" in the church encyclopedia. The Brunists embarrassed him. He felt exposed by them, as if his faith were being mocked by their nutty extremism. Miller in fact made a comment to him much to that effect. Debra was irritable with him—she still hadn't forgiven him for the Colin Meredith episode a few days earlier, would never—and stayed glued to the television after the service, finally going on out to help care for the injured. Fulfilling her Christian duty, as he thought of it at the time, though in truth, the rift between them was opening; she was finding a cause and he was not it. She visited Colin in the mental hospital every week or two thereafter, close to a hundred-mile drive each way, exchanged letters with him between visits, his being mostly protestations of his sanity and complaints about his treatment, sent him packets of food and clothing. Finally, after a year or so, she secured his release and brought him back to the manse, making it clear there was nothing Wesley could do about it. She openly mothered the boy, cuddling him in her soft bosom when he cried or got hysterical, feeding him when he seemed not to want to eat, washing his clothes and buying him new ones, reading to him from the Bible and saying his bedtime prayers with him, all of which Wesley indulged with Christian forbearance while expecting worse to come. Inevitably, it did, and it was back to the mental hospital for Colin. Debra tried to shield the boy, but Wesley had seen all and said no. The hospital visits resumed—"They're torturing him up there," Debra protested tearfully—but when Colin was released once more, Wesley put his foot down. In front of the front door. Debra was furious, screaming at him that he was worse than the Antichrist. Colin assumed his familiar pose of the sorrowful martyr and promptly vanished. Debra blamed Wesley for a catalog of imagined horrors, though, as it turned out, Colin had simply hitchhiked to California where some of his fellow cultists had settled. The letters resumed.

If Wesley's own fate has brought him here today like a severed head on a platter, whither now is it taking him? This dirt road may lead to the camp. Is he meant to follow it? To what end? Does he want her back? He does not. She took the car when she went. Does he want *it* back? It would be useful right now, it's a long walk back, but wet's wet, it hardly matters. But how is he going to fulfill his pastoral duties without it? He is not going to fulfill them, with it or not.

How will you get food and drink?

If I get hungry, I'll order out pizza.

And if they come to get you as they came for me?

Ah...good question...

Remember the old rule of the prophet, my son. When they persecute you in one town, flee to the next.

He pauses. He is standing in the middle of the road, worn away to hard greasy clay here at the crest of the little hump, staring out through the downpour on the vast barren desolation and the fateful mine hill beyond, and he feels a momentary horror in his heart. But also a thrill, and something like illumination. Am I a prophet then?

Have I not said? Why do you not understand what I say? I have appointed you! You only have I chosen!

A prophet. That is to say, a truth teller. His life, yes, is beginning to make sense. He has always felt some special mission awaited him. "You will do great things, Wesley," his mother often said. He has come here to this hillock in the rain to receive the news. He understands better now the nature of his recent crisis, his forty days in the wilderness of his own confused and troubled thoughts. They are still rather confused and troubled, but the pattern gradually being revealed is heartening. If he didn't invent it all himself. How could he have? He's not smart enough. But he is getting smarter. A kind of wisdom is descending on him. He has a purpose now; his self-confidence is returning. He's not sure what he'll have to say, but he is certain it will be important.

Let not your heart be troubled, my son. What to say will be given to you. I will be your mouth and teach you. I will give you words that no one can withstand! I will make my words in your mouth a fire! He knew this would be the Christ's reply. Such thoughts have been on his mind since this dialogue began. Not consciously, but underneath. That he might be being used by some power beyond him. Even if it does not exist. If that makes sense. The pride in that. But also the fear of losing control over his own thoughts. Prophets do not merely tell the truth, they are possessed *by* the truth. He has used all these lines in sermons and they have come back to haunt him. Or, as Jesus would say, perhaps is saying, they have come back to recreate him. Is he ready for this? He is still hopeful, but the sudden surge of self-confidence is draining away. He is cold and wet and tired. He had not realized how tired he was. He wants to return to the manse. Perhaps he can figure things out tomorrow. He can read Kierkegaard again.

No, says Jesus, listen to me. Forget the past. I declare new things. The old has passed away, the new has come. Let us proceed.

He glances back over his shoulder as if to survey that which has passed away and sees the banker's tall, lanky son a few hundred yards down the road, standing under an umbrella on a small plank bridge over the ditch.

They're after you. You should have paid heed to that line from Psalms: Muzzle your mouth before the wicked.

I know. But I don't seem able completely to control myself.

Even as he says this, or thinks it, he is charging down the hill straight at the boy, glaring fiercely. The boy staggers back a step, looks around as though pretending to be sightseeing or searching for some place to hide. "Crazy weather, eh, Reverend Edwards?" Tommy says awkwardly as Wesley storms up. "In arrogance the wicked hotly pursue the poor!" Wesley shouts in righteous fury, removing at last the pipestem from his mouth and pointing it at the boy. "Let them be caught in the schemes which they themselves have devised!" The boy looks somewhat aghast. "Really? I-I don't know what you mean, Reverend Edwards." The minister lowers his voice. "You are a wicked, boy, Tommy Cavanaugh. Beware. The wicked will not go unpunished. It's God's law." And he turns abruptly on his heel and strides back down the gravel road through the worsening storm toward town. Tomorrow will begin tomorrow. For now he needs a hot bath.

Wesley had left the manse in a state of egg-spattered squalor following upon three days of serious neglect and abuse, and it is that sad state which greets him when he returns, there being no magic in the world, though by leaving the lights off (nobody home) he is able to dismiss the worst of it to shadow. "Let there be dark!" he says. More than three days of neglect. Debra traditionally does her spring housecleaning the first half of Easter week, but this year those energies were devoted to getting the Brunists moved in. Likewise, all their supplies; he'd seen her empty out the cupboards under the sink and bundle the stuff to the car. So, that's right, he couldn't really clean the place up properly if he wanted to. Good, forget it. The prophet's drear unkempt hovel. Which he has entirely to himself now. There's a certain melancholy in this, and a certain elation. He runs himself a hot bath, strips off his wet garments and throws them on the pile of other wet garments, and—"I stand naked before the Lord!" he declares to the silent house, and Jesus replies good-naturedly (they are coming to an understanding): Nakedness will not separate you from the love of Christ, my son!—settles his cold shivering body (now, as it were, the humble abode of the Master) into the hot water for a long healing soak and a solemn meditation on the nature of his new vocation.

While walking home through the deluged town (the drains are clogged, the potholed streets are like running rivers, the desolate little town is in deep decay; no one cares), Jesus brought him the new evangel: the end has already happened. It was something Wesley already knew, has always known, and yet, walking through the cold rain down deserted streets in a numbed body, it was a revelation. He was thinking about the Brunists and their apocalyptic visions to which his wife has been drawn, and Jesus said: They are prophets of the past. That's old news. The world has already ended. In fact, it ended when it began. This is not merely a post-Christian or post-historical world, as some of those people you've been reading say, it is a post-world world. We are born into our deaths, my son, which have already happened. I am the first and the last, he said, acknowledging John the Seer who he said was blind as a bat, the beginning and the end, and so are you. We are not, but only think we are. Our actions are nothing more than the mechanical rituals of the mindless dead. This is the truth. Go forth and prophesy.

A prophet, Wesley knows (he has preached on this), does not see into the future, he simply sees the inner truth of the eternal present more clearly than others. He understands what Jesus is saying. He knows that he was born into death. Sure. This makes sense. Someone he read back in college said as much. All beginnings contain their own endings and are contained by them. It is his calling now to bring this truth to the world, or at least to this place on earth where he has been found, and to reveal all the hypocrisy and injustice and corruption and expose the madness of sectarian conflict which has no foundation. To what end such endeavor? There are no further ends; the question is irrelevant. Ignorance is sin and this town is full of it, for every man is stupid and without knowledge, as Jesus has reminded him. That's all one needs to know. Thus, his feelings of failure and unworthiness are being transcended by a new sense of mission. His life, thought wasted, is acquiring meaning. Direction. Procrastination, the cause until now of much regret, can be seen in retrospect as a patient waiting for the spirit to descend. He would perhaps prefer to continue his ministry as of old (it ensures the comfort of hot baths, for example), but it's too late for that. Actions have been taken, in particular his own, and, like Adam before him (Adam did not eat the apple, the apple ate him), he has to live with their consequences. If one can speak of consequences in a world that has already ended. He is somewhat overwhelmed by all this heady speculation and fearful that he might be inadequate to the charge laid upon him—he was only a B student, after all. But at the same time he feels he has indeed been chosen, if not by Jesus, then by his genes, and he knows that, either way, there is nothing he can do about it. Thus, he's a Presbyterian after all.

He also understands that he who has taken up residence within is not so much the Risen Christ, about whom there are still doubts, as the suffering Jesus who was betrayed and forsaken. He too has suffered and has been betrayed and forsaken. They share this. Which explains in part why Jesus has chosen him. I have chosen you out of the world, he said. I can see you are a prophet, for you bear the wounds of one.

With the Lord, Jesus says now, a thousand years are sometimes as one day, and sometimes a day is as a thousand years. This day has been more like the latter. One wonders if it will ever end.

I have often wondered the same each year on this day. Even now I should be doing baptisms, christenings, evening services, who knows what all. All in celebration of your rising.

What's there to celebrate?

Did you not arise from the dead?

No, Jesus says with what might be a sigh (it causes bubbles in the bath water). My time has not yet come. Is it not evident? What would I be doing lodged in here if it had? It has been one insufferable tomb after another.

Then it has all been a lie! A fabrication!

No, no, my son. Remember your *Golden Bough*. Truth is not fact. Don't confuse myth and history.

But the Bible says—

Wishful thinking. Mine, everybody's. You know better than to trust that book. I'm still waiting. Though I have no expectations. Perhaps waiting is the wrong word.

But they saw you! They said so!

Did they? People will say anything to draw a crowd.

"No, they didn't see me, Wesley. I promise. I was careful." It is not Jesus Christ who has said this. It is Priscilla Tindle standing in his bathroom door. Drenched, her wet hair in her eyes. "I have been so worried about you. I came here right after church but you weren't here."

"But how did you get in? I thought the door was locked."

"It was. I came in the back door. The garden gate was bolted, but it's easy to scale. Are you all right? Somebody has thrown eggs all over your kitchen wall."

"I know. I did. I was trying…to understand something…"

"I didn't mean to intrude, Wesley. But I had to warn you. I heard Ralph talking with Ted Cavanaugh. They're going to send you to a mental hospital. They plan to ask Debra to sign the committal papers. They're also recruiting the entire Board of Deacons as backup witnesses. That's why they talked to Ralph about it."

This is not a surprise. He and Jesus have surmised the same. Even now, Jesus is saying: Have I not so prophesied? All the same, it is an alarming prospect. He remembers Debra's tales of poor Colin. Electric shock treatments: What do they do to you? And what if that's not all? Is her signature enough to authorize a lobotomy? They will destroy his creativity and thwart his mission. How can he prophesy from inside a mental institution? Who will take him seriously? "Tell me. Do you think I'm crazy?"

"No, Wesley. You're different. But I believe in you. You're the most sane man I know."

"Who do you say," he asks speculatively, "that I am?"

"You are a saint, Wesley. A noble and kind and wonderful man. A teacher. When I came to you for help, you told me about the megalopsychoi. The great-souled ones. You are one of those." She is standing in the room now and removing her wet clothes. Jesus is remarking on her lithe, interesting body. She and her husband Ralph were both once dancers and she is still in good shape. When she came to him for religious counseling (she confessed: "I don't think my husband is completely a man…"), it somehow got a little too personal. Perhaps because he had tried to explain to her, in his best pastoral manner, the nature of the male erection. He remembers standing in his office in the middle of this well-intended disquisition, gazing meditatively out the window onto the church parking lot where some boys were playing kick-the-can, with his pipe in his mouth and his pants around his ankles, Priscilla passionately hugging his bottom, his penis in her mouth, and though he wasn't sure just how it had got in there, by that time it didn't make much sense to take it out again. The affair, though brief, was sinful and it pained him, but it was also hugely satisfying and was a deeply loving relationship. She really understood him in a way that no woman had before. I know what you mean, Jesus says. "I'm ready to do anything for you," Prissy whispers, peeling down her leotards. Jesus makes an Eastertide remark about hot cross buns that is not entirely in character. "I adore you, Wesley."

She steps into the tub and kneels between his feet and commences to wash them, one at a time. And then she lifts them and kisses them. "You are so beautiful," she says. "You are the most beautiful man I have ever known." When she says this, she is gazing affectionately past his feet at his middle parts, which are beginning to stir as though in enactment of the day's legend. It is not hard to prophesy what will happen next. Is he being tested? Be anxious for nothing, Jesus says. As it is written, no temptation has overtaken you that is not common to man. She has a car, she can be helpful to us. I, too, have known the company of helpful women of dubious morals. So, accept her gift with a willing heart, do not disparage it, for every good and perfect gift is, as they say, from above. Remember, as it is written in the scriptures, she who receives a prophet as a prophet should receive a prophet's reward.

# I.3

## Easter Sunday 29 March

The sumptuous baked-ham Easter feast at the International Brunist Headquarters and Wilderness Camp Meeting Ground has long since been consumed, but the rain, which has done what it could to spoil their morning, is still thundering down in the afternoon. There was talk at the meal about carrying on with the electrical work in spite of the rain and even though it was the Sabbath and the Easter Sabbath at that (but working for the camp is not working, as Ben Wosznik always says, it is a kind of devotion), and now the two recently arrived ex-coalminers from West Virginia, Hovis and Uriah, waking up in their camper from their afternoon snooze, are trying to remember whether Wayne Shawcross said that if the rain stops they will start working again, or if he said that they will start working again even if the rain doesn't stop. Certainly they still have a lot to do before tomorrow night's big ceremony and maybe Wayne is waiting for them. Wayne is a good man and they do not want to let him down. "I'll go ask him," Uriah says, and he leaves the camper. After he is gone, Hovis notices that Uriah left without his raggedy old rain slicker, so he takes it off the hook and goes looking for him. He finds him standing in the mud and rain, all alone, up by the darkened Meeting Hall, but when Uriah, surprised by his arrival, asks him what he's doing here, Hovis, with a puzzled glance over his shoulder, says he doesn't know. Uriah, peering at him through the curtain of cascading rain, admits he doesn't remember why he's here either. "I'm lookin' for somebody, I reckon," he says, peering about, "but they must of left. That my slicker?" "Yep. That's right, Uriah. I brung it to you. It's rainin'." "But where's yourn?" "Shoot. I must of forgot it." "Then you better wear mine." "No, you're older'n me, you git it on." "But your rheumatiz is worse'n mine, Hovis, you wear it." They argue about that, passing the slicker back and forth in the rain, until Uriah pulls out his gold pocket watch and gazes at it quizzically and says: "I recollect now. We was agoin' to see Willie Hall." "We was?" "Yup. Come along now. And put this old slicker on, Hovis, afore you catch your death."

The man they seek has just left the bedroom at the back of the Halls' mobile home and stepped forward into the lounge and kitchenette area, his suspenders hanging loosely from his belt loops, to announce to the ladies gathered around his wife in there: "And it come to pass meantimes, that the Heavens they was black with clouds'n wind, and they was a awful great rain! *First Kings 18!*" Then he returns to the bedroom. The women acknowledge this intrusion without remark, for they are well accustomed to Willie Hall's quirks and talents. The little fellow knows only one book, but he knows it well, as well as anyone, and, as it is God's book, they all agree he needs no other, nor for that matter do they. He also reminds them in his way that, although the things that happen in the Bible happened a long time ago, they are also, being eternal things, like those contained in Mabel's cards, happening right now.

It is Sunday and Mabel Hall does not, by a rule admittedly often broken, read the cards on Sundays. But yesterday, the day of the Harrowing of Hell—when the Lord, gone underground, is not among them—she did so, using the simple five-card spread she prefers when considering less personal questions. Yesterday's was, "What will happen three weeks from now on April 19th, the fifth anniversary of the

Day of Redemption?" And there was much there on her card table to feel cheerful about—the upright Sun appeared right off, smack dab in the middle, proud as punch, and the happy communal Ten of Cups showed up last as the wild card of the far future, boding well for their growing church—but there was also, inevitably, a hovering darkness (visible in this case in the figure of the Knight of Wands standing on his head), because, as Mabel often remarks in her quiet little girl's voice, the future, however rosy, always casts a dark shadow, that darkness into which all must descend, even if, hopefully, to ascend thereafter into glory.

A shadowed joy is how one might describe all the long month they've been here. When they first arrived—just six couples and their children in house trailers and caravans and the two office boys in their car—there was snow on the ground and the trees were black with ice and there was nothing here but utter ruin and desolation. The old summer camp cabins full of rot and excrement and vermin and broken glass, a main lodge with its roof half caved in, its old generator wrecked, no phone or proper toilet facilities, thick dead overgrowth and mounds of frozen rubbish everywhere. There was well water on the premises, but the pump handles were broken, and the cisterns and creek were frozen up; until they could get the pumps working, water had to be brought in in gallon jugs and old milk cans or melted from snow and ice. The abandoned camp had apparently been used for drinking parties, judging by the litter, and there were obscenities and blasphemies scrawled on the lodge and cabin walls and there were rotting mattresses on the floors and all the windows were busted out, even the screens. Its sorry state did not dismay them; they just set to work making a home for themselves in the wilderness. For, if anyone asks you to go one mile, as Jesus said, go two. They have done so. They had no end of volunteers wanting to come stand with them and help them build their new world center, but they feared drawing attention to themselves in a place where Satan's power is strong and people, so cruel to them in the past, hate them much as Jesus was hated. For sinners, the truth is a dreadful thing, as Clara has often said, and they will attempt to crush it by any means at hand. With Mr. Suggs' offer of extra workers, they have been able to keep their core group small and secretive and, except for the two Bible college boys managing the church office, limited to skilled construction workers with their own campers or mobile homes, for as it's said, with the help of God, few are many. Ever since they pulled in, they have been working from before dawn to after dark, working so hard it has sometimes been hard to stop and recollect what it all means that they are doing this. It was like something had got hold of them and wouldn't let go, and they supposed it must have been like that for the early settlers when they first came through.

They were met here at the camp on their Leap Day arrival by the West Condon Presbyterian minister's wife, Mrs. Edwards, who, working quietly with Mr. Suggs, had made it possible for them to acquire the campgrounds in the first place, bless her soul. She was not alone that night. It was the eve of the fifth anniversary of the Night of the Sign, the night that their Prophet set everything in motion—exactly seven weeks after his miraculous rescue from the mine disaster, seven before he led them up the Mount of Redemption; Willie has often recited Bible passages to let them know why this was so and how thereby it was prophesied in God's word—so it was like a sign from Heaven that Mrs. Edwards, her conversion itself a sign from Heaven, had in her company young First Follower Colin Meredith. He was, like Mabel and Willie, Clara and her daughter Elaine, one of the twelve witnesses of that fateful night (the Sign was a death, it was very sudden and very frightening and made Mabel's knees shake, nothing in her cards had ever alarmed her so), a boy unseen since his brutal kidnapping the week before the Day of Redemption and rumored to have been tortured and killed. Mrs. Edwards and the boy, holding up a gas lantern, were waiting for them at the front door of the old wrecked lodge with a hot cooked supper in a picnic basket, a trunkload of groceries, extra dishware and utensils, spare flashlights, linens and blankets, cleaning supplies, aspirin and cold tablets, and even a fresh-baked cherry pie. They looked like angels there under that lantern in that dark place.

The little advance guard of Brunists had been traveling all day and they were cold and tired and a trifle dismayed by the camp's state of ruin as they entered it, but the affectionate welcome warmed their hearts and turned gloom to festivity. Willie loudly recited verses from the Moses story about getting fed manna in the wilderness, and Clara hugged the woman and the boy and found herself near to tears because everything she'd dreamt of was coming true and her gratitude was overflowing. Mrs. Edwards showed them where to park their motorhomes down on the old baseball playing field and they all feasted together in great joy.

All this they have been explaining to Bernice Filbert, visiting from town, who has inquired about the presence among them of the rich folks' preacher's wife and the boy. "I know them Pressyb'terians is a biggity lot," says Ludie Belle Shawcross, still wearing her stained apron from preparing and serving the Easter dinner, "but that lady she works like a slavey and she's all heart. The boy he is a orphant and she has took him in like her own youngun. He calls her his mama, first he ever had."

Bernice nods but she does not seem satisfied. She is dressed, as she usually is, like a lady from the Bible. Because today is Easter, she has told them, she is wearing the same clothes that the Other Mary wore on the day the stone got rolled away and she witnessed the Miracle of the Empty Tomb. It is a simple sepia wrap with a hair clip pinning up one shoulder, a brown sash at the waist and a headscarf to match. Bernice has left her muddy galoshes and medical bag by the door, not part of her Other Mary getup. Her painted-on eyebrows are arched like she's just had a big surprise, like the surprise the Other Mary must have got when she stuck her nose in. "I was wondering if something was ailing the boy," Bernice says. "He seems all skittery, like as he might have some mental virus."

"He is strange," Mabel says softly, her fingers twitching faintly as if laying out cards, "but he is a chosen one."

"Chosen?"

"He knows things."

"His thin little hands is near as smooth as unwrote-on paper and a mortal task to cipher," says Hazel Dunlevy, the wife of the carpenter

Travers Dunlevy. Hazel is a palm reader, small and pretty with a drowsy way of speaking. She always seems to be just waking up. The driver's seat of the Halls' caravan and the seat beside it swivel to serve as extra chairs in the tiny sitting area, and she and Glenda Oakes are perched up there, their backs to the streaming windshield, Glenda's gold tooth gleaming in the shadow of her face. "They ain't a line on neither palm that's whole nor straight, just little choppy wiggly bits you cain't almost see, crisscrossing into each other like ghostly stitchery," Hazel says with a soft yawn. "The pore thing is purty ghostly hisself and don't seem hopeful to live long."

Bernice nods again, more satisfied. Her being among them is an exception to the rule about outsiders, as they have mostly avoided their friends from hereabouts so as not to give out too loud that they are here, but one day one of the little Dunlevy boys stepped on a rusty nail and needed a tetanus shot and when Hazel told Clara, she said: "Ask Ben to go find Bernice." Bernice is a practical nurse who works part-time at the hospital when she's not caring for sick folks at their houses. Like so many of their friends, like Clara herself, she is a woman widowed by the Deepwater mine disaster, and for a short time she was a Brunist and maybe still is, though it's hard to tell. She is what Mabel calls a trifle enigmatic. She gave the little boy his lockjaw shot, washed the nail puncture, painted it with mercurochrome, and dabbed it with her miracle water, and though you could hear him yowling all the way to the other side of the Appalachias while she was doing that, he was soon up and running around as if hunting out more nails to step on. Bernice comes out to the camp regularly now to treat cuts and bruises and the common fevers of the little ones, and to bring them gossip from town, which likely travels both ways. They try to be cautious in what they say but probably they are not. Bernice still goes to their old Nazarene church Bible readings, dressed usually for the reading of the day, and so almost certainly their secret is out. She also works as a home care nurse and at present is attending the critically ill wife of the town banker, whom all remember as the evil one who was the powerful cause of so many of their troubles. Bernice says Mr. Cavanaugh is truly a mean bully as wicked as Holofernes, but Mrs. Cavanaugh is an abused and pathetic creature with an aptitude for true religion, and they should pray for her.

The heavy rain, which washed out their sunrise service up on Inspiration Point, is still rattling steadily on the roof of the caravan when there's suddenly a loud knock on the door, as if it were the bridegroom knocking, which makes everyone jump, and when Mabel opens the door, there standing in the downpour are those two elderly ex-coalminers who drove in from West Virginia a few days ago in their camper. For some reason, one of them is carrying a raincoat instead of wearing it. Mabel invites them in, but the one with the raincoat says, "No, ma'am. We're jest soppin', we'd puddle up your place. We only come a-lookin' for Willie." "Tell him we're here," the other one says. "He's anticipatin' us." Mabel pads in her house slippers to the rear of the caravan, then pads back. "He must of forgot. He's dead asleep." The two old fellows look perplexedly at Mabel, at each other, at the sky, at her. One of them consults his fob watch, nods, thanks her, and they trudge off into the storm.

Those two old miners asked to be baptized by light this morning in the Brunist way, their church's most beautiful and particular ceremony. Wanda's man Hunk Rumpel had built a roaring fire in the great stone fireplace to stand against the damp morning chill and, though thunder cracked and rain pummeled the new roof high overhead and lashed the windows, there was much rejoicing as they prayed and sang together, snug and safe from the storm—from all storms—for they were met together to undertake a grand enterprise, a blessed enterprise, and the success of that undertaking could be seen all around them. It was Clara Collins-Wosznik herself, their Evangelical Leader and Organizer, who conducted the baptism with her martyred husband's mining lamp, using the occasion to recall the white bird that appeared to Jesus at the moment of his own baptism, and the white bird that came to her dying husband Ely in the mine to inspire his last words, the founding document of their young church, now hanging on the chimney wall, and also the white bird witnessed by all the early Brunist Followers on the Night of the Sacrifice, perched on a telephone cable over the ditch where the poor saintly girl lay dying, now the subject of a famous painting. Clara reminded everyone there in the lamplit morning dark of their late Prophet's commands to "Baptize with light!" and of Paul's admonition: "For ye were sometimes darkness, but now are ye light in the Lord: walk as children of light." "For the children of light," she declared in her clear strong voice, honed over the past half decade of missionary travels, "they *won't* have to *die!*" *"Praise be to Lord Jesus!"* the others shouted back and the thunder rattled the windowpanes. "This is the Easter message, it is Christ Jesus' message, it is Giovanni Bruno's message, it is Ely Collins' message, and it is *our* message! Give thanks to our Father, who has brung us together here *into* the wilderness, *outa* the wilderness—has brung us *home!*" And then her second husband, Ben Wosznik, stood up, his guitar strapped over his shoulder, to sing his glorious new Easter song, "When Christ Rose Up Death Died." *"And when the tomb was opened/Lord, it cannot be denied/There poured out the purest light/When Christ rose up, death died!"* Their hearts were wrenched with the beauty of it.

Now into their midst once more comes Mabel's husband Willie, suspenders dangling as before, shirttails out, his eyes swollen with sleep. He clears his throat and, scratching his narrow chest, declares, "And the Lord God a hosts is him what touches the land, and the land it'll melt'n rise up like as a flood! *Lord Jesus!* It's him what calls for the waters a the sea, and pours 'em out 'pon the face a the earth: The Lord is his name, ay-men! *Amos 9:5-6!*" When he is done, Mabel tells him that the two fellows from out east were here looking for him, and he nods and returns to the back, drawing up his suspenders. "Oh dear. Maybe I shouldn't of told him. Now he's gonna go out there in that rain."

"He'll be all right," Ludie Belle says. "It's easin' up."

Glenda and Hazel glance over their shoulders through the wet windshield and see that the rain has stopped and the men have come out in their heavy boots and are inspecting the channels they've dug for the underground wiring, tracking them through the mud up toward the Meeting Hall. The plumber Welford Oakes turns and sees his wife Glenda staring at him through the caravan's front window with her good eye, her glass eye catching the hazy light from the brightening sky, and he grins and blows her a kiss and she turns away. Hazel Dunlevy, sitting beside her, shrugs and waves at her husband Travers when he turns around, and then the two men continue on up through the dripping trees along with Ben Wosznik and Wayne Shawcross to see what the storm has done.

"I got tangled up with the pillow and waked up this morning from a nightmare in which Wayne here was a-tryin' to rip my head off," Welford says. "I made the mistake a sayin' so when Glenda asked what I was yellin' about, and she said that only means I got a way a dodgin' the truth and I act afore I think, and I said well, maybe, but it hurt more'n that."

"Your Glenda got Hazel in a tizz," Travers says, "by tellin' her that a dream about gettin' to Heaven and flyin' around with the angels was really about her knowin' down deep she ain't never gonna get there, and then she told her some scary stuff about them angels which Hazel won't even tell me about. Dang near ruint her. She ain't been able to sleep good ever since."

"My lady can be a trial and a terror," Welford says. "Basically, she don't believe in happy dreams, it's bad news whatever, somethin' her ole lady laid on her early. So I've learnt to shut up 'ceptin' when I forget."

They find that some of the trenches they'd dug for the underground wiring but had not yet sealed up are running with water, like canals seen from the sky, and the uncovered lantern bowls have pooled up, but, though the ground is soft and soggy, all the lamp posts seem to be standing true and nothing has shifted. Welford asks after Hovis and Uriah, and Wayne says he sent the old boys over to his house trailer for hot showers. "They wandered out into the rain and got lost somehow. Their rags was stuck to 'em like another skin. But it seems to've let up. Figger we can sweep out the trenches and carry on?"

"Whatever you say, Wayne. Sure as heck don't wanta get my head tore off."

The camp's new system of streetlamps is Wayne's pet project. He has installed circuit boards inside the janitorial supplies closet off the Meeting Hall entryway, fed with power from the old Deepwater mine, accessed by over four miles of underground and overground cable, crossing county roads, ditches, and wooded land; a massive challenge, but, thanks to Mr. Suggs, they have had outside help for that from his own strip-mine crews and their heavy equipment as well as from members of the private militia he sponsors, the Christian Patriots, who are mostly the same persons. The Meeting Hall with its kitchen, office, and spare rooms has its own circuit board and there is another for all the cabins, the carpentry shop, the new laundry room, and whatever comes next. But incoming cables have also been directly connected to a separate distribution board and from there they have laid wire underground through these foot-deep trenches to new tubular steel streetlamp posts, donated to them by their Florida congregations and set up throughout the camp. Wayne has strung wire through the posts and they have dug three-foot holes for them with a post hole auger borrowed from Mr. Suggs and planted them squarely on the bottom on beds of gravel and staked them there in their upright positions. When the lanterns are in place on top, it will be possible to turn the lights on all at once or by sections or from inside the lanterns one at a time. All that remains before tomorrow night is to pack the post holes tightly and pull the stakes, empty out the bowls and attach the lanterns to the tops of the columns, and finally test all the switches and circuits, and if they don't finish it today, they still have all day tomorrow before sundown. They are all looking forward to this camp-lighting ceremony with great excitement, amazed at their own accomplishments. It will seem like a regular little city then, bright shining as the sun.

In her cabin next to the old lodge, the minister's wife, watching them work with such enthusiasm, understands their excitement and that of all her other new friends, but she does not fully share it. She loved the camp just as it was. Just as it was ten years ago, that is. She is grateful that circumstances have made it possible to rescue her favorite place on earth from what had seemed terminal ruin, and she is infinitely happy here in their little cabin, far from the outside world, with Colin safe and under her constant care, but the camp that was wholly hers is no longer hers. When Wesley first took up his ministry in West Condon, they were still holding summer church camps, and she was out here year round, making it ready, welcoming young campers, overseeing its rentals to other denominations, cleaning up after they'd gone. Debra cared little for most church duties in town, though she got used to them, but she loved the camp, and she often came out on her own at this time of year to air out the lodge and cabins, clean up the litter of off-season intruders, do some weeding and painting and creosoting of the cabins and tidy up the picnic areas, feeling more at home here than in their own home, which was really not theirs at all but more like an annex of the church. She liked using the outhouses and bathing in the creek and picking berries and chopping wood for the fireplace and the old wood cookstove and, above all, just walking through the campgrounds, day or night, often wearing nothing but her working gloves and mosquito repellant. She even loved the rain, the chattery patter of it on the cabin roof, the thin tinny sound it made when falling on the creek like insects walking on glass. And the insects, she loved the insects, their hopeful abundance, the chittery songs they sang. She felt closer to God out here, and though in town she could be quite skeptical and lighthearted about ultimate things, out here she knew she was a true believer. And Wesley, too, seemed to love it and love her in it. He was so passionate out here—the way he *looked* at her then, all over!—she was sure they were going to have a baby. They bathed together in the creek, soaping each other up, and sometimes made love in broad daylight among the flowers in Bluebell Valley, the sun beaming down on them, warming their bodies with its excited gaze. Even peeing together thrilled her, walking naked hand in hand under the stars did. Of course she still had her figure then, and her nakedness thrilled her even when he wasn't with her. Well, it still does.

Wesley lost interest in the camp when he lost interest in her and that was when everything started to fall apart. The generator broke down, a fungus invaded the communal shower. Vandals toppled the outhouses, left a scatter of broken beer bottles. She did what she could, but he rarely helped, paid little attention to the work she did, and he looked away when her clothes came off. When he complained to the Board of Deacons about the malodorous unappealing condition of the collapsing camp and requested a complete renovation, she sensed that it was she he was describing. He was disappointed; she was also disappointed. They refused to meet his budget request and he peremptorily closed the camp. On health and safety grounds, he said. She got angry about that, but he just puffed on his little pipe and went off on his pastoral errands. For a time she continued to come out on her own to care for the camp, but it grew away from her and she gradually lost heart. She never stopped loving it, though. And now at last, in an unexpected way, if it is not exactly hers again, she is, as before, its residing spirit.

In her love, she mapped the entire campgrounds in her head and learned the names of the trees and flowers and when they budded and bloomed, and became acquainted with the songs and calls and plumage and even the migration patterns and nesting habits of the birds that pass through or live here, using their calls as her own clock, and she has that back again. The world, someone has said, is a book written by the hand of God in which every creature is a word charged with meaning; she believes that and lives by it, a devoted reader. There is everything out here from little wrens, finches, and song sparrows, to redwinged blackbirds, whistling bobwhites, woodpeckers, and the family of great horned owls, who have been here for years, helping to keep the vermin population down. Goldfinches, cardinals and bluejays have already been customers at her new bird feeders, painting the gray days with their primary colors, and on Good Friday she spotted a little tail-pumping silvery phoebe down by the creek.

On the excuse that she hopes to enlarge it and eventually turn it into her longed-for halfway house for troubled teenagers, Debra has appropriated for herself and Colin the old camp director's cabin on a slight rise overlooking the lodge, a bit larger than the others with a small extra room, though she told a little white lie and said it had been the cabin for the janitorial staff and their tools, not to seem too greedy. It is the cabin that she and Wesley always used, and that was her home out here, whether or not he was with her, he often feeling like her guest as she was his guest in the manse. She has paid for the restoration and furnishing of her cabin completely out of her own pocket, hers and Wesley's, has bought all the paint, tools, insulation materials, window glass, the space heater and linoleum, even the electric plugs, and has done much of the work herself. The men helped her replace the rotted steps and roof of the little front porch, built to accommodate the slope, and Welford Oakes has promised to plumb fresh water in straight from the cistern when they do so for the Meeting Hall, so she has also bought a small sink unit and faucets. "Get you connected up proper," he said with a wink. She scraped away the old mud dauber nests under the eaves, oiled the hinges of the awning window frames, tacked up insulating plastic over the window screens to keep out the cold and allow a little privacy, and hung all her favorite pictures from the manse on the walls. Not religious pictures, not in the usual sense, but pictures of rivers and mountains and fields, a robin on a tree limb, a toad at the edge of a creek, a shimmering lake hugged by a pine forest. Religious to her.

The rain has let up. Perhaps Colin will come home now. If he is still too restless to stay inside, they can put their boots on and take a walk down by the creek, which must be leaping its banks. They can see if the little phoebe is safe in her nest. The rain for Debra is like an extra cloak wrapped around her private space; for Colin it's more like a straitjacket, poor child. Except when sleeping, he is in constant motion, as though to escape the constraints so cruelly imposed upon him during his imprisonment in the mental hospital, and storms particularly unsettle him. "I'm sorry!" he cried after one thunderclap, and ducked as if warding off a blow. His anguish sometimes makes her cry. This afternoon he has dashed out through the mud and rain to the church office in the Meeting Hall to be with Darren and Billy Don, dashed back to make sure she was still here, then back again to the office, and here again and back, giggling faintly, but terrified, too. Everything so new, so exciting, so delightful, so frightening. It is certainly the strangest Easter she has ever spent, but she knows she has done the right thing. A new beginning, just what Easter means. She hid chocolate eggs this morning for Colin, but had to put them in obvious places for he quickly lost interest in the game. He bit into one of them, left the rest on her bed, was out the door. He was back in time to be cleaned up and dressed for the morning church service, which was beautiful, as was the Easter dinner which followed—intimate, warm, festive. She'd bought and baked the hams for it and had let Colin supply the dessert—his abandoned chocolate eggs—and they all gave him a round of applause, which so pleased him.

Though they have only been living in the cabin for three days, they have been part of the community all month. She and the boy greeted the first arrivals on Leap Day's Night with food and water and medicine, and since then she has brought them carloads of linens, blankets, pots and pans, brooms and dustpans, toilet paper and paper towels, bugspray, air fresheners, all the things she has collected over the years for the manse and no longer needs there. The day after they drove in turned out to be the anniversary of the Night of the Sign, "when six became twelve," as she was told (so much to learn!), and she attended her first Brunist service. She came out to the camp every day after that, Wesley too self-absorbed even to notice her absences. She worked feverishly on her own cabin so as to be able to move out as soon as possible and rescue Colin, who was temporarily sleeping on the office floor with Darren and Billy Don, but she also helped the others in every way she could, showing them around the grounds, explaining what things were for and how they were named, helping Clara with the composing of letters to the Followers, and making shopping trips, often with her own money. She has almost singlehandedly taken on the task of cleaning up the entire campsite after years of neglect and desecration, removing litter and rubbish to the dump in the trunk of her car or in Ben Wosznik's pickup, pruning bushes and dead tree limbs, raking the leaves and small branches out of the creek, clearing paths, and she has created a new vegetable garden on the sunny south side of the camp near the creek, which she has taken on as her own special responsibility. The ground was very hard—before it can be worked, clay soil rained on and baked in the sun has to be smashed up just like smashing a pot—but Mr. Suggs came in with heavy machinery to churn it all up and even moved in a load of rich bottomland dirt dug up from the edge of the creek below the camp and plowed it in, and she and Colin have taken over from there. She bought an ample prefab cedar toolshed for it, spades and shovels, forks, a hoe and wheelbarrow. She sketched out a design with paths and borders, set out rows with stakes and string and surrounded the plot with bean and pea trellises as a kind of fence, and this week she and Colin began the planting, starting with lettuce, tomatoes, cucumbers, and peppers, with such things as cabbage, radishes, beets, and squash to follow. There are some old fruit trees on the west side and wild blackberries and blueberries, and she has added raspberry and strawberry patches at the edge of the garden near the woods and planted a flower and herb garden outside their cabin. All of it has received a good soaking from the rain; though others have complained about the rain, she has not. In fact, if she were out here alone, she would have taken off her clothes and walked around in it, her face to the glorious downpour.

It's all like a miracle, really, and it was she who made it possible by working with Mr. Suggs to engineer the sale of the camp in the first place. When she first heard about Mr. Suggs' offer, she was horrified and put her foot down, vowing to stop this desecration with her own body if she had to, somewhat alarming Wesley with her vehemence. For Debra, the camp was holy land and J. P. Suggs with his hideous strip mine operations was a notorious destroyer of the wild. Wesley Edwards would rot in hell if he let this happen, she shouted. Wesley said Mr. Suggs had promised to restore and preserve the camp for church usage, but she didn't believe him, so she decided to go pay the man a visit and find out for herself. Though Mr. Suggs was coy about it, she eventually coaxed the truth out of him. His plans meant not the destruction of the camp, but its recovery from ruin and for a godly purpose, and so from then on they worked together. That it might bring Colin back was just a bonus. Using her old dream of a halfway house as the pretense for changing her mind, she got the negotiations back on track—the place was a nuisance to Wesley and he only wanted to get rid of it—and they bypassed the local board by going straight to the synod for permission. The deal was done before anyone knew what happened.

It will be time soon for supper, and then the candlelight evening prayer meeting, something Debra now feels part of and awaits with an open heart, a moment when she can feel at one with the universe and with her new life and not have to think about anything except her love for God. She was startled at first by the Brunists' emotional side, and for a time she felt out of place when all the crying and shouting and arm-waving and loud praying began, but she envied them their access to ecstasy and has learned to release herself into it as best she can and to weep and pray and clap and fall to her knees with the others, trying not to be too awkward, and tonight, the last without electricity, she will become at last, her soul surrendered, a true Brunist like all the rest: she has asked to be baptized by light.

In one of the boxes he is unpacking in the new church office, Darren Rector comes upon official documents describing the court decisions that led to the incarceration of so many of their Followers on the Day of Redemption, including that of First Follower and Apostle Carl Dean Palmers, jailed that day and not seen since. He is said to be serving a life sentence without parole in the penitentiary, though Darren cannot understand what he could have done to deserve such punishment. There's a rumor of a murder inside the prison, but he has found no evidence of it. At least once a week they pray in unison for

Carl Dean's release and his return to the fold, yet somehow it always seems more like a recitation than a heartfelt appeal, as if they don't really believe he will be released, or want him to be. He was a true hero, sacrificing himself to allow the others to escape; it should be a bigger deal than it is. He wonders if there is something he doesn't know. Something perhaps to do with those embarrassing pictures of him in his tunic in the rain. He will study them closely again. Clara is sitting at her desk nearby, sorting through correspondence and marriage and baptismal records from the opened boxes, and he has asked her about Carl Dean, but she only says that she didn't see what happened at the end that day and anyway all that was a long time ago. She is a great woman and Darren believes wholly in the church she has brought into being—at exactly the right moment in human history!—but even though the Brunist faith rests wholly on historical events, the past is of little interest to her. Instead: the day-to-day rhythms of practicing a faith and building a church. Which might have been how God wanted it, else this great movement might never have been launched nor his own life so dramatically changed by it; but for Darren, the present—existence itself—is an illusion. At best, it is a passing flow of concealed clues about what is really so and what is yet to come, a clouded window onto superexistence—God's place—where the truth resides and can only be glimpsed. A brilliant professor back at Bible college taught him that; he used heady words like "being" and "becoming," but Darren understood what he meant. And churches are also, like all other worldly things, mere illusions; they may represent a search for truth and provide a framework for it, but they are not the truth itself. The truth. That is what Darren seeks and all he seeks. It is his vocation.

Creating this new office has been their first task and accomplishment, the seed and model of all else, the vital center. They arrived in bitter wintry weather, and all the others had heated caravans and house trailers, but he and Billy Don Tebbett had only Billy Don's old green Chevrolet two-door, a tent and sleeping bags. So they were put up in a highway motel at the church's expense while everyone went to work on this room off the main hall of the old lodge, a room that was apparently part of a later extension with its own flat roof that only needed resealing. The rest of the lodge was something of a wreck, but Ben and Wayne were convinced it could be restored, and so it has been. They treated this first room as a kind of model exercise for the refitting of the whole camp, stripping it down to the timbers, cleaning up the wet rot, then insulating, plasterboarding, and plastering the walls, fitting double hung storm windows in place of the top-hinged awning windows, wiring it up for future electricity with wallplugs and ceiling fluorescents. They gave the walls a couple of coats of white paint and even pinned down wall-to-wall red carpet, said by their patron Mr. Suggs to have come out of the old derelict West Condon Hotel. They added a gas heater and a gas lamp and he and Billy Don have used the room ever since as both the church office and, with sleeping bags, a temporary dormitory, awaiting a restored cabin of their own. During their missionary travels, he and Billy Don bunked down under their small tent or on the floor of someone's house trailer; this room of their own is a luxury.

Colin Meredith has been popping in and out, running between here and Mrs. Edwards' cabin next door, or chasing about after Billy Don. Until a few days ago, they have shared this room with Colin, who joined them while waiting for his own cabin to be ready. Darren and Billy Don will be babysitting him tonight because he tends to get overexcited at prayer meetings and they will have to invent ways to keep him distracted. A game of water baptism down at the creek maybe. He is a strange boy, living at the edge of hysteria and given to terrifying nightmares, sometimes waking up the whole camp with his screams. One doesn't get much sleep around him. But he also seems to be in touch with something outside himself, even if he himself does not understand it. It was Colin who brought the news about the Prophet, and though he spoke of it as a memory it did not seem like one. He is one of the original twelve First Followers and Darren has been watching him closely, recording what he says, using a new tape recorder he has purchased with office funds. In fact it has been running now while he has been talking with Clara. He has not mentioned it to her, though perhaps he should.

Thanks to this new space, Darren is now, except for meals and church services, free to work the whole day long—and there is so much to do, so little time. The anniversary of the Day of Redemption is only three weeks away, falling on a Sunday exactly as it did five years ago. They are living through a mirrored cycle as if in some kind of fairy tale, the calendar amazingly shifting into synchronization on the very night of their arrival at the camp. A Circle of Evenings! Darren can feel the old vibrating in the new, the repeating days spinning toward…what? something glorious? dreadful? He must open up all these boxes of documents and read everything—more than that, he must try to read *through* everything. Billy Don, who flees office chores at every chance, is not as much help as he'd hoped. As soon as the rain let up, he went out to help Wayne and Ben with the new streetlamps, and Darren, standing to stretch, now watches him from one of the Meeting Hall front windows. Whatever they're doing, Billy Don is good at it, gets smiles of respect from the older men, smiles back under the drooping moustache covering his overbite. The heartwarming kind of smile Darren was not blessed with. Though it is still overcast, Billy Don is wearing dark glasses as he always does because of his strabismus, even at night or when naked. A tall, lean, sweet-natured boy, innocent and vulnerable. They met at college when Billy Don joined his Bible study group, which Darren had set up as charismatic opposition to the antiquated self-serving authoritarian orthodoxy of the Bible college. The old fools who ran the college recited Jesus' message but they didn't believe it. They spoke of the Rapture as if it were a school picnic. The world could end, Jesus could return at any moment and no one cared. His group cared. They sought ultimate answers. Urgently, for the day of the Lord so cometh as a thief in the night. The Dean called him in and warned him that he was flirting with heresy, just as Jesus was accused in his own time, and he might be asked to leave the college. It was a choice between truth and lies. Darren sensed that he was being pointed in some new direction. Which is when the Brunists came along. He recognized them, knew he had been waiting for them. And Clara needed someone just like him. The perfect fit.

Billy Don was studying to be a youth pastor and first attended the study group in the company of a twittery young girl who, thankfully, didn't last long. When she left, Darren begged Billy Don to stay on, and he did, becoming his most trusting follower. Which has its limits. Billy Don believes just about everything Darren teaches him, but rarely seeks insights of his own. They have had arguments—about the uses and misuses of dogma, about the interpretation of this or that verse, about the impermanence of the church and the nature of divine punishment—but ultimately Billy Don always grins and says Darren is too smart for him. Only on the subject of sin is Billy Don obtusely doctrinaire, unable to grasp that while for the common man the artificial concept of sin is essential to maintaining order, for those who by knowledge and understanding have risen above the mundane world, there is no sin. God and nature are one. Nature's desires are God's desires. In satisfying them, one is carrying out God's will. "Nothing is sin except what is thought of as sin," as a great man has said. "But what if what I wanted to do was to throw that cute girl in the front row onto the teacher's desk and rip her clothes off?" "Well, you'd probably be arrested, and it doesn't sound like the sort of thing a wholly free and knowledgeable man would contemplate, but it would not necessarily be a sin." But Billy Don doesn't get it. "I don't know," he always says with a grin, "sounds to me like just an excuse for raising Cain." Darren misses the challenge of an intellect comparable to his own and sometimes grows impatient, but is always instantly appeased by that affectionate grin of surrender.

The men have stopped working. They seem upset about something. Colin runs into the hall, yelping, eyes darting in all directions, arms flung about like he's trying to fly, runs out again. As Clara steps out of the office, removing her spectacles, Billy Don comes into the hall and explains that there are people driving past on the roads out at the edge, honking their horns, shouting insults and obscenities, throwing beer bottles and stinkbombs into the camp. A lot of them. "Yes, we been expecting them," Clara says, looking both calm and worried at the same time, fingering the medallion around her neck. "Don't pay no attention to them. They'll go away." But then three cars of young people swing into the camp itself. They crawl out of their cars, some of them carrying clubs and chains, which they swing about menacingly. Their leader is a cocky young fellow who wears an old black fedora tipped down over his Roman nose; he stands with his hands on his hips, legs spread, grinning icily like a Hollywood gangster. Ben Wosznik and the others walk down to meet them and tell them that this is now private property and they are trespassing, but they just laugh and shout out insults and tell them to pack up and get out, religious sickos are not welcome here. One of them gives Wayne Shawcross a push. Then big Hunk Rumpel comes lumbering up from the campsite below, cradling a rifle. He doesn't say anything. He just walks slowly up to them and stares solemnly into their faces. After a quiet moment, they get back in their cars. All but the one in the black fedora, who holds his ground, glaring at Hunk, baring his teeth. Hunk flicks his hat off, stands on it. "Hey, Naz," shouts one of his friends from inside his car. "Time to go!" "All right," says the one called Naz, "but this fucking asshole's gotta get off my hat." Hunk, staring steadily at the boy, slowly grinds the hat into the mud with his boot heel. The boy's eyes begin to water up. "C'mon, Naz. That dude looks like he might not be all there." "That was my dad's hat," the boy says, his voice breaking. "He...he died." Hunk stares at him without expression. Kicks the hat away. Then he turns his back on him and walks away toward the trailer lot below. The boy picks up the mashed muddy hat, wipes away the tears. "That fat fucking sonuvabitch. I'll get him," he mutters, his face still screwed up. He raises a finger to them all and stalks off to his car and, wheels spitting up mud, roars away.

While there is still a trail of pale late-afternoon light in the sky, Ben and Clara pull on their boots and raincoats, tuck flashlights in their pockets, and climb the muddy path up to Inspiration Point, Ben's old half-blind German shepherd, Rocky, padding along beside them. A habit they've learned: coming up to the Point to pray alone together and talk things through. They have a lot to talk and pray about. The anniversary of the Day of Redemption and dedication of the camp is close upon them, and there's still so much to be done, so many problems to face. Not least of all, the multitude of Brunist Followers believed to be on their way here. How will they ever accommodate them? God has been good to them and Ben and his crew have worked miracles, it is amazing that so few can have done so much, but it has also been a hard month, with flooding and sickness and construction setbacks and difficult living conditions, this little summer camp not being built for such harsh weather. And now today these new harassments and intrusions. They will have to speak to Mr. Suggs about it; maybe his friend Sheriff Puller can help. The sheriff's visits worried them at first, but Mr. Suggs assured them he could be trusted and would help protect them from the townsfolk if need be. The sheriff's deputy turned out to be an old Nazarene church friend, Calvin Smith, who became a Brunist Follower the same night Abner Baxter did, though he and his wife Lucy did not stay active after the Day of Redemption. Cal Smith is not one to show what's on his mind, but he did not seem unfriendly and gave the building work they were doing an approving nod. He told Ben he still listened to his records and hoped he would make some more.

With the skies slowly clearing, it is brighter up here than down in the camp, where the night is already settling in. Inspiration Point—they were calling it just "the higher ground" like in the song, until Mrs. Edwards told them the real name for it—is a small wooded rise with a granite outcropping some forty or fifty feet above the rest of the No-Name Wilderness Camp, their own mighty rock in a weary land, looking out across the trees and flat scrubby lowlands toward the old Deepwater No. 9 coalmine, long since closed. The abandoned mine buildings, with their skeletal tipple and rusting water tower, sit on a rise close by a sizable hill over there that is said to be, though not much higher than where they stand, one of the highest points around. The Mount of Redemption, as they have named it and as they know it and revere it. It was the discovery of this view during their first inspection tour in January that most convinced them to accept Mr. Suggs' offer and come back here in spite of the adversity that must inevitably follow. It seemed to say: This place is our place. A place in the wilderness, shown to them by God, to pitch their tents, wherein to make a dwelling-place for the Lord. Like young Billy Don Tebbett said when he saw the view: "It's awesome. Almost like a picture in the Bible." This morning's sunrise service up here got canceled by the rain, but it was just right for their Good Friday vigil two days ago, the sky blackening then with the coming storm. It made them feel like the Disciples must have felt in the Garden of Gethsemane on the Mount of Olives, which people who have been there say is not much higher than where they stand now.

So much happened over there on and under that hill, so much pain and grief and desperate hope, then pain again. Ben has been over a few times in his truck to help with the electric and phone cabling, to look for mine tools left behind, and to gather slate and cinders for the camp access road, ground coal for the new Meeting Hall stove. It is not too far off, but Clara has been reluctant to go back until something calls her to it. It is so bare and deserted, with nothing happening on it, or even looking as if something could. Like a forgotten burial mound. And so it can be said to be. Somewhere in the closed-off mine workings down below, Ely's leg is buried, never recovered, though friends searched for it. Bishop Hiram Clegg said perhaps it was transported straight to Heaven and that could be so, though it is not the sort of picture Clara has of Heaven and what might be found there.

It was down there that night of the mine explosion that her husband, trapped and dying, wrote the prophetic goodbye note that has so changed her life, and the life of the whole world. Ben's brother Frank Wosznik was killed that night, too. It was the tragedy that brought Ben and her together in a common bond, that and their mutual love of Ely, and their unshakable faith, and now, after so many dangers, toils and snares, here to Inspiration Point tonight. "On a cold and wintry eighth of January/Ninety-eight men entered into the mine/Only one of these returned to tell the story…" Ben's own famous "White Bird of Glory" song, which for a while the whole country was singing. That saved one, if there was to be only one, should have been Ely, whom God had clearly chosen and to whom He had sent the White Bird vision. But it was his partner who emerged instead, bringing Ely's vision up with him—as he himself announced: "From the tomb comes God's message!"—though everyone said Giovanni Bruno wasn't really himself anymore; they said he had died and his body was inhabited by Ely's spirit, because Ely's own body had been crushed and could no longer serve God. Which explained everything, even if Clara never quite felt it in her heart. The White Bird maybe, but not Ely. Wouldn't have been like him to take up residence in any body but his own. Then, just fourteen weeks after Giovanni was brought up from the mine, driven by prophecy and the urgent necessity that had descended upon them, and partly because of Ely's last note and how it had come to be understood, they all gathered over there on that hill to await the imminent Coming of Jesus Christ and the Kingdom of Light—the Blessèd Hope!—which seemed like such a certainty. Instead, they suffered only crushing humiliation and cruel punishment and a persecution that has driven them from their homes. A great movement has sprung up out of that persecution, for as Paul wrote to Timothy, you must endure suffering and do the work of an evangelist and fulfill your ministry, and maybe that was God's true purpose, but if their prophecies be true, it is not a time for new earthly orders, but rather a time for an end to all worldly concerns, a time, as Ben's song says, "to meet our dear Lord face to face."

"Please help us, O Lord, as you see fit, to understand Ely's death and message rightly," Clara says, praying aloud, and Ben says: "Amen." "Let us poor sinners *know* the right so as we can *do* the right. And keep that good man Ely always close to your bosom, dear Lord! In the name of Christ Jesus, who has rose up this day in glory, and in remembrance of our beloved Prophet, amen!" "Amen."

Although their Prophet is at the heart of their public prayers, all the more naturally so now that he is dead, in their private prayers both Ben and Clara always put in a particular word for and to Ely, who is always somewhere near, she knows, watching over them. Sometimes near enough to touch if he could be touched. When she doesn't feel him close by, she knows she is doing something wrong. Like thinking too much about everyday details and losing track of their main objectives. Which are not about next things, but about last things. It is Ben who often brings her back to what matters by asking her, "Where's Ely, Clara?" Thus, merely by his presence, near or far, Ely sanctions her mission and guides her in it. The Brunists are as much his creation as hers or Giovanni Bruno's, though not everyone in the movement is fully aware of that. It is more like a kind of secret knowledge that she and Ben share. And little Elaine, too, who also in her loneliness talks to her father and her brother in her prayers, and sometimes when she's not praying. Ely with that quiet look on him seems always at peace, but at the same time concerned about them. As though he were God's servant, unable to rest until all that must be had safely come to pass. Harold, their boy who died so young in the war, is always there with him, just behind his shoulder. He and Ely were always close. Now they seem closer than ever.

Only recently have they learned that their Prophet has been called unto the Lord, though Clara was not surprised. She has felt Giovanni Bruno to be gone since the Day of Redemption, if not in some sense even before, his mission—God's mission through him—having been fulfilled by bringing Ely's message up from the black depths into the light that it might be understood and acted upon. Prophecy's broken vessel, alive and not alive. There was only a spark left in him, mostly in his eyes. When he spoke it was as if from some cavernous depths, deeper than he was deep, and she was not sure his lips moved. He was in bed mostly; the First Followers met beside it. At first there were six of them, and then twelve, and of these first ones now there are but six again unless the Palmers boy returns some day; out in the world, however, they have expanded manifold. It was young Colin Meredith who brought the news of the Prophet's last hour in an ecstatic and dramatic manner not unlike that of speaking in tongues, shortly after he joined the encampment some three weeks ago. Wayne Shawcross had tried to get Colin to help with wiring up the cabins, and even though there was no current running through the wires, as soon as the boy touched one of them he fell to the ground in convulsions with his eyes rolled back and he began howling like an animal with its paw in a trap. When they finally freed his hand from the wire and got him calmed down and back to himself again, he explained around his sobs that he had witnessed Giovanni Bruno being killed with electricity. They had both been sent to the same place after the Day of Redemption, and one day, he said, he saw they had the Prophet strapped down and wired up and then they turned on the electricity and his body started bouncing and jerking and smoking. He saw them rolling him out on a hospital trolley afterwards, completely blue, and he never saw him again, and he knew then that he would have to run away or they would kill him, too. He still has nightmares. After that, they released Colin from construction work and let him clean up the campground litter and help Mrs. Edwards—Sister Debra—in the vegetable garden. Though the boy clearly has emotional problems, to Clara his witnessing rings true. The Prophet of Light crucified by light. And now God's message, having passed through Ely and Giovanni, is lodged in her. It is not a safe or easy thing to be God's messenger (already there is a lump where there shouldn't be one), and she hopes she has enough life and strength left to overcome the powers of darkness and accomplish God's will.

Sister Debra was not around when Colin had his fit, but she was very upset to hear about it and pushed harder than ever to finish up her cabin so she and Colin could move in. Clara doesn't quite understand Mrs. Edwards' whole story, especially as regards the boy, and whatever happened between her and her cruel husband, but the woman seems truly dedicated and is an important convert right from the very heart of those who have persecuted them. She has asked to be baptized by light tonight. Her joining them feels like a story straight out of the Bible, like one of Jesus' parables, or Paul's "remnant chosen by grace."

Rocky is rooting about in the wet underbrush nearby. Might be a rabbit he's after, though he has no teeth left to do anything about it if he finds one. Wanda's Hunk Rumpel, who was such a hero today, has already shot a few and skinned them and cooked them up for everybody. Everybody who likes rabbit, that is, she not being of that number. Across the way, the distant mine hill is slowly slipping into the overcast sky, though the tipple and water tower still stand out as if inked there (it *is* like a picture in the Bible, Clara thinks, like something flat on a page you can't walk into…). Sometimes in the late morning the low winter sun hits that water tower and turns it into a beacon so bright it hurts the eyes, and even now it radiates a peculiar glow against the dark sky. Though she has hesitated to revisit the Mount, it is likely that, if Mr. Suggs can get permission for them, and maybe even if he can't, they will all make a pilgrimage over there together three weeks from now during the anniversary and camp consecration ceremonies, for it seems like the right thing to do. Maybe even an urgent thing to do.

"I come from plain people," Ben says alongside her. "Us Woszniks never come to a place like this with just only the view in mind. Might check to see if it was a good position to hunt from, but otherwise we wouldn't give a hoot. I guess none of us ever had much imagination. Nor much brains neither."

"You got brains aplenty, Ben—and more than brains, wisdom. The kind the Good Book tells about, the word of wisdom as given to believers by the Spirit of God. I depend on you, Ben. You know I couldn't never do this without you." She is not flattering him. He is a good man, a righteous man, and with his quiet no-nonsense manner he has counseled her through many a vexation during their long exodus, and she knows that Ely has chosen him for her and for her task. Ben is slow to move, but when he moves, it is with right judgment, his humble steadfastness a model for them all. Still a handsome man, too, tall and big-shouldered, with a bushy salt-and-pepper prophet's beard grown on their travels, a man comfortable inside himself, if a bit stooped now, starting to get the settled look of men his age. And he surely can sing. "Now, why don't you sing me your new song you was telling me about?"

"Well, it ain't exactly a new song. I figured we'd be singing 'Amazing Grace' tomorrow night when we turn on the lights, so I only made a special verse to begin it with." His guitar is down below, so he sings without it, just as he did the night he turned up, almost like a miracle, at one of their first meetings all that time ago, his mournful voice floating out over the dripping trees and into the dying sky, rolling gracefully up and down through the stretched vowels...

*"It was da-hark a-ha-hand damp i-hin Wil-derness Camp*
*As we worked through-hoo the ha-hard winter days;*
*Bu-hut theh-hen cay-hame a flame fru-hum God's-a holy lamp:*
*Thu-huh light uh-huv Amay-zi-hing Grace!"*

"Oh, that's beautiful, Ben, and it says so much in so few words."

"I reckoned I'd sing the first part in the dark, and when I got into the last line, Wayne'd throw the switch, and then we'd all sing 'Amazing Grace' together."

"You're a showman, too, Ben. Sing it to me again. Sing me all of it. It eases me so." Which is something Ely always said about that song, and now it's as if he has just said it himself, talking through her as he sometimes does.

Bringing electricity to the camp is in truth an amazing grace. They will celebrate it and give thanks to God at tomorrow night's Coming of Light ceremony, and now that the word is out about their being here, Clara has decided to invite some of their old friends in the area. It seems like the right moment. With electricity, they will not only be able to light up the whole camp, they will also have a big commercial refrigerator in the kitchen and electric ovens instead of that old cast iron wood-burning cookstove left over from the Depression era. They'll have electric space heaters that can be plugged in wherever needed and dehumidifiers so the plaster will set proper, and they can use their power tools in the workshop, speeding up the construction work. There will be lights in the Meeting Hall and in all the cabins that can be saved—many of the sockets and switches and ceiling and wall lamps are already in place and wired up—and this afternoon Wayne and the others have been testing out the new streetlamps, a gift of

Florida Bishop Hiram Clegg's congregation. They have set the date of April 19 for the formal consecration of the new International Brunist Headquarters and Wilderness Camp Meeting Ground, and they hope to have all the most essential things done by then. Crowds of Followers will be flooding in, and they are not near ready, but the turning on of electricity will make it feel like they might have a chance.

The electrification of the camp could not have been done without Wayne Shawcross. The movement invested in a house trailer for Wayne and his wife Ludie Belle, needing his experience as a builder and electrician, and he has been worth many times the purchase price. Ludie Belle, who converted from a life of sin, is a willing worker and a lively presence, though, as Ben has said, when she gets the Spirit on her, she does throw it around a tad. Purchasing a mobile home for one of their Followers was something they had already done, out of necessity, for Wanda Cravens and her children. Her husband died alongside Ely in the mine, leaving the poor woman at loose ends, and for these past five years she has been tagging dumbly along with them, not knowing what else to do or where to go, finding herself pregnant about half the time, Wanda being a simple thing men take advantage of. As Ben says, sin is sin, but for some folks there's just not much built in to fence it out, though it doesn't exactly stay either, but just sort of blows right through. She and Ben had to share with Willie and Mabel Hall the burden of carrying along Wanda and her sickly brood, until they finally decided to buy her a used trailer home of her own, Willie at first doing most of the driving. And it did help her find a man, another man in a string of men, though this one may stick around. Wanda is not much help, and whatever she does usually has to be done over, but they use her to run small errands, do the washing up, and serve coffee and cookies at their church services and tent meetings, and that was how she met Hunk Rumpel, an army veteran who was otherwise homeless and happy to have a trailer to move into, relieving Willie of his driving duties, though he may or may not have a license. Hunk is not much brighter than Wanda but he is a stalwart Follower and he has some construction and survival skills picked up in the Army. Smoke is now pouring out of the Meeting Hall fireplace chimney down below; Hunk is probably banking up the fire for tonight's prayer meeting, while Ludie Belle lights the candles and sets out the folding chairs.

Their general all-purpose Meeting Hall—church, dining hall, school room, offices—was converted from the old camp lodge, built early in the century in the days of rustic grandeur with heavy beams and stone walls and foundations. It was solid still except for the roof, which needed to be stripped to the rafters and rebuilt, and it was up on the roof that Hunk proved as invaluable as Wayne Shawcross has been on electricity. Though a big man with a lot of belly ballast, Hunk is agile and fearless in high places and he can command work crews with blunt authority and can lift the weight of three men. Once the building was tight and could shelter them, Ben installed a coal stove at the back and hung Coleman lanterns from the beams. Their brothers and sisters from Randolph Junction, still in touch with Hiram Clegg, presented them with a fine old upright piano. Ely's final message in its gilt frame now hangs by the fireplace, alongside the Prophet's "Seven Words" on a wooden plaque, created by some South Carolina youngsters with a woodburning kit, and a framed near-lifesize photograph of their late Prophet standing in the rain on the Mount of Redemption, a mine pick over his shoulder, his hand raised in a blessing. The Meeting Hall is where their Easter service was held this morning, celebrating Christ's triumph over death, and where tonight's candlelight prayer meeting will be. It is beautiful and it is hallowed by their labor and it anchors them.

So much of this is due to Mr. John P. Suggs, his money, time, influence, and his good Christian heart, a man who gives, as it says in Proverbs, and who does not hold back. He has obtained many of the materials for them at wholesale and purchased some things for them outright, has provided his own workers and equipment for pipe laying, erecting light and telephone poles, and resurfacing the access roads, has seen to the repair of the fresh water pumps, and, with Welford Oakes' help, work has begun on a new cesspool and modern septic system. He has brought in trucks and heavy machinery to rip out underbrush, shovel up rubbish, demolish and haul away rotted structures, and to clear a half acre on the south side for Mrs. Edwards' vegetable garden. He used his connections with the mine owners and bankers to get electricity extended to the camp from the old mine and is now arranging for phone lines from there, something crucial for Clara in her evangelical work. In effect, they will be wired up directly to the Mount of Redemption, something Clara plans to remark upon during tomorrow night's Coming of Light ceremonies. Mr. Suggs is a saintly man who attributes his conversion to one of Ely's tent-meeting sermons, at which time he gave himself to Jesus and became a regular supporter of Ely's Church of the Nazarene. He loved Ely and took his death hard, saying it plunged him into doubt and despair, and he did not at first understand the Brunist movement with its Italian Catholic prophet and its talk about the imminent end of the world. He was a businessman and he did not have any particular end date in mind, and he had no sympathy for wine-drinking Romanists, being a reformed drinker himself. But the Nazarene church fell onto hard times, and after trying on other denominations without conviction, he started thinking again about the Brunists and the role that Ely had played in their origins and it all began to make sense to him. Whereupon he got in touch with them. He and Ben hit it right off, and together she and Ben dispelled his doubts.

Their main worry is what they will do with the crowds of Followers they anticipate will be rolling in here over the next three weeks. The Meeting Hall, so warm and ample a haven for the twenty or so living and working at the camp now, could seat a couple hundred at a stretch, and though there are a few more cabins that might be made livable and others could be built, it is hard to imagine many more people living here than are here now. Even if they come with their own mobile homes, the trailer park itself is full already, and the parking lot near the Meeting Hall, not yet cleared, is meant for visitors' cars only. They have always intended this place to be a religious center and church headquarters, not a place for people to live, but Clara knows that many of those coming for the dedication ceremonies three weeks from now have no notion how they will live when they get here and will have no plans for moving on. Word about the new Brunist Wilderness Camp at the edge of the Mount of Redemption has spread among the believers; she herself has helped to spread it. Many of them are selling up or giving away all they have to be here, fully expecting the Coming of the Kingdom of Light, and Clara cannot naysay it because it may be so. She has sometimes said as much herself, following their Prophet's own call and asking for such commitment as Jesus asked, "Leave everything and follow me!" The coincidence of dates seems to fulfill the Prophet's enigmatical prophecies of "a circle of evenings" and "Sunday week," making ever more urgent his call to "Come to the Mount of Redemption," and, moreover, this place has mystical overtones for those who have never been here, and they will want to see it for themselves.

So, they will have to set up tents in the fields about and use all the local motels and call upon friends to take in pilgrims. They cannot turn anyone away. God has led them here, He will somehow provide. Mr. Suggs has offered mine property land for Followers to pitch their tents on or park their cars and mobile homes, as well as temporary accommodation in his Chestnut Hills development at the edge of West Condon, partly emptied out since the closing of the mines and the general exodus. Ben still owns a small farm nearby with a one-room farmhouse, and he has been back to see if it might be useful for visitors, but found it vandalized and in worse shape than the camp cabins, the porch and walls partly harvested for lumber or firewood. In fact, he pulled some of the loose boards off himself and threw them in his truck for use in repairing the camp cabins. They will just have to hope that, if the day passes without God's intervention, these people will see for themselves what is possible and what is not.

Though some will be more difficult than others…

"I know. We been getting on so well. He'll just only stir things up again."

"Who will, Clara?"

She realizes Ben has left off singing some time back. There is still enough light up here to see each other's faces, but it is completely dark down below. Camper and trailer lights have been coming on, casting their thin yellow glow upon the darkening evening, and she can see people moving about with flashlights and candles. Soon it will all be so different down there. It's almost impossible to imagine. "Sorry, Ben. I was talking to Ely." The blackest patch is just below where they are standing where the land dips away toward a kind of shallow ravine that the creek runs through. Her daughter Elaine named it Lonesome Valley, the poor child expressing her own sad heart. Bernice Filbert claimed to see ghosts drifting about down there on foggy evenings, though she always was one for exaggerated fancies. "About Abner."

"What does Ely say?"

"God will judge, not us. Abner is a Follower and must be took in."

"All we can do, I reckon. But he don't need to stay here in the camp."

"No. But he surely minds to. Him and all his people." They have been worrying over this ever since Abner Baxter sent word he'd be at the consecration ceremonies and assumed they could house him and his family. Ely has been worrying, too. Abner hopes to arrive a day earlier for the Night of the Sacrifice, the night five years ago of his own conversion. They have told Abner the rules and limitations, but they know he'll pay no heed. He was one of their most important early converts, for he was one who persecuted them and then believed, like Paul did, and he became their first bishop of West Condon, staying on to take the punishment here when the rest of them scattered. Of course Abner has had many conversions, all the way from godless communism. But he is still one of those most loyal to the faith, as best she can tell from the reports reaching her, even if they don't agree on a lot of things, most things maybe, and there's not much hope they ever will. "I don't know what we can do."

"This ain't meant as a place for living in."

"Well, we're living in it."

"We're building something, Clara. And they ain't but a few of us. What does Ely say about Elaine?"

"That we should oughta care for her more." Which is not exactly what Ben meant with his question. The lopsided Easter moon hangs low in the damp sky like an orange balloon that's losing its air. When it looked like that, her grandmother used to call it God's ear. "You see? He's listening, child. Tell him all what you know." I am afraid, she tells Him now. Her daughter has grown up tall and rambly, coming to look like a kind of scrawny slump-shouldered version of her father, but with none of his natural friendliness. She hasn't been back to school since they went out on the road, has been traveling only with grownups, so she hasn't had a chance to be the age she is. There have been teenagers at all of their revival meetings around the country, and in the early days Elaine was able to run the Junior Evening Circle, read Scripture lessons, talk about her experiences as a witness of their origins and as one of the First Followers, but she has become more and more withdrawn, shying away from people, ducking her head and covering her mouth the way she does, retreating to their trailer when not absolutely needed. When Clara asks her what she's doing there, she always says she's reading the Bible. The poor child. She has known too much sorrow for one so young. She brightens up only when she gets a letter from Junior Baxter, and then sometimes Clara hears a smacking sound behind her door. She knows what that is all about and she doesn't like it. She still has a nightmarish memory of being caught up in the fever of the Day of Redemption and being unable to rescue her daughter, to protect her from what was happening. There was so much else she had to do. Just like now. It's like in a dream when you have to run but cannot. She has tried to talk to Elaine about that day, but gets no reply. Clara knows what it is to be at that time of life and to be alive to one's own desires, and frustrated by them. She wasn't the prettiest thing in the county either when she was Elaine's age, but she was patient and steady in her faith and what she eventually found with Ely was pure and beautiful and wholly satisfying in a godly way, and she wishes for something like that for her daughter. Junior Baxter is not going to answer that wish. And so she is afraid. Elaine is all the family she has left. "We'll just have to trust in the Good Lord," she says finally, flicking on her flashlight. "Grace has brought us safe thus far, and grace'll lead us home. Reckon we better go get our tunics on and make sure the candles're lit."

"Ho, Rocky. C'mon, boy."

* * *

In the flickering candlelight, the snow-white tunics of the Brunist Followers, assembled for their Easter night prayer meeting, cast a rippling otherworldly glow, adding to the awe and grandeur of this day of Christ's Resurrection. There is a divinity present here in the Meeting Hall tonight, and it is they. Ben Wosznik leads them in the singing of their traditional baptismal hymn, "I Saw the Light," his sweet country voice lifting their own—*"No more darkness! No more night!"*—and then the Brunist Evangelical Leader and Organizer beams the lamp of her dead husband's mining helmet upon the head and shoulders of their kneeling benefactress and newest convert and says that baptism in the Spirit, as Ely Collins always preached, is the outer sign of what's happening inside, going from being dead in sin to being alive in Christ, and Mrs. Edwards says, "I am a terrible sinner seeking salvation," and Clara replies that whosoever repents and believes on the Lord Jesus Christ is justified and regenerated and saved from the dominion of sin by the grace of entire sanctification, and Mrs. Edwards, who is beginning to weep, says, "Oh dear God, I *do* believe and I feel *so* sanctified! Thank you with all my heart for allowing me to join the saints in light and for delivering me from the dominion of darkness!" Willie Hall shouts, *"Colossians 1:12-13!"* and the others hug the new Follower and commence to weep and wail joyously and to give testimonies of redemption and of the infinite mercies of God and, led by little freckle-faced Hazel Dunlevy warbling away like a bird in the trees, to sing in the Spirit, accompanied by Ben on his guitar as best he can follow the spontaneous eruption. Willie's wife Mabel drops to her bony knees and, eyes closed, raises her hands toward the rafters as if grasping for something, then lowers them to the floor, doing this over and over, touching different spots on the floor each time as though setting a table or laying out cards, and others do the same or similar, waving their hands about ecstatically, slapping the floor and themselves, even as they continue to sing in their medley of voices. "The Lord He has warshed away my sins, warshed me in the blood a the Lamb, I been born again!" declares Wanda Cravens in her soft nasal whine, barely audible in the noisily prayerful hall. "I been livin' for Him ever since in glory hallelujah freedom!" Wanda's husband Hunk Rumpel is minding the little ones tonight, but the plumber Welford Oakes is here and he responds with "Glory! Hallelujah! *Freedom!"* and others echo him and Willie Hall declares: "And Paul he said, But I was free *born! Acts 22:28!"* "Amen, brother! Born free! Hallelujah!" Travis Dunlevy barks fiercely. "God is light and Bruno is His Prophet!" Whereupon his wife Hazel goes under the power, falling to the floor and speaking in tongues, which the plumber's wife Glenda Oakes, her glass eye reflecting the myriad candles, interprets as a prophetic utterance about the horrors of hell awaiting all unrepentant sinners. "I want so much to be part of you! I'm so sorry for who I am!" Mrs. Edwards bawls, heaving to the floor next to Hazel and rolling about (she is wearing nothing but her flowered underpants underneath the white tunic, and some approve of that and some don't), "I *love* you *all!* I truly *do*!" The West Virginia coalminers Hovis and Uriah, rocking back and forth, separately confess to unclean thoughts, while balding Wayne Shawcross grips the straps of his bib overalls and, eyes closed and head tipped back, bellows out: "I hear ye, God! I kin hear yore trumpet soundin'!" Which is another cue for Willie Hall: "And he'll up'n send his angels off with a great sound of a trumpet, and they'll go and gather his elect from out the four winds, sweet Jesus! from one end a Heaven t'other! *Matthew 24:31!"* "Ay-men, Brother Willie! From outa the four winds! We was lost but now are found!" They can feel the Spirit stirring. Clara Collins is on her knees, praying for guidance and strength and talking quietly to her first husband, her daughter Elaine beside her, hand at her mouth, whispering a plea to her father that he not forsake them. "I'm sorry, Pa! It's important! I know you can see me. But I have to do it!" Mrs. Edwards is sobbing and gasping and thrashing about and words are coming out that is likely some kind of speaking in tongues, like in all baptisms, though there's something about her husband and Easter eggs that is probably not. "Sin crep up on me, Lord," Wayne hollers, drowning her out. "Tell us about it, Brother Wayne!" shouts Welford

Oakes. "Tell us about your rassle with sin!" "I was cattin' around and cuttin' shines sumthin awful, Lord, but You walked with me and You talked with me and You even come along unto a house a sin and led me to my lady and my salivation!" His wife Ludie Belle, who has been shouting and crying and dancing and shaking like all the others, though perhaps with more abandon, now commences to recount the story of her own fall into sin and timely conversion, which has been often heard but is always appreciated and is never told the same way twice. "I was jist a harmless split-tail thing and I thought my frolicksome carryin's on was jist only doin' my do, but my body it misfooled me with its carnical desires and carried me off down the Devil's black alleyways!" As Ludie Belle traces her passage through the diabolical regions, her husband Wayne, eyes closed, nods at all she says and leads a chorus of "amens." Hazel Dunlevy, emerging from her holy trance, commences to clap rhythmically to the beat of Ludie Belle's story, the others clapping with her in unison and singing out phrases that catch their fancy. Clara claps along absently, but her head is down and her eyes are closed and her lips are moving in private dialogue. "But I never left off a-goin' t'meetin' nor beggin' off to the Lord for all my sins!" Ludie Belle exclaims. *"My body it belonged to Satan but my heart belonged to Jesus!"* All are aroused by this to a fever of prayer and repentance, and the newest Brunist Follower, still tossing about on the floor, cries out: "O dear God! Help me! *I don't know who I am!"* Ludie Belle, standing legs apart and arms out among the shouts and slapping of palms, pauses to gaze down sympathetically upon this suffering sinner. "It's the question I useter ask myself when I was a unsaved working girl!" she declares, just as young Colin Meredith, calling for his mother, comes through the front door behind her with the office workers Darren and Billy Don, all three of them with wet heads. "I was that nameless lamb what went astray, but Jesus He found me when Wayne done! And now I *do* know who I—*Oh no! It's him! It's Satan hisself! Look out!"* She throws her arms up as if to ward off an attack, tumbles to the floor, goes rolling about, bowling into people and knocking over folding chairs, screaming: *"No! Stop, you mizzerbul fiend! I know you're jealous a Jesus, but I ain't a-comin' back!"* It's as though someone has grabbed her in a private place and is dragging her violently around the room and she is trying to tear his hands away. Hazel Dunlevy screams and ducks as if under attack herself, and others cry out as well as the chairs and hymnbooks fly. Billy Don, eyes agog, watches, he watched in turn by his coworker and roommate Darren, hands pressed prayerfully, palm to palm, before his face. Colin, seeing his adoptive mother bouncing about on the floor in such agitation, commences to shriek madly and dash about the room as though possessed, banging into the walls and furniture and other worshippers. Ludie Belle grabs a table leg as if hanging on for dear life, shouting: *"Pray for me, brothers! Pray for me, sisters!"* She is ripped away and tumbles along as though falling into a pit, grabbing at ankles and reaching hands. *"I feel it! I feel it! I feel the ecstasy!"* comes the other voice from the floor, still sobbing. *"Law sakes!"* exclaims Ludie Belle, clutching the leg of a folding chair and dragging it along with her. She struggles to her feet, but falls again. *"He's wild as a rollicky boar in a peach orchard! Halp!"* She is on her back, squirming, twisting, her fists flying. Oh no! The Devil seems to be having his way with her! It's terrifying! Wayne strides through the room, swatting at the air, and snatches her up. Ludie Belle, clinging to him, kicks out at her attacker. *"Git outa here with yore ugly ole hoe handle, Mr. Satan!"* she hollers. *"I been saved!"* Clara emerges from her deep reverie and says sharply: "Stop that boy, Ben! He's gonna hurt hisself." Her husband captures Colin as he comes flying by and brings him, yipping and trembling violently, to his mother, now getting confusedly to her feet and blinking as if returning from some vast unearthly distance and pulling her tunic down. Clara announces with a brief closing prayer that the Sunday night prayer meeting is concluded. Wayne picks up the fallen chairs and Ludie Belle snuffs the candles, as the others, with a chorus of amens and goodnights, turn to make their way back to their trailers and caravans. At the door, Hovis remarks to Uriah: "Ifn that ain't the beatenest! You think Ole Nick was really there?" "Shore he was. I seen him."

# I.4

## Wednesday I April

On his way over to Lem Filbert's garage to hunt down some wheels after a fortuitous cheeseburger and beer at Mickey DeMar's Bar & Grill, Georgie Lucci stops in at Doc Foley's corner drugstore to check out the centerfolds in the magazine rack. It is a glorious April day, first of its kind, the sun's popped at last, he has money in his pocket, the birds and flowers are doing their hot-ass spring thing—it is a day in short for draining the old coglioni, for having one's ashes hauled, as they say in the Land of Oz, and Georgie is many moons overdue. His last fuck wasn't even one, just a tired blowjob in the front seat of his city taxi by an aging whore—*una troia turpe*, as his long-gone old man used to call his mamma while belting her about—which he had to pay for. He'd even make a play for the scrawny snatch behind the soda fountain, but he'd probably have to order something and he hates anything with cow milk in it and has a philosophical objection to spending money for coffee. He loosens the staples and slips the centerfold out of the magazine (if he wins a pot some day, he'll buy a camera and take up photography), tucks it under his jacket, and with a wink at the big-eyed jugless kid who has been watching him, strolls out into the sunshine.

It has been shitsville since his vomitous predawn return on Sunday, *un merdaio di merda* as his dear babbo liked to put it when speaking of his beloved family, but things have at last turned around. For the past two days he has been mostly slopping around in the cold wet weather looking for a job, getting nothing better from it than a sore throat. The post office, the lumberyard and iron works, the strip mines, the bowling alley, the flour mill, the power stations, the bars, the gravel pits. Niente. Main Street is like Death Valley. That scarred-up war vet who runs the bowling alley and talks out of a hole at the side of his mouth could be elected its beauty queen. Shops boarded up, jobless guys hanging about in the pool hall and barber shop trying to stay dry, the streets potholed and littered with garbage. No trains, few buses, newspaper now just a print shop, the old hotel looking like a war casualty. Even the bus station pinball machines have been permanently tilted. His old mine manager Dave Osborne apparently got suckered into buying the shoe store from the new mayor when he got elected, and Dave, gone gray, looked twenty years older. Georgie figured there were worse things to do than tickle young girls' feet and peer up their thigh-high skirts, but Dave just shrugged when he asked and gazed off into the wet gloom beyond the shop window. He looked in on his late cousin Mario Juliano's widow Gina at the mayor's office in city hall, and she snorted when she saw him and said he must be crazy, no one who leaves this town is ever stupid enough to come back. At the Piccolotti Italian Grocery Store, the kid now running the shop laughed in his face. "Fucking highway supermarket's killing us," he said. "Go try them." He did. Offered himself up as a stockboy, bagger, delivery boy, whatever. The manager wouldn't even talk to him. He stole some razor blades and a candy bar and left, wondering what the fuck had dragged him back here. He should have got back on the overnight bus the same day he arrived. Nothing has happened here since he left, nothing good anyway, and nothing ever will.

His mother was startled to see him when he turned up back on Easter morning in his filthy wet rags, as big a surprise as Christ crawling out of his tomb and about as fragrant. "Where have you been, Giorgio?" she asked. "I thought you was dead." She fixed him some breakfast after he'd showered while he rattled on about the high life in the big city, but then when she saw he was broke and jobless, she started putting everything back in the refrigerator and cupboards again and cursing him for being *un imbecille, un testone stupido,* same way she used to curse his old man. Another hand-me-down of a sort, his life story. She had shrunk up some since he had last seen her and had retreated into widowy black, though when Georgie asked if the old fellow was dead, she just shrugged and curled her lip and said she had no fucking idea, or Italianisms to that effect. Georgie was just a teenager when the evil old bastard took off, heaving a few chairs around and giving his mammina a thorough walloping on his way out the door. Except for his kid sister, all his other brothers and sisters had by then vanished over the horizon, and his sister was soon to follow, running off with a stock-car driver, but Georgie, pulling on his old man's abandoned boots, went down in the mines and was still there a dozen years later when Deepwater blew up, convincing him it was time to change careers. The only brother Georgie knows anything about is the one who became a priest and who still sends his mother a little pocket money now and then. Georgie saw a lot of stag movies up in the city, his favorite being one about monks and nuns having an orgy on the altar in a monastery chapel, and watching it, he couldn't help thinking somewhat enviously about his brother, though as best he remembers him, he was never very interested in ficas. Georgie discovered that his mother, poor thing, still distrusted banks and hid her money under her mattress, which helped him get through the next couple of days while he beat the streets like a puttana, looking for work. The old lady makes him feel guilty all the time anyway, he figured he might as well give her cause. And it's just a loan; he'll put it all back with interest when he hits a lucky streak.

Which may have just begun. Making his rounds this morning, he dropped by the police station to see Dee Romano, whom he's probably related to in some bastard way. Playing pinochle up at the Legion last night (not part of his lucky streak), he had learned that Old Willie had been losing what few wits he had (as Cheese Johnson said, "Old Willie has lost his marble…") and had been retired from the force, and though everybody at the table and no doubt half the town were applying for the job, Georgie decided to throw his own tattered sweat-stained cap in the ring. As he had expected, the chief, who had locked him up a few times in the days of his dissolute youth, only snorted at this prospect, but agreed to put him on his list of volunteer deputies in case of future need and suggested he go visit Mort Whimple at the fire station, he might have something. This cheered him up. He had always wanted to be a fireman, ever since he was a little kid. But Whimple said no chance, he was facing probable layoffs of his underpaid part-timers as it was, all he could offer him was a cup of coffee. Never say no. They sat in the sun by the firehouse door and gabbed about the disaster and the crazy evangelical doings back before Georgie left town, when Whimple was the town mayor, Whimple shaking his grizzled jowls and saying he couldn't wait to get his fat butt out of the fucking Fort and back here to the fire station. He had eyes too close to his big nose, one a bit higher than the other, giving him a clownish look that made everything he said seem funny. The chief filled him in on the town's nightlife—"After the Dance Barn burned down, whaddaya got? A coupla sleazy roadhouses, the old Blue Moon, and the Waterton whorehouses…"—and said that probably the worst thing he could do if the town were burning down was try to save it. Georgie spun him a line about the good times up in the city, hinting at important family connections and a debilitating sex life. Why didn't he stay? Well, you know, dear old mammina, all alone… Whimple seemed interested in that and asked about other folks in the neighborhood, and then got up and announced it was time for his weekly visit to the crapper. "But stay in touch, Georgie," he said. "If something turns up, I'll let you know."

Empty as that was, it was the first time Georgie had been treated with something other than derision in his job hunt, so it and the delicious weather lifted his spirits enough to go treat himself to a sandwich and beer at Mick's Bar & Grill. He didn't even have to dip into what remained of his mother's pile to pay for it, having picked up a few bucks in the pool hall over the past couple of days, cleaning up on the young fry a quarter at a time, so he ordered up feeling virtuous. A man of means like other men. Mick, a heavy guy with a high squeaky voice, was full of stories, too. Georgie sat at the bar and heard about what a sinkhole the town had become since he left and how Main Street was dying as if it had an intestinal cancer, about all the people who had left or had popped off, who'd married whom and split with whom and screwed whose wives, about Mick's troubles with his alcoholic Irish mother (they were trading bad mother stories), and about the decline of the high school football and basketball teams and how it all seemed part of the general decline of morals among the kids these days, not to mention the rest of the general population, which was going to hell in a hangbasket, whatever a hangbasket was. Georgie said he thought it was something they used to use down in the mines, back before they had mechanical cages. Mick had a good story about how the old guy who owned the hotel died right here in this room laughing so hard at a dirty joke about a priest, a preacher, and a rabbi that he fell backwards out of his chair and broke his neck. Mick pointed at a big table in the corner where he said it happened. "He just tipped back, hoohahing, and went right on over and—*snap*!—he was gone." "Well, at least he died laughing. Not the worst way to go." "That's what I always say. Even the guys with him couldn't wipe the grins off their faces." Georgie elaborated on the line he'd just given the fire chief about life in the big city, inventing a few cool jobs, furnishing himself a swank bachelor's pad, augmenting the bigwig connections, and throwing in a ceaseless parade of hot chicks. Mick, all agog, asked him what the hell he was doing back here then, and he began to wonder himself until he remembered he was making it all up. He shrugged and said he'd got in a little trouble and had to leave town for a while.

Mick was just telling him how, speaking of trouble, business was so bad a year or so ago he was at the point of having to close down, until the mayor stepped in and gave him a tax break, when who should walk in but Mayor Castle himself, along with Chief Whimple and a couple of others, including that snarling asshole Robbins, who runs the dimestore down the street. They took the same table where the old hotelkeeper keeled over. Georgie got a nod from the fire chief, who then leaned over and muttered something to the mayor, and pretty soon they were all looking him over. He grinned and raised his glass and they invited him over, bought him a beer, offered him a cigarette, while Mick retreated to his yard-square kitchen off the bar to burn some hamburgers. Georgie had had dealings with Castle and Robbins in the past, which he hoped they had forgotten, though as it turned out later, they hadn't. It didn't appear to matter, maybe even gave him an in. It seemed they were worried about the general flaunting of the fire regulations in town, and to avoid a senseless tragedy, they needed someone to help enforce them. What they had to offer was a sort of unofficial job both with the fire department as a part-time inspector and also with the mayor's reelection campaign, helping with fund-raising. "He knows how to talk to his own people," Mort said on his behalf, and the mayor explained that they didn't have enough money in the budget to pay a salary, but they could cover him on a sort of contract basis: five dollars for each preliminary visit he makes for the fire department, fifteen for actual inspections, and two percent of all the money he collects personally for the campaign. He grinned and nodded, tossing back his lager, and he was told to report down at the fire station on Monday. They even picked up his lunch tab. On his way out the door, Robbins called out, "Oh earthling Ralphus!" and the mayor boomed, "The Destroyer cometh!" "Makest thee haste, our spaceship awaits thee!" Georgie, ball cap tipped down over his eyes, hunched his shoulders, waggled his arms as though shaking a sheet, and whooed like a ghost, which set them all off laughing so hard there was some risk of a sequel to the hotelkeeper's demise.

When Georgie reaches Lem Filbert's garage, Lem is not in, but Georgie's old drinking pal and classmate, Guido Mello, is still working there, looking heavier and a lot soberer than he used to. Married now, couple of kids, as he says, he is showing the burden of that. Black grease on his fat nose where he's rubbed it, adding to his general down-in-the-dumps look. Guido tells him Lem is out test-driving a car whose shocks and wheel bearings they have just replaced, but if Georgie has come by looking for a job, forget it. Lem has plenty of business, these being hard times when people have to fix up their old cars instead of buying new, but they also don't pay their bills. "He's an ornery sonuvabitch to work for and he pays shitty wages for too many fucking hours, but what can I do?" Guido says, and smears the other side of his nose. "Little as it is, my kids would starve without it." "Maybe you should unionize," Georgie suggests, and Guido snorts and says, "Yeah, me and who else?" "Well at least you could be union president," Georgie says, but instead of laughing at that, Guido only shakes his round burry head and sighs. "Jesus, Georgie, we're halfway through our fucking lives and what have we got?"

Long tall Lem rolls in then in the battered purple Ford he has been test-driving. Georgie greets his old mine buddy and baseball teammate and they shoot the shit for a while, Georgie filling Lem in on what little he knows about Wally Brevnik and the other Deepwater refugees who fled town after the mine closed and letting fly with his by-now well-rehearsed tales of the big city, which for the first time fail to impress, Lem meanwhile unloading all his sour gripes about the garage, the fucking irresponsible mining company, this pig's ass of a town, and the whole stupid fucking world in general. No, there's no baseball team; he hasn't swung a fucking bat since Tiger Miller left town. Lem's brother Tuck was killed in the disaster and Tuck's wife Bernice is now living with him, doing the laundry and housekeeping and fixing him his lunch pail every day, just as if he were still working a mine shift. She is some kind of a nurse and Lem figures Tuck married her to have someone to massage his hemorrhoids. A peculiar cunt who wears Bible clothes and lives in some fucking crackbrained dreamland of her own, Lem says, and she has recently gotten involved with those evangelical wackos out at the church camp. They have been having rows about that, but he knows Bernice was always close to Ely's widow and needs a connection, and it suits her angels-and-devils nuttiness, so he'll just have to live with it. Georgie asks him why he doesn't just marry Bernice, and Lem says, "Nah. Then I'd probably have to fucking fuck her."

Georgie tells him he is back in town for a while and needs an old junker to bum around in, what has he got? Lem looks skeptically down his long nose at him, so Georgie, on the pretense of digging for a coin for the Coke machine, flashes his mother's roll and mentions that he's going to be working for city hall and might require wheels for that. Lem shrugs and takes him around to the back lot where a lot of old wrecks stand rusting in the sun. Lem recommends a small rebuilt Dodge coupe with about seventy thousand alleged miles on it, but Georgie's lustful eye falls on an old two-tone crimson-and-cream boat-sized Chrysler Imperial with Batmobile tail fins and gunsight tail lights, a fucking classic and perfect for his more urgent needs. Lem says it has had a rough life and he can't guarantee it will make it out of the lot without breaking down, but Georgie's heart is set ("Well, it's your money, go ahead and buy the goddamn thing," Lem says. "I could use the fucking repair business..."), so they haggle for a while and agree on a price, and Georgie talks him into letting him give it a run around the block, setting his half-finished Coke down as if planning to come right back to it.

Inspired by the baseball talk and the lush weather, Georgie takes a run out by the high school athletic fields, first closing the glove compartment door on the top of the centerfold so that it dangles there to cheer him on his journey. He has done a lot of driving up in the city, that being mostly what he did except jerk off, and it feels good to get back behind a wheel again, and on mostly empty streets and roads where he can open up. The old crate makes a lot of clunky noises, has no pick-up at all, the gear shift is tricky and the steering wheel is pretty loose, but what it has, he knows, is presence. In it, he is somebody, and, window down and arm out the window, he blows kisses and tips his cap to all he passes to let them know he knows it. He decides to name the fading beauty after one or another of his favorite blue movie characters like "Nympho Nellie" or "Sadie Sucker," but finally, given her colors, settles on "Red-Hot Ruby," who, as he recalls, also had a big thrusting creamy ass and lipsticked her anus. It was an old black-and-white silent, but they'd gone to the trouble to hand-color the lipstick red. It jiggled around going through the projector, like the rear end of this old car on a rough road.

He is in luck. The boys are having their first practice of the new season. He stops, keeping the motor running, to jaw with the coach for a minute. He volunteers his services to help the kids with their hitting, while they gather around to admire Ruby. Georgie could never field a ball for shit, but he was a natural with any kind of stick in his hand. He had quick wrists, could watch a pitch until it was nearly across the plate, then whip the bat around like a fly swatter, and the coach remembers that and says, sure, come along any time. Georgie, waving goodbye, feels like this day is turning into the best day of his life.

After that, he rolls around the periphery of the town, the centerfold's raised culo flapping merrily in the breeze, checking out the motels and roadhouses that the fire chief mentioned for later on. "Big night tonight, baby," he says, rapping the dash. "Gonna get it *on!*" He passes, chattering away to Ruby, or else to the centerfold, they're an agreeable blur in his mind, the Sir Loin steak house and abandoned drive-in movie, the sleazy old love-cabins motel which charged by the hour, the driving range and country club, a few golfers already out enjoying the first real day of spring. He's joining the in-crowd, maybe he ought to take up the game, pick up a few bucks once he's got the knack. He swings into the rootbeer stand with the intention of offering his bod to the short-skirted carhops, but there's not a one looks older than thirteen, so he blows them kisses and rolls on out, passing the new shopping center, new when he left town, the turn-off to the gravel pits and old swimming hole, the road to the Waterton whorehouses, and the burned-out ruins of the old Dance Barn where the big bands used to come and where they served anyone who could see over the bar. First got his cork popped by the hand of another under the table in a hard wooden booth in there, the hand belonging to a girl just fifteen years old like his green young self. At the time, he didn't really know what came next, or if he knew, didn't know how to make it happen, so he lost out with that chick. Never mind. Many more to follow. Georgie Porgie, pudding and pie, kissed the girls and made them sigh.

He pulls into a filling station to add a few dollars of gas, patting Ruby's provocative rear end while he's got the pump in her (a patch of deep rust back there, he notes, like some kind of fatal crotch disease), and sees by the gauge it's just a drop in her bottomless bucket. Ruby's the deep throat kind of girl—he could run through a pile pretty fast just keeping her juiced up. He cruises the strip of car dealers, most of them closed down, their vast lots vacated, but still flying their faded flags and streamers, then Chestnut Hills, the cheap prefab developments built mostly for mining families at the edge of town where there are no hills, no chestnuts, looking for who knows what. Some broad from the past probably. A lot of scabby abandoned houses, muddy yards, old cars and trucks on blocks. Potholes that jar the dust out of the ceiling fabric. Then it's the rich folks' side of town with their big houses and flagpoles and fancy shrubbery—though even they are looking pretty seedy and uncared for, and there are FOR SALE signs on some of them—and finally, after a clanking cap-waving spin down Main Street and a kiss blown to his new employers at the Fort, on past the white RR XING signs, over the rusty unused rail tracks, and into his own neighborhood. "Home, baby," he tells Ruby. Mostly painted frame houses in various states of dilapidation, many of them multifamily, overcrowded and depressed, but comfortingly familiar and welcoming in the warm afternoon sun. He tours all the houses where former girlfriends once lived, letting Ruby show them what they've been missing. Probably all married now, swarmed round with brats and gone to fat or worse.

He spies Vince Bonali rocking on his front porch with a beer in his hand, and, as Ruby's been getting overheated, he pulls over to the curb to let her calm down and invites himself up past the molded cement Virgin foot-soldiering the muddy front yard, thinking he might be able to hit his old faceboss up for a buck or two of gas money. He is an understanding guy. They have been through a lot together, had some great old times. He would do the same for Vince. He'd heard that Vince had sunk pretty low after his wife kicked off, and he finds him so, a morose old musone, too grumpy even to stand up and shake his hand, but after commiserations and family talk and a few reminiscences about the old section, Vince lightens up enough to offer Georgie a beer and pop another for himself. Vince is wallowing a dead cigar in his mouth. "Want me to try to light that mess for you?" "Nah. If I smoked it, I'd have to buy another and I don't have the dough. Eating it, it lasts longer." He turns his pockets inside out in demonstration before settling heavily back into the rocker. There went that idea. Vince nods toward the car. "Pick that piece of faggot junk up in the city?" "No. Here. Just shopping. Giving it a trial run. Gotta go turn it in soon." "Made a pile up there, did you?" "Well, hit it lucky a coupla times, but—" "You know, when I first seen you coming, Georgie, I had the funny idea you were looking for a handout. What a laugh that woulda been. All the spare cash in this town is at the bank. That's where this comes from," he says, holding up the beer. "That guy at the bank's supplying you?" "No, Angie. She works there. She buys the groceries now. She gives me an allowance, Georgie. A fucking beer allowance. You're drinking up part of my weekly allowance." That makes him feel just great. What is he supposed to do? Give it back? It doesn't even taste good anymore.

"You were smart to get your ass outa here, Georgie. Look at me." He does. The old man is staring morosely at his missing finger joint. He's got about as much life in him as his sodden cigar. "I haven't had a goddamn day's work since they shut the mine. It's been a long, hard five years. And it's gonna get worse. I don't know what the hell you're doing back here." He can't use his little mammina line, Vince knows better, and he doesn't want to suggest to his old faceboss (he's *still* the boss) that he has been in any kind of trouble (he hasn't really, other than the everyday). So instead he tells him about his new job as a fire inspector, thinking to earn a little respect. Vince snorts and shifts his wet cigar to the other side of his mouth. That thing really is disgusting. "They're using you, Georgie. It's a shakedown racket. You remember old man Baumgarten?" "The dry cleaners?" "Yeah. He was asked for a contribution to the mayor's so-called campaign fund, and when he didn't come across, he got a visit from the fire department. They found a lot of things wrong. So he fixed them. They found some more things wrong and he fixed them again. He was reminded that it was costing him more to comply with the regulations than to cough up the campaign fund donation. Still, he wouldn't go along, so one night his business burned down. The inspectors said it was faulty wiring and he'd been warned, he couldn't even collect on his insurance." "No shit." Georgie's good mood is sinking as the sun sinks. It's clouding up and there's a cold wind. It was a mistake to come up here and let this sick old man bring him down. "Robbins is in on it, too, right?" Georgie nods glumly. He really doesn't want to hear any of this. "It was those two guys who dropped us in the shit five years ago, you remember that?"

"How could I forget? That loony lawyer we spooked." A glorious night of masquerades and theatrical revelry (they were shitface spirits from another world), and then a would-be gangshag with an old buddy's widow and a drunken brawl, ending up in handcuffs down at the station with newsguys' flashbulbs popping. He, Vince, Cheese Johnson, and Sal Ferrero—though Sal had fallen away before the end. Georgie thought it was all hilarious, but Vince had big ambitions back then and that night fucked it for him. He turned bitter and weird after that, and it all ended in a daylight raid on the old lawyer's house while everyone else in town was out at the mine waiting for the end of the world and playing bingo. Their aim was looting, plain and simple, but the house was empty. Mostly empty. What Georgie remembers is all the dead cats. "I spun by Lee Cravens' old place a little while ago. Looked like nobody lived there. Whatever happened to old Wanda?"

"How the hell should I know?" It is clearly a touchy subject. Not much prospect of a second beer. Bonali has got his sulk back and is giving him a look like he wishes he were dead. Georgie glances at his wrist as if he had a watch there. "Well, shit, I better get the car back. I'll drop back and see you again soon, Vince."

"If you do, bring your own beer."

* * *

"Well, lookit what's fell down the shaft," says Cheese Johnson when Georgie walks in. Cheese is sitting at a card table with old Cokie Duncan, Steve Lawson, Buff Cooley, Georgie's cousin Carlo Juliano, and one-armed Bert Martini. Some kind of whiskey bottle on the table. Drained. Collecting cigarette ash.

Georgie has made the usual rounds, but it's midweek and drizzly, the lush spring day having turned cold and windy again, it is doornail-dead all over town, and still too early for the roadhouses. He has never seen streets so empty. Like some kind of nightmare movie. Even the bowling alley and the Legion Hall, where he'd found two of these guys last night, were deserted. Meeting of the geriatric society in Hog's Tavern: the old union boss Nazario Moroni, who once punched him when he caught him with a pack of cigs in his mine jacket, and a couple of others of like vintage, including a senile cousin of his nonna, others unknown or aged past recognition. Watching a small mute TV hanging behind the bar. Or more like the TV was watching them. The Eagles Social Club was his last shot. "I was wondering where all the action was."

"That you, Georgie? You must of forgot your hair somewheres. What drug you back to town?"

"Too much tail up in the city, Stevie. It was making an old man outa me. Had to come back for a rest cure."

"Well, you come to the right place. Sure won't find no tail up here."

"I'm disappointed, Coke. I figured you'd be amenable."

"Listen at the nasty fella with his city ways!"

"Talk like that," Bert Martini says, shaking his head. Bert lost his left arm in the mine accident, the one he used to catch baseballs with, so even in draw poker he leaves his cards face down on the table, tipping up their edges briefly to read them, then tossing his quarters into the pot with the one hand he has left in life. "Sign of how bad the times is got."

"You mean, when you're up shit creek," Buff Cooley says, "Georgie's what you find at the other end."

There is faint laughter at his expense and he grins his grin. "You turned up just in time, Giorgio," his cousin Carlo says. "I could use that five bucks I staked you Sunday."

"Lemme see if I can win it back, cugino. What's the game?"

"Dealer's choice, stud or draw, nothing wild. Cap's three raises, limited to a quarter each."

"A quarter!"

"If that's too high we can lower it."

"This ain't the big town, Georgie."

"Okay, high rollers. Deal me in."

He's keeping up a brave front, but Georgie's earlier euphoria has drained away. Visiting Bonali was a real bummer, and the betrayed promise of spring weather hasn't helped. A new front has moved in like a kind of sudden sickness of the air and there's even talk of snow. April fool. What little he's eaten (there's an empty pizza delivery box on the next table still giving off a spicy aroma, reminding him how hungry he probably is) hasn't set well, nor has the hip flask of cheap rye he has polished off; he should have picked up some antacids in Doc Foley's this morning when he was in there. Worst of all, he has come to the sinking realization that he'll never get enough money together to pay for Ruby, cheap date as she is. Certainly not up here. Even if he took all these guys' money, there's not enough between them for a pair of windshield wipers. Which he has discovered is among the old tart's many urgent needs. Had to drive her with his head out the window during the showers. For all his bravura, he does wish he were back in the city. He misses the action, even if it's an action from which he was mostly excluded for lack of the wherewithal. All he has here that he didn't always have up there is a room to sleep in out of the weather, and the price for that is his old lady's ceaseless scorn and fury. Which can get worse. He can only hope she has not looked under the mattress yet.

"All I'm saying is that for the mine company fat cats the disaster wasn't nothing more than one bad hand," says Buff, picking up on some conversation Georgie interrupted. These guys are all survivors of the explosion that blew out Number Nine's innards and closed it down, and they're still grousing about it five years later. And using the same lines. It's like time's stood still here. His life had been shit in the city, but not this bad. He borrows a cigarette from Bert and lights up with Cokie's lighter. Buff's real name is Bill, but when he was younger he was a wild man during union strike action, whooping it up like a rodeo rider, and they started calling him Buffalo Bill, which got shortened over time. "They pocketed their winnings, quit the game, and went home, or wherever they go to get their fucking done, and left the workers holding an empty kitty."

"What did you expect?" says Bert with a shrug. "Them was the cards we was dealt."

"At least you got your disability pension, Bert," Steve Lawson says. Like Georgie's cousin Carlo, Steve lost a brother in the explosion. Steve sees Bert's quarter and raises.

"That makes me the lucky one, hunh?" says Bert, waving his stump.

"Put that thing back in your pants, Bert," says Cheese, meeting the bet and asking for a pair, "and stop showing off."

"We're halfway through our fucking lives and whatta we got?" Georgie says, repeating Guido Mello's line.

"Well, the clap," says Cokie Duncan. "Hemorrhoids…" Cokie once had a wife, but she ran off during a stretch on the night shift so long ago no one around here remembers her anymore, Duncan included. Cokie was Bonali's assistant faceboss in Georgie's crew and on the night of the disaster was left in charge when Bonali went looking for a phone. Georgie was sure Bonali was not coming back and they were all going to die if they just stood there in that black smoky furnace, so he and Wally Brevnik took off on their own. It was Georgie's intention to claw his way out by his fingernails if he had to. They went through some rough stuff, but Wally had a cool head and they eventually reached the top and already had a cup of spiked coffee in their hands by the time the rest of the section came up. All but Pooch and Lee. Names on a T-shirt.

The best card in Georgie's rainbow hand is a ten of diamonds, but after Buff Cooley drops his two bits in, he raises a quarter, pretending to want to throw in all he's showing, and it is not so much a bluff as an act of frustration, wanting desperately for something to happen, any goddamned thing, even a fight. Betwise, not smart. After drawing blanks, he tosses, and Carlo wins the little pile of coins with low triplets, Georgie's dwindling roadhouse reserve now diminished by his contribution to it.

When it's his deal, to do Bert a favor he calls seven-card stud. "I seen Guido Mello today. He's not a happy man," he says, passing out the hole cards.

"Well, he up and married the Sicano girl, the one who was never quite right in the head, and one a their kids has a medical problem. Some sympdrome or nother. So he's sorta lost his sense a humor."

"Sicano? The one we all banged on the Hog pool table one night?"

"The same."

"Oh man. Well-buttered buns." A memorable night. Used to be a popular neighborhood spot, Hog's Tavern, but Hog Galasso is long dead and it has fallen on hard times. Dark and foul-smelling. A few ancient habitués like those he saw tonight. But back then he was still just a kid working his first mine shift, getting tanked in there with some older guys from his section, when one of them went out and came back with the Sicano girl, and Hog locked the doors. The pool table got knocked permanently ajar by what happened afterwards; you had to know how to play the slope. "What'd he go and do that for?"

"Il Nasone never had lotsa options amongst the ladies."

"He says Lem has turned out to be a hard man to work for."

"Who ain't? He should try that tightwad cocksucker Suggs for a spell."

Cokie and Steve, he learns, have got on part-time at one of the strip mines, but when he asks, he's told don't even bother—old man Suggs and his hardass mine manager are not partial to Italians. "They only like to abuse their own kind." Cheese and Buff also got hired out there, he's told, and then fired—Cheese for his fuck-off wisecracks, Buff for trying to organize the workers—and they add to the asshole portraits of J. P. Suggs and his site boss, a surly black-bearded gun-toting churchgoing westerner named Ross McDaniel. "McDaniel hates everybody and everything. He's one of them guys that if his feet don't carry him fast enough to where he wants to go, he's apt to shoot them off."

"He believes the Bible should be the constitution and law of the country, and wants to execute everbody who don't agree with him."

"Never seen a guy with a lesser sense a humor," Cokie says.

Buff lights up. "There was a day we'd of strung up guys like him."

Several of them have been out to the hospital to see Big Pete Chigi, who has black lung and is breathing his last through respirator nose plugs, and he hears about Ezra Gray, who was in Red Baxter's section and got out of Deepwater okay, but then went down in another mine a state over and got crippled in a roof fall that killed three other guys.

"Yeah, I seen him—broke his fucking back. He's on rubber wheels for the duration. Ez was working non-union, so no comp or insurance. A hotshot lawyer talked him into filing suit, but the owner faded away like he never was. Like he disappeared into the paperwork or something."

"Same as what happened here. The ruthless dickheads." Buff slaps his cards. "C'mon, Georgie, cheer me up. Goddamn make me something. Send me down sixth street singing."

"Fulla potholes, sixth street."

"Ez is completely off his nut now. One a them Brunist types. He travels some with Red Baxter, I hear tell. Out there ranting about the end a the world and all that."

"Is old Ez back? Is he out there at the camp?"

"He's in town," says Steve, "but I never seen him in the camp and he'd be hard to miss."

At first Georgie thinks Steve might have got mixed up with those crackpots somehow, but it turns out Suggs has been helping them rebuild the camp, using his own workers for some of the heavy jobs, so both Steve and Cokie have been putting in time out there. It's not clear what old man Suggs is getting out of the deal, but they're pulling their normal paltry wages, so no complaints. "So what's going on out there in the woods?" Georgie wants to know. "Are they wearing any clothes?"

"We ain't sposed to talk about it," Steve says, "but, yeah, leastways by day. We don't stay past quitting time, so I don't know whatall they get up to, but it's too fucking cold to go round bareass even if you're rolling round a lot. From what I could see, they're mostly just only working their butts off, fixing the place up. Generally I didn't reckanize no one nother than Ben—ole Ben Wosznik, y'know—him and Ely's widder. They kinda run things. And also Willie Hall's out there. Willie and big Mabel."

"That'd be a cute pair, butt-nekkid."

"And Lee Cravens' skinny little widder with all her brats, she's there, too."

"Wanda?" Georgie glances up and catches Johnson's wink and gap-toothed grin.

"She's shacked up with some bigass hulk. I mean, really big. A man who's dragging around a whole heap a excess mollycules. But he can move. I seen him dancing round on the open beams atop the old lodge like a man who don't know what fear is."

"He ain't never been down a mine then."

Georgie has dealt himself a second king over a pair of eights, and he risks a couple more quarters, but Johnson beats him with a club flush, so even his luck is bad. Buff gets back on the mine bosses again, so to change the subject and lighten things up, Georgie elaborates on some of the tales he has been inventing during his job hunt, including a new one about a highprice hooker named Ruby, red-hot Ruby, using anatomical details from the centerfold he's had hung in the car all day and personality quirks based on the old junker's clunky behavior. "Well, we're just getting warmed up, you know—really shimmying down the road, burning rubber—when her fucking eyelashes fall off and she gets so hot she starts making these really nasty noises down below..."

"Sounds a real beaut, Georgie," Carlo says, laughing.

"No shit, she was. Even posed for one a them centerfolds. She invited me along for the photo shoot. She said me watching got her hot. Sure got me hot. She was a sight to see. An ass-end to die for! I still have a copy somewhere, I'll show it to you someday."

"Hey, speaking a pitchers, show Georgie the ones you got, Cheese!"

Johnson shrugs, reaches into a paper sack, and tosses out a half dozen well-thumbed black and white photographs of two naked people doing a kind of sex manual thing on a leather couch. No hardcore shots and the light's bad, could be stills from a cheap stag movie, but the guy's well hung, they're both good lookers, and the beaver shot with the guy standing over her with a newspaper in his hand like he's about to swat her with it is good enough to make you want to poke her. Then he looks closer. "Wait a minute. Who is that? Is that Tiger Miller?" They're all grinning. All except Bert Martini, who says, "You shouldn't ought to be showing them photos around. She was a nice girl. And Tiger was a pal. When I was in hospital he come by to see me near every day. I figure there's more here than what meets the eye." The others laugh at that.

"And that's the Bruno kid, right? Marcella. The one who got killed. She was in school with me. A young kid, coming in as I was going out. These are a little different from what's in the high school annual. Where'd you get them?"

"You remember Jonesy, useta work at the newspaper, back when we still had one a them shitrags. We was playing cards and gitting blitzed together up to the Legion the night Jonesy split town. I walked him to his train and he give 'em to me as a see-ya-later present. Plumb forgot about 'em till them apocaleptics showed up agin."

"Sure you did," Carlo laughs. "You can tell by all the cum spots on them."

Something about the photos bothers Georgie. Not just the realization that something was happening back then and he'd missed out. He missed out on plenty. She always had a nice smile, but she was just a kid, he hardly knew her. Her brother was a complete psycho and he supposes some of that rubbed off on Marcella. He doesn't remember anyone ever dating her. No, it's something about seeing her so exposed like that. Not so much her naked snatch, he's seen his share of those, but all the rest of her, so laid open. Georgie has never seen that look on a girl's face before. She is looking not just with her face but with all her body, her snatch as much a part of her looking as her eyes. Her navel or her toes. Her mouth, half open. So it's like something terrible is being bared that shouldn't be seen, something that, once bared, can never be covered up again, and he hates it that these cackling shits are ignorant witnesses to it. And she's so still. And silent. It's like she has been spread out to be carved up. Consumed. Well. She's dead. Must have died right after these pictures were taken. It's like getting the hots for a corpse. He wants to cover her up. Close her eyes. "Her nutty brother was in my class," he says, feeling soberer than he wants to be. "Is he out there at the camp now?"

"Giovanni? Nah, they locked the loony away right after the world ended and he never come out."

"He's dead, I think," says Steve Lawson.

"Dead?"

"So I heerd."

So, Georgie decides, tossing in another losing hand, is this dump. He feels suffocated by the dead. He looks around the table. Even these guys are dead. The whole fucking town is a town of the walking dead, and he's going to be one of them unless he moves his ass. Besides, if he wants to score tonight, he should get on the road while he still has coin left to operate with. He had thought to invite these guys along, but he really doesn't want to be around them any longer. He glances at his empty wrist and announces he has a date waiting for him, gotta go. He had made the mistake of tossing some money on the table when he sat down and, as he gets up to leave, Carlo reaches over and snatches up a couple of loose skins. "Now you owe me three," he says.

"Ruby," he says, leaning his heavy head against her wheel, "Ruby… what I really feel like doing is shooting somebody." Georgie is sitting in the Blue Moon Motel parking lot waiting for the old girl to warm up, sucking on the joint the Moroni kid gave him. Soft wet snow is falling like a punchline for the stupid joke that is his life. On the travel office window this morning, he saw a sign advertising holidays at a beach place called Brazil. Where he ought to be. Where he deserves to be. Wherever it is. He's cold, wearing only a shirt and jacket, feeling miserable. The only way morning's promise is going to be fulfilled is in a Waterton whorehouse, provided they still exist and he can find an old puttana who will take what little money he—he and his mother—have left. Ever hopeful even in deepest despair, he assumes that, on a shit night like this, they'll take any trade they can get.

The motel was the last stop on his desperate but futile nightlong quest. For what? Cunt? More than that. Some kind of affirmation is what he was looking for. Some justification. Just a pleasant conversation with some pretty young thing would have been nice. He is full of sorrow and could have used an arm around his shoulder. A soft breast to nuzzle. The roadhouses weren't completely empty. Worse. Those few out on the crummy night were all juveniles. Drunken teenage high school kids. Boys pissing themselves with their own confused excitement, a few girls going bad. Well, that was all right. Hey, let's rock. Georgie felt like one of them—he *was* one of them. But they didn't feel like one of him. They called him an old pervert. Baldy, they called him. Gramps. In one place, an unshaven kid they were calling Grunge even threatened to take him outside and beat the shit out of him if he didn't fuck off. He would have welcomed a brawl, but his own team had a membership of one and those red-eyed boys with erections bulging their jeans didn't look like they would know when to stop. Then a short stocky guy with a fedora tipped down over his broken nose swaggered over and told Grunge to lay off. "Pal of my dad's," he said. "You worked out at Deepwater, right?" Georgie acknowledged that he did, and recognizing now the tipped lid, he introduced himself and said he was in the mine the night it blew up and killed his dad. "Been away since then. Just checking out the old haunts. Ran into your granddad today, too. At the Hog. Nonno Moroni's the toughest bastard I ever knew." "Yeah. Who I'm named after. But this is a private party, Georgie. Sorry." "I smell fresh-baked cookies." Young Nazario smiled faintly, fished out a joint and handed it to him. "On the house. Lemme know if you're in the market for more. Me or one of my boys will fix you up. With whatever. Ciao."

By the time he had reached the Moon, he was no longer looking for women; he was happy only to sink into a drunken stupor and let his life end that way. Just as well, for there were no women to be had, unless one of the two couples in the room should have a blowup and leave a partner behind. He had hoped to catch the old girl who used to play a melancholic piano in here, but she had been replaced by one of those twangy hillbilly types, a long loose assembly of bones with some skin on them, wearing a sweaty cowboy hat and a plaid shirt. Boots that looked like they might not have been off his feet since he grew into them. When Georgie took his stool alone at the bar, the hick was singing about dead mommies and daddies, which was a real pick-up. There were two older people in a booth back in a dark corner and a young couple on the dance floor sort of melted into each other, mouths together, the guy's big mitt on the girl's plump little ass, the other holding her hand and pressed against her boobs. The Georgie Porgie of old might have cut in on the young stud, he could still show the little cunt a trick or two, but he had taken enough knocks for the night. "...And each night as I wander through the graveyard, darkness hides me where I kneel to pray..." Holy shit. They're getting off on lines like that? When they parted mouths long enough to go into deep-gaze mode, Georgie recognized the girl from Sunday at church: Bonali's hotpants daughter. The one at the bank. The boy, who was at least a foot taller, looked familiar, but he couldn't place him. Everybody around here looked familiar. It was a kind of curse. Even the bartender turned out to be a punk from the neighborhood, a kid who was in grade school when Georgie was in high school. Only he wasn't a kid anymore either. Beardy. Already developing a gut. "White dove will mourn in sorrow," the hayseed whined, and Georgie, though suffering a deep grief of his own, decided if there was one more fucking chorus, he was going to trash the place. Gratefully, the song came to an end, though the lovers stayed in their swaying clinch on the dance floor, grinding away softly. The girl spotted Georgie past the boy's elbow

(Georgie winked, she ducked) and whispered something to the boy and they left, and the older couple soon followed them out. The woman was either a whore or somebody's wife. If he'd come here earlier, he might have made out. It was when everyone was out of the place that, looking around, you realized how filthy it was.

The singer did an Elvis imitation of "When the Blue Moon Turns to Gold," apparently the house theme and just for him, for him and the bartender, who applauded, then, setting down his guitar, came over to the bar, to try to cadge a drink maybe, and Georgie told him flat out he hated hillbilly music. "Go fuck a horse," he said. The guy only grinned faintly out of the side of his mouth and shrugged and said there wasn't much else he knew how to do except drink and split the beaver, maybe Georgie had a better idea for picking up enough small change to get by. He didn't. That eased things, and though neither could afford to buy the other a drink, they ended up trading tales, leaning there on the bar, Georgie finding himself telling the truth for a change about his fucked up family and fucked up life, while the singer, who introduced himself as Duke (Georgie gave him his Italian name, just to let him know where he was coming from), told him about the shit life of the country music road circuit, and the even shittier life of the bush leagues. He said, when asked, he used to throw a little, and Georgie said he used to hit a little but could never stay sober enough to go pro. Georgie even got around to telling about the girl who had been killed, the girl who was, he only realized this just now, the true love of his life. "One thing about country music," Duke said, "is they got a song for ever damn thing that ever went wrong. They ain't many differnt tunes, but some words is better'n others." "And some words are worse," Georgie said and asked him why he was singing that sick mommy and daddy graveyard merda when he came in. "The girl ast for it. It was the third time I'd done 'White Dove' for the moony little thing tonight. Probly has to do with the first night she got laid. Most usually does." Georgie felt warm enough toward Duke by then to ask him if he'd like to join him on a run to Waterton, go give the dog a bone, but Duke said it was still too early, he had to stay on until midnight in case anyone came in. "But I'll be around. Got no place to go. Drop in agin."

The fat unseasonal snow is still falling in thick clots as Georgie, hunched over the steering wheel, pulls out of the motel parking lot. After the warm day, it is mostly melting as it falls, though it is a nuisance without windshield wipers and the roads are greasing up. Ruby is making a farting noise; that cheap gas he bought was probably watered down. Ought to forget it. Way he's feeling, he may not be able to raise a boner anyway. But it's his last chance while he still has wheels. Lem will be pissed off enough about him keeping the car overnight, especially since he won't be buying it, so no chance for seconds—it's tonight or who knows. Another thing he should have picked up on his rounds, he considers, was a pack of Redi-Wets. Old Doc Foley used to give all the boys free rubbers and showed them with a broom handle how to use them. Could use some now, but he's not a boy any longer. Learned that tonight if he didn't know it before. And anyway, it's too late, he's already a VD donor.

"Goddamn it, Ruby," Georgie asks, "what's all this for? If life is such shit, why do we go on living it?" He answers himself: Because you're scared not to, asshole. And because there's always hope for one more piece of tail. He pats the dashboard (he's glad he didn't turn her in, he'd be all alone without her), his nose at the windshield, trying to see through it, thinking about dying. Or rather, trying not to, but unable to keep it out. Where was Marcella Bruno killed? On this road? No, out by the mine. "What's it like, Ruby? What happens when you die?" The Waterton road is empty, almost spookily so. Nobody else fool enough to be out. No risk of hitting anybody, but it is easy to lose the road altogether. Can't see through the window but when he sticks his head out he gets snow in his face. Maybe he should never let Ruby go, he's thinking. Just drive through Waterton and keep on rolling. Go somewhere warm, make some money, fix her up. Whitewall tires. Radio. Leopard-skin seat covers, soft to stroke. Then he sees it, a small dark thing scurrying across the snowy road out in front of him with glowing ruby dots where its eyes are. It startles him with its sudden challenging presence. Raccoon maybe. Cat. Squirrel. Whatever. It's dead meat. Georgie floors the accelerator. No pickup at all. If anything the old girl slows down. He knows if he can hit this thing, everything will be all right. "Come on, sweetheart, throw your hips into it! You can do it!" His fingers are snapping at the wheel as if working pinball flippers, his whole body twisting and pushing. The animal has frozen. He's got it! And then, just as he's about to score, Ruby starts to fishtail, he whips the wheel back and forth trying to straighten her out, everything is suddenly spinning around him, trees that weren't there wheeling about in front of his face, and he braces for the impact.

The whumping crumple of metal is not as loud as he'd expected, though in the silence that follows it echoes loudly in his mind. He has been thrown around, whacked his head on the window, but he's okay. He switches off the motor, leaves the lights on, crawls out. He has wrapped Ruby around a light pole on the passenger side, the old girl nearly cloven in half at the waist, her rear end at an angle to the rest of her. "Oh, baby. I'm sorry." He is. It is the saddest thing that has happened in a long sad day. He's even crying a little. For her. For himself. He walks around her in the falling snow, whispering his apologies. His farewells. He crawls back in on the driver's side to rescue the centerfold, looking a bit the worse for wear. He kisses the steering wheel, getting out. He has a long walk back to face. But first he clambers up on Ruby's hood and, kneeling there in pious homage, lowers his pants, and using the centerfold's taunting raised ass to arouse himself, jerks off on Ruby's cracked windshield, fantasizing a loving blowjob ("Marcella! I love you!" he whispers as he comes). His final blessing. He wipes himself with the centerfold, no doubt inking his dick colorfully, and, a mile or so down the snowy road toward town, tosses it in the ditch.

# I.5

## Wednesday I April – Friday 3 April

Her true love is wedged deep inside her as if trying to take root there. Oh, would that he might! She squeezes as hard as she can, gripping his muscular bottom tightly, her ankles locked around his thighs, wishing this moment could last forever. She feels like she is in Heaven, floating on silvery clouds (she will say so later in her diary), waves of ecstasy throbbing through her like a sweet angelic storm. Five years of a terrible emptiness, this is what he is filling. Her dark ages. Oh, oh! Her whole being is flooded with rapturous delight. Soft white snow is falling all about them like the feathers of a dove, curtaining them where they lie on her bed of dreams in the back of Tommy's mother's station wagon. "Oh, I love you, Tommy!" she whispers. "With all my heart! I do!" Tommy moves slowly in her as though he too wishes to prolong this awesome moment for as long as possible, and as he does so she can feel her whole body begin to vibrate with liquid desire. He raises himself up to gaze adoringly down upon her and she knows herself to be a glowing image of fire, passion, and love.

The day opened up warm and sweet, heralding a new awakening. Angela arose feeling blissfully happy, fully alive. No heroine she has ever read about ever felt more so. On her way to the bank, she saw a white dove perched on a telephone wire like a kind of miracle, and she crossed herself and prayed to it, and now what she prayed for has come true. Oh, thank you, God! Thank you, Santa Maria, madre di Dio, piena di grazie! "White Dove" is their song, a strange song for lovers, yet prophetic too, for their love is tinged with the sorrow of dead and dying mothers. It was playing on the car radio that night, when, as the only gift she had to give, she gave him her virginity out here at the ice plant. Where she insisted on coming tonight. A sacred place (now doubly so), a sacred day. His white dove, Tommy called her that night so long ago, kissing her breasts worshipfully. They were much smaller then, she was still just a child, immature in body and mind. She dried his beautiful organ with her own panties (there was precious blood), her head leaning against his chest, listening to his pounding heart. And this day (she is an April fool for love!) is now another for her secret calendar.

He picked her up at the bank, not in his father's car but in the family station wagon, which was now his own car up at college, his mother being too ill to drive. Angela had hoped to see the big Lincoln come rolling up front to receive her as it had in times past (she had told her friend Stacy to watch), but now she is grateful for the extra room. It had been her suggestion that he come to the bank so they could go for a ride first, for she really didn't want him to come to her house where her sour old grump of a father would be sitting in his front porch rocker in his dirty clothes like he always is, drinking beer and bellyaching, coming out with who knows what awful remarks. They drove out to the lakes and nearly got right to it—a breast was out and his hand was between her legs almost before she knew it, and she knew she was soaking wet down there and feared for a moment she had lost the power to resist—but she jumped out of the car, gasping for breath, and they went for a walk holding hands and other things (well, his hands were all over, he could not restrain himself), and even as she walked along, she was suffering little orgasms almost like hiccups.

It clouded over and a cold wind came up (her panties were off, she can't even remember how that happened), so they went to the Blue Moon Motel for supper. She had a chicken salad sandwich, but she could only eat half of it, she was too excited, and she kept having to use the bathroom. It turned out there was a country singer in the lounge named Duke L'Heureux, so they went in, and since they were almost alone they danced for a while. Duke L'Heureux was pretty awful and they whispered jokes to each other about him ("What do you expect, with a name like that!"), but they asked him to sing "White Dove" for them and he did, several times, and Tommy bought him some drinks, so it was really a nice time, though Tommy's hardness rubbing against her and his hands squeezing her breasts and pinching her nipples and stroking her bottom and crawling down between were driving her crazy. If he had asked her to take her clothes off and lie down on the dance floor, she would have done it. She wanted to get a room immediately in spite of all her romantic plans and she knew he was thinking the same thing, but then one of her father's stupid friends turned up and started ogling her and she pulled Tommy out of there. It was beginning to snow when they returned to the car. It was very beautiful, and she reached into Tommy's pants and took hold of him and kissed him hard on the mouth and asked him to drive to the ice plant, her head in his lap, kissing him all the way, and he had to stop for a moment to avoid having an accident.

Now he is sliding back and forth in her with measured strokes, still gazing down upon her with a look of intense fascination in his eyes, as though he cannot see enough. And then he kisses her, tenderly yet hungrily, his tongue licking her lips and exploring the recesses of her mouth, while his thrusts become more urgent and his fingers reach for her other opening down below, sending electric tremors of pleasure and mad desire racing through her, and she rises to meet him in a moment of uncontrolled passion, crying out in her delight. When she was a little girl she had once heard her parents say of a friend of theirs who was not married but was expecting a child that she had been touched by the finger of God, and though the grownups seemed to think that was funny, it made Angela recall that painting in St. Peter's in Rome of God's finger, the one touching Adam. There was something so mighty and awesome about that finger, frightening even, and she had never forgotten it. That's what it feels like inside her now. The finger of God.

Snow is falling outside her window, recalling for her a long-ago walk through a snowy campus, a night of such exquisite purity, the flakes dropping past the lamps overhead like big soft petals. It was the first night he said he loved her, and during the long goodnight kisses outside her sorority, she let his hands cup her breasts. Such strong masculine hands—as was he in all respects—and so handsome, so passionate, and yet so kind and gentle. So loving. In the spring, she accepted his fraternity pin (his brothers serenaded her, singing the song with her name in it) and, trusting him implicitly, she surrendered to him before they separated for the Easter holidays. Which were agonizing days for both of them. Mail was slow and phone calls difficult and expensive, so he drove all the way to her parents' house to see her, and they walked hand in hand along the river, and he made love to her standing up against a secluded tree, and though it was all so new to her, she was able to laugh at the awkwardness of it, and then, still joined together, she cried. As she is crying now, and without him here to comfort her. Nor wanting him, for he is no comfort. She shudders and calls for the home care nurse Bernice, asks her to bring her one of her photo albums. The long white one.

The Presbyterian manse lights are off and the curtains are open on this first night of April, and Prissy Tindle, who should perhaps at this moment be known by her stage name of Priscilla Parsons, is dancing the "Dance of the Annunciation" for Reverend Wesley Edwards by the pale glow of the unseasonable snow falling outside. She has been thinking about it and choreographing it in her mind all day, ever since she saw the shimmering white dove preening itself in much balmier weather outside her kitchen window this morning. Her horoscope encouraged artistic endeavor and suggested that she foster new relationships with imagination and transparency. Which she took to mean she should dance with her clothes off. Wesley's record collection leaves much to be desired (it is probably his wife Debra's, that silly woman, he seemed to know nothing about it), but at least she was able to find Debussy's *Nocturnes*, the "Clouds" piece being both texturally and thematically appropriate for the angel Gabriel descending from Heaven while the dove of the Holy Spirit casts its fertilizing beam upon the magical scene. The mystery of mysteries. Forget your risen Christ, this is it.

Priscilla has chosen to interpret that mystery, not from the perspective of one of the three protagonists, but as an expression of the exchange occurring between them, including the respectful but lordly intrusion of the messenger, Mary's bewilderment and disbelief, and the dove's sweet feathery aggression, focusing, as the album cover notes say about the nocturne, on "an instant of pure beauty," which is also of course an instant of pure terror. All of this is, simultaneously, in her dance. Further nuances of gesture have been suggested by other album notes regarding the melting of juxtaposed discords into impressions of lucent sonorities, the rich languorous tone of the English horn set against the undulating background of the other instruments (languorous undulation is one of her best moves), and Debussy's own remark that the music he desired "must be supple enough to adapt itself to the lyrical effusions of the soul and the fantasy of dreams," which describes perfectly her own lifelong aspirations as a dancer.

Suppleness perhaps comes less easily to her now, her body being less lithe than it once was, her feet no longer quite leaving the floor in her little springs, but time claims its little victories, what can you do. Not that she is any heavier, she has always been careful about that, dieting and exercising regularly, but her flesh has rearranged itself subtly, adding a touch of texture here and there, as she thinks of it, and in what she hopes is an opulent and intriguing way. And she can still touch the floor with her palms without bending her knees, a gesture that always gives Wesley particular delight (he has often kissed her then highest parts in respectful gratitude). Wesley, too, is naked, for she has explained to him that he will join her in her dance, or at least be part of it. And, semitumescent, he has been watching her and commenting on her performance and on her beauty with his indwelling Christ, who claims to feel quite abashed (Wesley's translation) at this celebration of his conception. With his, or their, eyes upon her she feels flushed with anticipation. The room is sweetly perfumed as if with incense, adding to the sacred aura, for the three of them have been using Wesley's briar pipe to smoke the marijuana she brought, the teeth marks on the stem giving her a sense of profound intimacy. Like sharing a toothbrush.

Priscilla can empathize with Wesley's Christ within. She herself has always felt there to be another dancer inside her, trying to express herself—or itself—in a body that is, alas, never wholly responsive to its demands. In effect, this inner dancer represents the distance between the way she imagines herself dancing and the way it actually turns out. Although Prissy has held no two-sided conversations with this dancer within, she has sometimes spoken to her, or it, usually in exasperation or apology, much as one speaks to one's conscience, and sometimes "listens" to it, too, if not literally or with much compliance. Her husband Ralph, with whom she danced in her early days, used to complain about her muttering while dancing, saying that it broke his concentration while communing with the music, which for him was a sacred connection, her muttering therefore a kind of sacrilege. All she could say to the pompous ass was he just didn't, or couldn't, or wouldn't understand, which is the sort of philistine incomprehension poor dear Wesley is now enduring in this town. Reviled and ridiculed, abandoned, expelled from his pulpit and facing eviction from his home and, as she discovered today when trying to bank for him what's probably his last paycheck (though she hasn't told him, won't, for fear of what he might do or ask her to do), pauperized by his traitorous wife, no doubt in collusion with his worst enemy, the bank owner. He has his rights, he cannot be evicted without due process, cannot be arrested for he has committed no crime, and he seems determined to stay put and fight his oppressors, but Prissy knows this is too dangerous. If the deacons can get him certified, as they intend, the men in little white suits will come to get him and he'll be straitjacketed and locked away where she cannot help him.

Immediately after her "Water Dance of the Megalopsychoi" on Sunday night, their hair still wet and shoes not yet on, Wesley wanted her to drive him out to the church camp so that he might confront Debra with all her crimes against him, including something having to do with his golfclubs which Prissy didn't understand, and to demand of her that she not sign any papers presented to her by the church deacons and that she give him his stolen car back. She felt complete sympathy with the poor man from the bottom of her heart, but she couldn't do it. She was afraid. Of the scandal, sure, and of having to face Debra, and of Wesley's currently explosive temperament which might land them in all sorts of horrible trouble, but mostly she was afraid of those strange violent people with their diabolic visions of ultimate catastrophes. She had been afraid to go out to the stormy mine hill when they were waiting for the end to come, though she had witnessed their bizarre frenzies on live television while doing her morning exercises, never having seen so much exposed flesh on the screen before. Later, the networks censored most of it, but that morning it was all on display, all the fat wet bottoms and flopping breasts and all the screaming and whipping and the mad muddy brawl that followed, the beatings and the arrests—it was a nightmare, she couldn't bear it, she had to turn it off. She'd had no idea until church on Easter morning that those awful people were back, so she was in a state of alarm and anticipation even before everything else that had happened. Her horoscope that morning had urged her to take bold advantage of any unforeseen circumstances, and, well, she did.

"No," says Wesley now to his inner Jesus, while slowly exhaling a pale plume of smoke, "that must have been the dove descending, not the Virgin fleeing the scene of the crime." She realizes that thinking about Sunday morning has made her dancing increasingly agitated and fluttery, quite out of character with the music, and she has completely lost the thread of her argument, an unfortunate tendency Ralph often complained about. But no time to think about that, for "Clouds" is receding, its grand vistas about to give way to the dazzlingly festive and more earthbound "Fetes" nocturne. "The Dance of Life," someone has called it, with its sensuous melodies and celebrative processions, and during it she will, as the adoring Virgin, receive, by the silvery light of the falling snow, the Holy Spirit on the living room carpet, which she has earlier vacuumed for just this purpose. In the silence between the two nocturnes, she stoops to Wesley's floppy little bird and puts it to her ear like an old-fashioned telephone receiver, and Wesley, his hand stroking her bottom as though to say you have found favor, explains to Jesus, "I think she's trying to hear you directly. Say something." No, he has misunderstood, but no matter, the power of her touch is having its usual magical effect and the bird is puffing up and pushing its beak against her ear as though to impregnate her as Mary was impregnated. The jubilant procession has begun. The Virgin, making herself prostrate before her Lord, lifts her voice and sings: "Here am I, the servant of the Lord; let it be with me according to your word."

"Somebody loves me," the town travel agent and current Rotary Club president Gus Baird croons, waltzing through the bank, winking at the giggling young tellers and passing out flyers advertising a special holiday rate for flights to Brazil. "I wonder who?" He knows who, even as he points to each of them. No one. It's a sad song. Gus loves everybody but no one loves him. "Who can she be? I wish I knew!" The girls are used to Gus and carry on; he's in here every day, telling his silly jokes, dancing his dances. By chance his old WCHS classmate Emily Wetherwax née Hopkiss enters through the front door, and he sidles up to her: "For every girl who passes me I shout, Hey, may-*be*," and he does a little shuffle around her, goes down on one knee, "you were meant to be my lovin' ba-*by!*" Emily laughs and does a plump turn of her own before continuing to the counter, shaking her head (she turned him down in high school, she turns him down now, it's a habit, everyone's habit), and the girls clap and laugh. "Hey, wow," one of the Italian girls says, "Brazil! Great! Where is it?" Gus strikes something like a bullfighter's pose or else that of a tango dancer, clicks his heels and sings: "South of the bor-*derr*, down Mex-ee-co way!" "Gene Autry does that better," says Earl Goforth, the scarred war veteran who owns the old movie house on Main Street, talking out of the hole in his cheek as he empties a canvas bag of coins at the business counter, "and he can't sing neither." The pretty kid from college who's interning—first newcomer in a decade—is watching Gus with a puzzled smile, so he twitches his shoulders like Jimmy Cagney and, with a glance at a bank calendar set out to help people date their checks and deposit slips, growls with what he hopes is a fair imitation of Bogie, "Don't mind us, kid. It's what we do on Thursdays." For some reason she blushes. That doesn't happen often. He blushes back.

"Just because some preacher's a kook, Sal, doesn't mean the whole religion is crazy."

"No. On the other hand, if the whole religion is crazy, then every preacher's a kook, right?"

Sally Elliott is sitting on the Cavanaugh screened-in front porch, having a beer and a toke with Tommy, discussing interesting topics of the day. She has managed to bump into him just about every day and this evening she found him babysitting his sick mom while his dad was away on a business meeting, the home care nurse having the day off, so he was feeling unhappy and more amenable to company than usual. The days are getting longer, the sun's still out, yesterday's freak snowstorm is ancient history. There are still a few dirty white spots in dark shadowy places looking like little blisters, but spring is sprung. She is wearing her dirty cutoffs, a faded rose-colored T-shirt, and her grotey trenchcoat, which is not really hers but her father's, rescued one day from the trash can, redolent with garbage and washed only once since, when her mother stole it from her and tossed it in with a load of golf togs. The shirt reads: THIS IS MY BODY. It's her hand-crafted Easter tee. Earlier, Tommy was staring at it thoughtfully and she wondered if, amazingly, he was admiring those little bumps he used to fondle. She stretched the shirt out so he could read it better, and what he said was: "I was just thinking: How would that look if my mother was wearing it?"

Well, he's depressed about his mother, she understands that and knows he's hurting. Little Boy Blue. He is feeling let down, as though the world has double-crossed him. His mother was not supposed to fall apart like this. All of which has led them to the meaning of life, or rather, the meaninglessness of it, and the way that religion steps in to provide a comforting madness (her word). Which is what has been happening to his mother, who has been moving toward the radical evangelical line, much to Tommy's dismay. He finds he cannot even talk to her anymore; she's gone completely wiggy. The end is at hand, Christ is knocking on the door, repent before the shit hits the fan, and all that. The problem is, ultimate things are not in Tommy the Jock's repertoire. The topics of religion and craziness have in turn led them to the lunatic Presbyterian preacher and his dippy wife, the scandal of the day. When the preacher freaked out Sunday morning and stormed out of the church, Tommy's dad asked Tommy to tail him to make sure he didn't do himself or others harm, whereupon Tommy ended up out in the country with the rain bombing down and a crazy preacher charging down upon him and sending him straight to hell.

"He kept waving his arms about out there and shouting at the rain. It was weird, man."

"Tommy Cavanaugh, private dick. Or not so private." That sounds like the making of one of her Tom and Sally stories. Tom and Sally Play Detectives. Like playing doctors but with magnifying glasses. Tom and Sally and the Case of the Disappointing Universe. "So, imagine, the guy has a gun pointed at his temple. What do you do?"

"I don't know. Probably look the other way and duck."

"Your dad asked my parents to visit Auntie Debra. They want her to sign some papers to get Reverend Edwards committed."

"So I've heard. They tell me she's shacked up out there with some kid."

"Colin Meredith. She is taking care of him. The blond cutie from the orphanage. The emaciated angel. Remember him?"

"Vaguely. A flake. A pal of Ugly Palmers."

"Carl Dean? They don't seem to have much in common."

"Ugly didn't have many pals. Meredith was just about the only guy who could stand him. A couple of fucked-up loners. Ugly ended up in the pen, your blond angel in the loony bin. The Reverend's wife must be even crazier than he is."

"That's what my dad thinks, though he only thinks whatever your dad thinks. As far as he's concerned, they're all nuts out there. They should just put a fence around the place and send the doctors in."

"He's probably right."

"Yeah, well, they're all nuts in here, too, and he hasn't figured that out yet. What do you think? Is he going to lose his Chamber job?"

"Nah, why should he?" Tommy says, but he's blushing, caught off guard by her broadside, and Sally knows it's true. Damn. The only hope is that it's too dumb a job and no one else will want it. "How about another beer?"

"Sure. More ganja?"

"Why not."

While he's gone, she takes her notebook out of her trenchcoat pocket and writes, thinking about his mother inside (she can hear Tommy talking to her): There's only now. And when that's insupportable, there isn't even that. She pauses, adds: The hardest thing in life is to face the fact of nothingness without a consoling fantasy: at the brink, no way back, unable to jump. The only thing left is to grow up. That's a bit heavy so she writes: Inspiration: His hand on my ass. It felt like God about to take a bite. There's a cartoon she has drawn on the page of a sleeping princess with a wicked grin and her hands between her legs. Absently, trying not to think about that stupid night at the ice plant, she defaces the sleeper with a mustache and beard and a rising dick, then writes: He's not asleep, he's just been hymnotized. It's a sick world, she thinks, but (she writes): With a bit of dope, there's always hope. And, stuffing the notebook back in her pocket as Tommy returns with the beers, she rolls a buddha. She's feeling good. Rising sweetly into the evening.

Let's see what happens. "So, how did we get here?" she asks, gazing out distractedly upon the technicolor neighborhood, gilded by the dipping sun, while licking her cigarette paper. "One day we're a kid, and the next we're not."

"And the next day we're a kid again."

"Some of us just never get it." She lights up, sucks in a lungful, passes him the joint. "When are you going back?"

"Sunday afternoon. Econ test Monday. But," he wheezes, exhaling slowly, "I'll be back from time to time because of Mom. Except during finals. How about yourself?"

"Not going. Just a lot of exams I'm not ready for. Taking incompletes. My dad's totally hacked, but what's the big deal about graduating? I'll finish up next year."

Tommy nods. "I just want to get this part over with, try on the next thing. While you're catching up, I'll be backpacking through Europe."

My plans exactly. Let's meet up. Share room costs. But what she says is: "How tall are you now?"

"Six two."

"That's pretty tall."

"Not enough for the courts. I have to play guard, and I'm not quick enough. They kept me on the team up at State through most of my junior year, but when I didn't grow, they dropped me. Which was okay. Too much like the army anyway."

She's heard otherwise, badboy stuff, but she lets it go. "Not so long ago, you know, I was taller than you. To prove it, we stood nose to nose and touched foreheads, do you remember? I could feel that little lump down there pushing against me. I was trying to figure out just what it was. That's why it took me so long to get the measurement right."

He grins and his expression suddenly turns warm and affectionate and she flatters herself that she has got something right at last. Cool. She feels a sweet glow in her chest and other parts. But he's looking over her shoulder. Angela Bonali has pulled up at the curb in a girlfriend's car. His old high school flame. Shit. She's been through this before. Tommy drops the spliff and trots down there, tail wagging. They kiss, glance up at her, laugh, kiss again. Out comes the notebook.

They have met some distance away, at the new motel out on the highway, where she has a room on weekends, for cocktails and dinner. With fresh oysters from who knows where, very nice, and a pianist quietly playing golden oldies. Their Thursday treat. They have avoided all the difficult topics at dinner, talking instead—when they weren't just holding hands and saying how much they loved each other—about the arrival of spring and the surprise snowfall, about the need for better public relations to draw new industry to the area, and about the threat to that hope apparently posed by the evangelical cult that originated in the town and has now returned, intentions unclear. She sympathizes with his worries (she loves the way his brows knot up when he's troubled, loves it more when his smile and love light smooth the knot away), but, not religious herself, or at least not in his way, there was not much she could say about the problem of the cult except to suggest that maybe the cheapest thing would be to buy them all one-way tickets and guidebooks to the Holy Land, which he said (there came the smile, there went the knot) he didn't think would work. There were presumably thousands of the cultists by now, a lot of whom he expects will be descending on the camp and the town over the next couple of weeks. It all seems quite remote to her, but she supposes it means she may see less of him until all that is over, so she is able to share his sadness. This affair has surprised her with its spongy intensity, filling her up as it fills up with itself, making all else irrelevant. Though she has tried to end it (it's not right), she can't. Now, in their room, though their kisses on closing the door were as tender and searching as ever, his strong hands under her skirt exploring her with the usual urgency, the knot has returned and he is taking his time about undressing and coming to bed. She puts her chin on her crossed hands and draws her knees up under her breasts, raising her bottom in the air, her little nightie falling down around her shoulders. She knows that he adores her young body and cannot look away. He likes to lick it all over, starting with the little pink butterfly tattoo on her tailbone, as she does his. "You'll catch cold like that," he says as if scolding, but she can see that he is excited, even before his shorts come down. Always a nice moment. She finds his softening belly endearing. He is such a powerful man, still very athletic, even a bit intimidating, and his soft fuzzy belly, which she likes to lay her head on while she's fondling him, makes him seem more human and vulnerable. "You know, when I was a little girl I used to pray like this," she says. "I had read the Bible stories and been told about the birds and bees and I put the two together: I wanted to be the mother of Jesus and I was, as you might say, opening my ear to the Angel of the Lord." His gentlemanly laughter thrills her. As does his tongued "I love you!" to her opened ear.

"Thank ye, lays'n gents! That song, as we like to say down to Nashville town, went out to some very special folks here tonight. I'm fixin' to take a short break now, but I got a mess more a heart-stoppin' boot-stompin' country tunes to lay on your ears, or noses, or whatsomever y'tune in with, so don' go way. Anybody lookin' to stand me a beer, I'll be parked right over here…

"…Whoa! Lookit what's landed at my table! You settin' to buy me a drink?"

"No, honey, I'm clean broke. Only popped in here to see if I couldn't find a nice gentleman who'll tempt me with one."

"Ifn I was a nice gentleman, purty lady, I might. What was wrong with that feller who was leanin' all over you at the bar, the one with the big lump on his forehead?"

"I seen by the way he was tugging at hisself and by the spots on his pants he's most probably got a dose. So I told him I was with you to shake him off. Hope it don't offend you."

"Nope. Wisht you'd worked a drink off him first, though. We coulda shared it."

"You the sharing type?"

"When it suits me. This where you sprung from?"

"Yeah. But I left here twenty some years ago when I was still a kid. Nobody knows me anymore. Patti Jo Glover, Duke. What's your handle? The real one?"

"I ain't tellin'."

"That bad, hunh? Hey, you got nothing on me."

"Patti Jo? What's wrong with that?"

"Well, it's not Patti Jo. I'll tell you if you tell me."

"Awright, you funny-names fans, git a grip. It's Armand. Armand Rendine. That's it, darlin', that's whom I am. Whaddaya laughin' at?"

"I'm not laughing. It's cute. Sounds like it must be French."

"I like to think I got some bayou in me. It's good fer the marquee. Thoughta callin' myself Bayou Duke. Probly jist commonplace everday downriver canuck, though."

"Bayou L'Heureux rhymes better. What was your mama's name?"

"Rendine."

"Uh oh. One of those, hunh? Why they call you Duke?"

"Picked it up back when I was pitchin' bush league, along with a messa other tags, mostly not usable in polite company."

"Well, that's me, all right. So, a baseball player, hunh? You don't strike me as the athletic type."

"Wasn't mucha one. I could throw a purty mean fastball but not mostly where I aimed to. Spent mosta my time out in the bullpen gittin' blisters on my butt and tellin' dumb jokes. To kill the time, I picked up a box in a pawn shop and fooled around with it out there, entertainin' the fans bored with the games, gittin' a bigger hand than any the players done. So I quit baseball and headed fer Oprytown."

"Yeah, I heard them announce you as coming direct from Nashville, Tennessee."

"Oh, I'm *from* there awright. 'Direct' might be stretchin' it. Left that town a whole long buncha years ago. But as I been driftin' round out in nowheresville without a address ever since, I spose y'could say 'direct.' It's jist took me a while to git here is all, bein' as I git lost easy."

"Did you ever play at Grand Ole Opry?"

"Got a backup gig at Ryman wunst when the flu was goin' round and they was a mite desprit. Had two weeks over to a bar in Madison singin' with a lady friend. But that was the sum total a my Nashville joys. They was nuthin fer it finally but to pack my cardboard suitcase and hit the road. So I'm still out in the bullpen, as y'might say."

"What happened to the lady friend?"

"She quit the racket and married a dentist."

"Smart girl. But you seem to have a lotta fans here."

"Friday night at the Moon. No place else to go. Most of 'em'd probly rather hear band music."

"Well, you don't make it easy on them. That was an awful song about dead mommies you were just singing. Who were the special folks?"

"Them kids over there. The ones puttin' on the floor show and excitin' all the patrons. It's a purty unwholesome weeper, and I ain't big on religious songs in genral, nor not religion neither, but they're new reglars and got a amorous hankerin' fer that tune and the boy sets me up with a beer ever now'n then, so what can y'do?"

"I been watching them. The boy's gonna dump her."

"Everbody dumps everbody. What's important is the moment. They're havin' a good moment. I better git back to it and see what I can do fer 'em. Any requests?"

"You say gospel's not your thing. What is?"

"Honky tonk mostly."

"Okay, so how about 'If You Got the Money, Honey, I Got the Time?' Or 'Honky Tonk Blues?'"

"You got it."

...

"Hey, I'm impressed! You can even yodel! Chased those kids right outa here, though."

"They ain't goin' far. Jist down the hall."

"And thanks for the beer."

"Thank the kid."

"Oh. He bought that one for you. I'm sorry."

"Did it taste good?"

"Best I ever had."

"There y'go then. Enjoy the moment, Patti Jo, and fuck the rest."

"I like your grin. It spreads all over your face. I like your singing, too. Didn't think I would at first. You can't hold a note for long so the slow stuff's not so great. 'White Dove' was a cooked goose. Likewise, 'He'll Have to Go.' It'll have to go. But if you can move your voice around, you got something."

"You sorta jist lean back and let fly, dontcha?"

"I'm nothing if not honest, Duke. If that's the word for mouthing off like I do. Can't hold it back."

"Yeah? Not me. I was a born liar. Who was y'talkin' to while I was up there?"

"Just to myself. Bad habit I got."

"Now *you're* lyin'."

"Mmm. Dead sister. It's a conversation we have. I just sorta keep hearing her like."

"All the time?"

"No, mostly only when I got troubles. Which I suppose is next thing to all the time."

"Well, we seem t'be playin' in the same ballpark, Patti Jo. How old was your sister?"

"Just barely borned. She died of diphtheria before I came along. But I happened next and I always felt like she got reborned in me."

"Reminds me of a guy I knowed in the bush leagues. He played second base and he was always yappin' away there behind the pitchers, drivin' us nuts. I ast him who he was talkin' to, and he said he had the whole St. Louis team inside a him and they was always goin' at each other and never give him a moment's rest. I tole him I understood now why they called 'em the Gashouse Gang, and mebbe all he needed was a bicarb. So whatsa funny name? Gimme a laugh."

"Patricia Josefina Petteruti. That's the short version."

"You sound half-cracker, but I thought you had the Eye-talian look."

"That a bad thing?"

"Hell, no. I love it. The cook in this bedbox is Eye-talian. Cep fer the garlic, I cain't git enough."

"My dad was a coalminer here. Got killed in the Deepwater disaster five years back. Ever hear about that?"

"Yeah, sometimes I sing that Ben Wosznik song about it, the one he done down at Grand Ole Opry. The one, y'know, that starts—y'begun to say sumthin?"

"No. Well...no."

"Well, probly y'don't like reminders. Sorry bout your ole fella."

"I'm not. I hope the sick bastard rots in hell. When I was about twelve or so, my mom packed up and left him, dragging us around with her. She had raised us Catholic because she thought she had to, but she dropped all that when we took up traveling. Left us all pretty mixed up on that subject. Only thing left is I still cross myself when I'm in trouble."

"So you took your ma's name."

"No. Well, yes, probably. Can't remember. Never went to school after that, so I never had to tell anyone my name. She did start calling me Patti Jo around then. When she was sober. Worse names when she wasn't. She took good care of us but she had a mean backhand and a temper that just took the top of her head off sometimes, especially when coming down or when a hangover'd got the best of her. Haven't seen her since I first got married, and I don't miss her."

"You've had a run at knot-tyin'."

"A few times. You?"

"Nope. When the Lord made me, he made a ramblin' man. Or else Ma did. She was a great disbeliever in the institution."

"I can feel for that. My first time was to an older guy when I was fifteen, maybe I got sold to him, who knows, it just kinda happened, and then later, when he kicked me out, to a coupla others, one of them named Glover, I forget which. I sorta blank out a lot."

"Y'been around the block, Patti Jo. Like them pore little honky tonk angels."

"Well, 'angel' might be like you coming direct from Nashville, Duke, stretching it a speck. Hung out mostly in trailer camps in those years of holy matrimony, washing dishes or waiting tables so as not to starve, picking up the way I talk. I was sick a lot as I remember. One of my husbands, Glover probably, liked to play cards and when he was short on cash he used me as his stake. He wasn't very good at cards, always drank too much, so I got passed around the camp a fair bit. Apprentice work, as you might call it. Then, when he was sober, he'd beat me for sleeping around. Knocked a coupla teeth out and cracked a rib. Finally one day I just got on a bus and went someplace else. And then just kept moving. Been to both coasts. All through the south. There's always a bus going somewhere, somewhere better than where you are. So from time to time I just buy a ticket and climb aboard. A bus is a cheap overnight hotel, sometimes you pick up a little trade, and you always wake up somewhere new."

"And that's how ye ended up in this burg?"

"Sort of."

"How'd y'git all the way out here to the Blue Moon Motel?"

"Well, no place to stay downtown. The old hotel's closed up and all its windows are busted out. They told me where this place was and I just walked out. Nice day. Even took a stroll through the old neighborhood. Which is just as ugly as I remembered. Only dirtier and more shrunk up."

"Memory lane. Ain't what it's cracked up to be. I got a song about it."

"You write your own material?"

"Sometimes. That song I just ruint bout a drunk mournin' his dead sweetheart fer a sample. Got that from that feller with the spotted pants who was introducin' hisself to you earlier on. So how long y'plannin' t'stay round?"

"Hard to say. Got a room here for tonight, but they're filling up. Those religious people. Everything's booked for next week. A coupla busloads from Florida."

"Yeah, I know. I gotta change my repertory for 'em. But they gimme a bunk'n mornin' grub here as part a the deal. You kin crash there a coupla nights ifn worse comes to worst."

"I sorta feel like that just happened, Duke. I had one real friend when I was in grade school here. She was a little older, like the big sister I never had. She was very pretty, not much bigger than me, a little strange, kinda poetical as you might say, but very sweet and loving. Well, she's dead now. I miss her a whole lot and I went around to all the places today we used to play and talk. Went by her house. It's all messed up and fenced off. Made me sad."

"That's what brung ye back here?"

"Not exactly. It's a long story. Sure you wanta hear it? When I get going I'm pretty hard to turn off."

"I got all night, Patti Jo. First, though, I gotta crank up another set. Anything y'wanta hear? I swear, no slow stuff. I know enough t'stick with my money pitch when my change-up ain't workin'."

"So, let's keep right on honky tonkin'. 'Lost Highway.' 'Walkin' the Floor Over You.' You into Elvis at all?"

"Who ain't?"

"How about 'Heartbreak Hotel' then?"

"Okay. I don't have his moves."

"Well, I wouldn't want you to."

. . .

"Hey, where'd the beers come from?"

"I figured I could stand us a round. Specially if I can start saving on my room rent."

"Mmm. That goes down a treat and a half. Y'hongry?"

"Haven't eaten since yesterday. Or maybe day before that."

"The cook always brings me a sandwich after my last set. One a them fat Eye-talian ones with the thick bread. I'll ask fer two. What'd your sister have t'say while I was away?"

"She said that's one handsome fella who can really sing his socks off."

"Your sister's got good taste."

"Well…it's really not my sister. That's the problem…"

"I'm waitin'…"

"When I was little, especially after we left town, I used to talk to my dead sister to beat back the loneliness. You know. Like other kids talk to their pets or stuffed animals. But I never had any pets or stuffed animals—all I had was this dead sister. I did sometimes have the weird feeling she was somehow living out the life she never had inside of me, like I owed it to her, or she thought I did, but mostly she was just somebody imaginary to tell my troubles to. Then, one day, she started talking back. Or it seemed like she did. Mostly saying she wanted me to come home. Now, from here on, it gets a little spooky…"

"I kin roll with it."

"Traveling around like I been doing, cut off from most everybody, you don't always get the news right away. It was only a year or so ago that one of those end-of-the-world preachers come through the town I was in and some working girls I knew talked me into going with them to hear him preach in a little storefront church nearby. And it was through the stories the preacher told that I learned that my friend from childhood, the one I was telling you about, had been killed. I didn't know that. I couldn't hardly believe what I was hearing. I just started crying and everybody thought I was getting religion, and maybe I was. She'd been killed and there was something important about it, almost like Jesus getting killed. When I got the dates sorted out in my head, I realized she'd died about the same time my dead sister had started talking back. And I knew then it wasn't my sister. It was my friend Marcella Bruno."

"Bruno? Y'mean this group that's gatherin' here now? The gal in that song Ben Wosznik useta sing?"

"Yes, and that's the really peculiar thing. When I finally got on the bus and come here like Marcella kept telling me to, I didn't know about those people moving back to town. I didn't even know who they were except for what that preacher told me or that they were from here or that they'd ever left. That so many more were on the way, like something was about to happen, was downright scary. I learned that here at the motel this afternoon and it almost took my breath away. It's like they all been listening to the same voice I been listening to."

"Well, doggone my soul, as Ma useta say. That's quite a story, Patti Jo. So you been wanderin' round town today, pickin' up vibes?"

"Yeah, and one thing Marcella said today, while I was walking through the playground at the grade school, was: That was *my* sister, Patti Jo. And then I remembered how I'd made it all up about my dead sister, that it was Marcella's sister who had died of diphtheria when she was just a baby, before Marcella was borned. I never had a sister... That sounds pretty crazy, right? Can I still use your room? I'm kinda scared and need company."

"You're on. It ain't no palace."

"Don't worry. I been in a lotta these places. It's almost like home. If I ever have a real home, I'll have to install ice machines, artificial potted plants, Gideon Bibles, old steam radiators that knock all night, and a macadam parking lot with fluorescent lights just to feel like I belong. I even got some grass to share, if you like. Picked it up from some kids on the bus."

"Hey now, that's the number one toppa the charts idea a the week, Patti Jo. I got my K's fer the night. Jist one more set, so's they'll feed us. I'll cut it short. Kin you sing?"

"I can almost carry a tune if it's not got any more notes than 'Jingle Bells.'"

"Okay, how bout 'Honky Tonk Angel'? It's silent movies in here. Let's jist have us some fun."

...

"I really liked singing with you, Duke. That was fun."

"Me, too. You ain't got a very big voice, but it's purty."

"Oh, I'm not a real singer. But you help. Best night I've had since can't remember when. I feel so good I almost feel bad. You're some kinda lover, too."

"Not mostly. I can genrally raise enough wood t'do the dirty, but cep fer the little spurt at the end, I don't git a whole bushel a kicks outa it. But you're sumthin special, Patti Jo. Took me clean outa my mizzerbul beat-down self. How long y'been doin' that?"

"Since I was twelve. My father did me in my confirmation dress. That's how I know I was twelve. I don't remember much about it, but I do recall the blood on the starchy white skirt and worrying how I was going to get it out before we had to go to church."

"And that was when your mama split."

"Well, yes, about that time, but I don't think him raping me was the main cause of it. She'd married this good-looking Italian high school football star who'd turned into a fat drunken bully like a prince into a toad, and finally after fifteen years or so had got fed up with him. Him and his quick fist. He always had this sick grin on his face when he hit you, and it was what you remembered even more than getting hit. She always said her only regret was that the mean sonuvabitch never got killed or crippled in a mine accident. But finally he did. I don't know if she was sorry about that or not, but probably not. Probably she went out and got drunk like it was a birthday party or something."

"I had this guy I useta play ball with. He was a pitcher like me, and though he couldn't throw as hard, he was trickier and sharper—he could smash a fly on a barn door at sixty feet—and he actually got a brief sniff at the big time. He was specially good at a inswingin' curve so sharp it could break batters' fingers on the bat, but that was his undoin' cuz them batters got pissed off and begun sendin' line drives straight back through the mound, aimin' at his dome. He was too quick fer 'em but eventually they nailed his pitchin' shoulder and he ended up workin' in a doughnut factory. But the point a my story is his ole man had been a sarge in the army, had got shot up and had, you know, one a them hinged meathooks fer a hand, and he used it to terrorize everbody, includin' the guy's ole lady, who went completely crackers from the thing and finally stuck her head in the oven, and his two sisters who was both somewheres round twelve or so like you was. He'd snap that claw over their shoulder from behind, push 'em to their knees and threaten to stick that hook up 'em and do a lot more damage ifn they didn't take it and shut up. Well, the guy noticed his old man was beginnin' to cast lustful looks his way, too, and he figgered it was time to git his little butt on the road. So he waited until one day the ole fella was humpin' one a his sisters and he had a good look at his backside with everthing floppin' and he took his baseball and sent in a hummer that crushed the ole guy's maracas. The sonuvabitch was in a unholy rage and come roarin' at him t'kill him, but the kid was waitin' fer him with a live wire that he calmly handed to the steel hook and walked away, leavin' the ole man dancin', and went off into the world t'seek his fame and fortune. Ain't that the berries? Whattaya laughin' at?"

"Your stories are always so funny, Duke. Why aren't my stories funny like that?"

"Probly cuz yours are true."

"Aren't yours?"

"Some parts. 'Djever have any kids?"

"I got pregnant a few times. A lotta miscarriages, if that's what they were. Had the weird feeling sometimes my dead sister was killing them off. Who I thought was my dead sister."

"Ain't none of 'em lived?"

"I don't think so. I think I would of remembered that."

"Well, I sure ain't fixin' t'make new ones, good lookin', but I wouldn't say no to encorin' our duet. I'd like t'try it agin, as the song goes. One more time."

"Sure. Move it on over, Duke, and come on in. You sing the high part this time, honey, I'll sing the low."

# I.6

## Sunday 12 April

"I don't like the man," John P. Suggs says plainly. "Never did."

"Well, his conversion seemed genuine," says Reverend Hiram Clegg, the plump silver-haired bishop of the State of Florida and president of the International Council of Brunist Bishops, who was present on the Night of the Sacrifice and witnessed that conversion. Reverend Clegg, the most successful of all the Brunist missionaries, has arrived at the Wilderness Camp today with two busloads of pilgrims from his Fort Lauderdale congregation, the first of hundreds of Brunist Followers expected later this week, and this little Sunday afternoon meeting in the church office has been called to talk about the logistics of all that and about the anniversary celebrations and dedication ceremonies next Sunday. It is, however, the imminent return of Reverend Abner Baxter, who is expected the day before those ceremonies that now has their full attention. Debra has been included in this meeting because of her knowledge of actions likely to be taken by city and state officials, and she is eager to exhibit the kind of thoughtful serenity that has been all too lacking of late (she doesn't know why she said those things at the Easter prayer meeting, it was as if she were under a spell—that holy ecstasy maybe that she'd been seeking, but it was terrifying, and she found herself suddenly coming like an impassioned bride in front of everybody). She has only the dimmest recollection of Reverend Baxter, though she has been aware of the anxiety he arouses and learned more about him during her shopping trips with Clara. "The man then stayed on here a time and suffered more than any of us from the persecution, escaping only when incarceration became imminent," Hiram continues. "And he has been intransigent in the vigorous propagation of the Brunist faith. He might not be the man you once knew."

"He was the one who struck that girl with his car and killed her, was he not?"

"That would seem to be the case," replies Hiram, whose people are presently getting a tour of the camp conducted by Darren and Billy Don. "If one ignores divine intervention. It could equally be said that God called her to His bosom and thereby launched our true religion, Abner Baxter merely His instrument of the moment, in the manner of Saul of Tarsus."

John P. Suggs grunts and shakes his burry head at that.

Ben would seem to agree with Mr. Suggs that Reverend Baxter is a troublemaker and apt to be disruptive ("There's no music in him," he says and Debra feels she understands exactly what he means), while Clara, like Hiram, is more inclined to be conciliatory and respect Baxter's loyal ministry on the grounds that not to include him, and with open arms, would amount to a failure of their mission, and that is Debra's thinking, too, though her only expression of this has been the occasional nod while Clara is speaking.

"I have known Red Baxter a very long time," says Mr. Suggs, whose own short-cropped white hair was probably once red, "since back when he was an atheistic God-hating communist. He has condemned me to hell or worse many times over. He is a power-grabber, a parasite, and a renegade firebrand. If he moves in here, he'll just bring trouble."

"Well, people moving in is surely a worry," Clara says. "And not just Abner and his folks. This is a home for our movement, but not a home for people. We are mighty grateful, Hiram, for putting your congregation into motels. You can tell by the way things are out there that we ain't set out for heaps of visitors. Soon as we're done, all us living here will be heading out again on our missionary travels, except for them who run the office and keep the place in order and receive visitors and the like." That's me, Debra thinks, a little shocked at witnessing her life, its critical turning turned, spread out before her suddenly like a dummy hand in bridge, a win still possible, but not hers to play, she at best a kibitzer. Tour guide. Outsider still. "But I know, no matter what we've told them, a goodly number of these folks coming to the dedication got no place to go afterwards. They ain't even sure there's gonna *be* a afterwards. They figure they're here till God calls them to glory. And I don't doubt but what Abner and his people are thinking the same way."

"I would not want to see that man residing here," says J. P. Suggs.

"Well, I don't know what we can do about it should he put it in his head to stay, seeing as how he's still the bishop of West Condon."

"That was a mistake," says J. P. Suggs. "I suggest you name a new one."

"Why are we so certain he wants to abandon his mission in the field?" asks Reverend Clegg. "He, too, may be inclined to think of this campsite development as a ceremonial home and central office, useful to him in the same way it is to the rest of us."

"I wouldn't count on it," says Ben.

The fear of Reverend Baxter's return leads to a discussion of the harassment of the camp the last couple of weeks by the locals, and Mr. Suggs says they'd best get on with fencing the camp off and patrolling it with armed guards. "I'll bring a work crew over. We'll use barbed wire." This idea does not find favor with Clara, for it does not fit her notion of the movement's frank openness and universality: "The Rapture ain't gonna happen only here at the camp. Them people need to be saved, too. Maybe they want to be. Maybe they're like little kids who say no when they mean yes." Debra too is dismayed at the idea of an armed camp, hating weapons of all kinds, but the men seem to accept it as inevitable, and Mr. Suggs explains how he will help. Clara glances her way as though to say: We shall see about this.

She and Clara did this week's grocery buying over at the shopping strip outside Randolph Junction in order to avoid West Condoners, but while her keys still worked, Debra wanted to make a quick trip to the Presbyterian manse, so they risked a drive into West Condon on the way back. Clara said that now the word was out, it was anyway better to meet them head-on and not be afraid, though she probably was afraid. On the way to the manse, they swung by the charred foundations of Clara's old home. Still much as it was five years ago, just more overgrown, the exposed basement filling up with weeds, leaves, litter, a sapling or two. "Like an untended grave," Clara said, gazing out the car window. "I loved that basement, and I miss it now. And the big porch we had out front. Ely would write his thoughts, setting out there in a old wooden rocker we had. That burnt up, too. They never found who done it. They left a burnt black hand in a shoebox by the door, and everbody said that was the name of a old Italian gang, while others blamed the Klan or the Satanists. At the time I imagined the hand was my dead husband Ely's and considered he mighta burnt our house down hisself as a hard message that all that was in the past, the Rapture was coming, Elaine and me we had to leave home and go out into the world to bring sinners to Jesus afore it was too late. Well, I was just so upset. Losing Ely was the worse thing ever happened to me, other than my boy getting killed in the war. Ely's hands was not burnt and he never lost one. Only the leg."

Mr. Suggs informs them now that, based on conversations he has had with the Deepwater mine owners, it appears the West Condon authorities have been anticipating they might try to gather on the mine hill next Sunday and are planning to bring the state police out to close off access as they have done in the past. Clara wonders if, given the growing hostility toward them in the area, they should hold their ceremonies here at the camp instead, but Hiram reminds them that his people are counting on gathering out there on the nineteenth; that is mainly why they have come here, to reach the Mount of Redemption and learn first-hand from personal witnesses about the events of five years ago. These are the Followers, mostly elderly retirees, who have raised much of the money for the electrification of the camp, and they have come a long hard way to be here. They have even brought along their own tunics, purchased from the company that, thanks to Hiram's initiative, now officially supplies them. Clara sighs and nods. "They're right. It don't make sense to be smack next to the Mount on such a day and not go there."

"Whose legal jurisdiction is that mine?" J. P. Suggs asks. "I think it must be the county's. I will speak to Sheriff Puller. Cavanaugh more or less owns the governor, but the governor is a weak man and I am sure he would like to stay out of this. We could give him cause to back off, leave it in the sheriff's hands. Besides, the owners of that mine are desperate to sell, and they know I am a prospective buyer."

"Well, we could simply finesse them," Debra suggests, aware, even as she speaks it, that that verb may not be familiar to the others. "I mean, we could all go out there the day before and just stay on. We could set up tents and have a big campfire and hold an all-night vigil like they used to do on Easter Eve. If we are already there, the very worst they can do is force us to leave, but they might not want the negative publicity of that."

This idea gets general approval. Saturday is after all the Night of the Sacrifice. They all gathered on the Mount around bonfires on that night, too, before what happened happened. Hiram says he's not sure all night on a hillside without adequate facilities is the best thing for his oldtimers, but once the hill is occupied, they could return to the motel, and if there is any sign of official resistance, they can be awakened and bused back out there. Mr. Suggs says he will see if he can get the washhouse latrines at the old mine reopened for the weekend. "Also," Hiram adds, "I think my good friend, the mayor of Randolph Junction, might wish to join us on the Mount on Sunday. There will be news media present. Any attempted arrests could then be the cause of much local embarrassment. He will be among us here tonight and we can discuss it with him."

On such a positive note, the meeting draws to a close, but not before Clara speaks, as she did on their shopping trip, of her dream of a proper Brunist tabernacle church to be built on camp land, or even on the Mount of Redemption if it can be acquired, something Mr.

Suggs is already working on. He acknowledges this news with a nod as all turn admiringly toward him, and points out that this weekend's ingathering is a valuable opportunity for fundraising to this purpose. He promises rough architectural sketches by Saturday, but swears all to silence about his negotiations for the hill, lest they be compromised. This is warmly agreed to and Clara says, "Hiram, do you reckon you could say a few words about it tonight at the special ceremonies?"

When Hiram Clegg smiles, he shows all his teeth, and they are very white.

After the meeting, Debra slips away from the busy Main Square and takes a walk along the creek to the arched wooden footbridge that in turn leads to a path through overgrown brambles and a thick stand of trees into an open weedy place full of high grass and wildflowers, a hidden corner of the camp she has so far kept secret from the Brunists. In the old church camp days, she used to come back here to get away from the children and collect her thoughts and on sunny days to open up her shirt and let the hot sky make love to her in the old creation myth way, in the same way that God made love to Mary: sweetly, gently, immaculately. With all the strangers voraciously prowling the camp, she can't risk that today (well, she undoes a button), but the sun on her, lying in the grass, brings back warm memories of it. Everything was so easy then, her life seemingly so sensibly and comfortably structured. An illusion of course, like so many that life throws up, projections on a screen that seem real but vanish when the bulb burns out. She is learning to free herself from such fantasies, to make her own life, redeem her own soul. Uncertain times lie ahead, but she's doing what's right and everything will work out—she feels certain of it. It has to. True, she has done a rather dangerous and scary thing, but the *world* is dangerous and scary, and, if anything, she feels safer out here among these kind people than in that cruel and stupid town, living with that cold unappreciative man.

Not that Wesley was not important to her. He was, and there was a time she loved him dearly, or thought she did. She was without direction until he came along, rescuing her from the tedium of boring college courses and giving her a role in life: the minister's wife. She sometimes felt like she was in a movie and that was her name, not Debra Edwards, who was merely the actress who played the part. Wesley back then was both fun and serious, always a bit distracted, but thoughtful and loving with a playful sense of humor, and she lived for the little games they played and the good deeds they did, waiting for the children to come. But they never did. And then the possibility that they might withered away as Wesley got more and more absorbed in his pastoral duties, his sermon writing, his engagement with the dismal insignificant affairs of the town, his golf playing, his locked-away whatever. As her body filled and sagged and her hopes for children faded, she had to make do with the church nursery, summer camps, her projects for troubled teenagers. Sometimes after christenings and baptisms, she had to slip into the cloakroom where the choir robes were hung and have a cry. But then came the April night her husband and his friends kidnapped Colin Meredith from the cult and brought him to the manse. She immediately recognized the tearful orphan boy as the beautiful and sensitive son she never had. It was she who found him later that night, lying naked in the bathroom with his wrists slashed, and saved his life. Wesley's decision after that to commit the boy to a mental institution, just when he most needed the sort of love and nurturing that only she could provide, was the beginning of the end.

She can hear a meadowlark somewhere, quite nearby, asking its persistent question, which sounds like "What more must I do?" Debra is determined to play her part to the full, to surrender utterly to the Brunist community and to what they call the Spirit, just as she did on Easter night, no matter where it leads her, no matter how embarrassing. She wants desperately to believe as they believe and do as they do and become wholly one with these people to whom she has pledged the rest of her life, yet she knows she still has not achieved it. She is still

Mrs. Edwards. When the Florida buses pulled in today after church, the visitors poured out to embrace old friends—Clara and her missionary team had visited the Florida congregation on more than one occasion in the past and had brought about many conversions—and, though she was politely introduced as the camp director, Debra felt very much excluded. Mrs. Hiram Clegg, another West Condon disaster widow, then joined other women in a visit to Mabel Hall's caravan, where, as Debra understands it, other forms of prophecy are entertained, and where Debra has never been invited. Not that she would know exactly what to do or how to behave, finding suchlike as horoscopes and tea leaves a bit silly. She shares this with Clara, who rarely goes there either, though Clara does trust Mabel's intuition and often follows her advice. But the snub hurts. Even Colin with his strange ways is more welcome than she. As one of the original twelve, he was warmly embraced by all the new arrivals, most effusively by Reverend Clegg himself, who came limping down out of the bus to hug him, his pale blue eyes atwinkle with tears. When they asked about Colin's friend, Carl Dean Palmers, Colin told them that he was still in prison, where he will be kept for the rest of his life in solitary confinement, and they all sighed and commiserated with him about that and promised to pray for Carl Dean and for his release. There are some young guitar-plucking teenagers in the Florida group and they immediately made friends with Colin and the office boys, and they all went off together, leaving Debra feeling ever more bereft even as the crowds welled up around her. Lonely amid the many: Is this part of her fate, too? What more must I do?

There are voices nearby. She sits up, rebuttons her shirt (there are three buttons undone; how did that happen?), gets to her feet. It is Cecil and Corinne Appleby, all in white, scouting out new places for their beehives. "Look at all the wildflowers!" Corinne says. The Applebys arrived a few days ago and set up hives by the creek near her vegetable garden in a patch of dogwoods and maples and wild roses. They are a pious soft-spoken couple to whom the entire camp has taken an immediate liking, and they are adding something valuable to the camp's economy, but Debra doesn't want them intruding on her private space, so she tells them that unfortunately the area is off-limits, having been designated as a building site, a white lie she hopes never comes true, and she recommends the bushy area with the webby tangle of sickly young trees on the far side of the garden. Cecil shakes his head. "Skunks," Corinne says. "Do skunks like honey?" "They like bees," Cecil says. "They have a clever trick for luring the guard bees out of the hive and eating them." "Really?" "It's a parable," says Corinne.

"Oh my friends, it is such a lovely spring evening, a *Heavenly* spring evening, and I feel such a wondrous happiness, standing here with you in the dusk of the twilight under this budding dogwood tree. As you all know, it is the wood from which Christ's cross was made, but that was long ago when the dogwood tree was as tall and strong as the mighty oak. It is said that the Risen Jesus, God be praised, decreed that forever after the dogwood should be stunted and twisted and unsuited for such dreadful purposes, thus blessing the tree with a seeming curse. Just so have we been blessed by the seeming thwarting of our hopes by the powers of darkness on the Day of Redemption and the persecution which has followed, for from its soil has sprung, like spring itself, this great spiritual movement of which we are all a living part. Soon this tree will be releasing its precious cross-shaped white flowers with their little stains of blood and their tiny thorny crowns in the center of each blossom, making us all think of Him who was once nailed to a cross from a dogwood tree and whom, we have every reason to believe, we will, in our own lifetimes, rapturously embrace in person and live with in holy bliss forevermore. In the words of Brother Ben's inspiring song, *We shall meet our dear Lord there face to face!* Oh yes! I hear you! Amen! Amen! We have come here this week to dedicate to the service of Christ in the name of our Prophet Giovanni Bruno our new official home, the International Brunist Headquarters and Wilderness Camp Meeting Ground, and all week long there will be special ceremonies and prayer meetings devoted to this consecration, climaxing on Sunday with a commemorative service on the Mount of Redemption. Yes, I knew that would draw gasps of hope and joy. Praise God that we are here and able to witness this holy event and to be there on the Mount on that great day and receive Jesus in our hearts. Amen! This is so magnificent a setting! I had no idea it was so beautiful. A veritable garden of God with a spring running through it as a river ran through Eden, a spring whose name is No-Name, as if to declare the purity of its source. It is a garden not unlike that of Gethsemane and is within view, as all of you who have been up to Inspiration Point know, of our beloved Mount. It is as if it were planted here for us and for us alone! Oh, thank you and God bless you, Brother John P. Suggs, for all that you have done to make this miracle possible! A large portion of Heaven awaits you! You have brought us home! For this, *this,* my fellow Brunists, is our home. Here, truly, He walks with us and He talks with us and He tells us we are His own! Here, truly, we shall find peace in the valley and glory upon the mountain! This is veritably a terrestrial paradise, as Mrs. Edwards calls it, a place she loves with all her heart and knows as no other knows it. On Wednesday she will be giving all of us a nature tour through it, an opportunity not to be missed to commune with God's creation. But it was not always so. These paths were not always so open and well-tended. Our Meeting Hall, where later this evening we shall break bread together, was not always so beautifully kept and secure against the weather, nor were the cabins habitable or free from vandalism and vermin nor was there heat or water or light or refuge from the ravaging elements. A heroic effort was required to create what you see here today, dear friends. I ask you all to try to imagine the disheartening scene of ruin and desolation that greeted the first small band of Brunist Followers who arrived here in the dark winter days less than two months ago. The branches all were black and bare. There was no life in them. The winds howled and the snows fell and the rains poured down. A veritable flood ensued, a flood of mighty waters overflowing, lapping at the foundations of our little ark. Still, our valiant brothers and sisters pressed on with their noble labors, day in, day out, whatever the hardships. Only three weeks ago, my friends, there was no roof over our Meeting Hall. Only two weeks ago, as night fell, this camp was still enveloped in darkness, a darkness you will soon experience, as we re-enact the moment of the Coming of the Light, a moment our own dear Evangelical Leader and Organizer has called one of the most inspirational moments of her life, and a moment that some of us here helped, in our small way, to bring about with our modest contributions, and which we shall ceremonially share tonight, so hold on to your candles, you will need them soon. Such was the time of darkness, but now, lo, the winter is past, the deluge is over and the waters have receded; the flowers appear on the earth; the time of the singing of birds is come—listen to their godly chorus! And, ah! can you hear the doves cooing just behind me?"

It's picture perfect, as if a painter had arranged it: the tree haloed in golden late afternoon sunlight, the two pure white doves preening on an upper branch. The doves arrived a week or two ago and took up residence on the ledge of the old cistern behind the dogwood tree. They are too white for mourning doves. Debra thinks they must be domestic white doves, the first she's ever seen at the camp. Escapees from a wedding party maybe, who lost their way. When she mentioned this to the others, the news was received with great excitement, and Clara said, "Or who found their way."

"And Jesus, when he got hisself baptized," cries out little Willie Hall, "he went straightaway up outa the water, and, lo, the Heavens was opened up to him, and he seen the Spirit a God droppin' down like a dove, and landin' right on him. And behold they was a voice outa Heaven, sayin', This here is my beloved Son, in who I am right pleased!"

"Thank you, Brother Hall! Oh, the scene is vivid before my eyes, my friends! The Lord Jesus, who is the Incarnation of the Word, has come to the Prophet, who in his time was named John just as he is in our time, Giovanni, as you all know, being the Roman name for John. John was the greatest man on earth at the time, Jesus said so. So here he comes, watch him now, here comes the Word, walking straight down to the water, straight to the Prophet. And John says, There He is, that's the One! Can you see it? The Word comes to the Prophet, they're both standing there, there in the water, two of the greatest who ever walked on earth, the Prophet and the Word, looking in each other's eyes. Oh, that's too much for me! The eyes of the Word and the eyes of the Prophet meeting in the water! It takes your breath away! I want you to baptize me, says the Word. And he does, and when the Word is raised up out of the water, there comes the message from Heaven on the wings of a dove, 'This is My beloved Son!' The Spirit of God descending in the shape of a pure white dove! Oh yes! Hear it cooing behind me! It knows who we're talking about! The sweet bird of God's grace, the sign of the Holy Spirit! Ely Collins saw it! Even in the pitchblack depths of the mine he saw it! A sign from above! Oh yes! He sends us His pure sweet love! Sing it with me! *On the wings of a snow-white dove...!*"

After leading them all in song (it might help, Debra is thinking, if she knew the words of the songs they sang), Reverend Clegg moves on to tell how doves were used for atonements ("You take a pair of doves, cut the head off one of them, turn it upside down and bleed it out on its mate, and then you set the living dove free, and when he flies he splatters the ground around with the blood of his beloved, and the blood cries out to God, 'Holy, holy, holy is the Lord God!' You see? Just so was *our* dying mate Jesus Christ killed and His blood sprinkled on us, my friends, so we might go free, crying out, 'Holy, holy, holy, unto the Lord!' Oh yes! Holy, holy! Amen!"), how the robin got its red breast, how Jesus as a young boy was said to have made sparrows out of clay that flew away when He clapped his hands, and how swallows, who blind their young before restoring their sight, represent the Coming of the Light and also, somehow, the incarnation of Christ. "We once were blind, but now we see!" Reverend Clegg's own little bird-watching tour.

Returning last week to the town she left only a couple of weeks ago was like landing on the moon, the real town she once knew now buried under the strange otherworldly one they were driving through. Clara, too, remarked that it felt very peculiar. "It is hard to think,"

Clara said, "that all our troubles come from here." The camp, which seemed a million miles away, had become their cloister, their universe. All outside it was alien, though not dangerously so; there was something pathetic about the town, and about the manse as well. Which was, as she'd hoped, empty, though it was in a filthy state. There were dried eggs splattered against the kitchen walls and cabinets, spoiled milk in the fridge, a countertop and sinkful of dirty dishes, heaps of dirty towels and linens everywhere, and the furniture was all shoved about helter skelter. Pillows on the floor. Stains? She sniffed at the rumpled linens. She didn't really want to do that but she couldn't stop herself. How could she have lived here all these years with that stupid uncaring man? Clara waited anxiously in the car while, feeling like a thief (she *was* a thief!), Debra hastily gathered up everything she could carry and loaded it into the back seat, the trunk already packed with her new galvanized steel washtub, filled with chicken and beans and sweet potatoes and boxes of Jell-O. She started with her favorite chair, a low nursing chair bought at a country auction and reupholstered, piling everything else in around it, including the photo of Colin she'd saved, hidden inside the stacks of church sheet music (which she also grabbed up), the one taken of him at the orphanage on his ninth birthday, so cute in front of his birthday cake in his little shirt and tie, such a hopeful wide-eyed smile on his tender face. Clara does not know quite what to make of their living arrangements and on the way back to the camp expressed her concerns. Debra answered those concerns, explaining that she thinks of Colin, not only as a patient, but as her adopted son; they took out papers to adopt him officially when he was still in the hospital, but then Wesley selfishly refused at the last moment to sign them. Which was nearly true, and something like that might have happened had not Wesley been such a pig.

Now, because Ben Wosznik's dog has wandered up to sniff his leg, Reverend Clegg pats Rocky's head and asks, "Do you folks know how Rocky here got his name? Brother Ben told me only today. The dog's real name is Rockdust, for, as Ben says, he and his brother wanted to name man's best friend after a miner's best friend." The dog wags its tail. It is almost as if it has known its cue. "It is rockdust that is spread in coalmines to prevent explosions, and had Rocky's namesake been in sufficient evidence five years ago, we might still have Frank Wosznik and our beloved Ely Collins among us!" There are moans amongst the worshippers in the darkening evening, and some tears. Reverend Clegg's eyes begin to water, and Debra, watching Clara and Elaine, feels her own throat tighten up. "Oh, I tell you, that was a dreadful night! That disaster that struck Old Number Nine! So many good decent hardworking Christian men died and died so young! But from that tomb, in the words of our 'White Bird' hymn, came a message of gladness, a message of *gladness*, though its author, so much loved and revered by us all, had passed to his reward. 'Hark ye ever to the White Bird in your hearts,' his message said, 'and we shall all stand together before the Lord!'" Elaine is as pale as her limp tunic, though her ears seem flushed, her dry-eyed gaze fixed on some far horizon. Clara is worried about her daughter, and after telling Debra a little about the scenes on the Mount with the Baxter boy five years ago and their secretive correspondence ever since, has asked her, as an experienced counselor for troubled teenagers, to try to draw her out, but so far the child has shied away from any attempt to befriend her. Elaine does her work about the camp—setting tables and washing dishes, emptying the new trash bins, weeding, sometimes minding the little ones—in more or less utter silence, her distant stare unsettling. She is so ardent a believer it is almost frightening, and it is maybe that intensity her more practical mother cannot quite understand.

"Oh, God's ways are surely inscrutable, my friends. Out of the horror of that black night, that incomprehensible tragedy in the depths of the scorched earth, has emerged a transcendent vision and a stirring prophecy, one destined to shake the world! For it is the *truth*, and the truth *is* world-shaking! Just as the Holy Spirit was pleased to dwell in Jesus, so did it take up residence in that holy man Ely Collins, bringing to all of us, through him, the White Bird vision, and then, upon Brother Ely's cruel death, the Spirit passed on into that disaster's sole survivor, Ely Collins' own underground workmate, our Prophet

Giovanni Bruno. The Chosen One. In Brother Giovanni, the Spirit worked, as we know, a most marvelous transformation, turning a quiet solitary Roman Catholic coalminer into the prophetic leader of a great evangelical movement, awakening deep within the miner's heart an unforeseen profundity, a remarkable visionary sensibility. It was our own Ely Collins who perceived this spiritual potential in Brother Giovanni. We know that the poor man had been taunted and abused by his fellow religionists, for a prophet, as is well known, is not without honor, save in his own country and in his own house, and we know that he had been ruthlessly driven from his church for standing up against the priesthood, just as Jesus had stood up against the Sadducees, and it was Brother Ely, we know, who took him under his wing and sheltered him and nurtured his soul. And to what wondrous effect! In the words of Brother Ben's hymn, my friends: *Think of Moses, discovered in a river! Think of Jesus, a carpenter's son! Think of Bruno, a humble coalminer! 'Tis the poor by whom God's battles are won!"* Whereupon—amid the cries of "Amen!" and "Yes, Lord!"—the gathered Followers, arms raised and waving, break spontaneously into another chorus of the song…

*"So, hark ye to the White Bird of Glory!*
*Oh yes, hark ye to the White Bird of Grace!*
*We shall gather at the Mount of Redemption*
*To meet our dear Lord there face to face!"*

Debra's arms are also raised and waving, she is singing, tears are streaming down her cheeks, she doesn't know why but it happens all the time now, it's as though for the moment the Spirit is lodged in her own heart, and she is no longer the camp director, she is only a humble believer, part of God's company, God's glorious company, it's all so vivid and real. "Yes, Lord!" she cries out. She wants this. "Amen!" she says. And yet at the same time she is watching herself and questioning herself, feeling a stranger even to herself, so she knows she is still not saved.

"Oh yes, how well I remember him and all that happened in that historic time! For, as you all know, I was here, yes, I was here and blessed to be a witness to all that transpired on that stormy Day of Redemption and the awful night before, the Night of the Sacrifice, which haunts me still. As you all know, my dear wife Emma was taken, over there on the Mount of Redemption, God rest her pious Christian soul, taken like the young girl Marcella Bruno, she was redeemed, they were redeemed, redeemed on the Day of Redemption, their souls were transported straight up to Heaven, leaving the rest of us poor sinners here on earth, pining to join them in God's Heavenly kingdom. For the days that remain to us, God in his great compassion brought me my dear Betty, one of our First Followers who has devoted her life to our calling and who is here with us tonight. God bless her. Yes, I was here. I was here at that remarkable infolding of the faithful at the home of the Prophet on the eve of the Day of Redemption, summoned, as were all, by the Spirit. I was struck by the imposing nobility of our Prophet, by his august silence, his sober poise, his simple but powerful gestures. Not the gestures of a mere coalminer, but those of a being inhabited by the divine. You have all seen his portraits and his photographs—there is a large one hanging in there in the Meeting Hall—wherein one can see at a glance that here was a holy man, a good man, an inspired man, a genuine vessel of the Lord. I say 'was.' Now, some of you may not know this, for I have only learned of it today, but our beloved Prophet has suffered the fate of so many prophets and saints before him. He has been ruthlessly executed by his captors, and by that element for which we celebrate his new New Covenant—by light itself! Probably shortly after his capture, though we have until now been denied the knowledge of it. Yes, he is gone—that's right! pray for him! I hear you! God bless him!—confirming what many of us had suspected all along, for his going began that night, that day, over there on the Mount of Redemption, he seemed already half-transported. I was here. I was here when the fateful decision was taken to visit the Mount, the night before, to acquaint ourselves with it for the great day to follow. Was this a decision we made, or did God make it for us? I was in that room when Sister Clara, as though herself possessed by the Holy Spirit, rose to declare: 'We go to the Mount of Redemption, not to die, but to *act!* The Kingdom is ours! It awaits us on the Mount of

Redemption!' Oh, how moved we were by this great lady's majestic bearing and the depth of her faith, echoing her dear husband Ely, for whom we all mourned! You have all read about this in our church pamphlets. And I was there, over there on the Mount that Saturday night, as we all gathered around a great fire and sang and prayed and confessed our new commitment. I was there as the Prophet strode among us in his flowing white tunic, tall and bearded as Jesus was bearded and manifesting a strength heretofore unseen, his dark cavernous eyes aglitter with firelight, his hand raised in solemn benediction, nodding from time to time as if to say, Yea, in thee I am well pleased! It was as if Christ were growing in him, filling him up with his presence. I was there when someone cried that there were lights on the mine road and we extinguished the fire and rushed to our cars and—and—and—oh, my friends, I can barely continue! Forgive me! But I was there, there in the ditch beside the old mine road which you can see from up there on Inspiration Point, standing there over the dying girl, the saintly sister of our Prophet, who had been fasting and seemed dreadfully frail, lying there—I'm sorry! I'm sorry! I cannot hold back the tears!—lying there in the wildly crisscrossing headlamps of wrecked cars, her little body in its white tunic broken and bleeding, yet somehow at peace, yes, at peace, we all saw that, and on the breast of her tunic, here where the cross in the circle is embroidered, a heart-shaped bloodstain—oh, God save us! God save us all and bless the soul of our beloved Sister Marcella Bruno! Amen! Amen! I was there. I was there when foe embraced foe and all enmity ceased and we became one unified and universal movement, God be praised! And I was there, my friends, oh I hear you, I was there at the Prophet's house at dawn the next morning, none of us had slept, when that heartbroken man of God, his strength failing him, rose up out of his grief and commanded us to baptize with light, the seventh of his famous seven words, and we did that, I was baptized by the Prophet himself, we all were. He was never to utter another word, for he had already, choosing his words one by one as if mining them from his very depths or as if extracting them from the beyond, said all that was to be said. We all marched out barefoot to the Mount and there began the day with which you are all so familiar."

Now has begun the night. Reverend Clegg, his white teeth and silvery hair seeming almost to glow in the dark, has preached them deep into the evening on this clear moonless night. Debra can see why there is talk of his running for the U.S. Senate, for he has the gift. Her heart is pounding and her cheeks are still wet, but after her momentary flight she is once again the camp director and her feet are on the ground and her elbows by her sides and she is ready to organize what happens next. Soon the candles they are all holding will be lit and they will parade down to the open area in front of the lodge, the Meeting Hall, under the darkened streetlamps. The candles, on cue, will all be snuffed, Ben will sing his new verse for "Amazing Grace" in the dark, and on the last line the lights will all come on, just as they did two weeks ago, and they will all sing the great song (she knows this one) together. Then, after prayers of thanksgiving, they will go into the now fully lit Meeting Hall to share a buffet supper. It was Debra who created tonight's ceremony. This is what she can do, and they admire her for it.

"As the light fades from the sky, I ask you now to light your candles. The young servants of the Lord, Brothers Darren Rector and Billy Don Tebbett, will pass among you with lighted tapers. While they are doing that, let me remind those of you who came with me that we have organized a bus tour of the area tomorrow, including the Mount of Redemption and the Bruno home in West Condon. We may encounter hostility; we must be brave. On Tuesday, Sister Linda Catter will be here at the camp for all the ladies who want their hair done, and on Wednesday is the Brunist Wilderness Camp nature walk. Each day we are here, we are all expected to lend a hand with the building work, under the direction of Brother Ben and Brother Wayne and Brother Welford, and we will all attend the evening prayer meetings before returning to the motel. You have all heard the rumors of the future Brunist tabernacle to be built here, for, as it says, there shall be a tabernacle for a shadow in the daytime from the heat, and for a place of refuge, and for a covert from storm and from rain. Brother John P. Suggs, God bless him, expects to have architectural drawings by the weekend for all of us to see. It is our hope that, when we depart once more for

Florida, we might leave behind a substantial gift toward this exciting project. Certainly Betty and I will give all that we can. And now that the candles are all lit—oh, what a sight this is! what a vast glimmering multitude of little flames all burning together, one feels such a joyous unity here, such a togetherness!—let us bow our heads and pray!" She feels Colin draw near. This is the time of day when he most needs her. Her frightened little boy. She takes his hand. "Dear Lord, we thank Thee tonight for the promise of the imminent coming of the Lord Jesus Christ, when we'll all be together in a great prayer meeting that will never end, as we praise You through the ceaseless ages that are to come! Whether He comes tonight, this weekend, or in the weeks and months to follow, Lord, we will be ready! Our lamps are trimmed! We ask You to bless these, Lord, who have come so many miles to be here; lay Your hand of mercy upon them. And now, may He Who makes the stars to shine bright at night to lighten up the path when it's growing dim, may He lighten your path with the Star of Bethlehem to guide you to a full surrendered life in His Word! Praise Jesus! Amen!"

Later that night, after Hiram Clegg and his Florida party have boarded their buses and returned to their motels and the others have gone back to Chestnut Hills or their campsites or wherever and everyone at the camp is asleep and the birds are silent, Colin wakes up from a terrifying nightmare in which he'd been dreaming he was hanging in the dogwood tree and the doves were pecking his eyes out, and he comes into her bedroom and asks to crawl in with her. She's quite sleepy from the long day and quietly agrees, making a kind of chair for him to nestle into. The poor boy. He's still gasping for breath and trembling like a leaf. She wraps her arms around him from behind and strokes his chest soothingly. Her own dreams are happy ones. The evening has been a great success. Reverend Clegg—Brother Hiram—even called her Sister Debra when lavishing praise upon her, and all beamed at that, and those who came up here with him called her Sister Debra thereafter, and some of the locals did, too. They even sang some songs she knew and she was able to join in. Colin likes to put his head inside her nightshirt and snuggle against her breasts, and he does so now. He has grown a funny little beard on his chin, wispy, like loose pale threads dangling, and it tickles her. She has been losing weight here at the camp, what with all the physical labor, and one day, alone in the garden, Colin shyly expressed his unhappiness about that. He loves her ample softness and wants her always to stay the same. This is my body. She and Wesley used to have a joke about that, one that usually led to oral sex, which Wesley seemed to like more than the real thing. Now it has a whole new meaning. Not her body as a sexual instrument or object, but as a maternal one, a nurturing one. Not a fetish, but a shelter. She knows her relationship with Colin may seem strange to many, but he is so innocent, she can only be innocent, too, and as protective as he is vulnerable. When he returned to the manse after his time in the psychiatric hospital, he was very fragile. She worried about him every minute of the day and kept as close an eye on him as possible. And one afternoon, peeking in through the half-opened bathroom door, she saw him with a knife at his penis, about to cut it off. She entered the bathroom in alarm, an alarm she tried not to show, and talked him into giving her the knife, and then she sat on the toilet seat and took him in her arms like a little boy and asked him why he was doing that. He was trembling then as he is trembling now. How do you explain such things to a troubled boy? She did her best. It is such a nice little thing, she told him, he shouldn't want to harm it. "It makes me afraid," he said. Which was when Wesley walked in and, without making any effort to understand the situation, just exploded and ordered the boy out of the house. Colin ran away in shame and was nowhere to be found and she was terribly worried that he might do himself harm, but he finally turned up in California with his old schoolteacher and began writing letters to her from there. "Mother," he addressed her. Now he guides her hand down between his legs. His underpants are damp and sticky as they often are. She often sees him pushing at his pillows and has to launder the pillowslips several times a week. While she is cupping his tender little pouch in her hand, he falls asleep like that, snoring softly under her nightshirt the way children sleeping soundly do.

# I.7

## Thursday 16 April

Ted Cavanaugh, aging fullback and team captain, sits outside their en suite bathroom door with toast and coffee and a morning cigarette, waiting to see Irene safely back to bed. He is thinking about his wife, as he does now so much of the time, and with pity in his heart, but he is thinking about much else besides. His life this winter had seemed so simple, but reality has shouldered in and blitzed him. He thinks of himself as efficient, rational, cautious, orderly, responsible, eye on the ball, but he has been none of these things. He has let problems at the bank and in the town slide, has not kept a close enough eye on his or the bank's investments, has let his young son go his own way without counsel, and through sheer heedlessness has allowed that virulent extremist sect to return and sink new roots. Their followers have been swarming in all week, tents are up in the fields, the motels in the area are packed out, and there are more rolling this way. Pat Suggs, with the collusion of the Edwardses, has outmaneuvered him, and with time running out, there's all too little he can do. Although that little will be done. All week he has been working on defense—injunctions, health and safety inspections, roadblocks and trespass regulations, anything to slow them down—and he has found that he can influence the town, even to some degree the state, but not the county. Did he give his support to Tub Puller in the election for sheriff? Can't remember. Probably. Ex-coalminer, disaster survivor. If he didn't oppose him, then same thing.

The church is without a minister, too, another headache. Connie Dreyer is helping them out over at Trinity, but the board must find a replacement for Edwards soon or they'll all end up Lutherans. They have advertised the position in the church bulletins and consulted with the synod and Ted has made his own inquiries, but West Condon is not an easy sell. Ted has tried to get Edwards committed to a mental hospital for his own good as well as the town's, but his wife, whose sanity is also open to question, has balked at signing the papers, and there are several on the board who are reluctant to get involved with controversial committal procedures. Probably have to wait until Wes does something crazy enough to involve the police and hope he doesn't hurt himself or others. He's thankfully out of the manse—they will have to send in a cleaning crew and the whole place will have to be redecorated—and is living now in the Tindles' garage-cum-dance studio. Ralph is unhappy about it but saying little. Is it charity or an affair? Most think the latter, and many believe that's what broke up the Edwardses' marriage. Ted is skeptical, but what does it matter? He has always thought of Wes as a considerate softspoken intellectual, friendly, reliable, a loyal Rotarian and decent golfer, good citizen, so, even though there were early signals impossible to ignore (but he ignored them), Wes Edwards' Easter crisis came like a bolt. No less so his wife's sudden move out to the Brunist camp around that same time. Fleeing a lunatic maybe, or off on some wild tear of her own. Debra never struck Ted as particularly religious, just a kind of liberal do-gooder, a nuisance but no fanatic. Until now. Ted is fully aware of their finances. He has peered into their accounts and knows what Debra has done.

The toilet flushes and the doorknob rattles as Irene braces herself on it on the other side; he sets down his cup, stubs out his cigarette in the saucer, waves the smoke away. He has learned not to open the door for her, but to wait patiently for her to work the knob and stagger crankily out on her own. She always resents his presence, not wanting him to see her as she is now. She should be in hospital under constant care, but she refuses to go and he does not have the heart to insist. She is being "selfish" as she dies, and really for the first time, having always bent quietly to his wishes. He feels it as a kind of penance he must perform for what else is happening in his life.

It was the loss of her hair more than anything else that broke her spirit. Irene had such pretty hair, which she wore when young in tight dark curls. He made a special effort up in the city to have a dark curly wig fashioned for her, using old photos, but in truth it looked heartbreakingly silly on her and in her bitterness she managed to get it to the stovetop one night when he was away and set it afire. Does she even remember the love they once felt for each other? When he asks her, he gets only a dark stare in return. Such a pretty thing she was, tall for a girl and slender with a shy winsome smile, always well-dressed, fun to be with, a Homecoming Queen and the most popular girl in her sorority. And so utterly and charmingly dependent upon him, a faithful helpmeet, quiet and elegant in public, sweet and passive as a lover when they were still lovers, given often to tears after—of gratitude, he always believed. When they were young and courting, their song was "Goodnight, Irene." Now that song is full of bitter irony. He made the mistake of humming it to her one night, meaning only to remind her that he still remembered and that he loved her, and she reached up and clawed at his face.

With her illness and the dread accompanying it, she has become increasingly religious in a more fundamentalist way, something that disappoints him but that he understands and tolerates, even if she calls it patronizing. It is distancing her from him and he doesn't like it, does not want their life together to end this way. Yesterday, in her scratchy voice, she told him when they say goodbye, they really have to say goodbye, because she won't see him in the afterlife, he's not going where she's going. He wonders if the home care nurse, Bernice Filbert, is influencing her. She's a licensed practical nurse, which is why he hired her, but she seems to have progressed to that office with minimal interest in medical science, preferring folk remedies, superstition, and prayer. One day he saw her wet her finger with a murky water from a little flask and dab Irene's forehead with it. When he asked her what she was doing, she said she was refreshing her patient's spirit. She speaks of the Bible as though it were the morning newspaper, and she dresses eccentrically in shawls and long floor-scraping skirts that might be in imitation of Florence Nightingale but probably are not. She is also Lem Filbert's sister-in-law, Tuck's widow. He'll ask Lem about her the next time he's getting gas. Probably he should look for other help. Italian Catholics maybe, who seem to take ultimate things more casually. Bernice and her helper Florrie Cox, who also does the housecleaning, are both good workers at modest wages, though, and if they make Irene happy for the time she has left…

"We looked into it, Mr. Cavanaugh. But it's unincorporated land. It's in Tub's jurisdiction." "We did this last time, Dee." "Well, we didn't know better. And the sheriff back then was a cousin of mine." He tucks the phone between his chin and shoulder and lights a cigarette. Through the glass panel that separates him from the bank floor, he can see Stacy talking with a customer. Looks like one of the mine widows. Mostly hard luck stories these days. Foreclosures and repossessions up, bankruptcies, loans to cover loans. He grants as much leeway as he can but finally the bank has no choice. Stacy is full of natural sympathy and handles these people well, even when the news is bad. A real find. She came as an intern on the recommendation of an old fraternity brother now teaching up at the business school, a guy he still has a drink with when they cross paths and whose university projects he has occasionally funded. A tight end with good hands and some speed in his day, still fit. He told Ted the girl was whip-smart in all their investment games, almost always raked in the pot, and he'd like Ted to do him the favor. Ted guessed he might have been sleeping with her and was passing her on, but he no longer thinks so. You wouldn't want to lose someone like this. Her investment expertise as a games-player faded as soon as she had to deal with real people, but her grace with them is an even greater plus. She stands, smoothing down her skirt (she probably knows he is watching), to walk the client to the door; Ted swivels around in his leather chair, turning his back on this spectacle, not to lose the thread. "But, damn it, Dee, we have a major problem here. Right on our doorstep. What are we going to do about it?" "Not much we can do." "Listen, part of the state highway runs through the town limits. Can we block it off?" "Not if the state don't want us to. Wouldn't do much good anyway." The police chief reminds him that with Old Willie gone, there's only Monk Wallace, Louie Testatonda, and Bo Bosticker left; he's at least a man short. "And Monk's getting on and Bo and Louie aren't much more than traffic cops." The banker sighs. Nothing will come of this. He used to have to deal with trade union militancy, an un-American foreign import, and there were a lot of brutal old-fashioned knockdown power fights with some pretty tough bastards, but at least it was clear and simple, a case of those who deservedly had against those who undeservedly wanted but thought otherwise; it was easy to understand each other in a dog-eat-dog sort of way. Not so, these militant evangelicals. It's like an imaginary conflict on some other plane, but locally just as virulent and disruptive. "They say Red Baxter is on his way back here, Dee. Could we arrest him on those old murder and property destruction charges?" "Sure, if he comes into town. Just rile them up, though." He knows that Romano, though cowardly and frustratingly unimaginative, is right. They have to hit hard, right through the middle, or not at all. And they're too damned late, too undisciplined. He is. Suggs has been better organized. Unless the governor commits state troopers on Sunday, all his work this week will have been nothing more than a meaningless scrimmage.

He hangs up and Nick Minicozzi calls from his office upstairs. When things got tight at the bank, Ted let his bank manager go and moved down here, renting out his second floor office to the city attorney, who has become his bank lawyer as well. Sharp young guy. And Ted is glad to be back on the bank floor. Keeping an eye on things. Nick has been pursuing the question of camping permits. None of these people living in the fields are likely to have them, but again it's a problem of jurisdiction, even if they are issued here in town by the county clerk at city hall. Ted, mulling this over, scribbles idly on his desk blotter. His straightline gridlike doodles have given way over recent months to rounder, softer, more complex and flowing shapes. More sensuous ones. He smiles inwardly at that, wheels round to steal another glance; can't stop himself. She has been watching him. She looks away. Lovable, you're so lovable...he's a hummer now. "If the sheriff won't cooperate," Nick says, "about the only way to force the issue is if a property owner complains." As the major non-absentee landlord in the neighborhood of the mine is John P. Suggs, that's not likely. Nick is developing a brief on Suggs, hoping to find something they can use. There are rumors of past links to the Klan and various rightwing militias, though even if true, they might do him no harm. Unless a crime can be found. So far, only a few meaningless bar brawls when he was young. Ted asks Nick to have a talk with the priest to brace him for possible problems on the weekend. "And, Nick, you and the accountant might take a look at the Presbyterian church finances, make sure all the money from the sale of the camp is accounted for." Nick says he'll do that and reminds him of their foursome at three. His requested call from the governor comes through.

When Ted walks into Mick's Bar & Grill for lunch, Earl Goforth, Burt Robbins, and Jim Elliott are at the back table, heehawing with the mayor and the fire chief, apparently at the expense of the scruffy character just making his exit, grinning but teeth clenched. Looks vaguely familiar. Might have been in the bank for a loan. Like everyone else. "That's Georgie, our new fire inspector," Maury Castle explains in his bellowing voice. "A coupla weeks ago, he took one of Lem's old junkers out for a test drive and never brung it back, totaling it that night out on the whorehouse run. Lem keeps a loaded shotgun in his shop and he's swore to kill Georgie if he ever shows his fucking face around there again. We just told Georgie his next fire inspection is Lem's garage." They all roar with laughter again, or at least the mayor roars; Robbins' laugh is more like a mean snicker, Elliott's a mulish snort, Mort Whimple's a gasping wheeze, Mick's a high-pitched hee-hee-hee, Earl's a wet whistle out the hole in his war-scarred face.

Ted smiles faintly, orders up the usual, bowl of soup and a grilled ham and cheese, asking Mick not to burn the sandwich. About what's edible in here, the soup not always. Where the elite meet to eat. "Why Lem's?" he asks. "It's not a public place."

"Well, it is," booms the mayor, still grinning. For Castle, the whole world is funny. Tragedy is funny. Death is funny. Power is. "We all take our cars there. There are oil spills everywhere, oily rags tossed about, welding torches going, sparks flying. And Lem's a smoker. He can't get insurance, or won't. It's almost sure to go up, sooner or later, and it'll cost the city a ton to put the fucker out."

"Lem's struggling to make ends meet."

"Ain't we all?"

He knows there is something wrong about this, people have been complaining, but he cannot think about it just now. Other priorities pressing. The Chamber of Commerce problem, for example. Elliott stands, weaving unsteadily. "Gotta go practice my putts," he says bleakly, swinging through on what looks more like an approach shot. "See you at three." Useless.

"How's Irene?" Robbins asks.

"The same." But he's not thinking about her. He's thinking about the people he's sharing a life with here. This is his town, he has devoted his life to it, and nothing's perfect, but sometimes, like now, staring at their dumb grins, he has the urge just to pick up his ball and leave the field. When Justin Miller, who ran the newspaper here some years back, left town (good thing he's not around now, hyping these nuts in his paper again; he sometimes misses the *Chronicle,* but closing it down and elbowing Miller out of here turns out to have been the smartest thing he could have done), one of the last things he said was, "Everything that happens, happens right here in West Condon. If it starts to look like nothing, then you're beginning to get the picture." Now Miller's out chasing that nothing around the world for one of the television networks. Ted used to hate that kind of cynicism, but love, if it is love and not just some kind of late-middleaged confusion, is making him rethink everything. "What you see in a place like this," Stacy has said in her soft plainspoken way, "is how sad everything is." Which sums up his present feelings. Even the cheese tastes stale today, the soup lacks salt. Sad soup. But damn it—Castle, who'll be running for reelection in a few months, is wheedling about the need for a new cop, especially with all this trailer trash rolling in—he's still the captain. He got cast for the part and he can't hand it off. And anyway, cheer up, it's a Thursday. "Well, better start interviewing," he says between bites. "And meanwhile let's see if we can get some help from the towns around. I've asked Dee to send out an alert. At this point we're expecting six or seven hundred cultists over the weekend. At least half that many are already here. Plus all the local sympathizers, at least another couple of hundred. Which means we could have a serious crowd control problem Sunday, especially if a lot of sightseers and hecklers turn up like last time." He casts an accusing glance at Castle, who was one of the perpetrators of that infamous carnival. Grinning nastily around his cigar. "We're getting zero help from the county, even though the hill is technically in their domain. We'd better be prepared to face this alone."

"I hear tell Baxter's coming back," says Whimple, who as mayor had to deal with all that madness. It was all too much for Mort, especially when all the big-time news media hit town. Baxter in particular was a constant thorn in his side. Funny-faced Mort was a reliable ally at the Fort while he was there, but he hated the job, was glad to get back to the fire station.

"That's the rumor. Baxter has been fulminating at every workplace accident in the country, and he may have gathered together his own little dissident army by now. The FBI tells me they're still keeping a dossier on him, have done since his commie days, but they don't have as free a hand with religionists, even dangerously kooky ones."

"Are we going to get any state troopers?"

"I don't know yet." Actually, the governor has told him the request has to come from the sheriff's office, but he doesn't tell them that. Must be some way to get at Puller. Unless Suggs has bought him. Probably. So the question is, how much would it take to buy him back? "There's bound to be some media coverage. I'd appreciate it if you'd drop by and have a strategic prep talk with Nick, Maury, make sure we hit 'em hard but don't break any rules." Castle laughs at this. "You might as well come along, Mort. You never know. They'll probably want to rake over the past."

"Maybe Lem loan me that fucking shotgun of his," says Mort, rolling his off-center beebee eyes.

As Ted has explained to Stacy (she thinks golf is funny), he loves golf as he loves every competitive sport, including banking and life itself ("And love?" she asked, and though ordinarily he would have laughed and said, sure, that most of all, he found himself momentarily voiceless—this is not a game, he was thinking), but there is something different about golf. Though she said she used to be a Quaker like the rest of her family, Stacy is not a religious person, so he couldn't explain it in those terms, and he had to fall back on the idea of beauty, with which he was anything but comfortable. Music, painting, books failed to move him. But a long completed pass or an explosive run through a swarm of tacklers, or watching his son sink a game-winner from the halfway line as the buzzer sounded, that was beautiful. And a golf course, when used as one, that is to say, purposefully, not merely as a park to walk in, is beautiful, can be. A revelation (he didn't say this) of God's bounty, His love of a moral order. Ted was not being frivolous when he proposed the rise at the sixth tee for this year's Easter sunrise service. It was while standing there at the sixth tee one day, about this time of year but many years ago, not long after the war, that he first understood the nature of prayer. A prayer was not a recitation. It did not even have words. It was a silent whole-body communion with the divine. In the way that a good golf swing is. The mechanics of a church service never touch him that way. He always feels that he's just going through the motions. Out here, it's the real thing. He may be a secular churchgoer, but he is a Christian golfer. I may be a cynical old bastard, Teddy, his father once said, having just hit a beautiful drive down the middle of the eighteenth fairway, back when they had eighteen fairways (it *was* beautiful, *this* was beauty—he said this to Stacy), but one thing I believe is that being a good Christian (left this out), a good banker, good citizen, good lover, good anything, is like being a good golfer: it's not something you do with just your head or your wrists, it takes your feet, your knees, your hips, your shoulders, your whole body and your whole concentration. Head down, stay focused, and swing easy. "Well," she said, smiling up at him, her breath coming in short gasps, "it seems to work."

Now, he's standing in the middle of the fairway on the dogleg fourth with a clear view of the pin. Chance for a birdie. In the old days he would have reached the green from here with a three-iron or even a four; now he'll probably use the three-wood again, the one he is using more and more as his driver, too. It gives him more loft and backspin, meaning it stays up in the air longer and so is still as long as it ever was, while his driver shots, though they still go further, have shortened—he feels younger than ever these days, but the length of his drives tells the true story—and are a little less reliable. The shorter shaft on the three-wood allows him to take a half step toward the ball, and that seems to help. Can take some of the wayward arc out of a slice, too, as he explained to young Nick Minicozzi, who has hit a couple already, because the backspin offsets the sidespin. Nick is over in the woods to the right now, debating between an easier shot back out onto the tee-side of the dogleg, or a tougher one through the trees and over the old cemetery toward the green. Nick, Ted knows, will settle for the sure thing; how they differ. Jim Elliott is on the other side of the fairway in the rough, looking for his ball. Which is about half his golf game. It wasn't a hook, just clumsily mishit off the heel of the club. He's got the swing of a heathen, as his father used to say. Elliott, after consulting his hip flask, will slash around a while, lie about his strokes, probably eventually send the ball—or *a* ball—straight across the fairway into the trees on the other side; he should have warned Nick to keep his head down. Connie Dreyer has just plunked his third shot into a water hazard and is now waiting for Ted to take his second before joining him for the walk to the green. The Reverend Konrad Dreyer is the very model of what he's looking for as a replacement for Wes Edwards: a thoughtful softspoken intellectual utterly committed to his mission. The voice of Christian reason and moderation. Too bad he's a Lutheran. Connie once told him he'd started out as a somewhat secular historian in search of what he called the "spirit of history" and with a fundamental belief in the creative force in the universe, that which orders and evolves and impels, what some people call "the ground of all being." Impressed by the incredible tenacity and power of the Judaeo-Christian tradition as an evident emanation of that spirit, he'd moved on into church history in graduate school, preparing for a life as a professor of theology and church history. But then he woke up one Sunday morning to the realization that in acquiring the athletic skills of the academic he had lost the fear of God. Which is when he entered the Visible Church, taking on a pastorate. Ted's shot hits the green, but too hard, and bounces off the other side. Should have used an iron after all.

On the walk to the green, he thanks the Lutheran minister again for all he's doing to help the Presbyterians in their crisis, and they talk about Wes Edwards. Wes often joined them out here on weekday and Saturday afternoons. Would that be good therapy for him? No. Lost cause. Though Dreyer is more hopeful. "Wesley has been a faithful servant of God. God will not abandon him." "Far as I can tell," Ted says, "that's just the problem—He's got inside him and Wes can't get Him out!" Connie smiles compassionately at that and goes on to explain the sources of some of Wesley's outbursts, including what seemed to be an Easter morning threat to destroy the church. "Mark 13.2," says Connie. "Don't worry. People with Christ parapathies often use that verse to assert themselves without even considering what it might mean." Ted tells Connie about Debra emptying out all their bank accounts to finance the Brunists. "Jim's wife Susanna says Debra told her she'd decided to lay down all she has and follow Christ. Only she laid down everything Wes has, too."

While Connie sorts out his problems at the water hazard, Ted studies his lie. Not too bad. He's played it before. About twenty yards beyond the pin in a clump of unmowed grass. It is technically fairway, so, with an unskilled parttime groundskeeper, it is within the club rules to clear the grass and debris around the ball, and he does so, then joins Connie on the bench beside the ball washer for a smoke while waiting for the others. He can still par the hole and plans to. Dreyer tips back his straw skimmer, strikes a match over his briar pipebowl, and asks about Irene. "A little better right now. Some kind of remission, I think." When he called home from the bank to check in with the home care nurse, Bernice said, "Well, she keeps trying to get up and walk around, Mr. Cavanaugh. I think she wants to up and fly like Elijah." "It has been hard, Connie." "I know. The children?" "They were all back at Christmas and we've stayed in touch. It would help if they could get back more often, but my oldest is in the State Department and posted to the Far East, where they really have their hands full, my daughter out on the coast has a legal practice and small children, and Tommy's finishing university, so I'm pretty much on my own. Tommy at least will be back for the summer." He needs Tommy, needs his help, his attention. Tommy's a bit lost right now, is even talking about going on to grad school, studying some subject other than business. Pointless. His grades are mediocre, way below his abilities. He got dropped from the basketball team, in spite of Ted's influence up there, apparently for flaunting training regulations. He seems all too loose and easy, as if life were just a passing joke—it's *not* a joke, damn it. Ted has only a B.A., all he has needed, and has always thought of business school as an excuse to keep fucking off, avoiding the hard decisions. But at least it might keep a kid like Tommy on track until he can grow up, so he'll push the idea. Tommy had wanted to work in the bank this summer, but Ted couldn't risk it—the boy has made a play for just about everyone in there, including Stacy—so he has managed to get him on the city payroll instead. They'll talk all this out when he's home for the weekend.

Nick Minicozzi's shot lands conveniently at the lip of the green. Must be at least his fourth. A tough couple of holes but he has a natural swing and, though not daring, is a stubborn competitor. When Nick sent the official foreclosure documents down this afternoon, Stacy brought them in and stood by his desk for a moment while he leafed through them. She seemed decidedly unhappy. Probably she had talked with most of these people at her desk. In the stack, along with the unpaid house mortgages and failed small businesses: Maury Castle's old shoe store. As the Deepwater night manager, Dave Osborne was something of a hero on the night of the disaster, so, with the mine closed, Ted helped him buy the store when Castle was elected mayor. He should have known better. Even Castle was losing money and he knew something about salesmanship. For a while, Osborne joined the others for lunch at Mick's, trying to fit in, but he has not been in for some time now. Except for small loans Ted granted him, he has had no money to buy in fresh stock, so most of the shoes for sale are the same ones as four or five years ago. Osborne is now deep in debt with no obvious way out; the bank has played along too long, the shop has to be closed and put on the block like so many others on Main. But Stacy was still standing there—"Look," she said, pointing: "New shoes!"—and he realized how much, just now, he needed her. He could not bear her censure. He set the documents aside. "These can wait," he said (was he growling? he was growling). "If the bank owns all the property in town, what the hell's it going to do with it?" "You're beautiful," she whispered as she left. Elliott's ball lands short of the green. He may have just picked it up finally and thrown it. If he announces it was his third shot, he'll fire him on the spot. When Nick arrives, cursing his slices, Ted says, "Your hips are moving forward before your hands are, Nick. At the driving range, try hitting a bucket of balls with your feet together. If your hips move first, you'll lose your balance."

* * *

The beautiful man is returning home in his beautiful car in a beautiful mood. It is late. He has stayed too long, and the drive from the distant highway motel where she stays on weekends takes more than an hour down dark two-lane country roads. But an immense peace has settled over him and he feels afloat on the night. Changes are taking place. Deep at the core. She has released something in him that he himself did not know was there. A buried self more open and lighthearted. Not frivolous, but possessed of a genuine lightness of being, one able to rise above (yes, he *is* afloat!) the cares and anxieties of the day-to-day world. The bank, the church, the Brunists, his so-called community have settled dimly into the background like two-dimensional markers of his new distance from them. And more loving, a self more loving. He had not known he could love as he loves now. Or be loved as she loves him. With all her heart, he knows that; she has touched him with her almost desperate confessions. It's a miracle. A touching of souls. Her young body, he loves that, too, is crazy about it, cannot keep his hands or eyes off it, and when he apologized for his abject adoration (he was undressing her, slowly, as if unwrapping her, as if revealing something holy, her emerging body—it *is* holy!—quite literally aglow under the bedside lamp), she smiled dreamily and said, "You have the hands of a poet." But it was not just her body—that was just, so to speak, the frosting on the cake (that is probably *not* the most poetic way of putting it, though he did like to lick it)—it was the young woman inside the body that most fascinated him: her good heart, her gaiety, her charming unpredictability, her fresh youthful wisdom. When he expressed his worries about the events of the upcoming weekend and all he was doing to confront them, she stroked his brow and said, "Maybe you're overreacting." "Could be. But I don't think so." "Listen, why don't we go somewhere Sunday? A drive...?" And though it seemed preposterous and irresponsible, it also suddenly seemed right. The nurse and cleaning lady have the weekend off; maybe they're going out to the mine for the ceremonies (are they part of that cult?), but Tommy will be home. It was possible. No, it was necessary. "Yes," he said. A weight seemed to be lifting. "We'll do that." And she kissed him, and then straddled his shoulders, presenting him her butterfly to kiss, and leaned down to stretch her body out over his, her head between his legs. You go to my head…their little joke about that. He was so glad he'd left the bedlamp on. Is this wrong? It cannot be, it is too beautiful, too pure, too profound. And life is short, its rewards few and precious, gifts of the passing hours to be accepted or forever lost. If not now, when? "It goes on and on," Stacy has said about life, "and then it stops." She's an agnostic. Or something else. But that's all right, maybe he is, too, he hasn't thought about it all that much. Probably not, but never mind. Love transcends all that. It's her religion, really. Love as God, God as Love. If it feels good, it *is* good. They can go over by the river, he was thinking as her thighs squeezed his cheeks, is thinking now, afloat in his big Continental, and also of her thighs and all between them (unbelievably, in spite of all the night's activities, he is hard again). That state park over there with the massive stone formations, hasn't been there in years.

There are lights in his rearview mirror. Another lover headed home? No, four lights. Two lovers, then. He's leading a parade of returning lovers. The lights do not seem to resolve into headlamps, spreading apart and drawing together again. Stacy has been introducing him to marijuana. Is it already affecting his brain? Probably just more tired than he thought. He slaps his cheek and looks again. He sees a fifth headlamp and knows now what they are. Before he can hit the accelerator, they are all around him, in front of him, behind him, roaring along beside him, five black-leather-jacketed motorcyclists, their metal jacket studs glittering infernally in the headlights, their ratty hair flying. They weave patterns around him, taunting him with obscene gestures and icy maniacal grins. One of them looks foreign, Hispanic. He pulls up alongside, spits on his window, smashes the side mirror with his gloved fist. An empty bottle caroms off his hood and windshield. On their jackets: skulls and crossbones, crosses, American flags with daggers in them, dragon-like serpents, the name WARRIOR

APOSTLES. It's unreal, a nightmare—indeed, he feels almost as if he has fallen asleep in the motel and is having an anxiety dream about getting home again. They continue to crowd him as if trying to slow him down, force him to the shoulder. They probably mean to rob him, even kill him. All right, team. Fuck this. Huddle time. The scrawniest one leans down and smashes out his left headlamp with a heavy wrench. Another roars up on his right and takes out one on the other side. The tail lights are going, too. He hits the brake, hard, forcing the two at the back into a spin, then, leaning on the horn like a war cry, barrels forward, head ducked, through the narrow space between the two peeling bikers in front. Driving a hole in their line. He hears the scrunch of metal against metal. Something thrown cracks his windshield. Not a lot of pickup in this cumbersome machine, it's a moment when he'd love to have the old manual gearshift back, but it does have power and he knows he can eventually outrun them. He only hopes they are not armed, or, if armed, don't shoot. And that, with only one dim left on the ditch side, he can stay on the black seamless road on this moonless night. It's like running the sideline to the end zone blindfolded.

When the banker reaches his house, he takes a moment to catch his breath, calm down. He's absolutely furious. He'll call Chief Romano, get him out of bed. The sheriff, too. Tell them he wants action and now, goddamn it. This is an outrage. Those shits should be run down tonight, captured and jailed. Or hung, preferably. He would personally like the pleasure of taking a sledge hammer to their fucking motorcycles. The innocent citizen strikes back. The more or less innocent citizen. He will have to explain what he was doing out on that road. Well, business meeting, possible investors, job interviews, etc. Could those guys follow him here? Do they know who he is, how to find him? He listens for the sound of their bikes, but the night is silent. To be safe, he puts the Lincoln in the garage, though not much worse could happen to it. Maybe he should leave it out in the driveway as bait and wait for them with his rifle. He could shoot them and they'd never be missed.

Inside, his mind still gripped by the hellish racket of crunching metal and shattering glass, he finds that Irene has taken a turn for the worse. "We didn't know where to reach you," Doc Lewis says, stepping out of the bedroom. Bernice Filbert is in there, sitting by the bed, head bowed, holding Irene's hand, her white head scarf curtaining her profile, spectacles dangling on a chain beneath her chin. They seem to be praying together. "We called the club…" "Sorry, M.L. An appointment. Lasted longer than I expected. And I got attacked on the way home." "Attacked?" "Motorcycle gang. They smashed up the car. I was lucky to get away. How bad is she?" "She's better. I gave her some morphine. Should settle her for the night. She should be in the hospital, you know, where we can monitor her." "Irene's pretty determined on that subject. And I tend to agree. Don't want her to die in hospital. She belongs here at home. With me." Lewis nods. He looks tired. Probably got dragged out of bed. A good man. Living proof that there *are* good men. The sort that, by who they are and what they do, ease despair. Something Stacy, expressing her love, once said about him. He didn't deserve it (love's like that), but Lewis does. As for the Sunday drive, forget it. What was he thinking of? "Should I call the kids?" "Not yet. Her heart's strong and her will seems intact. She could live on for months still. Let's see how she's doing tomorrow." "Bernice said she was so lively earlier." "Flush of euphoria probably. Often precedes a crisis." "Thanks for coming out, M.L. How about a nightcap?" "Well, that's kind, but…" "I need something to crank me down. Join me. The car's in the garage, go take a look. I'll let Bernice go home and say goodnight to Irene. Be with you in a sec."

That night, the banker dreams about the bikers. Only, it's not a nightmare. He's riding with them, matching their cool smiles with one of his own. The sun's shining and they're out on the open highway, blazing along. Nothing exists except the roaring machine between his legs and the exhilarating sensation of freedom as vast as the limitless landscape. No goal to reach, just the joy of life itself. One of the bikers pulls up alongside him. It's his fraternity brother, the one teaching up at business school. He has an ecstatic expression on his face. "This is beautiful," he shouts, and the banker agrees. The scenery is streaking past. "But once you get one of these things going," his fraternity brother asks, his expression metamorphosing to one of terror, his bike beginning to shimmy, "how do you get *off*?"

# I.8

## Saturday 18 April

When they arrive like returning heroes after their exhausting all-night journey, anticipating warm embraces, they find the steel gates at the end of the access road open, the camp abandoned. There are some trailers parked in a field with THE COMING OF LIGHT stickers on their bumpers and other evidence of recent occupation—in a cabin up from the main lodge, there are dirty dishes and muddy jeans, and the beds are unmade—but the atmosphere is one of a spooky emptiness. It reminds Franny of their father's pictures of the Rapture, which she used to think were photographs: the saved taken bodily up to Heaven dressed in wispy gowns like shower curtains, clothes left behind in castoff heaps. No fat people ascending. Which suits her fine. Her father wonders aloud if there has been a raid on the camp, everyone arrested. Maybe the Persecution has begun again. That suits her not at all. Franny Baxter is sick of being hated and chased about and wants to hear nothing more about the abuse of prophets and the suffering of the righteous. She hates her name that draws such bad feelings to it. She wants to be a nobody quietly living a nothing life in nowheresville, believing in nothing except her own crummy nothingness. She sure doesn't want to be back here. Their father has been in a state of repressed fury for days now, and sometimes not so repressed: little

Paulie has been whacked and swatted so many times this week, he can do nothing but scrunch up and snivel all the time. Not that he's capable of much more at his best, she thinks, though Paulie himself dreams of more. Like burning down the world and everything in it, for example. While roasting marshmallows over the flames. And he's not a nobody. He's Nat Baxter's brother. And he is going to be a Warrior Apostle. Nat promised him. They will cut him and mix his blood with theirs and together they will fight the war of the gods. Nat and Littleface have shown him pictures. The Apostles have roared here ahead of the rest and gunned their motorbikes up the hill to take over the high ground, and Paulie now follows after on foot. Amanda goes to tell her father what the others are doing, but he is standing in the big house, staring at all the folding chairs and the things on the wall and thinking about something. There's a big man on the wall, looking like God when He's mad. She is afraid, as she always is, it's all so frightening. Her oldest brother Junior meanwhile is on a come-and-see reconnaissance mission. Down in the trailer park, he finds the doors all left open as though their occupants had fled without time to lock them. Junior looks for Elaine Collins' trailer: he guesses the biggest and newest one, and he is right. For five long punishing years, he has been dreaming about her and about this moment. At times, it has been all that has kept him going, kept him believing. Their passionate togetherness in Christ, their dream of sainthood. He thinks she might be waiting for him in her bedroom, but she is not. In her underwear drawer, he finds his letters to her. And a man's leather belt. He leaves the letters, takes the belt and a pair of panties. In the kitchenette, he discovers an old cookie tin, too old to have cookies in it. Guessed right again. He pockets the bills, leaves the change. There's a shotgun near the back that's tempting, but too big. In a drawer behind it, though, he finds a handgun. When he returns to the camp, his father is just coming out of the lodge with a frown on his face. Nothing new. He always has a frown on his face. Their mother has not left the car, the sad old thing. She just sits there, staring into space. Nat, from overhead, shouts down, "There are a lot of people over on the mine hill!" That seems to cheer their father up. "Then we shall go there," he says.

Like Junior, Elaine has been waiting and praying for this moment for what feels like most of her life. Something happened to her out here on the Mount of Redemption, it was strange, she can't explain it. Just being back here today in her tunic, even with her other clothes on, makes her knees shake. It felt like, for a moment, she stopped being Elaine Collins and just rose right up out of herself. As if it really was the End and she was rising toward her Pa. It hurt but like leaving your body must hurt. Before that, she was standing all alone and the rain was pounding down and there was thunder and lightning and everybody looked almost naked like in the pictures when the Rapture happens. She was crying and trembling and she looked around desperately for her Pa, sensing him there, needing him, saw Junior Baxter instead. He was crying, too. He had torn a willowy branch off the little tree up there and he handed it to her. "Hit me!" he begged. "Please! *Now!*" Others were whipping each other or themselves and screaming for the Rapture to begin. She almost couldn't see through her tears, but she did as he asked. It started slowly, awkwardly, but when the pain began—he had a switch, too—it went faster and faster, like time itself was speeding up and it really was almost happening! If they could just hit hard enough and fast enough! She felt terrified and rapturous at the same time and she called out for her Pa and swung the switch, over and over, with all her might. And then suddenly everyone went mad and there was someone leaping on Junior and pounding him and bloodying his nose and mouth and she had to throw herself on top to stop him from being killed and her Ma was pulling her away and they were running, she was crying, they were all crying, her Ma too, it was as if they were running out of a new world back into the old one, which was no longer familiar or friendly, and then she was cuddled up in her Ma's arms in the car, her tunic muddy and her body stinging all over, and they were leaving West Condon behind. And after that day it was like everything had changed and for the first time she understood what it meant to be born again. Elaine grew up with religion, it was not something she chose or even thought about, so maybe what she had before wasn't really religion at all, just more like habit. Like most of these people up here today. A lot of praying and singing and saying things she has heard and said herself a thousand times, and then a snack in the food tent and polite smiles: You must be Clara's daughter. Her Ma probably thinks it's some kind of love between her and Junior, and it makes her Ma afraid of the Baxters, but what happened wasn't love, not for Junior Baxter. He's fat and has pimples on his chin, or did then, and he's not even very nice. Elaine knows about love. About Christian love and family love and other kinds, too. She loves Jesus and loves her Ma and she loved her Pa and her brother Harold with all her heart, still does, even though they're dead. She also loved Marcella Bruno. whom she's been thinking a lot about today. It's partly why they are all standing up here on the Mount of Redemption, remembering how she died on the road down below five years ago tonight. It was horrible, and remembering it still gives her a sick feeling in her stomach. Except for her own family, Marcella was the nicest person Elaine ever knew. Marcella loved Mr. Miller, but her Ma says that was the wrong kind of love, and that's why it ended the way it did. Elaine had a boyfriend once she loved for a little while in Marcella's way, or thought she did, Carl Dean Palmers, who was a nice Christian boy, a bit rough, but sweet to her and one of the original twelve First Followers like she was. Even though her Ma was not convinced, Elaine began to think that some day she and Carl Dean would get married. But all that stopped when Carl Dean went crazy up here on the Mount, and she saw the worst in him. The police took Carl Dean away and she hasn't seen him since and she doesn't want to. In their church prayers, they pray for his return, but she hopes that doesn't happen. She hasn't loved anyone since then, not that way, and she doesn't think now she ever will. So it's not Junior Baxter, it's something else. Something bigger than both of them, something they're just a part of, like a drop of water is part of a river. Again, the way religion is. She said that once in a letter to Junior, and he wrote back very excited that that was exactly what he was thinking, though he tended to think of it more like fire than water.

They call it a kind of sainthood, a reaching for it, because that's what Junior had been reading about in his Pa's books. She gave up love for that. What's strange is that it has to do with whipping each other. This was not something Elaine had ever experienced. Her Ma and Pa never raised a hand against her and her big brother Harold was always gentle and protective; she never got sent to the principal's office and she never did anything to make anyone mad enough to hit her. And she doesn't like pain, not at all. It's more like Junior has opened a door onto the real world, the world behind the world, showing her something she hadn't seen before. Something about God and what one has to do to get close to Him. What it means to be washed in the blood of the lamb. And so, yes, it's about love, after all. The most important kind. And it makes her heart beat like crazy just thinking about it. Earlier, she heard the roar of the motorcycles over by the camp. Everyone was afraid someone might be attacking the camp in their absence, and Ben and Wayne and Hunk went hurrying over there, but she knew. Her knees were shaking so, she had to go to the old people's tent and sit down on a chair there.

Before going over to the mine hill, Amanda is helping her father, Junior, and her fat stupid sister put up their big tent behind one of the cabins. Her father seems in an awful hurry to do this now. She knows she will have to sleep out here with her mother and Franny. The cabin is nicer, but the front door is missing and there is sawdust all around. Then some big men arrive and jump out of their truck, looking angry. Such moments, even though they seem to happen fairly often, always startle Amanda and make her squeak and hide behind her father. But it's not as scary as she thought because one of them turns out to be Mrs. Collins' husband, though she would never have recognized him with his beard on. And he's got so old. He and her father clap each other on the shoulder and shake hands, and Mrs. Collins' husband introduces the other two. "And you must be Amanda," he says, smiling down on her, and she gives him the smile she always gives everybody, the one that hides how scared she is inside. It's a flirtatious smile that Franny knows will one day be the little retard's undoing, though she wishes she had access to something like it, reduced as always to a deadpan nod when introduced (naturally, old Ben did not remember *her* name). One of the other two is pretty good looking and not so past it, but Franny is not interested in any man who has religion in any serious way. Enough of that for one lifetime. She wants a guy who goes fishing and falls asleep in front of the television, whether or not he even remembers her name. Her brother Junior is preening and sucking in his gut and stroking his silly little red mustache which looks more like fever blisters, pompously introducing himself as Young Abner, as he always does on formal occasions like this, wanting them to understand that he stands by his father and is his father's heir. "We have endured a great trial of affliction and suffering," he says, speaking as his father might, "but we have got here and didn't see you." Mrs. Collins' husband explains that they are expecting a police blockade of the hill tomorrow, so they decided to occupy it today and maintain an all-night vigil, and his father agrees wholeheartedly with this strategy and says he is prepared to do his part, and Young Abner nods solemnly. The men express surprise there's only their own family here, having expected the big numbers their father had written about. Their father explains that they have hurried on ahead to be sure to be here on the Night of the Sacrifice, so important to him personally, the others would be following later, though Junior knows, as do they all, that there are no others. Things have not been going well. Their father's message is a hard one and few can live with it. There also seems to be some problem about their tent. That cabin has already been allocated, and anyway the camp itself is not for personal residences. This confirms the worst for Franny, who assumes they will soon be on the road again in their beat-up old Plymouth Suburban, sleeping in it or in tents in parks and fields. Her father glances up toward the next-door cabin with the unmade beds and muddy jeans. "Except for working staff," says Ben. "That's for our camp director. And her boy." All three of them expect their father to explode as usual, but he only smiles sorrowfully, showing his weariness, and says, "Well then, we will only use it for the weekend, having no place else to go for now. Our tribulations have been many and we are footsore and heartsore, but happy are we thy servants to be standing here before you. Come, let us dress in white and put our tunics on." "You don't have to do that no more, just wear underneath whatever," says Ben Wosznik who is himself wearing boots and jeans under his tunic, but their father ignores him.

Darren Rector and Billy Don Tebbett interrupt their taped interview in the Florida tent of Reverend Hiram Clegg and his wife and follow them down the hill to the mine road, where Brother Ben and the others, returning from the camp, their arrival announced by the roar of motorcycles, have paused beside the ditch, alongside a squat barefoot man said to be Reverend Abner Baxter. He and his wife and four children are all in white tunics and not, it would seem, much else. The motorcyclists have moved over to the company parking lot under the water tower, sitting their bikes like sentinels, occasionally gunning their motors like smoke signals. One of them must be the fifth Baxter child. "Welcome," Reverend Clegg says, embracing Reverend Baxter. Reverend Clegg is not a tall man, but Reverend Baxter is even shorter. "We thank the good Lord that you have arrived safely and can be with us on this poignant day." Darren believes it is important to record the recollections of all the witnesses while they are still alive, starting with the Cleggs, who are not young and leave Monday to return to Florida. Not just to preserve the history, for history itself may not last much longer, but, more importantly, in the hopes of capturing a prophetic hint of God's plans for the end of things. The more he and Billy Don have learned about the origins of the Brunist movement, the more Darren is convinced that something truly profound and revelatory happened here five years ago, and their task is to understand it—to *read* it, as they used to say back in Bible college—and then to act according to that understanding and help others do so, too. While there is still time. While time still *is*. Both had become impatient at Bible college with the lack of respect for the prophetic impulse, the soul of all true religion, and with the school's diminished interest in the science of eschatology and the close reading of contemporary signs, their beliefs leading to accusations of heretical and disruptive behavior and threats of expulsion. And just then the Brunist missionaries came through. Their message, expounded so plainly and convincingly by Mrs. Collins-Wosznik, made perfect sense, it was just what Darren was looking for, and they have been traveling with them ever since, serving as the mission office staff. Now, at the ditch, Reverend Baxter has fallen to his knees. Darren and Billy Don know who Reverend Baxter is and why he has knelt just here, staring ashenly down into the ditch, for it is where, like Saint Paul, he was struck down with remorse for the death he had just caused and thereby became among the most fervent—and most punished—of all the early Brunists. Though others fled after the Day of Redemption, he remained defiantly in West Condon until driven out, threatened with arrest for disturbing the peace and for negligent homicide if not for murder, his local church wrecked, his home broken into and looted, black crosses painted on his door, his children attacked and beaten, his phone cut off, his mail filled with anonymous threats. They also know that Sister Clara's group has found fault with his interpretation of Brunism and think of him as an egoistic, ambitious and contentious man, endangering their movement with the threat of schism, and Darren is curious about that, fully aware that this is the moment in a religious movement before everything gets defined and codified and all still seems possible. He plans to interview him, for Reverend Baxter knows things no one else knows so well. He might, for example, know what happened to the girl's body. Nowhere in all the documentation from the opened boxes he has pored through has he found anything about her actual interment. Now, on his knees on the cindery mine road, Reverend Baxter declares in a strong quavering voice that can be heard all the way to the top of the hill: *"I was the greatest of sinners!"* And all the others fall to their knees and join him in prayer. "Yea, we were all born sinners," replies Reverend Clegg, going down on one knee only because of his bad one, "but by the obedience of one shall many be saved! He was not come to call the righteous, but sinners to repentance!" As the others chorus their "amens," Darren nudges Billy Don. "Turn on the tape recorder," he whispers.

Paulie knows that his brother Nat hates their older brother, and so he hates him, too. When Junior came up the hill to tell them they were going over to the Mount, Paulie stood behind him and did an imitation of him, puffing himself up and putting his finger against his upper lip like a moustache and waddling about, and had the Warrior Apostles grinning and cheering him on until Junior spun around to glare at him. Paulie smiled innocently, pressing his palms together as though in prayer, drawing more laughter. Normally, Junior would have boxed his ears, hard, hard enough to knock him down, but he knew Junior was afraid of the Warrior Apostles. Everyone was. Junior said there might be trouble over there, their enemies might be lying in wait for them, they needed the Apostles to provide an escort. That was different. They left their backpacks and loose gear to claim their territory, revved up. Nat told Paulie to go along with Junior, but he begged to ride with him ("Give Runt a break," said old Houndawg with a grin), and finally Nat gave in, provided Paulie got off when they reached the mine hill and stayed with the others. Junior had already started back down the path when they went blasting past him, making him jump into the bushes, all of them hooting and laughing and giving him dirty gestures, Paulie, too, pumping his fist like Juice did. Young Abner waited until they were out of sight, then turned and went back up the hill. A little something he had to do. Down in the camp there were some men with their father and sisters. Franny and Amanda were trying to get their tired old bag of a mother into her tunic. The men didn't seem happy to see the Apostles and backed off. Which suited Nat just fine. Not looking for approval, not from braindead old fossils like these. Just respect, man. Blessed are ye when men shall hate you, as his old man likes to say. A kind of power. He stared them down for a moment while his father scowled, then they roared away to wait for them at the exit to the camp access road. Now, astride his bike Midnight over by the mine tipple alongside Houndawg, Cubano, Juice, and Littleface, all five in black leather, he has watched the Collins people come waddling down the hill in their white tunics to greet his family, giving each a lot of playacting hugs. Nat has a clear notion of what the Last Judgment is all about, and it has nothing to do with those faggoty white nightshirts. His he has torn up to use as grease rags. After the hugs, they're into the praying, as usual. They do that like most people say hello. What they call praying. Really, just a way of showing off to each other that they're all in the same dumb club. Not Nat's way. He goes straight to the Big One. Raises his fist and tells Him what he needs and what he's going to do for Him. Short, snappy, in words that would fit inside a speech balloon. The Big One knows who he is, knows he can count on him, they can talk directly, no phony niceties needed. Just get the job done. The one useful thing Nat's ass-cracking old man did was push his nose in the Bible. Taught him about God's hatred of the sick world and what He plans to do about it. Armageddon. A final do-or-die rumble with Satan. No holds barred. Cool. He has seen images of it in his *War of the Gods* comics. Nat's ready. He'll be there. He will bring the fire. He has drawn the Apostles to this place with the promise of a rumble to end all rumbles. They won't be disappointed. Just two sides: the Big One and His Apostles against the rest. Get ready to choose. And die. Amanda knows which side she'll be on: her father's side, whichever. How he gets judged, she'll be judged. Anything else is too scary. Armageddon? Franny's just going to skip it. Let them do what they want. Her poor broken mother has not stopped bawling since she got here. Of course, this place has lousy memories for her. A miscarriage in a rain storm in front of all the cameras with everybody screaming like lunatics right when you think the world's ending—but unfortunately it doesn't—is about as bad as it can get. While her father and the silver-haired guy try to outpreach each other (her father is casting off the works of darkness, as he likes to say, and putting on the armor of light, and beseeching the others to do likewise), the women standing around mutter about how poorly her mother looks. "Pore Sarah 'pears to me pert nigh too weak to stand," one of the old ladies whispers. "She oughter be wearing shoes, her condition." "I have some days as bad as she looks," whispers another, "when I feel like jist layin' down and not never gittin' up again." "Yea, walk while ye have the light, lest darkness come upon you: for he that walketh in darkness knoweth not whither he goeth!" That's silvertop. Her mother perks up a bit when some other people turn up. Franny knows them. They all do. From their old church. More hugs, tears, prayers. Paulie is doing his little shake. He likes to pretend it's rock 'n' roll, but really it's just a panicky twitch that sometimes turns really bad, a kind of high-pitched whinny leaking out his nostrils like sound-snot.

Harriet McCardle is watching all this from the large food tent at the top of the hill. It is all quite remarkable, just as this entire week has been, and she wishes she could remember more of it, her very salvation may depend on it, but memory is no longer her long suit as it was in her championship bridge-playing days. It is why she is taking these photographs with her little box camera that one of her husbands gave her as a birthday present long ago, something to help her bring it all back when she's far away from here, provided she can remember to take the film in for development, which she often forgets until it's too late, the pictures then becoming mere teasing glimpses of a lost piece of her life, a mystery to go along with all the other mysteries. All of which, this problem of memory, has caused her to wonder about sin and redemption and the efficacy of grace. When they talk about washing away one's sins, she doesn't think this is what is meant. The scene down below, while dramatic, is quite confusing and she will have to ask Reverend Hiram Clegg to explain it to her later. He is down there with Clara Collins and her husband Ben, whose name is not Collins, and some other fellows, including a short reddish-haired man who shakes his fist a lot and seems to be arguing with them all, or perhaps they are just praying together, which these people often do in a quite vigorous and sometimes alarming manner. The hillside is filling up and the flat land down below by the road as well. Some of the new people seem to be members of this faith and are coming on up the hill, including one fellow in a wheelchair. He and the woman pushing him are met halfway up by several women who all seem to know each other and some men who help with the chair. She takes a photo. One of the women, the biggest one, is said to read the future with playing cards, just as Harriet McCardle once created the future with them in a more practical way. She has forgotten vast portions of her life, but she can still remember finessing a particular queen (it was a spade, held by a retired medical doctor sitting to her right who specialized in the inner organs and wore a toupee the color of a golden retriever) in a tournament she and her husband won, and, oh, many other such card-by-card details as well, including a hand she once was dealt which was nothing but diamonds, though she may only have fantasized holding such a hand, and then the fantasy became like a memory, something that further erodes her understanding of sin and redemption; she is convinced many of her remembered sins were about as real as that automatic grand slam hand, for as a young woman, she had a very lively imagination. So maybe that's what's being forgiven: her sinful imagination. Mrs. Collins' daughter Eileen, or Elaine, is also keen on whatever's happening at the bottom of the hill, watching it from behind Harriet's shoulder; whenever Harriet has tried to push her chair out of the way, she has moved with her as if afraid to face whatever's going on, wringing her hands and shrinking into shadows. Poor child. Perhaps Mrs. Collins and her husband have been too hard on her, though it seems unlikely for she and her mother are as close as any mother and daughter she ever saw. The mine tragedy happened just under their feet, and the girl might be afraid the hill will blow up again or just fall in on itself. Well, if that does happen, it probably won't happen today, more likely tomorrow, which is the anniversary of the End of the World, a concept that seems strangely paradoxical to Harriet, but one she will just have to accept, for religious faith is like that. Religion is something, thanks to her last two husbands, Harriet McCardle has come to quite late, at least in a serious way, and she is still, though years have probably passed, getting used to it. The sweet blond boy she first met in the vegetable garden seems quite agitated and his worried mother is trying to draw him back into the tent where she has been serving coffee and doughnuts. In his tunic, he looks just like an angel. She remembers to take his picture. The very nice Glover girl and the handsome man she sings with step out into the sunshine from the tent behind her to watch the proceedings below, the girl saying something about the ditch and how she can hear somebody down there talking to her. Harriet McCardle remembers the girl's name because she once had a six-grade geography teacher with that name. Why she remembers the six-grade geography teacher's name, however, she has no idea. The two of them perform religious songs for their group every evening at the Blue Moon Motel, using the bar area which has been closed down for their stay at Hiram Clegg's insistence, demanding peace and quiet for his religious community, and also no scandalous artwork on the walls or anything objectionable on the room TVs—something he could do since they are renting the whole motel. It was he who organized the singing, proud, he said, to be turning "a den of sin" into "a house of worship." He has been their Good Shepherd. And, oh, so successful. When he talks, you just have to believe him. Now, there are people who want him to run for political office and they have asked her for money for this and she will give it. Reverend Clegg has built their own little church into one of the largest in the city, the two busloads she traveled with being only a small portion of the congregation, and many of those he has converted have gone on to found churches of their own in other cities. Thanks to Hiram Clegg, she may not have to die. Being translated is a much nicer idea. Harriet McCardle is quite fond of Reverend Clegg and rather regrets she wasn't around when his wife died. Betty Clegg is such an uncultured person and not right for him at all. Harriet and Reverend Clegg have exchanged some thoughtful glances on this bus trip. Well, at their age, one never knows what might happen. Harriet McCardle has already been widowed three times and her fourth husband is not well. She remembers her first husband best of all and each one after less distinctly, though it was her second husband who was the bridge player. He was the one named McCardle, after which she stopped changing her name, as it got too confusing. As she imagines it will be when she gets to Heaven and they all try to sort things out. She hopes she doesn't get stuck with the first one. She and Mr. McCardle retired to Florida, mostly just to play bridge, and then he died and she married another man from the retirement home who was a good dancer but didn't last long. Best of all, she remembers her high school days when she was the toast of the town. She was less religious then, the end seemed impossibly far off, and she was a bit wild, she'd be the first to admit it, and has done from time to time in church during confession time. They used to sing "Swing Low, Sweet Harriet" about her, which was embarrassing, given that just about everyone knew what it meant, but she has no regrets. She loved those times and would have them back in a minute.

Climbing the Mount of Redemption, Young Abner Baxter has at last caught a glimpse of Elaine, standing behind an old lady sitting stiffly under a raised tent flap. He can't see much of her but he knows it's Elaine because the one eye he can see is staring right at him, and in a way that no one else ever would or could stare at him. He is momentarily stopped in his tracks by the intensity of that staring eye, and then, in a blink, it vanishes. Franny doesn't know what he's looking at, frozen there like that with his loose mouth gapping open, but she can guess. She has read some of Elaine Collins' letters to him. What they're up to is a bit odd, but then most people's relationships with other people are odd. Just look at her mother and father. And it might be useful. When her father came home from out here that awful night, he had changed into a different person, humble, repentant, almost tearful—like a little boy, Franny thought at the time, shocked by him and by the thought. For months her father had been railing against Clara Collins, calling her a vain deceiver and a false prophet, and suddenly she was a perfect saint who had helped him to see the light. The Bruno house was a Romanist den of iniquity, and yet he'd just come from there, praying with all the others. He had raised a little army to march against those Bruno people and suddenly they were all marching together. The change scared her and made her think something awful was going to happen. And of course it did. Only the next day on the march here, carrying a dead body, did they come to understand that their father had struck the girl with his car and killed her. Franny knew it wasn't right, but all she could think at the time was: Was that all? Her mother, despondent and heavy with a child she was about to lose, was also frightened half out of her wits, and sank into a depression she's still in. And now, after all the bitter years on the road, here they are again. He speaks admiringly of Clara Collins as a woman of spirit and great vision, but those two do not see things the same way and never will and so they're in trouble again. In one of the string of stupid high schools she was in during their travels, they read a play about two lovers from warring families called Romeo and Juliet, so maybe, she thinks, Junior and Elaine will do their own little Romeo and Juliet thing and somehow make them all loving in-laws. Franny smiles, thinking of Romeo and Juliet frantically switching each other while yelping out their love lines, lines the teacher made Franny recite in class just to make a fool out of her. Amanda sees her big sister smile and thinks she might be laughing at her in her tunic, which is too big and drags the ground. Later she will tell her father that Franny was laughing at them all and made her cry. Franny's always scolding and belittling her and calling her a sniveler and daddy's pet. Well, she *is* daddy's pet, and that's just too bad for Franny. Though she didn't understand everything, she knows her father has just done something very good and brave and everyone loves him for it, and it makes her happier than ever to be back here, walking up the sunny hill beside him, holding her tunic hem up above her pretty bare ankles, with people taking her picture. Her brother Junior sometimes gets in the way and she'd like to give him a kick in his fattest part, but at least he's never cruel to her like Nat and Paulie, who often hurt her or scare her and make her cry, calling her a fraidy-cat and a tattle and a dummy. Paulie sees none of this for his eye is on the mine entrance across the way. He can see Nat watching him and he wants to be with him and Houndawg and all the others. They call him Runt and he knows that that's a compliment, just because they've given him his own special name no matter what it is. He'd rather be Runt than Paulie Baxter any day. He does a little hop and gives them a wave, hoping his brother waves back. Nat's eye is indeed on the hill but focused on no one in particular, certainly not his kid brother. He is reading the lay of the land. Scouting the territory. Sorting the combatants. Who a lot of these people are he doesn't know, but it's easy to line them up. There are all those turkeys up on top belonging to old lady Collins and then there's his old man and his naked white feet and his fist in the air down below. He's a failure, but you wouldn't know it. There's the usual dumb swarm of gawkers and hecklers, some jerks with cameras. Disposables. A sheriff has turned up, so Nat has kept his distance. He has no papers on the bike, which he picked up on the run, and no license to ride it; he can't risk getting asked. Cubano says he knows someone who can fix that, but he's a long way from here. And finally there's that burly guy who came with the sheriff who seems to have them all on a string. Nat recognizes him. Mine owner. Longtime enemy of his old man, like most rich guys. He sensed the way they stiffened up when they saw each other. So the enemy list is growing. Nat points his finger at various targets and makes popping noises with his tongue. Like the heroes in *War of the Gods*, he has holy work to do here, and pals to help him do it. Though they have joined up just by crossing paths, they're close. They have signed blood oaths, which they call baptisms of blood (water and light are for pussies), tattooed their bodies with Bible phrases like "Terror of God" and "Destruction Cometh as a Whirlwind" and "My Name Is Dreadful," and have run missions of assault and plunder against the godless, who are just about everybody, considering themselves agents of divine retribution. And redistribution. Above the skull just over his left armpit, Juice has added the Brunists' mine-pick cross in a circle, signifying his commitment. The Warrior Apostles: Nat trusts them and they trust him. Totally. Otherwise, you're dead, man. Littleface is standing beside him while the others explore the mine buildings. The doors all have padlocks on them, but they can come back some night when no one is around. Growing up, he thought he'd be working out here, down a stinking hole, the rest of his life, they all would, like their old man. Funny how, if you don't watch out, your life gets made up for you without you knowing how it happened. Littleface has a head too big for his face. It's just a black ball of thick snarled hair with a small patch of pale flesh like a baby face in the middle, narrow beady eyes that sometimes look like they're crossed, a nose like a finger knuckle, a mouth barely big enough to work a spoon into. Almost no ears at all, just little buds. What's left, he says, after getting them torn off by some badasses who were coming after his brother and got him instead. He looks like a cartoon. Which is how he got his name. From a villain in a Dick Tracy comicstrip. "Look out for Dirty Dick," he likes to say, meaning the law. He wears an old army shirt with epaulettes under his leather vest and rides a bike no cleaner than he is, but one, rehabbed from a previous owner like Nat's, that is always in prime condition and finely tuned, tinkered with daily. Houndawg's best pupil. Everybody is everybody's pal in this gang, it's all even stevens, but Littleface is Nat's closest friend, having joined up with him the same day he appropriated Midnight. He saw Littleface tearing out of a liquor store with bottles in his arms and a wad of money in his fist and jumping on a bike that wouldn't start. Nat wheeled over, grabbed some of the stuff so Littleface could hop on behind him, and they roared off into the nearby hills where his family was camping out and they holed up there for a while. They hit it off right away. It was like they'd known each other all their lives, and Littleface said maybe they had met before in another life. "We don't die," he explained to Nat, "we just go into another body." Nat said that he'd seen something like that in a comicbook, but that he held more to the idea that when people died they lost their bodies but otherwise stayed the same, and that way they could sometimes come back to earth like in *Eternal Forces Comix* when Legions of the Holy Dead join the living in the battle against Evil. "I know that's how it's supposed to be," Littleface said, "but I can remember some of my past lives. Maybe it's, you know, like a bit of both. Like maybe some people aren't bad enough for hell or good enough for Heaven, but have to come back and try again in a different body." That made sense to Nat and he began thinking about other lives he might have led. They found another bike for Littleface and they've traveled together ever since, picking up Houndawg, Juice, and Cubano along the way. Houndawg is older and has taught them a lot; Cubano calls him El Profesor. Nat and Littleface call him B.O. Plenty, the name of another Dick Tracy villain, but not to his face. Juice is the wild one, a believer who joined up with them after turning up at one of Nat's father's tent meetings and recognizing Littleface from their days as strikers with a biker gang called the Crusadeers. "Weird!" Juice said, punching Face's shoulder when he saw him, and Face nodded and said: "Some things are meant to be." "Dirty Dick's cleared out," he says now. "Do we go back over there?" Nat shakes his head. Something is going to happen, but not right now.

"Well, I hear tell from Mildred," Linda Catter is saying, "that Sarah never got over what happened out here that day and has become a dead weight round Abner's neck. She don't even warsh herself proper, and mostly won't eat lest they set something in front of her. Then she'll eat anything and won't stop till they take it away again. Don't ask me about other things." "Some days," Wanda Cravens says with a weary sigh, "you cain't take no more'n jist want the Rapture to hurry up'n come." She is still the same old Wanda, Betty notes, though more beat down; she used to have nice little breasts, but no more, and she has gone slack in the britches and her belly is sagging, unless she's stumped her toe again. They have all crowded into Mabel Hall's caravan here at the foot of the Mount of Redemption to get out of the afternoon sun and catch up on each other's lives over the past five years and wait for the visit, promised by Mabel when it starts to get dark, of the young woman in spiritual contact with Marcella Bruno, who died right here on this road. Betty was here. At Clara's side. And the next day up there on the hill where the body was laid out on a lawn chair, pointing stiffly up at Heaven. Hazel Dunlevy wants to know what happened to Marcella's body afterwards, and Betty says it disappeared and folks reckon she got raptured straight to the other world. "She seemed to stand straight up and she ain't been seen since!" Betty had not met Hazel before. A pretty little thing with freckles and a dreamy look. She and her husband Travers, who is a plasterer and carpenter, are recent converts who have been here all winter. Hazel is a palm reader, and she read Betty's palm and everything she said was completely true: that she is a down-to-earth person with solid values, a practical outlook on life, a soft heart, and a pleasant romantic nature. Her money line and fame line cross, which means, Hazel said, that she will come into some money by surprise and luck, and her fate line means that her life will find its way into the public eye, but that already happened, which just shows how true palm-reading is, because Hazel didn't know that. Hazel wouldn't say anything about the health line, only that there was nothing to worry about, and so of course she has been worrying ever since. "Well, if this Patti Jo is talking to Marcella's spirit," Corinne Appleby the beekeeper says, "maybe she can just ask her." Sarah Baxter, who is not privy to these after-dark plans of Mabel's, has left, too miserable even to say goodbye, which gives them the opportunity to talk about her and her enfeebling illness. Sarah told Linda a long time ago that she saw the girl's head hit the windshield, she said her eyes were wide open, staring straight at her, and then *smack!* and that was what caused the miscarriage the next day, especially when the corpse just reared up like that, and Linda, who has given Betty a fresh perm this morning, relates that event to everyone now, goggling her eyes out at the staring part, and they all jump and gasp when the poor girl's face smacks the windshield, and they flutter their hands at their breasts and shake their heads at the tragedy of it all and how it has undone poor Sarah; it half undoes them, just imagining it. Glenda Oakes, who is another of Clara's new converts and is said to have the gift of interpreting dreams—having only one good eye, she explained to Betty, helps her to see into the fourth dimension, where dreams are—says she thought Sarah was just going to tip over into the ditch herself a while ago over at the mine road: "Her ankles look like her thighs has slid down round them." Truly, Betty has noticed, Sarah does look dreadful, her chin fallen to her breastbone, her eyes rheumy and hair all snarly, barely able to shuffle along by herself, her shoulders higher than her head. Bernice Filbert put some of her miracle water on her, but it didn't seem to do any good. She has been crying almost without stopping since they arrived, though Mildred said that was really out of happiness at seeing everybody again. It was the first sign of life she'd seen in the poor woman in years. Mildred joined them in the caravan for about five minutes, but could not leave Ezra alone any longer than that without him yelling for her and calling her names, mostly those of the devil and bad women of the Bible. She has dark circles under her eyes now and an unhealthy skinniness about her, probably from pushing the wheelchair around all the time, and she has adopted bitter ways. Why, after all that had happened, that man wanted to go back down in a mine again, no one can imagine, but there it is, you can't tell what's coming next in life. Unless, that is, you have someone like Mabel and her story cards. Mabel kept her husband Willie home from the mine on the night of the disaster because of what she saw in her thick little deck and she even foretold Ezra's accident for Mildred. "The five of spades come up flat against the Tower on its head, it was plain as the nose on your face," she said while Mildred was still here, and Mildred allowed as how all that was so, though just when this happened, neither of them could remember. Betty has already had Mabel read the cards for her, but without the best results, so she is hoping they will have another opportunity before they go back to Florida to see if they come out better, for Mabel has usually found good news for her. Betty, who is known here more as Betty Wilson than as Betty Clegg, realizes, talking with her widowed friends, how very fortunate she has been and how envious they all are of her, and how all this was prophesied long ago by Mabel, though she didn't exactly understand it at the time. Yes, she's been lucky, but nothing's perfect. As she admitted when the others kept remarking on what a fine man her Hiram is, "Yes, he's a mighty good talker and a holy man, and I'm right proud a him, but he don't do nothing for hisself," and they all laughed at that and said what man's not the same. It was a pretty short romance. Lasted about a day. Of course, Clara's the luckiest one of all, even if dear old Ben is showing his age. Betty still feels a twinge in her heartstrings when she sees him. "I hear tell Abner's people is baptizing with real fire," Linda says, and Betty is able to confirm this, for Hiram has spoken about it, saying that Abner has misread what John the Baptist said in the Gospels and that is sure not what Giovanni Bruno meant when he commanded them to baptize with light. "But how do they do that?" Bernice wants to know. Bernice is not exactly a Brunist either, having always been her own church of one. She dresses in long skirts with layers of things on top like shawls and capes and aprons, and today she is wearing bracelets and a pretty beaded headband. Hiram has spent some time talking with her about faith and prophecy and the afterlife and she seems interested in a deeper commitment. Most ladies are when Hiram talks to them. Bernice is providing home nursing care for the wife of the town banker, who is wasting away like the synagogue ruler's daughter, as she remarks, but she has the weekend off. "I mean," she asks, "when they do their baptizing, do they really burn theirselves?" Betty doesn't know, but she says she thinks at least at first they walked through fire, or else jumped over it like jumping over balefires. "Hard to say whether that's for saving souls or getting them used to the other place," says Corinne. The room is dimming as the twilight settles. All the talk about fire has reminded Mabel to light some candles and get out the folding card table she always uses. That girl who talks to the dead will be here soon.

Nat is sitting beside Midnight in the dark, under the mine tipple, watching the thickening crowds on the hill through stolen binoculars, most of them in those white gowns like old women at a dance. They're all making tent meeting noises now, mixed in with some twangy guitars and the tiny pops of flashbulbs going off. Usually, even at this distance, he could hear his father's voice above the racket, but not tonight. The old man has turned beggar. Not so many gawkers now as before; the sheriff's car has been parked more or less permanently down there, so people don't tend to hang around unless they want to go on up and be part of it. Anyway, it's boring. The sheriff himself is not there, but his number two is. Smith. Nat knows him from churchgoing days when his old man was the preacher. Smith marched out here that day with everyone else, but as soon as it was over he dropped out, just when his old man most needed him. Maybe he was a double agent, working for the other side. Another target. Pop. Midnight's chrome picks up flickering lights from the bonfires over there, making her seem alive and restless, burning from within. Like Nat is. He rests his hand on her frame, as though to calm her. He feels another headache coming on and needs to get himself in motion. The other Apostles have been making a swoop of the roads around, plotting out escape routes, casing supply joints, siphoning off fuel from parked cars, visiting roadhouses. Like Houndawg, Nat doesn't drink, but the others do. Houndawg calls it laying down roadslick. Juice says it keeps the machinery oiled. Midnight was green when Nat appropriated her, but Houndawg has helped him chop her down and rebuild her, bobbing the fender, wrenching in some scraps from the junkyard, reshaping the pipes, filing away all the ID numbers, and adding new engine guards, then repainting her body bits shiny black. Littleface calls her Nat's Batmobile. She's faster now and no way anybody could identify her. Houndawg himself rides a souped-up flathead with stretched downtubes and buckhorn handlebars, what he calls his old war horse. "Butt ugly, but fast and smooth." He's back, having a smoke in the darkness, Juice and Cubano are just rolling in, and Nat can hear the rumble of Littleface's shotgun pipes out on the access road. Have to do something about eating. There's food over there in the big tent and on a table set by one of the bonfires, he can smell it from here, but he doubts his pals would be allowed, and the Warrior Apostles travel together. Besides, the deputy sheriff is over there somewhere. "C'mon," he says as Littleface pulls in, "I'm hungry. Let's go." He stows the binoculars in his saddlebag, mounts Midnight and kicks her into life. Paulie hears the motors turn over and aches to be with them. Franny has tried to force some chicken and beans on him, but he's not hungry. He never is. There's some green Jell-O with marshmallows in it, and the twitchy little half-pint eats some of that. Franny thinks all the beatings may have stunted him, but he's only thirteen, he may not have started to grow yet. His not eating always makes their father mad, and Franny started getting fat eating up Paulie's leftovers so he wouldn't get another whipping. Now, eating is the only thing she feels like doing. Her kid sister, who is two years older than Paulie, is stunted in another way. She's got okay looks, a good figure, but she's got the brains of a seven-year-old. Amanda has taken her share of their father's beatings just like the rest of them, and still gets hauled in from time to time, but on her they seemed to have had a different effect. Maybe they weren't so hard. While the rest shy away from their father, Amanda clings to him. Thankfully, all that holy smiting of sinners' backsides seems to be passing away. In the early years of the Persecution, their father was more severe than ever, the laying on of the razor strop a regular family worship ritual, forcibly witnessed by all, but he has mellowed over time or else he is just giving up on them and has his mind on other things. The razor strop itself got thrown away or else Nat stole it. It was probably Nat who broke him. Nat was threatened with a thrashing when he stole the motorcycle, but Nat's near as big as her father and when Nat stood him down, her father just got older overnight. Franny often, out of pity, took beatings for the younger ones, but they didn't seem to appreciate it. Even, oddly, resented it. Well, the problem with big dumb Franny is, she just doesn't get it. She thinks her father's whippings were tough, wait till she gets to hell. Amanda knows. It's about the saving of souls, and Franny's will not be saved. Amanda can feel her own soul inside her, anxious for its fate, and she knows the body must be punished for it to be redeemed. She is, she knows, a sinful girl, and when she heard her father shout from the pulpit, "And if thy right hand offend thee, cut if off, and cast it from thee," and that if you didn't, your whole body would get thrown in hell, it frightened her so she could sleep only fitfully for weeks after, afraid the hand would do in her sleep what she refused to let it do awake, and sometimes it did. Not even to her father can she talk about this, she can only beg him to punish her for her redemption's sake. Her father, she knows, is going to Heaven, and the worst thing Amanda can imagine about hell is not the eternal torment but being all alone there. Junior, too, understands the relationship between the punishment of the body and the redemption of the soul, though he has a more generalized notion of sin—we are all born into sin—and consequently has a more traditional and communal notion of the need to punish the flesh to be free of the flesh. Mortification: this is a word Junior has taught Elaine. Whom he has been keeping an eye on, just as she has been furtively watching him. He has approached her, but under the watchful eye of her mother she has been very jumpy and unfriendly. But he knows. He has been in her underwear drawer. The belt he found there is buckled tightly around the tops of his thighs, under his tunic. He feels the tug of sin each step he takes. Like Paulie, Junior has also heard the motorbikes leave, and has heard Ben tell Elaine's mother that he's worried those boys are headed to the camp again and that he should get over there to check on things. So he's gone (Nat's an idiot, but a useful one) and Elaine's mother is dragged away to preach to everyone about the new tabernacle. Junior looks at Elaine and she looks at him.

Littleface and his fellow outlaws are throwing together a supper out of things found in the Brunist camp kitchen fridge and cupboards. Some cold fried chicken, milk, apples, cookies and crackers—a feast. Nat has told them to help themselves to the food, but to leave everything else alone. "If we wanta camp out here a while, we gotta stay cool." That makes sense like everything Nat says. He's just a kid but smart as hell. Even skinny old Houndawg looks up to him. Littleface loves him, has his name tattooed in tiny Gothic over his left nipple near his Warrior Apostles tattoo, though Nat doesn't know that. Religion is not a big deal for Littleface, but if Nat wants this scene, he wants it. He's mad at something, so Littleface is mad, too. Nat's old man is a preacher and Nat is a kind of preacher, too, but he doesn't preach *to* anybody. No stupid church services—that's for sissies, Nat says—no talk about sin, no praying. Nat just yells at who he calls the Big One from time to time, telling him what he thinks and what he's going to do, and the rest of them tune in and sometimes shout at the Big One, too. Face's pal Juice from Crusadeer days really gets into it, stomping around like he's marching and hooting and hollering along with Nat. Nat showed Face his *Classic Comics* version of the Book of Revelation to give him some idea of what's ahead. God and Jesus so damned mad they're going to destroy fucking everything, and the Apostles, Nat says, are going to be God's hit men. So all right, why not, let's at it. Littleface's old lady was an evangelical type, probably still is if she's alive, so he's heard the stories, but he never realized Jesus was such an awesome dude. He raises just one finger and the earth splits and swallows up all the howling and screeching sinners and then snaps shut on them again. Ker-*splat!* He speaks and the bodies of the enemies are ripped open and it's hard not to get hit by the flying flesh and blood. It's amazing! There's guys on horses and, even as they go galloping along, their flesh dissolves and their eyes and tongues melt away, the horses, too, and they end up just hideous skeletons, falling apart. Stories his old lady never told him. His old man got shot up and is no more and is not missed. Littleface does miss his brother whom he used to ride with, but who's in the federal lockup doing hard time and may never come out. Just as well. Lot of guys on the outside trying to kill him. His brother was a first-class gearhead and Littleface often argues with him when working on his bike. "Who ya talking to, Face," Cubano asked him, "to your asshole?" "No, to yours, Spic. Unless that ugly thing is your face." Nat is pressing his fingers to his temples: one of his headaches coming on. They usually hit him in the predawn hours, set him to howling like a wild animal. Can last for hours, days even. Why he says he doesn't drink. Whiskey, anyway. One day, when Nat was twisted up with headache pain, they came on a goat tied to a tree. Nat walked up to it, slit its throat, and put his mouth to the spurting blood. Did he want them to drink it, too? Nat didn't say, but Littleface and Juice took it as a dare and did. Houndawg chopped the head off and threw the body over his buckhorns and they left the area, and that night, after Houndawg and Cubano had skinned and cleaned the animal, they grilled it over an open fire. What was amazing was that Nat's headache had gone away, and that set off a pattern of his killing animals and drinking their blood, and it seems to work. Littleface has a bottle of bourbon he lifted from a shopping center liquor store out on the highway, in spite of all the eyes on him (he bought a pack of cigs and a beer to cover his exit), and he shares it now with Juice and Cubano. Beats blood any day. Juice rides what Houndawg calls a garbage wagon, a bike pieced together from boneyard scraps and very heavily loaded with saddlebags, chrome, accessories, and as covered with pins, stickers, flags, and Jesus paintings as his body is with tattoos. His Juicebox. He can do anything with it, spin it on a dime, walk it on its back wheel, leap cars with it. One of the stickers on its back fender says: "Watch your ass! Jesus is coming and He is as mad as hell!" He likes to say that he wants to get raptured doing a ton down an endless highway. Juice was very impressed when Nat showed them the big photo of Bruno by the fireplace. They all were, even Houndawg. "Look at that fucking mine pick," Juice said. "Cool, man! I want one a them." And he swung his arms like scything a wheat field. "You knew that dude, Nat?" Nat nodded, studying the picture. "The Man," he said. It was near lifesize and in the dim light it seemed to Littleface almost like the Man was alive and staring straight at them. Like something out of a horror movie. Go get them motherfuckers, he seemed to say. Like Jesus. Raise a finger and—*zap!* "Maybe they got some picks like that over at the mine," Littleface says now, gnawing a chicken leg, and Juice lights up and says, "Hey!" Cubano, sitting on an upturned crate, is showing them a trick he can do of throwing an apple into the air and slicing it in two with his switchblade as it falls, when old lady Collins' husband walks into the kitchen with his German shepherd. "What're you boys doing here? They's food over on the Mount." "We don't feel exactly welcome there," Nat says. Nat, Littleface knows, has taken a natural unliking to this beardy hayseed, though he looks like one of the good guys in that Revelations comicbook. Of course, in Nat's interpretation of that story, maybe the good guys are the bad guys. "We thought you wouldn't give a care if we ate up some old leftovers." "Well, I think it's better if you stay with the rest of us." He's seen the bottle of whiskey and he doesn't seem happy about it. Houndawg has called the dog over to him and is stroking him gently. "I do love dawgs," he says with his usual easy drawl, taking a grip on the dog's snout and peeling his lip back, "even old toothless ones. How d'ye call him?" "C'mere, Rocky," Ben says. But Houndawg has a grip on Rocky's collar in one hand, his open blade in the other. "Now just set still, Rocky. We'll find ye sumthin soft t'gum." Littleface realizes the man and his dog are all alone. Five to one, not much they couldn't do. He can see that Nat, gripping his forehead, is thinking the same thing. "C'mon," Nat says finally, rising with a fuck-you shrug. "Somebody here don't smell so good, and it ain't the dog. Let's cut out."

# I.9

## Sunday 19 April

Two children enter the garden. God's children. They have not chosen each other. God has chosen them, as He did the first stunned parents—whose initials they share, though they are not thinking about this. Nor are they thinking about parenting. It would make no sense. They are thinking about, not first things, but last things. Clad like forest ghosts, they step into the garden in the predawn dark, oblivious to its mysterious beauty, to say goodbye to this doomed human world, and to seek God's grace in His eternal one to follow. She does not like this world and will be happy to see it go away. She wants it to end so that she might be with her father and brother again and be freed forever from timidity and bad teeth. She wants it to end right *now*, and she believes that this day that's dawning might be when it happens. And if not, then very soon. Her father said so. Who is, as always, nearby. When she says the words, "Our Father which art in Heaven," it is her father she sees up there. No beard. Tall and wise and smiling down at her with love in his heart. She talks to him every day, and she promises him she is coming as soon as she can. An eternity without him is the most terrible thing she can imagine. And a life without him is nearly as bad. She *will* be redeemed and will do all in her power to be sure of it. That is why she is here. Her mother does not understand, but her father will. The Bible has taught her the relation of pain and suffering to salvation, and in a moment of inspiration—long ago, when they were both still very young—he with whom she walks has shown her the path. It was all quite new and baffling, but his letters (he's very smart) have explained things better.

Although in truth (and, it might be said, as his own father might say, in weakness), he is more reluctant to let go of this world than she, her instructor does feel he has at last returned to the source of the most rapturous moment of his life (only recently has he learned the word "transcendence," though not well enough yet to use it when he talks), and he is prepared to bear all consequences of its re-enactment. His own life, after all, has been difficult and mostly unhappy, and he is ready to accept a better one if that is what happens next. He is less keen than she on spending the afterlife with his family, but at least his infidel brothers will not be there and the others can be somewhere else. It's a big place. In fact, when he imagines it, he is all alone in glory with Jesus, standing side by side with Him over the fires of hell, punishing the wicked. Perhaps, because they are approaching sainthood together, she'll be there too.

It is she who has led them here. "I know a place nobody knows." Whispered behind the tent last night on the Mount of Redemption. They have met at the dogwood tree (the white doves were already cooing in the eaves of the Meeting House) and slipped stealthily past the cabins down the hill to the banks of the creek and across the little bridge there into the woods, the brambles snatching at their tunics. They wore shoes and jeans to come here, but now in the small clearing they kick them off, punishing their bare shins and feet as they will soon punish the rest of themselves, protected only by their cotton tunics and a few thin underthings. They are fearfully excited, their hearts pounding madly in their chests—hers feels almost like it has escaped her chest and is leaping about on top, like the heart on the statue of Mother Mary she once gave her mother—but there is no lust in their beating hearts, certainly not in hers. Her father is watching, she will do nothing wrong in his eyes. The boy's heart is perhaps not quite so pure. He has, for example, and for reasons not wholly religious and unbeknownst to her, stolen a pair of her panties; in fact, he is wearing them. But he too has his eye on the Eternal Kingdom, and if he has sinful feelings, well then they must be beaten out of him, and he needs her help for that. And to the extent that she excites him wrongfully, she too must be punished. There is no real love in their hearts for each other—nor for their own bodies (she hates hers), which must be chastised—but only for their souls, trapped within like caged birds, and for their Heavenly Father who must release them, receive them and clasp them to His bosom like all the preachers promise. They are each, for the other, a means to an end. *The* end.

In the Bible story, the garden was the serpent's own until the two people showed up. Naturally, the serpent was put out by their intrusion and he watched them closely and did all he could to get them expelled. These two children are also being watched. Not by a serpent, but by the minister's fascinated wife, a shadowy figure lost in shadows back in the trees. This was her secret garden, she its keeper, and she knows it will soon be a secret and hers no longer—look, it is already no longer a secret—and she has been paying a kind of wistful farewell visit to it this morning. Her ritual morning pee in the woods. She is wearing a loose frock and a cardigan, not her tunic. That was left back in the cabin where her boy sleeps fitfully. He was overexcited by the emotional crowds on the hill and she had to bring him back to the camp to calm him down. It was not easy. She is worried about him. He cries a lot and is increasingly given to nightmares and childish behavior and is spending as much time in her bed now as his own, desperate for solace. Out in the gloom of the clearing, the boy is giving the girl something. What is it?

"What is this thing?" the girl asks when he hands it to her, her voice barely audible in the damp dark. "My father's razor strop. It was what he used in our evening family worship." "Oh." Her father used to have one too. It hung on a nail in the bathroom. It feels heavy in her hands. Too short. She'll have to be too close. She'd rather have something like a switch, like the first time. There are plenty of them over there in the woods. Oh, the minister's wife is thinking. This is not what she has expected. The boy holds something, too. What is it they mean to do? What the boy holds (the girl knows this, he has shown it to her) is her father's old leather belt. The one she kept coiled up in her drawer and used sometimes on herself, feeling closer to her father when she did so. Though he never hit her, ever. Her own use of the belt was always a kind of practice; she never really got out of herself, but she has sometimes made herself quite dizzy and has hurt herself enough to cry. She does not ask how it came into the boy's hands. "We should pray," she says. She is a little frightened. She is alone in a dark field enclosed in a thick brambly forest, far from anyone who loves her, with a boy she hardly knows, who is bigger and heavier than she remembers, about to do something that, if it's like the last time, is a kind of letting go, when anything might happen. She has seen people lose control of themselves in tent meetings and fall down and pitch about and babble in tongues—there were people out on the Mount like that yesterday—and sometimes something like that seems to happen to her mother. But it has never happened to her, not completely, except for that one day on the Mount of Redemption, the rain storming down. "Dear God," the boy says. He has a soothing voice, but it doesn't stop her trembling. She who is watching is trembling, too. "Help us to do what's right. We only want to be with You. Forever and ever. Amen." "Amen," she whispers, and another whispers, "Amen." "I want you to hit me first," he says, also in a whisper. He's scared too. The girl senses that. "No," she says, "hit me first." "Well. All right. But when it's my turn, you have to promise to hit me hard." "I will." "Turn around." "Why?" "It doesn't hurt as much." "I want it to hurt." "I know. Me too. But first we have to get used to it." "Okay," she says, staring hard at him. His face has a mustache on it and isn't a young boy's anymore. "But don't touch me!" "I won't. And, no matter what, I want you to tell me when to stop." "Okay. You too." She turns her back and crosses her arms over her chest, squeezing the razor strop, bows her head. The keeper of the garden is somewhat horrified. Not only by what she realizes she is about to witness. But also by her own hand, snaking between her legs. "Help me, father," the child whispers. "Help me be brave." Somewhere, not far away, there is a flutter of awakened birds rising.

Evangelist and country gospel singer Ben Wosznik is a worried man. He is sitting on the fold-down steps of his mobile home, his twelve-gauge shotgun over his knees, gazing up at the faint first light of dawn just beginning to creep into the darkness up at Inspiration Point. They are up there; he heard them coming back about an hour or so ago. A sinister growl, like the night itself was growling. As a good hunter, he knows better than to rush upon his prey; he must think this through, anticipate what they might do. Especially now that they are armed. But Ben has been up all night, tending the campfires and steadfastly keeping the overnight vigil at the Mount, sometimes singing with the youngsters and praying with them and with Clara and the others staying up, or trying to. His weariness now is making it difficult to reason clearly. "How mean y'figure them boys is?" he asks. Rocky's answer is, as usual, noncommittal. But, tail wagging, he's ready for whatever.

Maybe he should wait for Abner Baxter to rise and talk to him about it first, but he doesn't know when that will happen. Could be halfway to noon, beat down as the man is, and Elaine meanwhile could be in bad trouble. The fellow, Ben has to allow, is much changed, and not just by the graying of his thick red hair. The missionary life on the road has tempered him. Certainly Abner said some very generous things about him and Clara in front of everybody at the Mount of Redemption yesterday, and it seemed to come from the heart. His middle boy's a heathenish little devil, though.

Ben feels uneasy being away from the Mount, even for a short time, for he is a strong believer in the imminence of the Rapture and the Second Coming—has been since he first heard Ely Collins preach—and he is fearful of missing it somehow. Not through faithlessness, but simple negligence. Bad luck. He knows what they have been saying about the seven years of tribulation—meaning there are at least two to go, if they've got their start date right—but he keeps feeling in his bones something is apt to happen today and he has to be on the Mount when it does. Maybe *so* it does. But there's nothing he can do. He has to wait for Elaine and work out these other problems, which he has been talking over with his dog.

He doesn't know where the girl is. Not on her bed where he left her, collapsed half-dead on top. She is often given to wandering around restlessly, talking or praying to her father, though she seemed almost unable to stand when he brought her back, so it's hard to figure. She kept going last night in her meek shrinking way until well after midnight, but she was looking peaked and was plainly giving out, and when he asked, she admitted she wasn't feeling very good. Maybe it's her periodicals. She is always shy to say so, even to her mother. So he drove her in the pickup back to her own bed in their trailer home, she begging him in her timid little voice to please come get her if the Rapture suddenly started up. The lot was empty except for a trailer or two, those like the Halls with caravans and smaller campers having driven over to the parking lot at the mine or the access road at the foot of the hill, and by now most had retired into them, though, at Clara's suggestion, they kept their window blinds open in case anything should happen during the night. Rocky was alone back here at the camp, tied to the hitching bar at the back of the trailer and feeling sorry for himself. Ben had had to leave him behind. Too many people around make the old fellow edgy, especially if they're all fired up with the Holy Spirit, like so many were; but by midnight the crowds had faded away and those keeping the vigil on the mine hill were mostly dozing, curled up in blankets and sleeping bags—even Abner and his family had come back to camp, worn out from their long hard journey to get here—so he picked up Rocky when he brought Elaine home and took him back to the Mount with him to feed him scraps from their hillside feast and exercise him a little and so as to have company through the rest of the night. And was he thinking about the possibility of his dog being raptured up and joining him up there in the presence of the Lord? He was. As Hiram says, God created animals and God loves them. Look into your dogs' eyes and see their soul. God will not forsake them. You will see them in Heaven.

Now he has returned, bringing Rocky back to camp to protect him from the crowds, which were already, before dawn, starting once again to assemble—coffee is on over there and there are fresh doughnuts—and to check on Elaine. When it turned out she was not in the trailer and nowhere to be found, he couldn't help but worry, not with those biker boys around. He is a man of peace, but if they did anything to little Elaine, he would kill them. Last night, when he walked in on them in the camp kitchen, the knives came out, so he figured, if he was going to pay them a visit, he'd better arm himself, and he went looking. His shotgun was there, but his wooden-handled three-screw Blackhawk wasn't. Had he misplaced it? He spent some time hunting for it and chanced on the can where they kept the slush fund for day-to-day camp supplies. They had been dipping into it pretty often, what with all the expenses of this big reunion and anniversary, but he had topped it up himself only three days ago, and now there was nothing in it but a few coins. So, though it took a few minutes, it finally registered on him that they had been robbed. The money, the handgun, maybe other things. Probably in retaliation for his breaking up their little kitchen party. When they left or when they came back? Was Elaine here? Various scenarios flicker through his worried mind, none of them comforting.

He stands. Has he heard something? Sort of like the muffled snapping of a dry branch. Down near the creek. Some animal probably. He hears it again. Was that a cry? Likely just a bird, or the squeal of a rodent—the owls often hunt down there. But now he's torn. Does he go down to the creek to investigate or on up to the Point to confront the bikers? He asks Rocky what to do, but Rocky doesn't know. He just wags his tail slowly in his melancholic way, as though he were worried, too. Ben could circle round but that might take too long. The direct path to both the creek and the Point bifurcates beyond the cabins. He'll carry his dilemma to the fork.

* * *

Maybe he is too weary from his journey, waxing faint like David among the Philistines. Or just overwrought by this homecoming and what it might portend. But, far from collapsing as Ben Wosznik has supposed, Abner Baxter, except for a thirty-minute doze, fraught with terrifying highway imagery, has been up all night, unable to put his troubled mind at ease. The Lord has directed him as Jacob was directed: Get thee to thine own house. Every man to his tents, saith Moses. Return unto the land of thy fathers, and to thy kindred; and I will be with thee. And so he has, with great effort and hope in his heart, returned to his origins and to the site of his spiritual rebirth. But he feels like he is home and not home, part of these people and this movement, and yet an outsider still, distrusted, misunderstood, resented even. Just as he was in his union organizing days. He has left the wilderness only to arrive in the wilderness. He understands the rules of the camp and wishes to abide by them, but they seemed uncommonly zealous about pointing them out. It was like they were intent on moving him on before he'd even alighted. He was hurt by that. For all their doctrinal differences, he does truly esteem and honor Clara Collins as a pillar of the faith, and even feels a certain Christian love for the woman unlike any he has ever felt for another, has since that night in the ditch when she reached across the horror to forgive and embrace him. "We are *all* murderers! Abner, join hands with us and pray!" He came late to the Prophet—almost too late. He was, as he has often declared, the greatest of sinners, for he not only denied the Prophet and his followers, he reviled and persecuted them. Then, on the eve of the Day of Redemption, God Himself intervened and the greatest of sinners was himself redeemed. To become—he knows this—the greatest of believers. That that night proved as decisive as the very Day of Redemption is a reminder that no date on the way to glory is without import. Abner believes that the day of the Christ's coming will fall at the end of the seventh year of the Tribulation that began five years ago today, in fulfillment of Biblical prophecy and that of the Prophet Bruno. But that does not make this day any less charged with potential meaning. Since his conversion, every day of his life from the best to the worst has been so charged.

Abner is well aware that there are many who call themselves Brunists but who remain merely plodding unchanged Christians, attached to their old beliefs and, even if convinced of the imminence of the Last Days, shy to profess Bruno as their Prophet. Abner has no such trepidation. He looked into the eyes of the Prophet on that fateful night as the man rose, gaunt and bearded, from his kiss of the dead girl, blood staining his lips and beard and even his brow, and he saw in those eyes the holy fire of divine possession. Bruno the coalminer, he barely knew, though they often worked the same shift. Bruno the Prophet, drawn up out of the fiery bowels of the earth, perhaps even resurrected from the dead, was transparently God's messenger, and he knew him instantly. Perhaps, as some proclaim, the Holy Spirit passed from Ely Collins at the moment of his horrible death into his partner Bruno; more likely, Ely Collins, for all his renowned goodness, was found unworthy. Bruno was the Chosen One. Was he once a Romanist? Well, Jesus was a Jew. All that night in the house of mourning and during their Sunday morning crusade through the papist temple, and then all day on the stormy Mount of Redemption, the Prophet strayed not far from Abner's side, and Abner felt anointed by him. Chosen by the Chosen. Bruno. Who, for Abner, has no other name. That the man is no more has come as no surprise. While others fled the Mount that day as the lightning flashed and the wind blew and the rain poured down, Abner stood his ground and railed against the attacking Powers of Darkness, and as they shackled the Prophet and led him away, Bruno turned to gaze one last time at him, and in that gaze Abner saw both a final farewell and a command: It was he, Abner, who must carry the sacred flame.

For much of the Tribulation that has followed in faithful and intransigent pursuit of that mission, Abner and his family have lived mostly in tents pitched in campsites, fields, parks, church grounds, back yards, and cemeteries—"alongside troubled waters," as he has often said—and they will no doubt have to do so again. Their travails have made vivid the Biblical accounts of the Israelites wandering in the wilderness, but they have been, in the high-speed rulebound modern world, a bitter hardship. He has often had to bite his tongue while the law forced him to strike his tents and move on. And jail they have known, too, and worse. They have been as if destined for affliction, like Paul himself as he wrote in his letter to the church of the Thessalonians. "For yourselves know that we are appointed thereunto." For the moment, however, they have this barren little cabin to rest within, if God so grants, their tent pitched as an annex at the back of it. He has collected a set of cots from the Meeting Hall for his family, most of which remain unused. Only those of his wife and daughters in the tented extension are being slept in, if his wife's nighttime misery can be called sleeping. Nathan and Paul are up in the motorcyclists' encampment and Young Abner left to use the privy and never returned. The minister's wife next door has also left her cabin—he saw her slip out into the night—but her whimpering boy is still in it. Abner heard them when they returned shortly after midnight, the boy having a hysterical fit, she shushing him; he hears him still. At a glance yesterday, Abner could see that the woman, though boasted about as an important convert, was not a true believer. A rich lady on a lark. And her boy, though one of the First Followers (and where was his mother then?), seems seriously disturbed. That they should be granted a cabin within the camp, even if she did pay for its repair, while he, the Brunist bishop of West Condon, is denied is an intolerable injustice, but one that he will have to learn, in this evil time, to tolerate. We glory in tribulations, we commend ourselves in afflictions, we are afflicted but not crushed.

A sullen dawn now muddies the sky, and out of the trees below the Main Square emerges a shadowy armed figure, stooped and menacing, bearded, his dog at his side. It is Ben Wosznik. A simple man of simple faith, slow and steady, but though Abner admires him and has tried always to ingratiate himself with him, there is a distance between them that seems hard to bridge, and he worries now why he should be approaching him in this manner. "Abner," he says, "I am glad to see you risen." "Yes, Brother Ben. Like Joshua, who rose up early at the dawning of the day to bring down the walls of Jericho." "Well, I hope you do not bring down these walls which has took a right smart a labor to keep standing. Abner, I got a serious difficulty. I come upon your middle boy and his friends last night in the camp kitchen, raiding the supplies and drinking hard likker. I asked them to leave, and afterwards my trailer got robbed. They took a handgun and all our emergency fund money. I don't know what all else, but I am worried." "That boy!" Abner feels his choler rising. Nathan has been a vexation since the day he was born, and all the whippings the boy has endured have not turned him from his innate wicked ways. He came into the world by the evil one possessed. Abner is already climbing the rise toward their encampment, his fists clenched, Ben Wosznik and his dog trailing along behind him.

On top, he finds his two sons and their despicable companions sprawled out in a thick heavy sleep in their filthy sleeping bags, a surly and angry lot when awakened. They arise with knives out and with blistering blasphemies and obscenities, but they see Ben's shotgun and back off, snarling like trapped animals. Ben circles around them, shotgun on his hip, peering into the undergrowth with a worried look. "They has been a robbery," Abner says. "A gun, some money. I want them things. Now. Empty out your bags and pockets." "I don't know what you're talking about, old man," Nathan says sourly and throws his backpack at him. "Empty them out yourself." He does so. Greasy unwashed clothing, rags really, tools, comicbooks, transistor radio, leather gloves. A gun. "Is this the one?" "It is," says Ben. Abner snatches it up, points it at his son. "The money." "Ain't got any. And I ain't never seen that gun before neither." Abner kicks through the miserable contents of the backpack. "All right. Then leave your motorcycle as repayment. And get out. All of you. You have shamed me." There is a pause when nothing moves. Except his own shaking hand with the pointing gun. Which Nathan ignores, glowering instead at Ben Wosznik. Then he gathers up his possessions, stuffs them back into his backpack, and mounts his bike. "I said, leave the motorcycle here." "Go to hell, old man," he says, raising his middle finger at him. "Paulie—?" "Hop up here, Runt," says the tall skinny one, and Paulie climbs up behind the older man with the gray braid down his back and raises his finger, too, and they're off. Abner swings round with the gun pointed at his middle son's head, but Ben Wosznik grips his arm and presses it down. "It's only money," he says quietly, taking the gun. "And I reckon that bike ain't worth nothing anyhow. Probly stole, ain't it?" "Yes." His will is breaking, his humiliation complete. He feels like the night he fell to weeping on Clara Collins' shoulder. No man should have to bear so much alone. The taunting roar of the motorcycles fades into the distance, punctuated by a final backfiring pop or two like snorts of cruel laughter, and then the morning songs of the birds return on this, the slowly brightening dawn of the Day of Redemption. He turns toward Ben Wosznik and opens his arms as though to offer an embrace and to say he's sorry, when there is a sudden rustling in the thicket below them, and deer hunters both, they turn toward it.

The bad brother has been sent into exile, but the reconciliation of the two patriarchs has been interrupted by the appearance in the valley below them of two spectrally white shapes fluttering separately through the trees and into the dimly lit clearing leading to the cabins. It is the two children, the children of God, tearfully departing the garden, clutching their talismans of leather, a kind of delirium possessing them still. The patriarchs stand as if frozen, high on a stony jut of land above them, beholding the scene. "My eyes ain't so good," whispers the bearded one. "Is that blood?"

# 1.10

## Sunday 19 April

"I've been thinking about the Holy Blood," Sally says. Is she just killing time or impatiently pressing her luck? She has talked Tommy Cavanaugh into bringing his cameras and tape recorder and joining her on a "research project" out here at the Deepwater mine hill in preparation for his new PhD career, doing her Girl Scout good deed of the day by luring him away from the bloodless banking life—"I'll be your R.A. and take notes," she said—and they are now mingling with the media folk and the crowds of the curious at the foot of the hill, watching the Brunists wander around up on top, about half of them in those white choir gowns. God's little lambs. His white corpuscles. The hill is aswarm with them, and there's a lot of coming and going and cheerful Heavenward gestures, but not much is happening, and Tommy is getting bored. Certainly no sign of the End of the World—though, who knows, maybe this is what it is like. The sheriff and his boys are out here, rocking around wide-legged like cowboys who just got off their horses and are trying to air out their crotches, but they seem intent only on keeping the townsfolk and reporters from pestering the cultists. She'd like to get closer, but there's no way up unless invited by a Brunist. They apparently pitched their tents up there yesterday to get the jump on everybody, as Tommy put it; he said he drove by last night (with whom? don't ask) and saw big bonfires blazing, and his dad, who had been working on ways to stop the gathering, bully that he is, was hopping mad when he heard about it. Tommy is sharing his mother's old station wagon with his dad now because the Lincoln got beat up by a biker gang and is in the garage having the the dents taken out. She has heard about these guys. They're some kind of Brunist tagalongs or security guards, but they're not out here today. "The Holy Blood was the blood that came spouting out of Jesus' side when that Roman soldier porked him with his spear. Later it got passed around to all the churches as a relic to work wonders with. Also whatever leaked out when he was scourged or squirted out from the nail holes. Like, you know, they had somebody there collecting it in little cups like you do when you kill a pig. It cured everything. Miraculous effluvia, they called it." She liked this phrase. Miraculous effluvia. It has gone into her notebook. Which today she is pretending is her steno pad for Tommy the Scholar. "It was a hot pharmaceutical product. There was a lot of money to be made and there were several enterprising bagmen trafficking in it, though the Church of the Holy Sepulchre cartel in Jerusalem cornered most of the market since they claimed to have all this stuff on the premises, the place being a kind of dead meat mine. They also sold his sweat, tears, hair, nail clippings, and foreskin, not to mention everything he ever touched, like rocks he stepped or sat on, raggy scraps from his loincloths and winding sheets, and even shards of the basin he used to wash the disciples' feet."

"His foreskin? C'mon, you're making this up, Sal."

"No, he apparently had several, actually. They're scattered all over Europe and displayed in jewel cases like little wedding rings. More than a dozen of them. Does that mean he had several dicks? I don't know. It's one of the unrevealed mysteries of the Christian faith." There is a festive atmosphere up on the hill, but also an undercurrent of fear. The cultists are spending a lot of time peering up at the sky, and the onlookers down here can't help following their gaze; when some-one yawns, everyone yawns. She looks up, too. After a sexy, summery week, it has turned cooler and the sky today has a dark woolly look, uncombed and knotted (she is thinking about her own neglect in this respect; epic rats' nest, as her mother calls it), and maybe it reminds everyone of the apocalyptic storm that pounded the hill last time. She remembers it. She was here. A giggler with other gigglers. Pathetic. "One big collectors' item for a while was a farewell note he supposedly left his disciples, writing with the nails he got tacked up with, using his blood as ink and his own skin as parchment. But, as we all know, his skin went to Heaven with the rest of him, even if he left his blood and other exudations behind, so that article got remaindered."

"I can see it coming. Next you'll be telling me they collected his shit."

"Well, there are rumors. I mean, if sweat, why not snot or vomit or ear wax, right? And what-all else. Dandruff? Dingleberries? That stuff under your toenails? I can just see all those guys chasing around after him, trying to grab up anything that fell off or out of him." Idea for a story: Jesus Has a Wet Dream. Sacramental consequences. "They also sold off all of Mary's bits and pieces, though her big item was her milk, which must have been more like cheese by the time it reached the customers."

"Oh my God! Spare me, please!" Tommy turns away with a pained grimace (she has grossed him out again, the tender little thing; why does she do this?) and, handing her his Polaroid, busies himself with his Nikon. The Brunists are a colorful lot, animated and emotional, lots of hugs and tears and emphatic declamations and occasional convulsions, and they dress funny, so there are plenty of great shots to be had—the amateur yodeler from the radio station, for example, in his matching white Stetson and white boots with red flames at the pointed toes and on the crown of the Stetson, a white jacket with fringes on the sleeves and tight white pants, blood-red tie like his throat has been cut, guitar over one shoulder and tape recorder over the other, picking up field recordings. Or that cluster of wailing worshipers in white tunics gathered around the pudgy silver-haired faith healer with the sparkling teeth, praying for the grumpy broken-backed man in the wheelchair to get up and walk. But Tommy ignores them (she has not; this has all gone into her notebook) and, shifting the bill of his baseball cap out of the way, points his lens at some young moonfaced kids with guitars wearing Brunist tunics. Well, one of the girls is cute, bare-legged and bosomy and wearing her shortened tunic like a loose nightie, the hypocritical little bitch, he probably has his eye on her. Or, more precisely, on what she's showing off between her legs. Come and see. Sally drops her cigarette and grinds it out. Fiercely. On edge. Can't help it. A lot of young kids out here, buying this craziness. It's scary.

"What I can't figure out, though," she says, hanging his camera over her shoulder and shoving her hands into her trenchcoat pockets, trying to stop herself from lighting up again, "is that, with all this emphasis on magical blood, there's no mention of hawking Mary's menses. I mean, hey, talk about miraculous effluvia."

"I suppose they figured it'd make you sick instead of better. The curse of Eve, right?" This said over his shoulder while clicking away. The little twit, knees still raised, is smiling at him.

"That's what the guys in charge called it. They used to chase menstruating women out of town and lock them up in a shed because they thought they'd ruin the crops or mess up the hunt—I mean, you could smell them from a mile off, couldn't you?—and they got blamed for everything from causing the milk to sour and the clocks to stop, to bringing on earthquakes and hailstorms and curdling the mayonnaise." That one about curdling the mayo she got from her Grandma Friskin. Who said it backwards a decade or so ago: "Well, at least I won't curdle the mayonnaise anymore." "But the magic sauce was also used to fertilize the veggies and fruit trees and chase off evil spirits, and they fed it to their pigs and chickens to spice up their bacon and eggs, so its rep was mixed. People even blended it with wine and drank it themselves for a longer life and for more kids and to pump up their spiritual powers and their dingdongs, which to guys is more or less the same thing. I mean, you know, good or bad, whatever the Ineffable touches, whammo. They believed the gunk could cure gout, warts, worms, the bubonic plague, epilepsy, and leprosy, not to mention fever blisters, buboes, and the whooping cough. Ragtime is a cosmic event,

Tommy. It swings with the moon and flows with the tides. The big red monster. Powerful stuff." Not that she believes any of this. It's a literal pain in the gut. "So you can imagine the market potential of Mary's monthlies, right? The *real* Holy Blood. In fact, the Blood of Christ is probably just a euphemism for it. Men are always trying to get in on the act. Take that wound Jesus got from the Roman dogface. Ever look at the paintings of it? It looks just like a bloody you-know-what."

"No, it doesn't."

"No?"

"No pubic hair."

She grins at that. He's listening. "Well, but he was still just a virgin, wasn't he? In that respect at least, with his little loincloth like a sanitary napkin."

"What's with you?" Tommy asks, a bit exasperated. "Are you on the rag or something?"

"How'd you guess?" What did she think? He'd feel sorry for her? Probably just makes him want to throw up. It always infuriates her when it comes on and it makes her lose her cool. Today it seems worse than usual. It feels like her ovaries are eating her intestines. Like maybe her uterus knows she is excited and is trying to claw the egg back in case something happens. *Is* she excited? Sure. Damn it. She takes a drag on her cigarette. (Another one. When did she light up? Doesn't remember.) "Cousin Tom, my roommate calls it."

"How did I get this honor?"

"Time. Of. Month."

"Oh. Very funny. Well, I'm just glad I don't have to deal with that."

"Too bad you don't. The world might be a better place if men had their turn. Monthlies keep you pegged to the earth. Men get lost in their own spacey heads and fly off somewhere, and that's how we got all this religious idiocy." She gestures up at the middle of the hill, where a huge theatrical fat woman with arms as big around as phone poles and stiff hair poking up like straw ticking out of an old mattress, her tunic riding up over her bulbous rump like a wrinkled slipcover, has knelt and started to moan beside an unfolded aluminum lawn chair with plastic webbing raised up on four cross-like stakes, which seems like some kind of weird altar or shrine. Others fall to their knees around her. The woman points up at the sky and shakes her head violently and all the others do the same. Some of them seem to have red crosses painted on their foreheads. "I mean, just look at all those wacky Christians! Looney tunes, man!"

"But that isn't real Christianity."

"Yes, it is."

He sighs impatiently, as though to say, oh shut up, and stares absently down at her shirt. She had tried this morning to pull on her old No-Name Wilderness Camp tee from when she was eleven, imagining it might be like a cool skin-tight top leaving a bare midriff, maybe tease out a romantic joke or two (hah), but she couldn't get her head through the neck of it. She decided it was not smart to wear anything too provocative, so she left her perversely illustrated JESUS LOVES ME tee at home and chose instead one of her noncommittal holiday shirts, the one from Yellowstone showing Old Faithful geysering. Figured it might give Tommy ideas. It does. "Reminds me. I need to pee. Time to go anyway. Dad will be waiting for me." See Sally smile. See Tom run. Off to feed the dummy. "We're taking turns with Mom. The home care nurse has the day off. In fact, that's her up there by the big tent. Bernice. The one in the headband, looking like an Arab refugee."

Nuts. "So how's your mom doing?" It's like her presence has somehow created her own absence…

"Better. That lady has been attempting some kind of faith cure, and it seems to be working. Sort of. At least Mom's in a better mood. Less bitter, somehow. She seems to have resolved something in her mind. So what the hell. If it works, all power to her." What can she say? That his mother would be better off suffering? "Here, Sal. Why don't you take the cameras, get us some more pix?"

"Nah. I'd just lose them. Before you go, though, could you let me use your car a minute?"

"Sure. What for?"

"I'm about to blow a fuse, Tommy. I need to change ponies." Is that a mixed metaphor, or what? I gotta sandbag the flood. Reload the rocket chamber. Feed the kitty. Diaper up. Ram a tam.

Make a list.

"Well, all right. But don't leave the old one in the ashtray, please."

"Don't worry. It's what trenchcoat pockets are for. Keeps the sniffer dogs away from the grass."

In his car, after making the change, she takes out her notebook and writes down that phrase about presence and absence. What does it mean? And what will she do with the spent bullet? Dracula's tea bag, as her roomie calls it. Where will Angela most likely poke around and find it?

Gods fucking mortals, whether as birds, bulls, dragons, or rain, are always stories of rape. Mary got bonked in the ear, so it was a kind of mind-rape. The Annunciation as an act of conceptual violence.

Words as random ejaculate. Potent. Diseased. Syphilitic. Mind rot.

Virtuosity alone is not satisfying, she writes. What is needed is the unmistakable crack of a hammer against glass.

Riding the Hood. Story about a chick who comes of age, dons the rag, and heads out into the world to make her fortune, delivering the goods to grandma. Who is juiced beyond redemption. A wolf tries to cut in on her territory, but he gets stoned on grandma. Red rules.

A woman's biological liquidity—blood, milk, tears: the emergence of life from a fluid medium.

There's a chinless little guy with big ears and buckteeth who passes through the food tent at regular intervals, spouting Bible verses. Mostly about last times. Death and destruction and the tortures of hell. God's playground delights. The verse-spouter doesn't look at anyone or speak to anyone. He is speaking to the world. Or some world. He reminds Sally of a sick polar bear she once saw in a zoo, striding compulsively back and forth between two fixed points. She draws a cartoon of him. "A city on a hill cannot be hid!" the little fellow cries out. For at least the fifth or sixth time. A line from the Sermon on the Mount. Most loathsome text in that loathsome book. He's probably talking about the plans for a temple up here. If he knows what he's talking about at all. "Sweet Jesus!" he exclaims.

City on a hill. Imagine. A wandering hill. A soft hill. A slippery hill: The city loses its footing. Oops. As the city slides toward the darkness below, the city fathers enact desperate ordinances against the decline. They float away like comicstrip balloons as the slide accelerates. This tent is perched on a hillside. Made of what? Coal slag maybe. She has to sit facing downslope for fear of tipping over, holding her place by gripping it with her butt. Facing upslope would be easier, but she might fall backwards.

Story idea: Struggling against invisible resistance up a hillside or mountain, like in a dream. What is on the other side? A destroyed town? Pleasure? The abyss? The feeling of persisting inside a negative force for no reason other than the need to persist. Ipsey Wipsyphus.

Sweet Jesus: a killer, dangerously criminal but given to endearing eccentricities. Pissed off at what they've done to him and out for revenge: Listen, you think I can forgive this? He shows his scars. When I think about them they still sting. I'm going to rapture the shit out of those dickheads! Dirty Pete as his enforcer. His ma: Big Mary. I Love to Tell the Story…

Maybe the easiest thing to do is found another church. She writes that, turns the page over, hoping no one demands to see what she has written. She tries to look like she might be praying. Her scribbling has drawn scowls, questions. But also beatific smiles. She's more comfortable with the scowls. To be sitting here among them is no doubt dangerous, but here she is. On one tagged page, which she can quickly flip to if someone comes to peer over her shoulder, she has written: The Brunists: an amazing movement! And it is. Almost like a magic act: something conjured out of nothing.

Two homely kids in tunics come into the tent, go out, one skinny, the other fat, looking stoned, careful not to touch, but never more than a foot or so apart. Not part of the others. Vaguely familiar. A rash of red fuzz on the boy's lip. They seem to share some dreadful knowledge. Or wrongful expectation.

One is deprived of full contact with reality by the flaw of hope.

Write about that. The woefullest thing. Hope.

As best she can understand these people, they hope the world is about to end, possibly even today, but are also afraid it might. Meanwhile, even as they get ready to fly away, they are building themselves a big spread for their headquarters and even a temple up here on the mine hill. Part of what that "city on a hill" cry is all about. The cathedral impulse: Is it an admission of failure?

There's a sad sack of a woman who can't stop eating. She picks up a sandwich, leaves the tent, tugging her tunic down at the back. A few minutes pass, she returns, picks up another sandwich, leaves, tugging her tunic down. She's not wearing any shoes. Chin sunk in her cleavage, mouth stuffed with sandwich. Often, she seems to be crying. She must have put away at least twenty sandwiches since Sally has been sitting here.

Time. Back to that. The shriveling of those foreskin relics. What time does. But: Christ preaching, riding a donkey, posing on the cross. Acting. In time, objects dissolve, but gesture is frozen forever. Sally Elliott's molecular law.

Words: somewhere in between. Their excessive superfluity. Like sperm. Now and then, after millions swim past and die, one sticks. Makes everyone sick for a while.

At first, people came over to speak to her, introduce themselves, invite her to come pray or sing or just walk about with them and she was able to put them off by saying she was waiting for someone, thanks; now they mostly leave her alone. Some asked what she was writing. "My thoughts," she said.

Her discomfort. Her stupidity. Her ugliness. Her blood sacrifice.

There's an old lady in the doorway, sitting upright in her chair as though bracing herself for an immediate ascent. Must be nearly a hundred. Can't come too soon for her, else she'll have to go through the burial, decomposition, and resurrection drill.

Idea for a story: The dead rise from their graves. Billions of them. Brief elation. And then they fall over and die again. A mess.

Now and then a helicopter rattles overhead. Five years ago, there were a lot of them. She thought of them then as pestilential, locust-like emblems of the last days. Today's loner is a distant melancholic echo of that day, like a marker on the grave of that lost time, of all lost time. But what time is not lost? Even future time is lost. What is different about the end when it comes: it cannot be remembered.

There are some snotnosed brats running around in the tent and a huge bald redfaced man in a split tunic gives one of them a sullen clout that sends him sprawling. Bawling. A lit cigarette dangles between the fat man's thick lips like a pea shooter. Darren and Billy Don said no smoking in the tent, but nobody is going to argue with that guy. A thin little woman with coarse sandy hair, a pooched belly, and a sad martyred look comes in and leads the yowling kid out. The big man takes up a fistful of sandwiches and follows them, brushing the tent flaps, making everything tremble. So much of him.

Flesh generates melancholy.

*Everything* generates melancholy.

That night in the back seat of his dad's car all that time ago. Boy Blue. His boner poking at her side like the legionnaire's spear. Knocking on the door. That she was ready to open but didn't know it.

Where is the little girl afraid to peep? She's behind the ice plant, getting in deep.

A pastoral romance.

She sighs irritably, folds up her notebook, stuffs it back in her trenchcoat pocket. She aches for a smoke, but if she leaves the tent she'll just have to walk on down the hill and home again. Her thirty minutes were up half an hour ago.

After Tommy split (when Angela tips down the sun visor to admire herself in the makeup mirror tonight: sur-*prise!*), she decided to try for an invitation up the hill. Fellow believers were recognized and led up past the sheriff's barriers, but she could never fake that. The reporters and camera crews, like the tourists, were restricted to the bottom of the hill, but cultists sometimes came down to talk to them. Two guys in particular seemed to be acting as spokesmen for the group; a tall slouching boy with handlebars covering an overbite, shaded pilot specs, burns and a hairknot, and his shorter friend, a more earnest and scholarly sort with a round face, granny glasses, and curly blond hair (she'd die for hair like that, she'd even brush it). She wandered over to tune in and it was clear they knew, in the way that baseball nuts know their stats, what they were talking about. They had the cult history down pat. Christian history, too. All the schisms and theories and prophecies and interpretations. Or at least they seemed to, what did she know? They had the Bible mapped in their heads as well. They could jump around in it at will, whip off quotes, name chapter and verse, draw parallels and morals. When some guy behind a camera asked if the Brunist movement wasn't heretical, they coolly said they didn't believe in the concept of heresy. All human efforts to grasp God's purposes have value. No one has a monopoly on the truth.

"Right on," she said over the reporter's shoulder, and the boys smiled benignly.

"The truth," said the blond one, "is more like something that exists apart in the intellectual space shared by everyone, not something bottled up inside this or that individual. All voices have to be listened to closely in order to catch a whisper of God's voice behind them." Whisper. Nice.

"The truth's more like the air we share," said the mustachioed one. "Not what you or I happen to have in our lungs at any moment. And like air, we can't see truth, but we know it's there and we can't do without it."

She could see problems with that metaphor, but she didn't say so. Instead, she waited until the reporters were out of the way, and then she said, "Hi. I'm Sally Elliott. You guys really know your stuff. I'm impressed." She knew she had a genuine expression of angst on her face because of the cramps. "I don't think I'm going to become a member or anything, but I'm really curious and I wondered if you could give me, like, a kind of guided tour and tell me what's going on?"

"Are you a Christian?"

"Well, a Presbyterian."

"Really? Here in town? The minister's wife is a member now."

"I know. Auntie Debra." Not really her aunt, of course. Was that cheating?

They looked at each other and nodded and introduced themselves and invited her up. Maybe her scruffiness helped. From what she could see under the tunics, or by those who lacked them, she fit right in. Probably a good thing she didn't have the cameras, though. Billy Don, the taller one, said this was hallowed ground and she could only stay for thirty minutes, unless she wanted to confess and become a member. There was still time. They were watching her uneasily (behind Billy Don's shades, she could see, one eye was askew), but they also seemed hopeful for a new adherent. Probably gave them status. Banking another soul.

The tour didn't take long. There wasn't much to see, but that wasn't the point. "Hallowed ground" was the point, and she its inquisitive intruder. When she asked, Darren and Billy Don explained that the lawn chair perched on the four waist-high roughhewn wooden crosses was like the one on which the dead girl (they said: "first martyr") was laid out on the Day of Redemption. Others passed by, pointing at the sky. She remembered the thin bluish corpse, whipped by wind and rain, only the second dead body she had ever seen. But she had forgotten the lawn chair. Probably too freaked out to notice. On the day, even while she laughed with her friends, she worried the Brunists might be right and she'd get left behind. She could still think that way. She'd been poised for a sprint up the hill if things started to happen. At the same time, she was afraid of getting struck by lightning. Billy Don asked her if she'd like to stop and pray, and she said she would like to meditate for a moment, and she assumed a grave expression and stared down at the lawn chair and had a rather ghoulish thought about Sleeping Beauty.

They walked her around behind the reception tent, as they called it, to the lone tree there, which had something to do with the invention of their new baptism ceremony with light instead of water. "It's like a new covenant—not replacing the old, but transcending it in the way that light transcends water." This ceremony awaited her if God granted her grace and understanding and she became a True Follower. They pointed to a large tent further up the hillside, whose open flaps revealed rows of folding chairs and said this could happen tonight if she were ready to confess her sins and give herself to Jesus. She asked more about this. Apparently there is a special "liturgical" flashlight they use just like the one from the first time. Or maybe it's the same one. The tree had a frail shaggy martyred look of its own, gaunt, leafy but without real branches, a wounded pole. Not unlike that of their leader Giovanni Bruno, as she remembers him from the day and from photos of the day. She asked about him and learned that he is dead. Not, apparently, from natural causes. Unless all causes are God's causes and therefore natural, she reminded them, hoping they didn't hear the irony, and they nodded solemnly at that, and seemed to relax just a little. They pointed out the place down on the mine road where the girl was killed and the area just below them where the Powers of Darkness gathered with their ominous yellow schoolbuses. Where she herself had stood. Full of darkness, to be sure. By the time things really got hairy, though, the Powers had to do without her and her friends. They'd earlier started for the bingo tent to get out of the storm when they heard a lot of screaming in there and that scared the pants off them and they ran all the way home and had to watch the rest on television.

Though some of the scowls she got suggested she was still oozing an aura of darkness, for the most part she was welcomed with smiles and praise-the-lord greetings, the two boys her ambassadors. The kids from Florida all gave her loving hugs, including the cute one (who, Sally was happy to note, had gapped front teeth and a lisp), and introduced her to others from their bus and people they'd come to know here. There were apparently over a dozen buses parked at the camp, and more down below here on the mine road. It was like being at a big school pep rally. On Homecoming weekend. She learned from the boys that the cult was now hundreds of times bigger than it had been. Something was happening. It was almost elbow to elbow up here. She met the radio announcer in the white cowboy togs, who was talking with a tall skinny dude with a guitar and his girlfriend about a gig at the station. She might have been part Mexican. When Sally asked her why she was here, she said she'd got called. Like someone called her on the phone. A lot of these people talked that way. Voices in their heads. In the wilderness of their heads. A dingbat with a rigid grimace and steely blue eyes under a peroxide blond toupee wandered past, trailed by admiring ladies in bouffants. He was lecturing them at full throttle on the meaning of the cross in the circle they were wearing on their tunics. Some numbers game involved, having to do with Christ's thirty-three years. "And, yea, there was give them to each one a white robe," he cried out. "Cause the spirit has took on flesh, a new day is come, brung by the White Bird, the Holy Spirit, and you are in it, my friends, a new day what will last to the end a the world!" There were people falling about in what her comparative religion textbooks used to call fits of divine madness, and other people strolling about with cups of coffee and beatific expressions, calmly watching the ecstatics as they might watch children playing in a sandbox. Weird. Tom and Sally at the Reality Border. "Do you guys ever do stuff like that?" she asked, and got only smiles in return, though Darren added, "God speaks with many voices."

That home care nurse in the beaded headband Tommy pointed out, his mom's faith healer, looked alarmed when she spotted her, and hiding her head under her shawl which might have been made out of an old bedsheet, quickly vanished, as did Aunt Debra, who did not seem happy to see her. She caught only a glimpse of Colin Meredith before Aunt Debra whisked him out of sight. A wisp of a fellow, rigid smile on his face, thin silvery hairs hanging from his chin. His goggle eyes were darting everywhere, and when they lit on her, they flashed with panic. Which, on seeing his, she felt, too. When she asked, Billy Don said, "He's a kind of visionary genius, like, and one of the first disciples and about the sincerest, most intense guy I've ever known.

He almost vibrates like a live electric wire, you know? Sometimes it kind of drives him crazy, but he loves his mother very much and mostly does what she says, and she keeps him from going over the top." Hmm. Something Sally's mother didn't tell her but hinted at: "The trouble with Debra…"

After consulting with each other, the boys showed her roughly where the new Brunist tabernacle temple is going to be built and said in a secretive voice that the great news of the day was that they had just received a really fantastic gift, nearly enough to build the whole thing. They didn't know where the money came from but supposed it was from their principal benefactor, Mr. John P. Suggs. He was pointed out to her. Not in a tunic. A burly big-skulled man in a gray suit and boots, plaid shirt, no tie, suspenders. He reminded her of the farmer who chased Peter Rabbit in a picturebook she had. Or the nursery rhyme man in brown who tried to net the flying pig, dickery dickery dare. The horsey, strong-jawed woman in the tunic beside him, she learned, was their evangelical leader, Clara Collins. "A saint." Sally had already noticed her. A bold lady, sure of herself. She didn't walk, she strode, and wherever she went, there were people around her. Mr. Suggs had unscrolled a large sheet of paper and was showing it to her. Darren said it was architectural plans for the temple, which would be formally presented tonight at their evening prayer service and dedication ceremonies. She asked them if there wasn't something paradoxical about building a new church when they were expecting the end of the world. Well, the Rapture could come any time, but they didn't think it would happen for at least two years ("Me and Darren are working on that," Billy Don said), and this gives them time to build a proper tabernacle wherein to receive the Lord, wherefrom to fly to Heaven. A kind of launch platform, as she later wrote in her notebook. A docking station.

Though they'd told her that the main events in the meeting tent wouldn't be starting until later in the afternoon, there was already a lot of preaching and singing going on all over the hillside, some of it broadcast over loudspeakers. That was to encourage anyone who wished to join them, Billy Don said, and he added that he sincerely hoped she would make such a decision. They accepted her thoughtful silence. These guys were easy. Clara Collins was a different story. When Sally was introduced to her, she asked bluntly, "Are you here as a believer, child?" "I am here as a seeker after truth, Mrs. Collins." "Well, so are them reporters down there." "No, ma'am. They only know their own truth and want you to confirm it. I don't know the truth and am on a quest for it." Got that right out of her medieval lit course. "Do you believe in Jesus Christ as your Lord and Savior, and in the resurrection of the body, and in the Bible as God's holy word?" "I wish to believe, but I am full of doubts. I am trying to resolve those doubts." "She's the niece of Sister Debra, Sister Clara." Clara gave her a stern look-over, gazing into her thicket of hair as though to search out there the demons who possessed her. "All right, child. But don't abuse your welcome."

An invitation to leave. But she wasn't feeling so great. She needed to sit down. The boys asked her if she'd eaten and she said she hadn't, so they led her in here under a tent where they had tables of food set out, found a folding chair in a corner, and brought her a white-bread lunch-meat sandwich and a cream soda, and that helped. Sometimes, it's true, it seems to her that she grasps or is embraced by a great cosmic mystery, and for a moment she enjoys a certain rapt serenity. But usually the mystery eludes her or it evolves into some familiar banality, like the cream soda burp she burped then, and it never comes close to happening when she's bummed out with the blahs.

A guy walks into the tent now wearing a chocolate Stetson and an unbelted white gown over jeans and dusty high-heeled boots. Looks like some kind of cowboy cross-dresser. Said to be a honcho politician and rich rancher from Wyoming and a bishop from there. She takes out her notebook again and commences a sketch. He grabs up half a sandwich, stuffs it whole into his jowls, and wallows it around in there like a chaw of tobacco. Suddenly, he topples over, knocking his hat off, and starts twitching and yelping out unintelligible noises, spewing half-chewed sandwich. When his tunic falls back, you can see that he's wearing holstered pistols—he *is* a cowboy! A crowd gathers. A woman with one dead eye and a gold tooth claims to be able to translate his gibberish. She says the Prophet is inside him and speaking through him. The Prophet says: Prepare! Christ is coming! They all know this, but they gasp and cry out all the same. A whispered chant: *Bru-no! Bru-no! Bru-no!* All this ecstatic communion: how the fantasy of soul gets made. After a while, the gunslinger gets up, dribbling chewed bread, looking dazed. He doesn't acknowledge those gathered around him. He straightens his tunic, brushes off his hat and leaves the tent. Singing ensues.

The Great Myth of the Rapture. She's sitting in it.

Nothing more certain, said Darren solemnly. "The Second Coming of Jesus Christ, his literal physical return and all that means, is referred to 1845 times in the Bible." She wrote the number down and factors it now just for fun. Three and five and one-two-three.

Another thing Darren said. About the religious calling. She flips back a few pages: An invisible form calling out for substance. One is conscious of this summons and its attraction, without knowing what it is that is calling. Something he read somewhere probably. Now she writes: The writer's vocation: An invisible form calling out for substance. One is conscious of this summons and its attraction, without knowing what it is that is calling. When she looks up Aunt Debra is standing there, frowning down at the notebook in her lap.

"I'm surprised to see you here, Sally. I didn't think you were a believer in much of anything anymore."

"You know me, Auntie Debra. I always have to know it all. How about yourself? I never thought of you as an evangelical sort."

"Well, I have changed." Certainly she seems to have lost some weight. In fact, like her mom said, she's looking pretty good. Settled into herself, at home in her tunic. Tanned and strong. But maybe not so soft and loving as before. More determined, somehow. In control. The opposite of what her dad says. He says Debra has blown all her money and her husband's too, and she is shacked up with a crazy kid and is completely *out* of control. Fruitcake is his word for gross dysfunction. She's a fruitcake. "These are good people who have suffered so much for their simple faith. I love them and have become one of them."

"But you seem so different from them, Auntie Debra. They're all so—well—so emotional."

"I know. I resisted that at first. Afraid of direct communion with God. All buttoned up like a good Presbyterian. I'm past that now. For the first time, I feel like I really have a personal relationship with God and belong in His world and am at last living a truly meaningful life. Everything is suddenly so *real*."

"Well, that's great, Auntie Debra. I mean, I guess it is. You're sure looking good. But Mom says your husband has turned kind of weird."

"I was slow to wake up, Sally. He was always kind of weird. And he knows nothing at all about true religion. He's a showoff without substance or faith or beauty. Like a strutting jay among meadowlarks." Do jays strut? She knows nothing at all about birds. "But," Aunt Debra adds, glancing skeptically at the tee and trenchcoat, into which she has hastily buried the notebook, "these people are very serious about their beliefs. You must be careful not to offend them."

"I am. But I have to be me. I saw that orphan boy before, Colin, is he…?"

"I'm taking care of him. I'm establishing that halfway house for troubled young people out here I once told you about, and he's like my first case. He's hanging onto life by his fingernails, Sally. He's been through a lot, more than you and I can even imagine, and I'm sort of keeping a grip on him, not letting him let go."

She wants to ask more about that, but Billy Don joins them, slouching up, hands in pockets. There's a red patch on the side of his face where he's been catnapping on it. "Are you staying?" he asks cheerfully.

"I think she needs more time, Billy Don," Debra says. "She was just leaving."

Well, she's ready to go. The cramps have subsided, but she desperately requires a cigarette, and she has had about all of this holy mania she can take in one go.

"Colin seems very frightened about something, Sister Debra. Darren's talking to him, but he probably needs you."

"Oh dear." She turns and gives Sally a brief but affectionate hug. "I love you, Sally. Come see me any time," she says, and hurries away, holding up the hem of her tunic, slapping along in her sandals.

"I better go help," Billy Don says. "Do you want me to walk you down first…?"

"No, downhill's easy, Billy Don. Like sin. Who's that mopey fat girl over there? I think I know her."

"That's Reverend Baxter's daughter."

"Right. Baxter. Frances Baxter. I was in school with her."

"Listen, if you change your mind…" He takes her hand in both of his and gives her a deep gaze through his sunglasses, at least with one of his eyes.

"Thanks, Billy Don. You never know. I may come out to the camp to see Auntie Debra and we can talk more about it."

"That'd be great." He squeezes her hand tenderly and leaves, pausing at the tent opening to toss her a wave.

Franny Baxter remains slumped in her chair when she passes, gazing up at her sullenly when she introduces herself. She's already looking like an old lady, bloated at the belly, round-cheeked, bespectacled. "Hi, Franny. I'm Sally Elliott. I used to see you at WCHS. I was a year or two ahead of you, but I think we had a history class together."

"What are you doing out here?" Her voice is flat, like it's been ironed.

"Oh, I'm just trying to figure things out. What do you think is going to happen?"

"I dunno. Nothing probably."

"You look pretty sad, Franny."

"What's it to you?"

"Oh, nothing, I guess. Sorry. But, hey, if you want to talk things out sometime, let me know." She tears a blank page out of her notebook, writes her name and telephone number on it, and gives it to her, Franny accepting it with a dismissive shrug.

At the tent portal, she pauses to add a note. Life's a story, she writes, and you either write it or get written. Accept somebody else's story and you're the written, not the writer. She smiles at that. That's me, she thinks.

"Pardon me, my child. Could you please hand me my cane?" It's the old lady sitting stiffly just outside the opening. Mrs. Mc-something. On the Florida bus with those cute Jesus children. Sally shook her frail blue-veined hand on coming in here. "It seems to have fallen."

"Sure. Are you all right?"

"All right? Well, for my age, I suppose I am." There's a mischievous knowing look on the old lady's face. "That boy's sweet on you, I do believe."

"Maybe. But I think it's only my soul he's after."

"You've been writing. Are you a writer?"

"Well, not yet. I want to be."

"What sort of writer? Love stories? Whodunnits?"

"Sort of both, I guess. I mean, I want whatever I write to be about finding out about things, you know, the way a detective solves a case. And love, well, everything's about love, isn't it?"

The old lady smiles at this, showing a pretty good set of teeth, assuming they're her own. Her skin is mottled, loose on her bones, her jaws are sinking inward, hands trembling slightly, but she's still clear-eyed and sitting up primly, straight as an arrow. "Yes, it is. Even when 'love' means zero."

Sally smiles back, imagining a tall trim debutante with bobbed auburn hair in white tennis clothes. A classic beauty. "I bet you were really something in your time," she says. "You're really something now."

"I was a bit wild."

"I'm a bit wild."

"But then, after a while, it all became something else. I started playing bridge."

"I don't want to do that. I want to stay wild."

"I think you probably will," says the old lady, and blesses her with a sly wink. And then she sort of blanks out, her expression goes flat, her eyes dull. "Ma'am?" There's a little windy sound. Oh my god. Time to go.

# I.11

## Sunday 19 April

The discovery of dear pious Harriet McCardle, sitting bolt upright in her folding chair just outside the food tent, staring down as if in judgment upon the multitudes gathered below her on the sunswept Mount of Redemption with eyes blinded by life's cessation, augments the probability in the minds of many that there will indeed be no tomorrow. As Brunist First Follower Eleanor Norton, presently a professional Spiritual Therapist on the West Coast (she now refers to herself as Dr. E. Norton) and the author of *Communing with Your Inner Voice* and *The Sayings of Domiron: Wisdom from the Seventh Aspect*, once famously announced on what in Brunist church history is known as "The Night of the Sign": "Death as a sign can mean only one thing: *the end of the world!*" A pronouncement absorbed by First Follower Mabel Hall (she was there in the Bruno house that night and heard it herself, saw the dead man in the living room) into her own systems of divination, which accounts for her solemn nods now to her friends on the hill who nod back.

Although Dr. Norton, seeking transcendence from all earthbound forms, is no longer an active Brunist or even a Christian and so is not present today on the Mount of Redemption, her influence on the early days of the movement was profound and has shaped the thinking of many here, not least her young acolyte and fellow First Follower, Colin Meredith, who, upon the discovery of the body, shrieked, *"I saw her! I saw her! The Antichrist!"* and, tearing wildly at his tunic, set off running at full gallop, pursued by his mother, all over the hillside. Since the Antichrist is generally presumed to be male, the boy was probably mistaken; perhaps he meant the Whore of Babylon, for the person he was referring to was the snarly haired young woman in the tattered trenchcoat (the Judas who betrayed them wore just such a garment!) who was the last person seen with Harriet McCardle when she was still alive and who then vanished as though she never was. A matter of concern to the church scribes, Darren Rector and Billy Don Tebbett, who were responsible for inviting her up and who now face intense questioning from their fellow believers. Was she wearing an inverted cross? Was that a picture of a writhing serpent on her T-shirt? *Was* it a T-shirt, or her very flesh? What was she writing? Did they notice any peculiar body odors? A burnt smell? Her figure was not particularly feminine—was she even really a "she?" They answer truthfully, describing her as, by outward appearance at least, a sensible Christian girl with a healthy curiosity, while at the same time acknowledging, while poor Colin goes clattering by, that, yes, the devil is a crafty dissembler, one cannot be too cautious, for they are serious open-minded students of redemptive history and are willing to consider all opinions and eventualities. Billy Don, for example, had watched her descend the hill until she reached the bottom, so she didn't really "vanish," not in his eyes, though he has to admit that what he witnessed may have been a diabolical phantasm since no one else shared in his witnessing.

On the original Night of the Sign, the Brunist Evangelical Leader and Organizer, Clara Collins, now Clara Collins-Wosznik, still distraught at the time over the recent loss in the mine accident of her husband Ely, was utterly undone by the sudden death of the Prophet's aged father in front of the TV set, and she fell to the floor sobbing and praying in the manner of many of those in and around the food tent now. But this afternoon her emotions are held in check by a more practical concern. To wit: What is to be done with the remains? What might be the ordinary passing of an old woman elsewhere is an extraordinary event here on the Mount of Redemption today, open to a variety of unwelcome interpretations by the civil authorities. The church has, in the past, been maliciously and unjustifiably accused of bizarre Satanic practices, and it could be again. Had she been privy to the notebook entry of the Elliott girl (she does not think that child is the Antichrist, the Whore of Babylon, or any other otherworldly creature—just a spoiled unkempt brat with more book learning than is good for her) about a city set upon a slippery hill, she would have understood it as an almost literal expression of her present anxieties. Sister Clara is tempted at first to conceal the death and, as Brother Hiram suggests, to try and get the body back to the motel, somehow, to be discovered there under less problematic circumstances. But one glance down at the foot of the hill, where reporters and gawkers still mill about in threatening numbers, tells her this would be impossible, even dangerous. Nor, as it's God's will, would it be right. She and Hiram and Ben talk it over with Mr. John P. Suggs, and together with the mayor of Randolph Junction, they inform Sheriff Puller. The sheriff, conscious of possible crowd trouble, says that he will call an ambulance and have her removed, announcing simply, if asked (of course he will be asked) that she has fallen ill and is being taken to hospital. They will take her to the Randolph Junction municipal hospital, not the nearby one in West Condon, but he will not say so. He will arrange for the usual county coroner's cause-of-death report and will not announce her passing until after the Brunists have safely left the hill. Or whatever, he adds, aware of the expectations of some. Meanwhile, they are to keep her out of sight and to turn off the public mourning and do something about that hysterical boy. The Randolph Junction mayor adds that, if her surviving husband agrees, she can be quietly buried in their city cemetery. "I am afraid," says Brother Hiram, "that the gentleman's youthful alacrity has abandoned him. He lacks the mental competence to understand even that she has died. With your permission, as the official leader and pastor of this pilgrimage, I shall, with the assistance of a lawyer in my congregation, secure power of attorney and sign the necessary papers on his behalf." And thus, thanks to her wise friends, a crisis is avoided.

Who is John Patrick Suggs, and what has led the wealthy coal baron and property developer, never known for his largesse, to become the Brunist movement's chief benefactor? Well, his hatred of the local old-family power elite with whom he has been at war all his life, for one thing. The movement's enemies are his enemies. For another: His view of redemption as a straightforward negotiation in the soul market. He is, as he thinks of it, buying into after-death shares. Does he believe that the End is imminent? It might best be said that, near the end of his own life and without heirs, he is betting on it. But above all, he is motivated by his loyalty to the late Reverend Ely Collins, who effected his conversion, and whose last prophetic message to the world as he lay dying in the scorched depths of the earth here below their feet launched this new evangelical movement. In his early days, Pat Suggs was known as a hard-living, hard-drinking, two-fisted hell-raiser. He has injured and known injury. Existence as a bruising contact sport: when young he lived such a life. Though his family traces its roots to Northern Ireland, he has always spoken of himself as an American patriot, a Calvinist, and a libertarian, and it was the Calvinist side of his nature that emerged as a consequence of a tent-meeting conversion upon hearing Ely Collins preach, he himself being the landlord of the field rented for the occasion. Though the pastor of a church with pentecostal tendencies, Collins himself was not an overtly emotional man, nor is John P. Suggs. Ely simply spoke from the heart and made good sense and Suggs felt an immediate rapport with the man and thought of him as wise and holy. He supported the Church of the Nazarene liberally while Ely was its minister, but loathed that smug hothead Abner Baxter who succeeded him after the mine disaster (he can see the man, standing not far off in his ill-fitting tunic, barefoot, glowering like the devil himself), a former communist labor organizer and unprincipled rabble rouser, a man who deserved to be shot for his radical anti-Americanism alone, and he abandoned that house of fools. He found no other church that suited him and eventually sought out the widow of Ely Collins who was, as he'd heard, carrying her husband's torch and had important tidings to tell. Clara Collins is no Ely (she is a woman, to begin with), but she is honest and forthright and devoted to the memory of her husband and the movement his vision has fostered. Sometimes Ely seems almost to be speaking through her, and perhaps he is. John P. Suggs did not think he would like this fellow Wosznik, with whom she took up so soon after Ely's death, but he has come to respect him, a simple man but arrow-straight, a true believer, hardworking, beholden to Ely Collins in the same manner as himself, and a valuable helpmeet to Ely's widow in the task of spreading, on what may be the very eve of the Apocalypse, this urgent new gospel. As he gazes about upon the activity on the hill (that stupid boy has thankfully been collared and removed from view), he feels good about what he has done and knows that Ely would be pleased.

The town banker, arriving now at the foot of the mine hill with the West Condon mayor, the police chief and officers, the Chamber of Commerce secretary, his own bank lawyer and other official personnel and civic leaders, speaks of Pat Suggs, often his business adversary, as an own-bootstraps sort of fellow, ruthless, decisive, shrewd, frank, unfriendly, an aggressive loner who accumulates all he can while contributing nothing to the community he is exploiting, a man he opposes on just about all issues: his countryside-destroying strip mining, his divisive anti-unionism, his unorthodox banking and investment procedures, his inflammatory white supremacist rhetoric, his simplistic but vicious anti-communism, his militant Puritanism. The feelings are mutual. To John P. Suggs, Ted Cavanaugh is an immoral liberal humanist, a country-clubbing hypocrite who uses religion cynically as a power tool, a legalistic destroyer of basic civil liberties who makes the rules convenient to himself that others have to play by, an unrepentant sinner and unscrupulous manipulator and usurer—in short, a damned banker like all bankers. He associates the persecution of the Brunists with atheists, Jews, Romanists, lawyers, politicians, and humanists like the banker, and would have needed no further reason to take up the

Brunists' cause than to do battle with him, even were he not motivated by his faith.

What the banker has come now with his team of city authorities and legal advisors to announce, is that the city is purchasing the mine property, including this hill, and that all these people are therefore trespassing on private property. He presents various documents and demands that the sheriff ask everyone to leave. Immediately. The sheriff glances poker-faced at the sheaf of legal-sized documents while the strip mine operator produces documents of his own: a written permit from the sheriff's office and a limited but binding two-day lease agreement from the absentee mine owners. The banker insists that, with the purchase, the circumstances have changed and the agreement is no longer valid, but John P. Suggs, whose own bid, unbeknownst to the banker, is also still on the table, only smiles icily, his thumbs hooked in his suspenders. He'd thought, from the astonishing earlier news, that the banker might have had an inexplicable change of heart, but he sees now that the reality is more amusing than that. The sheriff notes that he sees no deeds or purchase agreements amid the paperwork, and as the registry office is closed on Sunday, they will have to wait until tomorrow to present their case. Meanwhile, this is unincorporated county land under his jurisdiction. With a sneer aimed at the police chief, whom he regards as an ignorant foreigner, he suggests they not complicate his crowd control problems with their further presence, and some of his uniformed men arrive to back him up.

"What do you mean?" the outraged banker demands, jutting the jaw that intimidated a generation of state high school football players. There are news cameras focused on them now, and the crowds are pressing round, drawn here in hopes of a repeat of the entertaining events of five years ago. "If we don't leave, you're going to arrest us?" His demand is met by strategic silence.

"Well, I think this is absolutely ridiculous," says the Chamber of Commerce secretary.

The West Condon chief of police, one of the more flourishing members of the extensive Romano clan, and the principal supporter on his meager salary (and whatever else comes along) of eleven of them, had never thought that this would work and said so before reluctantly agreeing to haul his sad ass out here, dragging all these others with him. Chief Romano is uncomfortable around overheated evangelical types, so arrogantly full of false certitude, every man his own prophet and pope, and he is fully aware of the racist anti-Catholic biases of the likes of Puller and Suggs and that vicious firebrand Baxter, desecrater of St. Stephen's Church, who is standing off to one side and seems about to explode, damn his tormented soul. But, though he has no authority here, he had no choice. He likes to say that all the people of West Condon are his boss, but Dee knows from whose imperious hands comes his paycheck, and he knows the kinds of games they play, the cunning and meanness in their hearts. If truth be told, there's not a person in their party here not deserving of imprisonment if not hanging, himself included. But what can you do? Life is a crap shoot. He had one throw and this is what he got. "There won't be no arrests," he says flatly, fixing his gaze not on the sheriff but on his troops. Who are not, he knows, completely legal. Tub Puller's ambitious little warlord fantasies. The way Monk Wallace explained it to him down at the station, Puller is amassing this vigilante army and hoping for disturbances—even if he has to create them himself—that will justify this unit enough to draw state money to finance and arm it. For the present, the volunteers—no Italians among them—are not only unpaid, they even have to supply their own uniforms and weapons. In it for the action. They can't arrest anybody, though of course neither can he. John P. Suggs catches his drift. "If you want to stay," he says finally, "be our guests. Just don't stir up trouble. Last time, you let a mess happen. People got hurt. We're not going to let one happen today."

The West Condon mayor puffs out his fat cheeks and says in his booming voice, "We been told a woman was took to hospital. What'sa particulars?"

"She is Mrs. Harriet McCardle from Fort Lauderdale, Florida," Puller says, consulting his notes.

"But what's her problem?"

"Like I say, Mrs. Harriet McCardle from Fort Lauderdale, Florida."

There are hoots from the crowd. "That ain't what the man ast you, Tub baby," yells one of them. The sheriff knows him. A scrawny loudmouth coalminer named Cheese Johnson who sometimes worked his shift in the sheriff's own mining days, if what that ugly fuckoff did could be called work. The strip mine operator knows him as Chester K. Johnson, a ne'er-do-well whom he hired at one of his mines after Deepwater but who lasted only a week. Chief Romano as a drunken jawbox he has picked up off the street from time to time, a regular client in the free flophouse he runs at the city jail. The banker as the uncontrollable wiseass who horned in on his original Common Sense Committee and nearly wrecked it, beating up old Ben Wosznik in his own house. No one's happy that he and his shiftless pals are here. "No more stonewallin', my man," Johnson shouts in his nasal twang. "The ole girl's gone tits up, ain't it so?"

Clara Collins is watching apprehensively from a discreet distance. It was just such trouble that thwarted their gathering here five years ago, when it seemed certain that the Rapture was really going to happen, and she is afraid something like it might ruin her plans today. She tells Ben and Wayne to go get on the public address system with some good old-time gospel singing. "Let's loose the Holy Spirit on them and drown out all this ungodly bickering!"

Reverend Abner Baxter, seething with injured pride at having been excluded from all these exchanges and emboldened by the return today of some of his closest followers—including Jewell Cox and Roy Coates, standing beside him like stone pillars—now lets go his daughter's hand and, striding toward the banker and his minions, cries out: "*Enough* of these puffed-up babblings! Your deceitful words are *a loathsome abomination!*" Is he referring to the banker or to all parties present? Let them read it as they will. "There is no *truth* in your mouth, your soul is *destruction*, your throat is an open sepulcher! *Do you hear?* Look around you! Your land has become a desolation and a waste and a curse, your town an unholy emptiness! *Do you not see?* You have brought this evil upon yourself through your own sinfulness, and your unlawful persecutions of the just, and now *nothing shall never live here again!*" Old boss Suggs is looking unhappy. Good. Let the old sinner have ears. "Even him who led us to the Coming of the Light through his foreknowledge of God ye have taken away and by evil hands have ye slain him! *Ye are viler than the earth!*" "Amen!" calls out Jewell Cox, and Roy and Roy's boys and Ezra Gray and his own son, Young Abner, echo him, and others, too. It is spreading. The hillside is becoming *his* hillside, and the cameras are watching.

"That's enough now," says Tub Puller, hands on his gunbelt. But it is *not* enough. The Brunist bishop of West Condon is rediscovering his own lost self. The long, hard years on the road have taken their toll, but he is home again. He can feel within him once more the power of God, and that power, he knows, is of indignation and wrath. He brushes past the sheriff, raising his fist at the town dignitaries, just as Reverend Konrad Dreyer of the Trinity Lutheran Church, perhaps having hesitated a moment too long, touches the brim of his straw and steps forward to attempt to speak on behalf of the West Condon Ministerial Association.

"*But WOE unto the wicked! Your day of reckoning is come! That day is a day of wrath, a day of trouble and distress, a day of ruin and desolation! Your blood shall be poured out like dust, and your flesh like DUNG!*" Reverend Dreyer, who fully understands these apocalyptic yearnings and is eager to reassure the cult of the Association's basic support for the freedom of all Christian religion, and indeed other religions as well—the Jewish faith, for example—nevertheless finds himself somewhat overawed by Reverend Baxter's fiery passion and clenched fist (good Heavens, does he mean to strike someone?), and he staggers back into his own footsteps, banging into a cursing cameraman. It might have been better, he thinks, to have expressed the Association's views in a written letter. "*In the fire of His jealous wrath, all the earth shall be consumed, for a full, yea, sudden end He will make of all the inhabitants of the earth! As the whirlwind passes, so will the house of the wicked be no more! But the tabernacle of the upright shall flourish!*" Reverend Baxter gestures up the hill behind him, hearing the murmured "Amens" roll like ripples of subdued thunder as several drop to their knees. There are many new people here today, they have large expectations, he is speaking to them, telling them what they have been waiting to hear, he is *of* them, and they of *him*. He raises both arms like a conductor, whereupon strains of "The Battle Hymn of the Republic" can be heard, as if on cue, like a call to arms—though it is not "The Battle Hymn," it is one of the Brunist songs: *"O the Sons of Light are marching…"* Reverend Dreyer, who has been called here by his banker friend as a Christian leader, understands much of the present moment's dynamics, at least all that regarding religion, for he has made a study of sectarian conflict, which he believes to be due, at root, to a small but specific set of irresolvable philosophical paradoxes that need to be accepted as conundrums and not be allowed to divide men on the basis of what cannot be differing truths but only differing opinions—or, rather, like most seeming paradoxes, single truths identified by the very contraries they contain. This does not seem to be the right moment to explain this, however. *"For, verily, verily, I say unto you, the hour is coming, and now is, when the dead shall hear the voice of the Son of God: and they that hear shall LIVE! All that are in the graves shall hear His voice, and shall come forth; they that have done good, unto the resurrection of life; and they that have done evil, unto the resurrection of DAMNATION!"*

"Sounds as how Red here is fixin' to dump us all down the bottomless pit!" declares Johnson. The volume on the P.A. system has been cranked up too high and he has to shout over the screeching feedback.

"I done worked that shithole," calls out one of his companions, the ex-miner Steve Lawson, weaving about on his big feet. *"We shall see the cities crumble and the earth give up its dead!"* the Brunists are singing over the shrieking P.A. *"For the end of time has come!"* A state police helicopter, which has been coming and going all day, is back again, clattering overhead. The banker points up at it and speaks in the mayor's ear. "And, hell with it, boys," Lawson shouts. "I ain't a-goin' back down!"

That draws whoops and loud ay-mens from the drunken hecklers, but these fools are of no concern to Abner Baxter. Soon enough they will grovel. Nor does he have time for paradox or conundrums, did he know of such speculations; in fact, he has never used either word in all his long life, rich in high-minded rhetoric as it has been. His eye is fixed firmly on the end time, on the coming day of glory and of retribution, and thus on eternity. Has been since the day he abandoned godless communism—redemption not displacing justice, but simply redefining it. *"Hark ye to the White Bird of Glory!"* the Brunists are singing. Those who know the words are shouting along. *"Hark ye to the White Bird of Grace!"* There is less feedback now, but the helicopter is swooping lower, chopping up the sung words. Mouth-filling "glory" gets through the racket, "grace" does not. Abner does not have Hiram Clegg's silver tongue or Ely Collins' quiet persuasiveness, but he does have power. He has exhorted the multitude in vast open spaces and has been heard. He knows what they want to hear, because it is what he wants to hear: Blessed are the true believers for they shall enter straightways through the gates into the holy city, while outside the gates are dogs, and sorcerers, whoremongers, murderers, idolaters, and blasphemous foulmouthed imbeciles such as these, and do not doubt it, they shall know eternal torment! He raises his fist and cries out: *"And I heard a great voice outa Heaven, saying—"* but he is interrupted by another loud roar, this time on the mine road: it is his banished son and leather-jacketed friends, and little Paulie, too, and they stop him cold.

The motorcyclists, led by the redhead, leave the road and, heads down over their handlebars, dip into the ditch and up again as if rising from the bowels of the earth, then come gunning straight up at them over the patchy grass, as though to plow suicidally into their midst. None of them wears a helmet, except for the wildly grinning boy on the back of one of the bikes, his arms locked tight around the driver, an older man with a gray braid. The panicking crowds at the foot of the hill scatter in all directions, believers and nonbelievers and those who don't know what to think. Abner's daughter Amanda, squeaking in fear, has squeezed up behind him and is clutching his hand again. "Is that your son?" demands John P. Suggs. *"Whoopee!"* howls Cheese

Johnson, grinning his wide gap-toothed grin, as his pals abandon him at full boozy lope, Steve Lawson confusedly on his hands and knees. *"Hammer down, boys!"* And Cheese extends his arms to one side as though dangling a bullfighter's cape. "Those are the bastards who attacked me!" shouts the banker to the sheriff and police chief, pointing, while backing away and bracing himself. *"Hang on, Runt!"* shouts the biker with the gray braid, and all five hit their brakes simultaneously and skid into a screaming two-wheel slide, kicking up clouds of dirt, spraying the fleeing onlookers with shrapnel of slate and cinder, the short hairy one with the tiny face stopping just inches from Johnson's planted feet. *"Fucken A!"* Johnson laughs, and pumps his fist in front of his crotch, and the hairy biker returns the grin, but as if in miniature. The redhead rights his motorcycle and with a wide swing of his arm flings the head of a dog at Abner Baxter's feet. They all scramble out of the way as though the ghastly thing might explode—all but the impassive John P. Suggs and Abner himself, who is frozen to the spot, staring in horror at the bloody head his son has hurled at him. Ezra Gray, nose down, screaming at his wife to push faster, is being wheeled uphill, where the mayor and fire chief, wheezing heavily, are already standing amid the Brunist faithful in a state of dumb amazement. Two of the other bikers take aim and throw the decapitated carcasses of a pair of white doves like fluttery little footballs. Their wings open in flight and they come more to resemble tattered paper airplanes. "Help!" squeaks the Chamber of Commerce secretary, ducking, though ducking the wrong way and, as he falls, he catches one of the headless birds square in the face. "Gosh Almighty! What the heck is happening?!" The other dove lands in Ezra Gray's lap, a perfect throw. *"Touchdown!"* whoops the wild-eyed biker with the blue headband and the haloed skull tattoo on his bare shoulder. "Oh dang it to *shoot!"* Ezra cries and starts yelping hysterically, his wife Mildred plucking the dead bird from his lap and calming him down while he curses her bitterly. The Lutheran president of the West Condon Ministerial Association, who finds himself already some distance away from all these happenings and still moving at some speed across the open field, decides that, though he has contributed little to the day's proceedings, he will contribute no more, while behind him, back at the hill, the banker is yelling: "These are the sorts of people you have brought here, Suggs!" "They are not of us," replies the mine owner coldly. And then, with diabolical howls and raised fingers, the bikers roar away, Chief Dee Romano firing over their heads, to what purpose he does not know. Not to stop them, to be sure, maybe just to make them go faster. And as quickly as they came, they are gone, just a distant hollow rumble lost in all the other noise. John P. Suggs, turning to the sheriff, growls, "I don't care how you do it, Puller, but I want those hoodlums locked up or run out of here. And I want this hill secured. Now."

The loudspeakers are screeching and the helicopter, lifting away to follow the bikers, is still blanketing the hillside with its thuppety-thup rattle, but the songs and shouting have ceased. All are staring at the dog's head. Graybearded Ben Wosznik walks slowly down the hill, his somber wife following a few paces behind. He picks the head up and cradles it. He stands there a moment, gazing out on the distance into which the bikers have just disappeared, and the helicopter as well, his fingers absently scrubbing the dog's skull behind the ears. Someone turns off the squealing P.A. system and a sudden hush descends. People emerge quietly from the tents to gaze down upon the scene at the foot of the hill. Muttered prayers can be heard. A boy's hysterical whimpering. The mayor and fire chief, surprised to find themselves up among the believers, step gingerly back down the hill. The cameramen, their fallen equipment recovered, are filming the dog's head in Ben Wosznik's arms. "Rocky," someone whispers in answer to a reporter's question. "Oh, him, you mean? Wosznik. W-O-Z..." "Man, oh man," groans the Chamber of Commerce secretary, wiping at the blood on his face. "This is really crazy!" Which will be that night's area TV sound bite. "I don't think this is legal," the bank lawyer is saying to the sheriff. "See me about it tomorrow, mister. Right now, I got a job to do. You got thirty minutes and then we are gonna seal off the access road and arrest anyone who don't belong here."

* * *

Angela Bonali wants advice about giving in. "How much have you given in already?" her friend asks. They have decided to drive past the mine hill on the way home from the park to see what's happening. "Well, just about everything." "You might want to hold something back." The hill is still full of tents and little white spots all over it like cotton tufts, but they can see crowds streaming away from the bottom. Maybe everything is already over. Police car lights are flashing. Maybe not. Angie doesn't care. Tommy really *does* like to try everything, but she always just wants one thing: Tommy on top of her and inside her, his weight falling on her softly. She loses herself then, and it's magic. Everything else requires a kind of skill, and that means having to think too much. "Do you? Hold back, I mean?" "No, but I'm not trying to keep a man."

Angela had just had her second bath of the day and was applying blush and mascara for at least the third time when her friend from the bank called and invited her for a Sunday drive. "I had a date and got stood up," she said. Her friend is older, nearly twenty-five, but very sexy for her age, and Angela can't believe anyone would stand her up. But she could think of nothing else to do except have a third bath, and she had a whole afternoon to kill before her big date tonight, so she happily accepted, changing into jeans, sweatshirt, sneakers, and head scarf to protect her new hairdo and bouncing out to the car when it pulled up at the curb. Floating on air, she is. They drove over to the park on the river with the giant rocks. Angela felt like climbing up on them all and rubbing herself against them, especially after her friend pointed out one with a little bump on top that looked like a gigantic circumcised peter. "It's divine!" she said (a sinful thought about the founding of the Church occurred to her and made her giggle and cross herself), and her friend said, "Well, yes, I guess it is." Angela was just so madly, hopelessly, deliriously in love, and she couldn't stop talking about it. "It's just the greatest thing!"

Her friend smiled but did not seem convinced (well, she was having a bad day), so Angie changed the subject and told her the gossip going around that their boss has taken a lover. "I don't really blame him. His wife is in awful shape."

"But what if you were not at your best, and Tommy took a lover?"

"I hope I'm always at my best."

"Speaking of the devil," Angela says now, though it has been a while since they have done so, and points toward what her friend has just called "that sad little furor" over by the mine hill, where their boss can be seen walking away with the mayor and the police chief. He is very important. The most important person she knows. And he is also Tommy's daddy, which makes him nearly the most important man in the world. But he does not seem happy. Her friend decides it's time to drive on, not wanting to get mixed up in all that. "Can you imagine?" Angie says. "Those crazy people want the world to end!"

"I'm sorry," her friend says.

"What?"

"Oh, nothing. Talking to myself. I've been angry. I'm not angry anymore." She sighs, winks somewhat sadly at Angela. "I just wish the world were other than it is."

"Oh, not me! I love it and I never want it to change!"

Priscilla Tindle stops the car at the edge—herself also at the edge of something—of an open field across the way from the mine hill. She has so dreaded this trip, is full of dread still. Distantly, through the trees bordering the field on the other side, they can see crowds pouring away, police lights flashing, can hear the sirens. "Look, Wesley! Something bad has happened! We could get arrested!"

"Be strong and of good courage; be not afraid, neither be dismayed: for the Lord thy God is with thee whithersoever thou goest."

Jesus speaking. "Whithersoever" is a favorite of his. He likes to show off all that King James lingo, Wesley preferring the Revised Standard. She knows why Wesley wants to go there. He has been asking over and over and she has always found an excuse, afraid of those horrible people and of Wesley's horrible wife. He doesn't know yet about the money, but he wants to get his car back, and his ruined golf clubs, which were in the trunk. He wants to stop the woman from signing anything that would put him in danger. And when that grabby pig cleaned out the manse, she took the orange juice squeezer, and some of Wesley's favorite old shirts, which that crazy boy has probably inherited, and his hot water bottle, which he needs for his lower back pain, not being quite up to some of Prissy's routines. Prissy is helping him work that pain away with stretching exercises, but she has pushed him a little too hard and he could really use that hot water bottle now. For the past couple of days, he has been walking around in the sitting position. Her poor dear lamb. Lambs. But as to why his indwelling Christ wants to go to the hill, it's something of a mystery to her. He says he wants to tell everyone the Apocalypse has already happened, just as he said it would, and this is it, so they should all just go home.

There is a man hurrying toward them across the weedy field. It is the Lutheran minister Reverend Konrad Dreyer. He looks rattled and disheveled and is without the straw boater he always wears. "They're throwing dead animals around over there," he gasps. "It's getting pretty ugly." This is what she wanted to hear. She offers Reverend Dreyer a lift into town, Wesley thankfully not objecting, and on the ride the minister describes the wild scene he had just witnessed, Wesley listening with a wily, knowing, yet impatient look on his face, a look she has come to dread. "I must say, Wes, it does cause one to reconsider the whole ecumenical movement."

"Does it? I suppose, Connie, that you believe in the usual Christian notion of a benevolent God working His unfathomable will in Heaven and on earth, with worldly self-sacrifice the path to the Heavenly kingdom, spiritual peace lying on the other side of suffering, the whole idea of immortality being validated by our desire for it, like our desire for food and water." Prissy is impressed. She hasn't heard Wesley speak so sensibly since that memorable night she joined him in the bathtub.

"That, and the redemptive power of my sacrifice. *Christ's* sacrifice. Am I right?"

"Well, that's a simple way of putting it, but, sure, something like that."

"Well, all that's completely stupid. It's nothing like that. If that's what you think, you're as crazy as those people back there." Oh oh, thinks Prissy. "God's one tough hardballing cookie, my friend—about as benevolent as cancer. Just look what He put me through. His son, I mean."

Reverend Dreyer in the rearview mirror looks nonplussed. "Wes, is everything all right?"

"All right? Well, I've been driven out of my church and home and made more or less unemployable, they're trying to get me locked up, my wife has run off with a sick boy to live with those lunatic zealots and has taken our car and everything we owned, I'm reduced to sleeping on the floor in somebody else's garage, but other than that, sure, everything's fine. How about yourself, Connie?"

"I'm sorry, Wes..."

"If you guys in the Association had been doing your job, you wouldn't have let this happen. You would have protected my rights. You've let me down."

"Well, I'd heard..."

"You heard what those pharisaical church trustees, that brood of vipers, wanted you to hear. You have betrayed me to mine enemies, as the Good Book says. You've—no, I'm not going to tell him that."

"What?"

"I'm not talking to you, Connie."

"Who *are* you talking to, Wes?"

Oh oh. Here it comes. They are still three blocks from the Lutheran church. Prissy grips the wheel and tries desperately to think how to change the subject, but she's never good at that. Wesley has hesitated. He's probably thinking the same thing. "I'm talking to Jesus Christ," he says finally. "He...has moved in."

* * *

Franny Baxter has been scouting the crowds at the bottom of the hill for purposes of her own. She is, plain and simple, looking for a man. Also plain and simple. She wants out of all this. What will her family do without her? She doesn't care. She knows she has little to offer. She's homely, scrawny on top and hippy below, has nothing to wear but her mother's faded hand-me-downs, has pimples and hair where she shouldn't, has never read a book she hasn't had to, has a tin ear and is blind to beauty, both artificial and natural, has no interests she can think of, can't carry a conversation past hello and goodbye (look how she chased off that Elliott girl who was only trying to be friendly), has few job prospects other than housecleaning, laundering, diner waitressing, and dishwashing. She has pretty much taken over all the womanly family functions with the baggy collapse of her mother, but that doesn't mean she's much of a cook or has any talent as a housekeeper. The minimum does it for Franny. But she's also happy with little and can put up with anything except beatings and religion. She's had enough of both for one lifetime. But a jobless drunk? A lazy foul-mouthed atheistic womanizer who's never home? No problem. A dumb ugly cluck who doesn't know what his thingie is for? All the better. She had spotted a couple of promising candidates among the hecklers before they got chased off. One in particular—a guy she knows, if barely. The kid brother of the dead husband of a friend of the family, the widow a former Nazarene who used to be in her father's congregation, and now, if what she's heard today from gossip queen Linda Catter is true, not much of anything. Like Franny herself. Fed up. Tess Lawson was always nice to her and she figures now she'll try to get in touch with her and lay out her hopes and wishes and tell her she's more or less in love with her brother-in-law Steve, so what should she do next? In love? Sure, she is. Why not? Clumsy lunks with big feet who scare easy and fall down when they get drunk? Just her style. She knows most everything about boys, leastways their backsides, and what she doesn't know she'll ask that woman Ludie Belle they're all talking about.

* * *

"Well, I just don't know what to think, Duke. Those ladies want to hear a voice talk to them. Hel – lo – I – am – speak – ing – to – you – from – the – other – side…!"

"Oh yeah, honey! Hah! I believe! The growl's awesome!"

"Or else they want to see something weird, like something moving by itself, a card or a spoon, you know. Spookshow stuff. But it's not like that. I'm not reaching across any life-and-death divide or nothing. I don't hear any voices. Not like the way you're hearing me. I only sorta know what Marcella's thinking. I'm just, like, tuned in."

"Still, you musta blowed their minds, Patti Jo, callin' the shot on that ole lady expirin' like that."

"Yeah, well, but I didn't exactly, that's just how they want to think of it. It's that Mabel lady. She's the smart one, reads the cards and suchlike, has a kinda gypsy knowhow. She's the one who connects all the dots. I only just had the feeling all day yesterday, Marcella and me, that something worrying was gonna happen like it done before, that's all, and I told them that. Coulda been most anything. Like what just happened down there at the foot of the hill."

"They are sudden to read a lot in a little…"

"But you know, what if they're right, Duke? I thought it was kinda scary before, now I don't know *what's* happening. Why did I feel like I had to come here just now when all these other people were coming here, too? It was like we were all in touch with something, or something was in touch with us. I mean, what do you think, Duke? What's happening? What do you think I oughta do?"

"Well, it ain't my home ballpark, Patti Jo, but if I was your hittin' coach, I'd say you should jist hang in fer a pitch or two, swing easy, and see what they throw at you next. We're havin' some good innings, we got us a live audience, Will Henry's takin' us on his radio show, I'm cookin' up some new tunes to try out on the fans in the bleachers—and hey, I kinda like teamin' up with you, little darlin'. Wherever."

"You're really a sweet guy, Duke. And I'm so damned crazy. I don't deserve it."

* * *

Over at the Wilderness Camp up on Inspiration Point, Ben Wosznik is sitting beside his dead dog, a shovel and shotgun across his lap. He gazes across at the Mount of Redemption, where, distantly, under late-afternoon overcast skies, the Brunist Followers mill about, waiting for the evening's dedication ceremonies or else for the End. If the Rapture should happen now, he'd be a front-row witness to this spectacle, so inevitable yet so hard to imagine, but he might get overlooked in the gathering in of Christian souls. He should be getting back. He had set about to bury Rocky up here, where the old boy so loved to come when he and Clara used it as their own private chapel and talking-out place, but it still feels too polluted by the bikers' recent presence. He'll clean the area up tomorrow, but it will never be the same. Those cruel boys have probably spoiled it forever. Whatever forever is now in these last days. The scene up here at dawn this morning is still fixed in his mind, and he is only slowly coming to make sense of things. Abner's boy seemed genuinely surprised when they found the gun in his backpack, Ben saw that. So if the kid didn't steal it, how did it get there? "Why'd they do that to you, old fella? Must of been me they was after." That was probably it. They'd supposed he'd planted the gun on them to get them thrown out of the camp, maybe after he caught them in the camp kitchen, and they took their revenge. "But who really done it, then?" Who stole the gun in the first place? And the money? But left the shotgun? Somebody in a hurry. He may want to ask Abner about what happened when he first arrived yesterday, though that's apt only to put the man on the defensive again and stir up old feelings, never far from the surface, that the world is against him. Well, he's been going through a lot, that man. He only just gets his feet on the ground and his boys trip him up again. There was a tearful moment early this morning, standing up here, when, just for a second, Abner's vulnerability showed through, and his pain. A sympathy grew up between them—Ben felt it, too—but it hasn't lasted. Abner is no longer so alone, his old buds Roy and

Jewell having turned up today to egg him on, so he's recovering some of his contentious nature, and now, after what all else has happened, Ben's own forgiving nature is being sorely tested. Down below, the camp has been plundered. Cabin doors left gaping. Much of the food gone, medications. The lodge vandalized. Windows smashed. Vehicles in the parking lot and down at the trailer park broken into, though he'd hid his shotgun well and they never discovered it. But: Rocky's headless body on his kitchenette table. He found the doves' heads in the empty camp kitchen refrigerator, blindly staring out, beaks open as though begging for food or water. He tossed them down the hole in the men's privy. No need for people to have to see that. But he will have to tell them what has happened. Far across the way, the old tipple and water tower, silhouetted against the soft gray sky, stand like tomb markers over an old Indian burial mound. Which helps him think what it is he'll do.

*"When I was a lad*
*'N old Rocky a pup*
*Over hills'n meadows we'd stray,*
*Jist a boy and his dog,*
*We was both fulla fun,*
*We grew up together that way…"*

The sun, hidden all day, peeks out through a break in the clouds and casts a soft tender farewell ray on the back slope of the old mine hill. Ben Wosznik's beloved dog Rockdust is being laid to rest in a freshly dug hole there, wrapped in his own blanket, while Brother Duke L'Heureux, the famous Nashville singer, guitar around his neck, sings a special version of the classic "Old Shep" in Rocky's memory, bringing tears to the eyes of the mourners. For mourners they are, though it be but a dog. When that poor animal's head tumbled into their midst today, following so close upon the shocking passing of Sister Harriet McCardle, something of their past lives suddenly ended and they found themselves face to face with that which they have so often prayed for, yet cannot help but dread: the imminent end of time. This is what the horror of Rocky's severed head said to them, and it left them full of hope, and it left them full of fear.

*"When I come home from the mines*
*Or from workin' the land,*
*Old Rocky would be by the door,*
*Now them boys took a knife,*
*And ended his life,*
*I cain't believe he won't be there no more…"*

Many are kneeling, murmuring their own prayers, many more are crying, caught up in a grief that embraces not only Brother Ben and his martyred dog, but also themselves and the whole wide world. They can't believe it won't be there no more. But they *do* believe it. That is why they are here. As the lone ray of sun fades away, sucked back into the western sky like a withdrawn promise, and the song moves into the final verse, several others join in: Sister Patti Jo Glover, Sister Betty Wilson Clegg, Brother Will Henry in his fine white hat, those young folks from Florida, and then, invited by Brother Duke, just about everybody, even Brother Ben, the tears rolling down his craggy cheeks into his thick gray beard…

*"Dear old Rocky has gone*
*Where the good doggies go,*
*And no more with old Rocky I'll roam,*
*But if dogs have a Heaven,*
*There's one thing I know,*
*Old Rocky has a wonderful home!"*

A sad chorus of "amens" echoes up and down the hillside as people rise to their feet and wipe their eyes and dirt is thrown on the shallow grave. Before returning to the other side of the hill, Brother Hiram

Clegg remembers to say a word in remembrance of Sister Harriet McCardle, and then Brother Duke and Brother Will and Sister Patti Jo lead them all in the singing of "Precious Lord, Take My Hand..."

> *"Lead me on, let me stand,*
> *I'm tired, I'm weak, I'm alone,*
> *Through the storm, through the night,*
> *Lead me on to the light,*
> *Take my hand, precious Lord, lead me home..."*

Yea, lead me on to the light: This is their fervent prayer. It is the Brunist message of the new dispensation, the new covenant—the Coming of Light—and so they baptize by light as well, for that is who they are. The Army of the Sons and Daughters of Light. While ye have light, believe in the light, that ye may be the children of light, for God is light, and in Him is no darkness at all. How often have they heard that today! But when they return to the dusky eastern slope where all the tents are and where so much has happened on this momentous day, it is like stepping into the onrushing night, as if the burial has somehow brought the day to an abrupt end and plunged them all into what may be the final hours. Campfires are being built and lit against the encroaching dark and the apprehensive Followers are gathering around them, talking, praying, recounting the movement's origins and years of persecution, reading from the Bible, reciting the words of the Prophet, confessing, preaching, singing, trying to find their place in this epochal event that has never happened before and will only happen once in human history—and perhaps at any moment. A great cosmic drama, promised since the beginning of time, is being enacted, the hill whereon they stand its stage and they its chosen actors, all caught up in the fulfillment of prophecy in the way that Simon the Zealot or Thomas the Twin, Mary the wife of Clopas, the tax collectors Zacchaeus and Matthew, the Samaritan leper or the woman from Canaan, ordinary folk one and all, were caught up in the First Coming of Christ Jesus the Messiah, also anciently prophesied and glorious in its fulfillment. And did those feel something of the same rush of awe and anticipation and even something like stage fright felt by these here tonight, as history dissolves into eternity?

Throughout the day they have stood together in vast numbers against the enemies of the faith, spreading out over the hillside in their white garments of purity as though taking command of the earth itself, claiming it for Christ Jesus, and they felt great comfort in these numbers, which seemed to confirm the decisions they have taken and which gave them the sense, often verging on ecstasy, of participating in something far larger than themselves; this evening, in the dimming of the light, it is their aloneness that they feel, their smallness in the universe, and the strangeness of that universe, and, whatever their other differences, their shared courage in the face of that strangeness and that smallness, and their shared faith in God's goodness and His care and protection of His chosen ones, for the ways of man are before the eyes of the Lord, and he pondereth all his goings. God feels close by and people are talking to Him directly, like He's there in the air about ten feet over their heads, and sometimes passing right through them in the way that light flows through a window, say, or the way, as a Wisconsin schoolteacher in their midst puts it, that thought passes from neuron to neuron over the intervening synapses, or, to put it in words better understood by most (as she does), the way that thoughts go from head to head, and sometimes without a word being spoken. Oh yes, their heads are full of strange new thoughts that have reached them from who knows where.

Though for most, leaving the Mount of Redemption on this day is inconceivable (the Rapture—which is silent and sudden—can happen at any second), some have done so. Mr. John P. Suggs has been gone for several hours, though it is said he will be back for the tabernacle dedication service, and that his purpose was to deal with the threat posed by the banker. Will Henry returned to the radio station after the funeral service for all the evening programs, taking Brother Duke L'Heureux and Sister Patti Jo Glover with him. She is said to be in contact with the spirit of the Prophet's sister, and agreed to go only if she was back here by ten o'clock; meaning, the dead girl's spirit must have told her something, so they should be safe until ten. The sheriff also left the hill, though he is not a believer and once access was sealed off and troops posted, had no official reason to stay, though many have prayed for his conversion. But then he had to be called back when Brother Ben returned from the Wilderness Camp (another who seems to be coming and going incautiously) to report the raid on the camp by the biker boys. He and the sheriff went over there together, the sheriff angry with himself for not having left somebody to guard it, and he did so immediately. For most, the assault on the camp is yet another alarming sign that the end might be at hand, though for some it is also seen as retribution for the selfishness of their leaders, thinking too little about the plight of their most committed Followers.

For there are many here among the Followers who, fearful of the fate of Ananias and his wife, have sold or given away all they have, following the call of Jesus and of the Prophet himself to "Leave everything and follow me!" and "Come to the Mount of Redemption!" and for them, should God not rapture his church tonight, there is no clearly defined tomorrow. They have no place to go and nothing to do when they get there, as the saying goes. So, in spite of the general opinion that today is only the anniversary of a great historic moment, the true Coming not likely to occur for at least another two years, these Followers still believe strongly (they are scanning the darkening sky for the lights of spaceships or other unnatural and cataclysmic events, the children especially finding this an exciting adventure) that the Rapture *will* come tonight and *must* come, for tomorrow is unimaginable. Some are now camping out, often several families to a house, in the Chestnut Hills prefab development, thanks to Brother John P. Suggs, who built and owns much of it. But, being penniless by faith, they cannot pay the rents that begin tomorrow. Others are living like refugees in the homes of locals or in tents in the fields around, and this cannot go on. So, although they love and admire Sister Clara, they cannot agree with her (it's easier for her and her friends—they have reserved all the best places at the camp for themselves and won't let others in), and are drawn rather to those with a more urgent and immediate message, like Reverend Abner Baxter and his son Young Abner and all their followers. Though Brother Abner has largely been shunned by the official leaders and silenced by the gruesome acts earlier today of his wild younger sons (has Brother Ben Wosznik, as is rumored, done something unpardonable for which the killing of his dog was retribution?), he is attuned to their needs and convictions. He is not so lovable as Sister Clara or Brother Ben, but he is of one mind with them. He believes that the Tribulation has already begun, and they do too. He speaks boldly about the imminence of the Second Coming, interprets for them the mystery of the seven seals, the seven trumpets and the seven bowls (he is especially vivid on the topics of hailstorms, rivers of blood, mountains of fire, and loathsome sores), honors the Prophet more than any other, and preaches, as did the Evangelist Luke, that all in the movement are of one heart and soul and no one possesses anything of his own, but they all have everything in common; nor should there be a needy person among them, for those who have possessions must sell them and share the proceeds with all.

Others, though they too profess an eagerness for the Coming of the Kingdom of Light and look forward to flying into Heaven or embracing Christ Jesus here on the Mount of Redemption or whatever, are secretly relieved that this might not happen tonight, for the end of time is a frightening thought. It's like knowing you have to jump off the high diving board but are glad to learn that today the pool is closed. But if not tonight, when? This is a question that has perplexed millions before them, from St. Clement and his followers in the first century after Christ through all the centuries of millennial visionaries who followed right up to the likes of the Seventh-day Adventists, Jehovah's Witnesses, and Latter-Day Saints of their own day. Even Jesus and Paul spoke of the imminent end of time within the lifetimes of their hearers. Everything in the Bible is directly inspired by God. There can be no errors, they could not have been mistaken. But it did not happen. They were not raptured, the early church was not. So they clearly had something else in mind, something subtler and more obscure, as did the Gospel writers and John the Seer ("Behold, I come quickly!"...but He did not), a latent meaning waiting to be revealed perhaps centuries later. Perhaps tonight.

It is the revealing of that hidden intent that the two young Bible scholars and Brunist office managers, Brothers Darren and Billy Don, are attempting, and they believe they may find it in the accumulated *patterns* of the many prophesyings, interestingly sequenced through the centuries. Darren is an analyzer of texts, Billy Don is a mathematician, and together they have catalogued the origin of their own movement in detail, have examined all the contemporary newspaper accounts and photographs, have studied the life of Giovanni Bruno and that of his visionary predecessor, Ely Collins, have read Dr. Eleanor Norton's *Sayings of Domiron*, as well as secondary texts like the *Sibylline Oracles* and the *Scofield Reference Bible*, Jehovah's Witnesses' *Millions Now Living Will Never Die*, and *The Great Pyramid, Its Divine Message* (the Bible in stone!); they have analyzed all Biblical descriptions of the Last Times in both Testaments and all available interpretations of those descriptions, holding, as do all Brunist Followers, that Biblical prophecy is history written in advance and must be read as such, and they have prepared an intricate chart, entitled "Breaking the Code," showing the parallels and linkages with the Brunist chronology. Convinced that an important key lies hidden in this strangely resonant day, they have taped and photographed everything from the earliest sunrise service on the Mount when Brother Colin Meredith fell prostrate alongside the lawnchair bier, crying out that he could see Marcella Bruno lying on it, cold and blue and unmoving, except for her eyes which were looking straight at him in desperate appeal as she blew a horrible red bubble, through all the day's joys and outrages that have followed, all the comings and goings and declarations and disputations and confrontations, right up to the burial of the beheaded dog Rocky (they are well aware of Matthew 16.18, which some would see as ironic, but they do not) and the present anxious moment. Assuming there will be a tomorrow, as is their cautious but studied belief, they will need thorough documentation to pore over during the weeks to come in order to understand fully what has happened on this crucial full-circle day, and more importantly, what is likely to happen in the future and just when.

They are even willing to examine profane and scurrilous materials such as the book of photographs taken out here on the stormy hill five years ago by a local reporter and others by who-knows-whom in the dimly lit newspaper office in West Condon, photos now kept under lock and key in the church office and not for general distribution. The two young men have earlier questioned Reverend Clegg about the painting of Marcella Bruno dying in the ditch, pointing to Heaven, that they have seen hanging in his church in Florida. Since the painter was not present at this historic moment, who or what can he have used as his model? Is it possible he had access to the photo of the poor terrified girl on the newspaper office sofa? Reverend Clegg did not think so and he did not like the question; perhaps they pushed their inquiries too far. But there is nothing prurient about their close examination of these photographs, disturbing as they are if gazed at idly rather than searching them for purposes of historical veracity and for omens and portents of prophetic significance. The thrust of their question had to do with God's use of profane materials for divine purposes, and thus amounted to further praise of the painting, not a criticism. Even evil men serve God's purposes, must do so, in this world of God's invention. Above all, in the search for ultimate truth, no detail can be censored or overlooked. That uncanny image in Colin's vision this morning, for example, of the red bubble. It seemed to shock many, but so far no one will say more about it. Is there something missing from the painting in Reverend Clegg's church?

If nothing else, just as the growing worldwide power of the Christian faith is living proof of its undeniable truth (God Himself moving through human thought), so do all these apocalyptic expectations—even when seeming failures—participate in mankind's abiding, divinely inspired quest for truth and salvation, for oneness with God and His universe, and so are therefore true in some deeper, perhaps ahistorical—there is no history in eternity—sense. In eternity, as Darren likes to say, seeking *is* finding. The nobility of this inquiry into last things is best shown by those who have pursued it: all the great political and religious leaders through the centuries to the present day, the wise men, the holy men, the artists and the scholars, even the finest scientists who have tried and are trying to grasp the world's doom in their own limited ways. Christopher Columbus, who discovered what many hold to be the New Jerusalem, also authored a *Book of Prophecies* and predicted the impending Apocalypse, and Martin Luther, Cotton Mather, John Wesley, and Joseph Smith all envisioned specific end dates. Henry Adams did. It has to be assumed that the spirit of God spoke through them. As, they hope and believe, He is now speaking through those here tonight.

As the sky darkens, the baptismal lamps and flashlights come out, and those who have not yet done so, and many who have, now repent of their sins and pass through the signature Brunist ritual of baptism by light. Clara Collins uses a battered miner's lamp, said to be that of her first husband Ely, given to her at the time of his memorial service, but the flashlight made famous by the Prophet Giovanni Bruno, or one very much like it, is also used and by many preferred. The ancient issue of "sprinkling" versus "total immersion" arises with advocates for each, depending on the previous Christian denomination of the Follower, and there are some who, against Sister Clara's firmly expressed wishes, insist on being completely bathed in light, free of all garments (clothing casts shadows!), including the young musicians from Florida, who draw others, many squealing small children among them, into their immersive group baptism near the big bonfire. They sing "I'll Fly Away," and "There's a Light upon the Mountain," and some who surround them, in their holy fervor, forget they are naked, and some don't. "Let the Holy Ghost come in!" they are singing. Darren finds their heretical behavior disgusting, but Billy Don strips off to his sunglasses and joins them, as does pale, scrawny, wild-eyed Colin Meredith, his mother unable to hold him back as he flings himself ecstatically into their midst, crying out: "Oh Jesus! Jesus! Jesus! I *love* you!"

All of which infuriates Abner Baxter and his followers, Abner shielding his wide-eyed daughter from the sight and demanding that this sinful abomination cease immediately. Clara agrees (never mind the argument that this is how the Rapture will happen when they fly to Heaven leaving all behind, including of course their clothing) and, in the firm and commanding way she has, asks everyone to please put their clothes back on, the baptism ceremony is concluded. Reverend Hiram Clegg, though he had been singing along with them, arm in arm, joins her in her appeal, speaking directly to the young people in his fatherly fashion and helping them to find their scattered clothing. Reverend Baxter of course has his own rituals of baptism by light, which saying of the Prophet he interprets as baptism by fire, as first announced by John the Baptist—"I indeed baptize you with water; but One mightier than I is coming, whose sandal strap I am not worthy to loose; He will baptize you with the Holy Spirit and *fire!*"—and as experienced by Christ's disciples at Pentecost when they were lapped by tongues of fire as the Holy Spirit descended upon them, but though pain is not excluded from these rites, nakedness—or any other form of frivolous personal exhibitionism, including excessive gaiety—certainly is.

Clara, aware of the feverish expectations of many tonight and sharing their desires but not their convictions (she cannot explain this entirely, but perhaps Ely's calm sorrowful distance much of the day has been part of it), and consequently fearful of too great a disappointment at the end of the day's last hour, has wanted to finish on a cheering note, so she has delayed the official camp dedication and tabernacle announcement until later in the evening. The rising passions, however, and the risk of further disputes (altogether too much is being said about opening the Wilderness Camp freely to all believers; she knows this cannot happen though she has not yet thought how to stop it) compel her to get on with the ceremony now. Darren and Billy Don—with fourteen little white crosses, much smaller and whiter than those that support the lawnchair bier—set about mysteriously decorating the hillside, encircling the main meeting tent near the top of the hill. Then lighted candles are passed about and all are called upon to follow their Evangelical Leader as she parades them from cross to cross as if on a via dolorosa, as many of those present take it to be, singing and praying fervently at each station, led by the various preachers and ecstatics among them. There are so many little crosses, this takes a good time. Meanwhile Ben and Wayne light the kerosene lanterns in the meeting tent, setting it aglow like a beacon, calling all toward it. The tent is too small for this vast crowd of Followers, but Wayne has moved the tent-meeting microphones to the podium inside the tent with speakers outside to reach the overflow, as they have so often done on their missionary travels, and the side flaps of the tent are opened. After the Florida youngsters, their earlier excessive zeal forgiven, lead everyone in singing "Asleep in Jesus" and "The Ninety and Nine" and the melodious "Jesus Is Coming"—"*Jesus is coming! The dead shall arise! Loved ones shall meet in a joyful surprise! Caught up together to Him in the skies! Jesus is coming again!*"—Brother Hiram Clegg is asked to give the invocation, and at Clara's personal request, to say a few words to soothe, in his silvery tongue, the anxieties of the Followers and to prepare them, as it were, should the day pass without the hoped-for Rapture. Also, it will take a while as it always does with Brother Hiram, and perhaps it will allow Mr. John P. Suggs time to return.

"And I heard a great voice out of Heaven," cries Brother Hiram, his amplified voice carrying out past the tent and past the Mount into the night beyond, "saying, Behold, the tabernacle of God is with men, and he will dwell with them, and they shall be his people, and there shall be no more death, neither sorrow, nor crying, nor any more pain! Oh my brothers! Oh my sisters! No more death, neither sorrow, nor crying! No more pain!"

When he is finished, Clara will officially declare the International Brunist Headquarters and Wilderness Camp Meeting Ground open and present the architectural plans of what they are now calling the Brunist Coming of Light Tabernacle Church, sometimes the Brunist Tabernacle of Light, explaining that twelve of the little crosses they have just visited represent the actual twelve corners of the planned church which is in the shape of a cross, sitting on a large encompassing circle carved out of the top of the hill, thus imitating the cross-in-the-circle stitched on all their tunics and viewable as such when seen from on high (God will know who is here!). The other two crosses stitch the longer space between the arms and foot of the cross, the dimensions of which are seven units each for the arms and head, twelve units for the post, totaling thirty-three, the life in years of Christ and of their Prophet—which explains why she insisted on erecting the meeting tent just where it is, at the very altar of the tabernacle-to-be. She will then make the exciting announcement, which has floated up and down the hillside all day as rumor, that an extraordinarily generous gift from an anonymous donor has made it possible to get started immediately, so that the church will be built well before the seventh anniversary of the Day of Redemption, when all prophecies may well be fulfilled. The donor, she will be careful to point out, has specified that the gift is to be used for the new tabernacle and not for any other purpose, else they shall not receive it.

Meanwhile, Reverend Clegg has now launched into a lyrical evocation of the Seven Words or Sayings of Giovanni Bruno ("A humble man of the people, my friends! But spiritually pure and majestic of stature! A saintly man with riveting eyes, inhabited by the spirit of God!") in which the Prophet ("I am the One to Come") acknowledged the Forerunner Ely Collins and his vision of the White Bird ("Hark ye to the White Bird!"), and above all pointed to the prophetic message found in Brother Ely's hand upon his death ("The tomb is its message!"), announced the Coming of the Light on the Mount of Redemption involving time spans of a "Sunday Week" and "A Circle of Evenings," which led them to this hillside on the nineteenth of April five years ago today, and commanded that his Followers "Baptize with Light."

*"Bru-no! Bru-no! Bru-no!"* some in the back of the tent chant, and others on the hillside outside join in.

"Let us pray!"

In his prayer, Brother Hiram speaks once more of the decapitated doves and dog, assuring all present that animals do have souls and God loves them and there will be animals in Heaven for God, who watches over even the birds of the air, created them and loves them. "Dear Lord, we think of that song we have all just sung, 'The Ninety and Nine,' with its sorrowful resonances with the number who died beneath our feet in that terrible disaster. It expresses Your undying love of all living creatures, and not only for Your flock but also for Your strays. Even smelly dirty sheep are loved by You, their creator, and Your Son Himself became the sacrificial Lamb for us all. A homeless man brought hope and salvation to this world by becoming a lamb. All animals have a soul and are going to be with their maker and cared for in Heaven by those who loved them on earth—to say that animals don't go to Heaven when they die has no foundation in Scripture! The beloved Rockdust is in Heaven, wagging his tail, we know this and thank Thee for it!" He also says a prayer for Sister Harriet McCardle, whose death today has reminded them all of the need for a burial ground of their own, and after he is done, Sister Clara will be able to tell them that they have decided to consecrate the western slope of the Mount, facing the setting sun, for that purpose, so that the Brunist souls in repose will be easy for God to gather to his bosom. They will attempt to bring the bodies of all past martyrs and Followers to be buried here, along with those of the Prophet and his sister, even though, as she knows, there is some uncertainty among the believers as to whether such bodies even still exist, or whether they were both translated straight up to Heaven. Finally, she will take up a collection, not only for the new church, but also for the needy among them, for she agrees that all available unmarked resources should be used to help one another, and she knows that Brother Hiram's congregation will lead the way in this.

"Our movement has been blessed with many great visionaries," he declares after the chorus of amens, "and none less so than our inspiring Evangelical Leader and Organizer, Sister Clara Collins-Wosznik, to whom came one day, unbidden, as if the Lord were speaking to her directly, the glorious vision of a magnificent House of God to be built here on this site, about which you have all by now heard. Sister Clara will soon be telling you all about it and bringing new tidings of especial joy. We cannot say when the bridegroom cometh for, as Jesus said, such an hour as ye think not the Son of Man cometh, but if Jesus should come tonight and welcome us all to Heaven, my friends, we are ready! And yet if he should wait for a time and come a year from now or two years from now, we shall be ever more ready! We shall gather here then in a great new tabernacle church to receive him in all his glory and like the master of the house in Jesus' beautiful parable, we will be able to say: Come, for all things are now—!"

"We seen it! We seen it!" cries a child rushing into the tent, interrupting Brother Hiram at the height of his oratory. "A light! Over on the other side! A light in the sky! We seen a burning light in the sky! He's coming!" Oh sweet Jesus! It is happening! All thoughts of parables and tabernacles vanish and, with a communal cry, they all rush out to the top of the hill to await the coming of the Lord.

# I.12

## Monday 20 April

The new day dawns brightly, as if in mockery of last night's awesome imaginings, everything cheerfully aglitter from the light rain that has fallen in the early hours. Yet again, the world has not ended. This circumstance is met variously with disappointment, fear, relief, anxiety, indifference. Atop Inspiration Point, Ben Wosznik greets it with that grave equanimity for which he is known—whatever the Lord wills—and picks up empty beer and whiskey bottles, filthy rags, crumpled cigarette packs. In spite of all the exhausting events of yesterday and last night, Ben, who both as coalminer and farmer was always an early riser, has chosen the hushed predawn moment to climb up here with a trash bag to police the area, erasing as best he can all signs of the bikers' recent occupation. Those boys do some pretty heavy drinking. Across the way, the rising sun casts its first warming glow on the crest of the Mount of Redemption, where, just below it, the tents remain, containing many people in blankets and sleeping bags. Not just a new day for some of them. A whole new life. Ben remembers this feeling from five years ago, when he and Clara and the others had the same expectations many of these folks had last night, and how strange and dreamlike the next day seemed, like an imitation day hiding the real one. To keep their minds off their disappointment, Ben will try to busy them today with clearing the Mount—they must have everything removed by noon—and cleaning up the camp after yesterday's raid by the motorcycle gang. A lot of damage was done down below, but little that can't be fixed.

After a long hard day, once the troublemakers at the foot of the Mount were chased away and poor Rocky buried, things seemed to be going well enough last night, with Clara about to reveal to everyone the Brunist Tabernacle of Light plans (if his eyesight were better, he could probably see from here some of those little white crosses that pegged the corners) and to confirm the miraculous news about the large gift they have received, when those pesky Blaurock kids ran in shouting about lights in the sky and everybody rushed out. Probably just sparks from the fire on the front side of the hill, but it brought an end to the rest of the night's scheduled events. In fact, some blamed the distractions in the meeting tent and all the proud talk about a new church for the disappearance of the lights. Mr. Suggs arrived an hour or so before midnight and got an earful about that, which clearly did not please him.

Before joining the others on the top of the hill, the three of them, along with Hiram, gathered in the tent so hastily abandoned. Mr. Suggs told them he had been unable to close the deal on the old mine property as he'd hoped, one of the owners being away on a weekend fishing trip, but he was certain that would happen within the week. Meanwhile, he showed them a rough sketch of a new expanded architectural layout that incorporates the tabernacle and burial ground on the Mount, the Wilderness camp, his projected motel, and an additional adjacent trailer camp as part of a single Brunist headquarters and religious center complex, all connected by tree-lined access roads and camp meeting ground spaces, with living areas clearly designated, none at the camp itself. Ben was deeply impressed and said it looked almost like Heaven, and Mr. Suggs said, except there's no free admission. Those living in the camp buildings now would have to move, including Mrs. Edwards and the two young office managers, so as to give no one any justifiable claim to the right to live there, though the small trailer camp on the old athletic field down from the main buildings would remain for now, its available slots allocated to those already parked there, and those forced to move out of the official camp buildings, for whom small campers could be purchased with their new gift money. The front gates and the barbed-wire fence being erected around the camp to protect it from intruders will be completed at his expense, he said, reminding them that there should be someone manning the gates from sunrise to sunset as well as assigned night watchmen until an alarm system can be installed. Clara said she was worried about those who have given away all they have to be here and now have nowhere to go, but Mr. Suggs pointed out that most of those who have done so and now expect to be cared for by the community did not actually have all that much to give away in the first place, if their meager contributions were any indication, and the three of them, though perhaps more charitable than Mr. Suggs, had to agree that this was probably so. There were many ways, he said, they could earn their rent money, and meanwhile he'd begin developing the new trailer camp area this week, bringing in water and electricity, which will be metered.

The sun's rays are creeping steadily down the eastern slope of the distant Mount, falling now upon the tents, from which people start to emerge, scattering in various directions like ants from a disturbed anthill, some making their way over to the latrines at the mine buildings, others down to their cars on the mine road or coming this way on foot for the sunrise service or to use the communal showers. Still thirty minutes or so before the sun reaches the dogwood tree where this morning's service is to be held and many of the out-of-town buses have not yet arrived, though Ben can see folks beginning to mill about down below. Many more are coming, more really than the little camp can bear. After the service, he will visit Rocky's grave and help with the striking of the tents and the cleanup of the hillside over there, which has, even at this distance, a littered look, like after a church picnic. He wants to leave something at the grave. Flowers don't seem right. Then he remembers the brass dog tag Rocky used to wear when he was younger and running loose. Probably still back at the old farm house somewhere. Just the thing. He'll drop by when he makes his morning run to the rubbish dump. The bikers stole or ruined most everything edible, so he'll have to restock all that as well and pick up again the makings for a communal farewell lunch today for the busloads of visitors. Also some replacement window panes and more sacks of lime; the outdoor necessaries have suffered a lot of traffic and there will be a heap more today.

Billy Don Tebbett greets the first day after the last one with a vague but aching longing, having lain the night through, unable to sleep, almost unable to breathe, beside a beautiful young woman, herself asleep in her fellow's arms, the three of them huddled beneath the stars—though there were no stars, not until nearly dawn, and then there was a moon, too, a big one, that seemed itself like a revelation, even as viewed through his prescription sunglasses. Neither he nor Darren were of the opinion anything like the Rapture would happen last night, yet both had found themselves staring at the overcast night sky, almost afraid to look away, until well past midnight. Billy Don, lonely for friends his own age, had drawn close to the young people from Florida with whom earlier in the night he had danced in the altogether at the bonfire, immersed in light, and who were during the midnight vigil gently singing songs like "I'm Going Home" ("I'm glad that I am born to die…") and "Kum Ba Yah" and "Love Lifted Me." When the likelihood of any further drama in the sky faded away, they fell into a deep conversation about love and sin, deciding that the only true sin was unkindness, like what those mean boys did to that unfortunate dog—Darren disagreeing, as always, and insisting they had to return to the camp immediately to see what damage the bikers had done. Billy Don said that what was done was done and they should stay on the Mount to guard it until dawn, and Darren said that's what the sheriff's troops were for and anyway there was no longer any danger, and they had to get back. Right now. Billy Don was about to hand Darren the car keys when he was rescued by Mrs. Edwards, who was returning to the camp with Colin and offered Darren a ride, saying Colin was overexcited and she needed Darren's help to coax Colin into the car, and he stalked off with her in a wordless fury. Billy Don was rather hoping for a sleepy cuddle with someone through the night, but he could see that the young people had already paired off in various ways, and as there were anyway more boys than girls, there was nobody left for him. But then a young couple near the fire offered to share their blanket with him and he figured that was better than nothing and he was still wide awake, and so they crawled under together in their tunics, the girl between them, and continued their conversation about the meaning of life and the body's part in it, while they still have bodies, and about God's kingdom, to which they would all fly away by and by, as a kingdom of love and happiness and beautiful music. "Metaphorically speaking," the boy added, and the girl said, "No, *really*." As the fire died down and the temperature dropped, the blanket wasn't really enough, so Billy Don made a trip to the car for a quick pee (whoo, he was pretty excited) and his old sleeping bag, which they opened up and used as a comforter. The couple rolled into a sleepy hug, he lying beside them on his back, the girl's warm backside snuggled against his hipbone, and he supposed if you were asleep you wouldn't really be able to tell a hipbone from a hand, so, as they dropped off, or seemed to, he let his fall there as if by accident, full of wonder at the natural fit of those two parts. God is great. Until his hand was brushed by the boy's hand and he snatched it away and rolled over, faking a soft snore as though sound asleep and therefore not responsible for what his hand might have been doing. He and the girl were now bottom to bottom and it wasn't as good as before but it was enough to keep him awake all night, especially given his memory of it, unclothed, rosy, in front of the fire. It began to rain slightly, so they pulled the sleeping bag over their heads and curled up all the tighter, and he could feel the softness of her pressing against him as if trying to hug him back there, as he was trying to hug her. Whenever she shifted in her sleep, it felt like a tender caress, innocent as hand-holding, a caress that amounted, given the girl's interpretation of such things and increasingly his own, to a kind of communion with God. Now, as he pauses to pick up some morning stragglers on the road, headed for the camp, he is reflecting groggily (it will be a long day, and even if he finds a moment for a quick nap, he knows Darren in his spite will not let him have it) upon this divine caress, feeling even yet a kind of tingle down there like the way your lips sometimes feel after you've been kissing someone, and he realizes that that vague ache in his heart he awoke to is the ache of love. He is head over heels. But not with anybody.

For Lucy Smith, the new day, as every other day, brings with its arrival a certain wistfulness tinged with bittersweet regret at the way time keeps getting on, and like Billy Don, a vague longing for she knows not what. Something missed along the way or missing now. She did not spend the night on the Mount of Redemption or anywhere near it, for her husband Calvin, who has a paying job as many in town do not and who has a family to care for, as he often says, when he says anything at all, could not as a public official take the risk—in fact, he has already received a telephone call from a city lawyer asking about his three brief days as a Brunist five years ago. But what if? she asked when one of his officers came to drive her home, and Calvin simply shrugged and looked the other way. Everyone seemed so afraid; she was afraid. The dead white birds spooked everybody. A sign from above. She hardly slept all night, worrying about what might happen, but she assumes nothing did because she has risen at first light and found the world unchanged, no sign of the Kingdom of Heaven, and nothing about it on TV either, though they did show Susanna Friskin's husband sitting on the ground with blood on his face and looking amazed. Now, until it is time to wake the children, she busies herself with folding laundry and fixing the children's breakfasts and praying silently that she be allowed to understand the world before she dies.

She felt truly left behind yesterday when it started to get dark and all the others, feeling expectant and apprehensive, stepped out of

Mabel's caravan to climb the Mount together and she had to go home alone. But at least there were the hours before with all her friends from church, some not seen in years. Betty Wilson had come all the way from Florida (Calvin promised before they got married that they would go there someday, but he has probably forgotten) and Mildred Gray peeked in, too, though she could only stop in for a quick hello because of her crippled husband, about whom they all talked after she left, and less than favorably. He's driving poor Mildred into an early grave, they said. The way Mildred put it was that she hoped the Rapture would come that night because at least Ezra could fly up out of his wheelchair and she wouldn't have to push it anymore. Lucy had hoped to see again her old high school friend Wanda Cravens, but she was tending her youngsters up on the Mount, Mabel said, adding that there were several now, all about a year apart, no two looking alike. Like the old woman who lived in a shoe, said a lady named Ludie Belle, one of the many new people traveling with Clara's group. She had so many children because she didn't know what to do. Everyone chuckled at that, though in a loving and accepting way. They described Wanda Craven's new man and Lucy thought they were exaggerating until, later, she actually saw him.

The talk in Mabel's caravan, which had been going on before Lucy arrived, was about something mysterious that had just happened and what it might mean. Mabel had that look on her face with her head reared back that always signifies something very dramatic is about to take place, or else something she predicted has just occurred, but they didn't seem to want to tell Lucy what it was. It was because of Calvin's job, she knew, and she could understand that, but still she felt hurt. It was Florrie Cox who finally let the cat out, whether because she felt sorry for her or just because Florrie is always apt to blurt out things. It seems that some young female-like person, who may not have been a real person at all, had appeared and vanished all in a whisker, leaving a dead old lady in her wake, all of which signified many different possible things, depending in part on whether the phantasm, if it was a phantasm, was a godly spirit or a diabolical one, the prevailing opinion being the latter and generally supported by Mabel's cards. Bernice Filbert said that when she first witnessed the creature in her filthy garments hovering over the lawnchair that once held the cadaver of the Prophet's sister, she saw that while she—or it—was looking down at the chair, it also had a face on the back of its head which was staring straight at her. She said she did not think she was being singled out, but that the face was one of those, like in some paintings, in which the eyes follow you wherever you go, so in effect it was looking at everyone at the same time. Of course no one else saw this and Bernice has a very active imagination, but her stories are always interesting and you can't help listening to them. The amazing thing, they were all saying, is that a woman named Patti Jo, who is in communication with the dead, predicted exactly all this would happen, right there in Mabel's caravan the day before. It's true, many of them were here and heard it, and now Mabel's cards were saying there was more to come—maybe even the Rapture, or something like it. They were hoping Patti Jo would join them in case she had any new messages, but she didn't make it before everyone had to leave, though you could hear her singing religious songs on the loudspeakers.

Through the caravan window, Lucy could see her husband's boss, who appointed Calvin his deputy right after he got elected sheriff. His old partner in the mine. The man's thick shaved neck bulging out over his collar under his cap is what you saw. He was having an argument with some other people there at the foot of the hill, many of them wearing hats and looking important, but unknown to her. One she did recognize, even in one of those Brunist tunics, was Abner Baxter; she could tell him by his big mouth and his thick jowls, though his red hair had grayed and he was more sunk into himself. But he was carrying on in the old way, shaking his pudgy fist and looking as threatening as ever. Calvin has always been a little bit afraid of him, though he looks up to him, too, even if Abner is a foot shorter. He was Calvin's faceboss on night shifts. They all came up out of the mine together the night it blew up, Lucy waiting at the main hoisting shaft with the children, the two they had then, and her parents and Calvin's parents and his sister from Wilmer, and almost as soon as he reached fresh air and could catch his breath, Abner, his face all streaked with black, started preaching against the mine owners. She and the children and all of Calvin's family were just eager to get home and give thanks to the Lord and relax from all the tension, but Calvin wanted to stay and listen, so they had no choice. Later, poor Ely was found dead and Abner became their preacher at the church. His sermons were pretty scary and she wasn't sure her children should hear the things he said and some people left the church, but Calvin believed in him, and so she did, too. He's a good union man is what Calvin always said, and a fierce man of God, and when Abner Baxter told him to do something he usually did it. It was why he was out on the mine road that night the Bruno girl was killed and why they both marched out in the rain with the Brunists the next day. Sitting there in Mabel's caravan, looking out the window, which was like looking at a big television screen, brought it all back. That one night was as far as it went, though. She and Calvin knew Giovanni Bruno in high school, a peculiar Italian boy who seemed not to have any friends or want any and who stared at everyone like he hated them or was afraid of them. He looked like somebody who might get a gun and shoot everyone—that was what Cal and the other boys said—though they also sometimes teased him as if to see if he would. So when the state police started up the hill that day, they just ran like crazy and they threw away the tunics when they got home and went back to the Church of the Nazarene and never spoke of that weekend again, hoping that as few people as possible saw them there.

And then, while she was sitting there in the caravan, letting her memories roll over her, the most astonishing thing happened. Maybe it was what Mabel's cards had predicted. A bunch of men in black leather jackets came roaring right past on motorcycles. It was like they just popped up out of nowhere or came flying down from the sky. Several of the women screamed. Maybe she did. They went right down in the ditch and up again and straight at the people standing over there, many of whom started running away while others just seemed frozen to the spot. The riders skidded to a stop all at once and threw some things at the crowd, one of which Bernice said looked like an animal head, though Lucy could hardly believe that. One of the things struck Susanna Friskin's husband right in the face, and that's when he sat down. And then the men on the motorbikes came roaring straight back at the caravan, and someone was shooting, and she was so frightened, she ducked and fell right over onto the linoleum, clutching at the doilies on the armrests and dragging them down with her, and there was screaming and praying and crying and a terrifying rattle overhead, but Mabel and Bernice just stood at the window and stared out until they had gone past. Demons from hell. Everyone said so. Mabel said they had red eyes. Without pupils. And Bernice Filbert arched her penciled eyebrows and said in a whisper: You saw that, too! Betty Wilson whimpered she was having palpitations and had to lie down and she did, Linda making room for her on the sofa bed. After that, there was a lot of commotion on the hill and they were all drying their eyes and staring out of the caravan windows, trying to see what was happening, and that's when she saw Wanda's new man. It was true, he was everything they'd said he was. A television cameraman had apparently snuck up the hill to poke his camera into one of the tents, and he just picked him up like a rag doll and threw him into the ravine there! A giant!

She can hear the children squabbling. Her private silent time is over. Spats and tears, arguments about what to wear, fever blisters and runny noses. Couldn't be less like the Heavenly Kingdom. But she's grateful for it and thanks God and Jesus and sets out the cereal bowls.

Another who, like Billy Don, found himself last night enjoying the fit of palm to palmed—though in his case the cheek cupped was plumper and of a certain age—was the master plumber Welford Oakes. They were pressed together amid the crowds atop the Mount of Redemption, all eyes cast upon the Heavens in anticipation of the descent of Our Lord Jesus Christ in all His glory to establish Heaven on earth, and given the excited jostle, that his hand landed where it did could be seen as an accident, but not that it, without apology, remained there. She turned to frown up at him questioningly, and he smiled and murmured, "I thought y'might care to read my palm," figuring she'd either knee him where it hurts and walk away, or she'd stay and then something different would happen. What she said was: "I ain't never studied a palm before whose fate line cut clean acrost the life line like that." He grinned, gave her a gentle pinch. "That's what one a them other lines has to say about that," he said, and moved away. Now, at the sunrise service down by the flowering dogwood tree, they are exchanging frequent glances, trying not to. He understands the risks, but, like it goes in "Amazing Grace," "The earth shall soon dissolve like snow, the sun forbear to shine," and that being so, one has to make the best of whatever's left. Now the worshippers are burying those two headless birds and singing "Wings of a Dove," and when they reach the love line, he casts a meaningful glance her way. But she is staring fixedly up over her shoulder as if still looking to the sky for a sign of the Coming. He turns to look up through the trees at what she's peering at: Inspiration Point. When he looks back, she's already gone.

Hovis and Uriah have walked back to the camp for the sunrise service to find their camper gone. "Them bikers must of stole it," Hovis says with alarm. They are both alarmed. It's all they own. How can they get back to West Virginia without it? They search behind all the other trailers and caravans in the lot just in case it somehow got hidden. Uriah pauses, turns to look off toward the mine hill. "How did we git over there in the first place, Hovis? We must of drove." They both think about this. "Yup, we must of forgot. I'll go git it, Uriah. You're tuckered out. You go lie down." "How can I lie down if we ain't got our camper?" Hovis scratches his head, looks around again. No, it's not there. "Didn't think of that."

* * *

Debra Edwards knows more of the words of the Brunist songs now and can sing along when Ben selects numbers like "The Wings of a Dove." They are singing it in memory of their pair of nesting white doves so senselessly and barbarously slain yesterday. Ludie Belle Shawcross picked up the decapitated birds after they were thrown by the motorcycle gang and saved them for burial at this morning's sunrise service here at the foot of the budding dogwood tree. The heads could not be found. The camp is not yet in full flower, but it is already bursting with color and it is alive now with birdsong as if all the birds were participating in the honoring of the doves: lots of sparrows trilling away, and the newly arrived orioles and warblers with their pretty voices, the chats, buntings, and chirping dickcissels all joining in as they celebrate God's pure sweet love, sent down on the wings of a snow-white dove. Everyone had come to associate the doves with the "white birds" of Ely Collins' and Giovanni Bruno's visions, and the launching of their headless bodies into their midst on the Mount of Redemption produced a surge of fear among the Followers and prompted terrified predictions of dire events. Though Debra was not inclined to think of the bikers as demons, as many did, she herself felt this fear, and even more so on their return to their camp, which they found half-wrecked, her own home and Colin's cruelly trashed. The front screen door was torn off its hinges, two windows were smashed and the plastic insulation ripped away, their beds were overturned and urinated upon, their cookies and chocolates were stolen, the hot water bottle from the manse had been beheaded just like the dog and doves were, and her nursing chair, rescued from the manse, had had its pretty velvet seat slashed. Poor Colin, overwrought by all the day's excitements, went crazy on seeing it and ran out onto the camp road, screaming hysterically at the bikers, though by then they were miles away. Fortunately, she had brought Darren back to camp with her. He was the one person who could settle Colin down, and with a lot of coaxing he did so and, gratefully, took him to stay with him in the church office in the lodge, which, being locked and innocuous-looking, had escaped the gang's depredations; she was exhausted and could not have stayed awake another minute to comfort a distraught boy. She dropped, fully dressed, like a lead plummet onto the pungent mattress and did not regain consciousness until she awoke, startled and afraid, unsure of where she was until the early dawn light and birdsong relocated her, Abner Baxter next door, berating his wife and daughters.

Debra felt quite charitable toward the Baxters before she actually knew them, and agreed with Clara that they should be welcomed back, but they have been like a flock of predatory cowbirds descending upon a garden of songbirds. Nest robbers. And their followers are no better, demanding and bad-tempered and unappreciative and disruptive. As the beekeeper Corinne Appleby said, "Nary a one of them knows how to smile." Without any right, the Baxters have taken over the cabin next door, the one meant for Darren and Billy Don, and even though repairs on it have barely begun—it doesn't even have a front door—they don't seem inclined to leave it any time soon, which worries Clara and Ben. They put a tent up at the back to sleep the mother and daughters, Reverend Baxter and his three sons using the cabin proper, though now there's only the oldest son after the younger two were expelled. Already, they look like they've been living over there forever. Unloading their clunky old car was like emptying a moving van and they've taken whatever they wanted from around the camp. What's left of their family is here at the sunrise service, looking sullen and defensive, completely out of character with the beautiful day. Well, maybe they can't help it. Debra was born with a smile on her face, they were not. She has to try to understand them.

What's going on between Elaine and Young Abner is also worrying Clara, and if she'd seen what Debra has seen, she'd be even more upset. Clara has asked her, as a counselor for troubled young people, to have a talk with Elaine, but the girl has shied away from her, and now, after all she has witnessed in the garden, Debra might not know where to begin. Should she tell Clara what she saw? She should. But how? Clara would want to know why she didn't interfere, and she doesn't know the answer to that. Really, it's all too embarrassing.

"They have rejected God, creation, and morality! Oh, they don't call it humanism, they call it democracy, but they mean humanism, in all its atheistic, amoral, scientistic depravity!" The handsome bishop from Wyoming, invited to read from the Scriptures, is prefacing his reading with an attack on what he calls the devil's religion and "the most serious threat to our nation in its entire history! You can't be both a humanist and a true believer!" There are shouted replies and admiring gazes and soft *"Bru-no! Bru-no!"* chants from many of the gathered worshippers. The principal target of his denunciation is the false belief in evolution, one of the fables of her own upbringing, and one that has deprived her of the opportunity to help with the camp's home schooling, so she feels somewhat targeted as well. She's trying to unlearn all that to break down their distrust, so she also calls out an "amen!" or two, though she's probably not convincing anyone. But humanism, she has come to realize, is what's wrong with Wesley and all his stupid sermons, and that helps her to hate it as they hate it. The bishop puts on his spectacles and picks up the Bible, looking around at them all. "What are these which are arrayed in white robes? and whence came they?" he asks. *"We come from the dark, brother! Lead us to light!"* "And I said unto him, Sir, thou knowest. And he said to me, These are they which came out of great tribulation, and have washed their robes, and made them white in the blood of the Lamb!" *"Washed in the blood of the Lamb!"* they cry. And the *"Bru-no! Bru-no!"* chant begins again.

She knows that many of these people are feeling desperate today, having walked away from their livelihoods and given away all they own, and she knows what that's like. She too has impoverished herself to help their cause, abandoning the security of the life of a minister's wife to commit herself heart and soul to the Brunists. But though she feels for their plight, she wants them all to go away. Reverend Hiram Clegg, now preaching his last sermon before returning with his congregation to Florida—she will miss him and his warm kindly eloquence; like her, he always seems to see the bright side of things—is talking about those who have accepted voluntary poverty and the great sacrifices they have made and their need now to find further ways to support the community of Followers as it awaits the last days, quoting beautifully from the Bible and from the sayings of Giovanni Bruno as he always does, and she feels that though he is addressing the newly arrived multitudes, he is also talking to her. Well, she *will* work hard and continue to play her part and have faith and God will be pleased. She can sell things from the vegetable garden. Everything will be all right. It has to be.

Ludie Belle Shawcross has told her bluntly that she is out of her water here and should leave, but she could never do that, not so long as Colin stays, and now, like a lot of these poor people, she really wouldn't have anywhere to go anyway. The Wilderness Camp is now her home; she has and will have no other. Debra has always admired Ludie Belle's forthrightness in confessing her sins and has tried to emulate her, but yesterday, up on the Mount of Redemption, Ludie Belle shocked her by saying she makes most everything up when repenting. "I lean on history like a preacher leans on the Bible, sweetie. I select out a few juicy licks and stitch 'em together into a up-liftin' story, if you know what I mean." She said this after advising Debra she was getting too personal in her confessions, and she should learn not to give away so much. It's nobody's business, and they tend to hold it over you afterwards. "Anyways, it's more entertainin' with a little judicious resortin'." Just then Colin came by, sweaty and excited from all that had happened, and buoyed up by his new friendships with the young people from Florida—he had been bouncing about all afternoon as if the ground were hot and burning his feet—and he paused a moment to lay his head on her shoulder and catch his breath. And then, as quickly, he was off again. "Be careful, honey. You're playin' with fire," Ludie Belle said, and Debra, knowing she was red to the roots, could only walk away, not wanting to see that woman again.

Instead of hovering behind her back as usual, Colin is standing this morning with the cheerful youngsters from Florida, who have been so nice to him. Reverend Clegg uses the word "radiance," stretching it out in his resonant style (he is talking about the birds they are burying), and she thinks, yes, that's exactly what she sees in Colin, an inherent childlike purity, glowing innocence. Radiance. He is a receptor. She used to have to shave him, not wanting him near anything sharp, but he has taken to letting the hairs on his chin grow. There aren't many of them, no more than a dozen or so, and they are so blond they are almost like silver. It gives him a strange otherworldly look. Among his new friends, he has been tensely smiling, so rare for him, but they are leaving after lunch, so later he will cry again.

When Ben Wosznik hands out morning work assignments for cleaning and repairing the camp, Franny Baxter volunteers to help load the collected trash into his pickup. Ben has asked everyone to bag and drop all garbage and rubbish at the front gate of the camp where his pickup is parked and he will take it to the rubbish dump, and she posts herself there to receive it and toss it in the truckbed. When he starts up the motor, she gets in beside him on the hard bench seat and asks him if he could drop her off somewhere near the edge of town on the north side; she wants to have a talk with Tess Lawson. He says he's not going directly towards town, he's stopping off at his old farmhouse to pick up Rocky's dog tag and then proceeding on to the town dump. She can help him unload the truck and then he'll take her where she wants to go, and she says that'll do fine. He asks if she has asked her father and she says no, and don't tell him, but she's a woman now and doesn't need his permission for every little thing. If he finds out…? "All he can do is give me a larruping, and I'm plenty used to that."

"He beats you a lot?"

"Not like before. Nat sorta tamed him."

"Your father's skeereda Nat?"

"Everbody is. Junior's setting hisself up to take over, but Nat's the one with our father's fire." Ben doesn't say anything, so she says, "I think it's awful what they done to your dog. Junior is telling everyone you must of hid your gun in Nat's backpack to make us all look bad and get us moved out, and that made Nat mad."

"Well, it ain't so. Maybe Junior's trying to hide something."

"That's what I reckon." Pulling out of the camp gates, they had to thread their way through the crowds of people milling about, coming or going, and the fields they are passing now are littered with tents and trailers. The mine hill, too, only partially cleared, new smaller tents popping up there. The life she has known, wants to know no more.

"Your ma's looking poorly. She was crying a lot yesterday."

"This place gives her the creeps. After what happened, having a dead baby out there in the storm with nobody to help her but me, she didn't never want to come back. She should of stayed home in bed that day or gone to hospital, but my father drug her out there, saying if they was all transcended she would not wanta miss out, nor not the unborn baby neither. She was sick for a long spell after that, really sick, and she just never exactly got well again."

"That's too bad, Franny. Must be a burden to you."

"It can be."

"So why is it y'mean to go see Tess? Y'reckon they's a chance she'll come back to us?"

"Maybe."

"She knows you're coming?"

"Nope."

They are passing an old derelict farmhouse that would seem to be Ben's, but, after slowing down, they roll on by. Ben doesn't say anything, except a soft little grunt, but she saw what he saw: the wheel of a motorcycle sticking out at the back.

"We baptized it and raptured it, Mom, all at once," says Mark. "You ain't God, kid," Dot says, cuffing his big stuck-out ears. "I'll rapture your little britches if you try anything like that again. Now you and Matty get down on your knees over in that corner and pray for an hour that you don't get sent to hell for putting on airs and messing like that with God's handiwork." "Oh Mom, that's where the sandbox was!" "We didn't *mean* to rapture the cat, Mom," Matthew wheedles.

"We was only wanting to baptize it." "I *told* you not to put gasoline on it," says Luke, and Dot sends her to the corner, too. They have been sharing this unfurnished prefab in Chestnut Hills with a family from Alabama, who left in a huff when her kids burned their cat, no doubt heading straight out to the camp to tattle on them. Well, good riddance, she couldn't stand the stink of their homemade kitty litter dug up out of the back yard and the Blaurocks now have the place to themselves, though they don't plan on staying long. That family was just a bunch of ignorant, drawling rednecks who knew nothing about the latter days and were always complaining about keeping the place clean and about her kids bullying their kids and about little Johnny's dirty diapers and his whiny crying and about her loud snoring and Isaiah always hogging the bathroom. Well, her husband can't help it. He has a nervous stomach, and did they think they didn't snore, too? If God wanted her to snore, what could she or anyone else do about it? Not sleep? Get serious.

Dot and Isaiah Blaurock know everything there is to know about the Rapture and the Tribulation and the Last Days. They have been members of at least a dozen different churches and have been through what they went through yesterday any number of times. They believe in the general prophecy and whenever they hear about another specific end date, they try to be there. They find that they always cheer the other people up just by turning up and they get a lot of hugs, and that always makes them feel good. They first heard Clara Collins preach and Ben Wosznik sing in North Carolina, where Isaiah was working as an itinerant house painter, and they've been following them around, off and on, ever since. Not much Isaiah can't do. He has been a farmer, a blacksmith, a roofer, a factory worker, a ditch and grave digger, a miner, a garbage collector, a construction worker, a cook, and, even silent as he mostly is, a sometime faith healer. Other things, too, probably. Hard to keep track. He doesn't do any of these things particularly well, though his ability to keep their old Dodge on the road is a miracle by itself, but he's done a bit of everything and so he's valuable to any community like this one. Doesn't have much to say, her Isaiah, but God gave him a mighty engine and she's grateful. Clara has expressed her personal gratitude that they have come here to help out and she says there is a lot for them to do; Isaiah has lent a hand in putting the tents up on the mine hill and Dot has already showed that jellybean preacher's wife a few things about gardening. Dot grew up on a farm in upstate New York; she knows what she's talking about. They will be moving out to the camp this noon during the farewell luncheon for the busloads of old bluehairs from around the country, knowing they cannot be refused. They are penniless, and except for essentials, without possessions, having given up all for Christ, and they will be needed out there. This little house is something of a mess and doesn't smell good, but that's at least half the fault of the rednecks and no reason they should have to clean up after them, so they will just gather up their things and leave it as is, glad to get out of it. It's owned by some rich guy named Suggs who has bought the Brunists their camp and is building them a new church, so it's just pennies out of his pocket to get the place spruced up. In fact, maybe Isaiah can get the job.

Ben asked them to come out early this morning and help strike the tents and clean up the camp after what the bikers did to it, but you can't do everything, not when you have four excitable kids and a husband who can't get off the can until noon. Dot understands the rednecks' complaints—Isaiah is sometimes a nuisance to her, too. At least the camp has separate outdoor privies for ladies and gents, though she has trouble getting through the skinny wooden door. She and Isaiah like Ben better than Clara, who is a bit bossy for their taste, though she has a big church to run, so you have to give her credit, and both of them are two of the flat-out sincerest people she's ever known. They believe. You can feel it in everything they say and do. It was what most drew her and Isaiah to them. But they're both missing something, too, something that lets you know they are in touch with final things. They are, to put it plain, too down-to-earth. They are not *possessed.* That's what this group is mostly, a lot of sincere dedicated people, full of conviction, but without much pentecostal fire. They can do things like build camps, but they can't lift off. They've assembled a good team, though, with singers and preachers and bookkeepers, plenty of hard workers and even some prophets—those two boys don't look much like prophets, but that's probably what they are, and they're smart as a whip. Or two whips. Dot always thought there must be a scientific way to get at this mystery-of-all-mysteries, God being the master scientist after all, and if anyone can puzzle out when the Rapture is like to strike, it's those two, whatever might be their private ways. Dot looks forward to being interviewed by them as she figures she can set them straight on a few matters. That woman Mabel Hall seems like she's on to something, too, though it's not completely Christian. More gypsy-like. Old Goldenthroat from Florida has a great gift of the tongue and can really wind up the faithful, but he is something of a smoothie, you can't quite trust him. He was trying to do some faith healing out on the Mount yesterday but it was a complete washout. Isaiah has had better luck at that, and he can hardly string three intelligent words together. Still, old Hiram has gathered a real churchful around him and they pay their own way, so you can't complain. As for the rich man Suggs, he is like a kind of Joseph of Arimathea, more just part of the background plot than a main actor. He won't even wear the tunic. He might or might not get taken aboard when the Rapture happens.

The nearest thing to a man possessed she has seen is that short, jowly preacher, Abner Baxter. The women around him are pathetic and Young Abner is a spongy dimwit, but Abner Senior is full of beans; or, better said, full of fire. Holy fire. He knows the Bible forwards and backwards and has a voice that could knock down the walls of Jericho. His commie background is worrying to some, but it only shows he has always been on the side of the poor, even before his Christian conversion. He has raised some hard questions out there, questions that still need answering. Just why they are spending all that money on building a church, for example, when the end is coming anyway and there are needy persons who must be fed while they wait for it. He gets people's backs up with his rage and bluster and his biker boys are an embarrassment (Dot understands wild kids, he shouldn't be blamed for them), but he's a man driven by his calling and someone you have to listen to. That's what she and Isaiah think, and a lot of other people are thinking the same way.

Abner Baxter is also the one, even more than Ben and Clara, who seems most set on keeping Bruno in Brunism. His last conversion was a hard one and it has stuck. It's the words of their Prophet that makes these people different, but they don't all get it. Brunism is otherwise like a lot of the evangelical churches Dot and Isaiah have been members of: the Bible as the infallible word of God and its prophecies as future history, the creation of the world in a day by the hand of God, the deity of the Lord Jesus Christ with direct access to Him through prayer, the fall and salvation of man through adult baptism following the repenting of sins, speaking in tongues, faith healing, all that sort of thing that no one can argue with, plus of course a focus on the Rapture, the Tribulation, the millennial reign of Christ, and the Final Judgment, all announced by God in the Bible, all imminent. What Bruno delivers is a step past that. He has announced a whole new era, betokened by baptism by light (Isaiah and Dot favor Abner Baxter's reading of this as baptism by fire and have signed up for it), as though to say, this is it, it's coming now, get ready. And he has opened up a new window onto exactly when and where it's going to happen. You have to believe God is going to get some advance word out to the faithful, and that's what seems to have happened here. It's what the Mount of Redemption and all these dates they've been learning are all about and it's why Dot and Isaiah have come here. Jesus may turn up any minute.

Just who or what Giovanni Bruno was is more of a mystery. A man of the people, yes, from a humble family, who fought his own priests as Jesus did his, and was martyred. Above all, a man filled with a messianic fever—you can see it in the eyes of the pictures of him. But it seems like the real father of this movement was Clara's first husband. Ely Collins had the Holy Spirit in him, saw visions, converted a lot of these people, and was about to prophesy the end of the world, when he suddenly got killed in the mine as if the Antichrist were after him to shut him up. Before he died, though, he apparently passed the Spirit on, or God did, to his younger partner, who people said was like a son to him, so Johnny Brown, as many are calling him, wasn't really Johnny Brown, or Giovanni Bruno either, but more like a living transmitter for the voice of Ely Collins, and through him, of the Almighty Himself. Some say, especially those around Abner Baxter, that their Prophet, whom they call simply Bruno—*Bru-no*—actually died in the mine, too, but that his body, which still had both legs, was allowed to stagger on long enough like a kind of holy zombie to carry Ely Collins' spirit and message to the world. They say there was a bird did all this. Pretty weird, but Dot has known weirder and she likes the story. It adds up, and right now, it suits her.

It's time to get ready to move out to the camp. They'll be doing lunch out there in a couple of hours and there's nothing to eat here, all the food they hauled back from the buffet yesterday having long since vanished, so they can't be late. There will be crowds of hungry people; they'll have to fight for a place at table. No problem. She's good at that. The three kids have left the corner when she wasn't looking and are probably out terrorizing the neighbors' brats again. There aren't many toys in this slummy neighborhood, but they have managed to break or steal just about every one there is, what can you do. There's no tub out at the camp. She'll have one last hot bath and then pop all four in her bathwater for a quick scrubdown before leaving. Maybe she can get Isaiah to take a bath, too, though he doesn't often. She sniffs the air. Little Johnny's filled his pants again. The kid eats like a horse and poops like one, too. At least, when they get raptured, praise the Lord, there'll be no more dirty diapers.

While loading the food they have bought—for the second time—for today's big farewell luncheon into the trunk of Mrs. Edwards' car in the highway supermarket parking lot, the woman asks Clara if she's aware that her daughter may be practicing some form of flagellation. Clara knows what the word means and what this is all about, but the question has caught her by surprise and she asks anyway, and the minister's wife says it was the ancient religious practice of being whipped or whipping oneself as a purification rite. Clara has read about it and heard preachers preach about it. Punishment of the flesh as the corrupt prison of the spirit, the imitation of Christ's own sufferings, the flogging He took from Pontius Pilate, and so on, a kind of extreme penance. Sometimes not just to purge one's own sins, but those of the entire world. But she is skeptical. For the poor, Ely used to say, life is penance enough; we don't need to heap more pain on it. And there's something downright unhealthy about it. It's supposed to be an act of humility, a rejection of the body, but it's mostly just the opposite. And it can be something nastier. Ludie Belle Shawcross has stories. "How do you know about this?" she asks.

"Well, you asked me to speak with her and..."

"Yesterday morning Ben seen her coming from out the woods with Junior Baxter in their tunics and they was blood on them." There. It's out. Since Ben told her about it, she has been trying not to think about it, and therefore thinking about nothing else. She found the tunic before the girl could wash it and it was true. She has tried to talk to Elaine about it, but the child just ducks her head and says nothing. Clara felt herself growing angry—angry and fearful—and she had to back away and try to figure things out, but there was no time to do that; this weekend has taken all her time. Which has been true for too long. She is not the mother she used to be or ought to be. She has become instead the mother of a whole movement, something more important than just any one person, though she never asked for that, and her life is full up to the brim, often leaving her at the outer edge of her energy and abilities. "She sometimes does it to herself. In her room. A belt, I think." Clara is finding it very difficult to talk about this. Her chest feels like there's a big stone in it. She had not meant to tell anyone, but if it has to happen, it's probably best it's Mrs. Edwards. She has experience with young people's problems and maybe can help. "Do you...do you think they're doing anything they shouldn't oughta? I mean, taking their clothes off or...?"

"I don't think so. I've been watching them around the camp and up on the Mount. They never touch each other or even look at each other. It's more like a kind of serious compact between them, not anything romantic. That's my impression. But they are very cruel to each other."

"Cruel?"

"I mean, you know, if you saw blood…"

"Yes." Of course she has known all along, ever since that day on the Mount, what happened there, and then the letters Elaine and Junior have been exchanging and those sounds coming from Elaine's bedroom, often just after a new letter arrived. Knew but didn't want to know, and so kept on not knowing what she knew. She is standing in front of the open trunk, a package of chicken legs in her hands. Soft. Like a baby's thighs. She feels close to tears. "I am so afraid." Ben always says Elaine is a saintly little creature and he trusts God to take care of her, and that may be so, but it doesn't help in figuring what to do. Clara, who has lost her husband and her son, feels like she is losing her daughter, too, and it is tearing at her heart. Since Ely died and all this began, Elaine has been her close companion. They have been approaching the Rapture together hand in hand, prepared to spend an eternity together, but she has also been her anchor to the earth. She is all she has in this world, even if this world soon will be no more, more precious than life itself. "If anything'd happen to Elaine, I don't know as how I could bear it." She can hardly speak. That little Catholic statue that Elaine gave her of Mother Mary with her bleeding heart on her chest, that's what she feels like. What did Mary think when she held her dead son? What was the whole world to her then, and did she care if it was saved or not? "But what can I do?"

"I don't know. But maybe you could take the boy out of it by offering to take his place."

"What?" Clara is so startled by this suggestion she drops the chicken she's been squeezing. "You mean, get whupped half-nekkid by my own daughter?"

She has made a grave mistake talking with this woman.

"Well, I don't think she'll actually want to do that. But letting her think about it might show her what's wrong about doing this with Junior."

"Oh. I see." But she could never do this. Elaine would think she'd gone crazy. She picks up the chicken, packs it in, and slams the trunk closed. "I'll think on it."

Ben is going east soon to sing in some of the churches and maybe, she reasons on the ride back to the camp, she should go along and take Elaine with her. But can she leave the camp with all its problems? And she's worried about Ben, too. When he came back from his rubbish dump run, instead of taking over the cleaning up of the camp and starting on the repairs as he was meant to do, he got his shotgun and left again, looking moody. He'd also forgotten to pick up the day's groceries and replenish the supplies stolen by the biker boys, making it necessary for Clara to call on Mrs. Edwards for this emergency trip. That's so unlike him. And now she has the problem of the Baxters and all the people here with no place to go, and Hiram, who has been so much help, leaving her to solve all these problems herself. "We got a new plan for the camp and all the rest," she says suddenly, not sure just how she's gotten to this matter, though she's been meaning to bring it up since they left the camp, and she feels the minister's wife stiffen at the wheel, "including the new motel Mr. Suggs wants to build, like he showed us last night."

Mrs. Edwards turns the car radio on. "Will Henry said he was going to play some of the songs he recorded yesterday."

Clara feels irritated with the woman but knows there's no reason in it, and at the same time she feels beholden to her and sorry about what she has to say. "It means you and Colin and the boys will have to leave the camp buildings and move on down to the trailer park. We'll be buying campers for you."

"I had so hoped…" Mrs. Edwards says, looking stricken. "My halfway house…" She pulls over on the shoulder and stops for a minute. It's like she's having a hard time getting her breath. Clara wishes now she hadn't told her and wonders if there might be some other way. The poor woman has worked so hard, given so much. She put that cabin together near all by herself, and she has always been so cheerful and caring and only just now she was trying to help with Elaine. "Colin will be...just shattered..." She is sobbing into her sleeve. And now Clara is crying, too. She has tried to hold it back, but she can't. It's just too hard. On the radio Duke L'Heureux, Patti Jo Glover, and the Florida youngsters are singing "Let a Little Sunshine In." Clara is praying to Ely for guidance.

The Warrior Apostles are holed up in an old abandoned one-room farm shack, plotting their next move. In the comicbook Nat and Littleface have been reading, the villain is breaking into the U.S. Mint on the Fourth of July, while everybody's off watching the parade, and stealing all the gold. Nat wants to see what's behind the padlocked doors of the Deepwater mine buildings. He can't wait until the Fourth of July, but all those people will be off the hill today, may be off already. Nat figures it's best to hit the buildings after dark. Everyone will be exhausted and figuring all the excitement is over and they should be easy pickings. They'll approach them by the back route off an overgrown dirt road running alongside the old train rails scouted out Saturday by Juice and Cubano. Meanwhile, if possible, they should not turn over their motors today, draw attention to themselves. Until the job's done, let them think they've left the area. The shack is nearly falling down and is mostly stripped out, the front porch is gone and you can see through two of the walls, but it still has an old wood cookstove. Houndawg has brewed coffee on it, stoking the stove with part of the floor, and now he's frying up a breakfast made out of some of the food they took last night from the camp. Tons of stuff—more than they'll ever finish—including a quart of milk, which Littleface is chugging to the disgust of all, when Ben Wosznik turns up at the back door with a shotgun aimed at Nat's head. "Don't move," the old bird says quietly. "Don't even dare twitch or Nathan Baxter is history." They all have blades and Littleface found two guns at the camp yesterday, though they're probably in his saddlebag. Nat knows Littleface is prepared to die for him, but he shakes his head, staring straight at the old graybeard with the gun. "Though I'm dreadful sorry about what you boys done to poor old Rocky, who never hurt nobody," he says, "I don't aim to do you no harm. But I won't hesitate to shoot y'all dead if need be, and y'know that. You're trespassing on my proppity, and you got a bad reppatation round here, so no one'll blame me." "No shit," snorts Houndawg, grinning. "This your crib?" "I just wanta make one thing clear, Nat Baxter. If you didn't take that gun, and I don't think you did, I don't know how it got in your bag. I didn't put it there, even if that's what your brother's whispering round. Somebody else hadta done it. That's all." Paulie suddenly starts leaping about like he's trying to protest or dance or launch an attack and Ben swings the shotgun onto him. The knives are out. "Don't shoot him," Nat says. "My brother has fits." He goes over to put a knife handle in Paulie's frothing mouth for him to bite down on, and while he's doing that, the old guy quietly backs out the door. Littleface has a gun in each hand and is headed after him, but Nat says, "No, leave the old man be, Face. It's weird how you sometimes have to have somebody tell you what you already know."

Reverend Hiram Clegg, when called upon at the farewell luncheon in the vandalized Meeting Hall, expresses his heartfelt gratitude for the warm hospitality the members of his congregation and those of all the other congregations present have received at the beautiful Brunist Wilderness Camp this past week, shares with Brother Ben the sorrow of all for the tragic death of the noble Rockdust, and announces his congregation's substantial gift for the Brunist Coming of Light Tabernacle Church, a portion of which is to be employed for a memorial stained-glass window honoring Ely Collins, Giovanni Bruno, and Marcella Bruno. Though some might have hoped for prophecy's grand fulfillment on the stirring occasion of this great Brunist family ingathering, they have been witnesses, by way of the miraculous coincidence of the repeated calendar, of the fulfillment of Giovanni Bruno's prophecy of a "Circle of Evenings." He and all his fellow Followers will be returning to Florida with renewed commitment to the faith and hope for the future as designed by God, and, oh yes, they will be back, for their hearts are here with this great movement and its resplendent new home. Here where, one day soon, make no mistake, they shall all meet their dear Lord face to face. "Face to face, we will behold him, far beyond the starry sky; face to face in all His glory, we shall see Him by and by!" He leads them in prayer and in song and feels tears spring to his eyes at the thought of leaving, though in truth he is weary of the bus and motel life and is eager to be home again and away from the camp's problems and its gathering discord.

Hiram feels that Sister Clara has fumbled from time to time through the long hard week just passed, but today she has addressed those problems calmly and clearly, a true leader, and he has been reminded of Brother Ely Collins and his gentle force, which he himself has always tried to emulate but cannot quite. Clara has spoken of the work accomplished and that yet to be done, starting with the repairing and rebuilding of all the camp structures, which means, she said firmly yet kindly, that they will all have to be vacated immediately so that work can start up again tomorrow, the temporary exception being Sister Debra's cabin, which is more or less finished, thanks to her own money and labors, though she too will be moving to a caravan in due time. She has posted the new architectural sketches of the Brunist religious center complex next to the fireplace chimney, pointing out that none of the areas except for the motel and the trailer campsites are to be used for residential purposes. They are beautifully drawn and everyone is impressed. The golden-haired preacher from Lynchburg declares them to be divinely inspired, and this thought is amenned by many, though not by all. Brother John P. Suggs, who is present, announces that he has begun work today on a new campsite about two miles down the road, which should have water and electricity by the end of the week. Meanwhile he has extended by one week the free use of the designated houses in Chestnut Hills, with the stipulation that they be properly cleaned before departure, unless the occupants wish to stay, paying the modest rent. Brother Suggs is applauded. All who remain in the area are expected to help with the camp work at least six hours every day if not otherwise employed and they should let them know their construction and homemaking skills. One midday meal will be provided each day for the workers, Clara explains, but the church's resources have been drained by the week's events, so Followers will have to find their own means of further support.

Will some resist these directives? No doubt, for many who have stayed are helplessly indigent or inclined to radical views, but Hunk Rumpel is seated beside Clara like an unspoken modifier; no one argues with Brother Hunk. Only Abner Baxter cannot hold himself back, it not being in his nature. He speaks without his usual fire and after a generous encomium and an apology for his miscreant sons, but, with a low insistent chant of *"Bru-no! Bru-no! Bru-no!"* behind him, he goes on to observe that the church has not distributed to all what has been given to all. Clara replies calmly that the church has always shared its modest resources with everyone—indeed, though he himself has contributed nothing over the intervening years, she has often sent him support for his own mission—but now they must be careful to husband what limited funds remain, for they are faced with many serious expenses. If he is referring to the money earmarked for the Coming of Light Tabernacle Church, they are not free to use that for any other purpose or it will be taken back, a claim that Hiram supports though he is not certain that it is true. The bishop of the Eastern Seaboard and newly appointed director of the National Brunist Media Organization rises to quote from First Corinthians: "I beseech you, brethren, by the name of our Lord Jesus Christ, that ye all speak the same thing, and that there be no divisions among you," and he too is applauded. What with that large gift they have received, Hiram's own collection on behalf of the temple can be used partly, he feels, for his own church expenses and those associated with his duties as the president of the International Council of Brunist Bishops; consequently, he has turned over a little less than half of the sum to Clara, with the intention of forwarding all of it to her should it be needed. This morning he has seen to the temporary burial of Harriet McCardle in Randolph Junction and all the legal paperwork that it required; thanks to those documents, her own wealth and that of her husband will also reach the church in various installments, based on the health and longevity of the surviving spouse, though Hiram has not spelled this out yet to Ben and Clara. Mrs. McCardle has been buried in a simple grave with plans to move her eventually to the Brunist burial ground on the Mount of Redemption, for which Hiram has promised to cover the expenses. A three-line notice of her death in hospital by natural causes ("an elderly visitor to our area") has been discreetly announced in the Randolph Junction newspaper, placed there by the town mayor.

Now, Clara rings her water glass with her spoon and once more thanks all the brothers and sisters from around the country for making the long and arduous journey to join them here this week. She wishes them well on their homeward journeys, and she asks that the young people come forward and join Brother Ben and Brother Duke and Sister Betty and Sister Patti Jo in leading them all in singing "Will the Circle Be Unbroken," and they all stand because it feels right to stand and take one another's hand or put one's arm around a shoulder: "Will the circle be unbroken, by and by, Lord, by and by," they sing, and Hiram's heart is full and his cheeks are running with joyous tears…

*"One by one the seats were empty,*
*One by one they went away,*
*Now my family, they are parted,*
*Will they meet again someday?"*

*"Will the circle be unbroken,*
*By and by, Lord, by and by?*
*There's a better home a-waitin',*
*In the sky, Lord, in the sky!"*

# BOOK II

And when he had opened the second seal,
I heard the second beast say, Come and see.
And there went out another horse that was red:
and power was given to him that sat thereon
to take peace from the earth,
and that they should kill one another:
and there was given unto him a great sword.

*—The Book of Revelation 6.3-4*

# II.I

## Thursday 23 April – Saturday 25 April

"It don't make none a your common sense, Ted, and you know it. This penny ante town can't afford to fix the potholes or pick up the garbage—how we gonna get into a high stakes headbutt with old man Suggs over a useless goddamned artificial bump in the ground that ain't even genuine real estate?"

"Land is only useless, Maury, when it's not being used. It has electric and phone lines already in place, train rails and usable structures. With the flat land the town owns below it, it has industrial park potential, could be developed for housing or for a coal-burning power plant. Might even be turned into a profitable recreational facility." It angers him to have to wheedle with this irresponsible third-rate shoe salesman who is only the mayor because Ted has made him so. It angers him even more to think about spending so much money on that worthless piece of land, for which he is only inventing improbable uses. But he hates to get beat. If they lose the mine land and hill to Pat Suggs and those religious fanatics, they'll never be rid of them. He has heard rumors they plan to build on it and that Suggs may be buying up other property nearby. Creating a complex. His voluptuous doodles show signs of anxiety and irritation. Swirly lines flying off in all directions. Ted glances out onto the bank floor, catches her watching him;

she looks away. "And the city doesn't have to pay a nickel up front. You can float a bond and meanwhile the bank will loan the city the entire amount at bank rate."

"Nah, I'll never be able to sell this to the council. Let them fundamentalist loonies have their hill, Ted. Who the fuck cares? They're even bringing in a bit of business. If they turn up in town, we'll simply shoot 'em."

"They're already in town, Maury. Suggs is letting them occupy some of his prefabs in Chestnut Hills."

"Don't I know it. The handful of neighbors who still live out there are bellyaching about the filth and noise and overcrowding. It ain't clear who's paying the electricity and fuel bills. There are health and fire hazards. I've asked the chief to shut that operation down this week. By the way, Dee mentioned this morning there'd been a break-in in some of the mine buildings out there."

"Really? What got taken?"

"Dee don't know, says it ain't his jurisdiction, but figures it was more like vandalism than theft. Someone heard motorcycles, so it's probably them same shits who was throwing body parts around last Sunday. Unless the mine owners robbed theirselves to collect the fucking insurance."

"I'll see what I can find out."

"I am disappointed, Mr. Puller. I had supposed this matter would have been taken care of by now."

"Well, they been laying low, Mr. Suggs. And until now we never really had nothing on them to take them in."

"Was the slaughter of Mr. Wosznik's dog nothing? Their outrageous behavior Sunday at the hill? The attack on Cavanaugh's car? They probably do not even have proper licenses. I know for certain that at least one of them is too young. And some of their motorcycles may have been stolen. Have you checked into that? No, you have waited too long, Mr. Puller, and now we have a serious problem. The theft is undermining my negotiations with the owners for the purchase of the mine. They refer to those bikers as 'my people.' This will not do."

"They're at the top of our agenda now."

"I should very much hope so, Mr. Puller. We also need your assistance at the church camp. I promised them protection against threatened assaults until they could organize their own security, and I expect you to provide that. Our Patriots organization will be loaning them arms, and perhaps you can make the proper arrangements. You and Mr. McDaniel can provide training. But we have to be cautious. We don't want to put guns in the hands of unreliable people. And there is no need for powerful weapons, just enough to serve as a deterrent and protect the periphery."

"I can do that."

"And we have a possible problem of trespass. The rules of the campsite prohibit use of the main buildings for personal residences, but some of the persons who have come here from elsewhere are presently occupying them. If they do not leave voluntarily, they may have to be removed forcibly."

"My old faceboss, you mean. Just let me know."

"I will do so. Now either lock that motorcycle gang up or run them out of here. They are a dangerous threat to law and order. I expect results, Mr. Puller."

"Dave Osborne?"

"You got him."

"Dave, this is Ted Cavanaugh over at the bank. How's it going over there at the old footwear emporium?"

"I'm having a hard time beating away the traffic. Sold a pair of shoelaces just yesterday. Or maybe the day before. You calling for a look at the books?"

"No, this is something else, Dave. There's been a break-in out at Deepwater. From your time out there as night mine manager, what do you figure might have got taken?"

"Can't imagine anything worthwhile left behind."

"What was usually kept there?"

"Tools. Lamps and helmets. Tags. Electrical gear, that sort of thing."

"Any weapons?"

"I don't think so. Unless you call old mine picks a weapon. The mine managers on duty got issued a pistol, but I don't think it's there anymore."

Meaning, he took it home with him. "That's it?"

"Far as I can remember. Maybe some dynamite."

"Dynamite?"

"Yeah. For shot firing in the old days. It was how coal was loosened from the face. A few years back, we switched to compressed air. A lot safer. We probably got rid of the dynamite, though I remember seeing it on inventories."

"Dynamite. Holy mackerel."

"And then Jim got hit by a dead bird and ended up on TV. They're calling it the Headless Annunciation. God help us if he's pregnant." It is Sally's mother, spreading her daily evangel. "Well, you know Jim, Em. Always in the wrong place at the right time."

Em does know Jim. Back in high school her mom and dad and the couple who are now the Wetherwaxes used to double date. Only, with each other's present mates. Who came out best? It's a draw. Though Archie at least has a real job working for the phone company. They used to park out at the lakes and go for a moonlight swim together. Or anyway they did that once. The family legend. Now the two women talk about their men like pets they keep and clean up after. Sally writes: They were just having fun playing around in offbeat short stories, when suddenly they found themselves in the middle of a hackneyed genre novel. Written by the dim-witted little town whose covers they're clapped in.

"Jim doesn't know when to keep his mouth shut, especially if it's past eleven in the morning and he's had a couple. And Ted's got no sense of humor. Have I said that before?" Will she be able to write her own story? Will it be any better? She thumbs through the notebook to find her drawing of the sleeping prince, sketches in a black phone receiver by his ear, and above it writes: Hello? Hello…? "I suppose you heard about those bikers attacking Ted's car? He was coming back from a business meeting, and when he told Jim about it, Jim said it sounded like a gang of typical wildhair bankers to him and asked whether Ted noticed if anyone he'd been meeting with had any tattoos, and Ted blew up at him, called him a stupid goddamned you-know-what. Jim still doesn't know why, but since then he's started drinking at ten instead of eleven."

Telephones, she writes. The disembodied self as sown voice. Which is more real, speaker or spoken? The spoken can remain, the speaker cannot. Thus: back to gestures, foreskins.

"Yes, I know, Em, Archie can put it away, too. But at least he has to wait until after he's stopped climbing telephone poles." Once, when she had scarlet fever, Sally had to lie all day in the dark, her only entertainment the radio. The voices she heard seemed to hover in the dark like real presences. It's like that sometimes reading a novel. That weird thing called voice. There but not there, hovering over the text. But nothing is disembodied. That's a religious idea. Writing, radio, telephony: It's all just a vaudeville act. Like the first phone conversation. Come here. I want you. A novel in five words. "Yes, I heard that. She's got Wes penned up in her garage. What do you think's going on there? Oh yeah? Tell me, I'm all ears…" As an image would that be two big ears or a cluster of them, like that fire god who her anthro prof said was called "the thousand-testicled one"? Sitting bored in class, she tried to draw that, couldn't. A hundred maybe, max. Small ones.

"It has been a long time since the last inventory, Ted, but the mine owners promised to check it. They are probably nervous about it and may try to cover it up."

"Nervous?"

"Well, they still own the mine and could be held responsible for leaving such hazardous material unsecured. Especially if it were to be employed in a crime."

"That could be useful, Nick. The city is backing out of the purchase of the hill, at least at the current asking price, so we may have to try to stop this sale some other way."

"We have grounds for any number of temporary injunctions. I think we can keep them from taking the hill over for a year at least. Don't know, though, if we can keep them off it at the same time."

"And what about the sources of the cult's money? Where is it all coming from? Have you looked into our own church accounts?"

"I have. Mrs. Edwards seems to have funneled most of the church's income from the sale back into the camp. Presumably for a Presbyterian halfway house for troubled teenagers, which she's allegedly building out there. Should be easy to go after her. Getting the money back is another matter. She has also cleaned out her husband's accounts. Completely illegal. He could sue her."

"Wes is not part of the real world, Nick. I'm still working on getting him committed. For his own good as much as ours. But there's talk about their having the wherewithal to build a church on top of that hill. Where the hell did they get it? Can't be from the camp sale. Suggs again?"

"Well, I've hesitated to tell you, but you may be buying it for them."

"What do you mean?"

"I was asking myself the same question: How can they pay for this? So I went scouting around through accounts, looking for large withdrawals and I think I found what I was looking for. It's bad news, Ted. It's your wife."

"What? Irene?"

"Over the past few months she has been moving her funds into a separate account in a bank up in the city. And from there it has almost certainly gone straight into the cult account."

"But she's bedridden! How—?"

"Well, she has a telephone. Gave a corporate tax lawyer up in the city power of attorney, and he set it up for her. Know a guy named Thornton? Edgar Thornton?"

"Yeah, I know him. Thorny. Irene's old college beau before she met me. A Deke."

"A what?"

"Fraternity guy. Different fraternity. Jesus. I can't believe this. Can we put a restraining order on the transfer? Non compos mentis, and all that?"

"Probably too late. It's already gone. Some of it may have been handed over in cash."

"Or freeze the Brunist accounts?"

"We can try. It'll be a painful thing, you know."

"It's already painful, Nick. Right this minute, I'm having trouble breathing."

"Eh, ciao, bello. Howza lawr'n-order racket?"

"Had to shoot a stray dog week before last. How's things up in the big city?"

"Ah, you know, Demetrio, wine, women, and song, the usual stronzata. I miss the old neighborhood."

"Sure you do."

"Ascolta, cugino, I'm calling about a hometown boy there, see if I can't do him a favor since I owe him one. Un buon ragazzo, Charlie Bonali, Vince's boy—you know him?"

"I know him."

"He's a little hard up just now and could use a job. I thought you might have something there for him."

"Well, there is a police job opening up here, I think, but—"

"Now ain't that amazing! I thought there might be. And you got problems. You got some lunatic Jesus freaks down there."

"They're outside town and so far they mostly been only bothering each other. But—"

"But you never know, right? Those people are completely pazzo!"

"They're a bit weird."

"I know, I gotta deal every day here with spics and sambos and dumb hillbillies, all of 'em mostly bombed outa their dim little melons, either with dope or that yelling they call praying. Count yourself lucky! But you'll like Charlie. He's big and he's brave and he takes no shit from nobody."

"Well, he can come in for a—"

"Except you'n me, right? Shit from you'n me he takes like ice cream."

"There are other guys running this town. I don't have the final say who—"

"Right, you got that tinhorn ex-shoe salesman down there, what's his name, Cass-hole?"

"Yeah, the mayor."

"I hear he's been muscling in on our neighborhood, squeezing our people with some kinda fucking protection racket."

"He's been campaigning."

"Well, he won't be doing that no more, capitano. And you just tell him who you want. I got a feeling he'll be open to suggestion."

"I don't know. The mayor's got some powerful backers. The bank, for example. And the bank has recently hired a sharp new lawyer who seems to have his eye on just about everything."

"Nicky Minicozzi, you mean. Yeah, we call him Mini-cazzo. Nicky does what we tell him. Hang loose, cugino. Go to Mass. Pray for our souls."

"Sure, Dad. If it's important. I was hoping to stay up here at the fraternity house through graduation. There are a lot of parties going on this weekend. People I may never see again."

"I know, Tommy. But I do need your help."

"Is Mom worse?"

"Well, yes and no. But I've had to fire the home care nurse and the new one can't start until next week, so I'm all alone here."

"What did she do? Steal something?"

"I…I guess you could say so."

"Dad, you don't sound good. Are you all right? Dad?"

"I know. It's all right. Angela told me. She said she'd helped you find the new person." All week long she has been thinking about leaving. Ever since the night his car was attacked and he got home and found his wife so ill. It was her fault, really, and she has the feeling others think so, too. There is a scandal of some sort brewing and she is afraid of it. But now, just hearing his voice (he is apologizing for missing their traditional Thursday night together; he seems quite shaken and says he needs her more than ever, and she can hear the need and how much older his voice sounds, and it tugs at her), she knows she can't go. Not yet. Night of a full moon. She'll eat alone in her room, unable to bear the smirks of the motel staff. "Tomorrow's out, too, damn it," he says. "But Tommy's coming down from university, so Saturday looks good. We can take that drive we talked about." He looked absolutely stricken while talking on the phone in his office today, and when she brought in some documents for him to initial, she asked if something was wrong. He nodded, then shook his head sadly, as if it were all beyond him. Her heart was racing but he assured her it had nothing to do with her. He has asked her, more than once, about becoming the new Chamber of Commerce executive director, saying that he needed her business and personal relations skills in that job, her youthful enthusiasm, and, well, yes, her beauty, and though they might see a little less of each other, it would spare them the awkwardness of working together at the bank, but she has always made it clear that when her internship at the bank is over she is leaving. And then they both are sad for a while. "Hello? Stacy? Is Saturday okay?" She felt guilty about keeping him late that night, but she just couldn't let him go. Somehow it seemed like the last night, and at the door, when he was kissing her good night, she knelt and pulled his pants and shorts down and there went another half hour, and he probably didn't even know as he pressed his fingers into her hair that she was crying a little. She felt so awful the next day when she heard, she even packed her bags. But then just sat staring at them. The only god she has left from her Quaker childhood is love and he's not always a friendly god, sometimes even kind of scary, more like a demon, really. When little Angela asked her what she believed in, she joked that she was a holyroller for love, but what she didn't say was that if religious faith was a kind of dangerous madness, so too was love. "Hello? Are you there…? Stacy…?" "Yes. All right. Saturday then." "I'm doing all I can." "I know. I love you. And thanks for the flowers. They're beautiful."

"Mom? I've decided to come home for the weekend to see you. We're having a special Friday night supper tonight at the fraternity. One of my profs is a guest. I'll start down right after. How are you doing?"

"Well, I'm dying, my dear. Other than that I'm just fine."

"I tried to call last night, but the phone was busy or else just disconnected. I suppose you were asleep?"

"Yes, I am at peace in the Lord, Tommy. My soul has been saved and I rest easy."

"Where'd you learn to talk like that, Mom? It doesn't sound like you."

"It is not me, Tommy, not the me you knew. I have been born again. I didn't know what that meant. Now I do. I am someone new. I surprise even myself."

"Mom, what's going on? Dad seems very upset about something."

"Oh, you know your father, Tommy. If the world doesn't go according to plan, *his* plan, he gets all hot under the collar."

"Why did the home care nurse get fired?"

"Mrs. Filbert is a pious kind-hearted Christian woman. She has helped me through dreadful times in a way that no one else has and I miss her horribly. He has sent some silly little girl over here today in her place who talks to me like I'm three years old. I think your father did it for spite."

"He said you did something bad."

"I followed my own lights, as he likes to say and has done for over thirty years, without concern for me or anyone else. I am preparing to meet my Maker, Tommy, and He spoke to me and directed me to free myself of all earthly encumbrances, and I have been doing so."

"And me, Mom? Am I an earthly encumbrance, too?"

"All that is body is, Tommy. Not your spirit. Which I love more than you can know and hope to have near me through all eternity. The world isn't going to last much longer, which means at least you may not have to suffer what I am suffering. But you may not have much time. You must always keep Jesus in your heart, Tommy, and...(No, dear. Not now.)"

"Who's there with you now, Mom?"

"Groovy, Angie! But, hey, wasn't Tommy here just last *week*?"

"He says he simply can't stay *away* from me! He's just *crazy* about me, Ramona!" Angela knows this because of the way he looks at her, especially when gazing down upon her just before That Moment, his eyes ablaze then with adoration and awe (she is so beautiful! she *knows* this!) and tenderness and passionate desire. Tommy! She's so madly in love she's just wet all the time! "He *told* me so!"

"Oh, Angie, you're *so* lucky! Tommy's a fabulous hunk! And rich! And you mean you're really calling from his *house?*"

"Call me back if you like, and see for yourself. And I'll be here tomorrow, too." Tomorrow—Ramona knows this, but she is too stupid and shallow and jealous ever to understand the true deep meaning—she and Tommy will make love in this beautiful house (probably even under this very ceiling: she is calling from the phone in his bedroom, poking about, sniffing at things) which may one day be hers. April 25: She has already marked it on her sacred calendar. She's desperately close to her period, and that's scary, but hopefully it will not come until Monday. "Poor Tommy! He's hurting so! He needs me now." He's such a bad boy, though. Last weekend on the way to the motel, a used tampon dropped out on her lap. He made up some wild excuse, saying he'd loaned his car to a fraternity brother up at university who must have put it there as a joke, and he became very sweet in his embarrassment, but all Angela could think was: Did he have sex with a girl during her period? That sounds pretty gross, but if things go wrong this weekend, well, if he likes that, she might give it a try. "I still haven't got over my own mom passing away, so I know what Tommy's going through." Even if Mrs. Cavanaugh is really cranky and always complaining—nothing like her own mom who, even when she was dying, kept wanting to help somehow, and never said a word about her pain or fear, just how much she loved her. Thank goodness the old lady is asleep most of the time, lying there in her wrinkly old gown and plastic shower cap, or else looking through her photo albums with her little wire-framed glasses on the end of her skinny white nose. "When Tommy's father came to ask me yesterday to help out, it was just such a *thrill*! Especially when he said he specifically wanted a *Catholic* home care person. It was like he was reaching out to me, you know? I suddenly felt so much *closer* to him. He's a wonderful man, so kind, who has suffered so much, and he's the best employer in the world. I just *love* him!" On Tommy's shelves are his trophies and a personalized bowling ball and some framed photos, including a delicious one in his high school basketball uniform, holding a ball at his hip, which must have been taken about the same time they first did it. "Tommy's mother keeps asking for the other woman who was here. A Baptist-type nurse who did something bad, I don't know what."

"I bet she stole something. Those people are like that." Angela wants to steal that photo. Maybe tomorrow she'll ask him for it. He's so cute! She was just a dumb little kid then, but so was he. They are both so much more mature now. At the bottom of his socks drawer, she finds a stack of men's magazines and, while Ramona rattles on about the stupidity and immorality of Baptist hillbillies and all the craziness out on the mine hill last weekend, she thumbs through them. She recognizes the poses: Tommy asked her to pose the same way for his Polaroid. She loves him, so how could she say no? It made her feel funny, though, like her skin was not her skin but something she was actually *wearing.* But she could see it made him awfully excited, and it excited her, too, and she took pictures of him (he is so gorgeous!) and he used a timer to take pictures of them together, making love—"I know one should always keep one's dignity," her older friend Stacy Ryder once told her, "but really it's not much use in a love affair…"—and then he let her tear them all up and burn them after, all except one of them together, just kissing (you can't see the hands), which she let him keep to remember her by when he was away at college. "My dad said there's some really sick things going on out there, stuff you wouldn't believe! And those people are everywhere, the fields are full of them like herds of animals! I even saw somebody this morning who looked just like your brother Charlie, only he was ten years older."

"That probably *was* Charlie. He's back. He's going bald. He made some bad friends up in the city and I think he got into trouble, but you'd never know it. Swaggering around, snapping his fingers, acting the big cheese. He's already got into a fight with Dad and eaten up all the food in the house." She is, she knows, as beautiful as any of these women in the magazines, though she sees that her pubic hair is thicker than most of theirs; she will trim it, maybe make a little design. Tommy would like that.

"Angie, now that things are so cool for you and Tommy, can I have Joey Castiglione?"

"Sure, Ramona. He means nothing to me." She can be generous; she's not throwing anything away. Joey would never go for fat Ramona Testatonda. Ramona thinks she's such a big deal just because her dad is a town cop, but Joey Castiglione will still be waiting for his Angela a hundred years from now. She didn't let Tommy have his way in everything. She knew how to be both firm and gentle when she had to draw the line, like when he wanted to take a picture of her using the bathroom, for example. Absolutely not, Tommy Cavanaugh. Though he did take a picture of himself up close when he was in her other place and she wasn't looking—how could she be, on her hands and knees?—which was just too gross. No picture like *that* in these magazines. She asked her older friend at the bank if she ever let people take pictures when they're intimate like that, and Stacy said no, so maybe she has gone too far, though Stacy smiled and said anything really is all right when you're in love. And oh yes, she is! Her whole body is shaking and oozing with it.

"Bernice said he just stormed in last night and throwed her and Florrie out, Mr. Suggs. Said they weren't nothing but common thieves and they'd end up in jail. Bernice is a storyfier, but I credit her account. And his dying wife there in the room, Bernice said, whilst he was throwing his wrath around. She said the poor lady was brave and kept right on smiling, but her lip was a-quivering like a shook rag, and Bernice said she felt like her heart would break. I hope we done the right thing."

"Of course we have, Clara. The two women have saved another soul and found a way to do God's will in spite of that evil man. He will try to get the money back now, but I think we have made it safe for the Lord. Are you calling from the new office phone?"

"Yes, and we bless you for that, Mr. Suggs. It is so important to our work. I have used it to call other preachers and let them know we wish to live in peace among them like fellow Christians and I have invited them all to visit us and share in our services."

"It is good what you are doing, for we must, as they say, keep the dogs at bay. Which reminds me to ask: Has Abner Baxter left the camp premises yet?"

"No, they're all still here. And some others have been moving in. Using cabins that ain't even got electricity yet nor roofs nor windows neither, and setting their tents up in the empty spaces and out around the old fire grills. Folks are camped out in the Meeting Hall, too. And there are more tents over on the Mount of Redemption. Ben keeps making them move, but soon as he's gone, they pop up again. Mostly, though, they been behaving in a helpful and friendly if somewhat stubborn manner. The camp is still a dreadful sight from what them bad boys done to it, and most everbody's pitching in to fix it up again—even Abner."

"This won't do, Clara. If you need workers, I can send you some. Those people were all to have been gone by Tuesday. It is already Friday."

"Well, they ain't no place for them to go. They are waiting for the new campsite."

"They will find a place if you are firm enough. When the new campsite is ready, they will have no choice. I have spoken with Sheriff Puller. But for their own good and the good of the community, they must leave now. You will regret this delay."

"That may be, but it is a hard thing to do."

"That's a laughable offer, Ted."

"Well, think about it. We have some new problems here. Questions about the sources of the cult's money, whether or not there might be fraud and embezzlement involved. The mine's responsibility in leaving dangerous material unguarded—"

"Our inspectors are on the way. We're sure that stuff was removed years ago. And even if it wasn't, it has probably deteriorated over time."

"And if it hasn't? It's the sheriff's belief that the break-in was done by some of Suggs' people—"

"The sheriff said some renegade bikers."

"For all I know they are part of Sheriff Puller's illegal vigilantes. But there's also a rumor going around that the owners might have robbed themselves to collect on the insurance. I understand an insurance agent has been around asking."

"We didn't do that, Ted."

"All I'm saying is there's a rumor. It will have to be investigated."

"It won't go anywhere."

"It will take time."

* * *

John P. Suggs rocks back in his swivel chair in his South County Coal Company office, his thumb hooked in his suspenders, staring out upon the monumental landscape of narrow mounds and deep furrows that he has created. The spokesman for the Deepwater Number Nine owners has just told him that the city has raised its offer. There are some provisos, but they're tempted to go with it. Pat suspects a bluff. They're in trouble on the theft. He has had Puller call the company about it, asking difficult questions. He decides to take a chance and lower his offer by a third. The spokesman says that makes no sense in the face of the city's improved bid, and adds that there are rumors of fraud and embezzlement behind the Brunists' funds. "This is *my* money," John P. Suggs says, "and you know my money is good. What I'm offering you is still a lot more than the mine is worth. You'd better grab it while you can." There is a long pregnant pause. John P. Suggs smiles out upon his domain. He was right.

"Well, let us talk with your lawyers."

"I don't have any lawyers. You talk to me."

"Hi, Sally? This is Billy Don, you know, out here at the camp and all that? We just got a new phone line into the office and I'm, like, testing it out."

"Well, hey, Billy Don, it works."

"Yes, well, hah, I thought I'd give you a call, see if we could maybe sort of get together for a minute. There's something I need to…"

"Sure. Beautiful day. You want me to come out—?"

"No! No, I have to make a Randolph Junction mail run and pick up some, you know, typing ribbons in Tucker City. Can you meet at the drugstore there in about, like, an hour?"

On this beautiful day, the beautiful man, sitting all alone in his dingy bank office and feeling old and ugly, hangs up the phone, crumples his squiggly doodles and baskets them. Stacy has checked out of the motel. No forwarding address. Somehow, inexplicably, he has lost her, even as he has lost his wife, who has turned against him, betrayed him, and his town, which is abandoning him. As though the switchboard were fused, connections severed. A couple of nights ago, in the still of the night, he heard the bikers, or thought he did, and their distant grumble seemed to presage a nightmare, and that nightmare has come to pass. He decides to call home and check on the young Bonali girl, who is staying with Irene for the day, but the phone is busy. He imagines that Irene must be talking to that damned butt-in Edgar Thornton, so he calls him up in the city to see if his line is busy too. It is not. The secretary hooks him up immediately.

"Ah…Thorny, you're there. How are you? Ted Cavanaugh here, voice out of the past."

"Hello, Teddy. I thought you might be calling."

"Thorny, Irene is dying."

"She told me she was not well. She is a lovely lady. I am very sorry to hear it."

"I mean, she's not herself, goddamn it. You've helped her to do a very bad thing, Thorny."

"You mean give her money to a church? In my book, Teddy, that's a beautiful and virtuous act."

"Yeah, well, all right, to her own church maybe. But these people are not her people."

"Evidently they are now. I believe she has found a peace with them she did not find with her people, as you call them. No doubt meaning your—"

"Thorny, you have gone behind my back and taken advantage of a sick woman who is on a lot of drugs and mostly out of it, damn it. That was *our* money, not hers alone. I will hit you for your fees and all that you siphoned away, and goddamn it, I'll strip you of your license as well."

"I have spoken at length with Irene. She is a relatively young woman and plainly in command of her faculties. The accounts, perhaps for evasive tax reasons, were solely in her name so the transfers were legal. And I did not charge a fee. I did it as an old friend."

"Oh hell. But, hey, Thorny, aren't I an old friend, too?"

"Teddy, you were never a friend. Take care. I suggest you open your heart to Jesus and prepare for His imminent return and the final judgment which will follow."

"Omigod..."

"Well, that's a start, I guess."

"I am mighty beholden to you, Bernice, for gittin' summa that pennysilly for my boy to cure his nasty infliction. If Jewell'd found out, he'da got a awful whuppin'."

"Well, boys'll be boys, Florrie, and they's scads a wicked ladies ready to prey upon them. And upon older men, too, who should oughta know better, like that disgraceful reprobate we useta work for. You just *know* there's a woman somewheres.

"You mean, Mr. Cavanaugh?"

"Nobody else. Every week, come Thursday night, he's off and away, you seen that, and some other nights, too, when he gets a surge. He says he's on business, but there's only one sorta business gets done that time of day. You can smell it on him when he gets back worse than Ahasuerus's harem. His tie hanging like something used up and strange hairs all over him. And that poor knotty thing a-dying away in there in plain sight, her angel wings already half sprouted—you can see them poking out her shoulder blades."

"Who y'reckon—?"

"Not who, Florrie, but how many? Men like that, there's never only one. If he does get contentious, I figure we got something to bemean him with, though I misdoubt he's the sort who'd give a care."

"Oh, I wouldn't wanta cause no trouble, Bernice."

"Well, Florrie, sometimes like Judith, we just got to take history in our own hands."

"Oh no! You don't reckon on cuttin' off his head!"

"Oh, Florrie, course not! Why do you always take things so literal? Judith was maybe a smidge harsh, but the point is when she and her people were being persecuted by this rich powerful enemy, she just didn't set back and let it happen. She knew how to be a hero and save her people, and we have to try and do the same!"

"We want to thank you for joining us at the Mount of Redemption last Sunday, Mr. Castle, even if your purposes was not entirely friendly. But, as I'm sure you witnessed, we are peaceful folk; it's them others who's acting badly. We don't ask for your pertection, but we do ask for your understanding."

"Yeah, well, we'll do what we can, Mrs. Collins. Thank you for your call. (Hey, sweetheart, next time ask who's calling before you hand me the fucking phone, awright?)" Click.

"Hey, Nick. Wanted to catch you before you left for the afternoon."

"Beautiful day out there, Ted. You should be out on the course."

"I'd probably just ram my wedge up the butt of the first guy who told me it was a beautiful day. Right now, I have to head home to relieve the kid from the bank who's saint-sitting. I got nowhere with Thornton, Nick. What have you learned?"

"Well, the Brunist bank accounts are pretty fat but don't show large recent deposits. They've probably opened up another account somewhere for your wife's money. They've got phones out at the camp now. We can keep closer tabs."

"What? You mean tap them?"

"I think I can arrange it. I understand they have also instituted armed guards. And the rumor is that Suggs has closed a deal on the mine."

"Damn. Can we do anything about slowing that down?"

"Already in the works. One weakness Suggs has: he doesn't trust lawyers. We can run circles around him."

"And that motorcycle gang?"

"They've either left the area or are lying low. Not much we can do until they're caught, and that's something the county or the state will have to do."

"I've talked with the governor. Not very helpful. Says the sheriff seems to be doing his job. Maybe the possibility of stolen dynamite will wake him up." Not much hope of that. The mine owners will have got to the gutless bullshitter with their own soporific story. Elections are won, he once said, not by what you do, but by what you don't do. "Speaking of sleepwalkers, I ran into Jim Elliott on the street. Maybe he said something about a beautiful day, too. I'm afraid I really leaned into him. I may even have fired him."

"I know you've got a problem there."

"I was hoping to find some young blood for that Chamber of Commerce job, try to get this town moving again, but so far no candidates."

"The young woman here at the bank?"

"Doesn't want it." He stands, relieving the constriction in his chest. "You once mentioned the notion of a city manager instead of what we have now. I've been thinking about that. Of course, we couldn't dump the mayor without a lot of citywide restructuring. But I think the city council is fed up with him. There's even talk of an investigation. We might start with a job that relieved him of a lot of his day-to-day operational duties—taking care of the finances, for example—and adding in the duties of the Chamber executive director under some new title. A kind of take-over, make-over role. Would you be interested in that, Nick?"

"You mean as a job? I don't know..."

"Well, think about it. And what you'd need to make it worth your while. Meanwhile, I'd like to try to revive the old Common Sense Committee somehow. This was something we used back when the Brunist cult started up here. Involved the whole community. We need something like it again. Needs a new name, though. West Condoners for a Better Future, or something."

"Out of the Past and Into the Future."

"Something like that."

"A New Order for West Condon."

"Better."

"The acronym would be NOWC. Like Now West Condon."

"Hey, I like it. Maybe a New Outlook."

"Or New Opportunities."

"I think you have it, Nick. Let's call it that. New Opportunities for West Condon. NOW West Condon. Brilliant. I was going to be out of town tomorrow, but it looks like I'll be staying around. I'll get started on it."

"Don't call it that, Tommy. It sounds more like merchandise or something."

"What should I call it?"

"It doesn't have to have a name, Tommy. Just think about it."

"I do all the time. It drives me crazy. What do you call mine?"

"I've never called it anything."

"Do you like it?"

"Of course I do. I love it. I love everything about you, Tommy."

"Sure, but what about my ass? Go ahead, I can take it. Tell me what you really think."

"Your mom might be listening in, Tommy!"

"Oh yeah. How's she doing?"

"Well, it's very difficult for her, but your mom's the sweetest person. I just love her. It's so sad she's so ill."

"She's sounding pretty weird to me."

"Your dad says that's because of the people who were taking care of her before. That's why he asked me for a Catholic person and I found Concetta for him."

"I wish she could make it this weekend. I'm going to be missing a lot of good parties up here."

"Well, but you have me."

"Right. I know. You and your beautiful ass! I can hardly wait!"

"Please, Tommy..."

"In fact I'm looking at it right now. Gorgeous!"

"In your imagination, you mean?"

"No, in a photo. You know those Polaroids we took in the motel on that crazy end-of-the-world night?"

"Yes, but we tore all those up and burned them."

"All except one."

"The one of us kissing."

"Yeah, well, I switched. I kept the one where I asked you to say cheese upside down."

"Oh no! Not the one on my hands and knees!"

"Right! End of the world!"

"Tommy Cavanaugh, you bring that photo with you when you come and we'll tear it up while I watch!"

"I don't know if I can. My fraternity brothers asked for it for their meeting room, something to, you know, bow down to, and since I'm the chapter chaplain, how could I refuse?"

"Oh Tommy. You're such a tease. Do you love me?"

"Yeah, sure. You know that."

"Come home, Tommy. Skip the party. Come quickly."

Somewhere a phone is ringing, beckoning her from afar. A voice like that of Jesus. She wishes to answer the call—for eternity may depend upon it—but she cannot. She has been rendered immobile, her body existing in a different dimension, she rising from it, but inertly afloat, unseen. There is a problem. What's the matter? Something to do with her ability to transmit and receive. The lines are crossed, and there is nothing she can do. The Bible in her hands is like a phone book, its verses alphabetized and scattered among the white and yellow pages, hiding the destination she seeks. You know the father, someone says. She does, but even so she cannot find his name. How could she? Her eyes are closed. If, disembodied, she has eyes. She wants only to rise into the light. There must be an opening. If only she could reach the switchboard. But the switchboard has melted. Did she say goodbye? It doesn't matter.

"Resign? What do you mean 'resign'? Damn it, you can't do that, Maury." Ted doesn't like to be called at home. The ring can awaken Irene, doped up as she is, and set off a bad night. "I'm going to try to get you some help, but we can't have any instability while we have all these problems. What's the matter?"

"Well, for starters, some asshole up in the city with a scary accent is trying to stop me from campaigning in Dagotown."

"You get his name?"

"Are you kidding? I don't even *wanta* know it." When Castle speaks, the phone can be set down in one room and heard in the next. "And wait till you see our likely next cop. Know Charlie Bonali?"

"I know his father. Should be all right." He's had too much to drink and dozed off in front of the television, this jarring intrusion further souring his sour mood. It's a good thing the telephone separates them, else he might do serious damage to the stupid ass. Lem Filbert has been blunt about him. A crook. It's something he should get on top of. Soon. Outside, a fat moon is rising. Another sort of call. "His sister works for me in the bank."

"Yeah? How'd she get that job, Ted?"

"If you mean, did she have big-city sponsors, the answer is no. There was an opening, she was the most qualified applicant."

"Yeah, well, I got a feeling that's gonna be her badass brother's case, too."

"Hey, Tommy. Saw your mom's wagon in the drive this morning and knew you were back. Is everything okay?"

"I shouldn't even be talking to you. I don't want you ever in my car again. You are totally weird."

"I know it." Sally grins, thinking about the surprise that butterbags must have got when Riding the Hood's ruby bullet landed in her lap, and writes: Another first in the history of armed warfare. "Those religious people out on the hill apparently think I'm some kind of diabolical fiend in league with Satan."

"They're damn right."

"If they weren't all so stuck in their beefcake fantasies, they'd say I was the Antichrist, but that's too big a deal for a woman. You remember that wall-eyed kid out there with the pilot shades and cute hangdog look?"

"Sure. What awful thing did you do to him?"

"I bought him an ice cream sundae. He snuck away from the camp and met me over in Tucker City. At first he just wanted to warn me that I'd been demonized by the cult and that I should stay away from the camp for my own health, while at the same time trying to talk me into pulling on one of those nighties and becoming a member."

"What did you do to get so famous?"

"After you left Sunday, I got those two boys to invite me up the hill. Research for Professor Cavanaugh, you know. I got lots of notes for you, but I never quite fit in, I don't know why." She pauses to let him make a wisecrack about that, thumbing through her notebook and coming on that cartoon of Sleeping Beauty with the beard and boner and inked-in phone receiver. When he passes (he's probably scratching himself and yawning, pissed off by the call), she says, "And then a really creepy thing happened. While I was still talking to an old lady there at the tent, she winked at me and died. I freaked out and took off down the hill, and now they all think I sucked the life out of her." She liked that old lady. She'd felt blessed by her.

"And after that they still want you to join up? I thought it was that kind of outfit. Bunch of whacked-out vampires. You should fit right in."

"Poor Billy Don is pretty mixed up." Well, that hangdog look: he fancies her, give the boy his due.

"Billy Don?"

"That's the boy's name. When I said no thanks, he switched and made it clear he wanted out himself. It was getting too intense, he said, too unreal. His buddy Darren, that's the other one, apparently obsesses over the end of the world day and night, and it's beginning to drive Billy Don nuts." She understands that—it's hard to live around crazy people, especially when they don't know they're crazy—yet she almost envies this fascination with cosmic mysteries and wishes it didn't all seem so ordinary to her. She stubs out her cigarette. Maybe she should take up astronomy. She adds sunglasses to the bearded sleeper, and while Tommy makes what might be nose-blowing noises on the other end, writes: Beauty comes on a sleeping Prince Charming, lance in hand, and wonders whether or not she should wake him up. How will he behave when he has to give up his wet dreams? It might leave him with nothing to hold on to, so to speak. "He said he really wanted to get on that bus to Florida—you know, the one all those kids with guitars came on—but things are a mess at the camp after the bikers trashed it, and he couldn't let his pal and Mrs. Collins down just when they needed him." Beauty's own life in the world has been something of a mixed bag, as they say out in the briars. Why drag poor Charming into it? Like her father, he'd just be completely baffled and get drunk all the time. "Also, I think Darren made a play for him and he wasn't ready for that."

"Oh yeah?" Tommy perks up at that. "What'd he say?"

"One night he woke up and Darren was touching him."

"Yeah, well, did he like it?"

"I don't think he did. I think it scared him a little."

"But what did he do?"

"He didn't say."

"He liked it."

The telephone table is full of tiny black burn marks where her father—in one stupor or another, or maybe in a pique because of phoned abuse—missed the ashtray. He's in deep trouble, she knows, with Tommy's dad. He's going to lose his job, and then what will they do? It's not fair. He can't help it if he's about as clever as a broken pump handle and can only mimic the world in his friendly stupidity. He's the sort of guy who uses a whiskey-flavored toothpaste, a Christmas gift from his friend Archie Wetherwax, and has a cigarette lighter that plays "Smoke Gets in Your Eyes," which is his idea of high culture. Her mom is smarter—she's been known to read a bestseller or two and professes to adore Chopin's "Moonlight Sonata"—but she has been completely warped by this dumb town. "So how's your mom doing, Tommy?"

"About the same. If anything, when she's lucid, she seems better. More feisty. I'm home because dad had to fire the home care nurse and needs a break. Bad fucking story."

"What happened?"

"Can't say exactly. But it seems the woman stripped her out. All Mom's savings. The woman is one of those crazy cultists, it turns out, and I think they got it all. Dad's shattered by it. But it's also fired him up. He's getting up some kind of community action committee again, and he says he's going to throw the book at those freaks. That's what he's working on now down at the bank. Mom is teed off about all of this, of course, and not easy to get on with."

Growing up, Sally saw a lot of Tommy's mother. Their mothers often took them to the park or pool together. Back when the brain was just warm mud and didn't hold on to much, so it's all pretty dim. But she always remembered his mother as a sweet, passive creature, very quiet and unassuming. Pretty, even when she got older. Sally's mom always did all the talking. "It's sad, Tommy. Getting old is sad. How about if I drop by for a Saturday morning toke? I can say hello to your mom and give you my notes from last Sunday."

"Not today, Sal. I'm about to take a shower, get the day going. And then I've got company this afternoon."

For some reason, doodling, thinking about Christ's multitude of foreskins maybe, she has given the sleeping prince a second dick. Give Beauty a kind of kisser's on-off switch. And if she gets mad, she can bite one off and still have one to play with. Tommy's, if memory serves, is circumcised. This memory comes not from the ice plant—

she went blind that night—but from hairless childhood. To play it safe, she draws one with a foreskin, the other without. That way he'll be good to go, no matter which way it swings in the afterlife. "Well, let me know, professor," she says, trying not to sound hurt or angry, but no doubt sounding hurt and angry. "I'm only a phone call away."

"That's right. New Opportunities. You know, for West Condon. What do you think?" Ted's tenth or twelfth call of the morning. He can't even remember who he's talking to now. Probably someone on the city council. The voice on the other end sounds like it's coming out of a windy cave. Archie Wetherwax up a phone pole, maybe. Who will beg off so that he can stay home and play with his model train set. Nothing happening out on the bank floor this Saturday morning. Nothing at all. "We hope to acquire some new properties, see if we can lure some corporate and industrial investment to the area." He's still making swirly shapes with his penciled doodles like some kind of weird flowers, but now, whenever lines cross to create closed spaces, he finds himself blacking them in. Well, he's an old guy with a lot of history, and she's just a kid. He's known all along there'd be no long-term gain. It was more like a casino night: fast, fun, full of calculated risk, empty-handed at the end. But he hadn't realized her leaving, though it had to happen, would hit him so hard. "Yes, those fanatics are part of our concern, too." It's the priest he's talking to now. Key ally. So wake up. "They're responsible for a lot of our troubles here, Father Baglione, and we want them to move on before things get out of hand again." He's had his fair share of casino nights, but mostly out of town, while attending board meetings or sales conferences, pursuing investments, and the returns have been minimal but no debts or regrets, no troublesome residue. As a reliable donor to Republican party campaigns and a local organizer and counselor, he also gets invited from time to time to Governor Kirkpatrick's hunting parties (have to call him), and there are always lots of women around there, too. Short-term investments with little or no payback, just a pleasurable way to get rid of excess capital. That of the pocket, that of the loins. One of his upstate partners has shown him how to make most of it tax deductible. He even includes condoms among his promotional supply expenses, buys them by the carton. "You saw last Sunday the problems we face, Connie." The Lutheran minister has agreed to replace Wes Edwards at the Rotary Club and Ted wants him to focus his introductory remarks on the new action committee and its challenges. "We have to come together as a united citizenry, and we might as well start praying for it at the Wednesday luncheon." In all his previous affairs, it has always been easy come and easy come again. So what's different this time? Well, he has fucking fallen in love, that's what. "Goddamn it, Jim, that's stupid! I ask you what you think of our New Opportunities for West Condon idea and you can only make a lame joke about nude opportunities?" He hangs up on the drunken sonuvabitch with a bang, which causes the little Bonali girl out on the bank floor to start and glance his way. He shrugs and winks solemnly, turns away, recalling Stacy's mimicry. He'd brought up the idea of her taking over Jim Elliott's job, but she only laughed and then did an exact imitation of Elliott's stupid look, his dumb remarks. To prove, she said, she'd be perfect for the job. He's crazy about her. Never thought it could happen again, never wanted it to happen, and it did. She has brought something magical into his life. It's as though he's been spared from following poor Irene into the grave. An illusion, of course. Like religion, as Stacy would say. Though she believes in love like others believe in Jesus. He called his old fraternity brother up at the business school to ask if he'd seen her or heard from her. No, but he had another sharp student he might like. He was sorry he'd called. "Nick works for the bank, Burt. Guy I met at a business meeting up in the city. I don't think he even goes to church." It's nickel-and-dime Burt Robbins he's talking to. He's telling him about his city manager idea and Burt has asked him if he thinks it's smart to hand over that much power to the Italians. He says the mayor won't like it. "The mayor told me he wanted to quit." That surprises Burt, but Ted doesn't say more, changes the subject, says he has been on the phone to a couple of old profs and may have found a good candidate to replace Edwards at the church. "Young fellow named Jenkins. Something of a scholarly type, like Connie Dreyer, but said to be good at reaching out to the community and building consensus." Got the impression talking with him that he was something of a naïve ditherer and probably not even a golfer, but they've got to get a body in the pulpit soon, reopen the church before the doors rust shut. Ted has chewed his pencil through to the lead. He snaps it in two. Relax. She'll be back, she needs him, she can't stay away. He's arrogant enough to believe that. Meanwhile, the break is a good thing. Instead of an idle drive in the country, he's getting a lot of work done. He calls Lem Filbert to apologize for having to let his sister-in-law go, but it was a very serious matter. "She took advantage of my wife's incapacities." Lem says he hopes the crazy bitch ends up in the fucking clink and stays there, he's fed up with her religious wackiness and she needs to have her ass kicked. Lem's a good man and Ted tells him so while thinking about Stacy's sweet little behind, so arousing when she turns it toward him. Lit softly by the fading light coming through the motel window. To be kissed, not kicked. He asks when his car will be ready and Lem says he plans to finish the painting this afternoon. Should be dry by Monday, looking like new. "No hurry, Lem. No use for it until then." But, no, it's not a good thing. He's in pain. He imagines the drive. The sun. Her smile. Her hand in his lap. It's a long long way from May to December... He's not a hummer, but now he's humming. There you go. Though that one's about growing old. The days dwindle down to a precious few... He takes a deep breath and presses on with his NOWC calls (ah, damn the world and the way time fucks us!), trying to get his mind off her, and while he's got Judge Altoviti on the phone, he inquires about Concetta Moroni, the woman he has just hired, sight unseen, as a home care worker. Altoviti says she's a strong, reliable, big-hearted woman who was widowed by the Deepwater blast and could use the work; so, good, he'll stick with her. Not all news is bad. Irene has become an evangelical; now she can become a Catholic. Just to be sure, he calls Nick Minicozzi upstairs and asks him to do a background check. "And while you're at it, you might try to get me a rundown on the bank's investments in Deepwater or in any of its managers, outstanding loans, that kind of thing. I think we put some money into a gasification project of theirs. Bad field position, but until that deal is signed and sealed, we still might have a play or two left in our locker." September… November… When Nick asks, he says, "I may come out for a late nine." Vince Bonali's daughter, who gave him the Moroni connection, is doing some quiet housekeeping behind the counter, filling the time until they close at one. Then she's off to the house to help out with Irene. Ted's well aware he has set Tommy up with an in-house lay today, though he apparently needs no help. Consolation for dragging him back from university. The girl is cute, though far beneath Tommy. Should he call her father about NOWC? No. Lesson learned. He has just taken a grip on the phone to call Dave Osborne at the shoe store, thinking about Stacy showing him the shoes she'd bought there (even her feet he loves, and the way she stands and walks on them, the way she turns the soles up when—), when it rings. Almost as if by grasping it he has triggered it. If you hold the blackened doodles to the light just right, they shine like silver. He hangs up with a whispered I-love-you and calls the garage. "Listen, Lem, if its drivable, I might take the Lincoln out for the weekend after all and bring it back Monday. Yeah? Great." He signals to the staff to lock up. To fall so hard. And feel so good.

# II.2

## Saturday 25 April

On a slight rise on the way into what he knew when a boy as the Presbyterian No-Name Wilderness camp, within view of the artificial bump of land their little movement grandly called the "Mount of Redemption," Pach' Palmers stops to take a leak beside the panel truck that is his present home. It's his first time to see that goddamned mine hill since the day he got arrested on it. When he came back to West Condon after his release a couple of years ago, looking in vain for Elaine, he was able to pick up the old *Chronicle* delivery van, and once he got it running, he headed out here. But he turned back at the edge of town. He was starting up a new life. It seemed like bad karma, as Sissy would say. What a crazy time, what a crazy day. Life does throw up some fucking doozies. That one cost him a stretch in the slammer. Pach' lifts his cock and aims his stream toward the Mount, wishing he could piss away that awful day, the worst day of his life.

What was he really thinking that day? Did he think the end of the world was coming? That Jesus was going to come flying down out of the storm, superhero cape flapping, and whisk them all off to Paradise? He was so hot for Elaine's body, he didn't know what he was thinking. He was holding on to her hand, hoping to find some place they could at least kiss, last chance and all that, but they were on a barren hillside with one sick rickety tree, surrounded by freaked-out Jesus worshippers, the whole world watching, and nowhere to go. And, anyway, there was no budging her. Elaine was completely lost to the insane moment and stood there in the rain, her tunic pasted to her skinny body, rain and tears streaming down her face, looking out on the crowds or else up into the sky. Down at the foot of the hill, those they called the powers of darkness were massing up, including all the reporters and photographers and state cops, and overhead: the mind-rattling *yak yak yak* of police helicopters. All their own people, showing off all they had in their wet flimsy tunics, were praying, singing, crying, and flinging themselves about in holy fits, their tunics turning black and brown in the mud. It was pretty arousing. He had a massive hard-on impossible to hide under his soaked tunic, which not even fear of the impending apocalypse could shrink. He was able to bend his underwear elastic band down over the head, and belt it in somewhat with the rope they all wore at the waist, but it kept slipping, and when it did it stuck out a mile. He thought: Well, Jesus, here I am, take me, sins and all. Then the town newspaper editor showed up. Mr. Miller. The guy who'd pretended to be a friend and fellow believer, but who'd turned on them like Judas. Exposed them. Made them look like dumbass jerks. Everybody said he was why Bruno's sister went crazy, why she'd died in the end. So he was a killer, too. They were all charging down on him. The Antichrist. Or the Antichrist of the moment, anyway. He let go of Elaine's hand and joined them. It was something he had to do. He remembered pummeling the guy there in the pouring rain, hitting him over and over, wishing he could kill him, the girl's corpse somehow bouncing around in the middle of it all, pointing her blue arm at everybody. The guy's clothes got torn off, and in the end Pach' was pounding a lifeless naked body dressed in mud and blood. People were jumping on it. Somebody had an ax. Pach' thought they *had* killed him. Only some time later did he learn the poor sonuvabitch had somehow survived. Elaine's mother had had something to do with it. He was grateful for that. He was sorry about what he'd done. Doubly sorry, because when he went looking for Elaine again, he found

Junior Baxter whipping her with a switch, and he laid into the spongy tub of shit—second time that spring, throwing him into the mud and punching him with both fists—only to have Elaine start clawing him and scratching him and throwing her nearly naked body down on Junior to shield him and screaming at Carl Dean to go away, go away. And with that, he lost it. He turned and pitched himself like a howling maniac at the advancing state troopers, taking down a couple of them before they all piled onto him. He was sent up to detention for six months for that, though he doesn't remember anything after seeing Elaine's little body on top of fat Junior with blood all over his stupid face.

Anniversary last Sunday. The nineteenth of April. He might have made it here in time had it not been for a leaky radiator. Just as well not. They were probably all over on that hill again and he would only have repeated the whole mess or made it worse. Five years. Long time ago. Seems like a different lifetime. Fuck, it *was* a different lifetime. Pach'—he wasn't called Pach' then—was an ignorant young dickhead with a susceptibility for big total answers. He was president of the Baptist Youth Group and full of furious opinions (how easy it was to speak of God and Jesus then; they were like pals on the track team, and he was elbow to elbow with them, slapping butts) when his high school reading and writing teacher Mrs. Norton drew him and his friend Colin into her goofball Seventh Aspect fantasies, and then, after the coalmine disaster, they followed her when she got mixed up with the lone survivor, Giovanni Bruno, a weird lunatic like all so-called prophets, one thing following another with a kind of mad irresistible logic. Religion's appeal, no matter how nutty, to the down-and-out. He knows all about that, having been there all his life. The need for divine intervention to serve up just desserts, give the loveless something to love, cure the incurable, take revenge upon the wicked. Focused, God-sanctioned hatred. Oh yes, he felt all that, sometimes still does. He has an explosive nature; he knows that. He has learned to keep things in check, but as a kid he was just so damned angry all the time. He might have killed somebody and often wanted to. It was what made him let go of Elaine's hand. He let go of everything when he let go of that hand. Everything. He hated Miller at the time. Now he thinks of him as pretty much the smartest guy he ever knew. Sure dumb of him to turn up out there, though, after all he'd done. Must have been Bruno's sister who dragged him out. It was her body he was trying to reach when he got set upon. Pach' can understand that. Same with Elaine now. Why he's here. Except at least Elaine's still kicking.

Trying to track Elaine Collins down is mostly what he's done ever since they uncaged him. The six-month rap became a year for mouthing off and throwing his food on the floor and getting into fights with the other punks in detention, and they gave him another five in the state pen after he blew up and punched a sado guard. Laid the sick asshole out cold, sorry only that he hadn't broken his neck. They might not have let him go anyway. His fucked-up parents had split and left the cheap development at the edge of town and he had no idea where they were, nor wanted to know, so as a juvenile there was no one he could be sent home to. No other relatives wanted him. He was too ugly. After a row or two in the pen, he settled down into his old camp counselor ways and they finally let him go after a couple of years. He was supposed to keep in touch with a parole officer, but he never did. He boarded a bus and came back here. He couldn't have afforded the train, were it still running, but it wasn't. The closing of the coalmines had also meant the closing of the railroads. West Condon itself was like it had always been only more run down, needing a fresh coat of paint. He wasn't shopping, he was looking for Elaine, but she and her mother had left town along with most everyone else he knew, and, except for vague rumors of Brunist doings around the country, there was not much local news about them, so what he got out of the trip instead was his panel truck. He had wanted to apologize to Miller—tell him he was fucking right, they *were* all dumbass jerks, right on, man—but the *Chronicle* was closed. Miller had flown the coop, nothing left on the newspaper premises but a print shop run by an old schoolteacher and track coach he once had. Miller, the coach said, was reporting for network TV, something Pach' never saw except sometimes in bars. Where no one was looking at the news. The paper's rural delivery van sat out in the parking lot, its tires flat, battery dead, lights busted out, muffler falling off, hoses and fan belt shot, no shocks at all, but the body was not too rust-eaten and the engine looked repairable. The coach let him have it for a token dollar. A tall, sour ex-coalminer named Lem Filbert had a garage at the edge of town and he hired himself out to him in exchange for a tow, some used parts, a set of retreads, a meal a day, and Lem's mechanical know-how, serving as night watchman on the side for he was already sleeping in the thing, Lem's widowed sister-in-law providing him some old bedding. A part-time nurse of some kind who had plucked eyebrows and was so religious she dressed like women in Bible pictures. She joined their group around Bruno at the end, but he didn't remember seeing her out on the hill that day. Maybe she didn't want to get her clothes wet. She was the one who told him Elaine's mother was now married to the singer Ben Wosznik and was doing missionary work somewhere over near the Carolinas, and yes, far as she knew, her daughter was still with them. When he had the van rolling again, he headed east. Lem worked hard and demanded hard work, but he was good to him in the end, filling his tank and stuffing a few bucks Pach' knew he could not afford into his pocket.

The Brunists, he discovered when chasing around after them, had gone big time while he'd been locked up. They had churches all through that part of the country, radio and television programs, billboards and piles of pamphlet handouts, songs on the hillbilly stations, tent meetings said to draw thousands. Hundreds certainly. He saw them, looking for Elaine. The end of the world? Still on. Sometime. Soon. Patience, jackass, patience—that old church camp skit. Back in West Condon, nobody had seemed to know much about any of this. So much happens in this country that no one ever hears about. On their home turf, except maybe for Lem's sister-in-law, the Brunists were a joke. They'd all made fools of themselves, dancing around half-naked in the rain, waiting for a Rapture, as they called it, that never happened. It was embarrassing. They should have disappeared into jokes the next day, but instead they're a big religion. Hard to figure. Of course, Jesus Christ: same story. People are weird. Key apparently has been Elaine's mother. Old lady Collins is a powerhouse and an organizational genius and a saint. Everybody says so. He remembers her as a big, horsey lady with raw red hands, nearly six feet tall, dressed in print dresses and wide white pumps. She had a way of belting out battle cries like some kind of general or football coach and was at the same time given to throwing herself around and bawling like a stuck pig and talking to her dead husband like he was in the same room with her. Pach' was always afraid of her and knew she didn't like him very much.

The search for Elaine was mostly fruitless, but he didn't work all that hard at it either, even obsessed as he was. Something in him kept holding him back. Afraid of what he might say or do, maybe. Especially if she didn't want to see him, and why should she? So he took odd jobs slinging hash, working on the roads, making deliveries, and wandered about, following their trail, but fell into a funk and backed off whenever it looked like he might be getting close. Went to country bars instead. Got sloshed. Man of constant sorrow. He hadn't forgotten Elaine's Day of Redemption betrayal. How could he after what it cost him? But his sweeter memories of her and his hopes of winning her back were what had gotten him through these bad years, so he has kept chasing her even while shying away, fantasizing some kind of future with her and whacking off to the memory of her little body, just as he'd done all through his prison days, just as he is doing now, standing at the edge of a gravel road under the warm April sun, his fist pumping.

He especially liked to think back on that night on the way home from the mine hill with a carload of chicken feathers when he kissed her and grabbed her leg and more besides—and she wasn't mad after. It was Easter Sunday, a week before the day when the world was supposed to end, though it felt more like the world was just beginning. Wasn't that the point of Easter? He has had a good feeling about that day ever since, in spite of the stupid Jesus story that goes with it. Colin Meredith was along that night, and they parked on a side street, and by agreement, Colin got out to take a walk. They were coming from a service on the Mount and dressed only in their Brunist tunics and white underwear, and the feel of her flesh through the thin tunic is what he remembers, first her shoulder and armpit (the knotty edge of her little bra), then her leg, then her whole body as he pulled her hard against him, grabbing her tight little bottom through the tunic and cotton panties, her tummy against his, everything twisting and leaping and shivering, the gearshift somewhere in the middle of it all like an extra dick. He scared her, and he was scared too as she began to bawl and get hysterical, and he backed off, apologizing, starting to cry himself and cursing himself for his rough ways. He kissed her cheek softly, whispering his sorries to her, and blinked the lights for Colin to come back, and then, later, as they were walking from the car toward Giovanni Bruno's house, he told her he loved her, really loved her, and she smiled a trembly little smile—there was a chicken feather in her hair, like a pale flower petal—and his heart lifted. The next day at school, Elaine, tears running down her face, told him Junior Baxter had called her a whore, and he dragged Junior out of history class and thrashed him right there in the hallway in front of everyone and the principal threw him out of school, but Elaine took his hand and said if he had to go, then she was going too, and they walked out of there together, achingly in love, the only time he'd ever loved so hard or felt so loved in all his life.

Well, love. He doesn't know what it is, only what it isn't, and what it sometimes feels like. Back then, he was just trying to get into her pants, because he thought that was what guys were supposed to do. Now he knows that's the least important thing. Everyone and everything fucks. Can't help it, really. But, love: that's the rare thing. The hard thing. And not God love, which is just a fake way of loving yourself. Human love. For someone else. Like he loves Elaine, without knowing what it is or even needing to know. Only kind of redemption he knows now, all he can hope for. He pulls over again, gets out, stretches, combs his fingers through his beard, climbs back in, touches his "Elaine" tattoo through his T-shirt for luck, tunes the radio to the local country music station. Why all these highfalutin thoughts? Because he is closing in on her once more and all the old anxieties are back. The urge to stop, turn around, and forget it. All along, he knows, it has been like the going was more important than getting there, with the where of the "there" being uncertain enough to give him an excuse always to change direction. Kidding himself. But not this time. For once he knows exactly where she is and knows she's staying put. He has seen the fresh new sign pointing the way: "International Brunist Headquarters and Wilderness Camp Meeting Ground." He either goes there now or throws his life away again. "No Trespassing": that sign, too. Well, forgive us our trespasses, goddamn it to hell. He tosses his leather jacket in the back, takes down the plastic naked woman dangling from his rearview mirror and stows it in the glove compartment, starts up the truck again. Sniffs his armpits—fuck it, have to do. Pops some minty chewing gum in his mouth, which is mostly his way of brushing his teeth. The song on the scratchy old car radio is a religious one, sung by a bunch of young people. Sounds like a live recording not made in a studio. "Wings of a Dove." He thought he heard the radio announcer, old Will Henry (that dumb rube still there—some things never change), say something about the Brunists, but he may not have heard right through the static.

Elaine is always most on his mind during Easter, and it was Easter morning about a month ago (he would have blamed the coincidence on God, if he still believed in God; instead he attributed it to luck and the way wanting something badly keeps you tuned in to the world) that his trek back here began. He had picked up a kitchen job in a fancy eatery just off the Blue Ridge Parkway in southern Virginia, the trail having gone cold somewhere east of the Smokies, and at work on Easter morning he'd spun the dial looking for some good music. Something about heartbreak and rough traveling, for he'd awakened feeling melancholic, adrift in an indifferent world, going nowhere. Nothing on the radio, however, except fucking church services, one after the other. It was that part of the country. He was about to turn it off when he heard a congregation singing Ben Wosznik's old tune, "The White Bird of Glory," the one that starts with the mine disaster. It was a live broadcast coming from a Brunist church in Lynchburg, and when the song was over, the preacher sent around the collection plate, asking for contributions to what he called the new Brunist Wilderness Camp and Headquarters. He gave their local church address for mailed-in contributions. "We shall gather at the Mount of Redemption to meet our dear Lord there face to face!" he declared, quoting the lines of the song, and apparently that was exactly what they meant to do. On the nineteenth of April. Buses were being chartered. Pach' took off his apron and quit his job on the spot, thoroughly pissing off his employers, who were gearing up for their annual Easter buffet brunch. He headed to Lynchburg, intent on getting there before the service was over so he could talk to the preacher, that radio station tuned in the whole way. He made it in time to see a handful of fresh converts in Brunist tunics getting baptized by light and was able to corner the preacher after, but it wasn't easy to get anything out of him. He was one of those smug greasy fucks with peroxide blond hair and a smarmy style, and Pach' couldn't hide his loathing of him. His own beardy unkempt appearance also put the preacher off; he could tell by the way his eyes narrowed when he took him in. Probably didn't even smell all that good. It might have speeded things up to let it out that he was one of those twelve First Followers the preacher had blathered about in his sermon, but it would have taken too long to explain and he didn't want to risk having Elaine alerted. Luckily, he had a few bucks in his pocket, so he took them out and said he'd heard what the preacher had said about the Brunist camp and he wanted to contribute to it, and that softened Blondie up enough to get what he wanted out of him. He'd have made it here sooner, but he had to earn gas money along the way and he had a lot of breakdowns. And, well, maybe, also, sure, the usual cold feet.

Not cured yet. At the turnoff into the camp, he nearly drives right on by. As if distracted. Thinking about tomorrow. Feeling hungry. Needing to clean up first. Wash the van. Whatever. But he brakes (more tents over there in a field, beat-up cars, a camper or two) and makes the turn. The gravel access road dips down slightly into a fresh-smelling leafy space. The camp is located in a wet bottomland fed by the No-Name Creek, which gave the camp its original name. They sometimes had problems in wet summers. The Baptists rented this campground from the Presbyterians each summer for four weeks in August, and he was a regular, rising eventually to camp counselor by the time he was a high school junior. The best four weeks he had each year. He was somebody, then. Ugliness was good. It was strong and knew the ropes. He was good with the younger kids, took them on hikes, showed them how to do things. He could probably still walk the whole camp blindfolded. There are wildflowers along the side of the road, patches of daffodils, bluebells deeper in. It's a rich beautiful day. One of those days that makes you feel like you're going to live forever. A T-shirt day. He has rarely seen the camp this time of year, though they used to hold the Easter sunrise services out here on Inspiration Point when all the churches joined in, and he turned up at a few, mainly to check out the girls of the other denominations.

He is stopped at the gate by some burly guy with a gun. Didn't have those in his day. Didn't have those barbed-wire fences with the "Keep Out" signs either. All along, he's been afraid of being rejected. Or hoped to be. Now here it comes. In bib overalls, plaid shirt, and muddy boots. The guy wants to know his business and he knows he should say he is a believer and has made a kind of pilgrimage here, but he can't get it out. Feels too phony. Instead, figuring Ben Wosznik would probably be the most friendly, he asks for him.

"Yeah? Who should I say…?"

"Tell him the name's Palmers."

"Palmers? Hey. Not Carl Dean Palmers?"

"That's right."

"I'll be durned!" The guy rests his shotgun on its stock and a grin breaks across his weathered face. "Well, praise God, brother. Welcome home. We been praying for you. This is some surprise. C'mon, I'll take you to Brother Ben."

He leaves the van by the gate, follows overalls into the camp on foot. There are other changes. Telephone poles and electric streetlamps. Phone box in front of the old stone lodge. Which looks spiffed up. The weeds have been beaten back. There's a flower garden or two, bird feeders. The cedar cabins are under various stages of reconstruction. Some are missing, including the one he used to stay in as a camp counselor. Just the little cement support blocks left standing like miniature tombstones. Crowds of people milling about, busy with one thing or another. Lots of kids running around. Almost like a small town. They stare at him curiously, and his guide shouts out who he is and some smile and wave or come over to shake his hand, others frown or look confused or mutter amongst themselves. No one familiar, though five years is a long time. People change. He has. Elaine? He'd know her, no matter what, but no one like her in sight. Ben is working with a crew on one of the cabins. At first Ben doesn't recognize him (Ben's changed, too: thick gray beard now, fulltime spectacles, more of an old man's shape), and then he does, and he gives him a warm, firm handshake. "Mighty glad to see you, Carl Dean. We thought you was still in the penitentiary."

"Been out for a while. Heard you were back here and decided to stop by, say hello."

"Well, I'm glad you did, son. Can you stay?"

"Got no special plans for right now. Could you use a hand there?"

"You bet. First, lemme take you to Clara."

Walking alongside Ben toward the lodge, Pach' finds himself feeling like a kid again. Almost like he ought to take Ben's hand. Something about the old man. A kind of inner power. Certainty. Good guy to have at your side when trouble strikes. Serve time with. He can call you "son" and you don't feel offended. The sort of dad he wishes he'd had.

The old lodge and dining hall has been done up on the inside, too. Still smells of fresh varnish. Used to have dangling yellow bulbs powered by a generator at the back; now it has proper lighting but also gas lanterns hanging from the beams. There's a new coal stove at the back where some cots are stacked, piles of bedding. What most catches the eye, though, is a blown-up photograph hanging by the fireplace of Giovanni Bruno himself, standing out on the Mount in the rain, holding a coal pick like a mean cross, doing his ancient prophet act. Gives him a chill. Next to it is Ely Collins' framed death note, the one that started it all. The trigger. Rocketed him straight into the fucking pen. Pach' used to build the log fires in that big fireplace for their Baptist camp revival meetings, set out the folding chairs and put them back, clean up in the kitchen. Which, he can see at a glance, has also been modernized. Women are working in there. Large folding tables are being laid out for a meal. Ben explains that it's a luncheon for the workers and invites him to join them. Pach' tucks his ball cap in his back pocket, combs his fingers through his tangled hair.

Elaine's mother seems less happy to see him. "We thought you was still in prison in solitary confinement, Carl Dean." They are standing in a room off the main hall that has been fitted out with filing cabinets, desk, chairs, wire baskets full of paper, even a patterned red carpet. There are two young guys in there helping out. They seem excited he has turned up. "It's what Colin said."

"Colin likes to make things up, Mrs. Collins. I've been out for over two years."

"Do tell." Clara Collins seems hardly to have changed at all. A little bonier maybe, hair shorter and grayer, more business-like. Pants and sneakers instead of dress and heels. She casts a searching gaze over him, peering over her spectacles at his rags, his beard, his thinning but unruly hair. "Are you still a Christian, Carl Dean?"

"Well, I don't know what else to call myself, ma'am. But I don't have the same feeling anymore. It's one reason I came back here."

"What other reasons did you have?"

He knows he is turning red. He's afraid if he opens his mouth he'll just stammer something stupid. Finally, he says, "I wanted to see everybody again. I was lonely."

That softens her up enough to bring a faint smile to her face and she pushes her glasses up on her nose and says, "Looks like you could use a good clean-up."

"Yes, ma'am."

"I'm afraid we don't have room here at the camp to put you up."

"That's okay. I sleep in my panel truck."

"He's just passing through," Ben says. "He might could park down at the ballfield with us for a week or so while he thinks about staying on. Remember the parable of the hunderd sheep, Clara. It's a honor to have the boy back with us."

Mrs. Collins hesitates. Pach' can read her mind: That's too close to Elaine. But she sighs and nods. "Meanwhile, Darren and Billy Don here can show him about..."

Pach' remembers Inspiration Point as higher than this. Back in his days as a camp counselor it seemed to him that you could see the whole universe from up here, and then he felt like part of it, it part of him. Now the universe makes him feel like a spot of birdshit. Far across the way, he can see the Deepwater tipple and hoist, poking into the blue sky like a fairground ride, the water tower glinting in the sun. Also the Mount of Redemption, off to one side of it. Doesn't recall ever seeing that hill from up here but it must have been there. Goes to show that you see only what you're ready to see. Or want to see. It's the trouble with religious people.

He has managed to ditch Clara's two helpers, telling them he needed some thinking time on his own; they seemed to appreciate that, being heavy thinkers themselves. Bible school dropouts named Darren Rector and Billy Don-something. Or maybe they were thrown out; their story is ambiguous. They want to interview him for the Brunist church history they're assembling, a history they seem to think is going to unravel the mysteries of the universe. Something Pach' hopes to avoid; he'd have to tell them what he really thinks and blow what little cover he has. But it seems important to them, so he said maybe, after he's been here a while. This is his one shot at Elaine and he doesn't want to ruin it with his big mouth, but if he can get her to leave with him, maybe he'll let them have it just before he takes off.

The first thing they did was move his panel truck down to the trailer parking lot. The old softball field. He was sorry to see it being used like that, but he didn't say so. He asked who else was parked there, learned a few new names. Mobile homes with coming-of-light bumper stickers. He wondered if Elaine was in the Collins' house trailer but tried not to stare at it. Old bucktoothed Willie Hall came out to say hello and unleash a few welcoming Bible passages on him. He said his old mining injuries were plaguing him, which was why he couldn't help out with the construction work. He was just waiting for God to take him up into Heaven, that's all he had left now, and he held up his dogeared Bible to show him the weight of it. His big spooky wife did not come out. He saw her staring out their caravan window at him. He touched the bill of his cap to her, but no response. A filthy little kid who looked retarded stood a few yards away, not far from the Collins trailer, giving him a long dim look, snot running down his upper lip. Turned out to be Mrs. Cravens' kid Davey, and he learned something more from the two boys about that sadsack woman and her current fellow. He went over and squatted down in front of Davey to say hello, remember me? Smelled like he might have filled his britches. "I'm Pach', Davey. Let's be friends, okay?" The kid nodded and licked his lip. He could see the Collins trailer steps and door over Davey's shoulder. Should he go over and knock? No, he shouldn't. Patience, jackass. Later.

Does she know he is here? Probably. Scuttlebutt gets around quickly in shut-up places like this. A lot like a prison, he has been thinking since he was led in through that barbed-wire fence. Maybe she's hiding from him. Well, he can wait. He learned from the two boys that she and Junior Baxter still have something going, though they have only just got together again for the first time this past week, when the whole Baxter clan turned up for the anniversary celebrations over on the mine hill. Elaine is a very private person, they said. She and Young Abner, as he's called now, are often seen together, but they never hold hands or even talk to each other. It's more like a religious thing. It was the one called Billy Don who told him that, a talkative guy with dark shades, a ponytail, and handlebars; Darren is the more cautious one, a smart kid with blond curls and the bespectacled bright-eyed intensity of a zealot. The Baxter family are living in an unfinished cabin and were supposed to have left several days ago but haven't. They passed it on the path leading up here. A tent up at the back. Two of the Baxter boys have already been kicked out of the camp, he learned. Something about a motorcycle gang, a robbery, a gun. In retaliation, they came back and vandalized the camp when everyone was over on the mine hill praying, which explains the beat-up look of some of the cabins. But Junior and his two sisters are still here. One of the girls was pointed out to him as they passed the cabin. Cute. She was staring at him, and when he glanced back a couple of minutes later, beginning the climb up here, he saw she was still staring at him.

On the walk up to the Point, the boys filled him in on the years of the Persecution, the international following they now have, Mrs. Collins' plans for a tabernacle temple to be built on the Mount of Redemption. There was a lot of money being spent here, much of it apparently coming from a local rich guy named Suggs. But they were able to acquire the camp in the first place, they said, thanks to the Presbyterian minister's wife, Mrs. Edwards, who arranged for the sale and then became a Brunist Follower. This was unexpected news. Reverend Edwards was the guy who helped kidnap his friend Colin Meredith and kept him away from the Mount on the Day of Redemption. Pach' remembers him as a klutz in a porkpie. With a nervous smirk. All day on the hill, Pach' kept worrying that Colin would miss the Rapture. He learned later that Colin tried to kill himself in their house. "Mrs. Edwards is one of our most important converts," the boys said. "She's now the camp director." He remembers Mrs. Edwards very well. Nature girl. Fantasy stuff. When he asked, they told him she was probably working down at her vegetable garden with Colin. So Colin's here, too: also news. They offered to walk him over there, but he told them he knew the way.

Pach' once tried to kiss a girl up here on the Point when he was about ten, but she didn't like it and didn't kiss him back and told the camp counselor. Which ended his summer camp that year. He hasn't had a lot of luck with kissing. Elaine was always more a hugger than a kisser, being self-conscious about her bad teeth. But she's a good hugger. The most intense hug he ever got was over there on the mine road at the foot of the hill the night before the supposed end of the world—the night Bruno's sister was killed. He'd got turned on watching people in front of the bonfires they'd built to sing and pray around, the way their bodies were silhouetted inside the thin fluttery tunics when they passed in front of the flames. He was jealous of Elaine and hated it when she walked in front of the fires so others could see, but it excited him, too. Those were sinful thoughts, and on the very eve of what might well be the Last Judgment, so he tried not to look, but he couldn't stop himself. Not until Elaine's mother stood in front of the flames and he found himself staring at something he knew he shouldn't see. He turned away feeling hot and confused, as if his acne were erupting all over his body. Then the lights on the mine road, the rush to the cars, the awful thing that happened. He stood at the lip of the ditch, hugging Elaine, watching that poor girl die. Her smallness, her lips slightly parted, eyes closed, her fragile broken worried look. How many had hit her? Had he? Wrecked cars everywhere, lights pointed in all directions, some straight up into the sky as if trying to get someone's attention up there, his own car ditched somewhere behind him. Where it stayed until the county hauled it out weeks later and sent him a towing bill up in detention. Seeing his schoolteacher Mrs. Norton lying in the roadway as though dead, her fat-kneed husband fanning her face with his tunic hem, scared him even more than the struck girl. Was everybody suddenly dying? Was it really happening? Elaine was sobbing in his arms, her back to the ditch, and while he was staring down at Marcella over her shoulder, the poor girl's eyes suddenly opened and a red bubble ballooned out of her mouth, popped, dribbled down her chin. And that was it. His knees began to shake. Her brother stooped to kiss her lips and rose up with blood on his mouth, that's what he remembers, though his vision was pretty blurry, his head may have been playing tricks on him. Elaine wrapped her arms around him tight and held him close, close, dressed in almost nothing as they were, and whispered in his ear that she wanted to be in Heaven with him forever. Brought tears to his eyes as he, chastely, except for the club pressed against her tummy, couldn't do anything about that, hugged her back. Forever turned out to be less than a day.

He turns his back on all that shitty history and takes the path down to where he supposes Mrs. Edwards' vegetable garden to be, a trail somewhat overgrown, evidently not much used, in spite of the heavy traffic in the camp. Still a beautiful walk. Flowers, birds, trees, all kinds of sedges and grasses. Some of them pink now, this time of year. They all have names; he'll never learn them. Though, if he stays here, maybe he'll try. Mrs. Edwards had a thing for nature, as he recalls, she could teach him. She was a frequent visitor to the camp when the Baptists rented it. Came to see if they were taking proper care of it, he supposed, but always in a nice way. She was slim and pretty and dressed casually and he had fantasies about her, wishing for a mother like her, and sometimes he followed her around. One day, down in the wild place on the other side of the creek, she took her shirt off to sun her tits. He scrunched down in the weeds, stunned by the amazing sight, waiting and praying (yes, he was praying) for her to take the rest off. She never did, though over the years he saw other things. He used to wonder: What if he made himself known? Couldn't be done. She was from another world. It was like trying to step into a movie. There was only the watching.

The vegetable garden is amazing. A little farm. Mrs. Edwards is seeding a newly hoed patch when he arrives and introduces himself. She's older now, has a baggier look and a double chin, but there's still something fresh and girlish about her. She seems glad to see him, lights up with a cheerful smile. "Colin! Look who's here!" she calls out. Colin comes over from where he has been setting out stakes alongside a small freckle-faced woman. Colin was always odd looking, but now he's weirder than ever. Sickly pale and skinny with a wispy Chinaman's beard, wearing a floppy straw sun hat and rose-colored shorts, his silvery blond hair fluttering about his shoulders like a mad woman's. The way he moves reminds him of Sissy. Of course. Why hadn't he realized that before? Didn't understand any of this back then. A complete greenass. "It's Carl Dean, Colin!" Colin stops dead in his tracks, his eyes popping, his face twisting up like he's about to have a fit. *"No! It isn't!"* he cries and then runs away, screaming wildly for help. Mrs. Edwards throws down her garden gloves and starts after him, turning back just for a moment to cast Pach' a dark scowl. "Who *are* you really?" she demands, then returns to the chase. He shrugs at the freckle-faced woman, who only stares back at him. Well. There went his gardening career.

His building career shows more promise. With help from Ben and the others, all strangers to him, Pach' has been able to step right in with the crew this afternoon and work beside them. The cabin they are working on, which used to house eight kids in bunk beds, is being remodeled for use as a medical treatment room and two-bed sick bay. There are scores of people hanging about, most of whom seem to have come for last Sunday's ceremonies and just haven't gone home again. When they offer to help, Ben sizes them up quickly, assigns tasks to those who seem they might actually contribute something and sends the others off on pointless errands to get them out of the way. Even unskilled as he is, there's a lot Pach' can do. The cabin has already been wired up for electricity, and Wayne Shawcross, the overalled guy who let him in here, is showing him how to install wall plugs and light fixtures. Ben has also taken him on as a kind of apprentice carpenter. He's strong, and that's appreciated, too. He's enjoying it, more than any other work he's done since he got out, and in spite of the luncheon blow-up, he can already feel the urge to want to stay and work with all these guys whom he's quickly come to like. Get the job done. Be part of something bigger than himself. How much of religion, he wonders, is about this feeling?

At the luncheon earlier, over baloney sandwiches and potato salad, they made a big fuss over him, treating him as a kind of returning hero. It was embarrassing, given his intentions, and he only wanted out of there. Clara made a welcoming introduction and led them in prayer, thanking God for Carl Dean's safe return, and then prayed for all the other things they wanted. Darren Rector, reciting a little church history, praised him for his brave attack on the powers of darkness, which he said helped many others to escape arrest and carry on with their evangelical work (he didn't know that), and expressed everyone's sympathy for his suffering on behalf of them all. Which Rector compared to the ordeals of Daniel and Samson and Paul. Not at all how it was, of course. He supposed Rector was just buttering him up for the interview. Elaine wasn't there—still avoiding him, maybe—but just as well. He was glad she didn't have to listen to all that horseshit. Mrs. Edwards wasn't there either, nor Colin. The word about what had happened in the garden had evidently gotten around; the hero worship was not unanimous. There were surly mutterings here and there, and Junior's glare was so fierce it could have cut through steel plate, his short-cropped red head looking like it was on fire from inner rage. He's younger than Pach', but he's already getting an old man's soft heaviness in the jowls and belly and now wears a little red tuft on his upper lip. His kid sister, on the other hand, gave Pach' a sweet lingering smile. Somewhat vague. It just sort of stayed on her face. Her food had to be cut for her. Not all there.

Then an old fart in a wheelchair rolled away from the Baxter table and wanted to know in a loud voice if he really was Carl Dean Palmers like he said he was. His friend had not only not recognized him, he'd screamed like he'd seen the devil, scaring the whole camp. They'd all seen pictures. He didn't look like the pictures. So who was he really? Ben said he was Carl Dean, all right. They'd had a long conversation, talking about the last time they were together, couldn't be anyone else. "The devil is a great dissembler, Brother Ben!" Then Bernice Filbert, the widowed sister-in-law of the guy who owns the garage where he fixed up his van, the lady with the penciled eyebrows and the fancy way of talking who dresses up like Bible characters, vouched for him as well. "He has put on more beard and forehead since he stayed with us, but you can tell by his appetite he is who he is," she said, trying to lighten things up. "He has just put away his lunch quicker than Ezekiel could eat a scroll, as like I told him then." She's the camp nurse and is something of a celebrity today for having got fired a couple of nights ago as the home care nurse for the town banker's wife. All in some cause or other. Whatever, Pach' is on her side. It's enough just because the chump's a banker. Bastards who rule the world by making money off other people's money, a kind of legalized theft. They ought to be hung. Or sent to work in the mines. But also because the banker's dickhead son and his fatcat pals were the ones who laid the nickname of Ugly on him back in high school, getting rid of it being one of the few positives of his prison stretch. "That woman cain't talk 'thout lyin'," someone said, and someone else mumbled something about his driving the "devil's van." "What I'm asking," the guy in the wheelchair insisted, "is can he prove it?" Pach' tossed his driver's license out on the table and the cripple said that didn't prove anything, and then everyone started shouting, accusing the geezer of spoiling Carl Dean's homecoming and trying to sow discord in the camp. On the one hand, Pach' agreed with the old fossil; he sure as hell wasn't Carl Dean Palmers anymore, hadn't been for a long time. On the other, if the cantankerous sonuvabitch hadn't been in a wheelchair, he'd have popped him. He got up to leave, but Ben put a hand on his shoulder and reminded everyone of their Christian obligations to one another and then put his guitar around his neck and led them all in singing "Shall We Gather at the River?" After a moment, Abner Baxter stood up and joined in, and then, reluctantly, so too did the others at his table. All except the guy in the wheelchair, who spun it around, turning his crooked back on them.

Now, while Pach' works with Ben on the new sick bay, Baxter and his pals across the way are trying to hang a front door on their cabin, and neither crew is talking much to the other. People aren't getting along, just like before, and trouble is brewing. Ben sees him watching them with a frown on his face and says, "Let them be, Carl Dean. They ain't much good to us anyhow, so we at least get some work out of them for the time being. But that cabin has got other purposes. They ain't staying there."

Could he, he wonders? Stay here? Stay in this camp where he's always felt most at home, here with all these friends, more like family than his own family? Could he go all the way, put a tunic on again, win Elaine, help defend Ben and Mrs. Collins against the abominable Baxters and the local establishment, build something that will last? While he's asking himself that, Clara Collins comes rushing out of the lodge with big news: Mr. Suggs just called. The mine owners have accepted their offer for the Mount of Redemption. Papers are being drawn up. There are whoops and cheers and Wayne throws his painter's cap in the air. Time to bring out the beers! But, no, not here. Mrs. Collins falls to her knees there in the woodchips and closes her eyes and lifts her hands and launches into her full-throated God howl and all the others drop to their knees too and join in, waving their arms about and praying to beat the band. An old coalminer from out east declares it's a miracle, and that is noisily amenned. Mr. Suggs is grandly Godblessed. Nothing Pach' can do but follow suit, get down on his knees, take off his cap, and tuck his chin in, anything else would be an insult to these people, but he's feeling awkward as hell, a total hypocrite, the devilish reprobate they have taken him to be. Fuck. He could never do this.

When Pach' reaches the flowering dogwood tree a little before sundown for Saturday evening prayers, she is already there. Standing beside her mother. All these years gone past, mostly thinking about her, and suddenly here she is. He'd thought, after so much buildup, he'd probably be disappointed, and he'd arrived, hands in pockets, talking to others, trying not to look her way, staying cool. That lasted about a minute. She has grown up some. Taller now than he is. Gangly, but not big-boned like her mother. She's staring straight at him in a forthright way he has not seen before. He doesn't know what that stare means, but it cheers him to see her there beside her mother and not by

Junior Baxter. He nods to her as though in recognition, and when she doesn't nod back, he looks away.

"Looks like you brung us luck, Pach'," Wayne Shawcross says with a grin, passing by with his wife, Ludie Belle, and Pach' grins back, feeling a kind of twitch in his cheek (the grin's too wide, it's not something he does often), and says, "I can give it to others but I never keep none for myself." Ben and Clara still speak of him as Carl Dean, but he introduces himself to people as Pach', which is his name for his new life. "You mean like what you got there on the knees of your jeans?" Wayne asked this afternoon when told his name. "No. Like Apache." "You part injun?" "That's what they told me." "I think my granmaw was probly half Choctaw, but she wouldn't never admit it. It was like being half nigger back then." He'd got the new handle in prison. He'd lied and told them he had Indian blood, partly just to set himself off from the others, partly to shuck off the old life, be someone other than the self he'd come to hate. And who knows, given his old lady's careless habits, maybe it was true—didn't she like to claim when she was drunk that she'd got pregnant with him off a toilet seat? He was the only virgin in the men's prison, where rape was part of the new-boys break-in rituals, and he meant to stay that way (didn't quite), but he had to fight for it. Five guys, including a couple of trusties, grabbed him and ripped his pants down and the biggest of them said, "Bend over, Tonto, I'm gonna stick it to your holy huntin' ground." He was able to tear himself free and laid into the lot of them, starting with the fat asshole who called him Tonto, leaving him with less teeth in his mouth than he had before, and he was still holding his own against all five, even with his pants around his ankles, when the bulls finally showed up and broke it up with chains and truncheons. Lost him any hope for parole that year, but it earned him the nickname of the Crazy Apache, which over time got shortened to Pach', which most people hear as Patch. Whatever. Just so it's not Carl Dean. Or Ugly.

Elaine is still staring at him. He tries a smile this time. Same result. He has showered and laundered his rags in the new camp laundry, trimmed his beard, put on a T-shirt with only a couple of holes, and a denim vest. Combed his hair, even. Ben dropped a Brunist tunic by for him, but he decided not to wear it. There are others without tunics, so apparently it's okay. Two of those are a country singer and his woman, who are said to be famous singers from Nashville, though he hasn't heard of them. They're first on the program, because they have a gig after. At the bar in the old Blue Moon Motel at the edge of town. Can't be too famous. But a place to escape to maybe for a beer. What he misses most this time of day. They seem cool. The guy, anyway. The woman is mixed up with the fortuneteller, Mrs. Hall, and her flock of gossipy widows. Came to the prayer meeting in their company. She's said to be in touch with the dead.

The days are lengthening and the sun is probably still shining on Inspiration Point above them, but twilight has already settled on this little grove down here in the valley behind the lodge, oddly making the dogwood flowers seem to glow, and Elaine, standing under them, seems to glow as well. How beautiful she is in this strange pale light. Now he's the one staring and she's the one to look away. He can feel Junior Baxter's seething fury off to one side, but it means nothing to him. She's here and he's here. That's all that matters. On his way from lunch to the work site, Ben saw him craning about and said, "I s'pose you're looking for Elaine. She ain't feeling all that sociable today. Be careful, son. I think your coming here has gave her a fright. She'll be at the prayer meeting tonight. You'll see her there." All afternoon he has been plotting out what he'd say to her when they finally met, how he loves her, needs her, or else how he just wants to be friends again, have someone to talk to, whatever seems most likely to work, but all that has vanished from his head, and he knows it will all happen without a word or it won't happen at all.

There is apparently something sacred about the tree, which is why they are meeting here. The two country singers do a song about it. "All who see it will think of Me / Nailed to a cross from a dogwood tree..." The easy familiar singing mellows Pach' out (it was right to come here), and when they follow that with a singalong version of "In the Garden," he joins in. Old campfire standby. And the joy we share as we tarry there (he is watching Elaine, who is not singing; her head is down and she looks thin and fragile and he longs to gather her into his arms and take care of her), none other has ever known…

"Now, my son, the Lord be with thee, and prosper thou, and build the house of the Lord thy God, as he hath said of thee." This is Wayne Shawcross reading from the Old Testament, somewhat laboriously, his finger tracing the lines in the dim light, about somebody building a church. Could be referring to building the camp, but, after the news today, it's the tabernacle idea that has them buzzing. "Moreover there are workmen with thee in abundance, hewers and workers of stone and timber, and all manner of cunning men for ever manner of work." Sure. Cunning. Count me in. Wayne plows on in his wooden monotone: "Arise therefore, and build ye the sanctuary of the Lord God, to bring the ark of the covenant of the Lord, and the holy vessels of God, into the house that is to be built to the name of the Lord." There are a lot of amens and praise Gods now, people are getting excited, even though they probably don't know what arks and vessels Wayne is talking about. Elaine's head is up, a kind of startled expression on her face, but she is not joining in. A woman with a glass eye and gold tooth is watching her, head cocked, as if trying to decipher the expression. "The Lord hath chosen thee to build a house for the sanctuary: be strong, *and do it!*"

As Wayne looks up from his reading, pocketing his spectacles, the amens raining down, Elaine's mother steps into the ruckus and in her sharp clear voice starts to spell out what she calls the glad tidings about acquiring the Deepwater mining property and what that means to them. She gets about two lines out. "And I heerd a great voice outa Heaven saying, behold!" That's little Willie Hall interrupting. Can't hold him back, never could. "The tabernacle a God is with men, and he will dwell with 'em and they shall be his people, and God hisself shall be with 'em and be their God! Ay-men! *Revelation 21:3*!" People are shouting at him, goading him on. Clara can't get a word in edgewise. It's already turning into another one of those nights, just like old times, though now Pach' feels more like a self-conscious tourist. "Tell it like it is, Brother Willie!" "Let 'em bring me up onto thy holy hill," he cries, pointing, his big ears standing out like signal flags, "and to thy tabernacle! *Psalms 43:3*!" Abner Baxter raises his fist to speak, evidently keen to unload a few verses of his own, but the two singers take it as a cue to do another number: "The Sons of Light Are Marching." The song they sang on the march out to the hill that terrible morning. Pach' led the parade, walking backwards, bellowing at the top of his lungs so they could hear him all the way to the back. Hammering the ruts and gravel of the mine road with his bare feet as though to say goodbye to both road and feet. Must have hurt. Doesn't remember. Remembers Elaine marching right there at the front, watching him, almost desperately, singing with him in her timid little voice, the dead body they were carrying in the folded lawnchair rocking along above and behind her like a kind of canopy, the Prophet's gaga mother beside her being pulled over the bumps in a little red wagon, helicopters rattling in the sky overhead, photographers and newsmen and the curious trailing along beside them, the whole mad procession watched by state troopers in black uniforms and white visored helmets. "O the sons of light are marching since the coming of the dawn," Pach' sings now, joining in. "Led by Giovanni Bruno and the voice of Domiron!" But he's the only one who does it that way. The others sing: "Led by Giovanni Bruno, we shall go marching on!" So Domiron's out. The rest of Mrs. Norton's contributions as well, probably. He decides to shut up until he gets the whole picture. "So come and march with us to Glory!" Their own battle hymn. Not a song to tamp down the emotions, but it brings a certain order to them, makes them less dangerous, even as it stirs them up. Somehow it's the rhymes that do that, like little fasteners. Buttons. "For the end of time has come!"

When the song is over, Duke and his woman wave their goodbyes. "Peace!" Duke says. Pach' wants to leave with them, needs a beer, relief from all this shit, but he can't, wouldn't look right, and he still has hopes of connecting with Elaine. Runny-nosed Davey Cravens comes over and stands beside him, takes his hand. "You're my friend," he says, looking up at him. Big Hunk Rumpel, Mrs. Cravens' current man, rumbles forward in his split tunic and takes Davey up by the scruff. "It's okay," Pach' says, but Hunk just turns away and hauls the kid on up the path toward the lodge, the boy yelping and bawling all the way. Hunk never seems to say much, but at work today he took to Pach' right away and Pach' felt adopted by him. Respect of strength for strength. The old prison code. Maybe Hunk's done time too. Seeing what just happened to Davey, Hunk is not much improvement on the old man Pach' got stuck with, but he's someone you might want to have in your corner when things get tough.

Before Mrs. Collins can pick up where she got cut off, Abner Baxter starts up a rant of his own, like he's been threatening to do all along. He doesn't say so, but his Bible quotes seem to equate the temple idea with idol worship. That's how Pach' reads them anyway, and the look on Clara's face suggests it's how she reads them too. Elaine watches her mother with some alarm, her hand at her mouth, her shoulders hunched, while Baxter rails against pride and vanity and speaks up for the poor. "And therefore I command you, saith the Lord, thou shalt open thine hand wide unto thy brother, to thy poor, and to thy needy, in thy land!" He is getting a lot of shouted amens and some people start clapping in rhythm to all his "thy's." This probably has something to do with how their money is to be spent. It came up at lunch, too. People who want a place to stay, not another church. Pach' can only watch. He's on the other side of the world from these people now. Baxter turns toward his constituents, raising both arms. He is angry about the use of sheriff's troops to clear the tents off the Mount of Redemption and sealing it off and he thunderously says so. Pach' only wishes he could go take Elaine's hand and lead her out of here.

Who comes to take his hand, walking over in front of everyone, is Baxter's daughter, Amanda. She presses up beside him and says she wants to be his friend, too. In this half-light they may not notice how red his face is, must be, and how his acne's flaring up. He looks around in the sudden silence for help. He's afraid Elaine might get the wrong idea. Certainly Amanda's father seems to have got the wrong idea; he's sputtering and his face is puffed up like he's about to have a fit, his stupid son boiling up beside him. Luckily, the other Baxter girl, the older frumpy one, quietly takes charge. "She's kinda simple," she mutters by way of apology, and leads the girl away, and Pach' thanks her. All these crazy kids. Pach' is beginning to feel like the Pied Piper. Of course, people didn't like the Pied Piper either, did they?

Elaine puts her arms around him and hugs him close. She tells him tearfully how much she loves him, how she's missed him. Don't ever leave me again, Carl Dean. She calls him Carl Dean? Probably. Pach' doesn't seem right. She's such a tender fragile person, she can't even imagine savage Indians. When he slides his hand down to hold her little bottom, she doesn't complain. She presses closer to him and releases a little gasp, a kind of sob. He can feel her tummy pushing against him. "I love you, Elaine," he whispers, and she trembles and grips him tightly as the sweet night closes down around them. He tugs gently at her bottom to rub her tummy against his hard-on. He desperately wants her to take it in her mouth. But would she, could she? No, but Sissy does, lapping lovingly at it with his little puppy tongue. Pach' is somewhat alarmed by this, and he pauses to worry about it. He spent a lot of time and spunk jerking off in prison, but otherwise he stayed clean. Except for little Sissy, as they called him. Her. Sissy was more girl than guy and the men called him "she" and "her," and eventually Pach' did, too, but never in ridicule. Sissy had a little dick and it got hard like a pencil stub when he was excited, but he was curvy and cuddly with innocent blue eyes and puckery lips and a snow-white bottom, soft and round as a girl's. "Sissy" was for "Sister," both as in family and in nun: he liked to dress up like one, using prison blankets. Even the screws thought this was funny, and several of them were probably serviced by Sissy in that costume. He was in for drugs and as an accessory to murder, a murder committed by his boyfriend, whom he then tried to hide. His boyfriend died in a drug-crazed shootout with the cops, and Sissy was taken in. And one sad and lonely night when Pach' could not stop thinking about Elaine, Sissy took him in his mouth and he let him do that. Sissy said he'd never seen one that big and it almost frightened him. Eventually he had Sissy in other ways, too, but always while thinking about Elaine. And now, lying in the back of his van only yards away from her (he has been unable to take his gaze away from the lighted windows of their trailer, even though the blinds are pulled) and humping his pillow while fantasizing about her, it is Sissy who has taken *her* place. That's weird, and he doesn't think he likes it. Sissy eventually got a tattoo of a little heart with a large Indian arrow through it and the words CRAZY APACHE—not over his heart, but on his little white left cheek, otherwise without a blemish. Sissy cried when Pach' left prison and Pach' felt bad, too. Poor little Sissy. Oh, what the hell. Out of affection, Pach' lets him finish up.

The first time he blew his wad it was like an accident and he didn't know what was happening. He thought he'd been visited by angels. His old lady, who was not otherwise very religious, had a thing about angels and other supernatural creatures, and he was still pretty susceptible to all that. He sometimes thought he heard angels in his room, flying around like bats. Maybe they were bats. When he started getting serious about Christianity at the Baptist Church, it felt like growing up, and he looked down on his superstitious mother after that, though actually all he'd done was stop believing in Rudolph while sticking with Santa Claus. Then along came Mrs. Norton, who introduced him to Santa's big daddy Domiron off in some other dimension, therewith offering him access to possibilities beyond his pathetic fucked-up small-town life and making him feel like some kind of privileged highbrow. He finally got rid of all that crap in prison. Reading the Bible helped. One of the few books you could have in stir. He decided to plow straight through it, beginning to end. He read first with a certain awe (this has been *the* book for twenty centuries!), then with increasing irritation (who wrote this stupid thing?), finally with disgust and anger. A total swindle. Blaming God for writing it is a fucking sacrilege. Got interested in troublemakers instead. Which was just about anybody who got anything done. Jesus, for example, the wildass bastard. Before checking out, he got a pep talk in his cell from the prison chaplain, who interrupted him while he was saying goodbye to Sissy, and he let the bastard have it. "Jesus was all right," he said, "but Christ sucks." When the chaplain left, shaking his head, Sissy started giggling and bawling hysterically at the same time and told him he was completely crazy. His Crazy Apache.

Should he open another beer? He shouldn't. Only half a six-pack left and no easy way to get more. Not much money for buying it even if he should break out of this place for a time, and as long as he helps out here with the building, no way to earn more. He has at least been well fed. Wayne Shawcross and Ludie Belle invited him to stop by their house trailer after the prayer meeting for something extra to eat. She's in charge of the camp kitchen and has a well-stocked fridge. She probably keeps a bottle somewhere, too, but he didn't want to ask. Not yet. Same with telling them about Elaine. They are good people, and he wanted to talk with them straight out about his feelings—they'd seen what he did after the prayer meeting—and he even thought he might show them his tattoo, but when they asked him what he was doing here, he told them what he'd told Elaine's mother. Which is also true. He *has* been lonely. And both of them seem like pretty serious believers, Wayne especially, so he has to be careful.

The lights have gone out in the Collins trailer, which looms imperiously over him, aglow in the light of the full moon. In his imagination she sleeps in her Brunist tunic. The one she was wearing on Easter night all those years ago. When he thinks of her, that cotton fabric is what his fingers feel. Tonight, when the prayer meeting ended, he got up his nerve and walked over to her, his hands in his pockets, to say hello. It was an awkward moment with everyone watching and he knew his acne was flaring up. When he was actually in front of her, he couldn't think of what to say. He found it difficult to look into her eyes, but when he dropped his eyes, there was her body draped in the thin tunic, and that confused him all the more. Finally he just nodded and said, "Hi, it's me." Elaine only stared at him as if he'd just threatened to kill her, and without saying a word, left immediately with her mother. Well, he thought, at least she didn't tell him to go away. It's only his first day. He can be patient. Meanwhile, he has opened another beer. It's Easter night, the moon's filling up the sky, and they're in his car again. She's trembling, but she has been through this before, and is ready now. "Stay the fuck out of this," he says to Sissy. "Go take a walk and don't come back until I blink the lights."

# II.3

## Sunday 26 April – Wednesday 29 April

"Come on, Billy Don, how can you *not* hear it? It's right there, clear as a bell!"

"Well, that bell is just not ringing for me." Yet again, for the umpteenth time, Brother Abner Baxter says: "…cast off the works of darkness, and put on the armor of light." "Honest, Darren, all I hear is a kind of hissing sound."

"Exactly!"

"But it's not anybody saying anything. It's just a kind of noise. Might even be part of how Reverend Baxter is saying 'darkness.'"

"No, it comes *after*, Billy Don. It's her! I'm *telling* you!"

"Maybe you got better ears than me."

"Maybe I have." Sometimes Billy Don seems plain stupid. "But there's more! *Listen!*"

*Listen!* That's the whispered word Darren hears behind the powerful bass tones of the preacher: *Listen!* It is she. He knows it. The voice in the ditch. Marcella. They both have trouble saying her name. It is as though she has passed beyond the nominal, is mysteriously just "she." Less than she. Or more. An aura. The displaced voice of the mystical figure pointing to Heaven in the painting in Reverend Clegg's Florida church. A voice in pain. The recording, dated and catalogued, as are all their tapes, is the one from a week ago down at the foot of the mine hill during the arrival on the Day of the Sacrifice of Reverend Baxter and his family. Billy Don was holding the microphone, his own flat, ugly voice blocking out the others until Darren shushed him (maybe that's the sound Darren keeps hearing, Billy Don thinks: his own shushing). "Do ye likewise, my friends, while there is still time for your souls to be saved!" Abner Baxter is urging on the tape. There's a tiny pause between "friends" and "while," and Darren backs it up and plays it again. "Do you hear it, Billy Don?"

"Sure. Reverend Baxter wants everybody to put on the armor of light."

"No, I don't mean that. Pay attention!" He plays it again, growing impatient with Billy Don. He's doing this on purpose. It's that evil girl. She's corrupting his soul. "Between those two words, that girl's voice, saying 'to me.' It's just a whisper, but you can't miss it!"

"Yeah, okay, I hear it now." On the table between them is a blurry photograph of all the people on the mine road taken from the top of the hill, Darren having appropriated the dead woman's box camera before anyone noticed. The old lady's lens had been amateurishly aimed toward the sun and Darren presumably sees a ghostly presence in the consequent flare of light. "But why do you think it's a girl's voice? It's most likely one of those old women standing around, but you can't hear her except when Reverend Baxter stops to catch his breath."

"No, listen again. No one at the camp has a weird breathy voice like that. No one alive, anyway."

"'Do ye likewise, my friends...' (...to me...) 'while there is...'"

Okay, it's there. But so what? Ever since they met, Billy Don has shared Darren's scientific quest for eschatological truth, and he was just as curious as Darren was when Patti Jo said she could hear the dead girl speaking to her from the ditch that day, but Darren is losing him on this one. Darren has played and replayed these mine road tapes all week, hoping he might have picked up her voice, pressing on long after Billy Don had given up. At the Sunday service this morning, after Brother John P. Suggs had confirmed for everybody the final acquisition of the Mount of Redemption and the anonymous gift that will make possible the building of their temple on it, setting off a burst of rapturous praise-giving, Patti Jo got up with her friend Duke to lead everyone in singing "Higher Ground," and Billy Don, humming along in his tuneless fashion, found himself thinking about the way Patti Jo said she communicated with Marcella's spirit. "Marcella doesn't use words exactly. It's more like she's just thinking and I can sort of sense what she's thinking. I know that sounds weird, but it feels completely natural." So nothing really said, just a kind of shared thereness, and if that's so, he wondered, watching Patti Jo's breasts bob about under her white blouse (when they interviewed her, the poor woman had a lot of sad stories to tell—she's had a tough life and it shows on her face—but she still has a lot of bounce and it's fun to watch her sing), why did Darren think they would hear a voice when she didn't? We're not all mediums, Darren said. If it's important, like Patti Jo says the voice says it is, then the spirit has to get through however it can.

It's how he thinks. There's no answer, just belief or damnation. Like now, when Darren replays the "still time for your souls" bit and says, "If you listen close, you can hear her struggling to be heard while the others are carrying on, like a kind of strangled squeaky sound."

"I think that might be the little Baxter kid. He was having a fit or something."

"I don't think so, but even if it were, as I've tried to explain, Billy Don, that would only mean she might have been trying to reach us through him and it wasn't quite working."

"You mean like he was sorta possessed."

Darren sighs irritably.

Billy Don gazes out the window of their church office, which is still also their bedroom, the Baxters having commandeered their designated cabin with no signs of giving it up. No matter. Mr. Suggs has promised them a camper, which is a better deal anyway. It's woodsy and late-April green out there, a jean-jacket getup-a-ballgame day, not a day to be stuck in here. Darren is growing exasperated with him, he knows, but though Darren is smarter than he is and he's usually right, he's trying too hard to make something out of nothing. It's not just these mine road tapes. Darren has been puzzling through all their interviews and their field recordings of conversations picked up on the Mount and around the dogwood tree and everything else he thinks might contain secret messages. He had Billy Don set up the tape recorder in the ditch, where they left it overnight, hoping to pick up the ghostly whispering they could not hear by day, but the tape ran out and the battery died before they got anything. Darren claimed to hear strange rustlings, but when Billy Don said, "Rabbits probably," Darren just got mad. Darren has also been counting all the words and letters in the original sayings of the Prophet, as well as those in the slightly different versions preached by Sister Clara and the others, subtracting one from the other to see if there is any pattern in what he is calling "the residue of corruption." Darren is not as hot on Sister Clara as he once was. He has turned all the letters of each of the seven prophecies in both versions into numbers, has asked Billy Don to do a lot of adding and subtracting and averaging and figuring out ratios and square roots, then converted the numerical values of the differences back into letters again, and he has performed the same kinds of operations on Ely Collins' final death note, focusing especially on the words with improper capitals and misspellings. "If this message comes from God, Billy Don, and I believe that it truly does, for a great religion has been born from it, then we have to assume God makes spelling mistakes only on purpose!" Darren calls it the ancient Greek science of isopsephia, dating clear back to the Sibylline Oracles, which exactly predicted the birth of Jesus Christ centuries before it happened. This was amazing; Billy Don was impressed.

Now Darren is replaying "while there is still time for your souls to be saved," and at the end there is just enough of a pause to hear the word "week" or something like it. Billy Don has less trouble with this one, he just isn't so sure where it's coming from. Before he can say so, though, Darren has already moved ahead to the next break. Oh oh. Billy Don gets it now. "You hear it, Billy Don?"

"Yup."

"'Of Sundays!'" There's a kind of glow about Darren when he gets excited. His blue eyes seem to grow bigger behind his little round spectacles and it's like you can look right through them into the sparkly cavern of his head. He backs up the tape and plays it again. "*'Listen... to me! ...A week...of Sundays!'*" Darren whispers, imitating the voice. "That's what she was trying to tell us, Billy Don! Just like the Prophet!"

"Wait. Let me hear that again. Are you sure it's Sundays? Sounds more like it's got an 'm.' Like 'some days.'"

"Don't be dumb, Billy Don! What could that possibly mean? This makes complete sense. You can even hear her say 'again' a moment later. *'Listen to me! A week of Sundays...again!'* Hear it?"

"But, well, that's not exactly what her brother said. He said, 'Sunday week.'"

"That's right. 'Coming of Light, Sunday week.' But it turned out to be a week of Sundays, or seven weeks after the Day of Redemption."

"June the seventh."

"June the seventh. The Midnight Coming. When everybody gathered together five years ago all around the world. It was even bigger in terms of numbers than the Day of Redemption." Darren's voice has begun to sound like the wheezy voice in the ditch.

"Six weeks from today." Billy Don tugs on the end of his moustache. Could it be? Was the spirit of the dead girl really trying to reach them? It's possible. And scary. It means the Rapture might be even closer than they have been supposing. Nothing was to have happened for another couple of years at least. If it's true and not just something Darren is making up, he doesn't have much time to acquaint himself fully with the ways of the world and find a partner for eternity. It's like he's aged suddenly from twenty-two to eighty-two overnight. He pushes these doomsday thoughts aside and concentrates on the Prophet's sister instead. Though they never knew her, and she's a saint and completely dead, whenever Billy Don thinks about Marcella Bruno it is not her spirit that comes foremost to mind, or even the beautiful painting in the Florida church, but her radiant nude body in their secreted photos of her on the leather couch, photos he peeks at every chance he gets—as God's disciple and exegete, of course, seeking truth and understanding. As soon as Darren leaves, he'll get them out again, examine them for further revelations. And use the new office phone, give Sally Elliott another call. He wants to ask her about all this. And thinking about the end makes him feel bad (he's *not* eighty-two, darn it), and she always has something funny or smart to say that cheers him up. "So what do you think? Something's gonna happen that day?"

"I don't know, Billy Don. I'm kind of scared. I need your help."

When Darren asked Clara what happened to Marcella's body, she didn't know. "When things settle down here, we can maybe ask." Though some believe the Day of Redemption was the beginning of the Rapture and Marcella was transported directly to the Kingdom of Light, Clara, while allowing that it could be so, doubts it would have happened unwitnessed. Well, she is a good woman but she has a more naïve view of God's transparency than they do. "But why was the girl out there on the mine road all alone in the first place?" Billy Don wanted to know. "Why wasn't she with everybody else?" "She'd took sick, bless her soul. We was planning to take her out there the next day with us, but it was only the day before and we didn't want her to worsen. We probly oughter left somebody to watch over her, but I guess they was too much else to think on." "What kind of sick?" Darren asked. They didn't get an answer to that, though before she went back to Florida they overheard Betty Wilson Clegg say she believed the poor child really died of heartbreak. They feel fairly certain, after seeing the forbidden photos, what she meant by that, but they also think that Mrs. Clegg is something of a simpleton, and Darren in particular believes that such banalities trivialize God's operations among humankind. God is not a ladies' romance writer. They have conducted sit-down interviews with many of the Brunists in their effort to capture the early history of the movement, but Sister Clara is always too busy for long conversations, so Darren has made a habit of simply leaving the recorder running whenever she's in the office, and maybe she knows that and maybe she doesn't. She has said some things about Abner Baxter that suggest she doesn't, or else she forgets.

Reverend Baxter is one of those who believe the Prophet's sister and First Martyr was taken up bodily into Heaven. Billy Don has speculated that's because it relieves his guilt about the accident, but that just shows how earthbound Billy Don still is. The plain fact is that Brother Abner is a pre-Tribulation dispensationalist and Clara Collins is more post-Trib, so he would naturally expect Marcella to be taken immediately into the presence of the Lord, whereas Clara would suppose she'd have to wait for everybody else. It's as simple as that. Darren doesn't like Abner Baxter any more than Billy Don does, but he never lets personal feelings interfere with his pursuit of absolute truth, an attitude much like Reverend Baxter's, though Darren is more of a searcher, while Reverend Baxter is, well, a preacher. Darren and Billy Don are, as they like to say, dialoguing with history, but Billy Don believes there are as many histories as there are people and all of them are true, history being made up of memories and the recording of memories, which is why he is enthusiastic about their project. It also means the real truth will always elude him. Darren knows that they live in two kinds of time at once: human clock time and cosmic eternity. And though any understanding of the mysteries of eternity demands an accurate knowledge of clock time—history being a kind of obscure reflection of metahistory, as he likes to call it, having learned the word in Bible School—the seeming paradoxes of clock time are resolved only when absorbed as unities within timeless eternity. Reverend Baxter, in his blustery way, seems tuned in to that. He also adheres strictly to the original sayings of the Prophet, to the extent that they were written down or could be remembered. Darren is impressed by this faithfulness to prophetic utterance. Sister Clara has freely reinterpreted them, which is, frankly, disrespectful and a kind of corruption. Thus, Giovanni Bruno's "Circle of Evenings" is no longer even a prophecy but only a kind of blessing upon her Evening Circle church group. Sister Clara is thoughtful and caring, a deep believer utterly devoted to evangelism and the Brunist vision, and the sincerest person Darren has ever known, but she is also a stubborn pragmatist, a compromiser and a builder, her apocalyptic message watered down by personal beliefs in charity and brotherhood and the establishment of a new faith. He understands her motivations but finds something impure about them. Well, he is not himself a proselytizer. The truth is the truth. If only one person grasps it and is saved, that is enough. Brother Abner, contrarily, is more of a revolutionary, radically committed to the truth as it has been revealed to him, even if it is a terrible truth. Sins not expurgated by fire, he has preached, will be punished by fire in the life to come. If the Brunists are, as they call themselves, "the Army of the Sons of Light," Abner Baxter is the Army, Clara the Light. Darren is afraid of Brother Abner and loves Sister Clara but knows in his heart he belongs in Abner's Army.

Clara and Ben have also talked in a frank way on the tapes about First Follower Carl Dean Palmers, who turned up at the camp unexpectedly last Friday, calling himself Pach', or Apache. A strange, beardy, tattooed fellow in a tattered ball cap and engraved red boots who keeps to himself but is not afraid of hard work and who may or may not still be a Brunist believer. Ben mostly argues for him, but Clara seems full of doubts. Because of her daughter probably. Pach' seems to have his eye on Elaine, who is homely and spindly and a half foot taller than he is. Hard to figure, though he's no beauty either. He has been a wild and disturbing presence for many, seen as an apostate and a dangerous interloper, an ex-con with criminal ways, but Darren and Billy Don have found him something of a godsend—Darren because he is potentially a fount of information about the earliest days, Billy Don simply because he has needed someone like him at the camp his own age to talk to. They have seen his dark side in the somewhat obscene photos taken on the Day of Redemption, but Darren argues that his frenzy was a kind of divine frenzy. A hero who took a lot of punishment for others. And his arrival proved a good omen. The very same day he entered the camp, they received the amazing news that they were suddenly the new possessors of the Mount of Redemption and other lands about, and many credited Pach' with bringing them this miraculous good fortune by his return to the fold. He has been slow to open up and says he can't remember what the Prophet actually said, but he has told them some very vivid prison stories and what it was like down at the city jail the night after the Day of Redemption, and Darren is eager to learn more.

When Billy Don attempts to explain the Marcella tapes to Sally Elliott over a cherry-chocolate sundae in the Tucker City drugstore (she's buying as usual, knowing he's penniless), he is a bit disturbed by how funny she thinks it all is, but he appreciates the relief from Darren's fierce humorlessness, so he smiles his embarrassed smile and goes along. They are sitting at one of those old-fashioned wrought-iron marble-topped ice cream tables that he associates with the town he grew up in. He feels at home in here and is happy to be with this girl again. Sally wants to know how the voice ended up in the ditch, so he tells her the story of how the girl got left behind when the Brunists gathered on the Mount with box suppers the night before the Day of Redemption and how she came running out there all alone just at the same time that the Brunists' worst enemies, the followers of Reverend Abner Baxter, came driving out there to attack them, and how the Brunists, seeing the lights on the mine road and hoping to avoid the confrontation, jumped into their cars and with their lights off went charging down the hill toward the Baxterites, hoping to get past them before they could get turned around, and how there was a terrible pile-up (Sally is laughing again, but this is serious) and the poor girl got struck by six or seven different cars and died there in the ditch.

"That's *terrible*, Billy Don!" says Sally, still giggling. "And her voice just got stuck there and can't get out?"

"No, it's not like that. If she's God's messenger, she might be heard anywhere, any time, and even by different people in different places at the same time. But it was such a key moment. Reverend Baxter was converted and became a Brunist that night at the ditch, and there was a great reconciliation and they all marched together the next day to the Mount of Redemption, and that's really how the church was born. Right after that came the Persecution and everyone got split up and wandered about. And that Saturday last week was exactly five years after the Night of the Sacrifice, and it was when Reverend Baxter and Mrs. Collins and all their followers finally came together again, right there beside that same ditch. It was just natural something unusual might happen."

"That's what it's called? The sacrifice?" Sally plucks another cigarette from her pack, offers him one which he again turns down. "I only chew the stuff," he said shyly the first time, then worried she might have found that too hicksville and laughed it off as a joke, or tried to. "You know," she says, lighting up, "I remember my dad saying something at the time about her maybe being killed in a ritual sacrifice."

"That's an insane rumor. These are all just ordinary people like you and me. They don't do stuff like that. Your dad must have got mixed up with the Powers of Darkness."

He expects her to smile at that, but instead she turns melancholy. "You're not far off. My dad's in the dark all right, always has been. Less light in there than you can get out of a used sparkler. And mixed up? Absolutely. But power? He's had the stupidest job in the world and he just got fired from it. Now he's going to be filed away in some corner down at city hall. They'd make him the janitor, but he can't stay on his feet long enough to push a broom." She blows a long plume of smoke and watches it rise toward the tin ceiling of the old drugstore, then gets out her notebook and jots something down. He'd only meant to joke in his clumsy way, but he obviously touched a sore point, and he's sorry. Sally doesn't have all that much in the way of a bosom, just two soft bulges, but it's hard not to stare because she always wears T-shirts with funny things printed on them. Today there's a flying star and it says: IF YOU GET HIT BY A SHOOTING STAR, YOU'LL METEOR MAKER. That's probably sacrilegious, but he likes it that she gives him things to read there so he doesn't have to keep looking away. Maybe he should say he'd like to bookmark it and take it home with him. If he only had the nerve. As far as he can tell (she has a kind of shameless way of scratching herself), she doesn't wear a bra either. "So, the poor girl. Just bad luck, hunh? Went for a jog, wrong place, wrong time?"

"Well, we don't think it was just luck."

"Oh right. God's secret designs. Kill a kid to kickstart a new religion. And so now you guys are trying to crack God's code. Don't you ever wonder, Billy Don, why any god, if there were one, would want to play such silly games with people? If he wanted something, why wouldn't he just come out with it?"

"He did that. It's called the Bible. It's up to us to read it and understand it and live by it."

"Yeah, I've read the thing. Most of it. Skipped some of the dumber parts. If God wrote it, he's a crummy writer. He didn't, of course. A bunch of beardy guys with tight assholes did."

He knows he's gone red again. She's trying to provoke him and he should probably get up and leave, but the sundae is like the most delicious thing he's ever eaten and he can't help but linger over it. The sort of thing he has had to do without while traveling unpaid with the Brunists. If he or Darren need money for anything—new jeans or a pair of shoes—they have to ask Clara for it; no way they could ever ask for ice cream money, though Sister Ludie Belle sometimes buys tubs of commercial ice cream for the Sunday camp meals. Sally, watching him, says, "Hey, Billy Don. Would you like another?" He stares down into his empty bowl. He wants to say no thank you, but Satan (maybe she really is the devil incarnate like Darren says) has him by the whatsits and he can't.

And it's not just the sundae. Sally mostly makes fun of him, he knows that, but he likes to be around her and he finds himself confessing things to her he'd never tell anyone else. All his doubts, for example. How he still prays every day but feels more and more like he's just talking to himself, as if his involvement with the Brunists has cut him off from God and Jesus ("Well, there's *something* to be said for them, then," Sally said). How he wanted to get on that bus with the kids from Florida—they were a lot more fun than the crowd at the camp, and just as Christian—but how hard it would be to let down Darren and Sister Clara and Brother Ben. About how he woke up one night and Darren was touching him and how it scared him but he let it happen. In fact, maybe that was the scariest part. He didn't know what else to do until it occurred to him he could just roll over. The next day Darren told him about a dream he'd had about a beautiful woman who turned into Mabel Hall when he touched her and he wondered if it was some kind of omen. Billy Don believed him and didn't believe him at the same time. Mostly he didn't believe him, and it made him wonder about the wet dreams he'd had recently, though he didn't tell Sally that part.

And now these obsessions with words and numbers. When he told Sally about Darren's code charts and "sacred calendars" at their first meeting here last week, Sally said, "Numbers always have these weird magical properties—but it depends on where you start counting from, right? To add a millennium, you first have to locate zero and one." "I think we have worked all that out," he said with a smile, and she smiled right back at him and said, "I think we have not," and she told him about all the different calendars through history and how there have been thousands of prophets of apocalypse and all of them obviously wrong, the first being Jesus himself. "Well, Jesus was a special case," he said, "because Jesus didn't die. As for all the others, we can learn from them, and where they failed we can get it right." But a seed of doubt had been planted and he knew she could hear it in his voice. When she shook her head sadly and said, "Oh, Billy Don," he felt like he wanted to hug her and be hugged by her, and he worried then that he was succumbing to evil, and he wondered if he should just stand up and walk away as fast as he could.

It has been especially hard for him not to stand up for Darren. Becoming his friend was a turning point in Billy Don's life. He was morally adrift until then, confused, more interested in baseball than religion and in the opposite sex more than either. He ended up in Bible college because it was cheap and said to be easy and full of friendly girls. And because he needed to get on the wagon and stay there. He and Darren met in a New Testament seminar taught by an old fellow with soft dewlaps and a soft brain who dug at his scalp while lecturing as if trying to dip his fingers in it, and they started meeting outside of class for coffee or lemonade and boiled peanuts. Darren introduced him to the scarier side of religion—what it was all about, really—and opened his eyes to the underlying patterns of things, which are not really hidden so much as just not visible on the surface. Billy Don was always good at puzzles—Darren said it was a gift from God and at the heart of his calling (he'd not even *thought* about having a calling)—and Darren proposed some new ones of a seriousness beyond anything he had imagined before. Darren was the smartest and most intense person he had ever met, and when Billy Don was around him, he felt connected to the world—not just the world, the *universe*—in a way he had never known. But now, well, he's not so sure.

Today, when he brought up the Sibylline Oracles and how they prophesied the birth of Jesus, thinking to impress her, she only looked pained and told him they were a well-known sixth century fraud. Could this be true? "Such a desperate human thing," she said, "to look for mysteries where there are none." She often says things like that and it both thrills him and dismays him. That she treats him so seriously; that she mocks him so. But he likes to hear her laugh, so bold and free. He's never heard a girl laugh quite like that, and he sometimes plays the fool for the simple reward of it. Now he has been telling her more of the Marcella legends, about the heart-shaped bloodstain on her tunic, about how when she died she pointed to Heaven and kept that pose all the next day (the belief of many being that she was raptured straight to Heaven), about the white bird that flew overhead and some said right out of her mouth, and the crosses of blood that appeared on people's foreheads after. "Raptured? But there was a body. What happened to it?"

"No one knows."

"Well, it all sounds like a lotta phony baloney to me," she says, shaking her head and lighting up again.

"Yeah, that's sorta what Pach' said, too."

"Patch?"

"Carl Dean Palmers. He's one of the original twelve First Followers. He just turned up over the weekend. Drove in in an old beat-up van."

"Oh, right. Ugly Palmers. What we called him in high school. Poor boy, he was. A knobby-headed toad with acne all the way to his knees and a raging temper. How does he look now?"

"Okay. He's got a beard. Seems cool."

"I thought he ended up in the penitentiary."

"He did. He's out now He picked up his new name in prison. When we filled him in about Marcella, he said he was there that night, and all that was, well, he used a bad word, but, like you said, baloney."

Sally leans across the table and whispers conspiratorially, "What was the bad word, Billy D?" There's an embarrassed pause and he knows he has an idiotic grin on his face. "Bullshit…?" He nods. "So," she exclaims, leaning back, "Ugly Palmers said it was all bullshit. Good for him!" She raises her empty sundae bowl as if in a toast. *"Bullshit!"*

"Well, maybe," he says, trying not to look at the guy behind the soda fountain, "except for the part about her pointing to Heaven. You can see that even in the news photos."

"Hmm. You're right. I do remember something like that. Her arm sticking up like a petrified blue twig. I was so grossed out I could hardly register the details. At the time, I figured it must have been some kind of trick, but, really, I didn't want to look. I was pretty squeamish back then."

"There's a famous painting of her in a church in Florida, lying in the ditch, pointing to Heaven like that."

"With a blue arm?"

"No, she's very—"

"What's it based on? The painter's fancy, I suppose, like all the hokum Jesus paintings. I bet no one even took a photograph while she was in the ditch."

"Well, no…not in the ditch exactly…" Perhaps the whole conversation this afternoon has been aimed at this moment. There is something more he has wanted to share with Sally and he hasn't known how to bring it up, and now here it is. It's as if she knew just the question to ask. He reaches into his book bag and brings out the photos. He's brought two of them—before and after shots, so to speak. "These were taken just before she died. In the first one there, you can see her hand is pointing up just like—"

"Hey! Look at the gorgeous ass on that stud!" She runs her finger over it, grinning broadly. This might not have been the best idea. People's heads are turning. "Who is that? Oh right! I know! The newspaper guy. Miller. I heard my dad talking about these photos back at the time. And that's her, hunh? The voice in the ditch. Poor thing. She's cute. Except in this other one she looks absolutely terrified. She's clutching that choker around her neck like the guy's about to strangle her. Or maybe he's going to beat her with that newspaper. Do you suppose these photos have anything to do with her being out there on the mine road that night?" She thinks about that for a moment. "Sure they do."

"That might be a kind of simple way of looking at it," he says softly, recalling Darren's words. "God is not a ladies' romance novelist."

"No, you're right there. He works more in the horror genre. Do you love God, Billy Don?"

"Sure. Don't you?"

"If I thought he was really there, I'd hate him."

"Wow. Just like Darren says. You really *are* evil."

Sally grins and winks at him, stubbing out her cigarette, and he doesn't know if it's the wink of the devil or just a mischievous girl trying to be funny. "I wonder who took these photos. Do you suppose the jerk set up a camera at his back and took them himself?"

"Maybe. But we think it could be some sort of mysterious…you know…"

"God as a pornographer? Funny. I wouldn't be surprised. But tell me, Billy Don," she says, leaning across the table again in her bright orange T-shirt with the soft things floating in it and lowering her voice at last, "do these photos turn you on?"

"Well, sure. A little." He knows he's red to the roots (what a question!), but the conversation has come around to where in his fantasies he's always imagined it would, and he can tell she's pretty excited herself. He'd like to ask her how she feels about them, but he doesn't know how. He can only grin stupidly and read her shirt again.

"What does your friend think of them?"

"Darren? He says he feels as if he is staring upon the face of evil."

The expression on Sally's face is hard to read at first. It's like amazement, disbelief, expectation—but then she bursts into a whooping peal of laughter, nearly falls off her chair. Everybody in the drugstore is staring at them now and he knows he should hide the photos, but he can't move. "The face of evil!" she cries. "That's *beautiful!*"

"I think he meant, you know, the cruelty and—"

"He's *not* talking about the girl, I assume," she gasps, in and around her laughter.

"No—"

"What other face *is* there, Billy Don?"

When he stares blankly at her, she points to it. Oh. That's really embarrassing. It *is* funny, though, and he finds himself giggling in a hiccuppy sort of way. The guy behind the soda fountain is craning his neck to try to see the photos. Hastily, he slips them back into his book bag.

"Listen, Billy D," Sally says. "I've got an idea."

"Hey, listen to this one!" the Elliott girl calls out from behind an overgrown chokeberry thicket, putting Darren's teeth on edge, her very presence a desecration here. "'Buck Noone: Coalminer. Gone Below to Work One Last Shift.'"

"That's great," says Billy Don, grinning his clownish mustachioed grin. "But come here. Something really weird." The girl has twisted wildflowers into her snarly hair and is wearing an orange T-shirt with what looks like the Star of Bethlehem on it (black on orange, the devil's colors) and a two-edged slogan that could mean the birth of Christ connects you to God, but probably means that Christianity is lethal. "This headstone broke in half. See what it says."

"'A Broken Heart Lies Here.' Wow! That one wins the black ribbon! Except…" She kicks at a whiskey bottle and a couple of crushed beercans in the weeds nearby. "Probably not God's joke, but some drunk's. Party place."

The two of them are so engaged in their ghoulish amusements that they have forgotten the reason they are here. No matter. They will not find what they are looking for. Even did it exist, it would not appear before their blinded eyes. For this people's heart is waxed gross, and their ears are dull of hearing, and their eyes they have closed.

Darren does not feel he has come here of his own accord. He has been *brought* here, whether by some demonic force or by the will of God, he cannot be sure, but mindful of the messages he has been discovering of late, he too, though uninterested in the pointless search of his two companions, has looked and listened carefully, read the stony messages, watched for suggestive patterns in the arrangement of the tombs, especially here in this old municipal cemetery from early in the century, when the town was young. It was not far from the center when first laid out, but the town, instead of embracing it, grew the other way, almost as if in fear or revulsion, and over time other cemeteries of a more contemporary and sterile sort (they have visited them) were created while this one sank into its woodsy surroundings and was largely forgotten, its graves untended. "You Will Be In Our Hearts Forever," says a particularly melancholy gravestone lying in cracked ruin on its back, buried in weeds and dark green with moss, the deceased's name obliterated by the weather or else broken away. Vanity of vanities, all is vanity, saith the Preacher. Who did not know Jesus.

When Darren discovered both the photos and the car gone, he was seized by a convulsive rage, which may have been a holy rage, though it didn't feel like it. He felt personally betrayed and his eyes filled with tears. If Billy Don has shown that evil girl those photos, what else has he shown and told her? He had been working on his investigations into what he was calling "paranormal manifestations at the site of the first martyrdom" and additional esoteric implications in the patterns of text and number in other recordings and documents, such as "The Revelation to Reverend Ely Collins," and in his careful cut-and-splice isolation of the fragments from the ditch he had struck on something new and startling: the word "two" before "week" (so perhaps it was "weeks"). Did that mean the voice was suggesting that the critical date might not be June the seventh, but July the twenty-sixth? He had dashed out in search of Billy Don to get his opinion and out in the main square had run into Mrs. Blaurock, who told him she'd just spoken with Billy Don on his way over to the parking lot. She'd grabbed his arm in her big meaty fist and said, "There's a lotta people here think you boys're on to something. God bless you, son. You keep doing your good work." Their car was gone. He'd feared the worst. The missing photos had confirmed it.

It was all he could do to stop himself from exploding into a tantrum when a giddy, excited Billy Don returned to tell him the Elliott girl would be taking them on a tour of the town cemeteries in search of Marcella Bruno's grave. When he confronted Billy Don with his treacherous deception (his voice was trembling, he couldn't help it), Billy Don only blushed and grinned sheepishly and asked if he was going with them or not? No, he snapped. Certainly not. It was completely stupid—even if they found a grave marker with her name on it, they could not know whose the buried body was, or even if there was one—and it could be dangerous. He begged Billy Don not to go, but when Billy Don left, he left with him, in part to protect his deluded friend but mostly because he could not seem to stop himself.

They started in what the other two believed was the most likely place, the San Luca Catholic cemetery, and they did find the parents' grave with its small "Riposa In Pace" headstone, together with three other Bruno children buried close by—two boys just out of their teens and an unborn baby girl—but no sign of Giovanni or Marcella. Of course, they were probably excommunicated by then and not allowed in here. That was the girl's judgment, but just the same, they scoured the cemetery grave by grave, Billy Don squatting down to read the names and numbers, the Elliott girl sometimes taking notes. The place felt alien to Darren, full of open-armed Virgin Marys and tearful angels, and he did not believe he would learn anything here, so he trailed along behind the others, keeping a wary eye on the irreverent girl and on the other visitors wandering about, mostly old women wearing headscarves. In case anyone asked, they were presumably college friends of hers, working on a history project, but if they were found out, the consequences could be serious.

He did pause for a moment in front of a square blocky tombstone for two brothers who died apparently at the same time in 1931, an accident or something. There were two carved miners' helmets on top and a strange Italian inscription that read "Quello Che Siete Fummo, Quello Che Siamo Sarete." "Siete" might be "seven" and "fummo" "smoke," he thought, but he had no clue at all about "sarete" or "siamo." The helmets had lamps on them, just like the one Clara often uses for baptism ceremonies, and the four numbers of the year, he realized, added up to fourteen, twice "siete." Could "sarete" be some kind of tunic or something? The Elliott girl saw him studying it and came over to read the inscription over his shoulder, blowing her obnoxious "fummo" past his ear. "What's a 'sarete'?" he asked. Barked, really. He was finding it hard to be civil. "Well, my Italian is pretty lousy, but I think it's all a play on the 'to be' verb. Something like, 'What you are we were and what we are you'll be.' Couple of guys who wanted everyone to know we're all in the same club." He felt stupid and angry. He began walking toward the gate and eventually they followed, laughing at some private joke.

They went on to the Woodlawn, Our Savior, South Baptist Memorial (in which they recognized the names of several of the coal miners killed in the Deepwater accident, including Ben Wosznik's brother), and West Condon Municipal cemeteries, all out beyond the edge of town on one side or the other. In one of them the Elliott girl asked them about her aunt Debra. Had Darren any intention of replying to the girl's question (he had not), he would have said that she is a committed leader within the movement and one of its most selfless benefactors (this was mostly true), serenely (less true) awaiting God's next interaction with human history. He might also have told her that it was Colin, in a clearly visionary moment, who had recognized her as an emissary of the forces of evil—he mistakenly called her the Antichrist, though everyone knew what he meant—at the time of her brazen infiltration of the gathering last week on the Mount of Redemption. Colin, though desperately unstable, is a special sort of genius, attuned to vibrations beyond the ken of others in the way that certain high-pitched frequencies could be heard by dogs but not by the human ear, and Darren always listens carefully to everything he says. Billy Don did answer the girl and what he said was that Mrs. Edwards is "kind of upset" about all the new people in the camp and about having to give up her cabin and that she spends most of her time now down in the vegetable garden with Colin and Mrs. Dunlevy.

Here in the old city cemetery, where there does indeed appear to be a patch of graves marked only by rotting wooden crosses with obscure markings on them, the kind of place unwanted bodies might once have been dumped, Darren has found many small signs of possible relevance: several gravestones with encircled hands pointing to Heaven on them; somber quotations from the Book of Revelation; a flying bird, probably a dove, also in a circle on the tombstone of a woman named White; a carved bleeding heart on a broken stone obelisk ("The face of evil!" the wicked girl exclaimed, pointing at the heart, and for some inane reason the two of them fell all over themselves in hysterical giggling); several number combinations of seven and fourteen; and a dizzying quantity of letters, words and names lying about like the answers to a lost crossword puzzle. He feels he is drawing close to something but has not yet found it.

It was not easy getting in here. The Elliott girl knew where it was, but even so, it was hard to find, the paths overgrown, the cemetery itself hidden behind trees, brush, and bramble. She said there was an easier way in, but it was more public, the graveyard being only a hundred yards or so from one of the country club golf course fairways, and indeed they have come across a few gashed golfballs. It was while crawling through the thickest part on the way in, blackberry bushes snagging at his chinos, the sky overhead darkening, broodingly overcast, that Darren suddenly knew that he'd come to the place to which he'd been so mysteriously drawn, and he began to forgive the girl in the way that one feels inclined to forgive the Antichrist for doing what he has to do to bring on the Last Days. Until she said, "It's been a long afternoon, guys. Time for a pee. Ladies this way, gents that." Billy Don happily stepped behind a tree and relieved himself noisily into the dead leaves, but Darren left them in disgust and pushed on into the old graveyard on his own.

Billy Don now comes on a rectangular hole in the ground and he and the girl both assume it is an open grave, one that was either robbed or never filled. "Spooky!" Billy Don says, and in truth there is something unsettling about it, but Darren knows it is not what he is looking for, or what is looking for him. More like a kind of prefatory signal. It occurs to him that God's purpose in taking or hiding Marcella's body was to stimulate the very search he is undertaking, and that this insight itself is a kind of preparation. "Do you think it might have been hers?" Billy Don asks with a hushed voice.

"Just as likely it was dug by drunken kids on a graveyard dare," the girl says dismissively, but she seems nervous, too, and lights up another cigarette. "You know, who can spend the night sleeping in an open grave? It's so overgrown, I think this one must have been dug or disturbed a long time ago."

"Well, five years is a pretty long time..."

While the other two poke around in the hole like the disrespectful predators that they are, Darren moves among the gray stones as through a book with scattered half-erased pages, searching out the graveyard's hidden corners. The earth is soft underfoot, rising and dipping slightly (there is probably a webwork of old abandoned mines below and one day all of this could be completely swallowed up), the tombstones tipping and leaning in odd directions, many of them broken or fallen. The roots of maturing trees have reached into the graves themselves and upended their markers and no doubt stirred their bones. Darren is not disheartened by these reminders of time's ravages and the brevity of the human span. On the contrary, he finds the place unspeakably beautiful in its humble abandon and knows that God would find it so too, loving its buried denizens in a way not possible in those manicured grassy fields of grand self-congratulating monuments. He is happy he has come here.

And then, suddenly, there it is. Behind several small half-sunken footstones set in a kind of semicircle like boundary markers (like footlights, he is thinking, at the edge of a stage): a lone grave with a tilting stone and the name Gabriel J. Brown. Gabriel: the Annunciation angel. J. Brown: Giovanni Bruno. Died: age 33. Christ's age. The Prophet's own age on the Day of Redemption, and maybe the year he was killed, too. On the stone: the Brunist symbol of a cross in a circle. And an ominous warning: "Awake! Believe! Repent! Thy bones as mine are only lent!" He realizes the other two have gathered behind him. "Look at the date," he says. He is calm now, free from fear or loathing.

"That was a long time ago."

"No, Billy Don. I mean the day." There is a distant rumble of ominous thunder.

"Six, seven. Ah. Wow. June the seventh."

He feels the devilish girl shrink away. Was that a hissing sound?

# II.4

## Friday I May

I don't feel like I've come to the right place. How did you end up here?

"I don't know. It just seemed to happen." They are passing down West Condon's dark dripping Main Street with its facing rows of squat one- and two-story brick buildings staring sullenly at one another across a patched and repatched blacktopped street as if in chagrin or regret. Some are boarded up, others gaudily SALE-signed, the signs tattered with age. The rain has let up and there are breaks in the clouds, but there are still distant rumbles. It is Friday, a shopping day, and May Day on top of it, and there may be action out at the highway shopping centers, but nothing is happening here. The streets are empty but for a scatter of old rusted-out clunkers and muddy pickups looking as though they simply broke down where parked a decade or so ago, and were left to sit as monuments to ruin. The only shop doing any apparent business is a package liquor store down a side street. "A challenging ministry."

You can say that again. This place exudes sin like sweat. Those wet bricks stink with it, the gutters are running with it. Smell it? Like old socks. A seed of evildoers. These poor lost devils were shapen in iniquity, as the saying goes, and in sin did their mothers conceive them. What in my name are we *doing* out here?

A shoe store clerk steps out for a curbside smoke as they pass by. They exchange nods. He looks down at Wesley's shoes. "I was tired of being kept like a pet in a windowless cage," Wesley says. "I wanted to see daylight."

"I know what you mean," the shoe store clerk agrees gloomily, flicking his butt into the wet street, and Jesus says: I am the light of the world, son. What more do you need? "If you want to trade those old dogs in for some genuine vintage classics, come on in. I got a sale on. Whole damned store."

"Another time, thanks. Fresh air. I need fresh air."

"Suit yourself," says the shoe store clerk. Jesus says nothing, but Wesley feels a little tremor in his solar plexus or thereabouts, as though Jesus might just have shrugged.

Prissy seemed unusually excited and distracted this morning, and when she dashed off to do her shopping, she left the side door leading to the kitchen open, so he and his indwelling Christ just walked out. There was something very strange at first about the streets. As if they were not quite real. Eerie. It was raining lightly, but it was not the rain. Then it occurred to him. It was the daylight. The garage dance studio has only one window at the back, painted black, so there is not much difference in there between night and day, and he has somewhat lost his notion of diurnal time. Prissy sometimes brings him supper when he's expecting breakfast. Also there are no mirrors out on the streets, at least not in the residential neighborhood, the shop windows that remain here on Main Street having dimly restored the studio's ambience of replicative enclosure.

The Chamber of Commerce office looks closed, last autumn's high school football schedule still pasted up on its fly-specked window. A furniture and appliances store is offering its stock for rental as well as sale. Next to it, a bald-headed barber wearing a stained butcher's apron sits in his own chair, thumbing through a tattered magazine. He glances up at Wesley, raises his eyebrows in inquiry, shakes his head, returns to his magazine. Prissy cuts his hair now, shaping it, as she says, to suit his new image as a prophet. It is longer, he has sideburns now, and he has not shaved for a few days.

There is a bus pulled in at the corner station, which doubles as a juvenile hangout with its soda fountain and pinball machines. No one is getting on or off the bus, which is headed west according to the destination announced at the top of the front window. He has not told Jesus where he is going. There are no secrets between them, so he has also not told himself. But now the cat is out of the bag. He is going to the bank to get some money to buy a bus ticket. He can feel Jesus' sour complaints more than hear them. "You have told me to remember the old rule of the prophet," he says. "And you just said this place is so full of sin it smells like dirty socks." A bald guy in a bowtie leaving the bank—a member of his former congregation, best he can recall—seems about to object to that, then changes his mind, dances out of his way.

Well, I am not come to call the righteous, but sinners to repentance, and this is a good place for that.

"There are sinners everywhere," he reminds Jesus, pushing on into the bank. "If we stay here, we're just going to get into trouble. Wouldn't you like to hit the open road?"

Nah. I like it here, Christ says. There are three women in the bank behind the counters. Knowing Christ's preferences, he goes to the prettiest one. I think I'm in love.

"In *love*—?"

"I beg your pardon, sir?" the girl says, attempting a friendly smile, but flushing visibly as if he's found her out. Well, he's a prophet now. He probably has.

"Pardon is granted, my child." He returns her smile and hands her his checkbook. "I would like to make a withdrawal, please." She takes his checkbook with trembling hands and goes to check the account. Jesus says: It was her "Dance of the Seven Veils" that really got to me. She said it was a kind of requiem for my poor cousin, and I was deeply moved. "Perhaps we can take her with us," Wesley suggests, gazing at the young woman who has returned. She glances anxiously at the other women, who watch him now with big round eyes. Ah. Yes. There's an idea. "How much is there, my dear? I think I'd like to take it all."

"There's...there's nothing in your account, Reverend Edwards. The account is closed."

"Closed? *Closed?*" he roars, and the women all jump an inch or so off the floor. The young woman serving them crosses herself, and, inside, Jesus winces. It might be a good idea to ask who has done this, he says. "You let me handle this!"

"Yes, sir!"

"Who has done this? Who has closed my account?"

"I-I don't know, sir."

"Where is the thieving iniquitous money changer who runs this unholy establishment?"

"Who? You mean Mr. Cavanaugh? He's not here today, Reverend Edwards! I'll call the, uh, the assistant manager upstairs!"

Look, you've frightened her. It might be wise...

"No need to be frightened, my child. This is a mere business matter. Ha ha. Your soul is not in danger." He has meant that as a mere lighthearted jest, but she looks more terrified than ever.

"Charlie?" she is whispering loudly into the phone. "It's Angie. Come quickly!"

"Is Charlie the assistant manager?"

"Yes, sir, he'll—he'll be down in a minute."

I just have this uneasy feeling we should be leaving. Well is he, you know, that hath found prudence, et cetera. "Perhaps, miss, we'll come back another day."

Priscilla Parsons Tindle, returning from her highway shopping with a carload of flowers, decides to stop at the bank on her way through downtown to reprovision her depleted purse. She has amazing news for Wesley and she has decided to reveal it to him without words by way of a special May Day dance on a vast bed of flowers. Her May basket. She has chosen blooms with big velvety petals, which she plans to pluck and heap up in a great pile on the studio floor as a kind of aromatic nest, first dancing a vigorous bounding grand allegro dance of the joys of spring all around the studio to work up a good sticky perspiration, then plunging into the petals for the celebrative part of the dance, during which, now clothed only in sweet petals as if in full flower herself, she will, in effect, with movements she has been mentally choreographing on her drive, prophesy the extraordinary events of a few months hence. He may misunderstand her meaning and try to join her in the nest, but that's all right too.

She parks in front of Mrs. Catter's beauty salon and walks back toward the bank, just as two policemen come jogging across the street, their hands at their holsters, and with a great banging of doors and loud shouts enter into it. She decides perhaps it is not the right moment and returns hastily to her car.

I recognize the big one. The Roman legionnaire who speared me when I was nailed up and already dead and couldn't defend myself.

"He was a gum-chewer?"

No, but he worked his jaws in ominous ways. We can't let them get away with this. Do something.

The legionnaire has tipped his police cap low over his brows and is cracking his knuckles restlessly as though itching to inflict grievous bodily harm. The police station—counter, chairs, telephones, clock on the wall, notices pinned up—is much like the bank, but darker and dirtier and without any pretty girls. Would his money be safer here? It would not.

Oh oh. Get ready. I think we're in for a scourging. That guy coming looks exactly like Pontius Pilate.

Pontius Pilate introduces himself as Police Chief Romano.

Romano! What did I tell you!

Police Chief Romano asks why Reverend Edwards has been arrested, and the legionnaire snaps back in his hard blunt gum-popping way: "Public nuisance."

"What was he doing?"

"Scaring the pants off them girls in the bank," says the legionnaire's partner, releasing a gob of brown spit into a paper cup.

"Nonsense. I was merely checking my bank account. It seems I have been robbed."

"Robbed?"

"That's right, Officer. My personal account has been emptied out and closed."

"Was this an individual account or a joint account?"

"That hardly matters. It has been done without my knowledge or permission. The bank owes me an explanation, not to mention the missing money."

"Unh hunh." Police Chief Romano, who looks like a man who has seen everything, closes his ledger and pulls on his nose and says, "Let him go, boys." The legionnaire protests at that, smacking his fist in his palm, but the police chief says, "He's harmless, Charlie. Only a bit batty. It's his old lady has cleaned him out. Her and them people out at the church camp. You might say he's got a point."

While driving home, Priscilla has been rehearsing her "push-push" sequence for the nest of flowers dance, hammering the steering wheel with her pelvis, and she realizes that the climax of her May Day performance will be quite exciting and almost certainly misunderstood by dear Wesley. And by Jesus, too, probably, whom (if that is not stretching a pronoun), in some odd way, she has also come to love, though she believes he will be quicker to grasp the portent of her dance and be more approving of it. His story really. But now what to do with the flowers? They might wilt in the car or in the house or studio, and moreover she wants to surprise Wesley tonight and really does not want to have to deal with Ralph's tedious questions or even more tedious silence. She decides the best place for them is in the open air in the shade at the back of the studio under the blacked-out window, and all the better if it rains on them a bit, so she quickly improvises a little number she calls her "bundles of joy" dance, sweeping the precious blooms from the car to what she calls "backstage" in a series of little twirls and leaps that the neighbors will probably think of as quite loopy, though surely they are used to it by now.

This is, was for years, has become again of late, Priscilla's way. Life as dance else not life at all. It is her own special vision, her way of creating the beauty that life, left to do its own thing, so sadly lacks. In her professional years with Ralph, she preferred austere staging, harsh lighting, African percussion and Eastern wood and string instruments, and a minimum of costuming, finding even a body stocking too constrictive. Ralph was an elegant partner, always there, supportive, given to understatement, which set off her own passionate exuberance, but somewhat passive, waiting always for her to take the lead. Their dances seemed often to end without resolution, more like questions, really. He did not understand climax; he was incapable of it. He was something like a self-contained tango partner, formal (he even dressed in black with a pleated white shirt; only in the studio would he wear less), taut with an inner tension, but ultimately predictable. Priscilla had always aimed at the unexpected, for life, she felt, was all too predictable, and it needed something out of the ordinary for it to be experienced at all. It was, in effect, her way of praying to what she preferred to call the Life Force rather than God, though she was a believing Christian like most people were, simply too preoccupied or unsuited to figure things out on her own and trusting the wisdom of those whose vocation it was—Wesley, for example, various astrologers and philosophers, her great-aunt when she was still alive—and Priscilla addressed the Life Force wherever and whenever she could. She had dishwashing dances and laundry and ironing dances and shopping for Ralph's high-fiber breakfast cereals dances. Sometimes these were just spontaneous responses to the moment, a flash of sudden inspiration in a department store aisle or on a putting green, but she tried always to choreograph her dances, in retrospect when not possible before, choreography being her way of thinking about the world. Giving it, it being shapeless, shape. Being nameless, name.

Over time, however, trapped in this small town by the curse of a small family property inheritance and limited income, her vision slipped away from her, and the mundane became the mundane once more, her only dance the spiritless dance of the sorrowful housewife. The studio became a place to give classes to children, and her exercises, which she kept up without knowing were mainly a way to keep her weight down. She felt like such a fraud. She and Ralph became active at the church as a way, in her case at least, to keep a faint spark alive, her husband taking over Sunday School and the choir, she becoming the church organist and organizer of holiday pageants. And so the years went by. She and Ralph no longer danced together, though sometimes they gave little concerts, at the church mostly, Ralph singing, she accompanying him on the piano. She found herself increasingly focused on the mortal condition: If there was no further reason to dance, what was left except waiting for death? She would have created a dance to explore this question, but she was no longer creating dances.

And then there was Wesley. The great-souled one. What happened in his office that first time did not feel like a dance, it felt more like getting run over by a train. But that was because she had pretty much stopped dancing and had forgotten what it felt like. Of *course* it was a dance. It was *the* dance. Whereupon she returned with all her heart and mind to her abandoned art of choreography. The magic was back and she was alive again. *Really* alive. How could she not love this man?

Dropping the last load of flowers behind the studio, she sees that the light is on inside: the black paint has been scratched away in a tiny place at the lower right of the window pane and a spark of light is showing through. A kind of peephole, she thinks, and in the mud at her feet, though partly scuffed away: footprints other than her own. Ah. They have been watched. Well, she is used to being watched, if not exactly in this way. Just so he doesn't bring the neighbors. She leans forward to see what Ralph might have seen, and there is the pair of joined exercise mats in the center of the room, so often the site of their terpsichorean ecstasies, the various lamps with their colored gels set strategically about to provide maximum visual effects in the facing and overhead mirrors, the translucent silk cloths she used in her "Dance of the Seven Veils" draped over the barre, and the feathered headdress she has donned to play the eagle to his pinioned Prometheus, though they chose a different renewable organ than the liver for her to eat, and as she is studying the scene, it occurs to her that something is missing: Wesley.

You could at least have kicked his shins on the way out, Jesus says irritably. He is still in a rage about the legionnaire and Wesley's unwillingness to exact some token of revenge. They are sitting on a stool in Mick's Bar & Grill, Jesus having made a remark about having to feed the inner man when they passed it—I'd also be up for a quick snort, he added—communing over a beer and a grilled hamburger so overcooked it has an ashy taste even under a thick lathering of ketchup and yellow mustard. I've taken up residence in the wrong person again after all: a wimp and a fence-sitter.

"I would not object if you chose to reside elsewhere," Wesley replies.

"That seems to be the general opinion around here." This is the former Chamber of Commerce executive director Jim Elliott, sitting alone on the corner stool, his voice slurred with drink. Gin on ice with a twist of lemon. He's had three of them since they came in and was clearly well under way before that. Elliott is a Presbyterian and a Rotarian and a golfer of sorts. Wesley has suffered him on many occasions, and this is another. Because they have both been bullied by the same man, Elliott has assumed an affinity between them that does not exist, and has been unloading all his woes, everything from the general lack of recognition and gratitude for his selfless service to the city of West Condon to his deteriorating golf game, the termites in his basement, his irresponsible daughter, the sickening noise at the back end of his car, and his lack of a satisfactory amorous life, for which he uses a less delicate phrase, spicing his lamentations with groans and fist-bangs and curses. "Judas effing Priest!" he exclaims now, slapping the bar, and Wesley feels a sharp cringing deep in the gut as if his indwelling Christ, personally offended, has shrunk away. Judgments are prepared for scorners, and stripes for the back of fools, Jesus grumbles sourly, and Wesley asks the establishment's proprietor if he has any antacids. He has not.

"I know what you mean," Elliott says, apropos of nothing whatsoever. He raises his glass to Wesley in a toast, or perhaps to the villain behind the bar responsible for this travesty of a sandwich—the wretch's eyes are not focusing clearly. *"Bottoms!"* he exclaims, and tossing his head back, drains his drink, then slams the glass back on the bar, concluding with what is partly an *"Up!"* and partly a deep belch, a little act he probably practices. "Pour me another one, Mick! Gosh *darn* it!"

Mr. DeMars, who has been enjoying a sip or two himself—in memory of his dear old Irish mother, as he put it in his squeaky voice, though it turns out the lady is still alive, only somewhat non compos mentis due to a life of heavy drinking—does so, and with an apologetic glance and shrug in Wesley's direction, pours himself another while he's at it. Right, go with the flow. Wesley orders up another beer. Since he's sharing it, it's only half a beer, after all, and he needs it to keep the charred hamburger from getting stuck in his throat. Christ Jesus concurs. Thou hast put gladness in my heart, he says, adding a reminder that the Son of Man came eating and drinking, as it says in the gospel, and needs must continue upon his holy path. To every one, as they say, a loaf of bread, and a good piece of flesh, and a flagon of wine! Which calls to mind our own dear piece of flesh, Jesus adds postscripturally. I find I miss her.

"Yes, but she's very demanding."

"You can say that again! A real pain in the neck!" exclaims Elliott with crossed eyes. "Who're we talking about?"

"We must be talking about my mother again," says the big proprietor in his wee little voice.

"I feel freer out here."

Freer? Are you kidding? You nearly got us locked up!

"Me too, goddamn it! Let's drink to that! Feeling freer, whoever the heck she is!"

"Who you are in that airless box is who she says you are."

She has her little fantasies, Jesus says. But what a sweet tight little ass she's got.

"Ass? That doesn't sound like you."

"Did I say 'ass'? I meant to say 'neck.'"

I'm Jesus Christ, I can say what I want to say.

"But whatever I said, to heck with it! I meant it, and if you'll tell me what it was I'll say it again!" Whereupon Elliott snorts like a horse and lights up a cigarette with a musical lighter.

Wait a minute. That wasn't me who said that. There's somebody else in here.

"What—!"

"What?"

That's right. Move over, sucker.

Omigod! It's Satan!

"Oh no!"

"Oh yes!" says Elliott, rolling his eyes stupidly.

Get thee behind me, Satan, but no funny business back there!

"This is terrible! What's he doing in there?"

"In where?" Elliott asks, looking around in confused alarm.

No. Just kidding. It's really me.

"Damn you! Don't do that!"

"Hey!" cries Elliott, bristling and falling off his stool. He clutches the bar with both hands. "Don't do what? Why do I get the feeling that I don't know what the heck you're talking about?"

"I think he's talking to himself," the proprietor says.

"Oh." Elliott, with some difficulty, sits back down. He picks up his drink again, brings it and his cigarette to his mouth at the same time. "That's all right, then."

"Sorry," Wesley says. "It's a kind of...indigestion. Too much white bread."

"That'll do it."

"'I am crucified with Christ; nevertheless, I live: yet not I, but Christ liveth in me.' Something Paul said. I think he ate too much white bread, too."

"No shoot. That's really interesting. Paul, hunh? But I'm lost. Another round, Mick. And get another beer for the preacher and whoever."

"I know when I've got a good thing" is the subtext of one of Priscilla's repertoire numbers. It is one of her simplest routines. She could call it her "sex slave" dance, but she does not wish to demean in any way the grandeur and nobility of the relationship it celebrates. The name that Wesley knows it by is the "Glory Dance." He need only say the word. She adores this beautiful crazy virile man and is willing to do *anything* for him, and this dance expresses that. She knows she must work really hard to keep him here and keep him safe, which is not easy. Only she understands his special genius. Only she is capable of it. The others laugh at him or are afraid of him and they will try to lock him away and do dreadful things to him if she is not vigilant. Protecting this great-souled one is now her life's work, though she is fully aware it will bring her hardships and humiliation. As now. These men are laughing at her, she knows. But people have laughed at her before. She holds her head high. She is doing her dance of quiet pride. Her whole body is in motion, but they cannot see that.

When she saw the police enter the First National Bank, she should never have fled. She could not have known that Wesley was in there; she was only frightened of the policemen, those ominous authority figures who have been turning up in her nightmares. But why are they in her dreams? Because of her fears for Wesley. And so, in a sense, she *did* know he was in there. It was her dream happening in real life. When she arrived after racing back from the empty studio, the women clerks were still in a tizzy about "the crazy man." She didn't need to ask any questions, she merely did her making-a-cash-withdrawal dance, one she has rehearsed all too often, and listened to their chatter and that of the other women who had entered. He was shouting lunatic things about love and Jesus and calling the bank president vile names, they said. He wanted to abduct Angela. The cute one, who acknowledges this with her hand on her breast. We'll take her with us, he said. We? There were others? Probably outside in a getaway car. The women were waiting for him to draw a gun and try to rob the bank. There were no men in the bank now, so one of them admitted to having soiled her panties. Just a speck. It was so terrifying! But what happened to him? Angie's brother came running over and arrested him. The crazy man called the officers agents of evil, or something like that. Charlie looks so handsome in his new police uniform.

So she came here to the police station, fearing the worst. She knew she might never see him again. She was close to tears. Could she somehow choreograph a jailbreak dance? But they have released him. He is not here. It's a miracle. She feels a great wash of relief that makes her tremble, even though she is trying to appear calm and collected, like some sort of nurse or sister. She is surrounded by uniformed men who see her, she knows, as a ridiculous and wanton woman. In her worry and fear, she has been too transparent. But she can't help it.

"Where did he go?" she asks at last, her voice cracking.

They don't know. The burly one with the toothpick in his teeth has a vulgar little routine of his own, danced to the rhythm of his snapping fingers and popping knuckles with singular leering intent. He is standing between her and the door. She is already rehearsing in her mind her exit-stage-right dance. A casual farewell pirouette so she doesn't get her backside pinched. The older one who is chewing tobacco spits into the corner and says, "Not much open on the street. You might try Mick's. He was headed that general direction."

On his way to his unannounced destination (though Jesus has divined it: This is crazy! They'll be waiting for you!), Wesley has stopped to speak with his erstwhile friend and colleague, the Lutheran pastor Konrad Dreyer, whom he found tossing a ball around with his young boys in the churchyard during a sunny break in the weather. He wants Connie to call the Ministerial Association together to protest his unwarranted dismissal in the name of freedom of religion and freedom of speech, and Connie has said he would do that, though it also has its hazards because of sectarian differences, especially since Wes is claiming some sort of direct mystical connection to the Redeemer.

"It is not mystical."

He is in his old neighborhood, though he never thought of it as a neighborhood, more like some kind of accident that just happened, he but a passing witness. He had always known that his mission in life, as his mother had often reminded him, transcended neighborhoods, transcended towns, really, even nations, though sometimes it was hard to remember that during board wranglings or disorderly teenage Sunday School classes or rodent problems in the church basement. There are a lot of churches in this neighborhood, as there are in all others, here mostly made of stone or brick in accordance with the construction principles of the third little piggy. Trinity Lutheran is a limestone church with a heavy Teutonic entranceway, probably built about the same time as the lodge out at the church camp. Dark and damp inside, as he recalls, but pleasingly resonant for a preacher's voice.

"Paul said, Christ lives in me. Does he live in you, Connie?"

Connie meditates on that. He lights up a pipe, so Wesley does likewise despite Jesus' complaints that he is being asphyxiated. "Well, sure, Wes, in the sense that we all partake of the holy spirit. The ground of all being resonates through us all."

"That's not what I asked."

"I know, but I have to answer you in the way I best know how. I am less inclined to personalize the manifestations of the Absolute than are you. It is hard to speak of this, because as Dionysius the Areopagite has said: the finite cannot express encounters with the infinite. The created cannot do justice to the Creator. But I always feel that the spirit of God is within me, that God Himself is the ground of the soul and there is an inward way to Him. When I pray, I am not speaking to some outside other, but to the God within."

"Yeah, well, does he ever talk back?"

"I believe my prayers are sometimes answered."

"No, I mean, does he coach you in what to say and make you do things you weren't planning to do and say things like 'Where am I? Turn on the lights!' or 'Salute one another with a holy kiss,' or 'Hey, let me see your vengeance on them?'"

Connie chuckles around his pipestem. "What's that from? Jeremiah? Lamentations?"

"His remarks are not always original, but given the context, it's like I'm hearing them for the first time." The more words, the more vanity, Jesus is saying now. He has been grumpy ever since they left the studio. Is there no end to windy words? "Right now he is saying, Is there no end to windy words?"

"Job, probably. No, that is not the sort of conversation, if it can be called that, that I have with the transcendent cause of all things. It is more like the immersion of my finite self within the infinite self that is God."

"You know what? I think you're just kidding yourself, Connie."

Priscilla falters at the door of the Italian bar and grill. She can hear men hooting and barking with laughter inside and assumes they are laughing at poor Wesley. He is about all there is to laugh at in this town nowadays. She doesn't want to do this, but she must. Only she can rescue him. Her dance will be one of great suffering, but the suffering should not show on her face, for it would only be cause for more cruel laughter. She steels herself (she has a little dance for this) and pushes on in, half blinded by fear and shame. The mayor is in there, the former mayor, and two of the church trustees who voted for Wesley's incarceration, Burt Robbins and Jim Elliott, and they are looking at her with wild grins on their faces. That's the bad news. The good news is that Wesley is not among them.

"Hey, Prissy!" Jim shouts as though from mountaintop to mountaintop, then heehaws like a donkey and falls off his barstool, bringing fresh whoops of laughter from the others. That her name alone evokes such merriment means they've been talking about her.

"If you're looking for your loony loverboy," Burt says, unable to speak without snarling through his beak, "he and whoever he was talking to just left."

"Without paying," the mayor adds in his booming voice, and the big flat-faced man behind the bar, a squeaky piccolo to the mayor's bass, concurs.

"I'll pay his bill," she says, reaching into her purse, and they all think this is funny, too.

"So, how's Ralph, Prissy?" Burt asks pointedly, and she decides to ignore that, preferring that they laugh at her silence rather than anything she might say. Jim is still on the floor but able still to emit donkey sounds. "You guys all dancing together now?"

They all laugh at that, but the little roly-poly narrow-eyed ex-mayor with the big nose says, "Easy, Burt. That's enough."

Not quite: "I bet you look pretty cute all tangled up in your tutus."

"Did he say where he was going?" she asks, handing the barman a bill still crisp from the bank and pointing at the slice of lemon meringue pie in the glass case on the counter. She knows she will suffer more mocking laughter as she leaves, but perhaps she can deflect it somehow.

"For here?" the proprietor asks, and she nods.

"Said he needed a bath," the mayor bellows. "We let him know he could use a shave and a haircut, too."

"We told him he could also give that inner dummy he was talking to a good soaking," growls Burt through their sour snickering. "Maybe he could hold him under and drown the sonuvabitch."

She is somewhat alarmed by this news but hides her emotions behind a dancer's expressionless mask. She takes the slice of pie off the plate and holds it in the palm of her hand and gazes contemplatively at it as a mystic might gaze at a leaf or a feather, finding the mysteries of the universe contained within it, or as a jeweler might scrutinize a diamond or a pearl. Or Salome, the Baptist's head, its awesome truth.

Slowly she begins to sway, letting her upraised palm trail after her body motion as if it were the head of a snake, she its charmer, only hoping the wooziness she has been suffering of late doesn't return. She does an adagio glissade toward their table, still swaying, still focused on the pie, and there, while the men make self-conscious remarks about her nuttiness and back off, she mimes the effort to stick a finger from her other hand in it, though it always seems just out of reach. She leans toward it, her tongue out and doing a petit battement of its own, the hand pulling away whenever the tongue approaches. She straightens up, head high, attempts a little fouetté in her street shoes, and swirls gracefully to the opposite side of the room, where she begins to sway again, eyes closed, as though falling into a trance. The mayor applauds and guffaws, setting Jim off again, and once he finally stops his braying, she again glissades, swaying, toward the table, their eyes wholly on her now, watching her hips move, big boyish grins on their greasy faces. "She's stupid," she hears Burt say, though really she can hear and see very little, so intensely is she immersed in her performance. She mimes again the attempt to reach the pie with her finger and her tongue, leaning toward the mayor, so that he can see closely the teasing little dance her tongue makes with its étendre movement, quivering toward the elusive pie. He rolls his eyes comically, and as the other two lean close, trying to see what the mayor sees, she moves her arm fluidly from the third ballet position to the fourth and slaps the pie—*whop!*—in Burt Robbins' smirking face. He sputters and roars an obscenity and lurches blindly to his feet, the chair crashing against the wall, while she executes a rapid little pas de bourrée en arrière, tippytoeing backwards out of the bar, enjoying now the howling laughter she had earlier so dreaded.

As he steps into the bath, Wesley is thinking about Bergson's notion that all our perceptions are outside us in the things we perceive, not inside us. Connie Dreyer used it to illustrate the difficulty we have in glimpsing Being through the unreliable scrim of Becoming, which is the world of our sensations, but not the world itself, since our perceptions can never equal the perceived. The only way to see Being truly is by way of direct intuition or inspiration. Revelation. Connie's defense of faith by way of the likes of Plotinus, Augustine, that Areopagite character. Wesley was able to chip in a remark about John Scotus Eriugena, about whom he had once written a pretty good B-minus paper, but his heart was not in it, as his inner Christ has more or less disabused him of all notions of uroboric wholes common to these flaky Platonic dreamers. Faith, Connie said, is a kind of power: the power to appreciate revelations, which are facts in a way that what we call facts are not. Though one can reason about revelations, they are not a matter of reason but are simply received. In the way, Wesley asked, somewhat testily since he was not being taken seriously, that he has received his indwelling Christ? Connie puffed on his bent briar and said he was thinking of something a bit more abstract and all-encompassing. But the point is (his buttocks are now kissing the hot surface), Bergson uses the sensation of light as his demonstration of the distance between us and our own perceptions, seeing being the closest of the senses to thinking, and as Wesley sinks gratefully into the tubful of hot water (Jesus says: Yea, he warmeth himself, and saith, Aha, I am warm, I have seen the fire!), he concludes that there has been too little thought about the contiguous and instantaneous tactile perceptions of the flesh, which in the case of a hot tub bath anyway, come close to being the same as the perceived. And, if not, does that place our flesh outside us as well? The whiskey, he feels, is making him quite brilliant.

His route into the manse was via its nether regions, though not by choice. They had changed the locks, both front and back, but not the padlock on the old cellar door. Such a door on his father's farm led to their tornado and bomb shelter, and Wesley as a boy often used it as his hideaway. He kept secret provisions there in the way of candy bars and jawbreakers, and he did so here in the manse as well: a bottle of bourbon on the pantry shelves behind the paint tins, still nearly half full. While he was down there, he switched on the electricity and the hot water heater. The door at the top of the stairs was secured only with a hook and eye, easy to snap with a little push.

While he waited for the water to heat up, he strolled the darkening manse, stripped of all small and personal items, though still with most of its furniture, some covered with sheets, while outside the fresh rumbles of thunder drew nearer. The eggs, he saw, were gone from the kitchen walls, but not the yellow stains they left. No glasses, so he drank from the neck of the bourbon bottle, Jesus cautioning against it, lest he be filled with drunkenness and unable to find his way out of here and back to the studio again. "Well, you are right," Wesley said. "I won't have any. You may have it all." And he tipped the bottle back, Jesus remarking, with no little irony, Hah! the cup which my Father hath given me, shall I not drink it? Although everything in the manse was familiar, it was also unfamiliar, for his life had changed and was still changing and bore no relation any longer to these ancient philistine spaces. He could find no towels, but he pulled an old sheet off an easy chair which will do just fine.

The whiskey has indeed put Jesus in a mellow mood, that and Wesley's decision that they will, yes, return to Prissy and the studio. Jesus is now humming an old church tune, "Where the Healing Waters Flow," though he seems to be turning it into a kind of torch song: "O, this precious, perfect love! How it keeps the heart aglow!" Women were always important to Jesus and they are important to him now. His intimacy with prostitutes, whose sins he forgave as if they were not sins, got him in trouble with the Pharisees, and his ministry was benefacted by faithful women of means, all women who loved him one way or another. Some bathed his feet in their tears or splashed spikenard on his head, others just hung out with him like love-stricken camp followers. If two lie together, then they have heat, Jesus has said in his ecclesiastical style, speaking from within Wesley's recumbent body on the studio exercise mats that serve there as their bed (now here in the hot bath Christ has fallen blissfully silent), but how can one be warm alone? From Magdalene, his favorite, he expelled seven demons, and what he said about it was, Yeah, that was a lot of fun. We got on well. And now it is Priscilla. Wesley does not wholly understand his mission, but he knows that Prissy and her studio are part of it. That became transparent to him on his walk today through this hostile wilderness of a town in which he cannot survive alone and from which he cannot alone escape. For the moment he and Jesus are safe here in the manse, for outside a violent storm is brewing and no one will be out in it, but sooner or later they will have to brave it and make their way back to their mirrored refuge and to its peculiar rhythms. Which can be pretty strenuous. He sleeps a lot when Prissy's not around, just getting over when she is. Sleeps well. Better than he ever slept before.

Priscilla found Wesley's inner Jesus, whether real or imaginary (imaginary, she assumed then—symbolic, perhaps a way of expressing his prophetic insights), pretty disconcerting at first. Even with his head between her legs, Wesley would go on talking to him, describing what he saw there or arguing with Jesus' instructions about what to do with his hands or reciting passages from the Bible about perfumes and kisses and gardens ("His branch shooteth forth in his garden" was one of his favorites, his or Jesus'—it was hard to tell). But over time she has come to believe in this Jesus and to wish to please him and to desire him just as she desires Wesley, even if it does make their mating dances feel a bit like group sex. It also raises paternity issues. She is only a week late and she can be irregular, but she just *knows* through an inner knowing that cannot be denied. Her tender breasts tell her so.

That the conception almost certainly took place here that night of the freak snowfall, and that by chance or some kind of design beyond her understanding they are back here now, and that there is a storm raging outside as though to hide them from the world, all means that her revelatory May Day dance will probably be different than originally choreographed. A pity she didn't bring the flowers along, but she left in such a panic, fearing she would lose him to those who mean him harm. And, anyway, they will find a use for them back at the studio, perhaps in a kind of sequel, a ritual confirmation of the miracle (call it that: she had always supposed herself congenitally barren until now); dear Wesley is so responsive and so unflagging, a virility she now attributes in part to his ardent indwelling Christ.

Now, sitting on the edge of the tub, she watches the dance of his limp penis in the water as she stirs it (somehow the "Moonlight Sonata" seems right for this), dreaming of the future and of the child that will be borne to them all. The moment the mayor mentioned Wesley's desire for a bath, she knew where he had gone and she worried for him, exposing himself, brave but foolhardy, to such risks in broad daylight, though she appreciated his needs. In the studio there is only a shower and toilet in a corner behind a curtain, put there mainly for her students as a kind of dressing room, the corner having previously been used for a photography studio and so already plumbed, and the water is usually only lukewarm at best and sometimes little more than a trickle. She thought she might have to break a window to get into the manse before noticing the open cellar door and coming straight up here, where she found him sleeping soundly in the bathwater, snoring softly while the storm crashed outside. Is Jesus also sleeping, she wonders, or is he, in some manner, observing her? Just in case, she has taken her clothes off beside the tub, for she knows it pleases him, and she is excited by his pleasure.

Later, she will bathe Wesley (he has not washed himself, the water is clear, except for where his pipe has fallen into it and created a rather ominous little smudge) and perhaps he will bathe her in turn and she will dry him off and he will dry her off and she will dance her May Day dance for him and with him, and they will run to the car and she will drive him home through the rain and then they will have to take their clothes off again and dry off again and so on, but for now she is choreographing his awakening. She wants it to be gentle, for he may have forgotten how he came here, and be frightened when he first comes to. As much as anything, he likes her to do a grand plie over his face, cunnilingus being for Wesley—and for Christ Jesus, too—a kind of mystical religious experience (she calls it their "Dance of the Tongues" and it is best when they dance it as a pas de deux, or trois;

Wesley is a willing participant in all her dances, though he's not very athletic or flexible, so this is one of his best ones), but that's not easy in the tub, and it's probably not the best way to wake up. No, it will be a dance of the fingertips and she will whisper to him about his greatness and her love for him and she will also speak quietly to Jesus, tell him that she wishes to love him and to serve him and that he must guide Wesley and keep him safely within the sanctuary of the studio, lest he fall into the hands of his enemies. They must be prudent. For soon they will be four.

# II.5

## Saturday 2 May

Saturday night in West Condon and folks are restless and needful, but money is short and nothing much happens without it. Still, they go looking. The pool hall. The Elks Lodge. The roller rink. The bus station and the rootbeer stand. Neighborhood taverns. Mostly dead. The municipal ballpark. Table tennis at the youth center. With dented balls. Legion Hall. Filling stations. Drag-racing up and down empty pot-holed neon-lit Main Street. Making something out of nothing, trying to, a local skill honed by all the bad years. The young with cars end up at the lakes or the old ice plant or out at the edge of town in the abandoned movie drive-in lot or where the big Dance Barn was before it burned down. Listening to music on the car radio. Having a beer and a smoke. Of whatever. The old church camp on the Tucker City road used to be a beer party favorite, but it's occupied now by those religious idiot-sticks. Still, if you have nothing else to do, you can always drive by and shout out obscenities and throw bottles over the barbed-wire fence.

"I don't have big ambitions," an unemployed coalminer is grumbling up at the Eagles social club over a friendly game of pinochle. "Eat and shit regular. Fuck a whore wunst a week. That takes money. Not much. But some. Can't stand to have a whore look down her nose at me. So I need a job." The other three at table grunt in agreement, sorting their cards. "Have you thought of taking up whoring yourself?" one of them asks, wallowing an unlit cigar around in his jowls. "They tell me there's a market now." "They's probly a age limit." Now and then something opens up for a night guard or a short-order cook, a bouncer, debt collector, ditch digger. Shit jobs, but always a scramble for them. They hated the mines—the fear, the hard labor, the black greasy filth, the bad hours—but they miss them. They were a team then, union men. Now it's every miserable cocksucker for himself. There's work out at the strip mine, but it's non-union, and Italians need not apply, the owner and his mine manager being militant racists. They've organized their own Klan den, though they call it something else, some kind of holy legion or militia. Guys who work for him say old man Suggs keeps a huge horsewhip coiled over a nail in his office; it's the first thing you see if you go in there to bitch about something.

Not everyone's completely broke. The Sir Loin steak house, offering weekend specials (also available during the week), does a little business. Enrico's Palazzo di Pizza does. The chop suey joint out at the shopping center. The movie house with its pocked screen. The bowling alley. The Nineteenth Hole at the country club, which should probably be called the Tenth Hole with half the course long since gone to weed. Many of those eating and drinking in the Hole have played a round or two today and are now talking about their handicaps and missed putts and the deteriorating condition of the course and of life in general. Expressing their disgust at national politics, the injustice of the tax laws. Bemoaning the lack of downtown business. Wondering why, with all the unemployment, they can't find a decent cook out here. Commiserating with the former secretary of the Chamber of Commerce after the unexpected overnight restructuring of the city organization that has cost him his job. The town banker who engineered this move on the grounds of saving tax money and curbing corruption is not here tonight, being either at home with his terminally ill wife or off on another business trip, so they can speak freely about him and his bullying tactics, even if his motives are impeccable. The former Chamber secretary has not taken this change of fortune well, but the club members are tolerant folk who can put up with belly-aching drunks when there is cause. The bank lawyer, who will be taking over the Chamber duties and others as a kind of ad hoc city manager, was here earlier tonight, but left before the supper crowd arrived. He is a nice young man and will do a good job, but the ex-secretary is a local pal, even if he is pretty useless, and people feel sorry for him, while at the same time feeling sorry for themselves.

The Hole is accustomed to an early crowd and shuts down early, leaving a long night ahead. Some will meet up at a club bar, others in a neighbor's kitchen or over a bridge or poker table. Many will retire with a drink to a recliner chair in front of the box. A few, choosing to rough it, will head out to the roadhouses or take in a bit of country music at the Blue Moon Motel.

Sheriff Tub Puller is passing that popular Saturday night establishment and he decides to wheel through the parking lot to see who's up to what. Looks like a full night. Tub is returning from a Christian Patriots meeting out at John P. Suggs' strip mine offices, and he is feeling righteous and closely engaged with the way the world works and well equipped to do important deeds. Tub doesn't share the religious beliefs of most of the other Patriots, preferring not to think about any life after this one, mainly because no matter what comes next it's always a rough passage, but he is patriotic and he loathes Romanists and niggers and kikes and feels at home with Suggs' militia. They look up to him as a big man and a leader. And he's not just an immovable mass, he's a good marksman, too; people have to admire that. If Tub Puller shoots at somebody, he hits them where he wants to hit them. Suggs' mine manager, Ross McDaniel, is the only one who can beat him at target practice, and that's all he can beat him at, except maybe the hundred yard dash. McDaniel is an outsider brought to town by Suggs and even Tub is a little afraid of him. There's a rumor that his past targets might have included FBI agents and tax collectors and even a sheriff or two. Suggs knows Tub is not a very religious man, but he is cool about it, and Tub can appreciate where Suggs is coming from and respects it. Probably, in the end, he'll find his way there as well, for it's a hard, tough religion and the lines are clearly drawn and it has a certain manly appeal.

With a little help from Suggs' deep pockets, Tub has been putting together a volunteer police unit to deal with emergency situations in the county, and the core of it has been recruited from the Patriots. In fact, they are more or less the same thing. There haven't been any emergencies, but there are a lot of people around here who don't see eye to eye, so there are apt to be, and Suggs wants him to be ready. The church camp sect is one of Suggs' pet projects, and Tub's troops have already been called out there a couple of times to defend it. Some of his most reliable volunteers belong to that group. Tub's deputy Cal Smith is an evangelical, close to some of those people, and should fit right in, and for a while he did help out at training sessions, but since Red Baxter's return, he has begged off, using his family duties as an excuse. Baxter was their section boss in the mine. A man born angry. Tub could go along with the loudmouth's gobpile oratory back when it was about hours and wages, but then he got religion and became a rancorous pain in the ass. Suggs plainly hates the man and wants him run out of here. Smith, however, came from a family of pentecostals and only got closer to Baxter when Red shifted his hatred from bosses to sinners. In the mine, Tub was a shotfirer, using compressed air cylinders like dynamite to bring down walls of coal, a hazardous job, and Smith was his partner and driller. They hardly ever spoke to each other, but they were a team, so when Tub got elected sheriff, he appointed Smith his deputy, a good man to have at your back when there's dangerous work to be done. Now he's not so sure. There's been trouble at the camp since Baxter's return. If a line gets drawn, he may find his deputy standing on the wrong side of it.

Tub spots the Cavanaugh station wagon in the Blue Moon parking lot. The college kid's probably here. He'd love to haul the smartass in for whatever, smoking marijuana or fucking a minor or something.

His old man is a target of Suggs' fury, one of many, and Tub shares his dislike for the banker. For all bankers, for that matter. Fat cats living off the sweat of others. When mines shut down and men are thrown out of work, these are the ruthless decisions of the money-maggots. But Tub is not a vengeful man. In fact, he has few emotions at all beyond a cold scrupulous hatred of a more general sort, and as for the kid, he'd feel out of place going in there in his uniform and shiny boots unless he had specific charges and an arrest to make.

He's about to roll on out of the lot and back to his West Condon office when he sees them: three overdecorated motorcycles parked back in the shadows. They'd heard a distant growl tonight during the Christian Patriots' military exercises that was probably them and Suggs had turned his dark scowl on him. Since the break-in and theft at the mine, Suggs has been in a rage about these out-of-town shitheads. So he knows now he has something to do. He could disable the bikes. Or impound them. But he might need help for that. They could come out any minute and they're probably armed. It's a Saturday night, and Smith will be hard to find, and the guys who were at the Patriots will be scattered. But no problem. He can handle this on his own. There's a small secluded pull-off within view of the motel that he often uses to catch drunks and speeders leaving the motel, and after checking in with his radio operator, he pulls in there and turns off his car radio and douses his lights.

Cubano, Littleface, and Juice are sitting at the bar, knocking back whiskeys with beer chasers. Their pals Nat and Houndawg, who have stayed back at the base with Runt, are angry about it, but Juice and Cubano—penned up so long they're going stir-crazy—decided they needed a social moment before hitting the road again tomorrow, Littleface joining them to try to keep them out of trouble. And the sheriff is right: they're armed. The place is a miserable dive and the two country singers don't amount to much, but the Warrior Apostles dig the tunes, Juice bobbing his head to the beat and snapping his fingers,

Littleface meditating on the lyrics, which are making him feel sentimental about his life on the open road and about his pals and about his country. And besides, though they're cut off from the Brunists now, they saw these two yokels doing their act out at the mine hill and so they think of them as in some manner their own people.

There's a tough, beardy guy sitting alone at the bar dressed in leathers with APACHE painted on the back of his jacket. Might or might not be what his jacket says. Short stocky guy, kind of a buttless tube, losing his tread on top. Worn dusty red cowboy boots with buckled straps over the insteps and tooled scrolls up the sides, pinetrees on the front, which give him class. What class he has. He isn't flying colors, but he looks solid, so they ask him anyway, and he says no, he thought about buying a bike before he got sent up, but when he came out of the can, he went looking for four wheels, not two, needing something he could live in, sleep in, carry his shit around in. Juice tells him he admires his boots and he asks Juice if he ever did any time—he looks like a guy he'd seen up at the state pen. Juice says not in this part of the country, and asks, "What'd you get sent up for?"

"Laying into a buncha cops." Can't help but admire that and they all have another round. They ask him what he's doing here. "Chasing a woman."

"Not worth it, man."

"I know it. Bad shit. It's over. Moving on tomorrow."

"Yeah? So are we. If you weren't stuck in a cage you could join us."

"Where you headed?"

"Don't know. But it's like them two croonies there are singing, 'They's always a bus goin' somewheres.'" They ask what happens next for him and he says he doesn't know either, but there's another war brewing, and if they'll take an ex-con, he may join up. He feels like killing a few people.

They nod knowingly and Littleface says he tried to get into the airbornes but he flunked the physical. Just as well because there was a sergeant there who kept calling him Porky because of his hairiness and he knew he'd end up wanting to shoot that sonuvabitch more than the enemy. Cubano says he might like to fight to get his own country back some day, but he'd have to do it alone because he can't stand taking orders from anybody. Even his compañero, Houndawg—El Profesor—sometimes gets under his skin. Juice volunteers himself and the rest of the Warrior Apostles to help Cubano out if he decides to have a try, hoping some people there speak Christian English and not that weird spic noise that Cubano lets fly when he's cussing his bike out.

"So, hey, good lookin', whadja think?"

"It scared me a little. Especially those lines about back o' the bus gropes, rhyming with showing young boys the ropes and chasing lost hopes."

"Them was your lines, Patti Jo."

"I know, but like something left behind was suddenly real again and me right in it. But it helped to be singing it. Made it seem like it mighta happened to somebody else. And in a way it did. That me's not me anymore."

"I'm workin' on a coupla others. Hope y'don't mind."

"Like what?"

"Well, like 'Trailer Camp Blues,' fer one. What y'tole me bout bein' a stake in a poker game. And losin' your name."

"Well, I'm never one to stand in the way of genius, Duke. But I like it when you sing them to me in bed first, like with this back-of-the-bus one. It softens them up a little."

"Softenin' you up is my A-number-one priority, little darlin'. Nigh time fer another set. We got us a handsome multitude here tonight. The beers're flowin' and everbody's feelin' juicy and singin' to 'em is halfway like fun!"

"I suppose after the beers those two kids bought us we owe them that dead mommies thing, but honestly, if I have to sing it or hear it one more time, I'll throw up."

"No, I'll do 'Love Me Tender' and lean right over 'em with it and send 'em runnin' fer the nearest matteress holdin' on to theirselves. But right now, I reckon it's more like time t'rare back'n let fly some honky tonk'n a yodel or two. Unload a swot a whoopee. Sing 'em all, around the horn. Y'notice the fireplug over to the bar, by the way?"

"Fireplug?"

"Yeah, short and squat and hard t'pitch to parked on the far stool."

"Oh, you mean that Apache fellow. The one who turned up this week at the camp. He knew Marcella. He was there."

"Yeah. Wonder what he's doin' here, off from the camp, suckin' up the hard likker like that. That's some a them rough biker boys he's with. Looks as how he's one of 'em, don't it?"

"Might be. But he was sure paying a lot of attention when you were singing 'Take These Chains from My Heart.' Could be he's got romancing troubles. He's wearing a pierced heart tattoo with Clara's kid's name on it, but she didn't appear exactly over the moon to see him. Seems like little Elaine has turned a tad peculiar. They tell me she's got a whupping fancy. He probably wasn't ready for that and looks pretty cheesed out. In the next set, let's do 'Young Love' and see what happens."

"Give him a desprit case a the roarin' hurtin' wanta-git-laid long-gone lonesomes, y'mean."

"Maybe. You never know what a song might set off, though. I knew a guy once, this was out in Tucson, as I recollect, or somewhere in the desert thereabouts. A guy who told me he used to ride his own thumb around the country until some rich dude gave him his pickup truck camper for free."

"Ain't nobody gives his truck away free."

"I know. This guy was kinda scary and had very strong hands. He had the borrow of me for the night and we were having an oiling-up drink in this highway bar with old dollar bills nailed up on the walls, when somebody played 'Long Black Veil' on the jukebox. You know, 'Ten years ago, on a cold dark night, someone was killed, 'neath the town hall light…'? Well, he got up slowly and walked over there and pulled out a gun and shot that jukebox three times. Then he told everybody to get down on their knees and start praying for theirselves because they were all sinners with murder in their hearts who deserved to die and also to pray for that poor man in the song who was unjustly hung—just like Jesus Christ, he said—and he fired off another shot to make sure everybody was paying attention. So down they went and while they were all fallen on the floor like that, he grabbed me and dragged me out of there and back to his camp, hooting and whacking the steering wheel all the way, and he threw me down and done me every way he could think of. I was working too hard to be scared, but when it was over, he began bawling like a baby, and that's when I really started to panic and realized I was more religious than I thought I was, and that I totally believed in God and Jesus and the Virgin Mary and all the rest of it and just hoped they all had their eye on this poor little sparrow."

"Well, hah, somebody musta done cuz here you am."

"Yup. But one of the poor cops bought it who came to arrest him."

"That's some story, Patti Jo. Ifn we do sing that 'Young Love' song, I sure hope that injun feller ain't got a pistol, cuz I'd be his damn jukebox, wouldn't I? Oh. There's that guy Georgie, jist comin' through the door. The one who said Marcella Bruno useta be his sweetheart."

"Georgie…? Georgie Lucci maybe? It's been decades, and that ape's badly beat up. Looks like he's wearing his elbow on backwards, but it could be him. First guy who ever felt me up. In the church on the back stairs down to the basement. Don't know what I was doing there. Waiting for somebody to feel me up, maybe. I was just a kid then, eleven or something. I don't think I'd even got my period yet. He was older, already in high school or near to it, but still, basically, just a bad case of acne in pants. If it's him, he's a dumbass loudmouth clown. A total jerk. Marcella would not have let him get within a mile of her. Who's his pal?"

"I dunno. But he looks like one a them jugheads who was tanked up and givin' everbody a hard time out to the hill a coupla weeks ago."

"The one who kept standing up and falling down. Problem tonight is they look too sober. I doubt they got two dimes between them."

* * *

Two dimes maybe, not much more. Stevie's making good money, but he hasn't learned to count yet and he's got holes in both pockets. It has been Georgie's task to follow him around and catch it as it dribbles out and help him spend it in a more useful manner. But there's nothing more in there tonight. After the mayoral yuks, Georgie got compensatory hazardous duty pay for his visit to Lem's Garage, but that's also long gone. He winks hopefully at his scruffy potbellied ex-neighbor behind the bar, but the asshole doesn't wink back. Just glares. Probably Georgie walked out of here one night forgetting to pay. An honest mistake, shouldn't be held against him. There are some bikers perched there in black leather and ear studs, looking wired and vaguely dangerous, a dark-skinned greaseball among them, hair slicked back in a duck's ass. Also a very hairy punk who looks like an overgrown dwarf. If you got the money, honey, I got the time, those two rubes up at the mike are singing as though rubbing it in. It's party night at the Blue Moon Motel. First time Georgie has seen it as alive as this—they even have bouncers on the door now—and though he lacks the wherewithal to throw himself into it, it cheers him up, suggesting to him that, if they can bring this shabby wreck to life, the resurrection of the body is not an impossible crock after all.

His own will take some work. It's badly messed up: both eyes blackened, a tooth missing, bruises everywhere, and his shoulder feels like fucking Lem may have busted something when he laid the crowbar on him. Or else he's just stiffened up from sleeping on a thin mattress on the cold cement floor at the fire station after his old lady threw him out. His nose is running, his crabs are biting, and there's a clotty feeling at the end of his dick from the dose he picked up on his only foray into feminine flesh since he got back here. Blew his first little lump from his fire department job on her, needing a pro to do the right things, for in his depression he was having trouble getting it up. Turned out the woman was the sister of a guy he used to play baseball with, and though she did what she was paid to do, she was even more miserable than he was and inhabited by this virulent nastiness, which she obligingly shared with him. He'd just been to Big Pete Chigi's funeral, where old Bags was doing his Latin thing and the old birds were into their senseless twitter, and he felt like he was dying himself, starting with his shriveled coglioni. Carlo had dragged Georgie out to see Pete in hospital earlier in the week. Hooked up to some kind of green machine that was working his ruined lungs for him. It was hard for him to talk, but he managed to say, "This ain't no fun, boys. But what can you do? You just keep going on." And then a couple of days later he stopped going on. You come and you go in this world, but whatever that world was about, it didn't seem to be about Georgie. It was like big things were happening over his head from which he was congenitally and terminally excluded. Born to miss out. He felt like the little shepherd who had to stop to take a shit and missed the birth of Jesus. He was thinking a lot about Marcella Bruno at that time; those photos he'd seen had a grip on him. Back in high school, he probably saw her with clothes on, but he didn't remember them and didn't need to. They might have met here in St. Stephens, he was thinking, sitting there that day among the mourners, all knuckled into themselves and not saying much. In fact, she was probably the only reason he ever went there, to catch a glimpse of her or to bump into her in the nave. She always had a smile for him. Would have had. She was very young then, of course. Some years behind him. Probably why he never noticed her.

The reason he and Steve Lawson are out here at the Moon is to book Steve's stag party a month or so from now, a lone moment of happiness on the horizon, and to ask those two hillbillies, at Franny's request, to sing at the wedding, if they promise no religious songs. Georgie has had a beer or two with Duke, talked baseball, women, bad times they've been through. When you are sad and lonely and have no place to go, they're wailing now, call me up, sweet baby, and bring along some dough, and we'll go honky tonkin', honky tonkin' 'round this town. Sounds good to Georgie, and with an optimistic grin he scans the clapping, hooting, and boozing crowd in search of someone who might stand them both a beer while they do their business. But his gaze falls on Pete Piccolotti sitting in a booth with Vince Bonali's sexpot kid and two others, including that tall guy he's seen with little

Angie before, and his grin withers away. Young Piccolotti runs his family grocery store and it was Georgie's job today to do his fire inspector routine and hit the boy up on behalf of the mayor's campaign. Pete told him bluntly what he thought of him, and it wasn't nice. They got a gun to my head, Pete, I can't do nothing about it. I just don't want you to get in trouble. If you put me out of business, the kid said, you'd be doing me a favor. Now get the fuck outa here, dipshit. You're making me sick. Georgie feels hated and misunderstood and wants to change his life. He's a good guy, after all, and doesn't deserve all this abuse. All right. Lem was pissed off about the car, but Georgie explained to him he had to swerve to avoid a little kid on a sled. Out on the Waterton road? At midnight? Yeah, with all that snow there was a whole slew of brats with sleds out there. No shit. What was Georgie doing on that road in the first place? I took a wrong turning because of the snow, Lem. The goddamn window wipers weren't working. I couldn't see a thing. That was when Lem picked up the crowbar.

Duke and his woman are really wound up. Something about her is familiar. Looks like she's been around. Maybe he ran into her up in the city. Comb your hair and paint and powder, you act proud and I'll act prouder, they're hollering now. You sing loud and I'll sing louder, tonight we're settin' the woods on fire! The only thing on fire is his crotch. Georgie gives his cooties a scratch, feeling murderous. Like Il Nasone said: halfway through life and what has he got that's not infectious? His old lady was also a major disappointment, locking the screen door and yelling at him through it. Georgie let her know about all the big connections he'd made in town, how important he had become. But to get anything you had to grease some palms, she knew that, and he was only letting her invest in him. What was the matter? It was just a loan; she'd get it all back with interest. Sure, she said, when the goose pisses, and she told him she'd call the police if he ever turned up at the house again. By then she was screaming and all the neighbors were out on their porches. *Vaffanculo, testa di cazzo!* Mother love? Forget it. Tonight we're havin' fun, we'll show the folks a brand new dance, that never has been done! Yes, he'd like to dance a new dance, but he can't see how. He's completely fucked. All he has left now in his vanishing life are a handful of old jokes that nobody's laughing at anymore and his memories. Big Ruby, up in the city, bless her splendid creamy lipsticked ass. He thinks of her often. Should never have ditched her. And la bella Marcella. The only girl he ever really loved. The only one who ever understood him. He thinks about her now as he's last seen her in that photo (he would have busted in and rescued her from that vicious bony-assed scuzzbag, but how could he have known?) and wishes she were with him. I need you, baby, he says. I know, she says, and gently takes his hand. "Hey, whaddaya doin'?" Steve asks.

Tommy Cavanaugh's old pal and basketball teammate from high school, Pete Piccolotti, is unloading his woes. Business is bad, the supermarkets are eating him up, he's deep in debt and no way out, that beat-up flunky over at the bar has been trying to shake him down on behalf of city hall, his family grocery store will probably get either closed down or torched, this town is shit, life is shit. Tommy is sympathetic, but he's also thinking that's what you get for sticking around here, man, and he's been telling them about his own plans to avoid the family pressures and get a PhD in sociology and set himself up at a university somewhere far from here, travel around the world on research grants. That upsets Angela, he knows; she wants him right here and in the bank, but she's trying not to show it and is instead rubbing his cock under the table to remind him of the blessings of hometown life and gushing about how cute the Piccolotti kid is. They are squeezed into a booth across the floor from the singers, he and Angie and Fleet and his wife Monica, who used to be a looker but isn't now. The lips that used to thrill me so. Teeny Sabatini. Pete played point guard on their high school team, Tommy forward. Fleet and Kit, as they were known then. Fleet was a terrific passer, had great athletic moves, a good jump shot. He could receive a ball and shoot it all in the same move and seemed to have eyes in the back of his head. Though he wasn't tall enough for the big time, he might have made a college team if Monica hadn't got pregnant. A cautionary tale. He used to think of Pete as the smartest guy in high school, but the daily grind at the grocery store and getting married so soon, having a kid, have dumbed him down. And he has hardly smiled all night. Now he's into a really awful rap about putrefaction, Angela having just said she felt so alive tonight, Fleet replying that actually she's just a dead meat farm, nothing's really so alive as decaying flesh, which is its natural state. And he goes on to describe all the bruised fruit, clotted milk, rotten tomatoes and raspberries with blue mold, black lettuce, mottled bananas, and stinking gray meat he has to throw out every day at the store, dumping it all in the garbage buckets out back so it can really ball. Monica finally tells him to shut up, he's being morbid and spoiling the party.

The singers take another break, so Tommy pushes Angela's hand off his dick and goes to the bar for more drinks. He tries to avoid the bikers sitting there—are these the guys who tried to wreck his dad's car?—but one of them, the one with APACHE on his jacket, turns to him and says, "Hey, Moneybags."

"Whoa, that you behind all that face hair, Ugly? Goddamn, what say, man? What are you doing back in town?"

"Just making a cemetery run."

"Yeah, I know what you mean. Can I buy you one?"

"Nah. Might end up having to pay interest."

Same old Ugly Palmers. But he has aged a lot. Doing time has not been good for him. His mad-dog pals are glaring; Tommy decides this is his last night in the Moon for a while. "Well, let's get together, man, trade some cock and bull."

"Leaving tomorrow."

"Coffee or something before you split?"

"I'll be stopping by Lem's garage in the morning. Drop by there if you can get out of Sunday School."

Back at the booth, Angela is talking about the crazy man at the bank yesterday, and Tommy tosses in his own Easter anecdote about the mad preacher, which in turn leads them to the Brunists. Tommy starts to tell them about the research he is doing out there as part of his planned doctoral thesis, but the others say it's a mistake to pay any attention to them, those loonies all ought to be shot after what they did to their church, certainly run out of the county, their hatred reminding Tommy that he's the only non-Catholic at the table. He has his own beef: those leeches stole all his mom's money, but he and his dad aren't saying much about that, not wanting people to think his mom's not right in the head, while they try to get some of it back. With Concetta Moroni helping out at home now, his dad is able to catch up on some of his business meetings. Where he is tonight. Part of his ongoing effort, he says, to develop the new industrial park. Useless, but his dad keeps trying. Hometown hero. Or maybe he's just trying to distract himself from his wife's dying and her bitterness and her religious nuttiness and all that has led to.

Monica's mom is babysitting, and they have to get back, they say. "The joys of parenthood," Fleet says sourly, pulling himself up out of the booth like an old man, and Angela says, "I think it's great." Tommy sees that Ugly has his ball cap on and is also leaving. He tosses him a wave and mouths "tomorrow" and Ugly nods back, walks out with one of the other bikers, the funny-faced hairy one with the shirt-button ears. Angela's hand is squeezing his prick again. "Well, rootie tootie, Kit," Fleet says in grim farewell, quoting the song they all voted the worst of the night.

Juice, not trusting that fake Indian in the red cowboy boots, has stepped out to wing a wiz and make sure Littleface is all right. And has stepped right back in again, still putting his dick back. Nods at Cubano who leaves his drink to join him and they push out. "Face went left, the Apache went right, but I seen him flash his lights at a car racing up out of the bushes with its lights off. Wasn't a cherry top, but I think it was that fat sheriff at the crank and going like a bat outa hell." If they chase after on their bikes, they'll be targets, so they quickly hotwire a wooden-sided station wagon parked in the lot and leave their bikes behind. A couple of miles down the road, near a stone culvert, they come upon the car Juice saw, pulled off to one side, its headlamps blazing now. The fat man is standing over something in the field, kicking at it, rifle in hand, a wrecked bike nearby. "Stop the fucking car!" Juice is screaming, but Cubano neither slows down nor speeds up. "Ay, guapo, look at me, not him," he says quietly. "At *me*, coño! Don' show him your stupid face! We just only lovers rolling by, not seeing nothing." "But, fuck, man—!" "We got our little pistola against his rifle, man, we can' do nothing here. We go get some hardware and ask Nat what to do."

"If you guys had stayed here like I said," Nat says, his voice breaking, and there is a bad moment between them. Juice and Cubano know they've fucked up but cannot bring themselves to say so, though they are hurting and say they are full of God's fucking wrath and ready to do whatever has to be done. "We can take the asshole. He's all alone." "By now he won't be," Houndawg says. "There'll be fuckin' bulls all over the place. Was he live or dead?" They couldn't see much from the road, but it didn't look good, and the fat man was laying into him with his boot. "The bike?" "Looked hosed." "Was he wearing his brain bucket?" "Yeah, I seen him pull out in it," Juice says. "There was this so-called Apache fucker in the bar. Asked a lot of questions. I think he was fuzz. It was him signaled the cop in the bushes." "Whether he's alive or dead, they'll have to take him to the hospital," Nat says. "Yeah, right! We can rescue him," says Juice, "and blow away any motherfucker who stands in the way!" "Maybe," says Nat. "If he's alive. Let's go get your bikes before the cops grab them. You two come back here and take care of Paulie. Someone may have seen you. Houndawg and me will see what we can find out at the hospital."

What they find out is that Littleface's head has been stove in and his neck broken and he is no more. "Do we go shoot a few people?" Houndawg asks. Nat is crying and full of rage. Houndawg can see something of old man Baxter in him. A round blanched look under his shaved head with reddish eyes on fire. But his voice is ice. What he says is: "No. We'll get him, I swear. Face will be avenged. But right now we do like we said and bury what we got and leave this place. We need numbers. We'll take in some biker meets, look up Face's old gang. The Crusadeers. They'll want to be in on it. Juice'll know how to find them." Houndawg nods. "For tonight we can hang on to the wagon. That stuff is heavy, we can use the woodie to haul it, wreck it somewhere after we've buried it all."

# II.6

## Sunday 3 May

Once, many years ago, standing up here where he is standing now, waiting, then as now, for the buried sun to push away the stone and replay yet again its bloody crawl from the tomb, he had, like that lunatic John the Seer on Patmyass (a little joke of Sissy's in her nun costume), a kind of holy vision. It was his first year as a Baptist camp counselor. He was still just a kid, but older than most of the campers, and he had found himself suffering the pangs of first love, a bad case of the dizzying pittypat sort unlike anything he'd known before, for a pretty little girl with dark curls and big eyes and a warm friendly smile. Carl Dean was not accustomed to pretty girls smiling at him like that and it went straight to his heart. She was too young—twelve, thirteen, he not much more—but he projected a long ecstatic future together from that summer on. He couldn't speak of that, of course. He had to show his affection for her in other ways, teaching her things in a big brother way, obtaining special privileges for her, buying her presents like candy bars and craft supplies, even a little New Testament with wooden covers said by the salesman who turned up at the camp to be made from two-thousand-year-old trees on the Mount of Olives ("Jesus may have prayed under this very olive tree, children!"), and she was very attentive and kept giving him deep admiring looks and big smiles, though she never actually thanked him for anything he gave her. He ached to touch her, to kiss her, even just to hold her hand, but he couldn't. It wouldn't have been right. There was a line drawn between counselors and campers and he had to respect that, and anyway, even if it had been all right, he didn't have the nerve. He adored her and was afraid of frightening her or disgusting her. It was enough just to walk beside her on a nature trail and talk in a soft voice. And then one late afternoon, slipping into the camp kitchen for some leftover tapioca pudding, he chanced on her in a clinch with one of the older counselors, a jerk with scraggly chin whiskers who taught Bible study, bark painting, and volleyball. They were pressed up together against a sink in a passionate kiss with his hand between her legs. She was even raising one leg to try to wrap it around the scumbag's hip. Carl Dean wanted to scream and throw himself on them and tear them apart limb from limb, but he only backed out silently, almost unable to breathe, and returned blindly to his cabin and fell into his cot with his face to the wall. Where he stayed until the rest of the camp had eaten and prayed and turned in for the night. He couldn't sleep. Some time after midnight he crawled out and wandered the camp and the roads at the edges for a while, his heart still jammed in his throat, his acne on fire, the sound of their whimpering and grunting in his ears, and then, a little before dawn, climbed up here to Inspiration Point, pulling himself up the path as if dragging himself out of a soul-sucking quagmire. It was sick; they were all sick. He felt an unappeasable anger, a searing hatred, but it was larger than himself. It was a righteous anger, emanating as if from God Himself, he only its instrument, and he understood then that God created sufferers for this very purpose. To bear his anger. To vent it. It was midsummer. The sky was lighter than it is now (it is overcast this morning, dark as night, won't be much of a dawn), and from up here on the Point he could make out the church camp laid out in the gloom below, the boxy wooden cabins nestled among the trees, as indeed they are now, seen dimly through the budding branches. A deep dank crotch-like odor rising like an evil miasma. And as he peered down on the camp, he felt a strange power, as if, by simply wishing it, he could unleash God's wrath upon them all, bringing down a great destruction, and all those horrible plagues and woes would start to happen, hail and fire and seas of blood and earthquakes and scorpions like horses, even though he didn't know what a scorpion looked like when it wasn't a horse, except that it had a long tail like a coiled whip with a stinger at the end that could paralyze you. And that's what he wanted: everyone turned to stone. He could not think of a single person in the camp who should be spared. For a moment, though he was only imagining it, it was almost like it was really happening, as if he could actually *see* the horror—*yes!*—the camp reddening as if with an inner burning and about to explode (well, the sun was coming up), and all because of that loose little underage twat with the teasing smile; which, now that he thinks about it, was not all that unlike poor Amanda Baxter's imbecilic grin.

The sad fact is that he has never known how to read the other sex—a huge failing. They've always been a total mystery to him, one of the few left in his life, and given his skepticism about mysteries in general, he should probably let go of this one as well, get over all that dumbass awe and respect for girls that make him such a sucker. He'd thought Elaine was different. And, well, hell, she *is* different. No snatch-grabbing kitchen clinch for Elaine; no clinch of any kind. She's married to the fucking sky. He saw she'd changed the moment he laid eyes on her that night at evening prayers under the dogwood tree. For one thing she was staring straight at him, and she never used to do that. Not in hatred, but not like she was glad to see him either. Or like she even recognized him. More like: what is that awful thing? She's taller now, taller than he is, and skinnier than ever, hunched into herself like she always was, yet at the same time more fixed and sure of herself somehow, less afraid. Or maybe she's still afraid but accepts now what she's afraid of. A kind of haunted look. He couldn't quite put his finger on it, but when Darren and Billy Don showed him that book of photos from the Day of Redemption (it excited him to see her standing there on the Mount, near naked with the tunic pasted against her thin little body, but it also pissed him off that these guys could look at her like that), he saw again that wondering, tentative, nervous yet wide-eyed and tender innocence that he had loved. It said: Help me, I need you. What he aches for. Gone now. When he looked into her eyes yesterday while making a hash of trying to say goodbye, he saw someone else. Someone who wasn't someone exactly, but more like one of those religious statues with painted eyeballs. Scorpion-stung.

The damp predawn air is full of birdcalls. He recognizes many of them but doesn't know what names to attach to them. Except the robins, which are always first to start the breast-beating, if in fact they ever stop. Earlier, there were crickety sounds, but they've gone quiet. Now and then, the burp of a frog down by the swollen creek, where the trickle of water over its stony bed can be faintly heard. Muffled cracking sounds; some animal prowling about down there on the other side of the creek maybe. Once, he heard Colin crying out in the night. Not for the first time this week. Always sounds terrified. Colin finally opened up to him a couple of days ago. In a manner of speaking. Even though he seemed to have forgotten for the moment who he was talking to. Fucked-up boy full of wacky ideas, which some of the equally wacky cultists here take as visionary. He told him about a weird dream he'd had of Jesus on the cross with his dick lopped off and spouting like a garden hose, Colin holding himself all the while so as not to lose what he had. He also said he'd been talking with their old schoolteacher, Mrs. Norton, the flaky lady who lured them into this madness, and when Pach' expressed his surprise and asked where, Colin said here. She sometimes visits me at night. Oh shit, man, Pach' said, unable to stop himself. Colin froze, his eyes widening as if in terror, and that was the end of that. Luckily, he has the preacher's wife to take care of him, though that arrangement doesn't seem all that healthy either. She keeps Colin penned in most of the time, treats Pach' like an alien invader with a rabid disease. Someone was moving around down there in the dark. Might have been her. Also a light sleeper.

He hears a peep that sounds half human. Down in the valley somewhere near the creek. What they used to call Bluebell Valley. Lonesome

Valley now, for whatever reason. "Jesus Walked This Lonesome Valley" probably. Nobody else can walk it for us. Hell no. Maybe that animal down there just caught its Sunday morning breakfast. The other birds stop their racket for a second, the pause broken by the hoot of an owl. And it occurs to him in that brief silence what he's been missing: the wail of train whistles, the rumble of freight cars rolling along on steel rails. From the camp you could sometimes even hear at night the loading of the coal over at Deepwater No. 9. Instead, far off somewhere, those motorbikes, probably drifting away. Those trains just another reminder that time moves on, things change, you lose some things, get used to it. Kids born today will never know that they ever went through here. The sky has lightened just enough that he can begin to make out the contours of the mine hill. The Mount of Redemption. He doesn't want to look at it. Makes him sick. Time to piss and go.

Halfway down the hill he meets Ben Wosznik climbing up. They have often run into each other in the early dawn hours, Ben still living by his old farmer routines, Pach' unable to sleep more than a couple of hours at a time, prison having taught him never to lose consciousness completely. Inspiration Point is a place Ben and some of the others often come to pray, and he asks Pach' if he'd care to join him now. He'd like to tell Ben what he really thinks about prayer and religion, but instead, loving Ben and unable to hurt him, he only says he has to be by himself right now.

Which leads Ben to ask, "You been up here all alone?"

"Yeah. Who would I be with?" The question rankles him, hitting a sore spot—hadn't Ben seen the mess he'd made of things?—but it also troubles him. He woke up this morning from a hangover dream about Elaine in which she passed by his van like a ghost and disappeared, and he wonders now if that was really a dream. "Listen, Ben, I gotta tell you, though don't tell no one else till I'm gone. I'm moving on. I'm glad I came, and it was great to see you again, but I just don't feel like I belong here anymore."

"Well, I'm real sorry to hear that, son. We was all sorta hoping… If it's on accounta Elaine, maybe she just needs a little more—"

"Elaine? She hates me. She told me so. It's about the only thing she said to me all week. But it's not just her. You're about the nicest guy I know, Ben. I wish you were my dad. But I don't believe what you believe. Not anymore."

It's hard to read Ben's expression in the dark behind his beard. There's pained disappointment in it and a kind of old-man bafflement, but also resignation. And affection. "Well, Carl Dean, I hafta hope you'll come back to us. I'll pray for you and pray God takes care of you, wherever you are. We'll miss you, son." And he lifts his arms for an embrace. During which, Pach', trying not to break into unmanly tears as their beards entangle, his own still damp from the shower, thinks: Ben's a believer, the man can't think past that. Another week and he and Ben would have nothing to say to each other. Sad. Maybe it was better to have an old man who puts you off the whole idea of dads forever. The kind he had. Then you don't set yourself up to be let down.

It was the night before last when Elaine came over to his van on her way home from the Friday prayer meeting, which he'd skipped, to tell him to go away. He hadn't expected that. It was bombing down rain, and he'd thought he was safe. She caught him having a beer. Seeing her standing out there in her soaked tunic, hair streaming down her face, took him back to the last time they were together, really together, standing in the storm on the Mount of Redemption, holding hands and waiting for the end of the world, and he set the beer can on the dash and stepped out in the rain to join her. Felt apprehensive, yet vaguely hopeful. He couldn't think of anything else to say, so he said he was sorry. "Why did you come back?" she demanded. "Please go away!" What could he say? The beer drinking really didn't matter, he could see that. This was something else. He swallowed, and trying not to look down at her wet body, said he came back because he loved her and thought that she loved him. "That's stupid. I never did. I was shook up because of my dad dying and all that was happening and I didn't know what I was feeling. You took advantage of me." Her voice was breaking and she seemed to be crying, but maybe it was only the rain. There was thunder and lightning, wind in the trees. It was quite a scene. Finally, maybe because he was hurt and wanted to hurt back, he got up the nerve to say that he came back to try to rescue her from all this goddamned craziness. That she should leave it now and go away with him, and she cried out, "I hate you, Carl Dean! You're as bad as they say you are!" and ran away to her trailer, where her mother was watching from the steps, also getting drenched. Thunder crashed. A fucking nightmare.

His week was up, he should have left. But spent yesterday brooding about it. Teased himself into thinking maybe hate was love. Then, last night, he waited for her after supper. It was a beautiful evening after the storm the day before—not a cloud in sight, the lowering sun casting a soft movie glow on everything, as though promising a happy ending. He was supposed to be standing guard duty with Travers Dunlevy, but he got Billy Don, with whom he's been having man-to-mans on the subject of women, to sub for him, saying it had to do with what they'd been talking about and promising him it would be the last time he'd ask and that he'd tell him what happened. Elaine was with her mother. There were a lot of other people standing around, staring, but he didn't care. This was, he knew, his last chance on earth to get through to her. "Things are going to go bad for you, Elaine. When they do, think on me, and how I loved you and admired you. It will ease the pain some. And if you need me, just shout. Wherever I am in the world, I'll hear you." This was what he'd meant to say. He'd practiced it over and over. Didn't happen that way. He only got the first part out. Her mother asked "What?" and he stumbled on the word "loved" and choked up. Elaine was staring right past him as if he weren't there. Those dead eyeballs. He was halfway between crying and killing someone. In his desperation, unable to speak or to think what else to do, he lifted his T-shirt and showed her the tattoo over his heart. For a moment then, she did look at him. At it. She let out a yip of alarm and buried her face on her mother's chest. It was as if he'd pulled his dick out and shook it at her. They were both horrified and there was suddenly a lot of hostility all around. He felt like a complete butthead, hated himself, hated everything and everyone in sight and figured they all hated him back. Before they could move on him, he spun around, nearly stepping on little Davey Cravens who'd come up behind him to hang onto his pantleg, and strode away, fists clenched, charging straight at scaredy-cat Junior Baxter, knowing then he'd have an open path, and he did, fat Junior crashing into the light post in his effort to lurch out of the way. Down in the parking lot, he hauled his leather jacket out from under the tented tarp where he'd stowed it all week, jumped in his van and drove straight out to the motel where Duke and his woman do their singing, proceeded to get thoroughly scorched on the hard stuff, keeping back only enough money to fill the tank.

While Duke was singing "Take These Chains from My Heart," he made his mind up to stop back at the camp only long enough to pick up the rest of the gear he had stowed under the tarp and then drive off into the night without further ado, but the booze knocked him down and he fell out on the steel bed of the truck while he was loading up and didn't come around until an hour ago. He'd so absented himself from his body, it was like a kind of dying, as if something had ended and nothing mattered anymore. Hadn't even closed the van doors. From his headachy dream of the ghostly Elaine passing by, he awoke to utter darkness and a certain confusion of mind. His dream, if he remembered rightly, was also about being buried, and after the storm, there being still a damp earthy smell all about like that of a freshly opened grave, it took him a moment to be sure he was lying in his van and not in a coffin. He ached, rising, as if he'd been out cold for a year. Not used to that. He rarely dropped off that hard even when stoned. Felt sick and had to step into the bushes and throw up. Needed that cold shower and the walk up to the Point and back just to get the blood pumping again, clear some of the pain and thickness in his head. The shower was a smart idea. Last chance for a while, nothing ahead but wash-ups in filling station toilets.

* * *

He needs to finish the packing now and move his ass out of here before the camp wakes up and he gets asked too many stupid questions and he starts sounding off about the total craziness of these damned people and what they have done to his old sweetheart, fucking her mind like that as they'd once fucked his. Maybe she'll come to her senses some day just as he did, though when he said that to Billy Don a couple of nights ago on guard duty, Billy Don said, "I think she feels like she *has* come to her senses." He told Pach' some of the rumors about what she and Junior Baxter were up to. "They want to be saints," he said. Hurt him, but didn't surprise him. It was what drove him nuts out on the Mount of Redemption that awful day and got him sent up: she and Junior whipping each other with switches and then she turning on him, screaming at him to go away. There are pictures of that in that damned book, too, almost dirty pictures what with all those wet bodies rolling around and that old lady with her legs spread and him with his stiff prang slipping its bonds. The boys took the book back before he could grab it and rip it up. Well, he went away that day, all right. Away off to a different fucking world. So now the two of them are back at it. The world changes but stays the same. One of the old guys doing his third stretch in the pen told him that. Makes him wonder about those snapping sounds he was hearing earlier from up on the Point, and he turns his head toward the creek. Forget it, man. Not your problem. Pack up your shit and get out of here.

Billy Don is the one guy he's been able to talk to here, other than Ludie Belle and Wayne. Ben, too, if it's not anything important. But they're older and don't understand a lot of things, or don't want to. Billy Don is his own age and his gonads are on the boil like Pach's own. Wears handles over his overbite, shades even at night to hide his wall-eye, drives a battered coupe the color of green puke, is something of a Jesus freak, but he's easy to shoot the shit with. When Pach' offered him a beer, Billy Don said he hadn't touched a drop since he went a bit wild in high school before giving his life to Christ, Bible

College being the best thing that ever happened to him. Pach' could understand that and said he knew where he was coming from, but he offered it to him again anyway, reminding him that Jesus himself was a wino, and Billy Don didn't take it but he didn't say no either and there was a flicker of an embarrassed grin under his handlebars. He is one of Mrs. Collins' inner circle, but Pach' recognized him right off as a waverer and was able to open up to him, air out his own doubts and where they've taken him, confess the real reason he came here, and the hopelessness of it. Women. They ended up talking a lot about women. Which Billy Don knows even less about than Pach'. Like Pach', Billy Don has also had to deal with a lot of personal insults in his life, being homely and wall-eyed without much of a chin, but he was born with a cheerful nature the way Pach' was born with acne, so a lot of it rolled off him. Billy Don has the hots for some long-legged college girl with a dirty mouth who told him religion is for wussies who are too chicken to face reality, but in spite of that he can't stop seeing her, so he's pretty confused about things right now. Billy Don told him one night on guard duty about a busload of young Christian folksingers from Florida who visited the camp during the anniversary celebrations and underwent full immersive baptism by light, meaning they took off all their clothes and danced naked in front of a campfire, and Billy Don joined in and said it certainly made him feel close to God, if it also didn't win him any brownie points with Mrs. Collins. He said if he could sing worth a hoot, he'd go join them, and Pach' said, if you're going to get messed up in religion, that's probably the best way to go. When Billy Don asked him if he believed in God, Pach' told him, pointing up at the sky, "Sure. Look at him out there. He's what nature is. Big bastard. But he doesn't think. Only humans think. You could say it's what's wrong with them. God doesn't have that problem, but we like to think He does." Billy Don shook his head and asked him what he thought would happen to his soul after he died, and he said he didn't have one and hated the very word. "The only thing it's good for is as a cheap gimmick in a horror movie. Stop worrying about it, Billy Don. Go screw the college girl and forget the rest." Which caused Billy

Don to duck his head and finger his rifle like it was his own dingdong and grin sheepishly again.

The guard duty bull, like the periphery fence Pach' has been helping to put up, the barbed wire, the alarm bell, the secrecy, are all part of the sicko camp paranoia. As if the rest of the world cared fuck-all about them. Some of the people in town have been a nuisance, but the novelty is wearing off. And as for the bikers, they made it plain last night that they were clearing out and nothing to come back for. Secrecy. It's like it was at the beginning when they were meeting in the Bruno house and had all those secret passwords and signs and prayers about the One to Come that they weren't supposed to tell anyone about. At the Wednesday night prayer meeting, Billy Don took some stick from the older people for hanging out with the college girl, whom he said he was only trying to convert, staring daggers meanwhile at Darren for ratting on him. Elaine's mother (Elaine wasn't there; neither was Junior Baxter) said that even if his intentions were good, she did not believe that girl's were, and he should not risk the safety and security of the rest of the camp by exchanging private information with outsiders and unbelievers. All this was apparently because of a town cemetery tour the three of them had taken earlier that afternoon, looking for the grave of Marcella Bruno. They didn't find it, but Billy Don told him later they did find an empty grave that might have been hers with two golfballs in it like dropped eyeballs. The main subject of the prayer meeting was the announcement of June 7 as the date for the groundbreaking ceremonies for the new Brunist Tabernacle of Light to be built on the Mount of Redemption. Pach' will miss that one. The choosing of the date had something to do with one of Bruno's prophecies as well as something the boys saw that day in one of the cemeteries and what Darren called, rather ominously, "certain other developments." Nods around the room, muttered prayers. Crazy.

Darren's effort to break up Billy Don and the college girl made Pach' wonder, so he asked him if Darren had ever made a play for him and that so confused Billy Don that Pach' figured he had done and that Billy Don wasn't sure what to do about it. He told him a little about Sissy without admitting to anything, but Billy Don didn't want to hear about it and changed the subject. That's probably when he started in about those firelight skinny dancers from Florida, which Pach' also found tempting and wished he'd been around for, recalling those nights around campfires dressed in nothing but Brunist tunics and underwear. Once upon a time.

His own underwear is freshly laundered, thanks to Ludie Belle—she might have guessed he'd be heading off soon, she does always seem to know what's happening next—and he's wearing one of Wayne's warm hand-me-down flannel shirts with reinforced elbow patches. New patches on the knees of his jeans, too. When he took them off for Ludie Belle to mend, she remarked quite plainly on the size of his cock, which she called his Old Adam, saying she supposed it gave him bragging rights in the shower room, but probably it could sometimes be a nuisance, too, and he said that it was. Such conversations were never easy for him, but with Ludie Belle they seemed almost natural, and they didn't even cause his acne to flare up. She could talk about such things and about the love of Jesus all in the same breath, which she sometimes did at prayer meetings when things got dull. It was Ludie Belle who brought up Elaine without his even mentioning her name (this did cause his face to heat up), telling him he should not expect too much. "The child is greatly confused." She did not imply he should give up and leave, but she did not imply he should stay either.

He turns over the panel truck engine, giving it a bit of throttle, and while letting it warm up, scrapes the dead bugs off the windshield and hangs the toe-touching naked lady over the rearview mirror again. The old van has had some hard miles, but it's ticking along well enough, ticking being the right word for the sound the tappets are making. He'll drop by Lem's for a final tune-up and a cup of coffee before he hits the road. Lem has been letting him earn beer money this week at the garage whenever he's been able to break away from the camp, but there's not enough business there for a full-time job, as Lem never fails to lament, and anyway Pach' does not want to waste any more time around here; this story has ended. Some in the camp have probably wondered what he was up to, rolling out from time to time in this old newspaper rural delivery van they still associate with the cult's Judas (that evil rag is dead and they're not, as they like to point out), but the black grease on his hands and clothes told them clearly enough where he'd been, and he was able to bring back some gum and candy for the kids, a little act in part to impress Elaine, though it flew right past her. Pach' is a hard worker, always has been. Even in prison he worked hard. Lem appreciates that, as do Ben and Wayne out here at the camp. Main difference is that Lem's garage is a crossroads to everywhere—anybody might stop by, even people off the highway—while out here it's almost like crawling inside your own body, and it makes him realize how unnatural this past week has been for him. Being cooped up all those years has made him the sort of ramblin' man Duke and his woman were singing about last night at the motel, and of all his skills, moving on is what he does best. He came back here chasing a fantasy—a fantasy just as stupid as religion is. He got rid of that one, now he's done with this one as well. No more pipe dreams of any kind; he's a free man, freer than he's ever been. Or so (the light is on in the Collins trailer and he wonders if she's wondering where he's going) he keeps reminding himself.

Among Lem's customers yesterday was Moneybags' old man, in to pick up his Continental after its final paint job, Lem having told Pach' about the beating it took one night from the biker gang, pointing out where all the dents and dings had been. Couldn't see a single one. Lem's good. Not that he makes anything at it. He's keeping everyone's car on the road but barely ekes out a living, surviving mostly on bank loans. From the pit where he was lubing an aging Olds, Pach' watched the banker. Looked like a guy who never sweated. The sort who did all his work with a nod or two and people jumped. Strong hands, big shoulders, slumping a bit, thick neck and wrists, a guy comfortable with his weight. His brat's a wimp by comparison. Pach' ran into Moneybags himself at the Moon last night. The sonuvabitch called him Ugly as if they were still back in high school. Probably thought he was being friendly. Pach' wanted to paste him one, but the dumb fuck was not worth the trouble. Moneybags was there with his old high school piece and a couple of other wops. They made a date to meet at Lem's this morning, so if the jerk shows up maybe he'll get another chance to offer him a knuckle sandwich. For old times' sake. Certainly he has a few things to tell the smug bastard. Wake him up to the real world.

Pach' had been sitting there at the bar with three bikers, who were drawing a certain amount of attention. Warrior Apostles, as they called themselves on their studded black jackets. Decorated with dragons, swastikas, American flags, the face of Jesus. Wearing bandannas around their heads and ear studs. One of them had a patch on his jacket with what looked like Brunist symbols. Though the Baxter kid was not among them, he knew who they were, knew about all the trouble they'd caused, about their killing of Ben's dog, their trashing of the camp, and so on, but he was drunk and past caring about all that shit and settled for a quiet bull session, fantasizing for a moment about another kind of life. If somebody had tried to throw them out, he would have taken their side as another outsider, and he rather hoped that might happen. Needed a good brawl to get his head straight again. Take on the fucking world. Didn't care for the spic with the greasy duck's ass hairdo, reminded him too much of the prison trusty who called him "Tonto" and tried to rape him, and the one who did all the talking was like a raw nerve with a loose mouth at the end and an unwashed mop of hair on top, a cranked-up badass who'd as soon knife you as say hello; but the hairy one with the midget face and no ears was half real and they got on all right. Talking with him, Pach' could see that bikers had less lonely lives than he had, stuck as he was in his cage, as they called it. He asked them what they were doing hanging out in a shithole like this, and they said they were just passing through, be gone before sun-up. When the hairy one left, Pach', dough running out and well plastered, left too. They exchanged grunts out in the parking lot and headed off in opposite directions, Pach' passing a car that came barreling up the narrow road with its lights off. He flashed at it. Caught a glimpse of a fat guy hunkered over the wheel. Hard to tell. No lights on top but might have been heat.

The early morning light is leaking through the thick overcast sky. The camp will be stirring soon, but there's still time to swing by the lodge on his way out to make himself a couple of sandwiches from the camp kitchen. His week's wages, so to speak, well earned. When he turns off the motor and steps out of the van, he is struck by the moist dead quiet all around him, and it takes him back to Sunday mornings here at church camp all those years ago, when he'd rise before everyone else and walk into the more remote regions of the grounds to commune directly with God or nature or just with himself as he was then, green and hopeful. Suck up the morning dew. Jerk off. Deep into the summer, there'd be the sweet smell of vegetal decay, the ground hard underfoot, the promise of a hot sun; now it's softer and denser than that, the greens brighter against the creosoted cedar cabins, even in the gray light—or because of it. There were no postlamps or phone lines then. Looks almost like a small mountain village now, nestled in the trees like something out of a storybook. The minister's wife has planted a flower garden in front of the cabin next to the lodge that she and Colin are using and it's in full flower, and there are other sprinkles of color in the high grass, mostly the yellows and whites and pale blues of flowering weeds, which he's running through now, not knowing when he started, his heart pounding, a cry, a scream, shredding the silence, sounded like his name, his old one, the one she knows him by, racing past the cabins into the wet valley beyond, over tree roots and fallen branches, slashing through the shadowed ferns and sedges at the edge of the creek and splashing down into it in a single bound, stumbling on the stones there, turning his ankle, dropping to his knees in the water, everything slowing down, seeming to, his movements thickening as if in a dream, a terrified yowling, but pressing on, scrambling laboriously up the other side through the shrubs and brambles, losing his footing and sliding back down, clambering up on all fours, headed, he knows now, for that wild place where he used to spy on the minister's wife, the patch of meadow in the woods, where he can hear voices, stifled laughter, tearing through the thorny forest undergrowth, crashing at last into the clearing, where he expects to find his old nemesis Junior Baxter, and does, but not as imagined, two guys in leather pinning him down on his back, that wild-eyed loudmouth biker and a fierce burrhead, orange fuzz on top, must be Junior's kid brother, their knives out—are they killing him?—Junior gagged with the biker's blue dew rag, naked but for what look like girls' cotton panties stretched over his fat gut, his face bloody, mouth agape, maybe already dead, no sign of Elaine but a scatter of tunics that makes his heart sink, the biker and Junior's brother rising to meet him, and then he hears her, or hears something, sees her, must be her, a pale naked thing back in the trees, two other guys rushing out from there, the spic and an older guy, blades flashing in their fists, it's the fucker who set the fuzz on Face, cries the wild-eyed one crouched over Junior, and he knows that to get to Elaine he will have to go through them. His handgun's back in the van. All he has are his fists. Nothing to do but meet what comes next…

# II.7

## Sunday 3 May

Debra has left her panties in the woods but there's no going back to get them now. No going back there ever. It was her favorite place in the world, but she is afraid of it now. She sits in her nursing chair with the slashed velvet seat cuddling a distraught Colin, trying to stop her own crying because she knows it makes him cry, wishing she could seal up this cabin and never leave it. Debra has always been known for her cheerful optimism—Wesley himself used to say she came right out of a Hollywood movie—and even when times were difficult she could always see the positive side, but now she feels utterly destroyed, sunk in that slough of despond she once read about in a book in college and didn't really understand. In fact, it was just a joke—Wesley's joke, really. Let poor Christian Pilgrim into your slough of despond, he would whisper, back when he would still whisper such things and do such things, turning it into just a wet sticky place, not a dreadful condition of the soul. Such a place as cannot be mended, the book said: the joke after her hymen broke, thought funny then, terrifying now. An abyss has opened up and nothing is funny. Colin has stopped sobbing but is still trembling like a frightened rabbit, like the little bunny she once had as a child, the one her mother said died of too much loving, and she strokes his silky hair and presses his head against her bosom, which always calms him, trying, as her own tears flow, not to let her chest heave and set him off again.

The day had begun so peacefully, well before dawn. Her worries—about money (it is all gone), about the threat of having to leave their cabin, about Colin's daily ups and downs and the personal conflicts in the camp which upset him so—had seemed to drop away and a great contentment stole over her, as often happens when she is close to nature, which for Debra is the same thing as being close to God. The sky was overcast. There was no moon and the streetlamps had been turned off at midnight. She felt invisible as she slipped past the cabins and down through Bluebell Valley accompanied only by birdsong, the ground soft underfoot from the recent rain and the padding of long grasses. Instead of crossing the creek by one of the wooden bridges, she decided to take off her sandals and wade over, her toes and the soles of her feet scouting the rocky bed before taking each step like little prowling animals nibbling at the unseen stones. It was deeper than usual and there was an arousing rush of current against her ankles. She paused in the middle, and gathering up her skirt, knelt to scoop up a palmful of water, sipping a drop or two, then washing her face with the dampness that remained, feeling like an ancient priestess performing her holy ablutions. She prayed simply that nothing ever change, her prayer directed to the tender night more than to any being, then stepped on across and slipped her sandals on again. There was a small incline on the other side, and though it was pitch black in there under the trees, she seemed to know exactly where to plant each foot, and she felt full of grace as she rose up it.

She avoided the clearing, partly because the two young people sometimes came there, or used to before that strange ugly man who so frightened Colin turned up, and though she disapproved of their behavior, she did not want to seem to interfere with it, circling around through the trees until she found a little patch of pine needles behind some bushes where she could squat for her morning pee. Which she has always thought of, when able to avoid the suffocating outhouse and steal over to her private garden among the waking birds, as one of the most sacred moments of her day. Not the most Presbyterian of sacraments, but she loves it all the more for that very reason. She has sometimes gone there just as dawn was breaking, the sun's rays slanting gloriously through the thick trees then as though the divinity were joining her there in a kind of blessing. For fear of alarming the other campers, though she is not at all shy, she is forced to do this on the sly. But in the old days, between camping sessions, when the place was empty, depending on whether or not it was the mosquito season, she often wore no clothes at all around the camp, squatting whenever and wherever she felt like, bathing in the creek, sunning in the small meadow or even amid the bluebells and wildflowers next to the access road or right in front of the lodge on the patch of lawn there, putting her body in God's hands. And sometimes she didn't even care about the mosquitoes, accepting their stings like little love bites. The camp has never had a serious tick problem, though there is always a risk, adding an edge of danger to these excursions. People think that ticks drop from the trees, but actually they stay close to the ground and latch on from below. She did once get one and she had to bend over so Wesley could pull it out. He was so squeamish. Finally she had to bat his hand away and do it herself.

She so loved her body then, and Wesley did too, often joining her in the nude. But it never produced anything and Wesley wearied of it and it did start to fall apart and bag on her as bodies always do, and for years since, until now, it has gone largely unappreciated. But that place on the other side of the creek had always been her favorite, her secret corner where she could strip down, even when camp was in session, and lie back in the warm summer sun and close her eyes and listen intently to the musical language of the birds and insects, separating out their voices, deducing the meaning of their calls, and she lay so still that once a little wren actually landed on her and walked along her tummy. Colin's needs and agitations often make this pilgrimage impossible, but this morning she left him sleeping soundly, hugging his pillow, much buoyed of late by the attention paid him by Clara's two office boys and the general optimism of the camp. In a few weeks' time there will be a symbolic laying of the cornerstone of the new Brunist Tabernacle of Light over on the Mount for which there are already finished architectural plans, and the camp itself is becoming more beautiful and functional with every passing day. True, there are some who say that such projects make no sense if these really are the last days, but these are mostly people who are never really happy and who just want something for themselves.

She often leaves her undies back at the cabin, allowing the early morning air to whisper its whisperings without encumbrance, drying herself with her skirt afterwards but, like Colin, she has of late on warmer nights taken to sleeping in her underwear, so she had just pulled on a loose frock as she stepped out into the night, which decision was, as it turned out, dreadfully unfortunate. She had just lowered her panties to her ankles there in the nest of bushes, and bunching her skirt up around her midriff, had started sending a gentle hissing stream into the needles, when she heard hushed men's voices. There was someone else there in the woods and not far away. She turned off the flow or it turned itself off, stopping as her heart stopped. She was terrified, couldn't move, couldn't even lower her skirt. They were grunting and cursing softly and one of them turned on a flashlight for a moment and she saw it was the motorcycle gang. They had shovels and were burying something. A body? It seemed too small for a body. Had they killed another animal? She didn't see anything after that because she knuckled down behind a thick bush in the little depression there, trying to make herself as small as possible, fearful she was sticking out in all the wrong places, and began struggling, silently, with the tangle of underpants around her ankles, thankful for the racket of the birds covering her own fumblings and rustlings, but, doubled up as she was and stepping on them, she could neither pull them on nor get them off without standing up and making herself known to them. It would be getting light soon. Already she could make out the outlines of things, and she could see her own limbs clearly and knew they could, too, if they looked her way. She was in great danger, and if she had to run she couldn't. It would be like running in a sack race.

She doesn't know how long she stayed scrunched down there, her heart fluttering in her chest like a trapped bird trying to beat its way out, but the dark had been slowly lifting like a kind of dissipating fog and she knew she didn't have much time. She had managed at last to free one foot so she could run now if her legs would obey her and she took a deep silent breath and prepared to do that. They were faster, she knew, but they didn't know the woods as well as she did. She figured she had a chance by leading them through the most tangly part. Unless they had guns. Guns! The thought of being shot as she ran refroze her limbs, and she realized she was peeing again, it was trickling warmly down her thighs and into her sandals, doubled under her. She was praying now, not to nature or the night, which was all but gone, but to God and Jesus and the Holy Spirit and Mother Mary and all the apostles and disciples to please get her out of this somehow. While they worked, the motorcyclists were insulting one another in what they probably thought of as a manly manner, smoking and spitting and cursing the sheriff and other people and threatening to kill everyone. "Cover it up with dead leaves," she heard one of them say in a rattly growl. One of them, the one with the childish voice, was called Runt and another Jews or Juice and another Face, though he didn't seem to be there. Jews or Juice was the one who kept talking wildly all the time, often about the one called Face, and the others were always telling him to shut up or keep it down, which was why she knew his name. The voice that was giving the orders, telling the others what to do and how to do it, made a shushing sound and they all grew very quiet. Had they heard her? Maybe they'd heard her heart, which was thundering in her ears. No. Someone was coming. Through the trees she could see the two white tunics and she knew what would happen next. She wanted to warn them but couldn't.

Neither of them spoke a single word. There were no preliminaries, they simply turned their backs to one another in turn and smartly lashed each other, she with the razor strop, he with the belt—Debra had seen these things before, did not need to peek out at them to know what was happening. At first the strokes were measured and always, she knew, across the shoulders. But as the tempo picked up, the blows might fall anywhere, especially those of the boy, who seemed inclined to throw himself into it with more abandon. They emitted little grunts and whimpers as they swung, and once the girl—poor little Elaine, punishing herself for sins she could not even imagine—yipped in pain, unable to stop herself, a little squeak like that of a mouse caught by an owl. Whereupon the bikers, laughing cruelly, stepped out of the woods and encircled them, their knives out (Debra was watching them now, peeping through the brush, her heart in her throat). Elaine cried out, and then fell silent. The husky boy in the black leather jacket with the high collar, whom she recognized as Nathan Baxter, though he looked changed, rougher somehow, his head shaved nearly bald, took the belt and razor strop away from them and walloped his brother in the chest with both of them at once, flattening him out and leaving him gasping for breath. They stripped them both of their tunics, Elaine now stonily passive, staring off in another direction, as the older man with a braid sliced her tunic down the front with a knife, the downed boy struggling against them until he got a blow in the face from the razor strop. "Look," said one of the motorbikers, "he's wearing his chick's skivvies. Ain't that cute?" And they all laughed and kicked at him there on the ground with their boots. "What'll we do with her?" another asked, and Nathan Baxter said, "Whatever. She's with the enemy." "Don't mind if we fuck your girlfriend, do you, son?" asked the older man, his free hand clutching the girl between the thighs, and Young Abner said in a trembly girlish voice, looking like he was trying to smile and was about to cry at the same time, "She's not my girlfriend. I don't give a care what you do with her." Nathan Baxter took a fistful of his brother's hair and jerked his head up and laid the blade of his knife against his throat and said, "You got me in trouble, man, with that gun you stole. Maybe we oughta do to you what we done to the dog." And he drew a red line on the boy's forehead with the point of his knife. The boy started squealing in a high-pitched voice—"No! God! Please!"—and they gagged him with the blue bandanna the noisy one had been using as a headband.

This, Debra knew, was her moment to escape, had been, but she was still petrified, the long knives frightening her even more than guns would, and the moment was already gone because two of them were suddenly heading her way, dragging Elaine with them, still brandishing their knives, the noisy one called Juice or Jews or maybe Choose and a dark one with oily black hair who spoke with an accent, and she had to shrink down again, squeezing her eyes shut as if that could turn the world off. She could hear their hooting and sniggering, all their vulgar remarks about how scrawny the girl was as they exposed the rest of her and pushed her to the ground, then their grunts and heavy breathing, the noisy one complaining how tight she was, the other one telling him to break her open with his thumbs or the handle of his knife if he wasn't man enough to crack it on his own, and there was some dreadful thrashing about and slaps and cursing and laughing, while out in the clearing the gagged boy was whining desperately through his nose and seemed to be strangling and then he was silent. Debra, who could not have seen anything through her tears even if she'd been watching, was trying to stifle her sobs for fear of ending up like Ben's dog. What would happen to poor Colin if they rolled her head into the campground? The only thing she had heard Elaine say beyond a single gasp of pain was "Pa…?" which didn't seem right, but it was what she heard. Lookie here!" The noisy one was back out there in the clearing again without any pants on, his hair flying loose around his head like a nest of snakes. "He whupped her but he never fucked her!" She knew by the sounds behind her that the other one, cursing the child in his native tongue, was taking his turn. Would they kill her when they were done with her? They would. Oh my God. Out in the clearing, the one with the little boy's voice asked if the girl had hurt him, and the noisy one laughed and said, "Nah, that leaked outa her crankcase, Runt, not mine. A little somethin' got busted in there." The older one with the soft rattly voice said, "C'mon, Runt. Take your britches down and I'll show you how it works." Those two were now coming her way, too. Debra knew she could not take much more before she lost control and started screaming and it would all be over. The older one and the one with the accent were behind her showing the young boy what to do next, snorting with evil laughter and urging him to keep pushing and pushing, when there was a most horrendous howling out in the clearing like wild savages, maybe the gag had come off the boy, if he wasn't already dead, and she found herself on her feet, shrieking, bawling, unleashing her own savage howls, ready to die, but nobody was paying any attention, they were all out there in the clearing where there was a lot of yelling and violent cursing going on, only the boy had been left behind, still down between the poor child's legs, a scrawny redhead, couldn't have been more than twelve or thirteen, his bony bottom bouncing like a windup toy gone crazy.

And then, without even thinking about it, Debra did a very brave thing. She choked down her panic and picked up a thick branch, and just as the boy gave a surprised little yelp, gave him such a blow as might have bashed his brains out, grabbed up the lifeless girl, and half dragging her, half carrying her, screaming for help, hauled her away from there, stumbling through the undergrowth and over one of the bridges, afraid to look back for fear they were chasing her and she'd lose heart and fall down and they'd both be killed.

She was met at the edge of the camp by Ben and Wayne and Welford Oakes running her way, Ben with his shotgun, Hunk Rumpel just behind them in his white longjohns and carrying a rifle, Clara and Hazel and Ludie Belle in their bathrobes, everyone streaming out of cabins and the lodge and up from the camper parking lot, looking shocked and terrified. Clara swept her naked daughter into her arms, the child still stunned, wet eyes staring at nothing, mouth agape, her thin body oddly rigid like a stick figure, blood streaming down her sinewy thighs, her mother wrapping her bathrobe around her and hurrying her away. Debra's knees gave way as soon as she was free of the girl, and they were all suddenly crowding around her, asking her questions, who was it and what happened, but she couldn't think, she couldn't speak, all the tensions of her ordeal were exploding out of her in uncontrollable sobbing, she could only point toward the creek, and several of the men ran off in that direction (and, yes, she who'd always opposed the arming of the camp hoped they would shoot all of them), and then she was throwing up. She was gathered up in hugs and prayers from where she'd fallen, one of the women saying someone should call Bernice to bring out some nerve medicine, Ludie Belle whispering in her ear that it was all right, just fling up, honey, it'll do you a world, and guiding her toward her cabin, she should lie down a spell, she'll fix her a cup of tea.

She became aware then that someone else was wailing even louder than she was—it was Colin, running at full speed, round and round in wild circles in nothing but his underwear, yowling at the top of his lungs. At the door of the next cabin, Abner Baxter, the father of all those terrible boys, was scowling furiously at Colin as though it was all his fault and trying to push his youngest daughter back inside not to witness it. Darren and Billy Don tried to catch Colin, but he leapt right past them, and soon everyone was watching Colin or chasing him, and she herself had stopped her weeping. It was Hunk who finally collared him and lifted him up, his feet still churning, and brought him over to the cabin, where Darren and Billy Don and some of the women gathered to help restrain him and calm him down.

Before they could get him inside, however, there was the sound of anguished howls rolling up from below and the men returned, Travers and Wayne carrying Young Abner Baxter under his armpits, the boy dressed only in girls' panties with blood streaming down his face and hanging limp as a sack of butter from their grip, his toes dragging through the grass, but screaming in pain so at least he was still alive. They dumped him in front of Abner Baxter and Ben, who had a leather belt wrapped round his fist like tape, said, "Pack up your family and get out," and Colin fell down and rolled around in the twitchy way he sometimes does and started howling along with the Baxter boy.

"What's all this about?" Abner Baxter demanded over the racket.

"Ask your boy. You got thirty minutes or we'll do your moving for you."

He bristled and his neck reddened and he seemed ready to burst into one of his self-righteous tantrums, but then he looked around at all the armed men and at his bawling near-naked son and his chest caved in and his head seemed to sink lower on his shoulders. "But where will we go?"

"We don't rightly care. Just pack and git. Now."

"Ain't them letters writ there on his head?" someone asked.

"Looks as how somebody was tryin' to use his face for a notepad."

"Maybe it's the mark of the beast," someone whispers.

"Don't do nuthin rash, Wayne. Don't go killin' everbody."

"Ain't fixin' to, Ludie Belle. Only so long as these folks git trottin'."

And that was all of it she saw because the women bundled her and Colin, still yelping frantically and throwing himself recklessly about, into their cabin and closed the door on the outside world. The women managed to get Colin into his bed somehow and pin him down with his blankets, though he was still yowling. They steered Debra toward her own bedroom at the back, but she chose instead her nursing chair in the anteroom from which she could keep an eye on Colin. Glenda Oakes told him to stop fretting, it wasn't real, it was all just play-acting, and she cuffed him lightly to stop the hysterics, surprising him into a momentary stillness and shocking Debra just a little. Glenda had some hard candy for him in her pocket. She told him it was magic candy and to suck on it for five minutes and everything would be hunkydory.

There was no tea, so Ludie Belle made her a cup of instant coffee and then left for a while, but some of the others remained, crying and praying and talking to each other as if she and Colin weren't there, speculating on what might have happened. When Ludie Belle came back, she said she'd gone to the office and phoned Bernice and also Mr. Suggs and told him to bring the sheriff and then called Duke L'Heureux and some of the others to come out right away, and she shooed the other women out ("Something's on fire!" Glenda exclaimed, and Ludie Belle said, "Ain't nuthin but a little bonnyfire," shutting the door behind her) and closed the windows and tsk-tsked that Debra had let her coffee go cold. She said she should lock the door and get some private time, so as to recollect herself and settle the boy down. Before that could happen, Ben Wosznik stopped in still carrying his shotgun, to thank her and see how she was and to ask if there was anything she could tell him. She tried, but she still couldn't speak. She only started crying again, and Ludie Belle said Sister Debra was still in a state of shock, that they should maybe wait until after Bernice got out here, and she asked him if Young Abner told him anything. Ben said that the boy was out cold when they found him and the only thing they could get out of him after they'd dipped him in the creek to bring him around was that it was his brother Nathan who cut him. "What was he doin' with them bloomers on?" "I don't know. Was it them motorcycle boys down there?" Ben asked, turning toward her, and, still crying, she nodded. "Carl Dean's panel truck is parked out front and he ain't nowhere around. Was he there too?" She was confused about this, but she nodded again, and Ludie Belle said Duke told her on the phone that Carl Dean was drinking last night at the motel with the bikers and left with them. Ben stood there slump-shouldered for a moment, shaking his old head, and then he and Ludie Belle left, Ludie Belle giving her a sympathetic hug and telling her not to worry about church this morning, everybody would understand.

With everyone gone and the door locked, Colin, still trembling and whimpering softly around his jawbreaker, has crawled out of his bed and into her lap on the nursing chair. She holds him close and strokes his hair and tries to pray, but cannot summon the words for it, feeling more distant from God and Jesus than at any time since she first moved to the camp. Of course, she is grateful to have survived—it was a kind of miracle really, so it could be said her prayers have been answered. But why has she been obliged to witness such horror in the first place? She sees again the long knives, the snarling cruelty on their shadowy faces, hears the dismaying sounds behind her, the grunting, the sinister laughter, and finds that she is crying again. It was terrible, but there must be a reason. She has not always been a good Christian and has often been a doubter of the stories that get told, but that God is purposeful and that His purposes are loving she has never doubted.

She sees it in the birds, the flowers, the way a tree grows, the way the stars are born and take their places. If God is not purposeful, then nothing means anything, and that is an unbearable thought. And if He is not merciful, then He is a kind of monster, and that would be like saying the sun is cold and bad is good. God is God and cannot escape his own self-definition. I am that I am, He said so. Wesley taught her that. God, as he used to say, is not free, which is of course a very Presbyterian remark. From the Brunist point of view, God has a story to tell, but humans, through their actions, help him to write it. It's mostly a happy story, but it has its gruesome side, and maybe she has been given a glimpse of that. The basic plot is all laid out and irreversible—it's almost as though, in some other notion of time, it has already happened—but the details are obscure, only hinted at by prophecy, and the characters are interchangeable. One cannot choose to be among the communion of saints, but one can seek to be.

In her old life, her frivolous empty-headed one, the Book of Revelation was an inconvenient and somewhat hateful tag-on to the gospel of love, one that never fit her view of things, but it surges through Brunism like the swollen creek through the camp. God and His living metaphors: let him who has eyes see. She is learning. Loose the four angels, He said. Actually, there were five of them this morning. The fifth angel in Revelation is the one given the key to the bottomless pit, isn't that right? The one who bosses the other four and whose kingdom is full of darkness and pain? And there were more angels in the prophecy. More to come? Does this make any sense? Was God speaking to all of them through Elaine's ordeal with Debra as His witness? She thinks of herself as an unlikely receptacle for prophetic knowledge, but the same could be said of Giovanni Bruno. She will read that book again and think about it and share her thoughts with the two boys, who are better at understanding such things than she.

The shouting outside has died down. Deeper quieter voices have prevailed. The thought of leaving this cabin and facing the world again, even the little world of this camp, is almost unbearable, but she will have to do that. As for the larger world, it is beyond their reach, for they are penniless; what they have is this little cabin. Perhaps she will heat up some water and give Colin a soothing bath in the new washtub. Something worshipful to do in place of Sunday service. It would soothe her, too. Colin sighs tremulously or moans softly from time to time, but he has stopped shaking and may be asleep, and she has stopped crying, too. She has made a nest for him with her body, her broken-winged dove. Though he is cuddled up tight, gripping her breast as though to keep from falling, his thin white legs are asprawl, and she knows that they present an image not unlike that of Jesus being held by his mournful mother after His descent from the cross. Except that Colin, though as pale as the dead Jesus and not very well, is very much alive. He lets go of her breast now and takes her hand off his hip, where it had been resting, and slides it to his penis. He often sleeps this way when he crawls into her bed, his penis soft then, his underwear damp and sticky. It's not exactly right, but it always makes him feel calmer and she thinks of it as a necessary sedative and a kind of therapy. This morning, though, his underwear is dry and his penis is stiff, like a wooden clothespin. She wraps her hand around it as he wraps his hand around hers. He makes sudden little jerking movements, gripping her fist, and then there is a hot warm flow—"Mother!" he whispers, "Oh! Mother! I *love* you!"—then sinks away, sound asleep, dead to the world. Debra, cupping his wet pouch protectively as a mother might her newborn's tender little head, is crying again.

# BOOK III

And when he had opened the third seal,
I heard the third beast say, Come and see.
And I beheld, and lo a black horse;
and he that sat on him had a pair of balances in his hand.
And I heard a voice in the midst of the four beasts say,
A measure of wheat for a penny, and three measures of
barley for a penny;
and see thou hurt not the oil and the wine.

*—The Book of Revelation 6.5-4*

# III.I

## Thursday 7 May – Sunday 24 May

The King is in his counting house, but no money to be counted. The Wizards have it all. By magic? No, their magic couldn't pull a coin out of your ear. Probably he just left the back door open. He can't think of everything. The war is not going well. Treasure Mountain is under attack, its guardian dragon having wandered off in pursuit of succulent maidens. A serious error of judgment, but some things can't be helped. The forest has fallen to the Cretins, the King's counselors are bickering confusedly among themselves, and when the Jester, somewhat soused on the royal mead, remarks that the Castle has been caught out like a maiden with her drawbridges down, he is banished to the fields to practice his jokes on the sheep and share their mange and foot rot.

As for the Jester's daughter, the witless Goose Girl, she is slumped, desperately in need of a smoke, in the back row of the West Condon Township High School auditorium, scribbling idiocies in the notebook on her knees. This chilly spring day chances also to be (the world is suffocating in irony or else it's the imbedded transgenerational odor of child sweat) Ascension Day, though probably few here other than the Catholic priest, the Lutheran preacher, and herself even know that. Because Tommy Cavanaugh has asked her to, Sally is attending the inaugural meeting of the New Opportunities for West Condon citizens committee, the very one (irony is lost on Tommy) that, thanks to his dear dad, has cost *her* dear dad his job and condemned him to the donkey stables at the Fort. So do me a favor, Sal… It was Tommy's assignment to get the young people out to the meeting, and there are a lot of them in here—his old high school teammates and drinking buddies, all the stay-at-home losers, but especially Tommy's fan club, his exes and wannabes, she of the bouncing tits among them. Tommy himself is back up at university, having had to drive there in a beat-up tangerine-colored Buick Special rented from Lem after his mom's station wagon got nicked and wrecked over the weekend, so Sally is martyring herself unwitnessed, but she promised to send him her notes, and anyway it's all mill-grist, is it not? See here how her restless plume flies blithely o'er the welcoming page. Her dad's Chamber successor and new city manager (no one seems certain just how this has happened, least of all the mayor, who stares out upon the gathered citizenry from his marginalized seat at one end of the stage, his fat round face the very picture of bafflement; Sally makes a little cartoon sketch in her notebook: Simple Simon as a con artist) has just announced his first coup in office—he has interested a big-city consortium called the Roma Historical Society in the purchase and restoration of the derelict West Condon Hotel—and he has been duly applauded. Things are, on this day of Christ's liftoff, looking up. That's the message. The city manager is also the de facto chairman of this committee, and he goes on to describe in his crisp monotone all the legal actions they have taken against the illegal encampment of the cult at the edge of town, which is blamed for much that has gone wrong in recent times and which is now trying to steal the mine and its historic hill out from under their noses.

Backdropped by a huge banner in the school colors that says "NOWC" and surrounded by his varsity squad of preachers and politicians, Tommy's father assumes the podium to let it be known that if the city can acquire the Deepwater property, he will ask the state for funding for a new hospital to be built on it or else an industrial park or a state prison or some kind of recreational facility, maybe a monument to the fallen mine heroes, his very lack of a clear project (he asks the audience for their own ideas, setting off a general brouhaha) evidence that the hill is not his nor will it likely ever be.

This is one tough ballgame, he says—but what he doesn't say is that he is losing it. The Brunists already have detailed architectural plans for a big church up there—Billy Don has described them to Sally—with groundbreaking set for just a month from today, and apparently, thanks to mischievous Irene, they're building it mostly with Cavanaugh family money. Which, Tommy says, has left his dad, also not an appreciator of irony, pretty fucking depressed.

Now, as the citizenry argue noisily about how to use land they don't own and never will (some want to reopen the mine itself—there's a whole lot of coal down there still, they shout—all the mine structures have remained in place in hopes of its reopening, the city should take it over and run it, it owes that much to the hardworking people who have made this town what it is today), she can see the dismay setting in on the man's face like time-lapse aging, and he seems to be looking around for an exit just as she is. Somewhere she has written in one of her notebooks: It is the attempt to avoid fate which provokes the calamity. Now she opens her cogdiss page and writes: Calamity is the normal circumstance of the universe. Catastrophe creates.

This page was opened after her meeting earlier this week with Reverend Konrad Dreyer of Trinity Lutheran, now sitting onstage with the other city fathers, smiling that sad patronizing smile that preachers bestow upon the damned. Sally was there to try to find out what it was about him that so baffled her parents and their Presbyterian friends. Without a minister, they're obliged to go to church at Trinity Lutheran, which is damp and chilly and smells of mildewed hymnals, and that's bad enough without having Connie Dreyer put them to sleep with his fustian monologues. You should only have to take a metaphysical once a year, as her father put it, twisting the cap off his after-church Sunday morning "spirituals." Sally and the minister sat out on the church lawn where he'd been weeding dandelions and planting begonia and gladiolus bulbs alongside the broad front steps. He got out his pipe, meaning she was free to hit the cigarettes. Just to be provocative, she had worn her RELIGION IS MYTH-INFORMATION tee, even though it has a split seam under one armpit and wasn't completely clean—to which he replied, acknowledging the line with a nod, Yes, I can see that. But a myth is not a lie, Sally. It's a special kind of language used to symbolize certain realities beyond space and time. It *is* information. God's a symbolist, you mean. No, on the contrary. Everything he is and does is just what it is and nothing else. You know: I am that I am. We earthbound creatures use symbolism as one way of trying to understand God's thought, which for Him is the same thing as His actions. For we and all we think and do and feel are only shadowy and scattered emanations of divine thought, action, and passion. Whereupon, when she asked about passion, he explained God's love, quoting someone else to the effect that love, as experienced in eternity, is an incessant "dying to oneself" (she took a note, wondering if human love might not be something like that when it was really good), a prefiguring of which was provided by Christ's life, death, and resurrection, an act of divine love performed for us within the constraints of our own limited human perceptions of space and time, which are not those of infinity and eternity, but of mere extension and duration. He seemed so sure of himself. How did he know all that to be so? He gazed into his pipe bowl as though his thoughts were stored there, clamped the stem in his teeth, took a draw, then said: Well, Socrates would say by intuition, but for me it's more a matter of faith. And faith in divine governance is just that: faith. Everything else, including church dogma or Biblical interpretation, is achieved by reason and so is susceptible to human error. But so is your first principle, Reverend Dreyer. No, it may be true or false—in this world we'll never know—but it cannot be subject to error. He smiled. It is that it is.

She knew by then that it would be useless to question the historicity of the resurrection story or dispute the divine inspiration of the Bible or the prophecy of the Last Judgment and et cet, because he would just agree with her or say it could be so, we're only human after all, and smile his benign smile, the smile he is casting now upon the auditorium, as though to say God's love is flowing through him and he is sharing it with everyone. The smile of the terminally stoned upon the squares. So instead she asked him what he thought about the Brunists. Isn't it curious that their religion only got going after what they'd prophesied didn't happen? He saw through her instantly. You're going to say the same thing was true of the beginnings of Christianity, he said, and it was her turn to smile. Well, it was, wasn't it? Jesus told his disciples the end would come in their own lifetimes and it didn't. He let everybody down, his little cult should have died, but look what happened. Isn't that really weird? He nodded and said that it was and that there was now a quasi-scientific term for what causes that weirdness. It's called cognitive dissonance, which he explained as believing or wanting to believe two contradictory things at the same time, or acting or having to act in conflict with one's beliefs, and suffering the mental discomfort of that. Trying to resolve these conflicts and ease the discomfort releases a lot of creative energy, for the mind is forced to look for new beliefs or somehow transform the old existing ones. In the case of predicting an event that doesn't happen, for example, especially when you are publicly committed to it—when, not to seem a fool, you have to go on believing something that's contrary to the evidence, as with the Brunists or, yes, the early Christians—the dissonance aroused is alleviated by making it come true after all, perhaps by redefining it or rescheduling it, or just by getting more people to believe in the original prediction. So now I know what *you're* going to say, she said. If everything flows from God's head, then He planted this mechanism to make things like Christianity happen, whether or not there even ever was a Jesus. The minister laughed and tapped the ashes out of his pipe. Yes, the Spirit of God, which is everywhere, working from within to influence human imaginations to produce Christ-like stories, symbolizing the truths of God, as a great teacher of mine once said. And if so, it means that something good can come even from the Brunists, in spite of their naïve confusions and most folks' misgivings. Something intended by God—in effect, engineered by Him. And I will tell you something stranger, Sally. Studies have shown that the less the reward or the milder the punishment, the greater and firmer the change. When it's more like a voluntary decision, it sticks more. Thus, the failure of Moses' law tablets. He chuckled, pocketing his pipe. No wonder he had to break them: they were too extreme, too implacable, and didn't work. The Jesus generation knew better. And the most important lesson of cognitive dissonance is that to suffer is to love. People end up loving what they willingly suffer for, whether or not it merits either love or suffering. They don't want to suffer and so they have to find some sort of justification for having elected to do so. The more suffering we have chosen for ourselves, the greater the commitment to the changed beliefs that have led to the suffering and the greater the love toward the object of those beliefs.

Her present suffering may be having a similar effect. Chasing Tommy is an amusing diversion from what is now her writing life (yes, she has made that choice—this am who she am, bring on the dissonance and fuck the consequences), but putting up with nights like this, having to listen to her benighted townsfolk rattle insanely on in a suffocating school auditorium, suffering an infinite boredom sinking into total stupor, and not for Tommy's sake, as she likes to pretend, but merely for the sake of her futile pursuit of him, is ratcheting up that pursuit's value and her love for its object. Sally does not believe Tommy will ever show any interest in her, but she has to believe, against all odds, he will, else all she's putting herself through will have been for nothing—even if, on one level, she doesn't even like him, finding him an insensitive, spoiled, jock-strapped, self-centered nitwit. But, somewhat in the abstract, he's also beautiful and she loves him. Maybe all the more so since he took her to the brink five years ago, like the Brunists got taken on their stormy hill—and more or less at the same time—then dropped her. Another failed prophecy: They both thought it was going to happen and it didn't. And won't. But will. I believe. Such are her vain expectations and the punishments she must suffer in their anticipation. But there's a limit. When Tommy's father remarks that it is religion that holds this community together and asks the Catholic priest and the Methodist preacher to lead them all in prayer, she butts out.

* * *

A few days later, over ice cream sundaes in the Tucker City drugstore, Sally tries to explain this new concept to Billy Don Tebbett, leaving out the spooky divine engineering bit—the principle being, if you can understand the mechanism, you can escape it—but Billy Don only pretends to listen. He did seem genuinely happy to see her again when they met outside on the street, grinning his flushed awkward grin while pulling self-consciously on his droopy mustaches and squeezing her hand when she offered it, but now he has withdrawn behind his sunglasses once more as if regretting that he has come here. They are regulars now and evoke amused glances whenever they enter; the people all go silent and look the other way, busying themselves with this or that, no doubt hoping to overhear something scandalous again, and it's not in her nature to disappoint them. The fear of that may be what has made Billy Don apprehensive, or else it's her Mark Twain tee, IF THERE IS A GOD HE IS A MALIGN THUG, which he's staring at, though without the usual close-read. He's probably aware of the actions being taken against the camp by the city, and maybe he associates her with them. She asks if something is the matter and he only shrugs and says they've been working harder than ever at the camp and seem to be getting less and less done, and then he looks away. Though this is more an evasion than an answer, she decides to use it, and with her notebook open to her cogdiss page, she says that hard work might be a way of avoiding having to think about anything else, and he looks into her eyes with at least one of his and agrees with a nod that it could be. But when she suggests it might also be a way of inducing or reinforcing belief—that work is a kind of suffering, and the more of it you devote to some cause or other, the more you start to believe in it, *have* to believe in it—he says, no, it wasn't anything like that, it was just to prove they can carry on without Ben and Clara.

"You mean Mrs. Collins has left the camp?"

"Well, just for three or four weeks or so. Probably. She and Ben are on a, you know, like, tour of the East Coast churches or something. Ben's going to sing."

He's looking away again. Something's bothering him; he's not coming clean. He has made his methodical way down through his sundae, but the old voracity is not there. On a hunch, she says: "What I'm saying is, when you're only thinking about something—religion, say—you can take it or leave it. But when you start *doing* something, or have to, especially where people can see you, you get hooked. That is, you hook yourself. Doing creates believing. You know? Almost like it *is* believing. Or when, for example, something bad happens…"

"Something bad *did* happen."

"Oh yeah?" Heads turn in the silence, not to face them, but to position their ears. "Billy Don…?"

"I can't talk about it. I promised."

"Is it why Mrs. Collins and her husband left?" He doesn't reply, just glances up at her then drops his head. Maybe they got into it with somebody and things went wrong and they just ducked out. Which would be a total disaster. But what could have gone wrong? She had all her closest people around her; any fights, she'd have won them. And Mrs. Collins didn't seem like one to get caught out in any kind of scandal either. So something happened *to* her to make her leave. But she's used to trouble and she didn't look a quitter. You had the feeling she would have stood up against any…unless… "Did they take her daughter along when they left?" This time he doesn't even glance up at her. "Something happened to her daughter…oh no. Someone in the camp?"

He shakes his head. "No," he mutters, his head down, speaking so softly he almost cannot be heard. "It was those bikers. They…"

"The bikers? What—? Oh my god, Billy Don! They…?"

He nods and puts his finger to his lips, glancing uneasily around the drugstore. Nothing to be heard but the soft flutter of the ceiling fan overhead. "Your aunt was a real heroine," he wheezes, his hand in front of his mouth, and clears his throat. "She heard something and went down there and fought them all off with a big branch."

"She did? Aunt Debra?"

"But she's not the same now. She seems mad about something all the time, or else just sad. She gets very demanding and at the same time she cries a lot. *Nobody's* the same now."

"That's an *awful* story, Billy Don! It's *horrible!* Something has to be done!"

"No, they don't want anybody to know. You have to promise not to tell. They're afraid people around here will take it the wrong way. You know, like we're always getting accused of one sick thing or another. And the bikers have all left. One of them got killed. Sheriff Puller found his body and his wrecked bike out on the state road and he said they won't be back."

"I heard about that. Some guy driving drunk without a helmet. But their motorcycles are really noisy. You can hear them a mile away. How did they reach the camp without everyone knowing?"

"Well, it was very early, still dark. And they used a car."

"A car." Aha. "Saturday. Or Sunday. A week ago," she says. He looks up at her, surprised. "Friend of mine. His car was stolen that night. Later they found it trashed over by the mine." She saw Tommy that day. He'd gone out to the motel car park and found it gone. He said it took him a while to grasp that it had been stolen; at first he thought he must have parked it somewhere else, given someone the keys. But he *had* the keys. He said this happened "after midnight" which she translated to "the next morning."

"And Pach', he was there, too."

"Pach'?"

"Carl Dean Palmers. I guess he was one of them—everybody said so, but he really fooled me. Duke and Patti Jo said he was getting drunk with the bikers in the motel bar the night before. He loved her, but she wouldn't pay him any mind, so, I don't know, maybe he just…"

And so that, too. "My friend said he was supposed to meet Carl Dean that morning at the garage, but he got stood up. I guess after all that happened Ugly just took off."

"Well, not in his van he didn't. That got left behind. People set it on fire."

"They burned his car?"

"Everyone was pretty upset. Ben was the maddest I ever saw. He didn't raise his voice. He just got his gun and started laying the law down. The sheriff came, too. And Mr. Suggs. Reverend Baxter and his family and most all his friends got kicked out."

"But what did they have to do with it?"

"Well, two of the bikers are sons of his, and the other one was somehow mixed up in it too. They found him near-naked with his face all cut up. He was…"

"Was what?"

"Nothing."

He has set the spoon down. His hands are shaking. She reaches across the table to hold them for a minute. "Was what, Billy Don?" she whispers.

"He was wearing her underpants. He'd…he'd taken them off her… when…"

Cretin: 1779, from Fr. Alpine dialect *crestin*, "a dwarfed and deformed idiot," from V.L. *christianus*, "a Christian," a generic term for "anyone," but often with a sense of "poor fellow." The word Christian itself was not used in English until 1526. Good name for her Wizards in the woods. But the Castle is full of cretins, too. An internecine battle. Which in the time of knights and castles didn't mean an internal struggle within a group. It meant simply murderous, fought to the death. Characterized by bloodshed and carnage, a great slaughter. The Castle and the Wizards aren't there yet, but give them time.

All history as the history of language. A pathology of sorts.

Here's one for Tommy. There's an Australian myth in which the Primal Father swallows a lump of sago and shits it back unchanged, the turd then turning into a pig, which the Father names after himself. Look at me! I did this! The people hunt the shit-pig, which by now is confused with the Father, and the youngest son shoots and kills it. But then it's resurrected for a time, God is great, and it goes around opening women's pudenda and teaching people how to fuck. Who knows where the youngest son came from. Then the shit-pig dies again and people cut its flesh up and preserve it as "strong medicine." Some places have strips of dried human flesh they say are relics of the pig-father's body. Used for faith healing. No new religions, only heresies.

And where were you when the Incarnation hit the fan?

Humor does not displace the terror or hide it from us, but it deflects its immobilizing power. It says here.

Billy Don's story has left her shaken. She would like to do something about it, but she doesn't know what. This is all she can do. Write stupidities to herself. It's a kind of masturbation. Which, come to think of it, is a better idea. To be continued…

Sally is sitting in an old-fashioned oak swivel chair in what was once, she's been told, the *West Condon Chronicle* job room. Now it's used mainly for storage, including the newspaper archives, mostly unsorted. The print shop itself, job press and all—all that remains of the West Condon publishing industry—has been moved into the former editorial offices, where there are windows. They look bleakly out on a broken asphalt parking lot and the ruined backside of the old hotel, but they look out. This room, lit only by a flickering fluorescent, is a windowless storehouse of dusty old typewriters and telephones and other nameless junk, stuffed filing cabinets, stacked unlabeled boxes, and piles and piles of moldering paper, including yellowing newspapers and dimming photographs, one small stack now her own. The very disorder has helped Sally find some of what she has been looking for, the breakdown of the filing system having obviously worsened near the end—and then, once out of hospital, the editor himself was soon gone without, apparently, looking back, so whatever was left in the closed front offices just got dumped in here, helter-skelter. Thus, the more random the confusion, the more likely she is to find material related to the events of those tumultuous final days, almost as though, after the damp fizzle of the grand finale, that tumult shrank back into these stacks and continues to roil them.

Her medieval history class at college met early on Monday mornings, much to everyone's disgust, so she chose this post-Pentecostal one for her visit to the old newspaper plant in pursuit of what she described to the funny little toothbrush-mustachioed guy running the print shop as "thesis research." She remembers him vaguely as a teacher and some kind of coach at the high school. His current commission: a two-color mailbox stuffer outlining the goals of the New Opportunities for West Condon citizens committee, which he showed off proudly. He took her on a brief tour of the newspaper press and composing rooms at the back with their typesetting machines and antique flatbed press and soot-blackened windows and ancient Coke machine, the dusty concrete floor littered still with lead slugs (she pocketed one), then ushered her into this old job room, pulled on the lights from a dangling string, and clearing it of piled-up binders and ledgers, offered her the leather sofa. She said no—too quickly. She knows where she is. She's not superstitious, but if she were, she would have said it feels haunted. This whole boneyard of a room does, but especially that sofa.

The first thing she has come on in here is a large stack of the last issue of the paper. Last ever. April 18. The Saturday before the End. Monday didn't happen here. History stopped, just like the cultists said it would. Huge two-line banner: WE SHALL GATHER AT THE MOUNT OF REDEMPTION! The Brunist evangel to be shipped to the world. It's mostly a photo essay, as if it were by now all beyond words, or else the editor ran out of things to say. Her dad's in one of the pictures, standing alongside Tommy's father, some preachers, and Angela's father, who was apparently something of a bigwig at the time in what was called the

Common Sense Committee. NOWC père. Plus all the cultic stuff of prophecies and song lyrics and relics and doctrines, interviews, letters to the editor. Funny one from an old lady in her nineties who said she was getting a slip from the doctor to explain why she couldn't make it out to the Mount and giving her phone number. If something started to happen, they could give her a call and she'd ring a taxi.

She has dug around and come up with all the earlier issues back to the April 8 special edition, the one that first broke the news about the cult and created such a furor: BRUNISTS PROPHESY END OF WORLD! across all eight front-page columns. Amazing horror-flick pic of a charred black hand. The Prophet in a contrasty iconic mug shot. Photos of helmeted coalminers. The mine hill with nobody on it. The burned ruins of a house. Squibs about other cults used as filler. The editor was clearly fascinated, as is she, by the long, weird, and often violent history of apocalyptic movements, nowadays known euphemistically as evangelical or fundamentalist churches, and there's something in every issue, published without comment almost like contemporary news items: tales of millennialists, crusaders, ecstatics, flagellants, flat earthers and faith healers, naked adamists, hermits declaring themselves resurrected kings or sons of God, mystics, martyrs, messiahs, priestly rapists, ritualistic cannibals, visionaries (miraculous white birds flock past with the seasons), and other mythomaniacal eccentrics and criminals of the cloth. But also those who resisted these fantasies and the dire consequences they suffered, beheading the least of it. She sometimes thinks of herself as standing alone, breaking new ground. It's easy to forget that atheism is as old as theism. And that the ratios haven't changed much. Nor the power structure. According to the articles, end of the world gatherings seem to have happened several times a year over the centuries—some ending tragically, most comically. She learns, without surprise, that the Rapture idea was never mentioned in the Bible or in ancient times but was invented by a couple of religious charlatans in the middle of the nineteenth century and sold to suckers ever since. The *Chronicle* editor was obviously an atheist: to what extent was he St.-Pauling this crazy cult into a worldwide church with his deadpan epistles? Over her shoulder the Lutheran minister smiles, puffing on his pipe: God the Engineer at it again.

She also takes a moment to flick through the sports pages of the various editions until she finds a photo of the high school basketball team. Yes, he was cute. Wearing his hormones in plain view like another number on his shirt. Rascality written all over him. No wonder what almost happened at the ice plant almost happened…

After a prowl through the filing cabinets ("Street Repairs," "Rotary Club," "United Mine Workers," "Bowling Leagues"), she comes eventually upon the Brunist folders, including notes about each of the early cultists—some dated, some not. Full accounts of Bruno; Clara Collins; her husband, Ely. In Marcella's folder: a few typed scraps, photos, some job press proofs of her name in Old English, a couple of them with his name butting up against hers, rough sketch of the Bruno house floor plan. A handwritten background note speaks of her Catholicism, considers it to be more a kind of general mysticism—a thing of nature, not of doctrine. Therefore vulnerable to reinterpretation. To a change of heart. In one photo she wears a shawl or a light blanket as the Virgin often does in paintings, peering up at the camera with almost heartbreaking waif-like beauty. Already somehow looking martyred. Odd background structures. One print dated on the back that must have been taken out at the mine shortly after the disaster. Six different copies of this one. He put in some darkroom time.

Which probably explains that closet door with the small pane of glass. She looks inside: a small room, the cupboard-sized back half for development, plumbed and painted black with black curtains, the front, lit by a red bulb, for hanging wet prints. Lines and clips strung up just above eye level. A couple of curled prints still dangling there, including one of Angela's father in front of the police station. Looking fierce. The face of vindictive law-and-order. Instead of leaving the room, she pulls the door closed, peers out through the little square window. The sofa. The exact angle of those photos. Somebody must have been in here, either unknown to the editor or arranged by him. She goes to get one of the photos with the shawl, sets it against the far armrest, returns to the darkroom, stares out the window at the dead girl staring back. Could she ever imagine the world as that girl saw it? Get into the head of an otherworldly Roman Catholic, the innocent daughter of aging immigrants, modest and sweet-natured and accepting, as she herself is not? Her poor, working-class family is accustomed to a punishing life. Her older brothers are dead already. Their lives are presumably continuing somewhere else. In the sky. As will hers? The girl doesn't think about it. Like Reverend Dreyer's divinity: thought, action, passion, all one. Her brother Giovanni is ill, but miraculously he is alive and needs her. Miraculously? Yes, it was a miracle. The girl believes that. God is mysterious and unknowable, but he is not absent or uncaring.

Sally shakes off her spectral forebodings and stretches out on the sofa, staring up at the ceiling, the photo on her chest. White acoustic tiles. A kind of pocked movie screen. What did the girl see up there? Sally sees nothing. The blank face of the universe. Some cobwebs. She wishes she had a joint with her so she could relax into this. She feels big and awkward. The girl was small. With an enviable grace. Probably Marcella saw just what was in front of her: a strong handsome man who desired her. Whom she desired. What must he have seemed to her? God-like? No, but as one given her by God. What will happen next? It's like there's a force out there seeking to penetrate her. Not merely this naked man, but a transcendent force. As if she were uniting with something beyond either of them. She will accept it, for it is God's way and it is good. So what went wrong? Never know. Something profound. Because God's in the mix. A wholeness shattered. For now, he speaks her name. Like an endearment. Marcella. He's crazy about her. Of course he is. Sally has the urge to take her clothes off. She's a realist at heart. But she forgot to put the hook on the job room door. What the girl sees is the man's searching gaze, which she meets, more prepared for this probably than he is. What Sally sees is his nakedness, the urgent ferocity of his erection. She sits up abruptly, her hand between her legs. Those cloven Pentecostal tongues of fire. They descended, the Good Book says, into laps. Root and core of the problem…

* * *

In Doc Foley's downtown corner drugstore, picking up what her mother delicately calls her disposables, Sally runs into Stacy Ryder, the young intern at the bank. Sally knows her name because Tommy has remarked approvingly on the body the name belongs to. She introduces herself and Stacy asks what she's carrying.

"It's called a newspaper, an ancient human artifact, extinct in these parts." The fellow running the print shop said there were plenty, she could have it. She tucked into its pages, unseen, a few other items as well, including a print of shawled Marcella, that sports page with the team photo, the Black Hand issue, other photos. She could have taken anything. Would never be missed. If anything, she was rescuing these things from oblivion. She shows Stacy the gaudy headline. "Last of its kind."

"I've heard about that. Before my time here."

"Sort of before my time, too. I was just a clueless high school kid. Still dialing up Jesus in those days, so I was a bit scared these guys might have God's unlisted number."

Stacy smiles. A pretty smile, easy and friendly. She'll go far. "Pretty crazy. The world can be."

"You're not religious?"

"I gave up religion and the tooth fairy about the same time."

"One of the five percent. Did you know that eighty-five percent of all Americans, including Jews, Hindus, Muslims, Buddhists and atheists, believe in the Virgin Birth of Jesus, but less than thirty percent believe in evolution?"

"Sounds about right. But I have to tell you, Sally, when I gave up religion, I gave up thinking about it, too."

"Smart move. Not easy in this town, though. Sort of like not thinking about water when the ship's sinking."

"The main difference between religion and the tooth fairy was that at least I learned something from the tooth fairy. About money, marketing, the value of raw commodities. In the tooth fairy's world, baby teeth are an instrument of exchange. Currency. The tooth fairy gave me coin bankable in my world, took the tooth. Probably thought she was getting a bargain."

"Like the guys who bought this country from the Indians. The problem with teeth, I guess, is sooner or later the mine's played out…"

She flashes that easy smile again. Some are born with it, others aren't. "Exactly. So, ahead of that eventuality, I went exploring. Found a friend who didn't believe in tooth fairies and she let me have one of her teeth when it fell out, in exchange for a finger puppet. I put it under the pillow, waited for several days, but no one took up the option. I figured there must be some principle in play about rightful ownership. But I didn't believe it. I still don't. I knew there had to be a less scrupulous tooth fairy somewhere who would make an offer. So I kept the tooth. Still have it."

They're both laughing. Sally says: "That's the best kids' story I've heard since Grandma Friskin told me the one about the constipated Easter bunny."

"That shouldn't affect egg-laying."

"It does for kids, who start by believing rabbits lay eggs. How's the book?"

"This? It's pretty silly, I'm afraid. A friend at the bank loaned it to me. Listen. 'The smile in his green eyes contained a sensuous flame. His open shirt revealed a muscular chest covered with crisp brown hair. His stance emphasized the force of his thighs and the slimness of his hips. She wondered if his broad shoulders ever tired of the burden he was carrying.' Do you think he's the right guy for the girl?"

"If the girl's who I think she is," Sally says, "it should be the perfect match. She also has crisp chest hairs." That cracks Stacy up, but even at full throttle her laughter's of a wistful sort, her green eyes still melancholy. "Ever read *Madame Bovary*?"

"No. Is it good?"

"Well, it's about a woman who reads too many romance novels."

"I probably just said something stupid. It's a famous novel, right? I'm not much of a reader, I guess. Mostly I read stock reports and spreadsheets. When I read books like this, I tend to read them like financial statements, in terms of risks, margins, potential returns. Emotions as intangibles, collateral, character as intrinsic value. Winning the love game is knowing when to hazard your resources, take the plunge, make the crucial investment decision. Some win. Most lose."

"Is that how you play it, Stacy?"

"Me? No, I'm a spendthrift gambler. After a drink or two I'll bet the house on the next roll."

"Well, you can always pull back and reload. The emotions aren't finite."

"Yes, they are," she says sadly, and looks away.

Sally believes she's just heard something true. Straight out of one of those ladies' novels perhaps, but nonetheless true. But she doesn't understand it. "I guess I don't know much about the love game. I mostly throw snake eyes," she says. "Or the money game either, for that matter. What little I have from allowances and carhopping and babysitting you guys have in an account there. Every month you give me a few pennies of interest, which doesn't cover the resoling of my shoes from the walk to the bank and back. I suppose the bank is making a lot more than I am out of it."

"Yes, it is. Come in and see me some time and we'll see if we can't work out something better. Come soon, though, while I'm still here."

"Thanks. What's in that account won't last long enough to matter. But are you leaving town?"

She sighs. "I'm afraid I've already stayed too long. Oops," she adds glancing at her watch. "I've stayed too long on my lunch break, too. Have to get back and save the bank, which according to my boss is the same thing as saving the world."

"I'll walk you there. I'm going that way."

On this balmy mid-May early afternoon, after being buried all morning in an airless dead-paper morgue (more suffering, more love), that way was at first any which way, but now, sitting on a playground swing with her notebook on her lap, her *Chronicle* memorabilia on the swing next to her, Sally realizes, or discovers, or decides (who's running this life?) that she's on her way to the Royal Castle to visit the Dying Queen, as her mother has often asked her to do. She has not had to deal with a lot of death and has held back because she doesn't know what to say to a dying person. Probably she'll tell a lot of well-intentioned lies like everyone else. And how will she herself face such a moment when it's her turn? Better not to think about it. Not on a day like this.

She doesn't remember noticing the weather much as a kid, but this lush sexy day has reminded her of innumerable unspecific others, going all the way back to her childhood parks and playgrounds. Certain patches of sunshine. The smell and pale summery glow of a dusty sidewalk on which she was playing jacks, even the weedy grass growing in the cracks. The red dot on a spider. On a certain raggedy leaf. While she was squatting behind a bush. Because? Hide and seek? These memories, if they are memories, don't arise by trying to think about them consciously but bubble up spontaneously out of the unconscious the way dreams do and may have just as little to do with the real world. Probably stored and cooked in the same curtained niches of the mind. She has the feeling these are the sorts of memories useful to writers. Vivid, but imprecise and totally unreliable composites of a possible past, not that literal past itself. She wanted to write down these thoughts, but there was nowhere to sit. At college she'd have found a bench somewhere where she could jot notes, have a smoke, read a page of something. This town has no benches. Then she passed this empty playground offering her a swing. What from this scene will sink into her memory bank to return, unbidden, years down the road? The coaltown cinders underfoot maybe. Remember when…when she could rock on a swing and write to the world and still believe it was something meaningful to do…

She pushes off and swings back and forth a few times, a cigarette bobbing in her lips, her notebook in her lap, but finds she doesn't like it as she once did. She feels heavy, unbalanced. Her feet scrape the ground, even when tucked under. Didn't used to. She remembers how the boys would wander nonchalantly in front of the swings, hoping to get a glimpse under girls' skirts as they swung, thinking they were stealing something, not realizing that, for the girls, having their skirts fly up was fun, though you had to pretend you didn't see the boys out there. Is nostalgia about the past or only the past self? Whatever, she feels little of it, wants to leave this place, does not expect to miss it.

Riding the Hood, a.k.a. Raggedy Red, steps out of the forest, a.k.a., the dark night of the soul, leaving mother, grandmother, wolf, and woodcutter behind. Let them duke it out with each other.

Soul. As a slapstick comedian? Soul clowns it up: pratfalls of the dead image. Soul and Body as a comic duo on the vaudeville circuit? The vaudeville circuit: a.k.a., the self.

Something Dreyer said: We possess nothing but selfhood and that is on loan, as it were; the whole point in life is to realize this self wholly in the world. (She agreed. They shook hands on this note.)

But what about the little girl who thought the forest was her friend and was devoured by wolves? The Hood will remember her and show others how to avoid her fate. Thus, she too is an abuser of innocence.

History. Memory. Nostalgia for the dead past. Its illusions, falsifications. Documentations of the dead past. Their illusions, falsifications. Themes of the day. Here, it's Tommy's mother's photo albums. What she has of the life she is leaving. Her own bonneted childhood accompanied by doting parents and relatives, her transitions through carefully costumed adolescence and young womanhood, her European travels, her young family. Never doing much of anything, really—just being. Some photos gone astray from their tiny black corner pockets like memory lapses, others torn asunder. A kind of editing going on. A paring down. When Sally asks to see the wedding photos, Mrs. Cavanaugh waves her frail hand dismissively, gazes about absently, as if the album might be hiding somewhere. There are some photos of when she and Tommy were little. Sometimes his brother and sister are in them too, as well as other children and their mothers—but she and Tommy are never far apart. There's one picture of them in front of a bed of flowers holding hands. Two little kids, the girl taller than the boy. She doesn't remember that, but she feels it now as if it were happening. In another, Tommy is bawling, holding his arms up to the photographer, she off to one side with a guilty half-smile on her face. What has she done to him? Bad girl.

She wasn't sure what she'd say when she arrived, but what came out was, "I'm so sorry you're so sick, Mrs. Cavanaugh." Plain and from the heart. To which Mrs. Cavanaugh replied, her voice unfamiliarly harsh and gravelly: "The worst has been losing my hair, dear. I hate it. I'd rather have died sooner than to go through that awful treatment. And what good did it do? It made me awfully sick for a while and added at best a miserable month or two. Still, we do so desperately hate to give it up, don't we?" She sighed, looked up at Sally, looked away again. "I try not to cry, but sometimes I cry."

Most of her mother's friends, such as Aunt Debra and Emily Wetherwax, are like part of the family, people you joke with and call by the first name, but Mrs. Cavanaugh, though she's not that much older than her own mother, has always been either Mrs. Cavanaugh or Tommy's mother. And not just because of the man she's married to and how he runs everybody's life here, but because she has always been, though seemingly unassuming, such a person of quiet power herself—elegant, serene, president of just about everything at one time or another. It has been something of a shock to see her now in her plastic shower cap, scrunched up with her disease and melting into her bedclothes, her eyes dark and beady, spectacles on the end of her pinched nose, lips thin and unpainted, hands like tender claws. Her home care nurse, Concetta Moroni, Moron's mother, a happy round-faced lady widowed by the mine disaster, was here when Sally arrived and she brought her a glass of ice tea, then took advantage of Sally's visit to dash off to pick up a prescription and some fresh fruit. Tommy has told her that Concetta is turning his mother, after her crazy evangelical episode, into a Roman Catholic, and, sure enough, she crossed herself when Mrs. Moroni waved goodbye from the bedroom door.

Now she is showing Sally photos of her sorority house at college, telling her the life stories of each of the women in the pictures, whom they married or didn't but should have, which are divorced or deceased ("I will be one of the first!"), the famous ones, the infamous ones, the lost ones. There are lots of photos taken at school dances with many different guys on her arm—her beaus, as she calls them. Sometimes in funny costumes, sometimes in jackets and dresses, often in tuxedos and formal gowns.

"Is that Mr. Cavanaugh?" Sally asks, pointing at one of them.

"No, that's someone else." She glances up at Sally over her wire-rimmed spectacles with a little half-smile much like the one on her own little-girl face in the photo of bawling Tommy. "Bring me the phone, will you, please, dear?"

Mrs. Cavanaugh's mischievous look causes Sally to hesitate, but only for a moment. She winks (sisters!) and brings the phone on its long cord in from the hallway, waits until she puts the call through ("Is Edgar Thornton there, please? This is Irene Cavanaugh. That's all right. I'll wait..."), then slips away, peeking into the other rooms off the hall until she finds Tommy's. The usual boy stuff on the walls and shelves, probably not much changed since he went off to college. Virtually no books, except for a Boy Scout manual, some baseball annuals and comicbooks, plus a few books he probably had to buy for freshman courses and has never read. Plato's *Republic*, Homer's *Iliad*, Freud's *Interpretation of Dreams*, *The Golden Bough*. Not much to start a conversation with, except perhaps the Boy Scout manual. Mentally awake, morally straight should be good for a gag or two. She thumbs through for it and finds tucked inside a Polaroid shot of someone's shaggy pudenda. Guess whose. Why would someone want such a thing? Back to history, memory, nostalgia. Anticipated nostalgia. So: basically good news. If he had some grass somewhere, she'd steal it, but there's none to be found.

On her way back into the sickroom, she hears Mrs. Cavanaugh say, "No, she's not from around here; by my calculations, she lives about an hour and a half away," and she decides to wait in the hall. "A private what? Oh, you mean a detective. Well, thank you, Thorny, but I don't think I want to know. What in eternity, where we're all going, does it matter? Yes, I know. He told me he was going to do that. I'm sorry for you, Thorny, but we knew he wouldn't take this lying down. Bernice? That poor noble woman! Well, you must defend her, Thorny. No, I've been cruelly cut off from those kind Christian people. I'm becoming a Catholic now, you see. That's why I was hoping there was enough money left to go to Lourdes. My new nurse will take me. It won't be cheap. I'll probably have to be transported there on a litter." Sally hears Mrs. Moroni returning downstairs and goes in to warn Tommy's mother. "What? Oh, I have to go now. Yes, I know you switched to an evangelical church for my sake, Thorny. Now, for our sake, I'm asking you to switch again."

First tee. "That's a hook," he informs her when his drive ("Watch this carefully," he had instructed her) flies into the woods on the left. When he leans close to show her how to grip the club, Sally has to hold her breath. She misses the ball altogether on the first swing. "Keep your head down! Elbow straight!" The second follows his into the woods, though not so deep. She finds her ball then helps him find his. He explains that there is a course ground rule that allows him to put his ball back out on the fairway. That's the swath down the middle with the mowed grass. The trees and high weeds to either side is the rough. Which, to the left, is where her second shot again goes and his soon follows. She helps him find it. It is a long hole. Par 12 for beginners. Bogeyed.

Second tee. She thinks about the grip, makes an adjustment, sends the ball not very far but straight down the middle. "How did you do that?" her father asks. She shows him. He tries it. Same result: hooked into the rough. He can't find the ball. She goes to help but he gets impatient and throws another ball down in the middle of the fairway. "Charge me a stroke," he says. This time she's at the edge of the green in four, but it takes her another six to get it in the hole. He claims to be there in five, not counting the three times he moved the ball out of the rough, and says his four-foot final putt is a "gimme," and picks it up without hitting it, nearly toppling when he leans over.

Third tee. She suggests his problem might be he is standing too near the ball and is hitting it with the heel of his club, which is why it keeps flying left. "I think you should stand back a half step." "If I stand back any further, I won't be able to see the dadblame ball." But he takes a nip from his hip flask and has a try, teeing up the ball, assuming his stance, then stepping backwards. He trips over his own feet and sits down hard, which enrages him. He tells her to mind her own business. He struggles confusedly to his feet, takes a wild swat at the ball and knocks it into the woods again. His mood is worsening. Maybe this wasn't a good idea after all.

Fourth tee. The hole is called a dogleg, because it has a bend—in this case around the woods that hide the old city cemetery off to the right. Yesterday, Billy Don told her a weird story. Darren supposedly went back there on his own and discovered that the small empty grave they found with the golf balls in it had been filled in. Billy Don said Darren's face was completely white when he told him this. They both assumed it was a supernatural event, a kind of message from the beyond. "Like we got too close to the truth or something." She considers knocking her next drive over in that direction and going to take a peek while pretending to be hunting for her ball. But it's not in her nature to do less than she can do and she is beginning to enjoy swinging one of these dumb sticks with the ball-bopper at the end. Besides, another foursome is closing in behind them and her father will need help looking for his ball on the other side of the fairway. So she sends it down the middle again. By now she is beating her father even when he lies about his strokes.

Fifth tee. He finishes off the contents of his hip flask, and swinging loosely and more or less blindly, sends his drive deep down the middle of the fairway. She is strangely moved by the slow loft and arc of the ball. "Now that's how it ought to be done," he says. "But it takes practice." For once he'll be able to find his own ball. If he can walk that far. The other golfers are already approaching the green behind them: Tommy and his father, Reverend Dreyer in his straw boater, and the new town manager. The slicker who cost her father his job. She tries too hard to impress and tops her ball, sending it bouncing a few yards in front of them. Her father turns to the royal family and shrugs apologetically, what can you do, instructs her once more, loudly, on keeping her head down, eye on the ball.

Sixth tee. A climb to it from the green. One can see almost the whole course from up here—much of the old abandoned second nine just below, as well. They'd probably sell off that land if there was anyone to sell it to. After her flubbed first shot, she has still managed to reach the fifth green in fewer shots than her father, whose rage is building once more. Perhaps because the consoling hip flask is empty. Another long "gimme" has gotten them quickly off the green and up here. In the distance, one can just make out the Deepwater tipple and water tower, the top of the mine hill. Treasure Mountain. The foursome behind are growing impatient, leaning on their clubs as though in exasperation. Two holding up four. Her father hooks his drive into the rough again. "Heck fire," he says, and without looking for his ball storms off down the hill toward the clubhouse over on the far side of the distant first tee. Sally tees up, swats the ball cleanly down the middle, her best drive of the day (does she turn to see if Tommy is watching? she does not), then follows her father clubward.

"Well, I think Dad's offering her a one-way ticket, telling her that after the miracle she can swim back," Tommy says.

"It's that bad?"

"No, it's that cool. He's thoroughly pissed at what Mom has done and fed up with her religious yo-yoing, but he can see the humor in it, too." They are talking about Irene's fantasized pilgrimage to Lourdes. Sally wonders if they'd see the humor in his mother's organizing an afterlife affair with one of her old college beaus. The Christian illusion of spending eternity with one's nearest and dearest: it's such a smalltown idea. As Grandma Friskin says, What's wrong with Heaven is your damned neighbors. They are sitting at the bar in the country club's Nineteenth Hole after the disastrous Jester-and-Goose-Girl-on-the-Links Day, her dad, barely able to stand, having been whisked away by her mother. Archie and Emily Wetherwax offered Sally a ride home later if she wanted to stay, and she did. One place Angela Bonali will never show up. Babs Wetherwax and her gum-popping high school friends are at a table by the window drinking Shirley Temples and casting long giggly glances their way, but they're no threat. "And he's pretty sure he's going to get it all back and send a few people to jail at the same time."

"I know. Your dad's being awfully hard on Aunt Debra."

"The preacher's wife? Well, as I understand it, she sold church property and kept the money for herself. Most everywhere you go, that's a crime."

"I think she gave it to the cult."

"Same difference."

That she's drinking beer at a bar alone with Tommy Cavanaugh is both fortuitous and the result of strategic planning. She borrowed the family car while her parents were at church and drove past the Cavanaugh house. Not only was the tangerine junker in the drive, the new college graduate himself was on the front porch having a late breakfast and listening to something with a big beat coming out of the living room. Babysitting his mom. Though Tommy's welcome was underwhelming, he didn't chase her off. In fact, he had a favor to ask. When his dad gets back from church, could she follow him out to Lem's garage to turn in the rental, give him a ride back? His dad's buying him a red Corvair convertible with white sidewalls as a graduation present and as consolation for not being able to travel to Europe this summer with some of his fraternity brothers, and he's picking it up on Tuesday, the Lincoln available to him meanwhile as his dad has little use for it after tonight until an out-of-town business meeting on Thursday. Sally was feeling pretty grotty, still wearing the tee she slept in—her THERE'S A SUCKER BORN-AGAIN EVERY MINUTE shirt from her last ice cream parlor meet with Billy D—but she didn't want to lose the opportunity. Anyway, they say that cleanliness is next to godliness, and she doesn't really want to get that close. At the garage, after a ceremonial visit to the remains of Tommy's mother's wrecked station wagon, being harvested by Lem for parts, he and Tommy had a conversation about Carl Dean Palmers, Lem showing them Carl Dean's burned-out van he'd been asked to haul away. "Fucking insane," was Lem's judgment about the burning of it. Yes, Lem said, he'd heard from Bernice the rumor about Carl Dean joining the bikers and doing bad shit at the camp before taking off, but he didn't believe it. Not Carl Dean. Tommy said he didn't believe it either, but later, riding back with her, he said he did. He also said he'd agreed to join his father in a round at the club this afternoon, which explained her own father's gloomy gin-and-juice breakfast, he evidently having been bumped from his usual Sunday foursome slot by Tommy. So she decided it was time to do the father-and-daughter thing and ask him to teach her how to play the game, making him promise to stay off the sauce long enough to make it around the full nine—a promise he of course never kept. She showered, changed into shorts and a crisp white shirt—one of her dad's old ones, only partly buttoned, no bra—and after the abbreviated golfing tragicomedy, here she is. "Well, a crime maybe. But not immoral."

"There's a difference?"

"Sure. Crimes are defined by lawyers and politicians. In some societies, ripping off the rich and institutions like churches is not a crime, it's a public duty. Morality's a private choice. The custom is to obey the law, but to defy the law can be a moral decision."

"You think she did the right thing."

Sally laughs. "No, a moral decision can also be a pretty stupid one." She has been thinking about morality of late. The pursuit of aesthetic truth as a moral act. Concern with the trivial as immoral. Writing faults as moral failures. She's aware that some people think of golf in the same way.

Tommy excuses himself to go, as he says, drain the radiator, leaving her with her notebook. She adds his expression to her *scheisshaus* list along with "shed a tear" and "squeeze the lemon." On the way back from Lem's garage this morning, Tommy wanted to know what the bad shit was, and though she probably shouldn't have, Billy Don having asked her not to, she told him about the bikers and what they did. That was probably a moral lapse. What Tommy wanted to know when she told him was what was the girl doing there in the first place? You think it's her fault, you mean? she snapped. She loves this guy? What's going on? Of course, to be honest, she had wondered the same thing and asked Billy Don. He didn't know.

Billy Don was more upbeat when they last met, another two-sundae lap-up day. Still a lot of gloom and apprehension in the camp, but he also had a funny story to tell this time about the night Darren discovered he was sleeping with a prairie kingsnake. He screamed and ran out of the cabin yelping that the Devil was after him, and that set off Colin next door, and they soon had the whole camp in a stir. One of the men killed the snake and then the camp cook calmed everybody down with milk and cookies. This happened just after they moved into their new cabin, which has given Billy Don a little more breathing space, for Darren now views himself as a prophet and is very full of himself, more obsessed and bossy than ever. Aunt Debra is evidently now helping Darren with his prophesying career, having come up with some quirky notions about the bikers and the four horsemen of the Apocalypse that people are taking seriously, and Darren is now treating her as something of a seer like Colin, who Darren believes is, in effect, specially wired for divine transmissions. Why it is that dangerous schizophrenics are so frequently taken as holy prophets, she replied, is one of those timeless mysteries of the fucked-up human race. She likes to use expressions like that because they always make Billy Don grin sheepishly and duck his nose in his ice cream, glancing about the drugstore nervously from under his brows to see if anyone else has overheard her. She showed him the invitation she'd received to Franny Baxter's wedding and he said it was news to him. About all he knew about the Baxters was that they are said to be living in a field somewhere.

Babs and her friends have stopped lifeguard Tommy to ask him when the pool will open. Memorial Day weekend, everyone knows that, it's just a ploy to get his attention. It works. Maybe she has underestimated the lure of Babs' boobs. One of the girls drags a chair over and Tommy joins them. Babs glances over at her. Someone laughs. A schoolgirl titter. Who's going to pay for these drinks? she asks herself, rising. She's not.

# III.2

## Friday 29 May – Sunday 31 May

"She was dreaming that she was playing tag with other children. I didn't exactly recognize none of them, but you know how it is in dreams—especially someone else's dream. I was one of the other children and I almost hardly didn't recognize myself. Whenever she tagged someone, they fell down dead. Really dead. Their flesh melting off. I didn't run away, the one who was me. I said I wanted to be tagged, but she couldn't do it. She said that wasn't the way the game was played. If I didn't run, I couldn't be caught. Only it was like *I* was saying that to the person who was me, and I was impatient that she—I mean, me—didn't get it." The country and western singer Patti Jo Glover is telling them the dream that Marcella Bruno dreamt one night inside her own dream. Everyone in Mabel Hall's caravan sitting room is completely spellbound. Lucy Smith has never heard anything like it before, but the way Patti Jo tells it, it seems completely natural. Thelma Coates is sitting across from her and her jaw has literally dropped. Her bottom teeth are showing. Thelma had said she could only stay ten minutes, but it has already been much longer than that. Her husband Roy has forbidden her to come here, so what she does is hurry up her grocery shopping and dash by on the way home, hoping word doesn't get back to Roy. He's a mean man. She has a dark bruise on her cheekbone, and she probably didn't get that by bumping into something. Lucy's husband Calvin, who was upset at the way Reverend Baxter and his family were made to go out and live in the fields like animals, would also rather she stayed away from these people, but she always has lots of things to tell him when she gets home and he appreciates that, so he has not put his foot down. He only scowls when she brings him the news, even when it's funny, to let her know he doesn't really approve. When they first got married and she did things he didn't want her to do, he would turn her across his knee and spank her, and though it hurt and sometimes made her cry, it was also kind of fun and often ended better than it began. After a while he stopped doing that, but he can still be pretty severe and occasionally lashes out in a fit of temper that's not fun at all, though he always apologizes afterwards and they pray together, and when she asks him if he loves her, he says yes.

"Then everything changed," Patti Jo says. "She was still dreaming and she was still in my dream, but I wasn't in hers anymore. A man was. I could feel how happy she was at seeing him, and I wondered if it was Jesus she was seeing, but I don't think it was. For one thing, he didn't have clothes on and you could see everything and that didn't seem like something Jesus would do, even in a dream. He was standing in water, or else he stepped into it, and although I was enjoying her dream without thinking too much about it, I could feel Marcella begin to worry. The man dipped his hands in the water, like as if to baptize himself or her or someone, and when he raised them, they weren't there anymore, just the parts of his arms that hadn't touched the water. And then *I* started to worry on top of Marcella's worrying. The man stepped deeper in the water, or else the water rose up, and you just knew he was losing parts of himself. The business between his legs dipped into the water and when the water went away for a tick you could see that half of it was gone just like you drew a line through. The water got deeper, or else he sank into it, until there was only his head on top. He closed his eyes and his mouth gapped opened and the head floated away like that. And then Marcella woke up crying and I woke up crying."

There is a moment of absolute silence as they all watch that floating head, and then Thelma Coates puts her jaws back together and says, "That man musta been that newspaper feller."

"Or else her brother," says the beauty shop lady Linda Catter. "I mean, if all she felt was just only happiness, and not, you know…"

Bernice Filbert says it was like a dream of wasting away with only the head remaining like a kind of blind repository for the soul, what you might call a rapturing by water instead of by air, and it may be the sort of experience the Prophet's sister had when she died or else what she was afraid of. It's always interesting what Bernice wears, and today it's a one-piece dress that looks like it might have been made out of an old thin blanket, hanging loose in front for carrying things—the sort of thing women might wear in the field when they're gathering—with a sash around the waist and a scarf over her head.

"Losin' his hands like that," says Hazel Dunlevy, the palm reader, "that man in the water, whoever he is, it's like as if he's losin' his future, and I reckon that's how it turned out."

"But in dreams things are always the opposite from what they seem, aren't they?" Lucy reminds them. "So, maybe he's *finding* his future. Though it's not like it's a happy ending. Unless that's an opposite too. Crying meaning like she's really laughing, I mean."

"In some dreams that's true," says Mabel gravely, looking down upon them. "And in some it's not."

The others nod solemnly at this, and Hazel says: "As fer a naked man bein' Jesus, though, accordin' to what Glenda says, Jesus often takes his clothes off in people's dreams. Sometimes it's more like a halo down there and that's bad news, and sometimes it's only ordinary, like as he's one of us again, and that's good news. If Jesus makes love to you in a dream, she says, that's the best news of all."

"Well, I hope that never happens," says Corinne Appleby flatly. She rarely speaks at all, but when she does it's deadpan and straight out and always makes everybody smile.

"I guess we need Glenda here to explain it," Lucy says with a sigh. Glenda Oakes is watching the children, including Lucy's own, taking them on a nature walk along the creek bed to the beehives and vegetable garden and back, though she'll switch with Hazel and join them later when Mrs. Edwards arrives, because Glenda is the dream expert and Mrs. Edwards wants some help understanding her boy's nightmares.

"Actually, I told Glenda my dream of Marcella dreaming," Patti Jo says, "and she said possibly it was an old dream Marcella dreamt when she was still alive and she was only remembering it. But it didn't feel like remembering, it felt like it was happening right then for the first time. 'Well, how do we know what remembering is like for the dead?' Glenda said. 'It might be like dreaming.' She said that a head without a body could mean that Marcella no longer saw that person like she saw him before, so, if the man was Jesus or her brother, it could be saying she was losing her faith, and for that matter the naked man could have been both Jesus and her brother at the same time and others as well and not only men. Maybe her haunting days were ending and the man was just everybody, the head floating away signifying her own growing distance from this world, and she was crying about that. But Glenda said she couldn't be sure. She'd never interpreted the dream of a dead person before."

Everybody has an opinion about this, mostly having to do with the difference between a live dreamer and a dead one, all of which pretty soon has Lucy completely beflummoxed. Ludie Belle interrupts all these airy speculations by saying that what she wants to know is what the niggles atwixt his legs looked like before they got melted, and Wanda Cravens asks: "Why? Y'reckon y'mighta reckanized them?" This is quite rude and embarrassing, but her friend Wanda isn't really clever enough to be rude, it's just something that popped out, and maybe others are thinking it as well, and it's hard not to start giggling. But Ludie Belle only winks and says: "I was, you know, only wondrin' bout it bein' circumscissored or not, like as it might be a clue to who it was."

"Well, you know, Glenda asked me that same question, but she wasn't thinking about whether or not it might be Jesus," Patti Jo says. "She said that seeing a circumcision in a dream was a good luck omen, though it can also mean that the dreamer is worried about some forgotten detail that might embarrass them if it was found out, just as seeing one that has not been circumcised can mean that the dreamer is not thinking clearly and is refusing to see the truth. I said I didn't know which it was, or rather Marcella didn't seem to know—it wasn't like she was paying any attention to that part. It was just there like sometimes a face is there in a dream but you can't really see it."

All of which is finally too much for Thelma Coates, who gasps and says, "Oh my!" and flutters her hand in front of her face as though fanning it and says she has to get back or Roy will have a conniption. When she gets up to leave, Patti Jo also gets up and says she has to go back to the motel because Duke has a new song he wants to teach her for tonight. Thelma can give her a ride as far as the highway crossing and she can walk the rest. Everyone is sad about this; her story about Marcella Bruno's dream has been really exciting and they want to keep talking about it.

Instead they get back on about Abner Baxter and his family, who Thelma has told them are now living in an abandoned field next to that new campsite Mr. John P. Suggs is building, but without Franny who has left home, if you can call it home, to go live with Tessie Lawson, because she is going to marry Tessie's brother-in-law, Steve, who is something of a rowdy and a drunk and hollow between the ears, so not much of a catch, but if you're somebody as plain as Franny Baxter, what more can you hope for? This leaves Abner stuck with Sarah, who is so depressed she can't do anything except eat all day, and Amanda, who is subnormal and flirtatious and apt to get in serious trouble in a snap if you take your eye off her. They are living mostly off collections at Abner's preaching, which is not enough for one person, much less four, especially since most of his followers are even poorer than he. They discuss whether Abner's troubles are mostly his own fault or not, he being the sort of person who cannot keep his mouth shut, and Hazel says that, well, most saints are like that, aren't they, confessing Christ when they're told not to? Bernice confirms that the word carved onto Young Abner's forehead is "liar," she having read it before she put the bandages on, and Mabel points out that that's four letters, just like the four letters on Jesus' cross. Bernice counts them on her fingers and says that, yes, it calculates, though it's hard to credit the parallel.

Lucy is able to tell everyone about investigations into the mine break-in, which Calvin is helping the sheriff with, and that, in spite of the rumors, no dynamite has been found. Mabel says she asked her cards, and they were not completely clear, but the Magician and Pope turned up, side by side and upside down next to the Chariot, and she took the Chariot to mean their climbing of the Mount of Redemption, hampered by slickness and trickery and false propaganda, so maybe it really was just all a deception to try to keep them off the mine hill like Mr. Suggs says. They all shake their heads in astonishment at the world's wickedness and agree with that. Lucy is once again amazed at Mabel's gifts, wishing she had just a smidgeon of them so that the future didn't always keep surprising her so. The others remark on all the time Mr. Suggs is spending at the camp now with Ben and Clara gone, helping with the management and making sure people don't bother them. Talk about your saints. Mr. Suggs' halo is just waiting for him in Heaven, Linda says, and Lucy sees it there, hanging on a hook by the Pearly Gates like a ball cap. Lucy says that Calvin believes the motorcycle gang has split up since one of them got killed and they won't be seen around here anymore, and that's a blessed relief. But the damage has been done. It's so sad. Bernice says that, afterwards, she had tried to give little Elaine an inside wash as well as clean all the blood off the outside, and the girl had coiled up and snarled and spat at her like a snake or a trapped animal. Bernice, being a nurse, is the only one who even hints at what really happened, though everyone knows. And as if what happened to the girl wasn't tragic enough, now the camp has been all month without Ben and Clara, who are desperately missed by everyone. Will they ever come back? No one knows and many fear the worst, for they left in great despair. They all agree it's time for Mabel to consult her cards again and she gets them out and shuffles them in her strange sliding way, but before she can turn any of them over, Hazel Dunlevy, looking out the caravan window, says, "Here comes Sister

Debra. I reckon I better go'n mind the kids fer Glenda." As Mabel gathers up the cards, Lucy wonders what they might have said and whether or not this interruption means that a truth that might have been revealed will stop being true, changing the way the future will turn out, and thinking about so much terrible mysterious power sends a little shudder down her spine.

"Blue often stands in for spirituality, hope, positive thoughts. It's reckoned that a dreamer, dreaming of blue, specially a blue person, even a dead one, may be in the presence of his spiritual guide, and this would seem to be the case here, seeing who the dead man is and seeing as how he speaks wisdom even if it don't make sense when the boy's woked up. That he tries to stab the dead man with a table knife is not in itself a bad thing, because a table knife in a dream is a favorable sign pointing to succeeding at your life goals. That it ain't the right sorta knife for stabbing somebody might mean he don't really wanta kill the Prophet, but it's more like a, you know, ritual thing, and a way of loosing his anger that his spiritual guide has been killt. That he sets the body on fire don't look good on the surface, but fire is a symbol of change and growing up, specially for a boy, and may be trying to show a struggle for him to get control over something—to luminate it, like you might say. That the dead man keeps talking to him and keeps on being blue while he's burning means the fire must be symbolic and not real. That the boy tries to eat the roasted dead man and does eat part of him can signify he's just trying to take the Prophet and all his wisdom inside him, even if the part that he eats ain't normally the place where wisdom can generally be found. Just the contrary, in fact—but contraries are common as sin in dreams. That he seen worms crawling outa the dead man's flesh whilst he was eating him is a tad unsettling, but given the part he was eating, he mighta been seeing the intestines without recognizing them, and intestines are mostly a positive thing in dreams, indicating steadfastness and gumption, though sometimes they can remind you more like a maze you're lost in. That he woked up screaming was probably just due to the worms, or what he thought was worms, but the rest was not troubling to him or he woulda woked up before. To be safe, though, you maybe oughta check to see he's got worms or not, because sometimes dreams tell us practical things we should oughta pay attention to."

Alone in her cabin Debra has collapsed into tears as she has done so often over the recent weeks, though not in front of others if she can help it—certainly not in front of Colin, who is up at the office in the lodge, helping the two boys unpack boxes into the new filing cabinets. She is so grateful to Darren and Billy Don for taking Colin in as a friend and making him feel important, for he is all she has right now and when he is distressed and panicky she almost cannot bear it. She didn't think it would be like this. She worries she won't have the strength to see it through, not even knowing what "it" will be; though, whatever, it doesn't look good. She has heard others speak of life as a burden, but she has so loved life, she has never really understood until now how it could be. It's when you start being more afraid of living than of dying, and that awful Glenda is right, it does feel like an elephant sitting on her.

She prays a lot more now—it's the one time she can let go her feelings without embarrassment—tearfully confessing everything in front of everybody. Or, rather, having taken Ludie Belle's advice to heart, almost everything; she would never say anything to upset Colin, and she has to be careful not to overdo it, for her emotions can trigger bad episodes and complicate his therapy. But she has often described in her public prayers the terror and inadequacy she felt in the face of what happened that morning in the wild patch on the other side of the creek, thanking God for giving her the strength to do what she never could have done on her own, for she is a weak person and a cowardly one who, without God's help, would have simply run away or died of terror, rooted to the spot. She has always explained that she went there often for her dawn prayers because it was where she felt closest to God, which is true, but that she could never ever again return, for it has been irremediably contaminated with evil. Her account of events is probably a bit different from what really happened, but she can recall so little of it except as a kind of terrifying blur, it is probably as accurate as any other she could give. When she told Darren and Billy Don that the dark phantomlike figures who attacked the girl made her think of the four Horsemen of the Apocalypse and the four angels of horror and devastation, they were very impressed and Darren asked her to tell it again for his tape recorder. He especially liked the part about there being more black angels in the offing, for he said that was his interpretation too, and he has since often spoken of her in prayer meetings as having prophetic powers, so she is now esteemed for that as well as for her bravery, though she does not feel at all brave and all she can see of the future is the terrible trouble she is in.

Even though the place it all happened is now one of such utter horror to her, she nevertheless got up her courage one morning and snuck over by the back way from the vegetable garden to retrieve her abandoned underwear which if found would be hard to explain. Anyone who knows her would recognize them because she always wears panties with colorful flower patterns on them and she has hung them on the line often enough to dry and sometimes has gone around with little else on because they're not much different than swimming suits nowadays. But they weren't there. Those evil boys must have taken them. Or…someone did. She felt suddenly like she was being watched and she was too frightened for a moment even to move. The place where the body or whatever was buried seemed almost to start quivering. She thought she heard something behind her like the flutter of hawk or buzzard wings. Her heart raced and tears sprang to her eyes, for she recognized the sound as what she heard that morning behind her back as she scrunched down behind the tree here with her eyes pressed shut. But when she finally turned around there was no one there and everything was silent; only a few bees could be heard, a woodpecker high up in a tree. Afterwards, she thought of what she'd heard as the ghostly flutter of devils' wings, even though until recently she didn't really believe in devils, or ghosts either, and probably still doesn't, and she certainly doesn't know whether they have wings or not.

She has never dreamt about that morning in the garden, or about devils either, unless she doesn't remember. Most of her dreams are happy ones, and so after presenting to the women crammed into Mabel's caravan one of Colin's horrible dreams, she decided to balance it with one of her own, partly just to lighten her own heart. Colin's nightmares, from which he usually awakes screaming and trembling violently and needing her solacing embrace, worry her, for she is not certain she understands the difference in Colin's mind between his waking life and his dreams. Debra has never really believed in fortune-telling, horoscopes, and the like, but since she surrendered to the Brunist message, more things seem possible than before. After what happened that terrible morning, these women have, until today, been so protective and supportive and she has in turn wanted to accept their world and live in it to the best of her ability, to stay close to them. So, after Glenda was able to see Colin's nightmare about stabbing and burning and then eating the blue corpse of Giovanni Bruno in such a positive and heartening way, she was eager to show them that, even if sometimes she seems nervous and grumpy, down deep she remains the loving hopeful person she has always been. Only it didn't work out that way. Which is why she is crying now and can't seem to stop.

The dream she told them was such a pretty one and made her so happy when she dreamt it. At first there was something about flying that had mostly faded from her memory by the time she woke up, as dreams do; she could only remember being on a bridge and realizing that if she pushed against the air she could rise up and fly—it was so exhilarating! She flew to a peaceful meadow with glittery green grass the color of the synthetic grass in Easter baskets and hundreds of beautiful orange daisies as bright as coins, unlike any she'd ever seen, and she knew she had arrived in Heaven. It really exists! she thought in her dream. It was like a place inside a place and oh so colorful! The grasshoppers were a shiny emerald green with eyes like tiny sparkling rubies and the butterflies were all colors of the rainbow, their wings turning luminous when they caught the sunlight, and she remarked to herself how she loved all of God's creatures, even spiders and snakes and beetles. There were birds, too, and she named them all, though later she realized she had made up all the names, for these were birds with such rich plumage they would put a peacock to shame and were unlike any she had encountered before. She wanted to pluck some of the daisies and make the most beautiful daisy chain ever made, but she knew they would only wilt, so it was better to leave them just where they were, where they could be loved for their own sake. She knelt to kiss one of them. The earth they were growing in was a fertile black loam. How she wished she had some of that in her garden at the camp! Things would grow overnight in it! She dug her fingers into it, delighting in its soft moist texture. And then a funny thing happened. There was an elephant in the garden! It made her laugh to see it. She stood up and looked into its big sad eye and saw such wisdom there, so much knowledge, but how could it ever be revealed? Well, there was no reason it should be. It's impossible to figure everything out in the world, that's why one has to have faith. She felt that the elephant was her friend and, although it sort of disappeared from the dream, it would always be there in the way God is always there even if you can't see Him, and she awoke full of peace and contentment.

Glenda stared at her for a short time with her one eye, which reminded Debra all too much of the elephant's eye in her dream. The little sitting room was hushed except for the crowded breathing. Then, showing her gold tooth in a smile that was not really a smile at all, she said it was funny how the real innards of a dream get hid away in the pictures, like pride here in the peacock and shame about that or about something worse, what with all those unnatural colors, and the sadness of knowing too much or maybe having too much known about you and what a burden all this hidden knowledge was, as big as an elephant, crushing the pretty flowers with its big feet—Debra thought the elephant was funny!—but the relief of knowing that whatever the elephant knows will not be revealed, meaning the fear that it will be, which goes together with the secret lies when naming the birds, which usually stand for one's thoughts in dreams. And also how the most important things in dreams are not so much what is there as what is not there, like there are no human beings here in this Heaven, for example, and no children, or even any common animals like dogs or cats, they not being included with spiders and snakes amongst God's lovable creatures. There's a lot about money here, she went on to say, and Debra felt certain there was nothing about money at all, Glenda's remarks about the green grasses being the color of money and also the green grasshoppers with those beady eyes like little warning lights, or even sparks of hot hidden passion, being just completely crazy, even though Debra had to admit she herself had said the bright orange daisies were like coins she couldn't pick up. It occurred to her that the orange daisies might have been inspired by the flowers printed on her missing underpants, but she wasn't about to say so. Glenda went on about the orangeness of those daisies, saying that that color, as everyone knew, was associated with the reproduction, daisies themselves being signs of indecision and of being loved and not being loved, and then about her desire to string them together in a chain the way cells get strung together, but her inability to do so, if she tried they'd just die like they always do, and Debra simply had to tune out because she knew what the woman was getting at and it was very cruel. By this time she was close to tears and having a difficult time stopping her lower lip from trembling and was sorry she had come to the caravan and will never do so again. She could not look at the other women, feeling like they were seeing clean through her, like she didn't have any clothes on, or skin either, just a shriveled heart with pins in it. But Glenda, still staring at her with that one eye, and sliding her tongue over her gold tooth as if to polish it, went on about how feeling at peace with yourself in a dream always means just the opposite, and when she discovered Heaven was actually true, it really meant she did not believe it was, and when, like the daisies, she wanted to be loved for her own sake, it meant she felt she was not. As for the black soil, black always has to do with depression, sadness, and despair, she said, and sometimes hidden desires. "And, well, we all know what dirt means in a dream. And they's worse things, like what is it you are kissing and what's your hand doing down there in that wet black dirtiness, but I won't say them." But she already had. Debra mustered a kind of smile and a faint trembly thank you, and without looking at anybody, fled to her cabin.

Now, as the sobbing diminishes (Colin will be back soon, she has to get control of herself), she sits up on her bed and blows her nose and sees that Ludie Belle is sitting there on a kitchen chair; she must have forgotten to latch the door. "Go away," Debra whimpers, her voice just a squeak squeezing out of her clenched throat. "Please. Go away."

"I won't be a tiddly," Ludie Belle says. She holds what looks like an old tattered school notebook and is wearing her half-frame reading spectacles. "My Aunt Pearl gimme this on her death bed. It's her own way a thinkin' on dreams. It was near all she had and she desired me to have it. I don't hold to the belabored unpuzzlin' a nighttime fancies, which seems to me is mostly made-up stories that don't make no more sense than the dreams theirselves, so I ain't never hardly looked at this since she gimme it, but after that little opry over to Mabel's, I figgered it might throw some luminations on things, like them butterfly wings a yourn done to your purty garden. Aunt Pearl was a sweet ole thing who was always lookin' on the bright side, much like as you do. We all got doubts about what's gonna happen to us when we die, but your dreams a Heaven are like a way a reinfortifyin' your faith and hopes, and meadows and flower gardens is all about tranquility and happiness and bright promises for the future. That's how I parse out what she's writ here, for she had a trick a dreamin' a Heaven too, I only hope she got there. As for daisies, Aunt Pearl was simply crazy about 'em and always hopes to see 'em in her dreams, she says, on accounta they betoken innocence, simplicity, cleanliness, all them things we useta know and still hanker after, cleanliness bein' about the most we can respire to when the years've rid us of the rest. Orange ain't got nuthin t'do with makin' babies, not accordin' to Aunt Pearl, but signifies friendliness, courtesy, a lively personality, and a out-goin' nature, and that sounds like you down to the ground, don't it? Maybe she dreampt a orange daisies, too, cuz she was of the same type. And black ain't all bad neither. If the feeling in the dream is joyful, like it is in yourn, then blackness can signify a aptitude for godly self-sacrifice and seein' inta the future to go long with it. To dream of a kiss, Aunt Pearl says, betokens love, affection, harmony, and contentment—listen at that!—and what you're kissin' ain't nuthin dirty neither, it's nature itself, which you love more'n nobody I know." Ludie Belle folds up her spectacles and drops them in a skirt pocket and goes to the sink to get a glass of water. "Glenda was bein' spiteful and they warn't no call for that, but she has got difficulties of her own. Her husband Welford cain't stop hisself playin' round, you probly noticed, and so Glenda's got a natcherl gredge over most single ladies."

"No, I…" But then she recalls certain scenes in the garden, outside the public shower and privies, here in the cabin when Welford was plumbing in the running water, once down by the creek. She always thought of it as just harmless teasing, his way of being friendly, and she was flattered by it and usually joked back because that seemed the natural thing to do and because she is nice to everybody and does not like to disappoint them. Glenda was never far away…

"Here," says Ludie Belle, fishing a little white pill out of her pocket and handing her the glass of water. "Swaller this and see ifn it don't perk you up a tad."

Debra feels like throwing her arms around Ludie Belle and weeping again, but Colin comes in the door, and with one glance at her, his eyes start from their sockets in alarm like they always do and in his high-pitched voice he demands to know what's the matter, why is she crying? "I'm not crying, Colin. It's just the hay fever. You know, like sometimes down at the garden? Ludie Belle brought me an antihistamine and has just been helping me with the menus for next week. Put on your working shorts and we'll go down and pick some fresh lettuce and celery and spring onions from the garden for tonight. Also some carrots and new potatoes for the Sunday roast, and we'll see what else is ready."

"Fetch me up some cowcumbers and peas and slathers a young sparrowgrass, Colin," says Ludie Belle. "I'll see if I ain't got the makin's for my mama's sparrowgrass casserole." And she winks and blows a kiss from the door, Colin in his eagerness having already dropped his trousers where he was standing and rushed into his bedroom looking for his gardening shorts.

Pat Suggs is no dreamer. If you ask him if he ever dreams, he will say he never does. Nevertheless, he is dreaming. He is in his office at South County Coal, where he trains his Christian Patriots, and they are waiting for the Christ's arrival. Others are also present—fellow Disciples, or maybe interlopers. It doesn't matter. It will all get sorted. His humanist adversary, the moneylender, is here. Likewise, the ex-commie Red Baxter. Sent his boys in years ago to teach that splenetic troublemaker a lesson, but they came back with their own knees broken instead. Next time that won't happen. He is now Christ's warrior, not merely a patriotic businessman, and he will be ruthless. The moneylender is out of his water here and he knows it. He has withdrawn to a far wall and looks shrunken, a defeated man. But Pat knows he must not gloat or things could turn around. Pride before a fall. Pat knows the proverb, can quote it whole, even in a dream: Pride goeth before destruction, and an haughty spirit before a fall. He has used that line when bringing other proud men to their knees, and he will use it again as he quietly and humbly sees to the merciless scourging of the smug banker. Pat knows he is dreaming, so he reasons these things out as he goes along; that way, he'll be rid of it all on waking up, the lessons learned, but the dream forgotten as if never dreamt. Wosznik, Shawcross, Appleby, others from the camp are here as well. Disciples or friends of the Disciples. But which one, he wonders, looking around the room, will be the Betrayer? Baxter, Cavanaugh may be enemies, false apostles, but they are who they are, nothing up their sleeves. Puller? That new Patriots recruit, Dunlevy? His eye falls on Ben Wosznik. Constancy incarnate, so he's always thought. Not unlike the Disciple Peter. But there is something tainted about the man now. As if he were harboring a wickedness in his bosom. Or at least a weakness, which in holy battles can be worse than sin. That damaged girl. In Pat's mind, by choice or fate, she has become an agent of the dark side. What happened to her must have been deserved, or was at least necessary. Part of the divine plan. And for her now, Ben has abandoned everything else. So what is he doing here in the mining office? This dream suggests he will return to the camp, but his presence here may only be to reveal his true role. Having figured this out, Pat decides to erase the dream, wake up, get dressed, have his customary oatmeal breakfast, and go out to the camp. There's a meeting scheduled, a service, a Sunday buffet, plans to be made for next week's temple dedication ceremonies.

When he arrives at the camp, however, there's no one there. The place is a shambles. He checks the Meeting Hall: no buffet tables have been set out. It's as though the camp has been abandoned for some time. It's eerie, but there's probably an explanation. The Rapture? He discounts that. They might all be over on the mine hill, but why would they go there without telling him? Have they all been arrested? If so, he'll have work to do. Ely Collins' death message is still hanging by the fireplace. For some reason, that's reassuring. But then he sees the prophetic date has been changed from the 8th to the 30th. That was yesterday. He has missed it. For a moment his heart sinks. Then he realizes that the changing of the date is nonsense. He is still dreaming. Nearly got fooled. He wakes up again, dresses, has his usual bowl of hot oatmeal, waits until he is able to use his own toilet, and goes out to the camp in time for the Sunday morning service.

When he arrives, he feels like it's the second time he's come out here this morning; he dismisses the feeling. There's a cheery freshness to the place this summery morning, but they've fallen behind in their projects, he knows, missing the energy and discipline brought to them by Ben and Clara. That damned Puller. The sheriff waited too long to go after the motorcyclists, and see now the consequences. Puller has an official story about the death of that mop-headed biker, and then there's the one suggested by the since-repaired dent in the right front fender of his police car. No matter. They're gone. But so are Ben and Clara. He has an uneasy feeling about Ben this morning for some reason. Some new awareness dawning about where the man's priorities lie.

The church service, he learns, is being held up on Inspiration Point. After checking in at the Meeting Hall kitchen, where the ladies are busy preparing the Sunday buffet (he can smell roast pork), he makes his way up there, speaking with people as he goes. Both Wayne Shawcross and Welford Oakes acknowledge that they will see him later, before lunch, in the church office. Mrs. Edwards, about whom he is seriously concerned, will be there, too. No, no news from Ben and Clara. He remarks that there are more people here than he expected and learns that some of those chased out are drifting back by day, still feeling a part of things. Some help out, some don't. On his way past the cabin refurbished for the two office boys, he sticks his head in. Already looking too much like some kid's college room; he'll have to speak with them about that. There's something odd about the blond one, though he's smart and people seem to be taking his arcane decodings seriously, especially with regard to something that's supposed to happen next weekend. The other one is useful and willing but without much spunk and not completely reliable. Some folks, he thinks, are born to backsliding. Sooner or later they'll both have to leave the cabin and it will become the official church office.

Outside the sickbay cabin, he nods to Rumpel and Dunlevy, members of his Christian Patriots organization, but not of the camp executive committee; he keeps the two things separate. Both former soldiers, they were with him at the cemetery yesterday for the Patriots' Memorial Day services, a holiday too much ignored in this country. Dunlevy is a jack of all trades, useful in many ways, but only up to a point. Hard to know for sure what's boiling underneath Rumpel's thick skin, the one they call Hunk, but he is, at least on the surface, a simple man, blunt and mostly unthinking. He's strong and he takes orders well and is a good rifleman, has his own arsenal. Both men were useful in clearing illegal Baxterite squatters off the new trailer park and campsite a few days ago, and he has more projects for them this week.

Cecil Appleby, the beekeeper, conducts this morning's service on the Point. Reluctantly, as always; he's no showboat. When ye pray, use not vain repetitions as the heathen do—that's his style. Shawcross reads the scripture, Hall spouting a few spontaneous verses of his own, and that southern couple, L'Heureux and his woman, are there to lead the singing. Not sure about them. Especially the man, who croons religious songs like they're love songs and earns his living singing in bars. The woman is more interesting, has some kind of special connection. They may or may not stick, but for the moment they bring a certain quality to these occasions. While Appleby leads them in prayer, staring at his gnarled hands as though the text were written there, Pat gazes across the way at the mine hill glowing in the morning sun. He sees it not so much as a holy place now as a building site. He can see the temple sitting there, but there are still problems to resolve. Pat has learned a few things about Appleby. The man has known tragedy. Apparently he struck and killed a child one day while driving. He was in real estate then, beekeeping just a hobby, and he was on his way to view a new property, probably hurrying to beat a competitor there. He got jailed briefly for involuntary manslaughter, gave up real estate afterwards. Gave up driving, too—his wife does all of that now. He took up carpentry, what he calls the Master's trade, instead, and got good at it, it being part and parcel of his faith. Kept the hives, added to them, and the two of them became beekeeping nomads, chasing the seasons, picking up carpentry work on the side. Found his mentor in Ben Wosznik. Not because of Wosznik's preaching, which is minimal, but because of his singing. Appleby doesn't exactly preach either, he merely leads them in prayer, speaking quietly, sincerely, urgently to Jesus and God. Pat has taken a liking to him. Reminds him some of Ely Collins. Ely exhorted more, Appleby keeps more to himself, but he has Ely's quiet eloquence. Innate wisdom. Like Ely, he is who he is and is trustworthy to the core.

After the service, he joins Shawcross, Oakes, and Mrs. Edwards in the church office off the Meeting Hall where the lunch is being set out. Oakes offers Mrs. Edwards a chair and she refuses it a bit too sharply.

A little huffy recently, but there are a lot of pressures on her—pressures he can't do much about. There is much to talk about; too much for a one-hour meeting. Mrs. Edwards wastes some of that time expressing her gratitude to him on behalf of the entire camp for all the time and concern he is devoting to them in their present difficulties. He nods in acknowledgement, trying not to show his impatience, then takes reports on the various camp construction projects. Wayne Shawcross describes the completion of the cabin for the two boys and points out the new shelves and filing cabinets installed in the office. Welford Oakes says he is plumbing in a ladies' restroom with flush toilets in the unused storage room next door and the office where they are sitting is designated for future conversion into a men's room, so he's installing waste and supply pipes adequate for both facilities. Wayne reports there was another intrusion and vandalism in the camp yesterday. Somebody got in and tried to pull down one of the lamp posts, and there was an attempt to set Hunk Rumpel's chicken coops on fire, but they were chased away by gunfire. Mrs. Edwards says that although nothing has been stolen, intruders have also been inside her tool shed. "Probably Baxter's people," Pat says. "We chased them off the new campsite. They were retaliating. There's apt to be more of that. We're going to be making life ever more uncomfortable for them around here until they get the message and move on." Mrs. Edwards says that she will be putting a lock on the shed door and only she and Hazel Dunlevy, who has started helping her down there, will have keys.

They briefly touch on the legal harassments. The city's injunctions, he tells them, are dead in the water. If anything does stick, enforcement still has to go through Sheriff Puller and he has no intention of preventing the church from having free access to the hill. The threat of state and federal prosecutors is a red herring. Not going to happen. He says he has been working with a hotshot lawyer up in the city named Thornton who has taken a personal interest in their case and who assures him the charges of embezzlement and theft against the three women have no merit. What he doesn't tell them is that Thornton said the cases are similar, but the Filbert/Cavanaugh case is winnable and the Edwards one is probably not. Mrs. Edwards is one of their most dependable and enthusiastic workers; he could not have done without her during this absence of Clara and Ben. She has given her all, but she may have to be sacrificed. If she takes a personal hit, the church may be let off and they can perhaps avoid forfeiting any of the property. He assumes, if she gets sent up and the Rapture happens, being such a loyal and devoted servant, Jesus will find her. There's her troubled boy, but he'd be best off in an institution anyway. The one consolation is that their adversaries will never get the money. He hopes that will console her as well.

With what little time they have left, they talk about next Sunday's tabernacle groundbreaking and ceremonial cornerstone laying on the hill. He is bringing in heavy earth-moving equipment tomorrow. He plans to scar the earth in the shape of the temple ground plan with its encompassing circle and to fill the trenches with chalk. He is organizing aerial photography for news releases. Other ministries in the area have been invited, though few will attend. They'll have to plan on Clara and Ben not being there. So someone should organize the hour-by-hour events. "Young Darren is working on that," Mrs. Edwards says. They still have to decide which corner is the appropriate one for the stone, given its odd hillside construction. The back of the church, or top of the cross, will be buried in the hillside, while the front will have to be elevated. From the air, it will look like a Latin cross, but the shape of the building will actually be more like a squared-off Greek cross, each wing seven units long with the extra five units at the bottom part of the twelve-unit cross post filled out by broad full-width steps. Oakes wants to know what's being used for the cornerstone. "We'll be moving Ely Collins' remains to the spot and using his headstone, a solid block of granite," Pat says. "We won't need the body for the ceremony; it can be brought later. Mrs. Collins has approved this. We already have the headstone. We're adding a line to it with Sunday's date. It's with the engravers now."

There's a knock on the door. "Lunch is ready, folks! Come and get it!"

"Should start laying the foundations in a couple of weeks," he says, rising, "and be ready to begin the actual construction of the temple itself by the end of summer."

The others look at each other with raised eyebrows, faint smiles. The end of summer! "It's like a dream come true!" says Mrs. Edwards.

# III.3

## Sunday 31 May – Monday 1 May

The municipal pool has opened this Memorial Day weekend and the kids are nagging at her to take them, but Dot's pooped after the exhausting trip to the camp and back. Sunday dinners are a lot of work. Extra cots were brought in out there for last month's big weekend and they were probably just going to be dumped somewhere and left to rust, so they did them the favor of carting a few of them back here to Chestnut Hills. She has fallen out on one of them. God has blessed them with these small gifts.

"Come on, Mom," says Luke. "This is the last day it's free."

There's that to consider. Not much is free these days. That pork roast may be their last. It was overcooked like everything else they serve out of that kitchen and she let them know that, not for the first time; she could teach them a thing or two, but they're set in their southern ways. The rhubarb pie was sour, too, and begging for hot custard. You just don't serve rhubarb pie without it. What's wrong with these people? Then old man Suggs had the nerve to tell her that the meals and other privileges of the camp were for the workers only. If they are not there by 7:30 a.m. each day to begin work, they will not be able to share in the camp meals or other facilities. Is he kidding? How is she going to get Isaiah off the can at that ridiculous hour? Whatever happened to give to him who asketh you and the righteous showeth mercy to the needs of the saints? Is this a church, or what? Even *finding* all her kids in the morning, much less getting them washed and dressed, can take half the day. That old man should have a few to see what it's like, he'd be making fewer stupid rules.

"They got a big slide. Davey told me."

"Just let me get my wind, Luke." Somebody should wipe the kid's nose. Snot worming out of both her nostrils. Dot would make the effort but she has nothing to use except her skirt, which may not get laundered again soon. "Go get up a game of apocalypse in the back yard."

"Come on, Mom," her oldest says. "You're not tired, you just ate too much."

"I know, Mattie, but I figured if we weren't going to be invited back, I'd better store up enough for the rest of the week, and now I can't move." It was a good thing she was already well tucked in when Suggs dropped the edict. She managed to make it back for thirds and a half before they took everything away, and she was able to share a whole pie with little Johnny, fortunately not his favorite delicacy, he being still mostly on the bottle. Custard, though, he would have loved.

"Is that how it works? Storing it up?"

"I don't know. Probably not." She feels a good healthy snore coming on, Isaiah already at it in the back room of this little prefab—their fourth house since coming here, having used up the first three—but the kids won't let her drop off. They keep poking and wheedling. "All right, all right," she says finally, sitting up with a heavy grunt, and they jump up and down and let off squealing and whoopeeing sounds. Let them have their chlorinated dip—they're all in need of baths anyway, and the pool should sterilize them for a few days, save her time in the long run. Maybe they could somehow make it out to the camp at least one day a week in time to earn their lunches and bring home a few bags full of leftovers to get them through some of the other days.

* * *

How does a body survive in such a mean world? It's not easy, especially with this gang of Blaurock ragamuffins. But Isaiah is a hard worker and strong and fearless, and he's resourceful at picking up odd jobs, like taking dents out of fenders, lopping off dead tree limbs, pointing chimneys, caulking windows, getting squirrels out of attics and rats out of basements and on one occasion last week a cat out of a tree, though he did that one for free. He has a very Christian attitude toward dogs and cats and does not like to see them suffer, though in hard times past they have also sometimes eaten them. Isaiah's not inclined to say much, he just wanders the neighborhoods locating problems, points and gives his price. And he comes cheap, so they always invite him back. He brings the money home, she buys food with it. When they run out, they visit a restaurant out on the highway somewhere, walking out without paying, her kids, well-trained, asking loudly just before if they can go out and play. She keeps a list of places and ticks them off as they use them up. These people make such huge profits, it's a way of helping them tithe. Once, they made the mistake of going back to the same place twice, and on that occasion they had to check off not only the restaurant, but also the state. Which has been a nuisance ever since, it being one of those states in the middle that they always have to drive around to get somewhere else. Wandering one day through what the local Baxter people call Dagotown, Isaiah spotted an old Ford pickup on blocks, and after looking it over he offered to trade their Dodge for it, the old heap still running even if on its last legs, plus enough money to buy used wheels for the truck, part of which he earned by cleaning their gutters and unplugging their downspouts and getting rid of a tree whose roots were threatening the house foundations and sawing it up for firewood. A week or so later they had a vehicle twice as good, and one they could haul things in, though Isaiah had to make a few pieces out of scrap harvested from the truck bed, and visit some church parking lots to borrow the odd doobob or two he couldn't manufacture himself. Not much room inside for the kids, but riding shotgun at the back of the truck is a big adventure for them. Isaiah's next project is to build a camper unit for it. They can park it out at the camp somewhere. Meanwhile, they've been rotating through various Chestnut Hills properties, living among the cockroaches and mice, who seem to enjoy a comfortable life in this neighborhood, moving to a new house when the old one gets overtaken by filth and disrepair, trundling out to the camp for laundry, telephone, meals, prayers, and the occasional family shower. That will be harder now, though not impossible, she assumes. People having a way of letting her do what she wants if she's insistent enough. But it's no big deal anyway—anything that takes a coin Isaiah can make operate without. He can make slugs out of tin cans and roof lead and work magic with a bobby pin. Stuff they borrowed from the camp that they no longer need they have offered up in garage and yard sales, picking up pizza money. They also scrounge through other people's rubbish, occasionally coming up with a usable or saleable item, though it's a poor town and not much gets thrown away. They have better luck dumpster diving out at the shopping center; security's not perfect out there, meaning they usually come away with a few small store samples as well, which they feel they deserve by virtue of the abstemious Christian lives they live.

At the pool, they draw a lot of attention. Stares and giggles. Pointed fingers. The brat at the entrance who does the check-in and hands out the baskets for their clothes comes out now and tells them they can't swim in their underwear, they have to have swimming suits. Dot tells her those *are* swimming suits, the latest models, and a good sight more modest than what some of these other little heathens out here are wearing, so lay off. Of course, it would have helped had they been clean, but kids are kids, right? The girl looks for help from the lifeguard perched over there on his high chair at the deep end of the pool, but he is surrounded by fawning young things who keep falling into the water and squealing that they can't swim—save me, Tommy! The lifeguard's a pretty boy, tall and good-looking, and doesn't seem to care about little kids swimming in their underwear, and why should he, for pete's sake?

Now that she's in here, Dot is thinking about having a plunge herself, fairly confident that her drawers are more or less immaculate. She had a heck of a time getting through the turnstile at the entrance and was afraid she'd have to keep an eye on her kids from outside the pool's chain-link fence, but fortunately there was a gate in that fence, and when she insisted, the baskets girl found the key and let her in that way, though she didn't seem happy about it. Happiness is not something Dot tends to provoke in others, she has noticed, though she's a happy enough person herself. She sees that one of the half-naked creatures surrounding the lifeguard is that girl who is said to have sucked the life out of the old lady from Florida. Probably she ought to go over and pinch her to see if she's real. There's a pallor about her that does not look completely human, but then summer's just begun. A lanky underfed thing. No way she can compete with those other young beauties, whoever or whatever she is, though that may not be what she's doing there. She glances at Dot from time to time, maybe because she recognizes her, maybe for more sinister reasons, and once, while looking over at her, whispers something to the lifeguard. Like the devil whispering into the ear of the pious, though that's probably an exaggeration, in his case at least.

When Dot pulls her dress over her head, she catches a glimpse of the alarm on the face of the check-in girl, who goes ducking back inside the changing rooms building, and she sees that everyone has turned to stare at her. What? They never saw a fat lady before? Little Mark is standing at the edge of the pool with his underwear around his knees, peeing into the water. Markie never could hold it, was in diapers until only about a year ago. He's cute, like that fountain in France or wherever that she saw on a used postcard once in a junk shop, but these dummies probably won't make the connection, and most of them are scrambling out of the pool. The lifeguard steps down off his chair, no doubt intending to come over here, but just then Luke pushes another little kid off the top of the slide and he's drowning.

The lifeguard, there in a couple of strokes, plucks the spluttering creature out of the water and hands him up to an older kid, his big sister maybe. Which means that Luke, who is wheeing down the slide, is apt to have a problem of her own that the rest of them will have to share.

There are sirens outside and Dot realizes the check-in bimbo has called the police. She hasn't even got her toe in yet. The level of tolerance and understanding here is frankly disappointing. Mattie has taken another kid's green dragon float away from him and the sissy has gone wailing to his mother. So now everyone is watching them. They're the story of the day. Mattie is biting the rubber float, trying to puncture it. Two officers come in, sweaty in their dark uniforms, trying to appear officious but not succeeding. If there's anyone who looks out of place here, it's those guys, not her. The fat one with the Roman nose and three chins tells her to put her clothes on, dress her kids, and leave the pool. The older one tells him he thinks this is one of the families squatting illegally in Chestnut Hills. You know, Louie, he says. Them cultists. He's chewing something, but it doesn't look like gum. A nasty habit her own father had. It turns her stomach. She protests that it's a public pool and a free country, but they don't seem interested in this line of reasoning. Mattie, meanwhile, has successfully destroyed the green dragon. It floats flat on the surface like seaweed. Her kids are already up and moving toward the exit. They know when it's time to leave a place. "May the good Lord forgive you," she says. She tosses her dress and little Johnny over her shoulder, shoves Fat Louie into the pool, and stalks off toward the gate in the chain-link fence, which, she sees, the check-in brat has opened wide.

They stop by the new unfinished campgrounds on the way home to see how Abner Baxter and his people are getting on and to take the wet things off and let the kids dry off running around in the afternoon sunshine for a few minutes. There were no sirens chasing them after they left the pool—they were too busy hauling Tubby out of the drink. "Hey, help!" she heard a girl shout over the splashy floundering on her way out of the gate. "My daddy can't swim!" So Save-Me-Tommy had some heroics to perform, after all, if not the sort he might have preferred.

The new campsite is fenced off with a strand of shiny barbed wire, NO TRESPASSING signs dangling every twenty yards or so. There is some well-digging equipment standing idle, a small temporary worker's hut, some poles and big spools of wire cooking in the sun. Dot wonders if there's anything there Isaiah can use. The campsite is otherwise empty, though there are a few people still camped out at the edges, including Abner and his family, using a tented extension to their old Plymouth station wagon. Jesus will recognize his true disciples by the rusted-out clunkers they all drive. Just the four Baxters now, the mental girl at Abner's side, holding his hand; Young Abner behind his shoulder, sporting his new red bangs; Abner's wife Sarah off sitting in the passenger seat of the Plymouth, looking like she might have been there for several days. The defection of their oldest daughter is the cause of much bitterness. One wonders who's doing the dishes now. The big tent is still up from this morning's sermon and prayer meeting, with folding chairs set out which she recognizes from the camp.

Abner, scowling his scowl, says he is glad to see her, and others come to tell about their troubles and exchange God blesses. The sheriff has been demanding their driving licenses and car registrations or other proof of ownership on the grounds that there have been some recent car thefts in the area. This is absurd on the face of it because no one in their right mind would steal these cars. But some vehicles have been impounded and fines levied, jail threatened if the fines go unpaid. Some have just left the area, which seems to be the easiest way to get your car back. They have been made to move their tents and vehicles several times, sometimes only across the road—a kind of day-to-day harassment meant to make them want to give it up and go look for a friendlier location. The mayor of Randolph Junction, said to be close to Abner and a tent-meeting regular, has offered just such a place, though without any services, and many have already gone there, but Abner is determined to stick it out here and some of his pals are standing by him. Now there are threats of warrants being issued, which probably means anything resembling weapons will be confiscated, including kitchen knives, screwdrivers, and lug wrenches. Dot fills them in on developments at the camp and the new rules meant to exclude any but the inner circle. "Even the new lavatory is locked up," she says. "Can you believe it?" Ben and Clara and their daughter have not been seen since they left the camp over three weeks ago and will probably miss next Sunday's ceremonies on the hill, which, Abner says after dropping his head for a moment at the mention of the daughter, he and his son have been specifically ordered not to attend. Abner says he is not sure he will obey this order. Young Abner nods solemnly at this, his bangs flopping on his forehead, which still looks raw under there. It turns out his brothers and their gang kidnapped him and dragged him to that field to torment him and dressed him in the girl's underpants just to humiliate him. Dot adds a more detailed note about being excluded from the camp dining table, hoping someone will take the hint, but no one does. In fact, a couple of them have been nosing around the pickup and if there were anything there to steal, she figures it would be gone by now. Isaiah always sets a little money aside for shotgun shells and gas. Maybe there's enough for a pizza. If not, well, they'll have to test out the storage theory.

The next morning they awake to grim tidings. Not the writing on the wall, though there's that, too. "Aw, Mom," Mattie says after she swats him, "we only wanted to play Battleship and we ain't got no paper." "*Any* paper," she says. "You ain't got *any* paper." "That's what I said." "Well, that ain't no excuse to write on the walls. Now you take your erasers and see if you can't get some of that off." "Our erasers are all wore down." "Well, lick it and wipe it with your sleeve." Not that it matters much. They'll be changing houses soon.

But the really bad news, discovered a moment later, is that everything has been turned off. No electricity, no gas, no water. Which means, among other grave consequences, that the toilet won't flush. Isaiah who is headed in there now is going to be a very unhappy man. She goes door to door to the other houses in Chestnut Hills where people chased from the camp are living and finds it's the same story. Everything shut down. They can't do this. You can't deprive a person of water no matter how poor they are. She urges them to join her in a march down to city hall to demand their rights. Only a few buy into this plan and most of them drop away before they get there. In the end she's stuck with her own kids and a couple of yokels from Arkansas who can't seem to get it in their heads that the Second Coming didn't actually happen last month and they weren't somehow left behind. Democracy's a good thing, but it has its limits. On the steps of city hall, she also realizes she left Johnny at home. How could she have forgotten him? She sends Mattie to retrieve him and tells him to ask his father to bring them back here in the pickup because she might need his help.

The mayor's busy, but he's not so busy he can't hear her out. Dot pushes aside the fat girl out front and storms on in. The boys from Arkansas follow her as far as the door. *"What the hell is going on here?"* the mayor roars out, and then she's down to Mark and Luke. But it doesn't matter, she doesn't need numbers—right is on her side. She unloads her grievances on the mayor, a shady character if she ever saw one, telling him that she doesn't know who's responsible for the sabotage out there in Chestnut Hills, but it's unconstitutional and has to be put right or there'll be big trouble, and though he has been standing, he sits down again, wallowing a cigar around in his fat leathery cheeks, his beady eyes narrowing. She leans over and slaps her fist on his desk, reminding him that God is on her side and quite capable of serious devastation, and the mayor shrinks back into his leather swivel chair, nearly swallowing his cigar. At least she has his attention. He makes a circular motion around one ear and she thinks he's calling her crazy and is about to pop him one, but then she realizes he's signaling to the woman on the other side of the open door behind her to make a phone call. Probably to those clowns she met out at the pool yesterday. Little Luke has found a settee, something she hasn't seen in a long time, and it excites her. She's jumps up and down on it with gleeful yipping noises. Dot tells the mayor that children's health and lives are at stake, and to illustrate the subject, she lifts Markie up and stands him on the mayor's desk. Unfortunately, Markie uses that moment to let go again, puddling the scattered papers on the mayor's desk, and she tells him that's because with no running water they can't use the bathrooms and now look what's happened. The mayor can see what has happened. He's on his feet again and looks ready to make a run for it. Mattie comes in just then, dragging a squalling Johnny. He says, gasping for breath, that Dad wasn't home and he had to carry Johnny all the way here and he's too heavy and he dropped him a few times. He doesn't know where his father is, but probably he went to look for another bathroom—the one at home isn't any good anymore.

The mayor, outflanked, relents. "Take her over to the utilities manager and get this sorted out!" he commands, probably heard clear across town.

His secretary doesn't seem to know who the utilities manager is, being a typical underachieving government employee, but then she does know. Maybe the mayor mouthed something. Dot can hear the door slamming and locking behind her as they proceed down the hall. She carries Johnny now and drags along a reluctant Luke, who's howling that she wants to go back and jump on the bouncy thing some more. They are led to a back room which seems to be part of the city clerk's office. There's a guy slumped behind a dusty desk looking three sheets to the wind. "The mayor said to take care of this," the old girl squeaks and vanishes, not even explaining her case. Which Dot proceeds to do, though it's clear not much is getting through. It's still midmorning and this guy is gone for the day. Whatever she says, he just grins and winks. Consequently, the crisis she is describing becomes more of a monetary one, and what with her shouting and fist-banging and little Johnny crawling around on top of the desk and all three of the others now either whining or crying, he finally reaches blearily for his billfold, still grinning stupidly like she's telling him a funny joke, fumbles for a dollar bill. She snatches the billfold from him, finds three tens, hands it back.

"Hah!" he says and falls back into his chair, casting his grin upon the inside of his billfold.

"And tell the mayor to get those services turned back on or we're going straight to the Supreme Court!" she yells and leads the kids out of there.

Little Johnny is a load to carry, but Dot decides to toss him over her shoulder and go blow some change from their windfall on ice creams as a reward for her loyal little army, and while walking down Main Street, remarking as she goes on the street's boarded-up pot-holed post-Armageddon look, she passes a sorry-looking white-haired guy having a smoke outside a shoe store. "Looks like you got some ponies there need shoeing," he says.

"Well, I got ten dollars," she says and she shows one of the bills to him. "What can we get for that?"

"Come on in, have a look. Whole stock's on sale. Should find something you like for that price."

At first, all the shoes cost ten bucks each, but she says she can't buy shoes for just one of them, so the price drops to five, and then, when she shrugs and starts to leave, three pair for ten. "Look," he says, "I'll even throw in a pair of baby shoes for the little one. It's your lucky day. Line 'em up and fit 'em out."

Baby shoes. She hadn't even thought about that. First any of her kids have ever had. She picks out a pair that look a bit like his father's work boots. Mattie and Mark are easy enough, liking everything they try on and wanting them all, but Luke has her eye on some pink slippers high up on the wall of shoeboxes. "Not your size, little girl. Try these," the owner says, showing her a pair of patent leather sandals. But Luke is determined, it being her nature, and starts to climb the boxes, succeeding in bringing the whole lot tumbling down. The man's right, they're too big, but Luke wants them anyway. "I'll grow into them, Mom."

"When they fit, Lukie, I'll buy them for you. For now, come and try on these sneakers."

After that, Luke hates every pair she tries on, so finally Dot makes the choice for her, ignoring her loud, bad-tempered protests. Mattie and Mark are bringing down other stacks just for fun, trying to bury each other in falling shoes and boxes. "You know," the man says with a sick smile, "you're like somebody out of my nightmares." She asks him if he couldn't show a little Christian charity and lower the price enough to leave her change to buy ice creams for the kids, but by now, in his excitement, Johnny has pooped his britches again and the place is reeking and the store owner's free hand is closing. "No," he says, looking like he's about to gag. "Out. *Out!*" He herds them onto the street, following them out, locks the door behind him, and hurries away. Probably to go spend up the ten dollars, she assumes, and she wonders if somehow she got cheated.

The boys are jumping up and down in their new shoes on their way to the corner drugstore for ice creams (maybe little Johnny can win them a few more concessions if she fumbles a while for change), but Luke, Dot discovers, has stolen one of the pink slippers, though not its mate, and she's wearing it, dragging it along with a bare foot. She must have left the other sneaker back in the store. The boys have picked up some extra shoelaces, very colorful, probably for ice skates, and two shoehorns, which they seem to perceive as some sort of knightly weapon, attacking each other as they bounce along. She cuffs all three of them, reminding them that it's a sin to steal. If the man hadn't locked the store, she'd march them right back there. They're probably making Jesus very unhappy—whereupon, there on the corner of Third and Main, Jesus himself makes a surprise appearance, rolling down the street in a sky-blue automobile, driven by an ethereal creature who could be the Magdalene herself, though with makeup on! Dot falls to her knees in the street, fearing the worst (they shouldn't have stolen those shoelaces—"You see, Mattie, you see?" she cries), and she's ready to let rip with prayers and confessions and talking in tongues, whatever it takes, but the Master drifts on by and turns the corner at the next block and disappears. She remains there on her knees in the empty street for a few minutes reflecting upon this apparition, wondering if she saw what she just saw, until her kids get restless and ask her to stand up. Come on, Mom, let's go. They want their ice creams.

By the time they get home, Johnny has lost one of his new shoes. Well, give him a change and walk back and look for it. Not something anyone else would want one of. But there are new locks on all the doors; they can't get in. Locks are no problem for Isaiah, but he's not here—the truck's gone—so she breaks a window and passes Mattie through, and he opens up from the inside. Someone has taken all their stuff. The cots are still there, but without mattresses or bedding. Their clothes, collected possessions, the children's toys, kitchen utensils, the hotplate and electric fan, everything, stripped away. They have not bought any of these things, but still they miss them and feel like anyone else feels who has been robbed. It has happened to others in the neighborhood, she discovers. There have also been some forcible evictions. Some of the men, they say, had on uniforms or parts of uniforms, but they didn't look like city police. In fact, a couple of them wore bandannas on their faces like cattle rustlers in the movies. One of them was recognized as that big fellow from the church camp, so everyone knows who's behind this. One of the neighbors has been out to see Reverend Baxter and says they were raided overnight and many had their tents dragged away and ripped up. In protest, Reverend Baxter has cut the wire fence and installed himself in the middle of the new campground, with others positioned around him like encircling wagons, including people from town, and he welcomes all who'd like to come and help defend him. Many say they plan to go there.

Isaiah returns and she shows him what's happened and maybe he's angry and maybe he's not. Always hard to tell with Isaiah. He goes to work. He removes the locks and drops them in his tool box, and he does the same for other people who are still locked out. He taps a light pole directly for electricity supply and spends a good hour making the connection childproof. When it's connected, he turns on every light in the house even though it's still day. He visits the city dump and finds some of their stuff recently deposited there, including their mattresses, or some mattresses anyway, as well as some new things. A toaster, for example. Now all they need is some bread. He has also come back with a load of gallon bottles, milk jugs, and gas cans, and he and a couple of the men take these to a public fountain and fill them up, using the water to fill toilet tanks and allow everyone to flush. Praise God, they say.

As the day wanes, the neighbors gather in the Blaurocks' front yard, bringing along scraps of food to be cooked or warmed up on the recovered hotplate and shared around. The chosen people. Dot sends Mattie to the neighborhood grocery store to buy five loaves of white bread so everyone can have a slice of hot toast, setting aside one loaf for herself to help allay the hunger the day's exertions have brought on, and Isaiah goes to the pop machine in the movie house and gets cold drinks for everybody with his magic slugs. He had also brought a broken floor lamp from his dump run, and he now wires it up and sets it in the yard—a heart-warming thing to see there, a lonely beacon against the encroaching night. It provokes a round of preaching, praying, and gospel singing. Someone offers up a prayer for Reverend Baxter in his stand against the Powers of Darkness, and everyone joins in. Dot tells them all about her visit to the mayor and her encounter with Jesus on Main Street, and that leads to more prayers and the trading of miraculous visitation stories and speculations about the end times so near upon them, including the opinion that they have already begun, about which Dot is less skeptical than she was before. Little Luke comes shuffling up in her pink slipper and for no particular reason puts her arms around her, takes her thumb out of her mouth, and gives her a sleepy kiss on her cheek. The boys are already in their beds; Luke's always the last to quit. Isaiah lifts her up gently and carries her into the house. The way Isaiah has got things done this evening, God bless him, has Dot excited. Later she'll warm up some water on the hotplate, have a quick sponge bath, and then, praise the Lord, it's a bit of the old garden of Solomon.

# III.4

## Friday 5 June – Sunday 7 June

*"They're back! Ben and Clara!"* It's Willie Hall, banging on their cabin door. "Let the saints be joyful'n glory, let 'em sing out *loud* 'pon their *beds!"* And he's off to wake up the rest of the camp with his momentous news.

Billy Don pulls on his jeans and steps out into the drizzly June morning. A dismal day but bright in promise. They're back. He's surprised how good it feels. The camp has a rich murky smell. Funky. One of Sally Elliott's words. So different from the sweet toasty fragrance of dry warm days. Although there's something oddly exciting about this dense odor, something suggestive, almost sinful (it's the earth, Sally would say with her little one-sided grin—the earth is naughty, Billy Don), he's always glad when it lifts, especially after it has sunk in for several days. Billy Don likes the sun. Dusty baseball weather. Weather for lighter hearts. He feels it's the weather they now deserve with the return of Ben and Clara.

They must have rolled in overnight. Billy Don parked his Chevy down there yesterday at suppertime, after his midweek mail run, having met with Sally over ice creams and suffered his weekly dose of chagrin, doubt, and embarrassed longing, and he had paused to stare, as he often did, at the deeply indented space in the lot where their big house trailer had so long stood, anchoring the camp, thinking then, as often of late: Something has ended.

But now, as soon, renewed. Born again: Sally's T-shirt. A sucker. Yes, he can't shake his "appetite for hope," as she calls it. He wants to believe. In the way that Ben and Clara do.

He sees other believers, full of smiles, emerging from the dripping trees, some under umbrellas, coming up into the Main Square: Wayne Shawcross and Ludie Belle; Welford Oakes; Hazel Dunlevy. Mrs. Edwards steps out on her raised porch next door, Colin, still in his underwear, peering over her shoulder with his usual look of giddy alarm. "We'll wanta spruce things up, Billy Don," Wayne shouts, grinning broadly. He's wearing his bib overalls over a pajama shirt. Such a nice guy. Billy Don gives him a thumbs-up. He loves these people. "Take 'em on the grand tour! Show 'em what we done!" Old Uriah appears, Travers, Hovis, all trailing after Willie Hall, Cecil and Corinne Appleby hand in hand, the whole camp gathering, Willie hollering out: "And, glory be, they returned from searching out the land after forty days, *Numbers 12:25! Hallelujah!*" And there's laughter and some congenial amen-ing, and Ludie Belle says: "Come along now, I'll put some breakfast on! Wanda, go fetch up some fresh eggs from the coops! Davey, you scoot along with your mama and help out! Afterwards, Hazel, let's us go shoppin' for sumthin nice for lunch."

Back inside the cabin, Billy Don finds Darren still in his shorts, hastily clearing off his worktable. He tells him the good news, and Darren snaps back: "I know. Why do you think I'm cleaning up here?"

"I suppose we'll have to make the beds."

"I suppose we will."

Darren is clearly not as happy about the return of Ben and Clara as everyone else. He has been the center of attention and getting his way of late, and that's likely to change. Or else it's just him Darren's cross with. Billy Don has remained skeptical about the voice in the ditch, to say nothing of his roommate's fascination with Mrs. Edwards' dark angels story and Colin's crazy nightmares, which Darren believes to be windows onto the sacred, even if they have to do with killing and eating people. Now he has been finding signs that presumably pointed straight at Carl Dean Palmers' traitorous attack but that they'd failed to decipher until it was too late. Billy Don had guard duty with Pach' a couple of nights before everything happened, and Pach' did say things like they both had to learn to knock women off their pedestals, that they weren't worth it, and he told Billy Don about brutal fights he'd been in in which somebody might have been killed or at least crippled, but he also said at least there was the van. It was the one thing he had in this world, and though it was hard to tell what all was in there after it got burned, it seemed like just about everything he owned, including his driver's license. When Billy Don pointed that out to Darren, Darren only said: "Don't be naïve."

As for those voice-in-the-ditch tapes, Billy Don has listened to them more than anyone other than Darren himself, and he's pretty sure things are missing now from when he first heard them. Tiny snippets that might have muddied the clarity of the emerging "message." When he asked about this, Darren looked surprised and said that if anything was happening on the tapes, then it must be the Lord's doing and Billy Don should try to remember what has dropped out because what's no longer there might be more important than what remains. Or maybe it was the Devil's doing, Billy Don said, and Darren, without blinking, said that was possible, but, if so, that made trying to remember what has vanished even more important.

What Billy Don finds most disturbing is in spite of everything that has happened, Darren has drawn close to Abner Baxter. Two weeks ago on Pentecost Sunday he even underwent baptism by fire. Darren says he admires Reverend Baxter's principled intransigence and believes that he is the most knowledgeable of all the original Brunists regarding theology, history, and interpretations of Revelation. "He *knows*, Billy Don." Billy Don accompanied Darren on the first round of taped interviews, and it was true, Reverend Baxter did seem to have clear vehement answers for everything. He was more comfortable speaking of his faith in the divine mission of the Prophet Bruno than even Clara, and was quick to criticize her "softening," as he called it, of

Bruno's utterances, supplying Darren with what he claimed to be the Prophet's correct original sayings. He also gave them a blow-by-blow account of their visit on the Day of Redemption to the Roman Catholic Church, led by the Prophet wielding a mining pick—an event that Clara and Ben and most of their friends were not a part of and never talk about. Reverend Baxter described the Prophet's violent behavior and showdown with the old priest in glowing terms. He said he considered Bruno to have been a true vessel of the Lord, inhabited by the Holy Spirit. Billy Don then made the mistake of asking: "In the same way as Jesus?" Abner Baxter drew back, his face blooming with astonished rage. "Are you being serious, young man? Jesus was the Son of God!" Darren was furious with him and refused to take him along after that—though, later, Sally Elliott said he probably asked the right question.

Billy Don was curious about baptism by fire, just how they did it. Darren said it was a secret ritual and he wasn't allowed to reveal anything, though he said the ceremony was preceded by intense group prayers. People who were normally stern and stiff-necked seemed almost to melt, many of them becoming tearful and childlike, their group prayers gradually ascending into feverish chants, sometimes shouting the Master's name over and over, and he found himself surrendering utterly to them. "It was something like those hypnotizing experiments back in the Bible school dorms. I was told if I truly gave myself to Jesus, it wouldn't hurt, and I believed that." Darren fell into something of a trance even as he told about it, and watching him, Billy Don got the impression the ceremony had to do with circles of fire, maybe circles within circles, possibly while blindfolded, and was tied up somehow with the Brunist symbols of the Circle and the Cross. "Then, one moment, it hurt. But not really. It was like the hurt was happening somewhere else." Afterwards, Darren told Colin about it, and having his own turn is all Colin talks about now.

After breakfast—the prayers today will be thanksgivings: they're back!—he will clean up the office, which looks great with the new shelves and file drawers and their own mess moved out. Clara should be pleased. First, though, a trip to the can and a quick shower and shave.

Standing alongside four other men, splashing into the metal trough of the men's urinal, Wayne Shawcross says to the newest arrival: "How close y'reckon y'are to the new restroom being up'n running, Welford?"

"Well, it's running up right now, but down it ain't. The water's plumbed in, but not the waste. Still gotta finish that trench out back for the pipes. I wisht the space was ample enough to haul in some heavy equipment or that the Meeting Hall was closer to the sickbay so's we could hook up there. But we could turn the faucets on and do a flush to show when Clara and Ben come round and just drain it off out back somewheres if it's only water."

"Okay, but seems as how we might as well finish that trench while we're at it. The ground'll be soft with all the rain. Can you lend a hand, Billy Don? Uriah?"

"Sure, soon's I'm done perking up the office. I'll come round back."

"Diggin' is about the only perfession me and Hovis ever learnt, so, heck yes, let's git it done."

"Where does *this* stuff go?" Hovis asks.

"It don't go nowhere, 'cept prob'ly a pit dug out below. That's why it smells so sweet back here."

The others are peeling off and leaving, but Wayne holds back so as to be left alone with Welford. Welford's a happy-go-lucky sort, a skilled and willing worker and everybody's pal, but he's also a little too much like some old buddies in Wayne's past, back before he was saved. Not bad. Just restless. Reckless. "People ain't blind, y'know, Welford? Y'better watch out y'don't git inta hot water."

Even while he's saying that, Travers Dunlevy walks in and undoes his fly, and Welford grins and says: "You was saying, Wayne?"

"I was saying maybe we could try'n finish up them new hot water deposit tanks on toppa the showers."

"Yeah. Hah. Okay, Wayne. Good move."

* * *

Buffet style for lunch is always easiest—let folks help themselves—but with Dot Blaurock present, Ludie Belle decides to dish up the plates so as to be sure there's enough to go around for the forty or so who'll be here. Dot has a wild story today about seeing Jesus Christ on Main Street, which is entertaining, but which no one believes. Will Henry has also come out from the radio station on hearing that Ben and Clara are back, and Dot, who made it to the camp with Isaiah and her wild things about eleven this morning and evidently figures that was close enough to 7:30 to qualify for a free lunch, now asks loudly if Will has done any work today. What are the rules around here? She's a bully and a nuisance, but people laugh tolerantly and let her be, let her pesky kids be, too (the little girl is dragging a filthy pink slipper on one foot and has brought a stray cat to lunch), on account of they're all feeling so good, rising up today from the down times of the past few weeks. Wayne is near giddy with the joy of Ben and Clara's return and even erupted in a full-throated table blessing with no food yet on it, many of the others joining in and engaging in what could only be called holy laughter. Ludie Belle has been able to assemble a welcoming lunch of chicken legs, mashed potatoes with chicken gravy, spring peas from Sister Debra's garden, fresh buttermilk biscuits with honey from the Applebys' hives (now in full flow), a Jell-O salad with chopped up carrots inside and topped with mayonnaise and canned pears. She has even baked a blueberry cobbler for dessert. The flat-out ebullience of it makes everyone want to sing. "For the bountiful harvest, we praise thee, O Lord!" "Come, for the feast is spread, hark to the call!" "Down in my heart, I've got the joy, joy, joy!"

Mr. John P. Suggs arrives, having been called with the news, and while they're waiting for Ben and Clara, he tells Wayne and Welford they'll meet in the office after lunch to talk about Sunday, and then he huddles with Hunk and Travers. More mischief afoot, Ludie Belle reckons. She has heard about troubled doings at the Baxter encampment and in Chestnut Hills and Ludie Belle figures those two fellows are mixed up in it. Mr. Suggs' Christian Patriots. Wayne has been asked to join, but she has cautioned him against it. Too much like the sort of outfits her brother was in cahoots with back home, and he's in jail now. Doing a lot of Bible reading. Probably come out a preacher like so many bad boys. The camp has been vandalized a few times of late in retaliation or else in provocation, and one night a shot was fired, so things are ramping up in an unpromising way. There aren't a lot of people in the world who believe in this religion, and those who do can't seem to get on with each other. It's hard to figure. Creed. Where it gets sticky. For Ludie Belle, faith is part of the color of life. It goes with the horoscopes she reads, Mabel's cards, changes in the weather, game shows on TV, Sister Debra's nature love. Life would be a dull sad thing without it. After death? She doesn't know. Wait and see.

When Wayne asks her quietly if she spoke with Hazel Dunlevy, Ludie Belle says she did. "I says it ain't gone unnoticed, and she says, I know it, and she shows me the palm of her hand and says, see, it's been writ there since she was borned, ain't nuthin she can do about it."

"Well, there ain't neither of them got a spoonfulla sense, but maybe it'll cool off," Wayne says. They both know a lot about where such feelings can take a body and are slow to cast judgment.

Little Willie Hall bursts into the hall just then, crying out like that squeaky bellhop in the cigarette ads: "And when he gits home, he calleth t'gether on his friends'n neighbors, sayin' unto 'em—*Luke 15:6!*—Rejoice with me on accounta I have jist got back my sheep which was lost!" His wife Mabel comes shuffling in behind with Ben and Clara as people shout, *"Glory!"* and *"Praise Jesus!"* and there's a tearful rush toward them. Ludie Belle feels tears starting in her own eyes. It's like something hard and heavy they've been holding back can be let go of now. But though Clara and Ben greet everyone like it truly means something, they're both dry-eyed and Ludie Belle can see they're not the same as before. Scrawnier and road-weary, but more than that. There's something far off and broken about Clara, clenched up about Ben. Still in need of healing. Well, they can do that. Starting with fattening them up. She calls everybody to the table. Little Elaine, poor child, is not with them. That's about the first thing everybody has noticed. "She's ailing," Clara explains and says no more. Beside Ludie Belle, Wayne whispers: "Clara's bad hoarsed up and don't look right." Ludie Belle catches Mabel's eye and Mabel shakes her head as she does when a bad card turns up.

Ben, alone, is back where it happened, trying to figure things out. Everything here where the bloodying of Junior Baxter took place was beat down that morning, the grass and flowers torn up and trampled on and all of it darkly wet like it had been raining blood. Now everything's already grown back, this patch of weedy field wet today from summer rain and squishy underfoot, like nothing ever happened. Hard things happen and then become only ghosts of themselves. He and Clara have been visiting the Eastern churches, and most of the churches were full up and doing well and folks were good to them, treating Clara and him like heroes, hungry for news and eager to show they were all true Followers; but they were completely ignorant of the events at the camp, except those who'd come out for the dedication ceremonies, and even their memories were so different from Ben's he sometimes wondered if they'd been in the same place at the same time. As for the troubles since: no notion of them. Even the history of five years ago was changing. It has been told so many times and in so many different ways that it often seems to be happening in some other place, a magical place like a Jerusalem or a Bethlehem, and he has to admit that his own songs make that even more so. Ben sometimes tried to set them straight in his quiet no-nonsense way, and they were attentive, but he got the feeling they were mostly only being polite, listening to his side of the story because of who he is, meanwhile waiting for him and all the other original witnesses to die so they could get on with their own version of things.

Kicking about, trowel in hand, Ben finds a water-soaked blue bandanna. So this must be the spot, or near to it, where they found Abner Baxter's son, gagged by that bandana or one just like it. Probably came off a biker boy. Junior was out cold, his face running blood. They ungagged him and dipped him in the creek to bring him around. Only later did Ben learn from Bernice when she banded him up what was written there, and he knew then that it was probably his fault this had happened. What he told the younger one that morning when he caught them in his old farm shack, setting brother against brother. So he was in some way the cause for what happened to Elaine, too. Probably he should have just shot those boys when he had them in his sights. When he thinks about what happened here, he knows he could kill without remorse, and he knows that, even with God's commandment against it, the prospect of eternal damnation would not stop him. But how did they know they'd find Elaine and Junior here that morning? Junior must have told them, not suspecting what his brother had in store for him. When he and Wayne and the others found him, Junior was wearing nothing but girl's drawers. Elaine's, as it turned out, though she seemed ignorant as to how he got hold of them. He said the same, trying to put the blame on the bikers, saying they must have done that to him while he was passed out. Later, on the road, Ben got to thinking again about their trailer break-in the morning the Baxters arrived. The missing money and handgun. So: the underwear, too, probably. Sick boy. It might also explain the belt he found here in the grass that morning, which Clara said could have been Ely's. But Junior wouldn't have walked down here in front of everybody, even in the dark, in nothing but girl's underpants. Elaine was wearing even less, unless they stole her clothes. Far as he could understand her, they'd both had tunics on. Which made sense, given what they were apparently up to. But, if so, where were they? None to be found here that day and none here now. Whatever could those godless biker boys want with Christian tunics? There are a lot of things that Ben does not understand.

There was another pair of women's drawers, for example. Didn't see them at first that day. But, after they had hauled Junior up to the camp and cleared everybody out, Ben had come back here to look around, try to get a picture of what had happened. He found Carl

Dean's baseball cap at the edge of the woods, so that pretty much proved he was here, all right, hard as that was for Ben to take in. Then: a spot of bright color over there in the trees. He thought at first they must be Elaine's, but they weren't her size. Not her style, either: bright orange green-leafed flowers on them. When he realized whose they were, he also realized that she hadn't told them everything. That maybe it was worse for her than she had said.

So today, after the meeting in the church office, he asked Mrs. Edwards to stay behind and help him with some notes of thanks he wanted to send to the Eastern churches. Clara, feeling poorly herself, was not up for the meeting and had left with Bernice after lunch to go check on Elaine in the trailer. The poor child won't speak, won't eat, the flesh on her bones thin like a wax coating. Which is worrying Clara sick, sapping the pluck right out of her. The meeting was mostly for his sake, filling him in on the changes at the camp, including the fancying up of the office they were sitting in, roomier now with the two boys out of it (Ben had failed to remark on it when they entered, and he knows that disappointed them), the legal actions being taken against them ("Won't work," said Mr. Suggs), the troubles they were still having with Abner Baxter and his people, the cornerstone-laying ceremonies for their new Coming of Light Tabernacle Church over on the Mount on Sunday. But Ben was worn down and worried and the closed office was thickly scented with waxy smells, and his mind kept floating off onto other things. That awful day, mostly—so vivid to him since they returned. So many unresolved mysteries. Young Carl Dean Palmers, just for a sample: what he did and didn't do.

The first thing Ben asked Mrs. Edwards when they were alone in the office afterwards was what else she could remember from that morning. She began to tremble, and he knew it would not be easy for her. He apologized and said he and Clara would be grateful all their lives for what she did, but he was only trying to figure out some things and put his mind at ease, and he thought he'd start with what she could recollect about Carl Dean. Carl Dean is hated and reviled by near everybody. They'd all heard him tell Elaine the night before, like a threat, that things were going to go bad for her. And he'd bared his chest like a wild animal, scaring the child half out of her wits. He left the camp right after that, his wheels spitting up gravel, and Duke and his woman saw him in his leather jacket drinking with the bikers at the motel, leaving with them later on. Ben heard him coming home late, noisy, drunk. Fell asleep in his van with his feet sticking out. Then, like a taunt, he parked the van right in front of the Meeting Hall before leaving. With a vulgar obscenity hanging over the rearview mirror. But though he's what some would call rough trade, Ben believes Carl Dean is a good fellow at heart and he does not think it was in him to do what most people seem to think he did. They had a touching farewell up on the Point that morning and Carl Dean said he wished Ben was his dad, and he was sincere about it. Brought tears to Ben's eyes. He's not the only one with doubts. At lunch, Wayne and Ludie Belle said much the same, and Billy Don pointed out that Pach's handgun, driver's license, and utility knife were in the van when they burned it. Seems like he'd have taken those things along if he was planning on joining up with the bikers. He said Pach' was pretty ticked off, all right, and he might have liked to kill Young Abner, but he didn't think he would ever do anything to hurt Elaine, which was what Ben believed. And then Ludie Belle told him about Mrs. Edwards' apocalyptic angels story and pointed out there was no place for Carl Dean in that colorful gang. Like as if, in Sister Debra's lively imagination, he wasn't really there, no matter what she says to the contrary. So that's what he wanted to know about.

She said she was so terrified, it was like everything was speeded up and stopped dead at the same time, like it can happen sometimes in nightmares, but she did have the memory that that short bearded man with the pockmarked face, whoever he was, was there somehow, though sometimes it was like he wasn't. When they were burying the body, for example, he didn't seem to be there. Burying the body? I think it was a body, she said, though it wasn't very big. But it was heavy. An animal maybe. This was before what happened to Elaine. She stumbled upon them during her dawn prayers and just froze. She was so scared. But it was dark and they were drinking and didn't see her. They had shovels. Why had she never said this before? She didn't know. Somehow it was just coming back. Like she'd been too afraid to remember before. The ugly one with the beard may have organized everything and stayed in the background, so she didn't see him at first. Maybe he had always been one of them and had infiltrated the camp under false pretenses. Colin said he wasn't who he said he was. No, Ben told her gently. That was Carl Dean Palmers. Sure of that much. Ben had put her underwear in a plain brown envelope and he handed the soft packet to her now. She didn't open it, just started crying, couldn't stop, was soon hiccupping with her sobs. He said he was sorry and left her there. He had more questions, but they'd have to wait.

But that explained some things. Why they were burying the body at the camp, Ben has no idea, though, since they may have been lying in wait for Junior and Elaine, it might have been a two-birds-with-one-stone thing. The sheriff found a stolen station wagon later that morning over near the mine—apparently they'd taken the brake off and rolled it down the hill—and it was likely they used it to haul the body here. Made less noise than their motorcycles, too. Accounts for their quick getaway when he and the others rushed down there. Ben doesn't have much to go on, but he supposes from Mrs. Edwards' story that the burying must have happened near where he found the flowery drawers. The grave's probably not too deep, something they dug in a hurry. The trowel he has brought along should be enough. He's fearful of unearthing a decomposing body, only hoping she's right and it's just an animal. But where to start? Everything looks wet and settled, the ground back here in the trees covered with bushes and dead leaves. Could take him weeks, and even then he might miss it. Then he sees it. An area blanketed with dead maple leaves. But under an oak tree. He carefully clears the wet leaves away and finds the patch of disturbed earth where nothing new is growing yet, slightly sunken. About the size of Rocky's grave, too small for a grown person. A child? A severed head? The thought of digging up such a thing sends a shudder down his spine. Maybe he should turn this over to Sheriff Puller, he thinks, even as he begins to drive his trowel into the wet soil. But what he finds is not a child. Not a body at all. It all begins to make sense. He remembers now the rumors going round before they left. But why here? Because no one would think to look here. Which means they most likely didn't know Junior and Elaine would turn up, not wanting anyone to know they'd been here. It also means they're planning to come back. He could report it, but it would throw suspicion on him and the camp, might draw state and federal authorities to the area. They never said anything to any outsiders about the rape, wanting to protect Elaine, so there'd be a lot of explaining to do. They'd want to pin the theft on somebody, and the bikers aren't around, and they know he and the others have been seen over there around the mine buildings, not to mention the gatherings of all of them on the hill. Which weren't themselves completely legal, as he understands it from all the disputation. There are people who mean them harm and want to be rid of them and they could use this as an excuse. But he can't leave it where it is. What if they came back? It weighs too much to move any distance. He'd need help and that would mean telling somebody, and he doesn't want to do that. Not yet. It's hard work with nothing but a trowel, but he can shift it far enough that it won't be easy to find.

When he has done that and refilled and covered up the old place like it was before, he heads back to the house trailer. It's late in the day. The trailer's empty. Clara and Elaine are gone. He sees Mabel Hall through the kitchenette window hurrying over from her caravan looking fretful. His chest tightening, he steps outside to meet her.

I have not been a good mother. This is the despairing thought that Clara, seated beside her daughter's hospital bed, is thinking. I have not paid enough attention. Though it is to herself she speaks, praying the while for guidance and forgiveness, she hopes Ely is listening. She does not feel him nearby, has not for some time now, but she believes he must be, for Elaine's sake if not her own. They both need him now. Clara has given herself heart and soul to her church mission, which she has always thought of as Ely's mission, too, and Elaine's as well, her task to guide her daughter, hand in hand, toward redemption, the end so near upon them. But there was always so much to do, Elaine's hand was not in hers too much of the time—how much of her devotion to this sacred calling, she wonders, has been worldly pride and vanity?—and now see here, her emaciated child, broken, embittered, lost, her hands shackled, her nose violated by the tube that, seemingly against her will, is keeping her alive. Often during the past few weeks, watching her daughter's frightening decline, beset by doubt and weariness, Clara has thought she should ask someone else to take over. Hiram maybe. Or her new director of National Media, the bishop of the Eastern Seaboard. She even had a word with him about it. Did Jesus' mother, cradling her son's ravaged body, suffer the same doubts, the same regrets? What, at such a moment, does one care about the salvation of the world? She wishes she still had that little porcelain statue of Mary with her bleeding heart on her breast that Elaine gave her. It would speak to her now.

Purity of heart. Something Ely once said in a sermon, asking God he be granted it, and this has been her prayer as well and is now. What Ely meant by it was doing one thing in life and doing it right. It should be a grand thing and a noble thing and a holy thing, but one thing. It's what true devotion is. On the road out east, between one church and another, she talked about it with Ben. He said he couldn't define purity, but he knew how it felt. When they moved here to the camp they had it. Often, before that, in the early years, out on the road, too. But it was gone now. It's still gone.

Bernice lifted her spectacles and took only one look at Elaine back at the trailer and said they had to get her to the hospital. Now. That child is dying. Ben was nowhere to be found. They rushed here in Bernice's car, Elaine too feeble to resist. The doctor, too, was alarmed. The nurses took measures: emergency measures that Clara should perhaps have disallowed, but she was confused, ashamed, frightened, exhausted herself, the doctor taking note of that, asking questions, personal questions that she brushed aside or answered only in part, growing angry, then apologizing for that, trying not to break into tears, her daughter needing her strength, having so little of her own.

Her worst failing: Elaine has suffered so, and she has not known how to console her.

They left the camp, went east ostensibly to visit the churches there, sing and preach in them and bring the news, but primarily for Elaine's sake, to distance her from the scene of her ordeal, spend more time together, attempt a healing. Though it was good to get back on the road again, good for her and Ben, Elaine remained tucked darkly into herself, refusing to speak, eating almost nothing. It just takes time, Clara supposed. Time and love. The movement, she saw, was strong and healthy. There were large, enthusiastic crowds wherever they went, and they even thought about settling out there, turning the Wilderness Camp over to those folks still living here. Maybe trying to build this administrative center was a mistake, for them at least; they were missionaries, not office workers. That's how they were thinking. But word got around about Elaine wasting away and people began to get curious. They started comparing her to Marcella, only a legend to them, but a saintly one, and they wanted to see her, to pray in her company and to hear what she had to say. She had nothing to say, but that seemed to fascinate them all the more. Sick people turned up, asking to be cured. It got to be a little like a traveling freak show, which is how Ben put it one day in anger, chasing a crowd of them away from their house trailer, and they decided to return to the camp, fearful of the effect it might have on Elaine but not knowing where else to go. Besides, there was the Temple of Light cornerstone laying ceremony coming up; people would not understand why she who had brought all this about was not here. Even Ely, though mostly absent, seemed to be insisting on her return. The cornerstone was his tombstone, after all. But the trip back was long and Elaine, now refusing to leave her bed, worsened by the hour, as if the camp, as they drew nearer to it, were drawing the lifeblood out of her.

Ben arrives. He brings a chair over and sits beside her and takes her hand and asks clumsily how the girl is. He can see how she is. "How is it that something so good and holy can turn so bad?" he asks, not of her, just of the room. Of God. "I don't hardly know what to do," he says. And then he starts to cry. And she starts to cry. And they sit there for a while, two old people, weeping.

"Boy, this little lady kin sure flap, rare back'n cut down on a ballad! Jist give her a buncha words'n git outa the way! 'The Trailer Camp Blues!' So new it ain't hardly got notes yet and ye heerd it here first in the ole Blue Moon, hottest spot the back side a Nashville! 'Lost her name in a poker game!' But she ain't lost hers! Patti Jo Glover, folks, that's whom she am! That's right, give her a big hand, lemme hear it! I *love* her! And hey, ifn y'ain't lovin', y'ain't livin'! Am I right? So kiss a face there! Go ahead! Won't do ye no more harm'n a fever blister! And dontcha leave now, ya big sissies, hang in there to the end, cuz we got another big clump a Sattiday night honkytonk, hankypanky, hoedowns'n heartbreak a-comin' your way soon's we wet the whustle…

"That was beautiful, sweet thing! Y'really crunched it! Done me proud!"

"Well, I wish I could sing, Duke, and not only hoot and yip. Funny how you can make something just about bearable by only singing about it. And this one's kinda comical like I guess my life was, though it didn't feel like it at the time. Thanks for that. And thanks for the beer, too."

"Thank the feller who runs this flophouse. The beers're on him, and whatall else we hanker after. It's the big crowds we been pullin' in since we teamed up. Folks is comin' from all over the acreage. Kitchen's hummin' and the bar cain't stock in enough. Him and me we had a talk, and he's uppin' our wages, too. You ain't singin' fer free no more. And Will Henry says he knows a feller runs a record company who might wanta come fer a listen."

"Oh…"

"Whatsamatter, little darlin? Thought that'd set y'dancin'. Sumthin gotcha feelin' blue?"

"I'm happier than I ever been in my life, Duke. I'm so happy it sometimes makes me sad. But, well, I don't know, it just feels so unreal. You know. Life out at the camp, kneel down to Jesus, hooray for poverty, the end of the world and all that, and then us here in the Moon drinking beer and talking honkytonk careers. I'm sorta lost and I don't know if Marcella knows what to make of it neither."

"She been talkin' to ye?"

"Well, sure, in her way, most all the time. She's worried about all the problems out there, the way things are breaking up and turning quarrelsome, and about whether the little Collins girl is gonna live or die and just what's apt to happen tomorrow out on the mine hill, after all that young Darren has done to fever up anticipations and what with the troubles the Baxter people been causing, who knows what they may do next, but maybe that's just me worrying and she's worrying on account of I'm worrying."

"That's a most entertainin' notion, Patti Jo. A worried mind inside a worried mind. Ifn I knowed how t'write it in a song, I surely would."

"What I can't figure out is exactly why I'm here. Marcella must of drawed me back because she wants something, something to help her find peace, but I don't know what it is."

"She was your best pal, Patti Jo. Her family's all gone. You're what-all she's got now."

"You mean, she just wanted my company? She's not that selfish. Wasn't when I knew her anyhow. And anyway we were kinda keeping company already before I come back. Has to be more than that."

"Well, she mighta only wanted you to have a sweeter life than you been livin'."

"I thought of that. And I think it's partly true. It don't seem a complete accident you and me met up. But that's got done, and she still don't want to let me go. For one thing, I think I have to stay now till the Collins girl gets better, and the way she is, that may never happen. Bernice says she's real bad off, and Mabel is almost afraid to look at her cards. And it's like if I go, she'll surely die. I had a dream last night about her and Marcella. They were in a playground, playing like

Marcella and me used to do. Jacks and stuff. And then Elaine was in a swing and Marcella was pushing her. She kept going higher and higher and I could see if she went any higher she'd tip over and fall out. I was scared and I ran over and asked Marcella to please stop. She opened her mouth but nothing came out, she could only shake her head. She was as scared as I was, but she kept pushing like she couldn't stop herself. I knew she wanted me to help, but I couldn't. It was like my arms weighed a ton. I woke up all in a sweat, tied up in the sheets. I probably cried out and I was afraid I mighta waked you up, but you were sawing them off. Softly, though. It was kinda more like humming."

"I was probly conjurin' up a new song. Wisht I coulda wrote it down."

"You were laying on your stomach. Light from the parking lot was making your butt glow in the dark. It was beautiful. And a solace to me. I leaned over and kissed it for luck."

"That musta been when I got the rhyme. I don't recollect what it was rhymin' with, but the answer was Patti Jo."

"It helped me get back to sleep again. But now I keep seeing Marcella's face when she turned to stare at me. Like she's right in front of me. Her little gold cross on a chain around her neck, glittering in the sun. Her ears sticking out a little. The scared begging look in her eyes. Her mouth open, trying to talk. And Elaine way up above us, about to come falling down."

"Now, that's sumthin t'ponder. Not jist a fallen angel, but havin' one land on ye like a frigerator. Near as bad as gittin' stars in your eyes. Well, when you're low or feelin' fearful, honey, you jist keep smoochin' my butt, and I guarantee things'll turn up rosy!"

"It might help if I knew where she was resting. One thing I wanted to do right off when I got here was go put some flowers on her grave. But no one seems to know where it is. I went down to city hall and told them I was a friend of the family, a distant relative, but they said there wasn't much of that family left and they had no idea where anybody was. They kept eyeing me in a funny way, but finally said I should go ask Monsignor Baglione at the Catholic church. Father

Bags has been here forever, a disgusting old priest with an unwashed old man stink about him. He still doesn't speak much English and my Italian is mostly cusswords, but I was able to tell him directly who I was and why I was looking, figuring he was obliged not to tell anyone. He didn't know where she was buried neither, only that she'd been excommunicated and so wasn't in San Luca, and said I should ask down at city hall."

"They's some folks out to the church camp reckon she got dreckly transported."

"Took the body and left the voice behind, you mean? I've still got enough R. C. in me to find those rapturing ideas too much like something outa kids' comicbooks."

"Y'know, they's a gent sometimes comes in I could ask. Five-by-five squinty-eyed feller with a fat nose and a buncha chins, you may a seen him. He's the fire chief now, but he useta be the mayor some years back, so all that mighta probly happened on his watch. He mostly only turns up midweek when they's not so many people, usually with some wore-out ole bag or another. Got no idea what he does with 'em. On dead nights, when he's on his lonesome, he sometimes buys me a drink at the bar and gits t'talkin' in his sad comical way. I'll tell him a friend's inquirin' but I won't say who. An ole boyfriend or sumthin. But fer now, dear lady, the herd's a-gittin' restless. Time t'crank up another round."

"Okay. At least we don't have to do 'White Dove' anymore. Looks like that bird's kicked the bucket."

"No, them two kids're here. I seen 'em. He's drivin a sporty cherry-colored ragtop now. But they don't have time fer warmups no more. It's jist straight inta the dugout'n play ball!"

"Time for 'Baby, Let's Play House,' you mean."

"Or jist 'A Whole Lotta Shakin' Goin' On.' But you got me in a lovin' mood, Patti Jo. My butt's not customed to such tensions and it's still jist a-tinglin' like a little kid suffrin' first love. Let's do Hank's 'Baby, We're Really in Love.'"

"'I Love You So Much It Hurts.'"

"'I'm Losin' My Mind over You.'"

"'Lovesick Blues.' I really love to hear you yodel that one."

"Cuz it's bubblin' up from the heart, little darlin'. Or from somewheres in that genral neighborhood. You call 'em as we go. We'll close with the house theme'n let that rainbo-ho-ho turn the clouds away!"

Stealthily, they enter the camp just after midnight. Ten of them. On the blind side, near the Field of Transcendence, as he taught her to call it. Now that of his suffering, his mutilation. His Field of Affliction. He is the one who knows the routes in and out of the camp in the dark and is their leader. His father is not here, *he* is Abner Baxter. There are armed guards—he has warned them about that—but they are armed, too. They carry warning whistles that sound like owl hoots in case something goes wrong. It was how he and the girl called to each other. She who is nameless now. Who makes him sick for what happened to her. Angry. She didn't even try to stop them. It was like she wanted it to happen. The weather has been wet and drizzly the past couple of days. He can feel the damp working its way into his sneakers and socks, creeping up his pantlegs. But it provides a better cover for them. Sounds are dampened as well and the guards will be under shelter somewhere.

Their own encampment was a target last night. Each attack by old man Suggs' raiders has been more savage than the one before and last night's could have been bloody. His father had moved them defiantly onto the forbidden campground and many others had joined them. From town, from other campsites, from Chestnut Hills, Randolph Junction. Ready for whatever. Martyrdom maybe. But when a tip about the upcoming raid reached them, Young Abner suggested that they abandon the field for a few hours, hide their vehicles, return after the danger had passed. He had read about something like this in a Bible story. A tactic for a smaller force to frustrate an attack by a larger force without losing any ground. His father, his dander up, preferred a head-on collision, but the majority sided with Young Abner, and so they all melted away into the woods around. It worked. As soon as the raiders had given up and gone home, they were back and setting up camp again. There will be reprisals and there will not always be advance warnings, but last night was a kind of victory for them. And for him. Just desserts for the adversity he's been through.

He knows that, like Timothy, he must endure hardness as a good soldier of Christ Jesus and be strong in Jesus' grace, for if you suffer for righteousness, you will be blessed. But what he was put through was totally unfair. It hurt more than anything had ever hurt before. Then that humiliating scene up at the camp in front of everybody. They were so stupid, so uncaring, so wrong about everything. After that, the wounds on his head began to fester and he was sick for a while, and even now there is a nasty itch there that reminds him of his brother's cruelty. Baptism by the knife: He seems to remember hearing Nat say that and then laugh. Punishment was visited upon the entire family and many of their friends after that, they were all expelled from the camp and sent out into the fields, and for a time he was blamed. His father was especially upset about the girls' underpants, and he suffered anger and ridicule. He felt like Daniel in the lions' den. What if Daniel had got thrown to the lions in girls' underpants? What then? Would they have laughed and scorned?

Over time, however, they began to see his side of it. How he was victimized. Lured to the field. Ambushed. Tortured. Made to wear the underpants. Last night, Jewell Cox blamed it all on Clara Collins' pride, and Roy Coates said the girl was just asking for it. Young Abner should not have let her talk him into such wickedness, old man Coates said, but you could see how you could be tempted to whip the brat. He felt like whipping her himself. And his father, after pouring out his wrath on Nat and Paulie, acknowledged that the expulsion had strengthened them. There were more followers now, more true believers, more baptisms by fire. Many of these people had given up everything to make the journey here; they were faithful Brunists and did not deserve this treatment. His father above all. "He's the West Condon bishop and he ain't done nothing!" Ezra Gray declared last night, full of fury, rattling his wheelchair, and Jewell said, "Nat and Paulie is only boys. They must of fell under the evil influence a thet ex-con Palmers, or whoever he was." "They went bad a long time before that," his father said grumpily, his face scowling up like it used to do before meting out the family discipline. This was out under the tent, after the failed raid on their encampment, after they'd set everything up again and were feeling good and congratulating him on his shrewdness. It was when he proposed tonight's counterattack on the Wilderness Camp. His father was hesitant, but Roy and Jewell backed him, and pretty soon they had volunteers. More than they needed. There's a big ceremony out on the Mount of Redemption tomorrow, and they've not been invited. Has to do with those temple-building plans that have so outraged his father. The thoughts of those in the camp will be on that; good time to catch them unawares.

The plan is to cut off the phones and electricity. It might have been easier to do at the old mine, where the lines come from, but there have been workers over there on the mine hill all day—a lot of digging going on—and old man Suggs probably has people guarding the machinery, which is lit up. Hard to get up there unseen. So they accepted Young Abner's idea of sneaking into the dark side of the camp. The barbed-wire fence has been extended past where Nat entered, but there's a gap further down through which they've come, crawling through the thick growth of honeysuckle and high weeds. Young Abner has spent a lot of time mapping the camp out, knows its soft points. He'd like to do something awful to the girl, whom he thinks of as having betrayed him—whip her where it hurts—but the trailer parking lot is too exposed. At least with the lights on. The Coates boys, Royboy and Aaron, pushing at each other, have got into some kind of stupid argument and can't seem to keep their mouths shut in spite of everybody shushing them. Their father Roy gets fed up and gives Aaron such a fierce clout across the ears that he yelps out, and Young Abner has to blow his owl whistle to cover it up. Aaron mutters something and gets another blow from his father on the back of his head that sends him sprawling in the wet grass and this time he shuts up. They creep toward the creek. They can make out one or two of the post lamps through the trees. Maybe we should just knock out the bulbs, Royboy whispers, but Isaiah Blaurock shakes his head, puts his finger to his lips, and slips away into the trees, heading toward the center of the camp. Nobody moves. Dead silence. Even the Coates boys are holding their breath. Nothing happens for what seems like hours. A couple of their group have quietly backed out the way they came.

Suddenly there's a loud pop and fizz like a firecracker going off. Then darkness. It had seemed like darkness before, but they'd actually been able to make out something of the ground at their feet, the trees beyond, and he realizes the pale light they'd had before was from the camp lamps reflected in the drizzle. They're gone now and it's pitch black. "I cain't see nuthin," Royboy Coates complains and a shot rings out. "Dad, I'm hit! Oh shit!" It's Royboy's brother Aaron. "Oh! Oh! Help!" He's crying.

They all open fire. Young Abner is shooting, too, but he doesn't know what at. Just into the night, where the streetlamps used to be. He's blowing the whistle, as if anyone shooting will think he's only an owl. Somebody passes him silently on the way out. Isaiah. Tugs on his sleeve. Roy Coates stumbles by, his wounded son over his shoulder like a sack of meal. "C'mon! Let's get goin'!" he grunts. Young Abner's already on his way, the rest following his lead as more shots crackle in the night.

No one has slept all night. Except Willie Hall, who seemed not to know what happened. When told of the overnight attack on the camp, he cried out, "Lordy lord! The enemy hath smoten our life clean down to the ground! He's made us t'dwell in the dark like as those as has been long dead!" For some reason this recital seemed to cheer everyone up, and though somewhat shaken still by the explosive rattle and complete loss of power (the phone lines are out, too, as they'd discovered upon trying to reach the sheriff), they began to get on with the dawning day. Which is possibly the most important date in Brunist history. Or maybe not. Darren is beginning to see weak points in his calculations. Moments when he generalized or extrapolated or slid over difficulties. He was only trying to help. People expect too much. He may have made an error. He is looking for alternative interpretations of what he has collected so far, just in case.

It was what he was doing when the attack happened. Billy Don was on guard duty, so Darren could turn the lights on in the cabin, work at his table. He was listening again to the recordings of the Voice in the Ditch, and just as he leaned in close to the speakers, intent on hearing any least whisper, a sudden explosion dumped him to the floor and the lights went out. He couldn't see a thing. His heart was pounding. Was it after midnight? Maybe it was already happening! It felt like something in a dream and for a moment he thought that he *was* dreaming and he tried to wake up. He was startled by a loud knock on the window, like somebody hitting the closed wooden shutter with a hammer. Were they trying to break in? He heard shouts. He recognized some of the voices, crawled over to where the door should have been, and when he found it, opened it a crack and peeked out. Total darkness, but he could see movement. People running around in their pajamas and underwear—some of the men had rifles, which they fired into the woods, toward the creek. A mad hooting of owls somewhere. Flickering light in the cabin next door: candles. He slipped over there, ducking low, found Mrs. Edwards trying to soothe a distraught Colin dressed in nothing but his limp skivvies, howling something about black fire. Darren talked to Colin to calm him down and doing that calmed him down, too. He borrowed a candle from the grateful Mrs. Edwards and returned to his cabin, staying low. Black fire: Colin knew! Billy Don returned, wide-eyed, breathing heavily. "We hit one of them," he said. "But they got away." They stayed up the rest of the night talking about it. They sometimes dozed only to wake again at the slightest sound. He felt, in a sense, his prophecy had already come true. Except that it was not an act of God. Just hecklers. Vandals. More like a prelude. A fanfare. There had to be more to come.

When dawn leaked through the morning gloom, Darren discovered that the awning shutter had been struck by a bullet. The loud bang he had heard. Closing the shutter last night may have saved his life. The telephone lines had been cut and the electrical system shorted out. Wayne said the problem may go all the way back to the supply. He and his crew had already begun to work, but a lot of damage had been done, and he let people know it was going to take them a full day's work, which meant, with today's ceremonies over at the Mount, power wouldn't be back on until at least tomorrow. It was a setback, but they had lived without electricity until two months ago, they could live another day without it now. Ludie Belle announced that the Sunday dinner menu would be changed to include as many of the refrigerated perishables as possible. Billy Don said he knew of a pay phone in Tucker City where he could try to call the sheriff's office, and people chipped in some coins for him to use. The sheriff turned up soon after with some of his officers and they examined the sabotage and talked with Welford and Wayne about how it might have been done. A lot of shots had been fired and they found evidence of that. Darren showed them the window shutter. The sheriff sent someone to ask at the hospital if anyone had been treated for a bullet wound. One. A young man named Aaron Coates. A hunting accident. That was all Sheriff Puller needed. He and his troops swooped down on the Baxter encampment, and according to the reports now coming back to the camp, arrested several persons, including Abner himself. Also, in West Condon: Roy Coates and his two sons. They are being charged with trespassing, destruction of private property, disturbing the peace, and attempted murder.

In spite of the intrusion, the Brunists feel that God is watching over them, and they decide to go ahead with their plans to hold the Sunday morning church services over on the Mount of Redemption, followed immediately by the cornerstone laying. The sheriff has promised police protection and Bernice has agreed to stay with Elaine at the hospital to allow Clara to attend. Afterwards, they will return to the camp to continue to work together on the repairs. It's the Sabbath, but this is God's work, and everyone is eager to get on with it.

* * *

Mr. Suggs' crews have already dug a trench outline of the cross-shaped temple site on the hillside, marking the area to be excavated for the foundations, filling it with chalk, and it is larger than anyone has expected. It stirs excitement and people walk all around it as if for luck. Darren does, too. He notices the people watching him. He stands in the middle of the cross and looks around, trying to imagine the tabernacle church in place. Others do the same. They have also dug a special hole for the Ely Collins tombstone, which will serve as the church cornerstone, and an empty grave in front of it where his remains will be laid to rest. The tombstone will be brought later by Mr. Suggs, who will attend the morning service.

They feel somewhat exposed this morning on the Mount and are eager to get back inside the relative safety of the camp again, so they begin the church service as scheduled, even though Mr. Suggs has not yet arrived. Will Henry has joined them, and he and Duke and Patti Jo lead everyone in singing "I Shall Not Be Moved" and "Work for the Night Is Coming." They ask Ben to join them for his own Brunist hymn, "The Circle and the Cross," and he does so, though it's clear the old man's thoughts are elsewhere. There are over seventy people at the service, including Brunists from West Condon and Randolph Junction and other towns around, but they are not using any amplification, and even when they all stand and sing together, it's hard to hear anyone but oneself out here on the open hillside. "March on, march on, ye Brunists!" they sing, trying their best to lift spirits. "Forever shall we live! The Cross within the Circle will us God's glory give!" They give thanks to Jesus for the safe return of Ben and Clara and they pray for the rapid recovery of Elaine and for the protection of their Wilderness Camp, which has become a holy place for them all, sanctified by their own honest labor. Clara and Ben will conduct the cornerstone ceremonies, though Ben says the new song he promised for the occasion, "The Tabernacle of Light," is not ready. Darren has been asked to speak about the day's special meaning as a part of the dedication, and he listens carefully to everything sung and said, looking for some way to shape his remarks and prepare them all for another seven-week wait for…for whatever. The sign. He knows they are all desperate for justifying news. It will not be easy. Prophecy is not about what is wanted but what will be. A thought for his mental note pad—the sort of thought that must have gone through Jesus' head in his own time. Of course, Jesus was the Son of God, but so is everyone else, and Jesus, too, was known to have suffered doubts. Darren feels, as he has often felt, at one with Him. And he has been praying to Him now, asking for His help…

The carpenter and beekeeper, Cecil Appleby, reads from Paul's letter to the Ephesians: "Now therefore ye are no more strangers and foreigners, but fellow citizens with the saints, and of the household of God; and are built upon the foundation of the apostles and prophets, Jesus Christ himself being the chief cornerstone; in whom all the building fitly framed together groweth unto a holy temple in the Lord, in whom ye also are builded together for a habitation of God through the Spirit." He stares at his hands for a while, and then he commences to speak to God in his quiet prayerful way, which is his way of preaching a sermon. "Dear God. Hear us, Your humble servants. Our hearts are full today of hope. And fear. Of joy. And sorrow. Of certainty. And doubt. We thank You for the one, ask forgiveness for the other. We are only who we are. Sinners seeking Your eternal company. We are weak and ask for strength. We are slow of mind and ask for the grace of understanding. We are lonely and afraid and ask for Your protective love. We believe in You and in Your son and in the Holy Spirit, and in the resurrection of the body and life everlasting, as promised us by the Holy Scriptures and by Your son, Jesus Christ. In this, we have a simple and abiding faith. We believe that our own Prophet was granted by the Holy Spirit a vision of the last times, which we believe are soon, and we are preparing for them as best we are able. It is what has drawn us here to pitch our tent in the wilderness. When King David ordered the building of a temple for his son, Solomon, he ordered that it be exceedingly magnificent. We are not so proud. Our little

Coming of the Light Tabernacle Church will be an expression only of our humble love for You. We are grateful for having our Evangelical Leader here with us on this moving occasion. We miss her so when she is gone, Lord. Her faith and nobility anchor us. Please keep her well and always near us and give her strength and heart through this difficult time. We grieve for her child, o Lord, who has suffered so greatly, and who is now so in need of Your saving grace, Your close loving attention. Please, have mercy on her. Take whom You wish, but we beg You to spare the child. Take me, o Lord, but spare the child. We also ask mercy and forgiveness for the young man wounded last night. He was misled. No one should set brother against brother. Guide him to the truth, o Lord, and all those about him, and forgive them, as You guided and forgave the brothers of Joseph. They have rendered our little settlement powerless and without communication to the outside world; but You are our power, o Lord, and we need none other. It is to You we…"

Cecil Appleby pauses, raises his head. Has he heard something? He has. A voice at the bottom of the hill. It is Bernice Filbert, crying out. She is running up the hill, her long skirt pulled up to her knees, her car door flung open behind her. Clara blanches, staggers, takes an unsteady step toward Bernice. Ben rushes to Clara's side.

Bernice seems to hear the unspoken question, asked silently and in fear by all: "No, no!" she shouts, clambering up the hill. "It ain't Elaine! It's Mr. Suggs! He's had a powerful stroke! They think he'll die!"

So there it is. The terrible but justifying sign. All turn in awe and expectation toward Darren, where he stands, somehow apart, not far from the open grave. He remembers that cold wind he seemed to feel when he stepped across those half-sunken footstones in the old cemetery; he feels it again. He nods and knows he has nothing more to do or say. His nod suffices.

# III.5

## Monday 8 June – Wednesday 17 June

Money. What is it? He doesn't know. He defines himself by it, but it's still a mystery. Like the Holy Spirit. It exists and doesn't exist. You have to take it on faith. If it were more visible, more logical, it might not work. But it's completely irrational. We use numbers to mask that, make it seem to add up. Calculations as litanies, incantations. Credit as the dispensation of grace. A delusion that works. Stacy's definition of religion. Not his, but he can live with it. That people see money as the very opposite of the Holy Spirit, as something diabolical, also makes sense. Money as Mammon. Trying to do good with it is mostly a losing proposition. What's happening here in the bank. Big mistake. Or, rather, "good" in finance means something else. The Golden Rule doesn't operate here. Misguided generosity is a kind of wickedness. Loose morals. Failure to foreclose is an infidelity. But if "good" is not the same thing as the Golden Rule, it's not the opposite either. The system requires exchange to work, and exchange involves give-and-take. Some kind of honor code. I'll believe if you believe, I'll spend if you'll spend. It's how we keep ticking along, using up the world. Misers are sinners who constipate the system. To win it all is to lose it all. Sweeping the Monopoly board is like the end of the world; to continue, you have to redistribute and start over. Another Big Bang, so to speak. Expand and contract, expand and contract, the eternal cycle of the universe. Same as the business cycle. You can't legislate it—there's nothing there to legislate—but you can profit off the swings. If you're a believer. Like Paul said, you have to believe the unbelievable. Become a fool to become wise. A fool for Christ is not unlike a fool for money. That is to say a successful banker. Or a fool for love. Also a mystery. As Stacy wistfully said, laughing at his Monopoly board apocalypse. But also crying a little. Her longing for him is so intense it sometimes frightens him. Talk of leaving has ended. She now has no autumn plans. She has told Mrs. Battles she'll be staying. You must have noticed, she said, ducking her head and leaning into his chest, I've completely surrendered. As has Ted. Long since. Was only waiting for her to catch up. Never let himself be a fool before. Wiser now.

She enters the office with an application needing his signature. Displaying upright bank floor demeanor, knowing she is being watched. No eye contact. Only her flush gives her away. Deep into her throat. And the bluesy tune she is humming between closed lips. One of theirs. What is it? Hah: Baby, Knock Me a Kiss. Ted hopes his grin looks more like a boss's approving smile and flips the top page of the application over as though studying it. "It's okay, Mr. Cavanaugh," she says crisply. "Just sign it before my knees give way." She leaves primly, as though faintly exasperated, but twitches her hips slightly at the doorway like a backsided wink. What has he just signed? He doesn't know. Happy as a pup. Another of their songs.

One condition of surrender: give up his obsession with the cult. He can do this. The world's a crazy place, as unmanageable as economic cycles. Let it be. Suggs moved his heavy yellow backhoes onto the mine hill Friday, began chewing up the hillside. An outrage. There are pending legal actions, even their ownership of the hill is in question. It was like a dare: stop me if you can. Ted had learned they were having some kind of ceremony over there yesterday, the laying of a cornerstone or something. There must be a way. Stacy pleaded. Don't let it spoil our weekend. He hesitated. For a moment he felt that football in his hands again, had his fingers on the laces. But he smiled, shrugged, booted it out of sight. Felt good. That game's over. Whistle blown. With Tommy, Concetta, and her widow friend Rosalia sharing the home care duty, Saturday was a night in the city ("important meeting with investors"), yesterday a long drive in her car, a walk in the hills. Wet but beautiful. Maybe their most beautiful time together so far. They drove leisurely over into the next state, where they could wander around, hand-in-hand, unafraid of being recognized, then, somewhat more urgently, back to the motel. They got caught in a downpour between the parking lot and the room, so they shed their wet clothes, showered together, and spent a couple of delicious late afternoon hours in each other's arms, lit only by the soft forgiving light flowing in through the wet windows and falling upon them like a kind of benediction. Divine sanction. What divinity, he couldn't say. The days are long now. They dressed by that light for supper.

Nick Minicozzi drops down from his office upstairs, closes the door behind him when he enters. He has news. John P. Suggs is in the hospital. Intensive care. Catastrophic stroke. In a coma. Not expected to pull through. The Collins girl is there, too. She has apparently been starving herself to death. A kind of hunger strike against God for not bringing on the Second Coming, or something. And six men are in jail, charged by the sheriff with various crimes against the Brunist encampment. Apparently their power and phone lines got cut over the weekend. One of the arrested, a young guy, has a bullet wound, and another is Reverend Abner Baxter.

Even before he has fully absorbed it all, Ted is reorganizing his campaign. Breakthrough! He and Suggs have been playing "king of the hill" all spring and the coal baron has been beating him at every move; Ted had all but abandoned the field. Now things have suddenly changed. Pat is a stubborn autocrat, has no partners, only employees, disdains lawyers. It should be easy to tie up his headless empire in litigation, bring an end to the Brunist nightmare. And they seem to be fighting among themselves, making it even easier. He and Nick review all the legal actions they've been taking. Nick promises to follow up aggressively. Put on the blitz. "Especially hit hard on the money and property issues." Maybe they can not only wrest the Deepwater land away from them, but might even repossess the camp itself, reactivate it now that it's fixed up. Summer camp for the whole area.

"Who manages Suggs' mining company?"

"The site boss is a guy named McDaniel. Not from around here."

"See if you can reach him. Tell him he has to get those backhoes off the hill today or risk impoundment. Launch a suit that would force them to refill all the holes and trenches they've dug. And let him know you're doing it."

Even as he talks with Nick, he's on the phone. Getting the word out. Fashioning moves. Power plays. He makes one-on-one appointments with all the members of the West Condon Ministerial Association. Books announcement times with Rotary and the BPW, the Masons, the Knights of Columbus. The Fourth of July is coming up. In years past, they held an all-county parade here in town. Could revive that. Find some famous guests—like a pro ballplayer or a movie actor—try to lure the governor down. Book a carnival, organize picnics and ballgames, hold raffles, throw a spectacular fireworks display. Theme of Unity. Progress. New Opportunities for West Condon. Bring in that city group buying the old hotel. The Italian-American angle. Brighten up Main Street. Restore the community spirit. He asks the NOWC steering committee to meet Wednesday in the old Chamber offices. Starting late. They need six months, have one. Have to work hard at this.

Then it's off to the police station and jail, the hospital, see where the pieces lie. On the way out the door, his glance meets hers, sees the flicker of disappointment. The fool for love has lost his way again. He shrugs, shakes his head. Sorry. Can't help it. Have to do this.

"Numbers," Sally Elliott says, blowing smoke out over the porch railing, clouding the day. Ostensibly, she's here to borrow Tommy's cameras for a wedding she's been asked to photograph. "Mathematics." It's Monday, his day off from the pool. Summer coming all over itself.

Angela is working at the bank, he has the whole sweet top-down day out to himself. Maybe, first thing, once he's got rid of Sally, he'll drag Fleet Piccolotti out of his family sausage shop to go shoot some baskets or throw a ball around. Pete's down on life, a side of him he didn't see back in high school. It probably wasn't there. Marriage, family have infected him with it, shopkeeping has. No easy cure, but sinking a few might cheer him up. "A kind of wizardry built on the void. Starts with zero the way religions start with God. Neither exist, but you can build a whole system." She's trying to impress him with what she knows about the Brunists, mostly things she's learned from that wall-eyed kid with the droopy handlebars. If he can be trusted. Is she fucking him? Probably. There's a bit of a breeze. He can hear the flag flopping about lightly above the porch roof. Traditionally it was Tommy's duty to raise and lower it every day, but now he and his dad are both busy and preoccupied, so it stays up. When it comes down after Labor Day the house looks naked without it. Like it has lost its loin cloth or something. "Add in fantasy calendrics, a mysterious voice in a ditch, magic numbers and prophetic tombstones, and anything can happen, anything can be true."

He knows she'll turn all this into a thumbnail history of Christianity. She can be pretty funny, but sometimes it's hard to figure out what the joke is. Well, she reads books. Her T-shirt is about all he'll read today. He doesn't even know many who do read, not for fun. She may be the only person in town. Those he has known up at college were mostly pretty boring. Couldn't throw a ball or shoot the shit in an ordinary sort of way. Sally's different, but then she'd probably be different even if she didn't read books. On the porch table with their coffee cups and her ashtray are some old newspapers, one of which Sally says is the final edition of the *West Condon Chronicle*. She has explained all the pictures. He glanced at them. Ancient history. Vaguely remembered some of it, though at the time he wasn't paying all that much attention. Did remember that black hand. The Claw. A lot of sick jokes about it back then. All this info-gathering began with his telling her he was thinking about going on to grad school in sociology and using the

Brunists as dissertation material. That was months ago, while he was still up at school. Now he's thinking more about law school, but she only laughed when he told her and has carried on as before. Well, she's lonely—it gives her something to do.

"Now Darren has come up with a new idea," she says, lighting up again. "The preacher husband of the woman who founded the cult was killed in the mine disaster. They're apparently going to rebury him under one corner of their new church, and Darren wants to dig a hole on the other side and ask for Bruno's body back from wherever it is to put there."

"Bruno's dead? I didn't know that," he says. He's only half listening. He's wondering if he should take up pipe smoking.

"Meanwhile, he wants to fill the coffin with a tunic, a mining pick, and his seven sayings."

"His seven sayings," Tommy says, repeating her without thinking about it. A mistake. She goes on to quote them all and explain them, offering a few wiseass variants of her own.

The grass is high after the recent rain. Needs mowing. He owes his old man that much for his Bing Cherry gleaming in the driveway. Dandelions popping up everywhere, too. Have to behead the randy little suckers before they go to seed. His first sex: blowing dandelion seeds, impregnating the neighborhood. It's fun, but what's disappointing is the sad little nubbin that's left at the end, the wilt that overtakes the stem. Doesn't stop you from picking another, though, and having another blow. Maybe he should go for a drive today. Pick up a girl, someone new. A hand job on the highway with the top down, a fuck in the fields. He calls his new machine his Bing Cherry because, one, they're his favorite fruit and nearly as delicious as pussy, and two, being a poet at heart, he likes the connection to bang, bung, bong. But the car is actually more the color of pie cherries. Which are also delicious. His Cherry Pile? Fleet calls it, or him, Il Cardinale. He sometimes now calls him Holy Father. Sourly. Fleet's more like a sour cherry.

"So now, after what's happened, they're into their Hatfields and McCoys mode. Emily Wetherwax told my mother on the phone that

Archie is out at the camp this morning repairing the phone lines that got cut. Electricity's off, too. He called her from up a pole somewhere and said there'd even been some shooting over the weekend."

All in all, it's a wacky story, no doubt at least partly true. No wonder his dad wants to get rid of those wombats. The one image from her story that sticks in his head, even though it was probably made up, is of that redheaded fat boy dressed in nothing but girl's panties and dumped at his preacher father's feet like spoiled meat. Hi, Dad. Guess what? He and the girl were apparently in high school at the same time, both of them a couple of classes behind Tommy. She's a miner's kid, like Angela, but he doesn't remember her. Probably not his type. Though she was evidently Ugly Palmers' type, at least to the extent of gangbanging her with the others. Just as well the asshole didn't turn up at Lem's garage that morning; Ugly has just got uglier and was likely looking for an excuse to get into a fight.

"What if," Sally says, stubbing out her smoke, "all the madness is buried in the language and you can't get it out?"

He's not sure what she means (that voice in the ditch?), but as he finds himself staring at her FAITH IS BELIEVING WHAT YOU KNOW AIN'T SO T-shirt, he says: "In lines like that, you mean?" She stretches the shirt out away from her tits as if reading it for the first time. No bra under there. The shirt collapses back over her nipples, which are the sexiest thing about her. If Angela were wearing it, to read it you'd have to walk those hills a letter at a time. Though she never would. Not much wit in that girl. "Where do you find those funky tees, Sal? Different one every time I see you."

"I make them. But they don't hold up well in the wash."

"You made that up, too?" he asks, pointing.

"No, that's Mark Twain. Or at least he got credit for it. Goes back to the Greeks, I imagine, or more likely the Babylonians. Or the guys before them who didn't have anybody writing down what they said."

"Great. Mark Twain. You've finally named someone I've read."

"*Huckleberry Finn?*"

"No, I couldn't get through that one. *Tom Sawyer.*"

"A kind of role model, I suppose."

"I did think of him as pretty cool. And we had the same name. I especially liked the snuggle with what's-her-name in the cave. Lights out, pissing herself with terror, ready for anything. When you're ten years old, that's pretty hot stuff."

"You must have still been in your *Tom Sawyer* phase when you tried to scare the pants off me with that end-of-the-world line back in high school."

"Did I? Hah. Did it work?"

"Yes, it got me to praying. I was still in my Aunt Polly phase."

"You know, they always said that though Tom seemed like a rascal, really he was innocent. But that's not true. Really he wasn't."

"No, neither was Becky. They were both just dumb."

Ted pulls a chair up at the mayor's table in Mick's Bar & Grill and orders up the usual. Mumbled greetings around. His fellow civic leaders. They're a sorry lot, for the most part, but they're what he has to work with, and he somehow has to mold them into a team. Several of them are on the NOWC steering committee and he lets them know, over his bowl of thin flavorless soup and a grilled ham and cheese sandwich, about the meeting on Wednesday to work up new plans for the Fourth. "It's not a sure thing, but Governor Kirkpatrick is out on the hustings that day and said he'd try to fit us in." What the governor actually said was, "It's an election year, Ted. You've got problems down there. I don't want them to rub off on me." But he also needs Ted's annual contribution to his campaign fund, so he didn't say no. Mort Whimple, the fire chief, wants to know what the hell hustings are, and Elliott from his perch at the bar says muddily that it's where you graze sheep. "You know," he sings, raising his highball glass of iced gin, "'Home, home on the hustings…!'" Maury tells him Jim's workweek is now down to an hour a day, and that one not worth much. "The governor offered up some ways the state might help us out and he would use the occasion to announce them." What Kirk suggested was that they were looking for a location for a maximum security prison. It would take some selling. Doesn't exactly enhance the neighborhood, but it adds jobs. Ted replied that this was a good place for it. There was an available work force and they could also help fill it.

When he mentions inviting the new prospective owners of the old West Condon Hotel to the celebrations on the Fourth, Mayor Maury Castle mashes out his cigar and growls in his P.A. system voice: "The Roma Historical Society. Who are those guys? I got a feeling it was the Roma Historical Society just got us our new cop."

Whom Ted has seen this morning over at the police station. Vince Bonali's loutish son Charlie. Billed hat down over his nose like a Marine sergeant's, snapping his jaws and fingers, seemingly impatient with the slow pace of justice. Might be useful. Chief Romano is a weak man and things could get rough. Romano's number two, Monk Wallace, has been on the force forever and is reliable enough, but a slow-moving sort who likes to just sit and chew and watch the world go by. The other two officers are ex-miners, post-disaster charity hires—Louie Testatonda, a soft beanbag of a fellow, and the night duty cop, Bo Bosticker, a drowsy dimwit. They might need a guy like Charlie. By the time Ted arrived this morning, all those arrested Saturday night had already been released by order of deputy sheriff Calvin Smith, pending further investigations by the district attorney. All but Abner Baxter. Romano is holding him on old charges from five years ago, including jumping bail on murder charges and the destructive assault on St. Stephen's. Dee is still upset about that. Baxter could be heard railing at them from his cell, promising terrible retribution, if not in this world, then the next. When Ted asked what was going on out at the camp, the chief said that Baxter had been evicted a month or so ago over something involving his motorcycle son and his pals. That gang was gone, but the old man remained in the area and was still unloading his usual Bible-slapping crappola in the fields around. What happened Saturday night was apparently part of some kind of feud going on, and it has gotten to the point where they've started shooting at each other. One of the Coates boys ended up with buckshot in his backside and according to the sheriff a lot of shots were fired in both directions. Cause enough to close the camp down. If Puller won't do it, maybe the state will. Ted promised Dee a prosecutorial brief from the city to give him adequate cause to hold Baxter. He'd like to keep the preacher penned up and is disappointed the others have been let out. He wonders if there's some sort of discord in the sheriff's office and if there's some way to use it if there is.

Enos Beeker, the hardware store owner, asks him now if he'd heard about Pat Suggs' brain attack, and he tells them he's just come from the hospital. "He's out of intensive care and into a private room, but he has taken a crippling hit." When Doc Lewis emerged from Suggs' private room, Ted caught a glimpse of his former home care nurse, Bernice Filbert, dressed something like a World War I battlefield nurse, at Suggs' bedside. Bernice started when she saw him and hurried to close the door again. He glared at her, smiling coldly, as though to suggest she's in for it. And she is. Without Suggs' help, she's headed to prison for embezzlement and grand larceny. Burly plaid-shirted man with a thick black beard in there, too. Maudie, a nurse he knew from his own high school days, passed by and told him that was Mr. Suggs' strip mine boss, Ross McDaniel. "Hardshell libertarian," she said, inventing another sect. A cute freckle-faced kid back in school with a nice body who put out generously, something of a legend at the Baptist summer church camps out at No-Name, now as wide as she is tall, her dry hair thinning out, her freckles spreading. Still cheerful, though, as she always was, with a flair for the soap-operatic. Learned from her about the Collins girl. "When they brought her in, she looked like a skeleton with tissue-paper skin stretched over, and she's still bad off. She's trying to die. Has to be force fed."

He passes on some of this to the klatch in Mick's. Not all of it. Shaping the news to his purposes. Including in, including out. The way newspapers and news magazines work, inventing history. Something Miller said, some years ago. Probably in here, over a charred hamburger. He sure did that, damn him. His invented history is still being spun out. Miller did what he could to ruin this town and should have been tarred and feathered on his way out. Ted sometimes misses him, though.

Doc Lewis told him that Suggs had emerged temporarily from his coma, but the stroke was very severe. He asked if Ted knew of any surviving heirs. He didn't. A complete loner, far as he knew. Pat is mostly paralyzed, he learned, though he can twitch his left hand. He can open and close his eyes, but his face is frozen and he has trouble swallowing. No speech, but all the involuntary behaviors are apparently functioning, and though it's hard to be certain, deep down inside his insensible shell he still seems more or less alert. So far. As with earthquakes, there's always the fear of aftershocks. Was he a heavy drinker? "He used to be pretty wild, but he got religion. Now I hear he's a teetotaler." Lewis nodded at that. "We're starting rehab immediately, but the prognosis for recovery is not good."

Rehab is what Main Street needs, too, but same prognosis. It's a depressing sight out there. "We'll have to get rid of those boarded-up shops for the visitors on the Fourth, Maury." The mayor says sourly that it sounds like a job for the city manager. Ted expects that and ignores it. "Open them up free for craft and art shows, antique sales, club displays, get the shops that remain to put welcoming signs up for the holidays."

"Dave Osborne's already got started," says Gus Baird, the travel agent and Rotary president. "I dropped in Saturday and found him braiding all the shoestrings in the store into a single long strand. Very colorful. Says he has a birthday coming up and he's making decorations for the party. The strings are gone from all the shoes in the shop, including the ones in the window. Open boxes everywhere. Even the strings from the shoes he was wearing were gone."

The klatch finds that pretty funny. Ted has known for some time that Osborne is in trouble. At the hospital this morning, he was thinking that if Suggs died he might try to acquire the strip mine operations and move Dave out there to manage them, mining being more in his line of work. But he's evidently too late. He makes a mental note to drop by. He asks Mick for lemon meringue pie, hoping it's less than a week old, and that causes another explosion of hee-hawing laughter. He asks what's the joke and is told the story of Robbins getting slapped in the face with a slice of that pie by Prissy Tindle. Elliott clambers down off his stool to do a rubber-kneed hip- and head-wagging imitation of her performance, one hand on the bar to keep his balance. When he lets go to swing his hand through, he loses it. Hits his head on the way down, but doesn't seem to feel it. "Hoo hah!" he says from beneath the stools. "Crazy stupid cunt," Burt grumbles amid all the laughter. He still doesn't see what was funny about it, but everyone else does, including Elliott, still braying down on the floor. Beeker says he saw Prissy driving through town with a long-haired beardy guy who must have been Wes Edwards, but you'd never have recognized him. "Dancing with the dork," croons Gus Baird, rolling his eyes. Ted says his probable replacement, bright young fellow named Jenkins, would be here right after the Fourth. "We can put him up in the manse, Gus, get him used to his new home. His first pastorate. May take him a while to adjust." Elliott meanwhile has been hauling himself laboriously to his feet, grunting and farting, and he gets a round of applause when he succeeds, which he acknowledges by raising his arms and falling to his ass again and having to begin all over.

When Tommy arrives home after work on Wednesday, feeling down, the old priest is just leaving. His mom's latest holiness whim. Concetta and Rosalia are there, looking smug. He's just had trouble at the pool with Concetta's kid and his dickhead cronies. The town's bummed-out failures. There used to be mines to send them into. Now the only occupation left is street bully. The girls like to pretend to be drowning so Tommy will come out and rescue them, hug them to safety with his arm around their bosoms. He has sometimes played along, good practice, until some of the guys started imitating them, falling into the pool and floundering about comically, crying out "Help! Help! Tommy!" in falsetto voices. He tells them he's like God, it's up to him who lives or dies, and they're definitely not worth saving. Today, though,

Moroni's evil buddy, Grunge Grabowski, doing the falsetto routine, threw little Buddy Wetherwax into the deep end—and Buddy can't swim. He dove in and dragged Buddy—snorting and choking and beating on him blindly with his little fists, protesting all the way that he didn't need to be saved—over to the edge of the pool, where Babs, his big sister, squatted, waiting for him, her legs spread suggestively, a few curly auburn hairs peeking out at the swimsuit leg seams. So Tommy had to throw Moroni and his pals out. "Yeah? Let's see you try, scumbag," Moron snarled, cocking his fists, his buddies hovering close by. "Nah," Tommy said. "Not my job. I'll let the police do it. That's what they're paid for." And he went over to the emergency phone on the pole next to the lifeguard chair. With that, Moroni and his gang left, but not before Moron threatened to be waiting for him when he left the pool. He could handle Moroni, but probably not all of them, so he went ahead and called Chief Romano to tell him there might be trouble, it would be good to have someone just hanging around at closing time, and old Monk Wallace turned up and slouched at the fence, eyeing the girls and spitting into a tobacco tin.

"What's up with the priest, Mom?" He and his father both like Concetta's cooking and neither really care what religion his mother adopts next. There's no more money to squander, she can fly off to Heaven by any route she chooses. Tolerant flexibility is one of the advantages of being a Presbyterian. The priest has left behind a faint musty old man smell. "Been showing him your photo albums?"

"I was taking confession, Tommy, and having my catechism lesson. And, yes, I was showing him these pictures of my aunt's family on my mother's side who are Catholics by marriage. He looks grumpy but he's really quite nice. They call him Father Bags. Isn't that amusing?"

Those old albums have come to mean a lot to his mother in her illness, though she has also been doing a lot of damage to them, tearing up photos, sometimes whole pages. As best he can tell it's mostly his father who's getting ripped out of her story. Tommy has never paid any attention to these albums, but Sally Elliott has recently been given a tour and claims to have seen one of him at about age five with his pants down in the park having a wee wee; she was probably lying, but if it's there, he might figure out how to have some fun with it.

Fun is mostly what he's not having. Which is why he's feeling low. Not how he imagined his glorious summer after graduation. Except for the sporty new wheels with nowhere to go, sex with Angela is about it, and that's going stale. How do married people do it? Angela sets the agenda now and she doesn't give him a lot of elbow room. Babs Wetherwax lingered for a while after the pool closed this afternoon, having sent her little brother on ahead with a friend, and though it was a bit like robbing the cradle, he was tempted to invite her into the changing rooms, but Ramona Testatonda, Angela's fat spy, was also lingering, watching everything, and he wasn't yet ready to make the break. Not like that anyway. Not for a juvenile. But maybe it's about time to close down shop. He'll miss Angie's great body and all the things she does with it, but the world is full of great bodies. Bodies are the main thing it produces, and even the ones that are not great can be good for a romp, and what they don't know, they can be taught. Just thinking this way cheers him up. He'll spring it on her tonight. After the sex, of course. Thinking it might be the last time will give it a certain urgency. Might be the best night so far. Around the world in eighty ways. He's already hard thinking about it. First, though, he's overdue at Her Loins for his weekly supper with Dad. He has been skipping church. Probably in for a lecture.

Alone on a saddle stool at the steak house bar on a quiet Wednesday evening, communing with a double shot of Tennessee sour mash on the rocks. Waiting for Tommy, who is late. Coming from his lifeguard job at the pool. And probably from one pair of thighs or another. That unquiet time of life. Ted remembers it, not all that fondly. But at least he always knew who he was, where he was going, what he'd be doing. Tommy has a new plan for the rest of his life every week. Ted is concerned, sometimes irritated, tries to show neither, knowing how little it takes to set Tommy off. He needs him now. Close by. Needs him, loves him. Loves the others, too, misses them, but he feels there's a special bond between him and Tommy, something that's been there since the boy was born. If only he'd take life more seriously. Tommy loves his privileges but not their responsibility. Ted hates those who don't give a damn and worries his son is drifting down that alley. Probably just a phase. Still a kid. One day, he's certain, he'll be handing the First National Bank over to him and be proud to do so. No doubt his own father had the same worries.

Fatherhood was not something Ted thought about. It just happened. He has been grateful ever since. Three kids, all doing well. He doesn't pray much, but he thanks God for that. He has tried to talk about it with Tommy, what fatherhood means to him, but it only embarrasses the boy. He prefers to talk baseball instead. Cars. Travel fantasies. Tommy jokes about the life here. Calls the people out at the club a bunch of illiterate yoyos. Well, they are, but he hasn't earned the right to say so. He's even made some smartass remarks lately about banks and religion, calling both of them social parasites and partners in the power game. What college can do to a kid's core values. There's a sociology prof up there Ted would like to throttle. Tommy hasn't gone to church since he came home after graduation, either. Out most nights. Drinks a lot. Often testy, restless. Good with his mother, though. Patient in a way Ted finds difficult. Tommy is upset about what's happening to her, of course. It's a tough thing to deal with, part of what's making him edgy. Making them both edgy. Though with Ted there's anger, too. Instead of loving farewells at the end, there's this betrayal, bitterness, the religious madness, the shattering of their early dreams. If he were the first to go, it wouldn't be like this. His heart would be full of gratitude. Now Irene is tearing up her photo albums, their long life together apparently without value. The wedding album has disappeared altogether, the photos of him in his officer's uniform. Stripping it all away before the Last Judgment. At which, she assures him, he won't do well. Her end of the world is everybody else's end of the world. People, when they know they're going to die, can get like that. Then along comes a scheming woman like Bernice Filbert. Who's hanging out now at Pat Suggs' bedside. Someone else to get her hooks into.

Though he and Tommy are both on their own the rest of the week, usually eating at different times even when Concetta cooks up a pot of spaghetti and meatballs for them, they have set Wednesdays aside for supper together here, away from the golfing crowd, in West Condon's only claim to royalty. Sir Loin. Not that the food's much better here than it is at the Hole. The grilled steaks are usually edible after you cut away the fat, but that's about it. They come with iceberg lettuce blobbed with French dressing out of a bottle and potatoes that taste pre-baked a week before and reheated, all on the same oval platter. The dollop of sour cream and chives on the potatoes is probably the tastiest thing on offer. He always asks for extra. Well-stocked bar, though. Even a short wine list with the familiar classics. Beaujolais. Valpolicella. Liebfraumilch. Chianti in a basket. California Chablis. Mountain Red. And a pretty assortment of sweetly smiling waitresses in short skirts. Loins on view. The owner is a Rotarian, on the school board, a Methodist, has a sizable mortgage. He begged off from today's meeting of the NOWC steering committee but promised to help foot the bill for the fireworks on the Fourth. Ted feels like he's helping keep him afloat by eating here from time to time, as he and Irene used to do every other week or so. It's not far from the charred shell of the old Dance Barn just down the road. Seeing Maudie a couple of days ago reminded him of it. The big bands that came through. It was different here then.

Can't recover those old times, but things can be better. Will be. With Pat Suggs out of the way, Ted is feeling on top of the game once more. In control of the clock. Not that he wishes the man ill—tough thing, a stroke, he hopes he doesn't have to go through it himself—but before Suggs can get on his feet again, if ever, the cult will be out of here, some people will be locked away, the camp will be back in Presbyterian hands, the mine hill scramble will be ancient history, the town under Nick's sure hand back on a stable footing and free of corruption. He'll get something out of Kirkpatrick, a prison, National Guard shooting range, whatever, maybe state backing for a coal gasification project. There'll be more jobs, and more jobs make for more small businesses. Main Street will look like Main Street again. When Irene goes, he can set up Concetta with an Italian place on Main Street. She's a great cook, could feature fresh homemade pasta, give Mick some competition. One good restaurant breeds another. The street could get famous in this part of the state. Then, when the old hotel is back in operation, they could move her into it. She has kids; it could be a real old-fashioned family restaurant.

Tommy has ideas, too. Until the city consortium got interested in the old hotel, Tommy thought they should make a mining museum out of it, try to draw tourists. Ted regrets his response. What'll we have? he remembers snapping. Nothing but busloads of school children. The only new business we can hope for is a candy shop with postcards. And who gives a damn about mining history anyway except ex-miners, and they're jobless and pissed off and would just smear the place with graffiti. That was harsh. Tommy was probably hurt, though he only shrugged and walked away. Well, Ted was depressed at the time, and he apologized, told Tommy what some of the problems were. Later, they got to talking about the idea again in a new setting: How about the old mine? A tour of the horrific disaster with rides for the kids. Upgrade the hoists for a safe but scary drop into the darkness. Get the skips and shuttle cars rolling again down there and fancied up a bit like carnival rides. Everybody wearing mining helmets. Which can be purchased in the gift shop. Wax museum dioramas of the horrors of the disaster itself that light up as you pass. Empty miners' shoes and ownerless dinner buckets scattered about. Broken spectacles. False teeth. Sound effects: the explosion, the screams, the shouts. It could get famous enough to attract the whole nation. Tommy even suggested re-enacting the Brunist end-of-the-world scene on top of the hill, but Ted nixed that. Who knows what lunatics might turn up, thinking it was the real thing? Enough of that shit.

He chuckles, feeling loose and mellow, talking like a college kid. He orders up another double. Shouldn't, third already (where's the boy?), but he'll limit himself to a beer at supper. Also feeling, somewhat sweetly, melancholic. Maybe it's the tinny music on the cheap restaurant speakers. All the old songs. Nameless studio bands, but the tunes are enough. *Getting sentimental over you…* Yes, he is. Silently, he hums along. Stacy is alone tonight at Mrs. Battles' rooming house. He thinks about her there. All alone and feeling blue. She has admitted that she sometimes masturbates, longing for him when he isn't there. He imagines her doing that and it excites him—*things you say and do just thrill me through and through*—and he has to straighten up for a moment and adjust things, pretending to be reaching for his bill clip, which he sets on the bar. He has often thought to visit her there, but that would be too daring. And Mrs. B is a notorious gossip. They'll be together again tomorrow night. Soon enough. Keep it cool. What we do on Thursdays. Something Stacy says. Probably a line from some old movie. He hasn't gone to one for years, though they sometimes watch them now on the motel TV. Stacy seems to have seen them all, even the old ones. Knows the plots, likes to imagine alternative ones. That's what the movies are, she likes to say. Alternative plots. Not like life. Life has only one. That's sad. But true. Like all these songs. *All of you…* Never paid much attention to them before. Now he can name them, sing along on some of the lines. *I'd love to gain complete control of you, handle even the heart and soul of you…* Getting educated. Never too late.

Through the plate glass window with the restaurant name painted in reverse, he sees Tommy's red convertible pull into the parking lot and swing up near the window, where he can leave the top down and watch it from the restaurant. Tommy waves at him as he climbs out. A handsome boy—tall, lean, with the grace of a good athlete and a big infectious smile. Ted's chest fills with pride, love, a tinge of grief: all this will pass. He wants to hug him when he enters, and he stands, arms akimbo, meaning to do so, but instead finds himself shaking his son's hand and asking him why he's late and why he couldn't at least have changed out of his T-shirt and shorts for dinner. "Sorry, Dad. Stopped by to see Mom first and she wanted to chat. Why is she so mad at you?"

* * *

It was a mistake to come back here. Angela's idea. Another romantic Saturday night at the Blue Moon Motel with that happy couple, Monica and Pete Piccolotti, meant to stir the dying embers. More like pitching cold water on them. Fleet and Monica have been at each other since they arrived. The hayseed duo, who have gone over the top tonight with gross off-color songs about incest and bus-fucks and trailer park whores (who writes this back-alley crap? and why are all these jerks in here, including the hick in the cowboy hat who runs the local radio station, whooping it up and asking for more?), are now trying to make amends with "Have I Told You Lately That I Love You," or maybe Angela requested it. Probably. "He's cute," Monica says, nodding toward the beanpole singer. "He looks sort of like Jimmy Stewart after he's had the stomach flu for six weeks." Which is meant to be funny, but Pete, downing his beer, snaps back, "Have I told you lately that I'd like to stuff that goddamn guitar up that swamp rat's ass?" He belches loud enough for everyone in the Moon to hear and gets up to go to the bar for another round. Monica says, "That's enough, Pete," and he says, "Well, no, sweet mama, it is not."

Tommy rises to go with him, leaving the girls to talk about what sour ungrateful assholes they're both stuck with and why isn't there a nice place to go in West Condon where people dress up a little. Tommy is in a foul mood and Angela has picked up on it and has become snappish herself. And at the same time cloyingly affectionate. Trying to hang on. He fumbled the big midweek bye-bye and now here he is with it all still to do. He used their religious differences, why it was best to accept the inevitable, sad as it was, they belonged to two different worlds, they should call it off now before they got too deep and it became too painful; but, trying to keep the back door open in case he got desperate before this long summer is over, he softened it with too many I love yous, and Angela was convinced they could work it out. In fact, she took it as a kind of provisional marriage proposal and said they should go talk to the priest about it and he was too drained (what a night!) to argue. In fact, while he was brooding over what he might say next (tell her he had become an atheist and his kids would have to be raised atheist? no, a mistake to mention kids at all), he dropped off and didn't come to until after Angela had already left for the bank the next morning. She left a tissue with her lipstick-imprinted kiss on her pillow beside him. He blew his nose in it. His dad had more business meetings to attend out of town, something about seeing state officials in hopes of landing something big for the town before the Fourth, so after the pool job he had to stay home with his mother the next couple of nights, settle into summertime reruns. Which was a relief, in a way. It gave him time to think, and Angela could sense that and said on the phone he was just using his mother as an excuse not to see her, and like a fool he kept insisting otherwise and making his mother's condition out to be worse than it was.

But tonight's the night. Has to be. A clean break. He'd imagined tender farewells, lingering kisses; it's not going to be that way. He may not even get laid. *Tant pis,* as they say in Paris, which is where he should be tonight. Where it's a whole lot easier than this. The only other French he knows is how to ask a girl to lie down with him, and that's all you need. He had to coax Concetta into staying and to pay her overtime to get the night free, but she and her widow friends seem glad enough to get the work and the money his dad's been giving him as compensation for missing out on Europe more than covers the cost. Only it's a waste for a night like this. Except for Fleet, he hates everyone here. What is he doing in this stupid backwater? Naz Moroni was in here earlier with his demented Dagotown pals and there might have been trouble, but they had some women with them—breasty, big-nosed girls Tommy recognized from the pool—and they only made threatening and obscene gestures, which Angie insisted they ignore. If you want to take them on, Fleet said, let me know. Joey Castiglione was with them, or maybe he came on his own. Joey has the hots for Angela and Tommy wished he'd just grab Angie up and steal her away—it would have solved all his problems—but when Joey saw them there, he turned around and walked out again. Tommy thinks back on the college bars, the girls he knew up there, the class they had, and knows he doesn't belong here. He has to figure a way out. Now.

"You're trying to break it off with Angie. It won't be easy, Kit. You're her fucking be-all and end-all. You'll have a wildcat on your hands." The drinks have been made and paid for, but neither of them is in a hurry to return to the table. They drink them there at the bar and order up others. Fleet will be joining them on the golf course tomorrow afternoon, though he says he hasn't played since high school, can't afford the club membership or green fees. Tommy wants his dad to arrange some help for Fleet and the store, at least get him a complimentary trial membership at the club for the rest of the summer. "I suppose having babies is the sore point. The Catholic thing…?"

"No, Fleet, the problem is she expects too much. This is a summer fling for me and she wants more than that. Angela is gorgeous and awesome in the sack, but we've got nothing in common except for the sex."

"Well, anyway, that's something," Fleet says with a rueful sigh. And it is. Tommy has been taking a more open stance at the pool these days, wondering who might be next, but when Angela turned up after the bank closed this afternoon in her skimpy strands, she simply blew everybody else away. Eye-popping. In fact he felt a touch jealous that others could see so much of her. She's hot. And his. Does he really want to give that up? "But I know what you're going through, Kit. Happened to me several times with Monica. And I didn't even have the religion hangup. Still don't know if I did the right thing. Of course I was stuck here, had the family business on my back, didn't have your options. West Condon and a few of the towns around, none of them any better than this one. So one thing led to another and the next thing I knew I was doing the daddy act."

"Right. Babies. Nasty little boogers. No offense, Fleet, but they're not for me."

"Well, watch out, then. I'm sure Angie's already thinking about what to name it. One thing about Angie, though, she's like a lot of other Italian girls I know. Once they've got their name on your bank account and a bun or two in the oven, you can do pretty much what you like. My mother's like that. My old man is famous in the neighborhood for acting out all the butcher jokes with his lady clients. A salami Casanova. Why he only has one ear, though I don't know if it was cut off or shot off or just pulled off. But Mama doctored what was left of it, scolding him like she would a bad little boy, fed him some minestrone and a few shots of grappa and put him to bed, made him go to confession on Sunday, and things went on as normal. Not that great, never all that great, but normal. The missing ear became part of the family legend, the old man's ridiculous virility badge."

The radio station guy and his friends have left and the other two are singing "Always." Angela probably requested it. It means: Turn off the bull, heart of my heart, and come dance with me. When Duke told them "White Dove" was no longer in their repertoire, he and Angie switched to this one as their private theme song. Partly because of the pun that referenced their lovemaking: "I'll be loving you: all ways..." So here we go. Dance and yap a while, get potted, ship Fleet and Monica back to their babysitter, retire to the room at the back and get it over with. That's the plan. Doesn't work out that way.

Sunday is a day of prayer, of communing with the Maker of All Things, and Ted Cavanaugh is now approaching that weekly communion here on the gentle climb to the sixth tee. Church is a civic duty; here, faith is personal and real. His general feeling of well-being has been enhanced by a birdie on the fifth and what promises to be a splendid round on a splendid day, one that displays for all to see God's goodness. Others are usually aware that he likes to be by himself at this time and they draw back into conversations of their own, but this afternoon his son chooses to tag along, probably with the intention of asking some favor or other for his old high school teammate. Young Pete is a decent golfer and the Piccolotti Italian Market is doing about as well as any other business in town; Ted will probably grant it. They can become the chief supplier for Concetta's restaurant when it opens. She can feature the famous Piccolotti salomeats, as they call them, as an antipasto. He would rather Tommy put this off for another hole and allow him his traditional moment of quiet privacy here, but among his many blessings, in fact chief among them, is his youngest son. Maybe he can express to him something of the feelings aroused by this rise at the sixth tee; perhaps they can even pray together in a manly way.

Tommy skipped church again this morning, as has become his habit; his excuse has usually been that he has to stay home with his mother while Concetta is at Mass, but today Irene's new Catholic friends organized a wheelchair and transport for her and took her with them. More remarks to face down at Mick's, no doubt; she's becoming the town laughingstock and dragging him onstage with her. The boy came home late last night without his car. He hasn't yet told him why. He's doing a lot of drinking. Ted hopes he hasn't wrecked it. Probably just too drunk to drive. A rare act of wisdom. The Presbyterians gathered once more this morning in ever diminishing numbers at the Trinity Lutheran Church, where Ted was at last able to announce the arrival the week after the Fourth of July of their own new prospective minister, the Reverend Joshua J. Jenkins. Jenkins, trying too hard to please, told him on the phone his sermon that Sunday would be on "the intentional community," which he said was an old Presbyterian topic having to do with the role of churches in communicating "social location" in pluralistic, democratic, ethnically diverse, and loosely structured American society. Ted said he thought that would be over everybody's heads and suggested something more about what Reverend Jenkins hoped to achieve here in his ministry, and eventually they agreed the title of his sermon would be "An Old Evangel for a New Day." Much better.

The whole week has gone gratifyingly well. The backhoes have been removed from the mine hill, plans for the big celebrations on the Fourth have been launched at today's meeting, three of the boarded up stores on Main Street have been opened up this afternoon and a cleanup is underway, the governor has tentatively agreed to fit West Condon into his Independence Day schedule, and a sign has gone up on the old derelict hotel: Future Site of the Roma Liberty Hotel. A tourist attraction in the past, it could be again. He has met with most of the town's church leaders, encouraging them to focus their sermons during the run-up to the Fourth on West Condon as a traditional American Christian community, under the theme of "One Nation under God," and obtaining their tacit support for the moves the city is making against the cult.

The only setback has been Abner Baxter's attempted escape from jail last night. Back at the third hole, while Tommy was dealing with a difficult lie in the small copse dividing the third and seventh fairways and young Pete was over there helping him decide what club to use, Nick Minicozzi, the fourth of their foursome, filled him in on the events as he understood them. Apparently, when they brought Baxter his supper, he just pushed his way past everybody and stalked out, saying they had no right to keep him. When they tried to stop him, he became difficult and finally had to be physically subdued by Chief Romano and young Officer Bonali. In the process he took something of a bruising, mostly caused by his own thrashing about, and the doctor had to be called. An ambulance, too. Ted asked Nick about Bonali, Tommy having had some negative things to say about him, and Nick said that Charlie was a strong young lad with military training, a bit too aggressive maybe, but given the times it was probably good to have him aboard. "Yes," Ted said, "that's what I've been thinking, too."

The rise at the sixth tee is not very high, but the land is flat enough around here that just getting above the nearby treetops opens up inspiring vistas. One can see much of the course, including the abandoned second nine, the pale fields beyond, something of the West Condon outskirts, even the tops of some of the structures over at Deepwater, far in the distance. Soon to be back—thank you, Lord—in safe hands. Perhaps it will bring the old economy back with it. "There's something I have to tell you, Dad," Tommy says at his side, and he does. Ted feels his jaw tightening, his peace evaporating. Goddamn it. "She's lying," he says. "Drop her now."

* * *

The talk around the lifeguard chair near the high diving board has moved from flirtatious to outrageous thanks to Sally Elliott, who is getting her kicks out of shocking the younger set with talk about body parts and emissions and how to tell if a boy is a virgin or not. There are a lot of cute girls clustered around the chair below him. Word of his breakup with Angela has spread. "Ding dong!" Sally remarked, watching the eager Munchkins dancing around him. But most of them are pretty young and daughters of friends of his parents and he's not as keen on cherry-picking as he once was, so he is sitting coolly behind sunglasses on his elevated chair, smiling down on the giggly fuss as one might smile at a bunch of little leaguers worshipfully trying to copy your batting stance. Probably he ought to turn off the dirty talk, but Sally's pretty funny and the kids seem to be enjoying it. At dinner last week his dad got interested in some of the things Sally was telling him about the church camp, especially that blond kid's kooky idea of digging an empty grave for the missing Bruno body, and he asked Tommy to keep up the connection, so he is doing so. Easy enough. Sally is about the only person in town except Fleet he can have a real conversation with, even if she does tend to get wound up and go off the deep end. Getting anything intelligent out of Angela has been like getting a love song out of a whoopee cushion.

The split has been rough, but as far as he's concerned, it's final. He was pretty shaken by the act Angela pulled on him at the Moon Saturday night, but gradually he is shifting it into the picturesque past. Like Mom and her photo albums. Lesson learned. Angie got very cuddly on the dance floor, clutching his neck, his ass, pressing every inch of herself against him, like she was trying to push herself inside him; she seemed wistful, almost tearful, and he began to believe that reality was finally sinking in and he was going to get that sweet I'll-never-forget-you farewell he'd been hoping for. "I'm just so wet, Tommy," she whispered, stretching up to nibble at his earlobe. "I want to go to the room right now. I can't wait." So, even though they'd just bought a new round of drinks, they said goodnight to Monica, who was all smiles, and Fleet, who winked and shrugged and raised his glass, and off they went. Her clothes were already coming off before he could unlock the door. She tore at his clothing, kissed him all over when she'd stripped him, dragged him on top of her, grabbed his dick with her hot fist and plunged it inside her, locking her thighs around his butt, and started bucking wildly against him. When he tried to pull out, she whispered: "You don't have to anymore, Tommy. I'm so excited! I've wanted to tell you all night! We're going to have a baby!" He came instantly, almost in panic, but managed to shoot most of it between the cheeks of her ass, or he hoped he did. He freed himself from her, not easy, pulled on his clothes, told her brusquely to do the same, they were going home. And then she did start to cry. Great sobbing tears. What could he do? He put his arms around her, said please, he'd need some time, he was confused, he'd have to think what to do, they'd talk about it tomorrow, and he got her dressed as best he could and out to the parking lot, where they found the car with its tires and top slashed and ugly stripes down both sides, as if someone had dragged a coin across the paint. He heard Fleet and Monica arguing as they came out of the bar and he sent Angela, still sobbing, off with them, Fleet frowning, Monica glaring fiercely at him as he handed her the leftover clothes. He eventually hitched a ride home and spent a sleepless thick-headed night, recalling all the times he'd let her talk him out of wearing a rubber, claiming it didn't feel real, and how she liked to suck it, then jump on it at the last minute, all her sinister little tricks. What a fool. His dad was pissed off when he told him, but his opinion reinforced what he already knew: she was faking it. When she called, that's what he told her. That she was lying, just trying to trap him. After all they'd meant to each other, he was very disappointed, didn't ever want to see her again. Don't call back. She screamed at him from the other end of the line, but he knew he was right. And that was it. Concetta said the phone rang a few times, but the caller always hung up; it had to be her. It's over.

The conversation below his chair has moved from nudist jokes and the fine art of nose-picking to the subject of breasts and why boys can show their nipples and girls can't, and in demonstration of the absurdity of this inequality Sally strips her halter off and suddenly everyone else is very silent. She likes to say she's got breasts like goosebumps on a chilly day, but actually, after having spent so much time nuzzling Angela's milk jugs, Tommy finds them not unappealing—small, yes, less than a handful each—but sitting prettily on her chest there in the bright sunshine like overturned teacups, firm yet soft, their little pink nipples standing at attention, belying her pretense at cool. Pretty, but not permissible. "Put your top back on, Sally."

"I mean, what is it with nipples anyway?" she asks, and takes the finger of a boy standing there gawking and touches her breast with it. "Yeah, right, that feels okay, but I don't know what the big deal is. Did that turn you on?" The kid is too dazed to speak, can only stare.

"Sally, you are really crazy," says Babs Wetherwax, somewhat flushed, her hands covering her own breasts as though they were the ones on view. She probably wishes that they were. Certainly more to see.

"Seriously, Sal. There are little kids here. Cover up or I'll have to throw you out."

"And are guys' nips any different from girls'?" she asks and unexpectedly reaches up and tweaks one of his. It's like getting touched by an electric handshake shocker, nearly sends him right out of his lifeguard chair, and his yip releases the tension below him, setting everyone off to snorting and giggling again, and he can only grin as Sally blows them all a kiss and walks out, still topless, waving at the mothers and their children at the shallow end.

Tommy watches Babs follow Sally's exit, one hand still clasping her breast, and then she turns to gaze up at him with the sort of stunned look he hasn't seen since Angela first fell in love with him. Well, why not? Maybe just a drive somewhere, a friendly chat, try to find out how far along in the sex game she is. Even if she's still a virgin, girls that age are often into blow jobs and finger fucks, and after extreme sex with

Angela, that's probably enough for a while. Make it clear this time that whatever happens, it's just for fun. She's still staring up at him, still holding her breast. He winks and grins, calls out to one of the little kids to get back in the shallow end.

He has his weekly Wednesday date at the Loin tonight with his father and he's driving Lem's old tangerine junker again, his Bing Cherry in for new tires and top and a paint touchup, but there's still time and enough left in the junker to make it out to the lakes and back before supper. He figures she'll wait for him until he closes the pool, and she does. They've sent another cop over at closing time. Unfortunately, it's not the old guy—it's Angela's brother, Charlie. When he and Babs step out of the front gate and he has finished locking up, Charlie swaggers over, toothpick between his teeth, and says: "I'd like a word with you, punk. About your fiancée."

*These foolish things...* Ted's back in the Sir Loin saddle, ear tuned to the golden oldies, humming along silently. Second sour mash double on the rocks. Fatherhood, Tommy's recent crisis. Irene, the Dance Barn, the old days. Legal actions. Plans for the Fourth. Stacy alone, thinking about her. Is there a pattern here? Looks like it. What we do on Wednesdays. Waiting for Thursdays. While waiting for his son. The double now just melting rocks. Orders up a third. Also a pattern. *A cigarette that bears a lipstick's traces...* Though she doesn't smoke. Doesn't wear a lot of lipstick, either. But it feels right, brings her to mind. But then, what doesn't? He stubs his out (maybe he'll give it up), turns his gaze away from the waitresses and their switching little behinds to look out on the sunlit parking lot. Swirls the ice around in his glass as though stirring his thoughts. Days long now. Midsummer soon. Must be this weekend. *An airline ticket to romantic places.* Rio maybe. Baird has a special offer this summer. Advertised by a lady with fruit in her hat. Or Paris, Hawaii, Rome. A feeling of nostalgia, seeing her in those places. Though they haven't been to any of them together, of course not. Yet, as if. A late April drive to a river town on a bluff where, holding hands, she told him how desperately she loved him and how lost she felt: more like it. The pale beige cardigan she wore that day with the amber necklace he gave her. Walking past him in the bank, smoothing her skirt down over her rear, knowing he is watching. Pointing down at the shoes she bought from Dave Osborne. Foolish things. That window in the motel room where the milky afternoon light seeps in. The pink butterfly on her tailbone. *The ghost of you clings...*

He sighs. Feeling good. Sad in some sweet way, but good. Most things have been going his way for a change. The NOWC network is cohering around the plans for the Fourth of July celebrations. Bringing the community together again. Cleaning up Main Street. Poor Dave Osborne. He'll have to go. Stacy's purchase didn't save him. Will try to get him some help. What will they do with all those lace-less shoes? Props for their coalmine horror ride maybe. Pat Suggs remains incapacitated, though some of the city's court initiatives have been blocked as though the old brawler were pulling strings from his hospital bed. Probably that black-bearded hardshell libertarian. When Nick called him he said he didn't talk to wops and hung up on him. The backhoes are also back on the mine hill. *The ghost of you...* Probably just residual knock-on effects from his earlier moves, Nick explained. Good man. Though he wasn't able to prevent Baxter's release when some lawyer from Randolph Junction filed a complaint about the injuries the preacher sustained during his attempted escape. If it was one. Maury Castle said that Monk Wallace has a different version. "For one thing," Maury said dryly, "he says Baxter wasn't never out of his cell." Well, the mayor's a notorious racist, hates Italians, is resentful of Nick, is not to be trusted. Nick is working on getting Baxter rearrested, and the rest of that lot as well, has confidence in the chief and young Bonali. He believes Baxter's followers are getting counsel from someone on the inside; the chief thinks it might be the deputy sheriff, Calvin Smith. As for what's happening out at the church camp, Ted monitors things fairly well by way of Tommy's friendship with Jim Elliott's daughter, who is apparently having an affair with one of the young cultists. She's a wild kid, but useful. Her mother was pretty wild, too. Frisky, they called her. “Yeah, I don’t know why,” Tommy said last week at supper, “but Sally talks to me. She’s a kind of comedian, and I think those religious crazies provide her material.” Ted has learned about the rape, the schism, the temple construction, the ripple of new prophecies, and it’s how he found out about their plans to dig an empty grave for Giovanni Bruno’s body. Some sort of symbolic burial ceremony later this month or early next. Only one problem: Bruno isn’t dead. He called to check. So he’s thinking about that. Not such a good thing that the Elliott girl and Stacy have become friends, but in a place like this, everyone knows everyone, there are no airtight seals. He found out when Stacy began describing a racy French novel she was reading about a woman’s extramarital affair that she said Sally Elliott had loaned to her. Maybe, describing it, she was trying to excite him. He once read a French novel called *Lucky Raoul* that was pretty arousing, but he didn’t remember enough of the plot, if it had one, to tell her about it. Those French. The Elliott girl has also visited Irene a couple of times. So has the Bonali girl, of course. Also a friend of Stacy. Small-town webworks. Enmeshed in them.

What’s that one? Dum-da-da-da-da-dum-dum… *For sentimental reasons…* Mmm. *Think of you every morning, dream of you every night…* Moony old bastard. What time is it? Tommy’s later than usual. Maybe the old orange jalopy broke down. But he could at least call, damn it. Lem is taking his time with the convertible repairs and Tommy is clearly frustrated without it. He claims that Concetta’s son was responsible for the damage and he dragged her out to the car and railed at the poor woman until she cried. Have to caution him about that. Can’t afford to lose her. But Tommy had problems with that same boy at the pool, too—a kid they call Moron. Had to call the police. Says there’s a gang of them. It’s probably time to free his son up from that job. Too exposed. Hire him to work for the NOWC committee, maybe. At least until after the Fourth. The boy is full of good ideas. Would add some youthful energy. Tommy has been through a rough patch (past that now, good riddance), but getting his car back should help. Lem promised that it would look like new when he was done with it. Good old Lem. Works harder than anyone in West Condon. Except maybe the poor mechanic with the face full of nose who works for him. As a miner, Lem was a union hothead who railed against the bosses; now he's a boss himself and is learning it's not all haves and have-nots. But still he can't seem to turn a steady penny. Have to ask the bank accountant to look at Lem's books, such as he keeps, see if he can offer any advice. Probably mostly clients who haven't paid up. Lem deserves the best and should be one of the town's success stories. Da-dum-da-dum-da-dum... *The very thought of you.* Right. *And I forget to do...* something... Nearly an hour late. Too much. Irresponsible damned kid. Too much like him of late. Well, to hell with him. Eat without him. What? "Phone for you, Mr. Cavanaugh." Ah. At last. "Where the hell are you?" But it's not Tommy. It's the emergency room at the hospital.

# III.6

## Friday 19 June

One morning in the middle of summer he awakes to find himself in a strange place haunted by an infinite series of bearded men with hair down to their shoulders. The man sitting up in front of him in the blue purgatorial light and throwing off the comforter as he sits up and throws off his comforter is both familiar and unfamiliar, as are all his reiterations echoing out into the immeasurable distance. He thinks of days of fasting in the desert, when such hallucinations would appear commonly in the deranged euphoria of starvation, and full of self-understanding he rises naked to greet the naked phantasms as they rise, half to greet him, erect as he is erect, the other half their backs turned toward him. There is a stirring at his feet and the head of the woman appears as though by a conjuring, also in endless regression at the feet of all the other bearded men, gazing up at their splendid erections. He turns sideways that all his selves might display them in serial profile. "Oh, Wesley!" she says with a sleepy sigh. "You are so beautiful!"

"To whom, my child," he asks, looking around in consternation, "are you speaking?"

* * *

The good news: Wesley has stopped talking to Jesus. The bad news: he *is* Jesus. Prissy is frightened, not by this sudden rise to the surface of the being within, but by his expressed determination, now that he fully is who he is, to embark upon his worldly mission, which she is certain can only end in catastrophe, like it did the first time. Happily, Christ Jesus has not lost his lusty ardor and has agreed to start the new day by dancing again their "Dance of the Incarnation," which is of course all about flesh and the spirit. She has dashed away into the house, careful to lock the studio door behind her for fear he might launch his mission without her, to get her Magdalene costume, which is really just a cotton nightshirt the color of a gunny sack but much softer and which she has discreetly ripped here and there to suggest destitution (was she really a rich lady who bankrolled his movement, as Jesus likes to say? no matter, it's more fun like this) and offer a few provocative glimpses of the poor sinful body within. Unfortunately, she forgot about her husband Ralph and woke him when she rushed, somewhat underdressed, into the bedroom. The ferocity of his scowl as he reared up in alarm was enough to pulverize a person's spine, as if his rage were a kind of ray gun, and she did in fact go limp for a moment and had the mad desperate thought that she might ask him for his advice, even though he understands nothing at all about what she is presently going through and thinks of her as little better than a whore. Which part she is about to play, one she admittedly finds easier to perform than that of the Virgin Mary.

It is too dangerous to let Wesley out amid the rabble of West Condon, so to provide him some fresh air, over the past few weeks she has been taking him on drives into the country, where in secluded woodsy places they have danced the dances of the peaceable kingdom, the fall of the sparrow (a challenge to her choreographic ingenuity, which she rose to brilliantly, even as, paradoxically, the sparrow fell), and the parables of the hidden treasure, the persistent widow, and the ten virgins, sometimes mixing these things up for variety, which tends to suit Jesus more than it does Wesley, who is something of a stickler for textual exactitude. Too O.T. is what Jesus calls him, if she understands their conversations rightly. Which is difficult, because until now she has only heard Wesley's half of them and has had to guess the rest. Today her ingenuity will again be tested, for Jesus has already announced his intention to leave the studio and go forth and preach to the unenlightened and it will not be easy to dissuade him. Although both he and Wesley are stubborn, Jesus is the one more receptive to playful and adventurous notions, saying it takes him back to his carefree boyhood days in Galilee, and she believes she will find a way.

Dressed in his scarlet tunic and flowing midnight-blue robes, fashioned for him by the woman from styles of an era not his own, Jesus studies, somewhat in perplexity, the bearded apparition in the mirror that presumably is himself. How is it that he has been reborn in this confused and faithless Presbyterian preacher, whom he has been wearing these past weeks like a thick scratchy overcoat? A wrapping now shed, though traces remain. This is not his nose, for example, and these fancy rags, richer and cleaner smelling than his own ever were, conceal a lack of sinew and a pallor most unlike him. Perhaps that confused faithlessness is the very reason for his having landed here: soft mud for the planting of the seed rather than the thorny fields of orthodoxy, the stony ground of dogmatic certainty, as per his parable, that seed now become purpose incarnate. He strokes his beard. Too much has gone wrong over the centuries; it has been a history of error compounded by more error. Christianity, as he understands it, is a farce, an embarrassment, its professional advocates a pack of fools and charlatans—his current vessel no exception. He knows what he must do. But is this body he is in strong enough to do it? Though his memory is not clear, he feels certain he has attempted this many times through the ages, and clearly he has always failed or things would not be as they are.

The woman returns somewhat breathless. In her pretty rags. She is all his Marys, among them the Magdalene, dear heart, just as he is Jesus. Not exactly the same as the originals, but yet the same; each essence newly embodied. The substance of her "Dance of the Incarnation": that which has no body, no form or limits, made visible. Tactile. She puts on some music. Bach. A prelude. Meaning this will not be a quick exclamatory frenzy of the Word becoming flesh, but something more structured, more exploratory, explicative. A peroration.

"I have to go," he says, impatience overtaking him. "I must carry my message to the multitudes."

"No, you can't! Not yet! They're not ready for you, Wesley! It would be a disaster!"

He stares blankly at her.

"Jesus."

He nods. "But my time is now."

"No, it is…ah…tomorrow."

"Tomorrow?"

"Yes, at least! There are things we must do first!" Her hand is in his tunic. She is already dancing. "And then the temptation of Christ in the wilderness!"

It's true. He is still getting his new bearings. His reflected chrysalis-like pallor above the puddled robes at his feet is an eloquent reminder of the newness of his advent. She is right, as she often is.

Loose gravel rattles under their wheels as they roll along on small country roads, headed for the wilderness. It's a bumpy untended road, one Priscilla has never been on before, with scrubby ditches on either side, but at least they have left the billboards behind. They are on their way to premiere her new "Dance of the Temptation of Christ," in which she will play the parts of both the devil (wild, perverse temptation) and the ministering angels (tender, loving embrace), more or less at the same time, since she perceives this as an active battle for Christ's soul (did the Son of God have a soul? if so, does God?) with the outcome somewhat open-ended, even if that is not one hundred percent theologically correct. After all, they are skipping the forty-day fast as well, so this is only a creative representation of the general principles intended to show that Christ is above such petty squabbles and meant to be adored no matter which way it goes. In fact, since leaving the highway, she has already begun the dance, her bared breasts (whereon changes are taking place) bouncing as the car bounces over old unused railroad tracks. She steals a sidelong glance at Jesus to see if he is watching. He is not. His new state is confounding him. He has been like a troubled spirit these past couple of months, trapped in the shell of a stranger, and she realizes that subconsciously, for reasons mainly of performance values (no one had ever treated her to cunnilingus before, not like Wesley and Jesus with their doubled appetites, and she loves the feel of his beard nesting in her thighs, trimming it daily to her own pleasure), she has been refashioning that shell better to represent the rising spirit within. He has become what he seems to be.

"Stop the car, please."

"What—?"

"I wish to get out."

He opens the door while the car is still moving, perhaps trusting those ministering angels more even than did the Christ in the Bible, and she skids to a stop. Ah. She sees now. They are at the backside of the old mine, the tipple and water tower appearing up there through the scraggly trees. He is already clambering down into the ditch and back up the other side. By the time she has switched off the engine, grabbed up the raincoat she always carries in the car, and gone chasing after, he is striding toward the big yellow earth-moving machines parked on that infamous hill. All she can hope is that it is unoccupied and remains so until she can get him down off it. Whatever made her take this road? She hopes God isn't punishing her for her latest routines. Perhaps (look on the bright side) He is only giving her an unanticipated opportunity to devise a new one. It is a warm day, and even in her dishabille she is sweating by the time she catches up with her erstwhile dance partner and feeling somewhat light-headed. Undivided Christhood has given him new energy, but she is no longer undivided. Does he understand her delicate condition? She has danced her dances, but he has seemed oblivious to their import. Well, it's something that has never before happened to him—to either of them; one might expect a certain male obtuseness. She must learn to be more direct. Sometimes a simple two-step is more effective than an arabesque.

"But, Wesley," she gasps when she reaches him. "*Jesus*, I mean!" She feels like she's swearing all the time. "This is not a wilderness!" Strange trenches have been dug here on the hilltop, like mass graves lined with chalk, and she stumbles in and out of them, feeling exposed and vulnerable. Can they be seen up here from the church camp? There is a dance she must do, one that will get them back to the car, but she's too frightened to think how to start it.

"There's a tree. It will do. Anyway, I was not thinking of a dance exactly. The place inspires me to something more like a sermon." He spreads his arms like the beckoning Christ on mountaintops and in cemeteries. "Blessed," he declaims, "are the free in spirit, for theirs is the kingdom of Heaven!" There is a resonance in his voice she has not heard before, not even when he was in the Presbyterian pulpit. Maybe least of all then. Though of course this is a different he. "Blessed are the pleasure givers for they shall receive pleasure! Blessed are the demoniacs for they shall be invited to the dance!" Prissy realizes he is composing a love song for her and her heart softens and her fear subsides and she draws near. Perhaps this one tree *is* wilderness enough. They can use one of those backhoes for the pinnacle of the temple, whence Jesus is asked to leap but is restrained by angelic love. Her dance is taking flight. "Blessed are the lewd at heart for they shall see God! Blessed are the wanton for they shall not want! Blessed are the love makers for they shall produce the sons of God!" He knows. She is so thrilled she wants to cry. Her dances have not been in vain. She reaches for him, but he stays her hand. Something is happening down below. An old pickup truck rattles up on the dirt road, spewing black fumes. The doors fly open and a fat lady rolls out with a child in her arms—three other children scramble out of the truck bed. They come running up the hill. "Wait, Jesus! Wait for us!" the woman shouts. Prissy, shrinking behind Jesus, wants to flee, but he smiles down upon them. "The salt of the earth," he says and extends his arms in greeting.

* * *

"Soon as we seen you, Jesus," says the enormous woman fallen at his feet ("Rise with my blessing, my daughter," he told her, but she said it didn't seem right), "we run right over. We didn't wanta get left behind. It was Mattie spotted you from up on Inspiration Point, the little sweetheart should oughta be made a saint. I couldn't find my husband, but you can just reach out and bring him here. Isaiah is a righteous man and should not miss out. It wouldn't be fair. You know, like how you say anyone who follows you has got to throw off everything and live like the birds of the air and the lilies of the field? Well, he done that, Lord, I done that. These four children here they done that. You got six bona fide flat-broke disciples right off, Master, ready to go where you go." The three little ones have accepted his invitation to rise and are now circling him curiously, eyeing with suspicion the woman huddled behind him. "There was a whole bunch of us waiting for you up here a coupla months ago. We were dead sure you were coming then—we prayed like all blazes—but we musta got the date wrong. Forgive us for that, Lord. Those two college boys try hard, but they don't quite have it."

"Remember the parable of the self-righteous train engineer," he says, "for whom the timetable was his holy bible and as a consequence of his faith in it he ended up in a notorious wreck."

"I didn't know you had trains in your time, Lord."

"My time is all time."

"Let's see if it's really him, Mom," the older boy says. "I'm gonna fall in the ditch. If he's really Jesus, he'll save me." The boy stands stiffly at the lip and tips over, yowls when he hits bottom. "See? *See?*" he wails. Then his brother starts to cry too, and that sets off the baby.

"I had no intention of stopping you in your brazen foolishness, young man," Jesus says, having to shout over the racket. "For as it is said, Thou shalt not tempt the Lord thy God, or me either. Take it as a lesson learned."

"You heard Jesus, Mattie, get your little heinie out of there and stop your bawling or I'll box your ears so hard you won't hear for a week! You too, Markie. Look how you've got Johnnie going! Shut up now or we won't let you fly to Heaven with us!"

"Mom, he's not wearing any underpants!"

"Luke, you come out from under there. That's trespassing and you can go to hell for that!"

It is in his tradition to suffer little children, but there would seem to be exceptions. "If Jesus is God, Mom, shouldn't he have the biggest one?"

"Luke, I ain't telling you one more time! We been waiting all our life to get raptured, praying so hard our knees is half ruint, and I ain't gonna let you go and spoil it!" She drops the squalling baby and bounds forward on all fours, reaches under, and drags the girl out—dirty pink-slippered foot first—and then she has to grab the one called Markie, who wants his turn, and that one starts up again. The little girl hangs on to his ankles with both hands as her mother pulls and were it not for the woman behind him, he would be taking what in this unholy age in which he has landed is called a pratfall; he knows such things because he is all-knowing, but it's true, he has been slow yet again to appreciate the risks in mixing with the salt of the earth. "Forgive her her trespasses, Lord. She's a bit wild but—let *go*, Luke!—she was born that way, so it must be God's will." She pries the child's fingers away and he is free at last, though he has lost his sandal.

"I think it's curtain time," the woman behind his shoulder whispers anxiously.

"So, c'mon. Let's get going, Lord. Can't hardly wait to get there. Some folks didn't expect you until after the tribulation began, but I was always a pre-trib dispensationalist, except sometimes when it seemed like the tribulation had already started up, and then I was more like a mid-trib believer. But I was never a post-trib believer—you can ask anyone. I always said it would be like this. And I know everything about the four horsemen and the seven seals and seven trumpets and seven bowls and the abomination of desolation. Just ask me. Those other sinners back there, they didn't believe me when I hollered out you were over here, so it looks like we're all the holy remnant you got left."

"The perfect candidates, my daughter, given the fusty nature of the Heavenly Kingdom, so called," he says, speaking inside her own metaphors. The unmaking of those metaphors is at the very heart of his new mission. But they can be undone, he knows in his omniscience, only from within. "It would be interesting to see what your daughter made of the angels if she got inside their choir robes. But I'm afraid the time is not now. There is more yet to happen." He would like now to simply fly away, as the song goes, to vanish suddenly and reappear elsewhere—in the studio, for example—but he has received no favors from above nor does he expect any. Instead, they will have to step behind the backhoes as though into the wings and slip away down the hill behind them. "I must leave you now. But I shall return after a certain time. You must deliver that message to your fellow believers. Go forth, my daughter, and prophesy. Go! Go with my blessing!" It's a hard pitch and a tough house, but it works. He and the woman make their exit when all their backs are turned so that when they look back from the truck, they will be gone as if they never were.

The truth is, most of Priscilla's dances are improvisations, their design appreciated only after they have been performed. Because that's what life is. You visit your minister in his office for counseling and the next thing you're dancing the Second Coming with Christ Jesus, and suddenly a little self-enclosed pirouette en dedans becomes a grand jeté. You have to stay fit and supple and open to the unexpected. They haven't got around to the temptation of Christ today as they'd intended, and now they'll just have to skip past that. Her plan for the morrow, has been all week, is to create an erotic celebration of the summer solstice (the summer solstice *is* erotic), a "Dance of the Wedding of Heaven and Earth," with its story of the victory of sun and light over darkness and death while haunted by the simultaneous birth of the

Lord of Darkness, and not coincidentally Jesus' cousin John, followed by the descent toward the winter solstice. At which time her own child is due—a little lord of light—and everything starts up all over again. All this she has meant to script in, while turning the studio into a kind of symbolic forest, celebrating the unconscious, mother womb of dance itself, with Wesley and Jesus each playing their parts, their art their very artlessness. But now with the events of the day, she is having to make adjustments. What they do tonight will be a kind of rehearsal for tomorrow, but she will call it the "Dance of the Transfiguration" in recognition of Jesus' rise to the surface (but where did Wesley go? she has to admit she already misses him, the dear befuddled man), focusing on the element of radiance—"And his face did shine as the sun" is the text she has chosen—something transfiguration shares with the fires and fairy dances of midsummer. They will anoint their bodies with fragrant oils and use special gels on the spots and dance, after adagio preparations, to the summer storm of Vivaldi's *Four Seasons*. She hopes only that she's up for it. The day has taken something out of her.

Before returning to the studio they stopped at the shopping center on the highway to pick up some chop suey, Jesus complaining that he's had enough carryout pizza for an eternity—why can't those damned Romans leave him alone? She has never mastered the Dance of the Culinary Artist unfortunately, leaving most of that up to Ralph; she's too easily distracted, never getting past the burnt frying pan jig. Her contributions to the church Christmas bake sales have always been packaged doughnuts topped with pancake syrup and sprinkled with red and green colored sugar. And there aren't many carryout choices in West Condon; in fact, there's only one. They weren't dressed for a shopping trip, but she pulled on her car raincoat and dashed in to place their order, Jesus waiting back in the parking lot, shouting after her to ask for extra chow mein noodles. When she returned to the car he was gone. Can't leave him alone for a minute. She found him preaching to some lounging beer-drinking teenagers who laughed and made rude remarks as she led him away, but they can go to hell and almost certainly will.

She finds her appetite has vanished, the very smell of the chop suey making her somewhat nauseous, but nothing wasted, Jesus is ravished and eats both portions himself. The day's adventures have enlivened him. She had hoped he might be ready to go into retreat for a while, forty days and forty nights, for example, but he is already making big plans, reminding her that she told him his time is tomorrow. I think I was mistaken, she said, but he has paid no heed. Shedding Wesley has given him a new boldness; he is brusquer, more impatient, more demanding, but also more exciting, and a more eager and appreciative dance partner. Wesley was always polite and never took her for granted, but because of his natural diffidence, he often had to be coaxed into the more experimental aspects of the dance, Jesus urging him on from within. Now Wesley is gone as if molted (she has a serpent in her transfiguration dance, too, it's one of her best movements, and it tumbles neatly into the succulent uroboros position), and the dances are freer and more direct, but she will miss the playful complexities of their old ménage à trois. Jesus, spooning up the last of the chop suey, announces that tomorrow they will revisit Main Street and pass through city hall and walk the various neighborhoods, and he will bring his message to the swimming pool and playing fields and address the foursomes at the country club, and on Sunday they will visit all the churches, that the preachers and their flocks might look directly upon the subject of their hypocritical prattle. Dear Christ, she wonders with a shudder, how will I get through all that?

He looks up and grins around a mouthful of crunchy chow mein noodles, rice and bean sprouts ornamenting his beard, and asks: "Were you speaking to me, dear lady?"

"Oh dear. Was I speaking out loud? I am so confused and exhausted. And I think I may be about to throw up."

When the woman described her "Dance of the Incarnation" this morning as one of her most abstract (something is happening you can't quite see) and least abstract (flesh is flesh), she was closer to the mark than she knew, for this paradoxical coincidence of opposites is the very essence of the Incarnation, a moment when the unimaginable ineffable supposedly coincides with its material expression. Videlicet, yours truly—he smiles at himself in a mirror and picks some grains of rice out of his beard. The creator identifies with his creation even as he simultaneously transcends all creation, becoming both part and whole at the same time, a mathematical conundrum. Whimsical amusements of the millennia of theological charlatans who have imbedded themselves in this preacher whose poor carapace he occupies, leaving him with this riddling residue. They also came up with the notion of learned ignorance, which is a kind of unlearning, and there is something to be said for it, if taken seriously and starting with that ruinously falsified history which is the Bible.

Can the Son of God and/or the Son of Man (another teasing conundrum) feel guilt? Yes, he can and does. The bizarrely fanciful apocalyptic delusions suffered by those no doubt well-intentioned but hopelessly benighted followers of his over in the church camp and indeed around the world are largely his own contribution to world history. Such vengeful bloodthirsty ideas had been around for a good while before he came along, but he made them his own, and because of his rhetorical and teacherly talents (yes, he had a certain charisma, he acknowledges, posing magisterially before the mirror, then softening his gaze to a loving, protective and understanding one and reaching out with open hands) and not least his exemplary intransigence, he got others around him to buy in to his claim that the much-prophesied establishment of the Kingdom of God on earth was not only imminent but had already begun to happen and he was the guy with the inside track. Many alive here will see the day and will not have to die, he'd said. Follow me and you'll make the cut. Where did he get such megalomaniacal ideas? Well, they were in the air, but mainly it was the Baptist, wrongly said to be his cousin, who led him to it. Seduced him with his crazed evangel. Gave him the tools, the lingo, sent him off to round up a gang of his own. They were harsh times. He was pretty desperate. Everyone was desperate. If life were to be bearable, something had to happen. It did, but not what he'd foretold. No matter, people will believe anything. Enter mad Paul, the unscrupulous evangelist scribblers, the Patmos wild man, the remote muddle-headed church fathers (so called) plus a few ruthless tyrants and you've got a powerhouse world religion. And then down through the centuries: generations of other desperate people like those church campers out there, borrowing the spiel for equally fatuous end-times reruns of their own. All his fault.

The truth is you're a fraud.

I know it, but as my jailer once asked, or is said to have asked: What is truth? Anyway, if I'm a fraud, then, as all those coincidence-of-opposites philosophasters would say, I am therefore all the more genuine.

At least you never said anything about your own Second Coming.

Never occurred to me. Somebody else thought up that—"Wait a minute. Who is this?"

After her thin retch (nothing since breakfast, really), Prissy gargles and rinses and, aware that she may have left the studio door unlocked, hastens back, grabbing up Ralph's brandy bottle on the way and getting hit by his rage gun again. She stumbles (Ralph has been so surly of late; maybe it was a mistake to repaint the back window where he had scratched the peephole), picks herself up and hurries on, fearful Jesus might be on the loose again. He is not. He is standing before the mirror, hands on hips, looking put off with himself. "Why?" he asks, and answers himself: "Because you're too slow. That's why."

"No, no," she gasps, "I came back as quickly as I could!"

"I have a mission to fulfill! It is time for the Lord to act! If I'd waited for you, we'd be stuck in here until next Christmas!"

"Christmas?" She's confused. What is he talking about? "That's the other end of the year."

"Exactly." His reflection looks up at her, seeing her there as if for the first time. "Ah. Are you still here?"

"Who," she asks in a voice she almost cannot hear herself, "were you talking to?"

He shrugs, glares at himself. "Shut up," he says. "I'll handle this."

"I only meant—"

"I wasn't talking to you."

"Are you…are you still Jesus?"

"Of course I am," he snaps. "Who else would I be?" He is glaring at her as he was glaring at himself.

"But then…you were…is it Wesley?"

"Maybe." He belches, shrugs. "Probably it's just the chop suey."

Prissy feels a great sense of relief and joy. Her abdominal muscles relax and she allows the changes taking place there to proceed. They are a family again.

# III.7

## Saturday 20 June

Midsummer at cock-crow. The day that the earth hesitates in its nervous wobble, begins to tilt the other way again. The day, as they say, that the sun stands still. For lovers of the night it is the worst time of year, for there is so little of it. Few are up to greet so untimely a dawn. The night-duty police officer is. End of Bo's working day. Dee and Monk and Louie will be here soon, and he'll be able to go home and get some Z-time, Bo Bosticker's Zs being a town legend. He has been sleeping beside the phone all night, but that doesn't count. The garage owner Lem Filbert is another, greeting the rising sun fiercely, angrily, tools in hand, cursing his lazy mechanic in the same manner that he greets, at more or less the same hour, the midwinter dark. He is working on the Cavanaugh kid's topless fire-engine red fuck-machine, eager to get it done not only because the boy has been badgering him, but because he'll pay his bill when the job's complete, as too damned few in this town do. Guido Mello puts up with a lot of shit working for Filbert, including ten-hour shifts, but he's an old union man from his coalmining days and he won't start until his shift starts at 7:30, and Filbert, an ex-miner himself, has to respect that, no matter how it pisses him off. Not that Guido can sleep in; his kids wake him as kids do parents all over town and countryside, up with the sun, the little heathens, then cranky all day. And if it's not the kids, it's the TV, the telephone, alarm clocks, flushing toilets, banging doors, or just the light pressing in through drawn shades. For prodigal son Georgie Lucci, emerging unwillingly from a sick stupor on the firehouse floor (didn't quite make it to the mattress), it's his hangover that forces him into some kind of consciousness, or else its contrary. For Sheriff Tub Puller it's a nagging toothache, for Hovis out at the church camp his "rheumatiz," for Lucy Smith the need to fix breakfast for her early-rising husband Calvin and her squabbling offspring. Calvin is headed to the roadside Baxter encampment this morning ahead of his deputy sheriff duties to see how poor Abner is getting on and to let him know that the police officer who beat him up has been suspended. She has never seen Calvin so mad about something. The banker's wife, having risen before her husband and snuck off to the bathroom on her own, is not sure now she can make it back. Maybe she can just sit here until the home care nurse turns up. She crosses herself, hoping that, under the circumstances, it is not disrespectful. The ex-coalminer Salvatore Ferrero is awakened just as in the old days by what his mammina called *il canto del gallo*. Some of his neighbors are probably awakened by it, too, less nostalgically. They objected bluntly—"No fucking chickens, Sal!"—when he set up his backyard coops a few years ago to help his family through the rough times after the mine closing, but he has provided each of them with the occasional chicken and sack of eggs and they have grown accustomed to the reek. A rooster is crowing at the Brunist Wilderness Camp, too, displacing the hoots of the resident owls on this day that somewhere in the world is the Day of the Owl and thought of as somewhat sinister. The camp chickens are cared for by Hunk Rumpel and Wanda Cravens, layers mostly for the communal breakfasts, though the cull of cocks and unproductive hens brings meat to the table, too. The little ones always love to watch Hunk kill chickens, which he does by grabbing their heads and whipping them round and round in a great flutter of feathers until the necks snap off and the headless birds flop and stagger comically about the chicken yard. No one likes to pluck the things, though; the task in rough sketch usually falls to Wanda, designated chief chicken plucker, with Ludie Belle Shawcross and the other ladies cleaning up after her. The coops are kept downwind of the trailer park, out in what used to be deep left field of the old softball field, far enough away not to be a nuisance unless there's an unexpected easterly, but near enough to hear the cock's morning fanfare.

The bumptious crowing of the rooster was the first thing camp director Debra Edwards had heard as she slipped out of her cabin and set off on her sacramental morning trek, though as she stepped deeper into the woods it faded away, overtaken by the noisy morning chatter of her beloved birds overhead. In spite of everything that has happened, Debra has done her best to keep her chin up and adhere to her daily routines. She has tended her garden daily, weather permitting, harvesting fresh fruit and vegetables for the supper table; has assisted Ludie Belle and the other women in the kitchen and Clara and the two boys in the church office; has policed the entire campgrounds at least once a week; and has—with the help of Corinne Appleby, who brings fresh beeswax to the task—kept the woodwork and furniture in the Meeting Hall polished, all the while caring daily for Colin and their own cabin home. The Blaurock children massacred her herb and flower garden out front, playing some sort of apocalypse game in which her flowers were the condemned sinners, but she has been able to rescue the hardier plants and continues to provide fresh herbs for their daily meals. The cabin is fragrant with them today, for last night she gathered herbs and flowers from her garden and from the woods and hung them on the doors and windows and over the beds, something her Swedish grandmother used to do at Midsummer—for protection, as she said, and Debra so needs protection. She has taken comfort in the camp's dependence on her and the gratitude of all her friends here; she has also cried a lot. She is crying now. It's not just the dead bird, it's everything. She now avoids what was once her secret corner of the camp, but when she can, she still communes with God in her own special way each morning at daybreak, which up to today has been earlier and earlier every day. No matter. She hardly sleeps at all anyway, even when taking the little pills the camp nurse brings her in her shiny black bag. Debra used to pray for sleep; now she only prays she not be sent to prison, leaving Colin on his own.

This morning she has followed No-Name Creek downstream to an untraveled place halfway toward the beehives, and after spraying her under parts against mosquitoes, has squatted beside the creek at the foot of an old wooden footbridge canopied by small trees, out of sight from Inspiration Point, where Ben Wosznik often goes for his morning prayers, her skirt tucked up around her waist, staring in grief through her tears at the body of the little gray phoebe, no doubt another victim of the Blaurock children's BB gun. Bernice insists she has seen fairies down here at dusk, whispering to each other amid the fireflies and dragonflies and clouds of gnats, and this little phoebe was probably one of them. Do fairies live forever, or are they mere will o' the wisps, released like mayflies to dance one night and die? And if so, is one night, if beautiful, enough? Should they be grateful? The Blaurocks were here yesterday. Each Friday they turn up just before lunchtime, and each Friday Mrs. Blaurock is told not to come back, but she always does. It is hard to refuse such a big intimidating woman. And her silent, unsmiling husband also seems somewhat ominous. Yesterday, the oldest boy, Mattie, was shooting at birds with a BB gun and Debra took it away from him and scolded him, but his mother grabbed it roughly out of her hands, giving her a push that backed her right up against a cabin wall, and handed it back to the boy, saying she was interfering with his Second Amendment rights. He has no right to shoot my birds! she screamed, fearing she was about to break into hysterical sobs again, but Hunk Rumpel collared Mattie as he ran past, took the gun away, and snapped it in two over his knee. The children started to protest, but Hunk took one step toward them, the folded gun bits in one fist, and they scampered off. Later, they were up on the Point, throwing stones down at everybody in spite. Debra always longed for children of her own, but what if she'd got some like those? Well, the one she has is not all that easy either. She stifles her sobs, wiping her eyes and nose on her skirt hem. Colin, who collapsed after being up half the night from a nightmare about people walking around without any skin on, will be waking again soon and he will need her. Amen, she whispers, and letting her skirt fall, rises to her day.

Bernice Filbert, fairy watcher (they are so common, she doesn't know why everyone doesn't see them), has risen at dawn to prepare a lunch for her brother-in-law, just as she rose each dawn to fill her coalminer husband's lunch pail until that day the mine blew up, taking away a man she never knew beyond his mealtime druthers nor really wished to know. Now, with Lem out of the house, she is plucking her eyebrows and considering the expression she will draw there for the day, a day known for the otherworldly and the unexpected. Open-eyed curiosity perhaps, one brow arched slightly higher than the other, both slightly lengthened to suggest spiritual composure and a readiness to accept whatever might come her way. From Mr. Suggs' viewpoint: a combination of optimism and professional concern. Bernice has kept her eyebrows plucked since she was a young girl, just like her mother. "You ever seen any of them ladies in the Bible with hairy eyebrows?" her mother would demand, pushing Bernice's face into the *Illustrated Bible* pages. "It ain't lady-like!" And it was true—they did all seem drawn or painted on. Her mother scolded Bernice for everything from uncombed hair to scuffed shoes and just about all between (but not the personal parts, her mother was fiercely silent on the matter, and once, without any explanation, slapped her for flowering her dress before Bernice understood what was happening). But she scolded everyone, it was her mother's way. She was a permanently dissatisfied woman, as she herself often said. Start by thinking the worst, she would say, and you're already halfway there. By studying the women in the Bible pictures, Bernice also learned how to keep her hair braided and pinned up under scarves and shawls and how to stand in company and tilt her head just so in conversation and how to make some of the dresses the ladies wore. Today she has chosen a modest but becoming dress of the sort young Esther might wear at the well, though she is thinking more about Queen Esther and how through wile and diplomacy she saved her people, so she has added a lightweight shawl made of crocheted doilies dyed golden and a necklace of colored beads, which, for all others know, might be precious gems.

Her daddy was a miner, nicer than her mother, but easily bullied like Mary's Joseph was, and not much help when Bernice was being scolded. When he died of the black lung, her mother went to live with *her* mother, a crotchety old thing even bossier than she was, but by then Bernice was already a licensed practical nurse and married to Tuck Filbert, so she stayed here in West Condon. Tuck was an older fellow who knew her daddy in the mine and always admired the contents of his lunch bucket. She was well past the marrying age and no one else was interested when her daddy, who was already ill with the black lung, suggested it, so without much ado it happened, and there she was, like Ruth and Esther and so many ladies in the Bible, the young bride of an old man, arranged by another old man. Tuck did his duty by her a time or two, but he wasn't enjoying it and neither was she, so they stopped it, and that was it, and it was enough. Tuck was not much of a husband or even a friend, but leastways he never took hickory to her as she had feared, being forewarned, though she has sometimes said he did, speaking in parables as she often does, for even if he never actually hit her, all those Filberts do lash about fiercely with the tongue, and enough to draw blood. At least to the cheeks.

Her dowry was the wardrobe of Tuck's mother—who had gotten the flu one winter and passed away without anyone noticing until it was Sunday dinner time—together with a lot of old curtains, table cloths, and other frills the Filbert men had no use for. Bernice adapted all these things to her *Illustrated Bible* styles, creating interesting collars and puff sleeves and velveteen bodices made out of old pillows. She lengthened the skirts with decorative borders and used beaded cloth belts high up under the breasts with corset-like laces up the front of some of them, and added sashes and brass bracelets and head scarves and an abundance of simple flowing shawls and sashes, often cut from old bedsheets and dyed in primary colors. Her patent leather shoulder bag doesn't exactly fit, but she needs it in her career, just as she now needs her reading spectacles, which dangle on a plastic chain—an accessory Rachel and Ruth probably did without; at least, it's something you don't see in the pictures. Because sandals are not appreciated in this part of the world, she has mostly worn high-top nurses' shoes, though last week she found a pair of sandals in Mr. Osborne's shoe store and he was so surprised to see them there he gave them to her for a quarter each. She has been trying them out from time to time, watching the reactions of others. Won't do when winter comes, of course; in the Bible, it's always summer.

"So, whatcha reckon, old fella? Am I justified? Ain't we taught to hate evil and cleanse the world of it and ain't them biker boys worse'n devils?" In the past, when troubled, Ben Wosznik always talked things out with Rocky, and sitting alongside the dog's grave on the backside of the mine hill, having hiked over here from the camp as the midsummer dawn opened up the sky, he is doing so now, his dog as good a listener dead as he was alive. Though he misses the reassurance of Rocky's wagging tail. I love you, it had said. You are right. You are always right. But is he? He's not sure. Hating is one thing, already a sin, but acting on that hate? Doing something that can't be taken back? Even if it feels like a holy thing to do? "Catholic folks has a halfway place t'go, Rocky. Maybe they'll let us in and you'n me'll meet up there." He gazes affectionately at the grave and then notices that the small wooden cross he carved for it is standing there all right, but at the foot instead of the head, where he put it. And sideways. He gazes off past the big earthmoving machines (they went away for a day and came back again; old man Suggs must be getting better) toward the old tipple and mine buildings, thinking about this, and sees something he hasn't noticed before. A bone. They ate a lot of chicken up here, but that's not a chicken bone. His heart sinks. He knows he is going to have to open up the grave. He might be able to claw it away with his fingers, but if Rocky's still down there, it's not really something he wants to get his hands into. He wanders over to the mine buildings to see what he can find and under the tipple, where the old rusty railroad tracks pass through, leaning up against a timber, he comes upon a shovel. New one, still shiny. Like the ones he bought for the camp. He already knows what he is going to find.

"Yo, wake up, little Suzie. Let's think about livin'..."

"I am awake, Duke. And already thinking. You reckon we could maybe pay a visit to the old Bruno house?"

"Now that's a early mornin' cogitation t'stir the dust in the attic, Patti Jo. What's sparked it up?"

"A dream I just woked up from. Or else I woked up first and then I had the dream. It was about playing with Marcella in her bedroom, like we used to do. And there was something she couldn't find. She wants me to go look for it."

"Well, bless her little phantom heart, what was it?"

"I don't know. Just something. I guess I'll know when I get there. Since your fire chief friend told you where she was buried, it just seems something I gotta do. We can take it and put it on her grave."

"But didn't you tell me that Bruno place was fenced off?"

"Yes, but I don't think the fence is in very good shape. You can see people have been in there, messing around, wrecking stuff."

"So, a out'n-out burgle, y'mean. You kin tell what day a the year it is by the craziness it sets off. My ma useta keep me home such days. Said it was the day of the swamp demons. But, heck, why not? Sonuvagun, sounds like fun, so long's nobody don't start shootin' at us. Tonight though's our big night. The live recordin' session. Don't wanta die before we've played this ballgame to the last out."

"I know. Maybe afterwards, if we're on a high and feel like it. Or after Franny Baxter's wedding tomorrow. We still gotta choose our songs for that, too. Whaddaya think? 'A Stranger in My Arms'?"

"I was figgerin' on 'You Ain't Nuthin but a Houn' Dog.'"

"That should do it. Or how about 'Face on the Barroom Floor'?"

"'Sixteen Tons'?"

"Oh my! You do know how to hurt a girl. But we shouldn't make fun, I guess. Not everybody's so lucky as you and me. You know, I do admire this pretty thing of yours, Duke. It has always stood me in good stead, as you might say, reliable as the old Orange Blossom Special and quite a ticket when it gets up a head of steam. But it's got appeal when it's soft like this, too. Like a hank of warm rope."

"Won't stay thataway, you keep tryin' t'knot it."

"Mmm, yeah, look a-yonder comin'. Whoo-whoo! Up you go! The rush of the mighty engine! These eggs are something, too. Look at 'em! Never seen any hung so low and mighty."

"Don't know why them things should hang at all; never did find a pair a pants t'hold 'em right."

"Maybe you shouldn't ought to wear pants, honey. Just let 'em swing free like those Scottish mountain fellas do."

"Well, that's okay, I reckon, providin' it ain't freezin' out nor not mosquita season. But awright, all aboard, little darlin'. Ready t'git rollin' down the line. You tell your friend t'close her eyes now…"

Bride-to-be Franny Baxter has asked Duke and Patti Jo to sing "My Happiness" at her wedding tomorrow because it best describes the mood she's in, except for the lines in it about evening shadows make me blue, for her lover is lying at her side and she is not blue at all. "Whether skies are gray or blue, any place on earth will do, just as long as I'm with you," that's her happiness, a happiness she never thought would be hers. She was unlucky to be born a Baxter, unlucky to be fat and homely and redheaded and kept ignorant all her life, unlucky to grow up with God against her, humiliating her and whipping her for reasons she could never understand except maybe she had just been born bad and because she was a she. For a long time Franny did not think of it as suffering because it was all she knew, but you have to be as mental as her sister to stay dumb forever. And now her miserable Baxter life is over. Though she didn't think so at the time, coming back here to West Condon was the luckiest thing that ever happened to her. She doesn't believe in fate, doesn't believe in anything, but she almost could, so perfect has everything worked out. "I never knowed I could ever be so happy."

"Me neither, sweetie," says Tessie Lawson, and she squeezes where she has her hand. "Now all we need is a baby. Let's see if we cain't make us one. Startin' tonight after the stag party. I'll help out."

The Honey Moon—the full moon of midsummer—has just begun to wane and is still plainly visible in the early morning sky. Will they see another? the Applebys ask themselves on their way to their hives. Whether they do or not, Cecil says, he is certain the bees will; for what would the Heavenly Kingdom be without honey? Isn't that the Gospel promise: milk and honey? "I wonder," Corinne wonders, "if they will still have their stingers there?" It is the time of year when the hives are rich to overflowing, which is how the moon got its name. The camp table can use only a small portion of the bounty, so they sell the excess at local markets, tithing to the camp from the profits. Their hand-lettered labels this year say "Wilderness Camp Honey," and there is a simple line drawing of a cross in a circle. Cecil's artwork. Corinne has added her usual line from Proverbs: "Eat thou honey, because it is good; and the honeycomb, which is sweet to thy taste." On their way to the hives, holding hands as they often do, they come upon Mrs. Edwards, looking somewhat woebegone, poor thing, though she greets them cheerfully and they wish her God's blessings. When she has passed, Cecil remarks on her devotion to the camp and to the Brunist faith and the price she is paying for that. "Not all devotion is holy," Corinne says mysteriously.

* * *

For an interpreter of dreams to wake from a dream in which she is dreaming of the present reality—that her children are playing on the floor of their house trailer, building a toy church camp with blocks and sticks and scraps of paper and cardboard, and that her husband is brushing his teeth in the shower room, as each are—means that the interpreter's mind is rejecting the efficacy of symbols and her powers of analysis are fading. As she rises and pulls on her bathrobe and pads to the kitchenette to start breakfast, she realizes she has been dreaming about rising and donning a bathrobe and reaching for the skillet that she is now reaching for. It's as if she were still in the dream, though she knows she is not. It does, however, make her feel like she is living simultaneously within two realities, which are nevertheless the same in all respects except that they exist in two different places—one inner, one outer—and are running at slightly different speeds, neither more real than the other. This is not like double vision (she has only one eye, after all) but more like a single vision with two surfaces. And Glenda Oakes knows that she will be living in these paired realities all day, the longest and most testing of the year.

Welford emerges from the bathroom in his shorts and undershirt with a good-morning smile on his face, humming an old church tune, one learned in childhood, and she finds herself thinking about it as if it too were from a dream and not really happening. An omen of some sort… And He walks with me, and He talks with me… Perhaps it will not be a good day. But then, few are.

Stacy Ryder does not confuse dreams with reality any more than she confuses Alaskan goldmine stock with blue chips. Nevertheless, she is aware that dreams can leak into the real world and warp it the way that intangibles can infect the balance sheet, color investment. God is such a dream; a nightmare, really, an inherited liability from the infantile origins of the race. But love, too? A culturally sanctioned delusion layering raw unlovable instinct? Reason says it may be so, but maybe reason is the real dream stuff, the vaporous detritus of instinct no less than love is and of less intrinsic value. Such are her thoughts as she awakes alone on a sunny Saturday morning in the tower in which she is kept by love. Her dream was about loneliness, as is her waking. After the disruptions of the past two days, they will at last be together again tonight, though she knows her lover's presence, even here in this bed, will not completely take the loneliness away. In anticipation of his imminent absence, it may even make it worse, though there are moments—of tenderness, of sexual union—when love's illusions seem almost like realities, moments when time pauses, and the loneliness evaporates. Such a state, only partly made of orgasm but rarely without it, is what she strives for. Except for these ephemeral moments of ecstatic communion, however, love and the objects of love do not quite coincide but exist only as tantalizing possibilities. This, roughly, is her theology.

She is grateful that, in spite of everything, he kept his Thursday date. Even if only for an hour. He was in need of comfort, and though she felt the abyss between them (so much of his life she can never share), this was good, too, as he unburdened himself of his sorrow and fury, while, straddling his chest, she kneaded his brow and temples. The lovemaking that followed was more of consoling empathy than of passion, but sweet in its aching intensity, and she felt blissfully at one with her circumstances. Though her lover lives a life from which she is largely excluded—their own love less like life than theater, this generic motel room its principal stage, they two gifted strangers cast for parts in a show destined only for a short but brilliant run—she has grown accustomed to it and sometimes wonders if entering into his larger life would deepen their love or end it. If love is a fantasy, better that it be played out in fairytale spaces in allotted patches of time apart from time.

That Thursday morning had begun alarmingly. Her boss and lover had met her young friend Angela at the bank door, and handing her a final check, had brusquely dismissed her. Only later, called in for a brief "business meeting," did Stacy learn why. "The doctor said he'd only seen nasal trauma that serious after car wrecks, and then the victims were usually dead." Angela's vengeful brother Charlie. Wearing brass knuckles. "My son said the sonuvabitch was in his police uniform, fully armed, driving the squad car." He was soon on the phone to his lawyer, the police department, the mayor, pounding his fist on his desk as he spoke to them. His rage was understandable, but it unsettled her for the rest of the day, and only when he embraced her that evening and whispered that he loved her and needed her did her anxieties begin to fade.

He has much to do today, but will still join her for dinner. Meanwhile, after she has showered and breakfasted, perhaps she will drive over to that pretty river town on the bluff, where he took her two months ago and where he said he loved her and she said the like. A day of deepening mutual investment. A mortgaging of the heart. Angela will be free today, poor girl, and were things not as they are, she might ask her along for company. Angela could probably use a friend. Not to be, though. Angela gave all of herself, but never freely. Possession: the dark side of love.

She hates him. She loves him. She wanted to kill him, but she's so very sorry about what her brother has done. She wishes she could care for him, show him the depth of her love: that he could say such things and she could still forgive him in the spirit of her religion and of the Holy Mother, universal emblem of compassion, and could love him, even with his face such an ugly mess, and sacrifice herself for him. "You make me want to die, Tommy," she told him on the phone, "but I'll live for the sake of our baby." Her body under the thin white sheet does indeed look somewhat like a corpse in its winding cloth. If Tommy were to come in and see her, lying lifeless, it would break his heart. And then there suddenly appeared before me… Imagining him there at the foot of the bed, gazing down upon her, Angela V's her legs and smoothes the sheet down around her body that this last tragic sight of her might be seared into his memory. As she closes her eyes, she can see his brows drawing together in that agonized expression that overtakes him at the moment of climax, the deep sigh of contentment he always releases replaced now by a groan of sorrow and remorse, and she presses the sheet into her crack with one finger to remind him of what he is missing and will now miss forever. He will never find anyone like her again. So young. So purely in love. So passionate and giving. So beautiful. That stupid Wetherwax twit doesn't even come close.

Angela Bonali is not one to lie abed, yet she cannot bring herself to rise and face the long empty day. By this time on a Saturday morning she would be up and bathed and preparing herself for her job at the bank, drying and arranging her hair, applying blush, mascara, eyeliner, lipstick, dressing herself with that devotional care for which she is known. Her father (she can hear him now, up bumbling about) opposes her six-day work week, saying she is being exploited, but she loves the bank, would happily work there all her waking hours and for half the money. So different from the bitter prison of this dilapidated house, with its old man smells and bad plumbing and flaking yellow paint and muddy yard. Like a scabby old woman with her makeup cracking. In dirty underwear. She has often imagined Tommy in his father's office in the sort of tailored suits his father wears, she with an office of her own but mostly out on the bank floor, greeting customers and chatting with the tellers, making it such a happy place that it could not help but prosper and earn her husband's loving gratitude, and her father-in-law's too, if he is still with them and has not died of grief or retired to a golf course in some warmer place where they can visit him with the children at Christmastime.

Christmas makes her think of snow, so she opens the diary she keeps by her bed to revisit their night at the ice plant in April during the freak snowstorm. "I lay panting, my chest heaving, gasping in sweet agony," she wrote then. It was one of the most beautiful nights of her life. How his hands searched out every inch of her. It was a kind of delirium that sometimes overtakes her again, just thinking about it. "Over and over, my body melted against his in golden waves of passion and love and the world was filled with him!" It was, she was. She remembers the pure clean whiteness of the snow which fell all around them as they lay there in his mother's station wagon, and which she felt as a kind of divine purification, erasing the black sins of her Dark Ages, which were not sins against God or the Church so much as sins against herself. A pitiless demeaning of her own body, her own precious soul. When she remarked on the beauty of the snow, Tommy said, "Yes, but so short-lived." She has written that in her diary, because though it was not something she wanted to hear, she is always honest with herself. At least he didn't say it would soon get dirty. Which in turn reminds her of the Polaroid photo she keeps tucked in the back of the diary. Though they tore up and burned all the photos they took together (or at least most of them; Tommy has done a very naughty thing, unless he was just teasing), this is one she took of him while he was sleeping, stretched out on top of the motel bed, his feet dangling out over the foot, so tall is he, his delicious manliness fallen languidly between his open legs on its lumpy little pillow and nuzzled against one lean muscular thigh. The finger of God. Her only regret is that she did not find some way to get herself in the picture. When she confessed all this to Father Baglione, she did not tell him she kept the photo. She kisses it, hoping Tommy feels a certain mysterious tingle of desire down there as she does so, and tucks it back in its hiding place.

Tommy left her once when she was young and vulnerable and then returned to her, unable to resist the woman she had become. He will return to her again; she has to believe that. Her news frightened him, but he has a noble heart and he loves her, he has said so over and over; he will do what's right, and when he sees his son—she has already decided it will be a boy—he will be proud and will love her even more deeply than before. Perhaps she was premature in telling him, but she was afraid he was about to leave her, and she didn't dare to wait. If she is wrong (she is not, she *knows*, a woman's body tells her such things), she will say it was a miscarriage, and she will cry over the terrible loss and he will pity her and hold her close and beg for her forgiveness. And she will grant it. Pressing her hand against her belly, she can just feel the little heartbeat.

* * *

The first sinner to visit his confessional this morning, the Reverend Father Battista Baglione knows, kneeling before a crucifix for his morning prayers, will be, as always, the widow Signora Abruzzi. It is she who, seemingly sleepless, brings him at dawn and dusk each day the news of the neighborhood in the form of her confessed sins of ira, invidia, and calumnia. An incurable and cruel gossip. Not always reliable, but always interesting. What his mama used to call una tremenda pettegola. Last night it was mostly about the Vincenzo Bonali family, what is left of it, and their current catastrophes, including violence, lost employment, and mortgage foreclosure caused apparently by the end of the shameful affair between the daughter and the banker's son—the sordid details of which are all too familiar to him. A child utterly lost to the sins of the flesh but whose heart still belongs to the Church. The widow hinted at a pregnancy out of wedlock and recounted previous salacious episodes in the girl's life. Oh my God, I am heartily sorry, the widow said as usual in her prayer of contrition. But she is not. The priest adds a prayer for himself—"O Mary, Queen of the clergy, pray for us..."—then rises and enters the confessional to await the orange-haired widow's newest dispatches. This morning, however, she is not the first; another widow has usurped the honor. A good woman who has served her church, family, and community well, and who has found a new convert for the Holy Mother Church. "Forgive me, Father, for I have sinned," she says, then whispers that she has been stealing from her employers. "You must return what you have taken and repent of your sin," he says sharply. "But they have so much, Father, and we have so little." "God places such temptations before us, my daughter, to test our strength and our faith. You must do as I say. And you must pray for forgiveness." He assigns her a stiff penance. Father Baglione's parish is not blessed with great wealth. He does not want to lose such a valued convert.

* * *

It is in the early morning that Vince Bonali most misses his wife Etta. Even when times were hard—during the long winter mine strike, for example—she always had a hot breakfast ready for him by the time he reached the kitchen. Sometimes little more than her German potato pancakes and homemade applesauce, made from bruised apples she bought cheap, but always delicious and satisfying. He has long since realized that she often did without so he would not go hungry. The thought always makes him tearful and does so now. This house they shared… This morning all he could find was a stale piece of bread which he toasted and buttered with cooking lard, topping it with sugar and the last sprinkle from the dusty cinnamon shaker. Etta would have been proud of his resourcefulness. But he is still hungry. He has taken his morning walk around the block, sum total of his daily exercise. He has opened his last beer and sunk back into his old porch rocker, where he now passes his days, wishing them away. Earlier last week, while things were still going well, his son Charlie bought him a quality fresh cigar, now half smoked, and he tucks it into his jowls, pats his pockets for matches. None. Have to light it at the stove. Later. He remembers when they bought this house. Such optimism then. Good job, union officer, steady pay, low mortgage. Figured on paying it off in ten or twelve years. Handy with tools, he put a lot of time and energy into the place. Rundown now. Never finished that paint job he started five years ago; it all looks the same again. The little picket fence he made lies broken and trampled. The cement Virgin, a Christmas present from Angela, leans in the mud as if losing her footing. Inside, nothing works as it should. No matter. No longer his anyway. He has refinanced it many times over just in order to scrape by and owes more now than the original mortgage. Angie's job at the bank has protected him. That's over. He has been notified. Papers are being served. He's being locked out of his own house.

* * *

On his way out to the car, Ralph Tindle hears banging on the studio door. "Ralph? Ralph? Is that you?" he hears his dear helpmeet call out. He knocks on the door: "Hello? Hello?" "Ralph! He's escaped! He locked me in! Let me out!" He knocks again. "Hello?" "Ralph! What are you doing? Quickly! He may be in trouble!" He knocks again. "Anybody there?" "Ralph! Please! Don't be annoying! It's urgent! I have to find him!" He smiles, locks up the house, and, humming that old Salvation Army tune, "Let Him In," the frantic banging on the studio door playing in the background, gets in his car and drives away.

"Eh, cugino, what's this with our ragazzo? He called. He feels you are not protecting him."

"Charlie don't need protection, he needs discipline. You unloaded a lotta trouble on us. He's your fucking ragazzo, not mine. You should keep him in line."

"Ma che minchia…? He's apprehending a criminal, has to use a little force…"

"The kid he hit is the lifeguard at the city pool. He was just closing up."

"That's your story, hunh? Don't sound very helpful, Dee. There was a broad…"

"A young high school kid. She was the one who—"

"Sua puttana…"

"No, he's been seeing someone else."

"Charlie's sister, right? And he dishonored her. She's got a bun in the oven and he's dumping her for this new piece of ass. Hey, it's a family thing, Demetrio, what can you do?"

"Charlie was in uniform, armed, driving the squad car, used excessive force—even if there had been a crime, and there wasn't. He's got a mountain of serious charges on his head right now."

"So, what's the kid's price? We can take up a collection."

"It won't work. His father runs the bank here and everything else."

"So, all right, we call up the kid's old man, let him know how expensive this could be for him."

"I wouldn't. He's a pal of the governor, congressmen, has a direct line to the FBI through some old college buddy. Get him into it, he might have some more questions to ask."

"…"

"Charlie is suspended pending an investigation, but I have to fire him and bring criminal charges. If I don't, I'll be out of a job, facing charges of my own, and Charlie will get taken in anyway."

"Well. You disappoint me, compagno. Ma che cazzo, maybe we could use someone on the inside…"

"As I understand it, Nick, they assume Bruno is dead, some sort of mad doctor atrocity or other, and are planning a symbolic burial out on the hill in the next couple of weeks. I figured we'd ask to have him released to us for a day and take him to his own funeral. Things are boiling up again out there, and maybe this will give them something to theologize about for a while."

"They don't usually like to release mental patients."

"I think I can get the governor's intervention on this one. Kirkpatrick has been looking for an excuse to duck out on our Fourth of July parade. This would be a useful tradeoff for him."

"There are some risks."

"I think we should take them. Now, what's happening with that sonuvabitch who assaulted Tommy? The girl's been fired and mortgage papers have been served on the father. Why hasn't the city gone ahead with a criminal prosecution against the asswipe who's responsible for all this?"

"I'm still checking into all the legal issues, Ted. Meanwhile he has been suspended from the police force."

"What does that mean? I walked by yesterday and he was still in there."

"His movements have not been restricted. If he has friends…"

"Nick, that's not good enough. A cop in uniform beats up an innocent civilian: that's a crime."

"Well, I know, but it can be tricky. We can assume he'll put up a stiff defense. Want to have everything in place before we get involved with the courts. You also asked about getting a parade permit for the Fourth. That's been done. And the bank picnic will be set up out on the high school football field, with part of the raffle proceeds going to the school's athletic program. Working out the contract arrangements now."

"All right. People will want to use the unoccupied Main Street commercial properties to exhibit or sell things. Let's offer them small grants for fixing them up. Stick a notice up on the old Chamber of Commerce windows. I've put Tommy in charge of the parade and the fireworks. We'll have a small brass band for the parade made up mostly of school kids from here and the towns around, fire engines and police cars, at least one float built by the New Opportunities for West Condon steering committee, and some marching groups like the American Legion, Knights of Columbus, what's left of the miners' union, the Christian Patriots—"

"Isn't that J. P. Suggs' private militia? They're just the Klan under another name." "I know, Nick, but the request came through the sheriff's office, and it seemed better to fold them into the community on the day than to exclude them, especially with Suggs himself out of the picture now. We'll have an essay contest—what it means to be an American, that sort of thing—and I've got people rounding up raffle prizes."

"You can probably get a whole bunch of shoes from Dave Osborne."

"Yes, he's a problem. We have to close that embarrassment down before the Fourth. Wouldn't want the governor to see it, if he did turn up. I was also wondering if we might make some use of the old hotel? Display the town history in the lobby or something?"

"It's not in great shape, but I suppose it's doable."

"Maybe we can get the prospective new owners to put a little money into it. Nick, what do you know about that group, the Roma Historical Society?"

"Not much. Italian Americans. With money. I think one of them is from a family that used to live here twenty, thirty years ago."

"What family is that?"

"I'll ask."

"Unh-hunh. Nick, did the Roma Historical Society have anything to do with the hiring of Charlie Bonali?"

A guy comes in. Vaguely familiar. He's wearing some kind of scarlet desert smock with blue robes. He announces himself as Jesus. Yeah, that's probably who he looks like all right. "Son of God? That one?"

"Verily, my friend. The same yesterday, and today, and forever. All hail. But what is this? None of your shoes have laces!"

"Yeah, it's a kind of plague. One your old man didn't think of."

"I count it more a parable, whose meaning as yet escapes me, though I will search for it." Jesus points down at his feet, one sandaled, one bare. "Behold my feet," he says.

"First thing I noticed when you came in." Dave shows him one of his hand-painted CLOSING DOWN SALE signs, not yet up on the front door. "Perfect timing. First two pair free today."

"I was hoping only to match the one I have."

"All out. There's been a run on those things. My entire stock got wiped out in a single day. Must be the weather. But I may have just the ticket. What size is your foot?"

He lifts the bare one to look at it. "I'm not sure. It belongs to someone else. But nine and a half, I'd judge."

"I think you need to wash that foot, no matter who it belongs to."

"Well, it has had no rest. If you will wash it, my friend, I will make you a disciple, for he that humbleth himself shall be exalted, as I myself, in a foreign tongue, have been erroneously quoted as saying."

“That’s mighty generous, pal. I appreciate your pitch, but it’s not my line of work. Nor discipling neither, which is strictly against my principles. But, here, try these on. What do you think?”

Not far away, in the city firehouse, Georgie Lucci is pleading with the fire chief: “C’mon, Mort. Be a buddy, goddamn it. Lemme drive the engine in the big parade.”

“With your record, Georgie, I wouldn’t let you drive my kid’s tricycle, if I had a kid and he had a tricycle, which, thank God, I don’t and he don’t.”

“Is that a long way round of saying yes, Mort?”

They are drinking Mort Whimple’s double-strength coffee, Georgie sweetening it with the hair of last night’s mutt. Another big one tonight: Stevie Lawson’s bachelor party. Have to get braced for it. They’ve already dipped into Steve’s sister-in-law’s gift to them, which accounts for this morning’s hangover, but there’s plenty left. They’d hoped to book the Blue Moon Motel for the party, but he and Steve have been banned from there and they’ve got bouncers now, and besides, they’re dead broke and limited to the bottles of cheap rye supplied by Tessie, so it’s a B.Y.O.B. drift about town tonight. At least they’ll be welcome wherever they go.

Mort fills him in on all the raunchy new songs those hillbillies have been singing out at the Moon, songs about whoring in buses and trailer camps, a jukebox-killer sex maniac, and a new one called “The Night My Daddy Loved Me Too Much,” which Mort says so shocked the locals they couldn’t even clap or hoot afterwards, they all just sat there with their jaws gapping. But after a moment of dead silence everybody started hollering for them to sing it again. “The old beauty I was with started blubbering and couldn’t stop, like it had just happened to her. I never heard nothing like that before, not in mixed company.”

“That’s pretty wild,” Georgie says, sucking up coffee and wondering if he can hit Mort up for a plate of bacon and eggs over at Mick’s.

The pressure's off him now that the mayor has canceled his reelection campaign in the Italian neighborhood, but it also means most of the commissions have dried up. "I gotta hear that."

"Well, tune in the radio tonight. They're going live. Some big-ass record company is turning up. They're headed for the big time."

When Vince Bonali sees Sal Ferrero arriving with a bag of eggs and a plucked chicken, he nearly breaks into tears again, so he lurches to his feet, bites down on the cigar, and growls: "Hey, Sal. What the hell. Come for the goddamn wake?"

"Yeah, soon as I heard, Vince. That's rotten news. What's up anyway?"

"Oh, nothing special. Angela's fired and probably knocked up, Charlie's suspended and may get sent to the pen, and the bank's taking my fucking house away. I'm out on the street, Sal. Other than that..."

"Jesus, don't cry, Vince. Look, I've brought some eggs. Had any breakfast?"

"Lard on stale bread, Sal." He's not talking, he's croaking. "You can't beat that at the Ritz."

"Well, come on then, buddy, let's scramble up the eggs. I also snuck out some bacon. I'm starved."

At the stove, stirring the eggs with a fork while Vince brews up a pot of weak coffee from the last grains in the can, Sal says: "Listen, Vince, I can take out another loan on my house, and me and Gabriela, we can cover you for a few months and see if we can't get this sorted out."

"No, it's not the mortgage. They're after me, Sal. I won't let them drag you down too."

"Well, at least let me talk to Gaby's cousin Panfilo. He's a pretty good lawyer. Maybe he can fight this thing."

"For free?"

"Sure, for free."

Though he knows nothing will come of it, that somehow cheers him up, and he carries his coffee and plate of bacon and eggs out to the porch, feeling like he's getting control of his life again. This is my house, asshole. My whole life is in it—just try to take it away.

Dreamers often remark on the vividness of their dream worlds, which are not perceptions but are very much like perceptions (where does all that stuff come from?), and at the same time on their instability, their dissolving boundaries, their lack of continuity. John P. Suggs is not a dreamer, as he has often said, but were he, he might describe his waking life as like one. Lights come and go. Sounds and talk make little or no sense; it's like spinning a radio dial. The people at his bedside fade into one another. His personal nurse will be speaking to him in her yattery way and she will grow a beard and become his surly mine manager. This is not what really happens—he knows that, he's not crazy—but it's the way his damaged mind is processing the random fragments that it registers. His own thoughts are no better. He hears himself thinking things he doesn't understand himself. He's never quite asleep, nor awake, either. But he has these moments of lucidity, and he has to use them. He and the camp nurse—she's not completely stupid—have worked out a rudimentary eye-blink code. Voiceless, he must act; there is much he must do, and the only action left him is instruction. He waggles his working finger, his call for attention. She pulls a chair up to his bedside with pencil and paper in hand.

Down the corridor from Mr. Suggs and beyond the double doors in the women's wing, Clara Collins-Wosznik slumps despondently outside her daughter's room, consulting with the doctor on his morning rounds. He talks too fancy for her troubled mind, but she nods her head at whatever he says. While he is talking, they wheel a dead body by, sheeted head to toe. Clara says a little prayer for the dead person, for herself, for Elaine. Were the doctor not here, she would drop to her knees. So much sadness in God's world. It is getting her down. She has been able to resume her leadership duties at the camp, working several hours a day in the office in and around trips to the hospital, catching up on the budget and inventory and essential letter-writing, restoring all the weekly practices such as Bible study and Evening Circle, which had somewhat dropped away in her absence, and meeting with all the people out there individually to plan out the rest of the summer, but the old energy and concentrated attention are not there. She feels like a prisoner of her own creation, able to do what's demanded of her but no more. It's still only morning and she's dead tired. She knows it's just from worrying and told the doctor so when he remarked that she did not look well and would she like to visit him for a check-up, maybe some blood tests, an X-Ray? She said she didn't have time; she'd pick up again soon enough when Elaine started getting better. What she's most distressed about this morning is that the poor child has been put back on the feeding tube again, her hands strapped to her sides, ankles in shackles, head in a kind of brace, and that ugly coiling thing snaking out of her nose like her innards are being pulled out through her nostrils. It is an image to rival the worst of the punishments of the Last Judgment. Ben, who has been somewhat distracted and not his old easygoing self, said in the office last week that maybe they just ought to spare her this suffering and leave it all in God's hands, that they can't keep on feeding her that way forever. She was upset by this and told him so, though she knew he was in deep pain, loving the child as if she were his own, and fearing for her. Truth be told, Clara has had similar thoughts and did not object when they stopped using the tube for a time to see if Elaine would go back to feeding herself or at least allow herself to be fed, and she was not sure she wanted the tube back if she didn't. There's a nurse out here who has been able to talk to the girl a mite and she did get a few spoonsful down her, but then Elaine clamped her jaws shut and that was that.

"Of course, emaciated females often suffer from amenorrhea," the doctor is saying in his kindly but frustrating way, "but the urine samples seem to indicate..."

Clara doesn't know what the doctor is talking about but is too ashamed to ask and she certainly doesn't want to talk about urine samples, so instead she brings up the issue of forced feeding again. It was just such an awful thing, couldn't they maybe stop it?

"I'm afraid she seems determined to starve herself," the doctor says. "We could let her do that to herself, I suppose, but not to the baby."

What?

"Unless..."

"What are we gonna do about Elaine, Ben? She won't eat and won't talk and won't bestir herself. She probably wouldn't breathe if she could find a way to stop. I can't hardly bear to look on her with that thing up her nose."

"Maybe it ain't right to make her suffer so. Maybe we should just only leave her be. Let the Good Lord decide."

"How can you say that, Ben? She'd just go and die! *We can't let that happen!*"

"No...but then I don't know what."

"Maybe we shouldn't of come back here."

"It woulda been worse for her out on the road."

"I know. *(She sighs.)* But, well, it's not right to say it, Ben...but this don't feel like—"

Darren, hearing someone outside the door in the main hall, hits the pause button, hides the tape recorder under a loose stack of paper, goes to check. It's only Hunk hauling in a stack of wood for the partitions in the new women's restroom next door. Hunk grunts and nods and heads off to the kitchen for breakfast, which may or may not be his first one. He eats enough for three or four people, but then his wife and kids hardly eat anything at all, so it comes out even. Clara, Darren knows, is at the hospital, Billy Don is sleeping in after night guard duty, and Mrs. Edwards will be down at her garden by now. The only one he's not sure about is Ben, but he's not likely to come to the office unless Clara is here. So, unless Billy Don staggers over early, he should have the place to himself for another hour at least for this urgent task. Which is his alone. The Prophet's final resting place has been dug. The

Fourth this year is on a Saturday; Darren has scheduled the graveside ceremony on the Mount the day after. He is not sure exactly what will happen but he must know everything he can know before then. Ben is less involved since he got back. Darker in mood. God has been a little slow to act, he has said on these secret recordings. Clara said he mustn't talk that way, but she also seems full of doubt. Maybe those who opposed the temple were right, she allows at one point on the tapes. And now these thoughts that he's just been listening to from a week ago about abandoning her mission here. Darren, sitting in the office, door closed and locked, ponders this waning conviction, which may be part of a larger scheme of things. It's almost as though what happened to their daughter was ordained so as to weaken the present church leaders' resolve, or to expose their hidden weakness, make them more vulnerable to the rise of new, more intransigent leadership strong enough for the end times. Clara and Ben have been brilliant at getting the message out, creating a large movement, playing their part as Ely Collins in his martyrdom played his, but now a new phase has begun, and maybe—Jesus himself had no patience with family sentimentality—they're not up to it. Perhaps Abner Baxter should attend the ceremonial burial of the Prophet. It might be useful for him to hear these tapes. Darren punches the play button, leans his ear into the speakers, keeping the volume low.

"—home no more. Them Baxters has near ruint it for me…"

"When Clara cries, it sounds more like Balaam's donkey." Bernice Filbert, using the private phone in Mr. Suggs' room during one of his blanked-out times, is describing Clara's newest crisis to Florrie Cox. When Bernice took a break from her bedside duties in Mr. Suggs' room a while ago, she walked down the corridor to see how Elaine was doing, and she found Clara down on her knobby knees, looking red-eyed and broken. "Near worse off than her own child," she tells Florrie. Clara wouldn't say anything past the noises she was making, but Bernice guessed the problem right away, for she had picked up rumors from the nurses—and the girl's face breaking out like that, those tiny give-away bumps on her nubbles—rumors confirming what she had been worried about since the day it all happened. She tried to help that day with her nursing skills and miracle water, which does not work for everything, but which, if she could have used enough of it, might have worked for that, but Elaine fought back like a wild thing. Of course, she was scared to death and hurting, but it was more than that; something had got inside little Elaine and it was changing her. "Now the prognosis are that the child is on a straight path to the madhouse if she don't die first."

"That'd be a shame," Florrie says. "I hardly don't know what to think."

Bernice remembered that Reverend Hiram Clegg has worked some exorcisms, from what they were saying when he was here a couple of months ago, though when she said to Clara they should ask him back, Clara squeezed up her face like she was having gas pains and shook her head no. She hasn't told Florrie any of this, simply saying that Elaine has taken a turn for the worse, is back on the feeding tube, and Clara is in a dreadful state. Mr. Suggs is shifting out of his more or less silent seven-sleepers state into his lively speaking-in-tongues mode, which is sometimes followed by a short period of furious clarity, but more often is not. The one thing he seems to appreciate at those times is when she dabs his forehead with her miracle water and recites the magic words, something she did every day back when he was unconscious in his coma, and it does seem to make him better, if only for a moment. She also sometimes adds a drop of miracle water to his bath water, but this so far seems less efficacious. Florrie, hearing him carrying on in the background, asks after him, and Bernice says he's about the same, though some parts of him are shriveling up and some parts are getting longer. She can hear Florrie trying to imagine what parts she is talking about, so she adds: "His nose, for example," and doesn't say whether it's growing or shrinking.

"Mostly, he looks next thing to a dead man, Florrie. He's outa his head more than he's in it, but at them moments when he's got his wits about him, he's full up with notions, and he keeps me trotting." At such times, they use an eye-blink code, which she proceeds to explain to Florrie. "We got blinks for numbers and letters and all that, but mostly we do it by me asking him questions and him blinking once for yes and contrariwise not blinking at all. Like, I say does it begin with A, and he just lays there, and I try other letters and finally I say does it begin with F, and he blinks, and I try A again, and he just lays there again until I get to L, and he blinks, and I ask, you mean Florrie? And if he blinks we go on to the next word, and if he don't we keep working on that one."

"Really? He ast about me?"

"No, for goodness' sake, I was just giving a for sample, Florrie. Showing you how hard this is." When Mr. Suggs' brain attack struck him down, Bernice felt struck down too, for he was what stood between her and a life in prison. But one day a lawyer from the city turned up. Big ballooned-out gentleman with a bunch of chins, dressed in a tailored suit with a hankie in the pocket, and a tailored shirt, too, because all his buttons were fitting just right. Shiny shoes and shiny up on top as well, with just a few yellow-dyed hairs pasted down. He said he knew the sick lady she and Florrie had been caring for, but, no, he wasn't a friend of the family. It took a lot of eye-blinking, but eventually Mr. Suggs gave the lawyer limited power of attorney, witnessed by her and Maudie and the physical theropest who sits him up every day. The lawyer, whose name was Mr. Thornton, worked out a salary for her, saying she was sort of like a private secretary, taking dictation in this special way, and he seemed to hint that if all went well, there'd be more for her, though he didn't say exactly what "well" was. He also promised her he'd fight all the thieving and embezzlement charges against her and he did not expect any of them to even get to court because everything was on the up and up, he himself had seen to that. At first she'd thought he might be one of those rascally humanits, but now she knew who he was because she had helped Mrs. Cavanaugh place the calls. Mr. Suggs was so tired out by all these negotiations that he slept for a whole day after, and the first thing he asked when he woke up the next day was where did that lawyer go he was just talking to? "I only wisht I was a better speller, Florrie."

"I can't, Billy Don. I've promised a friend I'd go for a ride with her this afternoon. But let's meet up later. It'll be light until nearly midnight. My folks are going out with friends and have given me the car and supper money, so instead of ice cream, we can go share a pizza or something."

"Well, I'll have to miss the evening prayer meeting, but sure, why the heck not?"

"Okay. Tucker City, in front of the drugstore at eight. Got that hole dug for your prophet?"

"Yup. Two weeks tomorrow."

"Sounds like a crazy party. I may put on a party hat and sneak in."

"Well, huh, I wouldn't..."

"Yes, we heard from the governor, and I suppose we can do this, if proper precautions are taken. But, well, we, ah, treated him surgically to ease his anxieties, Mr. Cavanaugh. The patient won't give you any trouble, but he may not be of much use to you..."

When Debra opens up the garden shed, she notices that things have been moved around again, but the lock wasn't broken and nothing seems to be missing. Hazel Dunlevy, who sometimes helps out, has the only other key, so when she turns up, still looking half asleep, Debra tells her about what she found and asks if she saw anyone going in or out. "No, that was probly me," Hazel says, yawning. "I was jist only tryin' to ease the wheelbarra out." Hazel doesn't do much work, but she's good to Colin. He shows her his hands every day, and Hazel, with her dreamy freckle-faced smile, tells him something a little different each time. She likes to say that the way the lines cross in his palms is not like other people's, meaning that he will always have a life different from theirs, and certainly that is true and does not need a palm reader to prophesy it.

It's a lovely day, perfect for the year's longest, and her garden is overflowing, all their hard work of the spring now coming, literally, to fruition; but her spirits are not lifted by it. She awoke somewhat tearfully, and she is at the edge of tears still. She tries not to think about it, taking every moment as it arrives, but they could come after her, she knows, at any time. She has followed Christ's urgent command to the letter and she is about to be punished for it. Her friends here at the camp could not be more supportive, but they, like she, are mostly penniless and living by a different law from that of the world around them. That world, finding such earnest holiness impermissible, would punish them all if it could.

Mr. Suggs has warned her that if the Board of Deacons brings a suit against her and her husband for misappropriation of church funds, he would be happy to pay for her defense, but he did not think they could win. As an alternative, he offered her a flight to any destination of her choice, and enough to live on for a month or two. And she's ready to leave—the camp's not the same anymore, not since what happened to poor Elaine. She loved the time without phones or barbed-wire fences, without electricity, the deep woodsy nights unspoiled by artificial light, nothing to be heard but the owls and crickets, and all that is over, it's time to go. But when she asked, he did not offer money for Colin and she could never leave without him. And now it's too late. Mr. Suggs is no longer able to be of help to anyone.

She believes she could face this ordeal with a peaceful mind were it not for Colin. A few minutes ago he brought her a little bouquet of marigolds and oxeye daisies from the field bordering the garden, gazing up at her sweetly from under his funny straw hat, and she had to stop herself from wrapping him, weeping, in her arms; she wiped the tear that did escape and smiled, though she knew her lip was trembling, and told him they were beautiful and she loved him very much. And now what will happen to him when they take her away? Can he even survive without her? Having given herself to Christ, she would now willingly sell her soul to the devil to keep Colin safe and happy. Maybe she has already done that. The therapy that he demands and needs, she is well aware, is at best unorthodox, not something she could ever talk about with others, even Ludie Belle. But when, a trembling uncertain child, he slips into her bed at night and folds himself into her and, whispering, calls her mother, it is all so clear and simple, so pure, so innocent and loving. The end is coming. She and Colin will have to face judgment. She is not afraid. She is ready. It is the impending crisis that frightens her. Perhaps she needs to get away from the camp to think about it. Find ways to prepare him for it. Take him over to the state park for a hike, or out to the lakes. A picnic maybe. Yes, she'll pack a picnic. They'll take a walk through the bird sanctuary and nature preserve at the edge of the lakes, have an afternoon picnic together at one of the lakeside cookout areas. She looks over at him weeding the pea patch and smiles when he looks up. And he smiles back. Her funny little nuthatch. It will be all right, she thinks. Somehow.

Knocking out the little back window was easy enough, and she threw some towels over the bottom of the frame, but it has taken forever to get rid of all the jagged splinters on the sides and top so as to be able to crawl out of the garage without getting carved up, and even then, in her desperate haste, she misses one small shard, which snags on her artfully torn Mary Magdalene costume and adds an incidental rip down the back. Prissy Tindle races to the house for a quick change and also some chocolate cookies and a glass of milk, but finds the doors locked. That Ralph! Her car raincoat is in the studio, where she took it off last night, and she does not want to crawl back through that window, so she'll just have to worry about it later. No time to lose!

"The Brunists think their guy is dead, done in by the Jews and atheists who control mental hospitals, so they want to hold a ceremonial mock-burial for him. They don't know where the body is, so they're going to bury a mine pick and one of their tunics, a flashlight and other weird stuff that was never his but is now." They are rolling along through a countryside much prettier than that around West Condon, on their way to a river town on a bluff that Stacy has visited before, a favorite spot of hers and one of her present love's holy places, though she doesn't say so. Stacy has told Sally about Ted's plans to bring the brain-damaged prophet of the cult to his own funeral and said she wondered what all that was about. "The problem is: Mr. Bruno isn't dead," Sally says. "So your boss has got up the bright idea of surprising them by bringing the deceased to his own wake."

"The way you say it, you don't think it's going to work…?"

"They won't believe it. They don't want to believe it, so they won't believe it. They'll figure he's a ringer, just another dirty trick." She fumbles about in the glove compartment for a matchbook, lights up again, blows the smoke out the open passenger window. Sally is a tall, gangly girl, rather plain but in a dramatic way, with a darting gaze, no makeup, and snarly hair. She says she likes to wash her hair, rub it roughly with a towel, and then, without looking in a mirror, let it dry any which way. A new hairdo with every shampoo. Not your everyday romantic heroine. Her breasts under her T-shirt, which today reads GOD DOESN'T BELIEVE IN ME EITHER, don't amount to much, but she goes braless, unwilling to make them amount to more, as though to say she doesn't give a damn. But smart and funny. Certain guys would go for her. Some girls, too, probably. "So, tell me," Sally says, "how are you getting on with the big cheese you work for?"

"I don't think I can do that."

"I think you can, Maury."

"Why don't you have your fucking city manager bust him? I'll bet a nickel he's dragging his heels, too, ain't he, Ted?"

"Maury, you and Dee either arrest Charlie Bonali and bring criminal assault and battery charges, damn it, or I'll personally see to it you're jailed for corruption and racketeering."

"What the hell you talking about? Put in an honest day's work around there, what do you get? A knife in the back. Anyhow, I might prefer jail. Stay healthier that way."

"Let me warn you, Maury. This is becoming a federal case. The FBI is taking an interest. They'll have some tough questions to ask. I'll see you over at Mick's. We'll talk about this."

Jim Elliott, always Mickey DeMars' first customer of the day, is having an encounter with Jesus Christ, who has come in and introduced himself and asked for an egg sandwich. "Give us this day our daily eggs," he said. This is not something he has expected. Jesus does not call him Jim, he calls him Paul. Saint Paul? Good grief. This is ridiculous. Or maybe it is not. Is he Paul or was he ever? His memory is not too good, especially after a few. It's possible. What isn't? He decides to go along with Jesus, raising his glass of gin to him (hmm, empty; he signals Mick for another). Why not? No skin off his back, as the saying goes. Which is a strange one, now that he thinks about it. They flayed a lot of guys back then. Roman fun. Was Paul one of them? Is this guy dangerous? He is wearing shiny gold lamé slippers like foot halos, which definitely look right on him and convince Jim that he is who he says he is. More or less. What does that mean, "more or less"? Well, he looks the part, but what is he doing here? This is not his time and place. Is it? What the heck is happening? Jim sees that his glass is already half empty. Jesus must be helping himself. Good for him. He slides the glass toward him and asks Mick for another for himself. Mick does not know what to make of all this. Jesus calls him the Good Samaritan and Mick shrugs and rolls his eyes. "I got a feeling I ain't gonna get paid for that sandwich," he says in his squeaky voice. "Don't worry," Jim says grandly. "It's on me. Not every darned day you get to buy Jesus Christ an egg sandwich." Not that the fellow is all that appreciative. "You're the spooky con artist who invented all those lies about me," he says. "Who, me? Never!" "You repackaged me and sold me on the international market as some kind of alien-from-outer-space carnival act. Eat the flesh and drink the blood," he says, tapping his gin glass, and Mick refills it. "You made all that up, you deceitful quack!" "Listen, gosh darn it," Jim says, his dander rising, "I don't care if you are Jesus Christ. I'm not gonna take this lying down!" But, after his abrupt and ill-timed lurch from the stool, that's exactly the circumstance in which, a moment later, he finds himself, his head hurting from where he banged it on the way to the floor. He could get up. Probably. But it's not worth it. "Shut up," Jesus is saying overhead. "I know he's not Paul. You think I'm crazy? It just feels good to let fly from time to time." Mick says, "I didn't say nothing," and Jesus says, "I know that, I wasn't talking to you." Oh oh. Another one of those. This town is full of them suddenly. Is it catching? Jesus drinks off his glass of gin and then slugs down Jim's as well. Car doors slam outside. Voices. "I tell you the truth," Jesus says, hovering above him, his bright robes fluttering, "it is—to quote that whimsical mental case, John, who was pretending to quote me—to your advantage that I go away." And, sandwich in hand, he exits by the back door as the mayor and his pals come in by the front. "Well, if that's not the berries," Jim says, holding down the rising and falling floor with both hands, and is greeted by the newcomers in the affable manner that is their daily lunchtime custom.

"We won't have to do this soon, will we, you naughty little pooper?" says Dot Blaurock while changing Johnny in one of their many little Chestnut Hills homes. Jesus is already in the neighborhood, wandering around, appearing and disappearing. It's happening. The latter days, the end times: she's in them. And she has been chosen. "Go forth and prophesy," he said. Well, if Johnny could keep his diapers clean for five minutes she would. A kid with dirty diapers does not help to draw a multitude. When she raced back to the camp to tell everyone like Jesus told her to, no one believed her. What's that line about a prophet in your own county? It's true. Deaf ears. Well, tough luck for them. Out at the other campsite, Abner Baxter's people were more willing to listen. "I was watching them all the time," she said, "and suddenly they weren't there anymore." They nodded at that but wanted to know more about that woman who was with him. In all the pictures of the Rapture, Jesus is strictly on his own. She might have been Mary Magdalene, Dot said, but she wasn't sure. She didn't look well. Maybe she was somebody who'd just been resurrected from the dead.

Her older kids rush in now with the news that they saw Jesus at the shoe store downtown. "What were you doing in the shoe store?" she wants to know. She can't keep track of them. She should stand them in the corner for a while just to know where they are. But the corners in this place aren't all that habitable. Isaiah's going to have to open up a new one for them.

"We got a job! Look!" Mattie shows her a stack of flyers announcing a closing down sale. "When we've put the rest of these on everybody's porches, we get some candy and more new shoes! Gotta go, Mom!"

Doors open at noon, the fliers say. It's almost noon now.

When the banker reaches Mick's Bar & Grill, he finds it empty, except for the former Chamber of Commerce secretary on the floor, drunkenly crooning a Sunday school tune. Even the proprietor is gone. Then he spies the flyers on the tables. The sonuvabitch, knowing he's facing foreclosure, is spitefully stripping the store of any recoverable equity. The bank can put a stop to that.

It is noon in West Condon. The sun will never be so high in the sky again for another year. It drenches the town's unkempt streets in an all but shadowless light. As the solstice is associated with the birth of John the Baptist, it is sometimes said to be the day that Salome lifts her veil, and indeed nothing is veiled. One's own shadow is just a small black puddle underfoot, the size of one's girth. Children play at trying to jump out of it. Under this saturating midday light, a crowd is gathering on Main Street, where crowds have not been seen for years. Many are clutching flyers announcing a closing down sale at Dave Osborne's shoe store. First two pair free. Others are there by word of mouth or by announcements on the radio or flyers posted on shop windows and telephone poles, hoping they don't need the flyers as vouchers. There are large hand-painted signs taped to the door and front walls and a tumble of laceless shoes in the window, but the store is locked. People press up against the window, peer in under cupped hands, knock on the front door. More are arriving every minute, trying to squeeze in toward the front. The shop owner appears in the inner dimness, waves at them, points at his watch face, holds up two fingers. "Two minutes!" someone shouts over his shoulder at the restless mass, and his shout is repeated by others. The owner is standing on the stepstool he uses to get down shoe boxes from the top shelves, trying to adjust something overhead. Changing a light bulb, maybe. Or hanging decorations. His movements are explained by those in front to those behind. Tied and netted around his legs like clownish pantaloons are all the debris of his trade: shoe horns, foot measuring devices, boots, floor mirrors, shoeshine paste and fluids, and thick bouquets of shoes with their tongues hanging out. He is holding in his hand a colorful strand that some recognize as the rope he has been braiding out of shoestrings, and this amusing explanation is offered to the others pressing round. The shop owner steps down, pushes the stool back a yard or two, steps back up on it, loops the shoestring rope around his neck and jumps off. He swings toward the window, his feet belting the plate glass with a blow that causes the crowd to fall back, swings back into the dimness again, his hands reaching reflexively for his throat, then dropping away, swings forward and kicks the window again. At first his eyes bulge, staring fiercely at all those in the street as he swings, feet striking the window ever less resoundingly, then they cloud over. This seems to last forever and no one speaks under the noontime sun. There are soft thumps and then there are none. The banker arrives and kicks at the window and right behind him come the town cops. They smash their way in (people are screaming now, shouting, issuing astonished expletives, pushing forward for a better view or else backing away in horror) and cut the shoe salesman down. A siren can be heard like a howl of grief or anger. The crowd parts for the approaching ambulance. Inside the store, the police officer, Louie Testatonda, picks up a brown paper bag on the counter next to the cash register and asks: "What the hell is this?" A child rushes in, snatches it from his hands, dashes out again. "Stop her! She's stealing the evidence!" he cries, but the child is gone.

Lucy Smith was getting her hair done in Linda Catter's Main Street beauty shop when some noisy little kids came by with the shoe store flyers. Linda said she hadn't been able to afford new shoes for over three years and that this was her chance, so they dashed over, mid-perm, Lucy's hair still in curlers and wrapped with piled-up wet towels. Well, what they witnessed was not gratifying and certainly there were no new shoes to be had, though Lucy saw people running away with armloads before the police locked the place down. When the poor man kicked the window, Lucy nearly fainted, and she still feels sick. As soon as they cut him down, Linda ran back to her beauty shop to call everyone she knows, and Lucy followed her there on shaky knees, sinking back dazed and nauseous into her chair in front of the mirror. Where now she sits, staring aghast at the pasty white face staring back under its thick white turban and looking only half alive, listening to Linda tell and retell her grisly tale. Lucy recalls her last visit to Mabel Hall's caravan, when Mabel turned over the card of the Hanged Man, next to the Tower card. The Hanged Man was hanging by one foot, not his neck, and he looked quite peaceful with his legs crossed like he was sitting upside down watching TV, but the Tower was being struck by lightning and exploding apart and people were falling or diving out to die on the rocks below. It was quite terrifying, really. Mabel said it meant that there is a great calamity on the horizon, but one must surrender to the inevitable—something like that. But how does one know what's inevitable and what's not? If something is after you, can't you run away? Maybe it's like in dreams, when you want to run but can't. Lucy was frightened then and she is frightened now. Was what just happened the calamity? Or was it only the card before it? Between Linda's calls, she asks if she can please phone her husband. "I was so scared, Calvin," she tells him. "Pray for him," Calvin says calmly. "He was not a practicing Christian, but he was a good miner and a good man. I owe my life to him."

As do many men in town, guided up through the blasted and gaseous Deepwater mine workings by Osborne that night of the disaster that killed ninety-seven, Dave the night manager at the time, a miners' miner who had begun at the face and risen through the ranks. He knew Old Number Nine like the devil knows hell, as Cokie Duncan puts it, smoking and spitting with fellow miners out in the street in front of the store, squinting into a sun they still mostly avoid. Cal Smith's boss, Sheriff Tub Puller, now pushing grimly through the milling crowds to confer with the town police, is another who reached the surface that night thanks to Osborne. As is wheel-chaired Ezra Gray, who made his wife Mildred push him all the way here as fast as she could in hopes of a free pair of shoes, Dave's kicking of the window like a kick in the teeth. That's how Mildred would put it later to Thelma Coates. Some years back, before he was night manager, Dave was Ezra's faceboss, best he ever had. Ezra resented Dave becoming a downtown businessman, a kind of betrayal of his own kind, and now just see what it has come to. By the time Thelma Coates gets the phone call from Linda Catter, her sons Aaron and Royboy have already run back from town with the alarming news, and she and Roy set off for Main Street, the boys running ahead. Thus the word spreads and scores of others turn up in front of the shoe store, though the body is gone and the store is locked, the broken windows taped up with flattened cardboard shoe boxes. Witnesses of the suicide detail the event to the newcomers, and some who were not witnesses do, too. It's Ramona Testatonda who brings the sad tidings to the Bonali household in a call to her friend Angela, who in turn carries them to the front porch, where her father is sitting with Carlo Juliano. Mortgage foreclosure has been their bitter theme, the Juliano family also walking the edge, and is now more so, Carlo arguing that it's that which has brought Dave Osborne to such ultimate despair. "That goddamn bank is killing this fucking town," Vince says, biting clean through his well-masticated cigar. As his daughter runs back in to call Monica Piccolotti, his son Charlie comes out, digging at his crotch as though that's where the problem lies buried, and tells Carlo he plans to do something about the way things are and they should talk about it on the way to Main Street to see for themselves what has happened. There they run into Nazario, Ange Moroni's boy, with his hangabout pals, cigarettes dangling from the corners of their sullen lips. Moroni compliments him for busting the banker's son's ugly honker, and Charlie fills them in on the persecutions he and his family are suffering as a consequence from the bank, the city, the county, not to mention all the fucking heretic churches, including that maniacal god squad out at the church camp who once tore up St. Stephen's with mine picks. He pops his knuckles, and working a toothpick around in his teeth, nods his head toward the sheriff and his deputy, now in a huddle with the banker and the mayor, and says, "Look at them racist pricks over there bunched together. Dreaming up some new shit. See? The sheriff's eyeing us. They're all in cahoots. Fucking Klan all over again. We gotta do something about it before we're all mulched garbage." Moron grins icily under his rumpled fedora and nods at his pals. Moron's mother, Concetta Moroni, was here earlier, but is gone. She had slipped away from the Cavanaugh house for the shoe sale, witnessed the shocking scene in the store window, which she feared was some kind of divine admonishment for her own sinful greed, then fled when her employer showed up at the store and kicked the window in, and she is now, having told poor Mrs. Cavanaugh all about it, showing her patient, who is a bit dopey today from all the drugs she is taking, how to pray with the rosary she has given her—an old one that her husband Angelo received from his grandmother but rarely used, though it was in his jacket pocket when he died. She hopes God will perceive this gift of a family heirloom as penance and compensation for things she took and cannot give back. Later, she will call all her friends and they will meet after working hours in someone's kitchen to talk about this strange event and what it means to their sad little town and their own uncertain futures. At the hospital, Concetta's out-of-favor predecessor in the Cavanaugh household, Bernice Filbert, has heard the ambulance wheel in, and after she gets the news from Maudie, she hurries down to Elaine's room to let Clara know. Clara is still as woeful as those two wailing Marys outside the tomb of Jesus and she only half registers, but Ben has arrived and he takes the news sorrowfully. "He was a friend," he says in his tired rumbly voice, "and a good man. I'm mighty sorry to hear it." When she calls the camp, it is young Billy Don Tebbett who answers, and he promises to get the word to others, especially people like Willie Hall, who worked in the mine with Dave Osborne. The first person Billy Don calls, though, is Sally; her mother answers the phone and tells him Sally is not home, is there a message, and though he is somewhat confused by this unexpected connection with someone he has not ever really thought about before except in the abstract, he blurts out the story of the shoe store owner hanging himself in his own shop window, as understood by Bernice Filbert, who wasn't there. In Bernice's version, he was found hanging in the window with a closing down sale sign pinned on him, and it is that version that Susanna Elliott carries to Main Street and shares with others.

"His sidekick, Dirty Pete, is a thick-bearded docklands thug, dumb as a rock, as you might say, and Big Mary I see as a kind of badass guerrilla leader of the right, organizer of monks, nuns and popes, violent, ruthless, intransigent. A giant. Indestructible, but heartbreaking in her lonely grandeur. The real power behind the Sweet Jesus Gang." Far from the Main Street buzz of West Condon and ignorant of it, Susanna's daughter Sally is describing for Stacy, over Cokes and sandwiches, one of her new story ideas. They are sitting in the Two-Door Inn, a mawkish imitation of an English tea house with exposed beams and wall lamps with fringed red shades, paper placemats shaped like crocheted doilies and plastic menus—if you ask for tea, which is not on the menu, you get a grocery store teabag and a cup of hot water—but, silly as it is, it is dear to Stacy's heart. "Her krypton is her virginity: if she loses that, she loses all her power, so she is brutal in preserving it. I'll call the story 'Christian Love.'"

"You think that's the sort of person Mary really was?"

"I have no idea, but neither did the clowns who wrote the Bible. They made up one character, I can make up another. If she catches on, it'll change a lot of church art. A whole different comicstrip."

Stacy is laughing again, has been all through the drive and lunch, worrying only that it might edge into hysteria, for she's feeling quite giddy, unable to stop thinking about the time she was here with Ted and all they did and said that day. Today there are crowds of tourists with small chattery kids, but that day they were alone, or at least that's how she remembers it, the world around them little more than a painted backdrop, with the prettified melodies of old love songs tinkling away on the sound system, a kind of charm bracelet music she seemed to hear even when they were standing out on Lookout Point, hand in hand, staring dreamily down on the rich muddy river ripe with spring, and feeling the surge of it. Probably the same songs are playing now, but they're lost in the noisy chatter. She has had to fend off Sally's curiosity about life at the bank and outside it, about the amber necklace she is wearing and how she spends her weekends, and when they came in here Sally remarked that the place seems to have some special meaning for her, so Stacy made up a story about a teenage love affair consummated in this village, the amazement of discovering sex for the first time, partly based on a forgotten true story that actually happened at a ski resort, and she even found herself describing the boy's body, which was not at all like Ted's body, yet somehow reminded her of it. Just because it had all the relevant parts probably—all the "bits and bobs" as English tea house habitués might put it. She was tempted to tell Sally the real story, or something like it, especially when she realized Sally jealously suspected the young boy she was describing might be Tommy Cavanaugh—it would be the fastest way to disabuse her of *that* idea—and she so longed for someone to talk to about it, but she couldn't risk the scandal. It would end everything. So she has bit her tongue all day and kept changing the subject. It is how she has learned all about the Brunists—more than she ever wanted to know—but as told by Sally, it has been mostly an entertainment, full of amusing and horrifying and insane incidents. The terrible mine disaster, the lone survivor, the cult that formed up around him, made up of over-educated occultists and ignorant evangelicals possessed by the Jesus demon, their shy privacy shattered by the cynical local newspaperman who infiltrated the cult and then exposed them to the world, their naïve prophecy about the Second Coming and end of the world taking place out at an old slag heap which they called the Mount of Redemption, all of it becoming a huge international media event—a bizarre carnival, really—and ending in catastrophic failure. Out of which has grown this new religion with scores of churches and thousands of believers, while the little town itself, which purified itself by chasing everyone off, including the newspaper editor, has sunk into what Sally called the slough of terminal despond, probably quoting some book or maybe Shakespeare. "It's all so depressingly predictable," Sally said. "Round and round. It's like living inside a palindrome." Stacy already knew some of this, though not so pessimistically, for Ted is a market optimist and always has a positive outlook, but the story that was new to her was that of the prophet's sister, which Sally described in intimate detail, based on secret photographs she has seen, admitting to having found the couch of the girl's apparent deflowering and stretched out on it and felt the fire of that ill-fated romance. Stacy, who couldn't help but imagine Ted as the ravisher, remarked that it all sounded like the makings of a good novel, but though Sally agreed that it probably was, it was not, she said, the sort she'd ever write. Whereupon she began describing some of her story ideas, which have struck Stacy as sometimes pretty funny, but mostly way too weird. Stacy says she likes more realistic stories.

"Like those ladies' romances you read, you mean," Sally says with a grin, picking at her teeth with a fingernail. "The conventional way of telling stories is itself a kind of religion, you know, a dogmatic belief in a certain type of human perception as the only valid one. Like religious people, conventional writers follow hand-me-down catechisms and look upon the human story through a particular narrow lens, not crafted by them and belonging to generations of writers long dead. So conventional writers are no more realists than these fundamentalist Rapture nuts are. The true realists are the lens-breakers, always have been. The readers, like your average Sunday morning churchgoers, can't keep up with all this, so the innovators who are cutting the real mainstream often go unnoticed in their own time. It's the price they pay. They don't make as much money, but they have more fun." Sally brushes some crumbs off her chested slogan, causing GOD to wobble as though calling for attention. Or nodding his agreement. "Tight-assed little paragraphs laid out in order like snapshots in a photo album are not for me. I don't want a life like that either." Sally has been fumbling edgily with her pack of cigarettes. She needs to get out into the open air. Stacy asks for the bill. "Recently I went to visit Tommy's mother who's dying of cancer and is pretty much bedridden, the poor woman. We spent a lot of time looking at her photo albums. You know, the usual parade of bygone days lying like corpses against those funereal black pages: childhood, college, family, kids, travels, and so on. I'm in some of them, playing with little Tommy in the park, making him cry, that sort of thing. What's odd, though, is that she's mutilating them. Ripping people out of photos, trashbagging whole albums. As far as I could tell, it's mostly images of Tommy's dad that are getting edited out. Who knows why. Maybe she feels he isn't paying her enough attention, or she thinks he's playing around, or she's just mad that she's dying and he isn't. But, whatever, the more damage she does to them, the more interesting they get. They're an ugly mess, but there's passion now. Art." Sally is smiling. Stacy isn't, though she's trying. "I asked her if she had three wishes, what would she wish for? I expected her to say something like not to have cancer or maybe the end of all cancer in the world or else something vengeful to go along with what she is doing to the photo albums. But instead, she said she wished we were all better prepared for the disappointment that life is."

"Oh…! That's so sad…"

On West Condon's Main Street, the lunchtime klatch has reconvened at Mick's Bar & Grill. Georgie, tagging along with the fire chief, needs a drink badly after what he's just seen, but so far, no one has offered him one. Whatever made Dave off himself like that? Georgie can conceive of doing things that might leave him with limited chances of survival—he's seen all the old war movies and has imagined his own ill-fated heroics (after a consolatory fuck or two with the village darlings)—but jumping forever into the night like that for no better reason than love or money makes no sense to him. Old man Beeker of the hardware store, munching away, says if things don't get better on Main Street, he'll be the next to tear up his ticket, and others echo him, though Burt Robbins says the problem was that Osborne was just another blue-collar meathead who couldn't make the class jump. His snarling remarks always piss Georgie off, the more so when aimed at a solid guy like Dave, his body not even cold yet, but he keeps his peace and probably, because he can never turn it off, even has a stupid grin on his face. Is it bad luck to see a guy swing like that? Probably, but so is everything else.

The mayor, who dumped the shoe store on Dave in the first place, comes in and lights a cigar and orders up a soup and a club sandwich, looking both solemn and pleased with himself. They ask him what he was talking about with Cavanaugh, and Castle says in his booming, cheek-blowing way that the banker has been pressuring him to lock up Charlie Bonali for busting his kid's nose in a squabble over a girl, and he suggested to the banker if he wants to have a wop war he should get Puller and Smith to be his hired guns, knowing what they think of dagos. People laugh sourly at this. Just what is being laughed at is unclear, though Georgie has the idea it might be his own kind, so he orders up a plate of bacon, cinnamon toast, and three easy overs, and figures it's the mayor's treat. Stevie has told him that since old man Suggs' brain burned out on him, his manager has taken over and might be hiring again, and he might not share Suggs' grudge against the Roman church. McDaniel is an outsider, hopefully ignorant of Georgie's history, so maybe he'll go check it out, though it does sound too much like work.

The imbecilic spugna on the floor has been blabbering something about Jesus Christ being nothing but a deadbeat freeloader, so finally Mort Whimple asks Mick what the hell Elliott is talking about, and Mick confirms that the crazy preacher who thinks he's Jesus had been in earlier and polished off a sandwich and a few glasses of gin on Jim's tab. Earl Goforth says he saw Prissy Tindle out in front of the shoe store, running around frantically in the street looking for the preacher in nothing but a raggedy nightshirt and showing her ass out a rip at the back, and there are further remarks from other witnesses, not all complimentary, on this remarkable sight. Georgie, tucking into his eggs, wonders how he missed that. "In case she comes in here looking, Mick," Robbins says, "lemme have a slice of that lemon pie."

Who does come in is Elliott's wife. Nice-looking lady in a crisp lemony frock who knows everybody and gets friendly greetings. "Come on, Jim," she says, trying to haul her husband to his feet. So much dead weight. "Give me a hand, Maury," she grunts. "Whuzz happenin'?" Elliott asks. "Whereza party?" "It's naptime, Jim. The party's tonight. You have to sober up so you can start over again." Georgie pops the last bite into his mouth and helps the lady get the dipso off the floor and out to the street and into her car—a lot of people still wandering around out there in front of the shoe store—then just drifts off, figuring on a little sonnellino of his own somewhere in preparation for tonight's big stag party for Stevie. Maybe his old lady would trade him an hour on the sofa for the story of Osborne's suicide.

* * *

"I don't think you go anywhere," Luke says. "I think they just stick you in the ground like they did Gramma and you stay there forever. I think it's a big mistake to die. I don't ever want to do it."

"That's stupid, Lukie," says her big brother around his jawbreaker. "What about the Rapture? Mom's gonna get really mad if I tell her what you said."

"Go ahead. I'll tell her you thought Jesus is just some man in a fake beard."

"Like Santa Claus, you mean?" one of the other kids asks.

"Yeah," says Mattie. "But meaner."

"Well, Santa Claus can be pretty mean, too," Luke says, and some of the other kids agree with that.

"He gave Ma a black eye last year," one of them says.

Markie starts to cry and his jawbreaker pops out and lands in the gutter. Mattie wipes it on his cutoffs and gives it back to his brother to stop his crying. The three young Blaurocks are sitting on a curb in Chestnut Hills under the midday sun with all these other kids, peeling the rubber off their sneaker soles and sucking on the all-day jawbreakers given to them by the shoe store man who has just gone off to the other world—even if that world, as Luke would have it, is only a hole in the ground. Meanwhile, their mom is traipsing from door to door in Chestnut Hills with little Johnny in her arms, telling everyone about Jesus and the hanged man. Mattie is skeptical about these Jesus sightings, but Luke says their mom is seeing him because she wants to, and because of who she is, that makes it so. "If Mom wants something to happen, it happens." No one argues with that, not even Mattie. There are always people in and out of their house now. It's almost a kind of church, whichever house they're in, changing houses being about the most fun thing they do now. Most of the kids know that Luke is completely mistaken about what happens after you die. When some glad morning the roll is called up yonder, they're all going to fly away, fly away, to join the angel chorus and rest at Jesus' feet (won't it be so sweet), joyfully carried on the wings of that great speckled bird to gather at the river in that fair land where the soul never dies, at a better home awaiting over on God's celestial shore up in the sky, Lord, in the sky, where the silver fountains play upon the mountain high and the milk and honey and healing waters flow cleft for me. They know that. They have sung all the songs and heard all the stories and they know the truth. And Lukie does, too, she's just being contrary, as usual.

The fragrant Chester K. Johnson, chronically unemployed ex-coalminer, odd-jobber, smalltime thief, cardsharp when sober (not often), and unregenerate wiseass, contrarian by nature, rises, bearing the scars of many battles, from the stinking beat-up sofa in the American Legion Hall above the Main Street dime store where he has spent the morning after an all-nighter so heavy it has obliterated all memory of the day that preceded it. Perhaps there was a poker game up here at dawn; he doesn't recall. His empty pockets provide no clue, whereas a coin would be something like positive proof and also token for a coffee somewhere. The place is filthy but not so filthy as his own wretched waterless and powerless dirt-floor hutch at West Condon's hardscrabble edge, wherethrough have drifted, along with the multitudinous vermin, some three generations of Johnsons, if his restless fucked-up clan can be measured by generations, he the last of known whereabouts, known to him anyway, default inheritor of the family estate.

He stumbles off to take a leak and to check in the cracked mirror the hair on his face, which he scrapes off about once a week to stop the itching, the nearest thing he has to a calendar, the days otherwise passing without remark. He decides it can wait another day or two. When did something of sustenance last pass between his broken teeth? Nothing chewable comes to mind, his daily nutrition mostly provided these days by the froth of fermented grains, and that rarely of his own purchase. In short, he is hungry or probably hungry. Maybe he'll hitch a ride to Waterton. There are a couple of doddering whores over there, including the sister of one of his old mine buddies killed out at Deepwater, who have taken him on as a sort of charity case, and who may be willing to stir up a pot of beans and rice for him when they see his sad condition. Also, he can get his monthly bath and still be back in time for Georgie Lucci's stag party tonight for Stevie Lawson. Tomorrow, Stevie is marrying one of the Baxter girls, the fat ugly one, though the poor dingdong, who has the brains of a turnip, doesn't seem to know how it's happened. The thought of married life makes Cheese queasy, though he'd happily marry anybody's mother if she'd cook for him and wash and mend his clothes and give him a bit of money for booze and women.

Down on the painfully bright street he finds a lot of people milling about—too many, the town cops among them (what the fuck is going on?)—so he ducks down an alleyway, figuring he might as well check out the trash cans behind the Pizza Palace for a scrap of breakfast, and there encounters a bearded midday drunk in fruity gold slippers, a blue bathrobe, and a hiked red nightshirt pissing against a wall. He's so crocked he thinks he's Jesus Christ. "Behold, our belly's like wine which hash no vent and's ready t'burst iz wineskin!" he declares, letting fly. Chester Johnson knows this legendary personage primarily by way of his own fulsome and frequent curses, pronounced through his missing teeth as Cheese-us Christ, whence his nickname, his customary unwashed state also playing its part. "Where am I?" the drunk asks confusedly. "'Iz brick wall looks f'miliar." He leans forward, knocking his forehead against it, leans back. "Hah! Must be wunna the fourteen shtations. Back onna glory trail…!" What is he talking about? No idea. He looks like he might have escaped from that religious zoo out at the church camp near Deepwater. Which means he's open game. "It hash been said the 'vents of my life reveal the mind of God," he goes on, talking too loud as drunks do and sweeping his free hand through the stagnant alley air with its heaped-up rubbish and overloaded trashcans. "Look about'n wonder!" As he splashes against the wall, Cheese considers rolling him, but he sees the sucker has no pockets in that smocky thing and his legs under it are bare; might be a lark and a way to get the day started, but there would be no profit in it. It's like the loony is reading his mind, though, because the next thing he says in his thick-tongued slur is: "So, whish are you, my friend? Good thief'r bad?"

"Huh, gotta be the bad one," Cheese replies with his usual loose grin, feeling vaguely threatened by something beyond his ken but wondering at the same time if there might be some fun to be had in this, a story to carry with him to Waterton as entertainment for the girls. As an old carny barker uncle who took up preaching as a hustle once told him: Jesus Christ, buster, is the hottest fucking freakshow on the midway. Always envied that uncle; his women, his money. "Ain't never been a good nuthin nor never aimed t'be."

"A wise choice," this alley Jesus says, dropping his skirt and wheeling blearily around to look him over. How did he get so tanked without pockets? He must have a tab somewhere or else he has generous friends. Maybe he could tap into that. "The good thief got locked up for eternity inna Holy Kingdom, a bitter fate. You don' want that."

"Hellfire, no," he agrees, and spits through the gap in his teeth. His preacher uncle laid the whole Jesus story on him, at least the hairier bits, though Cheese remembers only the parts about the flood and the animals, the lady who got screwed by a bird, and then the weird zombie act at the end, which his uncle said was the real zinger and key to his good fortune. People are scared to die, he said, and they'll cough up anything if they think they can get out of it. He recalls nothing about thieves, but the Jesus character did gather a gang around him, and who knows what they got up to?

Chester is about to suggest, somewhat in jest, that, if Christamighty has no objection to a little healthy thieving, they ought to pal up, when the guy, with a wicked grin, says much the same thing (Cheese feels like the fly is open on his brain), declaring they could be "laborers together for God" against "iz 'bominable pit of c'ruption inna pois'nous grip of the moneylenders." Cheese can go along with that to the extent he understands it, but, holy shit, what the guy wants to rob is the bank. "Come along now! Returning to the people whuzz rightly theirs is not theft! Follow me!"

Against his better judgment, which is generally about the same thing as his worst judgment, he does so, and is led by way of the alleys into the back door of the downtown hardware store. Everyone is either out there among the crowds on the street or on the phone in the office—the store is at their disposal—but before Cheese can fill his pockets with some items of his own, his partner loads him up with a gallon can of black paint, picks up a wide house-painting brush and a screwdriver, and marches him out again. Weaving along tipsily in his golden slippers, he leads them right out onto the sunny street and over to the bank corner, where he pops the lid on the can Cheese is holding with the screwdriver, dips the brush in ("I know, I know, be not anxious!" he mutters, though it's not clear who he's talking to) and commences to write across the bank wall and window: He hath swallowed down riches, and he shall vomit them up again! He steps back, admiring his authorship, sticks the brush back in the paint. Cheese is a slow reader and is still trying to puzzle it out when he is grabbed by the town cops, Monk Wallace and Louie Testatonda. The drunk is gone. There's a crowd around, whooping it up, some calling his name.

"Hey, it wasn't me!" he protests. "It was fuckin' Jesus Christ!"

"Sure it was," says fat Louie, gripping his nape like you might a cat.

"And you're fuckin' George Washington!" says Monk, handcuffing him.

Never mind. They're applauding him. He's a hero of sorts.

Now she can't stop throwing up. It's okay. She wants everything that's inside to come out anyway, no matter how much it hurts. Something has got into her, something evil, and she has to punish the body that let it in in hopes it can be driven away. It's her own fault, she knows that. Even her Pa has abandoned her in her wickedness. Elaine used to talk daily with her Pa, but she is no longer worthy of him. She prays to him and to Jesus and to God, but she hears her prayers in her head like empty echoes. She must go looking for him and beg his forgiveness. If he loves her, and she believes he does—he *must*—he *will* forgive her. But to do that, she first has to die. Only it's so hard. Elaine has come to realize that crossing over is the hardest thing in the world. The sinful body just keeps fighting back. Her Ma is in the room with her. Her Ma's husband Ben. A nurse. Also the camp nurse. She hates them all, but she knows that the hatred in her heart is not her own, for there is a badly damaged self buried deep inside that loves them more than anything. There is also someone or something else in the room. She can't quite see it. It's a kind of shadowy hotness. She hopes it is Jesus or maybe her Pa, but she does not think it is. She thinks it is something horrible. That it is just waiting for her to die, unprotected. Unhealed, unsaved. And therefore unable ever to see her Pa again. Only the camp nurse knows what is really happening and she tells her quietly in her ear what she must do: There is something bad inside her and she must get strong enough that they can get it out while there is still time. Elaine understands: She must eat to die. If it makes her sick, that is only part of her martyrdom; she will welcome it. The thing inside her is resisting furiously, but, with a nod, she agrees to do whatever the camp nurse wants.

Things that get inside and change everything. Love, for example. Or something like love but less than it and worse than it. The palm reader Hazel Dunlevy sits alone, Mrs. Edwards having taken Colin for a ride, on a little wooden stool in the middle of the sunny vegetable garden staring, somewhat terrified, upon the earth's ripe vegetal wantonness. Animals, too, they just go at it, can't help themselves. Those flies: in midair. Men and women are caught between pure divine love and the sinful love that drives all nature. But even God's love can be excessive, can't it? Just look what He did to Mary. Is that a sacrilegious thought? She knows he is there before he speaks. A kind of shadow, not his own, that goes wherever he goes. "Well, lookie here," he says. "It's little Miss Muffet…all by her lonesome…"

Things that get inside and change everything. Fear. Appetite. The love of Jesus. Of Satan. Of Mammon. For Ben, it is unassuageable rage that has invaded him. Some might say that it is a holy rage and he sometimes wishes it might be, but he does not think that it is holy. It is a hellish black thing that fills him up, fattening itself on all that he once knew himself by. Blinding him, shutting up his ears. But there is nothing he can do except pray and have faith that God will not desert him in his darkest hour. Sitting beside poor little Elaine's bed, suffering her suffering, he made his mind up. Or it was made up for him. By what got inside. Now, after he drives Clara back to the Wilderness camp to get Elaine's room ready, he has work to do. The things he has to make he has used but has never made, but the principle is simple. Along the road back to camp, there are a lot of illegal roadside fireworks barns popping up, as usual this time of year. Never been legal, but nobody does anything about it. Should find something in one of them that can be made to work.

"So many things has gone so wrong," Clara says, as much to herself as to him. "I didn't never imagine it to turn out this way."

"No." Clara's faith is still intact, as is his, but her will is being tested. And her strength. It's like something vital has been sapped right out of her. She cries a lot more now, moves more slowly, often with her head down, is tired all the time. The latest bad news is that Hiram and Betty Clegg have been arrested in Florida and charged with something like what got Sister Bernice and Sister Debra in trouble. Has to do with that dead woman's estate. Mrs. McCardle. Hiram got hold of it through the doddery husband, somehow, but it turns out there are children, and they have brought legal action against them and the church. And it looks like only some of the money ever reached the church. Something has got into Hiram, too. "What does Ely say?"

"It's been a while. But today I felt him in the room, watching over Elaine. I think it was him. He didn't say nothing. He was just there."

What Ben felt in the room was utter hopelessness, but he doesn't say so. "I'll drop you off at the trailer," he says, pulling into the camp, nodding at Hovis at the gate. Hovis draws his fob watch out of his pocket and meditates upon it. "I got some errands to do."

Wayne and Billy Don are throwing a baseball back and forth in the sunshine in front of the Meeting Hall, and Wayne raises his hand and comes over to get the news about Elaine and to ask about what they should work on next. Ben answers him but feels he is growing distant from all this. Probably what he has just said has only confused the man. He tells Wayne they'll talk about it later, when he gets back for supper and tonight's prayer meeting.

Down in the trailer park, little Willie Hall hoists himself out of his heavy, redwood garden chair and comes over, Bible in hand, to tell them about the suicide—"Behold, I seen Absalom hanged in a oak!" he exclaims—and Ben and Clara nod and say Dave Osborne was a good man, it was a terrible thing, they must all pray for his soul, and Clara shows signs of tears again, though she hardly knew Dave. Willie asks about Elaine, and Clara says she's getting better, they're bringing her home, and Willie runs off, spouting good-news verses, to tell Mabel.

"What is it you gotta do, Ben?"

"I found some things. They make me figure we'll likely see more a them biker boys."

"What things?"

"Just things. Things they're gonna want back." Clara gives him a hard look, one mixed of pain and uncertainty. "I love you, Clara, and I love Elaine," he says, "more'n I ever loved anything in the world." Then he grins, feeling a little foolish. "'Cept maybe Rocky," he says.

"Why are you telling me this, Ben?"

"Well, sometimes I keep things too much to myself. I just felt like, whatever, you oughta know."

She leans toward him and rests a hand on his shoulder. And then her head. "Be heedful, Ben. I need you so."

Doesn't make things any easier.

Darren Rector has watched from the Meeting Hall windows as Ben and Clara's old muddy pickup rolled in. Not long after Mrs. Edwards and Colin, with that scared-rabbit look on his face, rolled out. In Clara's and Ben's grave faces he has seen no sign of good news. They are at the edge of cataclysmic events that will impact upon the entire universe, and Ben and Clara are still preoccupied with their little family tragedy. And it *is* a tragedy, as earthbound events go. Very sad. Poor Elaine is starving herself to death. Doing, as if obliged, the Marcella thing. Odd how exemplars create themselves without ever knowing they are doing this. Perhaps, unwittingly, he is doing so himself. Elaine will receive her reward in Heaven, and Ben and Clara are both good Christian souls whom God will surely take to his bosom, but they are no longer reliable leaders for the end times hard upon them.

Darren has not been standing at the window waiting for their return. He has been watching Wayne and Billy Don playing catch. As though nothing were happening. That peculiar unawareness of most of the world even when at the very edge of the end of things. It's almost a sign of it. A shying away from looming reality, which is awesome, and from one's personal responsibility before it. Jesus' ceaseless reminder, generally ignored, of the need for hourly preparedness. The virgins who kept their lamps trimmed in anticipation of the bridegroom, and those who didn't. Most didn't, don't. That's the very heart of the story. To be among the chosen, you have to work at it every minute of every day. It's the ultimate final exam. Billy Don has no excuse. He has been privy to everything. It's that demonic girl. Well, too bad for him. Darren is learning not to be angry about it. Sometimes he even feels sorry about the horrible fate that awaits his friend. Though not very.

Darren has spent the day devotedly poring through his tape recordings in search of further hints of God's ultimate intentions, planning his symbolic burial ceremony at the Mount of Redemption, and drafting an urgent open letter to the churches in the form of a mimeographed pamphlet. The letter is ostensibly from Clara Collins as the Brunist Evangelical Leader and Organizer, though in its pamphlet form it does not require a signature. He would show it to her, but he does not want to intrude upon her grief and worry. She has often relied upon him to produce such mailings for the church. The letter speaks of the recent history of the Brunist Wilderness Camp, including the many improvements and increased security made possible by member contributions, the presumed author's warmly welcomed return to the camp headquarters with her husband after their eastward travels (the author thanks the host churches for their kind hospitality), the carving out of the foundations of the new Brunist Coming of Light Tabernacle Church on the Mount of Redemption and the laying of the cornerstone; but it also tells of the ceaseless harassments and intrusions, the unjust legal actions being taken against them, the formation of a sinister organization in West Condon whose stated objective is to crush their movement, the brutal assault (not otherwise specified) upon her own daughter that has left the child at death's door, the ruthless beating while under police custody of the bishop of West Condon, and the armed attack on the camp, though without naming the perpetrators of the latter, it being Darren's firm belief that the event was driven by a divinely ordained internal dynamic, its protagonists selected from among those available. The camp has been stoutly defended, the letter says, by the county law enforcement agencies, by Brunist friends in the Christian Patriots, and by their own brave camp leaders, but is ever in need of stalwart and faithful defenders. After writing that line, Darren decided to capitalize Defenders, thereby, he realized, suddenly creating a new category of membership and one that might draw further numbers to this area in case of need.

The letter also describes, in the third person, his own prophecies and revelations and the church's current plans, organized by him, for a symbolic burial of their assassinated Prophet on the fifth of July, making it clear in the announcement that all Brunist faithful are invited to that memorial ceremony and urged at least to celebrate it in their own way wherever they are. But how, he wondered, should he refer to himself? "Prophet" and "visionary" seem too ostentatious, clerical titles like "church secretary" insufficient. He thinks of himself as the "church historian" or "scribe," but these have a stuffy academic ring to them. Finally he has settled on "evangelist," news-bringer, a general term that places him humbly among all "evangelical" believers (Clara would like this) and at the same time sets him among an elite and celebrated yet subservient Biblical company, capable of prophecy but not defined by it, sometimes allowing Sister Clara to add a qualifying adjective or two to add specificity and a note of approval. The pamphlets have been run off and the envelopes have been typed. All that remains is to fill the envelopes and seal them, which he must do now in time for the afternoon mail. Now that Clara is back, he will also have to hide away the tape recorder and his unedited working notes. Darren has a locked office file drawer with his own key, keeping there his secret tapes, his private copy of the book *On the Mount of Redemption* and those other disturbing photos used by Billy Don for improper purposes, and various personal items such as his diary, Clara's twelve-sided pendant, and the revolver he came upon a few days ago down where the rape and the armed incursion took place. What they call in the Western movies a six-gun. Though in principle he does not approve of firearms, and along with Sister Debra and others, unsuccessfully opposed their use in the camp, the startling discovery seemed more than mere coincidence; the gun lay glittering in the dark weeds like a personal, if somewhat foreboding, message from the beyond, dropped there specifically for him. When he picked it up, it seemed almost alive, vibrating with veiled purpose. He has fired it once, just to test it, shooting out a window at the back of one of the mine buildings over by the Mount of Redemption during the heat of day when the sound was less likely to carry. He found himself shamefully excited and could not resist a fierce moment of sin right there in broad daylight, under the very eye of God, repenting of the sin even as he was committing it, but reasoning later that it might not have been a sin at all but rather, given the nature of God's strange gift, a kind of symbolic prayer of thanksgiving.

"Hello, Nick. Calling from home. Here checking on Irene before heading out to the club with Tommy."

"Terrific day for it, Ted. Do you need a fourth?"

"Thanks, but Tommy and I have things to talk about."

"Is Irene—?"

"About the same. Concetta's here. But, Nick, I just heard that, after everything else that's happened today, the bank has been vandalized."

"Yes, graffiti painted across the east wall and window. Something from the Bible, I think. Getting someone to clean it up now. They've arrested a man named Johnson."

"Johnson? Chester Johnson, probably. Bad seed. In and out of jail so often he should be paying rent."

"That's him. But he seems all but illiterate. Everyone says it was really your mad preacher who did it."

"Edwards?"

"He must have sprung his cage. That dancer has been running around all afternoon like a headless chicken with her feathers up and tail showing looking for him."

"I think I caught a glimpse. Are we ready to make those arrests?"

"There are still some jurisdiction issues, but, yes, the warrants are prepared for our boys to enter the church camp and we know where the minister is being kept."

"So what's holding things up?"

"Well, I was going to do it early next week."

"Do it today."

In the melancholic penumbra of St. Stephen's, waiting for Father Baglione to turn up so she can take confession, Angela Bonali prays silently to the Virgin Mary, asking that the Holy Queen, Mother of Mercy, intercede for her in restoring Tommy Cavanaugh's temporarily lost affection. He is confused and frightened, O holy Mother, and does not understand his true self. There are many different images of Mary in the church—the pious Virgin, grieving Mother, triumphant Queen of Heaven; Angela has chosen to pray before a more voluptuous and youthful Mary, smiling sweetly, the curly-headed Baby Jesus at her ample breast. The sight of the infant nuzzling his mother brings tears to her eyes. I live my life in sorrow, she tells the Virgin, calling upon the White Dove song she shared with Tommy. Darkness hides me where I kneel to pray. I thank you, dear Mother, for your promise to help me in my need today.

Mary knows of course about the anal and oral sex and the dirty pictures and all the rest of it, and Angela can only hope that the Blessed Virgin in her Heavenly wisdom, for all her lack of experience, can understand and forgive. When she sees it through the Virgin's eyes, it does look a bit sordid. But from deep inside herself, when lost in his embrace, suffering shivers of delight, it is mysterious and beautiful. Cosmic. It helped us feel so much part of each other, O holy Mother. We became as one person, it was really divine in the true meaning of that word, and I felt closer to God than I've ever felt before. She can see how Mary might not be convinced. It's just so hard, she whispers, feeling a pain in her chest (and also in her rumbling tummy—she is starving!), to be a woman. Please don't let me fall back into my dark ages. You remember how awful that was. I couldn't bear it!

Gazing at Mother Mary looking down upon her so lovingly, no matter how sinful she might be, Angela is reminded of her own mother, whom she misses terribly. They came here often to pray together, though the last time she prayed alone. It was the day of her mother's funeral, the loneliest and saddest day of her life. Her dad always barks a lot and stomps around the house like the most important person in the world, leaving his cigar butts and ashes all over the place, but her mom, big and warm and kind, was just quietly there for her. Someone to talk to, to lean on. She let Angela know just how she felt but she never scolded her. Now Angela is the woman of the house, cooking and cleaning for a sullen old man and a despicable bully of a brother, earning until now the family's only steady income, and all her brothers and sisters expect this of her, so long as the old man is alive. A woman! It's hard to believe she'll soon be twenty! She crosses herself, feeling Death's chill blowing past. Sancta Maria, Mater Domini nostri, ora pro nobis peccatoribus, nunc, et in hora mortis nostrae. Amen.

In catechism class, Father Bags always insisted on learning the Latin prayers; Angela was good at it and still remembers them. Deus meus, ex toto corde poenitet me omnium meorum peccatorum…I am sorry for my sins. Which, in Latin, seem less personal, less shameful, more like just the way the world works. One night, when Tommy caught her crossing herself before making love, he asked in his joking way if she thought that would make the sex better. She said she was only asking that their love be blessed. But wasn't she sinning? No, not really, she said, gazing upon him, feeling almost feverish with desire. It was okay because she loved him with all her heart and would love him forever. That made him grin and blush, which was pretty unusual for Tommy Cavanaugh. His erection dipped slightly, so she knelt and kissed it as she might kiss the toes of a saint. And then, because one thing usually leads to another, not as she might kiss the toes of a saint. His manliness always thrilled her. Well, his whole beautiful body did, his handsome face, his excited gray-blue eyes, his smile of pleasure, his strong long-fingered hands and the way they gripped and stroked her. "His searching hand seared a path down my abdomen and onto my thigh." She has written that in her diary. Should she tell Father Bags that in confession? How would you say it in Latin?

She realizes that her thoughts have drifted away from prayer and she tries to return to it. Salve Regina, Mater misericordiae. Vita, dulcedo, et spes nostra, salve… But she is too hungry. Ad te clamamus, she cannot. All day she has been suffering a wild desperate craving for a banana split with scoops of strawberry and chocolate ice cream, hot caramel sauce, maraschino cherries, nuts, and whipped cream. It would be the worst thing ever for her diet, but these mad cravings happen to expectant women and she is almost certainly having to eat for two now, isn't she? And she hasn't had a bite all day—the refrigerator was empty, Charlie having cleaned it out—no wonder she's hungry. She could devour a pizza, too. With double cheese. But after the banana split. Father Baglione has arrived and is shuffling about by the altar with his shoulders above his head and his big nose in his cassock like an old buzzard. Perhaps this is not the best moment for confession.

She begs the Holy Virgin not to let her monthlies come—not yet, anyway—whispers another Salve Regina and prays that her father's house be saved, and leaves the church. Was the old priest scowling? He always scowls.

Father Baglione is known for his scowling sobriety. The scowl is a gift from his Lombard forebears; the sobriety he has acquired in consequence of it. If a playful spirit came naturally to him, as to most children, it did not sit well on his countenance and inspire playfulness in others, except at his own expense. He was known derisively from a young age as Bags and was often the victim of bullies and practical jokers. He therefore abandoned the playground and withdrew into scholarship—which he was not very good at, never having mastered his new language—but as a poor immigrant boy, he had few other options, and soon enough, relying on diligence, he found himself in seminary, where jollity was less of a virtue, memorization more useful than reason, and Latin closer to his mother tongue. His face was there deemed a pious one and he adopted that reading as the true one, achieving a reputation for humble self-denial and implacable orthodoxy. His father was a New York cobbler, but he had immigrant uncles who had taken up coalmining, and so willingly accepted a parish in coal country among natives of his own country, supposing it to be the first step into the ecclesiastical hierarchy. But Latin, he has come to learn, is not the persuasive language of accession in the American church, nor is humility its channel. So here he remains, dear old dour old Father Bags, a living portrait of the communal gloom. He knows that others, gazing into his face, sense that he has seen into the very depths of their sinfulness and is appalled by it, and they are intimidated by that, and reveal more than is probably their intention. Today his scowl is deepened by his sense of the impending danger posed by the cultists at the edge of town. The church must be protected against further criminal assault, and these deluded madmen operating under the guise of religion must be stoutly resisted. Resistance requires unwanted meetings with representatives of other local churches, who deem themselves—though unrepentant schismatics and heretics and ignorant beyond belief—to be Christians, and having to listen to their nonsensical pieties and tedious Biblical quotations. The translation of the Sacred Scriptures into vulgar tongues and thereby its transmission to the uneducated and inflammable masses, as Father Baglione has often remarked, was one of the great calamities of human history.

"Do you hear it, Colin? Listen! Tea-kettle-tea-kettle-tea-kettle-tea! That's a little wren calling. It's hard to see them because they're mostly down on the ground, hopping around in the tangle, looking for insects. But showing off up there, making sure you *can* see him, is what looks and sounds like a bunting. See? High up in that maple? Dark as a little ink spot but purply and gleaming in the sun. An indigo. That pretty warbling song, do you hear him?"

"I want to go back to the camp."

"I know. We're going back. But first we'll walk through here and see how many different birds we can find, and then we'll have a picnic by the lake. It's our little holiday. I've fixed your favorite peanut butter and jelly sandwiches, and have brought potato chips and cold sodas and chocolate chip cookies for dessert that Ludie Belle baked just for us and even some marshmallows to roast if you want to."

"I want to go back to the camp."

It has been his litany since they drove out through the camp gates, but it is so peaceful and beautiful here in the lakeside bird sanctuary, more like the church camp used to be before it got so civilized. Debra feels certain that if she is patient he will warm to it and begin to enjoy himself and be grateful afterwards for their little midsummer treat, and they may be able to talk a bit about what might happen next. He could even like being away from the camp so much he'll be willing to think about leaving it for good, just the two of them. The golden age of the camp has passed; it's time to leave. They can go somewhere where no one knows them and she can get a teaching job, or work as a social worker or a librarian, and take care of him for as long as she lives.

"Can we go back to the camp now?"

"Are you afraid? Don't be afraid. You're here with me." He only glares at her as if at a stranger. "Oh, look, Colin! Don't move!" she whispers. "A hummingbird!" She nods toward a coral honeysuckle shrub where the little ruby-throated bird with its hypodermic beak, hardly bigger than a June bug, hangs in midair, its pale wings an invisible blur, its tiny heart pounding away over a thousand times a minute. Success at last! Colin watches it with awed fascination. Her own heart is pounding, too. She so much needs today to go well. Colin reaches out as if to touch the bird and it darts away.

"I want to go back to the camp."

"Oh, Colin…" But he is already halfway to the car. She has to run to catch up. Overhead, a single bird sets off in alarm, arousing a flock and causing a ripple through the trees like a shudder down the spine.

"Help me, Lord. Show me what's wrongful and what's needful and what to do if something's both." Thus, under the shower, the penitent sinner, Christian songsmith, and unassuming man of peace, Ben Wosznik, weighed down with fury and awe and despair, pleads for illumination as the cold spray needles him. He has done what he can. He has run his errands and he has crafted the caps and fuses, saving the crimping of the fuses for such time as they might be needed. The old sticks are sweating their nitro and are dangerous, telltale crystals poxing some of them, but everything is buried safely out of sight and reach. The hard face they're to be used on is not a wall of coal, only history, but it's just as black and impenetrable and just as likely to blow out on you.

The camp's communal showers have a new electric hot water tank that is turned on for six hours each day. The tight little shower in their house trailer has no elbow room, so after the hot water is off and the others have gone, Ben sometimes likes to come up here for a cold shower on his own. Sometimes, on good days, he thinks up new songs here, sometimes he just hums old ones, listening inside them for the grace he seeks. "The darkness deepens, Lord with me abide…" He's humming that now. In the deepening darkness of a bright afternoon. A darkness poor Dave Osborne jumped into. Ben occasionally finds the young, curly-headed office fellow in here at this time as well, but the boy never stays; if he comes in while Ben is here, he always apologizes shyly and leaves immediately. That's what has happened today. Darren is a strange boy with strange ideas, but also smart in a way Ben is not, nor could ever be. Consequently, though Ben respects him and listens to him, they never have much to say to each other. Ben gets on better with the other one, Billy Don, who is also a good Christian boy with some Bible college ideas but more down to earth. Thinking about those two boys, he is reminded of Carl Dean Palmers and the last time he saw him, that terrible morning, just below Inspiration Point, wearing his leather jacket, ball cap, and red boots, the lad's beard still wet from a predawn shower. It was when Carl Dean said he wished Ben was his dad, filling Ben's heart, and then to Ben's sorrow he said goodbye and they hugged. Ben wishes now he knew how to reach him. He might be able to talk with him about this thing he's thinking of doing. Maybe even get some help. He wonders if he will see Carl Dean again if those biker boys come back. He does not think he will.

Elaine is taking food again, only a bite or two of dry toast and a swallow of milk so far, but it's a change of attitude, so they've agreed to release her today after the doctor makes his afternoon rounds. After his shower, Ben will take Clara to the hospital in the truck so she can ride back with Elaine in the ambulance. But the girl is not well. She does not look like she will ever be well again. A cruel punishment for such a pious child. And for her pious mother, too, who is near broken by it. About Bernice's idea of trying exorcism, Ben doesn't know. The child does not seem to be herself, it's true, and anything is worth trying. But it's not amongst his notions of how God works in the world and tends His souls, notions learned mostly from Elaine's father, that gentle righteous man who set Ben on the true path all those years ago and brought him home to Jesus. "Grace is not something you die to get," Ely used to say in his sure quiet way, "it's something you get to live!" Ben has been working for some time on a song with that line, to the tune, loosely, of the old church number, "I'll Go Where You Want Me to Go." Another melody he has been humming of late: "I'll do Your will with a heart sincere, I'll be what You want me to be." He may introduce the song tonight at prayer meeting, if he can get the second line right.

Though Ely's spirit seems to have withdrawn from his wife and daughter of late, Ben has felt him close by all day, and he is reassured by that. Ely seems to be saying, just by being there, that there is man's work to be done and Ben must do it, though he promises him no peace from the sin of it, nor does Ben expect such a promise. Contrarily, Ben has not felt Jesus close by, not for some time. Moses, more like. As he said to Clara at the hospital this morning, "I'm feeling more Old Testament than New." "I know," she said. "But we're New Testament people, Ben. We have to bear up." But she was crying and did not stop crying.

When Ben unearthed the first batch of dummies down where the attack on Elaine took place, he supposed he had found it all. Only when he chanced on the second smaller lot in Rocky's violated grave did he realize the bikers must have buried their haul in separate parcels. More than anything else it's that careful planning that convinces Ben they'll return. How much is there? Sheriff Puller told them what the old inventory showed, but it was assumed to be out of date, and at the time no one took it seriously. But maybe they should have. The two parcels Ben has found would be only about a fifth of that inventory amount, meaning, if the number's right, there may be five or six other locations—or even more, depending on how they split it up. After finding the heap in his dog's grave, he paid a visit to his old abandoned farm shack where the biker boys holed up while they were here, figuring it was a likely out-of-the-way place for them to stow such things. He rooted about and took up floorboards and followed all their tracks, but he turned up nothing. Now, though, under the sharp cold spray, it comes to him like a revelation: that pile of small unburnt logs in the old wood cookstove. Everything else a shambles and those clean logs stacked as neatly as a kid's building blocks. He'll stop by there on his way back from the hospital.

He's just drying off, thinking about this, when Wayne Shawcross comes running in. "Ben! It's the police! She ain't here, but they've come to arrest Sister Debra!"

"They put a full-court press on Fleet, Dad. Fleet said Charlie picked up a pear and ate it with his mouth open while leaning on him. He was pretty sure Moron and Grunge and the others were pocketing other stuff from the store, but Charlie was wearing his brass knuckles and had all his attention. When he told Charlie the pear cost a quarter, Charlie tossed the core at him and told him to keep the change and try to keep his arms from getting broken." They're on the fifth green, Ted putting for a par. Tommy is understandably struggling with his swing today, trying to see with blackened eyes past his smashed and bandaged nose. They're not keeping score. They're having the conversation they missed at the Loin on Wednesday, when Tommy ended up in hospital. Tommy has been telling him now about a phone call he got from young Piccolotti after Charlie Bonali and his gang, including Concetta Moroni's badboy son, visited his Italian grocery this afternoon, threatening him with dire consequences to body and business if he didn't join his Knights of Columbus Volunteer Defense Force and contribute to arming it. "They also call themselves the Dagotown Devil Dogs, Fleet said."

"Devil dogs. Old wartime nickname for Marines. Probably reliving his days in the military."

"Well, that's another thing, Dad. Charlie was only in the Marines a few weeks before he went AWOL. Something Angela once told me. He ended up doing brig time and getting busted out with a dishonorable discharge." Nick only said Charlie had military experience. But he must have known. When he gets back to the clubhouse, he'll call Nick and Dee and demand Charlie's immediate arrest. Now. You've got sixty minutes. Ted sinks his putt in spite of hitting it too hard, but after two tries and another long lie, Tommy gives up and picks his ball up.

"And that thing they have about the Corpse, it's like they're queer for each other, just like fucking priests and the corpse of Christ." The ex–U.S. Marine recruit Charlie Bonali is treating members of his newly-formed Knights of Columbus Volunteer Defense Force to afternoon beers in Hog's Tavern, a dark little bar in the Italian neighborhood once popular with coalminers but now a little-used relic of times past. Hog Galasso has been dead for over a decade, but subsequent owners have seen no need to change the name, nor for that matter to clean it up or improve its reputation. The Hog is what it is, a local legend and landmark, scarred and rank and joyless. Charlie picks up his bottle and sucks long from it, looking like he might bite the top off and eat it, then signals for another. "They're like a mob of sick monks who whip themselves all the time just to show how holy they are." At the request of his enrapt younger comrades, Charlie, popping his knuckles for punctuation, is recounting his brief unhappy life in what he calls the "Marine Corpse" with its "little tin soldiers in toy uniforms." "They're always horsing around, grabbing each other, and the ones who don't touch, they're often the weirdest of them all, vicious little jerkoffs who get their kicks out of seeing other guys get their balls twisted. Killing for them is a kind of faggoty flirting with the Corpse. Trying to make out." Charlie belches fulsomely, examines his fingernails, polishes them on his unbuttoned blue police shirt. He is being arrested today but only laughs about it. "For me, killing people is just a job. It's no different from stepping on ants. And I like having a piece in my hands. Makes me feel like I am who I am. I've erased a few suckers, had to. That's why I'm back here for a while. There was a hood on the south side of the city working for the Old Man who decided to set up for himself. He said he didn't see any need to continue the partnership any longer, they could just be friends. So the Old Man sent me and some other guys in to waste him, make him a lesson for others. Now I got nothing against this motherfucker, it's just a matter of politics and territory, like in the last war the old farts are always bragging about. The dude had trouble with piles, and he went to a private clinic every so often to get his asshole doctored. We ambushed him there, only it turned out he'd been expecting us and had brought a lot of artillery with him and we were the ones who got ambushed. The shit was really flying. Talk about getting your ass reamed! But one thing I'd learned from the Corpse was to stay cool and keep a steady finger. Soon as I saw the receptionist was not at her desk, I just ducked out of sight, snapped my Sten onto automatic, and then at the first lull, stepped back in and blew them all away. They were shooting back, but they missed. They were trying too hard, like the sarge used to say. Six of us went in there, but only three of us got out, and one of them was badly shot up. I carried him out on my shoulder and later him and the other guy told the Old Man all that had happened. I was a hero. I mean a real hero. Those candyasses back in the Corpse would have shit green to watch me. So I got a rep now, I got respect. The Old Man smiles when he sees me. The other big guys aren't so sure. They think I might try to take their place someday." Charlie smiles a crooked smile at the rigid glassy-eyed faces smiling back. "And, hell, they're probably right."

Reverend Konrad Dreyer of Trinity Lutheran, home from his pole-fishing excursion to the lakes with his two small sons (they have caught three little sunfish the boys will share at supper), is seated in a lawn chair in his sunny backyard, which is also the church's backyard, a stack of books, his briar pipe, and a pitcher of fresh lemonade on the table beside him. The boys are off to the city swimming pool with his wife; he has this delicious late afternoon to himself. All around him: the green lawn he has nurtured, the flowers and fruit trees he has planted. Butterflies. Songbirds. The midsummer sun is still high in the sky and warm—warm enough for T-shirt and shorts, but not yet smotheringly hot as it soon will be in the weeks ahead. On his return from the lakes, his wife told him about the suicide of the shoe store man and said that Police Chief Romano called and wanted him to please call back, and he did so. Officer Romano said the deceased listed his religious preference as Lutheran and he wondered if the Reverend knew him or his family, as they were looking for possible surviving relations. Connie said, sorry, the man was not a member of his congregation and he did not know him. That's not surprising, he was not known as a religious man, the police officer said, but he had received a request from the secretary of the United Mine Workers local asking if Trinity Lutheran could host a memorial service for the man as they regarded him highly and wished to honor his passing, and Connie said that they could and that they should call him personally to schedule it. During summer vacation time, activities at the church dwindle, it should not be a problem.

In tomorrow's sermon, it is his intention to take on some of the more contentious issues being raised by faddish theologians: the death of God; the supposed fabrication of a Jesus who never was by way of ancient mystery cults and pagan spring deity myths; the invention of Christianity by Paul and the later gospel writers, none of whom knew Christ (if he existed); the contrary "truths" hidden in the Apocrypha, suppressed by the church fathers; Herod's slaughter of the firstborn; the myth of John the Baptist; the "dubious" legends of the Virgin Mary, and so on. Thus his afternoon's stacked reading. He will not argue separately against these naïve opinions but will rather contest the appropriateness of approaching the sacred by way of profane reasoning. In his early days at university as a philosophy major, before Augustine and Aquinas led him into theology and eventually the ministry, Connie, thinking he might have talent as a writer, took a memorable English course in which the professor convinced him that well-made fictions were true in ways that history and scientific formulae were not. Amusingly, the professor used the "Three Little Pigs" story as an example and actually made a kind of theology out of it. This concept of lies that were truer than truths corresponded nicely with his own belief in the "spirit" of history as opposed to history's supposed facts and made him feel at one with what he was even then calling "the creative force of the universe." It helped him to see that myths were not falsifications of history, but rather a special kind of language for grasping realities beyond time and space, realities of the eternal order, and to understand Christianity as the gradual shaping of a sustaining human vision, one impervious to the aberrations of history and the pretentious intrusions of misguided scholars. As such, it is true, even if it is not "true."

He pauses, takes a note to that effect, then returns to the book in his hand, which examines the historical evidence behind the four Gospels, finding little, and none at all for the existence of any so-called Jesus of Nazareth. Whereupon, out of the blue and as if in manifest refutation, Jesus appears before him, dressed in a crimson tunic with a dark blue robe over his shoulders and accompanied by a flock of small children. It takes him more than a moment to recognize Wes Edwards. The transformation is quite remarkable. This is not the real Jesus, of course, but the one popularized by Western art: pale, straight-nosed and high-browed, with a well-trimmed beard and flowing auburn locks (has Priscilla been adding highlights?), and costumed straight out of the Renaissance masters and European cathedral windows. "Hello, Wes," Connie says, standing and offering his hand. Which is not taken. "How good of you to drop by. I was just thinking about you."

Wesley glances back over his shoulder, frowns. "I think it's you he's speaking to," he says, peering down his nose. "Yes, yes, I know he's a fool, and foolishness is a sin, but, as has been said, God hath chosen the foolish things of the world to confound the wise. He believes, as he says, in 'learned ignorance,' so let us help him along in his belief." His focus lifts to rest on Connie. He smiles. His gaze is steely and unwavering, yet mischievous. He picks up the book Connie has been reading, thumbs through it thoughtfully. Much has changed in Wes' demeanor. He has lost his old crinkly-smile, lip-nibbling manner, is more aggressive, self-assured. He almost *is* who he pretends to be. When Wes pauses at a page, Connie prepares for a discussion about Jesus' own existence in history. Instead, Wes tears the page out, folds it into a paper airplane, and tosses it into the still air. It floats gracefully for a moment before dipping to earth, and Wes rips out another page.

"Hey, wait a minute—!"

The children clamber about, tugging on Wes' robes, asking if they can make airplanes too, and he smiles and spreads his arms and says, "I place before you an open door." Whereupon, before Connie can stop them, the children snatch up his books, spread out over the back yard, and commence to tear the pages out. Connie manages to grab hold of the last of the books, but the child screams so bloodcurdlingly he lets go of it again.

"Wes! Please! This is terrible! Make them give them back!"

"Wes, I'm afraid, is indisposed. And I am disinclined."

"But how *can* you? This…this disrespect for…!"

"Nonsense. There is altogether too much mystification of the written word. Especially that insignificant branch of fantasy literature known as theology. It is right that, like fancy, these pages take flight. Think of them," he adds, as a paper airplane floats past right in front of his nose—Connie ducks and bats at it as if at a pestering moth—"as angels bearing such pompous human folly on their wings as to fill thy mouth with laughing."

The big children are showing the little ones how to fold the planes and set them dancing. Meanwhile, they help themselves to his lemonade, drinking straight from the pitcher. A little girl, her cheek bulging, offers him a sticky jawbreaker with her fingerprints on it from a filthy brown paper bag. He fears he might be ill. At which point Priscilla Tindle shows up in a breathless tizzy, wearing only a torn nightshirt. "Oh dear Jesus! Thank Heavens! I've been looking all over for you!" she gasps, tears in her eyes. *"Come! We have to go!"*

"Woman, why weepest thou?" Wesley asks with a faint self-mocking smile, winking over her shoulder at Connie. Connie can see that her gown is ripped down the back and she is wearing nothing underneath it.

"The police have been at the studio!" she cries. "They came to arrest poor Wesley! *Hurry! You must save him!*" The children gather behind her, pointing and giggling. One of the little boys sails a paper plane in that direction, but it veers away shyly. It immediately becomes a game like pin the tail on the donkey and they are all trying to hit the target with their paper planes. She turns to them. "The police are trying to put Jesus in prison! We have to stop them! Tell them he took a bus out of town! Tell them he ascended into Heaven! Anything! *But don't let them find him!"*

After they have all scattered, Connie, somewhat shaken (he was not made for life's rough and tumble), wanders his backyard collecting books and pages. He has decided to postpone his truth-in-fiction sermon. He is too disconcerted to carry on, and summer is anyway too frivolous a time for it. Besides, let's be frank: those in his pastorate prefer a simple—and brief—communion service with a few Christian homilies tossed in, caring nothing for these bookish disputes, which just put them to sleep. He is, as Wesley himself has reminded him, only talking to himself.

The drive back from the lakes is a disaster. Debra makes the mistake of trying one last time to talk Colin into leaving the camp with her, taking a sudden turn onto the highway as she's crossing it, and Colin in panic tries to leap out of the moving car; she has to hit the brakes and grab him. She tries to pacify him in the old way, but he slaps furiously at her hand, shrieking wildly. "Don't touch me! They won't let me into Heaven!" She promises him, crossing her heart, that they'll go straight back to the camp, just please don't try to jump out of the car again. She drives very slowly, her heart pounding, tears in her eyes, one foot on the brake, Colin glaring at her in terror and gripping the door handle all the way back. As soon as they reach the camp gates, he does jump out of the car, tumbling onto the road, then leaping up and running toward all the people rushing their way, gripping his crotch, screaming hysterically that she's been doing terrible wicked things. *"To this!"* My God, has he opened up his pants? She sinks into the car seat, leans her head against the wheel. She only wants to die. "It's the police!" people are shouting outside her window. "They came to arrest you! Darren kept them out, but they'll be back! You can't let them see you!" She doesn't move. She doesn't care.

"The Virgin Mary told her that the cancer was eating her mind. If she could kill the cancer in her mind before it was too late, the cancer in her body would just melt away." Concetta Moroni is in Gabriela Ferrero's kitchen with her friends, Bianca and Gina and Francesca. The kitchen smells like a chicken coop with a kind of perfume on top, but they are all used to it by now. The five of them have gathered, as they often do in one kitchen or another, for a late afternoon coffee, drawn together today by the shoe store man who hung himself in his shop window, which Concetta witnessed (she gasps and crosses herself each time that terrifying scene pops back to mind) and Gabriela, picking up her prescription, saw just afterwards, when they were cutting the poor man down, and then Francesca saw the body when they brought it to the hospital. They all agree that it was the bank's fault, and Concetta expresses her pity for poor Mrs. Cavanaugh, having to live with that cold heartless man who only knows about money and is holding the whole town to ransom. "Mrs. Cavanaugh said the Virgin Mary telling her that was like a dream even though she was wide awake, and I said, no, it was a miracle, a visitation." Her friends all nod at that, though Gabriela says maybe it's all that morfiend she's taking. Gina, who is the mayor's secretary, wants to know how you cure mind cancer. "Like you cure all cancer, Gina," Concetta says. "Prayer. The only thing that works. If God wants you to die, there's nothing you can do, but you can always ask. Mrs. Cavanaugh and I may go to Lourdes to ask up close." She opens a little silk pouch and shows them the woman's rings, including her wedding ring, which Concetta is supposed to sell to raise the money for their trip to Lourdes because Mr. Cavanaugh refuses to give her any. Bianca tells about a friend who went to Lourdes and got her hearing back, and Francesca says if the Virgin is visiting Mrs. Cavanaugh here in West Condon, maybe they don't have to go to Lourdes. Francesca works as a receptionist at the hospital and is therefore their expert on medical knowledge, and she says that the best thing for mind cancer is hot compresses.

"Look at all those wires and panels and dials those sound guys have set up. Looks like an execution chamber in here."

"Yeah, not that I ever seen one. Nor won't never, I hope, knock on wood. Ifn they was any wood around to knock on…"

"You can use my head, Duke. Nothing up there right now but wet sawdust. The way they've set us out on the floor like this is scary. I'm so nervous I have to pee every five minutes. I just only hope I can remember the words tonight."

"I ast about the setup and ole Elmer lifted up his Stetson to reset his hairpiece'n declared it was time fer us to step out inta the crowd'n *be* somebody."

"Elmer?"

"Elmer Jankowski. Happens that's Will Henry's real monicker, wudja believe? One a them recordin' fellers let the cat out. Always figgered Hank Williams backwards couldn't be his genuine tag."

"Oh. I see. Funny. Well, I'm changing my name, too, Duke. We gotta fix the sign out front and be sure it gets spelt right on the record label. I'm changing it to Rendine."

"That's my name."

"I know. I don't mean it like a married name. It's just who I am now. Who you made me. It's like that song of yours, the only good thing that's happened. I wanta mark it somehow. Patti Jo Rendine. It's the only name I want now for the rest of my life. And nobody knows it's your real name, not even those record company guys. Just only you and me and your mama. You can think of me like a kinda cousin. A kissin' cousin."

"Well, purty lady, gimme a smack to show me whom you am. Yep. I reckanize you now, Patti Jo Rendine. Gimme me another, dear cuz, jist fer ole times' sake."

"Mmm. That feels almost too good to feel good, Duke. I always thought I knew too much about love and the disappointments of love, but I've never known anything like this. And thanks, I do appreciate your not being mad about the name."

"Mad? Patti Jo, you're the best doggone thing happened to the fambly since great granpappy Rendine figgered out howta make likker outa swamp moss. But, y'know, them record fellers said ifn one of our songs take off, they wanta git us round to other radio stations'n agent us inta gigs in bigger places. We may hafta load up the ole Packard'n hit the road. You gonna be ready fer that?"

"Well…sure…"

"What does Marcella say about it?"

"Don't worry, it'll be okay. She'll let me know when it's time to go."

"Hey, that's a nice line for a song."

"What is?"

"She'll let me know when it's time to go. Like, they's this feller shacked up with a beautiful gal who's the restless sort, y'know, always havin' to try on a new man from time to time. She's beautiful'n he's gonna enjoy her while he can, even knowin'…she'll let me know when it's time to go."

"I can almost hear it now. But that's not me, you know."

"No, sweet angel. It ain't me neither."

It has been a long day for Police Chief Dee Romano, and it's getting longer. That mess over at the shoe store filling the streets with restless gawkers. Vandalism at the bank. He jailed that wiseass Johnson, put up with his shit for a while and let him go. Cavanaugh and Minicozzi on his back all day. He has been ordered to lock up Charlie Bonali before sundown or heads will roll. Charlie himself turned up at the station, still partly uniformed, snapping his fingers and ignoring Dee's orders to turn in his arms and equipment. When he told him that when the city attorney sends the charges over he'll have to arrest him, he only laughed. Bunch of younger pezzi di merda hanging on his elbow, chewing thick wads of gum and grinning malevolently, most of them wagging beer bottles and calling themselves the Knights of Columbus Volunteer Defense Force. Charlie's private army. Demands came in to arrest the Presbyterian minister and his wife, but when they took the phony warrant out to the church camp to pick up the wife, they got turned away by a blond kid needing a haircut; got a better one now. Monk and Louie, meanwhile, haven't been able to find the preacher, even though that loony has been staggering around in plain sight all day making mischief, his girlfriend chasing him with her tail on view. They're still out there, somewhere. The city attorney calls again to tell him Bonali is at Hog's Tavern and ready to turn himself in, letting him know that he has spoken with Judge Altoviti and bail will be granted, the money for it already in hand.

Louie and Monk return, finally, and he asks them where the hell they've been.

"Lookin' for that preacher. A little kid come in and says he seen Jesus over to the bus station and begged us not to let him go away so we run over there. Turns out they ain't been a bus through in more'n two hours and none due soon, but they was another kid there playing the pinball machine, and when we asked, he said he thought Jesus had gone to get a pizza while he was waiting for a bus."

"Whaddaya mean, playing the pinball machine? That thing's been tilted for years now."

"Well, he was pretending then. The crazy preacher wasn't at Rico's pizza joint neither, but they was a little girl playing jacks in the street who said she seen him and heard him talk about going to preach out in Chestnut Hills. She said some funny lady with a bare bottom was driving him and she pointed in the direction they went. We grabbed the cruiser and rolled out there, but Chestnut Hills is mostly a slum for the homeless nowadays and we couldn't find nobody who seen him—until we come on a coupla kids sitting on a curb, and they said they seen him at the big stone church in town where they was flying paper airplanes. That sounded pretty nutty and we was about to give up, figuring we was getting the runaround, but we supposed they musta been talking about the Lutheran place, so we stopped by there anyhow, and sure enough, the preacher there said the Jesus guy had been there, and the kids, too, making paper airplanes, and even the lady with the nekkid patoot. He didn't know where they'd gone."

"What are you sucking on, Monk?"

"Jawbreaker. One of them little kids gimme it."

Romano is beat and ready to call it a day, hand the station over to Bo, but before he heads home, he and his two lieutenants have one final run to make to complete the list of his day's failures.

It's that time of day: When shadows fall and trees whisper day is ending… An old song, as the country singer Duke L'Heureux would say, but a new virgin of it. The people of West Condon have been through this longest day countless times, and at the same time it has never happened before; they have often reached this tender time of evening, but not the tender time of *this* evening now softly upon them. The midsummer sun is still posted as high in the sky as it ever gets in midwinter, but it has begun to lodge in trees and duck behind buildings, offering a gentler, kinder light. Work for most, if they have work, is over, and they are, often with a drink in hand, considering the possibilities of the long twilight ahead. There are gatherings on front porches, at backyard grills, in the town's bars and eateries, over picnics at the parks and lakes, on baseball diamonds, cinder basketball courts, the golf course, on street corners. Dave Osborne's shop-window suicide has thrown a weird cast upon the day and much of the talk is about it. Those who have seen the rogue Jesus, believed by many to be an escapee from that crazy church camp sect, parading drunkenly about with his rascally troop of kiddies and that frantic lady in the ripped nightshirt have these tales to tell as well, and as with the day itself, everyone has heard such stories before, and yet they are all completely new. Those gathered on Vince Bonali's front porch have the additional treat of son Charlie's comical account of his arrest by the clowns who pass for town cops and his subsequent release on bail. Charlie's stories go down well, supplemented as they are by a case of cold bottled beer provided by him, and even his father knows better than to butt in. Their church organist running around in the streets with her behind on view was also witnessed by Emily Wetherwax, out shopping for hamburger and hotdog buns for tonight's picnic out at the lakes, and she describes the sight on the phone to Susanna Elliott. She and Susanna have agreed they'll take the Wetherwax car out to the lakes and both are excited by the old-fashioned wienie-roast fun ahead. "I even picked up some marshmallows," Emily says. Emily has been asked to help out down at the bank as they have lost one of their tellers and are shorthanded. Her husband Archie is somewhere up a telephone pole just now, Susanna's Jim is snoring on the couch, sleeping off one hangover to get ready for another. "Remember, Em, how on hot nights," Susanna says as her daughter Sally comes through the door, "when they wouldn't let us into the Dance Barn because we were too young, we used to dance in the parking lot, listening to the music coming through the open windows?" The banker, in from the links, hears from his bank lawyer and city attorney the story of Charlie Bonali's arrest and his release on bail, as granted by Judge Altoviti, and asks, "Did we contest it?" "We queried it," he is told. This is not the answer the banker wanted to hear, but he is into his second sour mash whiskey and is already thinking ahead to his upcoming night at the highway motel (the light outside the Nineteenth Hole windows, which face onto the putting green, is just right) and he lets it go. The nearness of you… The woman he'll be seeing has just dropped the Elliott girl off at home and is on her way out to the motel. She has not heard the stories of the man dressed like Jesus or even that of the suicide, but she has heard the story of the torn scrapbook photos and she remains gloomily haunted by it. Perhaps she will have to cancel tonight's supper date. The various stories, though not that one, are going around the pool hall, too, where the organizer of tonight's big stag party for Stevie Lawson is doing his best to scratch up some coin for the festivities by challenging the hangabouts in there to games, and Georgie has held his own, two bits at a time, but the truth is that he can't shoot for shit since Lem Filbert laid into him with that crowbar and crooked up his arm. Georgie damns the hothead many times a day, and he damns him now. Lem is still at work, one day like another, pissed off that his bonehead mechanic has knocked off early. He's having second thoughts about the big new loan he has just signed on for at the bank; he'll have to work twice as hard just to meet the payments and he doesn't know how he can do that.

It is late in the afternoon, shortly before supper, when the West Condon police arrive at the Brunist Wilderness Camp on their second attempt to arrest Sister Debra Edwards for appropriating all that money from her rich folks' church and giving it to the camp. The shadows are lengthening, the birds are into their evening concert, the fireflies are dancing their fairy dance down by the creek. Mabel Hall's friends have already gathered in her mobile home down in the trailer lot for today's reading of the tarot cards and have been idly gossiping in anticipation of the main event while waiting for Lucy Smith and Hazel Dunlevy. Things have been busy over at the Collins trailer which they can watch out of Mabel's caravan windows. Poor half-starved Elaine was brought home from hospital in the ambulance today, exciting everyone ("Let them through! It's little Elaine! Clara, Bernice, too!"), for Clara and Ben have not been the same since they got back and they reckon only Elaine's improvement, signaled by this release from hospital, will change that. Bernice, who is the only one who has been allowed in and out over there, has assured them that the girl is eating again, explaining that Elaine is possessed by the devil, maybe more than one, and that when she is strong enough to survive it they will attempt an exorcism, but Ludie Belle, who got a close glimpse of Elaine when they were unloading her from the ambulance, says she reckons "she's a-breedin'," and that stirs thoughts of a darker sort, though few get expressed. "Devils getting in do the same effects," Bernice explains solemnly, arching her brow. They have all wanted to go pray with her and see for themselves, but Elaine is too weak for visitors.

Then suddenly Mabel's husband comes busting in to tell them that the police have arrived to arrest Sister Debra. "Lord have mercy! The wicked is at the gates a the righteous!" Willie cries. Ludie Belle is the first one out the door, the others quickly following.

They see Ludie Belle's husband and Ben running up the hill ahead of them toward the Main Square, and when they get there several of the other men are there, too. The sheriff who was here earlier has left, so Billy Don has run into the Meeting Hall to try to call him from the office phone. The three policemen have paused at the gate, and Ben and Wayne go over to talk with them. It's a tense moment but people are being polite. The police read out the charges and show Ben the new warrant and Ben says quietly that he's sorry but it's his understanding that the camp is outside the town's jurisdiction. The police, who do not seem very intent on their task (it's Saturday night and they're working people too), point out that the warrant now covers the entire county and that if they wish to call the sheriff they may, but he will be obliged under the law to carry out the same arrest. Which explains to most who hear this conversation why the sheriff has gone away and why Mr. Suggs made a final offer to Mrs. Edwards to give her money to leave the area immediately, which she, in her distress and against the advice of her friends, has turned down.

Even now, while Ben and the police are talking, she steps mournfully out of her cabin wearing only a loose wrinkled summer smock and floppy thong sandals and walks to the gate to turn herself in. Her eyes are red and streaming still, and two or three of the women start to cry, too, including Lucy Smith, who has just arrived with two of her little ones and is watching all this from outside the gate, and then her children start to cry. Sister Debra has given so much of herself to this place they now call home, and if there is some question about where the money came from, there is certainly no question that Sister Debra has kept none of it for herself. She has been devoted to them as they now feel devoted to her. Ludie Belle and Linda and Corinne and all the others flock around and interpose themselves between her and the police, Ludie Belle berating the police fiercely for picking on the poor saintly woman, but Sister Debra says in a choked whispery voice that it's all right and she steps past Ludie Belle and through the gate. The police say she might want to take an overnight bag. She shakes her head and walks toward the police car, but Ludie Belle and Corinne run into her cabin and throw a lot of things into a canvas bag they find there and bring it and a cardigan out to the police, Ludie Belle still giving them a piece of her mind. Hunk and Travers have a word with the older policeman with the bent rusty badge, and the officer shrugs and spits a wad of chaw.

As if all this isn't bad enough, young Colin, without any pants on, bursts from the boys' cabin past Darren and starts screaming out the same dreadful accusations against his mother as before, somewhat alarming the police and everybody else, Darren trying to drag Colin back to the cabin, telling him if he carries on they're going to lock him up in an institution again. One of the police officers, the one in charge, sighs and asks Ben for the boy's name, and Ben hesitates and looks around at the others but finally he tells him, adding that the boy is Mrs. Edwards' adopted son but he is not completely right in the head. The police officer nods sadly and apologizes to Ben, saying sometimes there are things he has to do he'd rather not do, and Ben nods back gravely and the officers get into the car with Sister Debra and drive away.

In Mabel's caravan afterwards, the talk is mainly about the arrest of poor Sister Debra, bless her heart—she looked like something was completely broken inside—and about the terrible things Colin was saying. Could they be true? Ludie Belle will say only that he is a troubled boy with special needs and that Sister Debra is a loving and caring person. They can read that however they like but, as Christians, always with charity in their hearts. Bernice was not in the caravan when they got back. She has probably returned to Mr. Suggs' bedside at the hospital. She hardly ever leaves it. There are people who want to put her in jail along with Sister Debra, and only Mr. Suggs has the money and power to stop that from happening, so it's a "desprit needcessity," as Ludie Belle puts it in her extravagant way, to keep him ticking even if the tick is more like a t-t-tick now. Well, they all need him; God grant him a full recovery and a long life. Lucy remembers that last week Mabel turned up the Wheel of Fortune card upside down, along with that dark ace which could mean bad planning, and she wonders if that wasn't a prophecy of these latest events, and everyone agrees it may be so, and turn expectantly to Mabel. Sister Hazel Dunlevy has not arrived but they decide not to wait for her. They will have supper together soon, before the eight o'clock prayer meeting down at the dogwood tree, joined there by some old friends from the Church of the Nazarene who are becoming Brunists tonight. There is just time left for Mabel to spread and read the cards, which now she is shuffling expertly with her eyes closed in solemn meditation. They wonder if they will learn more about Sister Debra's fate or little Elaine's or even their own, God save us, and whether or not, on such a day, the Hanged Man card will reappear. "I have noticed," Glenda Oakes says, gazing with her one eye upon the fluttering cards now sliding into each other and coming to rest, "that Jesus is not in the deck." "No," Mabel replies in her soft feminine voice, so different from what one might expect from a woman her size. And then she opens her eyes to look at Glenda. "He *is* the deck."

"I reckon I shoulda went to Mabel's by now."

"Yeah. But it's too late. I skipped out on Wayne's crew, too."

Too late. Yes. It surely is. She shudders, sighs. Too late. Too late already that first time up on Inspiration Point. They have stepped out of the shed and walked the garden rows and picked a few weeds and wildflowers and eaten some berries and they have gone down to the creek to splash fresh water on their faces and private parts and they have even walked the path back toward the Meeting Hall a ways, but they keep coming back here. Like they can't help it. She looks at her palm. "I'm skeered about the next part. But I thank the Lord this part got wrote in before."

"Y'figger the Lord's had anything to do with it?"

"He has to do with everthing. All what signs they are—in people's hands, their dreams, Mabel's cards or tea leaves—is jist misty windas into God's mind. Who's thunka everthing already on accounta He's perfect'n all-knowin'. It's all been worked out. Back when time begun."

"What about this purty little part down here? Is that a winda into God's mind, too?"

"Has to be. It all is. Think y'kin read it?"

"It says your heart line'n fate line is seriously crossed up, but it don't matter none on accounta how splendrous it is."

"Yes. And how sad."

"Don't see that part. But here, lemme use my tongue'n turn a page…"

"Oh…!" We are, she thinks, making darkness our home tonight, and a warmth creeps through her, and another shudder. "Yes…"

"It's suppertime. Hungry?"

"No…"

When Sally Elliott suggested they bring their pizzas out here to the lakes, Billy Don had no objections. Neither did he object to the two six packs of cold beer Sally picked up at the liquor store around the corner. They took Sally's folks' car rather than his old pea-green Chevy, which they left parked at a broken meter back in Tucker City to save Billy Don gas money, and he appreciated that. He has appreciated everything. It's a gorgeous evening, sliding easily into twilight. The lake water is unruffled and the birds are singing and the crickets are doing their hiccuppy thing and the pizza is delicious and he's pretty sure he is in love, though he's new to the idea. Probably she could kick him in the shins and he'd appreciate that, too. He has filled her in on the arrest of her aunt Debra, which upset Sally a lot, and her sadness made her seem prettier somehow. Behind a man's frayed white shirt, open down the front and buttoned at the cuffs as protection against the mosquitoes, she is wearing a T-shirt tonight that says GIVE ME A HUG – I'M AT THAT AWKWARD STAGE BETWEEN BIRTH AND DEATH.

He'd like to do that and maybe he will if it's not too late (it probably is, darn it), but she jokes a lot and he's not sure she really means it, and he's even less sure she means it for him. She's friendly, but not friendly in that way, though maybe it's just the way she is with everyone and she really likes hugging and is trying to tell him so and he should stop being such a coward. It would help if she wasn't so smart. Tonight it has been how any dumb notion, no matter where it comes from and especially if it can be pictured, can become what she called a motif (he asked her to spell it) and then get borrowed and used around the world, notions like messenger birds and human sacrifice and magical virgins and holy mountains, which become the common currency of religions everywhere and contribute to the universal madness. Not everything catches on, of course. Back in the Dark Ages, she tells him, they used to celebrate midsummer with cat-burning rituals, and those aren't so popular anymore. When he tried to change the subject to something more in the hugging line by remarking that he felt like tonight was almost like living in a dream, Sally said that, yes, life was a kind of dream all right, but it's mostly a dream dreamt by others—the hard thing being to figure out how to wake up. He had told her about Glenda Oakes' dream interpretations, more or less in the same clumsy sentence, and she said that's what preachers and theologians were: charlatan dream interpreters.

Now, over pizza and beer at the lakeside picnic table, listening to the crickets and birds, distant boat motors, the occasional floating voices out on the lake, the dry crackle of firecrackers at other picnics, he has shown her Darren's latest newsletter to the church membership. It's the copy intended for Reverend Hiram Clegg, which he plucked out of the bagful before mailing them this afternoon. Reverend Clegg has problems of his own right now and is probably even in jail, so they may not even have the right address. "Sometimes I think Darren is completely crazy," he says, watching Sally read, squinting in the dimming light, "and sometimes I think he's the only one who knows."

"Right the first time, Billy D," she says around a mouthful of pizza and she punches open another can of beer. He sips his slowly, it being the first he's had since before Bible college; Sally has just finished off, with a wink, her third one. When she calls him Billy D, he doesn't know if that's a putdown or a come-on. "The 'remarkable prophecies of the brilliant young visionary evangelist Darren Rector' as revealed in all modesty by the brilliant young visionary himself."

"Well, the letter is from Mrs. Collins. Or, you know, that's what..."

Sally only smiles, lights up another cigarette, sets it on the edge of the table, and takes another bite of pizza, and with a happy shrug, so does he, trying to keep his moustache out of the melted cheese, and he also finishes off his beer and reaches into the ice for another one. He's sure she wants him to hug her. "Darren is living in the realm of the supernatural," she says. "The natural has dying in it, the supernatural doesn't, it's as simple as that. Dying is too much for most people. So what are you going to do if you don't live in the majority's crazy made-up world? Steer clear if you can and duck when they have guns in their hands. Speaking of which, any more attacks on the camp?"

"No, but everybody's pretty nervous. Including me. I had the watch last night with Welford Oakes and he said he thought he heard something and told me to sit tight until he got back. I suddenly heard all kinds of noises and thought I saw a whole army creeping around out there in the trees and I mighta fired off a shot but I was hunkered down behind a thick bush and didn't want them to know where I was. Besides, it mighta been Welford. I thought he'd never come back, and when he did he was smoking and humming to himself and said it was just some animal, rooting around down in the vegetable patch."

Sally is laughing. He likes to hear her laugh, even when she's laughing at him. It's a lot better than making him feel like an idiot just because he's a Christian. "Would you ever shoot someone?" she asks.

"I think I already did. Just buckshot in his rear, though."

"Got him while he was running away, hunh?"

"Well, I didn't know that. It was dark and the bullets were flying and I was hiding behind a tree and shooting backwards over my shoulder."

Sally laughs again (that wasn't exactly true, but he wanted to hear her laugh), takes a long drink, then belches noisily like a boy. "Whoo!" she says, and belches again. "I think I need some powdered toenails!"

"What?"

"Powdered toenails. Just the thing for heartburn. Grandma Friskin told me. Like chewing the bark of a tree struck by lightning when you have a toothache and eating twenty crickets with wine to cure asthma."

"I guess that would cure most anything." He'd like to know what works for a near-fatal case of raw throbbing horniness. Well, he knows what works…

"Mmm. Listen to the little buggers sounding off. It's like a mass protest. Maybe they think we took their name in vain." He's trying to figure out how to get back to the hugging idea, when Sally rubs out her butt on the sole of her sneaker, scuffs it into the earth, lights up another, and says, "Best folk-wisdom healer of all, though, is water. Especially on a night like tonight. A midsummer night's dip heals everything."

"Like baptism," he says. "Another, what you call it, motif." The word feels funny in his mouth but he's glad he can say it.

"Right on, Billy Don. So what do you say, after it gets dark, just for our health, we go for a little skinny dip?"

Her faith is in question, her heart is full of doubt. It is a faith that has sustained and protected her since she reached the age when she could think for herself, and now she is unsure of it. As it is the only faith she has had, she has become, she recognizes, something of a fundamentalist. She has trusted it absolutely as other people thoughtlessly trust their God, a kind of unconditional first principle, and she is losing that certainty. He arrives in his colorful golf clothes, carrying an overnight bag, and asks her to join him in the shower, and she hesitates, never having hesitated before. Undressing, knowing his eyes are upon her, she wonders if her apostasy is transparent. But under the cool spray and lathering hands, that sense of oneness with the universe common to all mystical religions returns, and she gratefully surrenders to it, lets her tears flow with the waterfall, and tries, eyes closed, to think of nothing but this unique sudsy moment of existence. After they dry each other off, he walks her over to the window, ostensibly to gaze out upon the fading midsummer evening, but in reality to gaze upon each other sweetly costumed in that soft light. He turns her to face away from the window and kisses her slowly from nape to heels, nipping her buttocks in his teeth as he passes by them, his large strong hands squeezing them gently, passing between them, his tongue licking at her anus and the backs of her knees, and what she sees in the full-length mirror across the room is her shadowy silhouetted presence, like someone only half-formed, the framing window glowing like a nimbus, the man she loves behind her, his features softly lit by her body's reflective glow, kneeling to kiss her feet before rising slowly to repeat the ceremony from heel to nape, his hands caressing the parts in front. He murmurs, as he kisses his way up her body, how exquisitely beautiful she is and how much he adores her and needs her, and she knows the reply to this but is silent for once. She has always thought of her first principles as something that came spontaneously to her—by inspired insight, as it were. But she probably had to learn them. All religions are learned, Sally said. To escape them, they have to be unlearned. Most people don't want to do that. She doesn't want to do that. Sometimes this unlearning comes from personal effort, what Sally calls the hard work of waking up. Sometimes it just happens.

"What does anything mean if dying's at the end of it?" asks Guido Mello, still feeling loose from his after-hours beers on Vince Bonali's porch and unwilling to go to his unhappy home yet. He is sitting at a lackluster round of four-handed penny-ante poker up at the Eagles Social Club with Cokie Duncan and Buff Cooley and one-armed Bert Martini, and they're blowing off about Dave Osborne's suicide. There is a pile of laceless shoes rescued from Dave's store on the table next to them, but none of them match. So it's a kind of memorial instead.

They are all ex-miners and knew and respected Dave, and Bert has just remarked that suicide sucks all the meaning out of life and he doesn't understand why anyone would do that. "Thing is," Guido adds, "thinking about dying can be worse than the thing itself. So, only two ways out: buy into some God-and-Heaven bull or knock yourself off. Anything else is chickenshit."

"God and Heaven ain't bull and you oughtn't talk that way," Bert says angrily.

"Count me in with the chickens," says Cokie Duncan, who rarely says much of anything at all, and spreads his hand, which has a jack and two kings in it. "Here's Jesus and his two fathers," he says morosely.

"I will say, if I ever did such a thing, and I wouldn't," says Buff, tossing his cards into the pot in disgust, "that I wouldn't waste the occasion. I'd take a few bigwig assholes with me."

"Why, Buff?" asks Guido, his nose still smeared with auto grease from his long day as a slave at Lem's garage. It's rumored that Guido's wife is pregnant again and he doesn't know how she got that way, though her own old man is a prime suspect. "You'd just be trying to paste meaning onto where there fucking ain't none." If he had the words for it, he'd say: Pure suicide is a mere cancellation of the self as a solution to an otherwise insoluble problem. But he doesn't have the words for it.

Just when they're feeling their most miserable and wordless, Georgie Lucci turns up with six or seven other disreputable drunks, including Stevie Lawson, whose stag party night this turns out to be, and some boxes of hot pizza from the Palazzo di Pizza. "Enrico give us these for the party," Georgie says, and they open up the boxes and screw the top off a new bottle of rye whiskey. They learn that Lawson is marrying one of Abner Baxter's girls tomorrow, though no one, including Stevie, quite knows how this has come about. "We're making the rounds. Rico's joining us when he turns off the ovens. Plan to end up in Waterton and get Stevie laid by three whores at once. It's our wedding present. Cheese has set it up."

Johnson grins, showing his scatter of teeth. His hair has been chopped back. He's bathed, shaved, and is even wearing a new silk shirt, gift of one of the Waterton ladies of the night. Johnson is famous for the graffiti he painted on the bank wall today and they all compliment him for it. "It was me and Jesus," he says, and they all laugh at that though they don't know what he means exactly, never having thought of him as a religious-type person.

They toast Lawson and his bride. "Is she good lookin'?"

"Well, there's plenty of her," Lawson says, and they all laugh again. They figure he must have got her pregnant somehow when he was working out at the church camp for Suggs. He doesn't deny that and they make jokes about the physical hazards of fucking holyrollers when they got the spirit on them. They aren't funny jokes, but everyone snorts just the same.

"I hear the place to be tonight is the Blue Moon Motel," Buff says. "They're recording them hillbillies live."

"We been there," says Stevie Lawson, his speech already slurring. "They throwed us out."

"We're letting the show out there get revved up and then we're going back with a squad big enough to open that door like Moses parted the red-ass sea," Georgie says with his usual me-ne-fotte grin. The Eagles Club is redolent with hot garlic and bakery aromas and nobody is thinking about suicide. "Give ole Duke and his lady some background hooting and hollering that'll drown out how bad they're singing. You guys come along. We got booze should last us till dawn."

"Grace is not something you die to get, it's something you get to live!" Ben Wosznik is singing, his guitar slung over his weary shoulder. Such a sadness in him these days; but his song is not sad. "Of all God's gifts, the gift a grace is the greatest He can give!" It's his new song using Ely Collins' famous line, and it's a good night for introducing it, for they have seven of their old Nazarene friends in their midst, all of whom were church members in Ely's day and loved him as man and pastor, and it makes them feel more at home. Clara has been speaking regularly with the Nazarene elder Gideon Diggs, and as they have been without a pastor for some years now and share close confessional ties, these seven have decided to join their fellowship in the Gospel and become Brunists, most of them asking to be baptized with light. Other old friends are known to be attending services led by Abner Baxter, so there is still hope they will all be together again someday. With the light lasting so long these days, the Brunists hold their evening prayer meetings, weather allowing, down here by the dogwood tree. Its blossoms are long gone but have been replaced by bright red berries—like drops of Christ's blood, some say—that help to feed the camp's population of squirrels and birds. The sky is a softer eventide shade of aqua blue now, wearing like a ghostly mask the waning moon, already palely risen, and a golden light has settled in as if the whole world were being haloed. The seven new Followers are a welcome addition tonight (Darren has invited them all to the consecration of the two graves on the Mount of Redemption on the fifth of July and they have all said they will be there), for several of their own camp regulars are missing—both Dunlevys, for example; poor Sister Debra, for whom they have all prayed; Welford Oakes (missing at supper, too; after the service Bernice will check to see if Welford has a problem she can medicate); Hunk Rumpel, who has a training session with the Christian Patriots this evening, which is probably where Travers Dunlevy is, too; also the gospel singers, Duke and Patti Jo, who are committed to a recording session tonight of Duke's new song, which may not be a completely Christian one; and young Billy Don as well. Maybe it's the good weather: not always worship's best friend. Billy Don's absence seems to have got Darren's dander up, probably because he needs help in coping with Colin, who has been more or less out of control ever since the arrest of his mother. When the song is finished, Clara walks over to Ben and takes his hand in both of hers and thanks him, and they all thank him and bless him, and then, with apologies and a prayer that the grace Ely spoke of and Ben sang about be granted, she takes her leave to return to their trailer to watch over Elaine. Poor

Sister Clara has been badly beat down by recent events, but there are heartening signs of renewed life in her now that her daughter is back home and beginning to eat again. In her wake there are spontaneous prayers for her and Elaine, who, their Nazarene friends are told, may be demonically possessed and needing all the prayers they can offer up. Gideon Diggs says he once knew a Hungarian lady over in the next county who did exorcisms and he'll try to find out if she's still around.

The Nazarene visitors are startled by a noise out on the periphery that sounds like repeating gunfire just as Ben is about to lead them all in singing a verse or two of the hit parade tune "Whispering Hope" ("If, in the dusk of the twilight, dim be the region afar…"), and Wayne explains that vandal-types have been driving by all week and tossing firecrackers and cherry bombs into the camp; it'll probably tail off after Independence Day. Meanwhile, Colin keeps crying out that he wants to confess. "Not out here under the tree, Colin," Darren urges. "It's not right." "I got something here to calm him down, Darren," Bernice says in a whisper that carries everywhere, indicating her patent-leather handbag, "but it has to be done with a needle, so if you can—" That sets the boy to screaming hysterically and running off toward the cabins, Darren chasing after to be sure he doesn't harm himself. Some of the women exchange knowing glances with Mabel Hall, for in her reading of the tarot cards before supper she turned up cards that meant either the destructive use of fire by the clash of opposites (Glenda asked what kind of fire was meant and Mabel said all kinds) or else chaotic unmanageable energy and loss of direction provoked by new family or community arrangements created by exigencies beyond their control, and they know now which was the right one. That's how it is: mostly bad news in the cards these days. Well, they can only hope…

*Hope, as an anchor so steadfast,*
*Rends the dark veil for the soul,*
*Whither the Master has entered,*
*Robbing the grave of its goal…*

*Whispering hope, oh how welcome thy voice,*
*Making my heart in its sorrow rejoice...*

After the song, Wayne steps forward to read the scripture lesson, which was to have been on the theme of "The present sufferings are not worth comparing with the glory to come," from Romans. But with the arrival of the visitors, he switched—with the help of his wife Ludie Belle, who is a faster reader—to the theme of togetherness. "For where two or three are gathered together in my name, there am I in the midst of them," he reads, and turns the page. "And then we which are alive and remain shall be caught up together with them in the clouds, to meet the Lord in the air: and so shall we ever be with the Lord!" is the next passage, announcing the Rapture and taken from First Thessalonians, but he just has them caught up together in the clouds without yet meeting the Lord when more pops are heard out at the edge somewhere, and Gideon Diggs interrupts to say, "I don't think them was firecrackers." In the brief silence—even the birds have stopped their evensong—they listen to hear if there are more, and there are—not many—and then they stop. They seemed not far away, but sounds travel easily at this time of evening. "Where you suppose...?" Ben asks, cocking his ear, and Glenda Oakes, her one eye staring off into the distance, says, "In the garden." "The garden?" She shrugs, draws her children closer and other children who have joined her own. "Go see, Wayne," Ludie Belle says, and Wayne, who has armed himself for guard duty later tonight, sets off toward Mrs. Edwards' garden, the other men following cautiously behind and, when no more shots are heard, the women follow too.

It is quiet down in the garden and there is no sign of intruders other than a few late-to-bed birds raiding the berry patch. Up in the trees, darkening now against a darkening sky, others are back at their lusty night-warble. The evening air is full of the rich midsummer fragrance of ripening fruits and vegetables. Such an abundance all about! They should get down here more often. And will have to, too, now that Sister Debra has been taken away. The only thing out of the ordinary is that the tool shed door is open. Inside they find Hazel Dunlevy and Welford Oakes with bullet holes in their foreheads. Neither are wearing much. In fact, they are not wearing anything at all. They seem quite peaceful. More souls to pray for, and some drop to their knees and commence to do so. Everyone knows who has done this. "We'll have to call the sheriff," someone says. People notice that their Nazarene friends have left. "Look at their hands," Corinne Appleby says. "Like Jesus' nail-wounds on the cross," Wayne Shawcross observes. Corinne shakes her head. "Looks to me like he shot away their life lines."

After the longest day: the shortest night. But one so steeped in legend, ritual, and superstition—or decayed religion, as superstition is sometimes called by those who do not see all religions as such—that it sometimes seems the longest one. A night of love oracles, fire festivals, fertility rites, and magical cures. Of witchcraft and drunken excess. Of dreaming awake. It marks the birth of the god of darkness, whose power now will wax as the sun god's wanes, and thus marks the birth of madness and death. The sort of thoughts the amateur folklorist Sally Elliott might be entertaining as she removes her clothes at the shore of the moonlit lake, the deepening sky still faintly aglow—her body, too, for anyone there to see. Even in a rational age, should such a thing improbably exist, these sorts of notions would die hard, nurtured as they are by the common imagination and its craving for solace and meaning in the face of the faceless abyss. Tonight, for example, Angela Bonali has tied nine flowers with pieces of grass (only scattered clumps of it to be found in their muddy unkempt yard, but fortunately long as weeds), and after asking the cement Virgin in the yard for her blessing on them, has placed them under her pillow, hoping to dream later of her future husband—namely, Tommy Cavanaugh, whose picture she has taken from her diary and also put under the pillow just to be sure—because she read about this in a magazine for young mothers loaned to her by Stacy last week before Angela got fired at the bank.

The magazine, the unreflecting carrier of these ancient fancies, also had astrology charts and hers told her to expect a change of fortune on the very day (or nearly) that the bank let her go. She is waiting at home tonight for Tommy's call, which she has thought about so much it's almost as though it has already happened. He wants to take her to the Blue Moon Motel and dance with her in front of all her friends, even with his face all bandaged up, so she has bathed and shampooed and done up her hair in a different way based on a picture she saw downtown this afternoon in Linda Catter's beauty shop window (it was wrong to have a double banana split and a whole pizza both on the same day, but she had a desperate craving for them so powerful that it has not abated even with the satisfying of it, and in her condition what can you do?) and tweezed her eyebrows and shaved her armpits and other parts seen only when everything is seen (she has created a kind of fern-leaf pattern down there) and applied blush and mascara and lip gloss and eyeliner and perfumed her bra and panties and put on her most summery and revealing dress and practiced what she will say when he apologizes and begs her to return to him.

In another part of town, Franny Baxter is in like manner preparing for her marriage on the morrow. Her prospective sister-in-law has fashioned a wedding gown for her out of her own old wedding dress plus a couple of yards of white satin, taffeta, and chiffon to accommodate Franny's more ample figure, and she is helping Franny now, after giving her a bath, with the applying of perfume and makeup (first time ever!). The groom will arrive home shortly before dawn, probably too drunk to stand and stinking of whorehouses and vomited rye whiskey and pizza. Tess will drag him under a cold shower and then present him with his bride, spread out on their marital bed like a lush prairie flower in full bloom, in her wedding dress but nothing else, hoping stupid Stevie has enough jism left after his night of debauchery to do the trick. In case he gets confused or falls asleep, Tess has a steel ruler close to hand to whack his backside and urge him on. Angie Bonali will fall asleep on top of her bed in her party dress, but not Franny Baxter.

Out on the Bonali front porch, Angela's father, headachy after the late afternoon beers, is talking into the gathering night with Sal and Gabriela Ferrero, mostly about their early married years, and about their working days down in the mine, how tough and dirty it was, Gabriela remembering when Sal would come home with his shoes full of coaldust and looking like a colored man, but how heroic and full of camaraderie those days were, too, and how they are missed now. They have also been talking about Dave Osborne, who hanged himself today, and their pal Big Pete Chigi, who died of black lung, and poor dear Etta, the town's dead hovering over them as if peering down on them from the chalky face of the moon, and Vince has been reminded of his old high school, mine, and union buddy, Angelo Moroni, how he used to wear his hat tipped down over his nose when he played pinochle, cracking wry one-liners, maybe it's the tipped lopsided shape of the moon that has brought him to mind, poor old Ange, killed in the mine that awful night like so many good men. And now the foreclosure on this house, the only one he's ever owned, the one Etta loved so much, he's getting near to tears again. "Next stop, Sal: a charity old folks' home. Good night, sweetheart. That's all she wrote."

This old family friendship is being perpetuated into the next generation tonight by the two friends' sons: Vince's boy Charlie and young Nazario, known to his pals as Moron, who are, along with a half dozen or so other members of Charlie's newly formed Knights of Columbus Volunteer Defense Force, on a reconnaissance mission at old man Suggs' strip mine, where the Christian Patriots (fascists!) are holding their bi-weekly pep session, parade drill, and target practice under the instruction of Suggs' black-bearded mine manager, who sleeps, it is rumored, under a Nazi flag. The Dagotown Devil Dogs, as they also call themselves, have climbed one of the ugly mounds thrown up by the strip mine and are watching the Patriots through a pair of binoculars they pass around. Charlie points his finger at them and makes soft thuckety-pop noises, which Moron and his buddies assume must be the sound of a revolver with a silencer on it. With hushed pow! and pock! sounds they follow Charlie's lead and knock off a few Christian

Patriots with their pointing fingers. When the sheriff comes banging out of the mine office and jumps into his squad car, the Dogs fade coolly into the night.

If it is a night of sudden death and dark omens, it is also a night of erotic festivity. The ecumenical stag party up at the Eagles is now in full swing and has been joined by another dozen or so revelers, few being of a mood on such a sweet summery night to say no to free whiskey and good-humored horseplay. Carlo Juliano has provided an old blue movie about a guy in an antique Model A Ford picking up two girls hitchhiking, but the film has come apart just as the girls were taking their pants down, so they are entertaining themselves by telling about the first time they got laid. High school virgins, Waterton whores, babysitters, stepsisters, friends' mothers. Georgie Lucci makes up a story that he swears is true about a nymphomaniac nun who took him under her habit when he was eleven years old to show him what she called the pearly gates and insisted on his reciting the Pater noster when she took a grip on him and transported him into Heaven. Just when memories and imaginations are drying up, laconic Cokie Duncan, who has said very little all night while nevertheless holding his own with the bottle, surprises them with a story about taking a sweet young thing out into the fields and just as he's humping her having her mother show up. "Haw!" snorts Stevie Lawson, slapping his knee. "What'd she say?" "Nuthin. She just went on eatin' grass." Which sets everyone off in drunken mooing. They're having a grand time.

Soon they'll be moving on to the Blue Moon Motel, where Duke L'Heureux and his partner Patti Jo Rendine, backed up on guitar by the local favorite Will Henry, are at this moment introducing, to enthusiastic cheers in a packed house, a new number written by Duke just this afternoon called "She'll Let Me Know When It's Time to Go." All Duke's and Patti Jo's songs have gone down well tonight—"There's Always a Bus Going Somewhere," "A Toybox of Tears," "Trailer Camp Blues," "The Potholes Down Memory Lane"—and the record company people have taut knowing smiles on their faces, but the hit of the night is "The Night My Daddy Loved Me Too Much," which may or may not ever get sold over the counter. No one has ever heard a song like that before—not in a public place. They don't know if they *like* it, but they keep asking for it over and over again, as if they can't believe their ears.

A quieter sort of celebration of the solstice is taking place in the Presbyterian church basement, where Prissy Tindle, after a quick visit home to freshen up and pick up costumes and props and her portable record player and the little rabbit-ear TV from the studio (Ralph was more petulant than ever, she had to push him aside to get into her closet), is mentally choreographing her advertised midsummer night special: The Dance of the Wedding of Heaven and Earth, hoping, after chasing Wesley all over town today, she has strength enough left to perform it. It was originally meant to be performed in the wild by moonlight, but it's now restricted to their hideout down here in the church basement by candlelight. It's an all-night dance (though on such a night as this that's not so long), and while Wesley and Jesus converse quietly but grumpily about the circumstances in which they find themselves, Prissy blocks out the main elements in roughly fifteen-minute segments and considers ways to enhance the performance space, which is mostly a cluttered concrete floor with bare walls, no mats and no mirrors, about which lack Jesus has already complained, whining wearily. It has been a long day for the poor man and his eyes are crossing, so she shortcuts her way to the finale (a majestic moment) so as to get started as quickly as possible, assuming her knack for improvisation will carry her through the unscored middle bits or maybe they'll just skip them. She is, of course, Earth, and he is Sky or Heaven, which means she will be obliged to dance the climactic scene on her back, so she sets out some dusty sofa cushions for the purpose. But first comes the Setting Sun and Rising Moon Dance, and, using the "Grand Canyon Suite" for dramatic effect and then "Claire de Lune" as a soothing closing movement (she has a yin/yang thing in mind here), she pours into it all the terrors and joys of the day, for the sun and moon also chase themselves about in a fiery manner, never quite finding each other. It is one of her best dances ever, but she succeeds only in dancing her audience and dance partner to sleep just at the most poignant moment, when his own participation is called for. Well, in a way, it's a relief. She rolls him over on his side to diminish the snoring, and regretting only that she forgot to bring a couple of jars of pickles and peanut butter to get her through the night, curls up beside him, dancing the Dance of the Exhausted Disciple.

Exhaustion has also at last dropped Debra Edwards into a heavy sleep in her hospital bed, that and strong medication. Worried about her unresponsive state of mind, Police Chief Dee Romano called the minister at Trinity Lutheran, which he understood from Officer Bosticker was the church being attended temporarily by the pastorless Presbyterians, and said he was sorry to bother him again, but would he be willing to come down to the station to provide some urgent spiritual counseling? Of course. Reverend Dreyer took one look at the woman there on the wretched jail-cell cot and said she was obviously suffering from dangerously deep depression and should be kept in hospital overnight, where she can be kept under medical observation. Her dreams there are of dreaming, with Glenda Oakes sitting at the edge of her dreams like a dark angel and commenting cruelly on them even as she dreams them, so she keeps trying to wake up to be free of the one-eyed harpie, but she cannot. Down the hospital corridor from her, Mr. John P. Suggs—who does not dream, as he says—is suffering his own kind of nightmare: he is trying to think. He has the sensation of being in a large empty house with hundreds of locked closet-sized rooms for which he has no key. Brute strength alone frees him from any one room, only to leave him in another exactly like the first. Bernice Filbert, sitting nearby in a lumpy hospital easy chair, dozing fitfully, can feel his struggle and it translates into her own fragmented dreams as its opposite: the desire to push herself down into sleep, free from the cares of the world; but those cares resist her and will not let her go.

Cokie Duncan has no such problems. He is out cold on the floor of the Eagles Social Club and he is not dreaming, his bombed brain cells are not up to it, but he is alone now under a scatter of playing cards randomly dealt upon him by his departing companions. They are now piling past the bouncer at the door of the Blue Moon Motel and entering the sound track of the final Duke L'Heureux and Patti Jo Rendine number, an upbeat Elvis-influenced rendition of one of the motel's theme songs, "When My Blue Moon Turns to Gold Again," the final number because the recording crew have quickly decided with the arrival of the whooping stag party that it is time to close up shop and get the hell out of here. Will Henry, too, is packing up his guitar and moving toward the door. The two singers are on a high, though—it has been the night of their lives—and when they get a clamorous request from the crowd pressing in around them on the dance floor for yet another refrain of "The Night My Daddy Loved Me Too Much," they cannot resist. It is into this festive congestion that tomorrow's groom-to-be Steve Lawson and his rampageous pals stagger, not meaning to throw elbows and knock drinks out of people's hands but not meaning not to either, too drunk for decision-making of any kind. Their goal is the tableful of drinks ordered up for the singers in the middle of the room and not yet consumed, their own supply exhausted, and, when reached, these are snatched up and passed around with a lot of hollering and cussing and laughing and generally obnoxious behavior. The freelance civil servant, Giorgio Lucci, the leader of this wild pack, gives a wave to his boss the fire chief who is just leaving, lets out a resounding coma-ti-yi-yippee-yippee-*yo* in acknowledgement of the hayseed performers, tosses back a tall glass of beer in one long guzzle and finds himself face-to-face with the female half of the singing duo, no longer singing. He blinks in recognition, belches, grins his stand-up comedian's grin. "'Patti Jo.' I'll be damned! Patricia Josefina! I never forget a nose! You nearly fooled me with that hayseed act, Josie. Remember me? I once had my finger up your little patonza." He grabs her in the crotch of her jeans, and sings: "So why not take all of me?" Doesn't get past "all" before her musical partner and former bush league bullpen pitcher comes in with some high heat for his big K of the night. Which is the signal everyone has been waiting for.

Out at the lakes, far from the bench-clearing brawl erupting at the Blue Moon, Sally Elliott steps out of the cold lake waters as she stepped in, mooning the moon and musing about the whimsical customs of midsummer. A distant voice, floating with silvery clarity over the still waters, has just cried out: "Omigod! What are we *doing*?" "That was my mother's voice," she says, drying herself off with her shirt. "Let's go." Billy Don, still wearing his sunglasses, lingers in the water at waist level, wanting to stay cool as she has stayed cool and consequently self-conscious about his telltale arousal—which, for fear she will laugh at it, he is trying desperately but unsuccessfully to detumesce with prayer and the recitation of mathematical formulae and also with moral fortitude, the sort his baseball coach used to urge upon him, with equal lack of success, to discourage the sin of Onan. They have been playing a game of water tag that should have been more fun than it was, but Sally has done too much pool time and he has been unable to keep up with her, or else it was the beer (he's not used to it), so he has rarely had his hands on her and then only fleetingly and not in the best places, which never seemed quite available. Like some kinds of knowledge he's been offered in his life, but that he's not been quite able to grasp, advanced calculus, for example. But just seeing her moonlit bottom bob up when she dove under water and feeling the swish of her as she passed suddenly between his legs have been enough to keep him in such an unholy fever it's a wonder the water around him hasn't started to boil. "Billy Don? Come on!" Still he hesitates. She seems to guess what's troubling him and tosses him her shirt, the one that says give me a hug, turns her back and walks over to pull her jeans on. Using his boner as a shirt hanger is probably even more ridiculous than leaving it exposed and bobbing stupidly on its own, but that's what he does, pretending to be drying himself off until he can reach his cast-off clothes. Still hasn't been able to give her that hug. He doesn't know why. Just too dumb, probably. This damp T-shirt between his legs, he's pretty sure, is as close as he's going to get.

His return from the dead is celebrated with libations spilled upon his countenance and welcoming bilingual oaths. Where is he? In hell, as the company suggests? *Who* is he, for that matter? He is staring up at a blinding light. Some say it's what people who have near-death experiences see. Are his eyes open or closed? Open. He is staring up at one of the lamps that overhang the Blue Moon Motel parking lot. "Maybe Georgie's got some words of wisdom for us from the other side," someone says. It might be his cousin Carlo. There are snorts of thick, drunken laughter. Georgie is sick. His head aches, his jaw hurts. There's a hollow place where a tooth used to be. The arm that fucking sorehead Lem Filbert wrecked is in pain; must have done something to it when he fell. "What happened to that long string of shit who hit me?" he asks, digging the words up from somewhere, not sure they come out as intended. He has a mouthful of stones. "The singer? Them people took off before you could see 'em go." His comrades are sitting around on their butts, swigging from an array of bottles. "Where'd all that juice come from?" "Inside. We managed to grab some on the way out. Beats what we been drinking all to hell." They tell him what happened. The historic brawl he missed. He sees now they're wearing shiners, split lips, bloody ears. They're all grinning shit-eating grins. "Wrecked the fuckin' place," young Nazario Moroni says. "The cops let us go. Just chased everyone out and shut it down." They offer Georgie one of the bottles. He has to suck from it lying down, though. He can't sit up yet. It might be whiskey, might not; it's wet and stings the wounded places. There's weed getting passed around as well, a wedding gift from Moroni. "We lost Guido Mello, though," cousin Carlo says. "As they shoved him out the door, he took a slow-motion swing at Louie Testatonda. You almost can't miss Louie, but he did. It was like il Nasone was desperate to get hisself locked up so as not to have to go home to his dimwit wife and mongol kid and whatever else is going down there. They probly took him in as a family favor." "Guido had our only wheels left. How're we getting to Waterton?" "Grunge here is driving us. Him and Naz have joined the party." "The brawl finished off the others," young Moroni says. So they're down to Johnson and Juliano, Stevie Lawson, and the two young toughs. And the resurrected hero who invented this monumental festa, much praised by all. The Sick Six. "One of 'em has two cunts, Stevie, and one of 'em don't have none at all," Cheese Johnson is saying. "We ain't tellin' you which is which—you gotta guess." Stevie says, "Huh." He stands up for a moment and falls down. They laugh and offer him another drink. Stevie has already forgotten he's getting married tomorrow. Or later today if it's got as late as that. From here the stag party goes to Waterton to share Stevie's wedding present with him. That's the plan. But Cheese and young Nazario have cooked up something else they want to do first.

So the next thing Georgie knows, they're all out at the Brunist church camp under a vast moonlit sky, being sung to by mosquitoes. The camp has a perimeter fence strung with barbed wire, but Stevie helped clear the garden and move topsoil in for old man Suggs, so he knows a back way in, an old two-track route to the creek from an abandoned farm. He also knows they now have armed guards at the camp, having been one a time or two, so you can pick up an assful of buckshot. Moroni says he wishes he'd known about this route. He and Grunge and some of their pals have also been out here, it turns out, wrecking gardens, sabotaging lampposts, trying to set some chicken coops alight before getting chased off with rifle fire, but they had to cut their way in. Doesn't seem like only anti-cult mischief. Carrying some deep grudge, more like, especially against the big stud Wanda Craven's living with now. Georgie gets the idea it's the way they've been able to recruit Grabowski's car. The plan is to kidnap Wanda and take her somewhere and gangbang her. A warmup for the whorehouse. The last time Georgie and Cheese tried group-fucking Wanda Cravens, they got beat up and arrested and it cost him a few bills. He grins to remember it and he's reminded how much his jaw hurts. Young Moroni tells them how to get to the trailer park without passing any of the cabins or other mobile homes by following the creek and coming in from the back side. Wanda and her guy live apart from the others because of their chicken coops. The moon's not full but bright enough it should be simple to find their way. Of course, that also makes them easier targets. They should stay in under the trees. First, though, they'll have to distract the big bastard, get him away from their trailer so they can grab Wanda. Cheese has brought along a big packet of stink bombs, firecrackers, and flares for the purpose, which he apparently stole from some place. Someone should take a different route, he says, and set all that stuff off and then tear ass, and the other four will snatch Wanda when everyone goes running toward the fireworks. Georgie volunteers for this diversional task or is volunteered, it's all the same to him. Me ne sbatto il cazzo, he says. His aching head's not working well, and it seems simpler and less dangerous, and it's always fun to light fireworks. How will he know when to set the shit off? Cheese will hoot like an owl. He shows him what he means. Sounds more like a night train with a broken whistle, but it should be easy to tell from a real owl hoot in case there are any out here. Cheese gives him the armload of fireworks in a gunny sack and some matches. Moroni says not to worry, he'll take care of the fat man if necessary. All in all, it seems like a good plan.

But they've just parted ways there in the woods and Georgie is alone in the dark when he sobers up enough to recognize how stupid it is. He and his pals are too drunk, the two boys are too sober. What did Moroni mean, "take care of"? Were they armed? There are strange sounds all around him. This is supposed to be fun. What happened to his happy stag party? He doesn't feel like he's in the real world anymore, but has got dropped into some nightmarish place where weird shit can happen. He tries not to panic, but he is panicking. He decides the only sane course of action is to beat it back to the car. First, though, he has to set off all these fireworks. Was that an owl hoot? Close enough. He has just lit a few fuses when the quiet night is torn open by a howling scream. It's Cheese Johnson. He's being attacked. *"Fucking Christ, they're killing me!"* Georgie is on the run, fireworks popping behind him. He hears shots. The sky lights up with flares. The screaming gets worse. And the others start yowling. There are desperate cries for help. Must have been an ambush. Georgie runs away from the wild screaming (what the hell are they doing to them?), his head full of confusion, suddenly smacks up against the periphery fence. Didn't see it coming.

He is down again, his shirt torn by barbed wire. Probably he's bleeding. His face hurts, his jaw hurts, his arm hurts, his gut hurts. There is a lot of noise in the camp now, shouts, Cheese and the others yowling, crackers popping, gunfire. The whole place is lighting up and coming alive. No place to turn. He is suddenly back in the exploded mine. Most terrifying moment of his life. His faceboss Vince Bonali told them to stay put while he went to phone topside, but some of them couldn't wait. He couldn't wait. He remembers the thick dust, the darkness, the fear of fire and of suffocation, Pooch Minicucci's panic, screaming with terror like Cheese Johnson is now, and how it got to him and Wally Brevnik, sending them off on a mad suicidal run. He has always bragged about getting out before Bonali did, but he knows it was a big mistake and he and Wally could have ended up dead like Pooch and his buddy Lee Cravens, the last of their air sucked up by that mental case Giovanni Bruno, the only bastard who was trapped and got out. The one this camp is named for. That thought sends a shiver down his spine. Has he come full circle? Is he being punished now for his stupidity that night? He's scrambling along the fence, snagging himself on it, trying to find the end of it, avoiding the moonlight when he can, feeling his own air getting sucked up. There are gunshots, more shouts: *"It's the murderer! He's back!"* He starts praying. First time since that night when he was lost in the black mine. C'mon, God, do me a fucking favor, for Chrissake! Some high-pitched voice way off somewhere is screaming about witches. What the hell is that about? *"Over here! This way!"* More shots. He seems to hear bullets ripping through the trees overhead. Something stinks. He has either shat his pants or kicked a skunk. He begins to cry, begs for pity. From God, the Devil, Lady Luck, whomever. The fence ends. He wipes his tears away. There's an open field dangerously lit up under the moon. He decides to risk it, doubled over so if he gets shot he'll get shot in the ass, not the head. Nothing happens. He reaches a copse, another creek, brambles, still running, a ditch, turns his ankle and goes down hard, more brambles, finally a paved county road. He recognizes it. Leads into town past shithead

Lem's garage. First he pauses to throw up and take a long sticky piss. He's full of rage, pain, terror, nausea, self-pity. He realizes he's been clutching the sackful of remaining fireworks to his chest the whole time like a lifejacket. He drops it, starts limping down the road back to town, then realizes he is turned around and going the wrong way, makes the correction, throws up again. Passes the dropped fireworks. Picks them up again. Long walk back on a swollen ankle. But still alive and out of there. So he should probably give thanks. But hey. God may have saved his ass, but why did He let him get in so much trouble in the first place?

"Ain't never burgled a haunted house, Patti Jo. Sure y'wanta do this?"

"I'm sure."

"Looks all boarded up."

"Yeah, but, see? The padlock on the door's been broke. I hear tell it gets used now for high school beer parties. If you stumble over any bodies, don't worry, it's just probably drunken kids passed out."

"I stumble over any bodies, little darlin', and I'll see ye later back at the Moon."

"It all looks so empty and busted up I can't hardly recognize it. But I remember you turn left here into the dining room and then left again. The stairs are off the kitchen. Shine your light a sec, Duke. Here, this way."

"What a hole. Worse'n the swamp I never growed up in. I cain't smell no beer, but them kids has been relievin' theirselves wheresomever it's took their fancy."

"It's so sad. Marcella's family had to get by on so little, but her mama always kept a neat house in a old-fashioned way. Now everything seems like either broke up or stole. C'mon. Marcella's bedroom is up here at the back, looking out over the porch roof and backyard. Marcella kept a flower patch down there. She talked to the flowers like they were little people."

"What are we aimin' t'find?"

"I don't know. But I'm thinking maybe that little gold cross she always wore on a chain around her neck, the one I saw in my—Oh...!"

"Whew! Nuthin in here, Patti Jo. Only scribblin' on the walls and a ole rotten matteress which the kids probly been usin' fer their party games."

"Her room was always so pretty. I just loved coming here. It's like something worse has happened to her than her dying. I feel like crying."

"This room has had a lotta rough traffic. You ain't gonna find any gold necklace here, angel."

"No...but shine your light over there under the radiator. There's something..."

"Lemme see...no, it ain't nuthin but a cheap plastic hair clasp."

"That's it, Duke! We've found it! It was one of her favorite things. Mine too! It's filthy now and all scratched up, but it used to be shiny, and if you got close you could see your face in it but warped in a funny kinda scary way. It was like another world and we made up stories about it. Right here in this room! Sitting here on the floor, next to her bed! I think she must of been wearing that barrette in the dream, too. And I think I even saw a face in it...but not mine. Let's take it to her, Duke."

"Whoa! Tonight? I ain't keen on dead a night graveyard romps, sweet cuz. Cain't we save it fer daylight?"

"No, let's do it and get it done. It's what she wants, I know. Anyhow, the moon's so bright tonight it's almost like daytime. I've picked up some grass from that bad boy they call Moron. We can set on a tombstone and have us a party. C'mon, Duke. If you wanta have fun, come along with me..."

...

"It's okay now, Duke. You've been a true pal. I'll never forget it. Does your hand hurt?"

"Some. It's swoll up a mite, but the weed's helpin'. And this dead people party gits your mind off other things. Won't throw another knuckleball for a while, though. Don't know ifn I'll be able to pluck a gittar right soon neither. Y'may hafta tape the pick to my finger splint."

"I'll do whatever you want me to, lover. I'm so grateful and proud. Nobody ever stood up for me like that before. You made me feel like a real person. And you did it with style. You really laid dumb Georgie out."

"That pore mizzerbul joker was borned to be stood up'n knocked down. He ain't even a number."

"Those record company folks were helpful, too, shielding us and hustling us outa there when the place started popping. They were real nice."

"Nice probly wasn't on their minds. I think they was more like pertectin' their proppity."

"I guess that's what we are now, all right. At least until they have a second listen and hear what noise I make and call singing. The Moon won't likely want us back, though. They looked to be getting seriously trashed."

"Sure, they'll want us back. Trashin' the Moon is like trashin' trash: you probly cain't tell the differnce. They ain't never had such crowds, and ifn our songs take off, with that 'Recorded Live at the Blue Moon Motel' printed on all the labels, we'll have put 'em on the map big time, and ole Will, too…hmm…damn if that don't sound like a song title. 'Trashin' the Moon.' Maybe I'll git sumthin outa this crazy night after all."

"I'm sorry I drug you into it, Duke. It *is* crazy. I know that. *I'm* crazy. But we made Marcella happy, so it was worth it."

"Just on accounta you left a old plastic hair clasp over there on her grave?"

"No. That I honored her by completing the task she'd set me. It was like some of the stories we used to tell when looking into the barrette. You know, princess offered up as a bride, princes given weird tasks to win her hand and the kingdom, the need for a tittle of magic and a friendly helper to get the deed done—that sorta thing. We sometimes had cemeteries and unmarked graves in our stories, too. So I can see how she set all this up. It was her way of us playing together one last time…"

"Well, settin' here in a paupers' buryin' ground under the hanged moon mongst the lonesome dead, jist the two of us, smokin' reefers'n cuddlin', is about as wild a party I been to since the wake fer Granpappy Rendine when his still blowed up, and I hate t'break it up, Patti Jo, but if the ole Blue Moon's still standin', we should oughta head back'n have us a beer outa the fridge'n move our cuddle twixt the sheets. I jist heerd a rooster soundin' off over there."

"Yeah, and we got a date in a few hours at a wedding, too. We'll have to be up for that. I suppose all those rowdy boys'll be there. One of them's supposed to be the groom."

"They'll likely be too sick to stand, but ifn they start actin' up, with my hand broke, you'll hafta pertect me, lil darlin."

"I will, lover. Anybody get close to you, they'll find out what a angry Rendine gal can do to anyone messing with her favorite cousin. They just better hang on to their goolies."

"Hmm. Must be even later'n I sposed. Lookie over there to the west. Looks like dawn a-breakin'."

"I see it. The problem is the sun don't come up in the west."

"That's right. If it's doin' that, them friends a ourn at the camp might be onta sumthin. Most probly it's a fire. Big 'un, looks like."

"We can drive past and see. Here. While you finish off the joint, I'll just go say goodbye to Marcella…"

…

"Everthing cool?"

"Yup."

"And now you're free? She says you kin go?"

"I can go. But she's not saying nothing. She's the one who's free. She's gone."

# BOOK IV

And when he had opened the fourth seal,
I heard the voice of the fourth beast say, Come and see.
And I looked, and behold a pale horse:
and his name that sat on him was Death, and Hell followed with him.
And power was given unto them over the fourth part of the earth,
to kill with sword, and with hunger, and with death,
and with the beasts of the earth.

—*The Book of Revelation 6.7-8*

# IV.I

## Wednesday 24 June – Friday 3July

J. P. Suggs looks like a dead man, the reddish gray frizz on his bony skull like some kind of sickly mold. Only his eyes and a finger on one hand work. No expression, just those eyes staring out from some awful depth. Gives Tub the creeps. Is he angry? Can't tell. He can blink and wag the one finger. Ask him a question, he blinks once to say yes, stares back icily for no. Sometimes he wags his finger to say no, and then it seems like he might be angry that he's having to work too hard, but mostly he either blinks once or stares back. Tub on occasion has remarked that he and Suggs see eye to eye, and that remark has now taken on a spookier meaning. But give Suggs credit, he's a tough old bird. Has been in and out of coma, reduced to a stalk of celery with eyeballs, but he refuses to give up. Tub admires that. Bernice, old Tuck Filbert's quirky widow, is here in the room, working as a private nurse for the old man. It's not charity and she's not doing it just for the money. Without Suggs, she's in deep shit. Like her patient, she mostly lives in her own head; if Suggs' head is a stone, though, hers is a swamp. She and Suggs have contrived this code of eye blinks and finger twitches, and she has been helping to move the conversation along. "I suppose I could deputize the Patriots." The man blinks. Suggs wants all the Baxter followers camped on his property arrested for trespassing and either jailed or chased out of the county once and for all. "Baxter has already had the stuffing knocked out of him by that gangster cop, but it has only made him meaner." The sheriff is talking more than is his habit, filling up the silence, doing Suggs' talking for him, as it were. Though Tub has used the Christian Patriots against the illegal Baxterite encampments before, he has not sent them in as official sheriff's deputies. Doing that will pit him against his own sidekick. "I'm having some trouble with Cal Smith." Suggs blinks once, which Tub takes to mean "I told you so." "I'm looking around for a new deputy. One of the Patriots probably. Though not many of them are near smart enough." Suggs' lids droop slightly as though to say "So what?" Or maybe he's passing out again. Tub can see all the forces lining up. His own volunteer unit and Patriots militia with the Brunist campers and Suggs' money. Next, Smith and the Baxterites, lawless drifters for the most part, many of whom are armed—and a lot more of them around than there used to be. Then the town establishment: Romano and his city cops, the mayor, the city manager, all under the banker's thumb. And now Vince Bonali's tough-ass kid and his Knights of Columbus Defense Dogs, or whatever they're called, together with all the rest of the Romanists. Mostly pissed-off, unemployed ex-miners who are apt to shoot at just about anybody as a remedy for unhappiness. And what next? State troopers, maybe National Guard, though so far Tub has fended off the governor. He has also heard rumors of the FBI getting involved, which means federal troops. Hot summer ahead.

Down the hall from Suggs' room, Lem Filbert is bellowing out his curses. They're aimed mainly at the West Condon fire chief, who is in a bed at the other end of the hall. Lem says he aims to fucking kill the fucker as soon as he's able to fucking stagger down there, and because he probably means it, Romano has his fat Italian officer posted outside his room. What's Lem going to do, strangle him with his IV tube? He says the fucking mayor is also in for it and everybody else at fucking city hall. He intends to fucking kill the whole crooked fucking lot. Tub does not hear himself mentioned but doubts he'd be excepted. When Whimple turned up at the fire station late last Sunday morning after being up all night hopelessly battling the oily blaze at Lem's garage, Lem was waiting for him with a crowbar. Bernice said the first thing she did when she saw the fire, even before calling the fire department, was hide her brother-in-law's guns, which was a good thing because the place burned to the ground and everything on his car lot caught fire as well, the biggest fire in these parts since the old Dance Barn went up, and Lem snapped. Apparently he'd gone storming down to the fire station looking for Georgie Lucci, who has been sacking out on a mattress there and against whom Lem has had a longtime grudge, but Georgie wasn't in. Lying low. Or maybe passed out in a ditch somewhere on the other side of town, as he later claimed. So it was Whimple who ended up in the hospital. Romano and his boys ran over to try to calm Filbert down, but when Bosticker got within a yard of him, Lem laid into him with a crippling crowbar blow to his knees. When he fell, Lem took his gun off him, at which point Romano decided it was time to stop fooling around and he shot him. Aimed at his gun hand, hit his bony wrist, shattering it, the bullet ricocheting off into his gut, and then, when Lem grabbed the gun up from the street with his good hand and kept coming, Romano shot him again, this time in the arm, and then again in the leg, finally bringing him down. Still, Lem fought them all the way out here to the hospital, and he has never stopped yelling even though they've kept him heavily doped. At first the mayor tried to blame the fire on Lem's own carelessness and his flaunting of fire regulations, but when they found the empty shells of Roman candles, he decided some drunken kids must have driven by and set it alight. His cops more or less confirmed that. An anonymous caller even phoned in to say he'd seen kids running away from there when it started to go up, but he couldn't see who they were.

Tub has his own notions. It had been a particularly bad Saturday night in the county. Mischievous kids on the loose, the usual drunken wife-bashing, the arrest of the Edwards woman (she's also here in the hospital somewhere; Suggs told him to forget about her, a lost cause), the weekly Patriots training session interrupted by the camp murders, a string of burglaries over in Randolph Junction, the trashing of the

Blue Moon Motel, and before the night was over, he'd got called out to the camp a second time after some drunks intruded and set off some fireworks down near where the murders had happened earlier. They had caught one of them—that stupid jackass, Johnson—when he plowed into the beehives in the dark. Tub, his mood worsened by the onset of a toothache, kicked him around for a time, asking him questions, trying to find out who had been with him and thinking he might even try to pin the double murders on him, but the jerk was so badly bee-stung—must have been hundreds swarmed onto him—Tub didn't have the heart to work him over as he might have done. His arm looked like it might be broken, so Tub shipped him off to the emergency room instead. Anyway, he knew who the others were, and if there were any sleepers, they'd be easy to spot by the bee stings. As for the fire, he figured Lem wasn't that far off when he first went looking for someone to batter to death. Those fuckups had been causing trouble all night, setting off a wild brawl at the Blue Moon before their assault on the Brunist camp; after collecting the fireworks debris at the camp, Tub wasn't surprised when more of it turned up later in the ruins of Lem's garage. Given everything else that had happened, he'd decided against filing any report about the camp break-in by those drunks, not to draw more unwanted attention to that place. He certainly doesn't want any state or federal forces moving in, taking over his job. But if Lem gets his sanity back, they'll have a talk.

When Governor Kirkpatrick called him to say he was under a lot of pressure from people to send in the National Guard, Tub figured he was talking about the mayor and the town banker who had been badgering him too, and he told Kirkpatrick that Castle and Cavanaugh were alarmists, everything was under control, and if there should be any trouble, which he doesn't expect, he could simply mobilize his volunteers, if the governor would authorize that, and the governor said that he would, that it seemed like the best solution. He'd even organize some sort of emergency budget for it if it turned out to be necessary, which is what Tub wanted to hear, saying that one thing he needed right now was more riot gear. The governor said he could do that. He was mainly concerned about some event the day after the Fourth, which Tub had heard about but without paying much attention. It seems the Brunists are organizing some sort of ceremony at the mine hill that day, Kirkpatrick said, and Cavanaugh is planning to spring a surprise on them that might backfire. The governor had stuck his neck out on this one and wanted to be sure the sheriff and his deputies would be out there that day, keeping an eye on things, and Tub said not to worry, they would be there. Tub has been explaining some of this to Suggs, choosing his words carefully, when he notices the old man is no longer focused on him, his eyes still open but without that fierce stare. Tuck's widow, checking his pulse just to make sure, says Suggs often sleeps with his eyes open and that that's what he's doing now.

"Dave Osborne stayed on the phone until everyone he could reach below had been directed to safety, then joined the first rescue crew. We needed him down there. It was black as only you guys know it can be and thick with hot coaldust, and no one knew the Deepwater workings and could move through them blind like Dave Osborne." It's Barney Davis speaking, the Deepwater company supervisor at the time of the accident, now employed by the State Mining Board, having been shoehorned into the job by the company owners to protect their asses up in the capital. The Barn's crew-cut hair is as white as it ever was, but he looks younger than he did five years ago; life in the capital suits him. Everybody else here in the church looks twenty years older, Tub included. He's standing at the back, near the doors, rather hoping there might be an emergency call that will get him out of here. He is short on patience with this sort of memorializing sentimentality, and what little he has is being ground away by his nagging toothache. Should go to a dentist, keeps putting it off. He associates these places with the dead, funerals being the only times he turns up in them. Tub is not a churchgoer just like he's not a flag waver. He is a patriot and a believer simply because this is the world he lives in and there is no reason not to be. He enforces the law around here, and it's American law and Christian law, and if he started questioning too much how it got that way, he wouldn't do a good job of it. He knows who he is, and that's enough. The world will take care of itself and doesn't need him for its ceremonies. But should he be wearing these guns on his hips in here? Probably not. Well, tough titty, as the saying goes in or out of a church. Without them he'd feel like he was not wearing pants. "We were anxious to find survivors and get them to the surface as quickly as we could, so we went below bareface with only wet rags against the dust and gases. What we found down there was a nightmare. Airlock doors blasted open, timbers the size of phone poles snapped like matchsticks, roofs down and piled on top of machinery and men, buggies crunched like sardine cans and blown up against the ribs, twisted rails looking like some kind of devil's 3D handwriting. Dave Osborne guided us through all that with nothing but our cap lamps, aiming straight for the worst of it, sometimes on our hands and knees." It was partly due to The Barn's negligence that the mine blew up in the first place. Everybody knows that. In a just world the sonuvabitch would be doing time, but no one's making a point of it. That's not why the union invited him back. They know Davis is trying to get some mines reopened and they want him to keep doing that. Though the Osborne memorial service organized by the union is being hosted by the Lutherans, there are people here from most of the churches in town, including the RCs, all sitting together over at one side of the church like at the back of the bus, and even a few of those evangelicals from the church camp. There was a buzz when they showed up. Tub assured them he'd watch out for them, but they don't really fit in here in this town anymore and they know it. They sit stiffly, looking like aliens wearing human masks, even more uncomfortable than the RCs. "Some of us started getting sick from the gas, so we turned back and brought up the first bodies we'd found. Dave didn't want to quit and we had to drag him along with us back up to fresh air. He got himself fitted up with an oxygen tank and tools and went right back down on the next crew, working straight through until dawn. Dave Osborne was probably the first live person some of you out there saw that night. A hero. He was."

Before the ceremonies, standing around outside having a smoke, Davis had to take some flak from miners, led by that gasbag Bonali, complaining about the sale of the mine to the holyrollers instead of reopening it and putting men to work again. The Barn reminded them, pushing his rimless specs up his thin beak, that he is no longer associated with that company, but it was his understanding the sale still had not gone through and so far it didn't include mineral rights. That's what he'd heard. Tub didn't know that and he wondered if Suggs does. Tub can appreciate Davis' situation now that he has been sheriff a while: the endless contrary demands, the petty criticisms, everybody trying to get your ear and bend it. He can imagine being sheriff for life—for one thing, it gets him free tailored shirts and pants—but he wouldn't want anything up the ladder from that. As for Osborne, the truth is he was easy to get on with—no ambition, so stepped on nobody's toes, good at what he did—but Tub knows he also let things happen down there in his good-guy way. The man knew about the shoddy inspections, the covering up of reports of faulty wiring, the lack of regular rockdusting and excessive coaldust on the haulage ways, the failure to seal off leaking marsh gas, and he grumbled about all these things like everyone else did, but he didn't pipe up like he should have. Osborne was at his best telling jokes. Sure came up with a zinger at the end.

Most of the Christian Patriots are here. They each nodded silently at Tub when they arrived. A passel of disaster widows, some still wearing black, looking gloomy. Maybe they're feeling guilty for not buying shoes from Osborne. The majority crammed into the pews, though, are miners who used to work with Tub down in Deepwater. Those with gumption have mostly moved on; these bums in here are the losers. Like Bert Martini, the one-armed grouser talking now. Martini was one of the guys carried out by Osborne and his rescue team, his arm sheared off when a shuttle buggy, knocked off the rails by the blast, rolled over it. He's up front, praising Osborne and waving his stub around and sounding off about the criminal irresponsibility of the mine owners. "Took their money and shut down our workplace and left us to rot and die! It's what's killed Dave Osborne! There oughta be some justice!" *"Amen, brother!"* Buff Cooley, another rescued miner, shouts out and others agree more secularly. Reminds Tub of union meetings past. Why he avoided them when he could. *"Go to now, ye rich men, weep'n howl for the miseries what'll come upon ye! James 5:1!"* That's cowardly Bible spouter Willie Hall, one of the Brunists from the church camp. Let him get started and this thing will never end. The little chickenshit's alive because, as he often did, he ducked the shift that night. Abner Baxter, Tub's old faceboss, is here too, flanked by some of his oldtime rough boys, like Coates and Cox, and still looking beat up from the last time Chief Romano got his hands on him. There's a five-year-old warrant out for that old gobpile orator's arrest if he turns up inside city limits, which is what Romano held him on for his midnight thrashing, but no chance he'll grab him again here in the church. Too bad. Tub would like to see the sonuvabitch get hammered and he doesn't care who does it. Baxter has been a pain in the butt since he came back and it would be better if he got the idea it might be healthier to move on.

Tub's deputy and old mine buddy Cal Smith is speaking now, telling everyone what a loyal and dependable guy Osborne was. "A man you had to respect." Cal Smith's own loyalty is coming up short. He and Cal worked together down in Deepwater for years—Tub the shot firer, Cal his driller and cutter, two of the dirtiest and most hazardous jobs in the mines. Tub took it on because it paid extra, and Smith probably did too. In the old days, when they first broke in, they had to use dynamite. Fused foot-long sticks poked into boreholes on the coalface. When they went off, they brought down a mass of wall for the loaders. A lot could go wrong, but he and Smith knew their job, and nothing ever did. Later, they started using compressed air. It was still dangerous, especially the flyrock, but not near so bad as the dynamite, and the pay stayed the same. Cal was as careful as Tub was;

Tub always appreciated that. So when he got elected sheriff, also a dangerous job, he wanted Cal there beside him doing the drilling and cutting. Now, he knows, Cal has been going behind his back, protecting Baxter against orders, playing by his own set of rules. The morning after Tub arrested all those assholes who attacked the Brunist camp, the sonuvabitch went down to the jail and set them free. Tub's going to have to find somebody else and has been looking over the audience for a possible replacement. The widows remind him that most of the good guys are dead, but maybe that's also just misplaced sentiment. Buff Cooley's up there now, into one of his union rants. A Patriot, comes to all the drills, tough as nails, but probably too inflammable. And he so hates the establishment, if he were a deputy sheriff, Buff would have to rail at himself. Even though Travers Dunlevy at the Brunist camp is not from around here, Tub had thought of recruiting him for the job—an active Patriot with an edge about him and a good eye with a weapon—but the chump apparently knocked off his wife and her lover out at the camp Saturday night, then skipped town. Dumbest reason in the world for getting yourself in trouble. Tub is getting a bit fed up with those clowns out there, truth to tell, but the money is still rolling into his account from Suggs' mine, where he is listed as a technical consultant, so he does what he has to do. When he got dragged out to the camp the first time that night, to keep the heat off, he called what he'd found a probable lovers' suicide, but it's not likely he'll get away with that. Already that sleazebag shyster Minicozzi down at city hall, throwing his puny weight around, has demanded from the city a public inquest and a second coroner's report. Meanwhile Tub has put out an all-points alert for Dunlevy but doesn't expect to find him and doesn't particularly want to.

When the union bosses running the show discover that the old bearded guy at the back of the church is the famous country singer Ben Wosznik and ask him, overcoming the general town-wide bias against the Brunists, to come up and sing Woody Guthrie's "The Dying Miner," Tub figures he can only bear so much of this teary-eyed horseshit. He'll let Smith watch over the campers; it's time to cut out.

* * *

Sheriff Puller has played enough double-deck pinochle to know how to finesse a trick. In fact he is beginning to think of pinochle as a patriotic American game, and a Christian one, and that maybe they ought to use pinochle as part of their militia training program. Tub has led low, telling his deputy Smith that Suggs has asked him to negotiate a conclusion to the problems at the new campgrounds he's been building out beyond the church camp so he can get on with its construction, and since Cal knows those people better than he does, he wants him to organize a meeting at the site for the two of them with all their leaders and see if they can't resolve the issues. Forcing a crawl, as one might say at table, and here they are. He is disappointed that Abner Baxter does not appear, but most of the others do, including Red's puffball son Young Abner, as well as Roy Coates and his boys and Jewell Cox and others from town. Most of the rest hang back, but as the talks proceed they come out of their tents and trucks and edge forward. Then he plays trumps. All his newly deputized officers from the Christian Patriots come roaring up in their cars, spitting gravel as they hit the brakes; they spring from their cars and surround the campsite, weapons in hand. Tub has been careful to deputize only those he could count on not to spill the beans to Smith or the Baxterites, and he can see by the flicker of surprise on Smith's otherwise stony face that he has been successful. A couple of big yellow school buses roll in behind the deputies' cars. Tub tells Smith not to worry, they've all been properly deputized on orders from the state governor. Then he puts a megaphone to his mouth and says: "I know you think of yourselves as religious people, but the truth is, you're all criminals. You are breaking the law, and you do not stop breaking the law even when you are told that is what you are doing, so I have no choice but to put you all under arrest." One of the men at the back makes a break for it, but two of the deputies fire shots over his head and he pulls up short. They lower their weapons and point them at his chest. He steps back with the others.

"Looks as how fatso has snookered us," Roy Coates says with a sneer, and Tub stares back at him. If he were a man who ever smiled, he'd be smiling. But if Roy calls him fatso again, the fucker will end up in the bed next to the fire chief.

"My deputies are ready to fit you with some nice shiny bracelets and bus you to the county lock-up, if that's your choice," he says into the megaphone, "though the law don't work so good around here and I don't recommend it. Your other choice, which is a lot easier on everybody, is to permanently and for all time leave the area. If them's your rathers, you got five minutes to pack up. Don't try driving away on your own—you're gonna be personally escorted outa here over into the next state. Anybody not got a vehicle and don't wanta go to jail, we'll be providing taxi service across the state line in them school buses over there. We're all gonna proceed together in a nice neat line, just like a parade. Anybody peel off, they'll get shot as fugitives from the law. You got little kids here. Let's don't let that happen. And if you try to come back in, you'll just be giving my boys target practice. We'll be patrolling all the highways and roads in the county, so don't even think about it."

"You cain't take us in," says Coates. "We live here."

"Aiding and abetting," he says.

"Bull."

He lifts the megaphone. "All right, let's get moving!" He's waiting for Cal to cross him so he can break him, but he doesn't say anything. Instead, a snot-nosed brat dragging a dirty pink slipper on one foot comes over and pokes her finger in his belly. He swats at her but misses. "It's real!" she shouts and other brats draw near with mischievous grins on their nasty little faces as if they all intend to have a poke.

"Luke, you come away from there and let the man be!" a woman calls out. "He's just doing his job!" Big woman, near as big as he is, a squalling fat baby over her shoulder. She waddles out of the crowd toward him and gets a grip on the girl's collar. "Sorry, Sheriff. We're town folk. We just come out to bring some food and comfort to these poor people. I feel sorry for them and I think you should oughta too, but I suppose you got your orders. Us Christians is used to getting beat up by the law. We'll be going now and leave you to it, but next time I see Jesus, I'm gonna tell him what you done."

"Wait a minute—"

"I recognize them," Smith says. "It's okay. They're living in the Chestnut Hills prefabs."

"Squatters."

"Maybe. But that's Romano's problem, not ours."

It's Suggs' problem, too, he owning most of that property, but Tub knows this is not an argument that carries much weight with Smith. A lanky unkempt man with deep hollow eyes has come up beside the fat woman, toting a rifle and looking seriously deranged. Tub should probably tell him to hand over his weapon, but he has the notion it would not be a smart thing to do. The little girl in the pink slipper takes her thumb out of her mouth and asks: "Mom, can I have that silver star? *Please*, Mom!" and her mother tells her no, she can't, it's what makes the big man big, that without it he'd be a runt to a flea, and Coates' sneer spreads through the crowd of faces like a kind of infection. Tub has somehow lost the thread of this game. "All you folks live in Chestnut Hills come with us now. This ain't about us," the woman says, and one or two follow her toward their cars, and then a few others, and then everyone. Now having Smith here is a bad thing. Tub might have shot a few of them, but with Smith as witness he has lost that option. All he can do is unholster his weapon and holler at them to stop in the name of the law and he does that. Some of his boys do fire warning shots over their heads, but the fat woman says: "Come along now! Don't worry, they ain't gonna shoot nobody. They ain't very happy, but they ain't crazy."

"Doggone my soul, how I love them old songs! Put your hands t'gether there, folks, fer our sidekickin' goddaddy, Will Henry! He has done so much fer us and he does pluck a mean box!" Tub Puller likes country music about as much as he likes any music (not much), so when he heard that tonight would be the last Duke L'Heureux and Patti Jo Rendine show at the Blue Moon, he decided it might be a smart idea to hang out for a couple of hours to prevent any repeat of the brawl and also to see what all the excitement is about, hoping only they weren't singing songs like he'd heard them sing with the Brunists out on the mine hill, which he understood they were not. Needed a break from all that religious in-fighting. None of those nuts in here. He let Tess back at the station know he was going to be out of radio contact for an hour or two and if there was an emergency she should call him at the motel. He found the lot packed out, the stuttery "No Vacancy" neon sign lit, and the front door locked, and he had to bang loud with both fists to rouse anybody what with all the noise inside. When they finally showed up, they apologized, explaining they'd closed up because it was a complete sellout, no room for another body, though of course they'd let the sheriff in, which was, as he knew they were thinking, like letting in another half dozen. He asked them if there had been any trouble tonight and they said there had not and he moved on into the bar area. Not easy, even with the badge on his chest, to carve a grudging path. Never saw such a jam-up at the Moon, or anywhere else around here, for that matter. A lot of familiar faces but also a lot of strangers. The owner, watching things from the doorway, said they'd been rolling in all week for this show, every room booked double. But though he was glad to have seen this happen at the Moon, he said he was sad to see the act close down, and it was clear he'd had a few to console himself. Tub has sometimes stopped in here on dead midweek nights to have a whiskey or two on his own, so the bartender, when Tub finally got that far, simply greeted him with a nod and quietly poured him a glass of Coke spiked with a couple of shots of Kentucky bourbon, Tub hoping it might dull the pain in his tooth. After the holidays: the dentist, for sure.

A guitar is still slung around Duke's stringy neck, but two of the fingers on his strumming hand are taped to a splint, so most of the guitar playing is being provided by his slack-britches partner and the local radio station announcer, Will Henry, playing backup on the night and adding his whine to the others. The woman doesn't sing all that well but she's got an earnestness about her that somehow makes her sound better than she is. So far it has mostly been twangy old standards like "I'm Movin' On" and "Night Train to Memphis," where they're apparently headed tomorrow for a big Fourth of July stage show and a string of downriver venues after that, but he's heard talk of some off-color songs and he hopes his uniform and the fact he knows them from the church camp isn't putting them off. He's had some rough weeks with more to come on this long beer-picnic weekend, and he doesn't mean to make a fuss about song lyrics; he's only in need of an easeful few minutes before the next call comes in. Of course they may not even have seen him, but that's unlikely as his size always gets noticed, people turning to stare wherever he goes, and even now a lot of them are watching him, sitting there at the bar on a stool that feels more like the top end of a fire hydrant, drinking off his Coke and bourbon and accepting another.

Now, after a medley of moon songs—"Tennessee Moon," "Blue Moon," "Howlin' at the Moon"—Duke announces that to mark the occasion tonight he has written a new number, "The Blue Moon Motel," and that gets a wild cheer and some applause and foot-stomping. Will Henry does some preliminary strumming and Duke leans into the mike…

*I was knockin' about out on life's highway,*
*All alone and livin' in hell,*
*Feelin' so bad I jist wanted to die,*
*Then I met my gal in the Blue Moon Motel!*

And then the woman and Will Henry join in on the chorus…

*It's the oldest story I ever heerd tell*
*When boy meets gal at the Blue Moon Motel,*
*So listen up, darlin', it ain't never too soon*

*T'git your butt off to the ole Blue Moon…!*

There's a lot of hooting and hollering and loud whistling at that and then Duke calls the owner of the motel to come forward and he does, somewhat sheepishly and unsteadily, glass in hand, and he is cheered like you might cheer a ballplayer, and Duke puts his arm around him…

*We sang us some songs and crooned us some tunes*
*'Bout huggin' and kissin' and life was jist swell,*
*We was makin' real gold outa all our blue moons*
*And we owed it all to the Blue Moon Motel…*

This time the woman, Patti Jo, steps up to the mike to sing the chorus on her own…

*It's the oldest story I ever heerd tell*
*When gal meets boy at the Blue Moon Motel…*
*So listen up, cowboy, it ain't never too soon*
*T'git your rocks off at the ole Blue Moon…!*

There's a lot of loud whoopeeing and clapping and heehawing laughter, and though this is an uncommon scene for Tub Puller, he is beginning to melt somewhat into it and feel less uncomfortable on his bar stool, and he may even be grinning, though perhaps that's not obvious to others. But then the woman from the motel front desk presses through the crowd to shout in his ear that he has a phone call from his office. He says to tell the woman he'll call back on the car radio, it's too noisy in here, and he slowly downs his drink, lingering for one more verse…

*Well, we had a grand time and it hurts like hell*
*T'be singin' farewell to the Blue Moon Motel…*
*But our hearts is still here and we'll be back soon*
*Cuz we cain't stay away from the ole Blue Moon!*

The stringbean cowboy-hatted singer shouts out through the uproar for everybody to join in on the chorus, and they do, each singing their own preferred versions, and if Tub were the sort of person to do that he'd surely do the same, but instead he swivels heavily about and puts foot to floor and shoulders his way out. Back to the face…

*It's the oldest story I ever heerd tell*
*When boy/gal meets gal/boy at the Blue Moon Motel…*
*So listen up, darlin'/cowboy, it ain't never too soon*
*T'git your butt/rocks off to/at the ole Blue Moon…!*

When Tub Puller took over the rundown sheriff's office from Dee Romano's do-nothing cousin who treated the job as a family perk, he completely revitalized it. He repainted the office itself, hung blinds and detailed maps of the county, put down new linoleum, brought in furniture sturdy enough to take his bulk. His predecessor hardly ever ventured out of West Condon, not many people even knew he was there, but Tub has expanded his territory to include the entire county and has been developing a volunteer force prepared to respond to any emergency. He also added a new two-way car-radio system. It meant hiring operators on a tight budget, but there were any number of unemployed miners' widows looking for a little extra grocery money and willing to put in long hours of light work for not much pay. He could not afford twenty-four hour coverage, so he set up two nine-hour shifts, keeping someone there from seven in the morning to an hour after midnight. After that, emergency calls are switched to his home phone. A lot more work, but sheriffing is about all he does or wants to do, and it beats coalmining.

Now it's an accident on the back road to Tucker City. He's not happy about having to leave the Moon, and his tooth still hurts, but routine is routine and he sticks by it as what he knows best. Tess said in her radio call that she had deflected a few nuisance calls, but this one seemed pretty bad and he should probably check it out. He asked her who called it in and she said it was Royboy Coates. She said his mother had called earlier to say he hadn't come home for supper and she was worried about him, but she reminded Thelma that Royboy has had a way of getting in trouble of late and has been seen at all hours in unsavory places with unsavory people and that she and Roy should have a serious talk with him, and Thelma said no matter how many beatings Royboy takes from his father, it doesn't seem to make a tittle of difference. Tess said Royboy told her on the phone that it was some young kid on a motor bike, a car or truck must have hit him, he wasn't sure if he was alive or dead, but he'd wait there until the sheriff showed up, though he was scared so please come right away. He asked Tess if she knew where Cal Smith was and she didn't. He asked her to try to reach him by phone and also one or two of the new deputies and to send them out there to join him in case he needs help. He'll also need an ambulance if it's as bad as Royboy says, so she should stay there until he calls back, but she reminded him tomorrow was a holiday and she was supposed to knock off early, so he told her to order the ambulance up now. She also reminded him about the Fourth of July parade tomorrow, which he'll have to ride in, suggesting he might want to take the newlyweds along in the back seat, now that he's hiring Franny in the office, and he reminded her he's supposed to ride a goddamned horse and then he got on the road. He considered driving past the Brunist camp and picking up Hunk or Wayne, but it's out of the way and they're probably already in bed.

As he rises over a little hump in the road, he sees Royboy there all right, just where he said he'd be—he waves frantically when he spots the sheriff's car coming—and there's the cyclist on the side of the road, his overturned motorbike another twenty yards further up where momentum must have taken it. Tub pulls his car over onto the shoulder and sits there for a moment, his lights on Royboy and the fallen biker, looking the scene over. There's a motorcycle parked beside Royboy. His own most likely. Royboy looks terrified, but then he probably hasn't seen many dead bodies, if it is dead. Tub is thinking about that biker gang with the death's-head and Brunist tattoos and patches who were here a couple of months ago. There are a lot of motorcycles in the county, it's a cheap way to get around, but you don't often see them out on the back roads this late at night. He hasn't dealt with a motorcycle accident since the night he created one down the road from the Blue Moon. He remembers the Cavanaugh station wagon rolling past that night, thinking at the time that it was the Cavanaugh brat and a girlfriend. They had more urgent things to do, he figured, so he finished what he was doing. But then he learned the next day the car had been stolen and trashed, probably by the bikers. If so, they'd seen him. They might have come after him right then, but they didn't. He supposed that they would and prepared for it, but it didn't happen, and instead they left the area. Ever since then they have been somewhat on his mind. There's a thick stand of trees over to the left beyond the ditch. Could be hiding someone. He turns his spotlight on it, leaves it and his brights on and the motor running, unsnaps his rifle from the overhead carrier, checks the ammo in the two pistols on his hips, dons his helmet, crawls out of the car cautiously, and looks around. Everything dead quiet. All he hears is crickets and the soft rumble of his car motor. Those assholes make a lot of noise; he's pretty sure he'd know if they'd come back. He's not wearing his steel-toed miner's boots tonight, but he doesn't expect to need them. Keeping his eye on the woods and the road in both directions, he approaches Royboy and the body, which looks twisted and lifeless. Royboy is so scared his teeth are chattering. "Why aren't you at home, Royboy?" he asks to break the silence, but Royboy only shakes his head and tries awkwardly to laugh. It's more like a sick whine. Tub pokes his toe at the body, then squats, asking himself if he's ever seen Royboy on a motorcycle and where is the phone he called from, to look more closely at it. Feels a chill. The greasy duck's ass haircut tells him all he needs to know. It's the darkie who rode with them, the one they called Cubano. The shit opens his eyes and winks at him. The sheriff is down there on one knee when they rise up out of the ditch and he more or less expects to die that way. The odd thought that comes to him is that now he won't have to go to the dentist. They strip him of his weapons and march him back to his car, where he can hear Tess on the radio signing off, telling him the ambulance will be out there in about fifteen minutes but she hasn't been able to reach Smith or any of the others, and reminding him again about the parade tomorrow.

# IV.2

## Saturday 4 July

Tommy Cavanaugh's hastily assembled, ragtag West Condon Fourth of July parade turns the corner out of Third, nearly two hours late, and heads up Main Street in the glittering sunlight toward the patient citizenry. Not much to do in this town. This is something to do. They can wait for it. Sally steps out of her "Four Freedoms" tee shop to watch it go by and wave a manikin limb at Tommy. Leading it is the West Condon mayor, riding in the back seat of Tommy's bright red convertible, the expression on his face that of a man listening to a dirty joke. He is accompanied by a supporting convoy of other area bigwigs and followed by a marching band of high school kids—long on drums, short on horns—tootling away at what is probably supposed to be "Stars and Stripes Forever," or maybe it's the high school marching song or even "White Christmas." Next comes the heaving and yawing "New Opportunities for West Condon" float with young girls in swimsuits hanging on for dear life, and behind it whooping police cars, ambulances, and fire engines, and finally all the marching groups Tommy has lined up, some with their own drum corps, from churches, unions, civic and social clubs, businesses, scout troops and sewing circles, including an armed mob carrying a Christian Patriots banner and some Italian neighborhood heavies led by

Angie Bonali's uniform-shirted brother Charlie, who busted Tommy's nose and is supposed to be in jail but isn't. They also have a banner: KNIGHTS OF COLUMBUS VOLUNTEER DEFENSE FORCE, it says. Also armed. People with childish ideas and grown-up weapons out to ruin the world. Tommy told her he had talked the sheriff into riding a white horse in the parade, but apparently he chickened out. Or maybe the horse did after seeing the sheriff. She once read in a pop psych book that parades were scarcely disguised representations of thrusting penises, drum majorettes at the tip wearing high plumed hats like French ticklers and twirling their batons in cocky foreplay, but on this dead street that would amount to a kind of necrophilia.

The corpse, however, is well-dressed for the occasion, with tricolor litter bins, ribbons on the lampposts, flags hanging from shop fronts, and a red-white-and-blue stripe down the middle of the street. Even the potholes have been filled in, if only with loose gravel. Sally has helped clean up and paint the empty Main Street stores for this weekend of rent-free entrepreneurialism, mostly taken up for rummage and bake sales, so-called arts and craft shows, charity drives, and town boosterism displays, and she has claimed this old once-bustling women's clothing store for her own showroom, celebrating freedom from pulpit, flag, marketplace, and FROM THE CULTURE OF WILLFUL IGNORANCE—which more or less includes everything else and is the theme of her current work-in-progress. This she has reshaped into "Living with the Cretins," in which she describes the town and nation beyond as a vast terminally Christianized loony bin, entering it into the first annual West Condon Fourth of July essay contest. The only other entry, no doubt at Tommy's urging, was by that dweeb Babs Wetherwax, "Why I Love My Country." Ah yes, let me count the ways. Sally got second prize, which was more than she expected even with the limited submissions. Boobs will read her winning essay at the bank-sponsored Independence Day picnic this afternoon; Sally has not been invited to do so, but she may read her own anyway.

On the shop walls and in the front window, she has pinned up hand-printed poster-sized quotes from the Founding Fathers—

Jefferson, Adams (THIS WOULD BE THE BEST OF ALL POSSIBLE WORLDS, IF THERE WERE NO RELIGION IN IT), Washington, Franklin, Madison—and such patriots as Tom Paine and Albert Einstein and Susan B. Anthony and Ambrose Bierce, all gathered for her Cretins essay, plus her own notebooked gems of wisdom (THE ENLIGHTENMENT: WHO HIT THE OFF-SWITCH?), even a few of her fiction fragments (literature! yay!). She put all her old unwashed T-shirts up for sale (once published, you don't repeat yourself), spreading them out on tables made of planks on sawhorses, and inked up some new ones for the occasion, including variations on her Four Freedoms and ones bearing messages like Mark Twain's SACRED COWS MAKE THE BEST HAMBURGER and H. L. Mencken's DEEP WITHIN THE HEART OF EVERY EVANGELIST LIES THE WRECK OF A CAR SALESMAN. The clothing store used to have a bargain basement where her mom always shopped and down there in the murk she found some broken manikins—headless torsos, loose heads, scattered hands and feet—and she used them in the window to model her shirts. Filthy creatures and grotesquely battered, but perfect for the occasion. She put the heads on the floor of the window, chins propped by their feet and gazing up admiringly (or abashedly, who could tell?) at the headless bosoms in their amazing tees, and she twisted the waists on some of those that had them so that they wore their bottoms at the front, then inscribed upon the glossy cheeks her own parodies of religious and patriotic clichés. When Tommy saw it, he said: "You're just trying to get people mad at you," and she agreed with him.

After the parade has stumbled past, her friend Stacy Ryder comes in, showing off a white ceramic elephant with its trunk broken off that she says she found in a white elephant sale and couldn't resist. "I mean, how often do you find *just* what you're looking for?" She's wearing shorts and a cut-off shirt that shows off her midriff. The sort of body that breaks hearts. "'Christianity is the most perverted system that ever shone on man,'" she says, reading one of the pinned-up placards. "Did Thomas Jefferson really say that?"

"Who knows what anyone said in the past? I can't tell you what I said yesterday. But it's in the history books, whatever history is. Jefferson was definitely no mindless Christian, though, nor were most of the founders. Different country then. Before the cults took over."

"My Puritan forebears should have sunk off Plymouth." She pauses in front of one of Sally's story fragments taped to the wall. "'A Place Called Suicide.' I hope you're not thinking of going there...?"

"No. A response to that shoe store guy." When they offered up the empty Main Street stores for temporary occupation today, nobody wanted that one. "I'm only a tourist, taking pictures. That's why I turned it into a place. So I could do that." There is a place, not so much at the center of the city as inside the center of the city; it is a place children cannot discover, though adolescents sometimes stumble upon it in their anxious posturing. That's the line Stacy is reading now. Maybe she shouldn't have tacked it up. But publishing it on the wall like that led Sally to another line she'd scribbled at the bottom: True travelers do not even see the boundary notices, but are there before they realize they have set out. Which will lead to another, already formulating itself in her head. She could never go to such a place, it's not in her nature, but the story can.

"When I was learning to ride a bicycle," Stacy says, "my mother always insisted I ride on the left, facing the traffic, so I could see what was coming. The way she put it was, Stay off the suicide of the road." Stacy smiles her smile, but a kind of sadness settles in. She doesn't think Stacy is going to stay around much longer. She picks up a rose-colored shirt that reads SUPPORT ATHEISM: A NON-PROPHET ORGANIZATION and holds it up in front of her. "Hah," she says, "it's my lucky day. Perfect thing for the bank floor. How much?"

"Given the slogan, I could hardly charge you for that one."

"I was thinking of it more like tithing."

"How about community service? I promised to help clean up the street after the parade. Want to give me a hand?"

"Sure. Then I have to go serve wienies at the bank picnic. I understand things are about as wobbly out there as that sinking float."

"Saw your boss pass by looking out of sorts. Is that what he was so agitated about?"

"My boss? No. Well, maybe. It was mainly about the sheriff, I think."

"You mean, why he didn't turn up?"

"Right. I think he's dead. That's what I heard."

"Oh wow! But how—?"

"I don't know. I heard people say his car might have caught on fire. Or got set on fire. And there was apparently some poor kid locked in the trunk."

"Holy shit! That's *really* scary! Who was the kid?"

"I didn't hear."

Later, at the bank picnic, Tommy tells her: Royboy Coates. Sheriff Puller was found in his burnt-out car, his wrists handcuffed to the steering wheel. The sheriff's radio dispatcher said she'd tried to reach him before she shut down, but he didn't answer and she figured he'd turned in for the night. She also said it was Royboy who apparently set the trap with a call about a highway motorcycle accident. "Royboy was just totally fucked," Tommy says, breathing noisily around his bandaged reconstructed nose. "The only odd thing at the scene was a Dick Tracy comicbook on the ground near the front bumper. It was old and beat up, but showed no signs of having been out in the weather, so they may have dropped it there as a kind of taunt to the cops. Maybe they can get fingerprints." For some reason that strikes Sally as funny in a sick way, but she doesn't say so. Tommy is pretty rattled. His dad tried to contact the governor to ask for troops, as he's been doing the last few weeks, but he was told the governor was out on a statewide tour of Fourth of July parades and couldn't be reached until Tuesday, and his dad said Tuesday was too late. "He was yelling at whoever he had on the phone, telling him this was an emergency, that the governor had to cancel his fucking joyride and get on top of this, order up the National Guard, we need them *now*, and the jerk at the other end said something about there being little he could do, it was a national holiday weekend and the available troops were all deployed at one parade or another. Dad shouted, 'Well, goddamn it then, *re*deploy them!' and slammed the phone down. He's mad as hell. He also called both senators, our congressman, and his pal at the FBI, yelling and swearing at all of them or whoever answered the phones. Answering service operators, mostly, who probably thought they were talking to a madman. And those armed Christian Patriots you saw today in the parade? They've all been deputized by the new sheriff."

Onward, Christian Soldiers. The real battle hymn of the Republic. Things are not going well for Captain America and his young masked sidekick. "I saw Charlie Bonali in the parade, too. He seems to have got up a gang of his own."

"The Knights of Columbus Volunteer Defense Mob, *alias* the Dagotown Devil Dogs. That vicious fucking asshole. Fleet said they turned up at his deli asking for money, pushed him around, threatened him, stole stuff. Romano tried to keep them out of the parade, and those fundamentalist Klan types, too, but couldn't. When the chief said they couldn't be in the parade if they were armed, they both said it was their constitutional right to bear arms and they'd just fall in behind the last lot and march anyway. Which would have meant they'd be marching together, and that seemed too dangerous. They were already eyeing each other like they couldn't wait to get at it. So the chief let them in and kept them separated, his own squad car and other marching groups, between them. Man. The whole day has just turned to shit. Things are fucking out of control."

"It's the Fourth, Tommy. An American holy day. What did you expect? Killing is patriotic."

"Killing cops isn't."

"Sure it is. Patriots are made by revolutions. Which are against cops and the guys who own the cops." She means that as a general historical principle, but he'll take it that she's slamming his father again. She lights up a smoke and tells herself to ease up. "What about your dad's resurrection circus tomorrow? Is that still on?"

"Dad's completely shot, about as low as I've seen him. Something's really got him down—Mom being so sick and all, maybe trouble at the bank, I don't know. I know he advanced Lem Filbert a lot of money, and Osborne too, and all that's down the tubes. And now what's happened today. He has worked so hard to try to turn things around, and this is what he gets. But, yeah, as far as I know he's going through with it. He figures none of this would be happening if those evangelical dingbats hadn't come back, so if he can get them to wise up and move on, the other problems may take care of themselves." Another Twain quote she found while composing her Cretins essay was "Against a diseased imagination demonstration goes for nothing." Twain wasn't talking to the diseased imaginations, they're a lost cause, something the human horde has to live with; he was talking to the fool who thinks he can do anything about it.

The whole town is out here at the high school playing fields, the nearest thing it has to a park. They used to have one in the center, but now it's a parking lot with a drive-in root beer stand on one corner. The townsfolk are lapping up the ice cream and free eats and soft drinks under the hot afternoon sun, and there's a lot of beer being passed around from personal coolers, but the mood is more apprehensive than festive. When the word got around, a lot of people dashed out to the Deepwater No. 9 access road where the sheriff's car was found to get a glimpse of his scorched body before it was taken away, and though they all thought they wanted to see it, after they saw it they knew that they didn't. It was like a sickening echo of the mine disaster and has brought the nightmares back. Sally follows Tommy's gaze and sees Stacy at one of the bank food stalls, where she's cooking up hotdogs and serving paper plates of potato salad and baked beans. Stacy waves and she waves back. She apparently lacked the nerve to wear the "non-prophet" shirt out here. Or maybe she didn't want to hide what she's got. Can't compete with that. "She's so cute," Sally says, and

Tommy turns away with a sad clownish grin under his swathed nose and says, "Yeah, but not very friendly."

The fat lady's family, the ones who cleared out the swimming pool, are all over there at Stacy's stall, grabbing up whatever's offered, pocketing what they don't eat. The little girl in the pink slipper is wearing Sally's stolen "sacred cow" tee backward, down to her ankles like a dress. It left her shop along with lots of other things while she and Stacy were cleaning up the street. That's okay. Spread the evangel. A fifth freedom. From the private ownership of the world. The girl and her brothers have been running about, throwing firecrackers at the squirrels and butterflies, trying to stamp out all the grasshoppers, helping themselves to the sports day prizes, shooting water pistols.

Sally has put on her John Adams "holy lies and pious frauds" tee for her Independence Day meeting with Billy Don, but maybe she should change to something more suggestive for later. Something straightforward like "Why Not?" Or "Ripe Fruit." Hanging by a thread from the Tree of Knowledge. My Cunt-Tree. 'Tis of thee. For thee. She drops her cigarette and grinds it out with her sneaker heel. Stupid. "I have to go, Tommy. I promised to meet that kid from the camp. But how about watching the fireworks together tonight? I'll invite Mary Jane along for company. I've got what's left of her stowed away somewhere in a dirty sock."

Tommy gazes at her thoughtfully with his discolored eyes. He's probably not seen a lot of action since he dropped Angela and had to get his busted nose repaired. It has been a hard week and he's tired and it shows. "Sounds just about right," he says. Her heart's pounding. She hopes it isn't making her tee bounce. Like in the cartoons. She feels like a cartoon. Goose Girl. Thump thump. She snaps a cigarette out of a rumpled pack and lights up again, trying to hang loose, as the boys say. "Dad has called an emergency meeting of the NOWC committee with the chief and the acting sheriff, and I still have to run the raffle and a couple of races, make sure the stage mikes are working, and play a game of ball on one of the teams Fleet has put together. But by the time they light up the sky, if we're not all dead, I'll be ready to cool out."

* * *

They meet at a pull-in near the path to the old abandoned municipal cemetery. Sally has ducked out of the town picnic, hoping to miss all the patriotic bunkum, go back after it's over with stash in her pockets and a better tee. Billy Don wants to show her the filled-in grave, the one that Darren holds to be an otherwise inexplicable signal that the Rapture, or something like it, has begun. Or maybe he only wants to get her alone in a dark place. Billy Don is alarmed when he sees the garden spade she has brought along and he stops in his tracks, so she shrugs, winks, and tosses it back in the car, gets out the sandwiches and sodas she has picked up at the picnic.

They haven't seen each other since their interrupted midsummer swim at the lakes two weeks ago, so on their walk down the overgrown path through the woods to the buried graveyard, both of them in shorts and having to pick their way carefully past all the thorns and scratchy bushes and poison ivy, they fill each other in on the recent town and camp news. Billy Don tells her that he was one of those who found the sheriff. The guards on night duty last night said they saw a fire over near the mine from up on Inspiration Point, but it died down and they figured it was probably just a brush fire or kids getting off to an early start on the Fourth, and decided to wait until daylight to go over there, especially since they'd been hearing motorcycles again and were worried that that gang might be back. So after breakfast Billy Don and some of the other fellows armed themselves and drove over—and came driving right back again to call the deputy sheriff on the office phone. They didn't open the trunk, only heard about that later. Billy Don says there's a lot of anxiety at the camp because of the loss of their two most powerful protectors, first Mr. Suggs and now the sheriff, and because of the possible return of the bikers, though Darren thinks these are just further signs of the looming End Days. "You know, the horsemen. In the Bible. Those bikers. It was your aunt who saw the connection." Billy Don tells her about Aunt Debra's arrest, what Colin said in front of everybody. No wonder Aunt Debra seemed so shattered. Billy Don says Colin is "a mischievous liar." Colin in turn now calls him Judas and screams accusations at Billy Don every time he leaves the camp. He is Darren's little buddy, and Darren has moved over to Colin's cabin. To take care of him, he says. Actually, that's the best part. Darren has taken his worktable with him and Billy Don now has the cabin to himself. He is turning it into a proper church office, he says, so they can close the other one and finish the men's restroom. After that, well, he doesn't know… He casts a sideways wall-eyed glance her way.

Sally hands him the hotdogs and sodas so she can pause to light a cigarette (she notices the matchbook is from some motel out on the highway; she doesn't remember where she picked it up but sees its ending up in her pocket as serendipitous) and recounts for him the story of the garage fire and Lem Filbert's crazed assault on the fire chief, which she says, according to her father, had to do with some sort of racket at city hall that Filbert was resisting. "Really, it's all pretty comical, in a dark torturous sort of way." When she asks about the reported lovers' suicides at the camp, Billy Don says it was actually a double murder, probably by the woman's husband who has disappeared. That was what Ludie Belle said, though he didn't see them himself. "It was, you know, that night…" He says they talked about burying them on the back side of the Mount of Redemption where the dog Rocky is buried, but there were objections that they had died in sin and it wouldn't be right to have them lying right next to the new tabernacle temple, so the sheriff organized a burial over at Randolph Junction, alongside that old lady who died a couple of months ago.

"The one whose soul I snatched," Sally says.

"Yeah. A lot of people still believe that."

Later that night of the murders, Billy Don tells her, after he'd got back from the lakes, there was an assault on the camp by a gang of drunks, but they made the mistake of bowling over some beehives in the dark. Sally laughs and says, yes, she saw a couple of them the next day at Franny Baxter's wedding, sick with hangovers, badly beat up, and covered head to toe with bee-stings—the groom included. "The best man apparently overslept and missed the wedding altogether. One of the guys, whose face was so puffy with bee-stings he was almost blind, had his skinny arm in a new white cast, on which others in the wedding party were posting lyrical obscenities. The writing bug can hit you anytime, anywhere. Then, during the ceremony, the groom threw up all over the bride's gown and passed out and had to be laid out on the sofa. I was supposed to *photograph* all that! Franny and her sister-in-law just giggled through it all like it was the funniest thing that ever happened." To keep the conversation lighthearted (they've reached the edge of the old burial ground with all its forgotten dead, and its shadowy melancholy is what they're both feeling), she tells him about the Blue Moon Motel singers who were there to sing hayseed love songs and who entertained everyone with a funny parody of "Frankie and Johnnie" that they made up on the spot, with lines about the bees and the Blue Moon brawl, and he asks if she knows what has happened to them, because they were Brunist Followers and always sang at their prayer meetings, but they seem to have left town. She doesn't.

When Billy Don leads her to the grave in question, it is more or less as she first saw it: open, empty, overgrown. But now there's a pile of fresh dirt nearby. Billy Don seems genuinely spooked, his mouth agape beneath his droopy handlebars, his eyes behind their dark lenses even less focused than usual. "I saw it! It wasn't like that!" he whispers, and she nods. "It was completely full, like there was a body in it!" She drops her smoke between her feet and steps on it, thinking about this. "Must be Darren," she says. "He's playing games with your head."

One's destiny in smalltown middle America: Death by submersion in a pot of boiling clichés. This great nation, under God… Is this what Jefferson and his coauthors had in mind? Sally has returned too early to escape the last of the Fourth of July oratory. All these self-styled, high-minded, sober, hardworking, patriotic, decent Christian swindlers. Billy Don told her that some of the Brunists believe that America is literally the New Jerusalem, and after they're raptured they'll all celebrate the Fourth of July there with God and His angels. "Nobody has never handed nothing to this town. We don't have mountains or oceans or famous buildings like a Awful Tower. I guess all we got is the corner bus station. But what we *have* got is quality of life. We got *heart!*" Hizzoner has the heart of a weasel. And the brain of a lizard. "If we got problems we can put 'em right on accounta this is America! People all over the world envy us what we got here! Right here in West Condon!" Much as they might want to believe it, people would have long since walked away from the mayor's horseshit, but Tommy has scheduled the raffle draw at the end of it all so as to keep them hanging in, clutching their little ticket stubs.

Her mother and Emily Wetherwax are sitting on folding chairs far enough from the speakers not to have to pay them much attention, having a smoke together, apparently having made up after what happened out at the lakes. A quiet moment of ciggyboo time, as they have called it ever since high school. Which her mother has never left. She's still that popular, carefree ball of fire called Frisky. Her own personal dreamtime. Which she revisits at every opportunity. Her dad's tanked as usual, but still staggering along, grinning idiotically and raising his hip flask to all he meets, mugging emotions. The Court Jester. He's especially good at stupefaction. Mothers and fathers, though lovable, are only useful up to a point. After that, they can go. She made the mistake of saying that to Tommy one day while they were cleaning out the vacated downtown shops together, still trying to rescue him from the plot he's been written into, and he called her a heartless bitch and said his mom and dad were the two most important people in his life and always would be. Wherein, alack, lies his eventual ruin. She was about to entertain him with the story of her parents and the Wetherwaxes getting drunk at their midsummer picnic and swapping partners, and all the funny anguished things she heard her mom saying on the phone to Emily Wetherwax the next day, but decided not to. In her effort to score with him, she has told him too many things. They wouldn't be springing Giovanni Bruno on the cultists tomorrow, for example, if she hadn't let him know about Darren's symbolic burial plans. Of course that's why Tommy has taken such a patient interest in what she has to say. He has been pumping her for information to pass along to his dad, using her much as she has been using Billy Don, and what's worse, she has been aware of it all along. Feeling guilty, and a bit pissed off, she told Billy Don about Operation Resurrection this afternoon while they were back at their cars having their afternoon snack, Billy Don being too shaken by the reopened grave to stay in there for their picnic. "What? Bruno? He's alive?" "Keep it to yourself," she said, knowing he wouldn't. It's like writing "to be continued" at the end of a story that's already over.

On the way out of the cemetery, Billy Don asked her a lot of earnest questions about life and death and how she manages it all without religion. She answered him the only way she knew how, but she was aware that what had begun as a kind of larky soda fountain game was becoming more like a responsibility, and she wasn't sure she wanted that. Who is she to unlock the mysteries of the universe? Strip an innocent kid of his fantasy consolations? "Well, you know," she said finally with a little shrug. "The truth, Billy D. Nobody has it all. My ears are open." But because she couldn't help herself, she went on to say he should leave the camp, that he was never going to figure things out in there. And without knowing exactly why, she suddenly feared for him. Maybe it was the bikers coming back, or Darren's craziness, or all the weird frightening things that have been happening, and she reached into her pocket and pulled out a twenty-dollar bill and pressed it on him. "Billy Don, I want you to do me a big favor. I've only got this twenty, but I want you to take it and go fill up your car and go back home, or go find those kids in Florida, whatever, wherever, but as far away from here as possible. Right now." He turned pale and gave her a look through his shades—two looks if you count both eyes—that could mean only one thing and shook his head and said thanks, but, well, she probably wouldn't understand, but he had to stay.

*Nobody's* innocent, she least of all. Remember that.

She sees Tommy over by the popcorn machine, leaning over Babs Wetherwax, peering rakishly past his plaster nose cast down the kid's cleavage. Sally has stopped by the house to put on a fresh tee (one of the free NOWC shirts, the C inked into a circle with a smiley face and an exclamation mark after) and one of her dad's throwaway white shirts, for its protective sleeves, open and tails out. She grabbed up some blankets, all the money she could find, and the last of her stash, saved for just this occasion; she even remembered the insect repellant and the cameras she borrowed. She has picked out a good place over on the slope to watch the fireworks, private enough to allow for the joints but with an open view of the sky, but she may lose the night after all. Some time ago, in a biology course she took for her science requirement, she came across the word "neoteny" and she wrote it down in her notebook. Adults of a species looking like juveniles and though retarded (as one might say) thought of as cute, and therefore more likely to get fucked. The way a lot of dogs get bred. The way American guys like their girls. Small, soft, fuzzy, dimpled, helpless, confused, naïve. Big eyes. Little noses. White baby teeth. Plucked pubes. A little tongue to tickle you with. Neotenic. At the same time, they like big motherly tits. The Hollywood starlet image. Boobs Wetherwax.

Why does it matter? Because Sally loves Tommy. Something she used to write in her high school notebooks then tear out in embarrassment, only to write it again. Not knowing what she meant by it. Not knowing now. Something to do with that last night at the ice plant. Meaning has to do with language. That didn't. No brain at all then, just body. Bare and burning. Her heart's in her mouth and her clothes are shorn. Says Boy Blue to Peep, come blow my horn. She was so scared, she started praying. The way she was then. Scared but desiring him—or desiring something—so much it hurt. Nothing like it since, really. In her masturbation fantasies, it's always Tommy, and more or less as he looked to her that night in the back of his father's car. Just a boy. Boy Blue. Pale, lean, luminous. In his fever, so enraptured by what he saw, enrapturing her; no one has ever looked at her—even if he only was looking at *it*, not her—like that before or since. His erection a shared magic between them. Right in front of her nose. First real one she'd ever seen up close. He seemed to want her to do something with it, but she didn't know what. Sniff it? At his urging she took hold of it, surprised at how cool it was. Well, and then more. But not quite enough more. She lights up another cigarette, cursing herself.

*. . . but then he leaves her alone and she goes home, dragging her tail behind her.*

*Blue never calls Bo Peep again, though he knows where to find her . . .*

And so the rest of the day goes, a catalogue of familiar disappointments, the author retreating after each into her notebook. Dog with her bone. She doesn't win the raffle and has no luck at bingo. Her best chance is the sack race, but she would have been the only contestant over four feet tall, so instead she referees it and gets everybody mad at her while Tommy puts the make not just on Boobs but a whole flock of bleating neotenics, some of whose bells, she knows, he has already rung, to speak in the classical tongue. Love is a sack race, she writes, in which not all sacks are equal. Tortoise truth: the hare always wins.

She needs a friend, goes looking for Stacy, but with the food gone, she's gone, too. Smart. Smarter than Sally, who could leave but can't.

The ballgame starts late and lasts less than an inning, ends badly. Baseball on the Fourth: as emblematic as hotdogs, beer, and car crashes. She sits on the grass with Monica Piccolotti and her baby, figuring that it gives her her best shot at crossing paths with Tommy, close as he is to Pete, and has to listen to the entire catalogue of the joys of marriage and motherhood while Monica feeds, burps, changes (turns out it's a boy), powders, nuzzles, bounces the kid. Also about how cruel Tommy has been to poor faithful Angela, especially after what he's just done to her. Sally doesn't know what that is, but she can guess. Did Tommy have Biblical knowledge of cute little Monica Sabatini? Probably. They used to call her Teeny—Teeny Sabatini—but no longer; Lotta Piccolotti's closer to it. The worst thing is what has happened to her complexion. Love's production line: high-maintenance baby-machines and the redesigning of mothers. Helplessly desiring what you can't possibly want. Evolution, not as fact, but as faith. That it's going somewhere. A promise forever withheld through the ceaseless tumble of new generations. In the first inning, two of the first three batters get on base, mostly due to bad fielding, and Tommy, swinging one-handed as the big guys agree to do, hits a home run. Using his golf stroke. Is that fair? The fielder is actually back far enough, but she drops it and then can't find the ball in the high grass. Tommy walks around the bases, encouraging the girl, but the throw never even reaches the infield. Tommy's team scores two more before the little kids at the bottom of the lineup strike out. Tommy, pitching underhand in the bottom of the inning, gets the first two out on balls hit back to him. But her dealer, Moron Moroni, swinging with both hands, smacks a ball that bounces between the little third baseman's legs and would have hurt if it had hit him. Moron slides into second, feet high, bowling over the beer-bellied Cox kid, standing there picking his nose and waiting for the ball to be thrown to him, and a fistfight breaks out. This is of more interest to the watching crowd, some of whom move toward the field to join in with cold grins on their faces. Another popular Fourth of July tradition. It frightens her, and that's another disappointment. It's the human comedy, so why isn't she laughing?

Tommy and Pete hurriedly exit the playing field, pulling some of the little ones out with them, Tommy remarking as he strides by that he needs a fucking beer, Pete offering him one from the cooler in the trunk of his car over at the parking lot. Monica throws her kid over her shoulder and apologizes, saying she'd better go keep an eye on the boys that they don't get into trouble, and leaves her. Down on the field, the fight ends when Angela's brother steps into it, slugs a few, and leads his troops out before the cops turn up. Should she wander over to the parking lot and invite herself to a beer? She shouldn't.

Consider, she writes in her notebook: the whole of the human environment as a pedagogic instrument, art as a particular technique for focusing attention, for teaching skills of close regard. Why you have to mix it up, keep people on their toes. See everything.

She thumbs through the notebook and her current mood of disappointment extends to what she has written. The sophomoric silliness of so much of it. The pretension. The self-pity. Those lines she has set down about Bo Peep and Little Boy Blue, for example. She crosses them out in disgust. Then regrets it. Leave it. It is what it is, she is who she is, even in her stupid infantile doodlings. The doodle as a form of meditation. Meditation as process, not product. Books, too. When they become product, they're dead. Writing is it, not the written. For all her disappointment, she still believes. Language makes and unmakes reality. There's an unfathomable gap between nature and culture, the infinite and the finite. Only the imagination can even try to bridge it. Its failures are what beauty is. And so on. The litany of Saint Sal.

As the sky darkens toward showtime, Sally spreads her blanket on the little slope she picked out, though out of the private spot and onto a more public one so Tommy can at least see her should he chance by. She lights up the joint she has rolled and stretches out to watch the stars appear. Tommy vanished from sight some time ago. Probably gone off with one or more of his groupies. Sprawled in his convertible somewhere with a view of the upcoming fireworks. Where they can time their orgasms with the bursts in the sky. In the beginning, she thinks, staring up into that sky (the sheer volume of it!): the fundamental error of giving form to the formless, thus creating time and the perception of space. God's famous parlor trick. But the notion that light—creation—is "good" will not stand the test of inquiry. Something like that. She'd write it down, but it's getting dark and she's tired of writing things down. She has worked at holding the earth together long enough for one day. Time to mellow. Beautiful summer night. New crescent moon like a glossy fingernail, brightening as the dark deepens, becoming a tiny rip in the sky, illumined from behind. On the horizon, the flicker of heat lightning. The birds are still into their nightfall bragging and seduction racket. The crickets and katydids. Crazy about love. Mosquitoes with grosser appetites. She sits up, already feeling the impact of the weed (whoo, nice), spreads repellant on her wrists, arms, forehead, and the back of her neck, buttons the shirt sleeves and covers her bare legs with the second blanket. She was wondering what would linger long after she left this place. This might be it, not a visual image at all, just the feel of summer. Before lying back again, she rolls a few more joints, her fresh supply courtesy of Moron. Feeling sad. But okay. How she wants it, really. Independence, it's the day for it, isn't it? Maybe she'll just smoke the entire lot and crash out here for the rest of the summer. Dream a little dream of you.

She has been recording her dreams since she came home from college, cataloguing their peculiarities. Take-home coursework of a sort. Dreamtime 101. Once she'd done it for a while, she found she could make them up, or at least imitate the form. At first she thought it was leading her into something disruptively new, a break from the conventional well-told tales of the day, but in the end it revealed itself as a definable and familiar form of its own with its own set of rules and limitations. Vivid imagery, and just about nothing but. Actions, not language, until trying to describe them. Then, simple declarative sentences, like movie scripts. But little or no continuity, things happening and then not happening. Like the fireworks beginning to explode in the sky above. Pop! this and then pop! that. Linked by as little as trailing color. Sensations of flow, flight, fall, heavy-limbed slowness, mazy disrupted travels. Odd lines of dialogue with hidden meanings. Or not. Lots of family stuff. Abrupt transitions and bizarre juxtapositions. Unstable settings. Sudden breaks and gaps of time and space, casual violence, fleshy landscapes, public nakedness, absurdist reasoning. Spectacularly illogical events that seem completely normal. Strangers you know but don't know. The threat of the Other. Feelings of powerlessness, vulnerability, masked by illusions of superhuman power, etc. In short, an awful lot like all those creation myths she read back in college, the main difference being that, while dreams are private, myths have been honed for the public marketplace. Invested with intentionality while hiding the original nonsensical flow. Just as the dreams she makes up with words are never as weird as the ones she actually dreams, which often defy inscription. Images in them she could never think up awake, and no idea where they come from or how they get into her dreams. Easy to see, then, how primitive minds would think of them as coming from outside themselves like visions from the beyond. Get doped up and let it flow in. Hello? God talking. First storytellers. Crazy zonked-out dream weavers. Establishing the fatal fetal patterns.

The dream she is having right now is of a drunk and/or stoned Tommy Cavanaugh sitting beside her, asking if she has smoked up all the grass. She doesn't reply, just passes him her roach, lights another. They do the cabbages and kings thing, Tommy explaining that his dad left him in charge of everything to go track down the governor personally to try to get troops here by tomorrow, and he's had to do everything from fending off the news guys asking about the sheriff's murder, to dismantling the stage and food stalls and getting the kids out from under foot so they could begin the fireworks display, she pointing out for him meanwhile the Andromeda constellation backgrounding the light show up there, because the story of a hero's last-minute rescue of a maiden chained to a rock seems to fit the dream narrative underway. He thanks her for all the help she's been over the past weeks, and she says, Sure, boss, any time. By this time, they're lying side by side on one blanket and under another, hand in each other's pants, passing a joint back and forth with the free one while the flying sprays of color burst overhead, and she's not quite sure how this has happened, but now that his hand's there, digging deeper, it feels just right. She slides the blanket away and unzips his fly to bring his erection out into the open so that she can—what? not sure, let's just see what happens—when Jesus turns up with a lady friend. Seems okay. Jesus has seen it all, what can he care? Tommy flinches, so she grips him all the tighter. Jesus is walking with a picturesque shepherd's crook, which appears to be an old man's cane with a taped-on extension made from a mop handle. There are a bunch of kids trailing along, too, but their eyes are on the sky, which is full of the rocket's red glare, the bombs bursting in air. Jesus makes a sign that could be a blessing or it might just be waving off what he sees or he might want a drag. She passes the joint up to him, and that's exactly what he wanted, yes. He sucks deeply, as if seeking ascension, and passes it to his friend for a toke, but she hands it back with a sad smile, patting her tum. She is wearing the tails of her blouse out over her slacks. There is a little bulge there. Jesus has been busy. Sally is thinking about Jesus' forgotten wife, poor red-eyed Aunt Debra, whom she visited in hospital before she was sent elsewhere, where they could supposedly deal with deep depression: when you're chained to a rock, the hero doesn't always come along. Aunt Debra had gone silent, except for a simple mantra repeated over and over: I'll be there. I'll be there. She leaned in to kiss her and Aunt Debra didn't move or kiss back, just said flatly, I'll be there. "Bless you, my children, and be of good cheer," Jesus says now, the smoke curling out of his mouth like cartoon balloons of speech. "God has so adjusted the body, giving the greater honor to the inferior part: lo *(cough!)*, it is given unto your hands."

"This is kind of public," Tommy says with a laugh when Jesus and his friends have moved on. "Maybe we should go somewhere."

"It's already booked," she says.

She yelps with pain. Tommy recoils, but she claps him to her. "No, stay where you are, don't move. It just hurt more than I thought it would." She's gasping, as if she's run a mile. She doesn't know if the pot has served as a partial anesthetic or has intensified her sensory apparatus. "Give me a minute."

"*What* hurt?" he asks in palpable confusion. "Wait a minute! Why are you so *wet*? Omigod, Sal!"

"It's all right, Tommy. It really is. Just hug me for a minute."

"But I always assumed—I wouldn't have—fuck! You should have told me!"

"Ssshh!"

To be naked with him. Holding him. Such a sweet thing. But awkward at first. She felt self-conscious, offering up all she had and fearful he might not want it. Thankfully he left his T-shirt on, so then she did too, and that seemed to help. When their pants came down, it all felt completely natural. Almost too natural, like when they were little kids jumping about under the garden hose. But this time he had a hard-on. She was so grateful for that hard-on. It meant he wanted her. Even if he was too stoned to be sure just who she was. It meant everything would really happen. She wanted to kiss him but was afraid to. She wasn't used to it, might do something stupid, and didn't think he'd want to, kissing being more intimate than mere sex. But no need to fear. He's an experienced lover. Did all the right things, made her feel desirable, desired. He was the one to turn the lights out. To put her at ease, she thought. He was so pleased about the room. Before switching off the lights, he thanked her for choosing a place with air conditioning, but he was looking out the window onto the highway and she knew he had been afraid she might be taking him to the Blue Moon Motel. She was staring at his bare backside as he stood there at the window. It was heart-breakingly beautiful. She wanted to nuzzle it. Wipe her tears on it. Bite it. Chew it. With the least encouragement, she would have done so. She was high as a kite. The cliché seemed right. All clichés did. Everything happening was a most wonderful cliché. When he did kiss her, his long-fingered ball-playing hands stroked her gently, lovingly, passed down her back, over her buttocks, between her thighs. Also a cliché. A creamy one. She was already coming before he lowered her to the bed.

Now he's moving in her again. This is okay, she thinks. This is really okay. Bring on the clowns. Even the pain's okay. Mostly gone now and overtaken by all the other physical stuff happening. Worth cataloguing, but not now. All the way to her throat she feels it. Her eyes, the roots of her hair. On her own, it was never like this. She clutches his undulating buttocks, her hands grasping what her eyes ate up, and as he drives harder and harder, she knows just how to respond, as though she has been doing this all her life, her hips rising to meet his thrusts, her thighs clamping him. She even—how did she know to do this? maybe she read it somewhere—while gripping his neck with one hand, fingers his anus with the other, then searches for the base of his testicles, some special spot there, pulling him deeper into her. At the last minute (for her, it's not the last minute, just another one, it's great, don't stop, her whole body an infinitely expanding orgasm), he grunts, jerks out of her, spills his seed on her belly, both hands cupping her buttocks, pulling her to him, whimpering softly, his body still pumping furiously, and then with a deep sigh he collapses gently on her. The right thing to do. But, oh, how she ached to have him stay where he was, explode inside her. What an ecstasy—even as chubby Monica with the bad complexion comes to mind—that must be! So much yet to experience, to try, to learn. He kisses her under the ear, his nose guard massaging her scalp. A kiss of appreciation. Not once but twice; leaves his lips there. She feels so rewarded.

They lie there a while like that, she holding him in place, caught in the parentheses of her thighs like a delicious thought to be squeezed of nuance. Like hugging a heavy pillow. The darkness is not so dark now. She can see his shoulders, faintly blue from the light outside, can hear beyond the hum of the air conditioner more fireworks going off, the distant drone tone of motors out on the highway, the world returning but not the familiar one she knew before. She's never been in a room like this, for example. Out by a highway. In a houseful of adventurous transients. Fondling a boy's testicles. He will ask her why she did this, and does. The answers she has rehearsed won't do. This is no time for her usual wiseass comebacks. No mention of that night at the ice plant, please. She tells him simply she had always wanted it to be him, even before she knew what "it" exactly was, and she has waited all this time until it could happen and she thanks him for it. No obligations, she says, but only to herself, happy when he hugs her tenderly in response.

And then finally he does slide off and stand up and turn on the light. "Oh man. They'll think there's been a murder. Why didn't you put something under you?"

"I always sign my work," she says, hearing her old self again, but proud of the body that his paired shiners are staring down at: it did everything it was supposed to do and it did it well, never mind what he might think of it as an aesthetic object.

"Just look at my dick," he laughs, holding the bloody thing up with his fingertips. She's afraid he might be angry or disgusted, but he grins and takes her hand and pulls her to her feet and says, "C'mon, let's get cleaned up."

And so they do that, and the shirts come off and there's all the fun with the soap, and more sex standing up and kissing under the shower, and then toweling each other off and back to bed—it's a big room with two beds, so they have clean sheets to crawl into—and one last joint to share (thank you, Moron, you dear little horse's ass). It's all very tender and loving and completely naked now, better than she could ever have imagined it, using their mouths as well as everything else, he punching her here and there with his funny nose, one position not unlike that dogleg at the fourth tee. My God what has she been missing? She even gets to realize that little fantasy of a while ago of nipping his bottom in her teeth. But also a certain melancholy is stealing in because she knows it can't last—he doesn't love her and her feelings, well, they're mixed at best. Much as this is, it may be all of it. Tomorrow it will already be a memory, a dream dreamt like all memories and fading as dreams do, and she'll be overtaken by a longing quite different from the sort felt until now. Humans. They think too much. "Are you hungry?" she asks. "I've only had a hotdog all day."

"Sure. But it's late."

"I checked. The bar has snack food and is open until one. You'll have to buy. I spent my last dime on the room."

"No problem. I've got plenty. We can shoot the moon."

So they start to get dressed and he pushes his hand between her legs while she's pulling her panties up and there's another delay, he taking her from behind this time. They're both still pretty high and it seems better than ever, like they've got dangling nerve ends in all the right places, their bodies are just having the best time in the world, and then they start the dressing again, finishing this time, even though there's a moment when she opens his fly and gives his penis a final kiss, his hands tangled in her wet snarls, before they head for the bar.

"Look," Tommy says, pointing toward an opening door down the corridor, "it's that cute chick from the bank!" He starts to call out, but then the guy she's with steps out behind her, and Sally understands that the night has just suddenly ended.

# IV.3

## Sunday 5 July

"Mom! Come and see!" It's the little Blaurock boy at the top of the hill. His mother lifts her mass up the slope. Her stretched tunic is split; it tears more as she climbs. Even before she turns with the news, Darren knows what it will be. He has been to the old cemetery this morning before church with Billy Don, has seen the vacated grave. *"It's Rocky!"* Dot Blaurock cries out. *"He's been raptured!"* Darren nods when others turn toward him. "I know," he says quietly, yet most hear. He watches them rush to the top of the hill to see for themselves. He didn't exactly know, but it fits. It's happening. Anything can be expected. These are the End Times. Just as he has foreseen.

He is calmer now, but when he first saw the empty grave at the old municipal cemetery he was frightened. Billy Don was watching him closely when he led him to it. To see if he was only acting, as Billy Don later confessed. He was not. His alarm, fear, awe would have been obvious to anyone. But why just this one? Billy Don asked. Why not all the others? Because it's a message, he whispered. A message especially for him. God's reader of signs. In the words of their Prophet: *The tomb is its message.* One talks about these things, imagines them, prepares for them, but always as somewhat abstract notions somewhere in the future, inevitable but not quite real. Like death. Then suddenly here it is. This ceremony today on the Mount of Redemption is taking on new meaning, one he can only partially intuit and hope he is prepared for. That feeling again of a cold wind. He knelt there in the long early morning shadows amid the forgotten dead to pray for guidance. To himself, silently, eyes closed; this was not for Billy Don.

Billy Don also told him about the city's plans to bring a person here to the Mount this afternoon whom they will allege to be the Prophet. Such tactics do not surprise him. False messiahs abound in scriptural depictions of the Latter Days; they are in effect further evidence that those days have arrived. "And many false prophets shall rise, and shall deceive many." How did Billy Don find out about all this? For that matter, how did the authorities know about today's unannounced ceremony? That evil girl. If she even is a girl and not a living manifestation of Satan himself—or herself. Everyone knows that the Devil, as a fallen angel, is sexless and can appear in any form. Billy Don's treason runs deep. It is far worse than mere apostasy. He has been warned and has ignored the warning. "What fellowship hath righteousness with unrighteousness? And what communion hath light with darkness?" It is such a tragedy, such a failure of understanding, with consequences to be suffered through all eternity. Darren has confided so much in Billy Don, ever since they were in Bible college together. He had such hopes. Now he realizes how wrong he was to do so. In the worldly realm of the body, of the senses, Darren has made some mistakes. The Devil has sometimes used Billy Don to tempt him away from divine things toward the worldly. He believed for a while—or chose to believe—that no man sins, for God does all things in him: "Nothing in a man's works is his own." An excuse for iniquity and folly. Such moral lapses are difficult to avoid here on this confused and sinful earth, but they are moral lapses just the same and he repents of them. Now they are entering upon a new stage of the human drama, and all that is in the past. In history, which is ending. Perilous times are come. He feels in his heart a great universal love, but he knows that Billy Don's besotted and corrupted soul cannot be saved.

Colin comes running down the hill in his tunic, scrambling over the trench marking out the floor plan of the tabernacle church, to tell him what he has seen. He is at the edge of hysteria again. Rarely is he not. "It's all right, Colin," Darren says. "It's good." Colin gazes at him through his wispy hair, looks back up the hill, looks at Darren again, perplexed but trusting. He is utterly faithful to Darren and will do whatever he asks, but he is also difficult, demanding, and so fragile. There is always the risk of sudden, erratic, even dangerous behavior. Colin had a similar relationship with Sister Debra and see what came of that. Still, this troubled orphan's spectacularly original visions provide a window onto things unseen by others—unseeable, really—even if they are not always easy to interpret. One night Colin told him that he dreamed he was in the Garden of Eden, lying in a soft pillowy place that was the giant body of the First Mother. Adam and Cain had already killed her. Her head was not there and something was flowing from her neck; not blood exactly, more like milk. It was causing wild vegetation to grow up around them, protecting him from Adam and Cain, but also giving them places where they could hide. Though the First Mother was dead, she wrapped him in her giant hands and he peeked out at the jungly garden through her fingers and saw atrocious things happening there, but believed they would not happen to him. Unless she let go. He awoke screaming because he thought she *was* letting go, and he came leaping into Darren's bed to tell him, trembling violently, what he'd been dreaming. Darren was not sure quite what to make of such a vision, beyond its obvious appeal for protection, but Colin later said it might only have been the First Mother crying, but everything was shaking. That made Darren think of the coalmine disaster and the feeling he sometimes had on the Mount of Redemption that the ground was quivering underfoot. Eerie. The local vulgar name for this hill, he knows, is C--t Hill. He was coming to understand it might be a strange local vision of the Last Judgment, and—the end is always in the beginning—has incorporated Eden and the First Parents into his own interpretations of the End Times. He feels that, thanks to his disciplined pursuit of the truth, the world is gradually revealing itself to him as an open book.

His relationship to Jesus has also been evolving. It was as a boy genius and courageous young man that Jesus won his heart, and he was moved then by Jesus' goodness, his love, his wisdom, the sufferings he endured for the sake of the truth he bore. As Darren grew older, Jesus' human life lost its importance, becoming merely an anecdotal preface to his eternal role as Lord and Redeemer, his image of the Savior moving as if from one plane to another, the human story remaining behind in the world to guide and solace the ordinary believer, but only as an insubstantial shadow of the timeless one, which exists in a dimensionless space, where all is One, and where even the very image of Jesus is absorbed and vanishes. But now the human Jesus has reemerged in Darren's thoughts, not so much as preacher, miracle worker, messiah, or martyr, but as prophet, for Darren, like the historical Jesus, is also living inside human time, experiencing the same hopes, fears, uncertainties as he did, struggling desperately to understand the enigmatic Father, and to help others to understand Him in time for their souls to be saved, and so feeling like a brother to him. His other self. They are stepping through history—it is the *same* history!—hand in hand.

At Darren's personal invitation, Abner Baxter and his followers have arrived, several wearing Brunist tunics. They are clustered together over by the mine buildings, reluctant to intrude upon the gathering on the Mount, although there are many more of them than are here on the hill, even with the addition of the new Defenders. Clara's presence, probably. She showed her clear disapproval upon noticing them. Abner feels a grave responsibility for much that has happened of late, most recently the horrific death Friday night of the son of one of his most loyal friends, almost certainly at the hands of his own wayward boys, so shockingly back among them. That friend is not here today. Most are appalled by these savage events; Darren is, but he is solaced by their fulfillment of ancient Latter Days prophecies. The dark angels have returned. The final tribulations have begun. He must be brave. It won't be easy. The Bible says so.

Clara was not happy about today's ceremonies—whose idea was it to dig an empty grave for Giovanni Bruno?—but she did not oppose them. After all, her deceased first husband is being honored and she admitted she could see the value of consecrating a future resting place for their martyred Prophet's remains before the temple's construction makes such decisions difficult. It was only that the ceremony seemed premature. She was even less happy about people arriving last night who said they were Brunist Defenders, answering her call and pledging their loyalty to her. She called Darren into the office, demanding to see the letter that went out over her name, and he showed it to her, reminding her that with Sister Debra's interpretive help, he had foreseen with such awful certainty the imminent return of the motorcycle gang, and in greater numbers than before. He had spoken about this at prayer meeting weeks ago and he was worried about Elaine, and he is right to have been. Clara was at the hospital all the time then; he felt he had to do something that she would do. Now, with the murder of the sheriff, their bulwark against a hostile world, they desperately need more help. Surely she can see that. They are in terrible danger. And these people are here to serve her and protect her. They will be able to double the guards at the camp now and they can help complete the periphery fence. Darren did not believe this would be done—there was no time left for it—but it pacified Clara. He was quite calm. He knew what was about to happen, even if she did not. She only nodded and went out to help organize cots for the newcomers to use in the Meeting Hall overnight. Many have been saying someone should tell her husband about the rapturing of his dog, but he is nowhere to be found, even though he promised to introduce his new song, "The Tabernacle of Light." Clara, Darren knows, is worried about him, too—so warm and reliable a man suddenly become so distant, so moody—so she is generally willing to let Darren have his way. Nevertheless, Darren now thinks of her as something of an obstacle.

At today's ceremony, it has been Darren's plan to place in the Prophet's empty grave several symbolic objects—a tunic, a miner's helmet and the mine pick on which he leans now as on the cross itself, the

Prophet's seven "Words" as scored by children of the Eastern churches onto a wooden tablet with a woodburning kit, a Bible opened to the Book of Revelation, all wrapped in oilcloth—while reading a selection of Biblical texts from both Testaments as elaborations on the Prophet's wisdom. Now that he has received the message of the emptied tomb and learned of the city's intentions, Darren will change slightly his scriptural selections, placing more urgent emphasis on the fearsome horrors ahead—the earth reeling to and fro like a drunkard (it *does* seem to be reeling), the stars plummeting from Heaven, the sun quenched and the moon turned into blood, the tortures of the damned—and adding in more about deception and false prophets. He intended to put in place today the headstone from Ely Collins' grave, picked up some weeks ago by Mr. Suggs, but it seems to have vanished. Bernice Filbert has asked Mr. Suggs what happened to it. He cannot remember. He tries so hard, she said, but some things just aren't there anymore.

Little by little, Abner Baxter and his followers have come drifting toward the Mount. Clara sends Wayne, Hunk, and Billy Don, along with three of the new Defenders to remind them they are not welcome, but her emissaries are met halfway by the acting sheriff, Calvin Smith. After a brief discussion (Wayne and Billy Don scowl up at Darren; he gazes back at them without expression), a compromise is reached, allowing the Baxterites to collect within earshot some forty or fifty yards below the tabernacle floor plan where the service is to be held. Down where a blackened patch marks the place where Sheriff Puller's car burned and not far from where Darren captured "the voice in the ditch." Perhaps the voice is there still. Or will now return. The acting sheriff, Darren has been told, has purged the newly deputized Christian Patriots of those alleged to have been involved in attacks on Abner and his people, and has added several new volunteers of his own choosing, mostly from among Abner's followers. Darren wonders if the death of Sheriff Puller, which has allowed this to happen, was somehow God's doing? Of course it was. Everything is.

No sign of the city authorities with their surprise visitor. Maybe they aren't coming, having realized how futile it would be. Or maybe the tip, given its unreliable source, was a trick, a way to unsettle him, deflect him from what it is he has to say. Hovis comes over to say he thinks he just heard a motorbike over Tucker City way. Not that far away. Hovis pulls out his old gold pocket watch and stares at it. Off on the horizon, a summer storm is boiling up, coming in from the west off the back of the hill, the blackening sky setting the two yellow backhoes off in bright relief. All the more reason to get on with it and back to the safety of the camp. Darren points at the storm clouds and calls out: "Let's get started! Trouble's brewing!" And, as if by his conjuring, a group of people appear there at the top of the hill in front of his pointing finger.

It is their tormentor, the town banker, flanked by armed police, city authorities, the old priest in his sinister black robes, others who are probably preachers and town leaders, standing above them on the crest in their ominous dark glasses like tyrants and judges. The powers of darkness. They have come up the backside of the hill, no doubt hoping to surprise them. Darren is not afraid of them. The banker raises a megaphone to his mouth and calls out, "My fellow Christians!" The Followers have gathered around Clara inside the outline of the tabernacle church, as if seeking sanctuary in a holy place. Well, they are right. It *is* a holy place. Darren, near the open grave intended for the Prophet's ceremonial burial, steps across the chalky trench to stand inside with the others and leans there on the mine pick, Colin quivering behind him. "We come to you in peace on this holy Sabbath, praying only that we might reach some understanding beneficial to us all. No matter which church we belong to, everyone here believes in the Lord Jesus Christ, God's only begotten Son, and in the Father and in the Holy Ghost, and that's the main thing." The banker is grinding his jaws in suppressed anger, even as he tries to appear conciliatory. Most of those with him look uncomfortable, bullied into being somewhere they don't want to be. "If we have our differences, they are minor compared to all that we have in common. Not only our Christianity, but this great country, too."

Clara's people accept this hypocrisy in silence, except for Willie Hall who lifts his Bible in the air and calls out: "These yere rich men is fulla violence, these inhabitants hereof is a-speakin' lies, and their tongues is deceitful in their mouth! *Micah 6:12!"* And that stirs some of Abner Baxter's people, slowly creeping up the hill below, to shout Biblical epithets and heap scorn of their own, though Abner himself remains silent. "God's agonna mizzerbly *destroy* these wicked men, deceivin' and bein' deceived!"

"No, no," says the banker with a forced smile. "It is precisely the truth that we seek and freedom *from* deceitful—"

"Please, please," says Darren, raising his hand and waving away this meaningless preamble. "I have the impression, Mr. Cavanaugh," he says, hearing his own voice crisp and clear in the midday quiet, "that, although he is hidden from us, you have brought someone to show to us."

That catches the banker off-guard, indeed everyone on the Mount, except maybe Billy Don. Who is probably frowning, poor boy. The banker draws back and studies Darren soberly. "Yes, it's true, young man," he says. "That empty grave you're standing beside is intended, I understand, for the remains of your founder, the lapsed Catholic Giovanni Bruno, whom you believe is dead. But he is not. You have been misled. He has been professionally cared for these past five years in the mental institution, where he was sent after the criminal outrages on this hill. Here he is. Mr. Giovanni Bruno."

The pathetic creature in hospital pajamas who appears at the top of the hill, held up between two burly white-coated male nurses, is shaved, nearly bald, pale as paper, thin and stooped, glassy-eyed. Clearly, he has been heavily drugged. His jaw hangs slackly, his naked big-eared head tips toward one shoulder, his knees sag. A poor bewildered man, whoever he is, being used cynically by corrupt authorities. An empty shell. Even if it is Bruno, it is not Bruno. People shake their fists and there are shouts of "Impostor!" and "Fake!" Colin runs hysterically at them—"That's not him! *I saw him die!"*—then runs away, runs at them again, runs away, in a wild shrieking toing and froing.

Several of those on the hilltop above them duck in alarm, but the banker solemnly holds his ground, watching Colin as if watching an animal in the zoo. Darren catches Colin as he staggers breathlessly by, pulls him under his arm. He is all a-tremble, as after his nightmares. There is a distant murmur of thunder. "Easy, Colin. It's all right. We'll make them go away now."

"I can show you proof," the banker says.

"Why don't you people leave us alone?" Clara asks plaintively.

"That's like asking the body to pay no attention to its cancers," the banker replies, and there are angry mutterings from both groups of Brunist Followers.

Darren hands the mine pick to Colin—"Hold this for me, Colin. Careful! Don't let it fall!"—and walks over to ask Clara's permission to approach the visitors. She nods and he climbs the hill toward them, clutching her dodecagonal medallion concealed under his tunic, feeling no fear but uncertain as to what he might do next. Each side of Clara's medallion stands for something, as defined by the First Followers—like ascent and descent, the disaster and rescue, etc.—with three sides representing illumination, mystic fusion, and transformation, which Darren has come to think of as the three final stages of the Rapture, something Clara is incapable of understanding, justifying his appropriation. Illumination is what he is seeking now, and he rubs that edge of the medallion, and as he does so, the old hill seems to wobble and darken and black bits in its soil sparkle as if to illuminate his path up the slope. Clouds have rolled in overhead; more distinct rumbles of thunder can be heard in the near distance. The banker has removed his sunglasses to glance up at the sky before gazing imperiously down upon Darren. A big man made bigger by the hilltop he commands. Darren returns the gaze calmly, finding power in those unblinking gray-blue eyes, but also a vast, soulless emptiness. Beyond redemption. Aware of it, and therefore disillusioned and embittered. "I only wish to speak to your prisoner," Darren says.

"He is not a prisoner." He nods at the two nurses and they bring him forward.

Darren senses a ghostly presence; the man exudes a chill. The sores on his arms could be signs of decomposition. A resurrected dead man? He thinks of that open grave at the old cemetery. The man's eyes flicker over Darren's tunic, the first signs of some kind of life, then over Darren's shoulder at the hill and the others on it. Perhaps in recognition: if it is he, he has been here before. Watching him closely, Darren realizes that though he will not say so to the others, almost certainly this is indeed Giovanni Bruno. Or was. A kind of ghostly shadow. He is expressionless on the surface, but something is stirring underneath. There is another rumble of thunder. Louder. Closer. The man looks up as though in anticipation. Or terror. They all look up. When they look down again, the man's eyes are closed and he is struggling to speak. "Dark..." he says. He sounds like he is strangling. He opens his eyes, his gaze fixed upon Darren. Darren feels momentarily pinned in space. "Light," he says in that same strangled croak, and Darren knows he has been privileged. Dark...light. A false vision? A paradoxical one? Or a true vision that is itself dark and fearsome? Blinding. Darren, his back to Clara, risks reaching into his tunic and pulling out the medallion. He shows it to the man. The nurses are unable to stop the man from crossing himself in the Catholic way and falling to his knees, his hands pressed together in worship. It is precisely the effect Darren was hoping for. Or, rather, that he supposed God would grant. Then the man's eyes roll back showing their whites, a kind of unearthly wail emerges, and frothy bubbles appear on his lips; he is trembling all over like a rag being shaken. Darren tucks the medallion back.

The nurses, cursing, their needles out, give Darren a hard shove, sending him staggering backwards, whereupon, with an angry shout, his friends from the camp charge the nurses and something of a scuffle breaks out. The banker imposes himself, threatening arrests in a bellowing voice. The police draw their weapons, and it is all over as soon as it has begun. The one they say is the Prophet Bruno is carried away, now completely lifeless. Is he even breathing? Was he before? As they turn to leave, the banker announces through the megaphone, his jaws clenched: "As a result of the barbaric murder of the county sheriff and the arrival in the area of dangerous elements known to be associated with your unlawful cult, let me advise you, the National Guard is being flown in tomorrow and state troopers are on their way. This hill will be off limits."

An open challenge, compelling response. But before one can be made, there is a powerful explosion. *"The camp!"* someone cries. *"They're attacking the camp!"* People break for their cars, clambering down the hillside, tunic hems lifted. Colin drops the pick and runs after them. Somewhere, a second blast can be heard. The police run too. Motors are turning over, wheels are spinning. There are shouts. The sirens start.

"Dark," Darren thinks, left alone under the turbulent sky, feet planted apart to stay the earth in its violent turning. It is beginning to sprinkle. "Light."

# IV.4

## Sunday 5 July

Spider says the chawing noises are making him sick, and the rest more or less share the ink artist's disgust. Not Nat's favorite grub, but he accepts what Deacon offers him. You have to learn to eat what's set in front of you, as his evil old man used to say, belting him one if he didn't. Deacon, stripped to his vast hairy pelt while his clothes dry near the fire, has danced around naked in the storm, netting a dozen or so small birds, sparrows and wrens mostly, huddling in the bushes. He has skewered them live and held them over the fire to burn their feathers off, then dipped them in and out of a barbecue sauce made of molasses and hot spices, cooking them crisp in several passes over the fire. He and Nat are eating them whole, crunchy heads and feet and all. Better than the grasshoppers Deacon fried up in the same sauce earlier, calling them crispies. Some of the others have gone off in the squally rain, looking for small game like coons, possums, chipmunks, squirrels—what Brainerd calls mountain boomers—which in truth don't taste any better or even as good and can be tough as old shoes, the best being the occasional family pet dumped in the park by their owners. Last night it was a pair of half-grown cocker spaniel pups down by the entrance, just squatting there waiting for them, their tails wagging. Let's give them a good home, Deacon said, lifting them tenderly by their napes.

The Wrath of God are bivouacking in a state park known for its giant rock formations, upheaval of another time, regrouping here after the bad hit they took, tending to their wounded, some grieving. Old Houndawg, for example. Alone, silent, his damaged leg wrapped with a bloody shirt, Paulie's head in his lap, still wearing its black eyepatch. Nat watches him and wonders at the hurt Houndawg is showing. Nat doesn't share Houndawg's grief, though maybe he should. The sheriff's murder of Littleface brought an end to that feeling—unless rage is a form of it, in which case he is grieving most of the time. People: they come and go in their garbagey way, always more following on. But when the End comes, this sick recycling of flesh stops. Nat plans to be in on that. The Big One put that nitro in his hands for a reason. He will do his part. The only real grief Nat feels is for the loss of his bike, Midnight. An impulsive decision, pushed into it by Deacon and Houndawg. But probably the right one. He'll get over it. Too much at stake for sentimental brooding. He has ridden hard over the past two months, dragging himself and his pals through tough and dangerous times, assembling the Wrath for a holy battle worthy of superheroes. Half of whom are either dead or have now abandoned him. He's angry about those who have ducked out, but there are still plenty for getting the job done. Fewer for the enemy to shoot at. The enemy is worldly power itself, he reminds himself, munching a bird; it's no pushover, you have to expect to take some losses. Sometimes you have to pull back, take off your cape, shake off the krypton factor, get your strength back. Something Face might have said. Might say: he still feels his presence. Hears him talking to him sometimes. Littleface had the idea that when you die you come back as someone else, like a comic superhero, or villain. Nat doesn't quite believe that, but he watches out for him just the same. He thought he saw something of Littleface in one of the Crusadeers. Wrong.

Together with the Crusadeer pals of Juice and Face and others they'd picked up, they rolled in Friday evening. Quietly: the detachable baffles Houndawg has fashioned for the pipes that work something like gun silencers mean they can now prowl like cats or roar like wild bears. Cool. They had numbers now. Power. Their first order of business that night was to avenge Littleface, but on the way in they picked up some of the stolen boxes of dynamite they'd buried. Before pulling out of the area two months ago, they'd divided the boxes into smaller parcels and scattered them about in different locations, figuring the cops might find some but not all of it. One of their pick-up stops was at the old cemetery, where Nat used to take Paulie and Amanda to play the Lazarus game because nobody ever came there. The hole they'd dug for their game was still there and they'd used it. Amanda was the one who usually got buried. Once he had her in the hole and unable to move with just her face peeking out, he'd scare her with stories about dead people coming after her, or pretend to be one himself, sitting on the grave so she couldn't get out, making horror faces and noises, brushing dirt toward her mouth whenever she tried to scream or bawl. Why did she keep going back for more? Because she was dumb. When she came home dirty, their old man would pull down her pants and spank her, and she never complained, but he never laid the strap on her the way he and Paulie got it. He always babied Amanda. The old derelict graveyard spooked Cubano, who refused to go in. Nat laughed and told Paulie to show Cubano how to be a man, but Paulie had a fit, the first since he got his head stove in. That crazy lady actually left a big dent in his skull. Blinded him in one eye, too. Popped his eyeball right out and they had to push it back in, though it didn't work after that. Did seem to cure his fits, at least until Friday night, but left him stupider than ever. That night, after they'd executed the sheriff, they holed out in the old man's abandoned farm shack, stowed what they'd picked up so far under the floorboards there. They peered in on the squibs they'd hidden behind small logs in the old wood-burning stove two months ago and everything seemed all right so they left them. Maybe everything wasn't all right.

Earlier that night they'd grabbed the Coates kid, out wandering around drunk, and before using him to set the trap for the sheriff, they pumped him for information, learning about the parade the next day and the Brunist ceremony on the Mount planned for Sunday, which

Royboy said his family wasn't invited to but were going to anyway. Meaning the town would be busy with the Fourth on Saturday, giving the Wrath a certain freedom of movement out at the edges, and then the camp would be vacated for a while on Sunday, allowing them to pick up the big chunk buried in the wild part down there, a little known corner of the camp discovered by Nat shortly after his family first arrived back. Which his fatass brother and the Collins whore also evidently discovered for their sick games. Or God led them there to get what was coming to them. The O.T. God. Nat's God. The Big One. The one at war with the N.T. wimp. Nat's theology. Though he has come to appreciate Jesus as a man of wrath. A comicbook in Nat's saddlebag shows how he was betrayed and rewritten, softened up to be sold to the crowd. They also learned from Royboy that Nat's old man had got kicked out of the camp after what they did to the Collins girl (Royboy was giggling nervously at this point) and that Junior had later led an attack on the camp in which Royboy's brother Aaron got a butt full of buckshot and everybody got arrested and Nat's old man got beaten up in jail by some wop cops. Didn't sound like Junior, but you never know what a little healthy scarring will do for you. Royboy also told them that the Collins girl was very sick and maybe possessed by the Devil, that old man Suggs had had a stroke and was in hospital, that some people had suicided themselves—one guy right in his shop window at high noon—and that there was a big fire one night at the used-car garage at the edge of town that didn't happen by itself but which was better than the Fourth of July. Deacon had grinned in his beard and said: "Whoa! I love this place!"

There were a lot of sirens on Saturday morning after they found the sheriff, so the Wrath kept their distance, using the day to gather up more of the nitro, case the area, deal with the defections. In spite of the blood oaths they'd taken, most of the Crusadeers who had joined them had split overnight, including Jesse Colt. Said they came to avenge their buddy Littleface, did that, they're moving on. They don't know dynamite and armageddons. So the Wrath is smaller, only a dozen or so, but it's hardcore. Nat's disappointed about Jesse. Dug his name, his style, thought of him as another Face. But he wasn't. When they're done here, they'll hunt those deserters down, take retribution. After the sheriff's car was hauled away, the mine hill was unoccupied for a time, so Nat, Juice, and Cubano took the occasion to roll in the back way and pick up the boxes buried under the tipple, but they discovered that the dog's grave had been cleaned out and refilled with dirt. Just a single putrefied leg bone in there, like they were being taunted. Which meant someone was onto them, at least partly. After sundown, they withdrew into this state park. Stored their assets. Laid plans.

Then today, once they'd made sure the Brunists were all over on the mine hill, they slipped into the camp quickly the back way they'd come before. There was a barbed-wire fence up, but they'd passed by and seen that and were ready with bolt cutters. Nat wanted them in and out of there in ten minutes. He led them to the place near the tagged tree where they buried the stuff, but it wasn't there. Didn't look like anything ever had been. Had he got the right place? Had the tag been moved? It was dark when they buried it; maybe things looked different. While he was puzzling this out, the old man turned up. Back in the woods some ways, half behind a tree. Cradling a rifle. "Over here, boys," he said. "You're looking for that nitro." The Wrath's guns were out, but Nat said, "Don't shoot!" "That's right. It ain't my aim to shoot nobody less I have to," the old man said. "I wanta make a deal. I don't figure this is all of it, nor not alla you neither, so I don't reckon I can stop whatever meanness you're up to. All I want, Nat Baxter, is for you to promise not to come back here to the camp again and not to bother the people here." "I can do that, old man." No problem. Nat doesn't want the camp. He wants the town. The world. "Awright. You're a mean young hellion, Nat Baxter, but I trust you when you give your word. It's back over here. I'll show you, but no funny business. Don't need your whole passel, just you and a coupla others. Maybe that one there in the fancy red boots and that older feller in the braid who looks sensible enough not to start up no trouble." Nat started forward with Juice and Paulie, who always jumped into everything, wanted or not, Deacon's pal Toad Rivers and old Buckwheat joining in as protection or just out of curiosity, but Houndawg hesitating, maybe because he'd been singled out, then Nat, too. "Wait a minute," he said, feeling one of his headaches coming on. Like somebody saying no. Something was wrong. What was it? He was squeezing his eyes shut against the sudden pain needling his head like black lightning and it was like Littleface was there with a lock on him—he reached for Paulie's shirt—"No, *stop!*" he shouted, and Houndawg's gun came up, aimed at the old man, and just as he fired, the whole world seemed to heave up and hit him in the face.

He couldn't hear anything for a moment, couldn't see, couldn't even breathe. Thought he might be dead. But then he saw Houndawg, his leg half blown away, limp over to where the old man was. He'd set his gun down, was praying. Houndawg was carrying the high-powered rifle they'd appropriated from the sheriff and he pumped bullets from it into the old man's head until he ran out, the head bouncing off the ground with each shot like a puppet. He started to load up again, but Deacon said, "C'mon, Dawg, you can't kill him more'n you already killed him. We gotta tear ass, man!" Nat had a headache still, but it was a different kind. In fact he hurt all over, like he'd just had a forty-foot fall. He was bleeding, he knew, just like those warriors in the comicbooks, but he was on his feet, ready for whatever. Buckwheat, Juice, and Paulie were just a splatter of torn-up meat lying there in the cratered earth and Deacon's tough old pal Toad was in bad shape, too, a big gaping hole in his middle parts. "I ain't gonna make it," he grunted. Blood was splashing out of him like from a broken hydrant. "Somebody fucken shoot me!" "He's your bud, Deac, whaddaya think?" Baptiste said. Deacon looked over at Hacker and the doc shook his head and Deacon shot him. "Grab up the guns!" he said. There wasn't much of Paulie left below the head; Houndawg sliced off whatever was dangling from it and took it with him. 666 wanted Juice's red boots and Deacon, who'd been rifling Toad's pockets, said, "You'll have to take them with the feet still in, Sick. Hear them whoops out on the highway? Here comes the man!" And then they were running. When they reached the bikes, Deacon pushed him toward Toad's new silver-and-blue-pearl ironhead with ape-hangers, like those on Houndawg's bike, shoved keys in his hands, and said, "Time for a new sled, kid. Your burnt-out old warhorse is ready for the boneyard. This one's bigger, faster, and it's legal." He only had a half-second to think. Glanced at Houndawg who was holding Paulie's head and dangling bits by the hair. Houndawg nodded. "I'll give 'em sumthin to chase," Baptiste said and he snapped off his silencer and went roaring off, hammer down, in the opposite direction from where they were headed. "You got any ident, kid, leave it with your bike," Deacon said, heaving his bulk into the saddle. "Toad is giving you his."

Goateed Hacker, his head capped by his goggles, comes by with some painkillers, stuff they lifted in a drugstore robbery a couple of states over. Nat waves him away. The wounds have been sterilized, bandaged, that's enough. He hurts, but he doesn't mind the hurt. Wants it while he thinks about what comes next. They've got some serious avenging to do. He refuses the whiskey getting passed around, too. Doesn't like it, never will. Houndawg does likewise, but takes the painkillers and also some penicillin. His leg is torn up pretty badly. Hacker says it probably ought to come off, but he doesn't know how to do that and won't do it, and Houndawg says that's just as well because he'd shoot him if he tried. Hacker's not a real doctor, but he has picked up skills on the road, needing them from time to time since mostly when you get in trouble, you can't use hospitals. Things like applying tourniquets, digging bullets out, stealing the right medicines. One thing he does is give Nat injections against his migraines. They help but can leave him feeling wasted until they wear off. Drinking the blood of sacrificed animals works better. Not much Hacker could do today about the wounded except clean and bandage a few cuts and hand out painkillers. Brainerd had been holding the front door of the old man's farm shack when it blew off and it broke some fingers, and Hacker, peering closely through his thick lenses, virtually touching the fingers with his nose, fitted the bones together and rigged a splint with whittled sticks and tape, Brainerd grinding a jawful of chaw and cursing softly all the while; that was Hacker's big job of the day. Luckily it's Brainerd's right hand, not the one he shoots with.

Teresita wants a second hole pierced in her right ear, and Hacker is able to do that. When Nat and the others raced away from the camp after the ambush, they made straight for the shack to warn Cubano's team, but they were too late. They met Teresita and Brainerd and the others on the road, Teresita alone on Cubano's bike. Got the bad news. They'd gathered up the dynamite they'd buried a couple of nights ago under the shack floorboards but forgot about the old stack in the woodstove. Cubano went back in to get it. "Musta been boobied," she said. "That choza ain' no more. Pile a fucken sticks." She saw the bike Nat was riding, the blood on his face, and asked about Toad, and they told her about the four guys who'd got killed back at the church camp. She was upset about it, especially about Runt, even though Paulie had been an aggravation to her with his sexual craziness. Houndawg showed her Paulie's head and she shook her head sorrowfully and crossed herself, though she's not much of a Catholic and is even said to have killed a nun when she was younger. With her bare hands. She had also pocketed a body part: Cubano's right ear, with the upside down cross in it. Now she's going to wear two in the same ear as a kind of memorial to him. She started to throw the ear away when she cut the cross out of it, but Chepe Pacheco asked for it as bait for a trap. "Catch me a coyote. Como Cubano." When Thaxton, trying to cheer her up, says she shouldn't let it get her down—Cubano is probably up in Heaven trying to get into the Virgin Mary's pants by now—Teresita says no way. "Cubano was a bad man. Beautiful, but bad. He gotta hope there ain' no afterlife." Teresita is a big-busted woman who wears tight sleeveless tees with pictures of a fierce Christ printed on them. She insists Jesus was a tough dude, a man of wrath who got turned into a creampuff by European faggots. That fits what Nat knows now. Littleface called Jesus the Joker, had a picture on his bike of the Joker with a halo over his head. When Cubano first brought Teresita around, Juice objected, saying he didn't "want no fender fluff in the gang." Juice was drunk, as he often was, and making jokes about fresh meat and back warmers and ground cover, thinking he was being funny, but he wasn't. It was only insults. Cubano said, "I suggest you don' fuck round with her, man." "Yeah? Whaddaya gonna do about it, spic-shit?" "Me? I ain' gonna do nothin'." Juice made a move in his direction and the next thing he knew Teresita had him and he was up in the air and sailing. He rose up shaken but angry and charged her and up in the air he went again, coming down hard. He was really mad now and pulled a knife and Teresita smiled and said, "Ven, hijo de puta. Gimme that puñal. I use it. I have your machitos for supper." Everybody was laughing by then and Juice was finally grinning too. "Praise Jesus, lady," he said and put the knife away, raised his arms in surrender. "I believe!"

Nat came to this park some years ago on a school trip. He remembered thinking at the time it was a great place to hide out, so he brought the Wrath here last night, figuring that going back to the old man's farm shack, where they'd stayed the first night, was too risky. The park is outside the county, and easier to defend, too. Guerrilla turf. The massive rock formations form above-ground caves of a sort, offering up places to hide and stay more or less dry. As a kid, he thought, if the Rapture comes, they won't find me here. He knows better now. As he should have known better about that old man. Some big mistakes today. Got sucked in. How many people would dig up a dead dog, looking for dynamite? He didn't ask that question, but should have. He would have answered that the cops might, but that was about it. But why would they refill the hole? Probably they wouldn't. So someone else was involved. They'd show it to the old man whose dog it was, ask him questions. They might have suspected him of stealing the stuff, hiding it there. But they'd see how straight he was, wouldn't do such a thing and wouldn't disturb his dog's grave if he did. Besides, everyone knew who'd broken into the mine buildings. So then let's say the old guy finds the pile buried at the camp.

His stepdaughter got banged down there, he'd be snooping around. He puts two and two together. That's the second lot, he figures, and there's probably more. There's some kind of strategy here, he thinks. Meaning they'll be back. So he sets a trap. Still not clear why he refilled the dog's grave, but maybe just respect for his dog. Or because he didn't want anyone else to know about the ambush he was setting. Probably. If the cops knew, they would have stopped him, wouldn't they? And it wasn't exactly a turn-the-other-cheek sort of operation, so he couldn't tell the other campers. If Nat had thought all this through, they might have avoided what happened. Or even turned the ambush back on the old man. Just didn't think. That's why all those guys left. Baptiste, too, who should have been back by now, his distraction maneuver just an excuse. They saw Nat as someone who walks his people into death traps. Out of carelessness and stupidity. Can't let that happen again.

Have to stay hard, too. Keep the purity. He had a soft spot for that old man. Thought they had an understanding of a kind. Made him too easy to con today. The old guy was trying to kill him and he couldn't see that. Couldn't see until it was too late how he was aiming straight at the old Warrior Apostles, who were down there in that field with Junior and the Collins bitch that day they did her. Four guys got killed because of that soft spot. Five. The old man got another of the Apostles at his old farmhouse, but he never knew it. Nat thought he knew that old man and what he was capable of and what not. Wrong again. Came close to making the same mistake with Royboy the night they brought the wrath down upon the sheriff. He didn't have much choice, but Royboy did everything they asked him to do and more. He said he wanted to join their gang; he hated his old man and wanted to get out of this dump. He didn't have a bike, but he'd steal some money and get one. Nat was tempted. He had known Royboy since grade school. They were in the same church. Their fathers were close and he knew what Royboy meant about hating his hardass old man and believed him. But he'd played slingshot war games in the street with Royboy, and because of that he knew him to be a bit slithery, and a coward when it came to a showdown. And now a loose-mouthed drunk. They were into something deadly serious here and they couldn't risk a betrayal. "Do we let him go?" Toad asked. "No," Nat said. "He's just going to shoot at us or turn us in." He was looking straight into Royboy's eyes as Sick brained him from behind; together, they stuffed him in the trunk.

And then last night he nearly went soft on those young kids. The Wrath surprised them when they turned up at the state park. They were still frantically trying to get back into their clothes. Everyone had a good laugh about it and made remarks about the girl's body, which was less than perfect. The two of them apologized sheepishly and hurried away, heading for the parking lot, obviously scared. Big Deacon watched them go and said, "We better not let them leave the park." "We can't kill everybody," Nat said. Deacon smiled his beardy smile. "Yes, we can." Probably he saw the hesitation on Nat's face. "I mean, it's Last Judgment time, right? Timer's running down. We're just only giving these nice kids a head start to glory. And if we don't, we gotta leave here now." Nat didn't say anything, so Deac nodded at Rupert and Sick and they drifted off together. Everything is God's will, Deacon likes to say. Even when that everything is something Deac has done or is doing. Great is the wrath of the Lord, he says with his Santa Claus grin, bringing the hammer down.

Rupert acts like a crazed rich man, talks like one, and maybe he is or was a rich man. He was riding with the Crusadeers, but he's a pal of no one. The legend that trails after him is that he murdered his parents and burned their house down. He wears carefully knotted ties over colored T-shirts, shaves and trims his moustache and sideburns every day, files his fingernails, has swastikas tattooed on his biceps—which Houndawg, who considers himself a patriot, complained about. Religious exercises for Rupe are like doing calisthenics. Like Nat, he is a believer in the War of the Gods, says it's why he stayed when the others left, but they don't seem to be gods out of the Bible. "Nothing in this universe lasts or is meant to last," he says in his precise tight-assed way. "We are the gods' agents, fulfilling the destinies they have assigned us." Sick's real name, the only one they know, is just the number he wears on both bony shoulders: 666. The number of the Beast. They took to calling him Sick for short, partly because he's even more psycho than Juice, and it stuck. A glazy look and a fixed grin with clenched teeth, not so chummy as Deacon's. Topknot wagging on top of his shaved head like a clownish hat. He and his pal X were survivors of a destroyed gang looking for a new connection, when the Wrath picked them up. Their old gang called themselves Avengers or Avenging Angels. Not clear what happened to the rest of them, Sick being too spaced out to be intelligible, X never speaking, just making guttural noises, an unshaven black-browed guy in raggedy black clothes, his staring eyes set wide on his cheekbones like they belonged to two different heads. What does X stand for? "It stands for I never learnt his name," Sick said, "and he's not talkin'." Some of the mystery was cleared up when Hacker told them X's tongue had been cut out. Sick said he didn't know how that happened. By the time they first ran into Sick and X, Nat had already changed the name of the gang and they had fashioned new patches, and Sick said he admired the name and it suited his religion. It was Deacon who had suggested the change, just after he joined them. He said Warrior Apostles was too much like kid stuff and Nat agreed. They were already wearing tats like "The Burning Wrath" and "Rod of His Wrath," and they were into something bigger and deeper. Something final. A great slaughter, like the Bible says. The sort vividly illustrated in the *Eternal Forces* comic. So Nat proposed The Wrath of God and nobody was against it. Deacon was especially pleased and from then on made sure whatever Nat wanted, he got. Their patch, which still has a mine-pick cross in a circle, also now has a fist with a bolt of lightning in it. When they added Spider to the gang, everybody got a fist and lightning bolt on their skin. Took to wearing upside-down crosses in the right ear. Rewrote their jacket studs. Swore fresh blood oaths.

* * *

The damp's bad in here under the giant rocks, but the fire feels good, for the sudden rain which caught them on their way here has brought a chill to the day, more felt in wet clothes. There's a nice smell, too. Chepe Pacheco in his blue-red-and-yellow headband and embroidered Mexican shirt is frying up green bananas. No idea where or when he picked them up, but they've all learned to like them. Nat is not completely stripped down like Deacon, who is still strutting around naked, reciting apocalyptic lines from the Bible (he claims to have once been a preacher, also an actor, a politician, a university professor, a lawyer, an auctioneer, a faith healer, a carny barker, and he may actually have been some of those things), but he has hung his dripping high-collared leather jacket from a jutting rock and his shirt is off and near the fire next to Deacon's, drying out. Red hair is sprouting on his chest now, as if having been shaved off his head it had to find someplace else to grow. His old man has chest hair like that, going gray now. The only guy in the gang carrying a clean dry change is Rupert, who has a bagful of colored T-shirts and loud ties to go with the satin-striped black pants he always wears. Right now it's a canary yellow shirt under a green and lilac tie. During house burglaries, Rupe likes to find an iron and press these things, then leave the hot iron plugged in and face down on the ironing board. His style is the very opposite of his pal Brainerd, who hasn't changed clothes or shaved or washed since the day he joined up. He says he doesn't think he has any socks left below the ankle, that they've just rotted away in there, but he hasn't taken his old muddy farm brogans off to check. City dude and mountain man. Hard to say which is meaner, though. Brainerd claims to know about a Colorado ghost town they could all go to after this is over. If he can be believed. He's a folksy bullshitter, now into a tall tale, thumbs in his suspenders, about a wild man of the woods who thought he was a bear and in most ways *became* a bear, and who was finally tracked down by his scat, which wasn't bearlike, and was caught in a net and used in a circus sideshow until one day he clawed himself to death.

Sick, wearing Juice's boots, which weren't his originally either (maybe that's how the old man picked Juice out; yeah, sure it was), says, "Y'know what? When I peeled Juice's feet outa these boots, I found out he only had two toes on the left foot and they wasn't next to each other." "Probably shot them off or else stobbed them fooling around on his bike," Thaxton says, and Nat adds: "Or got them caught in a paper cutter." Everybody laughs at that, thinking he's making a joke. But one day he did chop off part of a kid's finger with a paper cutter, and Juice's missing toes made him think of it. It was when his dad was the preacher at the Church of the Nazarene, and there was one in the office for trimming mimeographed church programs. The kid was a sissy-type piano player who sang in the choir and always made good grades, so you might say he deserved it. First it was just a threat, but then, almost not realizing he was doing it, Nat brought the blade down. *Zop!* End of piano lessons. Considerable trouble after that, but Nat threatened the kid with a lot worse ("If you rat on us, buddy, next time it's your weenie!") and the kid told everyone it was an accident, though later, when Nat's family was getting kicked out of West Condon, the story came up again and earned him another licking. Sick found the word "Apache" inked into the red boots on the inside, and has been collecting feathers from the birds they've killed and eaten, including bright-colored bluebirds, orioles, and cardinals, to fashion a waistband and necklace for himself, turning himself into a warrior brave.

Nat steps out onto the ledge at the mouth of the rock pile. There's a break in the rain, though it won't last long—hot and muggy and more thunder and lightning off to the west. Houndawg has left with Paulie's head and a mine pick. Nat can see him now limping into a marked trail in the woods. He needs Houndawg and wants him to get over whatever weirdness he's going through. Toad's bike, silvery, luminous in the cloudy light like the ghost of a bike, is parked just below him with all the others. It's a good moment to take it for a spin, get to know it, and at the same time make sure they're alone here in the park. While he's checking out the power plant (the kickstart ignition nearly took his leg off the first time, he'll have to get used to that), Deacon comes out with some of the stuff he took from Toad's pockets. The ugly photo on the license could be anybody; could be him. Toad's last name was Rivers and Deacon says they used to call him that before he got so big, and then he became Toad. "But you're still a kid." Deacon pauses to think about that. "That seems right. Kid Rivers." He grins. "Already a legend." He pats the rear fender of the bike tenderly as if it were a girl. "A pale horse," he says, and grins his whiskery grin. "Give her a run, Kid. See what she'll do."

He does, and after trolling the park's paved roads, he takes it up a hiking trail and back. It's not as heavy as Midnight, but it's longer and he's not used to the hanger bars; he takes a spill on a tight narrow turn. But no harm done. Beginning to feel good. It's powerful and easy to handle with its springer front end, and its popping growl gives him a thrill. And Houndawg will help make it even sleeker and faster, chopping it to fit him, making it his. The Phantom. One of Face's favorite strips. He'll find a Phantom comic, ask Spider to paint the character on the gas tank. Gray on gray. When he comes down out of the trail, Houndawg is waiting for him, leaning on his good leg. Carrying the pick but without the head. That's over. He pulls up and offers the bike to Houndawg for a test ride, and when he gets back—Houndawg, even driving it one-legged, shows why it's a great racer bike—they sit there on a bench and have a talk. About the bike, things they can do to it, but also about what happens when the rain stops.

When he gets back to the hideout, carrying Houndawg through the sudden violent return of the storm, he finds Deacon stretched out on his belly, getting his big butt tattooed by Spider by light from the fire and the lamp of one of the mining helmets they stole. Sick is stripped to a loin cloth and feathers and is doing an Indian dance around the fire, his topknot wagging. "Hey, it's Kid Rivers," Deacon says, grunting from the needle's pain. Others call him Kid in greeting. They're making fun but they're not making fun. Deacon has been preparing them. Nat Baxter is dead. It's how he likes it. Like a superhero emerging from his weakling disguise. The Kid. Juice's abandoned jazzed-up bike—what Houndawg called a garbage wagon and Face used to call "Juice's Jukebox"—had a sticker on its back fender that said "Watch your ass! Jesus is coming and He is mad as hell!" Deacon admired that and it's what he's having tattooed on his own backside. He says it's a kind of tribute to crazy Juice. Spider is even adding a small motorbike speeding across the top of the letters, the cyclist longhaired with a blue headband. Spider calls the body just a big web for catching things, especially things that matter to the body's owner and to nobody else, and he prefers original designs over the classic ones, often linking them up with thin threadlike lines. His own body is tracked by those crisscrossing lines. Maybe it's how he got his name, or maybe his name gave him the idea. When Chepe Pacheco joined the gang, he had only two tattoos: one a traditional rose with the word "Mamacita" under it, the other the badge of a previous gang with skulls and daggers and something written in Spanish. He accepted the Wrath of God tattoo somewhat reluctantly, but then liked Spider's work so much he began drawing pictures for him of things he remembered from his home country—which is a hot wet place somewhere south of what Cubano called May-hee-ko—for Spider to use as the basis for new designs, adding a new tattoo in and around the needle tracks every week or so. Spider likes to show off Chepe to strangers like a sort of walking gallery. Chepe thinks of it as a kind of personal photo album and checks the pictures out from time to time with his side mirrors. Too fancy for Nat, whose skin, bike, and jacket are kept relatively unmarked, except for the identifying emblems of the Wrath. And he has no time for the past.

Thaxton has come back from hunting with the prize quarry of the day: a wild turkey. Thax is a mean dude, has known a lot of trouble, done prison time, digs the holy war concept. He's not a comicbook reader, but he has that style, knows all the grisly ways the saints died, shares the Wrath's hatreds. Came with the Crusadeers, but Juice didn't know him, didn't think the others did either. They'll have the turkey for supper. Deacon offers to prepare it. He lets them know he was once a chef in a fancy New Orleans restaurant. They don't have an oven, but that's all right—he'll cook it over the fire in a whiskey sauce. Rupert asks for the feathers. To make a pillow, he says, which makes everyone laugh. Rupe can have them, Teresita says, if he'll pluck the bird. The Wrath are in a lot of trouble, but they're safe in here, the park empty, rain pouring down, thunder cracking; the Big One concealing them, preparing them. But there's also a lot of restlessness. When they were holed up in the shack, they called it cabin fever. What would it be called now? The storm has blackened the skies, turning the sun into darkness, like it says in the Bible; but for the miner's lamp setting Deacon's butt aglow, their rocky hideout is lit only by the wood fire and the occasional flash of lightning. Faces a spooky ripple of light and shadows. Nobody's saying anything. They're waiting for him to tell them what happens next. They have to wait for the rain to stop—can't light fuses in the rain—but it *will* stop. Maybe tonight.

"So, what's exercising you, Kid?" Deacon asks, sitting up. "Say the magic word."

Nat doesn't preach. He hates preaching. Anything that stinks of church services. He doesn't pray either, not in public, just shouts sometimes at the Big One. "I think we got some killings to avenge," he says now. "They gotta feel our anger." That's his way of explaining it to the others. In his mind, those killings have just been part of what's really happening. The war of the gods. What happens next was always going to happen, with or without the killings. He has his shirt and jacket back on now. He feels older in them. His head is clearer. Vengeance is part of it, of course. The Big One's way of motivating. He used to imagine being Robin after the brutal torture, disfigurement, and murder of Batman. The rage that would consume him purely put him above the law. That's what he has been feeling since the murder of Littleface during these long weeks on the road. The wrath. He has a detailed battle plan—who goes where and when, what to do if things go wrong—that he's plotted out with Houndawg. They'll start with the power plant and phone exchange. The radio station. Then the power centers, beginning with the schools and churches, followed by city hall, the police, jail, fire station, bank, and businesses. All carefully timed. He has hand-drawn maps with everything marked. Systematically destroy it all. Bring the sick town to its knees, like Deacon says. By his cruelty he will instill fear into the peoples. The dwelling place of the wicked shall come to nought. He had not planned to include the church camp, but after what happened today: it's another target. It will have to be annihilated. A word he learned only a year or so ago. His old man used it in a sermon. Hated the sermon. Digs the word. A great battle, and he will call upon the dead Warriors to be with them. He gets the maps out of his backpack, spreads them on the dirt floor. He also has marked the overland escape routes via the rail beds the Apostles discovered when they were here last time. But things still aren't just right. He's looking for a phrase, or for something to happen. Something does. Baptiste returns. "They chased me. Lots of 'em. And they was roadblocks." He is excited. They're excited. "But the weather was bad. They couldn't send up choppers, and the bike could go fuckin' anywhere, through any kinda shit. Finally I shucked 'em, left 'em off in the next state somewheres chasing their assholes. If we stay outa sight, they'll figger we're long gone." Flickering grins now on the faces around the fire. They're a unit. Everything's cool. "All right," Kid Rivers says quietly, moving toward the flames, gunbelt over his shoulder. "Here's the plan…"

This is war. They're ready for it.

# IV.5

## Monday 6 July

The rain drums oppressively on the Halls' little caravan roof. It has hardly stopped since yesterday afternoon. Willie came in wearing his visored cap down over his ears and declared, "That selfsame day was all the founts a the deep broke up and the windas a Heaven was opent and the rain was 'pon the earth forty days'n forty nights! *Genesis 7:11-12!*" And then he went back to his room again. He is terrified by what has happened and will not leave the caravan, rarely leaves his room. Mabel is frightened, too; they are all frightened. Nothing has prepared them for what they saw when they came running back from the Mount of Redemption yesterday. A scene of such horror as to make one's knees fold. They could not even be sure how many bodies there were, so ruined were they. Poor dear Ben was there, his head shot up so bad he could hardly be recognized. Clara collapsed with a terrible cry when she saw him. Billy Don raced back to the sickbay cabin to get the stretcher and he and Uriah carried her through the sudden storm to her house trailer. At first they thought there were only three bodies other than Ben's because there were only three heads and six feet to go with the three motorbikes parked by the back road, but there were enough other parts that what was left did not fit into just three bodies. Maybe, someone said, the ones who got away are cannibals. With what they have seen so far, one can expect just about anything, no matter how ghastly.

They have all been over to see Clara, one at a time, keeping a vigil. She is much changed, a frail and shriveled shell of herself. Ludie Belle said she looked to be a "pore thing on the down-go," reckoning her condition to be more problematical than just her present dismay. Bernice is back and has brought along a nurse friend from the hospital to help out, and the nurse said the same and said she must see a doctor. While she was visiting Clara, Mabel looked in on Elaine. The poor child is nothing but a skeleton. The startled look in her big eyes startled Mabel. If she is carrying a baby and not a devil, that baby is not getting nourished. Of course, if it is a devil, starving it might be the right thing. She didn't know what to say—to Elaine or to Clara, or to Bernice or the nurse either, who said that if the girl really wanted to go, they probably couldn't stop her. Mabel tried to be cheerful, but she only broke into tears. And prayer. They have all wept and prayed. Since yesterday they have not stopped praying and weeping, for they feel the hovering presence of death and the end of things, and praying is the only thing they can do. As for the weeping, they can't help it. Mabel's cards have been foretelling as much, but no one has wanted to believe it. Mabel has not wanted to believe it and has not always told them what the cards were really saying. The acting sheriff, Calvin Smith, was there where it happened because he'd been with them on the Mount and had run back when they did. He said it looked to him like the motorcycle gang intended to blow up the camp but Ben stopped them and it cost him his life. Ben was a hero. A hero and a saint. They have always known that. He apparently shot one of the bikers; the rest were killed in the explosion. Their gang leader died, that devilish middle son of Abner Baxter, the one responsible for what happened to little Elaine. His body was the one without a head, but his motorcycle got left behind when the others ran away. Calvin said that this was the dynamite stolen from the mine. It was a big blast, so he hoped it was all of it.

There are only five of the old regulars here in Mabel's sitting room this rainy Monday afternoon, all that's left—plus Bernice, who comes and goes from Clara's house trailer across the way, and Lucy Smith, who can stay because Calvin is investigating the explosion. They say a second explosion happened at Ben's old abandoned farm house. A dark fellow thought to be one of the motorcycle gang was killed. Maybe they had been camping out over there. Calvin says there were three or four dozen of them around here yesterday, but they have been scattering and leaving the area. He has been in touch with all the neighboring sheriffs. Two of the bikers had been detained for speeding, but they had paid their fines and, not knowing about what had just happened, the officers had let them go. That won't happen again. These are things that Lucy tells them. She is paler than usual today and her eyes are red and her hands can't stop fidgeting. "Calvin's very brave," she says softly, beginning to tear up. "But I'm not."

The thunder and lightning have eased, but the rain keeps pounding down, and sometimes the thunder comes back, too. Unexpectedly, like a blow to the heart, scaring everyone. Rain like this makes Willie's rheumatism worse and Mabel always gets a bad feeling in her sinuses and bowels. The camp is getting soggy, everything feels damp and sticky, puddles wherever you look. Everything on the other side of the creek is now an official crime scene and no one can go there. They have stretched a tent over the place where it happened. There's a big hole there, like a bomb has fallen. State troopers have arrived, their sirens howling all night long, and the newspaper reporters and TV cameramen are back, swarming around the tent and the black charred place in the mine road where the sheriff's car was found. The reporters are almost as frightening as the motorcycle gang, and for all who were here, they bring back the nightmare of five years ago. When it was also storming, as though this were God's way of decorating His catastrophes. Lucy's husband and his deputies—mostly Christian Patriots who have been protecting the camp all along, plus these new Defender people—have so far managed to keep these outside forces out of the rest of the camp, but they are also letting some of Abner

Baxter's people in. They are at great risk, Calvin says, and must be protected. It's the Christian thing to do. He is the sheriff now, what can you say? Most of them are camping out in the lodge or the parking lot, though tents have also begun appearing throughout the camp, especially down by the creek. A lot of them have guns. Abner isn't here yet, but they say he's waiting at the edge of the camp for the right time to enter. When Billy Don ran back to get the stretcher, he left the sickbay door unlocked and the Blaurocks have moved in there with their pesky children. "It's like they've walked in right over Ben's dead body," Ludie Belle says. They have to be quiet about these gatherings in case the Blaurock woman gets wind of them and barges in uninvited, for that's the kind of person she is. She claims to have seen Jesus walking around and to have talked with him. That's almost impossible to believe, but Darren says it might be so. One should not expect human logic in divine actions.

"I remember when Ben first come," Wanda Cravens says in her thin nasal wail. "There in that Eye-talian house. He was like a kinda miracle. He sung 'Amazing Grace.' Him and Betty Wilson. It made me cry." Wanda hardly ever shows any emotion. Things just happen to her and she lets them and doesn't seem to care. But she's crying now, just a little. Mabel was also there that night when Ben and Betty sang. Ben said he had read about them in the newspaper. Things were not going well, everybody was feeling depressed, but his comforting presence lifted spirits and his singing touched them all. It was very beautiful and Betty's voice had never been prettier. He was like a gift. They knew everything would be all right after that. A song sung well can do that. Through the years, Ben anchored them with his singing. When the Cleggs were back visiting in April, Mabel noticed that Betty was still carrying the torch. She will be much affected when she learns what has happened. Betty is out on bail now, but both she and Hiram are facing trial for stealing that McCardle woman's money—mostly for the church, though maybe not all. She called Clara long distance to tell her that it was all just an honest mistake and everything would be put right, but they needed some help to pay for lawyers because their accounts were frozen. Clara said the church would do what it could, though she made it clear to Mabel later that she was not happy with what the Cleggs had done and felt let down by them. But she also asked everyone to pray for them, because that's Clara's way. She is a woman of charity and peace and of deep abiding faith, sincere and giving. She is the best person Mabel has ever known. It hardly seems possible all this could be happening to her. And she drew to her side two of the best men the whole world has known. Both victims of horrible deaths. Her son, too, in the war. There is talk now about burying Ben in the grave opened up for Giovanni Bruno's symbolic burial across from Ely. Both men side by side on the Mount of Redemption, flanking the entrance to the new temple. But Clara isn't interested. She doesn't want to talk about the tabernacle temple.

At least Clara is talking to Ely again. Or Ely to her—he has been absent for a time, as Clara has confessed to her. Mabel believes this talking is real and is a good thing, and she hopes that Ben will be able to get in touch with Clara now, too. He and Ely will be good friends and together they can help poor Clara whom Mabel loves more than her own self. Ben has been distant for a while, just like Ely, and Mabel knows Clara has felt this and has worried about it. He seemed to lose interest in the camp of late, all the building they had been doing, even the day-to-day like taking the garbage to the dump. Something preys on him, Clara said to her one day. They realize now how much they have relied on him and how sorely he will be missed. Ludie Belle says that her husband Wayne is lost without him. He just mopes and shakes his head and "keeps a-backin' and a-forthin'." Bernice, who has popped in under her head scarf and umbrella from across the lot where she has been caring for Clara and Elaine, says she thinks Ben stopped taking care of things because he somehow knew he was going to die. "He had that way of peering in instead of out." Others agree that a certain gravity had overtaken him and that maybe he had some foreknowledge of his fate. His newest song used one of Ely Collins' famous lines. It was almost like he was preparing to join up with him. "Ben has gone to be with his dog in Heaven," Linda Catter says with a wistful sigh, referring to the discovery yesterday of Rocky's empty grave over at the Mount of Redemption, but Corinne Appleby notes there was a dog's bone left behind—"You wouldn't rapture a dog and not take his leg bone along, would you?" Glenda Oakes says she rather hopes you get a change of bones when you get raptured. She doesn't want to suffer her arthritis all through eternity.

Mabel did not witness the dog's empty grave. It was strange, but not the strangest thing. The strangest thing was the man they brought to the Mount. Was he really Giovanni Bruno? Nobody thinks so; he didn't look like him at all. Mabel knew the Prophet well, right from the beginning. He didn't say or do much, but he had a quiet stately way about him. This one was all jittery. Whoever or whatever he was, though, he certainly looked ready for a grave. If he hadn't been dug up from one. The powers of darkness are capable of tricks like that, as Bernice always says. If what it looked like happened had really happened, he's certainly in a grave by now, or back in the one where they found him.

There are mixed feelings about young Darren, too, but it's hard to deny his special powers. The way he prophesied the return of the motorcycle gang and more disturbing events for yesterday, the way he foresaw the rapturing of Rocky, the way he pointed to the barren empty hilltop and seemed to make all those people appear out of nowhere, the way he announced the appearance of the false Bruno when he was still not visible, the way he approached the strange man and made him fall to his knees just by his presence. The man seemed to shrivel and die at Darren's feet, or return to death. Like vampires do in the movies when you stake their hearts in the sun. Or in real life, too, probably, though to the best of her knowledge, Mabel has never known a vampire, and certainly has never seen one die. Then, as soon as the man fell down, there was the explosion at the camp. As if the dark powers, losing one battle, were determined to win another in a different place. Only Darren remained calm. It was like he knew all along what was going to happen.

Glenda Oakes has talked with Darren and she says he believes that, for a moment anyway, the spirit of Giovanni Bruno did inhabit that wretched creature and revealed to him a new eighth prophecy: Dark Light. This was just before he fell down. Like all of the Prophet's pronouncements, its meaning is somewhat obscure, but that's in the nature of all prophecy, as Mabel, a fellow practitioner in her modest way, knows well. Her cards predicted the disaster yesterday, for example, even the exact number of deaths down in the wild place where poor Elaine was so calamitously abused. Looking back she could see that, but she failed to interpret rightly. Darren says if Ely had lived it would all be much clearer, but the messages have had to reach them through a damaged medium, like through a thick curtain. Glenda says that Darren believes God chose these means on purpose, making His message unavailable to any except true believers with the will to seek understanding. And the gift to achieve it. She says this with a certain sadness because she doubts she herself has the gift. Of course, Glenda says everything with a certain sadness. Since the shooting deaths of her husband and Hazel Dunlevy, Glenda has lost the power to interpret dreams, but she is becoming a palm reader. She doesn't know how this is happening, but it is.

Ludie Belle is closer to the other boy in the office, Billy Don, and has a less admiring view of Darren. "I don't over-confidence that finicky young feller," is how she puts it. "He's swoll up with hisself and kindly snaky in his prophesyin' ways, bushin' up what's inconvenient to his hypostulations." True, Ludie Belle admits, Darren is the only one who seems able to handle "that fittified boy" now that Sister Debra's gone, but she is not certain in her mind if how he's doing that is "as healthsome as it should oughta be." She doesn't explain what she means, but the others can imagine what's on her mind; Ludie Belle has never quite left her scarlet past behind. Darren sending out a pamphlet over Clara's name when she wasn't looking was a sign of how pushy he's become, and Ludie Belle is pretty sure he's wearing Clara's missing medallion under his tunic, a kind of thieving of a spiritual sort. She considers him something of a Judas for turning away from Clara and toward Abner Baxter, with his fire baptisms and his violent sons and followers, and frets that it might have been Darren who set Colin against Sister Debra and so broke the mind and spirit of that poor honest woman. Bernice, who still goes out to the West Condon municipal hospital every day to help with Mr. Suggs, has told them Mrs. Edwards has become strange in her ways and has been transferred to a hospital for people with mental problems. Were the things Colin accused her of true? Is anything that crazy boy ever says true? Ludie Belle wanted to know. Their vegetable garden is mostly untended and overgrown now. Colin won't go back because he believes she's still down there somewhere. Hiding in the bean rows. When those men crashed into the Appleby beehives the night that Welford and Hazel died and the fireworks went off, Colin started screaming that it was Debra who was doing that. When they tried to calm him down, reminding him that she'd been taken away to jail, he cried: "She's a witch! She flew out! She came back!" Yes, it's true, they all heard this. "And now Darren cossetin' him like he's some kinder reborned Patmos John…"

So the chatter persists. Like the rain. Mabel's neatly stacked deck of cards sits on the table, awaiting its final shuffle. But she is not ready. Nor are they. They all want to know, but they are afraid to know. Even "innocent" cards on such a day as this will have their darker side. They talk instead about the grieving Coates family (poor Thelma!), the horror of the burned car, that man and boy burned alive. Lucy says Calvin says Roy is ready to kill and he doesn't seem to care who, and his friends are with him. Roy doesn't blame Abner, but he doesn't not blame him, either. There's some unease between them, and that has Calvin worried. "I'm so scared," Lucy says. Linda tells them that she always leaves the radio playing in her beauty shop and the other day she heard Patti Jo and Duke singing one of their songs. It seemed quite sinful to her, and as she had a client, she turned it off, but she understood from the introduction that they are quite famous now and Will Henry from the radio station is playing with them, which is why that station is off the air and their Brunist songs aren't being played around here anymore. They all admit to missing Patti Jo and her conversations with the dead Marcella. Patti Jo was a good storyteller and she was so plain and direct about the things that were happening to her. "It's like the bright has wore off out here without her," Ludie Belle says.

Mabel picks up her tarot deck and studies it, sets it down again. They all watch her, trying not to. Ludie Belle says, "We all know it's time t'go. We also know we cain't go on accounta we cain't forsake Clara. We're like soldier boys in the trenches. Stay'n get killt. Go'n get killt." "Well," says Linda, "we live here. It's not the same for us." "And anyway," says Glenda, "isn't this it? The end, I mean? Isn't it all just near over?" At this awkward moment, which seems like halfway between time and the end of time, Wanda Cravens begins to sing "Amazing Grace." She has a thin nasal voice, but there is something painfully compelling about it. Lucy and Corinne join in. And then they all do.

# IV.6

## Tuesday 7 July

At breakfast time in the Brunist Wilderness Camp Main Hall this wet Tuesday morning, kitchen manager Ludie Belle Shawcross is faced with what she calls a "rumbustious tear-out," as three or four hundred fractious people, most of them armed, try to get out of the rain and "scrooge in" to a hall that can stand only half that number. They finish off all the coffee, bread, and eggs in about five minutes and crowd into her cook-room, helping themselves to whatever they can grab and raising a clamorous ruckus. Ludie Belle takes off her apron and tells Corinne Appleby there's nothing more for them to do here, they'd better get down to the trailer park to defend their goods—"Them ramptious peckerwoods has a appetite up and is apt to plunder round our own kitchens if we don't take cautions!" She waves at Wayne and Cecil caught up in the packed crowds in the next room, and also Uriah, Hovis, and Billy Don when she manages to catch their eyes, and she and Corinne hurry out of there. Mabel and Willie aren't up at the Main Hall yet, nor are Hunk or Wanda, and Glenda, she knows, is down below overwatching her regiment of little ones.

Mabel is not surprised to hear Ludie Belle hammering on her caravan door and telling her to pack up—"We ain't stayin' more, Mabel, it's time to red up'n cut mud!"—for she herself has arrived, after her reading this morning of the cards, at the same conclusion and has already done the packing and secured the dishware and other loose objects for road travel. Knowing Mabel rises early, Glenda dropped over right after waking up from the two-camper complex she inherited with her widowhood to tell her about the dream she'd had in which she and Hazel Dunlevy were driving through mountains somewhere and Hazel was telling her what it felt like to be shot. The way she described it, it sounded more like what she was doing with Welford in the garden shed, but when Glenda said so in a mostly friendly way, Hazel, who was never famous for her sense of humor, took offense and said that Glenda didn't understand anything and that was the whole problem. Glenda said that made her feel guilty, like maybe she really was responsible for everything that happened, and she tried to say how sorry she was, but it wasn't Hazel anymore, it was Ben, just like they saw him Sunday with his eyes staring and his face all full of holes, and she wasn't driving, he was, or maybe nobody was, and she knew they were going to crash. Glenda, who has lost the power of interpreting dreams, asked Mabel if she had any idea what it meant and Mabel said she thought it signified the end of something, but it wasn't at all clear what was starting up in its place; it didn't seem promising, but on the other hand, it might foretoken the Rapture, which is often associated with car wrecks. She asked if there were any children in the dream and Glenda said she thought they were in the back seat, but they were being very quiet, which was unusual and in fact a little frightening, and she wished Mabel hadn't asked. When Glenda left, Mabel decided to read the cards for herself and when she turned up the Tower, signal of calamity, next to the Chariot and the three of spades, she knew it was time to go. She called Willie, who has rarely left his room since what happened to Ben, and told him to get the caravan ready for the road. Which, quoting from the perilous travels of the Apostle Paul ("What presecutions, sufferin's and afflictions I have indured, like as what come smack onto me at Antioch, at Iconium, at Lystra!"), he has done, removing the blocks, checking the tires, filling the tank from their spare canisters, then retreating to his room once more. They had planned to stay at least until Ben's burial, but they might all end up getting laid out beside him if they don't go now. She does not want to leave Clara behind, but she feels that God—who has guided her in her reading of the cards, which she accepts always as divine instruction (unless there is interference)—will somehow provide.

The trailer park is crammed with other vehicles that block their way out, but Ludie Belle says those folks will all be driving off to the Mount soon to try to take it by force, those being Darren's presumptions, and they can hightail it out of here then. The others turn up at Ludie Belle's calling, and while they all wait in out of the rain around Ludie Belle's kitchenette table, they talk about the routes they'll take, where they'll meet up if they get separated, and what to do about Clara. Wanda says Hunk won't be going; he's staying to tend his chickens, and she's too tired out to get on the road again and is probably having another baby, so they could leave Clara and Elaine in their hands. But the others fear for Clara here without Ben, and she and her daughter should anyway be out east where Brunist Followers who love them can take proper care of them. Glenda says you don't have to be a fortune teller to know that Clara needs a doctor, "she's so badly drawed up." Clara won't want to go, so Ludie Belle proposes they tell her a white lie that the police want to question Elaine about a possible illegal medical procedure, namely that of that back-roomer disguised as an exorcist who Bernice dug up somewhere, because even though Clara chased the old quacksalver off before damage was done, she won't want questions being asked. One look at Elaine and they may take her away, as this society cannot tolerate the irregular. Then Wayne can drive Ben's old truck and pull Clara's trailer while Ludie Belle hauls theirs. Billy Don offers to trade off shifts with her if she doesn't mind slumming in his old rusted-out Chevy, though first he has an errand to run and he'll join up later. The Applebys take careful note of routes and meeting-up places, because once they can leave the lot they'll have to hurry round the back way by the creek to load up their hives, and that can take a time as bees can turn exceptious if you rush them.

Homesick Uriah agrees to go with them, but his buddy Hovis has not turned up in the trailer park—he's a bit slow, probably he didn't understand what was happening—so Uriah goes trudging back up through the sticky brown mud in his old rain slicker and soft-billed cap to search for him. Outside the Meeting Hall, he finds big television trucks and tents and camera equipment and cars parked everywhere, even on the grass and in the flower beds, and crowds grown so thick he cannot squeeze into the hall, but he has a key to the kitchen service entrance off the back parking lot and he lets himself in that way. The kitchen is jammed up with people, too (his heart sinks a little, thinking about the hard labor they've put into this building, and how little these folks respect it), but over their heads he can see young Darren in the main hall addressing the gathered faithful, spelling out the peculiar signs that have marked this time and place for momentous events soon to happen and indeed already happening, as Uriah has often heard him do, though never so sure of himself as now. He speaks of the voice in the ditch and the headless biker and the double sevens and the emptied graves and the sightings of Christ Jesus, and along with everything else, he tells them what that sick man who was supposed to be the Prophet Bruno said last Sunday before the terrible explosion in the camp: "Dark…Light." He says it has many meanings but it was partly an astonishing prophecy of that blast itself just minutes before it happened, and this is because of what Uriah and Hovis told him later about dynamite used in the mines sometimes being called "black lightning." Darren was amazed. "Why, that just fits!" he said, and Uriah and Hovis felt proud, but of what they weren't sure. Darren, who has grown up some since his early days here as Clara's office boy, is wearing his belted white tunic with a golden medallion on a chain around his neck and carrying a mine pick like a kind of staff, just like the Prophet in the picture, the very image of a young holy man, his bright blond curls standing out around his ears like a halo. The boy has a quiet, spellbinding way of speaking, giving the impression he knows what he's talking about, even if there is some question about that among most of Clara's people who have known him longer. But these are not

Clara's people. These are the Followers who have been traipsing around in the fields after Abner Baxter, a whole army of them, brazen and hungry, wet, raggedy, and ready for whatever, including the Rapture and the violent upheavals of the Apocalypse, if that's what's next. Uriah supposes that if so many of his people are here, Abner cannot be far behind, and, sure enough, there's a parting of the masses at the main door like the folding back of the Red Sea, and to loud applause and cheers and *"Bru-no! Bru-no!"* chants, in strides the Brunist bishop of West Condon with all the fiery purpose of a short red-headed Moses, thick jaw a-jut, a few cameramen and photographers sliding in in his wake as though he were towing them, and in his booming voice he calls everyone to prayer. You could hear him all the way over on the Mount of Redemption. That man can squench thunder, as they say where Uriah hails from. Darren sometimes talks over Uriah's head in his college-boy way, but he can certainly follow Abner, who is more like those hellfire preachers and union organizers Uriah and Hovis had known and followed all their lives back home. Where now, though the weather's no better there than it is here, Uriah longs to be. If he's going to have to slop around in mud while waiting to get raptured, he'd rather it was West Virginia mud. He tries to remember why he came up here. He pulls out his fob watch to study it, but as usual forgets what time it is as soon as he pockets it again.

*"Are ye ready for the Glorious Appearing? Are ye ready for Christ to return?"* the Reverend Abner Baxter asks with his freckled fist in the air, his flushed face wet from the rain, and he is met with an affirmative roar. Abner's bitter years in the wilderness have come to an end. There were times when he would speak and no one would listen, times when his embraces would be met with blows. Times when, as Paul said, "no man stood with me, but all men forsook me." He has been hounded cruelly from town to town, has been shot at and pelted with stones and even with cow dung, attacked by night riders, betrayed, cursed, imprisoned, beaten, and deserted by family and fellow believers alike. About the only hardship he has not shared with the Apostle is shipwreck. On the other hand, Paul had no sons to lose or turn against

him. In his intransigent faithfulness to the awesome and punishing Word of God, Abner has suffered the abomination of desolation as spoken of by Daniel the prophet and has been brought close to utter despair, but now, tempered by adversity, his faith annealed, it is he who will lead the holy remnant to glory. It is a word that fills his throat: *Glory! "There must be a Day of Wrath,"* he declares in a voice trembling with urgency, *"when sun and moon and stars is darkened, and the Heavens is rolled together and the earth is shook!"* As he looks back on his years of tribulation, he understands the tender generosity of the Lord's wrath, the ferocity of His love. He can, like the Apostle Paul, now speak of these things with an eloquence born of terrible suffering and unyielding faith, and he does so here in the crowded Meeting Hall. *"Bru-no! Bru-no! Bru-no!"* the Followers chant. He recounts for them the horrors (another word that fills his throat) of the Final Days, many of which they have already suffered, and the blessings of the Heavenly kingdom that awaits them on the other side of their ordeals, which is not unlike the workers' paradise he once imagined before his conversion to the true faith. *"All things are cleansed with blood,"* he cries, "and apart from the *shedding* of blood *there is no remission!* These things saith the Son of God, who hath his eyes like unto a *flame of fire,* and his feet are like *fine brass!"* The Followers are shouting his words back to him, calling for divine judgment, and some commence to speak in tongues. The earthly kingdom of Christ is imminent; the assembled believers can feel it, they have only to go out and pledge their eternities to it.

"He will come in *power* and *great glory* and I tell ye, the time is *now! The Millennial Kingdom as announced by the Prophet Bruno is at hand!"* thunders Reverend Baxter and Dot Blaurock bellows back: "Amen, brother! I *seen* Him! He's walking around out there right now! *Hallelujah!"* Her kids all shout out high-pitched amens and hallelujahs, too, all except little Johnny who passes a bit of wind in his sousaphone way, young zealot that he is, and then begins to howl, his howls drowned out, however, by echoing hosannas and amens at full throat from all those around her, God bless them. Abner raises his fist and shakes it. "But the blessed Mount of Redemption, which is rightfully and needfully *ours*, has been sealed *off* from us! *The Antichrist is usurping God's rightful place of worship and is desecrating the Temple!"* There are shouts of outrage and dismay, and Dot joins in, even though the temple that is being desecrated is really only the idea of one. She has joined up with a lot of these revelational groups over the years and this is the best it has ever got. Young Darren now coolly lays out the plan of action: They'll leave here and form up at the base of the hill, where the mine road turns off from the main road. "Give others a ride if you can! But we'll wait for those coming on foot!" Then, with the Brunist Defenders serving as marshals (Dot has volunteered herself as a Defender, but they have not yet taken up her offer; well, they're busy, she'll just be one anyway), they will all march peacefully up to the tabernacle as outlined on the hillside, where they will hold a church service in memory of their fallen friend and saintly Brunist Founder, Ben Wosznik, so horribly murdered while heroically defending their Wilderness Camp home. And, yes, they can take their guns with them—this is America, it's their right. "We won't use them except in extreme self-defense, but we won't be intimidated either." Darren says they have spoken with the new sheriff and he will do what he can to ease their way, but if there is trouble they should follow the leadership of Reverend Baxter. Who—fist raised again, shouting out *"Glory!"*—bulls forward. With that, the crowd turns and follows him noisily out the front door. *"Glory!"* they shout. Maybe the television crews weren't expecting this, for some of them fail to get out of the way in time and are fairly trampled by the sudden brass-footed rush to the exit. Dot herself feels chunks of camera gear crunching under her boots as she clambers out of the hall, Johnny in her arms, Matthew, Mark and Luke following at her heels. "Christ Jesus, here we come!" she shouts, but then she has to pause for Markie to take a wee-wee in a rain puddle. Even with all eternity to go jump into, the boy can't wait.

The camp is suddenly aswarm with people piling into their vehicles and pulling out, wheels spinning in the mud and horns blaring. Down at the emptying trailer park, Ludie Belle looks out her trailer window and says, "There they go! The weather's still ketchy, but it's fairin' up.

Looks like it's time to shuckle outa here." Cecil and Corinne step out through the dying drizzle, start up their camper truck, and squeeze out through the congestion, waving at everybody. Hovis has turned up finally, but Uriah who went looking for him has not come back. Hovis remarks that Uriah is a mite slow and easily confused and may have got caught up in the general movement toward the hill, he'll go find him. He asks again where they are meeting up and he says he thinks he can remember that. Billy Don says he'll go along with him because he wants to use the office phone. Wayne and Ludie Belle take Mabel along to Clara's trailer to explain why they have to leave the camp, but when they get there, they discover that Elaine is gone. "She cain'ta got far," Wayne says and he goes looking for her. "Whatever passes," Ludie Belle calls after him, "you be back here in ten minutes, hear?"

When word gets back to town that the Brunists are on the move toward the mine hill, Police Chief Dee Romano informs the mayor's office, then calls Ted Cavanaugh at the bank to let him know, and he and Louie head out there, leaving Monk to mind the shop, lamed-up Bo Bosticker having gone home to get some shut-eye after his night duty. The mine hill is not really in Dee's jurisdiction, though it is no longer in the county sheriff's either—it belongs now to the state troopers who took it over Sunday night after the dynamite blast at the camp—but Cavanaugh expects it of him. He asked Dee to tell the troopers on duty there to hold their ground until he gets there, and to let them know the governor and National Guard units were on the way. Dee radioed ahead to be sure some troopers would actually be there when he arrived. As he'd anticipated, they were all over at the scene of the explosion, having coffee under the tent. They said they didn't understand what the connection was between the blast at the camp and the empty mine hill. Dee doesn't exactly understand it either but said he'd explain it to them when he got there, and meanwhile these were the official orders from the governor. There are a lot of cars on the road out to the mine, so he turns on the sirens and roars past them, thinking that if he were not a Romano and all that ties him to, he'd just keep on going.

The banker has arrived early after the long holiday weekend, while the tellers are still setting out their stalls. He'd planned to confront the backlog he had been avoiding, but now, after Romano's call, he'll have to holster up and get out to the mine. It has not been a good weekend. He has lost his intern (he is hurting, he'll get over it), his son is not speaking to him, his embittered wife is increasingly caustic and befuddled by drugs and religious confusions, private armies have been forming up, stirring old local ethnic animosities, his Fourth of July celebrations were something of a shambles, underscored by the brutal murder of the sheriff, and his attempt to reason with the cult fanatics was a fiasco. He has to hope that Bruno recovers from his seizure, or he'll have more problems on his hands. On top of all that, his fraternity brother in the FBI has confirmed Nick Minicozzi's underworld connections (knew that, damn it; ignored it); the goddamned news media are back in numbers, determined to make everybody look like idiots, lunatics and criminals; and his own weak policies and lack of personal oversight have damaged the bank's fiscal stability. Meanwhile, the violence is escalating and the various police units are incompetent in dealing with it, if not obstructive in some cases. The town has been overrun by a gang of vicious killers associated with the cult, and except for those who blew themselves up at the church camp and that abandoned farmhouse, they all got away without one of them being caught. Maybe they're being hidden at the camp by the cultists. As soon as Ted has that thought, he knows it to be true. Meaning they may have more dynamite over there. He'll demand a complete search and a shutdown of the camp, which is now a crime scene. National Guard units are at last on their way to support the state and local police, but they should have been here weeks ago; it took the murder of a lawman for Governor Kirkpatrick to take Ted's warnings seriously. The pompous ass is driving in sometime this morning with his political entourage; Ted intends to meet it. He sees by his desk calendar that the new Presbyterian minister is also due today. Can't deal with that. He calls Jim

Elliott and tells him to meet the man at the bus station, take him to the church, show him the manse, get him settled in. Name's Jenkins. Make him feel at home. Stay off the gin until you get the job done. He signs four foreclosure documents, approves the drafting of eight others, freezes all accounts with overdrafts, hauls on his shoulder holster, and calls Maury Castle at the mayor's office, telling him to arm himself and meet him out at the mine hill. Immediately.

Sally Elliott is also headed to the mine. By way of Tucker City. Billy Don has called from the church camp to say he's finally taking her advice and leaving, but he wants to see her before he goes. That's really great news, she'd said, and they agreed to meet in forty-five minutes, the time it will take her to bicycle to the Tucker City drugstore. He'd told her that the Brunists are now led by Reverend Baxter with Darren at his side, and they had just left the camp to march over to the Mount of Redemption and challenge the state police there. Billy Don and the others were taking Mrs. Collins and her daughter with them when they leave, only hoping (he said with a nervous laugh) they're making the right decision and the Rapture isn't really coming. She said, "Don't worry, Billy D—it's the right decision." Since the Saturday night downer when Tommy abandoned her to a night alone on bloody sheets, penniless and carless, blaming her for taking him to that hotel on purpose, cursing her loudly in front of all those opened doors as he stormed away, she hasn't felt like writing, has been drawing instead. Smoking till her lungs hurt and drawing. Hands and ears. Eyes, mostly angry. The kitchen coffee pot, her shirt hanging over a chair back, the family cat. She sat for an hour in front of a mirror and tried to draw her vagina, but it was too depressing and she tore the page out and burned it. Then, using the Polaroid shot she had taken of the bloody hotel bedsheet, she recreated the design with colored inks, looking for some larger scene to arise from it in the way that Vasari described the painting of epic battle scenes from studying the pattern of spittle on a wall. This led her nowhere. Spittle was apparently more inspiring. When Billy Don called, she had been thinking about hopping on her bike and doing some sketching around town—the corner drugstore, abandoned train depot, backside of the derelict hotel—and his call brought to mind the old Deepwater No. 9 tipple and water tower, and that has become her project of the day. She scratches about for all the money she can find to give Billy Don, stuffs Tommy's camera and some pencils and charcoals in her backpack, and gets on the road to Tucker City.

Charlie Bonali, founder and boss of the Knights of Columbus Volunteer Defense Force, is not privy to events out at the mine hill, he's only guessing, but with the area sealed off by the state coppers after the nitro blast, he supposes the Brunist crazies will have to contest that and they'll be protected by Smith and his white supremacist militia, who are Charlie's real targets. He calls young Naz Moroni and tells him to arm the Devil Dogs and get them out there for the party. Moron says his nonno died overnight, the old guy he was named after, and he'll probably get dragged into family stuff, but he should be free until something like suppertime. Before going out, Charlie will drop by St. Stephen's to have a word with old Father Bags. Charlie is not religious, but he understands the Church's power politics and identifies with it. From the Godfather Pope down, it's like the syndicate. He'll let Baglione know that the Brunists are on the warpath again and tell him about the K of C Defense Force in case the church might want to hire a couple of professional guards. He'll also offer to restart and manage Bingo nights at St. Stephen's and provide protection for it. Charlie's old man is already out on the front porch, watching the rain fall and jawing with Sal Ferrero, a fellow member of the losers' club, who nevertheless has brought breakfast by for them all, gift of his hens. They've been talking about the death of old Nonno, who was their dead pal Angelo's old man, but now the subject of the pending foreclosure comes up, as it always does with these two whiners. It's also a problem for Charlie. The money from the city has dried up, the rumor reaching him that they're pissed about his busting the banker brat's nose without first taking his badge off, and he's not sure where he can park his bod if his old man loses the house. As for his whore of a sister, sprawled half-naked at the phone in her nightshirt, she does indeed seem to be filling out a bit in the belly, so maybe there's some hush money to be made there.

Angela is on the phone to her friend Ramona, who has upset her by letting her know that Tommy was seen leaving the Fourth of July picnic Saturday night with Sally Elliott. She can't believe it, but Ramona says everyone saw them. "She's just an ugly smartalecky slut," Ramona says. "It only shows how desperate he is." Is that supposed to make her feel better? Ramona says her dad has had to go to the mine hill this morning because something is happening again. There was a big explosion at the mine on Sunday when some of them blew themselves up and now a lot of people are hurrying out there because they think it might be like five years ago. "You know, like, *wild?*" Well, not Angela. It was nice of Mr. Ferrero to bring them eggs for breakfast, but she doesn't really like eggs, and she's starving. Now that the rain's nearly over, she'll take a bath, put on makeup, and go to town for something more filling. Maybe Stacy will be in Doc Foley's drugstore and she can ask her a private question about what a miscarriage is really like in case she has to try to describe one. Well, not in case. That's what she's going to have to say, or something like it. White lies: her days now seem full of them. She's running out of money but feels certain she'll soon get her job back when Mr. Cavanaugh realizes how unfair he has been and how much he needs her. She tells Ramona she has to go, that she has an appointment at the bank and needs to get ready for it.

White lies. It's how Bernice Filbert thinks of the stories she tells the bedridden Mr. John P. Suggs. They began with the best of intentions. She didn't want to tell him that his friend Sheriff Puller had been murdered and in such a gruesome way, fearing it might give him another brain attack. This morning he asked why the sheriff has not come by, and she said, "He did. But you was…sleeping." So she also hasn't told him about the motorbikers and Ben Wosznik getting blown up either because it's all part of the same story. And she certainly hasn't let him know about the changes at the camp since Ben died, because she knows that would really upset him and he might stop giving them money. So Ben is still at the camp and everything is as it always was, except for the hosts assembled by Abner Baxter at the outskirts, which oppress them daily. Ben hasn't come to visit because he needs to stay to protect the camp and also because he has a bad summer cold he doesn't want Mr. Suggs to catch. She hasn't said what day it is. Maybe it's still the Fourth of July. She can revise the story of the Fourth a little and then tell it like it's a new one, just happening; he won't know the difference. As for Sheriff Puller, maybe he had to resign and move somewhere else. Or maybe he also had a stroke, or soon will have. Eventually he could also die heroically saving the camp from the Baxterites. It depends on what happens next. There's no one left to tell Mr. Suggs otherwise, except that unpleasant McDaniel fellow, his mine manager, and she can have Mr. Suggs fire him for siding with Abner's people and send him away. She has a cousin who could do that man's job at the mine, and without scowling all the time. When that fat city lawyer with the yellow slicked-down hair comes back, the one who is being so helpful, they'll have a chat about it. She hopes he will admire her strategy.

Now that her foul-mouthed brother-in-law has been jailed, there's a bedroom free to rent at their house; the hospital is expensive so home care might be the right thing. The hospital could loan her all the things she needs like blood pressure monitors and specimen bottles and bedpans, and the theropests could come by her house to exercise him. At the hospital, they sit him up and walk him around, but nothing's working, his feet just bend back and drag along on his toes. If she can find someone to help lift him, they could hire her extra for that task. At least he is swallowing his own food now if it's mashed up, and the hospital has a home catering service that Mr. Suggs can afford. That would cut her own food bills down, too, because he doesn't eat much. He is alert a couple of hours each day, but otherwise, he appears confused and strange grunting and whining noises come out of him, as if he were speaking in tongues, and maybe he is, or else he sleeps. In his alert moment this morning, after inquiring about Mr.

Puller, Mr. Suggs asked her in his laborious eye-blinking way to tell the sheriff that he should put some pressure on those drunks who invaded the camp by telling them they were under suspicion for the murder of those two fools in the garden shed, which happened that same night, and get them to implicate Baxter and his followers in everything that happened. All this thinking and blinking tired him out pretty fast. Leaving the hospital on her way out to the camp to check on Elaine, Bernice bumps into her friend Maudie, the head nurse, and tells her about the Hungarian exorcist turning out to be an abortionist and getting chased off by Clara. Maudie shrugs and says, well, it's a kind of exorcism and it would probably have been a healing thing to do.

Wayne returns with dire news. The police have Elaine. "They said she was a-slickerin' herself with a belt down in the rough nigh to where all the bodies was found, and they're arrestin' her for indecent exposure and takin' her in for a medical." Wanda Cravens and Hunk Rumpel have come to say goodbye. Without a word, Hunk walks away toward the creek and a few minutes later he returns, carrying Elaine, looking like an unstrung puppet made out of sticks, her eyes starting like an animal caught in a trap, her skinny little tummy bumping out under the soaked tunic pasted to it like she swallowed a mushmelon. Hunk doesn't say how he got her, but they suppose they'd better get out of here fast. They can already hear the choppy crackle of helicopters somewhere in the sky. More troops will be coming in. Everything will get closed off. Glenda says not to wait for her at the meeting place, that she may have to stay. So many children to care for, it might be easier here, and she'd have to leave one of her two campers behind unless Uriah or Hovis returned to drive it for her. Those two West Virginia fellows aren't back, nor Billy Don either, but the rest can't wait, they'll have to join up later. Mabel agrees to ride in Clara's trailer to keep an eye on Elaine. Wayne says he hopes it's not really the Rapture and they're not dragging Clara and

Elaine away from their own salvation, but Ludie Belle says, "God ain't stupid. He'll know where to find us."

Which is how it is that Billy Don returns from his call to Sally Elliott to find everyone gone. No matter. Tucker City is in a different direction; it would only have confused them to see him turning off. He doesn't know exactly what he wants to say to Sally, but something like he's never known anyone like her before, meeting her has been the most important thing that's ever happened to him, and he doesn't want their friendship to end. He has her phone number but not her address, which he plans to ask for and also for her permission to call her from time to time. He may tell her he loves her, but he hopes he won't blurt that out because he doesn't think it's something she wants to hear. But he does love her. He knows that, has known it for a long time, and his chest is tight with the thought of leaving, even if only for a short time. His immediate plan is to drive up to his cabin now that everyone has pulled out and throw a few things in the car before taking off, but the car won't start. Seems completely dead. He's about to step out to see what the matter might be when Darren appears at the window. "What are you doing here? I thought you were headed over to the Mount."

"I am. Some people are walking. I have time. But I can't let you leave, Billy Don."

"What do you mean, you can't let me?" Billy Don pumps the gas pedal again, turns the key. Nothing.

"It won't work. I disconnected a few things."

Billy Don slumps back against the car seat in exasperation. "You're crazy, Darren. You're really crazy."

"I love you, Billy Don," Darren says, and he starts to cry. Then he takes something from inside his tunic and points it at him.

Though it's drizzly still, the sky is finally brightening, casting a pale but mostly cheering glow on the wet black streets and brick fronts of quiet downtown West Condon. What businesses remain are opening and city hall is filling up, as are the pool hall, the post office, and the drugstore booths and soda fountain. The pawn shop has its customary "Sales Only" sign on the front door and may or may not be open. Most of the temporary Fourth of July weekend shops on Main Street have been emptied out or abandoned, but a few first-time entrepreneurs, having faint hopes and little else to do, have decided to linger with their "antiques" and knitted goods and homemade jams, so long as no rent is charged. Faint hopes: the town's weak but stubborn motor. Gus Baird, the president of the West Condon Rotary Club, having had no new travel or insurance business for over five months now, spends the morning in his office, planning tomorrow's club luncheon meeting, hoping to run into someone there who wants to get away for a week or two before the summer ends. At the liquor store they restock the shelves and bins after the usual Fourth of July run on beer and cheap booze; drier times ahead, though it beats owning a grocery or a clothing store. Down the street, Linda Catter's first beauty shop customer is due in thirty minutes and Linda tidies up the premises for her. One of her blue-hair trade. Not really blue. An old Italian widow who likes orange hair, and gossips endlessly about people Linda doesn't know. Bernice calls Linda from the Brunist Wilderness Camp office to say most everybody has cleared out. They seem to have gone over to the Mount, as if something was about to happen. She's going over to take a look. Linda hopes that if it's the Rapture, they don't forget her stuck here in her beauty shop. Certainly, the graves seem to be emptying out, just like it says in the Bible. After work, if today lasts that long, she should go check where her husband Tommy has been laid to rest. Maybe he has stopped resting. Not far away, Enos Beeker, haunted still by the shoe store owner's public suicide, uses the slow day to take unseasonal inventory at his hardware store. Thanks in large part to the new cut-price D.I.Y. store out at the highway shopping center, not much will have changed since the last one. He is grateful that most of his aging stock is at least not susceptible to rot, a daily problem for young Pete Piccolotti, manager of the family grocery store, especially after the long weekend. Pete bags up the refuse that only days ago represented vendible goods and sets out the fresh breads and sausages his parents have made. His role in life. Mind the shop. He and Monica have had another row this morning. He's not ready for the second kid. He shouldn't have said what he said, but he's getting sick of the dead-end life he lives. Not much in the till. Have to send Monica waddling over to the bank for some rolls of change, hoping (faintly) for the occasional cash-paying customer. Over there, one of the first customers this morning (along with Gabriela Ferrero, who is trying to organize a small loan to cover the funeral of her father, who died last night in hospital) is Pete's pal Kit Cavanaugh, the banker's son, who is emptying out his account, taking the bulk of it in travelers' checks. He tells them, when they ask, that he's going to Paris. "Oo la la!" one of the girls says, and everyone giggles. They tease him about his papier-mâché nose. He looks off in the direction of his dad's office and is told his father got an emergency call and has gone out to the mine hill.

Faint hopes. Giorgio Lucci wears the town signature pasted on his mug. A goofy loose-jawed grin that won't go away whatever the circumstances. It used to infuriate the old man when he was beating him. He'd keep yelling at him to wipe it off while he pounded him, trying to wipe it off himself with slaps to the face, but he would have had to break his jaw, and even then that might have just wired it in place. When Georgie meets other people, they grin back. Raising always: faint hopes. This morning, waking on the Legion Hall sofa, sickeningly hungover from cheap skull-crushing hootch, he can hardly lift his head and his bloodshot eyes won't focus. But he's still grinning. He had to sleep on the broken springs. The high life. He kicked semicomatose Cheese Johnson off the sofa, but then had to let Cheese have the cushions. That's okay. He couldn't stand their stink, inflated over the years with a million drunken farts. Not sure who got the best deal. Pointless anyway, because Cheese has rolled off them and is sleeping amid the butts on the wooden floor, his broken arm across his chest, hand of the other clutching his filthy crotch. Another grinner, Cheese. But with fewer teeth. More malice to it. Not everyone grins back. His cast is so begrimed with obscenities, inscribed there during bolts of inspiration by his pals, that it looks like he must have spent the last few weeks down cleaning out the pits with it. Should be fumigated when it comes off and donated to the Smithsonian. Georgie steps over him and staggers off to take a somewhat painful leak. He has avoided Mick's Bar & Grill since Mort Whimple left hospital—the fire chief hangs out at Mick's and is mad enough at Georgie to kill him, blaming him for the blaze at Lem's garage and all that happened to him afterwards, despite Georgie's protestations of complete innocence—but today has to be an exception. He has a desperate need for coffee and he hopes (always hopeful) Mick will give it to him on credit, or for free, just because he likes his grin.

He has awakened from a dream that was partly about Marcella Bruno. They were back in high school and she was leaning over the water fountain, her pleated skirt falling over her hips, between her legs. Georgie stepped up behind her, and though he'd never even said hello to her before, ran his thumb up the crack of her ass, just for fun, because he was always known as an easygoing misbehaving wiseacre with quick wrists, no reason to take offense, and she turned around to see who was doing that. To chew him out, he supposed. But her face was the face of a person long dead, with exposed bone and teeth and tatters of decomposing flesh and bulging eyeballs. All he could think to say was: Whoa. Not feeling well? He was grinning and she was grinning, but it was not the kind of grin you like to see. He had the idea, in the dream, that this grim apparition had something to do with his sick hangover, like so many of the confusing and headachy scenes that had gone before in a night that was not sleepless but that had no sleep in it. The thought worked because then she was normal, not dead, or at least not showing it, and they were walking through the old neighborhood. Heaven's not a place, you know, she said. It's just wishing. He thought that might be a come-on, all he had to do was pop back with the right line, something about angels maybe (she's one!), but they were in front of St. Stephen's and she said she had to go in. And then she was gone. They were holding a funeral inside. Hers? Couldn't be sure. Didn't want to know. He left there, and next thing he was on a baseball field. It was his turn to bat. But the bats were all too heavy. He knew if he could find one he could lift he'd get a hit and win the game. He told himself: Don't forget to wish. Heard his old lady echo before sending him off to school: Don't forget to wash. And woke up. And washed. Wished.

Down on the drizzly street, Burt Robbins, owner of the dimestore situated below the Legion Hall, is standing under the overhang at the front door having a smoke with the mayor Maury Castle. They don't seem happy to see Georgie and they don't seem unhappy, so he pauses to exchange deep thoughts about the weather. Which is showing signs of improving. They grin back at him because they can't help it, though Robbins' grin is more like a sneer. Maybe one of them will buy him a coffee. He mentions hopefully that he's heading over to Mick's. They're talking about the Brunists, who are apparently back on Cunt Hill this morning doing a repeat performance of their famous dance-in-the-mud end-of-the-world thing. People are headed out there. A helicopter clatters overhead, punctuating this news. Might be fun. After coffee. If the weather clears. If his bruised brain heals. If someone will give him a ride. Robbins says they ought to get up another carnival out there, and the mayor lets fly with his sour booming laughter (it makes Georgie's head hurt) and says that after what happened last time, he couldn't afford the insurance. The mayor asks Georgie if he knows Charlie Bonali. Sure. Tough prick. Heard he might have been a hired gun up in the big town. Right, says the mayor. The sonuvabitch should be in jail, but he's being protected. He's got up a gang now. Bunch of young hardass RC thugs. Making trouble. We might need someone on the inside. The mayor hands him a bill. Say hello to Mick. After you've had a bite, why don't you drop by the Fort and see me?

* * *

Out on the rain-soaked mine hill, Ted Cavanaugh asks his police chief to radio Monk at the station and have him call the Fort, try to find out where the hell the mayor is. "All these TV trucks and cameras, not like Castle to miss a grandstanding opportunity," he says. Doesn't ask the chief, orders him. Like the old army officer he once was. That's all right. Captain Romano has served worse. He sees the banker as a kind of wounded general trying to rally nonexistent troops. Only four state troopers have turned up here at the hill this morning, and they don't seem to have any clear orders beyond securing the site of the dynamite blast over at the camp. Dee saw it. Sickening. There are a couple more troopers over there still, but that's the whole army. Cavanaugh is someone they listen to, though, and when he tells them to block off the hill, they block off the hill. Instead of helping them, the new sheriff and his hayseed militia are shepherding Red Baxter and the crazies from the camp, a lot of drifters and riffraff among them. They are massing up in the mud down below by the scores, singing like their feet are hurting. Not far from the blackened spot on the road where Tub Puller's car burned with him in it. At least the rain has stopped and the clouds are breaking up in the west, though everyone's wet and feeling crabby. An unmarked helicopter has been coming and going. Might be army. Or police. Most likely newshounds. Dee has not been informed. Red Baxter is blowing off as usual, punching the air with his fist, the others hooting and hollering in their wild-eyed praise-Jesus way, cheering him on. The blond curly-headed boy who caused them so much trouble out here Sunday is among them with a look on his face like he's already half-transported, that crazy stringbean son of the woman they arrested clinging to him as though terrified by something. His own wild imaginings, probably. "Ain't that one a them old picks stole from the mine?" Louie Testatonda asks, pointing at the blond boy. Cavanaugh nods. "Obviously there's a link." Locals are also gathering at the edges, not all as idle spectators. Too many guns among them. That cheap hood Charlie Bonali is down there with some of his buddies, nasty grins on their punk faces. The police chief sees this thing playing out in several ways, almost all of them shitty. He has contacted other police forces in the area to let them know they may be needed. Also ambulance services and fire departments, taking no chances. When Wallace radios back, he says as far as they know at city hall the mayor is out at the mine hill. Left some time ago. Monk says he wasn't sure who told him that. Didn't sound like Dee's cousin Gina. More like a squeaky old lady. Probably the mayor himself. Hard to hide that carny barker voice. Dee passes the first part on to the banker, not the second. Cavanaugh, angrily flicking his cigarette several yards away, calls the mayor a loudmouth, yellow-bellied tinhorn, or swearwords to that effect. He is also ticked off at the governor, supposedly on his way here but taking his sweet time about it. Some National Guard units are being trucked in as well, so they say, as yet unseen and unheard from.

And what about the bikers? Smith said he chased them into the next state and only lost them at the state line, then alerted the forces over there. "They'll catch them," the wannabe sheriff said. Dee's not so sure. About them being caught, about them being chased out in the first place. Though the leader of that pack was the Baxter brat, and with him killed they might scatter. Unless, like a thorn in a bear's ass, it's just got them madder. Old Wosznik's achievement, but at a heavy price. Dee liked Wosznik in spite of his dumb beliefs. Honest straightforward man you could trust, uncommon species in this depraved sinkhole. Brave, too, as it turns out. Or maybe just stupid. Never know.

When Dee and Louie first arrived out here this morning, access to the mine road was already blocked by the cultists down at the crossroads. Dee told Smith he should clear the road, and he did. Still playing man of the law. There were only two state troopers on duty at the hill, though they said two others were on their way over from the camp. The senior officer was a Catholic, so he and Dee and Louie had some common ground. Dee explained that, directly or indirectly, those religious lunatics were responsible for the Sunday blast and other crimes in the area, including the murder of Sheriff Puller, immolating the poor bastard in his own squad car, and he pointed at the black spot in the road where it happened. Cop killers. They were also the same people responsible for wrecking their church, especially that big mouth preacher down there making all the racket. Used mine picks on it, stole stuff. White-lying, Dee added that this hill was private property and those people would be trespassing if they tried to march up it without permission. They agreed, though, that if the vangies, as the trooper called them, decided to do that, there wouldn't be much they could do about it, short of shooting them all. And that might not work because they're all carrying weapons and could shoot back and outnumbered them at least fifty to one.

By the time Cavanaugh arrived, two more troopers had turned up, a lot of TV and newspaper people had rolled in, and the Brunist mob, still growing and increasingly unruly, had moved up to the foot of the hill. Cavanaugh carried a rifle and wore, Dee noted, a shoulder holster under his rain poncho. He stormed right through the mob, grinning steely-jawed at their verbal abuse, daring them to do worse. Dee and the others were impressed. He introduced himself to the troopers, briefed them all on the situation, listed the crimes they were dealing with, said that there was to be no shooting unless shot at, and that, if need be, they'd let the cultists up here, but meanwhile they'd try to stall until the National Guard arrived. The key, he said, was the acting sheriff. Whether or not he'd play by the rules.

So, when Smith starts up the hill with the cultists, Cavanaugh and the state cops meet them and tell them the state is now occupying the hill, it's closed off and no longer under the sheriff's authority. The cameras are pinned on them and rolling. The reporters have their pads out and are pushing mikes in people's faces. The copter circles back overhead. Smith says he isn't sure about the jurisdiction issue, but he's only trying to reduce tensions. "These people wish to express their grief over the loss of one of their most beloved leaders, and they should be allowed to do that." Presumably, the Brunists want to hold their memorial service for Wosznik up in that cross-shaped space where they have floor-planned the church they want to build. An outline of trenches lined with chalk that looks like a gameboard layout for a war game. Which it is. Dee asks, if the service is for Wosznik, why aren't his widow and daughter here? Smith says he doesn't know, maybe they just didn't feel up to it. "Mrs. Collins is in shock, the girl is in fragile health." One of the troopers says he thinks they saw that girl this morning. They took her into protective custody. She was doing herself harm over at the crime scene, but one of the camp thugs kidnapped her and carried her off. Big bruiser. The sheriff wants to know what the town cops are doing out here where they also have no authority. "Just getting out of the big city for a little country air," Dee says. Cavanaugh makes a mistake then and feeds Smith a straight line. "I don't know who's bought you, Smith," he says, "but—" and Smith interrupts him. "God's bought me, Mr. Cavanaugh." It will probably make all the evening newscasts. "All right," the banker says finally. "We'll let the governor adjudicate it when he gets here. He's due any minute. Meanwhile, you're here to protect law and order, Sheriff, and I want to know what measures you have taken in case things get out of hand." "Things aren't going to get out of hand," Smith replied. "If they do, Mr. Smith," Cavanaugh said, "it'll be on your head."

Dee has to admit Cal Smith holds his own as a novice lawman, but ultimately he's out of his depth. He's no Tub Puller. And, in Red Baxter, he's backing an overheated rage machine guaranteed to cause stupid problems. Out of the cult's hearing, Dee tells Cavanaugh that it looks to him like there has been some kind of takeover at the camp. These aren't the Brunists he knew from his visits there. And just a month ago, some of these same people got arrested for attacking the camp. Cavanaugh, offering cigarettes around and lighting up again, nods and says he's demanding a thorough search of the site, but they don't have the forces here to do that yet. When they do, they'll get the whole story. "But you're right, Dee," he says, "something's wrong." He thinks they could be hiding the bikers over there, too. Dee doesn't say so, but he doubts that. He also doubts Cavanaugh's belief in an operational link between the cult and the gang, even though the bikers do wear Brunist symbols on their skin and leathers. There's a distance he's not reading. Same reality, different interpretations. Like religion. But only one is true.

* * *

The bees, subdued by the wet weather, have been cooperative. They seem ready to leave this place. The Applebys, too, are ready. Corinne and Cecil have loaded the hives into the truck and secured everything and are set to get on the road. Earlier, just as they were getting started, they caught a glimpse through the dripping trees of Billy Don Tebbett's car over on the county road, going the wrong way. Darren Rector was driving it. Alone. While they loaded the hives, they talked about what that might mean. They decided that Darren might be trying to stop Billy Don from leaving by stealing his car. Now, as he gets behind the wheel, Cecil asks: "Reckon we should stop by the trailer lot?" "Billy Don won't be there and we won't know where to start looking," Corinne says. "But he could be on the road hitching, knowing we might be coming along. We can keep an eye out for him." On the narrow two-track road out of the camp, Cecil spots something down in the trees and asks Corinne to stop. It's a large bunch of ten-gallon gas cans all lined up. At least a dozen of them. "Somebody must've dumped them here, but they feel like they're full," Cecil says. "Don't reckon they'll mind if we borrow one of them for the road." "Gift of God," says Corinne.

Georgie Lucci's dream, whatever it was, is coming true. Mick is heating the grill to fry him up a plate of scrambled eggs and Piccolotti salomeats. A handful of aspirins, washed down with a beer bought him by the drunk at the bar, has eased the apocalyptic chaos in his head and the coffee, with its sweet healing aroma, is just beginning to perk in sympathy with his awakening brain. The town lush is already tanking up for the day. He's drinking vodka on the rocks, the cheap domestic brand. He calls it wodka. "The boss said to stay off the gin," he announces agreeably in explanation, lifting his glass, then he bangs it against Georgie's and tosses it back.

Georgie helped ruin a few bottles of that brain-acid last night, spending up the last of Steve Lawson's money. Apparently Stevie is already on the way to fatherhood, and they celebrated that, but if his dick had dropped off, they would have celebrated that, too. A kind of stag party replay without the insane adventures, though someone did suggest that they go out to the church camp and salt the beehives in revenge for the stings the little suckers laid on them last time; but they couldn't decide who'd do the salting and the camp is said to be sealed off after the explosion out there, anyway. Rumor is they found five bodies after the blast but only four heads. Weird. Religion is. The world is. All the people in it. They all agreed on that and drank to it. Weirdness. Yay. They considered a scavenger hunt for the missing head but didn't know what they'd do with it if they found it. Georgie suggested they could leave it in Father Bags' confession booth, see how many Hail Marys he'd assign the head for going around shamelessly without its body on. Cheese didn't know who Father Bags was. Guido Mello, who has a lot of free time on his hands since the garage burned down but seems to be spending little of it at home, called Cheese a fucking heathen, and Cheese, grinning his gap-tooth grin, said he didn't know what that was either but he assumed it was a compliment, and Guido said it was.

As his head and the weather clear as if each were bringing about the other, Georgie begins to have doubts about the mayor's project. How tough, really, he asks himself, *is* Charlie Bonali? *Very* tough, he decides. Just getting smiled at by him is like getting shot. Bonali approached him about joining his Dagotown Devil Dogs, and Georgie, grinning his hapless grin, said, sure, he probably would. Since then he has stayed out of sight. Good reason not to go out and rag the Brunists at Cunt Hill, where Bonali probably lurks with more lethal notions.

He's trying to think of a way of eating the mayor's breakfast and without guilt (should be easy, so rarely is he struck down by that grim disease) turning his offer down afterwards, when the scumbag dimestore owner comes in with a couple of other sad sacks off Main Street. The guy who owns the last downtown clothing store says people are trying to return things they bought six months ago, and the old fart who runs the hardware store says the only things he sold all last week were six screws and a nail. And that was on credit. Tee-heeing, Mick dribbles a bit of oil onto the grill and cracks the eggs into a bowl, whips them with a fork and spills them onto the grill and the lights go out. The coffee stops perking and the eggs fail to sizzle. "You should pay your fucking bills, Mick," Robbins grumbles. "I can't be more than a month behind," Mick says in his squeaky voice. "They always send you a notice." Everyone laughs at that. "Well, you don't have to cook the wodka," the drunk says, already having difficulty keeping his seat on the bar stool. He pulls an imaginary Stetson down over his nose. "Hit me again, podnuh! I'll suck it up raw!" Georgie waits a few minutes to see if the power comes back on. It doesn't. In this town, a power outage can last weeks. And Whimple may be on his way over by now. Carrying a fireman's axe, if he has an inkling Georgie is here. Georgie wolfs down a gelatinous slab of week-old green apple pie, pockets the change for later, and steps out the back door on his way to the Fort.

Over on Treasure Mountain, repository of the Kingdom's stash of black diamonds, the King and a handful of Knights stand alone against the vast formation of Cretin Wizards and their enchanted puppets at the foot. The Cretins raise their tinny battle cry: Oh, come and march with us to glory! Though they are not marching. Not yet. Just getting up the nerve. For the end of time has come! It's a kind of rope-skipping song. Why is the King denying the Cretins? Because it's a Holy Mountain and cannot be desecrated by lunatic fake magicians? No, because he is a King and it's his mountain and this is what you do. It's fun.

Sally can still think in the metaphorical way, though her heart's not in it and her pen's in her pocket. The end of once-upon-a-time has come. Goose Girl, looking for an ending to an old story of love unconsummated, kissed the Sleeping Prince's dick (dicks) and woke him up, and now she's sorry. Go back to sleep. I didn't mean it. It was an accident. The important thing about stories is not to begin them. I'm never going to be happy, she thinks. Not really happy. Satisfied maybe. Sometimes. Not often.

At least Billy D is not among the belligerents. Nor are Mrs. Collins and her daughter, as Billy Don foretold her. Franny Baxter's father is making noise over there with Billy Don's wonky ex-roomie Darren standing beside him, posing as a saint with golden locks and a mad beatific smile on his face, his granny glasses glittering in the emerging sunlight like golden coins, Auntie Debra's failed orphan rehab project pasted against his side. Billy Don didn't turn up at the Tucker City drugstore either. Probably, once he got away, he decided to just keep going and not look back. She'll miss him. He has been good company this long strange summer. He has her phone number; maybe he'll call.

While waiting for him at the drugstore, she picked up some more film for Tommy's cameras, and she has been whiling away the time here at the mine, in and around her desultory sketching (a lot of thick black lines), photographing the mine tipple, hoist wheel, and abandoned equipment, rusting freight cars, signs and graffiti, the limp tattered windsock over the grimy brick office building, the bloated water tower. She has also taken a shot or two of the confrontation over on the hill and of the tent at the edge of the camp where the dynamite blast happened, but mostly she has stayed discreetly out of sight, not wanting to draw attention to herself. A.k.a. the Antichrist. They are crazy, and they have guns. Anyway, now that she is no longer Professor Cavanaugh's research assistant, her interest in all that weirdness is fading. Christianity is quite simply a shamanistic cult of monumental stupidity, chicanery, and willful self-delusion. A legacy of the infantile origin of the species. She should stop worrying her head about it. Let it swallow its own tail.

The old coal tipple, rising high into the brightening sky above her, is more appealing, a giant contraption of scaffolding and pulleys and ramps and what looks like a seedy, quirkily designed hotel squatting like an old dame with lifted skirts over three parallel railroad tracks. How did this thing work? The mined coal went onto a conveyor belt and was lifted up into those shed-like buildings, where the rocks and rubbish were separated out and the coal screened for at least three different sizes, finding its way down chutes into the train cars below, the obvious corresponding anatomical appurtenance functioning, as it were, in triplicate. From loose to constipated. Thus, the anthropomorphizing of the world, both in the way we read it and the things we make for it, the stories we tell about it. Mother Earth and Father Sky. She has learned that the Mount of Redemption, long before it was called that by the Brunists, was known by the miners as Cunt Hill because of its cleft ravine under the rounded belly of its summit. If this is an obscenity, so were the primitive Mother Earth folktales she read in college. And, well, they were, of course. Dirty jokes that have evolved into our world religions.

Over on that exposed lady's tum, now catching a sunbeam or two, things are becoming more agitated. The aroused cultists, inheritors of those elaborated dirty jokes, have crept forward and stand face to face now with the policemen and Tommy's father. They still sing their Christian soldier songs, marching in with the saints now (oh, when the moon turns red with blood, they're singing cheerfully, I want to be in that number…), though from here it's just a thin cacophony, more like children yipping on a playground. A phalanx of armed men in farm boots and suspenders encircles them, either for protection or to arrest them. All of this is apparently on live TV, with helicopters hovering overhead. Some of the cultists watch the helicopters apprehensively. What are they thinking? That they might be agents of the Rapture? Or of the Antichrist? Their famous Great Speckled Birds? Is this funny? Only if madness is. She takes another picture of the people on the hill, framing it between tipple support posts to shrink it to its rightful dimensions. Two yellow backhoes sit off to one side like grazing dinosaurs. Tommy's father is having a fierce argument with the sheriff, pointing his finger at him. He is an unhappy man, Sally supposes, and in a mood to take no shit. Stacy called Sally on Sunday to say goodbye and to apologize for what happened. She sounded like she'd been crying. Maybe she hadn't stopped since the night before. Both she and

Tommy's father had tearful faces when they stepped out of the motel room, looking stricken and washed out under those awful corridor lights. She said she never finished that French novel Sally loaned her but she knows it must have ended badly. She's leaving it for her at her rooming house. Stacy had talked about going away during their drive over to the river town a couple of weeks ago. It's the sadness, she said then. Staying or leaving, the sadness is the same. Sally didn't understand it then. Now it's her own metaphysic.

So what now? Well, she could go back to college and get her degree. Or at least, now that the door's open, get laid. God expels Adam, takes a rib out of Eve: new playmate, better design. Adam left to play with himself. She has a writing prof at college who has a lot of faith in her, he says. Is he on the make? Probably. Writers are like that. She can get an education, learn a few tricks. He's married, but so much the better. He'll be careful, and there'll be no residue. She has rather hoped that the sort of love the Lutheran preacher called a "dying to oneself" might happen to her, at least once, in her earthly transit—not mere orgasm, but the legendary madness of love—but too late, she knows now. Back at the ice plant in Tommy's car, in that moment of frightened adoration (of what? doesn't matter), it might have been possible, but now irony has gotten in the way. Call it irony. It's what she has really lost. If her prof starts talking about the future, she'll find somebody else.

The singing stops, the bombast and bluster. They're all turning toward the mine road, where what looks like a funeral cortege is arriving. Will the raising of the dead require the mortician's art to undo what's been done? For some reason, by morbid association probably, Sally is reminded of that old lady over there last spring who blessed her with a wink and died. She has thought of her as a kind of tutelary spirit ever since. Nothing spooky, just something she has internalized. The old lady's faith in her. She seems to hear her admonish her now in her elegant, straight-backed way to stop feeling sorry for herself. Grandma Friskin behind her shoulder, nodding her approval. No pains without gains, child. Use them. Sally finds a sunny perch on a step at the backside of the tipple, turns her back on the Cretins, pulls off her tee (feels good; maybe she should take her shorts off, too), lights a cigarette, opens her notebook, blows away the cobwebs, and (and on the third day…) writes: Because you are a writer and this is what you do. It's fun.

The march to glory has been suspended. All eyes are on the arrival of the governor in his shiny black limousine, other cars and media trucks trailing behind in a procession rolling quickly down the mine road. Limousines are not a common sight in this county. It's like having an elephant gallop into view, dust and gravel flying. The limousine skids to a stop on top of the charred place in the road and an aide hops out and unfurls an umbrella over the rear door as he opens it, although it is no longer raining. The governor grandly brushes it aside. He can presumably see the banker halfway up the hill, but he strides straight through the mud to Sheriff Smith. The governor has his own television crew following him, security people, his political team. The governor is in neither party nor statehouse mode. He is in his campaign costume: hatless, white shirt with sleeves rolled up, bootlace tie at half mast, open black vest. Boots that servants will clean for him later. Wherever he goes there's a bright unnatural light on him. Under that light, he calls a couple of his state troopers over to be in the picture, and narrowing his eyes in the heroic manner, his shock of white hair stirring in the light breeze, converses intently with the sheriff and with selected members of the religious group. The impression (for the cameras) is that of a man on the front line, firm-jawed, crisp of manner, in charge of things. Mr. Dynamic.

The banker drops his smoke under his toe and steps down the hill to enter the governor's movie. The West Condon police chief has come to feel like the banker's personal bodyguard and he follows at a short distance with his first officer, who moves his bulk slowly but with a certain authority. The chief has received a radio call from Monk Wallace back at the station that, one, the National Guard troops have arrived out at the high school and, two, the power seems to be off all over town. The station and city hall are now running on their standby coal-fired generator. Romano asked him what the hell the soldiers were doing at the high school, they were supposed to be out here, and Wallace said that's what he told them and they said they'd be there as soon as they unloaded their gear and set up their bivouac area. The chief said he'd better get Bo in to help, but Monk reminded him that when Bo drops off it's like off a cliff. You only know he's alive by his snore. He couldn't hear a train going through his bedroom, much less a phone. As for the power outage, the chief said the storm probably knocked something out, but Monk should call the plant to check. Wallace said he did that, but no one answers. He'll keep trying. As the banker steps into camera range, the governor looks up with a warm smile of greeting, as if discovering him there for the first time, what a surprise, then switches to an expression of deep concern. The chief could never do that. Why he'll always be nothing more than a poor cop. "Ted Cavanaugh! I'm so glad you could come, my friend! We're trying to find a solution to the problem here. Perhaps you can help."

"I'm afraid the problem you're trying to resolve, Governor, is your own, not ours," the banker says drily. "You're trying to figure out how to conceal your spineless failure in the face of this crisis. You are so concerned with your own image, you can't recognize a real problem when it's right in front of your nose—it's only something that's blocking your view of yourself in the mirror."

The governor staggers back an unscripted step. "Are you mad? You have let things get totally out of control here and now you're trying to blame *us* for your own incompetence? Even now, while you've been doing nothing, I've been organizing a law-and-order team here—"

"With these people? That's great. A local rightwing fanatic with the sheriff in his back pocket assembles an unlawful white supremacist militia and you come along in your ignorance and sanction it."

"Hold on! That's not fair!" The governor has to speak up over the outraged religionists and the slap-slap-slap of the helicopters hovering overhead. The new sheriff is doing what he can to mute the protests of the Brunist Followers, assuring them that now that the governor is here, things will work out, and the young kid with the long blond curls raises his hand magisterially, and then Reverend Baxter nods and crosses his arms and they lower the volume. "I have also sent state police to the area and ordered up National Guard troops—!"

"Too late, Governor. And too little. Since last April our community has been begging you for help in the face of this extremist cult's illegal occupation of the mine property and the first assault by the murderous motorcycle gang they brought with them, and you laughed us off, said we were overreacting—"

"I say you're *still* overreacting, Ted. We're here to keep the peace, not stir things up. These people, I'm told, only wish to hold a memorial service on top of this hill, which they consider sacred, for a deceased member of their faith. I do not see why they cannot be allowed to do so. Freedom of religion is a Constitutional right. I have spoken with their leaders—"

"But they are *not* the leaders, or weren't before today. The true leaders are not here and we don't know where they are. There have been several murders already. We're afraid something may have happened to them. Nor do we know what happened to their motorcycle death squad. Are they hiding out over there? We need to search the campsite immediately."

"Murders? Over where? What are you talking about? If you want us to inspect an area, I'm sure we can discuss—"

"There's no time for more talk, Governor. We need action, but that's apparently not within your competence." The governor's media team have stopped filming, but the news cameras still roll. "You have been informed over the past three months of the continued criminality of the cult, the massive influx of armed drifters, the rise in burglaries and robberies, the violence taking place over there at their campsite, the break-in at the closed mine and the theft of dynamite and other weapons, and last Friday the horrific murder out here of the county sheriff and an innocent young man by burning them alive, but when we tried to reach you, we were told you were out politicking and couldn't be bothered. Those killers are still on the loose. Anything could happen. But you're still politicking."

"Obviously, you are not in a reasonable state of mind to discuss these issues," the governor says. "It is you and your town police officers who are breaking the law out here. I suggest you go home and leave this to me and to the legal state and county authorities who are here." He turns to his senior state police officer. "We will permit these people to hold their service on the hill on the condition that they vacate the premises when the service is concluded."

"You're making a mistake, Governor," says the banker in a voice clearly heard. "Look around. There are too many weapons out here. I realize you're completely and willfully ignorant of everything that's been happening here, but surely even you can see that much."

"Nonsense, Cavanaugh. You're becoming hysterical." The state police have stepped aside and the cultists are on the move, singing their Brunist battle hymn, but the governor holds up his hand and they pause. He turns to the sheriff. But the sheriff is not there. He has been called away to his squad car for a message from his dispatcher. The helicopters are wheeling away. Captain Romano has also withdrawn. He calls the banker over. The reporters press forward with questions, but Lieutenant Testatonda keeps them at bay. It is Monk Wallace back at the station. Romano asks Wallace to repeat the message. Cavanaugh holds the walkie-talkie to his ear: "Some folks has heard a explosion out to the power plant. May be that dynamite again. They still don't answer the phone. Might be some dead people out there." "Better get those units you've alerted moving now," the banker tells the chief, "but try to keep quiet about it, so we don't stir a panic and block our own way out of here. And ask Monk to phone the bank, tell them to lock the doors." He turns and strides down the hill toward his car. The chief is already on his way, barking out orders to Wallace on his walkie-talkie, cameras and reporters trailing after. He's thinking about his young nephew, who just hired on at the power plant. Officer Testatonda spies his daughter Ramona among the spectators and he jerks his thumb at her to follow him.

"Ted…? What's happening?" the governor asks, his bravado evaporating. The reporters want to know, too.

"You win, Kirk. The hill's all yours."

Darren feels himself on a plane of existence beyond anything he has known before. Nothing seems quite real in the old sense, and yet everything is endowed with a kind of dazzling super-reality. The glittering hill above them beckons like a mother opening her arms to receive her children; the very sun, now emerging, is at his command. When he lifted his hand a moment ago, it was not merely to hush the assembled faithful; he knew he had the power—like Moses, like Jesus—to change reality itself. And now, in response to that gesture, all the obstructions to their goal are melting away. The governor and his lackeys are leaving as well, the prying cameras and insidious journalists, all fleeing as if for their very existence. Not all vanish peacefully. Some burly Romanists barrel right through the gathered believers, issuing threats, promising to return, but they too disappear, pushed along into oblivion by the Christian Patriots and Darren's Defenders. Young Abner Baxter has been knocked down by one of them, muddying his tunic, and he is grimacing with panic, his headband slipped down over one eye and exposing his scar. Darren helps him to his feet and suggests he could go back and guard the camp if he wished, for it is their home and it is vulnerable now (the occupants of several trailers that have pulled out down there are noticeably absent here at the Mount; they will not be missed), and Young Abner, chewing his little red tuft of a moustache, seems eager to do that. Darren, prying himself away from Colin, takes Young Abner aside and slips him his revolver. Young Abner says he already has a rifle but Darren tells him he may need more than that, for the powers of darkness are restless and afoot, and Young Abner takes it and thanks him and hurries away. One must sometimes destroy the demonic, Darren thinks, to save a soul and open a corridor for God's grace. And later tonight:

a moment of holy fire. He has spoken with Young Abner's father about it and the word has spread. When the summit is theirs and they are standing inside the cross of the tabernacle and the sky has darkened, should that time arrive—should time still *be*—they will offer to the uninitiated baptism by fire. Colin has been begging for it, and he will be satisfied. Others have approached him as though he were the conduit to this form of grace. Today is the day. He knows this. All those paired sevens causing him to wonder whether the date would be a week of Sundays or two weeks of Sundays. It's all so much simpler than that. It's today's date. 7/7. God has spoken with thunderous clarity. Reverend Baxter watches him, awaits a sign. Darren nods and Abner Baxter nods. *"For ye were sometimes darkness, but now are ye light in the Lord!"* Abner calls out to all. *"Arise and walk! Walk while ye have the light, lest darkness come upon ye! Arise and walk as children of light!"* And solemnly yet joyfully, full-throated, their way prepared by the Lord, together they climb, unimpeded, their Mount of Redemption. *Dark*, Darren thinks. *Light... Ecstasy!*

> *"Oh the sons of light are marching to the Mount where it is said*
> *We shall find our true Redemption from this world of woe and dread,*
> *We shall see the cities crumble and the earth give up its dead,*
> *For the end of time has come!*
> *"So come and march with us to Glory!*
> *Oh, come and march with us to Glory...!"*

With the electricity off in the beauty shop and her client's hair only half done, Linda calls the power company, but no one answers. They never do, it's so frustrating. So she calls the police. It takes forever, but finally Lieutenant Wallace answers and tells her he doesn't know what the problem is, but he's working on it. Just what you might expect! Even as she slams the phone down, it rings.

It's Tessie Lawson at the sheriff's office, asking for Lucy Smith, who has just walked in, and she hands her the phone. "What did you say?" Lucy asks. But the phone goes dead. "If it's not one thing, it's another," Linda says, taking a listen. Lucy is confused. "I think she said he said I should go home right now and stay there, but maybe she said he said *he* was going home, and I should stay *here*. I just don't know *what* to do!" "Well, why don't you come with me," Linda says. "I'm going to pick up some money at the bank, if they still have any, and do a little quick shopping. We can stop by the sheriff's office and ask Tessie personally. Would you like to come along, Mrs. Abruzzi?" "No, dear, I only wait for you here and read your magazines."

On her way to the corner drugstore for her second breakfast, the real one, Angela Bonali pauses for a moment in front of Linda's Beauty Salon to study the hairstyles pictured in the window. Perhaps that's what she needs to lift her spirits: a new hairdo. Something different. Life-changing. She remembers a phrase from a book she read (she wrote it down in her diary): "Loose tendrils of hair softened her face." How do you get that in a hairdo? The trouble is, most heroines have blond hair, light and silky, or at worst flowing auburn hair—it's the men who have stubborn black hair like hers. Women in books whose hair is said to be like shining glass or polished wood or the black of a starless night tend to be half-men or loose or wicked. Inside, she can see Signora Abruzzi sitting in the dark with her thin dry hair in curlers, her beaky nose in a magazine. She'd go in and turn the lights on for her, but that's the old tattle who got Angela in trouble during her dark ages. Hard to imagine Widow Abruzzi ever eliciting moans of ecstasy, but then that's true of anyone that old. It's just awful how the body lets you down. You only have a moment, and when it's gone… She shudders, crosses herself, and hurries on.

Further disappointments await her in Doc Foley's. Stacy's not there and the waffle griddle's not working because the power is out. Angela loves their blueberry waffles with strawberry syrup and ice cream and crispy bacon on the side. She has to make do with just the syrup and ice cream. Because they are afraid the ice cream will melt with the power off they're offering it at half price until it comes back on again, so she orders up a double portion. Stacy is probably over at the First National, but Angela doesn't have the nerve yet to go back there. She feels terribly guilty about something, but she doesn't know what, and it doesn't seem fair. *She's* not the one who has done anything wrong.

The shy, spindly soda fountain girl (what's her name? Becky?) lingers at her table when she brings the ice cream. She has added some chocolate cookies for free and Angela thanks her for them. She's not pretty, but at least she has no worries about weight. Of the magic numbers—36–24–36—she has only the middle one, straight up and down. Awkwardly, the girl asks about Tommy. Angela wonders what she knows and doesn't know and whether or not she's salting the wound. Well, surely she knows nothing; she's not part of Angie's crowd. She admires Angela the same way that Angela admires Stacy, and she's just trying to be friendly. Angela smiles and says Tommy's just great and she likes her bracelet.

"Oh, it's only a cheap thing I won in a carnival..."

"It's nice." Angela feels generous and wise, a beautiful woman of the world, a model for sweet homely girls like Becky, if that's her name. Angela does not seek worldly goods like money, power, fame, or even beauty. All she truly wants is to be regarded in some modest fashion as the Virgin is regarded. Vita, dulcedo, et spes nostra, salve! That's her model. Blessed art Thou amongst women and blessed is the fruit of Thy womb. Which thought—yet another disappointment—depresses her again. She got through her last period with difficulty, not wanting anyone to see her in here buying tampons after all the fuss she'd made. She still hasn't figured out yet how to catch up to her own history. The girl continues to stand there, so Angela, fishing about for something final to say, borrows a line from Stacy, which she has also written in her diary. "A friend once told me," she says, "that love is not an island. I liked that."

"Tommy was in earlier for sausage and scrambled eggs," the girl says. "He had that funny thing on his nose. The power was still on then. He said it was his last breakfast special. He said he was leaving town forever."

Angela smiles, hoping her makeup is hiding the flush. And that she won't get sick. "He was teasing," she says. "He had to run an errand today for his father. Because of, you know, what's happening out at the mine hill. Tommy is becoming very important at the bank." The stupid girl doesn't say anything. She just stares at her.

Should Angela decide to risk a visit, she would find the bank closed, for Officer Wallace has called to say that Mr. Cavanaugh wants the doors locked until further notice, and they have done that, continuing to serve only those customers who are already in the bank. It's like an extra day of holiday added to the long weekend, except that he asked them to stay until he got back. But why must they lock up so early? The bank often closes during power failures, but Mrs. Wetherwax, who is filling in for Angela and Stacy, took the phone call and she said the officer made it seem much more urgent than that. So many horrible things have happened of late, almost anything seems possible. And now the phones are dead, too. Just before they closed up, Mrs. Catter came in with Mrs. Smith, and she told them about it and they tried them, and sure enough, they are dead. Mr. Gus Baird, who almost always comes into the bank at this hour, does a little waltzing turn and sings: "All alone, by the telephone, waiting for a ring a ting a ling!" and they all laugh nervously. There's an irate gentleman speaking with Mr. Minicozzi in Mr. Cavanaugh's office about the foreclosure on his house (he can be heard plainly all the way out here on the bank floor, and his language isn't nice), and when he leaves they'll tell Mr. Minicozzi about the policeman's call and ask him what it means. He always seems to know what's happening. Mr. Beeker of the hardware store, just being let out of the locked front door, says he hopes it doesn't mean the bank is running out of money, and the city hall janitor leaving at the same time—he has been in making a withdrawal, which leaves his account almost empty because the monthly payroll checks are late—says that as long as they have Mr. Beeker's millions on deposit, there should be no problem, and they all laugh at that and feel a little less nervous afterwards.

Young Mrs. Piccolotti, who is in picking up rolls of coins for the family grocery (they have all had a turn cuddling her cute baby), says the trouble is probably the fault of that awful religious cult out at the edge of town; they're completely crazy and they don't belong here. That upsets Mrs. Catter and she says that many of them are friends of hers and have lived in this town just as long as Mrs. Piccolotti's family, and they are decent Christian people. Religion is a private matter between a person and her God, and no one should interfere with it or make fun of it, the Constitution says so. They all agree and apologize if they've said something out of place. Mrs. Smith says she thinks she wants to go home. Mrs. Catter says in fact maybe they should start praying and repenting of their sins, because something very important might be happening, just like it says in the Bible, and Mrs. Piccolotti sighs and says, that's just what I was talking about, and then she clams up because she's the only Catholic in the bank except for Noemi and Mr. Minicozzi. It's getting a bit warm without the air conditioner, and arguments don't make it any cooler.

Mr. Baird changes the subject by saying he'd really love to see them all in bikinis on a beach in Brazil, that he might make a trip down there himself just for the amazing sight (he rolls his eyes in his comical way), and since they're the only people in town with their hands on real money, they ought to consider one of his special end-of-summer holiday opportunities. Mrs. Wetherwax knows Mr. Baird as the rather tedious class clown, but to the younger girls he's the bald guy with a bowtie who runs the local travel agency and is president of the Rotary Club. He wanders in and out of the bank most days, looking for people to tell his silly jokes to.

Then the phone rings and everybody jumps. It's back on! No, it's only Mrs. Wetherwax's husband from the phone company, up a pole somewhere and tapping in. He tells them that the motorcyclists are back, what looks like three or four different gangs, and that they have blown up the power station and phone exchange and radio station. Armored trucks full of soldiers have arrived at the edge of town and there are more helicopters out by the county airport. They should all stay where they are and not go out on the streets. The motorcyclists might be converging upon the center.

In Mick's Bar & Grill on Main Street, a block or so from the bank, the former Chamber of Commerce secretary has just ordered up another iced vodka when he suddenly remembers why he is supposed to stay off the gin. "Tag that with my social security number, Mick. I'll be right back," he says and staggers toward the door, singing "Joshua fit de battle ob Jericho! Jericho!" But the walls do not come tumbling down, and after slapping up against one or another without the door ever finding him in spite of the ever-helpful directions shouted out by his fellow klatchers (to him? to the door?), it is he who succumbs at last to the remorseless force of gravity.

Consequently, the intended object of his quest, young Reverend Joshua Jehoshaphat Jenkins, prospective pastor of the local First Presbyterian Church, arrives after overnight travels at the West Condon bus station unmet. There are numbers he could call, but being a self-reliant fellow, he deposits his bag with the stationmaster ("I see you are planning to settle in here, mister, and have brung your own bricks," the stationmaster says sourly) and sets out upon the wet glittering streets on his own in search of his future place of employment, humming his favorite Sunday School tunes because he cannot seem to get them out of his head this morning. The downtown near the bus station is full of smiling people, young and old, emerging into the sunlight after the heavy rains. There are SALE signs everywhere, church bells are ringing—it's a happy day.

Joshua believes in the simultaneous veracity of various and even contradictory modes of discourse, and as he leaves the center and enters the residential neighborhoods, he chooses the descriptive one, which finds its truths in perceptive accuracy, not narrative coherence or moral judgment. Thus, while his observation that with the hot sun he is somewhat overdressed in his new three-piece corduroy suit remains within the descriptive mode, the reasons for his discomfiture (good first impressions!) do not. Not that the descriptive mode is without its own rationale. If everything in existence is God's handiwork, as Joshua believes it is, then close descriptive attention to one's surroundings is an approach to understanding God, and—reverentially—feeling His presence. In that respect, this sight of a bountiful garden of hollyhocks and sunflowers is equal to that of a dog squatting to relieve itself, and Joshua mentally records it all, finding in the activity, in spite of distant wailing sirens and a gathering awareness that he has forgotten to have breakfast, a profound peace and satisfaction. "He gave us eyes to see them, and lips that we might tell," he sings to himself, "how great is God Almighty, Who has made all things well!" Bright and beautiful, yes, all things certainly are, must be. Although, slipping momentarily out of the descriptive mode into the utilitarian one, he could do frankly with a little snap, crackle and pop.

As he thinks that, astonishingly, those are in fact the sounds he hears, as if conjured from his hunger, but caused, he sees, by the distant approach down this sunny tree-lined street of a procession of army trucks. Ah. The mere descriptive mode will perhaps no longer suffice.

Out at the city hospital, the head nurse, on her own up on the second floor, has just hung up from alerting the doctors, nurses, and hospital emergency team to the power blackout—must get the generators turned on to keep the life support systems running and the operation theater functional—when a busty foreign woman and four armed men, one wearing a black stocking mask, another a silk black tie over a luminous flame-red T-shirt, storm up to her station, poke guns in her face, and demand to know what room a man named Suggs is in. She points down the hall, gives them a number, and faints. Seems to. One of them gives her a kick—which seems to satisfy him, or her—and they dash off, their boots clocking on the polished floor. Shots are fired, hundreds of them seems like, as she scrambles desperately, heart pounding, into the restroom at the nurses' station and locks the door. When they come thumping back they notice her absence, shout death threats, not all in the mother tongue, and shoot up the place. Bullets come smashing through the restroom door, but she is as far away from it as possible, hunkered down behind the toilet. "Basta, Rupe!" she hears the woman say. "Don' waste your beebees!" *"Two minutes!"* another calls out. When the boots and voices rattle away and it's quiet again, Maudie peeks out through the bullet holes. They're gone. Just the same, she keeps her head below counter height as she hurries in a squat past the ransacked medicine cabinet (more shots below, an explosion), and grabs up the phone. The line's dead.

Mayor Castle snorts like a horse, roaring har-har sounds. He might be laughing. Georgie has been trying to weasel out of working as a mole for the mayor in Charlie Bonali's Dagotown Devil Dogs, but needing a job and having already eaten an indigestible bite out of the small bill the mayor gave him, he has been proposing alternative, less life-threatening schemes for keeping tabs on Charlie. "Hell, I didn't ask you to see me about that, Georgie," the mayor booms. "You drove a cab up in the city for some years, ain't that so? Well, I'm just a country boy and city traffic gives me the running shits. Besides, I lost my goddamn license. Something fucking wrong with a town when the mayor can lose his license just because he's had a few, but that's the kind of pisshole we live in, right? So right now I need somebody who can get me to the international airport fast and keep his fucking mouth shut. I can trust you, right?" Georgie grins and nods. Of course, he's always grinning. But now he means it. He can even start working on that lump of pie sitting like a stone in his belly. The mayor lifts a briefcase from the floor, sets it on the desk between them, opens it. It's full of money. More money than Georgie has ever seen. "There's over a mill here, Georgie. I'm thinking Brazil. If we make it, we'll split this pile 60-40. That's several hunderd Gs for you, minus expenses. Decent taxi fare. We'll take the official limo. You game?" Hell yes, he's game. Besides, it occurs to him that Castle didn't show him that money for nothing. It was to let him know that if he said no, he'd shoot him. "When are we leaving?" he asks. He's grinning, and the mayor grins back. "Now." That gives him brief pause. What is he leaving behind? Niente. "All right," Georgie says, "but I need an advance. Three-thirty, that's all. It's to pay off a loan. The thirty is interest." "Hey, Giorgio, you're outa here forever. Forget it." "Can't. La mammina. It's all she's got. We can drop it off on the way out."

When the Kid assigned him the high school, Houndawg said it was summertime, it would just be empty buildings, ditto the grade schools the others got assigned, and the Kid said, if it belongs to the enemies of the Big One, it's never empty. Sure enough, it isn't. There are three army trucks there, guys in summer khakis unloading gear, going in and out of the school gym. Jackpot! "We're disabling them three trucks," he says. "Don't worry about personnel less they get in your way." Houndawg handled explosives in the army, but this stuff is pretty crude. Just dangerous footlong firecrackers leaking their innards, really, that he and Hacker fused and partly bound in three- and five-stick packs yesterday while they were sitting out the rain. Thinking about Runt. Feeling the wrath. Things could go wrong. The timing has to be perfect. So far so good. Houndawg is a reluctant holy warrior, skeptical of the zealotry that motivates most of the Wrath, but they fill the aimless loneliness that had threatened to steal away what little life he had left in him, and he's grateful for that. He's having fun for the first time in a long time, not since the war—even if only for a short time, maybe just this one day long. He has the luxury of the ex-sheriff's high-powered rifle, but limited ammo, just what they found in the sheriff's trunk when they were stuffing the kid in there minus what he pumped into the head of that evil old cocksucker who killed Paulie. Silver bullets. He has to make them count. After knocking out the power and phones as a unit, the Wrath divided up into three teams of four to hit a sequence of separate targets simultaneously, synchronizing their moves with stopwatches, with the Kid roaming between the three. Houndawg's team is the least stable of them. Brainerd is cool, even with one hand disabled, but Sick has been shooting up and X has been eating uppers like they were a bag of Red Hots. It's the only time X ever smiles, but it's a twitchy smile and his set-apart eyes jiggle. Still, he's probably safer than Sick, who has painted his face red to match his boots and put on feathers and seems to be living in some other reality zone. Houndawg, on a heavy dose of painkillers himself, takes one of the trucks, assigns Brainerd and X the other two, explains to them how to pop the hood, and tells Sick to give them cover. "We got just two minutes. In and out. If you have a problem with the nitro, don't try to solve it. Okay, let's move." They have to take a guy out on the way in, catching him by surprise. Nothing personal. He can hear Sick firing away, who knows at what, while he's planting the squibs. "One minute!" he yells. Other people are shooting now, and he worries Sick may have taken a hit. "Now!" The three of them tear out of there, but Sick's not in sight. Then he comes backing out of the building, firing away, jumps on his bike and joins them as the building explodes behind him, the trucks blowing up as he guns past them, head down, wahooing like an Indian on the warpath, his topknot fluttering on his gleaming red skull like a raised flag. "Three fucking bells!" Houndawg laughs as they roar away. He can hear shooting, but they're gone from there.

Franny Lawson is keeping her sister-in-law Tessie company in the sheriff's office while her husband Steve is out at the mine hill with the Christian Patriots, doing his thing for God and country. They're talking about what to name the baby when Sheriff Smith radios in from his car to say he's on his way in but he's stuck in traffic. He tried to get away as soon as he got her call about the power plant but still got caught in the jam-up. Did they reach his wife Lucy? Tessie explains about the phone going dead so she's not sure Lucy got the message, but says that, yes, she was at the beauty shop. The sheriff tells them to shut down the office and go take cover. Gratefully, they do so.

It is a time for thanksgiving. The Brunists have reached the summit of the Mount of Redemption under a midday sun now sallying forth from the clouds as if joining their march and have entered into their outlined tabernacle church, though their numbers exceed its capacity and spill out over the hillside. Children are playing (they have got up a game down by the empty graves and are splashing in and out of them) and their elders are relaxing from the heightened tensions of the morning, when death and injury seemed all too near a prospect. There is still, however, an air of apprehension. The sudden dispersion of the authorities, releasing the Mount to them: was it God watching over them, shepherding them to higher ground, or is something more or other happening? Those ominous *ker-whumps* in the distance… But they are here now where they belong. Mr. Ross McDaniel, a man from the West of fierce faith and fortitude, has promised them that the Mount is theirs and they will not be moved, and they believe him. They all share the blessed hope of the rapturing of the church by Lord Jesus and the visible return of Christ with His saints to reign on earth for one thousand years, and today could be the day for that—as could any other, but as their young prophet and evangelist Darren Rector says, these days are overripe with omen.

A Brunist Defender and pastor who arrived this morning by bus from east Tennessee with two sturdy members of his congregation, rifles strapped to their backs, steps into the center of the outlined cross to add his voice to the exhortations and prayers of gratitude for their safe passage up here and to lead the assembled Followers in a prayer of remembrance for their fallen leader, Brother Ben Wosznik, a kind and holy man of unbending courage, tireless endeavor, and profound faith. He tells of Brother Ben's visit with Sister Clara three years ago to his "little church in the wildwood," as he calls it, and of all the souls that were saved that day through the mere power of the man's inspired singing. In his memory, they sing—joined by many of the sheriff's remaining deputies—some of the famous Brunist songs Brother Ben wrote and recorded, "The Circle and the Cross," "She Fell That We Might Live" (heads swivel thoughtfully toward the mine road, fingers point, the tale is whispered), and "The White Bird of Glory." This latter number, with its recounting of "the disaster that struck old Number Nine," reminds them that they are standing on ground hallowed not only by those members of the faith who stood here on the Day of Redemption and suffered death, incarceration, and persecution because of it, but also by all the brave hardworking men, friends and loved ones of many present, who perished beneath their feet in the worst mine disaster the area has ever known. There are many "amens" and "God blesses" and spontaneous prayers for the souls of the deceased, not excluding the saintly Ely Collins, whose leg is still down there somewhere. His widow, also Brother Ben's, is said to be too stricken by grief to attend, and she is remembered in their prayers, as are her unfortunate daughter and Brother John P. Suggs in his hospital bed. What a thrill to know he'll be raptured with an undamaged brain, and Brother Ely with his leg back on! Sheriff Puller, who was so supportive and protective, is also remembered, as is the oldest boy of Brother Roy and Sister Thelma Coates, both Royboy and the sheriff so cruelly murdered. Sister Thelma lets out a sad little wail. Sometimes the world seems completely insane, but they feel protected by each other, and by their faith, the truth they share. There are those who say they should also pray for the souls of the motorcyclists who died in the camp blast, for that is the charitable and pious thing to do, and Sister Sarah Baxter, who has lost her wayward middle son in it, especially seems to want this, but her husband scowls and turns his back, and this part of the Defender's eulogistic prayer is shortened to a passing mention of their youngest boy, Paul, who will hopefully return to them now that his older brother has passed away.

Reverend Baxter turns back, frowning at his wife in consternation. Where, he wants to know, are their two remaining children? She starts to cry. She doesn't know. Young Abner, Brother Darren explains, asked permission to go check on the safety of the camp now that it is emptied out except for a mobile home or two. Young Abner said he thought he heard the sound of motorcycles in that direction and Brother Darren proposed they send a team, but Young Abner was well-armed and insisted he could handle it on his own and would be back shortly. Brother Darren hasn't seen Amanda, but her brother was watching over her, and she might have followed him there. A further prayer is offered up for the safety of Young Abner Baxter and his sister, and another for the protection of the Wilderness Camp, where many here on the hillside will now be living, should this day be succeeded by another.

And where is Amanda Baxter? Far from the Mount of Redemption, sitting in her panties astride a motorcycle behind a biker known only as X outside the blazing West Condon Church of the Nazarene, and smiling her sweet winsome smile. "Hey, that's my sister," Kid Rivers says, pulling off his black stocking mask to give his face some air. He has just arrived from the hospital, leaving Hacker's team after finishing off Old Man Suggs and blowing up the ambulance, Hacker and the others meanwhile on their way now to leave the Wrath's signature at a couple of fat-cat churches. "She's mental, man."

"Yeah, well, X is mental. So what?" Sick says, speaking for his silent buddy. Both of them look dangerously spaced out.

"Why is she only in her underwear?"

"How we found her. Said she lived somewhere around here and was looking for her clothes."

"That was five years ago." The Kid doesn't like it and may have to take care of X when all this is over, but on the other hand, it can't be worse than living with the old man. He asks his sister where the others are and she only smiles dippily and points. The church camp, maybe. Or the hill. Probably why they've had such an easy run so far. His old man's moves have sucked everybody out there. Perfect. All falling into place, like it was meant to be. When the news about the Wrath gets to them, they'll be heading back in, but it has given them an extra minute or two. He raises a fist of gratitude to the Big One. Bells are ringing somewhere. Sirens off in the distance. Fire truck heading out toward the power plant. The bad guys are always dumb and do the wrong thing. He and Houndawg exchange quick notes on the hospital and the high school. Army trucks! Cool. And now his old man's church going up in flames.

Chopper rattling overhead. Doesn't look army. News creeps, probably. Trying to hang on to history when it's already too late. Could be a complication, though, when they try to get out of here. "Shall I take that whirlybird out?" Houndawg asks.

"Yeah. But not yet. There are more. Wait till we get downtown and they start flocking. Easier to shoot into a bevy than hit a single bird." Something old Roy Coates used to say. Coates will be browned off about his kid. He's a good hunter. Don't want to get within his shooting range. Kid Rivers glances at his sister (should he tell her something? maybe, but he doesn't know what) and at his stopwatch, pulls his mask back on. "We got less than twelve minutes. Deacon should be at the Baptists by now. It's big and brick and has a lot of steps. They may need help. See you at city hall."

But Deacon's team is not at the Baptist church and there's no sign they've been here. Rifle fire explodes from the doorway and The Phantom takes a glancing hit off the taillight mount—he rockets away from there. Word must be getting around. Those bells are banging away in Dagotown like a fire alarm. Catholic church bells. Where Deac was headed next. He's in trouble. The Kid heads that way, but through back streets, head down, expecting to be shot at. He reaches the asphalt basketball courts and parking lot behind the church. A guy jumps out of a car with a gun in his hand and The Kid shoots him, the shot drowned out by the headachy bells. He's not dead. And then he is dead. The Kid busts a window, crawls into the basement, his jaw clenched under his stocking mask, but he's grinning, too. He could fly if he wanted to.

* * *

In Mick's, Burt Robbins is venting his anger against the racket of the bells. While on the city council he got an ordinance passed forbidding the ringing of church bells except on Sundays. The Catholics were the main abusers. Rang them every day at dawn, noon, sundown. He stopped that. Toot sweet. Can't have a goddamned immigrant minority moving in and imposing their way of life on everyone else. He makes a few snarling remarks on the theme that affect none of Mick's customers, but ignore the fact that Mick himself is a Catholic, potato-famine Irish on his mother's side, who knows what bastardy on the other. Mick says it sounds more like something's wrong. Church bells aren't rung like that. Burt's lip curls in disdain. From the floor Jim Elliott can be heard crooning "The Balls of St. Mary."

Then Earl Goforth, who owns the skating rink and bowling alley and has a face grotesquely chewed up from the last war, comes rushing in and growls through the side of his mouth, "What do you make of *this*?" He is carrying a transistor radio, but the signal is so staticky nothing can be understood.

"What I make of it, Earl, is you need a fucking new radio," Robbins says with customary bonhomie.

"No, I just heard. It's a station from over in the next county. It comes in better out on the street." He holds the radio up to the one half-ear he has left; the other is just a button. "They say our power plant was blowed up. The phone exchange, too. People killt."

"I *told* you it wasn't my fault," Mick says in his squeaky voice.

"Also, there's something about the hospital and the National Guard, but I couldn't get it."

"National Guard!"

"It's them!" Robbins says in a voice that sounds like anger but is more likely fear. "They're still here! Lock the doors, Mick, don't let anybody in! And stay away from the windows!"

* * *

Vince Bonali and Sal Ferrero, gloomily shooting the shit on Vince's front porch not far from where the bells are ringing, also remark on them, wonder if they should wander over and see what's going on. Somebody getting married? But Sal's wife has the Ferrero car, needing it for the hospital, and Charlie has Vince's old wreck out at the mine hill—he takes it now without even asking—and that's excuse enough to stay where they are. It was raining when they first sat down here. The lights were on, the phone worked, and their coffee was hot. Now, except for the rain stopping, all that's changed for the worse. Their mood, though, has not; it couldn't. They've been sitting here, screened by the dripping of the clogged and rusted-out gutters, talking about the hard times they've been through, which are only getting harder. About this fucked-up town and those murderous lunatics out at the church camp, who have brought all this misery down on them. About the true religion, which is about all they've got and which should be of more help than it is, and about women they've known who have grown old, pals too, many dead, and how distant all that seems. Conversations they've had many times before. About all that's different this morning is the news about Sal's father-in-law, Nazario Moroni, who died last night in the hospital, not unexpectedly. Not the easiest guy to get on with; Ange had difficulties with his old man. Gabriela did, too. But in mean times, he was a guy you could count on, and Vince had always somewhat modeled his own life as a union man on old Nazario. Gabriela had to stop by the First National this morning to ask for a loan to pay for her father's funeral; if they turn her down the only hope left to avoid a pauper's grave is the mine union, which is in tatters. They gave Dave Osborne a big sendoff and he didn't even have the guts to see it out to the end; cranky old Nonno Moroni was worth ten Dave Osbornes, but except for a couple of senile old farts at the Hog no one will even notice he's gone. Several times already Sal has sighed and said he'd better get back and tend his chickens, they're all that's keeping them from starving, and he does so again, and Vince remembers to thank him again for the eggs and coffee he brought this morning and takes another sip from the cold cup. Sal says much as they love the Piccolotti salomeats, they're reduced nowadays to eating cheap breakfast sausage bought directly from a backyard pig farmer—who knows what's ground up in it, but they haven't got sick yet—and Vince says he couldn't even afford that. Sal actually stubs out his cigarette and gets to his feet and stretches and then Vince does too and says he'll walk Sal partway, wander past the church and see what all the bell-ringing is about.

By the time Gabriela Ferrero and her sister-in-law, Concetta Moroni, reach the hospital, senior staff have arrived and put some order to the chaos. The destroyed ambulance is still smoldering, there have been casualties, and the front lobby has been heavily damaged, but they have restored emergency power by way of the standby hospital generator and have cordoned off the building. Gabriela and Concetta have been told to go home or wait indefinitely in the parking lot or the basement canteen. The staff has secured two floors for receiving casualties, dispensed calmatives to the traumatized nurses, set up volunteer guards at the entrances, and they have moved quickly through the hospital to reassure patients in their darkened rooms, many of whom are terrified by everything they've heard, while others only complain about the television being off and ask them to please fix it or else give them a reduction in their bill.

The fire department, with its crew of four, stopped by the hospital on the way back from the power station (they brought in two bodies and three injured workers), but after a quick dousing of the blazing ambulance, they have gone on to the high school to deal with the fires and carnage at the basketball gym, serving now as both fire engine and ambulance. They used this gym after the mine disaster as a temporary morgue. It's one again. Governor Nolan Kirkpatrick, visiting what's left of the decimated National Guard unit, confers with school officials, looking like a man who has just learned he is suffering from a fatal illness. He has had the young officer in charge call up reinforcements and more state police on his orders and send an official plea for help to the federal government, which he always denigrates in his election campaigns. Now he commandeers some yellow school buses parked for the summer over near the football field, ordering the remaining troops out to the mine hill in some of them and sending the others to the county airport to meet the new Guardsmen being flown in. Fire Chief Mort Whimple picks up three more firefighters from among the troops, but he is beginning to feel the hopelessness of his task. The high school fire is not yet under control, he can see smoke rising from other locations in the town—can smell it in the air—and the water pressure is rapidly dwindling. On his way here, he saw flooding in the streets. Thought it was just from the rain until he saw all the open hydrants.

Much as Baptiste loathes the Catholic Church and disbelieves all its teachings, he still could not stop himself from genuflecting as he entered (Deacon laughed at him), laden with his grave tidings. He has paused in the narthex to peer in on what awaits him while Deacon and Spider clamber silently up into the choir loft to cover him, Thaxton standing guard out front on his motorcycle. The Kid's carefully mapped plans are ticking along like clockwork. It'll all be over before anyone knows what's happening. The nave looks empty, though there is a disturbing fragrance of incense, a banging of bells. Baptiste is not unfamiliar with the Kid's vision of a Holy War. He was raised Catholic in an illiterate dirt-poor Acadiana family, and he was first taught about the violent way the world would end by a mad French priest who wore a haircloth and shaved his head and went barefoot in all weather. When Baptiste was nine years old, the priest, after first scaring the pants off him with his fiery description of the Last Judgment—*Dies Irae!*—then fucked him, telling him it was the sacred route to eternal life and salvation from the horrors of hell, praying feverishly all the time he humped away, and making Baptiste pray, too, adding that his tears were holy and he should not be ashamed of them. This path to salvation was not a short one. It lasted almost four years before Baptiste, consumed by hatred of the stinking priest and inspired by a folktale his grand-père had told him, reached between his legs with a knife and did a little mid-fuck creative gelding. He told the priest his screams were holy and he should not be ashamed of them. Last time he was in a church, until now. His grand-père, Pépé Jules, was an old-time Bayou fiddler who spoke no English and taught him all the best Cajun swearwords, most of them as used against priests and nuns. Pépé Jules also fucked him. Called it making family music. Baptiste never liked it, but he never hated him for it, because there was no praying, just singing and laughing. Pépé bought him his first whore and his first motorcycle, on which Baptiste ran errands for him, learning the neige trade. When Pépé Jules died one night in a tavern knife fight, Baptiste hit the road and hasn't looked back since. Mostly lonely years, but he is finding a home now with the Wrath, who treat him with a respect he has not known before. He glances at his stopwatch and then, crossing himself again, pushes on into the aromatic church, moving quickly, intending to place the strapped packets of dynamite under the covered altar, but an ugly baggy-eyed priest rises up from behind it with a rifle, and before he can draw a gun or light the fuse, brings Baptiste to his knees with a shot in the gut. More shots ring out from the loft above him and the priest crumples. Without warning (where the hell is Thaxton?), the church is suddenly swarming with locals. Baptiste lurches to his feet, but meaty types barking in some kind of wop wrestle him to the floor and pound his head against it as if trying to crack it open. Can't reach the batons. Just inches away. Baptiste needs help. He's not going to get it.

The man above him in the Presbyterian pulpit, who says he is Jesus and looks and talks like Jesus and for whom young Reverend Joshua J. Jenkins has no other name, is explaining that the end of the world is not an event but a kind of knowledge, and has therefore already happened, at least for those in the know; and those who are not in the know are living in sin, are they not, for ignorance is itself sinful. Whether he is addressing Joshua or the anxious woman in the silky peach-colored gown who has come tiptoeing in or someone else altogether is not clear. Earlier, when introducing himself, the man said he was often spoken of as the Incarnation of the Word, an expression that has fascinated and solaced Joshua in the sense of the Word being the design in the mind of the Architect of the Universe, that Word made flesh at one transcendental moment in history, a concept grandly profound and nobly expressed, but Jesus, this person calling himself that, a madman probably, said that it was, as they say in the fairytales, *just so,* and that that word he incarnated was Oblivion. "Or sometimes Desolation, the Abyss, Vanity—there are synonyms." Said with the most unnerving of blissful smiles, marred only by the strange startled eyes, as if someone else were staring out through them.

This is not the interview experience Joshua had anticipated, that for which he has prepared by carefully reviewing church dogma and history, by assembling a vast array of Biblical and philosophical quotations as well as his own personal meditations, by outlining several possible inaugural sermons, and by attiring himself in this suffocating corduroy suit. Nor is he certain which mode of discourse he's now in. It is like that of dreams, but it is not that of dreams—unless he is still on that bus, and he does not think he is. It feels like a mode more in tune with all those Sunday school songs that have been running through his head all morning. Now it is the man's proposal that they all proceed out to some hill, one occupied—if the woman's opinion, frantically stated, is correct—by dangerous crazy people. "We shall take Mr. Joshua J. Jenkins with us," he says. "He is the grandson of a king. He will protect us. Come! Follow me!"

"But I can't!" the lady says. Her sorrowful gaze reminds Joshua of portraits of the Virgin, cradling the head of her crucified Son. "My condition!" She tightens the gown over the little bulge in her midriff in demonstration that she is expecting. Young Reverend Jenkins is not accustomed to such intimacies; his gaze flies to the ceiling then drops to his new shoes. But is Jesus…? he is wondering with alarm. Has he…? Well, of course, he is *not* Jesus. Is he? "Please don't go!" the lady pleads. "We could—we could go use the bath in the manse again?"

Whereupon Jesus pats her in a shockingly familiar way and says, "I have no choice, beautiful lady. I am who I am. Take courage! I will return again unto you, as is said. Come then, Mr. Jenkins," he adds, stepping down from the podium and taking his arm. "Off we go! Just a closer walk with me!"

"I was just…I was just humming that!"

"Of course you were. Let us set forth now to sow our tidings, short of wholly glad though they be!"

At the car (church bells are ringing somewhere, like a movie soundtrack), Joshua's companion pushes him in, slams the door, and hops into the driver's seat. He pulls his gown up over his bony knees and reaches for the key miraculously waiting in the ignition. By now, Joshua has not the faintest idea who the man is or if he is just a man. He cannot really believe he is Jesus Christ—that's absurd—but at the same time he finds it wondrous that a man of the first century knows how to drive this contemporary machine, a skill Joshua himself has not yet mastered. As though reading his thoughts, Jesus—or his impersonator—says: "If God had been the big deal they say He was, I could have ridden into Jerusalem in one of these instead of on a damned donkey! Right?"

They are about to pull out when four motorcyclists, three men and a woman, roar up in front of the church. Two of the men go running inside, then come running out again. As they watch in amazement, they are discovered. *"Down!"* Jesus commands and hauls him roughly below the dashboard. Bullets smash through the windshield. There is a loud crack like a thunderclap and fragments of glass strike the car, followed by louder thumps. "It is not Being that is ineffable," Jesus remarks, uncorking a bottle he has conjured from under the driver's seat and taking a long thirsty drink before offering it to Joshua, who can only shake his head helplessly, "but Becoming."

As the roar of the motorcycles fades away, the lady in the flesh-colored smock comes staggering out of the back door of the church and throws herself into the back seat. "Oh my *God!"* she cries.

"Yes?"

"What's *happening?"*

Young Reverend Jenkins has difficulty finding his voice. When at last he is able, he wheezes: "Could you just drop me off at the bus station, please?"

Georgie's mother slams the door in his face, but when she sees him waving the bills at her she opens it again. "Are you in trouble, Giorgio?" she asks, peering out at the mayor's fancy black car.

"No, Mama, my ship's come in, just like I told you. But I won't be seeing you for a while." She reaches one claw out for the money—"With interest," he says—and he blows her a kiss through the tattered screen door—"Ciao, bella!"—and bounces down the steps back out to the limo. He has just popped in behind the wheel when a loud explosion rocks the neighborhood and the church bells stop ringing. "Hey! That mighta been our church!"

"*Their* church, Georgie. We don't live here no more. Now let's get the fuck outa here while we still can! We've wasted too much time already. And don't go near the goddamned mine. Head over toward Wilmer on the Waterton road, pick up the highway at Daviston."

The Waterton road, a route (alas, poor Ruby) Georgie knows all too well. But they're already too late. Traffic approaches from both lanes, horns blaring, lights flashing, sirens wurping. Un ingorgo. They both swear simultaneously in their separate tongues. "Tieniti le palle!" Georgie shouts, and he throws on the brights and jams his foot down on the accelerator, heading straight at the oncoming traffic, dipping down at the last second into the muddy ditch, then racing along the edges of it, swooping from one side to another at top speed not to get stuck in the muck in the middle. Kicked-up mud, sticks and stones rattle on the underbody. Suddenly, just ahead: a culvert! Trees on the right, double lane of traffic up on the left! But they've reached the back end of the wrong-lane file, or almost. Georgie swings up onto the road at the last possible moment—"Eight ball into the top corner!" he cries—picking up a ding on the last car's bumper and a scrape off the culvert (in his imagination, la bella Marcella is showing her ass or else it's the Virgin Mary's and he is worshipfully kissing it), and they're on the way.

"Fucking Christ!" the mayor gasps, turned stone white. "Hope I packed some spare pants!"

The West Condon police chief, Dee Romano, trapped in the traffic heading into town on the Waterton road, has just witnessed the amazing maneuvers of the mayor's limousine, the madly grinning Georgie Lucci at the wheel, the terrified mayor sitting rigidly beside him, gripping the dashboard with white knuckles, and he wonders if he has just seen Castle being kidnapped. Some shit Dee's city cousins are up to? Dee, leaving the mine hill a few minutes too late to avoid the jam-up, has cut cross-country to a less-used road but found himself sucked up in a noisy congestion of police cars, ambulances, fire engines, and ordinary traffic—the latter headed in the contrary direction, the drivers utterly confused by the horns and bleating sirens. Except for a crossroad or two, there are no pullovers on this old road, just ditches to either side, so when cars stop in panic, everybody stops. His fault. He has called them all here. Only the state police motorcycles, weaving through the snarl, are getting through, and Dee flags one of them down, asks for a ride in, turning the squad car over to Louie Testatonda. "We're going to the Catholic church," he shouts in the state trooper's ear. He has just been on the squawkie to Monk Wallace back at the station, learning that the bikers have not only blown up the power plant and phone exchange, but the rumor reaching him is that they've also attacked the radio station and the hospital, done some serious damage to the National Guard at their high school bivouac area, and now seem to be targeting the churches. "St. Stephen's?" "Yup, purty sure," Monk said. "Big noise summers over there." Now Dee calls back to let Monk know he's hitching a ride in with a state trooper and to ask him to send somebody over to ask his cousin Gina Juliano if she knows anything about the mayor. "Send who?" Voice thin. Can hardly hear him. "I'm all alone here."

Four men are carrying the old priest out of the church and loading him gingerly into Vince Bonali's car, Vince's son Charlie giving the orders, just as Dee swings up on the back of the trooper's motorbike. Dust and smoke are still roiling out of the double front doors like escaping demons. "There's more people hurt inside," Charlie shouts, and two or three guys go running in.

Dee sends the state trooper into the town center, tells him how to find the police station. "If you have to shoot, shoot to kill," he says.

"Where's the goddamned ambulance, Romano?" Charlie wants to know.

"I don't think it is no more. Monk told me the hospital got hit too, and things are burning there. There's some rescue vehicles on the way from towns around, but it's a mess out there on the roads. What happened to the Monsignor?"

"Got here just too late. Old Bags was trying to win the war on his own and got badly shot up. Don't think he'll make it. Those holy-rollers out there on the mine hill were a diversionary tactic, dragging everybody out so as to give their fucking death squad free rein here in town. You can see that now." Maybe, maybe not. Dee has still not linked up the bikers with the cultists in his mind. Sometimes it seems just the opposite, though admittedly there's a family connection. That sonuvabitch Baxter. "We did reach the cunt with the explosives before he could set them off and were beating the shit out of him, and we had two or three of his buddies pinned down up in the loft when some motherfucker in a stocking mask popped up from behind the altar and set off the dynamite with gunfire. Blew the fucking hell out of the place. That did it for their bomber pal and two of our people, and there's others badly hurt in there." Dee peers in at the murky devastation. Bodies, a lot of wreckage. He can see that the rose window has been partly blown out. He should take control of this, but what's happened here has happened, and he's wondering where those godless bastards have gone now. Into town probably, unless they've shot their wad. They're bringing out another victim, still alive, moaning, badly hurt. Old one-armed Bert Martini. "He was brave as hell," Charlie says, "but he's short another peg now and will have to play pinochle with his teeth. Besides the asshole who got turned into hamburger there were at least three others. They got away when the explosives went off, but one of them made the mistake of trying to get back to his bike. His body's over there to the side. There's another stiff out back. Hate to tell you, I think it's your cousin Timo. There may be more. Coming in, we saw a chopper tailing somebody out of town, coming our way. We figured it might be one of those cocksuckers and we laid in wait for him. It was. You could tell by all the shit on his bike. He tried to surrender and kept crossing himself to show he was supposedly a Catholic. Didn't do him any good."

"You mean, you shot him?"

"He got shot." Charlie cracks his knuckles, gum snapping in his jaws. "Like it or not, Romano, you're gonna need guns. You gotta deputize us, give us the legal authority to bring them fuckers in—dead or alive."

"I got state cops here now."

"You don't own 'em."

They won't like it. Cavanaugh especially. But to hell with them. Survival, goddamn it. He nods—"Twenty-four hours," he says—and as Charlie goes loping off to rally his troops, he radios Monk to warn him that the bikers may be headed into town. He can see helicopters hovering there. "Somebody has to get here and get all these people off the streets," Monk says.

"I just sent a state trooper your way, Monk. Keep an eye out, and lots more reinforcements are coming," Dee says. "Did you get hold of Gina?"

"Gotta go. I think I'm gonna get busy here."

"Monk...?"

"Depart in peace, be ye warmed and filled," Jesus says as he drops young Reverend Joshua J. Jenkins off at the darkened bus station. Joshua bangs on the locked door. His precious books! Not far away, he hears the roar of approaching motorcycles. What he feels is the icy chill of the void. Where books are useless. Help! His hat flying, he goes running after the car, now a couple of blocks away, waving his arms frantically—it's like one of those dreams where he's trying to hurry through a sea of mud—desperately hoping Jesus can see him in his rearview mirror.

Out on the highway, far from West Condon, Tommy Cavanaugh's silvery spoke wheels are taking him back to his old university town as if by some will of their own, music blasting to beat back irresolution. He feels some regret, but once you start a move you have to see it through, even if it means committing a foul. Running out on his mother bothers him most. For all the religious craziness that has distanced him from her, he knows she is suffering and that he should not leave her. It's his father's fault. When he was a kid they used to sit around on street corners or front porches playing the what-if accident game: Suppose you were in a lifeboat after a shipwreck and both your parents fell half-conscious from the boat and were drowning and you could only save one of them, which would you save? He usually joined the others in choosing his mother, but he loved his dad, maybe even more, and was torn more than he wished to show. A rule of the game was that if you waited for more than five seconds to decide, they both would die. In his mind's eye, he could see them foundering and he always counted the seconds in his head to let his father live as long as possible. To hell with him now; he'll have to hack it on his own. He tried to reach Sally before pulling out to apologize for his obnoxious behavior at the motel—shouldn't have left her there, called her what he did—but only got her mother, who said Sally was not at home. Was there a message? There was none. He has met several Army trucks going the other way and now another convoy passes. Out of curiosity he switches to a news station. And, tires squealing, makes a U-turn.

Signora Abruzzi, reading the movie magazine for the third time, is shocked, shocked! The scandalous lives these people lead! You would think God would deal more harshly with such indecency. Make a public example of them. Thank Heavens for the Last Judgment! Though it's almost painful to think that they could repent before then and get away with all this sinning. Where's the justice in that? It makes her angry. A young man in uniform banging in through the beauty shop front door and asking for Lucy Smith startles her. She's not deaf, he needn't shout. She tells him that he should mind his manners. Then adds that Mrs. Smith went to the bank with Linda, and he runs out again without even thanking her. What the world is coming to!

The mayor's secretary, Gina Juliano, is waiting for a telephone call from the President. The mayor was in early today and more demanding than she'd ever seen him, sending her away on ceaseless errands, asking her to go bring him coffee after coffee which he just let go cold, barking at her if she asked him any questions. He grabbed up the phone whenever it rang and sometimes he shouted into it and sometimes he muttered like he didn't want to be heard and once she even heard him speaking in a high voice like an old lady. Then that ne'er-do-well Giorgio Lucci, a bad-apple second cousin on her mother's side, turned up at city hall with his stupid grin smeared all over his face, and the mayor said they had a very important meeting and on no account were they to be disturbed. *On no account, sweetheart,* he repeated, jabbing a finger at her. It's that crazy cult out on the mine hill, he said. They're at it again and he's having to do something about it. Something big. He told her he was expecting a very important call from Washington—from *Number One,* he said—so she mustn't leave her desk for any reason, but he let her go use the ladies' room before he locked himself and Georgie in his office. When that call comes, that's when she can knock on his door. What a thrill! She can see why he has been so jumpy. Even though you can't see people on the telephone, she freshened up her lipstick and combed her hair. She made herself busy at her desk, waiting for the call, but then the lights went out and her typewriter stopped working, so what could she do? There was filing to be done, but she'd have to leave her desk, and he told her not to, so she took up her knitting (a matching bonnet and booties; her teenage daughter has already gone too far, and there you have it) and thought about what she'd tell the President when he phoned. Of course she'd tell him how she admires him and voted for him (though voting is something she usually forgets to do, what difference does it make?), but she'll also mention her secretarial skills just in case.

The phone did ring, and her heart jumped, but it was only her friend Francesca out at the hospital, calling the mayor's office about the power outage. She said she'd tried to reach the power company but no one answered and can the mayor help? Gina said she was sure it was only temporary because of the storm and that the mayor was in a meeting. When Francesca started to tell her about old Nazario Moroni dying overnight, Gina had to interrupt to say that she was really sorry but she couldn't tie up the phone because the mayor was expecting a very important call. Then the phone went dead and she wondered if Francesca thought she was lying just to get rid of her and hung up on her, so she tried to call back, but, no, it really wasn't working.

So now how could the President get through? She wondered if she should tell the mayor. He said he was absolutely not to be disturbed and he could be very unpleasant if you did something he asked you not to do, but he was also waiting for a call that now could not be made. He is only her second mayor, because she has only been able to work at all since the mine tragedy when her husband Mario died. She liked Mr. Whimple better, but even though Mr. Castle uses bad language and talks very loud, he is easy enough to get on with and often lets her go home early. He is something of a rascal, but they all are. Probably the President, too, if truth be told. She loves the job, but Mario would never have approved. He wanted her to be a housewife and a mother and always to be at home when he wanted her, even though he almost never was there himself except to eat and sleep. They all had to go to Mass every Sunday, even the tiny ones, he insisted on that, too, even though he was sometimes too worn out to go himself. She and Mario spent more than a dozen years together, but though she washed his pit clothes, prepared his dinner buckets, and slept in the same bed with him, she can't say she really knew him. She keeps a photograph of him here on her desk beside a porcelain statue of the Virgin that he gave her once for her birthday, but it's a picture of a stranger.

Gina's mother was the wife of a coalminer and she always said, Gina, whatever you do, don't marry a coalminer, but then she did. Well, she was a coalminer's daughter, it was what she knew, but her mother was right. Gina kept trying to get Mario to better himself and to learn another trade, one that would keep him at home more, but he was not bright or disciplined enough, none of the Julianos are. He wasn't really good-looking either—he had the meaty Juliano face and big ears—but he was a good football player and that was a big deal back then. It still is. Her daughter's boyfriend is on the football team. Mario was also a good Catholic boy and when he learned he was going to be a father he did the right thing, and she has always been grateful for that. He was a little resentful about it, though, and didn't hesitate to play around if the occasion arose; Catholic boys don't take the sin of fornication very seriously. As she put on weight she could see that she was becoming less attractive to him and had no choice but to slim down or let him look elsewhere, and it was just too hard to lose so many pounds. And besides, she wasn't all that enthusiastic about having more babies, even if making them had, for a moment that was always much too short, its fun side.

Mario was one of the seven who barricaded themselves off the night of the mine accident and left an undershirt tacked up outside with their names on it. *COME AND GET US*, it said. But they came and got them too late and only Giovanni Bruno was still alive, though he didn't even have his name on the shirt, and that's why all those people are out at the mine hill today. If they only knew Giovanni Bruno like she knew him, they wouldn't be making such fools of themselves. Faith is a good thing, it never hurts anybody, but it would be better if people all believed the same religion and didn't keep inventing new ones. The undershirt is in the mining museum up in the state capital. As Mario's widow, Gina went up there for the presentation, and she was famous for a while and was interviewed on television in her black dress with her children around her. And she did miss him, though mostly because, with the children to raise, she needed his income, which is why, even though she could just see Mario scowling down on her from Heaven, she took this job in city hall, thanks to her cousin Demetrio in the police department and the child-minding help she gets from the family, especially her Aunt Delfina Romano, who never married and always said marriage was the ruin of women. For a while after the disaster, all the younger widows were competing for the same single men, but there weren't enough of them to go around what with so many getting killed in the mine, it was like musical chairs, and Gina had a weight problem that disadvantaged her. Also three small children. Men don't get excited about other men's children. She was briefly wooed by one or two guys who remembered her when she was cuter, but nothing came of it. Her heart wasn't really in it. Some of her friends did remarry, but mostly those have not been happy marriages.

It was still cloudy and dark when the lights went out, but now the sun is pouring through the high dusty windows. She'd clean them, at least from the inside, but her boss told her not to leave the desk. *Whatever you do, don't leave the desk!* What if the phone came back on and the President rang and she was up a ladder and couldn't get down in time to answer it? Though maybe all that was just a fib and she might as well go home like the sheriff's radio dispatcher Tessie Lawson, whom she saw walking through the corridor with her new sister-in-law, leaning into each other and giggling like schoolgirls. They are always laughing together over some private joke or other (now it was something about "taking cover"); it can be quite annoying.

City hall is a heavy stone building, often called "the Fort" for not much leaks in from the world outside nor is much distributed to it, but Gina can hear beyond its thick walls the muffled sound of helicopters and motorcycles and sirens. Is something happening? A distant boom rattles the windows. Could be a last clap of thunder, but you never know. It has been quiet in Mr. Castle's office for a long time, and Gina decides to risk the mayor's anger by knocking and telling him that the phone is not working and she has to go to the hospital to be with her cousin Concetta Moroni because Concetta's father-in-law has died. Whenever she says something like that her boss always says it's like everyone in town is one of her cousins—here he usually adds in a few swearword modifiers—and that's very nearly true, at least in her part of town. Her own children would be related to her in some way even if she hadn't given birth to them herself. She gets no answer and knocks again, louder this time, and calls out his name. Still nothing. She can hear running footsteps out in the corridors, doors slamming. She fishes her key out of the desk and opens his door: no one there. They must have left by the other door, the one at the back that leads out into the hall where the men's room is. The mayor was upset about what was happening out at the mine hill; maybe that's where they went. Or they're out there in the street where the noise is. But he could have let her know. If the President had called, what would she have told him? Well, that it was turning into a nice day here and he should come for a visit, she could show him around. The children will be at the pool by now, so with the mayor away and phones and power out, the afternoon is hers. The furniture store is having a summer sale, which is more or less a continuation of their winter sale. Maybe she'll make an offer on that pretty stuffed chair in the window with the orange-and-green flowered pattern, give her daughter the old red one now that she'll soon be setting up a home of her own. Paychecks are late this month, probably because of the holiday, but her credit is good. Desperate as they are, they'd probably sell it to her even if she had no credit at all. Then she'll go pick up some nice hamburger and fresh buns and a bag of charcoal and marshmallows to roast and have a picnic supper tonight in the backyard. Invite Aunt Delfina and her daughter's boyfriend, get him thinking in the family way, only hoping Aunt Delfina doesn't chase him off. The President is welcome to join them. He can wear Mario's old "Mister Good-Lookin' Is Cookin'" apron and grill the burgers. If she has time, she could haul the old baby crib out of the basement and clean it and repaint it. Decorate it with little colored stickers from the dimestore. She'll drop by there on the way home, and at the same time she can buy some more blue yarn (she's betting on a boy). The booties and bonnet are almost done; she can start a matching jacket. There's lots of time. She picks up her needles and knitting but, just as she tucks them in her bag, there is a sudden flash of light—

The blast rocks the Fort, followed closely by other thunderous bursts, one on top of another, as if in imitation of the fireworks finale on Saturday night: the fire station, the post office, the police station. There is shouting, screaming, the rush off the street for open shop doors before they're slammed shut, the crackle of gunfire peppering the gaps between explosions. Shopkeepers throw themselves down behind their counters, motorists press their accelerators to the floor, arriving reporters and cameramen turn on their heels, abandoning their equipment. Storefront windows shatter, streetlights and neon signs are blasted away. Somewhere a dog yips frantically. *"God is good!"* shouts a mountainous undershirted man astraddle a motorcycle bearing official government plates as he speeds away from the exploding courthouse.

Grinning a wide, whiskery grin he roars past the Chamber of Commerce offices, shooting out its plate-glass windows. A fish-eyed biker in fluttering black rags rolls down Main Street, the near-naked girl behind him splashing gasoline from a can on the hoods of all the cars and pickups they pass. They are followed by a strange glassy-eyed creature in red boots, loin cloth, and feathers with a wagging topknot rising from his shaved painted head, bearing the Number of the Beast tattooed on his bony shoulders and wielding a flaming torch he touches to the cars the girl has doused, setting the whole street on fire, mini-explosions counterpointing the larger ones. *"Five minutes!"* shouts a motorcyclist in a black stocking mask, as he takes aim at a bald chubby man in a stained butcher's apron rushing from the barbershop to try to douse the flames on an old beat-up Dodge coupe parked out front; he doesn't get that far. A dark stocky woman and a goateed biker with goggles, both wearing coalminers' helmets, leap off their motorcycles and smash their way into the corner drugstore, the woman covering for the man—there is a great crashing and tinkling of glass as she fires away, the mirror behind the soda fountain falling like a melting glacier—while he strips the shelves behind the pharmacy counter, dumping everything into his leather backpack. Out on the street, one of the burning pickups circles about, unbraked and driverless. It careens over a curb, caroms off a corner street sign and mailbox, and piles into a furniture store, setting it alight. At the liquor store, where the staff has taken refuge in the cellar, racks of bottles are tipped out and shot up and a lit cigarette is flicked into the mix. An elderly man in carpenter's overalls emerges from the hardware store with a shotgun, takes aim at the begoggled cyclist speeding away from the drugstore, the buckshot thudding into the rider's leather backpack, clanging off his mining helmet. The man turns to duck back into the store, but the masked rider following behind on a ghostly gray motorcycle draws a revolver from a hip holster and does not miss. He brakes to a stop, takes two-handed aim, fires five more times. *"Four minutes!"* he yells. The first out-of-town police units to arrive encounter heavy fire and the occasional hurled stick of dynamite. Even when taking cover, they find themselves being shot at; it takes them just a moment, but too long a moment for some, to discover the sniper up in the top floor of the town's derelict hotel: an elusive gunman in a golden guayabera and tight pants, colorful headband, who appears and disappears tauntingly from window to window as if there were a dozen of him, shouting out what are probably obscenities in a foreign language, then firing from where least expected. The troopers return fire but without conviction, staying hunkered down. A great many sirens can be heard approaching from all directions. They can wait until those guys get here. They were told there was trouble here, but nothing like this. The cyclist with the painted head, topknot and feathers smashes a ground-level window of the hotel with his rifle butt and springs lithely through with his weapons and backpack. An unmarked helicopter swoops low, drawing high-powered rifle fire from a biker with a gray braid. It lurches, continues to try to fly like a wounded bird, slowly loses altitude. The biker fires again, then swivels, leaning on his good leg, to aim at a second helicopter wheeling past overhead. More come clappety-clapping in from the east, where the county airport lies. Several attackers try to force their way into the First National Bank, kicking at the locked door, shooting at the lock, losing patience as time ticks away. The masked biker swings up, black head with eyeholes blackly framed by his high leather collar. He seems to be everywhere at once. *"Three minutes!"* he shouts, and hauls some packs of dynamite from the silvery saddlebags draped over his back fender and tosses them to the others. The acting sheriff has thrown himself down behind some trash cans in the back alley as bullets ricochet off the brick walls overhead and he now picks his way hurriedly down the alley, scuttling close to the walls, toward the bank's rear service door, hoping one of the skeleton keys on his key ring will open it. Inside the bank, the city manager, having abruptly dismissed the disgruntled client when the first blast was heard in the street and snapped at the women for not having warned him, races up the back steps to arm himself and to prepare for possible flight. The bank is solid and should be safe, but if he has to leave, there are things he must destroy or take with him. And opportunities may arise. The first emergency fire truck reaches the blazing street. It is met with rifle fire and a dynamite pack tossed through the cab window. The pool hall is hit. An Italian social club. When the movie house is dynamited, its antiquated marquee drops, biting the street like false uppers, letters flying like broken molars. Inside the nearby bar and grill, its walls pocked with the bullets that have crashed through the front window, they hear someone frantically banging on the back alley door, but after the loud overhead crash a few moments before—half the ceiling plaster fell: *"Holy Christ! We're being bombed!"* the dimestore owner wailed, scrunched down behind a table he had tipped over to hide behind—they are afraid and shrink back. The proprietor, hearing a woman shrieking, ignores the pleas of his customers and opens the door. It is the wife of the former Chamber of Commerce secretary. "Is Jim here?" she cries, staggering in. The scar-faced man squatting in one corner with a tray over his head points at the body on the floor. She screams. The body stirs. "Hello, dear," it says. Pushing in behind the woman before the proprietor can slam the door limps a grimacing man, fierce with rage, and the others duck behind their tipped tables again. There is a tumbler of vodka on the bar, its ice melted, sitting alone in its evaporating puddle like a minor miracle amid the shattered glass, and the man grabs it up and tosses it down, slams the tumbler back on the bar, explaining when he can get his breath that he's the pilot of the helicopter that has fallen on their roof and he thinks his leg is broken. "Those assholes were *shooting* at me! I don't shoot anything except *pictures* for fuck sake!" The bank's owner has at last fought his way through the clogged traffic, has parked behind the smoldering ruins of the bus station, and is making his way on foot toward the center, rifle in hand, when an out-of-town police car stops him, the officers pointing weapons at him, ordering him to drop his gun. He does so, tells them angrily who he is. "We're just losing time, goddamn it!" They ask for identification. "No, it ain't damp squibs," one of the bikers in front of the bank door is grumbling, a shaggy hayseed with yellow teeth, the fingers on his right hand in a splint, suspenders holding his pants up, "it's the fucken matches." A tall mustachioed man dressed in satin-striped tuxedo pants, a dazzling red T-shirt and a black silk tie, swastikas on his upper arms, produces a silver cigarette lighter. The sirens encircling the town are now as loud as the roar of the motorcycles in the center. Two military helicopters with multiple machine gun and rocket mounts have appeared and are hovering overhead, adding to the racket. Radio contact is established with them and they are asked by the police units on the ground to try to take out the sniper in the derelict hotel. The acting sheriff is pinned down on the back steps of the bank in a shootout with the masked motorcyclist, who is firing at him from behind the corner of the building, when he suddenly hears someone approaching from behind. He wheels round to blow the attacker away but sees in the nick of time that it's a young unarmed man in a grocer's apron with his hands raised. "My wife's in there!" he gasps. "Mine too," says the sheriff and tosses the kid his rifle. "Cover me!" In an instant, the kid is across the alley in a doorway, firing at the masked biker, driving him back. But none of the keys on the sheriff's ring seem to work. *"One minute!"* the masked man calls out, pulling away from the alley fire fight. *"Mufflers on!"* A scrawny unshaven straw-headed fellow with one arm in a sling ambles down out of the Legion Hall, where he has spent the night on the floor. Grinning his gap-toothed grin, he surveys the scene through the scrim of his piercing hangover. Biggest fucking bonfire he has ever seen, hairy dudes on motorbikes storming around, raising hell, bodies here and there like bundles dropped by rag merchants. Not far away, there's a man under a flaming store awning sprawled beside a prehistoric shotgun. He picks it up. Not easy to fire the thing with one arm, but he figures he might as well shoot a few people because that's what's happening and why not. There's a guy up a telephone pole watching the action down below. He shouldn't be up there. He gets him in his sights, imagines the fall (slow-mo, like in the movies), but does not pull the trigger. This old shotgun probably has such a kick it could break his other shoulder. Anyway, it's not his nature. "Bang!" he says and laughs, lowering the gun. The Woolworths under the Legion Hall is shot up and abandoned, the door agape, small fires erupting, so he goes in and raids the candy counter for breakfast, helps himself to a change of underwear and bright purple and green socks with white toes and other useful and redeemable items. As the police chief reaches the station, too late to be of help to his duty officer, the police and emergency vehicles he called in from other towns are beginning to arrive in large numbers and overhead the army helicopters are firing round after round into the old hotel. Along the way the chief has come upon the state trooper who gave him a ride in, his throat slit, his motorcycle missing. He watches as a patrol car driven by a friend of his from the next county blows up less than half a block away, and he spies the missing motorcycle, in its saddle a huge bearded man in a strapped undershirt and leather vest, now pulling away from the blast: a big target, but he gets off only a couple of shots before the street is rocked by a tremendous explosion on the bank corner, a signal for the city manager up on the second floor to head down for the back door, on the double. He slams out, bowling over a man knuckled down behind it, sending him tumbling into the alley. The city manager levels a revolver at his head, but the young man across the alley shouts out: *"No! No! It's the sheriff!"* The sheriff has drawn a revolver of his own and all three men have weapons pointed at each other. A blink. Recognition. The city manager jumps down into the alley, a bag and a bundle of folders under his arm, and sprints away while the sheriff and grocer rush into the bank. Outside the front door, which is no more, the masked man shouts: *"Time's up! Forget it! Let's go! Now!"* The tall biker in the black glasses, suspendered tux pants, tie and crimson tee, calmly raises his hand and says in a precise commanding voice: "Go, and may the Big One be with you!" The others hesitate, then leap on their bikes, tearing off in all directions, gunfire chasing them. The man combs his hair and moustache with his fingers, adjusts his black silk tie and sunglasses, and strides into the bank through the floating dust with the stiff erect bearing of a mechanical tin soldier, carrying under his arm neatly tied packages to which he is applying a small blue flame. The banker, freed at last from the bumbling cops, reaches Main Street. A vast devastation, blazing cars and buildings, a scatter of dead and wounded amid the glass and rubble, police swarming in, ambulances, fire engines, helicopters overhead slamming the old hotel with rocket fire, another copter fallen in a rumpled heap on the flat roof of the bar and grill. The tall man in the tux pants and luminous red shirt is just disappearing into the gaping hole where the bank door once stood. Too late and too far away, but the banker fires off a shot anyway. He catches a glimpse of a biker in goggles and miner's helmet streaking down an alley. Not in a position to shoot at him, but in the street where the alley opens out many are, including the chief of police, white with rage. The biker is gunned down in the percussive crossfire of nearly two dozen armed personnel, all banging away at once, while in the bank the terrified clerks and their customers shrink back from the robotic figure in black glasses who has entered through the hole that was once the front door. *"In the name of all that's holy and all that's unholy!"* he cries out, and like a newspaper boy tossing his folded papers onto front porches, he distributes his lit packages. This is what the sheriff's wife hears before someone lands on top of her and the world ends around her. As she crumples to the floor—an explosion! another!—she is thinking: They were right! It's really the end! Her poor children! One lit package is winging its way toward a woman huddled with her howling baby behind the water fountain when it is plucked out of the air by the young grocer and former high school basketball star, leaping high as if for a jump shot, and in the same movement flipped back at its thrower, terminating the assault with a final massive blast. A hot dusty silence descends, broken only by groans. Things are winding down outside, too. The bikers are dead or have vanished. The hotel has fallen silent after the helicopter fusillade. A senior police officer assembles an assault team to enter the building and they are gathered at the front door, trying to force entry, when the feathered biker with the topknot springing from his shaved red head appears on the damaged roof with an armful of strapped dynamite packets, which, while bellowing out his praise of God—some god, praise of an eccentric sort—he lights and drops on the state troopers and neighboring town police below, now frantically scattering. The army helicopters, distracted by the fleeing bikers, come clattering urgently back. The biker greets them with an Indian war dance, leaping and howling, beating his bared chest; the helicopters spare no firepower but obliterate him with rocket fire, leaving nothing on the roof except leg stubs in tooled red boots.

To while away the time on their way to the airport and out of the state and country, Georgie Lucci and the mayor have been trading whore stories. Which when real mostly depress Georgie, so he has been inventing a few bigcity yarns, borrowing on the plots of blue movie queens like Nellie Nympho and Red-Hot Ruby. "Ruby lipsticked her asshole and jiggled it around, and with your hands bound behind your back you were supposed to kiss it before poking it. It was like bobbing for apples."

The mayor's laughter booms. "You're fulla shit, Georgie, but your stories are better than mine. Christ. Since I got married, the occasional cheap whore is all I've had. Of course, all women are whores, so I guess that's *all* I've had or coulda hoped to've had. And I can't honestly say I've ever had a good one."

"I could introduce you to a few."

"Nah. What I need is some child sex slaves. They tell me Brazil is full of them. Dime a dozen. Ever fuck a little kid?"

"Not since I was one myself."

"Your kid sister or little cuz, you mean. Rec room romps when mommy's away. That don't count and can mess you up. I'm talking about sex market specialties. Clean, dressed, and prettily packaged consumables." Maury Castle's loud grating voice and nasty imagination are getting under Georgie's bark. "Like buying choice baby lamb in the meat market."

"Not my style, I guess. I go more for the fleshy bargains."

"Yeah, I know what you mean. I married one. Beachball britches. Ever think about getting married, Georgie?"

He hesitates. Shouldn't talk about this with a guy like Castle. "Yeah. Once." He seems to see her bent over a water fountain. His high school sweetheart. In a pleated skirt. Or a crisp yellow frock. Actually, in nothing at all. Her sweet little buttocks. His hand between them. Her terrible vulnerability. "She was…different." The way she looked up at him after he'd saved her from that newspaper fuck. So intense, so giving, a whole-body look, total surrender. But so still…

"What happened? Cold feet?"

"No." Can't stop himself. He's fucking starting to cry. "She died."

"Jesus, Georgie, sorry to hear that." That night out at the Brunist camp, the night of the bees and the fireworks when he was trapped and being shot at and he was pleading for mercy from everyone from God to Lady Luck—she was there. She *was* Lady Luck. He remembers this clearly now. "She probably did you a fucking favor, though. Did you get in her pants before she kicked off?"

What a question. He hates this filthy sonuvabitch. In his mind's eye, though, there were no pants he could get into. She was like Eve. Spread for him. La bella… "No. We were saving it for…you know…"

"Big mistake. Unless somebody else dicked her, the poor little cunt died without ever getting laid. What kinda fucking life is that? You owed it to her. You let her down."

Coglione. Maybe he should spin the car in front of a big semi so it gets hit broadside on the passenger side. But he might get hurt himself. And even if not, how would he get away with the pile of cash in the back seat? This vehicle is what he's got.

The fire chief has reached the town center with his exhausted crew and has half a dozen volunteer fire trucks from the towns around at his disposal, but water pressure from the sabotaged hydrants is low and some incautious units have suffered demoralizing casualties. It is a hot day, hotter here. They beat the small fires out or smother them with foam. A few of the larger ones are brought under control in city hall, the post office, and the fire station itself, but in the untenanted Main Street shops, the liquor store, the furniture store and pawn shop, the surging flames rage unchecked, spreading now from building to building, and torched cars and trucks, no longer worth saving, are allowed to burn themselves out. The police chief's hunting dog—retrieved from one of them and half-blind, its coat on fire—immediately attacks its rescuers and must be destroyed. Crews lift the dead off the street and deposit them temporarily on the tables of the bombed-out pool hall and on the sorting-room floor of the demolished post office, where they are covered with gray canvas mailbags, all of it recorded by grimacing television and radio reporters, many now wearing combat helmets and kerchiefs over their faces. Ambulance teams gather up the wounded and wheel them urgently off to the city hospital, guided by local townsfolk jumping aboard to accompany friends and relatives.

The banker, his face marked by flying debris when he rushed toward the bank at the moment of the final blast, grabs one of the ambulance crews and together they stretcher out the injured from the bank. Among them: Archie Wetherwax's wife Emily, pinned under a fallen desk. The Rotary Club president, Gus Baird, in bad shape, midriff bubbling. Tommy's young friend from the Italian grocery, out cold, his face bloody, his wife wailing over him. Also the acting sheriff and his wife, looking bruised and stunned though both on their feet, the wife staring blankly, muttering to herself, shrinking from everyone, even her husband. Smith must have left the mine about the same time Ted did but somehow beat him back. Smith tells him about Piccolotti's heroism and personally organizes an ambulance for him. Those who can walk are helped to police cars, which are also filling up with wounded off the street. Ted has a word of encouragement for each. For the moment, the dead in here are left in the rubble where they lie, ambulance blankets tossed over them. With a gaping hole where the front door used to be, the place is vulnerable to looting. He'll have to secure the tills and vault, gather up everything of value and lock it away in his office. Nail something up over the shattered windows and block off the door.

He's just starting the lockdown when Dee Romano stops in to check out the damage. He kicks at what's left of the bomber in tux pants, gives a terse angry report. Monk Wallace is dead. The mayor's secretary, Dee's favorite cousin. Others at the post office, county courthouse, hospital, phone exchange. A nephew from the power plant hospitalized with a bullet in his lungs. The mayor? He's gone, fled or kidnapped. Dee tells him what he saw out on the Waterton road, mentioning in passing that no one employed by the city has been paid yet this month. Father Baglione, he says, is in critical condition at the hospital. The church was dynamited, people killed and maimed. His second cousin, Timo Spontini, was shot down in the parking lot. Apparently the old priest defended the church with sheer bravado, facing the bombers on his own with bells and incense. Ted lights up, offers the chief one. The chief shakes his head. "None of this woulda happened if them goddamned holyrollers had not come back here," he says through clenched jaws. "But I'm taking care of that." He says nothing more when asked, just glares coldly. Ted likes Romano, trusts him, but feels a new distance between them. Almost as if Romano blames him somehow for the attack on his church. Ted thinks back on the scene at the mine hill. "Wait a minute," he says. "You mean, Charlie Bonali's gang?" Romano leaves him without reply.

Ted glances at his watch: barely past noon. Can it get any worse than this? It can get worse. He knows what Bonali is capable of. And the Brunists are in league with Suggs' rightwing militia. He saw something of a battle scene dress rehearsal this morning. Will he have to go out there again? How can he not? But who will care? Ted has never known despair, too much of a fighter for that, and a dogged believer in the prevailing power of the right, but standing there in the ghastly ruins of his family bank, he's at the edge of it. He has never thought of God as the Almighty but as something more mysterious than that. The ground of all being, as someone has said. Something like that. Well, the mystery has just deepened. A young teller lies a short distance away in a scatter of bills and coins. Daughter of friends of his. Might have been Stacy, had she still been here, so he has to be glad she's gone. But he has lost her just the same. Lost his wife, his son, and now his bank and all these innocent people. He has failed them. He has called the plays and none have worked. The bank is insured, of course. But is it covered for this kind of madness? Does it matter? Does he really want to reopen? He realizes how easy it is for lives to have bitter endings and is determined not to let that happen. This town is a mess, but it's his town and he can't walk away from it. He will not let himself be defeated, even when victory is hollow. That's what he tells himself, in the old way, team captain up against it, back to the goal line, standing firm, jaw a-jut, shoulders braced. But his heart is sinking. Fuck it, he thinks, wiping the tears away with his sleeve. It's finished. Then he feels an arm around his shoulder. "C'mon, Dad," his son says. "Let's clean this up."

The bank explosion sent night duty police officer Bo Bosticker leaping with a scream out of one of his coalpit nightmares, a persistent haunting from his mining days, the leap taking him out of his bed and onto his damaged knees and thence to his face on the floor. He lies there, wondering whether what he heard was real or part of the dream. For Bo, a leap from sleep is a mighty one from the abyssal deep and is violent by nature, for he is a heavy sleeper, known for his powerful snore. He has had a number of women move in with him over the years, then move out pretty quickly with bags under their eyes. He never leaves sleep with a light bounce—it's more like clawing up from a deepshaft grave—unless rocketed out in terror like today. A glance at his watch tells him it is still early in the day, that he should get in a couple more hours of shut-eye if he's going to last through the night watch, and he considers doing that right here on the floor where he lies. But his knees hurt and he is hungry and by now he hears the sirens, the helicopters, smells smoke in the air. Not slag smoke. Wood smoke. He also seems to catch a whiff of something that reminds him of entering the mine in the old days after the shotfirers had done their thing. So he pulls on his uniform shirt and pants and launches forth from his little house down by the old railroad tracks to limp into town on his wooden crutches. It is a hot sunny day—the sort Bo rarely sees at this hour o'clock—yet damp underfoot, and he remembers it was raining when he went to bed. Long before he gets to where he's going, he perceives that there has been a serious amount of vandalism while he's been sleeping: a grade school with its windows smashed, spouting fire hydrants, a church on fire. The military helicopters overhead seem to be firing at something right in the middle of town.

The closer he gets to the center, the worse the damage is, the thicker the smoke now clouding out the sun. The post office is a smoldering shell. He hobbles in on his crutches for a look. There are people on the sorting-room floor covered with gray mailbags and other people carrying on over them. Bo wants to ask them what's been happening, but they are mostly too hysterical. *"Everybody's dead!"* one of them screams, shaking her fist at him. An older cop he doesn't know stands guard over the place and Bo asks him what's up and the guy says he doesn't know, he just got here himself, something to do with a bunch of religious fanatics. He says he hasn't seen anything like it since the last war.

That's what it looks like. An old war movie. Main Street lit up with burning cars and trucks and many of the buildings on fire, their windows smashed, black graffiti sprayed on them. Fire trucks, police cars, ambulances parked at whatever angle, mostly empty inside, their lights whirling. Flat water hoses snaking about underfoot. The helicopters are pounding the old hotel for no clear reason. One of them is parked on top of Mick's Bar & Grill. The old moviehouse marquee is down, which makes the building look like it has dropped its pants. The bank has also been hit. Seems to have lost its front door, the whole corner just a big hole. Some of the police cars and motorcycles rev up their motors and pull out. Bo asks one of them where they're going. "Out to the mine hill! The ones who did it are out there!"

He runs into Charlie Bonali loading a bunch of weapons into some young guy's car. The guns look like they might have come from the station. He should ask about that, but Charlie is wearing a bent tarnished badge and Bo isn't sure of his authority or even exactly what is going on. "Where's Monk?" Bo asks. "You'll find him over at the pool hall," says Charlie, pulverizing a wad of gum in his jaws. "On one of the tables." "What the heck's he doing? Resting?" "Yeah. In peace." He's pretty sure he knows what Bonali means by that, but he doesn't want to ask.

He heads to the station to report in. Looks like it's going to be a tough day; they're going to need him early. It has already been a tough day. He figures he should fuel up first with some meatloaf or else a hot turkey sandwich, but at Doc's drugstore, which is one of the few buildings not burning, they're bringing a body out. "Dead," they tell him when he asks. "Shot down in cold blood." Well, maybe they can call the Italian grocery and have them send something over.

The first face that Angela sees, peering woozily up over her shoulder, is that of her friend Joey Castiglione. He's holding her hand, which is cuffed to the cot. They're in some kind of van. She hears a siren. "Take it easy," he says. "You'll be all right." All right? Why shouldn't she be all right? Where is she? Kicked. She feels like she's been kicked. Who did that? She's lying on her tummy, a pillow under her, her numb bottom raised. It hurts, other parts, too, but distantly as though they don't really belong to her. She can't move. She thinks her spine may be broken. "Where are we going?" she asks. "To the hospital. We'll be there soon. Ramona told me you'd gone downtown, so when all hell started breaking loose, I came looking." "Ramona?" She remembers something happening in the drugstore, people slamming in, she was trying to duck under the table, crawl somewhere. "Joey? Have I been shot?" He grins, gives her hand a little squeeze. "Yeah. But if it was going to happen, you got hit in the right place." She feels very sleepy. Her eyes keep crossing. "Joey? Thanks a lot, Joey. You didn't have to do this." "Hey. It's worth it just for the view alone."

When Vince Bonali learns that his daughter is being ambulanced in with bullet wounds, he breaks down in tears. He is down in the dimly lit basement canteen, sitting with the Ferreros and Concetta Moroni (no coffee, the percolators have been turned off to save electricity), and his old friend Sal wraps an arm around his shoulders and says, "Easy, Vince. Easy. It's gonna be okay." "It's too much, Sal!" he sobs. He feels foolish, especially in front of the two women, but he can't help it. "It's too *fucking* much!" He hauls out his handkerchief and blows his nose loudly. He and Sal have brought Father Baglione here in Vince's car; the old priest is in the emergency room with multiple bullet wounds and is not expected to pull through. Gabriela and Concetta are out here because old Nonno Moroni died last night, and both of them are in a fury about what happened to Nonno's body (Gaby tears up whenever it's mentioned) and are talking about asking Gabriela's city lawyer cousin Panfilo to take legal action. Lights pop on in one corner of the canteen, where Doc Lewis, looking shattered, is being interviewed live for TV news. When they bring Angie in, Vince is waiting at the ambulance door. Joey Castiglione is with her. That's good news. Joey winks unsmilingly and gives him a thumbs-up. He feels better.

Out on the Mount of Redemption, the self-appointed Brunist Defender Dot Blaurock feels woozy with hunger. Breakfast didn't amount to much. It's getting hot and there's no proper place to relieve yourself out here, though many have been doing so behind the backhoes or their cars or on the backside of the Mount or wherever. Young Darren Rector, still getting a lot of mileage for striking down the false prophet on this very spot two days ago, feels certain that they're here for a purpose as yet unrevealed, a purpose that may be thwarted if they desert the Mount, and he suggests they open up the mine building restrooms as they did on the anniversary of the Day of Redemption. A good idea, but no one has the key. That guy McDaniel, Mr. Suggs' strip mine manager and newly appointed deputy acting sheriff, says they should stay here. They could get trapped in the camp, and they're better off holding the high ground. But what if those helicopters on the horizon should come this way? They'd be sitting ducks on this open hillside.

No, Dot is one of those who is ready to call it a day. They've made their point, they've achieved the summit, they've held their memorial service—better to go back to the camp, try to find something to eat. Besides, she has squatter's rights to the camp sickbay cabin and she doesn't want anyone taking that away from her. "Take no thought for your life, what ye shall eat, or what ye shall drink; nor yet for your body, what ye shall put on," the preachers say, quoting Lord Jesus, the Son of Man, the one they're all waiting for, "for is not the life more than meat, and the body than raiment?" Sure. But they're starving, and they can't hold it much longer. The Son of Man never talked about what to do if you can't find a restroom. There's not much food left at the camp, but they can harvest the rest of the garden, eat it up before the Rapture comes. The camp is full of birds and animals that can be hunted. God will provide. One of her fellow Defenders says they could take up a collection and go pick up some hotdogs and buns and soda pop at the highway supermarket. Several of the women volunteer to do the cooking. Spirits rise. Then some terrified people arrive down on the mine road, jump out of their cars, and come running up the Mount to join them. *"It's the end of the world!"* they wail. *"It really is!"* Sobbing and blubbering, they tell them about the demons on motorcycles, the bombs, the guns, the fires, the slaughter, the destruction. *"They's hunderds of them!" "They're everywhere!" "They've blowed up all the churches!" "Ours is burnt plumb to the ground, Abner!"* People start praying in earnest. It looks like a long day. Maybe even an endless one. *"Now is the judgment of this world!"* cries Abner Baxter. "Mom, when is Jesus coming?" Mattie asks. "Soon," she says hopefully. And then He does.

With the improving weather, Glenda has taken the children—hers, Hazel's, Wanda's and a few others temporarily abandoned by people who arrived at the camp this morning—down to the garden to collect fruit and vegetables for their lunch and do a little weeding. Hunk has killed and gutted a chicken they will all share, hoping that the others over on the Mount of Redemption do not come back before they are done. Not even Jesus could stretch a chicken out among so many, and anyway, he's not yet around to work such marvels, were he able. She also has some canned and packaged goods that Ludie Belle Shawcross gave her before she left, but Glenda intends to save them for the hard times ahead that she foresees. This is not prophecy or fortune telling, it's just the stone truth they face. If Hovis or Uriah had come back, she would have had someone to drive the Dunlevy caravan and they might have left with the others, but those two fellows never showed and their house trailer is still parked in the lot. They both seemed more befuddled than usual this morning and they have probably ended up over on the Mount without knowing how they got there. She oversees the children's little harvest, making sure the plants themselves are not pulled up with the weeds, and leads them in singing while they work—children's hymns and nursery rhymes and popular songs like "Mairzy Doats" and "How Much Is That Doggy in the Window?" When she hears the roar of intruders coming up the back road, she hurriedly shepherds the children into the garden shed and closes the door and tells them they're all going to play the quiet game while she reads their palms. Everyone wants to be first and they all start shouting and she has to shush them, telling them that there is a little voice she listens to when she reads their palms and they have to be very quiet so she can hear it, and if they listen very very hard, they may hear it, too. She does not tell them what she really hears in here: rustlings of the flesh. For here the two of them were found naked with the bullet holes in their heads and here something of them remains. As Glenda examines the children's plump little hands, she whispers all the happy wonderful things she sees there. She sees dark things, too, but she keeps these to herself. Even if there's sadness ahead for them, they're only children and need not fret over it. And then, just as she hears the intruders sputtering along on the old two-track road on the other side of the creek, then pausing ominously, only yards away, one of the little ones starts to howl. Wanda's oldest, Davey, a boy not all there. He is hungry and thirsty and has made a mess in his pants and there's no stopping him. She claps her hand over his mouth and then the others start. Would God approve strangling one to save the rest?

Why did you bring us out here? Wasn't once enough?

It's my suffering Christ side. Being reviled we bless, being persecuted we rejoice, and all that. But now that I'm here, seeing this great multitude sunning itself on the hillside, I feel some more blesseds coming on.

Oh no. You've done that already.

I know, but I'm doing a rewrite. I shall open my mouth and teach the many, for it is my task to bear witness to the truth.

They're beyond teaching. Look at them. They're not sunning themselves. They're out of their minds with fear and religious frenzy.

They stand—their shared arms outstretched in iconic embrace—on the cusp of the mine hill above the chalky cross trenched into the side, gazing down upon the astonished followers of the coalminer Giovanni Bruno, the pale plump Jehoshaphat fellow sweating in his brown suit at their side, excited children scurrying around their feet like foraging rodents. Some of the cultists have fallen to their knees in the greasy mud in frenzied prayer, tearfully repenting of their sins, which are no doubt multitudinous and unforgivable, and begging for admittance into the kingdom of Heaven, while others, more skeptical, draw together, scowl and grumble. "What's goin' on here?" the one in the wheelchair asks, peering virulently up at them from between his hunched shoulders. They fear most those on their knees. And the children. That troublemaker dragging the filthy pink slipper, for example, who is at this moment describing for all her pals what she saw last time when she crawled under their robe.

"Can we go now?" the quivering creature at their elbow asks, sotto voce.

"In a moment, Mr. Jenkins. First, I have some devils of false expectations to cast out."

"Devils—?"

Well, if you're going to insist on acting out this mad charade, we should stop standing here with our arms out like a scarecrow and sit as Jesus sat.

As I sat, I know. But there is no place to sit here unless you offer me your knee.

My knee is your knee.

Sometimes in nightmares young Reverend Jenkins has found himself standing before a great throng in his underwear, obliged to give a speech or a sermon he has forgotten. Though he is now dressed in a handsome if slightly stained three-piece corduroy suit, he feels as naked and lost as in his nightmares. It seems a lifetime since his bus ride into this crazed community—crazed with religion, true, but in some ghastly medieval or else futuristic way, not at all the peaceful-valley pastorate he had imagined, more akin to his happy days back in his hometown Sunday School Brigade. Unimaginable catastrophe has followed unimaginable catastrophe like the turning of pages in a horror novel, with footnotes by Jesus' lady friend, who on the drive out here explained to him, among many other improbabilities, that Jesus, as he is known now, whoever he was before, is one of the true megalopsychoi of the world, and though Joshua didn't know what that was, he did know that "mega" meant big, so it probably meant something like a great huge psycho, a total raving lunatic, and that made complete sense even if it did cast a shadow on Jesus himself—in his own time, that is—especially when she drew the comparison. *"Blessed are those who learn by unlearning! who make by unmaking!"* the fellow is crying now, stirring devotion and hostility in equal portions among the cultists like contending fires. *"Who have faith in faithlessness and believe in unbelieving!"*

"Hallelujah!"

"What did he say?"

"He said, have faith and believe!"

"I *do*, Lord!"

Joshua knows this is not going to end well. He did not want to come out here, but everything was blowing up and people were shooting at him and there were thunderous crashing and booming noises, so he was grateful that they spied him chasing after the car and stopped to let him in, no matter where they were going. By then he was crying, couldn't help it. He is a modern man with modern beliefs who does not believe in Leviathan or Behemoth or the Whore of Babylon, much less the Four Beasts of the Apocalypse, beyond their usefulness as metaphors (when engaged in that mode of discourse), but back in that town he felt as if literally pursued by all of them, and he feared worse ahead. The woman did not want to come here either, and on the ride out she begged the man to drive away to some safe place, but the man seemed not even to hear her, singing loudly that he was going to go tell it on the mountain. When they arrived, he jumped out and commenced to climb what turned out to be the malodorous back side of the cultic hill, Joshua and the lady following, because what else could they do? Joshua's heart was in his mouth or else sunk in his sweaty new brown oxfords (blisters on both heels!), his terrified gaze taking in everything and nothing at the same time. As they drew near to the summit, they could hear people on the other side loudly reciting the Lord's Prayer—barking it out, really, like at a football pep rally. The lady gave a little cry as though she suddenly had a pain somewhere down where she was holding herself and ran back down to the car. Joshua tried to follow, but the Jesus fellow had an iron grip on his elbow, and arguing with himself all the while as if there were someone alive inside him, he dragged Joshua on up to the summit. And there they were, the infamous Brunists, spread out below them in the blazing sunshine, a kind of vast holy bedlam, hundreds of them, many in glowing white tunics sticking wetly to their bodies and belted with ropes, the wildest of them clustered behind a wet trench dug into the hillside as though penned up there. And guns, guns everywhere. As the helicopters clattered overhead, a preacher ranted about the children of the kingdom being cast into the outer dark with weeping and gnashing of teeth (*he* was weeping, *he* was gnashing his teeth!), and the Jesus person next to him, against whom he leaned, shouted: *"Blessed, my friends, is the outer dark!"* Whereupon there was a gasp of recognition, or else of alarm, and people fell to their knees in the mud, and there were howls and hallelujahs, and shouts of anger and disbelief. *"For it snuffs out the illusions of the inner light!"*

"Yea, Lord, punish the wicked!"

"Bring the light!"

"No! Cain't you hear? It ain't him!"

"Yes, it *is!* Praise Jesus! *He's come back!"*

*"Just like He promised!"*

Joshua was introduced to the gathered ecstatics as friend and disciple Jumping Jehoshaphat—"His father was a king!"—and his knees turning to jelly, he cracked his lips in a quivering imitation of a smile, pleading with his tearing eyes not to shoot. The man had released his elbow. He could run, but he couldn't run. He could only hold on. "Can we go now?" he whimpered into the man's armpit, but the man, after waving off the doubters and announcing to himself and the hillside what he is going to do—devils are part of it!—began unleashing his mad beatitudes. The language was familiar, but in the way nonsense in dreams is somehow familiar, and Joshua found himself grasping once more at the hope he might still be sleeping on the bus ride in. When the fellow in plaid shirt and suspenders who was riding the bus with him (so long ago!) removed his billed cap, stood his rifle on its stock, and started singing, "God sees the little sparrow fall, I know He loves me, too!" the man in the robes sang back (his singing voice was *not* divine), *"Damned are the fallen sparrows for they shall be eaten!"*

"Lord, save us! Don't let us be eaten!"

"Shut up, you fools!"

*"Hear me now! You must leave this wicked place! Go forth, be fruitful, and multiply!"*

"He said we are leaving this wicked place!"

"Save us, Lord! Take us to the Promised Land!"

In the distance, smoke rises from where the town must be—or have been—as warplanes swarm and explosive thuds resound, and it occurs to Joshua that the man beside him might really be who he says he is, that the Christian end times he always believed in—or *believed* he believed in—are really upon them in all their monstrosity after all, and that he is standing amid the Holy Remnant. But then the man says: *"Verily, I say unto you, blessed are ye that have seen, and yet have not believed!"* and though he can't think why—he can't think at all!—Joshua feels certain this is not right. He knows all the songs (that scary Sunday School tune "Too Late, Too Late!" is now pounding through his tormented head), but he has never been good at quoting the Scriptures. Understanding the varieties of human discourse is something he *is* good at, and he knows that, at such a critical moment, he should be employing—and *urgently!*—the analytical one in search of efficacious action but that mode has abandoned him and all others—even prayer!—as well. He is paralyzed with fear, fear and confusion, his mind turned to a hot burning coal (he is standing on black chips of coal, the whole hill may be made of nothing but coal; his feet are burning, too), even as his belly turbulently liquefies. Once able to hold several contrary notions in his head at the same time and act separately on each, Joshua can no longer hold one thing in his mind at the same time and could not act on it if he could.

A young white-robed fellow with long golden curls like someone out of a storybook steps forward and says: "I'm sorry, but that is not what Jesus said." A hush falls. The boy seems to have everyone's respect. Perhaps there is hope. There is another creature pasted to him like a pop-eyed Siamese twin, or else Joshua is seeing double. He may be. His eyes are misted over with tears and sweat. It is stiflingly hot. It's as if the torrid Bible lands have been transported here, or they there. His chest hurts. His feet hurt. He has a stitch in his side. His corduroy suit suffocates him. He envies that other boy perched over across the way on that strange rickety structure (a carnival ride?) with his shirt off. Probably a boy. "He said: Blessed are they that have not seen, and yet have believed."

"I know, young man. I already said that. A long time ago. I am saying something else now. The old has passed away, as I have also said. The new has come."

"But if you are who you say you are—"

"I say nothing. The words are yours."

Houndawg is also hurting. He can hardly walk, but he can still ride, his bike a kind of wheelchair operated mostly by hand. He once traveled with a pegless guy, a paraplegic shot up in the war. The guy taught him a few tricks that are useful now. None for stopping the pain, though. Hacker promised him meds from the hospital and drugstore raids, but he hasn't shown up out here at the Brunist camp. Teresita said she heard a lot of gunfire on the way out of town and she doesn't think the poor dude made it. There was a supercharged moment back there when Houndawg felt about as alive as he's ever felt, but it has sputtered out with the pain. Not running on all barrels either. A kind of fading in and out, like a loss of compression. Fever probably. His leg has a wrecked, ugly look and he leaves it mostly hidden away in his pantleg, not to be sickened by the sight and smell of it. And now Kid Rivers is talking about a head-on assault on the hill. Wherever the Kid goes, Houndawg will follow, the Kid being pretty much what's left of his fucked-up life, but he hopes he doesn't do that. Catch them by surprise, he says. Roar at them from all sides at once. The Big One's with us, he says. The Kid believes that. Even if "us" is only these six, all that remain of the Wrath of God. And anyway, you never die. The comicbooks tell him so. Cubano and Littleface and Spider and all the rest aren't really dead. "They'll be back, man." Houndawg doesn't think so. Another notion from the Kid's strips: the Legions of the Holy Dead joining the living in the final battle against the Forces of Evil. Houndawg heard him talking to himself one night and asked him who he was talking to. "Face. He's there, man. He's still there."

Who is the Big One? In the Kid's scheme of things, best Houndawg can tell, it's the Devil. The one who lost the first War of the Gods and now wants his own back. Which makes them all players on a bigger stage than the one Houndawg was cast for. In reality, the Gods' battleground looks a lot like Nat Baxter's hometown, the combatants his family and friends, imagined enemies. And who he wants now, of course, is his old man. His ass still smarts from all the whalings he took as a kid, and he wants his own turn. But the others have been up on that stony rise above the camp with their binocs and have seen everyone over there on the mine hill armed to the molars. They'd be so many birds at a turkey shoot, as Brainerd says. Unless they could get in behind the mine buildings unseen and hit them suddenly from the blind side. That's Chepe's idea. But how would they do that? It's all so naked over there. Unseen is a fantasy. Chepe himself looks like a fantasy today, dressed in bright colors as if for a party. Tight shiny pants and one of those lacy faggot shirts from south of the border the color of hot piss. He's been brilliant, though. Fearless. The Kid reminds them that he still has the two Brunist tunics saved from the day they buried the nitro here at the camp a couple of months ago, and there are a few sticks left. Someone could strap them around his body, he says, wear the tunic over the top, walk into their midst over there as a fellow believer and give them all a grand send-off into the Promised Land. The others glance Houndawg's way. He's half-dead anyway, they're thinking, so why not? Because he's no Juice or Sick or Rupe; he wouldn't be as old as he is if he were. And he doesn't buy the immortality wheeze. He leans on his good leg and waits them out. Then Deacon comes up with an idea that might work. Steal one of the campers left behind here and take the nitro in canvas bags around to the back side, climb the hill in the tunics and mingle with the believers, leave the shit with long fuses lit and drift back to the wheels again. "Have to be somebody they don't know," Brainerd says. Which excludes Houndawg and the Kid. So Houndawg nods and says he likes the idea. Chepe and Teresita don't fit in with the white trash over there and Deac is not of a size to pass unnoticed. Brainerd has just volunteered himself.

They probably shouldn't have come back to the camp at all. Wasn't in their original plan, which was to hit the town hard and fast, then scatter, gathering later at an abandoned Colorado ghost town Brainerd told them about. But then came the ambush on Sunday over in the woody patch the other side of the creek here. It was the same place they gangfucked that scrawny virgin, the killer blast a kind of awesome punctuation for it. Houndawg, crippled up by it and with little Paulie and his Apostle pals blown away, was feeling the rage and proposed they terrorize the camp and burn it down; the others bought into that, and during the rains they started collecting ten-gallon cans of gasoline and parking them in the woods off the old farm road at the far side of the camp. So it's his fault they're here. Though where else they could have gone except to hell is not clear. So maybe he did them all a favor.

As it turned out, the camp was empty, everyone having vacated the place to go sing Jesus songs on the mine hill. They could have strolled in, but that's never the Kid's way. If there's no action, it's not real. Doesn't fill the frame. So after picking up the gas cans, they rolled in, blasting away, shooting the place up. That the camp was at their disposal, the Kid, with his cosmic view of things, took as another sign of otherworldly support for their mission, as he calls it, which is one of severe judgment and devastation. Desolation is the word on the Kid's tongue these days. Utter desolation. That's the state they left the town in and how they will leave the camp. Since he stopped being Nat Baxter, he has come to sound more like his old man every day, though it would rile him if anyone said so. Beginning to look like him, too. Putting on weight, neck and shoulders thickening. And he has suddenly grown older. Though some ways yet short of twenty, Nat has always said he felt like forty, and now, with Toad Rivers' license in his pocket to confirm it, he is. Changing who he is has toughened him, smartened him. Young Nat Baxter might not have succeeded at this day's operation. For Kid Rivers, it has been a walk.

After "capturing" the old lodge, as the Kid put it, they'd gathered in it to wait for the others, but nobody showed. Deacon said he thought he saw X and the girl peeling off right after they torched the liquor store, and Thaxton may have double-crossed them. "I caught him doing that R.C. abracadabra stuff with his fingers as we were running into the church and he had a stony look on his map like he'd just written us off," he said. "And he wasn't there when we came out. Thax wasn't who he said he was." "Warn't even Thaxton t'begin with," Brainerd said, scratching his head with his filthy finger splint and spitting chaw. "Tole me that was the name of a bud a his who got killt by a sideswiper, and he tuck it as his own cuz his name was on too many bounty lists." They're not sure what happened to Rupe, but he's not back and has probably, as the Kid says, joined the Legions of the Holy Dead. Deacon told everyone how the Kid set off the dynamite Baptiste was carrying by shooting at it so that he and Spider could escape. "Didn't do Baptiste much good, but he had a bunch of angry papists piled on him and was already done for. The Kid saved my ass, and Spider would've made it too, but he went back for his bike, and they were waiting for him. Not smart. But Spider had all his inks and designs in his saddlebags, couldn't let 'em go. They were his life. A real artist, man. Right to the end." Deacon is the Kid's deputy, or maybe vice versa. They're both driven by the need to destroy something, but for Deac it's the system he hates and everything that holds it in place. The Kid knows the truth and is going to enact it; Deac knows the enemy and he's going to bring them down. Deac's enjoying himself in his dark grinning way; the Kid's in a holy rage. As far as Houndawg can tell, Deacon doesn't have a religious thought in his head. When he goes through the motions for the Kid's sake, it's like he's playing out a private joke. Right now they suit each other, though he can see Deac splitting when they get out of here. If they ever do.

The Kid walks over to the blowup of the Man hung up near the fireplace—an awesome sucker in truth, looking wild-eyed and dangerous, wielding a mine pick like some kind of Iron Age killer—and he goes down on one knee in front of it in a kind of stiff deliberate way, like he's trying to signify something. A kneeling knight, maybe. Chepe and Teresita do the same, adding in some genuflections, though the Kid doesn't seem to be looking for imitators. He's just into it. After he has done that and mumbled a few things about retribution and the end of things, talking maybe to the Man, he takes the picture down, smashes the frame it was in, and folds it up to take along. Then he says that Deacon's notion of delivering the nitro from the back of the hill via one of the caravans has given him an idea: They'll strip out three or four of the campers and trailers, stow their bikes inside, and drive them out of here, dump them later. Move slow, like old people, take different routes to throw off the guys in the sky and anyone else who might get curious. This seems pretty cool, though Houndawg, too wrecked to drive a cage with all its floor pedals, has to team up with somebody. He tells the Kid he'll ride shotgun for him with his rifle; still enough bullets to bring down a chopper or two, if they get chased. They choose their vehicles and throw out the shit inside them, setting aside what's edible or eating it, pocketing what's valuable. Not much. These are poor folk.

But then Deacon steps out of a house trailer, clutching by the scruff a bedraggled woman looking too tired and beat up to complain. "Look what I found," he shouts, grinning in his beard, and he lifts her off the ground like shot game. "We ain't got time for that," Brainerd says, and Deac says: "No, not now. I was thinking hostage." The others nod at that, but Houndawg figures she'd be more trouble than she's worth. Most women are. Better to tie her to a tree before setting the place alight. He's about to say so when a powerful big-bellied man with a gray burr around his puffy ears stumbles out of the trailer, still pulling his pants up. Must have been in the can. Deacon drops the woman and pulls a knife, as the fat man, faster than he looks, leaps forward and throws his arms around the Deac in a bear hug. Not easy to do. Deacon's a big man, too. They all unsheathe their blades and advance on the two of them, but the Kid holds his hands up to stop them, a dry hard grimace on his face. He seems fascinated by the sight of the two huge men locked in their fierce embrace, Deacon's knife deep in the other man's meaty back but, arms pinned, unable to pull it out and strike again. Like hulking giants in a death dance. Something the Kid may have seen in one of his superhero comics, acted out now before his eyes. Though in the strip the pants of one of them probably wasn't around his ankles, his hairy butt framed by unbuttoned trapdoor longjohns. There is a long quiet moment broken only by soft wheezing grunts as Deacon slowly presses back against the man's grip, the Brunist tattoo on Deac's shoulder with its skull and lightning bolt seeming to bulge and tremble as if about to pop. It's like time itself is slowing down and so motionless are they, eyes squeezed shut, they seem almost to have fallen asleep in each other's arms. Houndawg, leaning against a tree not to fall over, is taut, almost breathless, stuttering a bit in the brainpan himself. Deacon, feet spread and pushing against the earth as if to stop its turning slowly leans forward, trying to tumble his opponent to the ground, but then blood begins to leak from Deacon's mouth, nose, eyes, and there is a crackling sound. The Kid lurches forward, they all do, except for Houndawg, driving their knives into the longjohnned fat man over and over, turning white to crimson, Brainerd finally yanking the man's head back from behind and slicing his thick white throat. Too late for Deacon, whose bleeding eyes spring open at the end as though to witness their avenging. Teresita turns on the sadsack woman and is about to plunge her blade in her when Brainerd grabs her arm. "Leave her be, girl," he says, taking the woman by the hair and hauling her to her feet. "I kin use her."

*"Blessed are the fantasists for they shall not be dismayed by oblivion!"* the man who calls himself Jesus is declaring.

"Yea, Lord, save us from oblivion!"

*"But damned are they who project their mad fantasies upon others!"*

"Is it a parable, Lord?"

"It's a prophecy!"

"That's crazy! Don't listen to him!" Angry shouts, heard now as then, so long ago, growing ever fiercer, commingled with the wails of woe and worship, a cacophony of dissent and fervent prayer and threat and lament, and also the rackety flapping of the helicopters overhead, with which Jesus did not have to contend in his own time.

The rising anger might have turned to violence did not the man, swarmed about by small children as though costumed by them, look so uncannily like the image of Christ on their Sunday morning church programs, and had not Reverend Baxter—who at such a moment would ordinarily be railing at full throat against false prophets and other deceptive abominations of the sinful world—fallen, while gazing upon the intruder, into a dark contemplative silence, as if stilled by the ominous workings of the day; for, as he declared it would be, so it is, if what is seen can be believed. He does not believe it (who is this fool?), but he distrusts his disbelief. The announced hour of fulfillment—*he* has announced it!—is this it then? Is this He? He who will create a new Heaven and a new earth, the King of kings and Lord of lords, the one who always was, who is, and who is still to come? He can't be! And yet, for such are the mysterious workings of the Lord, he—He?—can. There is also the alarming apocalyptic testimony of those who have fled West Condon. No one can doubt the muffled explosions, the smoke billowing over the town, the hovering helicopters (are they firing rockets?), the wild chorus of sirens over there getting louder. Some say they have seen bodies rising into the sky, though none can be seen from here. Should they flee while they still can? Or is the same thing happening all over the world? Many have been urging a return to the sanctuary of the camp. But is it sanctuary or entrapment? They ask this Jesus who has appeared before them. He only smiles with glittering eyes and says: "*There is no sanctuary!*" Which is exactly what Abner would have said himself.

In the Meeting Hall below, when Abner called for this Holy March, he felt a surge of conviction more powerful than he'd ever felt before, and it's almost as though that very certainty has provoked its contrary. Torn between yea, yea and nay, nay. Abner is most himself when most righteously enraged, and as they climbed up here, that rage, which served him well in the camp lodge, began to evaporate under the brightening sun, giving way to a kind of awed anticipation. Has God spoken through him, as he so often feels He has? If so, is he ready? *Can* he be, assailed by doubt? He felt the first presentiments of this strange bafflement of mood when they arrived down on the mine road at the place where he struck and killed the girl that terrible night. He seemed for a moment to see her there or to feel at least her presence, and the road seemed to blacken under his feet, and he knelt to pray. Her shattered face against the windshield scrimmed his mind, hanging like a transparent curtain against the thinning clouds when he looked up. He thought that climbing the hill away from the road would free him of her, but she has risen with him, haunts him still. Young Rector has taught him to trust these mysterious impressions as fleeting experiences of the real world beyond the corrupted one of our senses, and he has learned to trust the boy; he has been so right about so many things, and more loyal to Abner than his own family. He is less certain about the peculiar bug-eyed orphan at his side, even if he is one of the twelve First Followers; there is something not right about him. But young Rector has assured him that the boy is subject to a kind of divine madness, which makes him particularly receptive to holy visions. "Illuminations." Glimpses beyond the veil. Where there is no dark and all is light.

Light.

And so Abner finds his voice. *"Ye are the light of the world! You do not light a candle, and put it under a bushel, but on a candlestick, and it gives light unto the world!"* he declares, though without his usual vehemence, hearing himself somehow echoing himself, and the man who says he is Jesus replies: *"Blessed are they who put their light under a bushel for they shall ignite a great conflagration!"* Whereupon the very mention of fire sets everyone on the sacred Mount of Redemption off again.

Not all hold the mine hill in such reverence, nor see the followers of the apostate Catholic Giovanni Bruno as anything but heretical, if not demonically possessed. Another of God's armies, the Knights of Columbus Volunteer Defense Force, who also call themselves, throwing insult back as pride, the Dagotown Devil Dogs, are even now gathering in the empty field near the hill, once meant as the site for an industrial park that was never built. They have been officially deputized by the city police chief and are turning to march upon the hill and arrest all those on it, with orders from their leader to shoot to kill, if necessary. Their church has been dynamited, friends and family killed or maimed, their priest hospitalized in critical condition. They are impatient to exact due justice; there will be no negotiations. In town, the police chief himself, as the reluctant de facto leader of all the volunteer police and rescue units from the region who have rolled in to help, has issued instructions to many of them to proceed toward the mine hill, and they are doing so. They too have suffered casualties and will brook no further resistance. More ambulances and medical teams arrive, and the chief sends them out there as well. The town banker, whose place of business, so central to the community, has been dynamited with a substantial loss of life and property, confers with the state governor before also heading to the mine. He demands that what remain of the troops called in by the governor be, for God's sake, dispatched out there immediately to secure the hill and prevent the outbreak of anarchy and further bloodshed. The governor, who has just told a network interviewer that the problems here "have nothing to do with religion, these are just evil people assaulting a decent Christian community," knows that no good will come of it. The young soldiers have been traumatized and are ill prepared for this sort of sectarian conflict, many of them being themselves believers of one or another of the contending persuasions, nor is it clear what exactly they will do when they get there. "Securing the hill" is probably an unexecutable command. But he also knows that he has no choice; he has made too many mistakes, the town is burning, and the banker has made it clear he will be held accountable. The swarming and increasingly hysterical news media, some of whose members have also been targeted, already hold him accountable. He has commandeered yellow school buses to replace the destroyed army vehicles and even now they are rumbling slowly out of town, bearing their whey-faced battalions.

* * *

From her grandstand seat high up on the mine tipple steps, Sally Elliott can see the buses in the smoky distance, rocking in tandem on the approach road like liverish elephants, trunks to tails, and she takes a photo of them. They remind her of the last time this happened out here, when they used those buses for the mass arrests they made. She ran home that day before all the bad stuff began, but she remembers the buses, how surreal they seemed, and sinister, parked there side by side in the rain with their blunt impassive faces, waiting to open their maws and eat the people. She has been scribbling in her notebook, shut off from the world, totally absorbed, willfully ignoring the carryings-on of the Brunists on the hill and the more disconcerting sounds coming from the direction of the town. New principle: Writing first, everything else second. But there's smoke on the horizon now, too. Helicopters wheeling about like chicken hawks. She worries about her mom and dad. Actually, she has been worried all along, but only now has she brought it forward into the thinking part of her head. Things may be turning out not so funny.

She stands to stretch. Over on the hill, the Brunists seem to be having a row. The wacky Presbyterian minister has turned up there in his Jesus outfit and is apparently stirring them up, a chubby little fellow in a brown suit beside him like a company lawyer, or maybe his agent. His lady friend, the church organ lady, is bobbing indecisively up and down the back of the hill in her flesh-colored nightshirt, like a terrified puppet on elastic strings. She's painted some of herself red. There's a new crowd marching toward the hill from a distant field in a kind of loose military formation. Can't see who they are, but the one out front in the blue police shirt might be Angie Bonali's brother. Sirens are approaching from all directions. In a ditch at the edge of the old county road that runs past the church camp, a shiny pea-green bump catches her eye. Almost everything is green over there, but the bump is brighter than the rest, reflecting the sun. Metal. Like the top of a car.

She has sat too long in the sun. She touches one finger to her chest, it leaves a white spot, then turns bright pink again. A helicopter buzzes her, the pilot grinning out the window, and she waves her shirt at him, grinning back. As she does so, she glimpses the weird golden-haired pal of Billy Don on the hill. Shielding his eyes. Staring over at her. That mental orphan at his side. He points. Uh oh. Time to go.

Prissy Tindle has carefully choreographed her "Save the Fathers Arabesque," a routine meant to whisk Jesus and his inner Wesley away from the danger they are in with a simple fluid and irresistible movement while paralyzing all those confused people with surprise and wonder. It would be better if she could pop suddenly from behind one of those big earth-moving things, but they're too far away to reach unseen. There's only one way and not much time. When they first parked down here behind the hill, there were a couple of muddy old junkers resting by the ditch with no one in them, but more people have been arriving by that road, several of them dressed in those white bedsheet things, almost all of them carrying guns and looking insanely dangerous. Jesus doesn't understand the trouble he is in, or else he's just *trying* to get killed. Which some say was Jesus' problem in the first place, back when he first made himself famous. She finds herself calling him Jesus all the time now, for it's the only name he answers to, and anyway it's like poor dear Wesley has sunk away somewhere beyond her reach. She felt more comfortable with Wesley on top, so to speak, for she still had some sway, but she has to admit that Jesus is sexier—so forthright and self-assured and virile. Thrilling, really. It's like Wesley has been saved after all. And for all their bold new style, they still need her—maybe more than ever. She brushes their hair, keeps their beard trimmed, creates and cares for their wardrobe, feeds them, and, when she can, shields them from trouble. If only they would stop arguing with each other! Down at the far end of the road, men are forming up and beginning to march this way. She does not know who they are, but she does not think they will be friendly. And those shrieking sirens! Like burning cats! She has to get him away from here! If only Jesus will cooperate! How can he not, seeing the danger she will be in? She wants only to be away from here, but old trouper that she is, she takes one determined but terrified step after another and arrives at the top and there they are again, spread out below her, all those wild mad people! They are shouting at Jesus and at each other—anything could happen! Be brave, her inner voice shouts. She has used up all her lipstick on herself, hoping she has created the right effect. She flings off her gown and opens her mouth to do her naked Whore of Babylon shriek. But nothing comes out. She's too scared. She's a dancer, not a singer. That panicky little preacher at Jesus' side with his hair standing on end and shirt tails out stares at her in abject horror, and his eyes roll back and he keels right over. *"It's the Antichrist!"* she hears someone scream. Hysterically, over and over. That orphan boy who so hates Wesley. Oh no! They all start shouting. *"Don't let her get away!" "She killed an old lady!"* What? There is a terrifying rattle of gunfire. But well in the background, for—that does it!—Prissy Tindle is already performing her "Leaping Gazelle Adieu" through a crowd of advancing armed men (there is rude laughter, a passing slap on her bare fanny) on her way back down to the car. Jesus is in great jeopardy, and she fears for him and she loves him, but he'll just have to miracle himself out of it somehow. She's retiring to the wings. Bring down the curtain and kill the lights. This show is closing.

Hovis, holding up what looked like a raggedy tarpaulin thick with mud, had just been showing Uriah the missing slicker he'd found—"It looks different," Uriah said, and Hovis said, "Gotta be it, Uriah. Ain't nobody else but you'd wear nuthin this old and ugly!"—when Sister Debra's strange boy interrupted Jesus' recitation of his newfangled beatitudes and started screaming about the Antichrist, and everybody commenced shooting at the old mine tipple like it was some kind of giant coming after them. Neither Hovis nor Uriah could see exactly what they were shooting at, but they fired off a few rounds because it seemed like the way this day was panning out. A day which—both have thought but not at the same time—may be the last of its kind. Even before Jesus turned up with his sweaty little pal in the suit, Uriah could feel it in his bones, like the onset of a thunderstorm, though the skies are clear. The end of things. Uriah had said as much to the scruffy fellow in the Brunist tunic from back home, pointing out that the very sun seemed stalled up there, right smack on top of the Mount, and the fellow, a friendly and poetical sort, had said, "Yep, know what you're sayin', brother. Like it's been a sweet ride, but bad curves a-comin'." Sister Wanda had come to the hill with him, and when people asked after the big fellow she stared at them like she was only half there and said he was feeling poorly, and people said they were sorry to hear that but they were glad that he had let her be up here with the Elect now that things were really starting to happen. Poor worn-out thing, her belly hanging low on her scrawny frame; Uriah hopes she'll be blessed with more smarts and gumption in the next world.

Isaiah Blaurock came past about then, just before the shooting at the tipple commenced, looking both fierce and quietly determined, like he always does, and Uriah thought he might have brought them all something to eat, but instead he just gathered up his three younguns from under the feet of Jesus and, without a word, carried them down to the foot of the hill where his pickup was parked. His wife Dot, who was just asking Jesus about the marriage supper of the Lamb, when could they start tucking in, seemed as surprised as everyone else and just stood there for a moment watching him go. Then she tossed her little one over her shoulder and went gallumphing after, shouting back over her shoulder: "Hold on! We're going for reinforcements!" Which was when that boy started screaming about the Antichrist.

Now, they're still blasting away at the tipple like it's the Fourth of July (and maybe it is, wasn't it supposed to happen sometime soon?)—*"I got her!"* someone shouts—when a number of armed men appear from different angles at the crest of the hill with rifles pointed down at them, and order them to lay down their arms in the name of the law; they're all under arrest. Italians by the look of them, though others cry out that it's the Powers of Darkness. And they could be both at the same time, because it was the Romans who crucified Jesus, wasn't it? "We are afflicted from all sides," Jesus says, seeming somewhat exasperated. The boy won't stop shrieking and somebody says, "Who is that crazy kid? Shut him up before he gets us all shot!" and somebody else says, "Sshh! He's one of the First Followers!" "What?" Young Darren puts his arm around him and he eases up and starts to sob softly and Darren leads him downhill, away from the center of things, toward the "doorway," as it might be called, of the outlined temple.

And then that mean cuss McDaniel from the Christian Patriots points his rifle straight at the armed men's leader, the one wearing a badge, and shouts back that he's the acting sheriff out here and is the boss and *he* is arresting *them* if they don't clear out immediately, or stormy words to that effect, not all completely Christian, and besides, he says, we got a lot more guns, so if you want to have a shootout, let's get started. Then for a moment they're all just standing there with their rifles and shotguns loaded, waiting to see who'll shoot or back down first, the overhead sun casting ominous shadows under their brows and noses. Down on the mine road, a parade of yellow school buses with soldiers in them are pulling in and also some police cars with their sirens cranked up. "Reckon it's time to go take a leak," mutters the beardy fellow Uriah has been conversing with and he looks for a place to toss his smoke, finally just stubs it out inside his canvas bag and hands the bag to Uriah and asks him to hold it for him until he gets back. Hovis asks who that was and Uriah says it was a fellow from their parts who was agreeable to talk to if you could get past his smell. "He knowed a lotta friendsa ourn, or said he did when I mentioned 'em. Said he seen us on the tellyvision and come a-runnin'." "Where's he gone now?" "Off to take a leak, he said." "With Sister Wanda? Don't seem right." "No. But you know Sister Wanda." "She looked purty skeered." "Well, I'm skeered, too." "Whaddaya reckon's in the bag?" "Cain't say. Didn't ask and t'ain't polite to—"

Far from all these apocalyptical doings and without access to any TV screens now broadcasting them internationally in all their entertaining horror (the blast on the side of the mine hill is so powerful it knocks back the cameras and the images go bouncing up to the sky and back and even end up sideways, and by now everybody's watching—wow! did you see *that*?), Georgie Lucci has just made his fortune. Long overdue and much deserved, beloved and noble faccia da culo, gran testa di cazzo that he is. At the airport, the mayor told him to wait in the car while he got the tickets. He left the briefcase in the back seat, but showed Georgie he still had the key: "No fucking funny biz, partner. I'll just be a jiff." Once the chump was out of sight, Georgie took off, barreling down the highway bat-outa-hellwise aiming for the state line, laughing all the way, pounding the wheel with his palm, jerking on his boner, blowing thankful kisses at la bella Marcella, his Lady Luck, his Virgin Mary, his Red-Hot Ruby, blowing kisses as well at his nonna, his mother, even the puttana who gave him his present dose, singing "Fly Me to the Moon" at the top of his voice, and imagining what he was going to do with all that money. He figures if that crook Castle said Brazil, that's the one place he's not going. He doesn't know where it is, but it did sound cool, full of naked young ficas lying around on soft golden beaches, all aquiver with pent-up desire. A kind of island paradise, how he pictured it. But, too bad, he'll have to miss it. He's not that stupid. There are other beaches, other hot women. When he's out of the state and far enough away to risk it, he pulls over beside some roadside picnic tables. The briefcase is a tough nut to crack; the mayor knew what he was doing when he bought it. His knife is as useless as a soft dick against a resistant maidenhead, so he takes the limo's crowbar to it, alternatively smashing and prying at it, one eye on the highway for cops or snoopers. He speaks sweet nothings to the briefcase while he beats it. "Spread, amore! Show me what you got!" The lock breaks at last and he jimmies the case open. What he finds inside is wadded newspaper. Old yellowing *West Condon Chronicles*. The ones with the old Cunt Hill photos that caused such a storm. Like the one raging inside him. He's grinning, can't help it, but he's murderously pissed. He leaves the newspapers to blow in the wind, hops back in the limo, pockets the revolver he'd noticed Castle hiding in the glove compartment, and guns it back to the airport. Where, after an emergency call from the mayor of West Condon, they are waiting for him. Caution. He may be armed.

When officer Bo Bosticker reached the police station at the end of his odyssey through the burning town, he found the front of it reduced to a pile of grimly decorated sticks and stones, though the unlit holding cell at the back was still intact and occupied. He himself had arrested Cokie Duncan the night before for loud-cussing, pissing-in-the-street, fall-down drunk behavior, and as the otherwise agreeable old fellow seemed to need a place to sleep it off where he wouldn't get stepped on, he locked him up there and supplied him with coffee and smokes until he passed out. Dunc, like Bo, survived the Deepwater mine disaster, so he feels a fraternal regard for him, and even a certain duty in that he has a job and Cokie does not. He stumbled on his crutches over the debris to the back, and found the old boy still in there, jawing with Cheese Johnson, who was sitting on a wooden chair outside the cell, one arm in a filthy plaster cast, the two of them sharing a bottle of some kind of whiskey of a good color with a charred label. "Well, lookit here," Duncan said, "it's ole Bo! If it ain't his ghost! Thought you was dead, Bo!" "Well, I was dead to the world for certain, and missed out on all the dramma." "Drop your props'n pull up a chair, Bo," Cheese said. "Have a wake-up snort." "They killt everbody else," Duncan said. "You're the only one left!" And so he sat down for a minute to rest his aching knees and Cokie told him about the blast out front—"I got hit smack in the face by a piece a pore ole Monk! It was like he was lettin' fly at me with one last gob!"—and Cheese filled him in on some of the wild doings out in the street while the bikers were still on it, including an illustrated account of the war dance of a Red Indian on top of the old hotel before he got blown away in a manner that Cheese called "outright magical." While Bo eased the pain of his ruined knees with a few medicinal breakfast swigs, a bunch of other killings and explosions were colorfully recounted and somehow that got them onto the mine disaster again, which always had a way of coming up regardless, ever more so when calamity was the theme, and then Cheese left to go rescue some more bottles out of the liquor store fire. When he came back with an armload, plus a couple of cartons of cigarettes in his sling, he said he heard something big go off in the direction of the old mine and now everybody was tearing ass in that direction, the word being that they're all shooting at each other out there, it's a fucking free-for-all, so the three of them now have the town pretty much to themselves, what there is left of it, though besides the smokes and whiskey there's not much they need. Risking the flames that are eating up the inside of the dimestore, Cheese has also retrieved a soft over-shuffled deck of cards from the Legion Hall above it. One thing leads to another and pretty soon the three of them find themselves quietly day-juicing over a wistful unfocused game of pitch, a particular pleasure for Bo, card-playing being something he has generally had to miss out on since getting hired for night duty and one of the few things he is somewhat good at. He has often thought that playing cards would be the way he'd most like to spend the afterlife, and, who knows, given the look of things outside, maybe the worst has happened and this *is* the afterlife. He says so and makes it clear that, if so, he is happy with their eternal company. Of course, he shouldn't be drinking on the job, but strictly speaking he's still on his own time, though with everyone else dead, it's probably up to him to take over. If he wants to. A circumstance that has never previously arisen and he is not comfortable with it. He asks, thinking aloud, if they ought to go out to the mine and see what's happening, and Cokie, peeing on the wall of his cell, says, "Some things, ifn you cain't do nuthin about 'em, ain't wuth lookin' at." "Your ugly pox-eaten dick, for example," says Cheese in disgust, and then he falls off his chair.

Bo's boss, West Condon Chief of Police Dee Romano, sits alone at the back of the bomb-damaged St. Stephen's Catholic Church, trying to imagine an alternative career and seeking divine counsel in the matter, when his lieutenant Luigi Testatonda, returning from a check on his family, piles in heavily beside him, settles his cap on his lap, and informs him that another big one has gone off out at the mine hill and it has reportedly set off a lot of reckless shooting. He has a worried look on his sad moony face and Dee says, "It's not our territory, Louie. We're not going out there." The worried look is nodded away and Louie busies himself with wiping his brow with a handkerchief and muttering a few prayers for the dead and dying. Of which they have seen their fill, need see no more. After organizing the volunteer units, they have toured the temporary downtown morgues in the post office and pool hall, where they said goodbye to what was left of their colleague Monk Wallace; have visited the various outlying targets, including the devastated National Guard bivouac area at the high school gym, where army medics, flown in by helicopters now sitting on the football field, are tending to the wounded and tagging the dead; have checked in on Father Baglione at the city hospital and some of the others who are out there. Dee's nephew is pulling through, though he'll have to give up smoking. The old priest is still touch and go. They have made consolatory house calls to the Juliano, Vignati, Spontini, and Lombardi families, most of them related, by one womb or another, to the Romanos. There were others, but they were both drained and could bear no more, so they stopped by to see that Dee's family was all right (large ingathering at the house, general state of mourning, wife organizing a vigil for the priest), and then he let Louie drop him off here, giving him the patrol car to go look in on his own family. Shock and worry, Louie says when Dee asks, but no calamities. His daughter hiked out to the hospital when she heard about the Bonali girl getting shot, but they turned her back. Only letting in immediate family. Ramona keeps picking up the dead phone, he says, listening for the dial tone to return. The early afternoon sun casts a bright dusty beam through the shattered rose window much like those often shown in pictures of saints, or the Virgin at the Annunciation, or the boy Jesus astonishing the elders in the synagogue, the sort of beam that makes you feel that, if you walked into it, you'd be transported straight up to Paradise. The only trouble is, it's falling on the blood-stained crater in the floor, not so much a welcoming beam as an accusing one. Step into it, you might get fried. The main impression it gives, though, is of the messy nothingness that it is beamed upon. Man's life on earth: there has to be something more, or it's not worth living it.

The doctor and nurses have come to Angela Bonali's room to take the bullets out. It's not that her case is urgent, they say—the bullet went deep and hit her hip bone, but there's no breakage or spinal damage—but that the operating room is in constant use and they need her bed. There are casualties coming in every minute, and from what they could see on the TV outside, there are soon going to be a lot more. She can hear the gurneys with their squeaky wheels constantly rolling by. The doctor says there will be a small scar but she should think of it as a beauty mark, and she is able to smile shyly at that. Once it stops hurting, it *will* be fun to show it off. Really, she's lucky. Her friend Monica Piccolotti stopped by for a moment earlier. In tears. Pete's head is wrapped, blindfolding him, and Monica can't bring herself to tell him that he won't notice any difference when the bandages come off. That made Angela cry, and Joey hung his head. Pete saved Monica and their little boy and their unborn baby, and Monica said that for the first time she really understood what marriage was all about and why it was ordained by God. She would love Pete now forever, and take care of him until they were in Heaven together and Pete could see again. Pete saved the life of Sheriff Smith's wife, too, and the sheriff has been in and out of Pete's room ever since, praying over him in his intense Protestant way, though now they say he has left for the mine hill again. Where something awful is happening.

"Somebody blew himself up along with a bunch of others and now they are all shooting at each other and there are bodies everywhere," Joey Castiglione says when he comes back after they've bandaged her up. He's trying to be cool but his voice is shaking. Because the emergency generator still runs the hospital, all the TVs are off, except the one at the nurses' station, and while they were digging out the bullets, Joey, who most people out here think is her brother, left the room and joined the crowd clustered around the set there. "It's really gross, Angie. I saw some people down on their knees praying and they suddenly just keeled over!" Angela hopes she didn't know them and is glad her dad is here at the hospital and far from trouble—and Joey, too. He says she ought to see it, but no, there are some things it's better not to look at. When bad things happen on the TV, even when it's just a made-up movie, she always closes her eyes or leaves the room. People go crazy, especially around other crazy people, and you can go crazy watching them. Joey also said some things about religion that she didn't want to listen to. A Baptist preacher out there in the hallway now is blaming everything on the sins of the town and has got people into an emotional prayer meeting right in the hallway, and that's the sort of thing, Joey says, though less politely, that gives him stomach cramps. Joey thinks he saw her brother Charlie right in the middle of everything. Well, Charlie was made for trouble, he can take care of himself. And if he can't she'll be sad, but mostly because her dad will be sad. Charlie is a total pain, and she doesn't want him to die, but she does wish he'd just go away and stay away. His latest idea was to take her to the city and make money with her in an evil way. Angela told him he was the most disgusting person she ever knew and he only laughed and popped his gum in her face.

When people die—and when *you* almost die!—it makes you think about things, so she and Joey have been having a very intimate conversation about how short life is and what it all means, and though neither of them have mentioned marriage, it seems like that is what they have been talking about. Joey is not any taller than she is and has the knobby Castiglione chin, and she's not sure she really loves him, certainly not in the my-heart-stood-still way, but she has always felt easy around him, in some ways he has been her best friend ever since they were little, and she knows he would do his best to make her happy. They could go visit the fountains of Rome on their honeymoon and have their marriage blessed by the Pope, even if Joey's not very religious. That's what she finds herself thinking. But then, out of the blue, he says something that makes her cry. He says not to worry about the kid she is carrying, he'll help her take care of it, and she breaks down in tears and tells him the truth but begs him not to tell anyone else. "I've made such a fool of myself, Joey!" she weeps. "I'm so *embarrassed!*" He smiles. "Hey. It's okay," he says. He kisses her. It's awkward, with her lying face down and her sore bottom in the air, but she likes it. Not a lot. But enough. The word "comforted" comes to mind. Like in some romances she has read, though usually about older women. She feels comforted. And now, if anyone asks, that stupid girl from the drugstore, for example, who is also somewhere here in the hospital with cuts from the broken mirror which crashed down, she'll tell them she is dumping that jerk Tommy because she has found true love with Joey, who is not such a spoiled selfish egomaniac and is ten times a better lover.

At the Brunist Wilderness Camp, Young Abner is standing up on Inspiration Point, sometimes also known as the Higher Ground, leaning on his rifle and gazing down in fascination upon the burning cabins beginning to snap and crack, and he asks himself if—should his father die—he is ready to take his place. He decides that he is. Why else has God spared him by sending him here to the camp away from the terrible punishments on the Mount of Redemption? He has much to learn, but he already knows a lot, too. You don't live all your life with a father like that without it becoming part of you. Since he is all alone here now, he has been reciting out loud some of his father's famous lines—"The moment of *holy* retribution and rivers of *blood* is at *hand!*"—and, with practice and a little more courage, he'll be able to sound just like him. "Ye shall *set* the city on fire!" Also, he's taller, so he'll be able to look down on people and not have to shout up at them like his father. He may be called on soon. Since the bomb went off over at the Mount, there has been a ceaseless poppety-pop of gunfire and a lot of people, he can see from here, are falling over, and that doesn't even count the ones who must have died when the bomb went off. He can't see his father, so he may already be dead.

Young Abner may have seen the making of that bomb. After Darren sent him back here, he patrolled the grounds, finding little of interest (a pair of cracked sunglasses that he is wearing because they make him feel more heroic, a jar of honey with a homemade label in a cabin cupboard which he ate) and there were still some pesky children running around, so he posted himself up here on the Point to guard the camp as he was asked to do. It's drier and the chiggers aren't so bad. He was resting against a tree, half asleep, considering what acts of retribution he might have undertaken had that jezebel's trailer still been down in the parking lot, and keeping a lazy eye meanwhile on the sky over the Mount just in case something started to happen, when his brother's motorcycle gang suddenly came roaring in below, guns out and firing into the cabins. That woke him up in a hurry, and he spread himself flat, peeking at them over the edge, his heart banging away at the stones under his chest. He recognized Nat immediately, even though he was supposed to be one of the ones who got killed. The one without a head, they said. Well, he was certainly still wearing it. And bossing everybody like he always does. Who was missing was his other brother, the little one. They left their motorcycles outside the Meeting Hall and charged in like storm troopers, kicking the doors open, blazing away.

After that it was quiet and they stayed in there for a while and Young Abner was just thinking about rising from his prone position and scuttling down the back way while he still could, when two of them came out and started prowling around and he ducked his head again. The next time he got up the nerve to look, there they were, the whole gang, coming up the path to the Point. He had to scramble behind some thick bushes, which were not much protection. Scared spitless, as that wall-eyed boy who worked for Clara Collins used to say. Then the worst possible thing happened: his family has been eating a lot of canned beans lately with the inevitable consequence and it was like the devil had got into his bowels and was just trying to get him killed. But Nat and the others kept studying the Mount through their binoculars and arguing and they didn't hear it (it was only the softest little poot), so God was still watching over him and answering his prayers. He saw now that Nat was wearing a leather jacket that said KID RIVERS on it in metal studs, and the main thing you'd say about him was that he didn't look like a boy anymore. But it was Nat. Or at least the head was. Maybe they sewed it onto somebody else's body. He realized, seeing him again up close, how much he hated him. And feared him. The big one in the undershirt, who looked like Goliath in Young Abner's *Illustrated Bible for Children*, had a shiny policeman's badge on his greasy leather vest, and the others wore bracelets and necklaces and upside down crosses in their ears like earrings. Not all of them were real Americans. Maybe none of them were. Some kind of monster aliens. Young Abner knew he could shoot them. That's probably what he was expected to do—but what if he missed? He didn't want to die! And if they weren't all human, it might not do any good to shoot them. Nevertheless, he kept the revolver Darren gave him pointed at Nat the whole time just in case they did see him there; at least, before they killed him or did other terrible things, he'd be able to get back at his cruel brother for scarring his forehead. Nat shouted and shook his fist in what might have been some kind of prayer but sounded more like cussing, and then at last they all went away.

Young Abner could hardly breathe, and when he crawled to the edge for another look, he saw that they had joined up with a sixth motorcyclist down below, an old crippled guy with a gray braid whom Young Abner recognized from the last time they were here, the one little Paulie was riding with when they left and the only one who looked like he might still be human, and they all went over to the emptied out trailer lot. He couldn't see well through the trees, but it looked like two fat men got into a fight in which they both fell down, or maybe they were killed by the others; they didn't get up again. One of the fat men was that big Goliath guy with the police badge. The others started vandalizing the few trailers and caravans still parked there while the old guy with the braid limped back up toward the Meeting Hall. He got some things from a sack that looked like big firecrackers, and he tied them up and settled them into a canvas bag. When the others came up to the Main Square, they were dragging along an older woman with scrawny arms and legs but a poochy belly. They must have found down in the trailer park. Did he know her? Possibly. From the old church. They dressed her in a raggedy Brunist tunic and one of the bikers put another one on like maybe they'd converted and he stowed his motorcycle inside the house trailer he'd driven up from below and the two of them drove away in it. The others stole other caravans and trailers and did the same, but before they left they splashed the buildings and grounds with big cans of gasoline and set everything alight. As they pulled out, he fired his rifle a few times in the general direction of the camp access road just to be able to say he had done what he was supposed to do. He will say they were shooting back, it was a real fire fight, he's lucky to be here, and he fired a few shots into the trees behind him as evidence of that. He didn't see what happened to the canvas bag, but now he can guess.

After they were gone and he was alone except for the two dead men, he could pass wind as much and as loudly as he wanted—he thought of it as a kind of exorcism, and God-blessed himself with each *ker-blatt!* Down in the camp the fires were dying out. One thing Young Abner knows all about is building fires—burning the trash being one of his main chores growing up—so he gathered dry kindling and firewood from the stacks by the fireplace in the Meeting Hall and paper from the church office files and added it all to fires that were still smoldering, crumpling the paper to let the air get through and building little tepees with the wood. He knew that to make big fires you had to start with little ones. He broke up some of the wooden folding chairs and made the tepees bigger with them. Some of the gas cans were not completely empty and he sprinkled what was left over his constructions, and also into the old upright piano in the Meeting Hall, tossing a burning splinter in (there was a sweet responsive *whoosh!*), and then he capped the empty cans tightly and left them on the fires just for fun. He also remembered the old creosoted half-rotten boards from the ruined cabins and piled up on the far side of the trailer lot, and though it was hard work, he managed to haul most of them into the Main Square and add them to the cabin and Meeting Hall fires and they caught right away. While passing through the trailer lot on the way to get another armload, he paused to study the two dead men (the bearded one with the police badge was especially scary with his bulging eyes, which seemed to be looking right at him and crying, but crying blood, and with little red blood-worms crawling out of his nose and mouth and ears) and he took out the revolver and shot them both in the head, killing them a second time. It didn't make much sense to shoot them both if he was trying to take credit, but he did. And that was when the huge bomb went off on the Mount of Redemption, and he hurried back up here to the Point to see what was happening. He saw the black spot where the bomb went off over there and all the crowds that had gathered and saw the helicopters and people shooting at each other and falling over, and he watched them for a while. They looked like white ants fighting black ants.

Down in the camp, the spreading fire is popping and crackling healthily now, thick smoke billowing. There are flames in the bushes. If it gets hot enough, he knows, everything will catch and burn. He ties his bandanna over his nose. The smoke will draw attention. He may have to leave soon. But not yet. It's an amazing sight. He can't take his eyes off it. A God-sized bonfire, only lacking the bodies of the wicked. But he can imagine them, God plucking them from across the face of the earth and bringing them here and tossing them in, watching them scream and claw at the air as they fall, and knowing that it is good because He is good. The way Young Abner used to throw ants into his trash fires. "Let them be *cast* into the fire, into *deep* pits, that they rise not *up* again! For a fire is *kindled* in mine anger, and shall *burn* unto the lowest *hell*, and set on fire the *foundations* of the mountains!" Texts he knows well, having often recited them over the dying ants. They will be at the heart of his ministry. "For our God is a consuming *fire!*" His voice is a little too high. He tucks his chin in and practices making it deeper. "For our God is a *consuming* fire!" Better. He fondles the revolver, points it at the continuing mayhem on the hill. It was fun shooting the two dead men. He wishes he had something else to shoot. Behind him, somewhere below, even as he makes that wish, he hears a cry. A girl, it sounded like. Maybe God has just answered his prayer, and appointed him His avenging angel.

The Brunist Followers on the Mount of Redemption are not sure whether it is the beginning of the Tribulation or if they are into the midterm Rapture and the dreaded Abomination of Desolation or if it's the Final Rebellion and the all-consuming battle of Armageddon, but, wherever they are in God's awesome plan, the End Times are as horrific as the Bible said they would be. There was a mighty explosion that rocked the world on its axis and, some say, caused the sun to bounce, followed by the unleashing of a great slaughter, which seems to have no end. Indeed, depending on how you read the Bible, it could last for a thousand years. In the mind of God, of course, a thousand years is just an instant, the seeming passing of time being an illusion of human existence. For God, all things happen at once, and that's exactly how it seems on the Mount of Redemption right now: eternity squeezed into one punishing explosive moment. They have heard the trumpet judgments, felt the earth quake under the scorching sun, been stung by the ice and fire raining from the cloudless sky, experienced within themselves the shattering of the bowls, for it is written that "as the vessels of a potter shall they be broken to shivers." "Send the fire!" they sang in genuine hope and longing, and now the fire has been sent and the bodies of the wounded and dead, as yet unraptured, litter the hillside. *Day of wrath, O dreadful day! When this world shall pass away, and the Heavens together roll, shriveling like a parchéd scroll!* They have known this was coming, all the shriveling and shivering, ceaselessly they have announced it, prayed for it, sung about it, and yet they have not known, could not have known. The paltry human imagination is not up to it. When the fire *(when the fire)*/Comes down from Heaven *(down from Heaven)*,/This old world *(this old world)*,/Will melt away *(melt away)*!/

Millions then *(millions then)*/Will cry for mercy *(cry for mercy)*/But it will be *(it will be)*/Too late to pray! Those with clear consciences smile with pious joy as they welcome their transport into the hereafter, their raised eyes ablaze with an inner light, while others, less certain of their fate, cry out in desperation to the Lord Jesus Christ for mercy, for forgiveness, for an end to the torment. Christ Jesus has indeed made his Glorious Appearance, returning as so often foretold, but he seems as stunned by events as the wailing believers who swarm about him, groveling at his feet, hands reaching out over other reaching hands to touch his garments, tug at them in supplication. All believe now. How can they not? He is, in the crushing horror, what hope remains. Children have crawled up on him, each trying to climb higher than the other, as if clambering up a crowded ladder to Heaven. As others have cried out, he has remained silent; as others have fallen, he has remained standing, overseeing what must be. Somewhere on his vesture and his thigh, they know, is written KING OF KINGS AND LORD OF LORDS, but under the clinging children this cannot be seen. His demeanor is stern, but composed. Bullets seem to have passed right through him!

Don't you have anything to say to these people?

What can I say that I've not already said? I am confused by their confusion, oppressed by their hope. It's all very sad. Yet I long for such innocent longing!

Then what are we *doing* out here? It's really *dangerous!* And we're not even ducking!

I know. Somehow that feels out of character.

But this is madness! Where is that wretched fellow who was with us?

Somewhere under all these others, I suppose.

Shouldn't we at least be protecting all these children?

No. They are protecting us.

Helicopters clatter overhead with hollow amplified voices like those of creatures from outer space. *"You must leave this property immediately! Put down your weapons! You are all under arrest!"* They go largely unheeded. Though many have been brought low, the remaining

Brunist Defenders and Christian Patriots, under the command of Ross McDaniel, the deputy acting sheriff and Patriot sergeant-at-arms, have managed to pin back the enemy forces at the top of the hill, using the excavated outline of the temple floor plan as a shallow trench bulwarked by fallen bodies, and they continue to exchange sporadic gunfire. At least, for the moment, the shooting has stopped from the base of the hill, where the town banker, exercising his wartime experience as a decorated senior officer, has pushed aside the state governor and the frightened young National Guard captain and ordered the rattled troops to stop firing and take cover behind the buses. With the megaphone wrested from the young officer, he turns to the outraged townsfolk, arriving now by the carloads, seeking revenge for the horrors visited upon them, and appeals to them to put away their weapons, warning them that they could face imprisonment or worse. They should return to their cars at once and clear the area. None do—it was the banker himself, after all, who urged them all to arm themselves—but at least, after his warning, they stop taking potshots at the tunicked zealots on the hillside. He moves through the crowd, seeking out law officers, firemen, medics, conferring with them, and as he points out various positions, they all spread out.

Although they think of themselves as righteous servants of God and country, the citizenry at the foot and those in the air are serving human laws, not divine ones, and thus are recognized by those fighting the Holy War of the Last Days as members of the legions assembled by Satan, it being in the nature of the Powers of Darkness that they do not *know* they are the Powers of Darkness, just as, though they are doomed, they cannot know that they are doomed, else they would not play the roles in God's grand scheme that they are obliged to play. Such are the beliefs of the ardent young Brunist evangelist, presently scrunched down in the puddled grave at the temple cornerstone intended for the last remains of the Prophet Giovanni Bruno, together with the hysterical First Follower and visionary who is his constant companion. As he once replied to the young woman accused by many of being the Antichrist—and perhaps she is indeed an unwitting manifestation of that enigmatic figure, so essential to the Apocalypse—when she protested that it seemed unfair of the deity to single out a chosen elite: "Well, too bad. That's how it is." Victims have fallen in on top of them, but they have been pushed out again.

"Can we fly to Heaven now, Darren?"

"No, we'll wait here."

"I'm afraid. I want to go sit in my chair."

"Stay down, Colin. We're safe here."

*"I want my chair!"*

"Here, this is *like* your chair."

"It's *wet!*"

"No, it's all right. Just sit on me. Raise yourself up a little so I can... there. Is that better?"

From the other empty cornerstone grave comes the stentorian voice of the spiritual leader of the Holy Remnant, the Brunist Bishop of West Condon. *"Sound the alarm on my holy mountain! Let all the habitants of the land tremble, for the day of the Lord has come!"* He has been foxholed there by his loyal supporters, who shield him from those who wish to kill him. He is staunch and unbowed still, fist raised in defiance of the stuttering gunfire around him. *"There has never been such a day before, and there won't be no other after it! The sun and the moon they'll go dark, and the stars will quit their shining!"* On top of the Mount of Redemption, intent on thwarting the will of the Almighty, is the Romanist villain who thrashed him so mercilessly when he was held, like the Apostle Paul, in captivity: It is all falling into place. Divine history is revealing itself. He is who he has always thought he is. *"Do you hear?"* he bellows, his voice resounding over the scorched hillside. *"Yea, God is fed up with the wickedness on earth and nothing will escape His fury!"*

His chief guardian, the black-bearded deputy acting sheriff, hunkered down in the trench next to him and firing at anything that moves up on top, is not so certain God has the upper hand. Through carelessness they have ceded the higher ground, and now they are easy targets out here on this barren hillside and risk total decimation. He turns to the Christian Patriot nearest him, the bishop's new son-in-law. "I want you to cover me, Lawson. Keep them pinned down up there. They're mostly just kids and scared outa their skins. You shouldn't have no problems. If they show more'n their cowlicks, put a bullet in their dumb brains to give 'em something new to think about. I'm gonna make a run for them backhoes." He selects two Brunist Defenders to go with him, and as they are about to attempt their run, another in a plaid shirt and billed cap, leaning on his rifle, struggles to his feet and begins to sing: *"Stand up, stand up for Jesus, ye soldiers of the cross!"* Yet another rises beside him, then another. *"Lift high His royal banner, it must not suffer loss!"* Soon there are half a dozen, then ten, twelve others courageously pulling themselves erect and raising their militant voices, rifles at their shoulders, their fusillades pounding the hilltop rhythmically as they sing. Even the old fellow in the wheelchair pushes himself forward and joins in with his sharp nasal caw. *"From victory unto victory His army shall He lead...!"* It works. The Patriot leader and his team run low behind them, sprint the final open yards, and reach the backhoes before the first shots are fired at them, bullets now whanging ineffectually off the backhoes' pressed steel bodies.

At the foot of the hill, the town banker and team captain, having positioned his gathered forces in preparation for wresting the hill away from the cultists and their adversaries, delivers his ultimatum to the governor. His price is a multi-million dollar emergency rescue fund for the town. "Otherwise, these cameras are writing your political obituary. You might as well go up there and lie down with the others." The governor, though clearly shaken by events, tells him to go to hell, his jaw thrust forward in political poster defiance. "Moreover, Governor, I can prove criminal negligence. I have all the evidence. Including recorded phone conversations." The governor cries out in exasperation as someone else cries: "*Look out!*"

A backhoe bears down on them like some long-necked prehistoric monster, head bobbing and smacking the earth, iron jaws agape, picking up speed as it careens down the hillside, rolling over the crippled and the dead, taking out the little tree, its lifeless black-bearded operator slumped over the controls. They barely have time to lurch out of the way, the banker shouting a warning to those huddled down behind the school buses, when the backhoe slams into them, overturning one of them, somersaulting over its own bucket and dipper stick and landing on top of the heap, belly up.

Shocked silence follows, broken only by scattered moans.

And then: *"Fire! Fire at the camp!"*

Pillars of smoke are indeed rising over the camp. *"It's the biker gang!"* The helicopters go wheeling urgently in that direction. "Yes, there's a motorcycle down there!" comes the crackly report from the sky. "And a couple of dead guys. One's wearing a badge, might be a cop. And—*wait!*—we do see movement! Over near some kind of shed! Looks like they might be shooting at us!"

"Whoever they are," the governor screams, "take them out! *Now!*"

"Careful, Kirk, there may be some innocent people over there."

"Out of my way, Cavanaugh! Captain! Mobilize your forces! Prepare to occupy the camp!"

The banker shakes his head, lifts the megaphone, and directs his own hastily assembled troops to move up the hill with him, drawing a net around the belligerents, just as the Knights of Columbus Volunteers appear at the top, weapons leveled at the cultists, ordering them not to move. Their leader, grinning around a thick wad of gum, waves the banker up, saluting him ironically. One last moment of suicidal madness, and then it is over. At least on the Mount of Redemption. Not far away, the camp is being shelled. And then that stops, too. It is not yet three in the afternoon.

The Brunist Tabernacle of Light, represented by the chalky cross carved out on the side of the hill, slowly empties out, its traumatized worshippers and their Defender and Christian Patriot guardians ported off to jails, hospitals, mental institutions, and the temporary morgue in the West Condon city hospital parking lot. Some at the foot have cheered the takeover of the mine hill and the humiliation of the cult, shouting insults at them as they are led away, but the majority, somewhat awed by all that they have witnessed, watch quietly, then they drift away, returning to their smoldering town. Most West Condoners, like people everywhere, even if church-goers of one persuasion or another, are content to live out their insignificant lives (ultimately, they console themselves, all lives are insignificant) within the conventions of human history, the modest everyday stuff as found on tombstones and in newspaper obituaries. It is for them that the many reporters and cameramen are recording all these happenings, looking always for those iconic moments by which large events are later remembered—the helicopter on the bar-and-grill roof, for example, the runaway backhoe, the present scatter of abandoned tunics on the hillside—and they find another now when the young Brunist evangelist with the blond curls rises peaceably from the empty grave at the foot of the trenched cross with his terrified friend clinging to his side. Though the young man respects human history as evidence, sometimes hidden, of God's entrammelment in human affairs (this is how the Christ story is to be understood), he himself lives within divine history, as best he understands it. Today that history has been full of a terrible violence, but, as he knows, it is not terrible to God, for whom death is only a kind of brief translation to a more glorious state and not to be feared. Both are handcuffed, and as the terrified boy is torn away from his side and commences to scream hysterically, the young man says, "Please. Don't hurt him. He needs help." There is a vulgar reply, which will be cut from the evening newscasts, and then he who lives in divine history turns to the news cameras on the slope below him, and with a sad, forgiving smile, raises his manacled wrists above his golden head, and this is the image that will appear over and over that evening across the nation.

* * *

Wait a minute, you can't leave me!

Of course I can. I am already on my way. Electric shocks, drugs, needles in the brain: who knows what terrible scourgings they have in mind? The baths probably aren't as much fun as the ones we've had either.

But what will I do? Who will I be?

You will be what's left when I am gone. You have to admit it wasn't a perfect arrangement. No man can serve two masters, as they say.

As you said, you thieving sophist. But where will you go?

Who knows? The foxes have holes, and the birds of the air have nests; but the Son of Man hath not where to lay his head…

There are NO VISITORS and RESTRICTED AREA signs posted on the taped-up hospital doors, but Ted Cavanaugh speaks with the staff, checks the admissions lists at the nurses' stations, looks in on employees, bank clients, people he knows. Too many. Some are in isolated intensive care; others have already been sent home. Some have died. In general, a scene of controlled chaos. More or less controlled. Rooms full. Loaded gurneys in the corridors. A lot of moaning and crying. Medics and nurses rushing about, strangers mostly, volunteers from the towns around somewhat lost but getting the job done. Many of the victims are out under Red Cross and army field tents on the hospital grounds and in the parking lot; he makes a mental list, will visit them before returning home.

Where he will be watching over Irene on his own tonight. When he stopped in on his way in from Deepwater, where he'd stayed until the mine hill was cleared and secured, he found Tommy alone with her, Concetta and her friends off doing their grieving—the whole town is grieving—and he promised to relieve him as soon as he has finished his hospital run. Ted told Irene a bit of what had happened at the bank, leaving out most of the details so as not to upset her, and what she said was, "Well, dear, you should be more careful." He saw by the snaking of the cord that the phone had been back in her room. Tommy said it was some friend and they were praying together in her new R.C. fashion. Meaning that conniving prick from their college days is still calling her. It was too early for a drink, but he poured one anyway. Tommy said that while one of Concetta's friends was still in the house, he had gone back to the bank as Ted had asked, and had found the office broken into and ransacked. "I think I surprised someone because I heard noises at the back and found the security door open back there. It's locked up again now, but probably too late."

No doubt in Ted's mind who it was. On a television screen over one of the nurses' stations, he sees him now, taking credit for overseeing the emergency operations in the unexplained absence of the mayor. Some fear, he says, that the mayor might have been killed in the powerful blast at city hall, where the search for survivors goes on. Nick knows damned well that the mayor has absconded and he may know where he is, may have been in on it. On the car radio driving here: a news bulletin from the city, where they have apprehended an armed criminal at the international airport said to be a man named Giorgio Lucci from West Condon, driving a stolen official vehicle and suspected of grand larceny. Rumors of mob connections. Ted knows Lucci. Town loafer, no scruples, no brains. A fall guy. Nick tells the reporter now that the city is applying for federal disaster relief funds, and the governor has personally assured him that emergency state funds will be made immediately available to them. He mentions in passing that Marine veteran Charles Bonali, "one of the heroes of the police intervention at the mine hill," has been appointed to the city force as temporary replacement for the murdered officer Monroe Wallace. Never knew Monk's real name before. That's what obituaries are for. Get to know somebody. Certainly he has gotten to know Nick Minicozzi. When the crisis is over, Ted has work to do. And he will do it. Kirkpatrick makes a cameo appearance. Ted heard the governor on the car radio complaining about the local corruption, arrogance, and incompetence that had forced the state to step in to prevent total anarchy. He lamented the local failure to heed his constant warnings about the perversion of traditional Christian values by a conspiracy of militant extremists with known communist histories. Now, however, they are showing images of the two small children killed during the shelling of the church camp, the only known victims, and he is more subdued. All he can say is that the camp was a closed-off area; the reporters who went in there were breaking the law.

Gus Baird, the Rotary president and travel agent, is on one of the gurneys in the corridor. He looks pretty far gone, but he winks at Ted and Ted grins and winks back. Gus is humming weakly. "Smoke got in my eyes," he wheezes. "You'll be all right, Gus." Gus shakes his head, winks again. "Something deep inside," he warbles faintly, a joker even in extremity, "cannot be denied…"

Doc Lewis comes down the corridor, stripping off translucent gloves, and instructs a couple of nurses' assistants to wheel Gus into the emergency room where doctors are waiting for him. Lewis fills him in briefly on who's dead, who's not, who's likely to be. "Not sure how long the old generator will hold out. We're beginning to move many of the less critically wounded to other hospitals around."

"Not been a great day." Ted realizes he has been thinking in tight abbreviated phrases. Like a lot of song lyrics. And repeating himself the way songs do. Someday, when I'm awfully low, when the world is cold… "One thing out at the mine hill, M.L., really got me down. There was a lot of shooting going on and people were getting killed. And down at the foot of the hill were all these people from town. Our fellow citizens. Cheering loudly whenever one of the cultists fell."

Lewis nods grimly. "I know. We've received phone calls from people saying we shouldn't be doctoring them, they deserve to die." M.L. looks as exhausted as Ted feels. He's ready to call it a day. Nothing to eat since breakfast. Go home, put a couple of steaks on the grill for him and Tommy, open a fifth of sour mash. Another way of communing with the higher powers. "By the way," M.L. says, "they brought in some preacher they picked up on the hill named Jenkins. Not from around here. But he mentioned your name."

"Jenkins! Christ! Our new minister! Forgot all about him! Where is he?"

"I'm going that way. I'll take you to him. I can't find anything physically wrong with him except that he's incontinent and rather badly bruised, probably from getting trampled on. But when we try to stand him up, he just falls down again."

On the way in, a nurse passing by shakes her head sadly at the doctor. "Mr. Baird," she says.

Jenkins is a pale puffy young fellow with startled wet eyes and unwiped mucus on his upper lip. Looks as if all his blood has just been sucked out of him. Damp, funky smell. Ted tells him he's sorry he wasn't there to meet him when he arrived, but it's not clear that the man registers anything. He is trying to say something, but it's inaudible. Ted bends down, asks him to repeat himself. "Don't..." Still can't quite catch it. The man stares at him as if at his worst nightmare. Ted closes his right ear with a finger, leans in with the left ear to the man's lips. "I don't think..." Reverend Jenkins whispers faintly, "...I want the job."

When Sally Elliott finally pulls herself out of the culvert in the ditch, dusk is settling on the camp behind her, and on the mine hill across the way, fast falling the eventide. She is stiff and sore, her knees are banged up, her breasts are raw from sunburn and the grit she's been lying in, her throat and lungs are raspy from wood smoke. But she's still here. Wasn't confident she would be. She's not hungry, but her belly is so empty it hurts. When she fell from the tipple, she dropped her notebook, cameras, T-shirt, backpack, banged her knees and most everything else, but the fall probably saved her life, the bullets dinging off the tipple supports above her. She crawled frantically toward her bicycle behind the mine buildings, expecting the worst, fearing they might come over after her, but by then there had been a massive explosion like a bomb had been dropped, and they were shooting at each other. She had apparently been forgotten. Her knees were shaky, but she was able to pedal away from the mine, always keeping the buildings between her and the cultists and not looking back, heart pounding, until she reached the old county road. That in turn, heading home, carried her past the shiny pea-green bump she'd seen from the tipple. Smoke was rising from the camp. She should have kept going.

Looking. Knowing. Her mantra. Big deal. There are some things she doesn't want to see, know. Sure. But she can't stop herself. She always has to look. It's a kind of systems flaw. She tried not to cry, but when she started, she couldn't stop. If she had eaten anything all day, she would have been throwing up. Instead, a kind of hiccuppy weeping that was worse than throwing up. Next thing she knew, somebody was shooting at her again, and she threw herself into the ditch. There was an open culvert there and she crawled in, still crying. She heard a bullet hit the car and break a window. Then suddenly there were much louder sounds. Helicopters rattling away overhead, shells exploding. Sirens. The loud crackle of a big fire. The culvert was the right place to be. By the time the shelling had stopped, so had her sobbing. A moment of relative quiet and then a lot of men running past overhead, shouting commands, discovering the car, shouting some more, obscenities mostly, then running on into the camp. Gunfire. Shouts: they found somebody. She stayed where she was.

Eventually they brought whoever it was over to the car and grilled him about the body in it. They called him names. It sounded like they were slapping him around some. He was whimpering and crying out each time they struck him. He was only guarding the camp for his father, he whined. He didn't do anything; it was the motorcycle gang. They asked him whose bicycle that was and he said he didn't know. That was probably the creep shooting at her, but he didn't give her away, she has to give him that much. More likely he really didn't know who she was or where she was and was maybe afraid, if they did find her, she'd tell them he'd been trying to kill her, or she'd already be dead, and he was in enough trouble already. She could have stepped out and answered a lot of questions for them, but she decided it wasn't a good idea. Especially being shirtless. There was a conference around the car, some walkie-talkie talk, and then an ambulance arrived and they took the body away and a police car came and took their prisoner away.

There were soldiers in and around the ditch for a while, so she stayed put. Taking mental notes. Thinking about teleological fantasies. The madness of "grand narratives": history going somewhere. Her theme of the day. Wishing she had her notebook with her. One of the soldiers told a dirty joke, but nobody laughed. They bitched about the smoke, the officers, the bizarre things they'd seen. Life and death got mentioned. Eventually they all left, and as the long summer day drew to a close, it grew dimmer, darkness descending. It seemed safe. She crept out.

They have taken her bicycle. Which means she'll have to walk home. Probably have to answer some questions. She'll tell them she ran away into the woods and just kept on going. She won't say anything about being shot at; fair's fair. Over the camp, black smoke is rising; still burning. Across the way the mine hill is empty except for a small patrol of soldiers at the foot. It looks sad and worn out. Abused. Cratered. A few abandoned tunics. A lot of wrecked vehicles. The little tree isn't there anymore. She wonders if her notebook is still over there somewhere under the tipple. Full of unforgettable musings she'll never remember. She'll go back tomorrow and look for it. Too tired now. Too tired to walk home, too, and her battered knees are killing her, but she has no choice, and so she sets out, humming along bravely. The darkness deepens…

Car lights. She considers throwing herself into the ditch again. But too late, they've seen her. It's all right. It's the family car. Her mother. Says she has been looking all over for her. Where's her shirt? And she starts to cry again. Her mother begins to get a bit hysterical, asks if it was those soldiers, did they do something, should they go see the doctor, which makes her laugh. So she's laughing and bawling at the same time and completely out of control, which is just about right if you've been through the Apocalypse and crawled out the other side.

# IV.7

## Wednesday 8 July and beyond

The first question Mr. John P. Suggs asks when he wakes up in Lem's bedroom the next morning is: Where am I? Bernice knows what's coming, all she needs is the W, but she takes her time, lets him work a bit, get his broken wits about him. "A safe place, Mr. Suggs," she tells him when she acknowledges at last that his eye-blink question has been understood. "Sheriff Puller arranged it through the secret service. Them evil Baxter people, they tried to murder you, but the sheriff he held them off long enough for us to get away." It is difficult to read his thoughts because his face is so frozen. Distrust? Fright? Gratitude? Mere confusion? "Abner has called his bad biker boys back. You recollect that dynymite they stole? The whole hospital got exploded and a lot of people was shot. But it was you they was aiming at. God spoke to me and I come a-running. We only got out barely just in time." When she found the Brunist camp empty early yesterday morning, even Clara's trailer gone, she drove over to the mine hill, where people were massing up at the crossroads. Those two old coalminers from West Virginia waved at her, and then the others did, too, but mostly they were not people Bernice knew. She didn't see Clara's trailer or Mabel Hall's caravan anywhere, but she did see ill-tempered Abner Baxter, and he seemed to be in the middle of things. She couldn't find a place to park without walking half a mile back, it was still rainy, there were a lot of guns, people weren't getting on, so she decided to return to the hospital to check on Mr. Suggs. Was God speaking to her? He was. Through Abner Baxter and her distaste for the man and his wrathful elocutions, which chased her off. "Sheriff Puller and his men they killed a lot of them, but them bad boys blowed up the sheriff's car. That made him mad. You might of heard that."

At the hospital, she found the doors blocked off by outsiders issuing commands in nervous high-pitched voices, but after she showed them her nursing credentials, they let her in. Near the entrance: an ambulance, still smoking, that looked like it had had a bad accident from the inside out. Which, it turned out, is what had happened, though it was no accident. Blood on the shattered windshield, and blood and wreckage in the reception area, too. A violent devastation. She couldn't help but be put in mind of all the End Times talk of recent weeks, talk she had a habit of not listening to, and she wondered, just for a moment, if she might regret having left the hill. Later, she learned about her friend Francesca and all the other unfortunate people who were in there when it happened. Two of them were dead and Francesca and a patient who came in with an earache were in intensive care. She describes this horrific scene for Mr. Suggs while feeding him a bite of soft-boiled egg, recounting her passage as if it were still blowing up as she went running through. She found her friend Maudie, the head nurse, on the second floor, dashing about among all the patients being wheeled in. Maudie told her about the bikers' attack and how they asked for Mr. Suggs' room and how, thinking fast, she sent them into the room of an old Italian man who had died overnight and that's who they shot so many times that, as Maudie said, "There ain't face enough left to name him by." Bernice tells Mr. Suggs how she got a young doctor to help her whisk him out of his bed and hide him in the nurses' restroom, even as they could hear Mr. Suggs' name being shouted out and the boots of the motorbikers clattering up the steps. "That poor nice doctor. He didn't make it." She describes the bullets smashing right through the restroom door and walls (Maudie showed her the holes and the pockmarks on the inside) and zinging around their heads. She started to say that they were helped, not by a doctor, but by one of God's angels. For that, though it certainly probably didn't actually happen, is what it feels like when she thinks about it, but she's not sure what Mr. Suggs understands about spiritual beings; he's only a man, after all, and a businessman at that.

Clearly it was time to move Mr. Suggs to a safer place and that's what Maudie thought, too, and besides, as the doctors said, if she was willing to take responsibility it would free up a badly needed bed, and they would be grateful for that. She had to wait for one of the out-of-town ambulances to find time to help her, so meantime she helped care for the injured, cutting away clothing and washing the wounds, giving pain injections and tetanus shots, hooking up transfusions, doing whatever Maudie and the doctors asked her to do. She even assisted a surgeon in taking a bullet out of a young woman's sitter. She had hoped to sprinkle some of her miracle water on Francesca, but the poor lady was in the operating room and she couldn't go in there. Caring for Mr. Suggs would be hard work, as Maudie warned her, for there isn't much the man can do for himself. Though he can swallow a morsel of food now, he can't do much chewing, so she'll need to mash everything up. The hospital will provide a catering and laundry service that Mr. Suggs can pay for. Theropests, too, who will visit at least three times each week as soon as the present crisis is over, and Maudie promised to drop by regularly. She doesn't tell Mr. Suggs any of this now. She only says he is being cared for by a team of the nation's top professionals who have been sworn to secrecy as to his whereabouts because those assassins are still on the loose.

Finally, two young men came to help her, though they didn't really know what they were doing and their ambulance wasn't one, just a rattly old station wagon with the back seats taken out, but something better than nothing. Mr. Suggs was not easy to shift, a heavy and lifeless old thing, and the two young fellows nearly collapsed under the bulk of him. On their car radio, she could hear that things were turning darksome out on the mine hill, and she was thankful that God had guided her away from there. At home, she treated Lem's bed with a spray Maudie said was for killing chinches and whatever other hatefuls might have got in there since the last laundering, and the two young men managed, grunting and snorting, to roll him into it and onto the towels she spread there, and she thanked them and gave them her blessing. Mr. Suggs was restless in the spirit after all this upheaval and making bubbly groaning noises with his eyes half rolled back, so, though it's maybe not the best thing for a stroke victim, after the ambulance had left, she injected him with a little something to relax him and guarantee him (and her) a night's sleep, she being completely beat down after the long and tempestuous day. "What's happening is they's a war on out there, Mr. Suggs," she says now in response to his laboriously eye-blinked question. "It's maybe just only a murderous feud, but most reckon it's a full-blowed Holy War, God and Americans against Satan and the humanits and everbody else, and famous Christian patriots like yourself are spang in the middle of it. Them killers, they knew who you was. They was calling out your name, and they pert nigh got you, but you got strong and reliable friends, Mr. Suggs, and I am one of them. We will not let them carry out their evil machineries."

In the afternoon, after Mr. Suggs has dropped off and she has washed and diapered him—he looks set for a long doze, and even if he does wake up, he's not going anywhere—Bernice returns to the hospital, which is still mostly frenzy and turmoil like yesterday, relatives having got in to add to the pandemonium. There are crowds of people on the grounds outside and she later learns they are mostly people from out of town, come to witness in person what they have seen on TV. Some of them take her picture as she enters the hospital, so she walks erectly with measured steps, a sister of mercy with work to do. The hospital staff is desperately stretched, many of the volunteers having faded away or been called back to their own hospitals. They are running out of things like bandages and linens and rubber gloves, and they're so tired it's easy to make mistakes, like forgetting people parked on gurneys or getting the medicines mixed up, so after she has gathered up the extra things she needs for Mr. Suggs, she helps out as best she can. She is glad to be here and to be useful and, above all, to be around human beings with whom she can have a normal mouth-and-ears conversation without having to worry about her spelling. There may have been hundreds of people killed and injured, she learns, worse than any mine disaster around here ever, most of the bodies now out in the hospital parking lot under the autopsy tent or else already in funeral homes. The hospital is chock full of shot and injured persons, and she is sorely needed.

One who has not made it through the night is her friend Francesca, the hospital receptionist. Bernice wonders if she might have saved her with her miracle healing water had they let her in, but she was so severely injured they say it's a blessing she didn't survive. It was Francesca who first told Bernice about the miracle water. She had an aunt, she said, who was suffering from a cyst so bad she couldn't sit down and she dipped her fingers in holy water and touched the place where the cyst was and it disappeared. It has also been known to cure rheumatic fever, dropsy, and psoriasis, and can sometimes remove warts. Bernice learned that this magic water was kept in a big stone bowl at the entrance of the Catholic church and it was free, so, though she had never stepped foot in there, she put on a long black dress like the old Italian widows wear and covered her head and snuck in and stole a little medicine bottle of it. It didn't take her wart away, but it did seem to help her heartburn when she touched her chest over her esophagus with it. When she went back for more, she was caught by the old priest who wanted to know what she was doing. She told him she was a poor widowed nurse who was thinking of converting to the Catholic religion and asked him to teach her, and he grunted and grumpily agreed. And thus, like many of her Bible heroines, she infiltrated the tents of the adversary and learned something of their ways. The first thing Bernice learned was that she was dipping the fingers of her wrong hand, which was what had given her away to the priest and was probably one reason the water wasn't working as well as it should. The second thing was that there was a faucet not far away marked HOLY WATER and she could take all she wanted, though for it to be more than only plain water she had to become a Catholic and learn certain incantations, which were the secret of its magical effects, so she continued with her lessons. She told the priest she had a strong belief in angels and devils and felt like they were all around her all the time (omitting any mention of the ghosts, fairies, demons, talking objects and creatures, and dream spirits who also populate her world). She might have carried her deception right up to the final baptism, but the old priest wearied of her and turned her over to a dotty old orange-haired Italian lady with bad breath, so she filled up two milk bottles from the faucet and left with what knowledge she had and did not return.

That old priest got thoroughly shot up when he tried to stop the motorcycle gang from blowing up the Catholic church, but he is pulling through. His people are saying it's a miracle. Maybe he went heavy on the water. They are showing the wreckage inside his church on the television at the nurses' station, along with other scenes from yesterday, and Bernice can see over the crowd clustered there that truly awful things happened, including a crazy scene of a backhoe gone berserk, barreling down a hill right over people like the Biblical Behemoth she has seen in pictures. West Condon is famous again and everyone all over the world is talking about it, but not in a flattering way. Watching all that cruel uproar, Bernice feels a headache coming on and takes the vial of miracle water out of her medicine bag and dabs her forehead and the back of her neck with it. When Maudie passes by, she asks her if she thinks people should be looking at such dreadful events, and Maudie says at least it keeps them out from underfoot.

Outside Roy Coates' hospital room, she finds his wife Thelma sitting on a chair, looking off into the distance with her usual doleful expression. Thelma says that Roy got shot and stomped on and their son Aaron has been arrested and they're coming to take Roy away to the prison hospital as soon as he's fit to be moved. She's afraid for both of them because they are talking about murder, like with Abner and

Junior Baxter. "Mostly they arrested the men and let the women go," she says. Bernice says she missed all that because of Mr. Suggs, and Thelma says, "Well, you was smart to do so, Bernice, and I dearly wisht I could say the same. I hear tell you got him to home now."

"They was trying to kill him here."

"That's what Maudie says. She's a good soul, Maudie, even if she is a Babtist." Thelma tells her in her flat sad monotone that the Cox boy got killed, and that brave McDaniel fellow and Franny Baxter's new husband—"She's a widder now, and she ain't even hardly married yet!"—and also Mildred Gray. "When the police started up the hill and them Eye-talians started down from the top, Ezra was hollering out his holy curses on them all, and Mildred she said, 'It's okay, Ezra, I'll go take care of it,' and she left his wheelchair and picked up a gun from the ground and started walking up toward the Eye-talians with this spooky smile on her face, and they all shot her at once, like they was at the carnival, shooting at one a them tin rabbits on a pull-chain. Meantimes, the church camp it caught on fire just like that boy Darren foresaid it would, and Abner he prophesied it, too, so I guess it was a thing ordained. When I seen the smoke, I was afeerd for Clara who had stayed back with Mabel and some a them, but either they got out in time or more likely they was taken prisoner. That's what they're saying. Them army heliocopters fired a lotta rockets into the camp on accounta they thought they seen some bikers over there, but so far as I hear tell only one biker got killt and he was maybe probably already dead, but two of Wanda's little ones got bombed on. The governor tried to blame that on the biker boys, but Maudie says it was them heliocopters of his done it. They searched all over but couldn't find Wanda. I'm sure I seen her up on the Mount just before everything turned so bad, but then she just plain disappeared."

"Maybe she was already dead and that was her ghost."

Thelma nods bleakly. "Nor else she got raptured suddenly, though she don't seem the likeliest choice. They arrested Junior Baxter over to the camp. They say he killt some people, I don't know who. The Baxters, they are in a ruinous state. Two boys run off and into deadly mischief, at least one of them dead and his head gone missing, the oldest boy in jail and Abner right in there with him, and little Amanda kidnapped and made to do wicked things—some say they witnessed her bare nekkid on the back of a motorbike and others say they seen even worse things. Poor Sarah, she is a lost soul, she don't even know what's happening, though I do hear Franny and Tessie has took her in, so that's a blessing. And our church, you know, the one in town, it also got burnt down, clean to the ground."

"I heard. I must of seen it just before."

"You was over there?"

"Just passing by on the way here." Driving in from the mine yesterday morning, Bernice spied the little Baxter girl walking on the side of the road in the last of the drizzle in her black dress, no raincoat or umbrella, so she pulled over and offered her a ride. The girl is simple, and perhaps she was lost. No, she said, her dress was too hot, and now it was all wet. She wanted to go home and change. Home? She only smiled like she always does. It might have been more proper to take her back to her mother, she was not a child to be left alone anywhere, but on the car radio they were reporting that the power was out in the town of West Condon and the phones as well and it might be sabotage. If that was so, the road behind her was going to fill up with people rushing back, so her best option was to take advantage of her head start and get on into town. She decided to drop Amanda off at the Church of the Nazarene, hoping there was someone there who could take care of her. On her car radio they were reporting trouble at the hospital and the high school, so it made her trip in all the more urgent. She told Amanda to stay there and she'd pick her up later, not knowing the trouble she was dropping the poor child into.

"Also Lucy Smith was in the bank when it blowed up and she is dead or nearly," Thelma says, continuing her drear litany. "And Linda Catter is passed on and they say they killt the barber, too." Thelma's voice has risen as though she is about to cry. And then she does cry. "Ain't nobody left in town to cut your hair," she wails. She gulps and wipes her nose and turns her teary gaze away. "God never does nothing wrong, Bernice," she says, the words catching in her throat, "and He always does the right thing. He's always loving, fair, honest'n pure, like the preachers say. He knows everthing and He's more powerful than anything else or anybody who's ever lived nor never's gonna live. I believe that. I got to. But sometimes, when things happen, it's all so hard to take in. Our brains is just too puny. And the question is"—she's sobbing now—"why didn't He make them *bigger?*"

"I know, Mr. Suggs, that there is some things you can't remember. When the Devil shot you with his ray gun, he was trying to melt your brains, and he come near to doing that, but your brains is strong and they did not give up and they will not give up. And meantime we got all the best doctors in the world working on an anecdote against them rays. At the Fourth of July parade—you was there, but you probably don't recollect this, not now, but some day it will come back to you—the governor called you a patriarch of the people just like Abraham and said that you was one of the country's greatest Christians and bravest patriots, and he would not let Satan have his fiendish way with you, and that is why he put the secret service in charge of protecting and rehabitating you. And, oh yes, did I tell you? The governor he is a Brunist now. He is a believer. Because of how brave and dignified you were, he come to realize you must be on to something important, so he confessed his sins, or a bunch of them anyways, right there on Main Street, and Clara herself baptized him. And Ben Wosznick, he took time out from defending the camp against all them hosts of ungodly Baxterites and sung a nice song about you. About how Mr. Suggs filled all them thugs fulla slugs and got lotsa hugs." She has worked hard on this, but Mr. Suggs looks skeptical and has one finger up as though to wag it. "Course it's not one of his best songs."

"Well, the governor's not stupid," is what Maudie said yesterday. "He can see which way the wind is breaking." After all Bernice's help at the hospital, Maudie wanted to have a coffee with her before she went back home to Mr. Suggs to thank her for all she'd done. "You made a big difference this afternoon, Bernice, and we are all beholden to you," she said, and Bernice said she was just as beholden to Maudie for saving Mr. Suggs' life. According to Maudie, that things got so out of control was at least partly the governor's fault for not acting sooner and then for overreacting in careless and arrogant ways, but TV news was exposing all that and he was backing down from his highhat ways and, thanks to the negotiations of the smart young city manager, Mr. Minicozzi, was beginning to come across with the disaster relief funds needed for the town's recovery. Mr. Minicozzi is in charge of West Condon, Maudie explained, because the mayor ran off with the city payroll. "They don't know where that bandit is and nor the money neither, but at least they caught his dopey sidekick, who thought he was on his way to Brazil, but didn't even have a passport, nor know what one was." They reminisced over lost friends like Francesca and poor brave Mr. Beeker and the beautician Linda Catter and the kindly pharmacist Doc Foley, who Maudie said was almost like part of the family. "Dr. Lewis, he is just desolated," she said, and Bernice thought about that old Bible word and how it fit so many things. Maudie also talked about Mr. McDaniel, who, Bernice learned, was the man in the runaway backhoe. He was an occasional Cornerstone Baptist like Maudie and Maudie said she took a fancy to him when he first turned up in town to work for Mr. Suggs, mainly because of his handsome black beard. "But then I noticed he never ever smiled, not even when he shook hands with the preacher or someone showed him their baby, and I figured there was a dark streak in him that could spoil things just when they might get interesting." Bernice is sorry he or anyone else got killed, but it means he can't turn up at Mr. Suggs' bedside and contradict her account of things, an account in which he can also now play a bigger part. A sign God still has his eye on her and on her needs.

"Abner Baxter and his people is a master plague, Mr. Suggs. They just keep on pestering the camp and won't let our people be. You can jail them and beat them and even kill them, and they just get up and keep a-swarming back, his boys carrying on their cruel killing sprees, his brash daughters seducting whomsoever chances in their neighborhood. Boy or girl, man or woman, it don't seem to matter to them. The middle boy he got mixed up with his own dynymite and blowed his head off, and now the youngest girl she has took over the gang and goes riding around naked as a jailbird, the wicked little sprite." Bernice feels like Rebecca at the well, refreshing Mr. Suggs with her stories as Rebecca refreshed the thirsty travelers with her water. Mr. Suggs' mind has been scoured out by the stroke and she is anointing it with balm and refurnishing it. "As you know, before he seen the light, or claimed he did, Abner used to be one of them commynest devils, everbody knows this. Well, it turns out, he never stopped being one. That's why he hates you so. His preaching is just only for covering up his evil acts. He's like one of the Devil's main captain generals." Mr. Suggs is frantically wagging his finger. He wants to ask something. She takes her time, drawing it out letter by letter, hoping he drops off before he gets it all out. The first letter is "W" again, and soon enough, she knows he is asking where is somebody. Sheriff Puller again. She misses the sheriff. She was impressed by him and put herself in the way of him somewhat like Ruth did before her boss (Tamar's way of catching Judah's eye might have worked better but is not within Bernice's talents), but he never took notice. Well, why should he, humble servant of God that she is? There are true stories about plain ordinary women being recognized by handsome young princes for the royal beauties they really are inside, but of course that fat homely man was no young prince and he saw everybody only as criminals or not criminals, with no affection for either and no appreciation of the soul within. "I have not wanted to tell you, Mr. Suggs, so as not to overworry you unduly, but Sheriff Puller, he has disappeared. There is fear that he has been kidnapped by the humanits, which would mean we might never see him again. Or we could maybe need some ransom money. But he is a man who is never afraid and who can stubbornly suffer a lot of pain so we are not giving up hope. A special secret service commander unit has been sent out to try and locate him and rescue him if possible. I can tell you about your mine manager Mr. McDaniel, though, or Mr. McDamniel, as we call him now in the secret service, in case you was about to ask. He is not who you thought he was or who we thought he was. With some money give him by the wicked moneylender Mr. Cavanaugh, he went and got him a backhoe bigger than a barn and it was fast and bulletproof and he set about attacking everbody and laid waste half the county. He was worse than Holofernes on the warpath tearing up Judea. The governor, he ordered up some bomberplanes to try and stop him, but that backhoe had a long claw that could reach up and snatch them planes right out of the air and chaw them up." Mr. Suggs is wagging his finger again. Maybe she has gone too far too fast. "Of course, I am speaking in parables, as I'm sure you reckanize, Mr. Suggs. I mainly wisht to say he become a threat and a terror, but it don't really matter now on account of he is dead. He attacked our people on the Mount of Redemption with his backhoe, killing I don't know how many of our genuinest believers, but he brung about his own desolation when he up and somersaulted his backhoe clean over some schoolbuses that had accidentally got in his way. And you can see that wicked Mr. Cavanaugh directing him all the way. If we ever get electricity back, I can show you pictures on the tellyvision because they never weary of showing them."

Without meaning to, she has let the story jump ahead. She was still at the Fourth of July parade. She hasn't told him yet about the gathering at the Mount of Redemption and all inbetwixt, she was saving that for later, and suddenly there's Mr. McDaniel careening down the hillside. Also she took that boy's head off before she'd really got around to *his* story, but that's all right, his wild naked sister will do as well and might appeal more to Mr. Suggs' imagination. And though things in her story are a little mixed up, they aren't half as scrambled as poor Mr. Suggs' blistered brains. If he questions her, she'll just tell him she told him already and he wasn't paying attention or he fell asleep in the middle. The point is to theropy his crippled mind, get it fizzing and popping best she can, and to keep reminding him why they need his money and to what sacred use they are putting it.

* * *

Later, after Mr. Suggs has been fed some beef bouillon soup and a bite or two of mashed potatoes and has sunk back into his common afternoon stupor, Bernice prepares him for his enema and his bath, stripping off his diaper and hospital gown, and with some difficulty, tipping him over on one side. She never does this when he is alert, for he is a proud man and offended at being seen in this condition. The enemas are her preferred way of keeping account of how much goes in and how much comes out, and it's convenient to give him his baths at the same time. Even when not emptying or washing him, she must roll him from time to time so as to prevent bed sores, but his heavy lifeless body is almost too much for her. The hospital food service has made its first delivery this noon, and though everything was tasteless and overboiled, it didn't matter to Mr. Suggs and Bernice has ways of making it more flavorful for herself. She is still earning a tittle each month as Mr. Suggs' personal secretary, but with the garage burned down and Lem in jail, her widow's pittance from the mine union having stopped altogether, and a cruel vindictive mortgage to pay at the greedy bank thanks to Lem's endless refinancing of the refinancing—she is already several months behind—the leftovers from Mr. Suggs' daily meals will be a budget blessing.

When she finishes scrubbing Mr. Suggs' back and his broad flat old man's backside, white as the sheets he's lying in, and giving it its daily alcohol rub, she turns him over and goes to work on the front side and is just sudsing up his floppy old prides when the doorbell rings. She rushes to the door, still carrying the soapy washcloth, thinking it might be Maudie come to help, but it is that portly city lawyer Mr. Thornton with the pasted-down yellow hair, tailored shirts, and shiny shoes. He says he saw the horrible events on television and he was worried about her and Mr. Suggs, and since there are no telephones, he felt it best to drive here and see her and him in person and make sure everyone is all right. He went straight to the hospital and the head nurse there told him something of the calamitous attack and sent him here. She sits him down in her front room and tells him to wait until she is finished with Mr. Suggs. She feels it is not proper for him to witness Mr. Suggs in such vulnerable circumstances, for it will weaken Mr. Suggs in his eyes, and moreover she herself has not finished dressing. She has her clothing on, but she has not yet made her eyebrows, and she knows her face must look half-naked. So she lets Mr. Suggs lie there for a moment in his suds while she does that, choosing an expression for today of both concern and cleverness; then she quickly rinses Mr. Suggs off and towels him, stuffs a diaper under him just in case, spreads the fresh hospital gown over him without putting his arms in, pulls the sheet up to his chin, and invites Mr. Thornton in, warning him that, should Mr. Suggs wake up, she has not, for the old gentleman's own good, told him everything that has happened—about Ben Wosznik, for example, or Sheriff Puller, or the motorbikers' attack on the town and all the people that died—so he should be cautious about speaking of any of that. "I also have not told him yet that Mr. Cavanaugh's bank got exploded," she adds, partly for Mr. Thornton's sake, because she has come to understand in some wise just why he is so involved, "but I may try and find a way to do that, because I believe it would please him."

Mr. Thornton smiles and tips his round self forward to peer more closely at the patient, noting with approval that Mr. Suggs has been freshly shaved and even his eyebrows have been trimmed, and he asks why she brought him here. She explains that with all the terrible things that happened, there was no room for him at the hospital, and he says, yes, that's what he understood. "Besides," she says, lifting her reading glasses to her nose, "he's better here. It's more…particular." Mr. Thornton gives her a comprehending gaze and nods his head and asks how much this private care will cost? She is prepared for this. She tots up the rent, her hours at theropest wages, breakfasts and suppers and hospital catering, cleaning and laundry, medical supplies, personal hygiene items, and extras, and Mr. Thornton says: "Let's drop the extras and I think it can be arranged. I will organize a trust fund to cover it, which my law firm will administer, though we will again need witnesses, which I hope you can arrange. Until all the paperwork is completed, Mrs. Filbert, it is important that Mr. Suggs stay alive and more or less competent, even if only in this limited manner. I am still locating his many investments, which he managed entirely on his own and which are therefore less than wholly transparent."

Over a pot of tea in the front room (Bernice, having donned an apron and rolled her sleeves up like in the pictures, serves him with the same quiet humility that Martha showed when Jesus came to raise her brother Lazarus, though her head is working more like Deborah's or Judith's), Mr. Thornton asks how Mr. Suggs is accepting his new circumstances, and Bernice tells him that she has not told him this is her own house and explains about her idea of the secret service protecting him from assassins in a hidden location. "Maudie, that head nurse you talked with, she saved his life when the bikers busted into the hospital asking exactly for Mr. Suggs and she sent them into the room of a man who had already died, but it was plainly him they wanted, and so I figured it was best to hide him for a spell, and that is what I told him." He says he heard something of that story at the hospital and he congratulates her on her strategy, adding that protection of their patient's health and well-being is their primary objective, and it is easier to discuss matters like this here than in the hospital with so many other people around, which was precisely what she wanted him to say. She shows him the white blouse on which, on the pocket, she has carefully stitched B.FILBERT SECRIT SIRVIS. He smiles in a kindly way over his triple chins and reminds her that people in the secret service do not usually advertise themselves so it might be best not to wear the blouse, and she agrees and puts it away again. "I was only beguiling the time," she says.

He tells her that it is his understanding that at least one hundred seventy people will be charged with unlawful assembly, trespassing, illegal possession of lethal weapons, disturbing the peace, conspiracy to disturb the peace, and who knows what-all, and that as many as seventeen or eighteen people are to be charged with murder or conspiracy to murder or accessory to murder. "I will send you a list when I know it. You should let me know if there are any among them who are friends of yours, and I will see what I can do." She says she will do that and asks if something can be done now for Mr. Roy Coates and his son Aaron, and Mr. Thornton shakes his head and says that he believes those two are among those charged with murder and are well-documented co-conspirators, so they are probably beyond his powers of influence. "Well, at least see what you can do for the boy," she says, "on grounds of compaction." She drops her spectacles to her chest and raises one brow to suggest a worried but considerate mind. Bernice feels more like the wilier mature Rebecca now, negotiating for her favorite son, though Aaron Coates is hardly known to her. She is thinking mainly about her friend Thelma and how impressed she will be if she is able to show how powerful she can be and is already imagining Thelma on the phone telling others. "He is young and still under his father's influence and he lost his brother when them bikers burnt the boy to death in the trunk of the sheriff's car which was a awesome desolation for him and mightily disturbed his spirit."

And then, even as that horrible scene comes back to mind, sobering them both, a useful thing happens. Mr. Suggs can be heard grunting and whining in the next room, the only sounds he seems able to make when he's awake, and she takes Mr. Thornton in there to introduce him. Mr. Suggs is alert and blinking away and wagging his finger. "I been telling Mr. Suggs, Mr. Thornton," she says, "about how them motorcycle killers came after him in the hospital, hollering out his name, and tried to shoot him, and how a lot of people died and things got blowed all to flanders, and also about how that Mr. McDaniel drove a backhoe through all those poor people on the hillside and crashed into some school buses, but it's all so terrible and peculiar, I don't think he quite credits me," and Mr. Thornton nods gravely and says, "I'm afraid it's all true, Mr. Suggs. And more you have not yet been told. We are living through strange, dangerous times. I assure you, you can believe everything that Mrs. Filbert tells you."

* * *

"The Cravens boy he had a wee nick cutting clean through his life line. I asked him how he done that. He didn't know. Then 'bird,' he said. It give me a chill." Staring into Glenda Oakes' solitary eyeball gives Bernice a chill. It is like staring into the middle of nothingness. Hazel Dunlevy, before she got shot and died, looked at Bernice's palm one day and said that there was trouble on her fate line but her life line was long and deep, and that was a mostly good thing. Bernice wonders what Glenda would say now that she reads palms instead of dreams, but she is afraid to ask. The woman has become gaunt and hollow-cheeked and seems to have taken a dark turning, or maybe it's just the darkness in her has risen to the top, stirred up by the cruel times she has been through. She wears a gun in a holster and is holding a child who has been crying but now is only hiccupping. Glenda doesn't know who the child is. His parents have not returned from the Mount of Redemption to claim him. "And then, when later I was trying to get all them children to leave the garden and head for the woods and away from the camp by pretending to have a little Injun race, Davey he started wailing in his bereft manner and crying out that he wanted his mommy, and I knew that something bad was going to happen. He run off with his sister afore I could stop them. The rest of us we wasn't more'n a hunderd feet away, in under the trees and running doubled-over like all get-out, when there was a thunderous racket and the garden shed wasn't there no more, nor not the two kids neither. And that night was when them two lovebirds come back. They been haunting the camp ever since. And they ain't sorry for what they done. They're just only missing their nest."

"Is that what the gun is for?"

"No, you can't shoot a ghost. But I think I may of seen Hazel's husband Travers sniffing around out there at the edge. If he tries to get in any closer, I aim to kill him."

The church camp does have an eerie haunted feel, even by day, the humid overcast adding to its gloom. When Lucy Smith's husband Calvin, who took over as sheriff when Mr. Puller was crematized, stopped her outside the hospital and asked her if she'd do him the favor of visiting a person who was badly hurt, she'd thought he was talking about her friend Lucy, who she'd heard had survived the explosions but was somewhat bedazzled by the blow she took when her head bounced off the bank floor. But instead he drove her out here to the camp, which seems a completely different place from when she last visited it only three days ago. There is a heavy smell of wet ash and lingering wood smoke and, under the blackened trees, a weedy overgrowth springing up, aswarm with wasps and mosquitoes, and thick brown tire tracks ripping through all the green parts. The desolation, she thought, moving through it. The desolation. Most of the cabins are just black skeletal ruins. She saw a toilet standing alone on its plumbing where her sick bay once was and the sassy little Blaurock girl was sitting on it, still wearing her pink slipper, thumb in her mouth and shorts down around her ankles, while others watched and giggled. Two of the children she recognized as belonging to Glenda Oakes, so she supposed that lady must still be here. The little girl's father was working on the ruins of the cabin next to the camp lodge, the one that used to belong to Sister Debra, making walls out of old blankets nailed to the charred corner posts and roofing it with tattered tarpaulins, and two others were helping him. Calvin asked her to say nothing about what she sees here, for he is under strict orders to clear the camp, and sooner or later must do so, but he wants to protect these few remaining people from further harm as long as he can. "If it was known they were here, people hate them so, some might try to take the law into their own hands." Bernice gave him her word. She asked after Lucy and he said she had not yet got over what happened three days ago, and if Bernice is able she might pay her a visit and prescribe something for her nerves.

Calvin led her past the guards at the door into the old camp lodge, made of stone and still more or less intact though mostly black on the inside, and there at the back of the room near the iron stove, under a hanging gas lantern, a man in raggedy underpants was lying on a camp cot with an ugly wound in his thigh. She was told he had been shot and had dug the bullet out with his own knife and had somehow managed to stagger away from the hill and escape arrest. Bernice washed the wound with fresh well water a woman brought her, sprinkled it with a few drops of her miracle water, applied mercurochrome (he screamed like a child and swore at her in an unChristian way, and Calvin scolded him for that), and bandaged it. She doesn't know why, but when she was helping with the tetanus shots at the hospital during the crisis that first day, she dropped a clean needle already filled with toxoid into her shoulder bag, and now she had a use for it, and she saw that all this was foreseen. After the injection, she gave the man the rest of her mercurochrome and bandages and told him to wash the wound and medicate it and change the bandage every day. He was full of a feverish rage and told her she only had to fix him up well enough that he can make it into town and have it out with those papist wops who shot him and murdered his friends. Thus she was saving one life to bring about the possible ends of others. Medicine is like that. It fixes little problems, not the way the world works. The man didn't even thank her, but Calvin did and said there were other people needing some help and asked her if perhaps she could come back with more supplies. She said she would do that, but in truth she doubted she would ever set foot in this strange, accursed place again.

The big Blaurock woman was whumping around the Meeting Hall in her elephantine way, in and out of Clara's old office, fat baby under one arm, shouting out commands and commentary, and wishing to avoid her, Bernice asked if she could see Glenda before she left and Calvin brought her down here to the old trailer lot where Glenda is living in a cluster of old vehicles with all the children, together with a handful of other people who escaped from the Mount, mostly women. Glenda's own two caravans were stolen, but whoever took them thankfully dumped out everything before they drove off, including most of the children's toys, and they left behind the small house trailer belonging to those two West Virginia miners who never came back, and that's where Glenda is living, as well as in some abandoned cars and trucks, set about in a kind of circle the way settlers used to do on the prairie.

She and Glenda now sit amid them, swatting at the mosquitoes. Bernice says she saw that Blaurock family up by the lodge, acting like they own the place. "Well, they don't let nothing nor nobody get in their way," Glenda says, "but the camp wouldn't work without them. Isaiah, he goes out every day and forages for food and soda pops and other useful things. Dot, she has found a post office box key in Clara's old office and has pointed herself the church treasurer and is writing to the faithful, asking for money. And her kids is out peddling souvenir stuff they have found in there that didn't burn up in the fire, old letters and tape recordings and suchlike, even somebody's diary, and including, they say, some dirty pitchers them two boys was hoarding, which her little girl sold for enough to buy carryout pizza last night for everybody. It was a kinda party after all the misery. The little girl called it their nekkid bottoms party on account of the pitchers that paid for it. Clara, she would never have 'lowed that, but most everybody thought it was cute and give her a big clapping. They were too hungry not to. They ain't nothing left to eat here. They have harvested the vegetable garden right down to the dandylines and crab grass and killt alla Hunk Rumpel's chickens, and they have cooked up a great many of the wild birds and small animals. They have even et the owls."

"I took notice it was quieter than usual."

"Sister Debra would be horrified at the slaughter, but she always did care more for birds than people. Isaiah also brings back whatever newspapers he finds, and Dot, she digs through them, looking for other end-of-the-worlders. She says she's found a feller up in Canada who's got it all figured out, so they're laying plans to migrate up there and invade that movement, and they are inviting everyone along."

"Will you go?"

"I don't know what choice I got." Glenda fixes her with her one eye and a little shiver runs up her spine. There's a faint breezy rustling all about even though the air seems still and she can't help thinking about the ghosts of Hazel Dunlevy and Welford Oakes fluttering about somewhere nearby. With the lights out and the birds dead, it must be a spooky place here at night.

She tells Glenda what she has seen at the hospital and around town—all those downtown buildings full of the spirits of the recent dead, the shoe salesman still swinging in his window—and about how she and the head nurse at the hospital saved Mr. Suggs from being murdered by the motorcycle gang led by the naked Baxter girl. She is taking care of Mr. Suggs now privately, and thanks to her miracle water, he is much improved. The doctors are all amazed. "He is setting up and eating normal and don't need diapers no more. Even his hair is growing back on top of his head—and it's red as a carrot."

Several of Glenda's collection of little ones have arrived, complaining that they're hungry, and that reminds her that she has to go find Calvin to drive her back; it's Mr. Suggs' feeding time. She fishes about in her shoulder bag and finds half a packet of cough lozenges and she passes those out to the children, promising to come back with more things. Just as she's about to leave, however, Glenda takes a grip on her hand and turns it over, palm up, and studies it, her head cocked so the eye stares straight at it as if shooting a beam into it, and it feels almost like it is burning. She flinches, but Glenda has a tight grip. "I suppose people have told you, Bernice, about your head line and your life line and how little luck there is between them, but I wonder if they have showed you the line of escape, sometimes called the line of fancy, running crosstways down here near your wrist?" The children are crowding around to look. They seem quite dangerous. "Not everybody's got one, but yours is plain to see, like to say it's a powerful influence on your nature. People with lines like that, they oft-times have arty lives, but when it crosses the health line like this…" she traces a line with a long horny fingernail from Bernice's fingers to her wrist and the sensation is that of being cut open, "they can lose control and end badly."

Bernice's heart is pounding. All she wants is to have her hand back and to leave this fiendish place immediately. "Badly…?"

Glenda turns her eye up to stare it at her, still gripping the hand, her gold tooth glinting in the dusky light. "A fatal confusion of the spirit," she says, and Bernice feels her knees go wobbly. "Madness."

* * *

"I am sorry to have to tell you, Mr. Suggs, but something evil has got into the Wilderness church camp. It is infested with the ghosts of murdered sinners and a brood of filthy-minded imps and a cannibal witch who is one of them cyplops with just one eye. Wherever she walks a fire breaks out behind her and they's no more birdsong because she aims her evil eye into the trees and the birds they fall like rain. Even the owls. Murderers are lurking out at the edge, and worse things, too, if you could see them, but there's like a thick smoky cloud has sunk down over the camp with a rotten smell like the Devil makes. And Sheriff Puller, he's come back, but he is blind and walks rocking back and forth the way dead people who crawl out of their graves do. Ben Wosznik has been doing all he can, praying and fighting and singing, but he is badly wounded in the thigh and we don't know if he will live or die. I was able to doctor it, but it is a ugly wound and has got infected and we fret for him in the secret service. Clara and her daughter, they have fell into a kind of coma trance, which is that evil cyplop's doing, and many people are losing their minds or are in fear of losing their minds. I wisht I had better news, but fear and trembling has got holt of me, and I am glad that we are safe here and far from all that sad desolation."

As the days pass and Bernice recovers from her scare at the church camp, she repents of the darkness that overtook her history and begins to move it in a happier direction, telling Mr. Suggs that Ben is much better, thanks mainly to her miracle water; that Clara and Elaine have waked up from their deep sleep though they're still very weak, it being said that it was the spirit of Ely Collins who came back and kissed them both that broke the spell; and that Mr. Puller was only pretending to be a kind of zombie so as to escape his kidnappers. Too late for the birds, though. She is sorry about turning Glenda Oakes into a wicked cyplops, partly because that gives her more power than she deserves, and, hoping Mr. Suggs has forgotten what she said before, speaks of her instead as a cranky old woman who is losing her mind even as everyone else in the camp is getting theirs back. Crazy as she is, you can't believe a thing she says.

Thinking of Glenda Oakes reminds her of her promise to Calvin Smith. On a day when the theropests come, she walks over to the Smith house to visit Lucy, stopping at the hospital first to fill up her shoulder bag. There she learns that Mr. Thornton has presented Maudie with a handsome little reward on behalf of Mr. Suggs, and also a gift for the hospital to help pay the costs of their emergency generator, and he is also arranging for a free load of coal for it to be delivered from Mr. Suggs' mine. "He's a real gentleman," Maudie says, and they all thank Bernice for her part in it, and she accepts their thanks.

On her way across Main Street to Lucy's house, she finds huge crowds gathered to watch cranes lift the fallen helicopter down off the bar and grill roof, and she tells Lucy about this when she arrives. "Folks had got climated to it and booed when it come down and cheered when it tipped sideways suddenly and busted one of its fan blades." She finds Lucy more distracted and nervous than before, and there is a big lump on her forehead, but she says she is feeling better and only needs a few good nights' sleep. Bernice tells her she has brought her some pills to help with that, and also some miracle water to put on the lump and make it go away; Lucy takes some pills right away and wets some cotton with the miracle water and holds it against her brow and they sit down for some cookies and a chat, Lucy saying that she can already feel the lump going down and apologizing that she only has an electric percolator, so she can't make coffee.

Bernice fills her in on the rescue of Mr. Suggs and her errand of mercy at the church camp, adding a few details that Lucy might appreciate, and Lucy tells her how the Piccolotti boy went blind saving her life and Calvin's—"He seemed to fly way up in the air and catch the dynamite and throw it back at the bomber all in one single motion, and that was the last thing I saw!"—and how Junior Baxter apparently murdered the Tebbetts boy and maybe some others as well because he got caught with the gun in his pocket still hot from being fired, and how Calvin, who is the most peaceful and honest person in the world, is being blamed for helping some of the people who are now being charged with murder and may get put in jail himself. "He says that Vince Bonali's mean boy, who is known more for breaking the law than keeping it, wants his job and is out to get him and that Italian city manager fellow is helping him."

The strangest story, though, is that of finding two more bodies buried out at the state park, two missing young people whose parents thought they must have eloped, and also a severed head and two feet, though the feet had been mostly eaten up by animals. Naturally, everybody thought the head would be Nat Baxter's missing one, but it turned out to be his younger brother's instead. Had both brothers been beheaded? What was going on? Then they remembered that Junior Baxter, when he was arrested, kept saying that the masked biker gangleader with "Kid Rivers" on his jacket was really his brother Nat, so now a nationwide manhunt for Kid Rivers *alias* Nat Baxter has begun. Or anyway that's what Bernice supposes Lucy meant to say, for what she actually says is "…s'crazy…notion…kid…ers…" and her eyes cross and she falls fast asleep while she's still talking, such that when Calvin comes home a few moments later, he finds his wife sprawled out on the floor snoring. He smiles and calls Bernice a miracle-worker and a heroine.

Bernice's first and most enduring life model was Martha, who labored quietly in the kitchen when the Lord came to visit while her flirtatious sister sprawled idly at the Master's feet to better show off her dinners, as her father's rude miner friends sometimes called them, and of course Jesus, like all men, couldn't get enough of her or of them, falling out of her half-buttoned blouse like fruit out of a tipped bowl, and He even scolded Martha when she complained that she could use some help setting the table. Though, yes, Bernice also did sometimes complain, she was a mostly polite and biddable child who always felt she was born to serve. The gratitude of others comforted her, even that of her unloving mother, and she knew before she was twelve years old that she was going to be a nurse. Over time, Bernice grew more interested in Miriam, who saved her baby brother Moses' life and stood by him faithfully on their long arduous journey but who questioned his absolute authority, especially as she was his big sister, and as punishment got struck down with leprosy and eventually died, the point being, one, that she *did* question his authority and, two, her lifetime of loving service availed her little when she did. A lesson learned, which led her in turn to other less servile Bible women like Esther and Deborah, Jael and Judith, women of wealth and power, capable of guile and subterfuge but also of bold action like beheadings and driving tent stakes into bad men's heads, even while pursuing selfless lives of service, and she has stitched a bit of each into the wardrobe by which she presents herself each day to the world.

It is these latter women who have guided her through her most recent trials in her care of Mr. Suggs. When they came to tell her that they were waiving bail and releasing her brother-in-law Lem because all the jails were full, she replied that she was very happy to hear it for she wishes to have him near to care for his needs, hoping only that his time in prison has tempered his violent nature, which he has used so often against her in times past. "Once when he got drunk," she told them matter-of-factly, "he tried to press hisself on me and I had to fight him off with a skillet, and he said he'd cut me up and have me for dinner. Of course he probably didn't mean it and things like that don't happen all the time." She said that, though he promised to shoot the fire chief and others at the fire station as soon as they let him out of jail, they shouldn't worry because she has taken the caution to hide his guns and she won't tell him where they are even if he beats her or tries to strangle her as he has done in the past, so where are the papers, she'll be glad to sign them. They apologized and said they had decided to delay his release while they looked into his case more closely, and just to make sure she went to see the old sinner and told him she'd done all she could to try to get him set free, even told a few white lies, but there is somebody in the jail who doesn't like him and is badmouthing him to the authorities and he should find out who it is and stand up for his rights, and she could tell by the expression on his face and the cusswords he used that he would not be coming home for a good while yet. Warrior types are easy pickings for the likes of Jael, Judith, and Bernice.

Mr. Thornton is smarter and wilier than Lem or those police people, so a different approach was necessary when the lawyer presented her with the trust documents. She knows that Mr. Suggs is a very rich man and that there is probably a way to get all that money herself, but she's not smart enough, and the law is like a secret code she'll never be able to cipher. So she needed the smooth tongue of a Rebecca or an Esther. She looked up a lot of words and memorized them as best she could, and when he came, she told him that Mr. Suggs could not accept such words as "unlimited" and "esclusive" and "perpintuity" and she took Mr. Thornton into the bedroom to show him that this was so, Mr. Suggs behaving admirably, especially the vigorous way he wagged his finger, though what he was saying was not exactly like her translation. Then they sat down in her front room for a frank discussion. She had dressed that morning like Queen Esther, in a fancy white blouse and a long dark satiny dress laced up the front like boots, with her hair braided and pinned up tightly and parted down the middle, drawing her eyebrows with a very slight frown to suggest a certain royal gravity and a troubled affection, and she could see that she had Mr. Thornton's respect. She said she understood that, as Mr. Suggs had no known heirs, his wealth was being absorbed into Mr. Thornton's law company so as not to let the bankers have it all. Maybe that's the best thing, maybe it isn't, but it was what was happening and she could accept it. If they wanted her help, however, she had two requests. One was that the trust provide a substantious gift to the Brunist church in the name of Mrs. Clara Collins-Wosznik, as this was probably Mr. Suggs' own intention and it should be honored. Besides, it will help her persuade Mr. Suggs to give his approval. The other is that to care for Mr. Suggs and in such a way as to be useful to Mr. Thornton's law company is a very difficult thing and she will need to be properly reinpursed. "I got a mortgage on this house. It's not very big, you will laugh when I tell you, but with the garage burnt down and Lem in jail I am in rears and I may not be able to pay it. You know how cruel Mr. Cavanaugh is and how he is ruining this town and taking people's houses away where they have lived all their lives. I don't speak of myself, but if he took my house, where would Mr. Suggs go then? If Mr. Suggs can pay off that mortgage and cover my expenses as long as he lives, I am sure he will find it in his heart to agree to the trust." "Is this Mr. Suggs' request, Mrs. Filbert?" "It is my request, Mr. Thornton." Mr. Thornton gave her a respectful look as though to acknowledge her wisdom and her courage and her acumen and after a moment he smiled. "Your needs will be met, Mrs. Filbert. The trust will continue to provide you a monthly stipend with enough extra to cover your mortgage payments, and when Mr. Suggs passes away, you will receive a lump sum payment of ten times the amount of the remaining mortgage due. My partners and I are very grateful for your kind and valuable assistance." This was much more than she expected and she had to clench her jaws not to show her excitement. If Judith had shown her emotions, it would have been she who got her head chopped off, not Holofernes. When Mr. Thornton stood to go, he took her bony hand in his plump one and thanked her again; then he glanced tenderly toward Mr. Suggs' bedroom and sighed. "The poor dear man. It is a terrible agony he is going through. And for what? It would almost be a mercy if he could peacefully pass on."

By the time the lights come on again and the phones finally work, Bernice's account of recent history has taken a more nightmarish turn. For one thing, she has blamed the need for candles on the Baxters' use of Leviathan to drink up all the power, putting the whole world, and certainly West Condon, at their mercy, and as she is rather proud of this development, she continues to use candles long after it is necessary. The candles, moreover, cast wavery shadows around the bedroom which she characterizes as demonical spirits, pointing them out to Mr.

Suggs in a harsh frightened whisper—*"Over there! in that corner!"*—knowing he can't bend his neck to look, can only glimpse the flickering light and dark. Sometimes she even frightens herself. She has introduced into the motorcycle gang the oldest Baxter boy, the one with the Mark of the Beast on his forehead whom everybody astigmatizes, and, remembering something that blond boy once said about the Horsemen of the Acropalypse. she has given them all individual motorcycle colors and specific woes and plagues to distribute. What they all did to Clara's poor daughter has now become a legend of horrific proportions that continues to happen night after night, as if it were some eternal punishment in Hell. She has even brought back the middle Baxter boy, the one who got blown up: "They took his head off but now he's riding round with that gruesome thing tucked under his arm, still yelping curses out its bloody lips and demanding everbody what to do! I wouldn't of believed it myself if I hadn't seen him with my own eyes!" She told how Sheriff Puller was seducted into his car by the naked Baxter girl and handcuffed to the steering wheel and how the biker boys set his car afire, and how they stuffed an innocent boy in the trunk as extra fuel. Mr. Suggs seemed very upset by this story, so when he asked the pointed question if Sheriff Puller was alive or dead, she said he was alive but he was so melted down to his blackened bones you wouldn't hardly recognize him. She looks into Mr. Suggs' heavy-lidded eyes, and sometimes she sees seething anger there and sometimes confusion and sometimes even fear. As Holofernes in his drunken stupor might have felt looking up at sober sword-bearing Judith, or Sisera foggily seeing Jael enter with her hammer and tent stakes.

Of course, Bernice has no such tools, nor would she likely be treated as a national heroine, as those women were, if she had them and used them as they did. There are, true, the subtler weapons of her own profession—the feeding routines, the medications—but Mr. Suggs is being monitored constantly by Maudie and the doctors, and they would not appreciate any creative tamperings with his regime, nor would it feel the right thing to do. For she is not Judith or Jael, she is only Bernice Filbert, LPN, of West Condon, the kindly long-suffering public servant and at heart a good person intent only on helping others, even Mr. Suggs, whose own life is a great burden to him and to her, and who fails to appreciate all that she has done for him. He could have blinked out at least one thank you. It is a harsh world, governed at least partly by malevolent forces, not all visible, and Bernice has only her nursing skills and her faith with which to defend herself. And her stories. Which are not always understood by others, though they are her chief remedy against the desolation. She is reminded of something Ludie Belle once said about her prayer meeting confessions: that by being partly true and partly made up, they were more true than if they had been completely true, because the plain truth hides a lot of things.

By coincidence, as she is thinking about this, the telephone rings in the kitchen, and it is Ludie Belle herself calling from out east somewhere, almost as though by thinking about her Bernice has conjured her up, the sort of coincidence that happens often in Bernice's life. And they both have so much to tell each other! Right off, Bernice asks about Clara and Elaine and all the others, where did they go, she looked everywhere for them and was scared they'd all been kidnapped, and Ludie Belle tells her how—for Clara's sake, and little Elaine's—they took off before all the troubles. They agreed on a meeting place near the state line, and they were waiting there for Cecil and Corinne and Hovis and Uriah and Billy Don to catch up, but somebody noticed the bumper stickers they'd forgot to remove, and they all got arrested. Ludie Belle was able to convince them that those stickers got pasted on without their acknowledge while they were passing through from out west, and she showed them Clara and Elaine in their sickbeds and said they were rushing them to a hospital in the east where specialist doctors were waiting for them, and the police got nervous not to have somebody die on them and let them go, provided they immediately crossed the state line. But that made them miss the others and she still doesn't know what happened to them but supposes the three fellows are back home by now and the Applebys and their bees are probably off chasing the pollens. Bernice says she hasn't seen the Applebys, but she's sorry to say that the two West Virginia coalminers were apparently blown up on the Mount of Redemption, though there's not much remains of them to tell for sure, and as for Billy Don Tebbett, he got murdered by Young Abner Baxter. Ludie Belle lets out a little cry and says she is wholly destroyed by this news, for Billy Don was one of her favorites, and she asks for all the details and Bernice provides her with all she knows, and then some.

Ludie Belle in turn tells her that her Wayne and the Halls are doing fine and have been telling their stories to the Eastern churches, and Elaine seems to have resigned to accept the baby she is carrying and isn't trying to kill herself or it anymore, "though I did ketch her a-swoppin' her belly with a flyswat as like to get the baby customed to what's in store for it, but, come grass, Clara's grandchild should be safely borned." Bernice wants to say that she hopes it will be completely human, but decides better of it for it might bring bad luck. Ludie Belle goes on to say she hopes Clara is still around for that occasion, for the poor woman is calamitously ill with a cancer in her chest that has mettasted to other places and there is not much confidence. Bernice says this is the worst news she has heard since all these troubles began but that, somehow, she already knew it. She is thinking about what she told Mr. Suggs about Clara's strange coma, and she worries that her stories might be invading the world. "I guess I had some apperhension." At least out here, Ludie Belle says, Clara is well cared for. "They give her a lotta reception and dote upon her like the saint she is." Bernice urges her to sprinkle some miracle water on Clara every day, but Ludie Belle says she has used it all up and that Bernice should send her some more. Ludie Belle likes to wear a drop of Bernice's water behind her ear like perfume, because she believes it might help her hear what people are thinking.

Ludie Belle has been following all the news on the car radio and now TV, plus what all the brothers and sisters in the Eastern churches have been able to fill in, but it's like news from the sky and she needs to get it from on the ground, so Bernice tells her all about how when she was out at the Mount looking for everybody she had a forenotion about Mr. Suggs being in trouble and raced off to the hospital just in time to hide him from the motorbikers who were coming after him, and how she has been privately caring for him ever since. "I am now receiving a special salary from the government."

"The government?"

"I can't say no more."

In fact, Mr. Thornton has been true to his word and he has got the wicked banker's lawsuit thrown out and she has been able to catch up her mortgage. When she received the statement, she multiplied the remaining amount due by ten to see what she would receive if Mr. Suggs were to expire that day, and it was quite thrilling, but he isn't likely to pass away for some time yet. When Maudie was last here, she noticed that Mr. Suggs had lost some weight and musculature, and Bernice acknowledged that he was getting easier to turn because there was less of him, but Maudie said this was normal, she shouldn't worry, Mr. Suggs could live on for years and he might even get better. Meaning more and more of the principle will be paid off and the final sum will be smaller. Something to think about, and she has been thinking about it. She goes on now to tell Ludie Belle how the Baxter motorbikers went roaring through town blowing up everything and shooting everybody and setting the whole town on fire. "That's when the heliocopter fell and Linda Catter got sent to glory along with all those other poor people in the bank, and the one they say was Carl Dean Palmers got rocketed clean off the hotel roof."

"I got a inkle a all that on the tellyvision replays later on. They kept showin' that red injun's execution for days after. He didn't look a dot like Carl Dean."

"Well, them evil sorts, Ludie Belle, they don't always keep to their same shape. Meanwhile, out at the Mount of Redemption, they was all this killing going on. I nearly got squashed when that crazy backhoe come somersaulting down at me, like something from straight outa the Book a Relevations—you must of seen that!"

"I thought you was at the hospital."

"I was, but by happen-chance they had a TV on at the nurse's station and I seen what was happening and knew I was needed out there, so while we was waiting for a ambulance to move Mr. Suggs, I went running out to help. If you look close, you can see me off to the left scrambling on all fours towards that ravine out there, just as that backhoe goes wheels up."

"Well, you're a better person than me, Bernice. Me, I see trouble like that a-comin', I'm hikin' my skirts'n skedaddlin' the other way at full pelt. Which is what we done, and why you're there and I'm here. I did hear on the news young Darren got hisself arrested, so what's become a Colin?"

"I think he must of run away or they took him in. He wasn't at the camp."

"The camp? I thought it got burnt down and closed off."

"Well, it did get seriously delapidated by that murdrous biker gang, but—I gotta swear you to secrecy, Ludie Belle, cause if it was to get out, more lives'd be in desprit danger—but people are still living out there. That mad Glenda woman and her passel of wild orphan kids, them audacious Blaurocks, and a whole bunch of poor people who come looking for redemption, women mostly whose husbands are in jail or worse. A lot of them was badly wounded, and I have had to doctor them on the sly. The camp is haunted by them two murdered adulterers and who knows how many other homeless spirits, and Glenda she says she seen the murderer hisself hanging round back under the burnt trees like he still had more work to do, though Glenda herself is suspected of those murders and of bewitching Hazel's husband and binding him up in a hollow tree. Old Hunk Rumpel, he died fighting off the bikers and got his throat slit like you butcher a pig, but he don't seem the haunting kind. Them two little Cravens kids who got bombed by the heliocopters, though, are probly still looking for their mother."

"Wanda's younguns? You don't mean little Davey?"

"Him and his sister. Glenda has the rest of them. Wanda she got kidnapped, or else she was raptured. They's different opinions."

"Little Davey! The sadness is just about more'n I can sustain. The most thing I recollect about little Davey is that pearl a snot always a-glistenin' on his upper lip. Like a kinder jewel a innocence. Lordy! I feel half-haunted myself!"

"The new sickbay is gone, so the Meeting Hall has been set up for bedding the wounded. It's all burnt out inside and they's a bad charred smell, but at least it's still standing. So is that old upright pianner, though it'd probly crumble to ash if you touched it. Looks like made of coal. When I passed it by, I heard sounds coming from it, but nothing like music, not real music—more like the strings were whimpering and falling gainst each other. It made me think of what you said about that old player pianner in that place you was once in employment, how it seemed habitated, not by the dead so much, but by their miseries and their lost gaieties, and I thought, this old pianner, it is lamentating about when everbody was here and praying together and was full of hope and happiness and now see what it has come to."

"'The Lamentatin' Pianner,' it sounds like a Duke'n Patti Jo song. You should oughter tell 'em the story, maybe you'll get famous like they are."

"Patti Jo and Duke? They're famous?"

"Sure, where you been? That song about the little girl who was overloved by her own daddy has been toppa the charts since they first let it out, and right behind it is a song about a crazy cowboy shootin' up a jukebox and a unusual cemetery lovesong which has something of the Prophet's dead sister in it. And they got other big hits, too. They're the hottest thing in country since Hank Williams died. They even been on Grand Ole Opry."

"I guess I missed all that. We don't have a radio station here no more." Ludie Belle asks her about the things hanging on the fireplace because Clara was asking about her husband Ely's final message, and Bernice says all that got burnt up, nothing left but ashes, and while she's telling her that, she hears someone at the front door. Maudie bringing that venal feeding apparatus, or else the exercise people. Maudie was complaining that Mr. Suggs did not seem to be digesting his food properly and was losing weight. "Come on in!" she hollers out, covering the mouthpiece. "I'll be there in just a breath!" She hears the screen door slap and turns back to Ludie Belle. "I have to go, Ludie Belle, the theropests is here. But call again soon! They's tons more to tell!"

In the bedroom, she pulls up short. It is not Maudie. It is the Antichrist. The one in female form. Right here in her own house. Wearing a T-shirt that says It's the Sadness. Face on face to Mr. Suggs, staring hard, like she means to suck his hidden story out of him. Or to snatch his soul like she did to that old lady out on the Mount that day. Bernice feels like she has just been struck in the heart and she can't move a muscle.

"Hi, Mrs. Filbert. I'm Sally Elliott. You may know my folks. Isn't this Mr. Suggs, the man who was bankrolling the cult?"

"It's not a cult," Bernice says icily with what whispery breath she has left, meeting the Dark One's challenge. It's almost as though she—or he (which is it?)—is changing shape before her very eyes. "It's a church."

"Sorry. I meant to say church. But I'm not here about that. I really hate to bother you, Mrs. Filbert, but there aren't many people left around here still alive and not in jail who can help. I have already talked with Mr. and Mrs. Smith and Franny Baxter and Mrs. Coates—who said to thank you if I saw you, by the way, for helping to get the charges against her boy reduced. She says there's even some hope now of getting him released altogether on compassionate grounds. I gather that's your doing."

"Well, yes, I know some people." Bernice has not heard this news, having lost touch with Thelma after she moved back in with her mother. It eases somewhat her anxiety. Her power is being acknowledged. She is able to take a deep breath, wondering if this has been a disarming tactic by the Dark One or if this is really just only a girl.

"You've done a good thing, Mrs. Filbert. There's too much hysteria out there right now. It's like people are caught up in a dangerously insane story and they don't know how to get out of it."

"Dangerous? Just only stories?"

"Most dangerous things there are."

"Do you mean…? Can they, you know, kill somebody?"

"Sure they can. What's the toll now from all this madness? You might say story has killed them all." The girl glances down at Mr. Suggs. He is in his alert phase and is taking all this in, wagging his finger for attention, but the girl ignores him, turns away. "But the story I'm interested in, Mrs. Filbert, is how Billy Don Tebbett died."

"Young Abner Baxter shot him."

"That's what they say. Did you see it?"

"No, but everbody knows."

"He told the police when they arrested him that he didn't do it, and I also have my doubts."

"How do you know what he told the police?"

"I was there at the camp. I heard him."

"Well, maybe it was you done it, then."

"Billy Don was my friend. I was hiding. Someone was shooting at me. I think it was Junior Baxter himself."

"Well, then…"

"But Billy Don was already dead. Had been for some time, I think. Looked like he'd been shot by someone up close. So many guns. Could have been anyone, I suppose. But, tell me, Mrs. Filbert, did Darren Rector ever carry a gun?"

"No, he wouldn't touch one. Wouldn't even do guard duty on that account."

The girl pauses to think about this, staring down at Mr. Suggs again. "What if there were an afterlife and that was what it was like?" she says, more to herself than to Bernice. "A kind of unending nightmare. And you can't die, not even if you want to…" Bernice feels a shiver run up her spine. Because she has thought this, too, or something near it. It's like the girl, who probably isn't a girl after all, is reading her mind. "Do you think Mr. Suggs would know anything helpful?"

"He's had a bad stroke. He can't talk. Probly can't think neither."

Mr. Suggs is wagging his finger vigorously and the girl sees this. "Do you hear me, Mr. Suggs?" He blinks. "Is your name Yankee Doodle?" He wags his finger. "That's usually a sign for saying no."

"No, he's just trying to wave at you and say goodbye because your questions is confounding him." The anxiety is back. The sense of imminent danger. A demonic presence.

"Is your name Mr. Suggs?" He blinks. "I think I'm getting somewhere. Are you being well cared for, Mr. Suggs?"

He wags his finger urgently and Bernice, gathering up her courage for this may be the last thing she does in life, interposes herself between the two of them and orders the fiendish intruder out of the house. *"Now!"* she screams, and she crosses herself in the Romanist way to further shield herself against the Evil One. *"Or I'll call the police!"*

When she has gone, vanishing as if she were never there, Bernice turns on her patient, her heart pounding. His ingratitude! Not well cared for? She feels utterly betrayed—after all she has done for him! But the secret's out. Scary's not enough. It has to be something worse than scary. And fast! "You shouldn't of done that, Mr. Suggs. What you got is you got me and you shouldn't do nothing to make me mad. Up to now I been nice to you, telling you the truth, most of the time, but not all of it. I still haven't told you, for example, that Clara and all them have turned the church camp into a casino full of wicked women. That's right. I was afraid you wouldn't like that, so I was holding back. Nothing you can do about it. Your money's all gone. That fat lawyer with the slicked-down hair has took it all. You won't see him no more. He don't need you now. You are a pauper, Mr. Suggs, and you will get buried thataway." Maudie will be here soon. She prepares a hypodermic. "You've not paid your taxes, so the banker, he's got your coalmine now. They say he's struck oil, worth zillions, but it's his, not yours. He's laughing at you all over town." She thinks of her new stories like tent stakes driven into the brain. Rebecca at the well: tying her visitors down and pouring buckets of water down their throats. She stabs the needle into his belly. "And Ben Wosznik? Well, he run off with another woman, a half-nekkid young thing who can sing a mite, and now they're out in the bars singing dirty songs, and it has just broke Clara up and she has took to drink..."

# EPILOGUE

## Two years later

Sally Elliott's first novel, *The Killing of Billy D*, receives mixed reviews, but the attempt by a state governor to obtain an injunction against its distribution does push it briefly onto the bestseller lists, both fiction and nonfiction in some publications, and draws national and even international attention once more to the notoriously bloody events involving the radical eschatological Brunist cult and the court cases that arose from them. The book's controversial mix of fact and fiction—dubbed "faction" in the press—disturbs many critics but is dismissed by others as imitative of a current fad among senior writers to "invade imaginatively" the lives of real living persons, typically criminals and politicians, if those are two separate categories. When she is accused of stretching the truth, she replies that it is a way of *seeing* the truth, for if you stretch something it tends to become more transparent. She worked hard on the prose in spite of the deadline pressures, the daily race against time, but that goes largely unremarked, except negatively by comparison to those senior writers, but her main goal is achieved: revived interest, at least on radio and television talk shows, in the death sentences passed upon Reverend Abner Baxter and his son and three others still on death row, enough to launch another round of appeals to overturn them. The talk shows are something new for her and at first she can't resist shocking her audience and interviewers just for the fun of it, but, with coaching from her husband, she has gradually acquired a cooler persona. Plenty of brass still, but tempered by the strings, as he says. She still leaves her hair in a wild tangle. That's who she is. But she wears shirts now instead of tees, sometimes leaves her old trenchcoat at home, and smokes without leaving the cigarette dangling in the corner of her mouth while she talks. May even, not to pollute the clean country air where now she lives, give it up altogether.

*The Killing of Billy D* was not the sort of book she had ever expected to write. She had thought she was going to start with something like "Against the Cretins" or "Riding the Hood" or a new western epic idea she had that summer, featuring Sweet Betsy from Pike as her lusty, journal-keeping narrator. But when she presented some of these pieces to the writing workshop upon her return to college in the fall, they were roundly ridiculed, not only by the class, which was largely made up of brainless Boobs Wetherwax-types with a few mad Christians disguised as writers thrown in, but by the professor as well, who scribbled dismissively on the copy he handed back: "A whimsical misuse of a vibrant imagination." While having oral sex with him on his office couch ("I wonder," she mused aloud around slurps, "if vegetarians avoid oral sex?"), he volunteered the further criticism, her vibrant arse bobbing in front of his nose in a room all too brightly lit, that she always adopts essentially the same point of view, namely her own, whether she calls it Goose Girl or Sweet Betsy or The Hood, and suggested (he had long hair and a cute little beard that tickled her thighs; she liked it) that she attempt a man's point of view just as an exercise, maybe something out of her what-I-did-last-summer adventures she'd been telling him about.

So, all right, she turned to look once more at what she saw that day in the ditch. It was unbearable, but she was a writer and she would bear it. She had spent the rest of that summer talking with anyone who might help her see clearly what had happened. There weren't many. Most of the Brunists had fled or been jailed, and those who had mingled with them tended not to trust her. All she knew for certain was that Billy Don was planning to exit the camp and meet her at the Tucker City drugstore before leaving the area altogether and that, before he could do that, somebody shot him in the head. She was convinced that person was his ex-roommate, Darren Rector, but she could find no one else who thought so. She revisited the place where it happened, but it was overrun with army troops and police and much of it was closed off. Even the ditch where the car was. She could only stare from some distance at the culvert where, sick with fear and grief and guilt, she'd spent that long afternoon. There were still wrecked school buses and an overturned backhoe at the foot of the mine hill the first time she went out there, but soon they were gone too. Eventually they let her up near the tipple to look for her lost things, and she did find her T-shirt, a colored rag half-buried in caked mud, and a lens cap, but her notebook was nowhere to be seen. Was someone reading it? Well, her first published work, so to speak.

By the end of the summer, the Mine Hill Massacre trials, as they were called in the media, were underway. An aggressive young district attorney, sniffing the possible fall of the governor and an opportunity to rise on the law-and-order issue, charged the cultists with murder and incitement to murder, as well as conspiracy to commit those crimes and others. It was a time of conspiracy trials, a popular current genre, a way to avoid having to prove the crime itself while maximizing punishment, no matter the offense. Simon calls it the worst law ever written. She herself was called on to testify about Billy Don's eight a.m. phone call, what she witnessed from the coal tipple, and what she saw when she peeked into Billy Don's wrecked car. She had to do a lot of explaining about why she was out there in the first place—developing a book about cognitive dissonance, she said (*that* kept them at bay)—and she confessed her fib about running away, admitting that she was lying in the culvert all the while, so scared she couldn't speak. To explain why she was so frightened, she had to tell them that someone was shooting at her. No, she didn't know at the time who it was, or who it was that shot Billy Don either, but when she started to tell them who she *thought* it was, they told her they were not interested in her opinion and dismissed her. The prosecutor pressed for the death penalty in over two dozen cases in addition to bringing similar indictments against an unspecified number of motorcycle gang members, the survivors thought to number between ten and twenty-five, for whom a nationwide hunt was on. In addition, over two hundred people were cited with disturbing the peace, resisting arrest, possession of unlicensed or stolen weapons, unlawful assembly, delinquency, trespass, and similar lesser crimes, and some of them were sent straight to prison, though most of the others were handed stiff fines, which, being indigent, they couldn't pay, so they were also sent to jail for a time. "Scab justice," as those who had been around earlier in the century called it. Jail them or shoot them.

By then it was clear that the forensic evidence against Junior Baxter in his more conventional murder trial was all but conclusive, the bullets in the heads of the two men at the camp trailer park matching the one in Billy Don's brain, all three coming from the gun in Junior's possession, still hot from firing at the time of his arrest, no prints on its handle or trigger except his. Moreover, when they arrested him within yards of the scene of the crime, he was wearing Billy Don's broken sunglasses. Probably couldn't even see through them. And he was certainly capable of it; he had shot at her, after all, and with even less reason. But she found it narratively more interesting to stick to her original assumption that it was, in effect, a dark love story, allowing her to get inside the warped mind of that megalomaniacal zealot and experience vicariously an act of impassioned yet cold-blooded murder. She named her victim Donny Bill, or Donny B and, stealing a famous name from the Anabaptists, called the killer Jan, a sexually ambivalent name for a pretty boy with blond curls, and one who, though eloquent and smart, was susceptible to spooky ideas, as in real life, so-called, both Darren's and Jan's. The Dark Lady who might have been responsible for Donny B's fatal defection went unnamed and was eventually omitted. Mere debris. She set the story at the church camp but made them all Bible college students on retreat, avoiding the complications of the cult while keeping the weirdness of their beliefs, especially as embodied by mad Jan. Since she was telling the story from Jan's point of view, she was able to use some of her research into the history of chiliastic sects and play with end-times language in suggestive sexual ways during Jan's attempted seduction of Donny B, and she even managed to include a paragraph in which Jan, in a pure and saintly manner, not unlike Santa Teresa, imagines making love to Jesus, an act mostly concealed by mystical religious speculations and revealed primarily by the self-evident fact that the boy has been masturbating throughout. Donny B finally gets fed up with Jan's mad touchy-feely evangelism and decides to leave the camp. Jan, jilted, is both enraged and grief-stricken and maybe afraid that Donny B might tattle on him, and he asks his friend to meet him up on Inspiration Point, away from the others, to say goodbye. Sally was losing sympathy with her crazed hero and his nutty apocalyptic imaginings and she had to work hard to make the genuineness of his emotions believable. Donny B was easier, a more or less commonsensical, good-natured guy who rarely said no to any request and so found himself up on the Point, all alone with Jan, with a gun in his face. His own, taken from his packed suitcase. The story ends: "'Close your eyes, Donny Bill, and pray.' Stubbornly he won't do that. He just stares back at Jan with an icy glitter in his eyes. Sad. Only one thing to do."

Sally didn't like the story very much, her favorite bit being the Jesus paragraph (she got excited by her own sensuous description of Christ's body and masturbated right along with Jan), but it was a big hit in the workshop. It was almost like being born again amidst well-meaning believers, and even the undercover Christians, with a few theological quibbles, praised it. Home at last! But then she followed it with a comicbook story about Sweet Jesus and his sidekick Dirty Pete, in which Sweet Jesus' basic magical stunt is resurrection and the bad guys are all trying to learn his secret or expose him as a sham, and she got hammered again. The professor gave her some credit for light satire, but then effectively trashed it as a frivolous and arrogant provocation (which, admittedly, it was; she was tired of this clubby little gathering), and she left both workshop and college. Broke and jobless, she had no choice but to go home, weather her father's drunken dopiness and her mother's sad frustrations, and get the writing done.

* * *

That winter, West Condon was enjoying a rare if illusory moment of prosperity rising out of the summer's horrors. Just about anyone who wanted a job had one, and a lot of out-of-towners were moving in to pick up the leavings. Her dad, unemployed and more or less unemployable, was an exception, though the new owners of Mick's Bar & Grill gave him occasional free drinks and a sandwich to sit on a bar stool and regale the tourists with anecdotes from that memorable day, most of which he had to make up, having spent much of the time in a stupor on the floor. They'd hired Mick to do the cooking to keep it authentically inedible at twice the price and even put a wrecked helicopter, though not the same one, back on the roof again. Tourism had tailed off some since the end of summer, but the ongoing TV coverage of the conspiracy and murder trials still drew out-of-state cars and occasional busloads, so rooms were often at a premium. All the area motels were doing full capacity business, and townsfolk were offering rooms with breakfast in their homes to take in the overflow. Her mom had planned to do just that, hoping for construction company officials, before Sally came home and reclaimed her space. They were embarrassed when she offered to pay for her room, but in the end they accepted her help. The Roma Historical Society, once interested in the now decimated West Condon Hotel, acquired a cheap derelict motel near the Sir Loin steak house, an old one that still had individual cabins, offering their guests a bit of rustic tin-shower nostalgia, plus slot machines in the office lobby, conveniently situated a few yards beyond city limits, and a ten percent discount at the Sir Loin next door, which was doing good business like all the area eateries that remained, Help Wanted signs in their windows for the first time she could remember. The gambling joints and whorehouses in and around Waterton were also prospering, it was said, thronged less with tourists than with locals, hard cash suddenly burning their pockets. Chestnut Hills had filled up again with squatters, hosting everything from poker games to prayer meetings, and roadside tents reappeared at the town's edges.

Old-timers said it reminded them of West Condon's boom time in the first part of the century, when coal was king and laws were few, when the town was three or four times bigger than it is now and workers were living in railway freight cars fitted out with bunks and stoves—zulu cars, as they were called—and fighting was more common than fucking. Not exactly how it got said, but that's how Sally wrote it in her notebook.

The big money was in construction, supported by state and federal disaster relief funds, and there were several companies in town vying for contracts, including two new home-based outfits, Bonali Family Builders and West Condon NOW, a consortium put together by the bank president and other local businessmen. The acting mayor/city manager favored the former, but the city council was still dominated by friends of Tommy's dad, and moreover, he was able to pull in a sharp young architect from a big-city firm owned by a fraternity brother of his, making it difficult for Bonali Builders to compete except by way of intimidation and backroom influence. Charlie had appointed his dad president, his sister bookkeeper, and had hired his private army of Dagotown Devil Dogs as construction workers; it wasn't clear where the start-up money was coming from. Angela was also the new secretary in the temporary mayoral office above the Knights of Columbus hall, occupied by the city manager. Sally, protecting her writing time, signed on three days a week with West Condon NOW to help write up proposals and pitch their designs, and was given a desk in the old Chamber of Commerce office where her dad once clowned about, bullet holes still in the Main Street windows, left there for the tourists to photograph.

When Tommy came home from business school for the holidays that year, he called Sally and asked her to join him out at the Blue Moon Motel on the night of New Year's Day to listen to their homegrown country star Will Henry celebrate the music of Duke L'Heureux and Patti Jo Rendine, who were that same night the feature attraction at

Nashville's Grand Ole Opry. Their songs had hit the top of the charts several times over, and three of them were still in the top ten that yuletide season, including their famous tribute to the Moon itself, making the motel the newest country music Mecca. "Old Will sings like he's got a sax reed up his nose," Tommy said, "but it should be worth a laugh." The night was fully booked, but his dad knew the owner, they'd add a table. She said okay, why not? Just the right night for such a reunion: day after the night before. She wondered what they would find to talk about. And then, in that week between Christmas and New Year's, she was gifted with grisly openers. A child had gone missing and his parents said he often played around the old abandoned Deepwater Number Nine mine, which was no longer being guarded—kids liked to light the gas leaking out of the mine through vents in the fields behind the slag heaps, more than one had got his fingers burnt and hair singed—and they were afraid he might have fallen down the closed shaft somehow. He hadn't (he was finally found out at the lakes, curled up beside his bike, lost and hungry, in the bird sanctuary), but the decayed unidentified corpse of a white male in his twenties or thirties was discovered at the bottom. All they could say about it was that it looked like it had been badly chopped up and had been there for a while.

So Sally asked Tommy over their first beer who he thought that body was, and he said he had no idea. Everyone's attention was on the murder trials just getting underway at the time, the networks replaying all the most violent footage from that catastrophic day, and Sally asked if Tommy had watched any of it. He had. Tommy had helped to identify the red boots left on the hotel roof when they blew away the biker who was wearing them as belonging to his former high school classmate Carl Dean Palmers. They had APACHE burned on the inside of them, which was Carl Dean's new chosen name, and that went along with the feathers and the red Indian makeup. But now that he'd seen him in the replays, Tommy said when Sally asked, that guy dancing on the hotel roof was definitely not Carl Dean. "That dude could have played basketball, but not Ugly. He's more the squat wrestler type. When he jumps, his feet probably never leave the ground."

"But then how do you think his boots got up there?" Tommy didn't know, didn't really seem interested. He was scanning the SRO crowd. Angela Bonali was there in a side booth, looking about ten or fifteen pounds heavier than the last time Sally saw her, squeezed in with Joey Castiglione and Monica and blind Pete Piccolotti. It was some kind of celebration. Tommy feigned bored disinterest, Angela excessive affection for her new partner, a loud gaiety. Sally watched from the wings. Will Henry was singing about a ghost in a graveyard. "That wasn't the first time that week a guy's feet got separated from the rest of him," Sally said to the back of Tommy's head. "A few days before, there was that dynamite explosion at the church camp which killed a bunch of people. One of the bodies was found without a head, another without its feet, which were discovered later out at the state park where the bikers were holed up for a night or two afterwards."

"Hah," said Tommy, turning toward her. "So you figure the guy was in a hurry and just cut the boots off with the feet still in them."

"Something like that. But the body without the feet was identified and that wasn't Carl Dean either. We know now how the boots might have got from the dead guy at the camp to the one on the roof. The question is: how did the first guy get them?"

Tommy stares at her a moment over his beer. "Ah, I get it. You think maybe the guy dumped down the mine was…?"

"He still had his feet on, but nothing on them except the tatters of rotting socks."

"How do you know?"

"I asked. Forget the socks. I made that up. But they said, yes, he was essentially barefoot. So, all right: the day of the rape. You were waiting for Carl Dean at Lem's garage, but he didn't show up. His truck was packed and parked in front of the camp lodge. He was on his way out of there, but something interrupted him. Unfortunately, the cultists set the van alight; they thought it was the devil's van or some such lunacy. The people I talked to last summer told me that both Aunt Debra and the Collins girl said Carl Dean was there at the rape, but they were confused about what part he played. They were both traumatized, especially the girl, so it was probably all just a blur. But Carl Dean was evidently in love with that girl and had come all the way back here to see her. And she was in trouble. What I'm trying to say is that it looks like your friend, whom everyone has vilified, was really a hero."

"Brilliant, Holmes. Good for old Ugly. But a dead hero."

"Longevity's not a goal for most heroes. They're going for something else. It's why we remember them and not much of anyone else."

"Mm. Poor old Pete over there's another. I've been by the store a few times to see him. He says he knows they're making a big deal out of what he did and everyone's talking about how he sacrificed himself out of love for Monica and her kid, but actually that wasn't on his mind at all. The ball was in the air, he said, and as soon as his feet left the floor, he was back on the court. Went up for the interception and follow-through jump shot and knew he had to sink it before the buzzer."

"Wow! I know that feeling. When the thing itself takes over and you're just its tool. Okay, here's another, not so scary. You know that Olive Oyl wallflower who used to pull sodas in Doc Foley's drugstore?"

"Beanpole Becky? Sure."

"Well, she turned up on TV the other day to describe the killing of Doc Foley and her own near-death experience. She said in that flat deadpan voice of hers that the whole thing has affected her orgasms, making the interviewer's eyes pop. He asked if she meant that it was, you know, interfering with…? 'No,' she said. 'I mean they're better.'"

Tommy thought that was hilarious, and the rest of the night, like Becky's orgasms, went better. Trading hero tales was a good idea. Tommy turned his back on Angela's party and over the next couple of rounds, in and around the over-amplified music, they talked about his mother's wacky trip to Lourdes with Concetta Moroni, paid for by an old boyfriend; the Bali postcard the ex-mayor sent the city council; and Christmas week's big news that Priscilla Tindle, who was back with her husband, had given birth to a daughter whom she was reportedly naming Mary after the child's grandmother, though maybe that was just one of her dad's jokes. Sally's mother had visited the preacher in the mental hospital and found him neatly shaved and barbered, smoking his pipe again, and completely sane, so far as she could tell. It was like the Jesus in him had sort of boiled off, or dropped away like the husk of a seedpod. His wife—Sally's "Aunt Debra"—was, and perhaps still is, in a women's prison, where she was apparently becoming something of a spiritual leader, talking with the birds and creating her own pollyanna branch of Brunism, and her adopted orphan had had, in her mother's words, "a very successful surgical intervention. Really, they've done a great job with the poor boy. He's very relaxed and pleasant now and he doesn't remember a thing about his mixed-up past. Of course, he doesn't recognize anybody either." Sally, her own brain wobbling a bit in her skull at the thought of this "intervention," took a mental note at the time about magic spells: You only hear about those who break their spells. Most don't.

Tommy said he was glad she was working for the West Condon NOW consortium and told her more about his dad's battles with the governor, the city manager, and Charlie Bonali, who had formed a kind of unholy alliance, the police chief part of it, his dad the common enemy. With the mayor absconded, there was a vacuum in town and Minicozzi and Bonali, both seen as heroes of a sort, were filling it. The governor was dumping money into the town, but it was all going through Minicozzi, and there were probably kickbacks. Bonali's building company got the big city hall restoration job without any competitive bids, Minicozzi claiming some kind of emergency powers. Already there were serious cost overruns, yet nothing seemed actually to have been done beyond fencing it off. The bank was robbed that day of the dynamite and the bikers were blamed, but his dad was pretty sure it was the bank lawyer. "Dad's determined to bring the governor down. He's putting his money in the next elections on the hotshot D.A. who nailed the Brunists." Tommy said he had no problem with that guy pushing for all those executions in order to make his name. "Look at how many people got killed because of those rabid freaks." Sally said that if they were freaks, then most of the rest of the country was, too, because a recent poll suggested over eighty percent of all Americans believe pretty much the same apocalyptic fantasies, it's only that not many have put a particular date on them. As for the absentee biker gang being the ones who terrorized the town, not those who had been arrested and charged, Tommy shrugged and said they were all part of the same family and the same fanatical cult. "They all wore Brunist shit on their leathers. Their tattoos. Their minds were fucked by their religious leaders, who have to be held responsible." The media often spoke now of the Baxter clan, referencing famous criminal families of the past. Old black-and-white photos of group hangings of captured bandit gangs were shown on television. Paul Baxter was on the original list of indictments until his head was found in the state park, whereupon he was replaced by Nathan, known now to be the masked gangleader advertising himself as "Kid Rivers." There were countrywide "Dead or Alive" posters up for him and he was number one on the FBI's "Most Wanted" list, the mug shots showing a mean-looking kid about fourteen years old.

A honey blonde in a red shirt and skirt with white fringes coordinating with Will Henry's red-fringed white suit had joined him to reprise the early L'Heureux-Rendine hits, "The Night My Daddy Loved Me Too Much," "A Toybox of Tears," "She'll Let Me Know When It's Time to Go," and "I Thought I Knew Too Much about Love," and then, by popular demand, for at least the fourth time that night, "The Blue Moon Motel," with its rowdy appeal to get it on. *"So listen up, cowboy, it ain't never too soon,"* they sang, *"to pop your cork at the ole Blue Moon!"* Tommy cleared his throat and said he was really sorry about his stupid badass behavior at the highway motel that night, he was out of control, a total jerk, and he hoped she could understand what he was going through and forgive him for it. She smiled and said sure (everybody in the joint was singing along now, bellowing out the lines, it was like church at its best), but when he told her he'd booked a room here as a kind of peace gesture—"It wasn't easy, there were no vacancies," he shouted over the raucous crowd, "but there was a last-minute cancellation!"—she smiled again and said no thanks. "Still holding a grudge?" "No, never did. But you're not as cute without your funny nose guard." He grinned and took her hand and said, "C'mon," but she shook her head. She realized she felt nothing at all for this young man, which surprised her. She placed her other hand over his. "I've moved on, Tommy. Don't take offense. But what can I say? You don't really interest me any longer." He seemed hurt by that and pulled his hand back, looking like he might revert to his badass jerk mode. Men are such sentimentalists.

And then, that winter, Sally's life took a surprise turn. Her workshop story, "Jan," was accepted by a prestigious national magazine. She hadn't even sent it to them; her old workshop teacher had. To show he was open-minded, he had also submitted one of her "Against the Cretins" fragments to an eccentric avant-garde literary magazine, whose only literary criterion, he told her when she called, was dirty language, and that one, too, was taken. It seemed forever before "Jan" appeared, but within days of its publication (her prof had made a few cuts and moved a couple of paragraphs about, so she was torn between gratitude and fury, elation and frustration, though never mind, it was only a workshop exercise anyway), she was getting calls from agents and publishers, asking to see more. She was sure she could bowl them over with her more imaginative writing, so she rushed some of it off special delivery, though with each submission, just in case, she also mentioned what she might do with "Jan" if she ever developed it further. One of these letters got her both a literary agent and then a book offer from a big New York publisher. The publishers were not interested in the experimental work. They wanted a further expansion of the published story along the more conventional *reportage* lines she had suggested in her letter with the events clearly linked to the Brunist cult and the Mine Hill Massacre, which, with all the scheduled executions, were still in the national headlines, and they wanted it more or less immediately so that the book could appear while the subject was still topical.

To the dismay of her new agent who had negotiated the contract, she turned it down. She regretted her cowardly cover letter. She wasn't a journalist. Breaking conventions is what she did. The agent said she was passing up an opportunity to launch her writing career, if the book was successful she could write how and what she wished thereafter, but Sally said that any book she wrote that she didn't want to write was unlikely to be successful. Her agent was not very enthusiastic about the more imaginative work either, so she sent her stories around on her own, having been bitten somewhat by the publishing bug. After some time, the little vanguard magazine appeared with her "Cretins" story and they took a second, a "Big Mary" fragment, but the others all came back, and the "Big Mary" piece never got published because the magazine folded. With a little inside push from her agent and her former workshop teacher, however, her two published stories and the book interest did win her a fellowship that fall at a writers' colony located in a mountain retreat far from West Condon, so she was able to give up her job with the construction firm. The architect friend of Tommy's dad, also using that unsettling word "career," offered her a full-time position at much higher wages either in West Condon or in the city if she wanted it, saying they were just about to break into big money, and she was tempted, but took a rain check, which she knew, unless devoid of writing ideas and utterly desperate, she'd never call in. He was a good-looking guy and, if he had come on to her, she probably, feeling lonely, would have accepted the offer and lived a completely different life, but he treated her more as one of the boys.

All of this had little impact back home. No one in West Condon was much interested writers who weren't on television or in the newspaper—which was rare, since the town didn't have a news station or paper of its own. Her only brush with fame was during the midsummer first-anniversary tourist surge when she spied a torn oil-stained copy of the magazine with her story in it on the floor of Rico's Pizza Palace, probably dropped by a disappointed visitor—the editors had referenced the Brunist cult in their authors' notes. She rescued it, has it still. The "big money" the architect spoke of was in anticipation of the imminent collapse of their local competitors. The year-long city hall ripoff erupted eventually into a full-blown scandal, due mostly to the relentless perseverance of Tommy's dad. Minicozzi was indicted, his mob connections exposed (the governor did not escape the implications), and the president of Bonali Family Builders—who was not Charlie Bonali, but his dad—was sent to prison. Charlie disappeared into the city, along with Moron Moroni and some of the other so-called Dagotown Devil Dogs. His sister lost her job at city hall and got married. The police chief was demoted and a new chief was hired in from upstate. The town had neither mayor nor city manager for a while and was run largely by the city council. The town had not had much luck with mayors and there was little appetite to elect a new one, nor did anyone seem interested in the job. Most of that happened after Sally had left town, but her mom kept her informed.

Before leaving West Condon for the writers colony at the end of August (forever, she felt), Sally paid a final visit to the Brunist file drawer in the *Chronicle* job room. Somebody, she discovered, had been poking around in the files since she was last there. The drawer was open and the "Abner Baxter Family" and "Millennial Cults" folders were out on top of the cabinet. She asked and the little mustachioed print shop owner said the only other visitor had been the mayor, who was in just before he disappeared, buying up a stack of the final edition of the paper at a nickel each "for the city archives," but he himself was in there with the fellow the whole time and he had no interest in the files. Does anyone else have a key? He didn't know. He'd never changed the locks, and the previous newspaper people might still have theirs. "No need for locks, really," he said with a cheerful, pink-cheeked smile. "This is a safe town where you can trust your neighbors."

It was hot and stuffy in that windowless room. She put the hook on the job room door, took off her shirt, and started with the "Cults" file, which she wanted to explore as fodder for her Cretin Wizards, and in it she found the scrawled note: "The great majority of men do not think with abstract ideas, only with colorful images or with concrete facts. Abstract spiritual ideas and principles must be clothed in some vivid and compelling form, even if, like this note, borrowed from elsewhere. Thus, the heroic journey, the parables, the miracles, the Easter story, the cross." Which she herself might have written, if not so succinctly. She copied the lines out in her notebook next to another thought she'd stolen from somewhere about imagination both illumining and darkening the mind, which she read as her kind of fiction *versus* the Christian sort, though she could see how it might work both ways. And then, without really registering the moves that got her there, she found herself stretched out on the leather couch again, smoking a joint and fantasizing about the new life that awaited her. It did not seem to include the cult or the town, not even as masked in the fairytale form of "Against the Cretins." It was grander than that, more heroic, and at the same time more modest, at least in scale: Wit. Bright and quick and unforgettable. Ever since her night at the Moon with Tommy and their exchange of hero stories, she'd been playing with the hero idea. She had returned home that night and written: "She did not know if she was a real hero or a false hero, but she knew the first thing she had to do was leave home in order to proceed to what the Saturday morning cartoons called the 'threshold of adventure.'" The new hero who emerged that night called himself or herself many names, but most recently Dawn, meaning lecherous, moist, wet, rutting; also graceful, but with the ancient sense of "one who has beautiful pudenda." Perhaps, she was thinking as she lay there, Dawn's first mind-opening adventure, sallying forth, radiant with purpose yet utterly in the dark, would be to awaken the Sleeping Prince in the Woods, that two-dick wonder (it was the circumcised one that mattered, though Dawn might not know that and have to try them both), then blithely send him on his way into the life of empty-headed princesses and ambitious chambermaids which were his destiny. Her hand by now was between her legs, hash in her lungs and behind her eyes. She was thinking about the Prince's beautiful backside while he stood at the motel window, his sturdy prick glistening with the stains of a ruptured hymen, the bathing of it under the waterfall of the shower—feet, she knew then, just a euphemism in the Jesus stories. Her eye fell on the darkroom door with its glass panel, behind which the photographer had been hidden. She stood, took off the rest of her clothes, and lay down again, staring tauntingly at the secreted photographer and remembering Billy Don, the flushed expression on his face in the Tucker City drugstore when he showed her the pictures of this couch and the violated Bruno girl upon it, and she spread her legs and took her hand away and raised her inside arm against the back of the couch in imitation of one of those photos (the difference was the roach in her other hand), wondering if she had the imaginative power to make herself come without touching herself. While the invisible photographer watched, stunned by what he saw, but greedily snapping away. She was close to it.

But her erotic imaginings were chilled by the lingering image of Billy Don, no longer that of him in the drugstore, but the final one: dead and bloodless in his wrecked car in the ditch at the edge of the camp, that hole in his forehead. She remembered suddenly that he was not wearing his dark glasses. This fact struck her at the time, it made him look so strange, he was never without them, even at night, but then she had forgotten it. Apparently Junior Baxter was wearing them when he was arrested, another strike against him. Junior had been found guilty of his murder and several other crimes on top, and had been sentenced to die in the electric chair. Arguing that charges of murder and conspiracy to murder seemed almost inadequate for the enormity of the crimes committed, the prosecutor secured death sentences for Junior's father as well and for his surviving uncaptured brother, plus four so-called "Brunist Defenders," two surviving Christian Patriots, and the entire membership of Nathan Baxter's "Wrath of God" motorcycle gang, all sentenced in absentia, however many and whoever they were. Presumably this was good for a lot of votes. Abner Baxter's closest lieutenant, Roy Coates, facing murder charges like the others, was given immunity for turning state's witness, providing critical evidence against many of the "armed criminals" on the mine hill that day, including Baxter himself. This might have been the same reason Darren

Rector only got a suspended three-year sentence; that and his pretty blond innocence. During the appeal process that followed, much of Coates' testimony was found insubstantial and contradictory and was discounted, resulting in lesser punishments for two of those sentenced to death and the outright release of another, but all that was later on. Clara Collins-Wosznik and others named with her were charged with conspiracy to foment violence and civic disorder, but as they were no longer in the state and were not on the hill that day, the charges were eventually dropped. Not long after the sentencing, Nathan Baxter *alias* Tobias Rivers *alias* Kid Rivers was killed in southeast Texas in what looked like a gang execution, along with others assumed to be members of the Wrath of God gang, who had apparently renamed themselves the Crusadeers. Baxter had been hideously burnt and was all but unrecognizable, identifiable only by his Tobias Rivers driver's license and wrecked motorcycle, making investigators cautious: Was this really Nat Baxter, or was he living on under yet another stolen identity?

Not only was the Billy Don murder case against Junior Baxter apparently all but watertight, Junior himself had in effect confessed, changing his plea to temporary insanity, the unfortunate tactic used by his court-appointed defense lawyer when things started to go against them. He was scheduled to be electrocuted in November. He did blurt out in his confused and inconsistent testimony that Darren Rector gave him the gun and told him to go guard the camp. Darren denied this, and the jurors chose to believe the one without "LIER" scarred on his forehead. But if Junior was telling the truth, when did that happen? Billy Don called her around eight that morning—that was in the trial record. He was probably killed soon after that. If it could be shown that Junior was at the mine hill at that time and for some time after, the verdict might have to be reconsidered. Might he have stayed behind in the camp earlier while the others marched over to the hill? No, he would have gone wherever his father went; no choice. Also, Billy Don was shot in the forehead from close range. No bullet holes in the car's front window, so he was unlikely to have been shot while driving. Where, then, did the murder take place? If not at or near the ditch, how did the car get there?

She sat up abruptly with the uncomfortable realization that this was a story she had to write. If for no other reason, because she owed it to Billy Don. He was coming to see her that dreadful morning. And that may have been the *reason* he was shot. It would also be a way of paying her dues to the literary tradition while yet making it a story of her own. Even as she sat there, bony elbows on bony knees, her bottom sweating on the leather cushion, the basic structure revealed itself to her. She has often described this moment in interviews, leaving out the dope and the sweaty butt. She would name everybody, risking whatever legal actions, while exploring each character, each scene, imaginatively, as if they were characters and scenes in a novel, trusting that her imagination would tell her more than the "facts" alone could. There would be invented characters, too, filling out the religious typology and enriching the story content. She would relate it in an exploratory first person, moving as author from darkness to light, while keeping Darren and Billy Don center stage, as in "Jan." The Baxters would be there, but backgrounded as part of the story of the cult. *The Killing of Billy D* was becoming a reality. Her body meanwhile had forgotten its appetites, overtaken by a mind on the boil. You think too damned much, she said irritably to herself, as she pinched out the roach and pulled her underwear on.

Mind erosion: the dust storms of daily excitement and triviality that blow away the sensitive topsoil of the spirit—the idea that attention-power is finite and precious, and that unless the individual is obstinate and cunning, this power may be dissipated, conventionalized. A note inspired by all that's presently eating up her life, the spent storms of birthday parties, poolside yatter, boy-chasing, and pop culture immersion now displaced by travels on behalf of the book, TV and radio talk shows, newspaper and magazine interviews, book and film proposals, teaching offers, rallies and protests, the daily froth of news and chatter, sex. Unless such notebook jottings as this be counted, Sally hasn't written a creative word of her own since the book came out.

Of course, to be fair, she has also been trying to save a few lives. The first routine appeals against the death penalties were turned down at about the same time she reached the writers colony, and she has spent most of the time since then fighting those judgments one way or another. They were what drove her through the research and writing of *The Killing of Billy D*, and at such an accelerated pace; forget the publishers' nagging deadlines, for her it has always been a race against the executioners, hoping to use the book as a circuit breaker. Not an easy one to write. Not only was it a different sort of writing than any she'd done before, she realized as soon as she'd settled into her cozy little cell at the writers colony just how much research she needed, and almost none of it in books. There were so many people she should talk to, now scattered around the country, so many places to visit, images to collect. But she had no car and was saving her book advance and West Condon earnings for when the writers' colony gig ended, so to get started she had to trust her memory and imagination. As a warm-up exercise, she developed character files for Darren and Billy Don, pouring into them all her memories and speculations, and then similar files for the Baxter family, the orthodox cult leaders, their opponents, all the secondary players in her drama. Who tended, threateningly, to multiply. Putting characters in was not what was hard, she realized. It was keeping them out. Moreover, her agent had, with difficulty, managed to sell her newest concept to the same publishers as before, and they continued to demand the full and true story of the cult, even if only as background, giving her a contracted deadline of six months for submitting the entire manuscript.

When her books arrived from home, boxed up with her notebooks, photos, drawings, and the Brunist files and newspapers she'd snitched from the *Chronicle* office, she was able to patch together a few paragraphs about the cult, its beliefs, its growth, its schisms, its relation to similar millennial movements of the past. All that was fine but, except as suggested by her "Jan" story, her book still wasn't on its way. She had always resisted that workshop bromide, "write about what you know," but she had no choice; not to be forever treading water, she launched the first rough draft with her own experiences that day in the culvert, the fall from the tipple being told in flashback as she lay there. Little research required, though it meant she was also, against her own outlined intentions, becoming a point-of-view character in the story. This character, she decided, would be somewhat like herself and yet not exactly herself. For one thing, she pasted an earlier version of the historical Sally on the fictional Sally, not the childish one who still believed, prayed, and fantasized an afterlife, but the one who lived unthinkingly in a world saturated with religion as one lived with air and water, using the Billy Don drama then as a way of freeing this character from a passive acceptance of the unacceptable, in much the same way that her imagined Sweet Betsy goes from innocence to bawdiness in her western epic idea, such that by the time she is cowering in the culvert she has come to understand that the real criminal that day was Christianity itself. Or, rather, the human mindset—in part, a susceptibility to made-up stories—that gives this dangerous nonsense such terrible power. Thus, a spiritual journey, after all, a remark she often makes in interviews or talk show conversations while explaining why that was not the book she ended up writing, each repetition gradually hollowing it out until soon she'll be free of it.

Some people at the colony were writing their socks off; for others, it was just a free-sex exercise pit. Sally allowed herself to get laid when the opportunity arose, for now that she'd got the hang of it, sex had become important to her, but she didn't let it get in the way of the writing. She had launched hundreds of stories over the previous year or two and had finished almost none. If this was going to be her life, she knew, she'd have to stop playing the dilettante. She had a book to write. She dedicated at least ten solid hours a day to the writing. Reading and writing. Plus two of hiking or roaming the hills on one of the colony's bicycles—another kind of writing. Or unwriting. She clocked herself, kept a chart, made sure there was no cheating. For the first couple of weeks before *Billy D* took over, she seemed to have time to do it all, work on the book, write new stories, revise the old, read voraciously, fill more notebooks. She felt good, as good as she'd felt in years. She smoked less (though always a butt lit while fingers were on the keys, even if left to burn itself out in the tray), immersed herself in the beauty of the surroundings, reveled in the meal-time conversations with other writers. Many of them came from money, had been to the best schools, had had lots of literary mentoring and friends who were editors and publishers; but they didn't intimidate her. She knew she had something they didn't. Coaltown grit, for one thing.

But she was facing a deadline, and there were things she had to know before she could continue. She described her research needs to a writer at the colony one evening, a somewhat older man with suave moneyed ways, and in particular her desire to interview Junior Baxter on death row somehow, there being some things she had to know that only he could tell her, and he said he might be able to help. He loaned her a car to take wherever she wished, a fast road-hugging foreign sports car unlike any she'd ever been in before, much less driven—she felt *hot* in it—and he introduced her to an activist lawyer friend from the city, Simon Price of Price & Price, whom she was able to convince to help her fight the Brunist death penalties. The other Price was Simon's wife, a lawyer who specialized in human rights cases—women's rights, in particular. "Looks a lot like Haymarket all over again," Simon said after studying her typed-up notes. Several routine gestures had not yet been made, so he was immediately able to get all the November and December executions delayed another six months while he prepared legal briefs and affidavits, and she brought this good news the next time she saw her wealthy friend at the colony. Though he seemed to know everything about literature, he didn't seem to be much of a writer, usually just smiled when she asked him what he was working on. When not talking about her book, they discussed music, art, literature, politics, and in provocative engaging ways she'd not enjoyed before. He was the coolest man she'd ever met, and he seemed to like her, too. He laughed generously when she was being funny in her wiseass way, listened carefully when she got serious. He liked her enough that he invited her to his house one evening, promising to get her back in time not to disrupt her writing rhythms. They drove for an hour or so through thick forests to a luxurious home with beautiful views, a lot of art on the walls, thousands of books, a grand piano in the middle of a room set aside for it. Everything in its place, but as though unused. Like Dracula's castle, she thought, but she didn't say it. The sex on satin sheets was easy and good—maybe not passionate, but fun—the wine he served her sensational. It turned out he was one of the writing colony's principal benefactors (an expensive dating club for him, she imagined) and a U.S. Congressman, wealthy enough to pay for his own campaigns, but a guy with a serious agenda, an agenda she mostly shared; she would vote for him. Much of the forest they had driven through was his, he said. They drove through it at least once a week after that and he always got her back to the colony by her usual bedtime. She was quite ready to stay over, to hell with the discipline, but he seemed to need her Cinderella hour even more than she did. Maybe there were other wives and lovers awaiting their turn, she thought, and her time was up.

Meanwhile, the writing rhythms he was protecting she was disrupting by note-taking travels through Brunist country, consultations with Simon, meetings with her agent and editors, prison visits, yet even so she managed to work on the book every day wherever she was, even if only for an hour or two. She had to. The days were dropping away like those calendar pages in the old movies, and she only had half-starts so far and a messy heap of loose notes. And the end of her fellowship loomed. What then? The peace of her studio and use of the car were each hers for only a short time longer, and she needed them both. So she drove back and forth a lot, reserving at least three days a week for her studio at the writers colony, the evenings with her wealthy friend unless he was in Washington—and once she met him there while traveling, and he seemed pleased, showing her off proudly (*she* felt proud) to his colleagues.

Her leash wasn't long enough for her to reach Florida or Alabama or congregations to the west, but she managed to visit over a dozen Brunist churches along the eastern seaboard, large and small, attending services for the first time in years, taking notes, keeping her mouth shut. In one of them the preacher stopped her as she was leaving and said she looked familiar, hadn't he seen her somewhere? She didn't think so. Possibly at the Mount of Redemption? Oh, maybe, she said, and he continued to stare at her, his eyes narrowing. She eventually learned where Clara Collins-Wosznik and her friends from the Brunist camp were living, but she was refused permission to speak to them or even get near. She was told that Mrs. Collins was quite ill, and prayers for her were often a part of the services she attended. She didn't know the name of either of the boys' hometowns, but she had a rough idea where Billy Don came from and spent some note- and picture-taking time in several small towns in the area until she grew uncomfortable with the grim, thin-lipped attention she and her jazzy sports car were drawing. She did know how to find the Bible college Billy Don and Darren attended and spent one of her best half-weeks there. The staff and faculty were aware of their former students' notoriety and were chillingly unhelpful (maybe her hair put them off; definitely not part of the local culture), but she was able to capture some of the school's atmosphere, became acquainted with several students, some of whom later entered her narrative pseudonymously, and located many of the places Billy Don had described. Which in turn triggered her first completely satisfying book chapter, in which, sitting in the student cafeteria (which really did have homemade lemonade and boiled peanuts, just like Billy Don said), looking out on an autumnal campus (how she saw it, what her camera recorded), Darren lays out, in his riveting soft-spoken way, his vision of the approaching End Times, and Billy D's life begins to change.

Simon had obtained all the trial transcripts and was studying them, and he passed on to her those of Young Abner's murder trial. A close read turned up a few minor notes, not themselves very significant, but possibly useful in conjunction with more substantial evidence. The arresting officer, for example, declaring that the accused, found hiding in the nearby woods, was sullen and only resentfully cooperative, said that when he handed over his weapons, the officer remarked: "Let's see if this gun matches the one that killed that kid in the ditched car," and

Junior, who said very little, said: "What kid?" The officer and prosecutor used the exchange as evidence of Junior's duplicity—"He was just playing dumb," the cop said. "You could tell by the cold-blooded look on his face." The defense attorney did not argue with this. Simon was enraged at the lawyer's obtuseness and the stupidity of the temporary insanity plea—"That sonuvabitch should be dragged into the dock on the same grounds!" he said—and by now, hoping to secure a retrial, had a list of some eighteen to twenty examples of ineffective counsel if not gross incompetence, including outright procedural errors by both lawyers. The unchallenged use of hearsay evidence, for example, as when a witness remarked that Junior was "a pal of the bikers, they raped a kid together," the judge, too, failing in his duty. That rape scene had become important to her after her rescue of Carl Dean Palmers from ignominy, and she was convinced and had convinced Simon that Junior was as much a victim as the girl was. "I suppose it's a problem with court-appointed lawyers," she said to Simon, and he replied: "Nah, I'm often one. He's just a shit lawyer. Maybe a chum of the prosecutor, doing him a favor. Probably how he got appointed an administrative law judge after the elections."

There were a lot of cultists still imprisoned back in her home state, many of them sentenced to twenty years or more, and most of them were eager to accept Simon's offer of free legal help in exchange for answering a few questions. Simon sent in a team of young legal volunteers with a list of thirty such questions for the first round, some of them meant to draw their cooperation by giving them a chance to explain themselves, others focused on what happened that day, with questions about Billy Don, Darren, and Junior Baxter mixed in, trying to pin down times and trace the movement of the handgun. When the answers came in, they compiled a list that suggested possible leads, and together they flew out for further interviews. By then she was married—a private civil ceremony in December, a brief ten-day honeymoon in San Francisco (they went to a lot of concerts) and wintry Yosemite—and was well installed in her new study, with the book finally taking shape. She had an outline for it, meaty yet succinct, which she was able to send to her publishers a week ahead of schedule. They were pleased, excited even, and began talking about jacket designs and book tours.

During the prison interviews, disguised as Simon's secretary, she filled notebook after notebook, not only with information, but also with character descriptions and sketches, idiomatic novelties, odd personal anecdotes and histories, but if she was somewhat duplicitous, Simon was not. He inquired into their individual stories of that violent day, listened carefully, took precise notes of his own, and indeed has managed to get many of their sentences reduced and some of them freed. It was decided that, with her reputation, she would stay away from the initial meeting with the two Baxters, but even so, Simon said, they were uncooperative, Abner ranting in his Old Testament style, Junior sullenly impassive. The only moment he showed any emotion at all was when Simon asked him about the torn tunic with his name stitched on a label at the neck, found on the backside of the mine hill, and that emotion was only momentary surprise and an embarrassed flush. At his trial he had first said that Darren gave him the gun and sent him over to the camp, but now he wouldn't speak of it at all. One prisoner told a volunteer that he did see Darren carefully cleaning and loading a handgun that might have been the one in the picture he was shown, though he didn't know what Darren did with it, and he said he told the defense lawyer that, though it never got mentioned at the trial. But when she and Simon interviewed him, he was adamant that he would not testify in court. If they dragged him there, they wouldn't get a word out of him. Never wanted to see the inside of a courtroom again until the Final Judgment, he said, and spat defiantly into a tin cup. After her own day in court, even if only as a witness, she was sympathetic. A weirder place than Wonderland, where the least thing you say can change your life forever. In the end it was a lot of work, and though she got material for her novel from it, it yielded little they could use in the capital cases. But she and Simon grew fond of each other on these travels, casually slept together in shared hotel rooms as though it was what grownup people always did, knew without having to say so that they'd be loyal friends for life.

Her marriage was a curious thing. Not at all what she'd expected. But expectations: what are they? Notions imposed by others. The stubborn entrenched ways of the tribe. He proposed to her by leading her to the west wing of his big country house and showing her the perfect study, fully equipped with picture windows looking out over the forest upon the mountains to the west, meaning that on sunny mornings she'd have an illumined postcard view of the mountains and often, in the evenings, spectacular sunsets. He said that if she married him this would be hers—the car, too, of course. In fact, just about anything she desired. She didn't know if she loved him (what was that?), but she really *liked* him and felt inclined to say yes, but first he wanted to show her another room. In this one, the Dracula image returned. Bluebeard's Chamber. It was windowless and full of instruments of torture: stocks, cages, velvet whipping stools, leg and arm cuffs in the walls, glass cases full of canes and belts and whips and paddles, elaborate ropes and pulleys meant for dangling victims, iron maidens, plus film screens and projectors and dance studio mirrors on the walls. "Scary!" she said. "Not for me. I'm just an old-fashioned squeamish all-American girl." "Oh, it's not for you. I wouldn't enjoy that. It's for me. And other men…" It took her a few moments to take it all in. She remembered his eagerness to show her off in Washington. This room would not win him a lot of votes. "You want me for cover. A kind of job." "I guess you could look at it that way. But what marriage isn't? This one's just a little different. And I do love you, Sally. Love your mind, your wit, your good heart, love your young body." It probably helps, she was thinking, that it's on the boyish side. "In a sense I've been waiting all my life for someone like you, just as in conventional romances. And you can step out of it whenever you want." Well, it was pretty weird, but somehow it made a certain sense to her, enough anyway that she smiled and said okay, why not. Try it out. Was the Chamber soundproofed? It was. While she was back in her home state with Simon, she remembered to call her parents and tell them she was married to a nice guy, a bit older, rich, a U.S. Congressman, and when she was more settled and the book was done, they could come visit.

"Oh, why don't you come here?" her mother said. "You know your father doesn't travel well."

The perfect study with the postcard views was waiting for her when she returned from the prison interviews (an immaculate snowscape: she couldn't resist, she ran out and *wrote* on it), and for the first couple of weeks everything seemed to be going brilliantly as she typed up her notes, papered the walls with clippings and photo blowups, revised her outline and the five completed chapters, and launched a sixth—well over half the book done, according to her outline. It was the legislative season and her husband was away in Washington most of the time, which meant that—though she found that she *missed* him—every minute of every day was her own, her meals and the house and laundry cared for by a French Canadian woman who came in five days a week and who sometimes regaled her with funny family stories, often remarking, "You should write it in a novel!" They were indeed the sort of stories most novelists feed upon, but Sally was determined not to do that; just get through this one obligatory project, then back to the good stuff, already developing under her left hand, so to speak.

And then, suddenly, two months before her deadline, everything under her right hand fell apart. It was a mere patchwork of lists and fragments, she saw. Nothing held together. The writing was pedestrian, her digressions were tedious and for the most part stolen, the characterizations fatuous and condescending. The only chapter worth keeping was the one set in the Bible college cafeteria. The two before that, the personal narrative of her afternoon in the culvert and an imaginary reconstruction of Billy Don's beer-drinking high school days were irrelevant and would have to be thrown out, and the one after it—an account of the boys' missionary travels with the cult—was totally unconvincing. As for the later chapter based on her "Jan" story, she could see now that, shorn of its climax, it was as trivial as any other conventional fiction. And hordes of new characters had come piling in, some real, some fictional. She was completely bogged down in the new chapter she'd begun—their arrival at the camp and its reconstruction—which she realized she knew almost nothing about, having only a fuzzy childhood memory of the church camp and having been banned from seeing what changes the Brunists wrought, all that now lost to the fire. Worse: what lurked just beyond it was the centerpiece Day of Redemption chapter, which she knew in her abysmal ignorance she could never write—what happened after the old lady died? she had almost no idea—and then the climactic holy war chapters and the murder. Impossible. And what if she were wrong about Darren's guilt? She was toying with a young man's life. In the trial transcript, Darren says: "I am a religious pacifist. I have never had a gun in my hand all my life and I never will." Numerous witnesses confirmed this about him. She was wrong. Junior did it. The "LIER." She had no story. The whole sorry project was a shabby, witless, rickety, undisciplined mess.

When her husband called, as he did almost every day, she told him, laughing, the latest of the maid's comical tales of family feuding and inbreeding, and said that she had decided to polish the Bible college chapter as a story and send it around and abandon the rest. He heard the panic in her voice, hired a plane for the weekend and flew home. He gently dragged her out of the trash heap that her study had become, first opening the windows to let out the sickening miasma of stale cigarette smoke, and led her into the bedroom, undressed her, and made love to her in a profoundly affectionate way of the sort rarely shown and then generally only after a punishing evening with his friends in the Chamber, leaving her crying softly on the pillow while he crafted a mushroom risotto with shaved truffles and cheese-flavored croutons in the kitchen. He tossed a green salad with garlic and lemon juice, opened a Barbaresco that even she with her nicotine-stunned palate could recognize as a serious wine, and put string quartets on the stereo system. Brahms? Mozart? She wasn't sure, her musical education only just beginning. She started to explain herself; he put his finger to his lips. "Just listen to the music," he said with a smile. After dinner he replaced the string quartets with big band music from the swing era and they danced for a while like lovers in an old movie and then went back to bed for another round of sex—slow, almost meditative in nature. "You're really good at this," she said, as he studied her from within and from above. "It's like a skill you have. I suppose you could do it equally well with old crones or chimpanzees or trained seals." "Probably," he said, smiling down on her. Appreciatively, she thought. "I do have quite a lot of sex. But only rarely the opportunity to make love."

She woke to find breakfast awaiting her and her study locked from the inside. Which frightened her. Perhaps, fearing for her sanity, he was destroying it all. She raised her fist to bang on the door, thought better of it, returned to her breakfast, hit the on-switch on the coffeemaker. Eventually he joined her, kissed her gently on that nice place behind the ear (she rather hoped he'd nip her lobe, but he didn't; what he might call consistency of style), and said he'd spent some time with her typescript, he hoped she didn't mind. She did, but at this moment she was too fond of him to say so. He praised it, found it "vivid, provocative, dark yet funny," etc. He had something else to say. She could wait for it. "I especially loved the high school beer party and the flagellation scenes."

"You would. But I've taken them out."

"Really? Also, I didn't find the cemetery story."

"It's gone, too. It didn't seem to fit in anywhere and I'd have had to explain too much if I used it."

"A pity. When you told me the story I remember laughing a lot and at the same time feeling a gathering anxiety, not so much because of the setting, but because of increasing apprehension about the blond boy. He seemed quietly and dangerously crazed. Not someone you'd want to be alone with in a cemetery or anywhere else. I think it would make a good first chapter. It sums everything up while keeping it all intriguingly mysterious."

"I have a first chapter." He smiled, sipped coffee, said nothing. "You don't think I have a first chapter."

"You have a kind of foreword. Or afterword, maybe. Not in the voice of 'the girl,' as you call her, but in your own. It is too argumentative for a novel chapter, but it works as a way of explaining how you got involved with this story and why you decided to write it. It's a place where you can summarize the cult history as you came to know it and comment on it in your own voice, and that saves you having to do that inside the novel itself. You're going to want to end the novel much like you ended the story, and you can use the afterword to fill in the rest of what happened that day and to report on the trials and sentences that resulted, which are part of the book's motivations. Also, in our very first conversation at the writers' colony, you unleashed some of your pet theories about cognitive dissonance and collective effervescence, and the afterword would give you the opportunity to indulge yourself a bit."

"Not my theories, I'm afraid."

"I know that. But they fit. Credit them if you think you must. But help us see what you see."

"This is going to take forever."

"Won't be easy, but you may be further along than you think." By now they had their coats and boots on, caps and gloves, and were entering the woods on a winter walk. About a mile further on, she knew, having been there before on her own, the land fell away and he or someone had built a rustic outlook with rough-hewn picnic tables for the summer. Always a surprise when one got there because neither the overlook nor the valley could be seen from the house. On the way, as they shuffled through the snow, stirring up creatures on either side of them, he pointed out that she already had enough for a book, though only half was probably worth keeping, and he encouraged her to rethink her removal of the flagellation and rape scene, because she probably wanted the boys with their alternating points of view to think more about Young Abner. When she protested he wasn't her character, Darren and Billy Don were, and besides he was totally unattractive, a stupid, sullen boy, he reminded her that Young Abner was the one on death row and said maybe she could try to make sullenness and stupidity interesting. "Make room for plain, ordinary ugliness. The everyday tragic drama of the impoverished spirit." She was thinking about this. She was resisting it. But he may be right, she was thinking. He *is* right, damn him. They emerged from the woods and reached the overlook. The air was exhilaratingly cold and clean. As they talked, the book settled into its new shape. It was as if she were gazing out upon it, metamorphosing before her eyes down in the snowy sunlit valley: the cemetery openers, the Bible college cafeteria meeting with some background bits cannibalized from the high school chapter, the two friends drawing together during their travels and establishment of the camp, their falling apart after the attempted seduction scenes of her short story, Darren moving toward the Baxterites, Billy Don staying loyal to the Clara Collins people. The cult schism: way to talk about that.

"Sounds good," he said. "What's left?"

"The end of their relationship. The murder." Six chapters, counting the afterword, three of them more or less written. She took off one of her gloves to pull out a cigarette, but he also took a glove off and held her hand and that was better. She felt spectacularly healthy.

Before her husband returned to the Capitol, he had one night with his friends in what he called the "library," but by then she was beavering away in her study once more, earphones on to stifle any sounds that might leak from the Chamber. The front two and back two chapters, she foresaw, would more or less write themselves; the middle two would be more difficult, but now that they were defined as coming-together and falling-apart chapters, all the peripheral material dropped away into the background, and her two characters rose to the fore. She was having fun writing again.

When he came to bed that last night, she hugged him and thanked him. He was trembling still from whatever it was he had just gone through. "You're like something out of a fairytale," she said.

"Think of me more," he murmured, "as a character from one of those Victorian novels you profess to hate. A kind of ambassador from them, as you might say."

"If it's your mission, Mr. Ambassador, to lure me into those tired woods, you will not succeed. It's the wildness I want." He laughed softly, sleepily, squeezed her hand.

* * *

In interviews she is often asked what she is working on now. When she tried to answer the question seriously, she only drew baffled stares and impatient interruptions: Didn't she have another *faction* in mind? So she finally learned to duck the question by pretending she didn't like to talk about work in progress and then, after she'd repeated it a few times, she was no longer pretending. To her agent, she has to be more specific. Gets an irritable sigh in return. Bad girl. The word "career" comes up again. When Sally dismisses it, the agent wants to know what, then, she needs him for. "To hold my hand when the rejections come in," she says with a smile, and he looks pained but shrugs and smiles back.

The interviewers also ask, inevitably, about her disputing of the trial verdict and her legally unproven assumption that the real killer, whom she names, was not the one convicted by the court. Isn't she liable to legal action herself? Yes, she is. But she is right. Or so she says when asked. Actually, throughout the writing, the doubt never went away. Doubt and the overcoming of doubt—it was like something out of one of those Brunist sermons she attended. Have faith, my daughter. Essentially Simon's message whenever she called him. "Don't worry. Darren killed your friend, then handed off the murder weapon to Young Abner just as he said he did and sent him back to the camp as the fall guy, everything points to it, and because the kid is naïve and stupid he fell for it. Might be hard to prove in a court of law if you got challenged, but I don't think Rector would want to take the risk. Expect Christian forbearance."

After they received the typescript, her publishers were also suddenly doubt-stricken. They sent her a list of requested alterations, and the first one was that she change all the real names to fictional ones, as in her published story. When she refused, they began demanding harsh cuts. What they seemed to hate most was her best writing. She sent a copy to her old workshop teacher and asked his opinion. A bit hasty, a few loose ends, but it's a well-made book with a compelling story, he told her. Don't give in. "The literary judgments of commercial publishers aren't to be trusted. They don't trust them themselves and will eventually back down." They did, but made her sign a statement accepting full responsibility for any legal actions against the book. Simon told her not to worry, she had a good lawyer on her side.

She was proofing galleys when Simon called to say he had managed to secure yet another stay of execution for all five of the remaining condemned—not including Nathan Baxter and his gang, who may or may not have died in the East Texas massacre—but that it may be their last opportunity. And he had good news for her. Through his contacts in the area, he had managed to obtain for her a ten-minute meeting with Clara Collins-Wosznik. Word had gotten around about his law firm's defense of the imprisoned Brunists and they were grateful. But Clara was said to be very weak, and ten minutes was all they could allow. He had made it clear that they should stop demonizing Miss Elliott, a talented young woman committed to their cause and an invaluable research assistant for his legal team. Moreover, she had something important to tell them. "I told them what you told me. That it was an act of redemption." It was another last opportunity: Once the book was out, that door would be slammed shut.

She was able to bring Clara a gift. Simon had asked to see again the things removed from Billy Don's car in case there was something there he could use that he'd missed before. There wasn't, but he found a framed document wrapped in a sweatshirt at the bottom of Billy Don's carrier bag which, according to the inscription on the back, was Ely Collins' last note before he died in the Deepwater mine disaster, something Billy Don apparently rescued at the last minute. The glass was cracked, but otherwise it looked undamaged. Simon was able to sign out for it on the condition it would be returned to the widow. Sally had a receipt for Clara to sign, which she did with a trembling hand. Might have been emotions, might have been her frailty. Her hair was gone and she chose not to cover her baldness. A kind of defiant nakedness with which Sally empathized. Brought out her gaunt masculine features, but her essential femininity was what you saw. The gentle matriarch. She was surrounded by other women who called her Sister Clara. All unsmiling, watching Sally. But moved, she could see, by the return of the death note. A red-headed toddler joined them. One of the prisoners they interviewed had said there was a rumor that Elaine's baby was not completely human, but this was a real kid, a bit scrawny but feisty and bright-eyed. His mother came out to snatch him up and Sally asked her please to stay, she had something to tell her. Elaine turned away in alarm but her mother called her over to her side and fearfully she went there, toddler in arms, her mouth pinched shut. Sally said there were three things she was trying to accomplish: to free as many of the jailed Brunists as possible, to get all the death penalties thrown out or reduced to prison time, and to find out how her friend Billy Don Tebbett got killed. "Junior Baxter did not shoot Billy Don. We know that now. So who did?" The women looked at each other. Something was being confirmed. But what Clara said was: "We don't know." They didn't know where Darren Rector was either and would say no more. Half her time was up, so, starting with the trail of the red boots, Sally told them the story of Carl Dean Palmers, looking straight at Elaine. "I just wanted you to know. He was so brave. One against a whole gang. All of them with guns and knives. He loved you. Enough to die for you. Few of us can say as much." Elaine's mother seemed to be wilting, her head dipping. "Ben always said…" she whispered, and one of the other women, nodding, said: "I knew it." "He is lying in a pauper's grave in the municipal cemetery. Not far from Marcella Bruno, actually." The girl showed no sign of emotion, other than the fear that seemed to reside in her. But who knows, maybe she touched her. And then Sally had to leave because Clara had to be helped back to bed. The woman who had spoken introduced herself as Ludie Belle Shawcross and accompanied her to her car. "Billy Don, he was a sweetheart," she said. "Not much of a believer and less a one as time went on. I reckon you maybe had sumthin to do with that. Which ain't a concern. But if you're thinkin' it was Darren mighta done him, well, you could be right. He's got a mighty high notion of hisself, like he's set above the rest of us and ain't obliged to play by the rules. He ain't none too poplar round here for the way he's took things outa Clara's hands. And now she's dyin' he ain't got no further use of her." They stood by the car, talking for a few minutes, but when Sally asked if they could stay in touch, Ludie Belle said, "Druther not. Done's done."

When she returned, she called Simon to tell him that both she and the district attorney were wrong about where the killing took place. In the courtroom version, Billy Don used the pay phone outside the main lodge and Young Abner, returning from the mine hill to guard the camp, surprised him there. Billy Don was betraying the sect, and Young Abner, no doubt on his father's orders, executed him when he emerged from the phone booth and dragged him into the car, or perhaps he shot him as he reentered the car. Young Abner then drove the car to the spot where it was found and ditched it. It was where he was found, hiding in the trees, wearing Billy Don's broken prescription sunglasses like a trophy. In her fictionalized version, Billy Don uses the free office phone inside, where he finds Darren locking up before heading to the hill. Darren chats amiably with him on the way back to the car, gives him a farewell hug, and once Billy Don is behind the wheel, shoots him in the head. But, according to Ludie Belle Shawcross, the camp was still full of departing traffic, so Billy Don left his car in the trailer park and walked up to the office and back. They had all agreed on a meeting place near the state line, and Billy Don had told them not to wait for him, that he had an errand to run. Thus, after the phone call, he returned to an empty lot, his friends gone, Darren waiting for him. That fit with Junior's claim that he'd found the sunglasses down there "where the two bodies were," which had been dismissed by the prosecutor as another of his lies. More importantly, Ludie Belle said there were two beekeepers who had passed through, following the blossoms, both cultists at the camp, who had stayed behind long enough that day of the murder to collect their hives and who told her they'd seen Darren driving Billy Don's car that morning. Probably hard to locate, but they check in with the cult from time to time during their migrations. Simon said, if they were believable and reliable witnesses, this could be the key; he'd try to find them.

Simon also mentioned he'd be flying out to speak with Abner Baxter and his son again, and she asked to go with him. It was too late for any major changes to her book, but she might be able to tweak her descriptions of Junior in galleys. And, anyway, she enjoyed Simon's company. He was quick to agree. He enjoyed hers. Both Abner and his son had always refused to meet with Simon if she were along, and that was still true of the father, but the fear of death had softened Junior up, and Simon felt sure he'd accept her presence. She had had a glimpse or two of Junior in the past, and remembered him vaguely from high school, but this was her first time to sit down with him face to face. She had described him to her husband, based on things Billy Don and Simon had said, as ugly, stupid, sullen. She did not misspeak. Though barely out of his teens, he was already heavy in the jowls, soft and lumpy looking, with a witless, baggy stare. Sally had always associated self-flagellation with a certain intelligence and imagination. He didn't seem bright enough for it, but there you go: no blanket judgments. His shaved head was a bright red where the new hair was growing, and she remembered that Billy Don had told her that after his humiliation and scarring, Junior had let his hair grow long to cover the scar and wore a headband, much as Billy Don hid his strabismus behind dark glasses. The exposed scar, looking raw as though he'd been scratching at it, somehow called to mind Billy Don as she'd last seen him—without his glasses and frighteningly vulnerable—and she felt a deflected tenderness toward the condemned young man in front of her.The scar, which could still be read, must draw a lot of ridicule from the other prisoners. Four letters like the four on Jesus' cross, declaring him a king. Another "lier." She didn't tell Junior that. She told her notebook. While she took notes and risked a sketch or two, Simon went over everything once more, searching for any detail that might have been overlooked, from the gathering early that morning in the Meeting Hall, through the mass move to the mine hill, the troubles there, Darren's hand-off of the gun, what Junior witnessed at the camp, and so on. Nothing really new, though Junior's confused embarrassment about the fire made Sally wonder. They got up to go. "By the way, Abner," Sally asked, not having thought of it before, "do you drive?" He flushed again, hesitated, looking guilty, shook his head. "You don't drive?" He stared at her sullenly as though facing another accusation. She looked at Simon. Simon looked at her.

In bed that night, sharing a smoke with her, Simon laid out his case. He'll go back to the trial judge with a motion for a new trial. He'll ask that the defense attorney be called to testify at the hearing. The prosecutor's scenario, starting from the phone booth outside the Meeting Hall, was almost completely wrong, but they would use it. All they had to show was that Junior could not move the car to the side road and ditch, no matter where one started from. That's the secret. Not the truth, but a good story.

By the time of the revised second edition, *The Killing of Billy D* is banded with the declaration THE BOOK THAT SAVED A MAN'S LIFE! and the afterword and jacket copy have been adjusted to include the story of Young Abner Baxter's release from death row and then from prison itself. His release, in turn, inspires a new round of talk show and news hour interviews, and on one of them the host, introducing the author, describes the book as an "affectionate portrait" of the title character, whereupon Sally breaks down in tears, as the pent-up grief for Billy Don, buried under all these strenuous months beginning to stretch now into years, bursts explosively to the surface. She has the presence of mind, when she recovers enough to speak, though blinded still by the memory of Billy Don standing waist-deep in moonlit lake water with his sunglasses on, to attribute at least part of her grief to that felt for Young Abner's father, the last remaining cultist on death row, whose execution in the electric chair is imminent—two of the other three having been granted clemency, the third having killed himself—and that felt for all other persons around the country and around the world, facing the barbarism of state-authorized human slaughter.

Though partly stimulated by Sally's book, Junior Baxter's release, and a general shift of public opinion toward sympathy for the condemned evangelicals, the two last-minute clemency decisions followed directly upon the grotesque suicide of the third of the condemned, a Brunist preacher from a small church in eastern Tennessee. The man first went on a hunger strike and then secretly, before being force-fed by the prison authorities on the governor's orders, swallowed the shards of a broken mirror smuggled in from the outside, the unspeakable horror of which, matched with the placidity of the dying victim, caused the prison chaplain and chief medical officer to resign or be asked to resign. The preacher's farewell note, penned in perfect Palmer Method script, gave thanks to God, Jesus, and His Disciples and Apostles, to the Prophet Bruno, his martyred sister, and the Brunist "saints" Ely and Clara Collins and Ben Wosznik, and above all to his "spiritual guide, the great incorruptible holy man Reverend Abner Baxter."

Unfortunately for Abner, such praise served as further condemnation, for the main charge against him from the outset has been his responsibility for instigating and directing that day's most horrific events, the final episode in a long history of unrepentant criminal behavior. His followers, roaming vagabonds for the most part, chronically unemployed and disoriented by despair and poverty, were obliged to pledge blind obedience to him, following wherever he might lead in his uncompromising militancy. Even murder could become not a sinful breaking of the divine commandment but a sacred duty. Soldiers in God's war to cleanse the earth of nonbelievers. That was the story about him, crafted by the prosecutor and the media. His three violent sons were believed to have been under his direct command—the motorcycle gang's immaculately coordinated assault was said by the district attorney to have been Abner's master plan, his march on the mine hill a sinister diversion to maximize the bikers' damage, their attack on the town in turn serving Abner's army on the hill by drawing away their adversaries, their final acts of murder and arson at the church camp aided and abetted by the oldest son standing guard for them (all right, he's free, but new charges will be filed)—and his inflammatory rhetoric was likened to his early days as a communist agitator during the mine union strikes and internecine wars. He still cursed the haves on behalf of the have-nots, now under the cloak of religion, and prophesied the eventual redistribution of all property equally to all people, no matter by what means, as Jesus Christ, he heretically proclaimed, preached and intended. He was heard by several witnesses and on more than one occasion to call for a "day of wrath," and the motorcyclists, led by his second son, wore "Wrath of God" on their leather jackets and tattooed on their bodies, as well as other cultic symbols. He was a major suspect in the death under suspicious circumstances five years earlier of young Marcella Bruno, sister of the founder of the cult (he has been heard to confess this crime), and was guilty of leading a destructive assault the next day on the St. Stephen's Roman Catholic Church, though he jumped bail before he could be brought to trial. More recently, he was believed to have masterminded an armed invasion of the Brunist compound, and when jailed for his crimes, he attempted a forcible breakout, injuring the two police officers who eventually subdued him, for which reason he has until now been kept under close observation at the prison, mostly in solitary confinement. The legal occupants of the church camp were chased out by him and his followers, and those who lingered were ruthlessly exterminated. And yet, the only witness to any actual death caused directly by Baxter himself was his former closest ally Roy Coates, and Coates' testimony, obtained in a plea bargain that spared him from a certain execution, was suspect. The specific victim in the Coates testimony was a member of the Knights of Columbus Defense Force and technically a deputized police officer, thereby adding cop-killing to Baxter's crimes, though this Defense Force was an irregular and probably illegal group, and any such shooting, if it even happened, was arguably in self-defense. The brutal assassination of the county sheriff, however, was unquestionably the work of his sons and their gang, and this too was laid by the prosecuting district attorney, now the state governor, at Abner's door.

Sally sees it all differently and says so on every possible occasion. While Simon files urgent appeal after urgent appeal, she uses whatever interview and talk show opportunities come her way as her bully pulpit, exposing the true realities behind the deceitful prosecutorial rhetoric, and continuing her assault on Christianity as the true culprit behind the crimes. She does her best to adhere to the cautionary guidelines laid down by Simon and her husband but never lets them get in the way of driving home a point with an imaginative flourish or two. Because she has become known for her reckless candor, interviewers and moderators often taunt her with questions meant to provoke another outrageous outburst. Both Simon and her husband have pointed out that letting fly with her unpopular opinions—she not only freely parades her atheism and her opposition to capital punishment and the conspiracy laws, she also vociferously champions all the liberal causes like civil rights, free speech, preservation of the wilderness, and prison reform, and rails against the inhumanity of corporate capitalism, the numbing banality of the networks, and the nation's insane wars—has the negative effect of lessening the impact of her criticism of the Baxter case, reducing it in the public mind to eccentric leftwing soapbox oratory. Even her quoting of Adams and Jefferson is often taken as an insult to the nation and a calculated assault on its enduring values. She knows that, and knows too that these people are just using her as entertainment, turning her into a kind of sound-bite clown to fill the gaps between commercials, and she does her best to stay cool as her husband has instructed her, but restraint is not among her inborn virtues. In this she feels a certain empathy with Abner Baxter, whose thunderous grandstanding makes defending him such a nightmare.

In the end, the nightmare evolves into real-time horror. The preacher is accused of many crimes but few in particular, so the only defense, finally, is against the law itself. The Supreme Court refuses to hear the case, but Simon does get it before the state Supreme Judicial Court. He gives it his best and the judge is sympathetic and takes note of Simon's eloquence, but tells him the court cannot change the law. "You should run for congress, Mr. Price," he says. That they are facing failure sinks in slowly. "Don't get your hopes too high," Simon said when they began all this, "we lose more than we win," but they both were certain they *would* win. They were right, and the right would ultimately triumph. When the last appeal is exhausted, they cannot accept it, but press on. And then—suddenly, it seems—the governor denies clemency, all options are closed, and the day of extinguishing Abner Baxter's life is upon them.

Organizations opposing the death penalty have been in touch with her, and they let her know that they will be holding a vigil outside the prison where the execution is taking place and ask her to join them. She and her husband fly out in a private plane, and her husband hires a limousine to drive them to the prison, where they meet up with Simon and his wife. Sally likes Simon's wife immediately. Passionate and smart. That ends that. But she and Simon will be friends still, and in this tribe of barbarians, that's something. Because he is a Congressman, her husband is interviewed by the hovering media. He says: "I am opposed to capital punishment. Period." She is proud of him. She hears him say so to the young newscaster and she hears him say so on the transistor radio she has pressed to her ear. The network she is listening to has a reporter inside the prison who will witness the execution and describe it for his listeners. Abner Baxter is said to be remarkably serene, having stoically accepted his fate, his blistering attacks on the faithlessness and corruption of those who put him here giving way to a quiet contemplative time. He is said to be reading the Bible. And writing.

Words. Their inscription. The pathos of that.

Night has fallen. They light candles as the hour draws near. They are not many. And they are not alone. A large parking lot has filled with cars and pickups, and tailgate parties are underway. Kegs of beer. Portable barbecue pits. A few musical instruments, blown or strummed randomly like an orchestra warming up. Someone is practicing a drumroll. They have rigged up a P.A. system to broadcast the reports from within and she can put away her transistor radio. They're making a lot of noise. It's like New Year's Eve in Times Square. "It's awful," she says to her husband, "to think that we might be alone in the universe and that this is what we are." Curious tourist-types gather, some joining the beer party, some coming over to their little group and accepting a candle, others approaching a larger mass of people, many of whom are now pulling on Brunist tunics. She has heard reports that they would be here. There are scores of them, and more arriving by the minute. What the occasional execution will do for a faltering movement. They also bring out candles. Abner releases a final statement, quoting Paul, which is read over the P.A. system by the reporter on the inside: "I have fought a good fight, I have finished my course, I have kept the faith." The Brunists groan and kneel to pray. There is some keening, but they are largely subdued in their mourning. They are witnesses to a martyrdom. The making of a saint. They can all write a book.

She spies the blond curls. The Evangelist. No surprise there. It is no doubt he who has gathered the Brunists here tonight. The surprise is that Young Abner Baxter is with him. Well, a surprise, and not a surprise. When Junior got the news of his release, he didn't thank them, just stared at them for a moment, then walked away, and she knew then that if the same circumstances as that day in the ditch should arise again, she'd once more be a target. Sally finds herself grinding her cigarette out underfoot and walking over to them. Is she feeling suicidal or what? The crowds around Darren stand and part. She hears hissing sounds. The Antichrist approacheth. Junior's hair is growing back. His moustache. He wears a headband, also white, hiding his scars. Menacingly expressionless. As are most here. Darren wears an expression of sorrowful bliss. Like he's high on something. A madman's smile. Eerie by candlelight. "I'm sorry about your father, Abner," she says. "We did everything we could." No response, not even a blink. She feels like the only moving thing in a fixed tableau. "I'm sorry, too, about Billy Don," she says, turning her gaze on Darren. He is wearing the dodecagonal medal Billy Don told her about, the one he stole from Clara Collins. It glitters in the night like something burning on his chest. His spectacles reflect the flickering candles like glowing half-dollars. She has not seen him up close or talked to him since that day on the mine hill, but Billy Don helped her to imagine him in his private ways, and she probably knows him better than he knows himself. Not probably; surely. "I miss him."

"Billy Don is in Heaven, waiting for me with open arms," Darren replies softly. She called his voice "quietly compelling" in her novel and it is, but his smug piety grates on her. "I do not think we will see you there."

"Don't be so sure," she says. She knows what he has done, even if he no longer does. He should be sitting in Abner's chair. But if he were, she's well aware, she would be out here, just the same. "Your Heaven exists only in your head, creep, dies when you do. But, meanwhile, Billy Don and I will haunt your fantasy world, so watch out. Our games may be cruel. We will make enemies of your angels. Listen carefully to what they sing. You will know no peace."

She feels suddenly exhausted. What has she said? She doesn't know. The parking lot party is in full swing, raucous and obscene, cheering on the executioner. She turns to leave, unsure of what might happen next, her knees wobbly, sees her husband and Simon waiting for her a few yards away. Her husband takes her hand, Simon her arm. The countdown has begun and solemnly they walk away to the drummed beat of it.

The Kingdom has been decimated by the black magic of the Cretin Wizards with their cult of the Living Dead. The King hangs those he can catch, but they are everywhere, ineradicable as cockroaches. Their magic is merely a clumsy sleight-of-hand that can only delude the stupid, but, alas, there is no scarcity of stupidity in the world, nor in his Kingdom nor in his Castle, either. A lesson for the Goose Girl as well, launching forth on adventures of her own. She is no longer a Goose Girl, having bade farewell to her flock, a bittersweet occasion, for she had to choose one of them for her supper before setting out (IT'S THE SADNESS is tattooed across her breasts), and she is no longer Beauty either, if she ever was, even in her own imagination. Inspired by the nightmares unleashed by the Cretin Wizards, she has taken up oneirophagy and will be known henceforth as Dream Eater, the tribal Dreamtime itself her chosen banquet hall. If indeed she is the chooser not the chosen. Is that enough for one life? No, but it beats bedding down in goose shit. Dream Eaters of the past have all been monsters. She will be a monster, too. *Is* one, born and bred. She flexes her talons, bares her steely teeth, and then, locking the gate and hauling up the drawbridge behind her, she's out of there. Done's done.

# ACKNOWLEDGMENTS

Excerpts from this book have been published in *Conjunctions, Harper's Magazine, Western Humanities Review, Kenyon Review, Five Dials, FlashPoint,* and *Golden Handcuffs*. Thanks to Brown University and, in particular, to Vartan Gregorian, Brown president from 1989 to 1997, supporter of endangered dissident writers, innovative digital literary arts, and iconoclastic tenure-rejecting professor-types in need of focused writing time. Bernard Hoepffner, Larry McCaffery, Alexandra Kleeman, Stéphane Vanderhaeghe, Dzanc Senior Editor Guy Intoci, my literary agent Georges Borchardt, and my wife Pilar provided valuable critical readings. Scott Burns, Gordon Pruett, and my son Roderick helped with specific research needs. The book's long decade of composition was sustained by daily late-afternoon coffees provided by innumerable neighborhood cafés in several cities, most notably by the Stella family and staff of the La Gaffe coffee and wine bar in Hampstead, London, where, in an isolated eyrie overlooking the city, much of the book's writing was accomplished.